THE LEGEND OF SIGMAR

• TIME OF LEGENDS •

THE LEGEND OF SIGMAR
Graham McNeill
(Contains the novels HELDENHAMMER, EMPIRE
and GOD KING)

THE SUNDERING
Gav Thorpe
(Contains the novels MALEKITH, SHADOW KING, CALEDOR
and the novella THE BLOODY HANDED)
(October 2012)

THE RISE OF NAGASH
Mike Lee
(Contains the novels NAGASH THE SORCERER, NAGASH THE
UNBROKEN and NAGASH IMMORTAL)
(January 2013)

AGE OF LEGEND
A short story anthology
Edited by Christian Dunn

DEAD WINTER
The first volume of the Black Plague
C. L. Werner

THE GREAT BETRAYAL
The first volume of the War of Vengeance
Nick Kyme
(November 2012)

NEFERATA
The first volume of the Blood of Nagash
Josh Reynolds
(January 2013)

TIME OF LEGENDS

THE LEGEND OF SIGMAR

Graham McNeill

BLACK LIBRARY

To DG. You taught me all I know.
This one is for Sawney, the newest recruit.
To Anita. For everything.

A BLACK LIBRARY PUBLICATION
First published in Great Britain in 2012 by
Black Library,
Games Workshop Ltd.,
Willow Road,
Nottingham,
NG7 2WS, UK

10 9 8 7 6 5 4 3 2 1

Cover by Stefan Kopinski.
Map by Nuala Kinrade.

A CIP record for this book
is available from the British Library.

UK ISBN 13: 978 1 84970 225 6
US ISBN 13: 978 1 84970 226 3

Printed and bound by CPI Group (UK) Ltd, Croydon, CR0 4YY

This is a dark age, a bloody age, an age of daemons and of sorcery. It is an age of battle and death, and of the world's ending. Amidst all of the fire, flame and fury it is a time, too, of mighty heroes, of bold deeds and great courage.

At the heart of the Old World lie the lands of men, ruled over by bickering tribal chieftains.

It is a land divided. In the north, King Artur of the Teutogens surveys his rivals atop the mighty Fauschlag Rock, whilst the berserker kings of the Thuringians know only war and bloodshed. It is to the south that men must look for succour. At Reikdorf dwell the Unberogens, led by the mighty King Björn and his fated son, Sigmar. The Unberogens seek a vision, a vision of unity. The enemies of man are many and if men cannot overcome their differences and rally together, their demise is assured.

To the frozen north, Norsii raiders, barbarians and worshippers of Dark Gods, burn, slay and pillage. Grim spectres haunt the marshlands and beasts gather in the forests. But it is in the east where dark forces are moving, and the greatest threat lies. Greenskins have ever plagued the land and now they march upon the race of man in their numberless hordes with a single purpose – to eradicate their foes forever.

The human kings are not alone in their plight. The dwarfs of the mountains, great forge smiths and engineers, are allies in this fight. All must stand together, dwarf and man, for their mutual survival depends on it.

CONTENTS

Our Land in the time of Sigmar
Salzenhus
FOREST OF SHADOWS
Brass Keep
Fauschlag Rock
CHERUS
Battle of the Berserker King
THURINGIANS
NORTH ROAD
Count Otwin's Castle
JUTONES
Jutonsryk
TEUTOGENS
THE GRE
FOREST
Reikdorf
Astofen
Marburg
BRETONII
ENDALS
UNBEROGENS
PALE SISTERS
GREY MTNS.

NORSII
ROPPSMENN
UDOSES
FRIKINGS
OSTAGOTHS
THE GREAT FOREST
DEAD WOOD
KOLSA HILLS
Hochergig
Taalahim
TALEUTENS
FÄRLIC HILLS
THE GREAT FOREST
ASOBORNS
HALFLINGS
Three Hills
To Black Fire Pass
Tomb of Rahotep
BRIGUNDIANS
Siggurdheim
Ubersreik
Ruins of Krealheim
MEROGENS
MENOGOTHS
Skaranorak's Lair

Introduction

IF YOU'RE GOING to choose a legendary character from the history of Warhammer to write a novel about, which one springs first to mind? For me it was always Sigmar, the mythical founder of the Empire who went on to become a living god. Who else in the panoply of heroes can lay claim to that kind of honour? Sure, there are High Elf heroes that saved the world and undying necromancers who tried to end it, but when you're already practically a god or have access to the most powerful magic in the world, it's perhaps not all that difficult to be legendary.

But when all you have is the strength in your sword arm and the fellowship of your brothers, a man has to dig deep within himself to become a hero. Sure, Sigmar has a magical warhammer, but that's not the source of his power, it only adds to what's already there. And that lies at the heart of what attracted me to the character of Sigmar. He was just a man. Nothing more, nothing less. Living in a land forever under the shadow of orc invasion from the east, raiders from the north and riven with tribal warfare, humankind existed on a precarious knife edge a hair's-breadth from extinction. Though Sigmar was the son of a mighty chieftain, he had none of the superlative qualities of long life, strength or skills with which many of the older races were blessed. He had something better, somethng no one else had. He had vision.

Sigmar saw that the internecine wars between the tribes would ultimately doom them. With foes in every direction, what hope could there be if every tribe counted the others as enemies? I loved this idea, and knew that there was real mileage in exploring what made a man cling to a vision no one else could see. Overcoming the entrenched notion that the tribes would always be enemies to one another and uniting such disparate forces as the frenzied warriors of the Berserker King or the warrior women of the Asoborns under one banner would be no easy task, but Sigmar had his sights set on nothing less than an Empire of Man ruled over by a powerful Emperor. Only then would the lands of men be safe.

Of course, as altruistic as this all sounds, let's not forget that Sigmar saw himself as that Emperor, and not everyone was going to share his vision. And those that didn't wouldn't be welcome in his empire... In telling the legend of Sigmar, it was immediately obvious that there was a lot of existing lore to incorporate into the novel, and I delved into the vaults of Games Workshop to uncover every morsel of information gathered in ancient issues of *White Dwarf*, old Army Books, role-play supplements and the like. A lot of the information I uncovered was fragmentary, contradictory or woefully out of date, but rather than seeing that as a problem, I looked at it as an opportunity. I had all this information about a heroic character who lived two and a half thousand years before the current Warhammer time period, and it was only right and proper that there would be elements of the narrative that didn't fit neatly together. The challenge would be to tell a compelling narrative that explored the nature of a man driven to bring an entire land under his control, and do it in a way that felt realistic and worked within what we knew of him. It's easy to write something in a broad swathe of hyperbolic description that represents incidents from thousands of years ago, but to actually write that scene in a novel, with real characters talking and interacting is quite different. This is a character about whom legends have been told and which have grown over thousands of years in the telling.

Heldenhammer was the first book that came out of this, and I'd always envisaged it as a stand-alone book, a telling of Sigmar's unification of the Empire and the awesome fury of the Battle of Black Fire Pass, with a postscript at the end telling what happened to him at the end of his reign. But that's not how it turned out, and the more I wrote of the story, the more I knew I wanted to tell stories beyond that battle. After all, winning an empire is only half the battle, *keeping* it is quite another. The existing timeline for Sigmar was teasingly dotted with one line references to other battles, other trying times and other legends. I wanted to tell those stories, and thus the postscript was jettisoned from *Heldenhammer*, and another book was planned. That book was *Empire*, and it dealt with how Sigmar coped with being Emperor, and whether it lived up to his expectations. And, more importantly, how *he* lived up to his people's expectations. After all, he'd promised them a great deal, and now it was time to live up to those promises of peace and unity.

But peace and unity are not the lot of men in the Empire, and as old foes rear their head and new enemies look upon what Sigmar has built with envious eyes, war is never far beyond the horizon. *Empire* went on to win the David Gemmell Legend Award in 2010, which was a huge thrill for me, and an honour worthy of Sigmar himself. As I type this, I'm looking up at the axe I won, and have a warm, tingly feeling in my fingertips. In case I didn't say it enough at the time, a huge thank you to everyone who voted for *Empire*.

God King is the final book in this omnibus, and it deals with a collision of legendary characters, a climactic battle to the (un)death between Sigmar and Nagash. This was the tale I planned to finish with, the culmination of Sigmar's legend where I'd finally get to use the postscript I'd written way back when I'd finished *Heldenhammer*. I was saying that all through the writing of *God King*, or at least until I realised I was leaving lots of breadcrumbs in my wake to be nibbled at later. I was setting up characters and plot lines that were just begging to be told in fresh stories, and by the time I got the Battle of the River Reik, I knew I wasn't done with Sigmar and the postscript went back in the drawer.

So, these novels are the first in what I fully expect to be an epic retelling of Sigmar's legend, which will go on to become a fitting saga for such a mighty hero. There will be more battles fought, more blood shed, more sacrifices made and more heroism before we finally get to that postscript.

For Sigmar and the Empire!

Graham McNeill
September 2011

HELDENHAMMER

BOOK ONE
Forging the Man

When the sun rests
And the world is dark
And the great fires are lit
And the ale is poured into flagons
Then is the time to sing sagas as dwarfs do
And the greatest of sagas
Is the saga of Sigmar, mightiest warrior.
Harken now, hear these words.
And live in hope.

ONE
Battle's Eve

THE FAINT SOUND of songs and proud boasts guided the two boys as they scampered across the hard earth of the darkened settlement towards the longhouse at its centre. Their movements were furtive and cautious as they negotiated their way between high, timber walled buildings, and past the fish drying racks and the warm walls of the smithy. Neither boy wanted to be discovered, especially now that guards had been set on the walls and night had fallen.

Despite the threat of a beating at this trespass, the excitement of their intrepid raid into the heart of Reikdorf threatened to give both of them away.

'Be quiet!' hissed Cuthwin as Wenyld clattered against a previously unseen pile of planed timber, stacked against the woodworking store.

'Quiet yourself,' returned his friend, catching the timber before it could fall as both boys pressed their bodies flat against the wall. 'There's no stars or moon. I can't see a thing.'

That at least was true, allowed Cuthwin. The night was utterly dark, the hooded braziers on the settlement's walls casting a crackling orange light out into the forests beyond Reikdorf. Sentries circled the settlement within the ring of light, their bows and spears trained on the thick forests and darkened shoreline of the Reik.

'Hey,' said Wenyld, 'did you hear what I said?'

'I heard,' said Cuthwin. 'It's dark, yes. So use your ears. Warriors aren't quiet the night before riding to war.'

Both boys stood as still as the statue of Ulric above Reikdorf's gate, and let the sounds and smells of the night wash over them, each one telling a story of the village they lived in: the groan of settling iron as Beorthyn's forge cooled and creaked from a day's work, producing iron swords and axe blades; the sounds of wives speaking with low, worried voices as they wove new cloaks for their sons, who rode to battle at daybreak; the whinny of stabled horses; the sweet smell of burning peat, and the mouth-watering aroma of cooking meat.

Over it all, Cuthwin could hear the open wash of the river as a constant rustle of water against the mud flats, the creak of wooden fishing boats as they moved with the tide, and the low moan of wind through the hung nets. It sounded sad to him, but night in the land west of the mountains was often a time of sadness, a time when the monsters came from the forests to kill and devour.

Cuthwin's parents had been killed last summer by the greenskins, cut down as they fought to defend their farmstead from the blood-hungry raiders. The thought made him pause, and he felt his hands curl into fists as he pictured the vengeance he would one day take on the savage race that had taken his father from him, and had seen him eventually brought to Reikdorf to live with his uncle.

As though feelings of anger concentrated his hearing, he heard a muted sound of laughter and song from behind thick timbers and heavy, fortified doors. Firelight reflected on the walls of the grain store at the settlement's heart as though a door or shutter had been opened, and from which spilled raucous sounds of merriment.

For a brief moment, the market-place at the centre of Reikdorf was illuminated, but no sooner had the light come than it was gone. Both boys shared a look of excitement at the thought of spying on King Björn's warriors before they rode out to do battle with the greenskins. Only those who had reached the age of manhood were permitted within the walls of the king's longhouse before battle, and the mystery of such a thing simply had to be explored.

'Did you see that?' asked Wenyld, pointing towards the centre of the village.

'Of course I did,' replied Cuthwin, pulling Wenyld's arm down. 'I'm not blind.'

Though Cuthwin had lived in Reikdorf for less than a week, he knew the secrets of the town as well as any young child did, but in such complete darkness, without any visual landmarks beyond knowing where they stood, the village was suddenly unfamiliar and strange, all its geography unknown.

He fixed the brief image the light had given him, and took Wenyld's hand.

'I'll follow the sounds of the warriors,' he said. 'Hold on to me and I'll get us there.'

'But it's so dark,' said Wenyld.

'Doesn't matter,' said Cuthwin. 'I'll find a way around in the dark. Just don't let go.'

'I won't,' promised Wenyld, but Cuthwin could hear the fear that crept into his friend's voice. He felt a little of it too, for his uncle was no slouch with the birch when punishment was to be meted out. He pushed the fear aside, for he was an Unberogen, the fiercest tribe of warriors north of the Grey Mountains, and his heart was strong and true.

He took a deep breath, and set off at a jog towards where the light had reflected on the walls of the grain store, following a remembered path where there was nothing to trip him or make a noise. Cuthwin's heart was in his mouth as he crossed the open market-place, avoiding spots where the light had shown him pitfalls or broken pottery that might crunch underfoot. Though he had only the briefest glimpse of the route he had to take, the image was imprinted on his memory as firmly as the wolves on one of King Björn's war banners.

His father's teachings in the dark of the woods returned to him, and he moved like a ghost, silently weaving through the market square, counting his strides and pulling Wenyld after him. Cuthwin pulled up and slowed his steps as he closed his eyes and let his ears gather information on his surroundings. The sound of merrymaking was louder, and the echoes of it on the walls were forming a map in his head.

Cuthwin reached out, and he smiled as he felt his fingers brush the stone wall of the longhouse. The stones were square-cut and carved, hewn by dwarf miners from the rock of the Worlds Edge Mountains, and brought to Reikdorf as a gift to King Björn when spring had broken.

He remembered watching the dwarfs with a mixture of awe and trepidation, for they had been frightening, squat figures in gleaming armour, who paid little heed to the people around them, speaking to one another in gruff voices as they built the longhouse for the king in less than a day. The dwarfs had stayed no longer than necessary, and had refused all offers of help in their labours, all but one marching into the east as soon as the work was complete.

'Are we here?' whispered Wenyld.

Cuthwin nodded before remembering that Wenyld wouldn't be able to see him.

'Yes,' he said, his voice low, 'but be quiet. It'll be a week emptying the privies if we're caught.'

Cuthwin paused to let his breathing even out, and then began edging along the length of the wall, feeling ahead of him for the corner. When it came, it was as smooth and as sharp as an axe blade, and he eased himself around it, glancing up as the clouds parted and a bright glitter of stars sparkled in the heavens above him.

The extra light glistened on the walls of the dwarf-cut stone as though they were filled with stars, and he took a moment to admire the incredible craftsmanship that had gone into their making.

Along the length of the wall of the longhouse, Cuthwin could see a wide doorway fashioned from thick beams of timber, and embellished with angular bands of dark iron and carvings of hammers and lightning bolts. Shutters above them were fastened tightly to their frames, not so much as a gap wide enough for a knife blade between the timber and the stone.

Through the shutters, Cuthwin could hear the muted sounds of carousing warriors, the clatter of ale pots, the sound of rousing war songs and the banging of swords upon shield bosses.

'Here,' he said, pointing to the shutter above him. 'We'll see if we can get a look in here.'

Wenyld nodded and said, 'Me first.'

'Why should you go first?' asked Cuthwin. 'I got us here.'

'Because I'm the oldest,' said Wenyld, and Cuthwin couldn't fault his logic, so, he laced his fingers together to form a stirrup like those used by the horsemen of the Taleuten.

He braced his back against the stone wall and said, 'Very well, climb up and see if you can work the shutter open far enough to see something.'

Wenyld nodded eagerly and set his foot in Cuthwin's hands, placing his hands on his friend's shoulders. With a grunt, Cuthwin boosted Wenyld up, turning his head to avoid a knee in the face.

He opened his stance a little to spread Wenyld's weight, and craned his neck to see what his friend was doing. The shutter was wedged firmly within its frame, and Wenyld had his face pressed against the wood as he squinted along the joints.

'Well?' asked Cuthwin, closing his eyes as he strained to hold Wenyld. 'What do you see?'

'Nothing,' replied Wenyld. 'I can't see anything, the wood's fitted too closely together.'

'That's dwarf craft for you,' said a strong voice beside them, and both boys froze.

Cuthwin turned his head slowly, and opened his eyes to see a powerful warrior, outlined by starlight, and as solid as if he was carved from the same stone as the longhouse.

The sheer physical presence of the warrior took Cuthwin's breath away, and he released his grip on Wenyld's foot. His friend scrabbled for a handhold at the edge of the shutter, but there was none to be had, and he fell, knocking the pair of them to the ground in a pile of acute embarrassment. Cuthwin shook free of his cursing friend, knowing that he was to be punished, but determined to face the warrior without fear.

He rolled quickly to his feet, and stood before their discoverer, his defiance turning to awe as he stared into the open, handsome face. Blond hair shone like silver in the starlight, kept from the warrior's face by a headband of twisted copper wire, and his thick arms were bound by iron torques. A long bearskin cloak flowed from his shoulders, and Cuthwin saw that beneath it the warrior was clad in shimmering mail, bound at the waist by a great belt of thick leather.

A long-bladed hunting knife was sheathed at his belt, but it was the weapon hanging beside it that captured Cuthwin's full attention.

The warrior bore a mighty warhammer, and Cuthwin's eyes were drawn to the wide, flat head of the weapon, its surface etched with strange carvings that shimmered in the starlight.

The warhammer was a magnificent weapon, its haft forged from some unknown metal and worked by hands older than imagining. No man had ever forged such a perfect weapon of destruction, nor had any smith ever borne such a fearsome tool of creation.

Wenyld sprang to his feet, ready to flee from their discovery, but he too was held rooted to the spot at the sight of the awesome warrior.

The warrior leaned down, and Cuthwin saw that he was still young, perhaps around fifteen summers, and had a look of wry amusement glittering in the depths of his cold eyes, one of which was a pale blue, the other a deep green.

'You did well getting across that market square in the dark, boy,' said the warrior.

'My name is Cuthwin,' he said. 'I'm nearly twelve, almost a man.'

'Almost,' said the warrior, 'but not yet, Cuthwin. This place is for warriors who may soon face death in battle. This night is for them and them alone. Do not be in too much of a rush to be part of such things. Enjoy your childhood while you can. Now go, be off with you.'

'You're not going to punish us?' asked Wenyld, and Cuthwin dug an elbow into his ribs.

The warrior smiled and said, 'I should, but it took great skill to get this far without being seen, and I like that.'

Despite himself, Cuthwin felt inordinately pleased to have earned the warrior's praise and said, 'My father taught me how to move without being seen.'

'Then he taught you well. What is his name?'

'He was called Gethwer,' said Cuthwin. 'The greenskins killed him.'

'I am sorry for that, Cuthwin,' said the warrior. 'We ride to do battle with the greenskins, and many of them will die by our hand. Now, do not tarry, or others with less mercy than I will discover you, and you'll be in for a beating.'

Cuthwin needed no second telling and turned from the warrior, sprinting back across the market square with his arms pumping at his side. The stars were out, and he followed a direct route from the longhouse towards the storehouse at the edge of the market square. He heard running steps behind him and risked a glance over his shoulder to see Wenyld swiftly following. The older boy quickly overtook him, a look of frantic relief plastered across his face as they rounded the corner of a timber-framed storehouse.

The boys pressed their bodies against the building, lungs heaving, and wild laughter bursting from their throats as they relived the thrill of capture and the relief of escape.

Cuthwin darted his head around the storehouse, remembering the fierce strength of the warrior who had sent them on their way. There was a man who feared nothing, a man who would stand up to any threat and meet it with his warhammer held high.

'When I am a man I want to be like him,' said Cuthwin when he had got his breath back.

Wenyld doubled up, the breath heaving in his chest. 'Don't you know who that was?'

'No,' said Cuthwin, 'who was it?'

Wenyld said, 'That was the king's son. That was Sigmar.'

SIGMAR WATCHED THE boys run off as though the Ölfhednar themselves were at their heels, smiling as he remembered attempting to sneak up to the old longhouse the night before his father had led the Unberogen warriors into battle against the Thuringians. He had not been as stealthy as the young lad he had just sent on his way, and vividly remembered the thrashing the king had administered.

He heard unsteady footfalls behind him. Without turning, he knew that Wolfgart, his closest friend and sword-brother, approached.

'You were too soft on them, Sigmar,' said Wolfgart. 'I remember the beating *we* got. Why should they not learn the hard way that you don't try to spy on a warriors' Blood Night?'

'We were caught because you couldn't hold me up for long enough,' Sigmar pointed out, turning to see a heavily muscled young man clad in mail and swathed in a great wolfskin cloak. A long-handled sword was sheathed over his shoulders, and unkempt braids of dark hair spilled around his face. Wolfgart was three years older than Sigmar, his features handsome and his skin flushed with heat, rich food and plentiful drink.

'Only because you broke my arm the year before with a smelting hammer.'

Sigmar's gaze fell upon Wolfgart's elbow, where five years previously, his rage had overcome him after the older boy had bested him in a practice bout and he had swung his weapon at the unsuspecting Wolfgart. Though long forgiven, Sigmar had never forgotten the unworthy deed, nor had he quickly forgotten the lesson of control his father had taught him in the aftermath of the bout.

'True enough,' admitted Sigmar, slapping a hand on his friend's shoulder and turning him back towards the longhouse. 'You have never let me forget it.'

'Damn right!' roared Wolfgart, his cheeks red with ale flavoured with hops and bog myrtle. 'I won fair and square, and you hit me from behind!'

'I know, I know,' said Sigmar, leading him back towards the door.

'What are you doing outside anyway? There's more drinking to be done!'

'I just wanted some fresh air,' said Sigmar, 'and haven't you had enough to drink?'

'Fresh air?' slurred Wolfgart, ignoring the latter part of Sigmar's comment. 'Plenty of fresh air to be had on the morn. Tonight is a night for feasting, drinking and giving praise to Ulric. It's bad luck not to sacrifice to the gods before battle.'

'I know that, Wolfgart. My father taught me that.'

'Then come back in,' said Wolfgart. 'He'll be wondering where you are. It's bad luck to be apart from your sword-brothers on a Blood Night.'

'Everything is bad luck to you,' said Sigmar.

'It's true. Look at the world we live in,' said Wolfgart, leaning against the side of the longhouse to vomit down the dwarf stonework. Glistening ropes of matter drooled from his chin, and he wiped them clear with the back of his hand. 'I mean, think about it. Everywhere a man looks there's something trying to kill him: greenskins from the mountains, the beast-kin in the forests, or the other tribes: Asoborns, Thuringians or Teutogens. Plagues, starvation and sorcery: you name it, it's bad luck. Proves that everything is bad luck, doesn't it?'

'Someone had too much to drink again?' said an amused voice from the doorway to the longhouse.

'Ranald shrivel your staff, Pendrag!' roared Wolfgart, sinking to his haunches, and resting his forehead against the cool stone of the longhouse.

Sigmar looked up from Wolfgart to see two warriors emerge from the warmth and light of the longhouse. Both were of ages with him, and clad in fine hauberks and tunics of dark red. The taller of the pair had hair the colour of the setting sun, and wore a thick cloak of shimmering green scales that threw back the starlight with an iridescent sheen. His companion wore a long wolfskin cloak wrapped tightly around his thin frame, and bore a worried expression upon his face.

The tall warrior with the flame-red hair, addressed by Wolfgart, ignored the insult to his manhood, and said, 'Is he going to be well enough to ride tomorrow?'

Sigmar nodded and said, 'Aye, Pendrag, it's nothing a brew of valerian root won't cure.'

Pendrag looked doubtful, but shrugged, and turned to his companion in the wolfskin cloak. 'Trinovantes here thinks you should come inside, Sigmar.'

'Afraid I'll catch cold, my friend?' asked Sigmar.

'He claims he's seen an omen,' said Pendrag.

'An omen?' asked Sigmar. 'What kind of omen?'

'A bad one,' spat Wolfgart. 'What other kind is there? No one speaks of good omens now.'

'They did of Sigmar's coming,' said Trinovantes.

'Aye, and look how well that went,' groaned Wolfgart. 'Born into blood, and his mother dead at the hands of orcs. Good omens, my arse.'

Sigmar felt a stab of anger and sadness at the mention of his mother's death, but he had never known her and had nothing but his father's words to connect her to him. Wolfgart was right. Whatever omens had been spoken of his birth had come to naught but blood and death.

He leaned down, hooked an arm under Wolfgart's shoulders, and hauled him to his feet. Wolfgart was heavy and his limbs loose, and Sigmar grunted under the weight. Trinovantes took Wolfgart's other arm, and between them they half carried, half dragged their drunken friend towards the warmth of the longhouse.

Sigmar looked over at Trinovantes, the young man's face earnest and aged before its time.

'Tell me,' said Sigmar, 'what omen did you see?'

Trinovantes shook his head. 'It was nothing, Sigmar.'

'Go on, tell him,' said Pendrag. 'You can't see an omen and then not tell him.'

'Very well,' said Trinovantes, taking a deep breath. 'I saw a raven land on the roof of the king's longhouse this morning.'

'And?' asked Sigmar, when Trinovantes did not go on.

'And nothing,' said Trinovantes. 'That was it. A single raven is an omen of sorrow. Remember when one landed on Beithar's home last year? He was dead within the week.'

'Beithar was nearly forty,' said Sigmar. 'He was an old man.'

'You see,' laughed Pendrag. 'Aren't you glad we warned you, Sigmar? You must stay home and let us do the fighting. It's clearly too dangerous for you to venture beyond the confines of Reikdorf.'

'You can laugh,' said Trinovantes, 'but don't say I didn't warn you when you've an orc arrow through your heart!'

'An orc couldn't skewer my heart if I stood right in front of it and let it take a free pull on its bow,' cried Pendrag. 'In any case, if it's the gods' will that I die at the hands of an orc then it will be with its axe buried in my chest and a ring of its dead friends around me. I won't be slain by some poxy arrow!'

'Enough talk of death!' roared Wolfgart, finding new strength, and throwing off the supporting arms of his friends. 'It's bad luck to talk of death before a battle! I need a drink.'

Sigmar smiled as Wolfgart ran his hands through his unruly hair, and spat a glistening mouthful to the earth. No one could go from drunken stupor to demanding more ale as quickly as Wolfgart, and despite Pendrag's worries, Sigmar knew that Wolfgart would ride as hard and skilfully as ever on the morrow.

'What are we all doing out here?' demanded Wolfgart. 'Come on, there's drinking yet to be done.'

Before any of them could answer, the howling of wolves split the night, a soaring chorus from the depths of the darkened forest that carried the primal joy of wild and ancient days as it echoed through Reikdorf. Yet more howls rose in answer as though every pack of wolves within the Great Forest had united in one great cry of challenge.

'You want an omen, my brothers,' said Wolfgart. 'There's your omen. Ulric is with us. Now, let's get inside. This is our Blood Night after all and we've blood yet to offer him.'

SPARKS FLEW FROM the cooking fire like a thousand fireflies as another hunk of wood was hurled into the deep pit at the centre of the great longhouse of the Unberogen tribe. Heat from the fire and the hundreds of warriors gathered in the great hall filled the longhouse, and laughter and song rose to the heavy beams that laced together overhead in complex patterns of support and dependency.

Dwarfs had built this longhouse for the king of the Unberogens in recognition of his son's courage and the great service he had done their own king, Kurgan Ironbeard, by rescuing him from orcs. Sturdy stone walls that would endure beyond the lives of many kings enclosed the warriors as they gathered to offer praise and blood to Ulric and carouse on what, for many, would be their last night alive in Reikdorf.

Sigmar threaded his way through the crowded hall towards the raised podium at the far end of the longhouse, where his father sat on a carved, oak throne, two men standing at his sides. To his father's right was Alfgeir, the Marshal of the Reik and king's champion, while on his left was Eoforth, his trusted counsellor and oldest friend.

The sights, sounds and smells of the great hall overwhelmed Sigmar's every sense: sweat, songs, blood, meat, ale and smoke. Three enormous boars turned on spits before a tall wooden statue of Taal, the hunter god, their flesh crackling and spitting fat into the fire. Though he had eaten enough to fill his belly for a week, the scent of roasting meat made his mouth water, and he smiled as a mug of beer was thrust into his hand.

Wolfgart immediately found more drink, and began an arm wrestling contest amongst his fellow warriors. Trinovantes fetched a plate of food and some water, watching Wolfgart with studied worry, while Pendrag sought out the squat, bearded dwarf sitting in the corner of the hall, who watched the revelries with unabashed relish.

The dwarf was known as Alaric, and had come down from the mountains with Kurgan Ironbeard in early spring with the cartloads of hewn stone for the new longhouse. When the construction work was complete, the dwarfs had left, but Alaric had remained, teaching the Unberogen smiths secrets of metalworking that had provided them with the finest weapons and armour of the western tribes.

Sigmar left his friends to their diversions, knowing that every man must face his Blood Night in his own way. Hands clapped him on his shoulders as he passed, and roaring warriors wished him well on the journey into battle, or boasted of how many orcs they would slay in his name.

He joined with their boasts, but his heart was heavy as he wondered how many would live to see another day like today. These were hard, sinewy warriors with the hunger of wolves, men who had fought beneath his father's banner for years, but would now ride beneath his. He looked into their faces as he passed, hearing their words, but not the sense of them.

He knew and loved these warriors as men, as husbands and as fathers, and every one of them would ride into battle by his command.

To lead such men was an honour, an honour he did not know if he was worthy to bear.

Sigmar put aside such melancholy thoughts as he emerged from the throng of armoured warriors to stand before his father. Raised up on his throne, King Björn of the Unberogen tribe sat between two carved statues of snarling wolves, and was as intimidating a figure as ever, despite his advancing years.

A crown of bronze sat upon his brow, and hair the colour of iron was bound in numerous braids that hung about his face and neck. Eyes of flint that had resolutely faced the many horrors of the world stared out with paternal affection at the warriors gathered before him as they offered praise to Ulric that he might grant them courage in the coming battles.

Though his father would not be riding to war with them, he wore a mail shirt fashioned by Alaric. The quality of the shirt was beyond the skill of any human smith, but had taken the dwarf less than a day to make. Across the king's lap was his feared axe, Soultaker, its twin blades red in the firelight.

As Sigmar approached the throne, Alfgeir gave him a brief nod of acknowledgement, his bronze armour gleaming gold, and his unsmiling face apparently carved from granite. Eoforth bowed to Sigmar, and took a step back, his long robes singular in a room full of armoured warriors, his sharp intellect making him one of the king's most trusted advisors. His counsel was both noble and fair, and the Unberogens had many times benefited from his foresight and wisdom.

'My son,' said Björn, waving Sigmar to stand beside him. 'Is everything well? You look troubled.'

'I am well,' said Sigmar, taking his place at his father's right hand. 'I'm simply impatient for dawn. I hunger to put the Bonecrusher to the sword and drive his army back into the mountains.'

'Curse his name,' said Björn. 'That damn greenskin warlord has been the scourge of our people for years. The sooner his head is mounted above this throne the better.'

Sigmar followed his father's gaze, feeling the weight of expectation upon him as he saw the many trophies mounted on the wall above the throne. Orcs, beasts and foul horrors with great fangs, curling horns and loathsome scaled skin were rammed onto iron spikes, the wall below stained with the blood of their deaths.

Here was the head of Skarskan Bloodhelm, the orc that had threatened to drive the Endals from their homelands, until Björn had ridden to the aid of King Marbad. There was the flayed hide of the great, nameless beast of the Howling Hills that had terrorised the Cherusens for years, until the king of the Unberogen had tracked it to its hideous lair and taken its head with one mighty blow of Soultaker.

A score of other trophies surrounded them, each one with an accompanying tale of heroism that had thrilled Sigmar as a youth, crouched at his father's feet, and which had stirred mighty, heroic longings in his breast.

'Any word from the riders you sent south?' asked his father, and Sigmar put aside the thought of trying to equal his father's deeds.

'Some,' said Sigmar, 'and none of it good. The orcs have come down from the mountains in great numbers, but it seems they are not going back. Normally they come and they raid and kill, and then they go back to the highlands, but this Bonecrusher keeps them together, and with every slaughter more flock to his banner every day.'

'Then there is no time to waste,' said his father. 'You will do the land a great service as you earn your shield. It is no small thing to reach manhood, boy, and as far as tests of courage go, this is a big one. It is only right that you should feel fear.'

Sigmar squared his shoulders before his father's stern gaze, and said, 'I am not afraid, father. I have killed greenskins before, and death holds no fear for me.'

King Björn leaned close and lowered his voice so that only Sigmar could hear him. 'It is not fear of death that I speak. I already know that you have faced great peril and lived to tell of it. Any fool can swing a sword, but to lead men in battle, to hold their lives in your hands, to put yourself in a position to be judged by your fellow warriors and your king: it is right you should fear these things.

'The serpent of fear gnaws at your belly, my son. I know this, for it twisted in my gut when Redmane Dregor, your grandfather, sent me out to earn my shield.'

Sigmar looked into his father's eyes, both a misty grey, and saw true understanding there and an empathy with what he felt. The knowledge that a warrior king as mighty as Björn of the Unberogen had once felt the same thing made him smile in relief.

'You always did know what I was thinking,' said Sigmar.

'You are my son,' said Björn simply.

'I am your *only* son. What if I should fail?'

'You will not, for the blood of your ancestors is strong. You will go on to do great things as chieftain of the Unberogen when the grass grows tall on my tomb. Fear is not something to turn away from, my son. Understand that its power over a man comes from his willingness to take the easy course of action, to run away, to hide, and you will defeat it. A true hero never runs when he can fight, never takes the easy course over what he knows is right. Remember that, and you will not falter.'

Sigmar nodded at his father's words, staring out over the warriors, who filled the longhouse with song and raucous merrymaking.

As if sensing his scrutiny, Wolfgart leapt onto a trestle table groaning with mugs of beer and heaped with plates of meat and fruit.

The table bent dangerously under his weight as he swept his mighty sword from its sheath and raised it high in one hand. The sword was aimed straight and unwavering towards the roof, an incredible feat of strength, for the weight of his weapon was enormous.

'Sigmar! Sigmar! Sigmar!' roared Wolfgart, and the chant was taken up by every warrior in the longhouse. The walls seemed to shake with the power of their voices, and Sigmar knew he would not let them down. Pendrag joined Wolfgart on the table, and even the normally quiet Trinovantes was caught up in the mood of adulation that swept the hall.

'You see,' said his father, 'these men will be your battle-thanes on the morrow, and they are ready to fight and die by your command. They believe in you, so draw strength from that belief, and recognise your own worth.'

As the chant of his name continued around the hall, Sigmar watched as Wolfgart lowered his sword and drew the blade across his palm. Blood welled from the cut, and Wolfgart smeared it upon his cheeks.

'Ulric, god of battle, on this Blood Night, give me the strength to fight in your name!' he shouted.

Every warrior in the hall followed Wolfgart's example, drawing blades across their skin, and offering blood to the harsh, unforgiving god of the winter wolves. Sigmar stepped forward to honour the blood of his warriors, drawing the long-bladed hunting knife from his belt, and slicing the blade across his bare forearm.

His warriors roared in approval, banging the handles of their swords and axes upon their chests. As the cheering continued, the table Wolfgart and Pendrag stood upon finally collapsed under their combined weight, and they were buried in splintered timbers and plates of boar meat, and drenched in beer. Roars of laughter pealed from the walls, and yet more mugs of beer were emptied over the fallen warriors, who took Trinovantes's outstretched hands and struggled to their feet with bellows of mirth.

Sigmar laughed along with his warriors as his father said, 'With such stout-hearted men beside you, how can you fail?'

'Wolfgart is a scoundrel,' said Sigmar, 'but he has the strength of Ulric in his blood, and Pendrag has a scholar's brain in that thick skull of his.'

'I know both men's virtues and vices,' said his father, 'just as you must learn the hearts of those who will seek to counsel you. Draw worthy men to you, and learn their strengths and their weaknesses. Keep only those who make you stronger, and cut away those who weaken you, for they will drag you down with them. When you find good men, honour them, value them and love them as your dearest brothers, for they will stand shoulder to shoulder with you and hear the cry of the wolf in battle.'

'I will,' promised Sigmar.

'Together, men are strong, but divided we are weak. Draw your sword-brothers close and stand together in all things. Swear this to me, Sigmar.'

'I swear it, father.'

'Now go and join them,' said his father, 'and come back to me after the fighting is done, either with your shield or upon it.'

TWO

Astofen Bridge

BOOMING WAR DRUMS beat the air with the raucous tattoo of the orc horde as they hurled their bodies at the log walls of Astofen. A seething green mass of armoured bodies surrounded the river settlement, the reek of their unwashed flesh and the primal ferocity of their battle-cries filling the air with a terrifying sense of impending doom.

'They can't hold much longer,' said Wolfgart, lying on his front beside Sigmar in the long grass of the gently sloping hill, a league to the east of the besieged town. 'The gate's already buckling.'

Sigmar nodded and said, 'We have to wait for Trinovantes.'

'If we wait much longer there will be no town to save,' said Pendrag, all but invisible, swathed in his scaled green cloak.

'If we attack before he is in position then we are lost,' said Sigmar. 'The orcs are too many for us to fight head on.'

'There's no such thing as too many orcs,' snarled Wolfgart, his hands balled into angry fists. 'We've ridden for days without sign of the greenskins, now here they are before us. I say we sound the war horns and Morr take the hindmost!'

'No,' said Sigmar. 'To fight such a host on equal terms is to die, and I have no intention of returning to Reikdorf upon my shield.'

Despite his words to Wolfgart, Sigmar longed to ride with his banner unfurled, the wind in his hair and the clarion call of war horns in his ears, but he knew he must restrain his urge to slay greenskins for now.

Concealed behind the ridge of the eastern hills, the Unberogen horsemen had the element of surprise, for the orcs' attention was firmly fixed on the embattled settlement before them, but surprise would not be enough to defeat this horde, for surely a thousand or more greenskins surrounded the town.

Astofen sat among a series of low, rocky hills on the banks of a fast-flowing river of the plains that poured from the towering peaks of the Grey Mountains to the south. To see such an open landscape had come as a shock to the young men raised in the forests, when they had ridden from the trees only a day previously, and Sigmar had not dreamed that the land in which he lived was so vast.

The town's palisade walls were formed from thick logs, the ends of which were sharpened into points, and which boasted defensive towers at each corner. Hoardings formed from planks and wetted hides protected a walkway that ran around the edge of the ramparts, and from here the men and women of Astofen shouted their defiance as they hurled heavy spears into the heaving mass of green bodies.

Sigmar watched with fierce pride as each missile felled an orc, but saw that such deaths were making no difference to the ferocity of the attack. The greenskins were an undisciplined rabble, fighting without apparent cohesion or plan, but one look told Sigmar that simple brutality and numbers would carry the day without difficulty.

Scores of spindle-limbed goblins sent flaming arrows over the timber walls of the town, and many of the closely huddled buildings within were ablaze.

Hulking orcs with green skin so dark that it was practically black waited beside a ramshackle battering ram that sat on splayed wheels, and looked as though a blind man had constructed it. Beside the battering ram, heavy wooden catapults lobbed a variety of missiles at the town: rocks, flaming pitch or even howling orcs with cleavers.

Thin lines of black smoke were etched against the sky from hundreds of fires, and grisly totems had been driven into the hard earth with crude fetishes and bloody trophies dangling from great, horned skulls. The orc horde was easily the largest force of greenskins any of them had ever seen. Each creature was heavily muscled, armoured, and armed with huge blades and a ferocious thirst for battle that was unmatched in all but the most frenzied berserker.

At the centre of the horde, an enormous orc in dark armour waved a monstrous axe, and even from this distance it was clear that the creature must surely be the host's master.

'Come on, Sigmar,' hissed Wolfgart. 'Unleash us!'

'Do you want to die?' asked Pendrag. 'We have to wait. Trinovantes will not fail us.'

Sigmar fervently hoped that Pendrag was right as he looked along the rutted earth road that led from Astofen's gate and followed the course of the river as it bent southwards towards a sturdy stone bridge a league away. Beyond the bridge, the road petered out past a line of trees, and the landscape opened into plains of hard, scrubby grass and scattered copses.

He shielded his eyes from the sun, and ignored Wolfgart's impatient bristling, hoping to see a waving banner, but there was nothing, and he silently willed his friend to hurry.

'As Ulric wills it,' whispered Sigmar, chewing his bottom lip as he watched the fighting unfold below, knowing that if they did not attack soon, Astofen would be lost.

Sigmar returned his attention to the town below as the orc leader hurled his great axe at the gate, and a roaring bellow of unleashed fury rose from the greenskin horde. The booming of the drums rose in tempo, and the armoured tide of orcs surged towards Astofen.

Grunting, sweating orcs pushed the wobbling battering ram forwards, its carved head wrought in the form of a giant fist. More flaming arrows arced over the horde, and the clash of iron blades against one another rang like a war cry to the brazen gods of battle.

'There!' cried Pendrag. 'Look! By the bridge!'

Sigmar's heart leapt as he followed Pendrag's shout and saw a green banner fluttering in the wind before a stand of trees to the east of the bridge.

'I told you!' laughed Pendrag, leaping to his feet, and sprinting back to his horse.

Sigmar pushed to his feet with a wild war cry, and followed Pendrag, with Wolfgart right on his heels. Two hundred Unberogen horsemen waited out of sight of Astofen, their mounts whinnying impatiently, and their faces alive with the prospect of battle. Spear tips gleamed in the noonday sun, and the bronze rims of wooden shields shone like gold. Pendrag vaulted onto the back of his horse, and swept up Sigmar's banner, a streaming triangle of crimson cloth with the device of a great boar emblazoned upon it in black.

The sunlight caught the richness of the colour, and to Sigmar's eyes it seemed as though the banner was a sheet of blood, bound to a spear. He gripped his dapple grey stallion's mane and swung himself onto its back.

Sigmar's heart beat wildly, and he laughed with the sheer joy of the waiting being over. The agony of watching his people suffer and die was at an end, and the orcs would pay for their ill-advised aggression. Sigmar slid a long spear with a heavy iron point from the quiver slung around his horse's neck, and accepted his shield from a nearby warrior.

He lifted shield and spear high as Wolfgart began chanting his name.

'Unberogens!' roared Sigmar. 'We ride!'

SIGMAR DUG HIS heels into his mount's flanks, and the beast surged forwards as eager for the fight as he. With a howling war cry, his warriors followed him, and lifted their own spears high as Wolfgart blew a soaring, ululating blast of the war horn.

His horse crested the rise before him, and he leaned forward over its neck as it thundered downhill. He threw a glance over his shoulder as his warriors came on in two ragged lines, one after the other. Their armour gleamed, and brightly coloured cloaks were streaming out behind them like the wings of mighty dragons.

The ground shook with the hammer blows of their hoof beats, and Wolfgart blew the war horn again and again, its valiant note easily carrying through the air. Sigmar rode hard and fast, urging his mount to greater speed as the tempo of the battle ahead paused and both orc and man turned to see what fate rode towards them.

Cheers erupted from the timber walls of Astofen as its defenders saw the hundreds of riders galloping to their rescue. Sigmar gripped the flanks of his horse with his knees, lifting his shield and spear high for his following warriors to see.

In disdain for the foe before him, Sigmar had eschewed armour, and rode without mail or plate to protect him. Like a savage warrior of a forgotten age, Sigmar rode tall in the wind, his hair a golden stream behind him, and the muscles of his chest pumped for battle.

The roaring of the orcs grew louder with every passing heartbeat. The wall of hard, green flesh and armour drew closer. Shields were turned to face them, each one decorated with leering faces, fanged maws or crude tribal symbols, and long spears were thrust towards the riders. Arrows and javelins flew from Astofen with renewed hope as the warriors rode onwards, and the giant orc at the centre of the horde bellowed and roared, his orders accompanied by sweeps of a great spear with a haft the thickness of Sigmar's arm.

The orcs were so close that Sigmar could smell the rank odour of their unclean bodies, and see the terrible scars of tribal markings worked into the flesh of their arms and faces. The eyes of the orcs were a hot red, deep-set in blunt, porcine faces with enormous fangs jutting from their lower jaws.

Just as it seemed that the thundering line of horsemen must surely crash into the jagged wall of iron, Sigmar hurled his spear with all his might. His throw was true, and the heavy iron tip smashed through an orc shield to impale its bearer. The sharpened tip exploded from the orc's back and plunged into the greenskin standing behind it. Both fell to the ground as a hundred more spears slashed through the air, and orcs fell by the dozen. Sigmar gripped his horse's mane, and pulled hard to the side while pressing his knees against its flanks.

The stallion gave a snort of protest at this harsh treatment, but wheeled immediately, and galloped along the length of the orc line, less than a spear's length from the enemy blades. Sigmar howled in triumph as black-shafted arrows leapt from goblin bows, but flew wide or over his head.

He heard a whooping yell, and saw Pendrag behind him, a trio of arrows wedged in the timbers of his shield, yet Sigmar's crimson and black banner was still held proudly aloft. His friend's face was alight with savage joy, and Sigmar gave thanks to Ulric that neither Pendrag nor the banner had fallen.

The orc line was still a solid wall of shields and blades, but already Sigmar saw that it was beginning to buckle as orcs sought to get to grips with the horsemen.

Another thunder of hooves announced the arrival of the second line of Unberogen horsemen, and Sigmar saw Wolfgart charging at their head. Each horseman carried a short, recurved bow, the strings pulled taut and arrows nocked as they controlled their wild ride with pressure from their thighs.

Wolfgart blew a strident note on the war horn, and a hundred goose feather fletched arrows flew straight and true into the orc line. All found homes in green flesh, but not all were fatal. As Sigmar wheeled his stallion once more, and drew another spear, he saw many of the orcs simply snap the shafts from their bodies, and hurl them aside with bestial roars of challenge. Another volley of arrows followed the first, before Wolfgart's warriors wheeled their mounts around violently and rode away.

This time the greenskins could not restrain themselves, and the line of shields broke apart as orcs charged wildly from their battle line in pursuit of Wolfgart's riders. Spears and arrows gave chase, and Sigmar yelled in anger as he saw wounded warriors fall from their mounts.

Wolfgart's horse pulled to a halt beside Sigmar, and his sword-brother put up his war horn to draw his greatsword from the sheath across his back. Wolfgart's face was a mirror of his own, with a sheen of sweat and teeth bared in ferocious battle fury.

Pendrag rode alongside, his war axe unsheathed, and said, 'Time to get bloody!'

Sigmar raked back his heels and said, 'Remember, two blasts of the horn and we ride for the bridge!'

'It's not me you need worry about!' laughed Pendrag as Wolfgart urged his mount forward, his huge sword swinging around his head in wide decapitating arcs.

Sigmar and Pendrag thundered after their friend as the pursuing mob of orcs drew near. The re-formed Unberogen horsemen followed their leaders, charging with all the fury and power they were famed for, a howling war cry taken up by every warrior as they hurled their spears, before drawing swords or hefting axes.

More orcs fell, and Sigmar skewered a thick-bodied orc, who wore a great, antlered helmet, the spear punching down though the creature's breastplate and pinning it to the ground. Even as the spear quivered in the orc's chest, Sigmar reached down and swept up his hammer, Ghal-maraz, the mighty gift presented to him by Kurgan Ironbeard earlier that spring.

Then the two ancestral enemies slammed together in a thunderclap of iron and rage.

The charging horsemen hit the orc line like the fist of Ulric that had flattened the top of the Fauschlag rock of the Teutogens in the north. Shields splintered, and swords cleaved orc flesh as the bonecrushing force of the charge crashed through the scattered greenskins.

Sigmar swung his hammer, and smashed an orc skull to shards, the thick iron of its helmet no defence against the ancient runic power bound to the weapon. He smote left and right, each blow crushing heads, and splintering bone and armour. Blood sprayed his naked flesh, his hair thick with gobbets of orc blood, and the head of his hammer dripping with the gruel of their brain matter.

Axes and notched swords rang from his shield, and his horse snorted and stamped with its hooves, kicking with its back legs to stove in the ribs and skulls of goblins that sought to hamstring it with cruel knives.

'In the name of Ulric!' shouted Sigmar, urging his mount deeper into the disorganised mass of orcs, and laying about himself with mighty sweeps of his hammer.

At the centre of the horde, Sigmar could see the enormous orc that led this furious horde, the warlord known as Bonecrusher. Its massive bulk was clad head to foot in armour forged from sheets of dark iron, fastened to its flesh with great spikes. A horned helmet covered its thick skull, and bloodied, yellowed fangs jutted from its oversized, pugnacious jaw.

It seemed that the beast was aware of him too, for it jabbed its thick spear towards him, and the press of orc warriors around the Unberogens grew thicker and more vicious. With every stroke of his hammer, Sigmar knew their time was running out, and he risked diverting his attention from immediate threats to see how his sword-brothers fared.

Over to his right, Wolfgart's greatsword swept left and right, hewing half a dozen orcs to ruin with every blow. Behind him, Pendrag's mane of hair was as red as the banner he carried, the curved blades of his axe cleaving through armour and flesh with deafening clangs and thuds. That Pendrag also carried Sigmar's banner seemed not to hamper him at all, and it too was a weapon, the iron point at its base smashing through helmet visors or punching through the tops of unprotected skulls.

Sigmar wheeled his horse, sending one orc sailing backwards with a mighty underarm swing of Ghal-maraz, and crushing another's chest with the return stroke. All around him, Unberogen warriors were cutting a bloody path through the orcs, but for all the carnage they caused, the orcs had the numbers to soak up such death without flinching.

Hundreds more were pushing forwards, and as the furious impetus of the charge began to diminish, Sigmar could see that the orcs were massing for a devastating counter-attack. Packed in like this, with their backs to the walls of Astofen, the orcs would eventually overwhelm them.

Unberogen warriors were being dragged from their mounts one by one, and horses fell screaming as goblins opened their guts with quick slashes. The noose was closing in, and it was time to make their escape.

'Wolfgart!' shouted Sigmar. 'Now!'

But a knot of howling orcs, their axes and swords tearing at his armour, surrounded Sigmar's sword-brother. Without a shield, Wolfgart's hauberk was battered, and links of chainmail hung dripping from his body in weeping sheets of iron rings. His sword hacked and cut, but for every orc that died, another two stepped in to fight.

'Pendrag!' cried Sigmar, lifting his bloody hammer.

'I'm with you!' answered Pendrag, urging his mount onwards with the banner held high.

Together, Sigmar and Pendrag charged into the creatures attacking their sword-brother, hammer and axe forging a gory path through the orcs. Sigmar's hammer smashed the head from an orc's shoulders, and he shouted, 'Wolfgart, blow the horn!'

'Aye, I know!' replied Wolfgart breathlessly, putting his sword through the chest of the last of his attackers. 'What's the rush? I would have killed them all in time.'

'We don't have time,' said Sigmar. 'Blow the damned horn!'

Wolfgart nodded, and switched to a one-handed grip on his sword, before lifting the curling ram's horn from the loop of chain around his waist and giving voice to two sharp blasts.

'Come on!' bellowed Sigmar. 'Ride for the open ground across the bridge.'

Barely had the echoes of the war horn faded when the Unberogen had turned their horses and were riding hard for the south with practiced skill. Sigmar waved his hammer, and shouted, 'For Ulric's sake ride hard, my brothers!'

The horsemen needed no encouragement, leaning low over their mounts' necks as the orcs howled in triumph at their enemy's flight. Sigmar held his horse from riding alongside its fellows as he scanned the battlefield to make sure that he left none of his warriors behind.

The ground before Astofen was littered with the detritus of battle: bodies and blood, screaming horses and shattered shields. The vast majority of the dead were orcs and goblins, but too many were armoured men, their bodies already being sliced apart by knife-wielding goblins, or bludgeoned unrecognisable by roaring orcs.

'Are we waiting for something in particular?' asked Pendrag, his horse nervously flicking its head, as the orcs gathered for the pursuit. Orc captains bellowed orders at their warriors, and lumbering mobs of greenskins with axes held in each fist set off towards the retreating Unberogen horsemen.

'So many dead,' said Sigmar.

'Two more if we don't move now!' shouted Pendrag over the roar of charging orcs.

Sigmar nodded, turned his horse to the south, and let loose a mighty curse on the heads of greenskins everywhere as a spiteful volley of arrows sliced through the air. He heard the despairing cry of the folk of Astofen as he rode south, their hopes of salvation dashed as cruelly as if they had never come.

'Have hope, my people,' said Sigmar. 'You are not abandoned.'

DEEP WITHIN THE shadows of the trees on either side of the bridge, Trinovantes watched the retreating horsemen with a mixture of excitement and sadness. Too many of the horses galloped towards his position without their riders, and he felt an aching sadness in his heart as he recognised many of the mounts and recalled which riders they had borne.

'Stand ready!' he shouted. 'And Ulric guide your thrusts!'

Beside him, twenty-five warriors in heavy hauberks of mail and plate stood with thick-shafted spears with long, stabbing blades. These were the heaviest, strongest men in Sigmar's force, thick of limb and stiff of back: men for whom the concept of retreat was as unknown as compassion was to an orc. Another twenty-five were hidden in the trees across the road: fifty men with very specific orders from their young leader.

Trinovantes smiled as he remembered the pained smile upon Sigmar's earnest face as Trinovantes had stepped forward when Sigmar had asked for a volunteer to lead this desperate mission.

'I'm counting on you, brother,' Sigmar had said, taking him to one side before the battle. 'Hold the orcs long enough for us to rearm and reforge our strength, but only that long. When you hear a long blast of the war horn, get clear, you understand?'

Trinovantes had nodded and said, 'I understand what is expected of us.'

'I wish–' began Sigmar, but Trinovantes had interrupted him with a shake of his head.

'It has to be me. Wolfgart is too wild, and Pendrag must ride at your side with the banner.'

Sigmar had seen the determination in his face, and said, 'Then Ulric be with you, brother.'

'If I fight well, he will be,' said Trinovantes. 'Now go. Ride with the wolf lord at your side, and kill them all.'

Trinovantes had watched Sigmar return to his men, and raised his sword in salute before swiftly leading his men around the eastern hills, hidden from the orcs, until they had reached this place of concealment on the other side of the bridge.

Looking at the faces of the men under his command, he saw tension, anger and solemn reverence for the fight to come. A few men kissed wolf-tail talismans, or blooded their wolf-skin pelts with cuts to their cheeks. There were no jokes, no ribald banter or ludicrous boasts, as might be expected from warriors about to do battle, and Trinovantes understood that every one of them knew the importance of the duty they were about to perform.

Retreating Unberogen horsemen rode south towards the bridge in ragged groups of three or four, scattered and tired from the frenetic battle. Their arrows and spears were spent, and their swords bent and chipped from impacts with orc weapons and shields.

Their shields were splintered and their armour torn, but they were unbowed, and rode with the soul of the land surging through them. Trinovantes could feel it, a thrumming connection that was more than simply the thunder of approaching horsemen.

In the last few moments left to him before battle, he instinctively understood the bond between this rich, bountiful land and the men who inhabited it. From distant realms they had come in ages past, and carved a home amid the wild forests, taming the earth and driving back the creatures that sought to keep them from what the gods had seen fit to grant them.

Men tended the land, and the land returned their devotion tenfold in crops and animals. This was a land of men, and no greenskin warlord was going to take that which they had worked and fought to create.

The sound of hooves rose in pitch, and Trinovantes looked up from his thoughts to see the first of Sigmar's warriors riding hard across the timbers of the bridge. The structure was ancient and dwarf-made, the timbers pale and bleached by the sun, laid across stone pillars decorated with carvings long since worn smooth by the passage of centuries.

Horsemen rode across the bridge, pushing hard for the fresh weapons that Trinovantes and his men had stacked beyond the trees further south. Scores rode past, their horses' flanks lathered with sweat and blood.

'Who would have guessed Sigmar would be the last to quit the field of battle, eh?' shouted Trinovantes as he saw Wolfgart, Pendrag and Sigmar riding at the rear of the galloping horsemen.

Grim laughter greeted his words, and Trinovantes snapped down the visor of his battle helmet as he saw the orcs pursuing the riders with relentless, single-minded purpose. Obscured by the dust clouds thrown up by the riders, they looked like misshapen daemons of shadow, their bodies hunched, and only the inextinguishable coals of their eyes distinct. Despite their graceless, thick limbs and monstrously heavy iron armour, their speed was impressive, and Trinovantes knew that it was time to perform his duty to the king's son.

He hefted his axe, the blades polished and bright, and kissed the image of a snarling wolf worked into the spike at the top of the shaft. He lifted the weapon towards the sky, and felt a cold shiver as he saw a single raven circling above them.

The last of the horsemen rode across the bridge, and Trinovantes looked down in time to see Sigmar staring straight at him. As the moment stretched, he felt the simple gratitude of his friend fill him with strength.

'Unberogens, we march!' he shouted, and he led his men onto the road.

SIGMAR SPAT DUST as he halted his horse with a sharp jerk of its mane, and circled the cache of spears and swords left beyond the bridge by Trinovantes. The weapons were stacked in such a manner as to naturally form the horsemen up into a wedge aimed at the bridge, and Sigmar saw Trinovantes's touch in the cunning of the design.

'Hurry!' he cried, leaping from his horse and accepting a skin of water from a warrior with bloody arms. He drank deeply, and emptied the rest over his head, washing the blood from his face as he heard the roar of charging orcs and the clash of weapons behind him.

Sigmar wiped a hand over his dripping face, and pushed through his warriors to better see the furious combat raging at the bridge.

Sunlight flashed on stabbing spears, and Sigmar saw the proud green of Trinovantes's banner borne aloft in the heart of the battle. Orc war cries rose in bellicose counterpoint to the shouted oaths to Ulric, and though the spearmen fought with iron resolve, Sigmar could already see that their line was bending back under the fearsome pressure of the attack.

'Get fresh spears and swords, and remount!' shouted Sigmar, his voice filled with fiery urgency. 'Trinovantes is buying us time, and we won't be wasting it!'

His urgings were unnecessary, for his warriors were swiftly hurling aside their bent and broken swords, before rearming themselves with fresh blades. Every man knew that this time was being bought with the lives of their friends, and not a second was wasted in idle banter.

The name of Ulric was roared, warriors offering the kills they had made to the fearsome god of battle, and Sigmar let them rejoice in the exultation of battle and survival.

Pendrag nodded to him, Sigmar's banner stabbed into the earth as he ran a whetstone over the blades of his axe. 'Trinovantes?'

'Holding,' said Sigmar, angrily wiping the head of Ghal-maraz with a ragged scrap of leather, unwilling to allow the orc blood and brain matter to foul its noble face a second more.

'How much longer?' asked Pendrag.

Sigmar shrugged. 'Not long. They must sound the retreat soon.'

'Retreat?' asked Pendrag. 'No, they won't be retreating. You know that.'

'They must,' said Sigmar, 'or else they will be lost.'

Pendrag put out his hand, and stopped Sigmar's furious cleaning.

'They won't be retreating,' repeated Pendrag. 'They knew that. As did you. Do not dishonour their sacrifice by denying it.'

'Denying what?' bellowed Wolfgart as he rode to join them, his expression eager as though they fought a skirmish against disorganised bandits instead of blood-maddened orcs.

Sigmar ignored Wolfgart's question, and looked deep into Pendrag's eyes, seeing an understanding of what he had ordered Trinovantes to do in the full knowledge of what that order entailed.

'Nothing,' said Sigmar swinging the heavy length of Ghal-maraz as though it weighed nothing at all.

'King Kurgan's weapon is earning its name,' said Wolfgart.

'Aye,' said Sigmar. 'A kingly gift, right enough, but there're more skulls to be split before this day is out.'

'True,' agreed Wolfgart, hefting his greatsword meaningfully. 'We'll get to them soon enough.'

'No,' said Sigmar, swinging back onto his horse, and looking north to the battle raging at the bridge, 'it won't be soon enough.'

BLOOD POOLED IN Trinovantes's boot, a deep wound in his thigh washing blood down his leg, and sticking the wool of his tunic to his skin.

An orc cleaver had smashed his shield to kindling, and cut into his leg, before he had gutted the beast with a swipe of his axe.

His arms felt as though they were weighted down with iron, his muscles throbbing painfully with the effort of the fight. Screams and roars of hatred echoed deafeningly within Trinovantes's helmet, and sweat ran in rivers down his face.

The warriors with him fought with desperate heroics, their spears stabbing with powerful thrusts that punched between the gaps in the orcs' crude armour and into their flesh. The pale, dusty ground beneath their feet was dark and loamy with blood, both human and orc, and the air stank of sweat and the coppery promise of death.

Spears and axes clashed, wood and iron broke apart, and flesh and bone were carved to ruin with no quarter asked or given from either side.

The warrior next to Trinovantes fell, an orc blade smashing through his shoulder and cutting deep into his torso before becoming stuck fast in his chest. The orc fought to drag its weapon clear, but the jagged edge of the sword remained wedged in the man's ribs. Trinovantes stepped in, his leg on fire with pain, and swung his axe in a furious two-handed swing that smashed into the orc's open jaw, and cleaved the top of its skull away.

'For Ulric!' shouted Trinovantes, channelling all his hatred for the orcs into the blow.

The body swayed for a moment before dropping, and Trinovantes screamed as his injured leg threatened to give way beneath him.

A hand reached out to steady him, and he shouted his thanks without seeing who helped him. The noise of battle seemed to grow louder, the cries of dying men and the exultant roars of the orcs sounding as though they were bellowed right in his ears.

Trinovantes stumbled, dropping to one knee as his vision greyed, and the clamour of the fighting suddenly diminished from its previous volume to something heard as if from a great distance. He planted the blades of his axe on the ground as he tried to force himself back to his feet.

All around him, the warriors of the Unberogen were dying, their blood spurting from opened bellies or torn throats. He saw an orc lift a wounded spearman and slam his body down on the stone parapet of the bridge, almost breaking him in two before hurling his limp corpse into the river.

Goblin archers on the bridge loosed shafts into the midst of the battle, uncaring of which combatants their arrows hit. Trinovantes felt the warmth of the wet ground beneath him, the sun on his face and the coolness of the sweat plastering his body beneath his armour.

However, for all the death around him, there was heroism and defiance too.

Trinovantes watched as a warrior with two spears punched through his back spread his arms, and leapt towards a group of orcs forcing their way past the flanks. He knocked three of them from the bridge to drown in the river. Sword-brothers fought back to back as the numbers of Unberogens thinned, while the orcs pressed across the bridge with even greater ferocity.

A spear thrust towards him, and instinct took over as the sights and sounds of battle returned with all their vicious din. Trinovantes's axe smashed the blade from the spear shaft, and he pushed to his feet with a cry of rage and pain. He swayed aside from the blunted weapon, forcing down the pain of his injured leg, and swinging his axe at his attacker.

His blade cut the orc's arm from its body, but its charge was unstoppable, and its sheer bulk carried him to the ground. Its blood sprayed him, and he spat the foul, reeking liquid from his mouth.

Too close for a proper strike, he slammed the haft of his axe against the orc's face, the fangs splintering beneath the blow. The orc's head snapped back, and Trinovantes rolled from beneath it, rising to one knee, and hammering his axe into its skull.

Shrieking pain exploded in his back, and Trinovantes looked down to see a long spear jutting from his chest, the blade wider than his forearm. Blood squirted from either side of the metal, his blood. He opened his mouth, but the weapon was wrenched from his body, and with it any breath with which to scream.

Trinovantes dropped his axe, strength and life pouring from him in a red flood. He looked around at the scene of slaughter, men dying and torn apart by orcs as they finally could stand no more.

His vision dimmed, and he slumped forwards, his face pressed into the bloody ground.

His axe lay beside him, and with the last of his strength, he reached out and curled his fingers around the grip. Ulric's halls were no place for a warrior without a weapon.

The squawking cry of something out of place penetrated the killing sounds of slaughter, and he lifted his head to see a large raven sitting on the stone of the bridge, the depthless dark of its eyes boring into him with an unflinching gaze.

Despite the carnage, the bird remained unmoving, and Trinovantes saw his banner flutter in the wind behind it, the green fabric bright against the brilliant blue of the sky.

The pain fled his body, and he thought of his twin brother and older sister as he lay his head down upon the rich earth of the land he had fought and died to protect. He heard a distant rumble through the ground, a rising thunder of drums, a sound that made him smile as he recognised its source: the sound of Unberogen horsemen on the charge.

SIGMAR SAW TRINOVANTES fall to Bonecrusher's spear, and let out an anguished howl of anger and loss. The orcs were across the bridge and had fanned out past the trees in a ragged line of charging bodies. After the hard fight at the bridge, any cohesion to their force was lost, and though Trinovantes and his men were dead, they had reaped a magnificent tally of orc corpses.

The orcs were in the grip of their battle lust, and Sigmar saw Bonecrusher desperately trying to form his warriors into a fighting line before the horsemen reached them.

However, it was already too late for them.

Riding at the tip of a wedge of nearly a hundred and fifty horsemen, Sigmar rode with fire and hate in his heart, Ghal-maraz held high for all to see. The ground shook to the beat of pounding hooves, and Sigmar scented the sure and certain tang of victory.

Pendrag rode to his right, the crimson banner snapping in the wind, and Wolfgart was on his left, his blade unsheathed and ready to take more heads.

Sigmar gripped the mane of his stallion tightly. The great beast was tired, but eager to bear its rider back into battle.

Arrows leapt from bows, and spears filled the air as the Unberogen riders loosed one last volley before impact.

Orcs fell before their spears and arrows, and cries of triumph turned to bellows of pain as Sigmar's charge hit home.

The wedge of Unberogen horsemen cleaved through the orcs, weapons flashing and blood spraying as they avenged the deaths of their brothers in arms. Sigmar's hammer smote orc skulls, and crushed chests as he screamed his lost friend's name.

Strength and purpose flowed along his limbs, and whatever he struck, died. No enemy in the world could stand before him and live. Ghal-maraz was an extension of his arm, its power incredible and unstoppable in his hands.

Blood sprayed the air as the Unberogen riders trampled orcs, easy meat now that their numbers were thinned and they were scattered. With room to manoeuvre, the horsemen were in their element, charging hither and thither, and killing orcs with every spear thrust or axe blow. Orcs were crushed beneath iron-shod hooves, smashed into the ground as the horsemen circled and charged again and again, now that they had the open ground in their favour.

Sigmar killed orcs by the dozen, his hammer sweeping out and crushing the life from them as though they were little more than irritants. His stallion's flanks were drenched in orc blood, and his iron-hard flesh dripped with their gore.

At the centre of the host, Sigmar saw the mighty orc who led the greenskins. Unberogen warriors surrounded Bonecrusher, eager to claim the glory of killing the warlord, but its strength and ferocity were unmatched by any orc his men had fought, and all who came near it died.

'Ulric guide my hammer!' shouted Sigmar, urging the stallion towards the furious mêlée surrounding Bonecrusher. He leapt piles of orc bodies, smashing aside those greenskins foolish enough to get in his way with wild, magnificent sweeps of his hammer.

The battle around him faded until it was little more than a backdrop to his charge, a muted chorus to accompany his performance. His every sense turned inwards until all he could hear was the roar of his breath and the frenetic pounding of his heart as he rode towards his foe.

Bonecrusher saw him coming, and bellowed a challenge, bloody foam gathering at its fanged jaws as it spread its arms wide. Its spear was aimed towards Sigmar's horse, and as the stallion leapt the last pile of corpses, Sigmar released its mane and hurled himself from its back.

His mount veered away from the thrusting spear as Sigmar sailed through the air, taking his hammer in a two-handed grip.

Sigmar loosed an ululating yell of ancestral hate as he swung his hammer at the warlord.

Ghal-maraz smashed down on Bonecrusher's skull, and destroyed it utterly, the hammer driving on through the body, and finally exiting in a bloody welter of smashed bone and meat. Sigmar landed beside the body before it fell, and spun on his heel to deliver a thunderous blow to the headless warlord's spine.

The greenskin chieftain, who had once been the scourge of the lands of men, toppled to the ground, its body pulverised by Sigmar's fury.

He swept his hammer around, slaying the orcs who stood close to their chief in a furious, unstoppable carnage. Within moments, the largest and most powerful orcs of the horde were dead, and Sigmar bellowed his triumph to the skies, slathered from head to foot in blood, his hammer pulsing with the light of battle.

A horse drew to a halt before him, and Sigmar looked up to see Wolfgart staring down at him with a look of awed disbelief and not a little fear in his eyes.

'They've broken!' shouted Wolfgart. 'They're running.'

Sigmar lowered his hammer and blinked, his senses turning outward once again as he took in the scale of the slaughter they had wreaked upon the orcs.

Hundreds of corpses littered the ground, trampled by horses or cut down by Unberogen warriors. What little remained of the orc horde was fleeing in disarray, the power of their lust for battle broken by the death of their leader.

'Chase them, brother,' spat Sigmar. 'Ride them down and leave none alive.'

THREE
Morr's Due

From her vantage point in the hills surrounding Reikdorf, Ravenna thought the view towards the south quite beautiful and, for a moment, she could almost forget that the young men of her settlement had ridden there to war and death against the greenskins.

Below her, Reikdorf sat on the mud flats that spread from the riverbanks, squat and unlovely, but home nonetheless. The high wooden palisade wall looked bare without the usual complement of warriors, and Ravenna sent a prayer to the gods to look after those who had ridden south.

She shielded her eyes, looking for some sign of Reikdorf's warriors returning.

'I can't see them, Gerreon,' she said, turning towards her younger brother, who walked beside her on the rutted track that led from the cornfields around Reikdorf to its fortified gate.

'I'm not surprised,' said Gerreon, shifting the leather sling that bound his broken wrist to his chest to a more comfortable position. 'The forest's too thick. They could be almost home and you wouldn't see them.'

'They should be back by now,' she said, stopping to loosen her knotted headband and run a hand through her dark hair.

Gerreon paused with her, and said, 'I know. Remember, I should have been with them.'

Ravenna heard the bitter note of regret in her brother's voice, and said, 'I know it was your time to ride to battle, but I am glad you did not.'

He met her gaze, and the anger she saw in his pale-skinned face surprised her. 'You don't understand, Ravenna, they already make fun of me as it is. Now I've missed my first battle, and no matter how courageously I fight from this day on, they'll always remember that I wasn't with them the first time.'

'You were injured,' said Ravenna. 'There was no way you could have fought.'

'I know that, but it will make no difference.'

'Trinovantes will not allow them to mock you,' she said.

'So now I need my twin brother to look after me, is that it?'

'No, that's not what I meant,' she said, growing weary of his petulance, and moving off down the path once more. Her brothers were dear to her, but where Trinovantes was quiet, thoughtful and reserved, Gerreon was quick-witted, handsome and the terror of mothers with pretty daughters, but he could often be cruel.

Like her, his hair was the colour of jet and worn long as was the custom of the Unberogen, and was his pride and joy. Only the previous week, Wolfgart had teased him about looking like a Bretonii catamite, such was the care he lavished on his appearance, and Gerreon had attacked him in a fury.

Gerreon was no match for the older boy, and had ended up flat on his back, nursing a cracked wrist. Trinovantes had stopped Gerreon from making any further rash mistakes, and helped him from Wolfgart's booming laughter to Cradoc the healer, where his wrist was set and a sling fashioned.

When the time had come for Sigmar to earn his shield and ride out to do battle with the greenskins ravaging the southern territories of the Unberogen, Trinovantes had made it clear that Gerreon could not ride with them.

'What use is a warrior who cannot hold onto his horse and bear a weapon?' Trinovantes had said gently, and Ravenna had been glad, for the thought of both her brothers riding off had worried her more than she cared to admit.

Ravenna scanned the trees across the river as she made her way home, looking for a telltale glint of metal, but again she saw nothing.

Early evening sunlight scattered bright reflections from the sluggish river as it meandered along the edge of the village and, despite her worry, she could appreciate the beauty of the place.

Since dawn, she and Gerreon had been amongst those bringing in the summer harvest, him wielding the sickle with his good arm, and her with the basket upon her shoulders. It was hard, thankless work, but everyone had to take their turn in the fields, and she was grateful for Gerreon's presence, despite his foul mood. Though he could not ride to war with the others, he could still wield a sickle and help in the fields.

Now the day's work was done, and she could look forward to resting for the evening and eating some hot food. The harvest had been plentiful, and thanks to the new pumps installed by Pendrag and the dwarf, Alaric, many acres of land that had previously been thin and undernourished were now irrigated and fertile.

The storehouses were full to bursting, and surplus grain left every week in wagons escorted by armed warriors for the east, to be traded with the dwarfs for weapons and armour, for no finer race of metal-workers existed than the mountain folk.

Gerreon caught up to her and said, 'I'm sorry, Ravenna, I didn't mean to make you angry.'

'I'm not angry,' she said. 'I'm just tired and worried.'

'Trinovantes will be fine,' said Gerreon, his voice full of pride and love for his twin. 'He's a great warrior. Not as elegant a swordsman as me, but handy with an axe.'

'I'm worried for them all,' she said, 'Trinovantes, Wolfgart, Pendrag...'

'And Sigmar?' asked Gerreon with a sly grin.

'Yes, for Sigmar too,' she said, avoiding his teasing smile as she said Sigmar's name for fear of blushing.

'Honestly, sister, I don't know what you see in him. Just because he's a king's son doesn't make him special. He's like all the rest of them, boorish and just one hot meal away from being a savage.'

'Hush!' said Ravenna, rising to his bait, and cursing herself for it when he laughed.

'What? Afraid Wolfgart's going to come and break my other wrist? I'll gut him first.'

'Gerreon!' said Ravenna, hearing genuine venom in his voice, but before she could say more, she saw her brother's eyes fix on something behind her. She turned, and followed his gaze across the river, her brother's harsh words forgotten in an instant.

A column of horsemen was emerging from the trees, their pace weary, but voices triumphant. Spears and banners were held high, and the warriors cheered at the sight of Reikdorf.

Answering cries came from the settlement's walls, and the men and women of Reikdorf ran to the gates as word spread that the warriors had returned.

Ravenna felt relieved laughter bubble up inside her, but it died in her breast as she saw a group of warriors in full battle armour leading the horsemen and carrying a litter of shields, upon which was laid the body of a fallen hero.

'Oh no,' cried Gerreon. 'No... please, by all the gods, no!'

Ravenna's heart sank as her first thought was that the fallen warrior was Sigmar, but then she saw that the king's son helped to carry the litter, and that his crimson banner was still held aloft.

Her relief at Sigmar's survival was then crushed savagely and heartbreakingly as she recognised the emerald green banner that covered the dead warrior: Trinovantes's banner.

THE WALLS OF Reikdorf loomed large ahead of them, stark and black against the faded ivory of the sky, and Sigmar looked forward to his return home as much as he feared it. He remembered the cheering folk of his home as they had seen the warriors off in glory, shields bright and spears shimmering in the sun.

Now they were returning in glory, the greenskin menace from the Grey Mountains defeated and its warlord slain. All told, they had burned just under two thousand orc and goblin corpses in great pyres, and by any normal measure, the victory had been magnificent.

The chieftain of Astofen, a distant cousin of his father, had welcomed them within the town's walls following the battle, his people tending to Sigmar's wounded men, and feeding the victorious warriors with the choicest meats and finest beers.

Sigmar had joined with his men in celebrating the victory, for to stand apart from them in melancholy for the slain would only have insulted their courage. In his heart, however, he mourned the death of Trinovantes. He mourned him and felt the ache of guilt that his order had sent him to his death.

Ahead, the land sloped down to the Sudenreik Bridge, a grand construction of stone and timber that Alaric and Pendrag had designed and overseen the construction of barely two months ago. Sigmar and his fellow litter-bearers followed the course of the dusty road as it wound down the hill towards the bridge, each step measured and dignified as they brought the honoured dead home for the last time.

The notched edges of the shields bearing his sword-brother bit into his shoulder, but he welcomed the discomfort, knowing that the burden of Trinovantes's death would be his long after he put down the litter and his friend was interred within his tomb on the edge of the Brackenwalsch up on the Warrior's Hill.

The ground levelled out, and the litter bearers passed between carved pillars topped with howling wolves that reared to either side of the bridge. Stone panels on the inner face of the bridge's parapet were carved with images of battle from the legends of his people, each one a heroic tale that had thrilled Unberogen children for years.

Heroes such as Redmane Dregor and his father battled orcs and dragons on the panels, and across from the image of Björn slaying a great, bull-headed creature was a blank panel where Sigmar's tale would begin. No doubt some graven image of the victory of Astofen would be rendered in stone, forever marking the birth of his legend.

Sigmar watched as the heavy gates of Reikdorf swung outwards, pushed by groups of straining warriors. The walls of Reikdorf were taller than those of Astofen, encircling an area far larger, and home to over two thousand people. King Björn's city was one of the marvels of the land west of the mountains, but Sigmar already had plans to make it the greatest city in the world.

The arch above the gate was formed from interlaced beams of timber, and at its apex stood a statue of a grim-faced and bearded warrior swathed in armour and wolfskin, who bore a huge, two-handed warhammer. A pair of wolves sat beside him, and Sigmar bowed his head before the image of Ulric.

His father stood in the centre of the open gateway, accompanied as always by Alfgeir and Eoforth. Sigmar felt intense joy at seeing him, knowing that no matter how far he travelled or how great his legend might become, he would always be his father's son and grateful for the fact.

Men and women of Reikdorf clustered around the gates, but none ventured from beyond the walls, for it was every warrior's right to march back through the gates of his home with his head held high.

'A fine welcome indeed,' said Pendrag, marching beside Sigmar, and also bearing the weight of Trinovantes's body.

'As well it bloody should be,' pointed out Wolfgart. 'The tribe hasn't seen a victory like this in decades.'

'Aye,' said Sigmar. 'As it should be.'

Their steps shortened as the ground rose, and they climbed the slope towards the walls of Reikdorf. Sigmar felt his spirits rise as he saw the crowds arrayed to welcome them home, feeling a great surge of affection for his people. Through everything this world could throw at them on the road to Morr's kingdom: monsters, disease, hunger and hardship, they survived with dignity and courage.

What force could halt the progress of a race such as his?

Yes, there was pain and despair, but the human spirit had vision, and dreams of a greater destiny. Already the seeds of Sigmar's vision were bearing fruit, but no growth was achieved without pain. Sigmar knew there would be much hardship in the years ahead, before he could realise the grand ambition that had filled him upon his dooming day amid the tombs of his ancestors.

Sigmar led his warriors through the gates of Reikdorf, and roars of approval and joy swelled from hundreds of throats as their people welcomed them home. Parents rushed to greet their sons with tears; some shed in joy, others in sadness.

Heartfelt welcomes and aching cries of loss filled the air as Unberogen mothers found their sons either riding tall upon their horses or laid across them.

Sigmar kept walking until he stood before his father, the king as regal and magnificent as ever, though his face spoke of the simple joy at seeing a son return from war alive and well.

'Lower him gently,' said Sigmar, and he and his sword-brothers slipped the shields from their shoulders and laid Trinovantes's body upon the ground.

Sigmar stood before his father, unsure as to what he should say, but King Björn solved his dilemma for him by sweeping him up in a crushing bear hug and embracing him tightly.

'My son,' said his father. 'You return to me a man.'

Sigmar returned his father's embrace, feeling his love for the brave man who had raised him without a wife at his side as a powerful force within him. Sigmar knew that he owed everything he was to the teachings of his father, and to have won his approval was the finest feeling in the world.

'I told you I would make you proud,' said Sigmar.

'Aye, that you did, my son,' agreed Björn, 'that you did.'

The king of the Unberogens released his son, and stepped forward to address the warriors that had returned to his city, his arms raised in tribute to their courage.

'Warriors of the Unberogen, you are returned safely to us, and for that I give thanks to Ulric. Your valour will not go unrewarded, and every one of you dines like a king tonight!'

The riders cheered, the sound reaching the clouds, and Björn turned to Sigmar and his fellow litter bearers. He looked down at the banner and said, 'Trinovantes?'

'Yes,' said Sigmar, his voice suddenly choked with emotion. 'He fell at Astofen Bridge.'

'Did he fight well? Was it a good death?'

Sigmar nodded. 'It was. Without his courage the day would have been lost.'

'Then Ulric will welcome him into his halls, and we shall envy him,' said Björn, 'for where Trinovantes is now, the beer is stronger, the food more plentiful and the women more beautiful than any in this world. In time, we will see him again, and we will be proud to walk the halls of the mighty with him.'

Sigmar smiled, knowing his father spoke truly, for there could be no greater reward for a true warrior than to be honoured with a good death and then welcomed into the feast halls of the afterlife.

'I had always believed that it was the loneliest thing to lead men in battle,' said Björn, 'but now I know that a father's loneliness as he awaits his son to return safely is far worse.'

'I think I understand,' said Sigmar, turning to look at distraught parents as they led away the horses that bore their dead sons. 'For all its glory, war is a grim business.'

'Then you have learned a valuable lesson, son,' said Björn. 'A victory is a day of joy and sadness in equal measure. Cherish the first and learn to deal with the second or you will never be a leader of men.'

Björn turned to Sigmar's sword-brothers and said, 'Wolfgart, Pendrag, it fills my heart with joy to see you both returned to us.'

Wolfgart and Pendrag beamed at the king's praise as three wagons bearing barrels of beer rumbled along the road from the brew house stores. Alaric the dwarf rode in the lead wagon, and a mighty roar went up from the warriors as they recognised the angular, runic script on the side of the barrels.

'Dwarf ale?' asked Wolfgart.

'Nothing but the best for our returning heroes,' smiled Björn. 'I had been keeping it for my son's wedding feast, but he seems determined to keep me waiting. Better to use it before it goes flat.'

'I heard that,' called Alaric. 'Dwarf ale never goes flat.'

'Figure of speech,' said Björn. 'I meant no offence, Master Alaric.'

'Just as well,' grunted the dwarf. 'I can head back to my people any time, you know.'

'Stop being such a dour misery guts,' laughed Pendrag, taking the dwarf's hand in a firm grip of friendship, 'and get pouring!'

Wolfgart nodded to Sigmar, and the king quickly made his way to Pendrag and the beer barrels.

'Not joining them?' asked Björn.

'I will,' said Sigmar, 'but I should wait with Trinovantes until his kin come for him.'

'Aye,' agreed Björn, with a knowing grin. 'Right enough, but until they do, tell me of your adventures and leave no detail untold.'

Sigmar smiled and said, 'There's not much to tell, really. We tracked the greenskins south and west, and then routed them before the walls of Astofen.'

'How many?' asked Alfgeir, with his customary lack of embellishment.

'Around two thousand,' said Sigmar.

'Two thousand?' gasped Björn, exchanging a proud glance with Alfgeir. 'Not much to tell, he says! And Bonecrusher?'

'Dead by my hand,' said Sigmar. 'Ghal-maraz drank deep of his blood.'

'Thousands,' said Eoforth. 'I had not dreamt such numbers of greenskins could be gathered under one warlord. And you killed them all?'

'That we did,' said Sigmar. 'Their corpses are ash in the mountains.'

'Ulric's blood,' said Björn. 'Then I hope Eadhelm gave you a hero's welcome in his little town, I'll have words with him if he didn't.'

'He did,' said Sigmar. 'Your cousin sends greetings to his king, and swears to send what warriors he can spare should we ever need them.'

Björn nodded. 'He's a good man is Eadhelm. Takes after old Redmane.'

Sigmar saw a warning look enter his father's eyes, and turned to see a girl with midnight dark hair walk stiffly through the gates of Reikdorf. His mouth suddenly felt dry as he recognised Ravenna, her long green dress and proud beauty sending his stomach into a loop of unfamiliar feelings.

Her face was lined with sadness, and Sigmar felt as though his heart would break at the sight of it. Her younger brother, Trinovantes's twin, followed her, tears of grief spilling down his pale skin.

She walked towards her brother's banner-shrouded body, and nodded to Sigmar and his father, before kneeling beside her dead sibling and placing her hand upon his chest. Gerreon slumped beside her, wailing and shaking his head as great sobs wracked his thin frame.

'Be silent, boy,' said Björn. 'It is women's work to weep for a fallen warrior.'

Gerreon looked up, and his eyes locked with Sigmar's.

'You killed him,' wept Gerreon. 'You killed my brother!'

THE FIRES OF the king's longhouse burned low, the peat and timbers smouldering, and the soporific heat had sent many a warrior to his bed. The revelries of victory had gone on long into the night, with offerings of choice meats and beer made to Ulric and Morr; the first to be thanked for the courage the warriors had shown in battle, and the second to guide them to their rest.

The longhouse was quiet, the sounds of perhaps a hundred warriors as they slept wrapped in animal skins and the creak of settling wood all that disturbed the silence. Those warriors with families had returned to their homes, while those without wives, or too young to know their limit of beer, lay passed out, face down on the long trestle tables.

As was customary on a night when fighting men returned home, the king and his heir watched over their warriors to honour their courage. Sigmar sat on a throne next to his father, a throne that had been carved by his father's hand in readiness for his coming of age, when he would sit beside the king as a man. A long wolfskin cloak hung from Sigmar's shoulders, and Ghal-maraz rested on a plinth, created specially for the dwarf-crafted weapon.

A small herd had been slaughtered for the feast, and when the dwarf ale had run out, the brewmaster's reserve had been brought out. Oaths of brotherhood had been renewed by veteran warriors, and new ones sworn by those who had earned their shields on the bloody field of Astofen.

Sigmar had celebrated along with his warriors, but could not rid himself of the image of Ravenna's strained face and Gerreon's weeping as they knelt by the body of Trinovantes. He knew the Battle of Astofen had been an incredible victory, but it was soured for him by the death of his friend.

Part of him knew that such thoughts were selfish, for did the deaths of those warriors he had not been sword-brother to not matter? Trinovantes had been a good and a trusted friend, quiet and thoughtful in his counsel, but never less than honest and true. Where Wolfgart would advise violence and Pendrag diplomacy, Trinovantes's counsel often combined the best of both arguments. Not compromise, but balance. He would be sorely missed.

'You are thinking of Trinovantes again?' asked his father.

'Is it that obvious?' asked Sigmar.

'He was your sword-brother,' said Björn. 'It is right you should miss him. I remember when Torphin died in the Reik Marshes, that was a sad day, so it was.'

'I think I remember him. The big man?' asked Sigmar. 'You haven't talked of him much.'

'Ach... you were only a boy and his death wasn't a tale for young ears,' said Björn, waving a hand. 'Yes, Torphin was a giant of a man, bigger even than me, if you can believe that. Carved from oak he was, and strong as stone. He was the best sword-brother a man could ask for.'

'What happened to him?'

'He died, as all men must,' said Björn.

'How?' asked Sigmar, seeing that his father was reluctant to be drawn on the matter, but sensing that perhaps he *wanted* to be coaxed into telling him the tale of his sword-brother's death.

'It was four or five summers ago,' began Björn, 'when we marched to war alongside King Marbad of the Endals. You remember?'

Sigmar tried to recall the encounter, but his father had left Reikdorf to fight so many battles that it was hard to remember them all.

'No?' said Björn. 'Well, Marbad's a good man and his people were scratching a living on the edges of the marshes at the mouth of the river. They'd settled there after King Marius of the Jutones drove them from their homeland after the Teutogens had taken *their* lands. I suppose it's possible to live there, but why anyone would want to, I don't know. The marshes are dangerous places, full of sucking bogs, corpse lights and daemons that drink the blood of men.'

Sigmar shivered, despite the heat of the longhouse, remembering terrifying tales of dead-eyed things of pale skin and needle teeth that lurked in the haunted mists to feast on the unwary.

'Anyway,' continued his father, 'Marbad and I go back a long way. We fought the orcs of the Bloodmaw tribe that came over the Grey

Mountains twenty years ago, and he saved my life, so I owed him a blood debt. When the mist daemons of the marshes rose up to threaten his people, he called in that debt, and I marched out to fight alongside him.'

'You marched all the way to the coast?'

'Indeed we did, lad, for when an oath is sworn you must never break it, ever. Oaths of loyalty and friendship are all we have in this world, and the man who breaks a promise or whose word isn't worth anything has no place in it. Always remember that.'

'I will,' promised Sigmar. 'What happened when you got to the coast?'

'Marbad and his army were waiting for us at Marburg, and we walked into the marshes as though it was some grand adventure, all us warriors out for glory and honour.'

Sigmar saw his father's eyes take on a glassy, distant sheen as though the mists he spoke of had risen up in his memories, and he once more walked that long ago trodden path.

'Father?' asked Sigmar, when Björn did not continue.

'What? Oh, yes... Well, we set off into the marshes, and the mist daemons rose up around us like ghosts. They took men down into the bogs, drowned them, and sent them back to fight us, all bloated and white. I saw Torphin snatched by one of them, I'll never forget it. It was white, so white, so very white. Like a winter's sky it was, with eyes of cold blue. Like the fires in the northern skies at winter. It looked at me, and I swear it laughed at me as it took my sword-brother to his death.'

'How did you defeat them?'

'Defeat them?' asked Björn. 'I'm not sure we did, you know. It was all we could do to get out of the marshes alive. Marbad possessed a weapon crafted by the fey folk, a blade of power he called Ulfshard. I don't know what manner of power was bound to it, but it could slay daemons, and he wielded it like a true hero, cutting us a path through the mists, and slaying any daemon that came near us. That wasn't the worst of it, though.'

'It wasn't?'

'No, not by a long way. Just as we got to the edge of the marsh, I heard someone calling my name, and I remember the joy I felt when I recognised it as Torphin's voice. Then, there he was, walking out of the mist towards me, eyes rolled back in their sockets, skin all waxy and dead, and black water spilling from his mouth as if his lungs were full of it.'

Sigmar's eyes widened, and he felt his skin crawl at the terrible image of his father's sword-brother and the horror of what had been done to him.

'What did you do?'

'What could I do?' asked Björn. 'Marbad offered me Ulfshard, and I cut Torphin down and sent him to Ulric's Halls. Being drowned is no death for a warrior, so I killed him with a sword, and if there's even a shred of justice in the wolf god, he'll let Torphin in, because there was no truer man than he that walked this land.'

Sigmar knew that his father would have had no choice but to kill his sword-brother to allow him to enter Ulric's Halls. The idea that he might one day have to fight one of his own sword-brothers was anathema to him, and he decided there and then that he would gather those closest to him and make an oath of eternal brotherhood with them.

'We left the marshes, I returned Ulfshard to Marbad, and we became sword-brothers. That's why when we or the Endals call for aid, the other is oath-bound to answer. In the same way, the Cherusens and the Taleutens are our sworn allies after the battles against the monstrous beast-kin of the forests. It's all about oaths, Sigmar. Honour those you make, and others will follow your example.'

Sigmar nodded in understanding.

RAVENNA CLOSED THE button of her brother's tunic and pulled the lacing tight, before smoothing the soft wool over his chest. Dressed in his finest clothes, Trinovantes lay on the cot bed he had risen from only a few days ago to ride to war. Since their mother and father were dead, it fell to her to wash his body and clean his hair in preparation for his interment in his tomb, upon the rise of the new moon the following night.

She ran a hand along the side of his cold cheek and through his fine, dark hair, so like her own and Gerreon's. His features had softened, but the lines of care and worry that had forever creased his handsome face remained imprinted upon him.

'Even in death, you still look sad,' she said.

His axe lay on the bed next to him, its edges sharp, and the blades gleaming in the firelight. She reached out to touch it, but pulled her fingers back at the last moment. It was a weapon of war, and she wanted nothing more to do with it. War was a fool's errand, a game to the warriors of Reikdorf, but a game that could have only one outcome.

Gerreon sat opposite her at their table, his head buried in a curled arm as he wept for his lost twin. On her deathbed, Ravenna's mother had confided to her that when Trinovantes and Gerreon were born, the hag woman who had birthed them said they would forever have a connection to one another, but that only one would grow to know the greatest pleasure and the greatest pain.

She had never spoken of this to Gerreon, but wondered if the death of his twin brother was the greatest pain of which the hag woman had spoken. What then might be his greatest pleasure?

Ravenna longed to take her brother in her arms and rock him to sleep as she had done many times when they had been growing up and the older boys had teased him for his thin frame and beautiful face. That, however, was the impulse of an older sister, and he was beyond such simple remedies.

She rose from her kneeling position beside the bed, and crossed their low dwelling. Smoke from the fire gathered beneath the roof since there was no vent, for the hot smoke kept the roof warm and dry. The smell of boiling meat from the king's herd rose from a bubbling pot hung on iron hooks above the fireplace, although she suspected that the meat would go to waste, for neither of them had much of an appetite.

Ravenna reached out, and placed her palm on her brother's head as she sat next to him. Ignoring her earlier thought, she slid her arms around him and drew him close to her. His arm slipped naturally around her waist, and she gently rocked him back and forth.

'Hush now,' she said. 'We'll have no more tears in this house, Gerreon. You'll attract evil spirits, and your brother does not want to go to Ulric's Halls with your sorrow as the last thing he hears.'

'I can't help it,' said Gerreon, lifting his head from her shoulders. Tears and snot mingled on his upper lip and chin, and his eyes were bloodshot from crying.

He wiped his free arm across his face. 'My brother is dead.'

'I know,' said Ravenna. 'Trinovantes was my brother too, Gerreon.'

'But he was my twin, you don't know what it's like to lose someone who's like a part of you. I could feel the same things he did as though they happened to me.'

'Trinovantes was a warrior,' said Ravenna. 'He chose that life, and he knew the risks.'

'No,' said Gerreon, 'I don't think he did. I've asked around.'

'What does that mean?'

'It means that Sigmar caused his death,' snapped Gerreon. 'I spoke to the warriors who came back, and they told me that Sigmar sent Trinovantes to hold Astofen Bridge. He ordered him not to retreat, no matter what. What kind of a choice is that?'

Ravenna slipped her arm from around her brother, taking him by the shoulders, and turning him to face her. She too had desired to know how her brother had died, but she had asked Pendrag and knew the truth of the matter.

'No, Gerreon,' said Ravenna, 'Trinovantes volunteered to hold the bridge. I asked Pendrag and he told me what happened.'

'Pendrag? Well, of course he's going to back up his sword-brother, isn't he? They've sworn an oath or something. He'd say anything to protect Sigmar.'

Ravenna shook her head. 'Pendrag may be many things, but he is not a liar, and I believe him. A greenskin killed Trinovantes, and Sigmar slew the beast.'

Gerreon pulled away from his sister. 'How can you defend him at a time like this? Is it because you can't wait to spread your legs for him? Is that it?'

Ravenna slapped him hard, her palm leaving a vivid imprint on his cheek.

'So it's true,' he said, and she drew back her arm to slap him again.

His hand snapped out, and caught her wrist in an iron grip.

'Don't,' he said.

Ravenna pulled her arm free as Gerreon stood, his hand balled into a fist, and the veins in his neck stark against his pale skin.

Ravenna scrambled back, frightened of her brother's sudden fury.

'I'm sorry I said that, sister,' said Gerreon, 'but you won't change my mind. Sigmar killed our brother as surely as if he'd driven that spear through his heart!'

FOUR
Sword Brothers

A COLD WIND blew over the grassy slopes of the Warrior's Hill, and Ravenna pulled her green cloak tighter around her body as she watched the snaking column of warriors make their way from Reikdorf. Sigmar led the procession, dressed in his gleaming bronze armour and iron helm. The king walked beside him, with Pendrag and Alfgeir following behind them, one carrying Sigmar's banner, the other carrying the king's.

Armoured warriors carried her brother on a bier of shields, his green banner draped across his recumbent form, and Ravenna felt a cold lump of grief settle in her throat at the sight of her brother's body.

Gerreon stood to her left, stiff and tense as the procession approached. She spared him a glance, his handsome features set as though carved from stone. He wore his finest tunic of scarlet wool, and had left his arm unbound from its sling. His sword was belted at his waist, and his good hand rested on its pommel.

She reached out and took his hand from the weapon, slipping her hand into his. He frowned at the gesture, but relaxed as he saw the sorrow in her eyes.

'Don't worry, sister,' he said. 'I'm not going to do anything foolish.'

'I didn't think you were,' she lied.

He squeezed her hand, and returned his gaze to the approaching men, who were already halfway up the hill. Ravenna watched as the warriors passed the tomb of Redmane Dregor, both Sigmar and his father bowing to their ancestor as they did so.

The king's father had been long dead before Ravenna's birth, but his stories had thrilled many of the settlement's children over the years, and his heroic deeds were known the length and breadth of the Unberogen lands.

At last, her brother's funeral procession climbed the winding path to the place set aside for Trinovantes, a barrow cut in the side of the hill, framed by tall pillars of weathered stone. As one of the guards of the King's Hall, Trinovantes was entitled to such honour in his final resting place, on a stone shelf beside their father. A heavy boulder lay to one side, a muddy crease marking where it had been rolled aside in preparation for her brother's interment.

King Björn halted before the opening of the barrow, and Sigmar gave her and her brother a solemn nod of acknowledgement. For long moments, no one moved, and the sigh of the wind around the hillside was the only sound, a mournful howling that captured the feelings of those present more eloquently than any could manage with words.

At length, King Björn stepped towards the barrow, and dropped to his knees with his head bowed beside the darkened entrance. His cloak of deep blue flapped in the wind, and the bronze crown upon his brow shone in the afternoon sun.

'A warrior is laid to rest in the land he fought to protect,' said the king. 'His name was Trinovantes, and he died a hero's death, his blade wet with the blood of his enemies and all his wounds to the fore. Know him, mighty Ulric, and grant him a fitting welcome.'

The king drew a bronze knife and slashed the blade across his palm. He made a fist, allowing droplets of blood to splash the ground before the black opening of the tomb.

'I offer you the blood of kings,' said Björn, 'and the honour of his sword-brothers.'

Sigmar led the warriors who bore Trinovantes past the king, and ducked down as he led them into the musty darkness. Ravenna felt Gerreon's hand tighten on hers, but she did not take her eyes from the sight of her brother's body as it was carried within.

She felt tears welling as she heard the scrape of metal and hushed words from the tomb. At last, the armoured warriors emerged into the light, taking up positions behind the king with their shields carried proudly before them. Eventually, Sigmar emerged from her brother's tomb, Trinovantes's shield carried before him like a platter. The leather stretched across the wood was split, and several of the brass studs around its rim were missing.

Sigmar walked slowly towards her and Gerreon, his face a mask of anguish, and her heart went out to him, even as she grieved for her own loss. She felt Gerreon tense beside her as Sigmar lifted the shield and offered it to her brother.

'Trinovantes was the bravest man I knew,' said Sigmar. 'This is his shield, and it passes to you, Gerreon. May you bear it proudly and earn honour with it as your brother did.'

'Honour?' spat Gerreon. 'Sent to his death by a friend? Where is the honour in that?'

Sigmar showed no outward sign of anger, but Ravenna could see the smouldering, grief-born rage behind his eyes. The king's son continued to hold the shield out, and Ravenna released her brother's hand that he might take it.

'He was my friend, Gerreon,' said Sigmar. 'I mourn his death as you do. Yes, I gave him the order that led to his death, but such is the way with war. Good men die, and we honour their sacrifice by living on and cherishing their memory.'

Ravenna willed Gerreon to take Trinovantes's shield, but her brother seemed determined to savour the angry confrontation, and steadfastly refused to receive the shield from Sigmar.

Both men's eyes were locked together, and she wanted to scream in frustration. Instead, she reached up, took hold of her brother's shield, and bowed her head to Sigmar as she slid it onto her arm and bore it before her.

Sigmar looked down in surprise as she hefted Trinovantes's shield, but she could see his anger diminish and the light of understanding in his eyes.

'Thank you,' said Ravenna, her voice strong and proud despite her grief. 'I know you loved our brother dearly, and he loved you in return.'

Sigmar said, 'He was my sword-brother and he will not be forgotten.'

'No,' agreed Ravenna, 'he won't be.'

Gerreon stood unmoving, but with the shield accepted, Sigmar turned away, and returned to stand beside Pendrag, and the crimson banner that snapped and rippled in the wind.

The king stood and glared at Gerreon, but said nothing as he took his place beside his champion. Sigmar and Wolfgart now stepped forward to stand beside the boulder that would cover the entrance to her brother's final resting place. Pendrag handed Sigmar's banner to another warrior, and joined his sword-brothers.

They placed their shoulders against the boulder and heaved, the muscles in their legs bunching as they strained against its weight. Ravenna thought they would not be able to move it, but it began to shift, slowly at first, and then with greater ease as its momentum built.

At last, the boulder rolled across the entrance, and Ravenna closed her eyes as it slammed into place with a thud of rock and a dreadful finality.

DUSK WAS DRAWING in as Björn sat on a rock staring at the tomb of Trinovantes, the sack containing the bull's heart on the ground before him. He was impatient, and the small fire before the tomb did nothing to dispel the cold wind that stole the warmth from him like a thief. This part of the funeral rite always unsettled him, despite its necessity, but as king, it fell to him to perform it.

He looked up at the slowly emerging stars as he waited for the other to arrive, seeing them as faint spots of light in the dusky sky. Eoforth said they were holes in the mortal world, beyond which lay the abode of the gods, from where they looked down on the race of man. Björn did not know if it were true, but it sounded good, and he was prepared to bow before the wisdom of his counsellor.

He tore his gaze from the stars as he heard soft footfalls from the other side of the hill, and his hand stole towards Soultaker's haft. He could see nothing in the gloom, but dusk was a time of shadows and phantoms, and his eyes were no longer as clear as they had been in his youth.

'Be at peace, Björn,' chuckled a low, yet powerful voice. 'I mean you no harm this night.'

A hunched woman, swathed in black robes, emerged from behind the mound of the tomb, but Björn did not release his grip on the weapon as he saw her. She walked with the aid of a gnarled staff, and her hair was as white as a mist daemon's hide.

The comparison unnerved him, but he stood to face her, determined that he would show no emotion before the hag woman of the Brackenwalsch.

'You bring the offering for the god of the dead?' asked the woman. Her face was ancient and wrinkled, yet her eyes were like those of a maiden, bright and full of mischief.

'I do,' replied Björn, bending to lift the sack from the ground.

'Something unsettles you, Björn?' asked the woman.

'Your kind always unsettles me,' he replied.

'My kind?' sneered the old woman. 'It was my kind that protected you when plague came to your lands. It was *my kind* that warned you of the great beast of the Howling Hills. Thanks to me, you have prospered, and the Unberogen are now numbered among the mightiest tribes of the west.'

'All of that is true,' said Björn, 'but it does not change the fact that I believe darkness clings to you like a cloak. You have powers beyond those of mortal men.'

The hag woman laughed, a bitter, dry sound. 'Does it bother you that my powers are beyond mortals or beyond men?'

'Both,' admitted Björn.

'Honest, at least,' said the hag woman, settling on her haunches before the tomb. 'Quickly now, bring the heart.'

Björn tossed the sack to the woman, who caught it before it landed, and upended it into the fire. The heart began to sizzle quickly, and the pungent aroma of burning flesh rose as it began to burn. The crackling organ spat fat and blood as it smoked, and Björn felt his mouth water at the scent.

'The god of the dead is also the god of dreams,' said the hag woman. 'He sends sleeping visions to those who guide the souls of the departed to his realm.'

Björn did not reply, having no wish to bandy words with this conjurer of dead things. She looked up at him. 'Do you wish to hear of my dreams?'

'No,' said Björn. 'What would you dream of that I would wish to know?'

The hag woman shrugged, moving the heart around in the heat of the fire. Its surface was blackened and shrivelling as the flames consumed it.

'Dreams are the gateway to the future,' she said. 'Vanity, pride and courage are no shield against the lord of the dead, and all journey to his kingdom sooner or later.'

'Is the ritual done yet?' demanded Björn, irritated by the hag woman's prattling.

'Nearly,' she said, 'but you of all people should know better than to rush an offering to the gods.'

'What is that supposed to mean?' asked Björn, looming over the hag woman. 'Damn your riddles, speak plainly!'

The hag woman looked up, and Björn felt an icy hand take hold of his heart as surely as the flames had taken the bull's heart. Her eyes shone with reflected light from the fire, and the heat from the flames vanished utterly.

The cold wind howled, and his cloak billowed around him like a living thing. He looked up to see that the sky was black and starless, and the light of the gods obscured. Björn had never felt so alone in all his life.

'You stand on the brink of an abyss, King Björn,' hissed the hag woman, her voice cutting through the still of the night like a knife, 'so listen well to what I say. The Child of Thunder is in danger, for the powers of darkness move against him, though he knows it not. If he lives, the race of man will rise to glory and mastery of the land, sea and sky, but should he falter the world will end in blood and fire.'

'Child of Thunder?' asked Björn, tearing his gaze from the lifeless heavens. 'What are you talking about?'

'I speak of a time far from here, beyond the span of your life and mine.'

'If I will be dead why should I care?'

'You are a great warrior and a good man, King Björn, but he who will come after you will be the greatest warrior of the age.'

'My son?' asked Björn. 'You speak of Sigmar?'

'Aye,' nodded the hag woman. 'I speak of Sigmar. He stands poised at a threshold of Morr's gateway, and the god of the dead knows his name.'

Fear seized Björn's heart. His wife had been taken from him on a night of blood, and hearing that he might outlive his son was to have his greatest fear realised.

'Can you save him?' pleaded Björn.

'No,' said the hag woman. 'Only you can do that.'

'How?'

'By making a sacred vow to me when I ask it,' said the hag woman, taking his hand.

'Ask it!' cried Björn. 'I will swear whatever you ask.'

The hag woman shook her head, and the wind lessened as the

stars began to shine once more. 'I do not ask it yet, Björn, but be ready when I do.'

Björn nodded as he pulled away from the hag woman. He looked around the hillside, seeing that the sky had returned to its normal dusky colour. He let out an anguished breath, and turned back to Trinovantes's tomb.

The fire was extinguished, and the heart burned to ashes on the wind.

The hag woman was gone.

SIGMAR WATCHED THE tiny flickering glow on Warrior's Hill wink out, and hung his head, knowing that the last of the funeral rites for his friend was over. He could not make out his father on the hillside, but he knew that he would not neglect his duty to the dead.

A shiver passed through Sigmar, and he looked into the west and the setting sun. Soon it would be dark, and he could already see wall sentries lighting the hooded braziers that illuminated the open ground before the walls of Reikdorf. Night was a time to be feared, and the monsters that lived in the forests and mountains claimed dominion over the land in its shadow.

No more, thought Sigmar, for now is the time of men.

'I will push back the darkness,' he whispered, placing his hand on a heavy square stone laid in the centre of the settlement. The rough surface of the stone was red and striated with thin golden lines, quite unlike anything west of the mountains.

The last of the sun's rays had heated its surface, and Sigmar felt a warm glow from the stone as if it approved of his sentiment. He looked up as he heard footsteps approaching.

Wolfgart and Pendrag, still clad in their bronze armour, strode through the town, their heads held high and proud. Sigmar smiled to see them, feeling a kinship with these brave souls who had fought and bled alongside him.

'So what's this all about?' asked Wolfgart. 'There's drinking to be done, and plenty of women who still want to welcome us back properly.'

Sigmar rose from his haunches and said, 'Thank you for coming, my friends.'

'Is everything all right?' asked Pendrag, catching a measure of his tone.

Sigmar nodded, squatting down next to the red stone. 'You know what this is?'

'Of course,' said Wolfgart, kneeling next to him.

'It is the Oathstone,' said Pendrag.

'Aye,' said Sigmar. 'The Oathstone, carried from lands far to the east by the first chiefs of the Unberogen, and planted in the earth when they settled here.'

'What of it?' asked Wolfgart.

'The town of Reikdorf was built around this stone, and its people have flourished, the land opening up to us and returning our care tenfold,' said Sigmar, laying his hand on the stone. 'When a man plights his troth to a woman, their hands are fastened here. When a new king swears to lead his people, his oath is taken here, and when warriors swear blood oaths, their blood falls upon this stone.'

'Well,' began Pendrag, 'you are not yet king, and I'm assuming you're not planning on marrying either of us?'

'He'd bloody better not be!' cried Wolfgart. 'He's too skinny for my tastes anyway.'

Sigmar shook his head. 'You're right, Pendrag. I brought you to this place because I want what happens here to be remembered by both of you. We won a great victory at Astofen, but that is just the beginning.'

'The beginning of what?' asked Wolfgart.

'Of us,' said Sigmar.

'Maybe you were wrong, Pendrag,' said Wolfgart. 'Maybe he does want to marry us.'

'I mean "us" as in the race of man,' said Sigmar. 'Astofen was just the beginning, but I see something greater for us. All year, the beasts of the forest attack our settlements, and greenskins from the mountains plague us, yet still we fight each other. The Teutogens and Thuringians raid our northern lands and the Merogens our southern settlements. The Norsii and the Udoses are in a state of constant war, and the Jutones and the Endals have fought each other for longer than any man can remember.'

Wolfgart shrugged. 'It's the way it's always been.'

Pendrag nodded and said, 'Men will always fight one another. The strong take from the weak, and the powerful will always want more power.'

'Not any more,' said Sigmar. 'Here we make an oath to end the wars between the tribes. If we are ever to make more of ourselves, to do more than simply survive, then we must be united in common purpose.'

Sigmar pulled Ghal-maraz from his belt and laid it across the Oathstone.

'On my dooming day, I walked amongst the tombs of my forefathers and saw our land laid out before me. I saw the sprawling forests and scattered towns within it, like islands in a dark sea. I saw the strength of men, but I also saw frailty and fear as people huddled together behind high walls that separated them from one another. I felt the jealousy and mistrust that will forever be our undoing in the face of stronger enemies. I have a great vision of a mighty empire of men, a land ruled with justice and strength, but if we are ever to stand a chance of realising that vision, we must put such petty considerations behind us.'

'A lofty goal,' said Pendrag.

'But a worthy one.'

'Worthy, yes,' said Wolfgart, 'but an impossible one. The tribes live for war and fighting, they have always fought, and they always will.'

Sigmar shook his head, and placed his hand on Wolfgart's shoulder. 'You are wrong, my friend. Together we can begin something magnificent.'

'Together?' asked Wolfgart.

'Aye, together,' said Sigmar, placing his hand on the head of his mighty warhammer. 'I cannot do this alone; I need my sword-brothers with me. Swear with me, my friends. Swear that everything we do from this day forth will be in service of this vision of a united empire of man.'

Wolfgart and Pendrag looked at each other as though thinking him mad, but Pendrag turned to him and smiled. 'This oath, will it require blood? We've all shed enough these last few days.'

'No, my friend,' said Sigmar. 'Blood is for Ulric, your word will be enough.'

'Then you have it,' nodded Pendrag, placing his hand on the haft of the warhammer.

'Wolfgart?'

His friend shook his head with a smile. 'You're both mad, but it is a grand madness, so count me in.'

Wolfgart placed his hand on Ghal-maraz, and Sigmar said, 'I swear by all the gods of the land and upon this mighty weapon that I will not rest until all the tribes of men are united and strong.'

'I swear this also,' said Pendrag.

'As do I,' said Wolfgart.

Sigmar's heart swelled with pride as he looked into the eyes of his sword-brothers and saw the strength of their faith in him. Wolfgart nodded and said, 'Now what? You want the three of us to march out and conquer the world tonight? We'd have our work cut out for us.'

'We three are just the beginning,' promised Sigmar, 'but there will be more.'

'Many will not want to walk this road with us,' warned Pendrag. 'We will not forge this empire of yours without bloodshed.'

'It will be a long, hard road,' agreed Sigmar, 'but I believe that some things are worth fighting for.'

Wolfgart looked up from the Oathstone, and said, 'Aye, I think you might be right.'

Sigmar followed his sword-brother's glance, and his heart beat a little faster as he saw Ravenna standing at the edge of the square. She was wrapped in a green shawl, pulled tightly around her body, and her black hair lay unbound around her shoulders. Sigmar knew that he had never seen her look more beautiful.

He turned back to his friends, torn between the solemnity of the oath they had sworn and the desire to go to Ravenna.

'Go on,' said Pendrag. 'You'd be a fool if you didn't.'

THEY WALKED TO the river, and watched the sun as the last curve of its light slipped further beyond the horizon. Darkness was creeping in from the east, and only the metallic rustle of sentries' armour and the splashing of the river broke the silence of the world.

Ravenna had said nothing as he approached, and they had walked in companionable silence towards the river, the dark waters churning past like fast-flowing pitch. Sigmar felt awkward in his armour, his every footfall loud and ungainly next to the grace of her poise.

They walked past the boats, pulled up onto the banks of the river and the drying racks, coming eventually to a small jetty where tall logs were driven into the river to shore up the banks. Ravenna stepped out onto the jetty, and walked to the end, staring out over the waters of the Reik as they flowed towards the coast far to the west.

'Trinovantes used to love swimming in the river,' said Ravenna.

'I remember,' said Sigmar. 'He was the only one strong enough to swim to the other side. Everyone else got swept downstream, and had to walk back to Reikdorf.'

'Even you?'

'Even me,' smiled Sigmar.

'I miss him.'

'We all miss him,' he said. 'I wish there was something I could say that would lessen the pain of his death.'

She shook her head. 'No words could do that, Sigmar. Nor would I want them to.'

'That doesn't make sense,' he said. 'Why hang onto pain?'

'Because without it I might forget him,' she said. 'Without the pain I might forget that it was war and men like you that saw him killed.'

'You blame me for his death,' said Sigmar.

She turned away from him, and the dying rays of the sun shimmered in her hair like molten copper. 'An orc drove that spear through my brother, not you. I do not blame you for his death, but I hate that we need men like you and my brother to protect us from the world. I hate that we have to build walls to hide behind and make swords to fight our enemies.'

He reached out and touched her shoulder. 'The world is a dark place, Ravenna, and without warriors and swords we would all be dead.'

'I know,' she said. 'I am not naïve. I understand the necessity of warriors, but I do not have to like it, not when it takes my brother away from me, not when it might take you away from me.'

Sigmar laughed. 'I am not going anywhere.'

Ravenna turned back to him, and the laughter died in his throat as he saw the tears springing from her eyes.

'You are a warrior and the son of a king,' she said. 'Your life is one of battle. You are unlikely to die as an old man in your bed.'

'I'm sorry,' he said, reaching for her.

She fell into his arms, and wept for her brother now that the rites were concluded. She had been strong for long enough. They stood together on the edge of the river as the sun sank beneath the horizon and the stars finally came out in all their glory. The night was cloudless, and Sigmar looked up at the star pictures, seeing the Great Wolf, the Myrmidion Spear and the Scales of Verena shining against the darkness.

There were others, but he did not want to move and spoil this moment to look at them. Ravenna wept for her lost brother for many minutes, and Sigmar simply held her, knowing that to try to speak would be to intrude on her grief. At length, her tears stopped, and she looked up at him, her eyes puffy, but as strong as when she had taken Trinovantes's shield from him on the Warrior's Hill.

'Thank you,' she said, wiping her eyes on the edge of her shawl.

'I didn't do anything.'

'Yes, you did.'

Mystified as to her meaning, he said nothing until she eventually pulled away, wrapping her arms around her body again.

'That looked serious,' she said suddenly, moving the subject away from her brother. 'with Wolfgart and Pendrag I mean.'

Sigmar hesitated before answering. 'We were swearing an oath,' he said at last.

'An oath? What kind of oath?'

Sigmar wondered if he should tell her, but then immediately saw that if his dream of a united empire were to come true then it would need to take shape in the hearts and minds of the people. An *idea* was a powerful thing, and it would spread faster than any army could march.

'To bring an end to war,' he said, 'to unite the tribes and forge an empire that can stand against the creatures of darkness.'

She nodded and said, 'And who would rule this empire?'

'We would,' he said, 'the Unberogen.'

'You mean *you* would.'

Sigmar nodded, 'Would that be so bad?'

'No, for you have a good heart, Sigmar. I truly believe that. If you ever build this empire, it will be a place of justice and strength.'

'*If* I build it? Don't you think I can do it?'

'If anyone can do it, you can,' she said, stepping forward and taking his hand. 'Just promise me one thing.'

'Anything.'

'Be careful,' she said. 'You don't know what I'm going to ask.'

'That doesn't matter,' said Sigmar. 'Your wish is my command.'

She reached up with her free hand and stroked his cheek. 'You are sweet.'

'I mean it,' said Sigmar. 'Ask and I will promise.'

'Then promise me that the wars will end some day,' said Ravenna, looking him straight in the eye. 'When you have achieved all you set out to do, put down your weapons and leave it all behind.'

'I promise,' he said without hesitation.

FIVE

The Dreams of Kings

WINTER CLOSED IN on Reikdorf like a clenched fist, each day growing shorter, and the temperature falling until the first snowfalls blanketed the world in white. The River Reik flowed slow and stately, the water cold and filled with drifting ice floes that came all the way from the Grey Mountains far to the south.

The Unberogens hunkered down to wait out the season, their grain stores filled with the fruits of a bountiful harvest; bread was plentiful and no household went hungry. King Björn sent wagons of grain westwards to the lands of the Endals, for the soil there was thin, and evil waters from the marshes had poisoned many of their crops.

Armed warriors travelled with the wagons, for the forest was a place of danger, even in the depths of winter. Brigands might cease their raiding while the snow lay thickly on the ground, but the deathly cold held no terror for the twisted beasts that hid in the darkest depths of the forests.

Wolfgart led the Unberogen warriors to Marburg, riding at the head of a column of warriors armoured in new hauberks of linked iron, fresh from the forge-work of Alaric and Pendrag. Wolfgart had been loath to part with his bronze breastplate and cuirass, but when Alaric had shown him the strength of the iron armour, he had tossed aside his old plate and happily donned his new protection.

He and his warriors would winter with the Endals to return in the spring, and Sigmar missed his friend greatly as the days passed with gelid slowness.

The cold weeks dragged on, and each one weighed heavily on Sigmar. He longed to make good on the oath he had sworn with his sword-brothers, but while winter held the land in its grip, nothing could be done. No army could march in winter, and to set out in such bone numbing cold was akin to suicide. Daily life continued as normal, with the folk of Reikdorf turning their hands to work that could only be undertaken when the days were not filled with the backbreaking labour of farming.

Artisans crafted fine jewellery, weavers created great tapestries, and craftsmen trained apprentices in woodwork, stone carving and dozens of other trades that would have been unthinkable without the luxury of a crop surplus.

Alaric's forge rang with hammer blows, and hissing clouds of hot steam billowed from the high chimney. Pendrag had become a daily visitor to the forge, learning the secret of blending metals to produce iron swords that held a superior edge for a greater span of time, and did not shatter after continued use.

As winter dragged on, the flow of trade into and out of Reikdorf dwindled to almost nothing. Only dwarf caravans dared to travel during the winter, squat, unlovely things pulled by equally squat and muscular ponies. Each caravan came loaded with ore from the mines, finely crafted weapons and armour, and barrels of strong ale.

Dwarfs encased in gleaming surcoats of mail and heavy plate trudged alongside the caravans, apparently untroubled by the deep snow. Their faces were hidden, and only their long braided beards were visible beneath bronze faceplates. Alaric would greet each caravan personally, talking in the gruff, yet lyrical language of the mountain folk, while the Unberogens watched from behind shuttered windows.

No sooner were the wagons unloaded than they would be filled with grain, furs and all manner of goods unavailable to the dwarfs in their holds. Messages would be exchanged between King Björn and King Kurgan Ironbeard, each passing on what news of the world they knew to the other.

Sigmar spent much of the winter training with the warriors of the Unberogen, honing his already fearsome skill, and instilling a sense of camaraderie in the warriors with his quick wit and loyalty.

Of course there were still battles to be fought, and both Sigmar and his father led their warriors into the forest several times to fight marauding groups of beasts that preyed upon outlying settlements. Each time, the riders would return to Reikdorf with skulls mounted on their spears, and each time it would be longer before the beasts attacked again.

Nor were beasts their only enemies. Teutogen raiders rode brazenly into Unberogen territory to steal cattle and sheep, but were hunted down and killed before they could return to their own lands. Gerreon finally rode to war in such a skirmish, earning the respect of his fellows for his deadly skill with a blade, though as he had predicted, his absence from the Battle of Astofen had created a gulf between him and those who had fought in the desperate battle with the orcs.

As the days lengthened, Unberogen warriors began riding further afield, maintaining a close watch on their borders. With spring's approach, border skirmishes became more common, and time and time again, Unberogen horse archers would turn back feints from laughing reavers, who whooped and hollered as they threw spears and loosed arrows.

The days passed, the people of Reikdorf survived the winter, and the hearts of men lightened as the days grew brighter. The sun stayed in the sky a little longer, and as the snows began to retreat, the green and gold of the forest grew more vivid with each passing day.

Farmers returned to their fields in preparation for the spring sowing, armed with Pendrag's seed drills as new mills and granaries were built throughout the land. The elders of Reikdorf proclaimed that the winter had been amongst the mildest they could remember.

No sooner had the first flowers of spring begun to push their way through the snow than a party of horsemen was spotted riding along the northern bank of the Reik towards the town. Armoured warriors rushed to the walls, until a familiar banner was spotted and the gates thrown open. Wolfgart led his warriors beneath the grim, unsmiling statue of Ulric and back into Reikdorf to cries of welcome.

The homecoming was joyous, and a great feast was held to celebrate the safe return of every warrior who had set out. Folk clamoured for news from the west, and Wolfgart revelled in his role of taleteller.

'King Marbad,' said Wolfgart, 'the old man himself, is coming to Reikdorf.'

* * *

THE AIR IN the forge was close and heavy, sparks and hot smoke gathering in the rafters as the bellows furiously pumped air into the furnace. The bricks closest to the fire glowed with the heat, and the charcoal roared as the air was forced over it.

'It must blow harder, manling!' shouted Alaric. 'The furnace must be hotter to remove the impurities!'

'It can't get any faster, Alaric,' said Pendrag. 'The tide is too low, and the pump can't get enough speed for the bellows.'

'Ach, they were going fine this morning.'

'That was this morning,' complained Pendrag, letting go of the crank handles on the mechanical bellows. 'We are going to have to wait until the tide rises again.'

He stepped away from the contraption of bladder airbags and leather straps that made up the bellows, and which derived its power from a fast-flowing channel of surging water diverted from the River Reik to pass through the forge.

When the river was in spate, the water spun a great rotary paddle that in turn powered the bellows, which heated the furnace to the incredible temperatures required for the production of iron.

Until only last spring, when Alaric had first come to Reikdorf, the Unberogen warriors had wielded bronze swords and spears, but following the dwarf's instructions, Pendrag had been the first man to forge a sword made of iron.

Within a season, every warrior had an iron blade, and every day, more hauberks of mail and leather were being produced as the smiths of Reikdorf learned the ancient techniques of metalworking known to the dwarfs.

'Tides,' said Alaric, shaking his head. 'In Karaz-a-Karak we care not for tides. Mighty waterfalls from the peak of the mountain plunge into the heart of the hold day and night. Ah, manling, you should see the great forges of the mountains. The heart of the hold glows red with the heat, and the mountain shudders to the blows of hammers.'

'Well, we don't have waterfalls like that here,' pointed out Pendrag. 'We have to make do with tides.'

'And the engines,' said Alaric, ignoring Pendrag's comment. 'Great hissing pistons of iron, spinning wheels and roaring bellows. Gods of the Mountains, I never thought I'd miss the presence of an engineer.'

'An engineer? What's that, some kind of smith?'

Alaric laughed. 'No, an engineer is a dwarf who builds machines like that there bellows, but much bigger and much better.'

Pendrag looked at the hissing, wheezing bellows, the concertinaed bladders expanding and contracting as the rotary pump spun in the channel. With help from Alaric, it had taken him and the finest craftsmen in the village an entire month to build the water-powered bellows, and it was a marvel of invention and cunning.

'I thought we did well building the bellows,' said Pendrag defensively.

'You manlings have some ability, it's true,' said Alaric, though Pendrag could see even such faint praise was given grudgingly, 'but dwarf craft is the best there is, and until I can persuade an engineer to come down from the mountains, we will have to make do with this… contraption.'

'You helped us build the bellows,' said Pendrag. 'Are you not an engineer?'

'No, lad,' said Alaric. 'I'm… something else entirely. I can fashion weapons the likes of which you cannot imagine, weapons similar to the warhammer the king's son wields.'

'Ghal-maraz?'

'Aye, the Skull-Splitter, a mighty weapon indeed,' nodded Alaric. 'King Kurgan blessed your people when he gave it to Sigmar. Tell me, lad, do you know the meaning of the word *unique*?'

'I think so,' said Pendrag. 'It means that something's special. That it's the only one.'

Alaric nodded. 'That's right, but it's more like saying that *it has no equal*. Ghal-maraz is like that, one of a kind, forged in ancient times with an art no dwarf has been able to reproduce.'

'So you couldn't make something like it?'

Alaric shot him an irritated glance as though he had impugned the dwarf's skill. 'I have great skill, lad, but not even I could craft a weapon like Ghal-maraz.'

'Not even if we had an engineer?'

The dwarf laughed, the tension vanishing from his bearded face. 'No, not even if we had an engineer. My kind don't much like to live without a roof of stone above our heads, so I doubt I'd be able to persuade one of them lads to come down from the mountains to stay.'

'You stayed,' pointed out Pendrag, watching as the glow of the furnace faded from a golden orange to a dull, angry red.

'Aye, and do you know what they call me back in Karaz-a-Karak?'

Pendrag shook his head. 'No, what do they call you?'

'Alaric the Mad,' said the dwarf, 'that's what they call me. They all think I've gone soft in the head to spend my time with manlings.'

Though the words were said lightly, Pendrag could sense the tension behind them.

'So why do you stay with us?' asked Pendrag. 'Why not go home to the mountains? Not that I want you to go, of course.'

The dwarf walked from the furnace to pick up one of the blades from the pile that lay on a low wooden bench running the length of one the forge's stone walls. The metal was dark, and a hilt and handguard were still to be fitted over the sharpened tang.

'You manlings are a young race, and you live such short lives that many of my folk think it a waste of time to try to teach you anything. It would take the span of several of your lifetimes before a dwarf was thought simply competent as a smith. Compared to dwarf craft, manling work is shoddy and crude, and hardly worth bothering with.'

'So why do you?' said a voice from the door to the forge. 'Bother with it I mean.'

Pendrag looked up, and saw Sigmar, silhouetted in the doorway, his bearskin cloak pulled tightly around his body. Cold air flowed into the forge, and the king's son shut the door behind him as he entered.

Alaric put down the sword blade, and sat down on a thick-legged stool next to the bench. He nodded in welcome to Sigmar, and said, 'Because you have potential. This is a grim world, lad – orcs, beasts and things best not spoken of seek to drown us all in blood. The elves have run scared to their island, and it's only the likes of men and dwarfs that are left to stop these creatures of evil. Some of my kin think we should just seal up the gates to our holds and let you and the orcs fight amongst yourselves, but the way I see it, if we *don't* help you with better weapons and armour, and teach you a thing or two about making them, then your race will die and we'll be next.'

'You think we are that weak?' asked Sigmar, walking across to the bench with the unfinished sword blades, and picking one up.

'Weak?' cried Alaric. 'Don't be foolish, lad! Men are not weak. I've spent enough time amongst you to know you have strength, but you squabble like children, and you haven't the means to fight your enemies. When your ancestors first came over the mountains they had bronze swords and armour, yes?'

'So the elders tell us,' agreed Pendrag.

'All the folks that lived here already had was stone clubs and leather breastplates, and look what happened to them: dead to a man. I've seen the orcs east of the mountains, and there's so many of them, you'd think you were going mad to see them all. Without iron weapons and armour they'll destroy you.'

Sigmar turned over the blade in his hand, and said, 'Pendrag, can you make one of these iron blades without Master Alaric's help?'

Pendrag nodded. 'I think so, yes.'

'That's not good enough,' said Sigmar, dropping the sword back onto the bench, and coming over to where Pendrag stood. The king's son's skin glistened with sweat from the heat of the forge, but his gaze was unwavering. 'Tell me truly, can you make such a blade?'

'I can,' said Pendrag. 'I know how to sift the impurities from the ore, and now that we have the bellows working, we can get the furnace hot enough.'

'At high tide,' grumbled Alaric.

'At high tide,' agreed Pendrag, 'but, yes, I can do it. In fact, I've been thinking about how we can better remove the–'

Sigmar smiled, held up a hand, and said, 'Good. When the snows break fully I will gather every smith from across the Unberogen lands, and you will teach them how to make such things. Master Alaric is right, without better weapons and armour we are lost.'

Pendrag said, 'You want *me* to teach them? Why not Master Alaric?'

'With all due respect to Master Alaric, he will not be with us forever, and it is time we learned to do these things on our own.'

'Quite right,' agreed Alaric. 'Besides you could die tomorrow, and then where would you be?'

Pendrag shot Alaric an exasperated look as Sigmar continued. 'The king has decreed that by the end of the summer every Unberogen village is to be forging iron blades. You and Master Alaric have done magnificent things here, but you two alone cannot hope to produce enough weapons, fast enough to equip our warriors.'

Pendrag stood, and spat on his palm, offering his hand to his sword-brother.

'By the end of the summer?'

'Think you can do it?' asked Sigmar, spitting on his palm and taking Pendrag's hand.

'I can do it,' said Pendrag.

KING MARBAD ARRIVED barely a week after the snows broke, riding towards the Sudenreik Bridge with his raven banner unfurled and pipers marching before him. The pipers wore long kilts formed from leather straps, and gleaming breastplates of layered bronze discs.

Each musician was a youth of extraordinary height, and the pipes they carried resembled wheezing bladders stuck with wooden pipes, one of which was blown into, while another was played with the fingers.

The music carried across the river, and the fishermen on the far bank clapped in time to the infectious melodies when they saw the raven banner, and who rode beneath it.

The king of the Endals was well known to the Unberogen, a grey-haired man of advancing years with a lined and weathered face. His frame was lean and spare, though his bronze armour was moulded to resemble the muscular physique of his youth. He wore a tall helm with feathered wings of black that swept up from the sweeping cheek plates, and a long dark cloak was spread over the rump of his horse. A score of Raven Helms rode alongside their king, tall warriors with black cloaks and winged helms identical to their king's. These were the best and bravest of the Endal warriors, men who had sworn to protect their king's life with their own.

The folk of Reikdorf paused in their labours to watch the procession of warriors, cheering as they welcomed these friends from distant lands. Unberogen scouts rode with the Endals, and the warriors manning the walls of Reikdorf passed word of the arrival of Marbad.

As the king of the Endals crossed the Reik and began the climb towards the settlement, the gates opened wide, and King Björn walked out to greet Marbad, with Sigmar at his side. Alfgeir and the Guards of the Great Hall followed close behind, wolfskin pelts draped over their shoulders and long-handled warhammers held at their sides.

Sigmar watched the riders with a practiced eye, seeing the discipline in their ranks as the grim-faced Raven Helms kept their hands near their sword hilts, never relaxing their guard, even in this friendly territory. They were powerful men, wolf-lean and tough, though the horses that bore them were thin, and not the equals of wide-chested Unberogen steeds.

'Damn, but it's good to see you again, Marbad!' bellowed the king of the Unberogen, his powerful voice easily reaching down to the river. Sigmar smiled at the genuine pleasure he heard in his father's voice, having found it absent for much of the winter.

Ever since Trinovantes's funeral rites had been completed, the fire in his father's eyes had dimmed, and he had taken to looking at him strangely when he thought Sigmar was not aware of it.

King Marbad looked up, and his previously grim face broke apart in a wide grin. The king of the Endals had visited Reikdorf many years ago, but Sigmar had only vague recollections of him. The black-cloaked riders made their way to the gates of Reikdorf, and fanned out to halt in a line with their king at the centre. The pipers took up position at either end of the line, while the bearer of the raven banner remained beside Marbad.

'Good to see you're still alive, Björn,' said Marbad, his voice powerful despite his lean physique. 'You've been having some hard times of it, I hear.'

'Wolfgart exaggerates,' said Björn, clearly realising where Marbad's information had come from.

Marbad swung his leg over his horse's neck and dropped lightly to the ground, and the two kings embraced like long-lost brothers, slapping each other hard on the back with their fists.

'It has been too long, Marbad,' said Björn.

'It has that, my friend,' replied Marbad, looking over to Sigmar, 'and this cannot be Sigmar! He was but a lad when last I saw him.'

Björn turned, with his arm still around Marbad's shoulders. 'I know! I can't believe it either. It seems like only yesterday he was suckling at the teat and shitting his cot!'

Sigmar masked his annoyance as Björn marched his sword-brother towards Sigmar. Though it had been years since the two kings had seen one another, both men looked so at ease that it might as well have been a day. As Marbad approached, Sigmar's eyes were drawn to the sword sheathed in a scabbard of worn leather at his side, the handle wound with bright silver wire, and a blue gem burning with a harsh light at its pommel.

This was Ulfshard, a blade said to have been forged by the fey folk in ancient times, when daemons stalked the lands, and the race of man had lived in caves and spoke in grunts and howls.

Sigmar tore his gaze from the weapon, and held himself straight as King Marbad placed his gloved hands on his shoulders, his face full of pride.

'You have become a fine-looking man, Sigmar,' said Marbad. 'Gods, I can see your mother in you!'

'My father tells me I have her eyes,' replied Sigmar, pleased at the compliment.

'Aye, well it's a good thing you take after her, boy,' laughed Marbad. 'You wouldn't want to look like this old man would you?'

'Just because we are sword-brothers, he thinks he can insult me in my own lands,' said Björn, leading Marbad away from Sigmar and towards Alfgeir.

'My friend,' said Marbad, taking the king's champion's hand in the warrior's grip. 'You prosper?'

Alfgeir nodded. 'I do, my lord.'

'As talkative as ever, eh?' said Marbad. 'And where is Eoforth? That old rogue still dispensing his gibberish and calling it wisdom?'

'He begs your leave, Marbad,' said Björn. 'He is no longer a young man, and it takes him time to get up from his bed these days.'

'Ach, no matter, I'll see him tonight, eh?'

'That you will, old friend, that you will,' promised Björn, before turning to Alfgeir, and saying, 'Food and water for the Raven Helms, and make sure their horses receive the best grain.'

'I shall see to it, my king,' said Alfgeir, who began issuing orders to the Guards of the Great Hall.

Marbad turned to Sigmar again and said, 'Wolfgart told me of Astofen Bridge, but I think I'd like to hear it from the horse's mouth. Maybe this time I'll get to hear it without all the dragons and evil sorcerers, eh? What say you, lad? Would you indulge an old man in a bit of storytelling?'

Sigmar nodded. 'I'd be happy to, my lord,' he said.

ONCE AGAIN, THE longhouse of the Unberogen was filled with carousing warriors, the ale and roasting meat in plentiful supply. Sigmar sat at the trestle tables with his warriors, drinking as his father and Marbad sat and talked at the end of the table. Serving girls circled the table, bearing platters of succulent meat, skins of wine and jugs of beer.

The atmosphere was fine, and even the Raven Helms had relaxed enough to remove their armour and join the warriors of the Unberogen as they feasted. Earlier in the evening, Sigmar had spoken at length with a warrior named Laredus, and had found much to like about the Endals.

Having been forced from their ancestral lands by an influx of Jutone tribesmen driven west by the warlike Artur of the Teutogens, they had carved a home from the inhospitable lands around the Reik estuary.

Sigmar had never journeyed that far west, but from the description of Laredus, and his father's tale of the battle against the mist daemons, he decided he had no wish to. The description of Marburg, however, made it sound magnificent, its earthen ramparts built atop a great rock of volcanic black stone that reared above the marshes, and the tall, winged towers of the Raven Hall constructed on the ruins of an outpost of what was said to have once been a coastal outpost of the fey folk.

Marbad's pipers filled the hall with music, and though the strange, skirling wail was not to Sigmar's taste, the warriors in the hall plainly disagreed with him, linking arms and swinging one another around a cleared space in the hall to its rapid tempo. Wolfgart danced like a madman, working his way along a line of young girls, who clapped and laughed at his antics.

Sigmar laughed as Wolfgart and his latest partner spun into a serving girl, and sent a tray of roast boar flying through the air. Cooked meat rained down, and the king's wolfhounds bounded into the mass of dancers to snatch up the tasty morsels. Laughing anarchy erupted as the barking hounds tripped dancers, and men and women helped each other to their feet.

'He never was very light on his feet, was he?' said Pendrag, taking a seat opposite Sigmar.

Sigmar turned away from the chaos of the dance and said, 'Aye, sometimes I wonder how he manages to swing that big sword of his and not take his own head off.'

'Blind luck, I assume.'

'There's something to be said for luck,' said Sigmar, draining the last of his beer, and banging his mug on the table for more.

'I'd prefer not to rely on it just the same,' said Pendrag. 'She's a fickle maiden, one minute by your side, the next deserting you for another.'

'There's truth in that,' agreed Sigmar as a pretty, flaxen-haired serving girl refilled his mug and smiled seductively. As she moved away, Pendrag laughed, and said, 'I don't think you need worry about finding a bed to hop into tonight, Sigmar.'

'She's nice, but not my type,' said Sigmar, taking a deep drink.

'No,' said Pendrag. 'You prefer girls with dark hair, yes?'

Sigmar felt his face redden, and said, 'What do you mean?'

'Come on, don't play the fool with me, brother,' said Pendrag. 'I know you only have eyes for Ravenna, it's as clear as day. Anyway, did you think I'd be so busy teaching old men how to make iron swords that I wouldn't notice that golden cloak pin Alaric is making for you?'

'Am I that obvious?'

Pendrag frowned as though he was deep in thought. 'Yes.'

'My thoughts are filled with her,' admitted Sigmar.

'So talk to her,' said Pendrag. 'Just because her brother is a serpent is no reason to avoid her. I've seen how she looks at you.'

'You have?' asked Sigmar. 'I mean, she does?'

'Of course,' laughed Pendrag. 'If you weren't so hung up on this vision of an empire, you'd see it too. She's a fine lass is Ravenna, and you *will* need a queen someday.'

'A queen?' cried Sigmar. 'I hadn't thought that far ahead!'

'Why not? She's beautiful and when she took that shield from you, I think I even fell a little in love with her.'

Sigmar said, 'Oh really?' and reached over the table and emptied the last of his beer over Pendrag, who spluttered in mock indignation and then returned the favour. The two friends laughed and clasped hands, and Sigmar felt a great weight lift from his shoulders.

He sat back on the bench, and looked over to the head of the table, catching his father's eye as the king beckoned him from across the room.

'My father asks for me,' he said, pushing to his feet, and running his hands through his beer-soaked hair. He looked down at his sodden jerkin. 'Do I look presentable?'

'Every inch the king's son,' affirmed Pendrag. 'Now look, when Marbad asks you to tell the story of Astofen, remember to make my part in the battle sound exciting.'

'That won't be a problem,' said Sigmar, slapping a hand on his friend's shoulder, and turning to make his way through the feasting warriors to join the two kings.

'You know you're supposed to drink the beer, not wear it, eh?' said Marbad, laughing as he saw the state of Sigmar.

'My son surrounds himself with rogues,' said Björn.

'A man *should* surround himself with rogues,' nodded Marbad. 'It keeps him honest, eh?'

'Is that why I keep you around, old man?' cried Björn.

'Could be,' agreed Marbad, 'though I like to think it is because of my winning personality.'

Sigmar took a seat beside Marbad, his eyes once again straying to the sword belted at the Endal king's side. He longed to see the weapon of the ancient fey folk, wondering how such a weapon would differ from one crafted by the dwarfs.

Marbad saw his glance, and swiftly drew the blade from its scabbard, offering it to Sigmar. The blue gem in the pommel winked in the firelight, and the reflected glow of the torches rippled as though trapped within the smooth face of the blade.

'Take it,' said Marbad.

Sigmar took the proffered weapon, amazed at its lightness and balance. Compared to his sword, Ulfshard was a masterpiece of the weaponsmith's craft, entirely different, yet filled with the same ferocious power as Ghal-maraz. The blade shimmered with its own internal light, and Sigmar knew that with such weapons nations could be forged.

'It's magnificent,' he said. 'I have never seen its like.'

'Nor will you again,' said Marbad. 'The fey folk made Ulfshard before they passed from the lands of men, and unless they return, it will be the only one of its kind.'

Sigmar handed the weapon back to King Marbad, his palm tingling from the powerful forces bound within the blade.

'Your father has been telling me of your grand dreams for the future, young Sigmar,' said Marbad, sheathing the sword in one smooth motion. 'An empire of men. It has a ring to it, I'll give you that, eh?'

Sigmar nodded, and poured more beer from a copper ewer. 'It is ambitious, I know that, but I believe it can be done. More than that, I believe it *needs* to be done.'

'How will you begin?' asked Marbad. 'Most of the tribes hate each other. I have no love for the Jutones or the Teutogens, and your people have fought with the Merogens and Asoborns in recent years. The Norsii are friends to no man. Did you know they perform human sacrifices to the gods of the northern wastes?'

'I had heard that,' nodded Sigmar, 'but the same thing was once said of the Thuringian berserkers, and that was just tall tales.'

Sigmar's father shook his head. 'I have fought the Norsii, my son. I have seen the carnage left in the wake of their invasions, and Marbad speaks the truth. They are a barbarous people without honour.'

'Then we will drive them from the lands of men,' said Sigmar.

Marbad laughed. 'He's got courage, I'll give him that, Björn.'

'It can be done,' persisted Sigmar. 'The Endals and the Unberogen are allies, and my father has ridden to war alongside the Cherusens and Taleutens. Such alliances are the beginnings of how I will bring the tribes together.'

'What of the Teutogens and the Ostagoths?' asked Björn, 'and the Asoborns and the Brigundians, and all the others?'

Sigmar took a long drink of his beer and said, 'I do not know yet, father, but there is always a way. With swords or words, I will win the tribes to my side, and forge a land worthy of those who will come after us.'

'You have great vision, my boy, great vision!' cried King Marbad as he clapped a proud hand on Sigmar's shoulder. 'If the gods smile on you, I think you might be the greatest of us all. Now come on, eh? Tell me of Astofen Bridge.'

SIX

Partings and Meetings

KING MARBAD AND his warriors stayed with the Unberogen for another week, enjoying the hospitality of King Björn and his people, and repaying it with tales of the west and their struggles against the Jutones and the Bretonii. The land around the Reik estuary was a place of battle, with three tribes of men squeezed into an area with only limited fertile land.

'Why did Marius not stay to fight the Teutogens?' Sigmar had asked one night as he and his father dined with Marbad.

'Marius was humbled by Artur in their first battle,' said Marbad, 'and the king of the Jutones isn't a man who likes to be humbled. Artur's Teutogens are fierce warriors, but they're also disciplined and have learned much from the dwarfs who helped them burrow up through that damned mountain of theirs.'

'The Fauschlag Rock,' said Sigmar. 'It sounds incredible.'

'Aye,' agreed Björn. 'To see it you'd think only gods would dare live up so high.'

'You have seen it?' asked Sigmar.

'Once,' nodded Björn. 'It reaches the sky I think. The tallest thing I ever saw that wasn't a mountain range, and even then it was a close run thing.'

'Your father has the truth of it, young Sigmar,' said Marbad, 'but living up high on that big rock changes a man's perspective. Artur was once a good man, a noble king, but looking down on the land he became greedy and wanted to be master of all he could see. He led his warriors west and smashed Marius's army in a great battle on the coast, driving the Jutones south to the Reik estuary. Masons followed in the wake of this victory, and built towers of stone and high walls. Within a few years a dozen of these things were spread across what had once been Jutone land, and Artur's warriors could attack at will across the forest. Much as I hate to admit it, Marius is a canny war leader, and the Jutone hunters are masters of the bow, but even they could not prevail against Artur's stratagems. To survive they had to come further south.'

'Into your lands,' finished Sigmar.

'Aye, into my lands, but we have the Raven Hall, and they'll not soon take that from us. We still hold the lands north of the river's mouth, and we'll fight to hold the Jutones from taking any more ground for now, but they'll keep coming. They don't have a choice, for the coastal region is little more than a wasteland, and few things will grow there.'

'You have our swords, brother,' said Björn, reaching out to clasp Marbad's hand.

'Aye, and they are welcome,' nodded Marbad. 'And if ever you need to call on the Raven Helms, they will ride to your aid.'

Sigmar had watched his father and Marbad offer their oath of aid, and knew that through such alliances might his grand vision of an empire be realised. It was with a heavy heart that he gathered with the rest of the Unberogen warriors to bid Marbad farewell from Reikdorf.

The sun was high, and the spring morning was crisp and bright. The last of winter's cold still hung in the air, but the promise of summer was in every breath. The Raven Helms in their dark armour rode through the gate, flanked by the tall pipers, and the king's banner was borne proudly aloft.

Marbad mounted his horse, grunting as his stiff limbs made the task arduous.

'Ach, I'm not a young man, eh?' he said, settling his cloak over the back of his horse and altering his sword belt to have Ulfshard sit more comfortably at his side.

'None of us are anymore, Marbad,' said Björn.

'No, but 'tis the way of things, brother, the old must make way for the young, eh?'

'That's supposed to be the way of it, aye,' said Björn, casting a curious glance at Sigmar.

Marbad turned to Sigmar and leaned down to offer him his hand. 'Fare thee well, Sigmar. I hope you achieve your empire some day, though I doubt I will be alive to see it.'

'I hope you are, my lord,' said Sigmar. 'I can imagine no stauncher ally than the Endals.'

'He's a flatterer too, eh?' laughed Marbad. 'You will go far indeed. Any you cannot defeat with swords, you'll win over with words.'

The king of the Endals turned his horse, and rode through the gates to join the waiting Raven Helms. As they rode off, the cheers of the Unberogen, who had gathered to watch their departure, followed them as they began the long journey home.

The riders crossed the Sudenreik Bridge, past groups of men building new homes and buildings on the other side of the river. Reikdorf was growing, and fresh walls were even now being raised to expand the town across the river.

'I like Marbad,' said Sigmar, turning to his father.

'Aye, he is an easy man to like,' agreed Björn. 'Back in the day, he was a mighty warrior. In his prime he would have attacked the Jutones and driven them away. Perhaps it might have been better for the Endals had rulership passed to one of his sons, to someone with more thirst for battle.'

'What do you mean?' asked Sigmar, walking back into the settlement with his father as the people of Reikdorf returned to their labours.

Björn put his hand on Sigmar's shoulder and said, 'In a wolf pack, the leader is always the strongest, yes?'

'Yes,' agreed Sigmar.

'While it is strong and can fight off challenges from the younger wolves, it remains the leader,' said Björn. 'All the while, the other wolves know that one day the leader will get old, and they will tear out his throat. Sometimes the leader senses when it is his time, leaving the pack and heading into the wilds to die alone with dignity. It is a terrible thing when age makes us weak and we become vulnerable or a burden. Better to leave while there's still some strength left to you than die uselessly with no legacy to call your own. Do you understand me?'

'I do,' said Sigmar.

'It is a hard thing to do,' said Björn. 'A man will cleave to power as he will a beautiful woman, but sometimes it must be set aside when the time is right. Everything has its time in the sun, but a thing that goes on beyond its allotted span is a terrible thing, my son. It weakens everything around it and tarnishes the memory of what glory it once had.'

'WHERE ARE WE going?' asked Ravenna as Sigmar led her through the trees towards the sound of rushing water. Sigmar smiled at the nervous excitement he heard in her voice. She was scared being blindfolded this far from Reikdorf, but pleased to be here with him on this perfect spring morning.

'Just a little further,' he said. 'Just down this slope. Careful, watch your step.'

The day was bright, the sun not yet at its zenith, and the forest was filled with birdsong. A soft wind drifted through the trees, and the gurgling of the water over rocks was soothing.

Spring had restored Ravenna's spirits, and the energising optimism that filled Reikdorf in the months following the snows had helped lift her from melancholy. Once again, she smiled, and it had been like a ray of sunshine in his heart to hear her laughing with the other young girls of the tribe as they came in from the fields.

Since the night he had told her of his grand dream, Sigmar had thought of little else other than Ravenna: her night-dark hair and the sway of her hips as she walked. As much as he had vision for greater things for his people, he was still a man, and Ravenna fired his blood.

They had seen each other as often as time had allowed, but never enough for either of them, and only now, as the touch of summer began to warm the ground, had they found time to escape for an afternoon together.

They had ridden along hunters' paths deep into the woodland, through open clearings and along rutted tracks identified with marker stones. Eventually, Sigmar had led them from the path and into the forest, where they had dismounted and tethered the horses to the low branches of a sapling. Sigmar had taken a hide pack and cloth-wrapped bundle from his horse's panniers and slung them over his shoulder before taking her hand and leading her onwards.

'Come on, Sigmar,' said Ravenna. 'Where are we?'

'In the forest to the west of Reikdorf, about five miles out,' he said, taking her hand and guiding her down the worn path that led to the river. With her eyes covered, he was free to look at her openly, taking in the curve of her jaw and the smoothness of her skin, so pale against the ochre yellow of her dress.

Her hands were tough, the fingers callused, but the warmth in them sent a flush of excitement through him.

'Five miles?' she laughed, taking tentative steps. 'So far!'

Though they were well within the borders of Unberogen land, it was still not entirely safe to travel so far into the forests alone, but he did not want any worries for their safety to intrude on this day.

'This?' he said. 'This is nothing, soon I will take you to see the open lands far to the south, and north to the ocean. *Then* you will have travelled far.'

'You haven't even seen those places yet,' she pointed out.

'True,' said Sigmar, 'but I will.'

'Oh yes,' she replied, 'when you're building your empire.'

'Exactly,' said Sigmar. 'Right... we are here.'

'I can feel the sun on my face,' said Ravenna. 'Are we in a clearing?'

'Watch your eyes,' he said. 'I am going to take off your blindfold.'

Sigmar moved around behind her, and undid the loose knot with which he had secured the strip of cloth across her eyes. She blinked as she adjusted to the light, but within moments her face lit up at the beauty of the sight before her.

They stood on a grassy bank at the edge of a river, its waters crystal and foaming white as it gambolled over a series of smooth boulders buried in the shallows of the riverbed. Sunlight glittered on the fractured water and silver-skinned fish darted beneath the surface.

'It's wonderful,' said Ravenna, taking his hand and heading to the riverbank.

Sigmar smiled as he revelled in her enjoyment, dropping the hide sack and cloth bundle to the grass, and happily allowed her to drag him behind her. Standing at the river's edge, Ravenna took a deep breath, her eyes closed as she took in the unspoiled scents of the deep forest.

Jasmine was heavy on the air, but Sigmar had no sense of the beauty around him, save that of the young woman beside him.

'Thank you for bringing me here,' she said. 'How did you know of this place?'

'This is the River Skein,' said Sigmar, 'where we met Blacktusk.'

'The great boar?' asked Ravenna.

Sigmar nodded, gesturing to a point on the opposite bank of the river near one of the rounded boulders. 'Yes, the great boar himself.

He came out of the woods just there, and I remember Wolfgart nearly dropped dead of fright when he saw him.'

'Wolfgart, afraid?' laughed Ravenna, glancing nervously across the river. 'Now *that* I would have liked to have seen. Is the boar still alive?'

'I don't know,' said Sigmar. 'I hope so.'

'You hope so? I heard Blacktusk was a monster that killed an entire hunting party.'

'That's true enough,' admitted Sigmar, 'but he was a noble creature, and I think we sensed something in each other that we recognised.'

'What did you recognise in a boar?' laughed Ravenna, kicking her boots off and sitting on the riverbank. 'I'm not trying to flatter you, but I do not think you look much like a boar.'

Ravenna dangled her feet in the cool waters and tilted her head towards the sun.

'No,' he said. 'I didn't mean that, though you should see me with a hangover.'

'Then what did you mean?'

Sigmar sat next to her and undid the thongs holding his boots in place. The water was cold, and he felt his skin tingle pleasantly as he immersed his feet in the fast flowing river.

'I meant that we were both one of a kind.'

She laughed, and gave him a playful shove before seeing that he was serious.

'I'm sorry,' she said. 'I don't mean to laugh.'

'I know, it sounds arrogant, but it is what I felt,' said Sigmar. 'Blacktusk was enormous, the biggest animal I have ever seen, legs like tree trunks and a chest wider than the biggest horse in the king's stables. He was unique.'

'You are right,' said Ravenna. 'That does sound arrogant.'

'Is it? I don't think so, for I am the only one who seems to have a vision of anything better for us than what we have at the moment. The kings of the tribes are content with their lot, squabbling amongst themselves, and fighting the orcs and beasts as they are attacked.'

'But not you?'

'No, not me,' agreed Sigmar, 'but I did not bring you here to talk of war and death.'

'Oh?' said Ravenna, flicking a spray of water towards him. 'So what *did* you bring me here for?'

Sigmar pushed himself to his feet and retrieved the items he had brought from his horse's panniers. He laid the hide pack beside him and handed Ravenna the cloth-wrapped bundle.

'What's this?' she asked.

'Open it and find out.'

Ravenna eagerly unfolded the cloth protecting the bundle's contents, turning it over as she uncovered what lay within. The last covering fell away, and she gasped as she saw a folded emerald cloak embroidered with curling spirals of gold. Silver thread intertwined with the gold, and the collar of the cloak was edged in soft ermine.

Sitting on the folded garment was a tapering golden cloak pin adorned with an azure stone at its thickest end, set in the centre of a circle of glittering gold worked into the shape of a snake devouring its own tail. The workmanship was exquisite. Small bands along the length of the snake's body were engraved with the symbol of a twin-tailed comet.

'I... I don't know what to say,' said Ravenna. 'It's wonderful.'

'Eoforth told me that the snake eating its own tail is a symbol for rebirth and renewal,' said Sigmar as Ravenna turned the pin over in her hands, staring in open-mouthed admiration at the incredible piece of jewellery. 'The start of new things... and the coming together of two into one.'

'Two into one,' smiled Ravenna.

'So he tells me,' said Sigmar. 'I had Master Alaric fashion the pin for me, but I think he only agreed so he wouldn't have to make any more mail shirts.'

Ravenna traced her fingers around the gold circle. 'I have never owned anything so beautiful,' she said, and Sigmar heard a tremor in her voice. 'And this cloak...'

'It was my mother's,' said Sigmar. 'My father said she wore it when they were wed.'

Ravenna placed the pin back on the cloak, and said, 'These are exceptional gifts, Sigmar. Thank you so much.'

Sigmar blushed, happy they had pleased her. 'I am glad you like them.'

'I love them,' said Ravenna. She nodded to the hide pack beside him. 'And what is in there? More presents?'

He smiled. 'Not quite,' he said, reaching over and opening the hide pack to lift out some muslin-wrapped cheese and a number of slices of bread. A wax-sealed clay jug came next, followed by two pewter goblets.

'Food,' she said. 'You thought of everything.'

Sigmar broke the seal on the jug, and poured a crisp liquid the colour of pale apple juice. He handed her a goblet. 'Wine from the slopes of the Reik estuary,' he said, 'courtesy of King Marbad.'

They drank together, and Sigmar enjoyed the refreshing bite of the wine. A more refined taste than the beer he was used to, it was, nevertheless, enjoyably crisp.

'You like it?' he asked.

'I do,' said Ravenna. 'It's sweet.'

'Be careful, Marbad warned me it's quite strong.'

'Are you trying to get me drunk?'

'Do I need to?'

'That depends on what you're trying to achieve.'

Sigmar took another mouthful of wine, feeling as though he was already drunk, but knowing it had nothing to do with the alcohol.

'I know of no clever way to say this,' said Sigmar, 'so I am just going to say it.'

'Say what?'

'I love you, Ravenna,' he said simply. 'I always have, but I am not skilled with words and have not known how to say it until now.'

Ravenna's eyes widened at his declaration, and he feared he had made a terrible error, until she reached out with her free hand and ran her fingers down his cheek.

'That is the nicest thing anyone has ever said to me,' she said.

'You are in my thoughts every day,' said Sigmar, his words coming out in a gabbled rush. 'Every time I see you, I want to sweep you up in my arms and hold you.'

She smiled and halted his ramblings by leaning forward to kiss him, her lips tasting of the wine and a thousand other flavours he would remember for the rest of his life. Sigmar kissed her back, sliding his arms around her and lowering her towards the grass.

Ravenna's arms slipped naturally around his shoulders, and they kissed for many minutes until their hands found each other's belts and buttons. Their clothes slipped from their bodies with ease, and though Sigmar knew it was foolish to be so exposed this far into the forest, all thoughts of caution were banished by the sight of her naked flesh beneath him.

Her skin was pale and smooth, and her flesh lean and hard from days spent working the fields, yet soft and supple and flushed with excitement.

Sigmar had bedded his share of village girls, but as his hands explored her body, he felt as though this beauty before him erased the memory of them. His every touch was experimental, tentative and deliciously new. Likewise, her hands touched the hard, corded muscles of his chest and arms with unabashed pleasure.

They kissed fiercely as they made love, their every movement gaining in confidence. Sigmar wished that the moment would never end. The chill feel of the wind on his back, the rushing of the river and Ravenna's rapid breath rang like thunder in his ears.

At last they were spent, and lay wrapped together on the banks of the river, all thoughts of the world beyond this moment forgotten.

Sigmar rolled onto his elbow and ran his fingertips along the length of her body.

'When I am king, I will marry you,' he said.

Ravenna smiled, and his heart was snared.

THE CAVE WAS dark and filled with echoes of the past: grand deeds, villainous betrayal and horrifying carnage. Some had been plotted and some had been prevented, but as with all things, they had their origins with men and their desires.

The hag woman sat in the centre of the cave, a cauldron of black iron hissing on a low fire in front of her. Evil-smelling smoke rose from the skin of murky liquid at the base of the pot, and she sprinkled a handful of rotten herbs and mildew into the hot metal.

Hissing smoke rose from the mixture, and she took a deep draught into her lungs as she felt the power that blew from the northern realms fill her body. Men knew little of this energy, fearing its power to transform and twist creatures into vile monsters. In their ignorance, they called it sorcery or simply *evil*, but the hag woman knew that this power was simply an elemental force that could be shaped by the will of one strong enough.

As a child, she had been cursed with visions of things that later came to pass, and could perform miraculous feats without effort. Fires could dance on her fingertips, and the shadows would obey her commands, carrying her wherever she desired.

For this she had been feared, and her parents had pleaded with her to stop, to keep her abilities to herself. They had loved her, but they had dreaded her coming of age, and she could hear them as they wept and cursed the gods that had delivered them such an afflicted child.

She was young, however, and the temptation to make use of her ability was too great. She had entertained the other children of the village with dazzling displays of light and fire, sending them squealing home with tales of her wondrous powers.

She had told her father of this, and her heart had broken as she saw the anguish etched into his face. Without a word spoken, he had taken up his axe and led her from their small home and into the dusk-lit forest.

They had walked for hours until she had fallen asleep, and he had carried her against his chest. If she tried, she could still recall the smell of his leather jerkin and the peaty aroma of the marshes as he splashed through the shallow bogs of the Brackenwalsch.

With the green moon high overhead, he had set her down amid the reeds and black water, the drone of insects and distant splashes of marsh toads loud in the darkness. His axe had come up, moonlight glinting on the sharpened blade, and she had cried as he had cried also.

The hag woman felt her anger grow and viciously suppressed it. Anger would cause the north wind to surge with fierce power and send her into a dark spiral of hate. To soar on the currents of power, the mind needed to be clear. Anger would only cloud her thoughts.

Her father had held the axe aloft, his arms shaking at the terrible thing he was about to do, but before it descended to end her life, a strong voice rang out, carried across the bleak fens with fierce authority.

'Leave the child,' said the voice. 'She belongs to me now.'

Her father had backed away, dropping his axe to the waters with a heavy splash.

She cried for him, but he had vanished into the darkness, and she never saw him again.

She had turned to see a withered old crone in ragged black robes making her sure-footed way through the marsh towards her. Her fear was instantly multiplied as she sensed a dreadful familiarity and awful inevitability steal over her, but her feet were rooted to the spot, and she could not move.

'You have the gift, child,' said the crone as she stood before her.

She had shaken her head, but the crone had laughed bitterly. 'You cannot lie, girl. I see it in you as my predecessor saw it in me. Now come with me, there is much to teach you, and already the Dark Powers are conspiring to see me ended.'

'I don't want to go,' she had said. 'I want to go home. I want my papa.'

'Your papa was going to kill you,' said the crone. 'There is nothing for you to go back to. If you return, the priests of the wolf god will burn you as a practitioner of the dark arts. You will die in pain. Is that what you want?'

'No!'

'No,' agreed the crone. 'Now give me your hand and I will teach you how to use that power of yours.'

She had wept, and the crone's hand, fast as a blade, snapped out and slapped her hard across her cheek.

'Do not cry, child,' snapped the crone. 'Save your tears for the dead. If you are to use your power and live, you will need to be stronger than this.'

The crone offered her hand. 'Now come. There is much to teach you and little time to learn it.'

Stifling her tears, she had taken the crone's hand and been led deep into the marshes where she learned of the mighty wind of power that blew from the north. The long years had taught her much: the power of charms and curses, the means to read portents and omens and, perhaps most importantly, the hearts and minds of men,

'Though they will hate you for your powers, men will ever seek you out to cheat what the world has decreed should be their fate,' explained the crone, who had never told her a name.

'Then why should we help them?' she had asked.

'Because that is the role we play in this world.'

'But why?'

'I cannot answer you, child,' said the crone. 'There has always been a hag woman dwelling in the Brackenwalsch, and there always will be. We are part of the world as much as the tribes of men and their towns. The power we tap into is dangerous; it can twist the hearts of even the noblest person, turning them into a creature of darkness. We use this power so others do not have to. It is a lonely life, yes, but the race of man is not meant to wield such powers, no matter what others might one day decide, for man is too weak to resist its temptations.'

'Then this is our fate?' she had asked. 'To guide and protect while being feared and hated? To never know love or family?'

'Indeed,' agreed the crone. 'This is our burden to bear. Now we will speak no more on it, for time is short, and already I can feel my doom approaching in the tramp of booted feet and the sharpening of cook's knives.'

A year later, her teacher was dead, boiled alive in her own cauldron by orcs.

She had watched as the crone was killed, feeling no sadness or need to intervene. The crone had known of her death for decades, just as she too knew the day of her death, and the time she would seek out an unwilling child of power to become her successor.

A group of men had come upon the orcs in the midst of a terrible thunderstorm and destroyed them. The leader of these men had slaughtered the orcs with deadly sweeps of his two-bladed axe as the woman who travelled with them screamed in pain. As the battle drew to a close, the woman's screams ended, and the screams of a newborn cleaved the air.

Anguished cries came from the men, who discovered that the woman was dead. She watched the grieving axeman lift a bloody baby from the ground as a roaring peal of thunder split the sky and a mighty comet lit the heavens with twin fiery tails.

'The Child of Thunder... born with the sound of battle in his ears and the feel of blood on his skin,' she hissed. 'Yours will be a life of greatness, but one of war.'

Over the years, she had found her thoughts ever drawn to the child born beneath the sign of the twin-tailed comet, the currents of power that flowed around him, and the twisting fates he shaped simply by existing.

More and more, she knew that great powers had been unleashed with this child's birth, but that they had left their work undone. To achieve his potential, much had yet to happen to him: joy, grief, anger, betrayal and a great love that would forever change the destiny of this land.

She allowed her spirit to fly free of her body, leaving behind her wasted, skeletal frame, and soaring on wings of the spirit, where all flesh was meaningless and strength of spirit was all. Invisible currents filled the air, stirred by the warlike hearts of mankind and myriad creatures of this world, and these currents blew strong, bathing the land in unseen thunderheads of roiling power.

The marshes of the Brackenwalsch seethed with ancient energies, the ground saturated in the raw power that bubbled up from the world's centre. She could see the world laid out before her like a great map, the great mountains of the south and east, the mighty ocean of the west and the lands of the fey beyond it.

The great wind of power blew in variegated clouds from the north, a mixture of powerful reds and purples with only a few spots of white and gold amongst the ugly, warlike colours. The darker colours were growing stronger, and war was looming like a vast shadow covering the land with its promise of destruction, famine and widows.

Her sight swooped low over the world, seeing the lone, trudging figure she had been waiting for as he made his way carefully through the marsh. His green cloak was pulled tightly around his lean frame, and she was mildly irritated that he had reached the hill where she made her home without her becoming aware of him.

Swirling colours surrounded him, vivid reds, shocking pinks and lascivious purples. An instrument of the Dark Powers, to be sure, but one with a purpose that suited her own for now.

She returned swiftly to her flesh, groaning as the weight of her years settled upon her after the freedom of the spirit. When her kind died out, none would remember how to soar on the winds of power, and the thought saddened her as she heard wet footfalls beyond the mouth of her cave.

She blinked away the harsh smoke, and awaited the arrival of the young man with vengeance and betrayal on his mind.

He was startlingly handsome, and his finely sculpted, slender physique stirred a longing in her that she had never before known. Handsome to the point of obscenity, his features were the perfect combination of hard masculinity and feminine softness.

Dark hair was gathered in a short ponytail, and a sword, sheathed in a black leather scabbard, was belted at his side.

'Welcome to my home, Gerreon of the Unberogen,' she said.

BOOK TWO
Forging the King

Mighty is Sigmar
He who saves a dwarf king
From dishonour
How can I reward him?
A hammer of war
A hammer of iron
Which fell from the sky
With two tongues of fire
From the forge of the gods
Worked by runesmiths
Ghal-maraz is its name
The Splitter of Skulls.

SEVEN
All our People

FIRELIGHT ILLUMINATED THE faces of the warriors around him, and Sigmar nodded to Wolfgart and Pendrag as he saw the shadowy forms of Svein and Cuthwin making their way downhill through the thick undergrowth. Both moved in silence, their skill in blending with the landscape making them Sigmar's most valued scouts.

'Here they come,' whispered Sigmar.

His sword-brothers peered through the twilight gloom. 'You have keen eyes, brother,' said Wolfgart. 'I can see nothing.'

Pendrag nodded towards a line of trees and said, 'There. By the elms, I think.'

Wolfgart squinted, but shook his head. 'Like ghosts they are,' he said.

'They'd be poor scouts if they let themselves be seen,' pointed out Pendrag.

The two scouts stepped from behind the trees they had been using as cover and Sigmar waved them over to the group of horsemen that lurked in the tangled bushes at the edge of the crater. The terrain here was steep and heavily wooded, the ground underfoot earthy and strewn with jagged, black rocks.

Legend said a piece of the moon had fallen here centuries ago and smashed a hole in the ground. Sigmar did not know if that was true, but the land around this place was barren, and nothing good grew here. The air had a foul reek to it and the trees were twisted as if in pain. The bushes that sprouted along the edges of the crater were wiry and barbed, the thorns weeping a greenish sap that imparted fever dreams to any man unlucky enough to be scratched.

The sound of muffled drums and guttural brays drifted over the rocky lip of the crater, accompanied by a dark tongue issuing from throats never meant to give voice to language.

Fifty warriors wrapped in wolfskin cloaks awaited the scouts, and Sigmar prayed that the ground was favourable, for he could feel the need for vengeance burning in every man's heart. The butchery inflicted by the beasts on the settlements straddling the borders of the Unberogen and Asoborn lands had been unprecedented.

'What did you see?' he asked when the two scouts drew near enough to hear his whisper.

'Around sixty or seventy beasts,' replied Svein, 'drunk and bloody.'

'Captives?'

Svein's normally jovial face hardened and he nodded. 'Aye, but none in a good way. The beasts have made sport of them.'

'And they have no idea we are here?' asked Wolfgart.

Cuthwin shook his head. 'I brought us in downwind of their encampment. None of them are looking outwards, they are too... busy... with the captives.'

'You're sure?' pressed Wolfgart.

'I'm sure,' snapped Cuthwin. 'If they find us here it will be because of your bloody noise.'

Sigmar hid his smile from Wolfgart as he remembered the night when he had discovered Cuthwin sneaking towards the longhouse in the centre of Reikdorf, nearly six years ago. It had been the night before they had ridden to battle at Astofen Bridge, and Sigmar remembered the lad's stealth and defiant courage, traits that served him well as one of Sigmar's warriors.

Wolfgart bristled in anger at the young scout's words, but kept his mouth shut.

'Pendrag,' said Sigmar, 'take fifteen warriors and ride eastwards for three hundred paces. Wolfgart, you do the same to the west.'

'And you?' asked Wolfgart. 'What will you be doing?'

'I'll be riding over the ridge charging into the heart of the beasts' encampment,' said Sigmar. 'When they come at me, you pair will ride in from the flanks and crush them.'

'Sound plan,' said Wolfgart. 'Nice and simple.'

Pendrag looked as though he was about to argue, but shrugged and turned his horse to gather his men. Sigmar nodded to Wolfgart, who followed Pendrag's example and rode off to gather the warriors he would lead into battle.

Sigmar turned in his saddle to face the warrior behind him as the tempo of the drums from within the crater increased, and said, 'Gerreon, are you ready?'

Trinovantes's twin rode forward to join him, and grinned wolfishly. 'I am ready, brother.'

SIGMAR AND GERREON had made their peace six years ago.

Sigmar had been sparring with Pendrag upon the Field of Swords at the base of Warrior's Hill, practising with sword and spear, when Trinovantes's brother had sought him out. The Field of Swords was the name given to a wide area of ground within Reikdorf's walls where the veteran warriors of the ever-expanding town trained the younger men for battle.

Wolfgart had argued that it was bad luck to learn the skills of war before a place of the dead, but Sigmar had insisted, claiming that every warrior needed to know what was at stake if they faltered.

Scores of youngsters learned to fight with sword and spear under Alfgeir's merciless tutelage, while Wolfgart instructed others in archery. Targets carved to resemble orcs had been set up, and the *thwack* of accurately loosed arrows and the clash of iron swords filled the air.

Every man in Reikdorf now owned an iron sword, and Pendrag and Alaric had travelled throughout the Unberogen lands over the years to ensure that every smith laboured in a forge equipped with a water-powered bellows capable of producing such weapons. Few warriors now wore bronze armour, and most riders were equipped with mail shirts of linked iron rings or hauberks of overlapping scales.

Emissaries from the Jutones, Cherusens and Taleutens had observed the great leaps the Unberogen were making, and King Björn relished the thought of his tribe's strength being known far and wide throughout the land.

'Here comes trouble,' said Pendrag as Gerreon approached.

Sigmar lowered his sword and turned to face Ravenna's brother, already tensing for harsh words and the handsome warrior's outrage at his behaviour with his sister. It was no secret that he and Ravenna were becoming closer, and only a blind man could have missed their obvious feelings for one another.

He was just surprised it had taken Gerreon this long to approach him.

As always, Gerreon was immaculately dressed, his buckskin trews of the finest quality, his black jerkin stitched with silver thread and his boots crafted from soft leather. His hand lightly gripped the hilt of his sword, a sword Sigmar had seen him wield with terrifying, dazzling skill in numerous practice bouts and battles.

Sigmar was a fine swordsman, but Gerreon was what the Roppsmenn of the east called a *blademaster*. He tensed, expecting furious indignation, and felt Pendrag move alongside him.

'Gerreon,' said Sigmar, 'if this is about Ravenna...'

'No, Sigmar,' replied Gerreon. 'This is not about my sister. It is about you and I.'

Surely Gerreon did not mean to challenge him to a combat? To challenge the king's son was madness. Even if he won, the king's guards would kill him.

'Then what is it about?'

Gerreon removed his hand from his sword hilt. 'I have had time to think since Trinovantes's death, and I am ashamed of the things I said and did when you returned from Astofen. He was your friend and you loved him dearly.'

'That I did, Gerreon,' said Sigmar.

'I just wanted you to know that I do not blame you for his death. As my sister said, it was an orc that killed him, not you. If you will offer me your forgiveness, then I will offer you friendship as my brother once did.'

Gerreon smiled his dazzling smile and offered his hand to Sigmar, 'And as my sister now does.'

Sigmar felt his face reddening as he took Gerreon's hand. 'You are Unberogen,' he said. 'You do not need my forgiveness, but you have it anyway.'

'Thank you,' said Gerreon. 'This means a lot to me, Sigmar. I did not know if I had forfeited any chance of friendship.'

'Never,' said Sigmar. 'What kind of empire will I forge if there is division within the Unberogen? No, Gerreon, you are one of us and you always will be.'

They shook hands, and Gerreon smiled in relief.

WOLFGART AND PENDRAG had been suspicious of this sudden contrition, but in the years that followed, Sigmar's trust had been vindicated, and Gerreon had earned their respect in dozens of desperate fights. At the Battle of the Barren Hills, Gerreon had saved Sigmar's life, neatly beheading an orc war leader that had pinned him beneath the body of its slain wolf.

Against Teutogen raiders, Gerreon had also despatched an archer ready to loose a point-blank shaft into Sigmar's unprotected back.

Time and time again, Gerreon had ridden into battle alongside them, and each time, Sigmar was thankful for the strength of character that had driven the warrior to seek forgiveness. Ravenna had been overjoyed, and Sigmar had spent many pleasant times with her and Gerreon, hunting, riding the forest trails or simply talking long into the night of his dream of uniting the tribes of man.

Now, with the darkness all around them and his sword-brothers riding away from him to circle around the crater, Sigmar was grateful for Gerreon's presence. He counted a hundred heartbeats before urging his stallion forward, the twenty warriors who remained with him following swiftly behind.

The sound of the drums grew louder as the horses climbed the rocky slopes of the crater, and Sigmar twisted in the saddle to address the riders behind them. Each wore a mail shirt, and many sported iron breastplates and shoulder guards. Red cloaks flowed from their shoulders, and every rider carried a long spear and heavy sword.

'We hit them hard and fast,' said Sigmar. 'Make lots of noise when you charge, I want them all looking at us.'

He could see in their faces that every man knew what to do. 'Good hunting,' he said.

The ridge at the top of the crater drew nearer, limned in starlight, and the clouds above glowed orange from the fires below. A scream tore the night, and Sigmar felt his anger grow at the terror and unimaginable pain it conveyed.

'You realise the risk we're taking,' said Gerreon.

'I do, but we cannot wait,' said Sigmar. 'If we do not attack now, the beasts will vanish into the deep forest and we will lose any chance to avenge the dead. No, they die tonight.'

Gerreon nodded and slid his sword from its sheath.

Sigmar hefted a heavy, iron-tipped spear from the quiver slung behind him.

'Unberogen!' he yelled, raking his heels along the stallion's flanks. 'Ride to vengeance!'

The stallion surged over the crater's lip, and his riders followed him with a roaring war cry.

Below was a scene of bedlam. Flames roared skyward, and packs of monstrously twisted beasts filled the basin of the crater, carousing and drunk on slaughter and vile spirits.

Freakish monsters of fur and hide, the hideous creatures were the bastard gets of man and beast, shaggy goat heads atop muscular torsos and twisted, reverse jointed legs. Red-skinned creatures with horned skulls and whipping tails capered amid mounds of the dead, while lumbering beasts that resembled a dreadful fusion of horse and rider lurched drunkenly around the edges of the campsite.

A great black stone reared above the gathering at the crater's centre, a spike of obsidian carved with hideous runes that spoke of slaughter and debauchery. A huge, bull-headed beast in a ragged black cloak tore the heart from a still-living captive as mad creatures of no easily identifiable heritage slithered and capered around the stone in lunatic adoration.

Their howls mingled with the drumbeats of huge, wolf-headed creatures that hammered their taloned paws on crude hide drums.

Bound men, women and children were spread throughout the camp, their bodies abused and beaten. Many were dead, and all had been tortured. Others had simply been eaten alive, and Sigmar's anger, already white-hot, threatened to overwhelm him as he felt a red mist descend upon him.

Sigmar was no berserker, however, and he focused his rage into a burning spear of cold anger.

His stallion pounded down the slope, and a wordless cry of hatred burst form his lips. An Unberogen war horn sounded, the strident notes of each blast seeming to carry them towards their foe with greater speed.

The creatures were rousing themselves, though their debauched revelries had left them lethargic and unprepared. The bull-headed beast let loose a deafening bellow that echoed from the sides of the crater, and the relentless tattoo of the drums ceased.

A handful of the red-skinned monsters hurled spears at the riders, but they were poorly aimed, and none of the riders were troubled. Sigmar hurled his own spear, the heavy missile punching through a beast's back and pinning it to a stunted tree. His warriors cast their own spears, and the air was filled with grunting roars of pain.

Cuthwin and Svein loosed arrows from the crater's lip, and each goose-feathered shaft felled another beast. With no time to hurl another spear, Sigmar took up Ghal-maraz and swung it at the snarling, bestial face of a shaggy, bear-headed monster.

The warhammer cleaved the beast's skull, and Sigmar rode deeper into the press of enemies. Snapping jaws and yellowed talons flashed towards him. His horse screamed in pain as a stabbing spear tore into its haunch. Sigmar backhanded Ghal-maraz into his attacker's chest, crushing its ribcage and hurling it through the air.

The Unberogen smashed through the beasts' campsite in a trampling fury of blades. Spears stabbed and swords hacked clawed limbs from powerfully muscled shoulders. The centaur creatures bellowed in defiance as they charged in, long axes and spiked clubs raised.

Sigmar saw one of his riders battered from his steed by such a weapon, the man falling to the ground broken and dead, his armour no defence against the brute strength of the monster.

The reek of the creatures was a potent mix of wet fur, blood and excrement. Sigmar gagged as a cackling devil-creature leapt onto his horse and buried its needle fangs in the muscle of his arm.

Sigmar slammed his elbow back, smashing its lupine features and dislodging it from his flesh. He drew his dagger with his free hand and stabbed backwards, plunging the blade into his attacker's belly. The beast fell from his horse, and he stabbed the dagger through the eye of a snarling creature that charged him with a wide-bladed axe. The blade was torn from his hand, and he heard more cries of pain as the beasts finally overcame the shock of the Unberogen charge.

The great beast in the centre of the camp stood with its arms outstretched, lightning dancing in the palms of its hands. Sigmar looked up to the east and west as he heard the war cries of his sword-brothers. First Pendrag appeared and then Wolfgart, leading the remainder of his warriors in the charge.

'Unberogen!' he yelled, riding into the thick of the fighting.

Sigmar swung Ghal-maraz left and right, slaying beasts with every blow, and roaring with the release of battle. The thunder of horses' hooves echoed around the crater as Wolfgart and Pendrag charged into battle, the clash of swords and axes deafening.

Then the lightning struck.

As though hurled by some malign god, a sizzling spear of blue-white light slammed into the ground in the midst of the Unberogen. The bolt exploded, and men, horses and beasts were hurled through the air as its deadly energy tore through them.

The reek of burned meat filled the air, and Sigmar blinked away dazzling after-images, horrified at the awesome destruction. Another bolt of lightning crashed into the earth, ripping a zigzagging trail of destruction as the blinding light split the sky.

Screams of pain sounded, and horses thrashed madly on the ground, their legs blasted to stumps by the power of the lightning. Roaring monsters fell upon the downed riders, stabbing with crude spears and knives. Crackling arcs of energy danced in the air, zipping from rider to rider, and pitching them from their horses.

Sigmar saw Wolfgart hurled through the air as yet another whipping bolt of light exploded amid the riders. Pendrag's warriors smashed into the beasts, scattering them before their blades and spears. Arrows thudded into bestial flesh, and terrified brays from the smaller beasts echoed as they sought to flee the slaughter.

The riders spared them no mercy, crushing them beneath the hooves of their charging steeds or bringing them down with hurled spears.

Yet more lightning stabbed from the sky, and the ground rippled with flickering blue fire as it struck. Arcs of power crashed into the crater, and Sigmar heard the bull-headed monster's glee at the destruction it had unleashed. The beast kept one clawed hand flat on the mighty herdstone at the centre of the crater as it called down the lightning, and Sigmar urged his horse towards it. He raised Ghal-maraz high as another snapping, fizzing bolt of lightning hammered downwards.

Instead of striking the ground, however, it struck the mighty head of Sigmar's hammer.

Sigmar felt the awesome power the great beast had called upon, and a terrible heat built in the shaft of Ghal-maraz as it fought to dissipate the dreadful energies. He cried out as a measure of those energies pulsed through him, filling his veins with elemental fire.

Arcs of blue light flashed around Sigmar and flared from Ghal-maraz in buzzing, crackling arcs. The lightning blazed in Sigmar's eyes as he struggled to contain energies that could tear him apart in an instant.

The creature saw him coming and barked out a series of guttural commands to its followers, who swiftly rushed to defend it. The freakishly twisted creatures shambled to block his path, but a host of arrows flashed, felling a number of them.

Sigmar let loose an ululating war cry, and his stallion leapt into the air.

The beasts howled as Sigmar sailed over them, drawing back his hammer and hurling it towards the lightning wreathed monster.

Ghal-maraz spun through the air, crackling with energy. Sigmar's horse landed as the weapon struck. With one hand fastened to the herdstone and the other locked in place with the lightning, the great beast was powerless to avoid Sigmar's throw.

The monster's skull split apart as the mighty warhammer struck, its head exploding in a welter of blood and bone fragments. A jet of blazing energy fountained from its headless corpse, and its body jerked spasmodically as the power it had summoned erupted from its flesh.

Sigmar wheeled his horse as the beast died, its seared body reduced to a withered husk of burned meat. The fire in his eyes dimmed, and the last of the caged lightning fled his body at the death of its creator. Sigmar took a juddering breath and turned his attention back to the battle raging behind him.

The beasts howled at the death of their leader, the last of their number being ridden down by Unberogen warriors. Wolfgart stood in the midst of the crater, hacking his enormous blade through the last of the slavering, wolf-headed drummer beasts, while Pendrag loosed shaft after shaft from his horn bow into the fleeing creatures.

Sigmar smiled grimly to himself. Within moments, not a single beast would remain alive.

He slid from the back of his horse and patted its flanks.

'Gods, that was a mighty leap, Greatheart!' he cried, rubbing a hand down its neck and ruffling its mane.

The horse whinnied in pleasure and tossed its mane, following him as he stooped to retrieve his warhammer. The lightning it had briefly carried within it had faded, though the runic script across the head still shone with power.

'That was perhaps the most foolish thing I have ever seen you do,' said Gerreon, riding up behind him.

Sigmar turned to face the warrior. 'What was?'

'Throwing your hammer like that. You just disarmed yourself.'

'I still had my sword,' said Sigmar.

Gerreon pointed to Sigmar's waist, where a broken strap of leather was all that remained of his sword belt. Sigmar had not even felt the blow that had cut the leather, and felt suddenly foolish for hurling Ghal-maraz.

'By Ulric!' cried Wolfgart, jogging over to join them. 'That was a throw, Sigmar! Amazing! Took the bastard's head clean off!'

Gerreon shook his head. 'And here is me telling him what an idiot he was for throwing it.'

'Not at all!' said Wolfgart. 'Didn't you see? I've never seen anything like it. The lightning! The throw!'

'What if you had missed? What then?' asked Pendrag, riding to join the gathering.

'I'd have beaten it to death,' said Sigmar, assuming a fist-fighter's pose.

'Didn't you see the size of it?' laughed Pendrag. 'It would have gored you before you could land a punch.'

'Sigmar?' said Wolfgart. 'Never.'

'Now if you had a hammer that came back to your hand once you'd thrown it,' said Gerreon, 'then I'd be impressed.'

'Don't be stupid,' said Pendrag. 'A hammer that came back after you threw it? How would you even make something like that?'

'Who knows?' said Wolfgart. 'But I'm sure Master Alaric could do it.'

Pendrag shook his head, and said, 'Leaving aside Gerreon and Wolfgart's tenuous understanding of the world for the moment, we should get these bodies burned and leave this place. The blood will bring other predators, and we have our own wounded to deal with.'

'You're right,' said Sigmar, all levity forgotten. 'Wolfgart, Gerreon, have your men gather up the dead beasts and build a pyre around that stone. I want them burned within the hour and us on our way. Pendrag, help me see to the wounded.'

THE JOURNEY BACK to Reikdorf took the riders six days through the forest, their route taking them past many scattered villages and settlements. Before reaching the inhabited areas of the forest, Sigmar led the survivors of the beasts' raids back towards the shattered ruins of the three villages that had been attacked.

The walls surrounding each were broken and ruined, hacked apart with heavy axes or simply torn down with bestial strength. When Sigmar's riders had come upon the smoking charnel houses of the villages there had not been the time to attend to the duty to the dead and, together with the hollow-eyed, weeping survivors, they buried the corpses and sent them on their way to Morr's kingdom.

As Sigmar stood beside the graves, he felt a presence beside him, and looked up to see Wolfgart. His friend's eyes were red-rimmed from the smoke of fires, and he looked weary beyond measure.

'A grim day,' said Sigmar.

Wolfgart shrugged. 'I've seen worse.'

'Then what troubles you?'

'This,' said Wolfgart, waving his hand at the graves they stood before. 'This slaughter, and the men we lost avenging it.'

'What of it?'

'This village is in Asoborn lands and the people we brought back are Asoborns.'

'So?'

Wolfgart sighed and said, 'They are not Unberogen, so why did we ride to their rescue? We lost five men and another three will not ride to battle again. So tell me why we did this. After all, Queen Freya would not have done so for our people, would she?'

'Maybe not,' admitted Sigmar, 'but that does not matter. They are *all* our people: Asoborns, Unberogen, Teutogen… all of them. The night we swore that everything we would do would be in service of the empire of man… did that mean anything to you, Wolfgart?'

'Of course it did!' protested Wolfgart.

'Then why the problem with aiding the Asoborns?'

'I am not sure,' shrugged Wolfgart. 'I suppose because I assumed we'd be making this empire by conquering the other tribes in battle.'

Sigmar put his hand on Wolfgart's shoulder and turned him around to face the work going on in the village. Burial parties dragged dead bodies from ruined homes, while warriors worked alongside farmers as they gathered up the dead, their hands and faces bloody.

'Look at these people,' said Sigmar. 'They are Asoborn and Unberogen. Can you tell which is which?'

'Of course,' said Wolfgart. 'I have ridden with these warriors for six years. I know every man well.'

'Assume you did not know them. Could you then tell Asoborn from Unberogen?'

Wolfgart looked uncomfortable with the question, and Sigmar pressed on. 'They say that all wolves are grey at night. You have heard that expression?'

'Yes.'

'It is the same with men,' said Sigmar, pointing to a man with sadness imprinted onto his face as he carried a dead child in his arms. 'Beneath the blood and grime we are all men. The distinctions we place on each other are meaningless. In the blood, we are all the same, and to our enemies, we are all the same. Do you think the beasts and orcs care whether they kill Asoborns or Unberogen? Or Taleuten or Cherusen? Or Ostagoth?'

'I suppose not,' admitted Wolfgart.

'No,' said Sigmar, suddenly angry with Wolfgart for his short-sightedness, 'and neither should we. As for conquering the other tribes... I do not want to be a tyrant, my friend. Tyrants eventually fall, and their enemies tear down what they built. I want to build an empire that will last forever, something of worth that is built on justice and strong leadership.'

'I think I understand, brother,' said Wolfgart.

'Good,' said Sigmar, 'for I need you with me, Wolfgart. These divisions are what keep us apart, and we have to grow beyond them.'

'I'm sorry.'

'Don't be sorry,' said Sigmar. 'Be a better man.'

FIVE DAYS LATER, Sigmar watched from the walls of Reikdorf as yet another barge eased against the docks that had been built along the northern bank of the river. This one was a wide, deep-hulled craft with tall sides formed from hide-covered tower shields, and was marked with the Jutone heraldry of a skull emblazoned across two curved sabres.

The upper deck of the barge was filled with barrels and timber crates, the lower hold no doubt filled with heavy canvas sacks and bundles of furs and dyes. The marshlands around Jutonsryk provided many ingredients for dyes, and merchants who could afford to pay warriors willing to venture into the haunted marshes could return with many vivid pigments that did not fade over time.

He could see another ship further up the river, this one bearing the raven emblem of King Marbad. He made a mental note to remind the night guards to keep an eye on the alehouses beside the river, for wherever Endals and Jutones gathered there was sure to be violence.

Sigmar's gaze spread from the newly constructed docks to the buildings on the far side of the river. The Sudenreik Bridge was already one of the busiest thoroughfares in the town, and work had now begun on a third bridge across the river, for the second, a simple timber structure, was mostly used to transport building materials to the newer southern portion of the town.

Taking what he had learned from Master Alaric, Pendrag had set up a schoolhouse in the new area where, twice a week, Unberogen children came to learn of the world beyond Reikdorf and of the means by which they lived in it.

Many of the parents of these children had complained to King Björn of the time being wasted on schooling when there were crops to plant and chores to be done, but Sigmar had convinced his father that only by educating the people could they hope to better themselves, and the lessons had continued.

With the clearing of the southern forests for crop fields and the establishment of new ranges for herd animals, a new granary and slaughterhouse had been built. More and more people had come to Reikdorf over the last few years, drawn by the promise of work and wealth, and the town was growing faster than anyone could have believed possible.

New homes had been set up within the southern enclosure of the walls, and a multitude of tradesmen had followed soon after: cobblers, coopers, smiths, weavers, potters, ostlers and tavern keepers. A second market had also sprung up within a year of the completion of the tall timber walls protecting it from attack.

Portions of the northern wall were already being improved, the logs uprooted and replaced with stone blocks dragged from the forest, and shaped by newly trained stonemasons under the watchful eye of Master Alaric.

Many of the buildings in the centre of Reikdorf were already stone and as more quarries were opened in the surrounding hills, yet more were being constructed to ever more elaborate designs.

Sigmar had not yet laid eyes on King Marbad's Raven Hall or King Artur's Fauschlag, but he doubted the settlements surrounding either were as populous as Reikdorf. The river and fertile lands surrounding the Reik had brought great prosperity to the Unberogen, and the time was fast approaching when they would need to make use of the great bounty the gods had bestowed upon them.

The coffers were filled with gold from trade with the dwarfs and the other tribes, and the grain stores were swollen with the fruits of the fields. The morale of the warriors was high, and with every smith in the Unberogen lands labouring to equip them, each man had a shirt of iron mail, a moulded breastplate and pauldrons, shoulder guards, greaves, vambrace and gorget.

To see the riders of the Unberogen on the march was to watch a host of glorious silver warriors glittering in the sun. Master Alaric had even suggested fashioning armoured plates for horses, but such protection had proven too heavy for all but the biggest steeds.

Even now, Wolfgart was buying the heaviest, strongest workhorses and the most powerful warhorses in an attempt to breed a beast with enough strength and speed to wear such armour. Within a few years, he was convinced, he would have bred such a steed.

Soon it would be time to take Sigmar's dream of empire beyond the borders of the Unberogen lands.

Sigmar's twenty-first year was approaching, and as he looked out over the thriving town of Reikdorf, he smiled.

'I will make this the greatest city of my empire,' he said, turning from his vantage point on the walls, and making his way back down to the longhouse at the town's centre.

He crossed the main market square of Reikdorf as the sun set over the wall. Most of the traders had already broken down their wagons and hauled them away, leaving the square a mess of scraps and scavenging dogs. Sigmar made his way past Beorthyn's forge, keeping to the centre of the street to avoid the muddy puddles that gathered at the buildings' edges.

Beyond the longhouse, he could see the armoured form of Alfgeir upon the Field of Swords, still training Unberogen men in swordplay despite the late hour. On a whim, Sigmar changed course and made his way towards the training ground.

A dozen young men sparred on the field, and the evening sun reflected on Alfgeir's bronze armour, making it shine like gold. Of all the Unberogen warriors, the king's champion was the only one still to wear armour of bronze.

Gerreon stood beside Alfgeir, for there was no better swordsman amongst the Unberogen and no better man to teach the next generation of warriors. Sigmar spared a glance to Trinovantes's tomb on the overlooking Warriors' Hill. Then he returned his attention to the training before him, relishing the clash of iron weapons as they struck sparks from one another.

He watched as Alfgeir shouted at the furthest pair of his pupils, and gave one a clout around the ear. Sigmar winced in sympathy. King's son or not, he had received a few such blows in his time learning upon the Field of Swords.

Sigmar watched with the practiced eye of a warrior born, noting the boys who were quickest, the most dextrous and the most determined, and which of them had the look of heroes, a quality that Wolfgart had been the first to give a name to.

'You can see it in their eyes,' Wolfgart had said, 'a perfect blend of honour and courage. It's the same look I see in your eyes.'

Sigmar had searched his sword-brother's face for any sign of mockery, but Wolfgart had been deadly serious, and he had accepted the compliment for what it was. In truth, once given a name and an idea, he had seen the same look in the faces of every one of his friends, and he knew that he was truly blessed to be surrounded with such fine companions.

Gerreon spotted him, and jogged over to join him at the edge of the field.

'They are coming along well,' said Sigmar.

'Aye,' agreed Gerreon. 'They are good lads, Sigmar. Give it a few years and they will be as fine a body of warriors as you could wish for.'

Sigmar nodded, and returned his attention to the sparring warriors as one of the boys gave a cry of pain and dropped his sword. Blood washed down his arm from a deep cut to his bicep, and he sank to his knees.

Immediately, Gerreon and Sigmar set off across the field towards the boy as Alfgeir shouted, 'Get the surgeon,' his words clipped and curt.

Sigmar knelt beside the wounded boy and examined the cut on his arm. The wound was deep, and had sliced cleanly through the muscle. Blood pulsed strongly from the cut, and the boy's face was ashen.

Sigmar said, 'Look at me.'

The boy turned his head from his bloody arm. Tears gathered in the corners of his eyes, but Sigmar saw his determination not to shed them before the king's son.

'What is your name?'

'Brant,' gasped the boy, his breathing becoming shallower.

'Don't look at it,' ordered Sigmar, putting a hand on the boy's shoulder. 'Look at me. You are Unberogen. You are descended from heroes, and heroes do not fear a little blood.'

'It hurts,' said Brant.

'I know,' said Sigmar, 'but you are a warrior and pain is a warrior's constant companion. This is your first wound, so remember this pain and any other wounds will be nothing compared to it. You understand me?'

The boy nodded, his teeth gritted against the pain, but Sigmar could already see that the boy was drawing on his reserves to conquer it.

'There is iron in you, Brant. I can see it plain as day,' said Sigmar. 'You will be a mighty warrior and a great hero.'

'Thank you... my lord,' said Brant as Cradoc the healer ran across the field with his medicine bag held before him.

'You will earn a scar from this,' said Sigmar. 'Wear it well.'

Sigmar wiped his hand on his tunic and picked up Brant's sword as Cradoc squatted beside the boy. He tested the edge, not surprised to find it was razor sharp. He turned to Alfgeir and Gerreon.

'You make them train with swords that are not blunted?'

'Of course,' said Alfgeir, his tone challenging. 'You make a mistake and get wounded, you will not make that mistake again.'

'I never trained with sharpened weapons,' said Sigmar.

'It was my idea,' said Gerreon. 'I thought it would teach them the value of pain.'

'And I agreed,' said Alfgeir. 'As does the king.'

Sigmar handed Brant's sword to Alfgeir. 'You do not have to justify yourselves. I am not about to berate you for this. As a matter of fact, I agree with you. The training *must* be as hard and real as it can be. That way, when they face battle, they will know what to expect.'

Alfgeir nodded and turned back to the other boys, who watched as their wounded companion was led from the Field of Swords.

'No one said you could stop!' he roared. 'Training does not finish until I say so!'

Sigmar turned from the king's champion to face Gerreon.

His friend's face was as pale as Brant's had been. 'Gerreon? Is something wrong?'

Gerreon was staring at him, and Sigmar looked down at his tunic to see a bloody handprint in the centre of his chest. Sigmar reached out to his friend, but Gerreon flinched.

'What is it? It's just a little blood.'

'The red hand...' whispered Gerreon, 'And a wounded sword.'

'You are not making sense, my friend,' said Sigmar. 'What is wrong?'

Gerreon shook his head as if waking from a long slumber, and Sigmar saw a coldness enter the swordsman's eyes.

Before Sigmar could ask more, the urgent sound of warning bells sounded throughout the town, and he reached for Ghal-maraz.

'Gather the warriors!' he said, turning on his heel and sprinting for the walls.

EIGHT

Heralds of War

SIGMAR RACED THROUGH the streets of Reikdorf, his hammer gripped tightly and his heart beating against his ribs. It had been years since the wall guards had felt the need to ring the alarm bells, and he wondered what manner of threat would have driven them to take such a measure.

He skidded around the corner of the central grain store, his mad dash joined by Unberogen warriors pulling on mail shirts or hastily buckling sword belts around their waists. The flow of warriors increased as the sound of the bells continued.

Sigmar ran to the ladders that led onto the ramparts. He slung Ghal-maraz to his belt and swiftly climbed the ladder. Curiously, he saw no urgency or fear in the men gathered on the ramparts. No bows were drawn and no spears were poised, ready to be hurled at an attacking enemy. Sigmar reached the rampart and made his way to the spiked logs of the battlements.

'What's going on?' he demanded.

'Scouts just brought word of them,' answered a nearby warrior, pointing over the wall. 'Hundreds of them are coming south along the Middle Road.'

Looking out over the walls, Sigmar saw a long column of people trudging towards Reikdorf. Hundreds of men and women in filthy, travel stained clothes wound their way from the forests to the north of Reikdorf. Many dragged wagons and litters, laden with canvas covered bundles, children and the elderly.

'Who are they?'

'Look like Cherusens to me.'

Sigmar transferred his gaze to the column of people as they marched warily up to the gate and the great, wolf-flanked statue of Ulric. He peered closer as he recognised a dark-haired woman walking beside the column. Supporting a woman with white hair, who carried a screaming child, Ravenna walked alongside these people, her long green dress stained with mud.

'Open the gates,' he said. 'Now!'

The warrior nodded and shouted orders to the guards stationed at the base of the wall. Sigmar returned to the ground as a handful of armoured warriors began pulling the mighty portals open.

As soon as it was wide enough, Sigmar moved through the gate and made his way along the length of the column, feeling the weight of their pleading looks.

Reaching Ravenna, he said, 'What is this? Where have these people come from?'

'Sigmar!' cried Ravenna. 'Thank the gods! We were finishing work in the high pastures when we saw them coming south.'

'Who are they? They look like Cherusens.'

Ravenna placed her hand on his arm, and Sigmar could see that she was exhausted. 'They are survivors,' she said simply.

'Survivors of what?'

Ravenna paused as though afraid to give voice to the terror that had driven these people from their homes.

'The Norsii,' she said. 'The northmen are on the march.'

THE MOOD IN King Björn's longhouse was ugly, and Sigmar sensed a growing anger and need for retribution fill the hearts of every warrior present. He had felt the same anger when they had found the carnage the forest beasts had wreaked amongst the villages on the eastern borders of Unberogen lands.

The Norsii...

It had been years since the bloodthirsty tribes of the north had come south, bringing death, destruction and horror in their wake. The lands of the far north were a mystery to most of the southern tribes, few having had cause or desire to venture from their own lands, let alone travel beyond the Middle Mountains. Tales were told of great dragons that roamed the forests and flesh-eating tribes of ferocious warriors, who gave praise to dark gods of blood.

Decades had passed since the Norsii had marched south, but the elders of Reikdorf still told tales of the foe they had once faced: brutal warriors in black armour and horned helms, with dread axes and kite shields taller than a normal man, towering horsemen on black steeds with burning red eyes that breathed fire.

Masters of the fearsome Wolfships, Norsii raiders were the terror of the coastline, killers who left nothing but smoking ruins and corpses behind them. Few had faced them and lived.

It was said that slavering hounds and twisted monsters fought in the armies of the northmen, and the elders whispered of foul necromancers, who could summon terrifying daemons from beyond the known realms and hurl spears of flame that could burn a host of armoured warriors to death.

Sigmar had no doubt that many of these tales were exaggerated, but the threat of the northmen was taken seriously by every man in the lands west of the mountains.

Nearly four hundred people had been brought within the walls of Reikdorf, with a further two hundred camped outside in makeshift tents and canvas shelters. Fortunately, the worst of the winter had passed and the nights were mild, so few were expected to perish without a roof over their heads.

Alfgeir had raged at the guards for opening the gates, and had threatened to flog the skin from their backs until Sigmar had explained that he had ordered them opened.

'And how will we feed these people?' raged the Marshal of the Reik.

'The grain stores are full,' said Sigmar. 'There is enough to go round if we are careful.'

'You assume too much, young Sigmar,' said Alfgeir, striding away.

Within the hour, the warriors of the Unberogen had gathered in the longhouse to hear the words of two men who had come with the refugees, emissaries from King Krugar of the Taleutens and King Aloysis of the Cherusens.

King Krugar's man was a lean, hawk-faced warrior named Notker, who bore a curved cavalry sabre and wore his hair shaven save for a long scalp lock that hung down his back to his waist. His clothes and slightly bow-legged walk marked him as a horseman, and his every movement was quick and precise.

The emissary from King Aloysis was named Ebrulf and was a giant of a man with powerfully muscled shoulders and an axe of such weight it seemed impossible it could ever be swung. Sigmar had instantly liked the man, for his bearing was noble and proud, but without arrogance.

Sigmar stood beside his father, who sat on his oak throne, his face grim and regal as he heard the words of his brother kings' emissaries. The news was not good.

'How many of the Norsii are on the march?' asked Björn.

Notker answered first. 'Nearly six thousand swords, my lord.'

'Six thousand!' said Alfgeir. 'Impossible. The northmen could not possibly muster that many men.'

'With respect to your champion,' said Ebrulf. 'It is not impossible. The lost tribes from across the seas march with them. Hundreds of Wolfships are drawn up on the shores of the northern coast and more arrive daily.'

'The lost tribes?' gasped Eoforth. 'They return?'

'They do indeed,' said Notker. 'Tall men on black steeds, with long lances and armour of brazen iron, who serve the forsaken gods, with shamans who call on the powers of those gods to slay their enemies with sorcerous fire.'

A gasp of horror rippled around the longhouse at the mention of the lost tribes, terrifying, bloodthirsty men who had been fought in the earliest days of the land's settlement. The hearthside stories told of brave heroes of old, who had driven these savages across the seas and into the haunted wastelands of the north hundreds of years ago.

'It was said that the lost tribes had died in the desolate wastes,' said Eoforth. 'The land there was cursed by the gods in ages past and none can live there.'

Ebrulf patted the haft of his axe, and said, 'Trust me, old one, they live. Neckbiter here has taken more than a few of their heads in battle.'

'I am assuming that you come to my longhouse as more than simply bearers of this news,' said Björn. 'Ask me what it is you have come to ask.'

Notker and Ebrulf shared a glance, and the Cherusen gave a curt nod to the shaven-headed Taleuten, who stepped forward and bowed low before the king of the Unberogen.

'Our kings have despatched us to offer you the chance to join a mighty host being mustered to face the northmen and drive them back to the sea,' said Notker.

Ebrulf continued. 'King Aloysis draws fighting men to his banner in the shadow of the Middle Mountains, and King Krugar marshals his riders at the Farlic Hills. Our army numbers nearly four thousand swords, but if you were to add the strength of your warriors, we would meet the northmen on equal terms.'

'An offer to join your host?' snapped Alfgeir. 'What you mean to say is that you face defeat and will be dead by winter unless we aid you.'

Ebrulf glowered at Alfgeir. 'You have a viper's tongue, king's man. Show me such disrespect again and my axe will bite at *your* neck!'

Alfgeir took a step forward, his face flushed and his hand reaching for his sword.

Björn waved Alfgeir back with an irritated wave of the hand. 'Though Alfgeir speaks out of turn, he is right to say that this is a great thing your kings ask of me. To send so many warriors north would leave my lands virtually undefended.'

Notker said, 'King Krugar understands what it is he asks, but offers you his Sword Oath if you ride north.'

'King Aloysis makes the same pledge, my lord,' said Ebrulf.

Sigmar was amazed at such oaths, but his father seemed to have expected it, and nodded.

'Truly the threat from the north must be great,' said King Björn.

'It is, my lord,' promised Notker.

THE EMISSARIES WERE thanked for their news and dismissed, taken by the king's servants to lodgings befitting the messengers of kings for food and water. The Unberogen warriors were likewise dismissed, their mood dark and filled with thoughts of war.

King Björn gathered Alfgeir and Eoforth to him, and Sigmar sat next to his father as they debated how the threat from the north should be met. The Marshal of the Reik was in a belligerent mood, his normal brevity rankled by the arrival of the refugees and the emissaries.

'They are desperate,' said Alfgeir. 'They must be to have sent those two to beg for our help. To offer a Sword Oath… that is not a thing given lightly.'

'No,' agreed Eoforth, 'but the northmen are not a threat to be taken lightly either.'

'Pah, they are just men,' said Alfgeir. 'They bleed and die like any other.'

'I have fought the Norsii once before,' said Björn. 'Yes, they bleed and die, but they are strong, ferocious warriors, and if the lost tribes indeed march with them…'

'I always thought the lost tribes were a dark tale to frighten children,' said Sigmar.

'And so they are,' said Alfgeir. 'They are just trying to scare us into helping them.'

'I do not believe so,' said Eoforth. 'Nor do I believe that either of those men were lying.'

'They were not,' said Björn. 'Sigmar? You agree?'

'Yes, father. I sensed no deceit in them. I believe they are speaking the truth and that we must march out to the aid of your brother kings. To have the Sword Oaths of two such powerful kings would greatly benefit us. Much of our northern border would be secure, and to have Taleuten cavalry and Cherusen Wildmen as allies is no small thing.'

'Spoken like a true king!' laughed Björn. 'We will, indeed march out. If the Cherusen and Taleuten are defeated then the Norsii will surely fall on us next.'

'I wonder,' said Eoforth, 'why Aloysis and Krugar have not turned to the Teutogens for help?'

'They probably have,' said Björn, 'but Artur will think himself safe atop the Fauschlag, and no doubt plans to invade his neighbours' lands when the Cherusens and Taleutens are defeated and the Norsii are weakened.'

'Then it is even more imperative that we march now,' said Sigmar.

'What of our own lands?' asked Alfgeir. 'We will strip them bare of protection if we send that many warriors north. The beasts grow bolder each day, and the greenskins are always on the march with the spring.'

'We will muster as many warriors as we can, but we shall not be leaving our lands undefended,' said Björn. 'I shall be leaving our greatest warrior to keep our homes safe.'

'Who?' asked Alfgeir, and Sigmar felt a leaden lump form in the pit of his stomach as he feared the answer his father would give.

'Sigmar will defend our lands while our army marches north.'

THE MOON WAS reflected in the Reik, and the sound of drunken revelry from the alehouses carried across the water to the dimly illuminated dwellings on the southern bank. Gerreon stood on the edge of the river, his thoughts in turmoil as he relived the incident on the Field of Swords.

Accidents were not uncommon under Alfgeir's harsh tutelage, but the blood spilled this evening had reminded him of a day he had almost forgotten. He closed his eyes as he pictured the smeared red handprint on Sigmar's tunic, and the sudden clarity of memory as he heard the hag woman's words echo in his head as though he had heard them only yesterday.

When you see the sign of the red hand in the same breath as a wounded sword... that is the time for your vengeance. Seek out the water hemlock that grows in the marshes when no king rules in Reikdorf.

He had left the hag woman's cave in a daze, his thoughts wreathed in fog from the opiates that burned in her fire and the implications of what he desired. Gerreon remembered little of the journey back through the Brackenwalsch, save that his steps had carried him unerringly through the darkened fens, and that he had awoken in his bed the next morning with a pounding headache and a dry mouth.

As he lay there, the hag woman's voice had whispered to him, and terror had kept him pinned to his bed as her words had flowed like honey in his ear.

Be the peacemaker... hold to your vengeance, but cloak it with friendship. Remember, Gerreon of the Unberogen... the red hand and the wounded sword.

He had risen from his bed, feeling as though he was walking through a dream as he made his way through Reikdorf. The sun shone and the sky was a wondrous shade of blue. He had stopped by the Oathstone in the centre of the settlement and felt a sick sense of unease as he made his way towards the Field of Swords.

There he had found Sigmar and made his peace with the future king of the Unberogen, though the words had almost choked him. For six long years he had held his hate close to his heart, nurturing it with each passing day, and picking at the scab of it whenever it threatened to diminish.

And yet...

As each day passed and Gerreon became one of Sigmar's friends, he found his grip on his hatred slipping as though the pain of his twin's death were somehow lessening. One morning he had realised, to his horror, that he actually *liked* Sigmar. Even Wolfgart and Pendrag, men he had loathed in his teens, had become likeable, and he was forced to admit that, seen without the petulance of youth, there was much to like.

He had soon slipped into the easy camaraderie of warriors who fought shoulder to shoulder and saved each other from death time and time again. As the years passed, he and Sigmar had become like brothers, and the future was golden, his hate vanishing like morning mist.

And now this...

Now he had seen the signs of which the hag woman had spoken, and the dark memory of Trinovantes's death surged back into his mind like a swollen river over a broken dam, the venom and anger and hurt of Sigmar's betrayal as strong as it had been the day they had brought Trinovantes's body back.

The wounded sword...

He had not known what such a sign might be, but as he watched the bleeding boy on the Field of Swords it had suddenly become clear. The boy had said his name was Brant, an old name from the earliest days of the tribe's migration from the east, a good name with a proud heritage.

In the early tongue of the Unberogen the name Brant meant sword.

And Reikdorf without a king? How such a thing might come to pass when the Unberogen were at the height of their power and influence seemed a far-fetched idea, but now King Björn had issued a call to arms

Horsemen had been despatched throughout his lands, summoning all those who had sworn allegiance to him to make their way to Reikdorf within ten days. Each man was to bring a sword, a shield and mail armour, and was to be ready to march into the north for several months of campaigning.

Sigmar would rule in his father's absence...

Leaving Reikdorf without a king.

Dark thoughts of blood and the pleasure he would gain from avenging Trinovantes warred with the bonds of brotherhood he had formed over the last six years. He looked away from the water, and turned towards the grey silhouette of Warrior's Hill where lay his twin.

'What would you have me do?' whispered Gerreon, tears rolling down his cheeks.

FOR TEN DAYS, Reikdorf became a gathering place for warriors from all across Unberogen lands. Sword musters from settlements along the river and fertile valleys of the Reik made their way to the Unberogen capital, drawn there by their king's command, and by ties of duty and honour that were stronger than dwarf-forged iron.

Camps were set up in the fields to the east of the town, long rows of canvas tents gathered for the hundreds of men that arrived daily from all corners of the king's lands. Grim-faced warriors with heavy axes, swords and lances marched over the Sudenreik Bridge, accompanied by lightly armoured archers with leather breastplates, bows of fine yew and quivers of arrows with shafts as straight as sunlight.

Wolfgart set up makeshift paddocks to the north of the town for horsemen to stable their mounts as Sigmar organised the warriors into fighting groups. The host swelled with each passing day, and soon the task of keeping records of the gathering warriors fell to Pendrag.

Traders had long used tally marks and simple script to keep track of their dealings, and with help from Eoforth, Pendrag borrowed ideas from the concept of dwarf runic language to develop a rudimentary form of written instruction. Quick to see the benefit of this, Sigmar commanded Pendrag to further refine this new form of communication and have it taught in the schoolhouses.

When the time came to marshal the army to march, Pendrag's head count indicated that King Björn would lead an army of just under three thousand swords, with each man and his village recorded faithfully by Pendrag.

Between them, Sigmar, Wolfgart and Pendrag worked organisational wonders with the assembled army, readying it for march, and ensuring that it would leave Reikdorf with enough supplies to sustain it through the campaigning season. A long train of wagons, and the tradesmen necessary to keep the army ready to fight, was soon assembled and made ready to accompany the warriors.

King Björn took little part in the organisation of the army, instead spending his days tirelessly with the men with whom he would ride into battle. Every day, Björn would tour the growing camp and pass a few words with as many of the men as he could manage in a day. Sometimes, Sigmar would accompany him, enjoying his father's easy banter with the warriors, all the while trying to hide his disappointment that he would not be marching to war with them.

He had made his way from the longhouse to Ravenna's home, following his father's pronouncement that he would be staying in Reikdorf, angry beyond words that he would be denied this chance to march out against an enemy of such power.

Ravenna had needed no woman's intuition to see his dark mood, and had immediately sat at her table and poured two large measures of Reikland beer. Sigmar paced the floor like a caged wolf, and she waited patiently for him to sit.

When eventually he did so, she reached out and placed a goblet in his hand.

'Speak to me,' she said. 'What is the matter?'

'My father insults me,' stormed Sigmar. 'The army is to march north and do battle with the Norsii. The kings of the Cherusen and Taleuten beg for our aid and my father has decided to answer their call.'

'And this insults you how?'

'I am to have no part in this campaign,' said Sigmar, taking a great mouthful of beer. 'I am to be left behind like some forgotten steward while others earn glory in battle.'

Ravenna shook her head. 'You have such vision, Sigmar, but sometimes you are so blind.'

He looked up, his expression a mix of anger and surprise.

'Your father honours you, Sigmar,' said Ravenna. 'He has entrusted the safety of all he holds dear to you while he is away. Everything he has built over the years is in your care until he returns. That is a great honour.'

Sigmar took a deep breath, followed by another mouthful of beer. 'I suppose.'

'There is no "suppose" about it,' said Ravenna.

'But to fight the Norsii!' protested Sigmar. 'There is glory to be had in battles such as these! There is–'

'Foolish man!' snapped Ravenna, slamming her goblet on the table. 'Have you learned nothing? There *is* no glory in battle, only pain and death. You speak of glory, but where is the glory for those who will not return? Where is the glory for those left upon the field as food for crows and wolves? I told you I hated war, but I hate more the fact that you men perpetuate it with talk of glory and noble purpose. Wars are not fought for glory or freedom or any other golden foolishness. Kings desire more land and wealth, and the quickest, easiest way to get it is by conquest. So do not come to my table and talk of glory, Sigmar. Glory saw my brother dead.'

Sigmar saw the hurt anger in her face and weighed his next words carefully. 'You are right, but there are some battles worth fighting,' he said. 'Fighting the Norsii is such a battle, for it is not fought for riches or glory, it is for survival.'

'And that is the only reason I am glad you are not going with your father.'

'Glad? What do you mean?'

Ravenna softened her tone, and said, 'Do you believe that the dangers we face every day will lessen while our warriors march north to face the Norsii? There are still beasts, reavers and greenskins to fight, and the other tribes will not be ignorant of your father's departure. What if the Teutogens or the Asoborns or the Brigundians try to seize Unberogen lands while the king is away? The warriors who march with your father fight for our survival, and I thank the gods that you remain here to do the same. I think you will find no shortage of battles to fight while your father is in the north.'

NINE
Those Left Behind

FIRES HAD GUTTED the village of Ubersreik, and the scent of charred wood still lingered on the smoky air. A hundred people had made their homes here, and now they were all dead. Scavenging wolves padded through the deserted village, and crows perched on every rooftop. Sigmar rode his grey stallion into the village, an immense sadness weighing heavily on him as he took in the scene of devastation.

The smell of corruption was a sickly tang on the air, and Sigmar spat a wad of unpleasant phlegm to the trampled ground. Wolfgart and Pendrag rode alongside him, and thirty riders followed them into the village, a quarter of those left behind after the king's army had marched north a month earlier.

Everywhere Sigmar looked, he saw death.

Families had been butchered in their homes, stabbed to death in a frenzy of blades, and then dragged outside and dismembered. Animals lay in rotten piles, skulls crushed, and half a cow lay in the centre of the road.

'Who did this?' asked Wolfgart, his anger and anguish clear. 'Greenskins?'

'Sigmar shook his head. 'No.'

'You sound sure,' said Pendrag, his voice less emotional, yet Sigmar could still sense the outrage beneath his friend's control. 'This looks like the handiwork of orcs.'

'It's not,' said Sigmar. 'Orcs do not leave bodies behind them when they are this deep in human lands. They feed on them. And there is no spoor or orc daubings. As vile as this is, it is too neat for orcs.'

Pendrag's face was a mask of disgust, and he turned away from the blackened, brutalised bodies piled in the doorway of a burnt-out home.

'Then what?' asked Wolfgart. 'You think men did this? What manner of man kills women and children with such savagery?'

'Berserkers?' suggested Pendrag. 'The Thuringians are said to field warriors that drink firewater that drives them into a maddened frenzy during battle.'

'I do not believe King Otwin would have allowed such slaughter,' said Sigmar. 'He is said to be a hard man, but nothing I have heard of him makes me think his warriors had any part in this... butchery.'

'Times have changed,' said Pendrag. 'Does he even still rule the Thuringians?'

'As far as I know,' replied Sigmar. 'I have not heard of any other taking his throne.'

'Then perhaps some new bandit chieftain is making an example of this place,' said Pendrag.

'There's too much left behind,' replied Wolfgart. 'Bandits would have cleared this place out, and why burn it to the ground? You can't rob people next season if you kill them.'

Sigmar halted his horse in the middle of the devastated village, turning in his saddle to take in the full measure of the slaughter and destruction around him. Despair settled on him as he thought of the people who had died here. How they must have screamed when the flames and the enemy took them.

'Why didn't they fight?' asked Wolfgart, riding alongside him.

'What do you mean?' asked Sigmar.

'There are no swords in the wreckage. No one tried to fight them.'

'They were only farmers,' pointed out Pendrag.

'They were still men,' snapped Wolfgart. 'They could still have fought to defend themselves. I see axes and a few scythes, but nothing to make me think that anyone fought. If a man comes into your home with murder in mind, you kill the bastard. Or at least you fight him however you can, with a carving knife, an axe or your fists.'

'You are a warrior, my brother,' said Sigmar. 'To fight is in your blood, but these were farmers, no doubt exhausted after a day in the fields. The attackers came on them at night, and our people had no chance to defend themselves.'

Wolfgart shook his head. 'A man should always be ready to fight, farmer or warrior.'

'They counted on us to protect them,' said Sigmar, 'and we failed them.'

'We cannot be everywhere at once, my friend,' said Pendrag, removing his helmet. 'Our lands are too vast to patrol with the few warriors left to us.'

'Exactly,' said Sigmar. 'It was arrogant of us to assume we could protect our lands ourselves, but Wolfgart is right, every man *should* be ready to fight. We have made sure that every warrior in our lands has a sword, but we should be making sure that every *man* has a sword.'

'Having a sword is all very well,' said Wolfgart. 'Having the skill to use it... that is something else.'

'Indeed it is, my friend,' replied Sigmar. 'We need to begin a system of training throughout our lands so that every man knows how to wield a sword. Each village must maintain a body of warriors to defend against such attacks.'

'That will take time,' said Pendrag. 'If it is even possible.'

'We must *make* it possible,' snapped Sigmar. 'What use is an empire if we cannot defend it? When my father returns, we will draw up plans to institute a system of raising troops, training them and equipping them in every village. You are right, our land is too big to defend with one army, so each village must look to its own defence.'

The discussion was brought to a halt when Cuthwin and Svein emerged from the forest on the north edge of the village and made their way towards the three warriors.

From Svein's expression, he could see that the suspicion forming in his mind had been correct. The two scouts approached, and Sigmar slid from the back of his horse as the craggy-featured Svein squatted on his haunches and sketched in the dirt.

'Perhaps fifty riders, my lord,' said Svein. 'Came in from the west just as the sun was setting. They drove through the village, burning as they went. Another group came in from the east and caught any who fled. Most people were killed in the open, but the rest were driven back to their homes and burned to death inside.'

'Where did the raiders go after they had killed everyone?' demanded Sigmar.

'West,' said Cuthwin, 'following the line of the forest to the coast.'

'But they didn't keep to that line, did they?'

'No, my lord,' agreed Cuthwin. 'After three miles or so they cut north following the river.'

'Good work,' said Sigmar, standing and rubbing ash from his woollen leggings.

Pendrag said, 'You know who did this. Don't you?'

'I have an idea,' admitted Sigmar.

'Who?' demanded Wolfgart. 'Tell us, and we'll descend on them with swords bared!'

'I believe the Teutogens did this,' said Sigmar.

'The Teutogens? Why?' asked Wolfgart.

'Artur knows the king has gone north with his army, and he is taking advantage of my father's absence to test our strength,' said Pendrag. 'It seems like the logical conclusion.'

'Then we burn one of his villages to the ground,' snarled Wolfgart, 'and show him what it means to attack the Unberogen!'

Sigmar turned on his friend, anger flashing in his eyes as he waved his hand at the burned and mutilated bodies. 'You would have us do this to a Teutogen village? Would you kill women and children in the name of vengeance?'

'You would leave this act of barbarism unanswered?' countered Wolfgart.

'Artur will pay for this,' promised Sigmar, 'but not now. We have not the numbers to punish him, and we will not give him an excuse to come against us in greater numbers. While the Unberogen army is in the north, we must swallow our pride.'

'And when your father returns?' demanded Wolfgart.

'Then there will be a reckoning,' said Sigmar.

KING BJÖRN PULLED his white wolfskin cloak around his shoulders, numbed to his very bones by the northern cold and biting wind that found its way through to his skin no matter how well he wrapped himself in fur. This far north, the climate and landscape were as different from the balmy springs and crisp winters of his lands as night was from day.

Here, the people dwelled in a land of dark pines, rugged valleys and windswept moors, where only the most determined would survive. The people of the north endured wet summers, and winters of such ferocity that entire villages died overnight, buried in snowstorms that wiped them from the face of the world.

Such harsh climes, however, bred a hardy folk, and the inhabitants of the north had impressed Björn with their courage and tenacity in the face of the Norsii invaders.

The king of the Unberogen made his way through the camp of the allied armies, smiling and praising the courage of every group of warriors he passed. Cherusen Wildmen, naked but for painted designs on their flesh and armoured loincloths, danced around fires that burned with blue fire, and Taleuten warriors drank harsh spirits distilled from grain as they spoke of the many heads they had taken.

Nearly seven thousand warriors had marched into battle. Nearly a thousand of them had remained on the battlefield, food for crows and the earth. Hundreds more were screaming in agony as the surgeons did the bloody work of saving the wounded. Ragged lines of tents filled the valley, though most warriors slept rolled in thick furs beside the hundreds of campfires that dotted the landscape like stars fallen to earth.

Alfgeir walked beside the king, clad head to toe in bronze armour and a helmet with a raised visor fashioned into the shape of a snarling wolf. Björn's champion wore an identical cloak of white wolfskin, a gift from King Aloysis when the Unberogen army had crossed the Talabec and ridden into the land of the Cherusens.

The two men were followed by ten warriors armed with heavy warhammers, their breastplates painted red, and their long beards woven in tight braids, in the fashion of the Taleutens. These men were so sure of their skills that they disdained the wearing of helmets and carried no shields. Björn knew that such confidence was not misplaced.

At least three times on the field of battle, these men had saved his life, crushing Norsii skulls or felling great monsters with their mighty hammers as they closed on the king. Each of Björn's retinue wore the white wolfskin cloak, and already it was whispered that these were warriors blessed with the strength of Ulric.

The forces of the northmen had penetrated far inland, and the capital of King Wolfila of the Udoses was still besieged in his coastal fortress city. Much blood had yet to be spilled to force the Norsii back to the sea. Thus far, they had been driven back, but these encounters had been mere skirmishes, foreplay before the great battle that had been fought in the rocky foothills east of the Middle Mountains.

The armies of the Norsii were wild and ferocious, but lacked the discipline of the southern tribes. The three kings had formed their armies into a great host and led by example, riding to where the battle was at its most fierce and exhorting their warriors to undreamed of valour.

The seven thousand warriors of the southern kings gave battle against six thousand cold-eyed killers from the northern realms and the black-armoured marauders from across the seas. Hordes of berserk warriors caked in painted chalk and blood, with spiked hair and whirling chains, had begun the battle, charging from the ranks of the enemy, screaming terrible prayers to their dark gods.

Volleys of arrows cut down these madmen, but the slavering hounds with blood-matted fur, and the howling beasts, had not fallen so easily, wreaking fearful havoc amongst the allied line with yellowed fangs that tore out throats, and bladed appendages that hacked a dozen men apart with every blow.

Björn remembered the terrible moment when a charging wedge of dark horsemen atop snorting steeds of shimmering black had crashed into the gap opened by the hounds. Scores of men had died beneath their black lances or were crushed beneath the unstoppable fury of their charge, but Cherusen Wildmen had charged heedless into the mass of armoured horsemen, and had torn them from their saddles, while Unberogen warriors had grimly despatched the fallen warriors with brutally efficient axe blows.

Back and forth the battle had waxed furiously, with each moment bringing a fresh horror from the enemy ranks. However, the courage of the men of the south had held firm. As the day wore on, the attacks from the Norsii became less severe, and Björn had sensed some give in the enemy line.

The allies had advanced in a silent mass of axes and swords, Taleuten horsemen riding around the flanks of the enemy, harassing them with deadly accurate bowfire from their saddles. Unberogen warriors hammered the Norsii line and bent it back like a strung bow, killing enemy warriors by the score. Realising the moment had come to make his presence felt, Björn had ordered his banner forward, and had charged in with his great axe raised high above his head for all his warriors to see.

The kings of the Taleutens and Cherusens saw Björn's charge, and the air filled with horn blasts and drum beats as the kings of the south rode to battle. Hundreds of horsemen crashed against the army of the northmen, killing them in droves and scattering them like chaff.

A great cheer had filled the valley, and it seemed as though the fate of the Norsii was sealed, their warriors doomed. Then, a Norsii warlord in red armour with a horned helm had ridden through to the front lines of the battle beneath a blood-red banner. He sat atop a dark steed with eyes like undimmed furnaces, and had restored order to his army, which then fought a disciplined retreat from the valley.

The allied army had not the strength or cohesion to pursue, and Björn had listened with a heavy heart as his scouts informed him that the northmen had regrouped beyond the horizon and were falling back in good order to a thickly wooded ridgeline.

That night, the armies of the three kings had rested and eaten well, for they all knew there was still fighting and dying to be done.

For days the allies had harried the northmen, seeking to goad them into charging from their defensive bulwark, but fear of the great warlord had kept their natural ferocity in check, and not even the wild, challenging taunts of Taleuten horse archers could dislodge them from their position.

The question of how to pursue the campaign against the northmen was one that vexed the commanders of the allied army greatly, and it was to a council of war arranged to answer this question that Björn now marched.

'Krugar will want to attack with the dawn, as will Aloysis,' said Alfgeir as they approached the tent of the kings, ringed by armoured warriors and blazing torches.

'I know,' said Björn, 'and part of me wants to as well.'

'Attacking up that slope will be costly,' said Alfgeir as they reached the tent of King Aloysis. 'Many men will die.'

'I know that too, Alfgeir, but what choice to we have?' asked Björn.

SIGMAR REALISED THAT time was not a constant thing, unbending and iron, but as flexible as heated gold. The weeks since his father had left Reikdorf had passed with aching slowness, whereas the hours he was able to snatch with Ravenna between his journeys around the Unberogen lands had flashed past like lightning.

No sooner had he ridden back through the gates of Reikdorf and fallen into her arms than it seemed he was once again donning his hauberk and shield, ready to do battle. The raids against outlying settlements were continuing, but none had yet repeated the savagery of the attack on Ubersreik.

Sigmar had sent wagonloads of swords and spears to every Unberogen village, along with warriors to help train the villagers. In addition to these weapons, the grain stores of Reikdorf had been depleted to feed the women and children, while their menfolk learned to be warriors as well as farmers.

Eoforth had devised a rotational system where each farmer's neighbours tended to a portion of his fields while he was training to defend their village. Thus each man would learn the ways of the warrior without the worry of his land going untilled or his crops ungathered.

With the Unberogen lands looked to, Sigmar's thoughts turned outwards to the lands beyond the borders of his father's kingdom. As the summer months passed, orc tribes were on the march in the mountains, with word coming from King Kurgan Ironbeard of great battles being fought before the walls of many of the dwarf holds. Sigmar had wanted to send warriors to aid the beleaguered dwarfs, but he could spare no men from his own lands.

He paced the floor of the king's longhouse, tired beyond measure as he awaited news of his father and the course of the war in the north. He drank from a mug of wine, the potency of the alcohol helping to dull the headache building behind his eyes.

'That will not help you,' said Ravenna, watching him from the door to the longhouse. 'You need rest, not wine.'

'I need sleep,' said Sigmar, 'and the wine helps me sleep.'

'No, it doesn't,' said Ravenna, coming into the longhouse and taking the wine from his hand. 'The sleep of the wine sodden is not true rest. You may fall asleep, but you are not refreshed come the morn.'

'Maybe not,' replied Sigmar, leaning down to kiss her forehead, 'but without it, my mind whirls with thought, and I lie awake through the long watches of the night.'

'Then come to my bed, Sigmar,' said Ravenna. 'I will help you sleep, and in the morning you will awake like a new man.'

'Really?' asked Sigmar, taking her hand and following her towards the longhouse's door. 'And how will you work this miracle?'

Ravenna smiled. 'You'll see.'

SIGMAR LAY BACK on Ravenna's bed, a light sweat forming a sheen over his body as she draped an arm over his chest and curled a leg over his thigh. Her dark hair spilled onto the furs of the bed, and Sigmar could smell the rose perfumed oils she had worked into her skin.

The fire had burned low, but the room was pleasantly warm and comfortable, with the fragrance of two people who had just pleasurably exerted themselves hanging in the air.

Sigmar smiled as he felt a delicious drowsiness stealing over him, a drink of wine and Ravenna's company having eased his troubled brow and made the cares of the world seem like distant things indeed.

Ravenna ran her hand across his chest, and he stroked her midnight hair as the events of the last few days washed through him, and in so doing, eased their weight upon him. He longed for news of his father and the men of the Unberogen who fought in the north, but as Eoforth was fond of saying, if wishes were horses then no one would walk.

'What are you thinking?' whispered Ravenna dreamily.

'About the fighting in the north,' he replied, and then flinched as Ravenna plucked a hair from his arm.

She folded her arms across his chest and rested her chin on her forearms as she stared up at him with a playful smile.

'What did you do that for?' he asked.

'When a woman asks you what you are thinking, she doesn't *actually* want to hear what you're thinking.'

'No? Then what does she want?'

'She wants you to tell her that you are thinking of her and how beautiful she is, and of how much you love her.'

'Oh, so why not ask for that?'

'It's not the same if you have to ask for it,' pointed out Ravenna.

'But you are beautiful,' said Sigmar. 'There is no one prettier between the Worlds Edge Mountains and the western ocean, and I do love you, you know that.'

'Tell me.'

'I love you,' said Sigmar, 'with all my heart.'

'Good,' smiled Ravenna. 'Now I feel better, and when I feel better… you feel better.'

'Then is it not selfish of me to simply tell you what I think you want to hear?' asked Sigmar. 'Am I not then saying it to feel better myself?'

'Does it matter?' asked Ravenna, her voice dropping as her eyelids fluttered with tiredness.

'No,' replied Sigmar with a smile, 'I suppose not. All I want to do is make you happy.'

'Then tell me of the future.'

'The future? I am no seer, my love.'

'No, I mean what you hope for the future,' whispered Ravenna. 'And no grand dreams of empire, just tell me of us.'

Sigmar pulled Ravenna close and closed his eyes.

'Very well,' said Sigmar. 'I will be king of the Unberogen and you will be my queen, the most beloved woman in all the land.'

'Will there be children in this golden future?' murmured Ravenna.

'Undoubtedly,' said Sigmar. 'A king needs an heir after all. Our sons will be strong and courageous, and our daughters will be dutiful and pretty.'

'How many children will we have?'

'As many as you like,' he promised. 'Sigmar's heirs will be numbered amongst the most handsome, proud and courageous of all the Unberogen.'

'And us?' whispered Ravenna. 'What becomes of us?'

'Our future will be happy, and we will live long in peace,' said Sigmar.

TEARS STREAMED DOWN Gerreon's face as he all but fled into the darkness of the Brackenwalsch. His fine boots of softest kid were ruined, black mud and water spilling over the tops of them and soaking his feet. His woollen trews were splashed with tainted water as his footsteps carried him deeper and deeper into the bleak and cheerless fens.

A low mist wreathed the ground, and the ghostly radiance of Morrslieb bathed the marshes in an emerald light. Glittering wisps of light, like distant candles, floated in the mist, but even in his distressed state Gerreon knew better than to follow them.

The Brackenwalsch was full of the bodies of those who had been beguiled by the corpse lights and wandered to their doom in the peaty bogs around Reikdorf.

His hand clutched his sword, and his anger grew as he pictured Sigmar rutting with his sister in his own home. The two of them had returned as Gerreon had been sharpening his blade, and it had been all he could do to smile and not cut the Unberogen prince down.

Sigmar had placed a hand on Gerreon's shoulder and he had all but flinched, the hatred in his eyes almost giving him away.

He had read Sigmar and Ravenna's lecherous intent in every word they spoke, and though they had asked him to join them for a meal, he had excused himself and fled into the darkness before the firelight would illuminate his true feelings.

Gerreon stumbled through the shallows of a sucking pool, dropping to his knees as the mud pulled at his boots. His hands splashed into the reeking liquid, and black tears dripped from his face as he stared into the water.

His face rippled in the undulant surface of the pool, grotesquely twisted in the shifting water. The breath caught in his throat as he saw the reflected image of the moon over his shoulder, its face bright and constant, inexplicably unwavering in the water.

Gerreon lifted his hands from the water, his fingers coated in a thin layer of oily, black liquid that dripped from his hands. In the dark of night it looked like blood, and he shook his hands clear of it in disgust.

'No... please...' he whispered. 'I won't.'

He looked up from the water as the moonlight shone upon a tall plant that grew at the edge of the pool, its stems dotted with many tiny, white flowers in flat-topped clusters. A sickly smell exuded from the plant, and with a heavy heart, Gerreon recognised it as water hemlock, one of the deadliest plants that grew in these lands.

A whisper of wind shook the plant, and for the briefest instant, Gerreon felt it was beckoning him. As he watched, its stem sagged and broke, an oily liquid dribbling from the hollow interior.

Gerreon looked into the darkened sky, seeking some escape from the future the fates seemed determined to force upon him.

The moon glared down at him, its cold light unforgiving and hostile.

Common belief held that it was ill-luck to stare into the depths of the rogue moon for any length of time, that the Dark Gods saw into the hearts of those who did so, and planted a seed of evil within them.

As he looked into the shifting light, it seemed that he could see a pair of shimmering eyes, cunningly hidden within the ripples and contours of its surface, eyes of indescribable beauty and cruelty.

'What are you?' he yelled into the darkness.

The depthless pools of the eyes promised dark wonders and experience beyond measure, and Gerreon understood with sudden, awful clarity that the strands of his fate had been woven long before his birth and would continue long past his eventual death.

He stood and waded across the pool towards the drooping hemlock plant.

'Very well,' said Gerreon, 'if I cannot escape my fate then I embrace it.'

⤙ TEN ⤚

Red Dawn

The sun rose through golden clouds, the rays of light striking the bronze armour of the Norsii and making it seem as though the tree-lined ridge was aflame. Defiantly gathered on the slopes of a wide, rocky ridge, the fearsome northmen battered their axes upon the bosses of their shields, and roared terrible war cries of blood and death.

Björn sat upon his horse at the base of the ridge next to Alfgeir, surrounded by his personal guards, the White Wolves as they were now dubbed. His wolf banner fluttered in the icy wind that blew from the north, and he looked left and right to see the flags of his fellow kings held high along the line of the army.

Of all the gathered warriors, Björn took pride in knowing that the Unberogen were, without doubt, the most fearsome and magnificent. Lines of spear-armed warriors awaited the order to advance, and tribal sword-brethren answered the Norsii's battle-cries with no less fearsome roars of their own.

Cherusen Wildmen bared their backsides to the Norsii, and Taleuten horsemen galloped with glorious abandon before the enemy army.

Spirits were high, and the frozen wind was seen as a good omen by the priests of Ulric, a blessing of the god of winter and a portent of victory.

Björn turned to Alfgeir, his champion's bronze armour polished to a golden sheen. His visor was raised, and he sat motionless beside the king, though Björn saw a tension in his features that he had never seen in the moments before battle.

'Something troubles you?' asked Björn.

Alfgeir turned to face the king and shook his head. 'No, I am calm.'

'You seem unsettled.'

'We are about to go into battle, and I must protect a king who rides into the heaviest fighting without thought for his own survival,' said Alfgeir. 'That would unsettle anyone.'

'Your only thought is for my life?' asked Björn.

'Yes, my lord,' said Alfgeir.

'The thought of your own death does not trouble you?'

'Should it, my king?'

'I imagine most men here are at least a little afraid of dying.'

Alfgeir shrugged. 'If Ulric wants me, he will take me, there is nothing I can do about it. All I can do is fight well and pray he finds me worthy to allow me entrance to his hall.'

Björn smiled, for this was about the longest conversation he had ever had with his champion. 'You are a remarkable man, Alfgeir. Life is so simple to you, is it not?'

'I suppose,' agreed Alfgeir. 'I have a duty to you, but beyond that...'

'Beyond that, what?' asked Björn, suddenly curious. Alfgeir claimed not to be concerned about death, but the coming battle had loosened his tongue in a way nothing before had. Even as he formed the thought, he knew that it was not his champion's tongue that was loosened, but his own.

'Beyond that... I do not know,' said Alfgeir. 'I have always been your champion and protector.'

'And when I am dead you will be Sigmar's,' finished Björn, his mouth suddenly dry as he realised that his desire to talk and connect with another human being was born of the need to ensure that his people would be safe after his death.

'You are in a dark mood, my lord,' said Alfgeir. 'Is there something wrong?'

It was a simple question, but one to which Björn found he had no answer.

He had woken in the middle of the night, his keen sense for danger awakening him to a presence within his tent. How such a thing could have been possible with Alfgeir and the White Wolves maintaining a vigil around it he did not know, but his hand quickly found the haft of Soultaker.

He opened his eyes, and felt a chill enter his heart as he saw a silver mist creeping across the floor of his tent, and a hooded shape swathed in black hunched in the corner.

Björn swung his legs from his cot bed and raised his axe. The ground was cold, and tendrils of mist clawed at him as the dark figure drew itself to its full height.

'Who are you?' roared Björn. 'Show yourself!'

'Be at peace, King Björn,' said a sibilant voice that he knew all too well. 'It is but a traveller from your own lands, come to claim what is hers.'

'You,' whispered Björn as the dark figure pulled back its hood to reveal the wrinkled face of the hag woman of the Brackenwalsch. Her hair shone with the same silver light as the mist, and a cold dread seized Björn's heart as he knew what she had come for.

'How can you be here?' he asked.

'I am not here, King Björn,' said the hag woman, 'I am but a shadow in the deeper darkness, an agent of powers beyond your comprehension. None here have seen me and nor shall they. I am here for you and you alone.'

'What do you want?'

'You know what I want,' said the hag woman, coming closer.

'Get away from me!' cried Björn.

'You would see your son dead and the land destroyed?' hissed the hag woman. 'For that is what is at stake here.'

'Sigmar is in danger?'

The hag woman nodded. 'Even now a trusted friend plots to destroy him. By this time tomorrow your son will have passed through the gateway to Morr's kingdom.'

Björn felt his legs turn to water, and he collapsed back onto his cot bed, terror filling him at the thought of having to see Sigmar's body pass into a tomb upon Warrior's Hill.

'What can I do?' asked Björn. 'I am too far away to help him.'

'No,' said the hag woman, 'you are not.'

'But you... you are still in the Brackenwalsch, yes? And this is a vision you are sending me?'

'That is correct, King Björn.'

'Then if you know who plots against Sigmar, why can you not save him?' demanded Björn. 'You have command of the mysteries. You can save him!'

'No, for it was I who set the assassin upon his course.'

Björn surged to his feet, Soultaker sweeping out and cleaving through the hag woman, but the blade hit nothing, her form no more substantial than fog.

'Why?' demanded Björn. 'Why would you do such a thing? Why set his murderer in motion only to attempt to prevent it?'

The hag woman drifted closer to Björn, and he saw that her eyes were filled with dark knowledge, with things that would damn him forever were he to know them. He turned from her gaze.

'A man is the sum of his experiences, Björn,' said the hag woman. 'All his loves, fears, joys and pain combine like the metals in a good sword. In some men these qualities are in balance and they become servants of the light, while in others they are out of balance and they fall to darkness. To become the man he needs to be, your son must suffer pain and loss like no other.'

'I thought you said I had to save him?'

'And so you shall. When we met upon the hill of tombs I told you I would ask you for a sacred vow. You remember?'

'I remember,' said Björn, a bleak dread settling upon him.

'I now ask for that vow,' said the hag woman.

'Very well,' said Björn. 'Ask me.'

'When battle is joined on the morn, seek out the red warlord who leads the army of the northmen and face him in battle.'

Björn's eyes narrowed. 'That's it? No riddles or nonsense? That makes me uneasy.'

'Simply that,' answered the hag woman.

'Then I give you my oath as king of the Unberogen,' said Björn, 'I shall face this Norsii bastard and cut his damned head from his shoulders.'

The hag woman smiled and nodded. 'I believe you will,' she said.

The mist had thickened, and Björn had awoken with the morning sunlight prising his eyelids open. He sat up, the substance of his encounter with the hag woman etched on his memories with terrible clarity.

Björn opened his fist, and found he clutched a bronze pendant on a leather thong. Turning it over in his palm, he saw that it was a simple piece carved in the shape of a closed gateway. His first thought was to hurl it over a cliff or into a fast-flowing river, but instead he looped it over his head and tucked it beneath his woollen jerkin.

Now, sitting before the enemy army, the pendant felt like an anvil around his neck, its weight threatening to drag him to his doom.

Alfgeir pointed to the ridgeline. 'There's the bastard now.'

Björn looked up. The warlord of the enemy host was riding at the front of the Norsii army, his armour a lustrous crimson, his dragon banner proudly held aloft. The warlord's dark steed reared up, and sunlight shimmered on the warrior's mighty sword as he held it aloft.

Drums and skirling trumpet blasts sounded, and the army of the southern kings began to march forward, thousands of swordsmen, axe bearers and spear hosts ready to drive the Norsii from these lands.

A wolf howled in the distance, and Björn smiled sadly.

'A good omen do you think?' he asked.

'Ulric is with us,' said Alfgeir, extending his hand.

Björn took his champion's hand in the warrior's grip. 'May he grant you strength, Alfgeir.'

'And you also, my king,' responded Alfgeir.

King Björn of the Unberogen looked up towards the red-armoured warlord, and gripped the haft of Soultaker as the ravens began to gather.

SIGMAR AROSE REFRESHED and alert, the last remnants of a dream of his father clinging to him, but hovering just beyond recall. He took a deep breath, and looked at the sleeping form of Ravenna beside him. Her shoulder was bare, the fur blanket slipped away in the night, and he leaned down to kiss her tanned skin.

She smiled, but did not wake, and he slid from the bed to gather his clothes.

Sigmar lifted pieces of cut chicken from a plate on the table before the hearth, suddenly realising how hungry he was. He and Ravenna had prepared some food, but when Gerreon had left them alone, their thoughts had turned to other appetites that needed satisfying, and the food had gone uneaten.

He sat at the table and broke his fast, pouring himself some water and swilling it around his mouth. Ravenna stirred, and Sigmar smiled contentedly.

His mind was less filled with thoughts of war and the worries for his people, but the business of ruling a land did not cease for any man, king's son or not. Briefly, he wished for the simpler times of his youth, when all he had dreamed of was fighting dragons and being like his father.

Such dreams of childhood had been put away, however, and replaced with grander dreams where his people lived in peace with good men to lead them and justice for all. He shook his head free of such grandiose thoughts, content for now to simply be a man freshly risen from sleep with a beautiful woman and a full belly.

Ravenna turned over, propping her head on an elbow, her dark hair wild and looking like some berserker's mane. The thought made him smile, and she returned it, pulling back the covers and padding, naked, across the room to pick up her emerald cloak.

'Good morning, my love,' said Sigmar.

'Good morning indeed,' replied Ravenna. 'Are you rested?'

'I am refreshed,' nodded Sigmar, 'though Ulric alone knows how, you didn't let me get much sleep, woman!'

'Fine,' smiled Ravenna. 'I shall leave you alone next time you share my bed.'

'Ah, now that's not what I meant.'

'Good.'

Sigmar pushed away the plate of chicken scraps as Ravenna said, 'I feel like a swim. You should join me.'

'I can't swim,' said Sigmar, 'and, unfortunately, I have things to attend to today.'

'I'll teach you,' said Ravenna, pulling open her cloak to flaunt her nakedness, 'and if the future king cannot take time for himself then who can? Come on, I know a pool to the north where a tributary of the Reik runs through a secluded little glen. You'll love it.'

'Very well,' said Sigmar, spreading his hands in defeat. 'For you, anything.'

They dressed swiftly and gathered up some bread, chicken and fruit in a basket. Sigmar strapped on his sword belt, having left Ghal-maraz in the king's longhouse, and the pair of them set off, hand in hand, through Reikdorf.

Sigmar waved at Wolfgart and Pendrag, who were training warriors on the Field of Swords, as they made their way towards the north gate. The guards nodded as they passed through the gate, making way for trade wagons pulled by long-haired Ostagoth ponies and travelling merchants from the Brigundian tribes.

The roads into Reikdorf were well travelled, and the warriors at the walls had their hands full inspecting those who desired entry into the king's town.

A wolf howled in the distance, and Sigmar felt a shiver down the length of his spine.

SIGMAR AND RAVENNA soon passed from the road and sight of Reikdorf, moving into the forest towards the sound of falling water. Ravenna's steps were assured as she led them into a secluded valley, where a slender ribbon of silver water spilled from the slopes around Reikdorf towards the mighty Reik.

The trees were widely spaced here, though they were still out of sight of the road, and a screen of rocks jutted from the ground like ancient teeth before a wide pool that sat at the base of a small waterfall.

The pool was deep, and Ravenna slipped out of her dress and dived in, cutting a knife-sharp path along the surface of the water. She surfaced and shook her head clear, treading water as she pushed her hair from her eyes.

'Come on!' she cried. 'Get in the water.'

'It looks cold,' said Sigmar.

'It's bracing,' said Ravenna, swimming the length of the pool with strong, lithe strokes. 'It will wake you up.'

Sigmar set the food basket down at the edge of the clearing. 'I am already awake.'

'What's this?' laughed Ravenna. 'The mighty Sigmar afraid of a little cold water?'

He shook his head and unbuckled his sword belt, dropping it beside the food as he pulled off his boots and removed the rest of his clothing. He stood and walked to the edge of the water, enjoying the sensation of misting water from the small waterfall as it speckled his skin.

A raven sat on the branch of a tree opposite Sigmar, and he nodded towards the bird of omen as it appeared to regard him with silent interest.

'Trinovantes saw a raven the night before you all left for Astofen,' said a voice behind him. Sigmar reached for his sword before realising he had left it with the food. He turned and relaxed as he saw Gerreon standing at the edge of the clearing.

Immediately, Sigmar saw that something was wrong.

Gerreon's clothes were muddy and stained black. His boots were ruined, and his leather jerkin was torn and ragged. Ravenna's brother's face was pale, dark rings hooded his eyes and his black hair – normally so carefully combed – was loose, and hung around his face in matted ropes.

'Gerreon?' he said, suddenly conscious he was naked. 'What happened?'

'A raven,' repeated Gerreon. 'Appropriate don't you think?'

'Appropriate for what?' asked Sigmar, confused at the hostile tone in Gerreon's voice.

Out of the corner of his eye, he could see Ravenna swimming back towards the bank, and took a step towards Gerreon.

His unease grew as Gerreon moved to stand between him and his sword.

'That you should both see ravens before you die.'

'What are you talking about, Gerreon?' demanded Sigmar. 'I grow tired of this foolishness.'

'You killed him!' screamed Gerreon, drawing his sword.

'Killed who?' asked Sigmar. 'You are not making any sense.'

'You know who,' wept Gerreon, 'Trinovantes. You killed my twin brother, and now I am going to kill you.'

Sigmar knew that he should back away, simply leap into the water and make his way downstream with Ravenna, but his was the blood of kings, and kings did not run from battle, even ones they knew they could not win.

Gerreon was a master swordsman, and Sigmar was unarmed and naked. Against any other opponent, Sigmar knew he might have closed the distance without suffering a mortal wound, but against a warrior as skilled and viper-fast as Gerreon, there was no chance.

'Gerreon!' cried Ravenna from the edge of the pool. 'What are you doing?'

'Stay in the water,' warned Sigmar, taking slow steps towards Gerreon. His route curved to the left, but Gerreon was too clever to fall for such an obvious ploy, and remained between him and his sword.

'You sent him to his death and did not even care that he would die for you,' said Gerreon.

'That is not true,' said Sigmar, keeping his voice low and soothing as he approached.

'Of course it is!'

'Then you are a damned coward,' snapped Sigmar, hoping to goad Gerreon into a reckless mistake. 'If your blood cried out for vengeance, you should have come for me long ago. Instead you wait to catch me unawares. I thought you as courageous as Trinovantes, but you are not half the man he was. He is cursing you from Ulric's hall even now!'

'Do not speak his name!' screamed Gerreon.

Sigmar saw the intent to strike in Gerreon's eyes, and leapt aside as the swordsman lunged for him. The point of Gerreon's blade flashed past him, and Sigmar spun on his heel, his fist swinging in a deadly right cross.

Gerreon swayed aside from the blow, and Sigmar stumbled. Off balance, he felt a line of white fire score across his side as Gerreon's blade slashed across his hip and up over his ribs. Blood flowed freely from the wound, and Sigmar blinked away stars of pain that bloomed behind his eyes.

He spun, and ducked back as Gerreon's sword came at him again. The blade passed within a finger's breadth of spilling his innards to the ground, and as he fought for breath, a sudden dizziness drove him to his knees.

Ravenna began climbing from the water, screaming her brother's name, and Sigmar forced himself to his feet as he fought for breath. Gerreon bounced lightly from foot to foot, one arm raised behind him, his sword arm extended before him.

Sigmar balled his hands into fists and advanced towards the swordsman, his breath coming in short, gasping heaves.

What was happening to him?

His vision swam for an instant, and the world seemed to spin crazily. Sigmar felt a tremor begin in his hand, a palsied jitter like that which plagued some unfortunate elders of Reikdorf.

Gerreon laughed, and Sigmar's eyes narrowed as he saw an oily yellow coating on the swordsman's blade. He looked down and saw some of the same substance mixed with the blood on his ribs.

'Can you feel the poison working on you, Sigmar?' asked Gerreon. 'You should. I smeared my blade with enough to kill a warhorse.'

'Poison…' wheezed Sigmar, his chest feeling as if it were clamped in Master Alaric's giant vice. 'I… said… you were… a coward.'

'I let myself get angry at you earlier, but I will not make that mistake again.'

The tremors in Sigmar's hands spread to his arms and he could barely hold them still. He could feel a terrible lethargy stealing over him, and he staggered towards Gerreon, his fury giving him strength.

'What have you done?' screamed Ravenna, running at her brother.

Gerreon turned, and casually backhanded her to the grass with his free hand.

'Do not talk to me,' snapped Gerreon. 'Sigmar killed Trinovantes and you whore with him? You are nothing to me. I should kill you too for dishonouring our brother.'

Sigmar dropped to his knees again as the tremors became more violent and his legs would no longer support him. He tried to speak, but the enormous pressure in his chest was too great and his lungs were filled with fire.

Ravenna rolled to her feet, her face a mask of fury, and threw herself at her brother.

Gerreon's instincts as a swordsman took over, and he easily evaded her attack.

'Gods, no!' screamed Sigmar as Gerreon's sword plunged into her stomach.

The blade stabbed through Ravenna and she fell, tearing the sword from her brother's grip. Sigmar surged to his feet, pain, anger and loss obliterating all thoughts save vengeance on Gerreon.

The red mist of the berserker descended on Sigmar and, where before he had resisted its siren song, he now surrendered to it completely. The pain in his side vanished, and the fire in his lungs dimmed as he threw himself at Ravenna's killer.

His hands closed around Gerreon's neck and he squeezed with all his strength.

'You killed her!' he spat.

He forced Gerreon to his knees, feeling his strength flooding from his body, but knowing he still had enough to kill this worthless traitor. He looked into Gerreon's eyes, seeking some sign of remorse for what he had done, but there was nothing, only…

Sigmar saw the crying boy who had wept for his lost brother, and a screaming soul being dragged into a terrible abyss. He saw the razored claws of a monstrous power that had found a purchase in Gerreon's heart, and the desperate struggle fought within his tortured soul.

Even as Sigmar's hands crushed the life from Gerreon, he saw that monstrous power reach up and claim the swordsman entirely for its own. A terrible light built behind Gerreon's eyes, and a malicious smile of radiant evil spread across his face.

Sigmar's hands were prised from his foe's neck as Gerreon pushed him back. The berserk strength that had filled him moments ago now fled his body, and Sigmar staggered away from Gerreon as his body failed him.

Gerreon laughed, and dragged his sword from his sister's fallen body as Sigmar lurched away from him.

'You are finished, Sigmar,' said the swordsman, his voice redolent with power. 'You and your dream are dead.'

'No,' whispered Sigmar as the world spun around him, and he fell backwards into the pool. The water was icy, and cut through the paralysis of the poison for the briefest moment. He flailed as he sank beneath the surface, water filling his mouth and lungs.

The current seized him, and his body twisted as it was carried down river.

Sigmar's vision greyed, and his last sight was of Gerreon smiling at him through the swirling bubbles of the water's surface.

ELEVEN
The Grey Vaults

Horst Edsel was not a man given to reflection on the whims of the gods, for he had accepted he was but an insignificant player in their grand dramas. Kings might lead armies to fight their enemies, and great warlords might conquer lands not their own, but the sweep of history largely passed Horst by, as it did many men.

He was not a clever man, nor was he gifted physically or mentally. He had married young, before the women of Reikdorf had fully realised the limited nature of his abilities, and his wife had gifted him with two children, a boy and a girl. The girl had died with her mother during the difficult birth, and a wasting sickness had taken the boy three years later.

The gods had seen fit to bestow these gifts upon him and then take them away, but Horst had not thought to curse them, for the joy he had known in those brief years was beyond anything he had known before or since.

Horst pushed the boat from the edge of the river, using an oar to ease it through the long reeds and thick algae that bloomed this far down the river, away from the timber jetties of the town. The meagre pickings he caught in the river were enough to feed him and provide him with a few fish to sell on market day, but little else, and certainly not the mooring fees charged by King Björn.

His nets and rods were safely stowed along the side of the small fishing boat, and his cat lay curled in the stern. He had not given the animal a name, for a name meant attachment, and no sooner had Horst ever become attached to something than the gods had taken it from him. He did not want to curse the cat by giving it a name and then having it die on him.

The sun had already climbed a fair distance into the sky, and he said, 'Late in the day, cat.'

The animal yawned, exposing its fangs, but paid him no attention.

'Shouldn't have put away the rest of that Taleuten rotgut,' he said, tasting the acrid bile in his throat from the cheap grain alcohol peddled by the more disreputable traders. 'We've slept past the best time for fish, cat. Earlier fishermen than us will have plucked the river by now. It's going to be another hungry day for us both. Well, for me anyway.'

Clear of the reed beds, Horst set the oars in the rowlocks and eased the boat out towards the centre of the river. Trading boats further up the river were sailing towards Reikdorf, and Horst continually checked over his shoulder to make sure he wasn't about to be rammed.

Shouts and curses from various ships chased him, but Horst ignored them with quiet dignity, and eased his boat towards a spot where a tributary that ran from the Hills of the Five Sisters flowed into the Reik. This had often proven to be a good spot for fish to gather, and he decided to give up on the main body of the river today.

He dropped the rope-tied rock that served as his anchor over the side of the boat with a satisfying splash, earning him a look of disdain from the cat, and then baited his hook with a scrap of rotten meat that he'd scavenged from the butcher's block.

'Nothing to do now but wait, cat,' said Horst, casting his line into the water.

He dozed in the sun, leaning against the gunwale of his boat, the line looped around his finger lest a fish should actually bite.

It felt as though he had barely closed his eyes when something tugged at the line around his finger. From the heft of the pull, it was something big.

Horst sat up and took hold of the fishing rod, easing it back with some difficulty, and looping the twine around a cleat on the side of the boat. Even the cat looked up as the boat swayed in the water.

'Something big, cat!' shouted Horst, dreaming of nice, fresh trout or mullet, or perhaps even a flounder, though this region of the river was a little far from the coast for that. He pulled on the rod again, and his hopes of dinner were dashed as he saw the body.

It drifted on its back towards him, the hook snagged in the skin of its chest. Horst squinted, seeing that the body was that of a naked man, powerfully built, but leaking blood into the water. Flaxen hair billowed around his head like drifting seaweed, and Horst reached over to pull him close to the boat.

With some considerable difficulty, Horst dragged the man's body into his boat, grunting and straining with the effort, for the man was muscular and powerful.

'I know what you're thinking,' he told the cat. 'Why bother when this poor fellow's obviously dead, eh?'

The cat uncurled from the stern and padded over to examine Horst's catch, sniffing disinterestedly around the wet body. Horst sat back to recover his breath, until his heart rate had slowed enough to tell him that he wasn't about to drop dead from the exertion.

Then he noticed that blood was still flowing from the long cuts to the man's side.

'Ho ho, this one's not quite dead yet!' he said.

Horst leaned over and brushed the sodden locks from the man's face.

He gasped, and reached for the oars, rowing for all he was worth towards the jetties of Reikdorf.

'Oh no, cat!' he said. 'This is bad... this is very bad!'

'WILL HE LIVE?' asked Pendrag, afraid of the answer.

Cradoc ignored him, for what was the point in offering an answer that the warrior would not understand and would not want if he did? The young prince was poised at the very threshold of Morr's realm, and no knowledge of man could prevent him from passing through.

He had been tending to a young warrior with a broken arm, another casualty of Alfgeir's harsh training regimes on the Field of Swords, when Pendrag had rushed in, his face pale and frightened. Even before the man opened his mouth, Cradoc had known that something terrible had happened.

Cradoc had gathered his healer's bag and limped after Pendrag, his aged frame unable to keep up with the young warrior. By the time they reached the longhouse, Cradoc was out of breath and his mouth was dry.

His worst suspicions had been confirmed when he saw the crowds gathered around the king's longhouse, their faces lined with fear. Pendrag had forged them a path and, though he had been prepared for the worst, he felt a chill as he saw Sigmar lying on a pallet of furs, his body wet and pale like a corpse.

Sigmar's sword-brothers and Eoforth knelt beside him, and a group of warriors stood to one side, their blades bared as though ready to fight. A hunched man in a tattered buckskin jerkin waited nervously to one side, and a small cat curled around his legs, looking nervously at the king's wolfhounds.

He had immediately shooed everyone out of the way and begun his examination, already fearing that the prince was beyond help, but then he saw that blood still pulsed weakly from deep cuts along his hip and ribs.

'I asked whether he would live?' demanded Pendrag. 'This is Sigmar!'

'I know who he is, damn you!' snapped Cradoc. 'Now be silent and let me work.'

Sigmar's colour was bad, and his body had clearly lost a lot of blood, but that alone could not account for the symptoms that Cradoc was seeing. Sigmar's pupils were dilated, and a faint tremor was evident in his fingertips.

Cradoc peered at the wounds in the prince's side, wounds clearly caused by a sword.

'What happened?' asked Cradoc. 'Who attacked the prince?'

'We do not know yet,' snarled Wolfgart, 'but whoever it was will die before this day is out!'

Cradoc nodded and bent closer to the injured Sigmar as he saw the faint yellowish deposit of a resinous substance coating the skin around the wound. He bent to sniff the blood, and recoiled as he smelled a sour, vegetable-like odour.

'Shallya's mercy,' he whispered, prising open Sigmar's eyelids.

'What?' asked Pendrag. 'What is it, man! Speak!'

'Hemlock,' said Cradoc. 'The prince has been poisoned. Whatever blade wounded him was coated with hemlock from the Brackenwalsch.'

'Is that bad?' asked Wolfgart, pacing the floor behind Pendrag.

'What do you think, idiot?' barked Cradoc. 'Have you heard of a *good* poison? Stop asking stupid questions, and make yourself useful and bring me some clean water! Now!'

He turned from the gathered warriors. 'I have seen hemlock

poisoning in livestock that eats too near the marshes, or drinks water in which its roots have found purchase.'

'Is it fatal?' asked Eoforth, giving voice to the question everyone feared.

Cradoc hesitated, unwilling to take away what little hope these men had for their prince.

'Usually, yes,' said Cradoc. 'The poisoned beast usually has trouble breathing, and then its legs fail and it begins to convulse. Eventually, its lungs give out and it breathes no more.'

'You say usually, Cradoc,' said Eoforth, his voice calm amid the panic that was filling the longhouse. 'Some survive?'

'Some, but not many,' said Cradoc, rummaging in his healer's bag to remove a clay vial stoppered with wax. 'Where is that water, damn you!'

'Do what you have to,' said Eoforth. 'The prince *must* live.'

Wolfgart appeared at his side, and Cradoc said, 'Clean the wounds. Be thorough, wash the blood away and don't be squeamish about getting inside the wound. Clean everything out, and leave no trace of the resin within him. You understand? Not a trace.'

'Not a trace,' said Wolfgart, and Cradoc saw the terrible fear for his friend in the warrior's eyes.

He handed the clay vial to Wolfgart. 'When the wound is clean, apply this poultice of tarrabeth, and then get someone with steady hands to stitch him shut.'

'And he will live? He will be all right then?'

Cradoc laid a paternal hand on Wolfgart's shoulder. 'Then we will have done all we can for him. It will be for the gods to decide whether he lives or dies.'

Cradoc moved aside as Wolfgart got to work, his joints flaring painfully as Pendrag helped him to his feet.

'Where was Sigmar found?' he asked.

'Is that important?'

'It could be vital,' snapped Cradoc. 'Now stop answering my questions with questions, and tell me where he was found.'

Pendrag nodded contritely and indicated the hunched man in the buckskin jerkin. 'Horst here found the prince in the river.'

Cradoc's eyes narrowed as he saw the worried looking man. He smelled of fish and damp leather, and the healer recognised him from some years ago. He had treated the man's son for a sickness that stripped the flesh from his bones, but despite Cradoc's best efforts, the boy had died.

'You found him?' asked Cradoc. 'Where?'

'I was out fishing by the edge of the river when I saw the young prince,' said Horst.

'Where exactly?' demanded Cradoc. 'Come on, man, this could be vital!'

Horst shrank back from Cradoc's sharp tongue, and the cat's ears pricked up.

'My apologies,' said Cradoc. 'My joints are aching, and King Björn's son is dying, so I do not have time for politeness. I need you to be precise, Horst, tell me where you found Sigmar.'

Horst's head bobbed in an approximation of a nod. 'Out by one of the north channels, sir. The one that flows from the Five Sisters. I was out fishing, and the prince went and snagged on my hook.'

'You know this place?' asked Cradoc, turning to Pendrag.

'I do, yes.'

'Sigmar was naked, which tells me he was swimming and did not fall into the water until after he was attacked,' said Cradoc, rubbing the heel of his palm against his temples. 'Is there a pool further up that channel?'

Pendrag nodded. 'Aye, there is. It is a favourite place for young lovers to swim.'

'Take me there,' said Cradoc, 'and if you wish to avenge yourselves on the prince's attacker, bring your finest trackers.'

'What is it?' asked Pendrag. 'What do you expect to find?'

'I do not think it likely that Sigmar will prove to be our only victim today,' said Cradoc.

SIGMAR OPENED HIS eyes to a bleak world of ashen grey. Rocky plains stretched out all around him, withered and dead heaths over which blew a parched wind. Twisted trees dotted the landscape, rearing high like black cracks in the empty, lifeless sky.

He was naked and alone, lost in this deserted wilderness with no stars above to guide him and no landmarks he recognised to fix his position. He did not know this land.

A range of mountains reared up in the distance, vast and monolithic, easily the biggest things he had ever seen. Even the distant peaks of the Grey Mountains were nowhere near as mighty as this great range.

'Is there anyone here?' he shouted, the sound as flat and toneless as the colours around him. The silence of the strange landscape swallowed his shout, and he felt a strange sense of dislocation as he set off towards the mountains in the absence of any better direction to travel.

His memories of how he had come to be here were confused, and he had only fleeting memories of his life. He knew his name and that he was of the Unberogen tribe, the fiercest warriors west of the mountains, but beyond that...

Sigmar walked for what felt like hours, but he quickly noticed that the sky above was unchanging, the dead sun motionless in the grey clouds. A moment or an age could have passed, yet his limbs were as strong as they had been when he had set off. He had no doubt that he could walk forever in this lifeless realm without feeling tired.

He stopped as a sudden thought came to him.

Was he dead?

This strange landscape was certainly bereft of life, but where was the golden hall of Ulric, the great feasting and the warriors who had fallen in glorious battle? He had lived a valourous life had he not?

Was he to be denied his rest in the halls of his ancestors?

Fear touched his heart as he felt shadows gather around him at the thought. Where he had stopped was as empty and desolate as any other place he had seen in his travels, but he could sense a gathering menace.

'Show yourselves!' he roared. 'Come out and die!'

No sooner had he spoken than the shadows coiled from the ground and shaped themselves into dark phantoms of nightmare. A pair of huge, slavering wolves with red eyes and fangs like knives stalked him, and a scaled daemon with a horned head, forked tongue and a dripping sword hissed words of his death.

Sigmar wished he had a weapon to defend himself, and looked down to see a golden sword appear in his hand. He lifted the blade, and imagined himself in a suit of the finest iron armour. He was not surprised when it appeared upon his body, the links gleaming and oiled.

The creatures of darkness surrounded him, but rather than wait for them to make the first move, Sigmar leapt to attack. His sword cleaved through one of the shadow wolves, and it vanished in a swirl of dark smoke.

The second wolf leapt at him, and he dropped flat to the dusty ground, his sword sweeping up a disembowelling cut. Again the beast vanished, and the daemon rushed in with its sword raised.

The blade slashed for his throat, but Sigmar ducked and rammed his sword into the creature's side.

Instead of vanishing, the creature let loose a screeching howl, the pain of it driving Sigmar to his knees. He dropped his weapon, which vanished as soon as it hit the ground. The daemon bellowed in triumph, its sword sweeping down to take his skull… to be met by a great, double-headed axe that blocked the blow.

Sigmar looked up to see a mighty warrior in a glittering hauberk of polished iron scale, with a winged bronze helmet and kilt of linked leather strips reinforced with bronze. The warrior's axe swept aside the daemon's blade, and the return stroke smote its chest, sending it back to whatever hell it had come from.

With the daemon despatched, the warrior turned and offered his hand to Sigmar, and even before he saw the warrior's face, he knew whose face it would be.

'Father,' said Sigmar as Björn took him in a crushing bear hug.

'My son,' said Björn. 'It does my heart proud to see you, even as it grieves me to see you in this place.'

'What is this place? Am I dead? Are… are you?'

'These are the Grey Vaults,' said Björn. 'It is the netherworld between life and death where the spirits of the dead wander.'

'How did I come to be here?'

'I do not know, my son, but you *are* here, and I mean to make sure you return to the land of the living. Now come, we have a long way to go.'

Sigmar indicated the barren emptiness that surrounded them. 'Go? Where is there to go? I have walked for an age in this place and found nothing.'

'We must reach the mountains. There we will find the gateway.'

'What gateway?'

'The gateway to Morr's kingdom,' said Björn, 'to the realm of the dead.'

THE BATTLE WAS won, but as Alfgeir had feared the cost had been high. The Norsii had fought like daemons against the armies of the southern kings, their shield walls like impregnable fortresses atop the forested ridgeline. Time and time again, the axes and swords of the Taleutens, Cherusens and Unberogens had hammered the northmen, until shields had splintered and spears had broken.

Inch by bloody inch, they had driven up the slopes and pushed the

Norsii back, but for each yard gained, a score of men had been lost. As the army of the southern kings finally took the top of the hill, the Norsii fought in smaller and smaller circles, defiant to the end and asking for no quarter.

Truly, these men were iron foes.

King Björn had fought like a man possessed, launching himself into the thick of the fighting from the outset, his mighty axe cleaving northmen dead with every stroke. The White Wolves had tried to keep up with him, but the king's progress had been relentless.

Alfgeir had seen where the king had been headed and tried desperately to follow, but a blood-maddened hound had leapt upon him with its fangs snapping shut on his gorget. He had killed the beast, but had been powerless to follow his king as the press of fighting bodies blocked all passage forward.

Alfgeir closed his eyes as he remembered the glorious sight of his king standing before the red-armoured warlord of the enemy host. Never had he been prouder to serve Björn of the Unberogen than the moment he had seen his liege lord's axe cut the head from the enemy leader. The dragon banner had fallen, and a cry of dismay and anger had arisen from the Norsii, their vengeful eyes turning to he who had toppled it.

The Marshal of the Reik turned from his memories and approached the fire where the healers worked. Screams of the dying filled the air, piteous cries for wives and mothers tearing at the hearts of those who attempted to make their last hours more comfortable.

Victory fires were even now being lit atop the hill, the mounds of dead northmen burning as offerings to Ulric, but the victory tasted of ashes to Alfgeir, for he had failed in his duty.

King Björn lay on a hastily erected pallet bed, his armour in a bloody and torn pile beside him. The king's flesh was grey, his body wrapped in bandages that covered the many sword blows and spear thrusts that he had suffered. Blood pooled beneath his body and dripped through the linen of the bed.

No sooner had Björn slain the Norsii warlord than his dark-armoured champions had fallen upon the king to wreak their revenge. Alfgeir could recall every sword blow and spear thrust, feeling them as though they struck his own flesh.

'Will he live?' asked Alfgeir.

One of the healers looked up, his face streaked with tears.

'We have stitched his wounds, my lord,' said the healer, 'and we have administered bandages treated with faxtoryll and spiderleaf.'

'But will he live?' demanded Alfgeir.

The healer shook his head. 'We have done all we can for him. It will be for the gods to decide whether he lives or dies.'

SIGMAR AND BJÖRN walked further through the Grey Vaults, the landscape remaining unchanged no matter how far they travelled. To Sigmar's eyes, the mountains appeared to draw no closer, yet his father assured him they were on the right path.

Though the scenery appeared unchanging, they were not without company on their journey. The dark shadows that had assaulted Sigmar flitted on the edge of perception, only ever seen from the corner of the eye, as though they escorted the travellers, yet were afraid of being seen directly by them.

'What are they?' Sigmar asked, seeing another darting shape at the edge of his vision.

'The souls of those damned forever,' said Björn with great sadness. 'Eoforth said that the Grey Vaults are inhabited by the souls of the unquiet dead, those whose bodies are raised by necromancy and who cannot pass into Morr's realm.'

'So nothing that dwells here is truly dead?'

'As good as,' said Björn. 'Though those consigned here may have been virtuous while alive, here they have been twisted into terrible forms by their hatred for the living. Our warmth and light reminds them of what they once were and what they can never now have.'

'So why aren't they attacking?'

'Be thankful they are not, Sigmar, for I do not think we have the strength to oppose them.'

'All the more reason for them to attack.'

'Perhaps,' agreed Björn, 'but I feel they are directing us to somewhere of their choosing.'

'Where?'

'I do not know, but we might as well enjoy the walk until we get there, eh?'

'Enjoy the walk?' asked Sigmar. 'Have you seen where we are? This is a terrible place.'

'Aye, true enough, but we are getting to walk it together, father and son, and it has been too long since we spoke as men.'

Sigmar nodded. 'There's truth in that. Very well, tell me of the war in the north?'

Björn's face darkened, and Sigmar sensed his father's hesitation in answering. 'Well enough, well enough. Your men fought like the Wolves of Ulric, and the Cherusens and Taleutens fought well too. We drove the Norsii from their lands and back to their own frozen kingdom. When you are king, you must do honour to Krugar and Aloysis, son. They are honourable kings and staunch allies of the Unberogen.'

Sigmar could not help but notice the phrasing of his father's answer, but swallowed the feelings growing within him. Instead he asked, 'This gateway we are heading towards? Morr's Gate? Why exactly do we want to get there?'

'Ask me when we get there,' said his father, and Sigmar read the warning in his voice.

They walked in silence for another indeterminate length of time, until Björn said, 'I am proud of you, Sigmar. Your mother would have been proud of you too, had she lived.'

Sigmar felt a tightness to his chest, and was about to reply when he saw that his father was looking at something ahead of them. He turned from his father, and the breath caught in his throat at the sight before him.

Though the mountains had been as far away as ever the last time he had looked, they now towered overhead, monstrous black guardians of an undiscovered country beyond. As Sigmar watched, the flanks of the mountains seemed to shift and twist as though the power of a god was reshaping the rock into some new design.

Entire cliffs shook themselves free of the mountains, grinding together to form terrifyingly huge pilasters. Towering ridgelines compressed with tectonic force, and splinters of rock and billowing clouds of dust rose from the mountains as a huge lintel took shape across the roof of the world.

Within moments, a vast portal had formed in the side of the mountains, wide and tall enough to encompass the lands as far as the eye could see. A yawning blackness swirled between the pilasters, darkness so complete that nothing could ever return from its midnight embrace.

An aching moan of desire arose from the landscape, and the shadows that had dogged their steps arose from the ground in a great swell. More of the dread wolves and daemon things appeared, accompanied by other beasts and creatures too terrible to imagine.

Black beasts with wicked fangs and gleaming coals for eyes rose on pinions of darkness, slithering drakes with teeth like swords, and skeletal lizard things with axe-blade tails and hideous skulls for heads.

Whatever these had been in life, they were monsters in death.

The army of shadows drifted through the air, forming an unbroken line between them and the gateway in the mountains. A tall warrior stepped from among the ranks of monsters, he alone of the shadow creatures imbued with a hue beyond black.

The warrior was tall and armoured in blood-red plate armour, his helmet carved in the shape of a snarling, horned daemon. A mighty two-handed sword was held out before him, the blade aimed at Sigmar's heart.

'You,' hissed Björn. 'How can that be? I killed you.'

'You think you are the only one able to bargain with ancient powers, old man?' asked the warrior, and Sigmar recoiled as he saw that the daemonic visage had not been wrought from iron, but was the warrior's true face. 'Service to the old gods does not end in death.'

'Fine,' said Björn. 'I can kill you again if that is what it takes.'

'Father,' said Sigmar, 'what is it talking about?'

'Never mind that,' snapped Björn. 'Arm yourself.'

With a thought, Sigmar was armed once more, though not with the golden sword of before, but with the mighty form of Ghal-maraz.

'The boy must pass,' said the red daemon. 'It is his time.'

'No,' said Björn, 'it is not. I made a sacred vow!'

The daemon laughed, the sound rich with ripe amusement. 'To a hag that lives in a cave! You think a dabbler in the mysteries can stand before the will of the old gods?'

'Why don't you come over here and find out, you whoreson!'

'Either give him to us, or we will take him from you,' said the daemon. 'Either way, he dies. Give him to us and you can return to the world of flesh. You are not so old that the prospect of more life does not appeal.'

'I have lived enough life for ten men, daemon,' roared Björn, 'and no cur like you is going to take my son from me.'

'You cannot stand before us, old man,' warned the daemon.

As Sigmar looked up at his father, savage pride swelled in his breast, and though he did not fully understand the nature of this confrontation, he knew that a terrible bargain had been struck in an attempt to save him.

The army of daemons advanced, wolves snapping their jaws, and the flying monsters taking to the air with bounding leaps. Sigmar lifted Ghal-maraz and Björn readied Soultaker as the masters of the Unberogen prepared to face their doom.

Sigmar felt the air thicken around him, and looked left and right as he felt the presence of uncounted others join him. To either side of him stood a pair of ghostly warriors in mail habergeons carrying a long-hafted axe each. Hundreds more filled the space behind them and around them, and Sigmar laughed as he saw the daemon's face twist in disbelief.

'Father,' gasped Sigmar as he recognised faces amongst the warriors.

'I see them,' said Björn, tears of gratitude spilling down his cheeks. 'They are the fallen warriors of the Unberogen. Not even death can keep them from their king's side.'

An army of daemons and an army of ghosts faced one another on the deathless plain of the Grey Vaults, and Sigmar could not have been prouder.

'This is my last gift to you, my son,' said Björn. 'We must break through their lines and reach that gate. When we do, you must obey me, no matter what. You understand?'

'I do,' answered Sigmar.

'Promise me,' warned Björn.

'I promise.'

Björn nodded, and turned a hostile gaze on the red daemon. 'You want him? Come and take him!'

With a deathly war cry, the red daemon raised its sword and charged.

≺ TWELVE ≻

One Must Pass

THE DAEMONS RAN towards the Unberogen with screeching bellows and hoots, their attack without strategy or design, and their only thought to destroy their foes by the quickest means possible.

'With me!' roared Björn, and charged headlong towards the daemons. The ghosts followed their king in silence, forming a deadly fighting wedge with Björn and Sigmar at its tip. When the armies met it was with a spectral clash of iron that sounded as though it came from a far distant place.

The army of ghosts cleaved into the daemons, swords and axes cutting a swathe through their enemies as they fought to carry their king and prince towards Morr's Gateway.

Sigmar smashed a daemon apart with Ghal-maraz, the hammer of Kurgan Ironbeard more deadly than any sword. The power worked into the weapon by the dwarfs was as potent, if not more so, in this place as it was in the realm of the living. Every blow split a daemon's essence apart, and even its presence seemed to cause them pain.

Björn fought with all the skill of his years, the mighty Soultaker earning its battle name as it cleaved through the enemy ranks. The daemons were many, and though the wedge of Unberogens pushed deeper and deeper into the horde, their progress was slowing as the daemons began to surround them.

For all its ferocity, however, this was no bloody battle. Each of the combatants disappeared when vanquished, the light or darkness of their existence winking out in a moment as a sword pierced them or fangs tore at them.

The battle raged in the shadow of the great gateway, and Sigmar saw the darkness of the portal shimmer as though in expectation, its urgency growing with every passing second.

Sigmar and Björn fought side by side, pushing the fighting wedge deeper into the daemon horde. As the turmoil between the mountainous pilasters of the gateway grew stronger, Sigmar saw a golden glow emanating from a pendant around his father's neck.

'I see you, Child of Thunder!' shouted the red daemon, cleaving a path towards him.

Sigmar turned to face the daemon, transfixed by the abomination of its very existence.

The daemon's sword slashed towards him, and he overcame his horror at the last second to sway aside from its attack. The deadly blade came at him again and again, each time coming within a hand's span of ending his life.

In that moment, Sigmar knew he was hopelessly outclassed, and that this daemon warrior had spent centuries perfecting its fighting skills. In desperation, he knew he had only one chance to defeat it.

The daemon launched another series of blistering attacks, and Sigmar fell back before them, appearing to stumble at the last as he desperately blocked a strike that would have removed his head.

With a roar of triumph, the daemon leapt in to deliver the deathblow, but Sigmar righted himself, and spun on his heel to swing Ghal-maraz at his foe's knee. The warhammer smashed against the armoured joint, and the daemon screamed as it collapsed to the ground.

Sigmar reversed his grip on his weapon, and swung it in an upward stroke into the daemon's howling face. The head of Ghal-maraz obliterated the daemon's skull, and with a shriek of terror, it vanished into whatever hellish oblivion awaited it.

With the death of their daemonic master, the shadow horde recoiled before Sigmar, and he pressed forward, the ghostly warriors of the Unberogen following behind him.

Sigmar turned to see his father surrounded by a host of daemons, desperately fending them off with wide sweeps of his axe. Without thought, Sigmar launched into the fray, and struck left and right.

Daemons fell back before him, and together, he and his father fought their way clear of the monsters to rejoin the fighting ghosts of the Unberogen.

The daemons were in disarray, their line broken and their numbers dwindling with every passing moment. Sensing victory, the Unberogen warriors pushed onwards into the daemon horde, and Sigmar and Björn once again took their places at the fighting point of the wedge.

The combat was no less fierce, however, and at every turn both daemons and ghosts vanished from the field of battle. Nothing, however, could halt the inexorable advance of the Unberogen, and as Sigmar crushed a daemon wolf's skull with his hammer, he saw that no more enemies stood between him and the portal.

'Father!' he shouted. 'We are through!'

Björn despatched a nightmare creature with dark wings and a barbed tail before risking a glance towards the mountain. The black portal rippled like boiling pitch and, for the briefest moment, Sigmar fancied he could make out the faint outline of an enormous, beckoning figure swathed in black robes, standing just beyond the gargantuan portal.

Far from being a figure of fear, Sigmar sensed only serene wisdom from this giant apparition, a serenity born from the acceptance of death's natural inevitability. He lowered Ghal-maraz, and knew now what had to happen.

Sigmar stepped towards the towering gateway, knowing that the Hall of Ulric would be open to him, and that he would find peace there. A rough hand gripped his arm, and he turned to see his father standing before him, the army of ghosts at his back and the horde of daemons defeated.

'I have to go,' said Sigmar. 'I know now why I am here. In the world above I am dying.'

'Yes,' said Björn, lifting the glowing pendant from around his neck, 'but I made a sacred vow that you would not.'

'Then you… you are… dead?' asked Sigmar.

'If not now then soon, yes,' said Björn, holding up the pendant. Sigmar saw that it was a simple thing, a bronze image of the gateway they stood before, though this portal was barred.

His father looped the pendant over Sigmar's head. 'This kept me here long enough to aid you,' said Björn, 'but it is yours now. Keep it safe.'

'Then this was supposed to be my time to die?'

Bjorn nodded. 'Servants of the Dark Gods conspired to make it so, but there are those who stand against them, and they are not without power.'

'You offered your life for me,' whispered Sigmar.

'I do not understand the truth of it, my son,' said Björn, 'but the laws of the dead are not to be denied, not even by kings. One must pass the gateway.'

'No!' cried Sigmar as he saw his father's form growing faint, becoming like the ghostly Unberogen warriors that had fought at their side. 'I cannot let you do this for me!'

'It is already done,' said Björn. 'A great destiny awaits you, my son, and no father could be prouder than I to know that your deeds will surpass even the greatest kings of ancient days.'

'You have seen the future?'

'I have, but do not ask me of it, for it is time you left this place and returned to the realm of life,' said Björn. 'It will be hard for you, for you will know great pain and despair.'

Even as his father spoke these last words, he and the army of ghosts were drawn towards Morr's gateway.

'But also glory and immortality,' said Björn with his last breath.

Sigmar wept as his father and his faithful warriors made the journey from the realm of the living to that of the dead. No sooner had they passed beyond the gateway than it vanished as though it had never existed, leaving Sigmar alone in the empty wasteland of the Grey Vaults.

He took a deep breath and closed his eyes.

And opened them again to searing agony.

THE TOP OF Warrior's Hill was exposed, and the wind whipped around it with cruel fingers that lifted cloaks and tunics to allow autumn's chill entry to the body. Sigmar made no attempt to pull his wolfskin cloak tighter as though daring the season to try its best to discomfit him. The cold was his constant companion now, and he welcomed it into his heart like an old friend.

No sooner had Sigmar opened his eyes and awoken to pain than the memory of the bloodshed by the river had returned, and he had screamed with an agony born not from his near death, but from his loss.

He remembered telling the wounded boy of the Field of Swords that pain was the warrior's constant companion, but he now realised that it was not pain, but despair that dogged a warrior's every moment: despair at the futility of war, at the hopelessness of joy and the foolishness of dreams.

Six armoured warriors accompanied him, his protectors since Gerreon's attack nearly five weeks ago. Fear of assassination had made old women of his sword-brothers, but Sigmar did not blame them, for who could have foreseen that Gerreon would turn on him with such savagery?

He closed his eyes and dropped to his knees, tears spilling down his face as he thought of Ravenna. His grief at seeing the paleness of her flesh, stark against the darkness of her hair was as fresh now as it had been the moment he had seen her lying lifeless upon the pallet bed.

Gone was the vivacious, intelligent girl who had shone sunlight into his heart, and in her place was a gaping, empty wound that would never heal. His hands balled into fists, and he fought to control the anger building within him, for with no one to strike at, Sigmar's rage had turned inwards.

He should have seen the darkness in Gerreon's heart. He should have trusted his friend's suspicions that Gerreon's contrition was false. There must have been some sign he had missed that would have alerted him to the treachery that was to rob him of his love.

With every passing day, Sigmar drew further into himself, shutting out Wolfgart and Pendrag as they tried to rouse him from his melancholy. Strong wine became his refuge, a means of blotting out the pain and visions that plagued him nightly of Gerreon's sword plunging into Ravenna's body.

Nor was Ravenna's death the only pain he carried in his heart, for he knew that his father, too, was dead. No word had come from the north, but Sigmar knew with utter certainty that the king of the Unberogen had fallen. The people of Reikdorf eagerly awaited the return of their king, but Sigmar knew that they were soon to experience the same sense of loss that daily tore at him.

A secret part of him relished the thought of others suffering as he did, but the nobility of his soul knew that such thoughts were unworthy of him, and he fought against such base pettiness. He had not spoken of the Grey Vaults and his father's fate to anyone, for it would be unseemly for a son to speak of a king's death before it was confirmed, and he did not want his rule of the Unberogen to begin on a sign of ill omen.

Reikdorf would learn soon enough the meaning of loss.

In the weeks since his awakening, he had learned that his body had lain cold and unmoving, not living, but not truly dead, for six days. His life had hung by the slenderest of threads, with the healer, Cradoc, at a loss to explain why he did not awaken or slip into death.

Wolfgart, Pendrag and even the venerable Eoforth had sat with him for all the time he had lain at the threshold of Morr's kingdom, and he knew he was lucky to have such steadfast sword-brothers, which made his forced estrangement all the harder to rationalise.

Grief, as Sigmar had learned over the years, was a far from rational process.

He had tried to reject what his eyes had seen on the riverbank and looked for retribution, but even that was denied him, for neither Cuthwin nor Svein could find any trace of Gerreon's passing. The traitor's meagre belongings were gone, and he had vanished into the wilderness like a shadow.

With Sigmar's awakening, Wolfgart had readied his horse to ride into the forest and hunt the traitor down, but Sigmar had forbidden him to go, knowing that Gerreon had too great a head start and was too clever to be caught.

Gerreon's name was now a curse, and he would find no succour in the lands of men. He was gone, and would likely die alone in the forest, a nothing and an outcast.

Sigmar shook his head free of such thoughts, and scooped a handful of earth from the summit of the hill, letting the rich, dark soil spill from between his fingers as he felt something turn to stone within him.

He looked over his domain, the ever-growing city of Reikdorf, his people, the mighty river and the lands spread out in a grand tapestry as far as the eye could see.

The last of the earth fell from Sigmar's fingers, and he reached up to his shoulder and brushed his hands across the golden pin he had given Ravenna by the river, and which now secured his own cloak.

'From now on I shall love no other,' he said. 'This land shall be my one abiding love.'

THE BREATH HEAVED in Sigmar's lungs as he made the last circuit of the Field of Swords, each step sending bolts of fire along his tired limbs. He could feel the fire build in his muscles, but pushed on, knowing that he had to build his strength up before the Unberogen army returned to Reikdorf with the body of the king.

The guilt of keeping this from his people still gnawed at him, but the alternative was no better, and thus he kept the bitter truth locked deep within his heart.

Once, this run would have barely taxed him, but now it took all his willpower to keep putting one foot in front of another. His strength and endurance was returning, though at a rate that still frustrated him, even though it amazed old Cradoc.

Every day, Sigmar fought to regain his former vigour. He sparred with sword and dagger to restore his speed, lifted weighted bars of iron that Master Alaric had forged for him to develop his strength, and ran a dozen circuits of the Field of Swords to build his stamina.

It had been Pendrag's idea that Sigmar train within sight of the younger warriors, claiming they would see him grow stronger and take hope from the sight.

Privately, Sigmar knew that Pendrag's suggestion was as much to do with giving *him* the edge he needed to succeed as give his warriors hope. Training alone, he had only himself to disappoint if he gave up, but failing in full view of his people would disappoint everyone, and that was not Sigmar's way.

Sweat dripped into his eyes, and he wiped a hand across his brow as he approached the end of the run. He jogged to a halt beside Wolfgart, who looked barely touched by the exertion, and bent over to rest his hands on his thighs. Pendrag looked similarly untroubled, and Sigmar fought down the bitterness that rose within him.

'You have to give your strength time to return,' said Pendrag, guessing his mood.

Sigmar looked up as his vision swam, and sank to his haunches, taking a series of deep breaths and stretching the muscles of his legs.

'I know,' he said, 'but it is galling... to know... I am not as fit... as I should be.'

'Give it time,' said Pendrag, offering him his hand. 'Six weeks ago you were on the edge of death. It is arrogant to think you will be your old self so soon.'

'Aye,' said Wolfgart. 'You're a tough one, my friend, but even you are not *that* tough.'

'Well, I should be,' snapped Sigmar, ignoring Pendrag's hand and rising to his feet. 'If I am to be king, then a poor king I will be if I cannot exert myself without wheezing like a toothless old man!'

He immediately regretted the words, but it was too late to take them back.

Wolfgart shook his head and planted his hands on his hips. 'Ulric preserve us, but you are in a foul mood today,' he said.

'I think I have cause to be,' retorted Sigmar.

'I am not saying you don't, but why you have to take it out on us is beyond me. Gerreon, may the gods curse him, is gone,' said Wolfgart, 'and so is Ravenna.'

'I know she is gone,' said Sigmar, his tone hardening.

'Then listen to me, brother,' implored Wolfgart. 'Ravenna is dead and I grieve for her, but you have to move on. Honour her memory, but move on. You will find another woman to be your queen.'

'I do not want another woman for my queen!' cried Sigmar. 'It was always Ravenna.'

'Not any more,' said Wolfgart. 'A king needs a queen, and even if her brother had not killed her, Ravenna could never have been your wife.'

'What are you talking about?'

Wolfgart ignored Pendrag's warning look and pressed on. 'The sister of a betrayer? The people would not have allowed it.'

'Wolfgart,' said Pendrag, seeing Sigmar's face purple.

'Think about it and you will see I am right,' said Wolfgart. 'Ravenna was a wonderful lass, but who would have accepted her as queen? People would have said your line was tainted with the blood of traitors, and don't try telling me that isn't bad luck.'

'You need to watch your tongue, Wolfgart,' said Sigmar, stepping close to his sword-brother, but Wolfgart was not backing down.

'You want to hit me, Sigmar? Go ahead, but you know I am right,' said Wolfgart.

Sigmar felt his grief and anger coalesce into one searing surge of violence, and his fist slammed into Wolfgart's jaw, sending his friend sprawling to the ground. No sooner had the blow landed than the shame of it overwhelmed him.

'No!' cried Sigmar, his thoughts flying back to childhood when he had smashed Wolfgart's elbow with a hammer in a moment of rage. He had vowed not to forget the lesson of control he had learned that day, but here he was standing with his fists raised above the fallen body of a comrade.

Sigmar's hands unclenched from fists and the bitterness melted away.

He knelt by his friend. 'Gods, Wolfgart, I am so sorry!'

Wolfgart gave him a sour look, rotating his lower jaw and pressing his hand against a flowering bruise.

'I do not mean to lash out at you. I just...' began Sigmar, trailing off as he found he had not the words to express the emotions simmering within him.

Wolfgart nodded and turned to Pendrag. 'Looks like we've still got our work cut out for us, Pendrag. He punches like a woman.'

'It is just as well our sword-brother is not back to full strength or he would have taken your damn fool head off,' said Pendrag, helping them both to their feet.

'Aye, maybe,' agreed Wolfgart, 'but then I knew that.'

Sigmar looked into the faces of his sword-brothers, and saw their fear for him and their acceptance of his grief-fuelled anger. Their forbearance humbled him.

'I am sorry, my friends,' he said. 'These past few weeks have been the hardest I have lived through. I cannot tell you how hard, but knowing that you are always there gives me the greatest strength. I have treated you badly, and for that I apologise.'

'You have suffered,' said Pendrag, 'but you do not need to apologise to us. We are your sword-brothers and we are here for you through happy times and evil ones.'

'Pendrag has the truth of it, Sigmar,' said Wolfgart. 'Only true friends would stand for you being such a royal pain in the arse. Anyone else would have just walked away by now.'

Sigmar smiled at Wolfgart's earthy truth. 'That is exactly why I *do* need to apologise to you, my friends. You are my brothers and my closest friends, and it is beneath me to treat you the way I have. Since Ravenna's death... I have become closed off, creating a fortress for my soul. I have let none enter and have attacked those that tried, but those trapped in a fortress with a barred gate will eventually starve, and no man should remain apart from his brothers.'

Sigmar felt new strength filling him as he spoke, and for the first time since his return from the Grey Vaults he smiled.

'Will you forgive me?' he asked.

Pendrag nodded. 'There is nothing to forgive.'

'Welcome back, sword-brother,' said Wolfgart.

THE FOLLOWING MORNING began with rain, and Sigmar drifted towards wakefulness in the king's longhouse with the remains of a dream slipping from his mind. Its substance was already fading, but he clung to it like a gift from the gods.

He had been walking alongside the river where he had faced the boar Blacktusk, the grass soft underfoot and the wind redolent with the scents of summer. His father had been standing at the riverbank, tall and powerful, and clad in his finest suit of iron mail. The bronze crown of the Unberogen gleamed upon his brow, the fiery metal catching the sunlight so that it shone like a band of fire around his head.

Björn radiated power and confidence, and as he turned to face Sigmar, he lifted the crown from his head and offered it to Sigmar.

With trembling hands, he accepted the crown. As his fingers touched the metal, his father had vanished, and he felt the weight of the crown upon his brow.

Sigmar heard laughter and turned, smiling with joy as he saw Ravenna dancing on the grass with the wind catching her hair. She wore the emerald dress he liked and his mother's cloak, which was secured by the golden pin Master Alaric had fashioned for him.

Though he could not remember the substance of their words, they had spoken for an age and then made love, as they had done the first time Sigmar had taken her there.

For the first time since Gerreon's attack, he felt no sorrow, just love and an enormous feeling of thankfulness to have known such a beauty. Never would she grow old to him. Never would she become bitter or resentful as the years passed.

She would be forever young and forever loved.

Sigmar opened his eyes and felt more refreshed than he had in weeks, his eyes bright and clear, his limbs powerful and lean. He took a deep breath and ran through his morning stretches, pondering the meaning of the dream. To have dreamed of his father and Ravenna would normally have brought pain, but this had been different.

Priests taught that dreams were gifts from Morr, visions allowing those blessed with them to glimpse beyond the fragile veil of existence and see the realm of the gods. To have such a vision was seen as an omen of great significance and an auspicious time for new beginnings.

Was this dream a last gift from the gods before he was to embark upon the great work of forging the empire of man? If so, it could only mean one thing.

Sigmar finished his stretches and dunked his head in the water barrel in the corner of the longhouse, drying himself on a linen towel before pulling on his tunic and trews. He could hear the sound of shouting from beyond the walls of the longhouse, and knew what it must be.

He lifted his mail shirt and pulled it over his head, rotating his shoulders until the armour lay properly. Then he ran his hands through his hair, and tied it back in a short scalp lock with a leather thong.

More raised voices came from outside as Sigmar lifted his crimson banner from beside his throne in one hand and took up Ghal-maraz in the other. He marched towards the great oak doors of the longhouse, the king's hounds padding after him, and Sigmar reflected that these beasts were now his.

He pushed open the door to see a solemn procession of warriors marching towards him through the rain, carrying a body on a bier of shields. Hundreds of people surrounded the shieldbearers, and on the hills around Reikdorf, Sigmar saw the Unberogen army watching their king's last journey home.

Alfgeir waited before the bier, his bronze armour dulled and dented. His head was downcast, but he looked up as the doors to the king's longhouse opened.

The Marshal of the Reik's eyes told Sigmar what he already knew.

Rain fell in misty sheets, dripping from Alfgeir's armour and lank hair. The Marshal of the Reik dropped to one knee, and Sigmar had never seen a man look so wretched or ashamed.

'My lord,' said Alfgeir, drawing his sword and offering it to Sigmar, 'your father is dead. He fell in battle against the northmen.'

'I know, Alfgeir,' said Sigmar.

'You know? How?'

'Much has changed since my father left to go to war,' said Sigmar. 'I am no longer the boy you knew, and you are no longer the man you were.'

'No,' agreed Alfgeir. 'I failed in my duty, and the king is dead.'

'You did not fail,' said Sigmar, 'and you should keep your sword, my friend. You will need it if you are to be my champion and Marshal of the Reik.'

'Your champion?' asked Alfgeir. 'No... I cannot...'

'There was nothing you could do,' stated Sigmar. 'My father gave his life for me, and no skill at arms in this world could have saved him.'

'I do not understand.'

'Nor do I entirely,' confessed Sigmar, 'but I would be honoured if you would serve me as you served him.'

Alfgeir rose to his feet, the rain streaking his face like tears, and he sheathed his sword.

'I will serve you faithfully,' promised Alfgeir.

'I know you will,' said Sigmar, moving past his champion to the bier of shields. His father lay with Soultaker clasped to his breast, his armour bright and burnished. His noble features were at peace, the fierceness of the scar across his face somehow lessened now that his soul had departed.

Sigmar stepped away from the bier and said, 'Carry my father within his hall.'

The procession of warriors marched through the mud and into the longhouse, and Sigmar turned to address the hundreds of mourning people gathered before him. He saw many friends among his people, and every face was a face he knew.

These were his people now, the Unberogen.

Sigmar planted his banner in the mud before the longhouse as a shaft of sunlight broke through the storm clouds and bathed it in light. The crimson fabric rippled in the wind, and Sigmar raised Ghal-maraz above his head as he shouted to the crowd, his voice carrying all the way to the thousands of warriors gathered on the hills beyond the town.

'People of the Unberogen! King Björn has passed from the land, and now wields the great axe Soultaker in the Halls of Ulric with his brothers Redmane Dregor, Sweyn Oakheart and the mighty Berongundan. He died as he would have wished, in battle, with enemies all around him and his axe in his hand.'

Sigmar lowered Ghal-maraz and cried, 'I will send riders throughout the land and let it be known that at the rise of the next new moon my father will take his place on Warrior's Hill!'

THIRTEEN

A Gathering of Kings

WITH THE RETURN of the Unberogen warriors to Reikdorf, a great feast was held to honour their courage and the deeds of the dead. Saga poets filled the alehouses, and gathered at every corner to entrance audiences with blood-drenched tales of the battles against the cruel Norsii and the glorious death of King Björn.

As epic and lurid as such tales were, Sigmar knew they did not – could not – capture the nobility or sacrifice of his father's final battle, when he had walked into the underworld to save his son.

Sigmar felt no need to add to the legends being woven around his father's deeds, knowing that the ages would want the desperate heroism and tragic inevitability of his death rather than the more intimate familial drama that had played out in the twilight realm of the Grey Vaults.

The days following the return of the army were joyous, as wives and mothers were reunited with husbands and sons, but also heartbreaking, for many families had suffered the death of a loved one, and the loss of King Björn was a grievous blow to the Unberogen.

The fallen were honoured with pyres upon the hills surrounding Reikdorf, and as the sun set the following day, a thousand fires banished the night. The northmen had been driven back to their frozen land, but Sigmar knew it would only be a matter of time before another warlord arose and fanned the smouldering coals in their warlike hearts.

For all that, the mood of the Unberogen was not downcast, and Sigmar could feel the confidence his people had in him as surely as he felt the ground beneath his feet. His skills in battle were well known, as was his honour and integrity. He could feel their pride in him, and knew that it was tempered by their sadness at the loss of Ravenna. No one dared mention Gerreon, his name unspoken and soon to be banished from memory.

Everywhere Sigmar walked in Reikdorf, he was greeted with warm smiles and the easy friendship of people who knew and trusted him.

He was ready to be king, and they were ready for his rule.

THE KINGS OF the tribes arrived in Reikdorf the day before the new moon.

King Marbad of the Endals was among the last to arrive, accompanied by his Raven Helms and bearing a banner dipped in blood in honour of the fallen Björn. With Pendrag by his side, Sigmar watched them arrive to the music of the pipers, and was once again impressed by the martial bearing of Marbad's warriors.

The last time Sigmar had seen these magnificent fighters was six years ago, when the ageing king had accompanied Wolfgart from his lands in the west to pay a visit to his brother king. Marbad had aged in the years since then, his hair now completely white and his spare frame painfully thin. Yet for all that, Marbad still carried himself proudly, and greeted Sigmar warmly and with strength.

The Raven Helms were as fearsome as Sigmar remembered, and just as wary of their surroundings, though Sigmar allowed that this time they had reason to be wary. Across the river, a series of bronze-armoured warriors with feathered helmets and colourful pennants streaming from their lances watched the arrival of the Endals with undisguised hostility. These were the brightly clad warriors of the Jutone tribe, emissaries from King Marius, who had not deigned to travel to Reikdorf.

Nor had King Artur of the Teutogens come, not even bothering to send an emissary to the funeral rites of his fellow king. Sigmar had not been surprised by this and, in truth, had been glad that no Teutogen would set foot in Reikdorf, fearing reprisals for the raid on Ubersreik and the other border villages and settlements on the edges of Unberogen lands.

Both kings that had fought alongside his father against the Norsii had come in person, King Krugar of the Taleutens and King Aloysis of the Cherusens. Both were men of iron, and had impressed Sigmar with their sincere praise for his father.

Queen Freya of the Asoborns had come in a whooping procession of chariots from the east, terrifying the people tilling the fields and sending a wave of panic towards Reikdorf until their intent was confirmed. Riding atop a bladed chariot of dark wood with inlaid gold flames, the beautiful copper-haired queen had presented herself before Sigmar with a wicked grin, and had planted her trident spear in the earth before him.

'Queen Freya!' she had announced. 'Destroyer of the Redmaw Tribe, conqueror of the stunted thieves and slayer of the Great Fang! Lover of a thousand men and Mistress of the Eastern Plains, I come before you to pay homage to your father, and to sup from your strength to measure it against my own!'

She had then snapped the trident spear and hurled it to Sigmar's feet, before pulling him forward to kiss him hard on the lips while grabbing him between the legs. Pendrag and Alfgeir had been so surprised that neither one had time to react, but as they reached for their swords, the queen released Sigmar, throwing back her head and laughing.

'The son of Björn has his father's strength in his loins,' said Freya. 'I will enjoy making the beast with two backs with him!'

With that, Freya and her Asoborn warriors, fierce women daubed in paints, who rode their chariots naked, had ridden from Reikdorf to make camp in the fallow eastern fields.

'Gods above,' said Sigmar later as they ate in the king's longhouse. 'The woman is mad!'

'Well, at least she said you were strong,' said Pendrag. 'Imagine if she had not been impressed with your... strength.'

'Aye,' grinned Wolfgart. 'If I were king, I wouldn't mind a night alone with that one.'

'It would certainly be an interesting experience,' agreed Pendrag, 'if you lived.'

'You are both mad,' said Sigmar. 'I'd sooner take a rabid wolf to my bed than Freya.'

'Don't be such an old woman,' said Wolfgart, clearly relishing Sigmar's discomfort. 'It would be an unforgettable night, and think of the battle scars you'd get.'

Sigmar shook his head. 'My father always said that a man should never bed a wench he couldn't best in a fight. Do either of you think you could take Freya?'

'Maybe not,' said Wolfgart, 'but it would be fun finding out.'

'Let us hope you never have to, my friend,' said Pendrag.

BY THE TIME the sun dipped into the west on the night of King Björn's funeral rites, the tension in Reikdorf was palpable. A great feast had begun in the longhouse when the sun had reached its zenith, with great quantities of beer and spirits consumed, as the assembled kings and warriors drank to the great name of King Björn. Hundreds filled the longhouse, men and women from all across the land, and Sigmar was thrilled to see so many from so far away.

The finest animals from the Unberogen herds had been slaughtered and hundreds of loaves of bread baked. Barrels of beer from the riverside brewery and scores of jugs of wine from the west lay on trestle tables along one wall. The central firepit heated the longhouse, and the mouth-watering smell of cooking meat swamped the senses.

Endal pipers filled the hall with music, and drummers thumped their instruments in time to the melody. A festive, yet strained, atmosphere danced on the air, for this was a time to remember the great deeds of a heroic warrior, a chance to celebrate his epic life as he took his place in the Halls of Ulric. The king lay in the House of Healing, his body tended by the acolytes of Morr, men who had walked from the Brackenwalsch the previous week to watch over his body before it passed the doors of his tomb.

Thus far, the atmosphere in Reikdorf had been tense, but free of violence, the warriors of each tribe respecting the banner of truce that the kings of men gathered beneath, and Eoforth had been careful to keep the warriors of those tribes whose relations were fractious as far apart as possible. To further safeguard the peace, Alfgeir and the White Wolves roamed the halls with their hammers carried loosely at their belts and their goblets filled with heavily watered wine.

The loud buzz of conversation and song echoed from the rafters, and Sigmar cast his gaze around the hall as he sat upon his throne, his father's throne empty beside him.

King Marbad told tales of the mist daemons in the marshes, and Unberogen warriors clamoured to hear of the battles he had fought in his youth alongside Björn. Krugar and Aloysis told of the war against the Norsii, and of how Björn had charged the centre of a shield-wall and cut the head from the enemy warlord in single combat.

Every ruler had a story to tell, and Sigmar listened as Queen Freya told of the final destruction of the Bloody Knife tribe of orcs, a battle that had seen the power of the greenskins broken in the east for a decade. Many of the Unberogen warriors gathered in the longhouse had been present for this victory, and the hafts of axes were slammed upon tabletops as they relived the fury of the battle.

As Queen Freya concluded her tale, Sigmar was shocked to hear her tell of his father's sexual prowess, now understanding that lying with the queen of the Asoborns had been the price of her warriors' aid in the battle against the orcs. He wondered if he would be called upon to share Freya's bed to win her to his cause, and the thought made him shiver.

Sigmar saw where the trouble would begin the instant before the first insult was hurled, seeing a Jutone tribesman with a forked beard, braided hair and a heavily scarred face swagger up to where the Endal pipers were gathered.

Though the young boy playing the pipes was much taller than the Jutone tribesman, he was much younger and clearly not yet a warrior.

'Gods, my ears hurt from this din! It sounds like someone rutting with a sheep! Why don't you play some proper music?' yelled the Jutone, ripping the pipes from the young lad's hands and hurling them into the firepit.

The rest of the pipers ceased their playing, and a handful of Endal tribesmen surged to their feet in anger. A handful of Jutone warriors in brightly coloured jerkins rose from the benches across from them. Alfgeir saw the confrontation gathering momentum, and strode through the crowds to reach the warriors.

The Jutone and Endal tribesmen glowered at each other, and King Marbad nodded to the remaining pipers, the music beginning once again.

'That *is* proper music, Jutone,' cried one of the Endals, dragging the charred remains of the pipes from the fire, 'not the ear-bleeding nonsense you listen to.'

The Marshal of the Reik finally reached the Jutone and spun him around, but the man had violence in mind and was not about to go quietly. His fist lashed out at Alfgeir, but Sigmar's champion had been expecting the attack and lowered his head. The Jutone's fist cracked into his forehead and the man roared in pain.

Alfgeir stepped back and thundered his hammer into the man's belly, doubling him up with an explosive whoosh of breath. A pair of White Wolves appeared at his shoulder, and Alfgeir quickly handed the incapacitated man off to them.

Spurred into action, the rest of the Jutones hurled themselves at Alfgeir, fists arcing for his head. He rode the punches, and slammed the haft of his hammer into a snarling Jutone warrior's face, breaking his nose and snapping teeth from his jaw. The Endals leapt to Alfgeir's aid, and soon fists and feet were flying, as long-standing grudges and feuds reared their heads.

Sigmar leapt from his throne and ran the length of the firepit, angry at the folly of this senseless brawl. Warriors rose to fight throughout the hall, and Sigmar pushed his way towards his champion. Belligerent cries followed in his wake, but were quickly silenced when it was realised who pushed his way through.

The fighting at the end of the longhouse spread like ripples in a pool as warriors further from its origin were swept into its orbit. Queen Freya leapt into the fray like a banshee, while Taleuten warriors fought with Jutones, and Cherusen men grappled with shrieking Asoborn warrior women.

Thus far, no one but Alfgeir had drawn a weapon, but it was only a matter of time until a blade was rammed home, and the gathering would break apart in discord. Without conscious thought, Sigmar hefted Ghal-maraz and leapt towards the heart of the struggling warriors.

The weapon swept up and then down, slamming onto a tabletop and smashing it to splinters. The hammer struck the ground, and a deafening crack spread from the point of impact as a powerful wave of force hurled every man from his feet.

Sudden silence fell as Sigmar strode into the centre of the fallen warriors.

'Enough!' he yelled. 'You gather under a banner of truce! Or do I have to break some heads before you get the idea?'

No one answered, and those closest to Sigmar had the sense to look ashamed of the fight.

'We gather here to send my father to his final rest, a man who fought alongside most of you in battles too numerous to count. He brought you together as warriors of honour, and this is how you remember him? By brawling like greenskins?'

Sigmar said, 'The old sagas say that the people of this land are those that the gods made mad, for all their wars are merry, and all their songs are sad. Until now I did not understand those words, but now I think I do.'

The words poured from Sigmar without thought, his every waking dream of empire flowing through him as he paced his father's hall, the mighty warhammer held before him.

'What kind of race are we that would draw the blood of our fellows when all around us are enemies that would gladly do it for us? Every year more of our warriors die to keep our lands safe, and every year the hordes of orcs and beasts grow stronger. If things do not change, we will be dead or driven to the edge of existence. If *we* do not change, we do not deserve to live.'

Sigmar raised Ghal-maraz high, the firelight glittering from the runes worked into the length of its haft and its mighty head.

'This land is ours by right of destiny, and the only way it will remain so is if we put aside our differences and recognise our shared goal of survival. For are we not all men? Do we not all want the same things for our families and children? When you strip away everything else we are all mortal, we all live in this world, breathe its air and reap its bounty.'

King Krugar of the Taleutens strode forward and said, 'It is the nature of man to fight, Sigmar. It is the way things have always been, and the way they always will be.'

'No,' said Sigmar. 'Not any more.'

'What are you suggesting?' asked King Aloysis of the Cherusens.

'That we become one nation,' cried Sigmar. 'That we fight as one. When one land is threatened, all lands are threatened. When one king calls for aid, all must answer.'

'You are a dreamer, my friend,' said Krugar. 'We swear Sword Oaths with our neighbours, but to fight for a king in distant lands? Why should we risk our lives for people not our own?'

'Why should we not?' countered Sigmar, his voice carrying throughout the silent longhouse. 'Think what we might achieve if we were united in purpose. What great things might we learn, were our lands always kept safe from attack? What new wonders might we discover if scholars and thinkers were free from the burden of feeding or defending themselves, and bent their entire will to the betterment of man?'

'And who would rule this paradise?' asked Aloysis. 'You?'

'If I am the only one with the vision to realise it, then why not?' cried Sigmar. 'But whoever would rule would be just and wise, a strong ruler with the support of his chiefs and warriors. He would have their loyalty and in turn they would have the protection of every warrior in the land.'

'You really believe this can be done?' asked Aloysis.

'I believe it *must* be done,' nodded Sigmar, holding out Ghal-maraz. 'I believe that no problem of our destiny is beyond us. We must unite to fight for our survival, it is the only way. The High King of the dwarfs gave me this hammer, a mighty weapon of his ancestors, and I swear by its power that I will achieve this within my lifetime.'

A cold wind whistled through the longhouse, and a gruff voice, sonorous and deeply accented said, 'Fine words, manling, but Ghal-maraz is much more than just a weapon. I thought you understood that when I gave it to you.'

Sigmar smiled and turned to see a squat, powerfully muscled figure standing silhouetted in the doorway of the longhouse. Fire-light gleamed on shining armour of such magnificence that it took away the breath of every warrior gathered to see it. Gold and silver hammers and lightning bolts were worked into the shimmering breastplate, and links of the finest mail covered the warrior's short legs.

A full-faced helmet, worked in the form of a stylised dwarf god covered the warrior's face and he stepped into the longhouse as he reached up to remove it.

The face revealed was aged and pale, barely any flesh visible thanks to the swathes of braided hair and silver beard that covered the dwarf's face. The eyes of the dwarf were aged with wisdom beyond the ken of men, and Sigmar lowered Ghal-maraz as he dropped to one knee.

'King Kurgan Ironbeard,' said Sigmar, 'welcome to Reikdorf.'

EVERY EYE IN the hall was fixed upon the High King of the dwarfs as he paced before the assembled warriors upon the raised dais next to Sigmar and Eoforth. News of the dwarfs' arrival had spread quickly, and the hall was packed with warriors gathered to hear the king of the mountain folk speak.

Master Alaric had come from his forge, greeting his king like a long-lost friend, and they had spoken briefly in the language of their people before the High King had nodded sadly and turned away.

The king's guards were powerful dwarfs in elaborate armour, fashioned from a metal that shone brighter than the most polished silver, and which threw back the torch light of the hall in dazzling brilliance. Each of the warriors bore a mighty axe, easily the equal of any carried by the strongest Unberogen axemen, and their eyes were guardedly hostile. No man had yet dared speak with any of them, for they seemed like otherworldly beings, strange and dangerous to approach.

King Kurgan had returned Sigmar's greeting, and marched through the men gathered in the longhouse, parting them like a ship parts the water as he marched towards the dais before the throne of the Unberogen kings.

'You remember the day I gave you that hammer, manling?' asked the High King.

'I remember it well, my king,' replied Sigmar, following King Ironbeard.

'Clearly you do not,' growled Kurgan. 'Or you'd remember that it was Ghal-maraz that chose you. I saw something special in you that day, boy. Don't make me regret giving you the heirloom of my house.'

King Kurgan turned to the gathered warriors and said, 'I expect you know how this young one came by Ghal-maraz?'

No one dared answer the king until Wolfgart shouted, 'We've heard it once or twice, but why don't you tell it, King Kurgan?'

'Aye,' nodded Kurgan, 'mayhap I shall. Looks like someone needs to remind you of what it means to bear an ancestral weapon of the dwarfs. But first I need some beer. 'Tis a long way from the mountains.'

Master Alaric swiftly produced a firkin of beer, the mouth-watering aroma of fine dwarf ale drifting to those nearby as a tankard was poured for Kurgan. The dwarf king took a long swallow of the beer, and nodded appreciatively before setting the tankard down on the armrest of King Björn's throne.

'Very well, manlings,' began Kurgan. 'Listen well, for this is a tale you will not hear from a dwarf's lips again for as long as any of you shall live, for it is the tale of my shame.'

A hushed sense of expectation pressed upon the walls of the longhouse, and even Sigmar, who knew the tale of Ghal-maraz better than anyone, felt a breathless sense of excitement, for he had never dreamed that he might hear the dwarf king speak of his rescue before a hall of tribesmen.

'Was barely yesterday,' said Kurgan. 'The blink of an eye to me, so close I remember everything about it, more's the pity. Me and my kin were travelling through the forests to the Grey Mountains to visit one of the great clans of the south, the Stonehearts. Fine workers of the stone, but greedy for gold. Loved it more than any other clan of dwarfs, and that's saying something, let me tell you.

'Anyway, we were crossing a river when the thrice-cursed greenskins fell upon us, led by a great black orc monster named Vagraz Head-Stomper. Cunning as a weasel that one was, waited until we were ready to stop for the night and break out the beer before they attacked us. Black arrows took my kinsman, Threkki, in the throat. Stained his white beard as red as a sunset, I'll never forget it. Our guards, dwarfs I'd known longer than twice your eldest's span of years, were cut down without mercy, and our ponies were hamstrung by goblins. Friends from hearth and home were murdered by the greenskins, and I remember thinking it were an evil day when they took us prisoner and hadn't just killed us.

'They robbed us of our gold and treasure, and of our weapons. A black day it was for sure, and I remember thinking to myself, "Kurgan, if you ever get out of this, there's going to be a grudge as long as your arm…". But I'm getting ahead of myself, and my throat's dry reliving this here story.'

The dwarf king stopped for another mouthful of beer, his audience enraptured by his tale and his iron-hard voice. It was a voice of supreme confidence, but was not arrogant, for the king had tasted defeat and, in doing so, had gained humility.

'So, there we were, tied to stakes rammed into the ground and nothing but sport for the orcs. All we could do was try to break our bonds and die with honour. But even that was denied us, for we were tied with our own rope, good dwarf rope that even I couldn't break. All around us, Vagraz and his orcs were sitting like kings on our treasure, drinking five-hundred-year-old beer that was worth an army in gold and feasting on the flesh of my friends. I struggled and I struggled, but I couldn't break them ropes.

'I looked that big black orc right in the eye, and I'm not ashamed to say that he was a damned fearsome beast. It was his eyes, you see… red, like the fires of a forge that had burned low, filled with hate and anger… so much hate. He planned on torturing us, one by one, letting me watch all my friends and kin torn apart for the fun of it. He wanted me to beg, but a dwarf begs to no one, least of all a damned orc! I vowed right then that I was going to see that beast dead before the morn.'

Spontaneous cheering erupted, and Sigmar found himself joining in, swept up by the defiant turn in Kurgan's tale. Every man in the hall was standing straighter, pressing forward to hear more of the dwarf king's story.

'Brave words, manlings, brave words indeed, but as my old counsellor, Snorri, was dragged towards the fire, I don't mind telling you that I thought my time for this world was done, that I was all set to join my ancestors. But it was not to be.'

Kurgan walked over to Sigmar and placed a mailed fist in the centre of his chest.

'The greenskins were getting ready to torture old Snorri when suddenly the air's filled with arrows, human arrows. At first I didn't know what was happening, then I saw this young lad here leading a scrawny looking pack of painted men into the orc camp, whooping and yelling, and screaming like savages.

'Half of me thinks that we're still not out of the pot, that we're just going to get robbed and killed by this lot instead of the orcs, but then they starts killing the greenskins, fighting with courage as hard as an Ironbreaker's hammer and just as deadly. Never saw anything like that before, humans fighting orcs with such heart and fire. Then this lad jumps right into the middle of an orc shield wall, cutting and stabbing with a little sword of bronze. Madness I thought, he'll never walk out of there alive, but then he does, not just alive, but with a ring of dead greenskins all around him.

'Now I'm not a dwarf that's easily impressed, you understand, but young Sigmar here fought like the spirits of all his ancestors were watching him. He even lifted the stake old Borris was tied to right from the ground, and I'd seen three orcs ram that stake into the earth. Course by now some of us are being freed, and as my bonds were cut, I turns to young Sigmar and tells him that his warriors are all going to die unless they gets some help. Now my lads and I, well, we had some powerful rune weapons with us when we were taken, and I knew exactly where to find them.'

Kurgan paused as he shared a guilty look with Sigmar. 'Well, maybe not exactly, but not far off. I knew that Vagraz would keep all the weapons in his tent, close by so he'd have all the best stuff, because even an orc knows good weapons when he sees them. By now, Sigmar here's fighting the monster, and they're going back and forward, hacking lumps from one another, only Sigmar's having the worst of it on account of Vagraz's axe and armour. Now, I don't know what kind of enchantment the orc shamans work, but whatever dark spells they wield must be powerful. Black flames flickered around the beast's axe, and, no matter where Sigmar stuck him with his sword, he couldn't even scratch the warlord.'

Sigmar shivered as he remembered the battle against the hulking orc. Every killing blow was turned aside, and each stroke of his enemy's axe came within a hair's-breadth of ending his young life. Even six years later, he sometimes awoke in the night, bathed in sweat with the memory of that desperate struggle fresh in his mind.

'So anyway, I runs to the warlord's tent and I'm hunting high and low for my old friend, Ghal-maraz, but everything's scattered and heaped all over the place. I found my armour, but nothing to fight with save a man's sword, which – and no offence here – wasn't much use since the blade was so poorly forged. So I'm looking for something useful, but I'm not finding anything, and every second I'm looking, Sigmar's men are dying, and I can hear Vagraz's laughter as him and his black orcs are set to kill us all.

'Then I found Ghal-maraz. I was cursing the orcs with every swear known to dwarfkind when my hand closed upon sturdy stitching wound around cold steel. I knew what it was by touch alone, and I pulled it from the heap of loot.'

Sigmar held out the mighty warhammer and Kurgan took it from him, running his hands along the length of the great weapon. The runes sparkled, though whether that was the light of the fires or the touch of its maker's race, Sigmar knew not. King Kurgan's eyes lit up at the touch of the warhammer, and he smiled ruefully as he held it out in front of him.

'I hold out Ghal-maraz and I'm ready to charge into battle, even though I'm fit to drop with pain and exhaustion, but a dwarf never lies down when there's battle to be done unless he's dead. And even then he'd better be really, really dead or his ancestors will be having words with him when he gets to the other side! But even as I lifted the warhammer, I knew it wasn't for me to carry it into battle. You see, the power in Ghal-maraz is ancient, even to us dwarfs, and it knows who is supposed to bear it. Truth be told, I think it's always been your warhammer, Sigmar, even before you were born. I think it was waiting for you, down the long, lonely centuries. It was waiting for the moment you would be ready to wield it.

'So instead of charging in, I throws Ghal-maraz to Sigmar, who's on the back foot, with Vagraz about to take his young head off, and damned if he doesn't catch it and meet the orc's axe on the way down. Now the odds are even, and suddenly Vagraz doesn't look quite so cocky, and starts running his mouth off, gnashing and wailing his big fangs. But young Sigmar here isn't fooled, he can see the bastard's worried and he lays into him with Ghal-maraz. Piece by piece, he takes the orc apart until he's down on his knees and beaten.'

Sigmar smiled at the memory, remembering the warmth and feeling of fulfilment that had enveloped him as he hefted the great warhammer and closed with the warlord to deliver the deathblow.

'You remember what you said to it?' asked Kurgan.

'I said, "Is that really the best you've got?",' said Sigmar.

'Aye,' said Kurgan, 'and then you smashed his skull to pieces with one blow. And I don't think there's many could have done that, even with a dwarf hammer. Now the battle's turned. Orcs don't like it when you kill their big boss, it breaks their courage like brittle iron, and they went to pieces when Vagraz died. When the battle was over, I remember you tried to give Ghal-maraz back, an honourable gesture for a man, I thought, but I looked into your eyes and I saw that they were smouldering with an energy like I'd never seen.'

The light in the longhouse seemed to dim as the dwarf king closed in on the ending of his tale, as though the structure built by the craft of his kind sought to enhance the telling.

'The rest of young Sigmar's face was in darkness, and as the flames flickered in his eyes, I swear they took on an eerie light. Even the gaze of the greenskin warlord didn't have the raw power of that stare. Right then I knew there was something special about this one. I could feel it as sure as I know stone and beer. I looked down at Ghal-maraz and knew that it was time for me to pass this great weapon, this heirloom of my family, to a *man*. Such a thing has never happened in all the annals of the dwarfs, but I think a gift such as Skull Splitter is worth the life of a dwarf king.'

Kurgan marched across the dais and once again presented Ghal-maraz to Sigmar, bowing to the young prince before turning once again to the rapt audience.

'I gave Sigmar this hammer for a reason. True enough, it is a weapon, a mighty weapon to be sure, but it is so much more than that. Ghal-maraz is a symbol of unity, a symbol of what can be *achieved* through unity. A hammer is force and dominance, an honourable weapon and one that, unlike most other weapons, has the power to create as well as destroy. A hammer can crush and kill, but it can shape metal, build homes and mend that which is broken. See this mighty gift for what it is, a weapon and a symbol of all that can be. Men of the lands west of the mountains, heed Sigmar's words, for he speaks with the wisdom of the ancients.'

King Kurgan stepped from the dais to thunderous applause, but the venerable dwarf raised his hands for silence, which duly followed after yet more cheering.

'Now let us drink to the memory of King Björn and send him to his fathers in glory!'

BOOK THREE
Forging the Legend

Then fame and renown
Of Sigmar, hammer bearer
Of the High King of the dwarfs
Spread far and wide.
Sigmar the chief mighty lord
Of the Unberogen and other tribes
Of mankind.

FOURTEEN
Vengeance

FIRELIGHT FROM THE burning ships lit the underside of the clouds with a glow like the hells the Norsii were said to believe in. Sigmar watched from the cliffs above the vast expanse of the ocean as thousands of men died before him, burned to death on their ships or dragged below the surface of the water by the weight of their armour.

He felt nothing for the men he was killing; their barbarity rendering them less than nothing to Sigmar. Hundreds of ships filled the wide bay, the night as bright as day as Unberogen and Udose archers sent flaming arrows into their sails and hulls as they jostled to escape.

'Great Ulric's beard,' whispered Pendrag. 'Do you mean to kill them all?'

Sigmar bit back a sharp retort and simply nodded.

'They deserve no less,' snarled King Wolfila. 'The bloodgeld of my people demands vengeance upon the northmen.'

'But this…' said Pendrag. 'This is murder.'

Sigmar said nothing, for how could he make his sword-brother understand? The Norsii were not part of his vision and could never be part of it. The northern gods were avatars of slaughter, the Norsii culture one of barbarism and human sacrifice. Such a people had no place in Sigmar's empire, and since they would not accept his rule, they must be destroyed.

The firelight reflected on Sigmar's face, throwing his handsome, craggy features into sharp relief, his differently coloured eyes hard as stone. Twenty-five summers had passed since his birth upon the hill of battle in the Brackenwalsch, and Sigmar had grown into as fine a figure of a man as any could have wished.

The crown of the Unberogens sat upon his brow, his for the two years since his father had been laid to rest in his gilded tomb upon Warrior's Hill, and a long cloak of bearskin billowed around his wide and powerful shoulders.

Thousands of warriors lined the cliffs in wide blocks of swordsmen and spearmen. Udose clansmen cheered as they watched the Norsii die, while Taleuten, Cherusen and Unberogen warriors watched with awe as an entire tribal race died before them.

No sooner had King Björn's tomb been sealed and Sigmar crowned king of the Unberogen by the priest of Ulric than he had ordered a sword muster for the following spring. Pendrag, and even Wolfgart, had argued against a muster so soon, but Sigmar had been immoveable.

'We have great work ahead of us to forge our empire,' Sigmar had said, 'and with every day that passes, our chance to realise it slips further away. No, with the break of the snows next year, we march on the Norsii.'

And so they had. Leaving enough warriors to defend the lands of the Unberogen, Sigmar had gathered three thousand fighting men and marched back into the north, calling upon the Sword Oaths sworn to his father by the Cherusen and Taleutens. Both Krugar and Aloysis were reluctant to honour their oaths so soon, but with three thousand warriors camped before the walls of their cities, they had little choice but to march out with the king of the Unberogen.

As expected, King Artur of the Teutogens had refused to pledge any warriors to Sigmar's cause, and so his army had continued north towards the beleaguered lands of the Udose tribe, a realm that suffered daily attacks from northern reavers.

King Wolfila's capital was a soaring granite castle atop a jagged promontory of the northern coastline, pounding waves booming far below. Sigmar had liked Wolfila from the moment he had seen him riding through the black gates of his fastness. With braided hair the colour of the setting sun and a plaited kilt, Wolfila carried a sword almost as big as Wolfgart's and his face was scarred and painted with fierce tattoos.

The northern king had been only too willing to join Sigmar's campaign, and wild, kilted and painted men and women of the clans with great, basket-hilted swords were soon coming down from their isolated glens and hilltop forts to join the mighty host of warriors.

The Norsii had fought hard to protect their lands as Sigmar had expected, but with eight thousand warriors marching on them, burning and destroying as they went, the northmen could do nothing to stop them.

The weather battered the armies of the south, fearsome storms and barrages of lightning, smiting the heavens with leering faces and howling gales like the laughter of dark gods. The morale of the army suffered, but Sigmar was unrelenting in his care, ensuring that every warrior had food and water and understood how proud he was to lead them in battle.

The final outcome of the war had never been in doubt, for the Norsii were outnumbered three to one, and their men were starving, and had seen their lives destroyed by the vengeance of their previous victims.

Sigmar had been careful always to allow the Norsii to fall back to the northernmost coastline, where their ships were beached. Though the northmen were fierce warriors, they were also men who wanted to live.

When they boarded their ships, Sigmar unleashed the newest weapon in his arsenal.

From the cliffs around the bay, huge catapults unleashed great flaming missiles that arced through the air to smash onto the decks of the tinder-dry ships. Strong winds fanned the flames, and as yet more missiles rained down from the cliffs, the entire Norsii fleet was soon ablaze.

Here and there, a few smouldering vessels limped clear of the inferno, but they were few and far between. In less time than it had taken to assemble the war machines, an entire tribe of man had been almost entirely exterminated.

Sigmar watched the slaughter below with satisfaction. The Norsii were ended as a threat to his empire, and he felt no remorse at the thousands dying below him.

King Wolfila turned to Sigmar and offered him his hand. 'My people thank you for this, King Sigmar. Tell me how I can repay you, for I'll be in no man's debt.'

'I need no payment, Wolfila,' said Sigmar, 'just your oath that we will be brother kings, and that you and your warriors will march beside me as allies in the future.'

'You have it, Sigmar,' promised Wolfila. 'From this day, the Udose and the Unberogen will be sword-brothers. If you want our blades, all you need do is ask.'

The two kings shook hands, and Wolfila marched away to join his warriors, his sword and shield held high above him as the flames turned his hair the colour of blood.

'They will not forget this,' said Wolfgart as the king of the Udose departed. 'The survivors, I mean. They will come back one day to punish us for this.'

'That is a problem for another day,' said Sigmar, turning from the carnage below.

Pendrag gripped his arm, his eyes imploring and forcing Sigmar to face the blazing sea. 'Is this how it is to be, my brother? Is this how you mean to forge your empire? In murder? If so, then I want nothing more to do with it!'

'No, this is not how it is to be,' said Sigmar, shrugging off his sword-brother's arm. 'But what would you have me do with the Norsii? Bargain with them? They are savages!'

'What does this act make us?'

'It makes us victorious,' said Sigmar. 'I listen to their screams, and I remember the people that died beneath their axes and swords. And I am glad we do this. I remember the women raped or carried into slavery, the children sacrificed on altars of blood, and I am glad we do this. I think of all the people who will live because of what we had to do today, and I am glad we do this. Do you understand me, Pendrag?'

'I think I do, my brother,' said Pendrag, turning away, 'and it makes me sad.'

'Where are you going?' asked Sigmar.

'I do not know,' replied Pendrag. 'Away from this. I understand now why it was done, but I have no wish to listen to the screams of the dying as we burn them to death.'

Pendrag walked down the cliff path through the ranks of armoured warriors, and Sigmar made to follow him, but Wolfgart stopped him.

'Let him go, Sigmar. Trust me, he needs some time alone.'

Sigmar nodded and said, 'You understand we had to do this don't you?'

'Aye,' said Wolfgart. 'I do, but only because I have not the heart

Pendrag does. He's a thinker, that one, and at times like this... well, that's a curse. Don't worry, he'll come around.'

'I hope so,' said Sigmar.

'So what now?' asked Wolfgart.

'Now we make offerings to Ulric and Morr. The end of battle brings duty to the dead.'

'No, I mean for us. Are we going home now?'

Sigmar shook his head. 'No, not yet. I have one last thing to take care of in the north before we return to Reikdorf.'

'And what's that?'

'Artur,' said Sigmar.

THE ARMY OF the Unberogens turned from the destruction of the Norsii to march along the northern flanks of the mountains, heading for the ancestral domain of the Teutogen. The journey through the forests north of the mountains had been fraught, and Sigmar had sensed inhuman eyes upon him as if an army of monsters watched from within the haunted depths.

Finally traversing the roof of the world and emerging from the shadowed forests, Sigmar had seen the Fauschlag rock from which Artur ruled his people.

Though yet a hundred miles distant, the great mountain stood alone and enormous, humbling the landscape as it reached into the sky. Its towering immensity defied belief, the great spire standing apart from the towering mountains that rose like grim sentinels to the east as though banished from the company of its fellow peaks. The presence of such a host of warriors had not gone unnoticed by the Teutogen, and Sigmar had felt the eyes of his enemies upon him with every step that brought them closer to the Fauschlag rock.

A well-travelled road curled southwards into less threatening woodland and, at last, their route brought them to the base of the great northern fastness, the scale of its enormity hard to credit, even when standing before it.

So great was the Fauschlag's height that no sign of the settlement atop it could be seen from the ground, but curling plumes of smoke had guided them to the castle at its base.

Towers of polished granite reared up to either side of a wide gateway of seasoned timber, banded with dark iron and studded with thick bolts. Scores of armoured warriors manned the walls, their spears gleaming in the sunlight, and blue and white banners fluttered in the wind.

Heavy chains hung from the top of the Fauschlag, guided down the face of the immense drop by vertical lines of iron rings hammered into the rock. In the days since his army had arrived, Sigmar had seen enclosed carriages travel up and down the Fauschlag, transporting men and supplies between the ground and the summit.

Sigmar had ridden towards the castle with Pendrag carrying his banner lowered as a sign of parley, and had announced his intention to call Artur to account for the Unberogen blood his warriors' had spilled.

Days had passed without answer, and Sigmar's frustration had grown daily as he awaited word from King Artur. At last, as the sun set on the third day since they had arrived, a messenger rode from a concealed postern towards the Unberogen army.

Sigmar rode out to meet the messenger, Wolfgart and Alfgeir beside him, and Pendrag, who had barely passed a word with him for a fortnight, carrying his crimson banner.

The rider was a powerful warrior, his breastplate and shoulder guards painted the white of virgin snow, and his red hair thick and braided. A great wolfskin cloak hung from his shoulders, and a long-hafted hammer was slung across his horse's shoulders, a great beast of some seventeen hands.

'You are Sigmar?' asked the warrior, his voice coarse and thickly accented.

'*King* Sigmar,' corrected Alfgeir, his hand sliding towards his sword hilt.

'You bring word from your king?' asked Sigmar.

'I do,' said the rider, ignoring Alfgeir's angry glowering. 'I am Myrsa, Warrior Eternal of King Artur of the Teutogens, and I am here to order you to leave these lands or face death.'

Sigmar nodded, for he had expected such a response and could see that it sat ill with the warrior that Artur had not come himself.

He leaned forward and said, 'Marbad of the Endals once told me that Artur had grown arrogant atop his impregnable fastness, and having seen this lump of rock, I can well believe it, for who would not feel above all other men with such a mighty bastion to call his own?'

Myrsa's face reddened at the insult to his king, but Sigmar pressed on. 'A king who skulks behind walls grows fearful of leaving them, does he not?'

'These are Teutogen lands,' repeated Myrsa, keeping his voice level. 'If you do not leave, your warriors will be broken against the Fauschlag. No army can breach its walls.'

'Walls of stone are all very well,' Sigmar pointed out, 'but I have enough men to surround this rock, and I can seal Artur's city until every man, woman and child has starved to death. I do not want to do that, for I wish the Teutogen to be our brothers and not enemies. Ask the Norsii what becomes of my enemies. Tell Artur that he has one more day to face me, or I will climb that damned rock and break his head open in front of all his people.'

Myrsa nodded stiffly and turned his horse, riding back towards the castle at the base of the Fauschlag. The main gates swung open and the Warrior Eternal disappeared within.

'You didn't mean that did you?' asked Pendrag. 'About starving the city out?'

'No, of course not,' said Sigmar, 'but I needed him to think that I did.'

'Then what do you intend?' asked Alfgeir.

'Exactly what I told him,' replied Sigmar. 'If Artur does not come out, I'm going to climb that rock and drag him out from wherever he is hiding.'

'Climb the Fauschlag?' asked Wolfgart, craning his neck to look up at the towering rock.

'Aye,' said Sigmar. 'How hard can it be?'

WITH SWEAT STINGING his eyes and his muscles burning with fire, Sigmar had cause to revise his earlier boast of the ease of climbing the Fauschlag rock. The forest stretched away below him in a great green swathe, the mountains of the east rearing from the trees in a series of white spikes, and the sea a distant glitter far on the horizon.

The exhilaration of seeing the world from this vantage point was offset by the terror of clinging to a rock face by his fingertips, knowing that one slip would send him tumbling thousands of feet to his death.

Powerful winds whipped around the Fauschlag, and, checking his handholds, Sigmar craned his neck upwards, but the top of the rock was still out of sight. Birds circled high above him, and he envied them the ease of flight.

His sword-brothers and Alfgeir had tried to talk him out of this foolhardy venture, but Sigmar knew he could not back down from this challenge. He had told Artur's champion that he would climb the Fauschlag, and Sigmar's word was iron.

Sigmar risked a glance down, swallowing hard as he saw his army spread out on the rocky haunches of the Fauschlag, little more than dots as they watched their king climb to glory or death.

'Still with me, Alfgeir?' asked Sigmar, shouting to be heard over the wind.

'Aye, my lord,' said Alfgeir from below, his voice strained and angry. 'Still think this was a good idea?'

'I am beginning to think it might have been a little foolish, yes,' admitted Sigmar. 'You want to climb back down?'

'And leave you here on your own?' spat Alfgeir. 'Not bloody likely. I don't think either of us is getting down unless we fall.'

'Don't speak of falling,' said Sigmar, thinking of Wolfgart. 'It is bad luck.'

Alfgeir said nothing more, and the two warriors continued their climb, dragging themselves up the rocky face of the Fauschlag, inch by inch. Hand and foot holds were plentiful, for the surface of the rock was not smooth, but the energy required to maintain his grip was fearsome, and Sigmar could feel his arms cramping painfully with the unfamiliar exertion of climbing.

Neither warrior was armoured, for to attempt such a climb in heavy mail would be even more suicidal than his warriors already believed it to be. Ghal-maraz hung from Sigmar's belt, and Alfgeir's sword was slung around his shoulders, for neither warrior desired to reach the summit of the Fauschlag without a weapon.

Several times during their climb, Sigmar had heard the clanking sound of metal on metal, and had looked over to see the wooden carriages being raised on their long chains. One such carriage was being lowered towards them, and Sigmar's eyes narrowed as he considered the practicalities of such a means of transport.

'No amount of men could haul these carriages and that amount of iron the full height of the Fauschlag,' said Sigmar. 'There must be some form of windlass mechanism at the top.'

'Fascinating,' gasped Alfgeir, 'but what does it matter? Keep climbing. Don't stop or I won't be able to start again.'

Sigmar nodded, and ignored the carriage as it passed onwards towards the castle far below. Once more, the climbers set off, clambering up the rock face until Sigmar felt as though he could not move another inch.

He heard Alfgeir climbing beside him and took a deep breath, his lungs heaving and on fire with the effort. An age passed for Sigmar, and he cursed the pride that had sent him on this foolhardy errand.

Sigmar remembered a time when he had been a young boy and his father had first shown him how to set a cook-fire in the forest. He had wanted to build a great bonfire, but Björn had shown him that the art of setting a fire was one of balance. Too small a fire would not warm you, but too large a fire could easily get out of control and consume the forest.

Pride, Sigmar was learning, was like that, too little and a man would have no self-belief or confidence and would never achieve anything with his life. Too much... well, too much might see a man clinging to the side of a towering rock, inches from death.

Still, it would make a fine addition to his growing reputation, and might even warrant a panel on the Sudenreik Bridge. The thought made him smile, and he hauled himself upwards once again, methodically reaching for another handhold and forcing his tired body to keep going.

The wind threatened to tear him from his perch at every turn, but he kept himself pressed to the rock, holding tighter than any lover had held the object of his desire.

Lost in the pain and exhaustion of the climb, it took Sigmar a moment to realise that the angle of his climb had lessened, and that he was clambering up a slope rather than a sheer rock face.

He shook his head and blinked his eyes free of sweat to see that he had reached the top. From here, the ground rose in a gentle slope towards a low wall built around the perimeter of the Fauschlag's summit.

Sigmar reached back to help Alfgeir, whose face was grey with effort, and who nodded in gratitude.

'We did it, my friend,' gasped Sigmar. 'We are at the top.'

'Wonderful,' wheezed Alfgeir, looking up. 'Now, we just have to fight our way in.'

Sigmar turned, and saw a line of Teutogen warriors in bronze hauberks appear at the wall, their swords bared and bowstrings drawn back.

SIGMAR UNHOOKED GHAL-MARAZ from his belt, and then helped Alfgeir to his feet. The two Unberogen warriors stood proudly before the armed Teutogens, exhausted, but defiant and exhilarated at the sheer impossibility of their incredible climb.

Myrsa, the Warrior Eternal, stood in the middle of the line of warriors, and Sigmar climbed towards him, expecting the line of bowmen to loose at any second. Alfgeir followed him and whispered, 'Please tell me you have a plan.'

Sigmar shook his head. 'Not really... I hadn't expected us to survive the climb,' he said.

'Wonderful,' snapped Alfgeir. 'I am glad to know you thought this through.'

Sigmar reached the wall and stood before Myrsa, looking him straight in the eye. He had expected Myrsa to be waiting for them, and hoped he had read the man's heart correctly when they had spoken on the ground.

'Where is Artur?' asked Sigmar.

A tightening of the jaw line was the only sign of tension in Myrsa, but it spoke volumes of the conflict within the warrior.

'He prays to Ulric's Fire,' said Myrsa. 'He said you would fall.'

'He was wrong,' said Sigmar. 'He has been wrong about a lot of things has he not?'

'Perhaps, but he is my king and I owe him my life.'

'If I were your king, I would be honoured to have a man like you in my service.'

'And I would be proud to offer it, but it is foolish to dream of that which cannot be.'

'We shall see,' said Sigmar. 'Now, unless you plan on cutting me down, take me to Artur of the Teutogens.'

THE BUILDINGS ON the Fauschlag were as finely constructed as anything in Reikdorf, and Sigmar could only wonder at the dedication and determination it must have taken to get the materials to build them lifted to the summit. He saw the artifice of dwarf masons in some of the buildings, but the majority of the structures were crafted by the skill of men. Man's ingenuity never ceased to amaze Sigmar, and he was more determined than ever to see his people united in purpose.

The walk through the settlement soon attracted a great following, with people emerging from their homes to see this strange king who had climbed the Fauschlag. Myrsa's warriors ringed Sigmar and Alfgeir, and though they could be killed at any moment, Sigmar felt curiously light-headed and confident.

Everything he had seen of these Teutogens spoke of a fierce, pragmatic pride, and his early notions of them as savage and murderous raiders vanished as he saw their ordered society. Children played in the streets, and women gathered them up as the swelling procession made its way towards the heart of the city.

The priests of Ulric claimed that the god of wolves and winter smote the mountain with his fist in ancient times, flattening the summit for his faithful to worship upon. It was said that a great flame burned at its centre, a fire that burned without peat or wood, and Sigmar felt a childlike excitement at the thought of seeing such a miraculous thing.

No words passed between the warriors as they made their way towards the centre of the city, and Sigmar felt a growing tension as they neared their destination.

At last, Sigmar, Alfgeir and their escort emerged from between tall buildings of granite with clay roofs into a space cleared at the centre of the Fauschlag rock.

A great stone circle of menhirs had been erected in a wide ring, with flat lintel stones balanced precariously on top. Each stone was glossy and black, veined with lines of red gold, and in the centre of the circle a tall plume of white fire blazed from the ground, the light dazzling and pure.

The fire burned cold and was taller than a man. A warrior in a wondrously crafted suit of armour with a sword held point down before him knelt in its glare. He prayed with his hands wrapped around the hilt of his sword, the pommel resting against his forehead, and Sigmar knew this must be Artur.

The plates protecting his back and shoulders shone like silver, and the bronze mail that fringed them was as finely crafted as any dwarf armour Sigmar had seen. A winged helm of bronze sat on the ground next to Artur, and as Sigmar approached, the king of the Teutogens rose smoothly to his feet and turned to face him.

Artur was handsome, his dark hair threaded with silver, but his weathered face was strong with the easy confidence of a warrior who had never known defeat. The king's forked beard was braided, and his power obvious.

It was to Artur's sword that Sigmar's eyes were drawn, however: the Dragon Sword of Caledfwlch, the shimmering silver blade said to be able to cut the hardest iron or stone. The legends of the Teutogens spoke of a mysterious wise man from across the sea, a shaman of the ancient lore, who had fashioned the blade for Artur at his birth, using a captured shard of lightning, frozen by the breath of an ice dragon.

Looking at the long-bladed sword, Sigmar could well believe such tales, for a glittering hoarfrost seemed to cling to the weapon's edge.

'You are the king of the Unberogen?' said Artur as Sigmar entered the stone circle. Four dark-robed figures appeared at the cardinal points of the circle, and from their wolfskin cloaks and wolf tail talismans, Sigmar recognised them as priests of Ulric.

'I am,' confirmed Sigmar, 'and you are King Artur.'

'I have that honour,' said Artur, 'and you are not welcome in my city.'

'Whether I am welcome or not is unimportant,' said Sigmar. 'I am here to call you to account for the deaths of my people. While my father made war in the north, Teutogen raiders destroyed Unberogen villages and killed the innocents that lived there. You will answer for their deaths.'

Artur shook his head. 'You would have done the same, boy.'

'You do not deny this?' said Sigmar. 'And, call me boy again and I will kill you.'

'You are here to do that anyway are you not?'

'I am,' agreed Sigmar.

'And you are here to challenge me to single combat I suppose?'

'Yes.'

Artur laughed, a rich baritone sound of genuine amusement. 'You are truly the son of Björn, reckless and filled with ridiculous notions of honour. Tell me why I should not simply have Myrsa and his warriors cut you down?'

'Because he would not obey such an order,' said Sigmar, advancing towards Artur holding Ghal-maraz before him. 'You may have forgotten the meaning of honour, but I do not believe he has. Besides, what manner of man would refuse a challenge before the eyes of the priests of Ulric? What manner of king could retain his authority were he to be proven a coward?'

Artur's eyes narrowed, and Sigmar saw a towering anger and arrogance behind his eyes.

'You have just climbed an impossible climb, an impressive feat, but one which has drained you of your strength,' hissed Artur. 'You are at the very limits of your endurance and you think you can best me? You are nothing but a beardless boy, and I am a king.'

'Then you have nothing to fear,' snapped Sigmar, raising his warhammer.

'The Dragon Sword will cut your flesh like mist,' said Artur, picking up his helmet and placing it upon his head. Sigmar did not reply, but simply circled towards Artur, studying his enemy and watching his movements. Artur was powerfully built, with the wide shoulders and narrow hips of a swordsman, but he had not given battle in many years.

For all that, he moved well, smooth and unhurried, his balance and poise almost as perfect as Gerreon's had been. The name of Sigmar's betrayer appeared unbidden in his mind, and his step faltered at the memory.

Artur saw the flicker in his eyes, and leapt forward, the Dragon Sword cleaving the air with a whisper of the winter wind following in its wake. Sigmar recovered in time to dodge the blow, but the chill of the blade passed within a finger's breadth of taking his head with the first blow of the challenge.

Sensing weakness, Artur attacked again, but Sigmar was ready for him, blocking with the head and haft of Ghal-maraz. Each block sent white sparks shivering through the air, and Sigmar felt the great warhammer grow colder with each blow he deflected.

Artur's reach was much greater than his, and only rarely could Sigmar close with the Teutogen king to attack. He spun around a thrust of the Dragon Sword, and Ghal-maraz slammed into Artur's side. The clang of metal echoed from the ring of black stones, and Sigmar swayed aside to dodge Artur's return stroke, amazed that his blow had not smashed the armour aside and splintered his enemy's spine.

Seeing his surprise, Artur laughed, and said. 'You are not the only king to make allies of the mountain folk and make use of their craft.'

Sigmar backed away, seeing the dwarf handiwork in the fluted scrollwork of the armour and the sheen of dwarf metal. The runic script on the haft of Ghal-maraz burned with an angry light as though displeased at being forced to inflict ruin upon another artefact of its creators.

The two kings traded attacks back and forth in the shadow of the blazing plume of Ulric's Fire, and Sigmar felt his strength fading with every passing moment. He had struck Artur several blows that would have killed a lesser warrior three times over, but the king of the Teutogens was unbowed.

He saw the triumph in Artur's eyes, and desperately brought Ghal-maraz up as another blow arced towards his chest. Once again, the weapons of power met in a ringing clash of metals unknown to man, and Sigmar felt the impact numb his arms. Artur spun in and thundered his mailed fist against Sigmar's chin.

Sigmar stumbled away from the force of the blow as light exploded in his skull.

He heard Alfgeir cry out, and looked up to see a roaring wall of white before him.

Sigmar threw up his arms as he fell through the searing Flame of Ulric's Fire, the light filling his bones with blazing ice. He screamed as he fell, the aching cold of somewhere far distant and unknown to mortals like nothing he had ever known.

Even the vast emptiness of the Grey Vaults seemed welcome compared to the harsh, pitiless power encapsulated in the fire. For the briefest instant, a moment that could have been a heartbeat or an eternity, that power turned its gaze upon him, and Sigmar felt his life's worth judged in the blink of an eye.

Then it was over, and he tumbled to the ground on the far side of Ulric's Fire, rolling to his feet with fresh vigour and energy. Gasps of astonishment rippled around the circle, and Sigmar shared their amazement, for there was not a mark on him, and the flame had left him untouched.

No, not quite untouched, for a fading cloak of shimmering wolf-skin hung from his shoulders, and ghostly tendrils of mist clung to his body as though he had freshly emerged from the depths of the deepest glacier. White fire wreathed Ghal-maraz, and Sigmar felt a furious energy fill him, wild and untamed, as though he were the fiercest animal in the pack.

Sigmar threw back his head, but instead of laughter, the triumphant howl of a wolf tore from his throat, the echoes of it racing around the circumference of the stone circle.

White lightning flashed in Sigmar's eyes, an endless winter's landscape in their depths, and he saw the legendary deeds of the past and future spread before him. The heroes of the past and the leaders of the future surrounded him, their epic deeds and courage flowing together, filling his heart with the glory and honour of their lives.

Without conscious thought, he raised Ghal-maraz, and felt the ringing blow of the Dragon Sword as it slammed into the war-hammer's haft. Sigmar dropped to his knees as though he moved in a dream, and Artur swung his ancient weapon once more.

Sigmar raised his weapon, and the head of Ghal-maraz met the blade of the Dragon Sword in a cataclysmic explosion of force. Unimaginable energies exploded from the impact, and Artur's blade shattered into a thousand fragments, the blade dying with a shriek of winter and the death of seasons.

Artur fell back, blinded by the explosion, and Sigmar surged to his feet, Ghal-maraz swinging in a murderous arc towards the Teutogen king's head.

The ancestral heirloom of Kurgan Ironbeard slammed into Artur's helmet, crumpling the metal and smashing the skull beneath to shards. Artur's body flew through the air, landing in a crumpled heap before the blazing fire at the heart of the stone circle.

Sigmar stood over the body, his chest heaving with the power that filled his veins and the exultation of victory. He saw the priests of Ulric bow their heads and drop to their knees. Not a breath of wind or a single voice disturbed the silence as Sigmar turned to face those who had borne witness to his defeat of Artur.

'The king of the Teutogens is dead!' cried Sigmar, holding Ghal-maraz high. 'You have a new king now. The lands of the Teutogen are mine by right of combat.'

Even as he spoke the words, Sigmar could feel the *rightness* of them, the conviction that this was the will of the gods. He closed his eyes as he pictured the Unberogens and Teutogens going on to achieve great things. This was but the first step towards that goal. So vivid was this vision that Sigmar did not notice Myrsa approaching, until he spoke.

'You claim rulership over the Teutogens?' asked the Warrior Eternal.

Sigmar opened his eyes to see Myrsa standing before him with a dagger held to his throat. The Warrior Eternal's eyes were as cold as Ulric's Fire, and Sigmar knew that his life hung by a thread. His eyes flicked to the edge of the circle, where he saw Alfgeir surrounded by armed warriors, his sword taken from him.

'I do,' said Sigmar. 'I have slain the king, and it is my right in blood.'

'That it is,' nodded Myrsa sadly, 'for Artur's sons are dead and his wife is long gone to Morr's kingdom, but here I am with a blade at the throat of the killer of my king.'

'You said you would be proud to serve me if I were your king,' said Sigmar. 'Does that no longer hold true?'

'That depends.'

'On?'

'On whether I believe you mean to make us slaves to the Unberogen,' said Myrsa.

'Never,' promised Sigmar. 'No man will be a slave of Sigmar. You will be my people, brothers to me, valued and honoured, as are all who hold true to the bonds of loyalty.'

'You swear this before Ulric's Fire?'

'I swear it,' nodded Sigmar, 'and I ask again, will you join me, Myrsa?'

The Warrior Eternal lifted the dagger from Sigmar's throat and dropped to his knees. Myrsa bowed his head, and said, 'I will join you, my lord.'

Sigmar placed his hand on Myrsa's shoulder. 'I need men of courage and honour beside me, Myrsa, and you are such a man.'

'Then what would you have me do?'

'The lands north of the mountains are infested with the dark beasts, and one day the Sea Wolves from across the ocean will return,' said Sigmar, offering his hand to his latest ally and hauling him to his feet. 'As your king, I need you and your warriors to guard the northern marches and keep these lands safe.'

Myrsa nodded, and glanced over to the dead body of the king he had once served as the priests of Ulric came forward to retrieve it.

'Artur was a good man once,' said Myrsa.

'I do not doubt it,' said Sigmar, 'but he is dead now and we have work to do.'

FIFTEEN
Union

THE PATH WOUND through the hills east of the River Stir, the earth rutted and obviously well travelled by wagons, and war chariots, Sigmar remembered, looking to the rolling green slopes around their caravan, and half expecting to see a host of Asoborn warriors descending upon them.

Around Reikdorf, the roads were stone, formed from flat-faced boulders placed in shallow trenches, rendered level with sand and hard-packed earth. Before departing the lands of men to return to his king's hold in the mountains, Master Alaric had helped Pendrag devise a means for constructing roads that could survive the rains and winter. As a result, Unberogen trade caravans travelled with greater ease and speed than those of any other land.

Sigmar dearly wished for some of those Unberogen roads now, for the wagons he and Wolfgart had brought from Reikdorf were travelling slowly, and needed to be dragged from the sucking mud on a regular basis.

A spring storm had flooded the land a week ago, and the eastern lands were still waterlogged and muddy. A journey that should have taken only a week had already taken nearly a month, and Sigmar's patience was wearing thin. Behind him, a hundred warriors of Reikdorf, a mix of White Wolves and Great Hall Guard, marched in perfect formation, and another hundred riders surrounded the four carts of weapons and armour.

Hunting dogs darted between the wagons and a string of six broad-chested horses and a dozen outriders roamed the countryside further out, alert for any danger to the travellers. Cuthwin and Svein moved ahead of the procession of warriors and carts, and Sigmar trusted them more than any other precaution to keep them safe.

Alfgeir and Pendrag had reluctantly remained behind in Reikdorf to protect the king's lands, while he was away on this mission to win the tribes to his banner. The column of warriors had only recently left the lands of the Taleutens, where Sigmar had renewed his oaths with King Krugar with four cartloads of weapons and armour, some of which were crafted from fine, dwarf-forged iron and beyond price.

Now, Sigmar was travelling south to the land of the Asoborns to further strengthen the ties with the fierce warrior queen, Freya. The Asoborns and the Taleutens were allies, and had sworn Sword Oaths, but no such bond existed between Asoborn and Unberogen.

With these gifts, Sigmar hoped to change that.

Wolfgart rode alongside Sigmar, his chequered cloak and bronze armour dull and muddy.

'We'll never find their settlements, you know that?' said Wolfgart. 'Even with Svein out front.'

'We will find them,' said Sigmar. 'Or, more likely, the Asoborn hunters will find us.'

Wolfgart cast a nervous glance to the hills around them and the thin copses of trees that crowned their summits.

'I don't like these lands,' said Wolfgart. 'Too open. Not enough trees.'

'Good farmland though,' said Sigmar, 'and the hills are rich in iron ore.'

'I know, but I prefer Unberogen lands. This is altogether too close to the eastern mountains for my liking. Lots of orcs are on the move in them, and it's bad luck to go looking for trouble.'

'Is that what you think we are doing? Looking for trouble?'

'Aren't we?' countered Wolfgart, shifting the weight of his greatsword on his back as water dripped from the pommel. 'What else would you call riding into Asoborn lands without permission? Oh it all sounds wonderful, I grant you, a land full of buxom warrior women, but I've heard of the eunuchs they make of trespassers. I plan to hang on to my manhood, and to have many sons.'

'Weren't you the one who thought it would be fun to spend the night with an Asoborn woman? I seem to remember you being very amused when Queen Freya... handled me.'

Wolfgart laughed. 'Yes, that was priceless. The look on your face.'

'She is a strong woman, right enough,' said Sigmar, wincing as he remembered the power of her grip.

'All the more reason not to be here then, eh?'

Sigmar shook his head and waved a hand at the wagons. 'No, if we are to make allies of the Asoborns then they need to see that we are serious.'

'Well, we are certainly giving away enough weapons for that,' said Wolfgart with a bitter shake of his head, 'and the horses are some of my best stallions and strongest mares.'

'It is not tribute, Wolfgart,' said Sigmar. 'I thought you understood that.'

'It feels wrong. With what we just handed the Taleutens, this is more than we can afford to give. Our own warriors could use these weapons and should be wearing this armour, and do we really want the Asoborns breeding stronger, faster horses?'

Sigmar held the angry response he was forming. Even after all these years, Wolfgart could still not grasp the concept of all the tribes of men working together. The tribal rivalries were still strong, and Sigmar knew it would be many years before the race of men could truly break their small-minded associations of geography to come together as one.

Without giving Wolfgart an answer, Sigmar rode to the vanguard of the column, passing his warriors and wagons to join the outriders. Lightly armoured in cured leather breastplates and hide-covered helmets of wood, these warriors were expert horsemen and carried short, recurved bows.

The contours of these lands were dangerous, for an attacking force of hundreds could be hidden in the hollows and dead ground without them knowing it. Ahead, the path curved around a waterfall in full spate on the hillside, and numerous bushes and boulders were scattered around the edge of the track.

It was open country, the sky somehow wider, and pressing down with grey clouds upon them. Rain was coming in from the mountains, and as Sigmar looked towards the vast wall of dark rock that reared up at the edge of the world, a shiver of premonition passed through him.

Wolfgart was right, it was not good to be so close to the boundaries of the land, for terrible creatures lurked in the mountains, entire tribes of greenskin warriors, who just awaited the rise of a warlord to lead them down into the lands of men.

All the more reason to make allies of the eastern tribes.

Little was known of the Asoborns, save that their society was fiercely matriarchal, ruled over with passionate ferocity by Queen Freya. Of the tribes further east and south, the Brigundians, the Menogoths and the Merogens, even less was known.

This journey into Asoborn land *was* dangerous, but it was necessary. Nothing provoked fear in people like the unknown, and, despite the danger, those other tribes would need to become known to Sigmar if his dream of empire was to become a reality.

Satisfied that the outriders and scouts were as alert as they ought to be, Sigmar halted his horse to give the rest of the caravan time to catch up as the threatened rain began to fall.

No sooner had Wolfgart and the caravan reached him than a great whooping yell arose from hundreds of throats, as the ground itself seemed to come alive with figures where none had been before.

Naked and semi-naked warriors leapt from concealment, clad in cloaks pierced with ferns and tufts of grass, which had hidden them from sight amid the brush and boulders.

'To arms!' shouted Sigmar as he heard a rumble of chariot wheels from beyond the curve in the track ahead. He lifted Ghal-maraz from his belt as his warriors splashed through the mud to form ranks in the road ahead of the caravan.

Spears were thrust forward, and archers took up position to loose shafts over the heads of the spearmen. Sigmar spurred his steed along the line of Unberogen warriors, expecting a deadly volley of arrows from their ambushers at any second. Unberogen warriors drew back on their bowstrings, but as the Asoborn warriors made no move to attack, Sigmar knew that for them to loose would be folly of the worst kind.

This was an ambush, but not one designed to kill.

'Wait!' he cried. 'Ease your bowstrings. Nobody loose!'

Confusion spread at his order, but Sigmar repeated it again and again. The rain rendered everything grey and blurred, but Sigmar could see that the strange figures surrounding them were women, naked but for loincloths, iron torques and bronze wrist guards. Each carried two swords and was painted with fierce war-tattoos, their heads crowned with a mix of wild cockades and shaved scalps.

Every one of them stood utterly immobile, their stillness more unnerving than any war shout would have been. Sigmar guessed that at least three hundred warriors surrounded them, and could scarcely credit that he had walked into the middle of such an ambush. What had happened to Cuthwin and Svein?

Wolfgart rode alongside him, his mighty sword held before him, his expression accusing.

'I told you this land was dangerous!'

Sigmar shook his head. 'If they wanted to kill us, we would be dead already.'

'Then what do they want?'

'I think we are about to find out,' said Sigmar as a score of war chariots appeared on the hillside and rolled towards them, the tripartite standard of Queen Freya billowing in the wind from spiked banner poles.

SIGMAR BLINKED AS the blindfold was removed and he found himself in a great, earth-walled chamber, illuminated by hundreds of lanterns and a great fire pit. The smell of wet earth and damp cloth was strong in his nostrils, and he ran his hands across his face and through his hair.

Wolfgart was beside him, similarly startled by the change in their surroundings.

The rain had eased as the charioteers surrounded their procession, and though they made no overtly aggressive moves, the tension was palpable. A tall, broad shouldered woman, naked but for her long cloak and tattoos, had leapt down from the lead chariot and stood defiantly before them.

Cuthwin and Svein were bound on a chariot behind her, and Sigmar could feel their acute embarrassment in their refusal to meet his gaze.

'You are the one the Unberogen call king?' asked the woman.

'I am,' confirmed Sigmar, 'and this is my sword-brother, Wolfgart.'

The woman acknowledged them with a curt bow. 'I am Maedbh of the Asoborns,' she proclaimed. 'Queen Freya has declared you a friend of her tribe. You will come with us to the settlement of Three Hills.'

'And if we don't want to?' called Wolfgart before Sigmar could respond.

'Then you will leave our lands, Unberogen,' replied Maedbh. 'Or you will die here.'

'We will come with you,' said Sigmar hurriedly. 'For I much desire to see Queen Freya. I bring gifts from my land that I wish to present to her.'

'You desire her?' asked Maedbh, waving a pair of her warriors forward. 'That is good, it will be less painful that way.'

'Painful? What?' asked Sigmar as the painted Asoborns unwound cloth bindings from their wrists and made to blindfold them.

Wolfgart lowered his sword to point at the Asoborn woman's chest. 'What is this for? We will not be rendered blind.'

'The secret paths to the halls of the Asoborn Queens are not for the eyes of men,' said Maedbh. 'You travel in darkness or you turn back.'

'You're going to blindfold us all?' snarled Wolfgart.

'No, just you and those who bring your gifts. The rest of your warriors will remain here.'

'Now just hold on–' began Wolfgart before Sigmar silenced him with a gesture.

'Very well,' said Sigmar. 'We accept your terms. I have your word that no harm will come to my warriors?'

'If they remain here and do not try to follow us, then no ill will befall them.'

Wolfgart turned towards Sigmar and hissed. 'You're going to let these damned women blindfold us and take us Ulric knows where? Without any warriors? They'll have our balls for breakfast, man!'

'This is the only way, Wolfgart,' said Sigmar. 'We came here to see Freya after all.'

Wolfgart spat on the ground. 'If I return and am unable to provide my father with a grandson, then you will be the one to explain this to him.'

The blindfolds had been tied tightly, and amid the protests of his men, the Asoborn warrior women had led Sigmar and Wolfgart away. As a parting order, Sigmar had shouted over his shoulder to Cuthwin and Svein.

'Make no attempt to follow us! Remain here until we return.'

They had been led into the forest, that much Sigmar knew, but beyond that, he could make no sense of their route, for it ventured over hills and through sheltered valleys and dense undergrowth. Though Sigmar tried to hold true to their course, he soon hopelessly lost his bearings and any sense of how far they had travelled.

At last he had heard the sounds of people and could smell the scents of a settlement. Even then, this was not the end of their journey as they had travelled through a long, enclosing space of echoes and wet, earthy smells. Sigmar had felt the heat and smoke of a fire, and had a sense of a great space above him.

The blindfolds had been removed, and Sigmar had found himself within the hall of the Asoborn Queen. It was like nothing he had seen before, the walls curving upwards as though they were in some giant underground barrow. Snaking tree roots laced together on the ceiling above him, and a timber-edged hole penetrated the roof to allow smoke to disperse.

Hundreds of warriors of both sexes filled the hall, dressed in striped leggings and long cloaks. Most were bare-chested, with bronze torques ringing their arms and swirling tattoos covering their chests and necks. Sigmar noticed that they were all armed with bronze-bladed swords.

'Ulric preserve us,' whispered Wolfgart, seeing the fierce queen presiding over the assembly on her raised throne.

Queen Freya was a striking woman at the best of times, but here in her own domain, she was extraordinary. She sat draped across a graceful curve of fur-lined tree roots, the wood carefully shaped over hundreds of years by human hands to form the throne of the Asoborn queens.

Her flesh was bare, save for a golden torque around her neck, a split leather kilt and a cloak of shimmering bronze mail. A cascade of hair like flaming copper spilled from her head, held from her face with a crown of gold set with a shimmering ruby.

Freya swung her legs from the throne and stood facing them, lifting a trident spear from the warrior woman Maedbh, who stood next to her. Muscles rippled along her lean, powerful arms, and Sigmar did not doubt the strength in them.

'I knew you would come to me before long,' said Freya, descending from her raised throne, and Sigmar could not help but admire her full, womanly figure. The cloak of mail partially covered her breasts, but what lay beneath was tantalisingly revealed with every sway of her hips and shoulders as she approached.

'It is an honour to stand in your halls, Queen Freya,' said Sigmar with a short bow.

'You have come from Taleuten lands,' stated Freya. 'Why do you enter my domain now?'

Sigmar swallowed and said, 'I have come with gifts for you, Queen Freya.'

'Armour of iron and dwarf-forged swords,' said Freya, tilting her head to one side. 'I have seen them, and they please me. Are the horses mine too?'

Sigmar nodded. 'They are. Wolfgart here is a horse breeder of no little skill, and these steeds are faster and more powerful than any others in the land. These beasts are among his finest studs and will give you many strong foals.'

Freya drew level with Sigmar, and he felt his pulse quicken as he took in the scent of the oils applied to her skin and hair. The queen of the Asoborns was tall, and her eyes were a fierce, penetrating emerald that regarded Sigmar with a predatory gleam.

'His finest studs,' repeated Freya with a smile.

'Aye,' agreed Wolfgart. 'You'll find no finer in the land.'

'We shall see about that,' said Freya.

THE SUN WAS approaching midday when Sigmar emerged from Queen Freya's Great Hall, tired and glad to feel the breath of wind on his face. His limbs were scratched and tired, and he felt as weak as when he had awoken from the Grey Vaults.

Golden light bathed him, and he turned his face to the sun, enjoying the blue of the sky now that the storm had broken. A great hill rose at his back, perfectly round and crowned with red-barked trees that flowered with a sweet smelling blossom. The queen's halls lay buried beneath the tree, the entrance hidden to all but the most thorough search.

Though he had just emerged from the hall, Sigmar found that even he could scarcely tell how to gain entry within. Looking around him, laughing Asoborns went about their daily duties, and here and there, Sigmar could see wisps of smoke from buried homes or perhaps a smithy.

The people of the east were long-limbed and fair of skin, their hair blonde or copper, and their bodies heavily tattooed. Though there was a mix of sexes moving through the cunningly concealed settlement, Sigmar noted that it was predominantly women who bore weapons and walked with the confident swagger of the warrior.

A fierce pride burned in the hearts of the Asoborns, and to harness that was to tie oneself to a maddened colt, but the bargain was sealed, and he and Freya had exchanged Sword Oaths after numerous bouts of furious lovemaking.

His back felt as though he had been flogged, and his chest bore the imprint of Freya's sharpened teeth from collarbone to pelvis. His leggings had chafed against his groin as he had dragged them on and finally climbed from her bed.

Sigmar walked amongst Freya's people and saw the steep, thickly wooded slopes of the other two hills that gave the name to the Asoborn settlement. He saw dwellings constructed atop the trees and among the tangled roots of their trunks. A mill had been fashioned in the body of a tall oak, the sails turning slowly and turning a millstone that Sigmar suspected must lie beneath the hill.

A tumbling stream wound its way through the settlement, and Sigmar knelt beside it, dipping his head in the fast-flowing waters, letting the sudden cold wash away his tiredness and the taste of the potions that Freya had made him consume, claiming they would prolong the act of love.

Sigmar knelt back on his haunches and threw back his head, letting the water pour down his chest and back. He blinked away the last droplets on his face and ran his hands through his golden hair, pulling it into a long scalp lock and securing it with a leather cord.

'So could you?' asked an amused voice behind him.

'Could I what, Wolfgart?' asked Sigmar, rising to his feet and turning to face his sword-brother. In contrast to his own appearance, Wolfgart looked fresh and well rested, his eyes full of wicked amusement.

'Could you beat Freya in a fight? Surely you remember your father's advice about only bedding wenches you could best in a fight?'

Sigmar shrugged. 'Maybe. I don't know. I don't think Freya sees much difference between rutting and fighting. I certainly feel as though I have been in a battle.'

'You look like it too, brother,' said Wolfgart, turning him around and inspecting the flesh of his back. 'Gods alive! It looks like you've been mauled by a bear!'

'Enough,' said Sigmar, pulling away from Wolfgart. 'Not a word of this when we get back. I mean it.'

'Of course not,' smiled Wolfgart. 'My lips are sealed tighter than a virgin's legs on Blood Night.'

'That's not very tight at all,' pointed out Sigmar.

'Anyway,' said Wolfgart, relishing Sigmar's discomfort and ignoring his glare, 'are we allies with the Asoborns? Did they accept our gifts?'

'Aye, they did,' said Sigmar. 'The gifts pleased the queen, as did your horses.'

'I should damn well think so!' said Wolfgart. 'I gave her Fireheart and Blackmane, the finest stallions of my herd. You could strap a hundredweight of armour to them and they'd still outpace the ponies the Asoborns use to pull their chariots. Give them a few years and they will have warhorses worthy of the name.'

'Freya knows that, and that's why she gave me her Sword Oath.'

Wolfgart slapped his palm on Sigmar's back and laughed as he flinched in pain. 'Come on, brother, we both know the real reason she gave you her oath.'

'And what is that?'

'When the sap of an Unberogen man rises there's not a woman in the world can say no.'

SIGMAR AND WOLFGART were returned to their warriors later that day, though as sworn allies of the Asoborns, they were not blindfolded this time. As they led their horses over the ridge before the gathered Unberogen, a great cheer went up, and Sigmar cast a withering glance towards Wolfgart, who affected an air of supreme nonchalance.

Sigmar was glad to see the Asoborns had been true to their word and none of his warriors had been harmed, but they were clearly relieved to have their king return to them.

Once again, their guide had been the warrior woman, Maedbh, and she rode alongside them in a chariot of lacquered black wood and bronze edging. A pair of hardy plains ponies pulled the chariot, and the wheels were fitted with glittering scythe blades. Remembering the ripple of fear that had passed through his men at the sight of the chariots, Sigmar knew that when they were pulled by powerful Unberogen horses, they would be nigh unstoppable in battle.

Maedbh halted her chariot and stepped down from the fighting platform to stride over to Sigmar and Wolfgart. She shared her queen's tempestuous beauty, and Sigmar hid his amusement as he guessed the reason for her approach.

'You leave our lands as a friend, King Sigmar,' said Maedbh.

'We are one people now,' replied Sigmar. 'If your lands are threatened, our swords are yours to call upon.'

'Queen Freya said you were a man of stamina. All Unberogen men are like you?'

'All Unberogen men are strong,' agreed Sigmar.

Maedbh nodded and moved past him to stand before Wolfgart. Before his sword-brother could say anything, Maedbh hooked one hand behind Wolfgart's neck, the other between his legs and pulled him close for a long, passionate kiss.

Another mighty cheer erupted from the Unberogen warriors, and Sigmar laughed as Wolfgart struggled in the grip of the fearsome warrior woman. At last she released him and climbed back onto her chariot.

'Come back to me in the summer, Wolfgart of the Unberogen,' called Maedbh as she turned her chariot. 'Come back and we will fasten hands and make strong children together!'

The chariot swiftly vanished around the bend in the track, and Sigmar put his arm around his sword-brother, who stood speechless at what had happened.

'Looks like I am not the only one to have made an impression,' said Sigmar.

CORMAC BLOODAXE STOOD on the shore of a sea as grey as iron, and stared at the ruin of what had become of his people. His anger made him gnash his teeth as the berserk rage threatened to come upon him once more, but he savagely quelled the rising fury. Sigmar of the Unberogen and his warriors had all but wiped them out, driving them from their homeland to this forsaken place across the sea.

The southern shores of the cursed land were bleak and swept with snow, a wind like the breath of the mightiest ice daemon howling across the string of makeshift settlements that dotted the coastline.

There was nothing of permanence to the settlements, for they had been constructed from the cannibalised remains of Wolfships, an ignoble end to the mighty vessels that had carried the Sea Wolves of the Norsii into battle for years.

Those same ships had brought them here from the lands of the southern kings, but few men were left that knew the skills of the woodworker and the builder. Draughty lean-tos and caves now sheltered the pitiful remains of all that remained of the proud Norsii people, where once they had dwelled in mighty halls of fire and warriors.

Cormac stood beside Kar Odacen, the stoop-shouldered mystic that had advised his father, the slain king of the Norsii, on the will of the gods. Cormac despised the man and had wanted to kill him for the disaster that had overtaken their people, but he knew better than to anger the gods, and had reluctantly allowed him to live.

Kar Odacen had counselled the warrior kings of the north for as long as Cormac could remember, and it had been whispered by the elders that this Kar Odacen was the same man who had stood at the right hand of his great grandsire.

Certainly, the man looked old enough, his pate shaved and his flesh wrinkled like worn leather. The man's frame was skeletal, and his features were hooked like those of a raven. Cormac shivered, despite his thick woollen leggings and the heavy bearskin cloak he wore wrapped tightly about him. Though Kar Odacen's dark robes were thin and ragged, he appeared not to feel the biting cold of the wind.

'Tell me again why we are here, old man?' snapped Cormac. 'You will see us both dead with a fever if we remain here much longer.'

'Have some patience, my young king,' said Kar Odacen, 'and some faith.'

'I have precious little of either,' snapped Cormac as a freezing gust of wind blew through him like a thousand icy knives. 'If this is a fool's errand, I will cut the head from your shoulders.'

'Spare me your empty threats,' said Kar Odacen. 'I have seen my death a thousand times and it is not by your axe.'

Cormac swallowed his anger with difficulty, and stared out to sea once more. Far to the south, through the banks of fog and across the dark waters of the ocean, lay the warm, fertile lands of the south, lands that had once been theirs.

Lands that would one day be theirs again.

Cormac could still taste the ash in his mouth from the burning ships and men as Sigmar's strange war machines had hurled balls of flaming death from the cliffs. Thousands had died as their ships burned beneath them, and thousands more as they sank to the bottom of the sea.

Sigmar and his allied kings would one day pay for these deaths, and Cormac vowed that he and all who came after him would once again sail across the water and take the songs of war southwards.

Cormac knew, however, that these were dreams for another day, banking the flame of his anger in his heart. Last night around the fire, Kar Odacen had promised him that the days of blood would begin again soon, and that Cormac must accompany him to this desolate shoreline upon the dawn.

Cormac could see nothing to make him believe that this journey was anything other than a waste of time, and was just about to turn and make his way back to the settlement when Kar Odacen spoke once more.

'One comes who will be mightier than us all, even you.'

'Who?'

'Look yonder,' said Kar Odacen, pointing a bony finger out to sea.

Cormac shielded his eyes against the glare of the pale sky, and saw a small boat bobbing helplessly in the swell of the surging waves. The tide was carrying it to shore, and the wind gusted uselessly through a torn and flapping sail. Such a boat was never meant to cross such an expanse of ocean, and Cormac was amazed that it had survived at all.

'Where does it come from?' he asked.

'From the south,' answered Kar Odacen.

The boat continued to approach the shore, and as it tipped forward on the crest of a wave, Cormac saw that there was a man sprawled in its bottom.

'Go,' ordered Kar Odacen, when the boat had closed enough to reach. 'Fetch it in.'

Cormac shot the mystic a hostile glare, but waded into the sea nevertheless. The cold hit him like a blow, his legs numb within seconds. He waded in past his waist, already feeling the cold sap his strength with every passing moment.

The boat came near, and he grabbed the warped timbers of its gunwale, quickly turning and heading back to shore. He heard the man within the boat groan.

'Whoever you are,' he hissed through gritted teeth, 'you had better be worth all this.'

Cormac struggled to shore, pulling the boat up onto the grey sands with difficulty. The cold was threatening to overcome him, but he saw that Kar Odacen had prepared a fire on the beach.

Had he been in the water so long?

Kar Odacen approached the boat, his face twisted with grotesque interest, and Cormac turned to the man in the boat as he rolled onto his back and opened his eyes.

Midnight dark hair spilled around his shoulders, and his face was gaunt. Though unshaven and malnourished, the man was startlingly handsome. A scabbarded sword lay in the bottom of the boat, and as the man stirred, he reached for the weapon.

Cormac reached down and plucked the scabbard from the man's weakened grip. He drew the blade from its scabbard, holding the weapon aimed at the man's throat.

'Be careful,' warned Cormac. 'It is a bad death to be killed by your own sword.'

As he held the sword out before him, Cormac admired the shining iron blade, its balance flawless, and its weight matched exactly to his reach and strength. Truly it was a magnificent weapon, and he had a sudden urge to lower the blade.

'Who are you?' he demanded.

The man licked his lips and tried to speak, but his mouth was parched from unnumbered days at sea, and his voice was an inaudible croak. Kar Odacen passed him a waterskin, and the man drank greedily, gulping down great mouthfuls.

At last, the man lowered the waterskin and whispered, 'I am called Gerreon.'

Kar Odacen shook his head. 'No. That is the name of your past life. You shall have another name now, a name given to you in ages past by the gods of the north.'

'Tell me...' begged Gerreon.

'You shall be called Azazel.'

SIXTEEN

To be a King

THOUGH THEY WERE nearly a mile away, the strident cries of the berserker king's battle line could clearly be heard from the Unberogen camp. Sigmar felt the weight of all his twenty-six years upon him now, hating the fact that his enemies on this battlefield were a tribe of men and not the greenskins.

The sun was bright and the air chill, the last of the snows still clinging to the peaks of the mountains to the north and the winter winds blowing in from the western coast. Nearly twelve thousand Unberogen warriors were camped in the wilds of the lands of the Thuringians, ready to do battle with the painted warriors of King Otwin.

Since dawn, the lunatic howls of berserk warriors had echoed through the forest, and the Unberogen men made the sign of the horns to ward off the evil spirits that were said to gather in the forests and drive men to madness.

Hundreds of sword bands gathered around fires, and men exchanged raucous banter, sharpened already honed blades or offered prayers to Ulric that they would fight well. The smell of cooking meat and boiling oats hung in the air, though most warriors ate frugally, knowing that a full bladder and bowels were not desirable before going into battle.

White Wolves tended to their mounts, rubbing them down and

tying their tails with cords in preparation for the charge. The steeds did not yet wear their armour, for they would need all their strength in the battle to come, and it would needlessly tire them to have it lifted onto their backs too early.

The army was mobilising for war, the leaders of each sword band rousing his men and dousing the fires with handfuls of earth. What had once been a mass of men gathered without semblance of order, swiftly transformed into a disciplined army of warriors, and Sigmar's heart swelled with pride to see them.

He turned as he heard footsteps behind him, and saw Wolfgart, Pendrag and Alfgeir approaching. All were arrayed for battle, and Pendrag carried Sigmar's crimson banner. The Marshal of the Reik's face was grim, and even Wolfgart seemed uncomfortable at the nature of the battle they were about to fight.

'Good day for it,' said Wolfgart acidly. 'The crows are already gathering.'

Sigmar nodded sadly, for the outcome of the battle was surely not in doubt. Barely six thousand warriors opposed the Unberogen, and Sigmar's army had never known defeat.

'There is nothing good about this,' said Sigmar. 'Many men will die today and for what?'

'For honour,' said Alfgeir.

'Honour?' repeated Sigmar, shaking his head. 'Where is the honour in this? We outnumber Otwin's warriors at least two to one. He cannot win here and he must know that.'

'It is not about winning, Sigmar,' said Pendrag.

'Then what is it about?'

'Think on it, if our lands were invaded, would we not fight?' asked Pendrag. 'No matter how badly we were outnumbered, we would still fight to defend our lands.'

'But we are not invaders,' protested Sigmar. 'I have done everything in my power to avoid this war. I offered King Otwin my Sword Oath and a chance to join us, but every emissary I sent was turned away.'

Alfgeir shrugged, tightening the straps of his breastplate. 'Otwin is canny; he knows he cannot win here, but he also knows that he would not remain king for long were he not to oppose us. When we defeat his army he will seek terms, for honour will have been satisfied.'

'Thousands will die to satisfy that honour,' said Sigmar. 'It is madness.'

'Aye, perhaps,' agreed Alfgeir, 'but I can't help but admire him for it.'

Wolfgart dragged his mighty sword from his shoulder scabbard. 'Ach, let's just get this over with and go home.'

Sigmar smiled, guessing the cause of Wolfgart's irritation, and grateful for a chance to change the subject. 'Do not worry, brother. We'll keep you safe and get you home for Maedbh.'

'Aye, she'd have our guts if we didn't,' said Pendrag.

Despite the danger of travelling in the snow, Wolfgart had journeyed back into the east soon after their return from their mission to Queen Freya's lands, and had spent the winter with the Asoborns. When he had returned in the spring, he had proudly sported a tattoo upon his arm, a sign of his betrothal to Maedbh. When this bloody business with the Thuringians had been concluded, he would be joined to the Asoborn woman over the Oathstone in Reikdorf.

Sigmar was happy for his friend and looked forward to the revelries that always followed a hand fastening ceremony, but melancholy touched him as his thoughts inevitably turned to Ravenna. Many years had passed since her death, but not a day went by without Sigmar thinking of her.

Even when he had lain with Freya, it had been Ravenna's face he had pictured.

He shook off such thoughts, for it would attract ill-luck to think of the dead before battle.

The blare of Unberogen horns sounded, the army ready to march to battle, and Sigmar shook hands with each of his comrades.

'Fight well, my friends,' he said. 'If we must fight this battle for honour, then let it be fought swiftly.'

SIGMAR CRASHED HIS hammer into the chest of a Thuringian warrior, spinning on his heel as he blocked a thrusting spear with the sword in his other hand. His elbow hammered the wielder's face, and he leapt the falling body to shoulder charge the man behind him. A berserker's axe had splintered his shield and he bled from a score of shallow wounds.

The sound of screaming warriors filled the air, thousands of battle-hardened tribesmen hacking at one another with axe and sword, or stabbing with spears and daggers. King Otwin's army was disintegrating before the charge of the Unberogens, Alfgeir's White Wolves smashing into the left flank and crushing the lightly armoured warriors there. Nimble outriders encircled the right flank, while unflinching spearmen and swordsmen met the furious charge of the berserkers in the centre.

Sigmar had waited with Pendrag and Wolfgart as the screaming Thuringians charged towards them. Most were naked and covered in colourfully painted spirals, their hair pulled into stiffened spikes with chalked mud. They swung enormous swords and axes, their eyes maddened and their mouths foaming.

A giant warrior came at Sigmar, his face pierced with spikes of metal and heavy rings. His body was enormous, packed with muscle and bleeding from deep, self-inflicted cuts. Sigmar ducked a whooshing sweep of the man's axe, the blow hacking the warrior next to him in two. The return stroke was blindingly swift, and the edge of the axe caught Sigmar's shoulder guard, and tore him from his feet.

Sigmar rolled in the mud, desperately trying to find his feet. A spear stabbed for him, and he deflected it with his forearm. The point hammered the ground, and Sigmar kicked out at the wielder, cracking his kneecap and driving him back. The ground slid beneath him, churned to mud by the battling warriors, and a sword slashed across his chest as he rose to his feet, the iron links parting beneath the powerful blow.

The padded undershirt he wore was cut, but the mail had robbed the blow of its strength. He headbutted the swordsman, and then slammed his hammer into his groin. The giant axeman swung at him again, and Sigmar threw up Ghal-maraz to block the blow. The ringing impact numbed his arm, but he spun around the warrior's guard, and stabbed his sword into his gut.

The sword was torn from his hand, and the giant slammed the haft of his axe into Sigmar's face. Blood sprayed from his burst lip, stars exploded behind his eyes and he reeled at the force of the strike.

Though dealt a mortal wound, the axeman came at him again, apparently untroubled by the sword in his belly. The man howled as he swung his axe, the madness of battle overcoming his pain. Sigmar ducked beneath a killing blow, stepping in to ram the head of his hammer against the hilt of his sword. The impact drove the blade further into the man's flesh until the hand guard was pressed against his skin.

The warrior reached out and took hold of Sigmar's hair, wrenching his head back to expose his neck. The axe rose, and Sigmar reached down. He took hold of the sword's handle and planted his foot in the giant's belly.

Sigmar twisted the sword and pulled. The blade slid free and Sigmar spun, chopping it down with all his strength on the side of the giant's neck. Blood spurted from the wound, the squirting power of the crimson stream telling Sigmar that he had struck an artery.

The warrior staggered, and Sigmar swung his hammer in an upward arc, knocking the giant to the ground. The mail shirt was dripping rings to the ground, torn and useless, so, in the few moments of space he had created, Sigmar shrugged it off, leaving his upper body bare. His hair was unbound and wild, his face a mask of blood, and Sigmar hoped none of his warriors would mistake him for a Thuringian berserker.

A breathless Pendrag appeared at his side, his axe bloody and his mail shirt battered, but his grip on the banner still strong. 'Gods, I thought that big bastard was never going down!'

'Aye,' gasped Sigmar. 'He was a tough one all right.'

'Are you hurt?' asked Pendrag.

'Nothing serious,' said Sigmar, seeing a furious melee erupt deeper in the ranks of the Thuringians, beneath a banner bearing a design of silver swords against a black background.

'Come on,' said Sigmar. 'I see Otwin's banner!'

Pendrag nodded as Unberogen warriors formed a fighting wedge around their king and, without further words, Sigmar led his warriors towards the centre of the battlefield. Sigmar's practiced eye could see that the Thuringian army was doomed. The White Wolves were crushing the flanks and pushing towards the centre, their dreaded hammers rising and falling bloody as they pounded a path towards the king's banner.

The right flank had collapsed into isolated shield walls. Only the centre held firm against the Unberogen attack, and if the battle was to be ended, Sigmar must reach the king.

Blood-maddened berserkers threw themselves in front of the Unberogen king, and all died before his warhammer or sword. Gathered around their king, Sigmar's warriors were unstoppable, fighting with stubborn courage and ferocity. Yard by yard, the Unberogen pushed through the screaming mass of Thuringians, hacking a bloody path and howling the name of Sigmar.

Sigmar saw Otwin fighting in the centre of his battle line and felt a shiver of superstitious dread seize him. The king of the Thuringians was a giant of a man, even bigger and more powerful than the axeman Sigmar had killed. Otwin's naked body was festooned with tattoos and piercings, his crown a patchwork of golden spikes hammered through the flesh of his temple. Blood coated his body and he wielded an axe chained to his wrist with twin blades more monstrous than those of Sigmar's father's weapon.

A clutch of similarly fearsome warriors gathered around their king, their howling cries like a pack of rabid wolves. Sigmar saw Otwin register the fighting wedge of Unberogen warriors and turn to face them with a leering grin of insane fury.

One of the king's champions leapt forward, unable to contain his battle lust, and Sigmar swung his hammer at the warrior. The warrior ducked and dived beneath the blow, rolling to his feet with his twin swords extended before him. Sigmar leapt above the thrusting blades and spun in the air, hammering his heel against the warrior's chin.

The man's neck snapped with a hideous crack and he fell as yet another warrior attacked. Sigmar raised his sword to strike, but hesitated as he saw that this champion was a beautiful woman with a whip-thin physique, golden hair and tawny eyes. Her body was powerful, but fast. Sigmar's hesitation almost cost him his life as the twin swords she bore slashed towards him in a blur of bloodstained bronze.

'I am Ulfdar!' screamed the warrior woman. 'And I am your death!'

Sigmar parried one of Ulfdar's swords as the other sliced across his shoulder in a line of fire. He deflected another blow with his blade, and rammed his forehead into Ulfdar's face. She staggered and spat blood, laughing maniacally as her sword stabbed for his groin. Sigmar swayed aside as the blades of his warriors finally met those of the Thuringian king's retinue.

The warrior woman's second blade slashed towards his neck, and Sigmar stepped into the blow, her hand striking the iron torque at his neck. Sigmar heard her fingers snap, and the sword spun away from her. He swung his hammer towards her stomach, the heavy head driving the breath from her body. His knee drove up into her jaw, and he heard it crack as she fell to her knees before him. The berserk light was fading from her eyes as the pain of her wounds overcame the red mist upon her, yet still she glared up at him in defiance.

Sigmar knew he should kill her, as she would have killed him, but some unknown imperative stayed him from delivering the fatal blow. Instead, he hammered his fist against her cheek, knowing that were she to remain conscious she would only try to find another weapon and get herself killed.

The battle flowed around Sigmar like a living thing, the tide of screaming warriors a rising crescendo of pain and fury. He saw a knot of enemy warriors forging a path towards his crimson banner, and shook his head free of the combat he had just fought as the mighty berserker king bellowed his challenge to him in blood and courage.

Sigmar lifted Ghal-maraz high for all his warriors to see, and answered with his own challenge.

The two kings met in a clash of fire and fury, Otwin's mighty axe cleaving the air in a bloody arc as Sigmar rolled beneath the blow to smash his hammer into his foe's side. The king of the Thuringians grunted in pain, but did not fall, the haft of his axe hooking down, the blade stabbing into the muscle at Sigmar's shoulder.

Sigmar cried out in pain and dropped his sword. Otwin thundered his fist against Sigmar's face, and he fell back, feeling his cheekbone break. The Thuringian king pressed forwards, his axe slicing up to take Sigmar under the arm and drive into his heart. Sigmar spun away from the axe and let the momentum of his spin carry Ghal-maraz into Otwin's hip, the powerful blow driving the Thuringian king to his knees.

Sigmar shook his eyes free of blood, and leapt to attack his foe once more. Otwin's axe swept out, but Sigmar was ready, and hammered Ghal-maraz against the king's wrist.

Hot sparks erupted from the chain that bound the axe to Otwin, and the links parted before the fury and craft of the great warhammer. Sundered links of chain flew through the air, and the enormous axe spun from Otwin's grasp.

Sigmar closed the gap between them, and his hand closed on Otwin's throat, crushing the breath from him. The berserker king's eyes bulged and he struggled to rise, but Sigmar kept him on his knees, his grip like iron upon his neck. Otwin clawed at Sigmar's arm, but the choking grip was unyielding. Sigmar lifted Ghal-maraz above his head, the rune-forged hammer poised to split the Thuringian king's skull.

All movement on the battlefield ceased as the warriors of both armies sensed the import of this clash of giants. The outcome of the battle was being decided in this one moment, and the clash of blades died as all eyes turned to the struggle at the centre of the field.

Sigmar lowered his warhammer and lifted Otwin from his knees, keeping his grip firm on his foe's neck until he saw the light of battle-madness driven from his eyes. The berserker king drew a rasping breath into his lungs as Sigmar released his grip and met his gaze without fear or shame.

'It is over, King Otwin,' said Sigmar, his tone brooking no disagreement. 'You have a choice now: live or die. Swear your Sword Oath with me. Become part of my brotherhood of warriors, and together we will build an empire of men to hold back the darkness.'

'And if I refuse?' growled Otwin, blood leaking from the edge of his mouth where he had bitten the inside of his cheeks.

'Then I will drive you and all your people from this land,' promised Sigmar. 'Every man gathered here will be slain, your villages will burn, your heirs will die and the lamentation of your women shall be unending.'

'That is not much of a choice,' said Otwin.

'No,' agreed Sigmar. 'What is it to be? Peace or war? Life or death?'

'You have a heart of stone, King Sigmar,' said Otwin, 'but, by the gods, you are a warrior to walk the road to Ulric's Hall with!'

'Do I have your oath?' asked Sigmar, offering his hand to the Thuringian king.

'Aye,' said Otwin, taking Sigmar's hand, 'you have it.'

MUSIC FILLED THE king's longhouse, and dancers spun and laughed as they wove in and out of each other's path in time to the drums and pipes. Garlands of flowers hung from the rafters, and the scent of jasmine and honeysuckle was a fragrant blossom on the air. Sigmar watched the wedding dances with unalloyed joy, relishing seeing his warriors at play instead of at war.

With the victory against the Thuringian host, the majority of warriors in Sigmar's army had returned to their homes, while the standing fighting men had marched back to Reikdorf in triumph. Though many men had died to secure the Sword Oath of King Otwin, Sigmar had been pleased, and not a little relieved, to see that many of the wounded would live.

Alfgeir had taken a lance to the side, but his armour had prevented the weapon from disembowelling him, and Pendrag had lost three fingers on his left hand when a Thuringian axe had struck the banner pole and slid down its length. Despite the loss of his fingers, Pendrag had not let the banner fall, and Sigmar had never been more proud of his sword-brother. The healer, Cradoc, had saved the rest of Pendrag's fingers, but he would always bear the scars of the battle to win over the Thuringians.

Wolfgart had come through the battle unscathed, requiring little more than a few stitches across his forearms and legs, and had immediately set off ahead of the main body of the army to Reikdorf.

Maedbh had been waiting for him, and on the day following Sigmar's return, he and Maedbh walked the flower-strewn path to the Oathstone, where the priestess of Rhya had fastened their hands with a spiral of mistletoe and taken their pledges of faith and fertility.

Sigmar had blessed the union and Pendrag had presented the fastening gifts: a gold torque of wondrous workmanship for Maedbh and a mail shirt embossed with a silver wolf for Wolfgart.

Sigmar had opened the doors to the king's longhouse and all were made welcome within, the wines and beers free to everyone who desired to be part of the festivities. The square before the longhouse became a gathering for feasters, and it did not take long for singers, minstrels and taletellers to begin the entertainments.

Sigmar had danced with many of the village maidens, but he had excused himself before becoming too entangled with the dancing, and returned to his throne to watch over his people. Now, with the pleasant glow of wine and grain spirits warming his stomach, Sigmar felt as though his dream was on the very cusp of completion. Only the furthest tribes remained aloof from the advances of the Unberogen, the Jutones and Bretonii in the west, and the Brigundians and Ostagoths of the east.

Further south-east were the Menogoths and the Merogens, but whether they even still existed was a mystery, for their lands were dangerously close to the mountains, where all manner of bloodthirsty tribes of orcs and beasts made their lairs.

Sigmar smiled as he watched Maedbh and Wolfgart dance with their arms linked in a circle of their friends. Seated at a table nearby, Pendrag tapped his foot in time with the music, his hand wrapped in spiderleaf bandages.

Even Alfgeir had been persuaded to dance, and old Eoforth was dancing lustily with the maiden aunts of the town. Laughter and good cheer were the common currency of this day, and Sigmar's people were spending it freely in the spirit of shared friendship and plenty.

Reikdorf had continued to grow over the years, and with the discovery of fresh gold and iron ore in the hills, its prosperity had been assured. Tanneries, breweries, forges, clothmakers, dyers, potters, horse breeders, millers, bakers and schools could all be found within Reikdorf's walls, and its people were well-fed and numerous.

Over four thousand people called Reikdorf home, and though much of the town was still protected by timber stockade walls, the majority of the foundations had been laid for an encircling wall of stone that would protect the Unberogen from attack.

Sigmar was not yet twenty-seven, but he had already achieved more than his father, though he was canny enough to know that he had stood upon the shoulders of giants to reach such heights.

The music shifted in tempo, slowing from the furious drive of the previous tune to become a haunting lament that spoke of lost love and forgotten dreams. The dancing slowed as couples held each other close, and friends drank fresh toasts to the honoured slain who walked with Ulric in the halls of the dead.

Sigmar rose from his throne and, unnoticed, slipped from the longhouse through a door at the rear, making his way from the festivities to a dark place to the north of the town. The night was warm and the light breeze was pleasant on his skin after so long in armour.

Both moons were bright and high, and his shadows were short as he walked alone through the streets. A few of his hounds followed him from the hall, but Sigmar sent them back with a curt whistle and a chop of his hand. The further Sigmar travelled from the centre of the town, the fewer stone buildings he passed, the majority well-formed from timber and thatch. The buildings were tightly packed, and he passed unnoticed towards the section of wall he knew was unfinished.

The wall was patrolled, but Sigmar knew the town and its rhythms, the pace of the guards and their movements better than anyone. It was a simple matter for him to pass the walls without detection and vanish into the forests around the city.

Free of the walls, Sigmar felt a strange sense of liberation as though he had been confined within the city as a prisoner, but had not realised that all his gaolers had long since vanished. Sigmar climbed the paths that led through the hills surrounding Reikdorf, looking back to see his home as a glittering, torch-lit beacon in the darkness.

Laughter and music were carried to him on the wind, and he smiled as he pictured his peoples' revelries. Sigmar's dream of empire had kept Reikdorf safe, and his preparations had allowed the Unberogen to become the pre-eminent tribe of the lands west of the mountains, but he knew there was still much to be done.

Scouts were already bringing word of an increase in orc raids from the mountains, and it was only a matter of time before the greenskins ventured from their lairs in a roaring tide of destruction and death. That, however, was a problem for tomorrow, for tonight was a night for Sigmar, a night for remembrance and regret.

Once within the forests, the tracks and paths were all but invisible, but as well as Sigmar knew Reikdorf, he knew the land better, and it knew him, welcoming him as a man would welcome an old and trusted friend.

Sigmar made his way through the dark trees, retracing the steps of a day long ago when he had walked into the future with only golden dreams in his heart. He heard the sound of rushing water ahead, and was soon descending into a peaceful hollow, where a shallow waterfall poured into a glittering pool that shone as if strewn with diamonds.

'I should have wed you sooner,' he whispered, seeing the moonlight reflecting on the simple grave marker at the side of the pool. Sigmar knelt before the carved stone, tears of regret spilling down his cheeks as he pictured Ravenna's dark hair and joyous smile.

He rested his hand on the stone and reached up to touch the golden cloak pin he had given her the day they had made love by the river.

'The king of the Unberogen does not celebrate with his people?' asked a voice from the edge of the clearing. 'You will be missed.'

Sigmar wiped a hand across his face and rose to his feet, turning to see an ancient woman, her hair the colour of silver and her eyes buried within a wrinkled face that spoke of dark secrets and forbidden knowledge.

'Who are you?' he asked.

'You know who I am,' said the woman.

'My father warned me of you,' said Sigmar, making the sign of the horn. 'You are the hag woman of the Brackenwalsch.'

'Such a graceless title,' said the hag woman. 'Men give vile names to the things they fear, which only serves to feed that fear. Would men be afraid of me were I called the Joy Maiden?'

Sigmar shrugged. 'Perhaps not, but then you bring precious little joy into our lives. What is it that you want, woman? For I am in no mood for debate.'

'A pity,' said the hag woman. 'It has been some time since I had the chance to speak with someone who appreciates grander things than a hot meal and a soft woman.'

'Speak your piece, woman!' spat Sigmar.

'Such hasty words. So like your father. Quick to anger and quick to promise what should be considered carefully.'

Sigmar made to walk away from the crone, tired of her ramblings, but with a gesture she halted him, his muscles rigid and the breath frozen in his lungs.

'Stay awhile,' she said. 'I wish to talk with you, to know you.'

'I have no such desire,' said Sigmar. 'Release me.'

'Ah, it has been too long since I walked among people,' said the hag woman. 'They have forgotten me and the dread I used to inspire.

You will listen to me, Sigmar, and you must listen well, for I have little time.'

'Little time for what?'

'Events are moving quickly and history is being written minute by minute. These are the days of blood and fire, where the destiny of the world will be forged, and much now hangs in the balance.'

'Very well,' replied Sigmar. 'Say what you have to say and I will listen.'

'The victory against the Thuringians was honourably won, but there is still much to do, young Sigmar. The other tribes must come together soon or all will be lost. You must set off once more. The Brigundians and their vassal tribes must swear their sword oaths to you before the first snows or you will not live to see the summer.'

'My warriors have only just returned from the west,' said Sigmar. 'I will not muster the army again so soon, and even if I could, we would not reach the Brigundians and defeat them before winter.'

The hag woman smiled, and Sigmar was chilled to the bone. 'You misunderstand me. I said that *you* had to set off once more. The tribes of the south-east will not be won over by conquest, but with courage.'

'You wish me to go alone into the wilderness?'

'Yes, for agents of the Dark Gods goad the orcs of the mountains to war. Without enough of the tribes beneath your banner, the greenskins will destroy everything you have built.'

'You have seen this in a vision?' asked Sigmar.

'Amongst other things,' nodded the hag woman, glancing towards Ravenna's gravestone.

'You saw her die?' hissed Sigmar. 'You could have warned me!'

The hag woman shook her head. 'No, for some things are carved in the stone of the world and cannot be changed by mortals or gods. Ravenna was a brief, shining candle that was lit to show you the path and then snuffed out to allow you to walk it alone.'

'Why?' demanded Sigmar. 'Why give me love just to take it away from me?'

'Because it was necessary,' said the hag woman, and Sigmar almost believed he could detect a trace of sympathy in her voice. 'To walk the road you must travel requires a strength of will and purpose beyond the reach of ordinary men, who only crave the comfort of hearth and home. That is what it takes to be a king. This land is yours, and you promised to love it and no other. Remember?'

'I remember,' said Sigmar bitterly.

SEVENTEEN
Chains of Duty

THE LAND SPREAD out before Sigmar, more open than the domain of the Unberogen, and even flatter than the wide plains of the Asoborns. The weeks since leaving Reikdorf had been liberating, and though his departure had provoked furious arguments in the longhouse, his decision to travel alone was proving to be the right one.

'It is madness,' stormed Alfgeir, when Sigmar had announced his intention to go alone into the lands of the Brigundians.

'Insanity,' concurred Pendrag, and once Wolfgart had been dragged from his marriage bed, looking like a whipped dog, he had added his voice to the naysayers. 'They'll kill you.'

Sigmar had listened patiently while all manner of alternatives had been voiced: diplomatic missions led by Eoforth, a quick war of conquest, and even a lightning raid into Siggurdheim to assassinate the Brigundian noble house.

He had listened to every suggestion, but made it plain that he intended to go alone into the wilderness, no matter what his friends and advisors said. As much as it rankled to listen to the hag woman's counsel, the moment he had made the decision to follow her words, a great weight had lifted from him, a weight that he had not even realised was upon him.

As the day turned from morning to afternoon, Sigmar gathered his supplies and marched towards the eastern gate of Reikdorf, passing from his capital and onto the roads that led towards the future.

His brothers had watched him from the walls, and that evening as he prepared a large meal of hot oats and rabbit meat, he had called out to the darkness, 'Cuthwin! Svein! I know you are out there, so I have made enough for three. Come in and take some warmth from the fire, and some food.'

Minutes later, his two scouts emerged from the woodland and wordlessly joined him for the meal. After it was finished, Cuthwin cleaned the pot and plates and the three of them had lain down to sleep in their blankets as the stars emerged from behind the clouds.

By the time the scouts woke, Sigmar was long gone, and neither could find his trail.

Walking through the landscape was an awakening for Sigmar, the sheer immensity of the vista before him expanding the horizons within him. He had been too long in the company of his fellows, and to walk alone in the world with the sun on his skin and the wind at his back was a rediscovered pleasure.

Unberogen lands had changed more than he could imagine in the last ten years, new fields in the lowlands, and herds of cattle, sheep and goats in the hills around Reikdorf. The discovery of new mines had changed the landscape beyond recognition, and a man could walk for days still seeing signs of habitation and no sign of true wilderness.

It was different here. This was the world as it was shaped by the gods: wide plains with rocky hillocks and great sweeps of open grassland. Dark, lightning-wreathed mountains flickered in the far distance of the south and east, and the raw, vital, quality of the land spoke to Sigmar on a level beyond words and mortal comprehension.

The sense of freedom out in the open, separated from all ties of brotherhood, family and responsibility was incredibly liberating, and as Sigmar watched a herd of wild horses thunder across the plains, he suddenly envied them. Ties of iron duty bound him to the Unberogen people and the future, but out here, with only the land for company, Sigmar felt those bonds loosen, and the tantalising prospect of a life lived for himself drifted before him.

A life with Ravenna had been denied him, but he was still young, and the world was offering him a chance to leave behind his life of war and blood, to step from the pages of history and become... become nothing.

Even as the temptation came to him, he knew he would never

succumb to it, for he could not simply walk away from his place in the world and his duty to his people. Without him, the tribes of men would fall and the world would enter a dark age, a bloody age of war and death. In any other man such conceit would be monstrous arrogance, but Sigmar knew that it was simply the bare, unvarnished truth.

He also knew enough to know that ego played a part in his decision, for who would not wish to be remembered down the ages? To know that future generations of warriors might, in ages yet to come, give thanks to his memory, or tell tales of his battles over a foaming tankard of ale?

Yes, he decided, that would be fine indeed.

DAYS AND WEEKS passed beneath the wide skies as Sigmar walked deeper into the south-east, and the dark peaks of the mountains drew ever closer. Though still many miles away, the threat from these colossal, soaring spires at the edge of the world was palpable as though a million spiteful eyes peered out from beneath gloomy crags and plotted the downfall of man.

A spear of purple lightning danced across the heavens, and Sigmar gave thanks to Ulric that his lands were far away from these brooding mountains.

No man would choose to live in such a place without good reason, but Sigmar had seen that the land was rich and dark, and loamy with goodness. To survive and prosper in a land so close to these threatening peaks would take great courage, and Sigmar found his admiration for the Brigundians growing with every step he took towards the heart of their realm.

Sigmar knew next to nothing about Siggurdheim, save what merchants who came to Reikdorf had told of it. The seat of King Siggurd was said to dominate the land around it from a natural promontory of dark rock with a wall of smooth stone around it. Traders spoke of King Siggurd as a wily ruler of great cunning and foresight, and Sigmar looked forward to meeting his brother king.

He had thought to check his route at the few villages he had passed through to buy supplies, but quickly found he had no need to ask, for many trade caravans were travelling south and all were bound for Siggurdheim. The one fact that *was* known of the Brigundians was that they possessed great wealth, trading food and iron ore with the Asoborns and the southern tribes, and even, some claimed, grain with the dwarfs.

As night fell on the fourth week of his travels, Sigmar set up camp next to a small stream, at the base of a jagged hillock that stood proud of the landscape like a lone barrow, its slopes composed of tumbled slabs of masonry and wild, rust-coloured ferns. A family of foxes bared their teeth at him as he set down his pack amid a collection of pottery fragments and began to prepare a fire, but he ignored them and they retreated into their den.

In the shadow of a fallen slab of rock, Sigmar set his fire and prepared a meal of roast deer with meat he had purchased from the last village he had passed through. The meat was tough and stringy, the hunter clearly having loosed his killing arrow while the beast was on the run, but it was rich and flavoursome nonetheless. He scooped some water into a shallow bowl and drank deeply, before washing his hands in the stream.

He lay back on a pillow formed from his armour wrapped in his travelling cloak and gazed up at the stars, remembering looking at these same stars with Ravenna in his arms. Where before such a memory had caused him pain, he now held to it as a precious boon.

Sigmar glanced over at the slab he sheltered behind, seeing patterns in the weathering that he had not previously noticed. The fire threw shadows on the rock, and grooves that Sigmar had thought natural now bore the hallmarks of a deliberate hand.

He sat up and leaned close to the slab, seeing that it had in fact been carved by some ancient hand in a language unknown to him. There were elements of similarity with the script Eoforth and Pendrag had devised, and Sigmar wondered who had written this forgotten message.

He brushed away some of the earth that had collected around the slab, and pulled up the ferns closest to it, seeing more fragments of pottery and the rusted heads of spears. The more Sigmar cleared, the more he saw that he had made camp amid a treasure trove of ancient artefacts, and a chill stole across him as he realised that what he had thought *resembled* a barrow in fact *was* a barrow.

Sigmar shifted a pile of pottery fragments, bronze arrowheads and broken sword blades with his foot, noting the unfamiliar design of the weapons. The swords were curved at the end, but straight at the base, though the handles had long since rotted away, leaving the corroded remains of the tang visible with scraps of leather still clinging to the metal.

Who had this tomb belonged to? Clearly a warrior or someone who wished to be remembered as a warrior. Hundreds of years must have passed since this warrior's interment, and Sigmar wondered if anyone remembered his name. In ages past, this might have been the resting place of a king or a prince, or a great general: a man who thought his fame would live on past his death into immortality.

Here amid the cold winds of the Brigundian plains, a lone man sheltered in the ruins of what might once have been a magnificent memorial to a forgotten ruler. Any dreams of immortality or eternal remembrance were as dead as the barrow's occupant. Such was the vanity of men to believe that their deeds would echo through the ages, and Sigmar smiled as he remembered thinking such thoughts earlier in his travels.

Would anyone remember Sigmar's name in a hundred years? Would anything he had achieved be remembered when the world finally fell? Might some young man in a thousand years camp in the shadow of Sigmar's tomb and wonder what mighty hero lay beneath the earth, little more than food for the worms?

The thought depressed him, and he crouched down beside the slab once more, determined to learn who lay within this tomb, offer a prayer to his spirit and tell him that at least one man remembered him.

Perhaps someone would do the same for him one day.

The script on the slab was faded and hard to make out, but the stark shadows cast by the fire helped pick out the strange, angular shape of the writing. Sigmar had learned the Unberogen script quickly enough, and, while this shared a number of similarities in construction and shape, there appeared to be a great number of pictographic representations that formed the words within each grouping of characters.

Sigmar's lips moved soundlessly as he attempted to read the characters, tracing his fingers over the carved letters. A warm and arid wind whispered through him as he squinted at the writing and the plaintive cry of a night-hunting owl echoed over the plain. Sudden dread seized his heart as he felt a terrible hunger emanating from deep within the mound, a dormant rage born of thwarted ambition and eternal suffering.

Sigmar groaned as he saw the image of a skeletal king in golden armour, lying within a casket of jade and clutching a pair of the strangely curved swords. A cold blue light burned in the eyes of the skull, and a name whispered on the winds that billowed around him.

Rahotep... Warrior King of the Delta... Conqueror of Death...

Sigmar fell back from the slab as though it were afire, the image of the skeletal king at the head of a monstrous army of the dead burning in his mind. Giant warriors of bone and serried ranks of dry, dusty revenants filled the horizon, and the same, terrible, unnatural light burned in the lifeless eyes of every warrior that marched for eternity under the spell of their master's dreadful will.

The hot winds of a far-off kingdom of endless sand and burning sun gusted around him, and Sigmar felt a nameless dread and horror at the thought that this army of the dead had marched across lands that were now home to men.

And might one day march across it again...

Sigmar quickly gathered his possessions and fled from the ancient barrow, the sick feeling of terror in the pit of his stomach fading with every yard that he put between himself and the resting place of the terrible skeletal king. Fear was not an emotion that Sigmar was used to, but the sight of these long-dead warriors had touched the part of him that was mortal, and which dreaded the cold emptiness of being denied his final rest.

For a warrior of the Unberogen, it was the greatest honour to be welcomed within the Halls of Ulric upon a glorious death, but to be denied that for all eternity, and to be forced to walk the earth forever as a mindless thing of death...

Sigmar ran through the night until dawn spilled over the eastern mountains.

SIGMAR HAD WALKED swiftly for four days since making camp in the shadow of the dead king's barrow, passing many farms and villages before finally arriving at Siggurdheim. Numerous rutted earth roads led towards the capital of the Brigundians, and a multitude of laden carts made their way towards the city.

Siggurdheim was as impressive as Sigmar had been led to believe, rearing above a river valley like a jumbled pile of knucklebones that might topple with the slightest push. The town was large, but constrained by the crag it was built upon, and what Sigmar could see of its defences impressed him, though its ruler had unwisely allowed the city to grow beyond the walls.

Many of the trades associated with a town of such size had spilled down the rocky slopes, with mills, tanneries and temples perched on narrow ledges, supported by a dangerous looking arrangement of wooden spars, or jutting precariously from overhangs.

Sigmar joined the road that led up the slopes by the most direct route, and soon found himself amid a press of men and women from all across the lands. He recognised Asoborn tattoos, painted Cherusens and the plaid cloaks of the Taleutens.

Mixed in with those tribes he recognised were several others he did not, harsh-faced men with dark clothing and sullen demeanours. Perhaps these were the Menogoths or Merogens, for who would not be morose living so close to danger?

As Sigmar drew close to the gate, he pulled off his travel cloak and swapped it for a clean red cloak from his pack. He draped it over his shoulders and fastened it in place with his golden cloak pin. Many passers-by admired the pin, and Sigmar glared at a number of would-be thieves until they fled.

Though many of the men were armed with short iron blades or hunting knives, none had a weapon of any significance, and Sigmar lifted Ghal-maraz from beneath his cloak and rested it across his shoulder. As he had expected, gasps of astonishment and whispers of his name spread like ripples in a pool as those around him saw the incredible weapon and pulled away.

Ghal-maraz was known and feared as the weapon of King Sigmar, and few who dwelled in the lands west of the mountains did not know of its great power.

Within moments, Sigmar was marching towards the gate alone, the wonder and majesty of his presence and that of his warhammer clearing a path for him as surely as a hundred trumpeting heralds.

The guards at the gate wore fine hauberks of iron scale, their bronze helmets polished and obviously well cared for. Each bore a long spear with a flaring, leaf-shaped blade, and a short, stabbing sword. Sigmar fought down a smile as he saw their suspicion turn to surprise and then awe as they recognised him.

Few, if any, of these folk would have laid eyes on Sigmar, but the force of his presence, the red cloak, dwarf-forged cloak pin and great warhammer could only belong to one man.

Sigmar halted before the gates of Siggurdheim.

'I am Sigmar, king of the Unberogen,' he said, 'and I am here to see your king.'

'You have come alone from Reikdorf?' asked King Siggurd, his flowing robes brightly coloured and edged with golden thread and soft fur. A golden crown sat upon his brow, its circumference studded with precious stones.

The Great Hall of King Siggurd was a far cry from the fire-lit austerity of Sigmar's longhouse, its walls inlaid with gold and painted with bright frescoes depicting scenes of hunting and battle. Tall windows lit the hall without need for torches or lanterns, but rendered it unsuitable for defence.

Scores of warriors filled the chamber, and Sigmar had been impressed by their discipline as they had escorted him through Siggurdheim towards the king's hall. The town was noisy and thronged with people, its heart alive with shouting voices and ad-hoc markets, selling everything from expensive gold and silver jewellery to fresh meat and brightly dyed cloth.

Every aspect of the town was given over to trade, and every street was packed with merchants and carts transporting their goods to and from the gates or docks. Despite the intense atmosphere, Sigmar had sensed a subtle undercurrent of fear as though the inhabitants kept themselves deliberately busy to avoid dwelling on some nameless fear lurking behind the smiles and shouted haggling.

King Siggurd was an impressive figure, his bearing martial and his build that of a warrior. His long hair was dark, though streaked with white, and his eyes were as cunning as Sigmar had been told they were. His guards were well armoured and carried themselves well, but Sigmar could see fear in their eyes, though of what he could not tell.

'I have indeed walked from Reikdorf,' said Sigmar in answer to King Siggurd's question.

'Why?' asked Siggurd. 'Such a journey is perilous at the best of times, but on your own? With the orc tribes on the march?'

'We have seen no orcs in the Unberogen lands for some years,' answered Sigmar.

'Of course not, for you are far from the mountains, but we are not so fortunate here.'

'I am not surprised,' said Sigmar, 'and it is for that reason that I travelled to your hall, King Siggurd. The lands of men stretch from the mountains on the south and east to the oceans of the north and west, and the tribes of men that dwell within it are the blessed people of the gods. We farm fertile land, we raise our children and we gather around the hearth fires to hear tales of valour, but there will always be those who seek to take what we have from us: orcs, beasts and men of evil character. In the north, I have forged alliances with many tribes, for we were like packs of wild dogs, fighting and scrapping while the wolves grew stronger around us. It is madness to allow petty divisions to keep us apart when our common ancestry should bind us together. In any settlement, all men must aid their neighbours, or they will perish. When one calls for aid, all must answer.'

'A noble sentiment,' said Siggurd, stepping down from his throne and walking towards Sigmar. 'Altruism is all very well, King Sigmar, but it is the nature of man to serve himself. Even when one man helps another, it is usually in the hope that he will receive some reward.'

'Perhaps,' agreed Sigmar, 'but I remember when a fire started in a barn at the edge of Reikdorf last year. The barn was beyond saving, but the owner's neighbours still bent every effort to prevent its destruction.'

'To prevent the fire spreading to their own properties,' pointed out Siggurd.

'No doubt that played a part, yes, but when the fire was extinguished, those same neighbours then helped to rebuild the burned barn. Where was the gain for them in this? Everyone in Reikdorf knows they can count on the people around them to support them in times of trouble, and that shared community is what gives us strength. It is the same with the tribes. I have sworn Sword Oaths with six kings of the north and all our warriors fight as one. When the beasts of the forest kill the settlements of the coast, Unberogen horse archers ride into battle alongside Endal spearmen. When the orcs of the east raid Asoborn villages, Taleuten warriors and Unberogen axemen drive them back into the mountains.'

Siggurd drew level with Sigmar, and he saw that the king's eyes were drawn to Ghal-maraz. Sigmar held the warhammer out for the king of the Brigundians to hold.

'The strength of your sword arm is well known to me, as is the power of your allies,' said Siggurd, taking hold of the warhammer and hefting it in a powerful grip. 'You keep your lands safe with thousands of warriors, who fight with the courage you give them. By strength of arms are your people defended, but we Brigundians prosper more by trade and diplomacy. Brigundian farms provide food for the Asoborns, the Merogens and the Menogoths, and our grain goes to the breweries of the dwarfs. These people are our friends, and through such alliances our lands are made safe.'

Sigmar shook his head. 'There will come a time when diplomacy will avail you nothing, when an enemy comes in such numbers that no tribe can stand before it alone. Join with me in swearing a Sword Oath, and our people will stand together as brothers. Together with the tribes of the south, we will finally be united as a people.'

'All men must stand together?' asked Siggurd, handing Ghal-maraz back to Sigmar.

'Yes.'

'And all men should answer their neighbour if they call for aid?'

'No man of honour would refuse such a call,' said Sigmar.

Siggurd smiled and said, 'Then as your brother king, I ask for your aid in fighting a great evil that plagues my lands.'

'My strength is yours,' said Sigmar. 'What manner of evil troubles your lands?'

'A beast of the ancient times,' said Siggurd. 'A dragon ogre.'

THE PEAKS TO the south of Siggurdheim were dark and hostile, the rocks jagged and the clouds drawn in tight to the mountains' flanks. The air was cold and, within a few hours of climbing, Sigmar was coated in clammy wetness. The hairs on his arms stood erect, and flickering embers of ball lightning danced from the rocks around him.

No sound of wildlife nor cry of birds disturbed the silence, and the only sounds were the skitter of loose shale beneath Sigmar's feet and the echoes of stones falling down the slopes and splashing into dark, silent tarns.

The wind sighed through clefts in the rock, and Sigmar had the uncomfortable feeling that the mountain was groaning in some dreaming pain. His hands were bloody where the razor-edged rocks had cut his palms, and his leggings and tunic were torn open.

Sigmar had left King Siggurd and his warriors in the foothills far below, by the banks of a fast-flowing river that rose in the heart of the mountains. A fair-sized village had been built beside the river, but nothing lived there now. Every building had been gutted by fire or torn down, and the wanton devastation reminded Sigmar of the ruins of the Asoborn villages raided by the forest beasts.

The main road through the remains of the village was dotted with blackened craters that resembled powerful lightning strikes, and Sigmar felt a growing sense of nervous anticipation at the thought of facing a creature that could call upon such power. Then he remembered the leader of the forest beasts and how it had used dark sorcery to hurl deadly bolts of lightning.

It had fallen to his warhammer, and so too would this creature of evil.

A drizzling rain had cloaked everything in grey, and the bitter sense of abandonment was palpable. Sigmar saw that many of the houses had been smashed down instead of burned, not by axe or hammer, but by brute strength.

'This was once Krealheim,' explained Siggurd, sadly, 'one of the many settlements destroyed by the beast. Many believe this to be the first settlement of the Brigundians. It was where my mother and father were raised.'

'And the dragon ogre did all this?' asked Sigmar, aghast. 'One creature?'

'Aye,' nodded Siggurd. 'The dwarfs call it Skaranorak. They say that its strength can crush boulders and its claws can cleave even rune-forged armour. My trackers believe it was driven from the depths of the mountains by the mountain king's slayers and now seeks to prey on us.'

'You have sent hunting parties to destroy the beast?'

'I have, but none have returned,' said Siggurd. 'My son led the last expedition, and I fear greatly for his life.'

'I will slay this Skaranorak for you, King Siggurd,' vowed Sigmar, offering his hand.

'Kill it and you shall have my sword oath,' promised Siggurd, 'and the oaths of the Menogoths and Merogens.'

'Their oaths are yours to give?'

'They are,' said Siggurd. 'Kill the beast and we shall be part of your grand empire.'

Sigmar had found a small fishing boat that was just about sea-worthy, and made his way across the river to begin his climb. Now, with the icy wind slicing down through deep, vertical crevices in the rock, Sigmar was chilled to the bone and his body felt like it was wrapped in freezing blankets.

He found some shelter in the lee of a jutting overhang of black rock, the shadowed hollow beneath it mercifully free from wind and water. Sigmar gathered together the little wood he could find and set a fire, the flickering flames barely warming his numbed body at all. Despite the cold, he slept, tiredness, and the pressing despair that hung over the mountains like a shroud, conspiring to overcome his watchfulness.

When Sigmar awoke it was approaching dawn, the stars invisible above him and a mournful howling coming from far away. No wolf this, but something far more dangerous and unnatural. He had not idea how long he had slept, but the fire was virtually dead and his limbs were frozen in place. He added some kindling to the fire and stretched his legs, massaging the tension from his thighs, and stretched his arms behind his head when the blaze caught.

With his limbs loosened, Sigmar warmed his cloak over the fire and chewed a little cured meat he had brought with him. He drank from a leather waterskin, for he was unwilling to trust the dark streams that tumbled down the mountainside.

'Time to be on my way,' he said, the mountain throwing back his voice in a mocking echo.

Weak sunlight lit the clouds, casting a diffuse glow over the bleak and inhospitable peaks, and Sigmar's spirits fell as he saw how little he had climbed. The low clouds obscured the full height of the mountains, but allowed him a perfect view of the lands below. The greens and golds of the fields and forests seemed to call out to Sigmar, and he ached for the feel of grass beneath his feet and the scent of flowers.

Looking at the sweep of wondrous land below him, it was little wonder that the beasts that dwelled in these forsaken peaks desired to take them for themselves.

For the rest of the day, Sigmar climbed higher and higher, pushing his body past the point where he knew he should turn back. Each time he came close to the edge of endurance, he heard his father's voice in his ear.

'It's all about oaths, Sigmar,' whispered Björn from the Halls of Ulric. 'Honour those you make and others will follow your example.'

And so, Sigmar would climb onwards.

As dawn broke in sheeting rain on the second day of his travels, Sigmar heaved his battered body through a jagged cleft of boulders, every breath like fire in his lungs. He slumped to his knees, breaking clusters of wood beneath him. He was grateful for the brief shelter from the thieving wind, and took a moment to rest before setting off once more.

As his breathing returned to normal, he realised that the pile of splintered wood he knelt upon was in fact brittle, bleached bones. With the realisation came alertness, and Sigmar reached for the reassuring feel of Ghal-maraz. The haft of his warhammer was warm, and he could sense a smouldering anger burning within the weapon, as though some ancestral foe was close by.

Keeping as still as possible, Sigmar took stock of his surroundings: a wide, lightning-blasted canyon formed from great slabs of glistening rock that had collided in ages past and formed a multi-layered plateau filled with an army's worth of shattered bones and skulls.

To Sigmar's left, the side of the mountain fell away into a darkened abyss, its base lost to sight beneath swirling clouds of yellow vapour. Ahead was a yawning cave mouth with a dozen corpses scattered before it. Most were missing limbs, some were missing heads, but all had been partially devoured.

A crackling energy filled the air, fizzing the rain, and Sigmar could see rippling lines of blue fire wreath the head of Ghal-maraz.

He heard a heavy crunch of splintering rock and looked up to see a monstrous creature from his worst nightmares, emerging from the darkness of the cave: Skaranorak.

EIGHTEEN
Skaranorak

A DRAGON OGRE, one of the most ancient races of the world. Sigmar had heard the elders tell tales of the dragons of the deep mountains, and had once even seen the preserved corpse of a hulking warrior that a travelling showman had claimed was an ogre, but nothing had prepared him for the awesome sight of Skaranorak.

It was a thing of flesh and blood, to be sure, but it seemed harder, older and more solid than the mountains it called home. A cloak of winter trailed it, and lightning crowned its head, but its body was a horror of warped, iron-hard flesh. Its lower body was the colour of rust, scaled and hugely muscled like a giant lizard, with powerful, reverse-jointed legs, gripping the rain-slick rocks with yellowed talons like sword blades.

A serpentine tail slithered behind the beast, blue sparks leaping from the iron spikes hammered through its end. The dragon-like form of the beast's lower half merged with the upper body of what resembled a massively swollen man, layered with muscles like forged iron, and pierced with rings and spikes. Great chains dangled from its thick wrists, and Sigmar could only wonder what manner of fool would try to keep such a dreadful beast captive.

Tattoos of dark meaning slithered across its chest as though writhing beneath its skin, and a mane of matted fur, stiffened with blood, ran from the back of its bestial skull to the middle of its back.

The monster's head was horrifyingly human, its features grossly exaggerated and widely spaced across its face, yet altogether recognisable. Its nose was a squashed mass, and its lips were kept forever open by a jutting pair of bloodied tusks.

Beneath a heavily ridged brow of thick bone, eyes of such infinite malice and age that Sigmar could scarce credit they belonged to a living thing surveyed its domain.

With utter certainty, Sigmar knew that the monster was aware of him and was even now seeking him out, its flattened nose wrinkling as it sought to separate his scent from the myriad foetid odours before it.

The monster reached down and lifted a massive, double-bladed axe from the ground next to it, and Sigmar felt a tremor of fear as he saw the enormous size of the blades. Such a weapon could fell an oak with one blow!

'Ulric grant me strength,' he whispered, and regretted it immediately as he saw the beast's head snap towards his hiding place, though it could surely not have heard him over the relentless hammering of the rain and distant booms of thunder.

The dragon ogre let loose a deafening bellow that echoed from the canyon's sides, and charged. It crashed over the rocks, its speed phenomenal for such a large creature, and Sigmar saw a raging fire in its eyes.

He rose swiftly and leapt to the side as Skaranorak's weapon smashed down onto the rocks, the force of the blow sundering boulders and cleaving rock. The axe swept to the side, and Sigmar pressed his body flat against the ground as it whistled over him, a hand's span from splitting him from crown to groin.

Sigmar rolled aside, and swung Ghal-maraz against Skaranorak's exposed flank. The hammer rebounded from the beast's iron hide. He scrambled to his feet and slammed his weapon into the paler flesh above the scaled skin of the dragon, but this blow was just as ineffective.

The dragon ogre lashed out with its foreleg, and Sigmar was hurled through the air, landing on top of a mangled, half-eaten body. He rolled from the bloody corpse and shook his head free of the ringing dizziness that threatened to swamp him.

Thunder boomed, and a jagged fork of lightning slammed into the ground, sending leaping blue flame spinning through the air. The rain beat the earth, and Sigmar swore he could hear hollow laughter in the wake of the thunder.

The dragon ogre came at him once more, but Sigmar was ready for it this time. Again, he swayed aside at the last moment, letting the monster's axe hammer the ground next to him. As the blade bit into the rock, Sigmar leapt towards Skaranorak, slamming his hammer into its chest and drawing a bellow of pain from it.

He landed badly, and lost his footing on the slippery rocks, tumbling to the ground as Skaranorak's axe slashed over him. Sigmar slithered over a jutting overhang, and dropped to a lower level of the plateau as the monster's foot smashed down, leaving a clawed print hammered into the rock.

Sigmar ran for the cover of a jumbled collection of rocky spires, gathered together like a forest of dark stalagmites in a cave. Perhaps here he could find some advantage, for out on the plateau he had none.

He turned as he felt a gathering pressure in the air, and fell back as a colossal peal of thunder roared like the bellow of an angry god, and a spear of vivid lightning ripped the sky apart with its unimaginable brightness.

The bolt struck the dragon ogre full in the chest, and Sigmar's initial elation quickly turned to horror as he saw the creature swell with the terrible energies. Its eyes blazed with power and fire writhed beneath its flesh, as though its very bones were formed from the fury of the storm.

Skaranorak leapt down from the plateau, and the earth seemed to quake at its touch. Sigmar had never known a foe like this, and his every instinct was to flee before its terrible power, for surely no man could stand before such a creature and live.

Sigmar, however, had never once fled before his enemies, and the very fear he felt gave him strength, for what was courage without fear?

He stood straighter and hefted his warhammer as the great beast advanced towards him, its prowling pace deliberate, like a stalking wolf.

Seeing he was standing unyielding before it, the dragon ogre roared and charged once more, its axe sweeping out and smashing one of the stalagmite towers to splintered rock. Sigmar backed away from the beast as it hacked again, splitting yet more of the rock to jagged shards.

Sigmar risked a glance over his shoulder as he led Skaranorak deeper into the forest of stalagmites. He saw that the depthless chasm was close by, noxious yellow tendrils of smoke reaching up from below.

He also saw that he was running out of room to withdraw.

The monster's roars drowned out the peals of thunder that were coming so rapidly that it was like some daemonic drummer hammering on the roof of the world. Flickering lightning lit the skies with an unceasing barrage, and the rain hammered the mountains as though an ocean had been upended from the realm of the gods.

Sigmar gripped his hammer and knew that he would need to make his move soon, for his reserves of strength would only last for so long. The climb from the lands of the Brigundians had left him almost spent, and to fight this monster at the end of such exertion…

The dragon ogre smashed through a pair of stalagmites with brute force, its axe raised high to strike him down. Sigmar vaulted towards a tumbled spire of rock as the axe swept down, and hurled himself towards the beast as the blades passed beneath him.

Sigmar slammed into the beast's chest, his free hand scrabbling for purchase and finding one of the iron rings piercing its flesh. Gripping the ring tightly, Sigmar braced his feet against the monster's stomach and smashed Ghal-maraz into its face.

Skaranorak's howl of pain sheared avalanches of rock from the mountain, and it bucked furiously as it sought to throw off its attacker. Sigmar held fast to the iron ring and slammed his warhammer into the beast's face again, drawing a fresh bellow of rage.

Scalding blood spattered Sigmar, and he roared in triumph as he saw the terrible damage his weapon had wrought upon Skaranorak's face. The flesh around its eyes was a gory mess, blood spilling like tears down the shattered bones of its skull. The monster reared up, and Sigmar hung on for dear life as its clawed forelegs tore at him.

White-hot fire lanced through Sigmar as the monster's talons ripped into his back. He fell from Skaranorak, and cried out in agony as blood flowed from him. The dragon ogre thrashed madly above him, its bulk toppling stalagmites, its howls deafening.

Gritting his teeth against the pain, Sigmar pulled himself upright, swaying as his strength sought to desert him. The blind monster thrashed madly in its agony and rage. Sigmar turned to climb the nearest jagged spike of rock as his vision greyed around the edges. He climbed higher, the rain hammering him and the wind threatening to dislodge him at any second.

A clawed hand slammed into the rock beside him, the talons gouging deep grooves in the stone, and Sigmar lost his grip. He spun madly in the air, hanging by one hand as the rock trembled at the impact.

Skaranorak's bloody face was inches from his, but he had no leverage to strike the monster. It clawed at him, and Sigmar swiftly clambered above its questing hands as they scored the rock in quest of his flesh. More lightning shattered the sky, but the bolts were slamming into the ground without direction, as though without the dragon ogre's guidance they could avail it nothing.

Sigmar hauled himself onto the flat top of the rock spire, and lay flat on his belly, the rumbling quakes of Skaranorak's madness causing it to shake like a reed in the wind. Blue fire crackled around the head of Ghal-maraz, and Sigmar remembered the lightning that had struck it before he had killed the leader of the forest beasts all those years ago.

The power had flowed through him, and he had felt the energies of the heavens surge in his bones, filling his muscles and masking the pain of his wounds.

Below him, Skaranorak tore at the air with its claws, its blindness rendering its attacks haphazard and random. Sigmar felt no pity for the monster, for it was a creature of unnatural origin, its flesh a fusion of warped beasts that were utterly inimical to his kind.

Sigmar lifted Ghal-maraz and rose to his full height as thunder crashed from the sides of the canyon, and a fork of lightning spat from above.

The howling dragon ogre below him was illuminated for the briefest second, its roaring face turned up towards him.

With a roar of anger, Sigmar leapt from the rock, Ghal-maraz held high as Skaranorak's axe struck the spire and smashed it apart. Sigmar landed on the beast's shoulder, and swung his hammer two-handed against the side of its skull.

Driven with all Sigmar's strength and rage, the rune-encrusted head of Ghal-maraz smashed through the thinner bone of Skaranorak's temple and buried itself in the monster's brain.

The dragon ogre's howl of agony died, stillborn, and its enormous bulk crashed through the few spires of rock that still stood. Sigmar gripped the matted hair at the beast's spine as it careened forward, and its body registered the fact that it was dead.

The monster crashed to the ground, the impact splitting the rock beneath it, and Sigmar was thrown clear, his body skidding through the shattered debris of their epic battle. Blood flowed in the rain from his many wounds, and Sigmar groaned in pain as the full weight of his victory settled upon him.

The last breath sighed from the tusked jaws of the dragon ogre, and as it died, the rain and thunder died with it. As Sigmar lay battered and bruised amid the rubble of the rock spires, the rain ceased, and the dark, purple-lit clouds began to disperse.

Sigmar rolled onto his front, groaning with the effort, and using the haft of Ghal-maraz to push himself to his knees. The body of the dragon ogre lay still, and despite the pain, Sigmar smiled. With the beast's death, he had won another three tribes to his banner.

'You were a worthy foe,' said Sigmar, honouring the spirit of so mighty a beast.

The sun broke through the clouds and a shaft of golden light shone upon the mountains.

SUMMER SUN SHONE on rippling fields of corn, and Sigmar felt a deep sense of contentment as he rode along the stone road that led through the hills to Reikdorf. In the two months since his departure from his capital, the fields had grown fruitful and the land had returned the care his people had lavished upon it.

Many farms and villages dotted the landscape as the sun warmed the backs of farmers with their faces to the earth. Sigmar was proud of all that he and his people had achieved, and though there were sure to be hard times ahead, the land was at peace for the moment, and Sigmar was content.

He had returned to the ruined village of Krealheim to find Siggurd and his men camping forlornly by the side of the river. The Brigundian king had wept with joy at the sight of him and the trophies he dragged behind him. After resting on the mountains for a day to recover his strength, Sigmar had cut the great tusks from the dragon ogre's jaw, and had taken his long hunting knife to skin the iron-hard hide from its flanks.

'We thought you were dead,' said Siggurd when Sigmar had crossed the river.

'I am a hard man to kill,' replied Sigmar, breathless from his trek down the mountain.

Sigmar held out the bloody tusks and offered them to Siggurd, who took them and shook his head in amazement and regret.

'Alone you have achieved what our best warriors could not,' said Siggurd. 'The tales of your bravery and strength do you no justice.'

Sigmar reached into a pocket sewn in his cloak, and removed something small and golden. He held it out to Siggurd and said, 'I found this in the beast's lair and thought it should be returned to you.'

Siggurd looked at the object in Sigmar's palm, and his face crumpled in anguish.

'The ring of the Brigundian kings,' he said. 'My son's ring.'

'I am sorry,' said Sigmar. 'I too know the pain of losing a loved one.'

'He was our best and bravest,' said Siggurd, fighting for composure before his warriors. The king took the ring from Sigmar and drew himself upright, squaring his shoulders and looking into the mountain as he drew in a deep, shuddering breath.

'We Brigundians are a proud people, Sigmar,' said Siggurd at last, 'but that is not always a good thing. When first you came before me, I saw an opportunity to be rid of you, for I had no wish to be drawn into what I believed to be your quest to enslave all the tribes with pretty words and high ideals. But when you accepted the task of slaying Skaranorak, I realised that you spoke true and that I had acted selfishly.'

'It does not matter now,' said Sigmar. 'I live and the beast is dead.'

'No,' said Siggurd. 'It *does* matter. I thought I had sent you to your doom, and I have waited here tormented by the guilt of that base deed.'

Sigmar offered his hand to the Brigundian king and said, 'Then our sword oath will mark a new beginning for the Unberogen and the tribes of the south-east. Let us measure our deeds from this point onwards as friends and allies.'

Siggurd's face was pained, but he smiled. 'It shall be so.'

They had left the shattered ruins of Krealheim and returned to Siggurdheim where the giant tusks of the slain dragon ogre were mounted on a great podium in recognition of Sigmar's mighty victory. He had rested and recovered from his wounds, and a week after his return from the mountains, the kings of the furthest tribes had come to Siggurdheim.

Henroth of the Merogens was a barrel-chested warrior with a long, forked beard of red and a heavily scarred face. Thick braids hung from his temples, his eyes were hard as napped flint and his grip strong. Sigmar liked him immediately.

The Menogoth king, Markus, was a shaven-headed swordsman with a lean, wolfish physique and suspicious eyes. His initial manner was cold, but when he saw the tusks Sigmar had taken from the dragon ogre, he was only too eager to obey Siggurd's directive to swear a sword oath with Sigmar.

The four kings crossed their blades over Skaranorak's tusks, and sealed their pact with an offering to Ulric that was witnessed by the priests of the city. After three nights of feasting and drinking, Markus and Henroth had departed for their own kingdoms, for the orcs were on the march, and they had battles of their own to win.

Sigmar had promised Unberogen warriors to their battles, and he watched from the highest tower of Siggurdheim as they and their sword-brothers galloped towards the mountains. At dawn the following day, Sigmar took his leave from his brother king and prepared for the journey back to his own lands.

It had taken him nearly five weeks to reach Siggurdheim on foot, but the journey home would be shorter, for King Siggurd had gifted him a powerful roan gelding with a gleaming leather saddle fashioned by Taleuten craftsmen.

Unlike the horsemen of the Unberogen, who rode their steeds bareback, Taleuten riders went into battle on saddles fitted with iron stirrups, which allowed them to better guide their mounts and fight more effectively from horseback.

In addition, the armourers and garment makers of Siggurdheim had worked together to create a shimmering cloak of scale from the hide that Sigmar had cut from Skaranorak. It was a wondrous thing, and could turn aside even the most powerful sword blow without a mark.

Amid cheering crowds and the sound of singing trumpets, Sigmar rode north for his own lands once more, enjoying the sensation of riding with a saddle, and relishing the prospect of seeing his friends again.

The journey north was uneventful, and Sigmar had once again enjoyed the solitude of travelling through the open landscape. He rode without the sense of liberation that had gripped him as he had left Reikdorf, but the chains of duty that had seemed constricting on the journey south were now welcome.

Sigmar had hoped to arrive quietly and unannounced in Reikdorf, but he had been challenged by Unberogen scouts at the borders of his lands, and word of his return had swiftly travelled back to his capital. He had refused the offer of an escort, and had ridden for Reikdorf through a pastoral landscape of golden cornfields and peaceful villages.

He passed a marker stone in the road that told him he was three leagues from Reikdorf, and urged his horse to greater speed as he saw many lines of smoke etched on the sky, too many for Reikdorf alone.

At last, he came around the side of a rolling embankment and saw the smoke curling from the city, and from the hundreds of cook fires spread in the fields and hills to the north. The flanks of the hills were dotted with makeshift shelters, and thousands of people huddled together beneath canvas awnings or in shelters dug from the earth. From the colours of their cloaks and their dark hair, Sigmar could tell these people were not Unberogen, but who were they and why were they camped before the walls of Reikdorf?

Warriors manned the walls of his capital, and afternoon sunlight glinted on hundreds of spear points and links of mail shirts. The city – it could no longer be called a town – was his home, and the life-giving River Reik glittered like a silver ribbon as it wound around the walls and meandered towards the far distant coast.

Sigmar guided his horse along the south road, and joined the many trade wagons as they made their way towards the city. As he approached the gates of Reikdorf, a great cheer went up as the warriors on the wall recognised him. Within moments, the entire length of the wall was a mass of cheering men, who waved their spears or banged their swords against their shields in welcome.

The gates of the city swung open, and Sigmar saw his closest friends awaiting him.

Wolfgart stood alongside Alfgeir and Pendrag, who held his crimson banner in a gleaming silver hand. Beside Pendrag was a short bearded figure, clad in a long coat of shimmering scale, who wore a winged helm of gold. Sigmar smiled as he recognised Master Alaric and raised his hand in welcome.

Another man Sigmar did not recognise stood behind his friends, a tall, rangy warrior with a bare chest and a single scalp lock trailing down his back from the crown of his head. The man wore bright red leggings and high-sided riding boots, and he carried an ornate scabbard of black leather and gold.

Sigmar put the stranger from his mind as Wolfgart clapped a hand on his horse's neck.

'You took your bloody time,' said his sword-brother by way of a greeting. 'A short journey you said. At least tell me it was successful.'

'It was successful,' said Sigmar as he dismounted. 'We are now brothers with the tribes of the south-east.'

Wolfgart took the horse's reins and gazed quizzically at the arrangement of saddle and stirrups. 'Brigundian?'

Sigmar shook his head. 'Taleuten, a gift from King Siggurd.'

Alfgeir came forward and looked Sigmar up and down, taking in the fresh scars on Sigmar's arms. 'Looks like they didn't join peacefully,' he observed.

'It is a fine tale,' said Sigmar, 'but I will tell it later. First, tell me what is going on? Who are these people camped beyond the walls?'

'Greet your sword-brothers first,' said Alfgeir. 'Then we will talk in the longhouse.'

Sigmar nodded, and turned to Pendrag and Master Alaric. He took Pendrag's silver hand, and was surprised when the fingers flexed and gripped his own.

His sword-brother smiled and said, 'Master Alaric fashioned it for me. Almost as good as the real thing, he says.'

'Better than the real thing,' grumbled Alaric. 'You won't lose *these* fingers if you're clumsy enough to let an axe strike them.'

Sigmar released Pendrag's hand and gripped the dwarf's shoulder. 'It is good to see you, Master Alaric. It has been too long since you visited us.'

'Pah,' grunted the dwarf. 'Was just yesterday, boy. You manlings have such poor memories. I've hardly been gone.'

Sigmar laughed, for it had been nearly three years since he had laid eyes on Master Alaric, but he knew that the mountain folk counted time differently to the race of men, and that such a span of time was as the blink of an eye to them.

'You are always a welcome visitor, my friend,' said Sigmar. 'King Ironbeard prospers?'

'Aye, he does. My king sends me to you bearing grim tidings from the east. Much like this young fellow,' said the dwarf, nodding towards the bare-chested man who stood apart from Sigmar's captains.

'And who are you?' asked Sigmar, turning to face the stranger.

The man stepped forward and bowed before Sigmar. His skin was smooth and his features soft, but his eyes were haunted.

'I am Galin Veneva. I am Ostagoth and come from King Adelhard. It is my people who are beyond your walls.'

* * *

SIGMAR GATHERED HIS warriors in the longhouse to hear Galin Veneva's tale, and it was with a heavy heart that he sat upon his throne and rested his warhammer beside him. The journey home through the peaceful fields and golden sunshine seemed now to be a last gift from the gods before what he knew would be days of blood and war.

The Ostagoth tribesman's voice was heavily accented, and he told his tale haltingly, the memory of the horrors his people had suffered weighing heavily upon him.

Orcs were on the march in greater numbers than had been seen in living memory.

They had come in a green tide from the eastern mountains, burning and destroying all in their path. Entire Ostagoth settlements had been razed to the ground. No plunder had been taken and no captives hauled away, for the greenskins had simply slaughtered the people of the east for the sheer enjoyment of the deed.

Fields were burned and all the forces that King Adelhard could muster were swept away before the might of the orc host. Braying, chanting orc warriors in patchwork armour offered no mercy, and the scattered Ostagoths were no match for the brutal killers.

The men of the east fought on, their king rallying as many men to his banner as possible, while the survivors of the swift invasion fled into the west. Some were even now camped around Taalahim, seat of King Krugar of the Taleutens, but fearing the greenskins would drive onwards, many refugees had continued west to the lands of the Unberogen.

Sigmar well understood Galin's bitterness at being in Reikdorf while his kinsmen fought and died to defend their homeland, but his ruler had tasked him with a solemn duty to meet with King Sigmar and present him with a gift and a request.

Alfgeir tensed as the Ostagoth approached Sigmar's throne, holding a black and gold scabbard out before him.

'This is Ostvarath, the ancient blade of the Ostagoth kings,' said Galin proudly. 'King Adelhard bids me present it to you as a sign of his truth. He pledges you his sword oath, and asks you to send warriors to his lands to fight the orcs. Our people are being slaughtered, and if you do not aid us, we will be dead by the time the leaves fall from the trees.'

Sigmar rose from his throne and accepted the scabbard from Galin, drawing the blade and letting his eyes linger on the fine workmanship of the sword. Ostvarath's blade was polished and smooth, both edges honed to razor sharpness. This was truly a blade fit for a king, and for Adelhard to have sent his own sword was a sure sign of his desperation.

'I accept your king's sword oath,' said Sigmar, 'and I give mine to him. We will be as brothers in battle, and the lands of the Ostagoths will not fall. I give you my word on this, and my word is iron.'

The relief in Galin's face was clear, and Sigmar knew that he wished to return to the east and the battles being fought in his homeland. Sigmar sheathed Adelhard's blade and handed it back to Galin.

'Return Ostvarath to your king,' commanded Sigmar. 'Adelhard will have need of it in the days to come.'

'I shall, King Sigmar,' said the tribesman with relief, before withdrawing from the throne.

Sigmar said, 'Master Alaric? What news do you bring?'

The dwarf stepped into the centre of the longhouse, and his voice was laden with grim authority as he spoke.

'The lad there spoke the truth, the orcs are indeed on the march, but the greenskins attacking his lands will soon retreat to the mountains.'

'How do you know this?' asked Sigmar.

'Because my people will stop them,' said Alaric. 'The warriors of the Slayer King and Zhufbar are even now marching to meet them in battle. But word has reached Karaz-a-Karak of a great horde of orcs, moving up from the peaks of the south and from the blasted lands east of the mountains. A host of greenskins that will make the army ravaging King Adelhard's lands look like a scouting force. This is an army that seeks only to destroy the race of man forever.'

The atmosphere in the longhouse grew close, and Sigmar could feel the tension in every warrior's heart at the news. The greenskin menace had been a constant threat for as long as any man could remember, killing and rampaging throughout the lands of men, but this was no mere raiding force.

Sigmar lifted Ghal-maraz, and his gaze swept over the warriors gathered before him: proud men, courageous men. Men who would stand beside him and face this threat head on: Sigmar's people.

'Send riders to the halls of my brother kings,' ordered Sigmar. 'Tell them I call upon their sword oaths. Tell them to muster their warriors and prepare for war!'

NINETEEN
The Swords of Kings

FROM WHERE SIGMAR stood on the banks of the River Aver, it appeared that the southern lands had been set ablaze. Pyres of dead orcs sent reeking plumes of black smoke into the sky, and what had once been fertile grassland was now a charred, ashen wasteland. The advance of the greenskins had been merciless and thorough, no settlement going unmolested and nothing of value left intact.

Sigmar's anger smouldered in his breast, banked with the need to avenge the last two years of war. He had aged in these last years. His face was lined and tired around the eyes, and the first streaks of silver were appearing in his hair.

His body was still strong, the muscles iron hard, and his heart as powerful as ever, but he had seen too much suffering ever to be young again. His body ached from the days and nights of fighting to hold the bridges over the River Aver, and his many stitched wounds pulled tight as he walked through the Unberogen campsite.

Sigmar was bone weary, and wanted nothing more than to lie down and sleep for a season, but his warriors had fought like heroes, and he spent some time with each sword band, praising their courage and mentioning warriors by name. Dawn had been but a few hours old when the battle had been wón, and now the sky was dark, yet still he could not rest.

Priestesses of Shallya and warrior priests of Ulric also made their way through the campsite, tending to the injured, easing the passing of the mortally wounded, or offering prayers to the Wolf God to welcome the dead into his halls.

Since Master Alaric's warning of the orc invasions, Sigmar had hardly seen the lands where he had grown to manhood. He had returned to Reikdorf only twice in the last two years, but no sooner had he washed the orc blood from his armour and hair than the war horns would sound and he would lead his warriors into the fire of battle once more.

The dwarfs had been true to their word, holding the greenskin tribes from advancing any further into the lands of the Ostagoths, but the warriors of the High King had been forced to withdraw to defend their mountain holds. The time bought with dwarf lives had not been wasted, for King Adelhard had rallied his warriors and had linked with Alfgeir's White Wolves, Cherusen axemen, Taleuten lancers and Asoborn war chariots. In a great battle on the Black Road, Adelhard smashed the orcs and drove the bloodied survivors back to the mountains.

By the time Sigmar had mustered the hosts of his fellow kings to march south-east, the lands of the Merogens and Menogoths were all but overrun, their kings besieged in their great castles of stone. Orcs roamed the lands with impunity and laid waste to the lands of men.

Brutal, green-skinned savages destroyed villages and towns, burning what they could not carry. Thousands died, and only the natural internecine violence of the greenskins had prevented them from spilling west and north with greater speed.

Thousands of refugees flooded the lands of the Unberogen, and Sigmar had given orders that all were to be given shelter. The grain stores were bled dry, and kings from far off lands sent what aid they could spare in an effort to relieve the suffering. The days were dark and filled with despair, and it seemed as though the end of the world had come, for each day more howling warbands of greenskins descended from the mountains, while the armies of men grew weaker.

Sigmar paused by a lone, fire blackened tree atop a small hillock and looked out over the flood plains of the Aver, where the armies of Cherusens, Endals, Unberogen and Taleutens camped. Nearly fifty thousand warriors rested beside their campfires, eating, drinking and offering thanks to the gods that they were not food for the crows.

A limping figure climbed towards him, and Sigmar saw the aged form of the healer, Cradoc, the man who had helped bring him back from the wound Gerreon had inflicted.

'You should rest, my lord,' said Cradoc. 'You look tired.'

'I will, Cradoc,' said Sigmar. 'Soon. I promise.'

'Oh, you promise, do you? I was told always to beware the promises of kings.'

'I thought it was their gratitude?'

'That too,' said Cradoc. 'Now are you going to get some rest, or am I going to have to beat you over the head and drag you?'

Sigmar nodded and said, 'I will. How many?' He did not have to qualify the question.

'I will know for sure in the morning, but at least nine thousand men died to hold these bridges.'

'And wounded?'

'Less than a thousand, but most will not live through the night,' said Cradoc. 'A man felled by an orc rarely survives.'

'So many,' whispered Sigmar.

'It would be more if you hadn't held the bridges,' said Cradoc, wrapping his arms around his frail body. 'I shudder to think of it. The greenskins would have killed us all, and would be halfway to Reikdorf by now.'

'This is just a temporary respite,' said Sigmar. 'The orcs will return. They have an unquenchable thirst for battle and blood. The dwarfs say an even larger host of greenskins gathers east of Black Fire Pass, awaiting the spring to pour across the mountains and wipe us from the face of the world.'

'Aye, no doubt that's true, but that is for another day,' said Cradoc. 'We are alive now and that is what matters. Tomorrow will look after itself, but if you do not rest, then you will be no use to man nor beast. You are a powerful man, my king, but you are not immortal. I have heard you fought in the thick of the battle, and Wolfgart tells me you would have been killed at least a dozen times, but for Alfgeir's blade.'

'Wolfgart talks too much,' said Sigmar. 'I have to fight. I have to be *seen* to fight. I do not wish to sound arrogant, but few men are my equal, and where I fight my warriors fight that much harder.'

'You think me a simpleton?' snapped Cradoc. 'I have fought in my share of battles.'

'Of course,' said Sigmar. 'I did not mean to patronise you.'

Cradoc waved away Sigmar's apology. 'I know the sight of a king risking his life in battle lifts the courage of men. But you are important now, Sigmar, not just to the Unberogen, but to all the tribes of men. Imagine how terrible a blow it would be if you were slain.'

'I cannot simply watch a battle, Cradoc,' said Sigmar. 'My heart is where the blood sings and death watches to take the weak.'

'I know,' said Cradoc sadly. 'It is one of your less appealing characteristics.'

WITH THE ARMIES already gathered in the south, King Siggurd had offered his allies the hospitality of his city, and a council of war was convened. The king of the Brigundians greeted the rulers of the tribes as they arrived at the golden doors of his great hall, and Sigmar's heart swelled with pride as he knew he was witnessing a gathering such as had never before been seen in the lands of men.

A great circular table had been set up in the middle of the hall, and a brazier of coals burned brightly at its iron centre. Sigmar, Wolfgart and Pendrag stood at their appointed places around the circle and watched as the arrival of each king was announced.

Marbad of the Endals was first to arrive, flanked by his eldest son, Aldred, and two tall Raven Helms in black cloaks and fine mail shirts. King Marbad nodded a greeting, and Sigmar frowned as he saw the venerable king of the Endals turn pale as he noticed Pendrag's silver hand.

Marbad was followed by Aloysis of the Cherusens, a lean, hawk-faced man with long dark hair and a neatly trimmed beard.

Next to enter were Queen Freya and Maedbh. Sigmar felt Wolfgart stand taller behind him at the sight of his wife, for it had been many months since they had been together. The Asoborn queen favoured Sigmar with a sly smile, and ran her hand across her belly before seating herself across from him.

King Krugar of the Taleutens was announced, and he marched into the hall with two hulking warriors in silver scale armour at his side. King Wolfila of the Udose tribe, clad in his finest kilt and pleated sash, entered the hall and offered a raucous greeting to the room. Two bearded clansmen of fearsome appearance accompanied the northern king, their beards and hair wild, and their broadswords carried lightly over their shoulders.

Representing the forces of the northern marches, Myrsa of the Fauschlag rock led a pair of warriors armoured in gleaming suits of plate, and Sigmar nodded to the Warrior Eternal as he took his place at the table.

Otwin of the Thuringians arrived next, and Sigmar did a double take as he saw who had come with the berserker king, for it was none other than Ulfdar, the warrior woman he had fought before facing Otwin. Both were virtually naked, clad only in loincloths and bronze torques.

King Markus of the Menogoths and Henroth of the Merogens arrived together, and Sigmar was shocked at the change in them since he had seen them two years ago. The sieges of their castles had only recently been lifted. Both men were painfully thin, and the dreadful suffering of their people haunted their eyes.

Adelhard of the Ostagoths was last to arrive, accompanied by Galin Veneva, and Sigmar liked the look of the eastern king immediately. The Ostagoth king stood tall and broad, his pride restored after the great victory on the Black Road, and his gratitude evident in the respectful nod he gave Sigmar before taking his seat at the table.

With all the oath-sworn tribal rulers gathered, Siggurd closed the doors of his hall and took his place at the table as a host of servers stepped forward and placed a silver goblet of rich red wine before each ruler.

Siggurd stood to address the gathering. 'My friends, I welcome you to my hall. In these dark days, it fills my heart with joy to see rulers from all across the lands beneath my roof.'

The Brigundian king lifted his goblet and said, 'This wine is valued above all others by my warriors, for it is only ever drunk in celebration of the greatest of victories. After two years of fighting, we have won such a victory, and driven the greenskins back to the mountains. Savour its sweet flavour and remember it, for a great battle awaits us at Black Fire Pass in the spring, when you will taste it again. Welcome, all.'

Fists were banged on the table as Siggurd took his seat, and Sigmar stood with his own goblet raised.

'Fellow kings,' he began.

'And queens!' shouted Maedbh good-naturedly.

'And queens,' smiled Sigmar, nodding towards Freya. 'King Siggurd speaks the truth, for it is a grand thing to see you all here. We are all bound together by oaths of loyalty and friendship, and it gives me hope to know that such warriors of courage and heart are gathered here.'

Sigmar pushed his chair back and began to walk around the circular table, his goblet still held out before him. 'These last years have been dark indeed, and doomsayers walk the land, tearing at their flesh and wailing that these are the End Times, that the gods have turned from us. The gods have abandoned us to our doom, they say, but I do not accept that. The gods have given us many strengths. They have given us the wit to recognise those strengths, and also the humility to see our weaknesses. What are these if not gifts from the gods? I say the gods help those who help themselves, and this gathering is another step towards final victory.'

As he reached Marbad, Sigmar placed a hand on the Endal king's shoulder.

'Since my father's death I have travelled these lands and seen those strengths first hand. I have seen courage. I have seen determination. I have seen fire, and I have seen wisdom. I have seen them in the deeds of every man and woman in this hall. I have fought alongside many of you in battle, and I am proud, so very proud, to count you as my sword-brothers.'

Sigmar lifted his goblet high. 'Oaths of man have brought us together, but ties of blood bind us even closer.'

The gathered rulers lifted their goblets, and as one, drank the victory wine.

'NEVER!' SHOUTED THE king of the Taleutens. 'Surrender command of my warriors to another? The gods would strike me down at such cowardice!'

'Cowardice?' retorted King Siggurd. 'Is it cowardice to recognise that we must fight as one or else be destroyed? I know you, Krugar, it is not cowardice that stays your hand, it is pride!'

'Aye,' nodded Krugar, 'pride in the courage and strength of the Taleutens. The same pride my warriors have in me for leading them in battle these last twenty-three years. Where will that pride be if I am to stand idly by while another leads them?'

'Whisht, man, it will still be there!' cried Wolfila. 'Any man who's fought alongside Björn's son knows there's no shame in granting him command. When the wolves of the Norsii were hammering at the gates of my castle, who was it drove them away? You were there, I grant you, Krugar, and you too Aloysis, but Sigmar it was who scattered them and drove them across the sea!'

'I share Krugar's unease at surrendering command,' put in Aloysis, 'but if we each fight as individuals, the greenskins will destroy us one by one. I am a big enough man to allow my Cherusen to fight under Sigmar's strategy.'

Sigmar nodded to the Cherusen king in thanks for his support.

'I will be no spectator in battle,' said Adelhard, drawing his sword and laying it on the table. 'Ostvarath hungers to be wetted in orc blood.'

'You will be no spectator,' snapped Freya. 'Like a true warrior, you will be in the fire of battle, where Ulric's wolves await to take the dead to their rest. I will fight alongside Sigmar, for I know the strength in his blood. If any one of us is to take command, it must be Sigmar.'

'And what of the Bretonii and the Jutones?' asked Myrsa. 'Their kings do not join us?'

'Marius?' spat Marbad. 'The man is a snake. I'd sooner have the Norsii on my flanks than that conniving whoreson. At least with the Norsii you know where you stand.'

'Be that as it may,' said Sigmar. 'I will send emissaries to the Jutones to offer King Marius another chance to join us.'

'And when he refuses?' asked Marbad. 'What then? His lands will be kept safe by the deaths of our warriors, but he will shed no tears for them. He will wring his hands and think us fools. Such a man has no honour, and does not deserve a place within the lands of men.'

As much as he loved the aged king, Sigmar knew that Marbad's hatred of the Jutones ran too deep to be assuaged.

'Then we will deal with Marius when the threat of the orcs is dealt with,' said Sigmar.

One by one, the remaining kings spoke up, and the debate swung back and forth as they danced around the issue of command. Though each king spoke highly of Sigmar, and expressed their respect for his deeds and vision in gathering them together, few were willing to surrender command of their warriors to another.

Sigmar felt his temper fraying with every hour that passed, the same arguments swirling around the table time and time again. He could see everything he had tried to build over the last decade and more slipping away.

At last he rose and placed Ghal-maraz heavily on the table before him. All eyes turned to him, and he leaned forward, placing both hands palm down on the tabletop.

'So this is how the race of man will die?' he asked softly. 'Bickering like old women instead of standing before our enemies with bloodied weapons in our hands?'

'Die? What are you talking about?' asked Siggurd.

'This,' said Sigmar, contempt dripping from his words. 'A lesser race stands poised to destroy us, and we *still* find it in our hearts to fight amongst ourselves. Orcs are brute savages, creatures that live only for destruction. They build no farms, they work no land and they murder any who stand before them. By any measure of reckoning they are less than us, and yet they are united while we are divided by pride and ego. It grieves me to think that all we have achieved and the great strides we have made to bring our peoples together will end in such petty squabbles.'

Sigmar stood straight and lifted Ghal-maraz, holding it out before him. 'King Kurgan Ironbeard told of how I came by this hammer at my father's funeral, and he reminded me that this great warhammer is not just a tool of destruction, but one of creation. The blacksmith's hammer forges the iron that makes us strong, but Ghal-maraz is much more than a blacksmith's hammer. It is a king's hammer, and with it I dreamed of forging an empire of man, a realm where all men could live in peace, united and strong. But, if we cannot put aside our pride, even when it means our doom, then I will have nothing more to do with this gathering. I will return to Reikdorf and prepare to fight any orc that dares to venture onto Unberogen lands. I will expect no aid from any of you, and will offer none if asked. The greenskins will come and they will destroy us. It may take them many years, but make no mistake, they will do it. Unless you stand behind me in battle.

'Fight under my command, do what I say and we may live through this trial. Make your decision now, but remember, united we live, divided we die.'

Sigmar sat back down and placed Ghal-maraz back on the table before him. None of the tribal kings dared break the cold silence that followed until Marbad rose and moved to stand beside Sigmar. The king of the Endals drew Ulfshard, the shimmering blade forged by the craft of the fey folk, and laid it beside Ghal-maraz.

'I have known Sigmar since he was a lad,' said Marbad. 'I fought alongside his father and his grandfather, Redmane Dregor. All were men of courage, and it shames me that I ever doubted the wisdom of his course. I welcome the chance to fight at Sigmar's side, and if that means placing my warriors under his command, then so be it. How many years have we spent at war with one another? How many sons have we buried? Too many. Our strength was divided until Sigmar united us, and now we want to shy away from allowing him command of our armies? No longer will I stand apart from my brothers.

The Endals will fight under Sigmar's command.'

Marbad gripped Sigmar's shoulder, and said, 'Björn would be proud of you, lad.'

Adelhard rose from his seat and circled the table, drawing Ostvarath as he walked. He too placed his blade beside Sigmar's weapon. 'My people owe you their lives. How could I not stand behind you?'

Next came Wolfila, who placed his great broadsword beside the other swords of kings.

One by one, each of the gathered rulers set their weapons beside Sigmar's warhammer.

Last to place his weapon was Myrsa, the Warrior Eternal of the Fauschlag rock, placing a heavy warhammer with a leather-wound grip and iron head in the shape of a snarling wolf next to Ghal-maraz.

'I am no king, Lord Sigmar,' said Myrsa, 'but the warriors of the north are yours by right and by choice. What would you have us do?'

Sigmar stood, honoured and humbled by the faith his brother kings had shown him.

'Go back to your lands, for winter is almost upon us,' said Sigmar. 'Allow your warriors to return to their families, for it will remind them why they fight. Gird yourselves for war and march your armies to Reikdorf in the first month of spring with sharpened swords and hardened hearts.'

'And then?' asked Myrsa.

'And then we will take the fight to the greenskins,' promised Sigmar. 'We will destroy them at Black Fire Pass, and secure our lands forever!'

TWENTY

Defenders of the Empire

'Leave me, boy,' gasped Svein, blood bubbling from the corners of his mouth. 'You... know you... have to.'

'Hush up there, old man,' snapped Cuthwin, hauling his friend and mentor's body around a loose tumble of snow-covered rocks, and propping him upright. Blood coated Svein's leather jerkin and stained his woollen leggings. The wound was plugged with a strip of cloth, but blood still leaked from the hole, leaving an easily followed trail of red dots on the snow.

Cuthwin was exhausted, and he took a moment to regain his breath as he scanned their back trail. There was no sign of pursuit yet, but there would be. The smell of blood would draw the goblins, even if they were somehow unable to follow the trail he had been forced to leave while carrying his wounded friend.

The goblin's arrow had come out of nowhere and struck the older scout in the small of the back, punching through his jerkin and jutting from his belly. A host of the squealing monsters had leapt from the darkness, serrated knives and stabbing swords bright in the moonlight.

Tiny hooded things that smelled of animal dung and rotten meat, the goblins were darting figures clad in ragged black robes that hid their cruel, pointed faces and needle-like teeth. Cuthwin killed the first two, and Svein had killed a third before they had closed in a flurry of rapid, slashing squeals.

Their weight had borne Svein to the ground, but Cuthwin had kicked them clear, stabbing with his sword and hunting knife. Even wounded, Svein had fought like a hero, snapping necks and gutting the foul little creatures with quick twists of his knife. More arrows had clattered against the rocks, and the struggling goblins had shrieked in terror at their fellows' lack of care for their lives, turning and fleeing into the darkened crevices of the mountains.

With the goblins fled for the time being, Svein had dropped to his knees, and Cuthwin had rushed to his friend's side. The arrow piercing his body was a crude thing, and Cuthwin snapped off the stone head and quickly slid the shaft from Svein's body.

'Ach... they've done for me, lad,' said Svein. 'Leave me, and get on back to the armies.'

'Don't be daft,' he said. 'You'll be fine. You're too big and ugly to die from this little pigsticker.'

Cuthwin swiftly plugged the wound, and hooked an arm under Svein's shoulder before hauling him to his feet. Svein grunted in pain, but Cuthwin could not afford to waste any time, knowing that the goblins would return when their fragile courage was bolstered by numbers.

Throughout the night, he bore his friend westwards to the gates of the mountains, and safety. Winter's grip had finally loosened on the mountains at the edge of the world, but the armies of the tribal kings were camped far from the mouth of the pass. If Svein could survive long enough, Cuthwin could get him to the apothecaries who would heal his wound.

As the night dragged on, however, and the wound continued to bleed, Cuthwin feared that the goblin's arrow had pierced one of his friend's kidneys and that he was bleeding internally. He also knew that goblin arrows were often coated in animal faeces, and it was more than likely that Svein's wound was already infected.

Morning's light brought little hope to Cuthwin, for Svein's colour was terrible, his face ashen and his cheeks sunken. Looking at him, he knew that his friend would be lucky to live another hour, let alone return to their fellow warriors.

Cuthwin felt tears prick at his eyes, and angrily wiped them away. He had known Svein for over half his adult life, and the big man had taught him the deepest mysteries, fieldcraft and survival, becoming the surrogate father he had never known since the greenskins killed his family many years before.

In the months they had spent in the mountains, the two scouts had encountered many goblin bands, and they'd had the best of all those encounters. Cowardly creatures, the goblins would attempt to strike from ambush, but Cuthwin and Svein had craft beyond the cunning of mere goblins, and had evaded all such ambushes.

The mountains at the eastern edge of the world were home to all manner of foul creatures, goblins among the least of them, and three times they had been forced to hide to avoid the attentions of trolls and, once, a lumbering giant. The danger was incredible, but Sigmar had tasked them with gathering information on the movements and strength of the greenskin horde gathering in the mountains.

When they had reached the eastern mouth of the pass, they had seen the full extent of the orc army. Though he had seen it with his own eyes, Cuthwin could still scarcely believe the size of the orc horde, a swelling ocean of green flesh that filled the ashen plains beyond the mountains as far as the eye could see. Thousands of tribal banner poles dotted the plains, and the smoke from the greenskins' fires cast a dark shadow over the entire landscape.

The boom of war drums echoed from the mountainsides, and the shouts and bellows of chanting orcs was like the roar of an angry god. Giant idols had been erected, enormous wicker effigies of foul orc deities, and Cuthwin's anger had threatened to overwhelm his sense when they were burned, and he saw that each one was filled with screaming men, women and children.

Following the burning of the idols, a huge winged creature with a serpentine neck and loathsome reptilian skin took to the air, a monstrously armoured warlord astride its back. Even over the tramp of marching feet and bellowing roars of the orcs, Cuthwin could hear this mighty beast's roar of hatred.

The horde began its march into the mountains, its movement fitful, and without the cohesion of an army of men. Packs of wolves roamed ahead of the seething host, and hideous monsters lurched alongside the tens of thousands of orcs.

Despite the snow that still lay in thick drifts, the greenskins were marching for the pass.

Both Cuthwin and Svein knew that unless Sigmar was warned the orcs were on the move, the greenskins would be through Black Fire Pass before the armies of men could stop them.

Haste had made Cuthwin and Svein incautious, and as they rested on the tenth day of their travels west, the goblins had finally caught them.

Svein would now pay with his life for their carelessness.

The news they carried was of vital import to Sigmar's force, yet Cuthwin found that he could not leave his friend to die alone on the mountains.

'You have to go,' said Svein, as though guessing his thoughts.

'No, I can't leave you here,' protested Cuthwin. 'I can't.'

'Aye, lad,' said Svein. 'That's exactly what you have to do. This wound is the death of me, and you know it.'

Cuthwin heard a soft scrape, as of rough cloth on rock, and knew that their pursuers had found them. Svein had heard it too, and he leaned forward to grip Cuthwin's tunic, his face creased in pain and determination.

'They're coming now and if you don't get to Sigmar, then I died for nothing, you understand me?'

Cuthwin nodded, his throat constricted and his eyes tearful.

'Give me that bow,' said Svein. 'You won't need it... and you'll be quicker on your feet without it.'

Cuthwin quickly strung the bow he carried, and handed it to Svein, propping a quiver of arrows against the rocks as his friend drew his sword and laid it on the ground next to him.

'Now, be off with you, eh?' said Svein. 'And may Taal guide your steps.'

Cuthwin nodded, and said, 'Ulric's hall will be open to you, my friend.'

Svein nodded. 'It'd bloody well better be. I don't plan on dying a hero's death for nothing. Now go!'

Cuthwin turned and slipped through the rocks, leaving a trail that would take more cunning than any goblin possessed to follow.

He had travelled less than a hundred yards when he heard the first squeals of dying goblins, followed swiftly by the clash of blades, and then nothing.

THE MEROGENS CALLED them the Worlds Edge Mountains, and Sigmar knew that the name was well deserved. Grim sentinels at the very edge of the known world, there was little beyond them that was understood, and much that was feared. Towering peaks of grey rock soared above the landscape, reaching to the heavens and piercing the sky with their immensity.

Snow lay in thick shawls over the slopes, and stands of pines scented the air with a freshness that Sigmar found welcoming after the stench of thousands of warriors on campaign.

Spring's boon was upon the wind, and with it the promise of a year of blood and courage.

The sun was low on the eastern horizon, shimmering through the haze of early morning and framed by the towering escarpments that marked the sheer sides of Black Fire Pass. The day Sigmar had been preparing for all his life had finally arrived, and he could feel the potential of it pressing against the inside of his skull.

Today would see the race of man doomed or triumphant.

Eoforth had woken him from a dream in which he had supped from a cup of blood with Ulric himself, and eaten meat ripped from the bones of a freshly hunted stag. A pack of wolves with bloody snouts circled him, and their howls were music to his ears.

He had told Eoforth of the dream, and the old man had smiled. 'A good omen, I think.'

Sigmar's silver breastplate sat upon an armour tree, gleaming and embossed with a golden comet with twin tails of fire. His winged helm shone as though new, and his greaves of bronze were worked with silver wolves.

Eoforth had helped him don his armour, and as Sigmar lifted Ghal-maraz, he felt a thrill of excitement pass through him. The ancestral weapon of King Kurgan also appreciated the significance of this day. Eoforth then handed Sigmar a golden shield, rimmed with iron, with a carved boss at its centre, depicting a snarling boar's head.

Sigmar emerged from his tent, and a great cheer erupted from hundreds of throats as the warriors camped nearest saw him. The rest of the army soon took up the cheer as word spread, and soon the mountains shook with the deafening roar of thousands of warriors.

The land of the wide plains before the gates of the mountains were filled with warriors, horses and wagons, for Sigmar and Wolfgart had travelled throughout the lands of men to ensure that the other tribes were keeping to the pledge they had made in King Siggurd's hall.

Their travels took them to the far corners of the land, and both men were pleased to see that there were no dissenters. Even those kings who had not attended were approached afresh with promises of honour and glory, but to little avail.

Each emissary to King Marius of the Jutones had been rebuffed, and King Marbad of the Endals brought word that the Bretonii had also refused to send any aid, leaving their homes and marching south across the Grey Mountains to distant lands. As unwelcome as the news was, Sigmar knew that the departure of the Bretonii was a blessing for the Endals, who now had fresh land into which their people could expand.

As the first month of spring had drawn closer, an ambassador from the west had presented himself before the gates of Reikdorf with word from the king of the Jutones.

Sigmar's heart had been full of hope for the meeting, but it had been cruelly dashed when the ambassador, a thin, stoop-shouldered man named Esterhuysen, had presented him with a bow of wondrous quality, the wood golden and shaped with such craft as only the fey folk across the ocean were said to possess.

'King Marius offers you this token of his best hope,' said Esterhuysen, bowing low. 'Regrettably, he can spare you no warriors for your war in the south, but he hopes that this magnificent weapon will bring you luck in all your endeavours.'

Sigmar had taken the bow, a truly wondrous artefact of incalculable worth, and broken it over his knee.

He hurled the broken pieces at the shocked Esterhuysen's feet. 'Leave my city,' said Sigmar. 'I need no luck to defeat the greenskins, I need warriors. Return to your miserable home, and tell your coward king that there will be a reckoning between us when this war is won.'

The ambassador had been all but hurled from the western gates, and it had taken all of Sigmar's self-control not to order an immediate attack on Jutonsryk.

Though the refusal of the Jutones to fight was a crushing disappointment to Sigmar, every ruler who had attended the Council of Eleven – as men were calling the momentous gathering in King Siggurd's hall the previous year – had been true to their word, and had marched to Reikdorf with their glittering hosts of warriors.

Like spring itself, it had been a sight to lift the hearts of all who saw it, and was a potent symbol of all that had been achieved over the last year. Throughout the winter, the forges of the Unberogen and every other tribe of men had worked night and day to craft swords, spears and arrowheads, and lances for the Unberogen cavalry.

Vast swathes of forest had been felled to provide fuel for the furnaces, and every craftsman, from bowyers and fletchers, to clothmakers and saddlers, had worked wonders in producing the less martial, but no less essential, supplies needed for an army about to march.

Winter was normally a time of quiet for the tribes of men, when families shuttered their homes and huddled around fires as they waited for Ulric to return to his frozen realm in the heavens, and his brother Taal to bring balance to the world in the spring.

With the prospect of war looming, however, every household had spent the cold months preparing for the coming year, ensuring each of its sons was equipped with a mail shirt and sword or spear. Entire herds were slaughtered, and the meat cured with salt to provide food for the thousands of warriors who would march into the fires of battle.

Within a week, the armies of the kings had mustered, and a host unlike any seen before had prepared to march to war. The Blood Night feasts were raucous and full of good humour, but also sadness, for many of those leaving in the morning would not return, leaving wives without husbands and children without fathers.

Sigmar and his brother kings had made sacrifices to Ulric, and offerings to the Lord of the Dead and the goddess of healing and mercy, Shallya. All the gods were honoured, for none dared anger even the least of them for fear of dreadful consequences in the battle ahead.

As the kings gathered on the morning of departure, Sigmar presented each one with a golden shield identical to his own, the design and workmanship exquisite. Pendrag had laboured long over the winter to create the shields, forging one for each of the allied kings of men. The outer circle of each was decorated with the symbols of the twelve tribes, and as Master Alaric had promised, Pendrag's skill with metal was greater than ever before.

'As you pledged me your swords last year,' Sigmar had said, 'I now give you each a shield to defend your body and your lands. We are the defenders of the land and this gift symbolises our union.'

Amid great cheering, the kings had renewed their oaths of loyalty, and the march south had begun to the sound of war horns, drums and boisterous pipe music.

For the first few weeks, the journey was made in high spirits, but as the shadow of the mountains grew darker, the easy banter soon petered out. The enormity of what was to come was lost on no one, and every man knew that each mile brought him closer to death.

The pace had not been forced, for the mountains were still cloaked in snow and the passes blocked, but that had changed when Cuthwin had staggered into the camp bringing word that the orcs were already on the march and that the snows were thinning in the pass. Sigmar was grieved to hear of Svein's death, but had put aside his sorrow to galvanise his warriors to greater urgency.

That urgency had been understood, and the men had marched with a mile-eating stride that saw them climbing into the mountains beneath a cold spring sun. Wrapped tightly in fur cloaks, the men of the tribes made no complaint or oath as they climbed higher and higher to where the air was thin and wind whistled down from the rocks with teeth like knives.

Sigmar looked up into the mountains, the craggy peaks dwarfing him and uncaring of the great drama about to be played out in their shadows.

This was Black Fire Pass.

This was where everything would be decided.

SIGMAR, ALFGEIR AND Wolfgart rode out ahead of the army of men as the sun rose higher, bathing the mountains in gold, and shining on over a hundred thousand glittering weapons. The ground was hard-packed and sandy, trampled flat by uncounted marching feet over the centuries.

Since the earliest days, Black Fire Pass had been the main route of invasion over the mountains, and it was easy to see why. Even this, the narrowest point of the pass, was nearly two miles wide, hemmed in by sheer cliffs on either side.

Black Fire Pass was a natural corridor from the blasted landscapes of the east to the fertile lands of the west, and Sigmar paused to look back on the assembled host of men.

The breath caught in his throat as he took in the awesome scale of the army of men: his army.

Warriors filled the pass from side to side without interruption, great blocks of swordsmen, standing shoulder to shoulder with spearmen and chanting berserkers.

Thousands of snorting horses stamped the ground, and Wolfgart's skill as a horse breeder was evidenced by almost all of the riders' steeds wearing iron barding. Most of the mounted warriors also carried tall lances, long lengths of wood with sharpened iron points. Heavier than a spear, these lances were deadly weapons, only made possible by the addition of stirrups to the Unberogen saddles. Clad in heavy plate armour, the riders were iron giants that would ride over the orcs in a roaring thunder of hooves.

Only Alfgeir's White Wolves had refused to take up the lance, for they were men of fiery courage, who desired to ride through the heart of the battle with their hammers crushing the skulls of the foe in honour of their lord and master.

Hundreds of Asoborn chariots were drawn up on the left flank, Queen Freya at their head, resplendent in a breastplate of gold with her wild, red hair unbound and pulled into great spikes of crimson. Maedbh rode beside her, and both women raised their spears as Sigmar and Wolfgart passed.

Taleuten horsemen ranged ahead, riding energetically along the line of the army, their crimson and gold banners trailing magnificently behind them.

The Raven Helms of King Marbad surrounded their king and his son, ready to take the fight to the orcs as soon as the word was given. Kilted Udose clansmen drank distilled grain liquor from wineskins, and waved their swords like madmen as a group of warriors armoured from head to foot in gleaming plate looked on with grim amusement. Myrsa, the Warrior Eternal, led these warriors, some of the strongest men in the west, men who fought with enormous greatswords said to have been forged by the dwarfs.

In the centre of the army were Sigmar's Unberogen warriors, fierce men who had fought for their king since Björn's death. No finer warriors existed in the land, and even the frothing, berserk warriors of King Otwin accorded them a nod of respect as they took their position in the battle line.

Merogens and Menogoths stood side by side, eager to take their vengeance upon the enemy that had ravaged their lands the previous year, their swords and axes blessed by the priests of Ulric to seek orc throats. Brigundian warriors in gaudy cloaks and intricate armour stood alongside their southern brothers, and King Siggurd shone like the sun in a suit of magnificent golden armour said to have been enchanted in ages past.

A forest of coloured banners fluttered and snapped in the wind, and as Sigmar saw the multitude of different tribal symbols, he smiled and whispered a short prayer to the spirit of his father. Almost overwhelmed by the spectacle of so much martial power, Sigmar turned away and rode on towards the warriors waiting by the ruins of a crumbling watchtower.

The warriors of Kurgan Ironbeard, High King of the dwarfs, were grim and unmoving, without the animation and cheering that echoed from the men behind Sigmar. Fully encased in hauberks of shimmering silver metal and plates of gleaming iron, the dwarfs appeared as immovable as the mountains through which they passed.

Thick beards and long braids were all that indicated that they were living creatures of flesh and blood at all, such was the weight of metal protecting them. The warriors carried mighty axes or heavy hammers, and Sigmar raised Ghal-maraz in salute of their bravery as he rode towards the watchtower.

The ruined state of the watchtower spoke of the battles that had been fought there, but Sigmar knew that what was to occur here today would eclipse them all. The forces gathered here were beyond comprehension, and the thought that such a host of men was his to command left Sigmar breathless.

Sigmar dismounted, and tethered the roan gelding to a withered tree. He ducked beneath the low lintel of the doorway and made his way to the stairs, the rise of each step smaller than he was used to. Wolfgart and Alfgeir followed him inside the dwarf-built tower, which, despite the ravages of time and battle, was relatively intact within.

He emerged onto the roof of the tower to find King Kurgan Ironbeard awaiting him, flanked by two stout dwarf warriors with mighty axes, and the silver armoured form of Master Alaric. The dwarf king sat on a wide firkin and slurped from a tankard of ale.

'You came then?' asked Kurgan.

'I said I would,' replied Sigmar, 'and my father taught me to be a man of my word.'

'Aye, he was a good man, your father,' said Kurgan, taking a great mouthful of ale and wiping his beard with the back of his hand. 'Knew the value of an oath.'

The dwarf king nodded his head to the east. 'So what do you think?'

Sigmar followed the king's gaze, seeing a desolate plain that began to slope downwards, becoming progressively rockier the further eastward it fell. He looked to his left and right, and said, 'It's good ground, and this is the narrowest part of the pass is it not?'

'Aye,' said Kurgan. 'That it is, young Sigmar.'

'The greenskins will not be able to use their numbers against us, and the cliffs will prevent them from flanking us.'

'And?'

Sigmar struggled to think what he might have missed.

'And the slope will slow them,' put in Wolfgart. 'They'll be tired when they get to the top. Gives our archers more time to shoot the greenskin bastards.'

'And there's that rock further back, Sigmar,' said Alaric. 'The Eagle's Nest, we call it. It would be a good place from which to direct the battle, elevated, yet safe from attack.'

Sigmar let the suggestion hang in the air for a moment before answering.

'You are suggesting I do not fight in the battle?'

'Not at all,' said Alaric. 'Merely that you direct the battle from safety before deciding where best to strike when the time comes.'

'Would you do this?' asked Sigmar of King Kurgan.

'No,' admitted Kurgan, 'but then I'm a stubborn old fool, lad. My fighters tend to get a bit lost without me there to show them how to kill grobi.'

'I shall not skulk behind my men,' said Sigmar. 'This battle will not be won by stratagems and ploys, but with strength of arms and courage. I am king of the Unberogen and master of the armies of men. Where else would I be but in the forefront of battle?'

'Good lad,' said Kurgan, getting up from the firkin and leading Sigmar over to the foreshortened battlements of the tower. 'Listen. Can you hear that?'

Sigmar looked out over the rocky pass, the landscape more rugged and inhospitable the further east the pass went. Some half a mile away, it curved to the south around a spur of fallen stone that had once been a mighty statue of a dwarf god, and Sigmar could hear a faint rhythmic tattoo thrown back from the rocky walls of the mountains.

'It's the drums, lad,' said Kurgan. 'Orc war drums. They're close. We'll be knee deep in greenskin blood by midmorning, mark my words.'

Sigmar felt a flutter of fear at the thought, and quashed it viciously. All his life had been leading to this day, and now that it was here, he did not know if he was ready for it.

'I have fought many foes, my king,' said Sigmar, his eyes taking on a faraway look as he gazed into the future. 'I have killed beasts of the forest, my fellow tribesmen, orcs, the blood drinkers and the eaters of men who dwell in the swamps. I have faced them all and defeated them, but this… this is something else. The gods are watching, and if we falter even a little, then all I have dreamed of will die. How does a man deal with such awesome responsibility?'

Kurgan laughed and handed him the tankard of ale. 'Well, I can't say I know how a *man* would deal with it, but I can tell you how a dwarf would. It's simple. When the time comes, hit them with your hammer until they're dead. Then hit the next one. Keep going until they're all dead.'

Sigmar took a drink of the dwarf ale. 'That's all there is to it?'

'That's all there is to it,' agreed Kurgan as the sound of orc war drums grew louder. 'Now, we'd best be getting back to our warriors. We have a battle to fight!'

TWENTY-ONE

Black Fire Pass

THE FIRST RAGGED line of orcs came into view less than an hour later, a solid wall of green flesh and fury. They filled the pass before the army of men, the booming echoes of their war drums and monotonous chanting, working on the nerves and heightening the dread every man felt.

Great, horned totems waved above their heads, festooned with skulls and fetishes, and the wind brought with it the reek of their unclean flesh: spoiled meat, dung and a sour, fungal smell that worked its way into the back of every man's throat.

Though Sigmar had heard of the enormous size of the orc host from the dwarfs and Cuthwin, the unimaginable vastness of their numbers still took his breath away. He looked to either side, and saw the same awe in the faces of his sword-brothers.

Wolfgart tried to look unconcerned, but Sigmar could see past the bravado to the fear beneath, and Pendrag looked like a man who had just seen his worst nightmare come to life.

The orcs were like some dreadful, elemental tide of anger and violence, their every action taken in service of the desire to wreak harm. This was unthinking violence made flesh, the aggressive impulse of a violent heart without the discipline of intellect to restrain it.

Were a man to walk from one side of the pass to the other upon the heads of the orcs, he could do so without once setting foot on rock. Sigmar smiled at the absurdity of the image, and the spell that the orc numbers had upon him was broken.

The greenskins carried huge cleavers, axes and swords, the blades rusted and stained with blood. Goblins scampered between the ranks of orcs, disgusting, cowardly creatures, swathed in dark robes and clutching wickedly sharp swords and spears. Fangs gnashed and shields were beaten in a manic rhythm, and it seemed as though every band of orc warriors strove to outdo the one next to it with its volume and ferocity.

Snapping wolves, wide-shouldered beasts with frothing jaws, pawed at the earth on the flanks of the great host, and more goblins riding loathsome, dark-furred spiders scuttled over the rocks. Towering above the orcs, groups of hideous troll-creatures lumbered through the army, wielding the trunks of trees as easily as a man might bear a cudgel.

'Ach, there's not so many of them, eh?' said Wolfgart, undoing the strap holding his greatsword in place and swinging the enormous weapon from his back. 'We fought more at Astofen, don't you think?'

'I think so,' agreed Sigmar with a smile. 'This will just be a skirmish by comparison.'

'By all the gods, they're a ripe bunch,' said Pendrag as the rank odour of the greenskins washed over him.

'Always stay downwind of an orc,' said Sigmar. 'That's what we always said wasn't it?'

'Aye, but I'm beginning to regret it.'

'No time for regrets now, my friends.'

'I suppose not,' said Wolfgart. 'How's that warhammer of yours?'

'It knows that the enemies of its makers are here,' answered Sigmar. Since dawn, the mighty weapon had sent a powerful thrill of anticipation through him, and he could feel its hatred of the greenskins coursing through him, filling him with strength and purpose.

'Aye,' said Wolfgart. 'Well, swing it hard, my friend. Plenty of skulls to split today.'

A mob of greenskins, more armoured and darker skinned than the others, stepped from the rippling battle line of orcs, a tall, bull-headed totem held proudly above them. They began roaring in the guttural tongue of the orcs, brandishing their axes and swords in some primitive ritual of challenge or threat.

'Holy Ulric's beard,' said Pendrag as they all saw the huge winged beast appear above the orcs. Sigmar's eyes narrowed, and he shaded them from the eastern sun. Riding the flying monster was an orc of such colossal size that it must surely be the leader of this army.

The warlord was huge beyond imagining, and was protected at least as well as Sigmar's most heavily armoured riders, with thick plates of iron fastened to its flesh. Its axe was taller than a man, and rippled with green flames.

The beast it rode was a wyvern, and, though Sigmar had never seen such a monster before, he had heard them described by his eastern allies enough times to recognise one. Yet, as much as the sight of it filled him with dread, he longed to match his strength against it.

'What do you think?' he shouted. 'Shall I mount that beast's hide on the longhouse wall?'

'Aye!' shouted a warrior from the ranks behind Sigmar. 'Skin it and you can use it to make a map of the realm!'

'I may just do that,' answered Sigmar.

The warlord swooped low over his army, and the orcs redoubled the fury of their roars, clearly eager for the slaughter to begin. The booming of cleavers and axes on shields rose to a deafening crescendo, the metallic ringing echoing from the sides of the pass, until it seemed as though the very mountains would crumble and fall.

The front ranks of the orc host began shaking, and just as it seemed as if they were having some horrific seizure, a terrifying war shout erupted from every orc throat in unison.

Immense and powerful, the sound was torn from the heart of their violent core, an ancestral expression of hatred and fury that had given birth to their race in blood and fire.

As the primal roar continued, the orcs began to jog towards the army of men, hatred gleaming in their eyes, and their tusked jaws bellowing for blood.

'Here they come,' said Sigmar, hefting Ghal-maraz in one hand and his golden shield in the other. 'Fight bravely, my friends. Ulric is watching.'

ULFDAR WATCHED THE advancing line of orcs through a haze of weirdroot and hemlock, their movements appearing sluggish as though they charged through sucking mud. Beside her, King Otwin beat his bare breast with spiked gauntlets, drawing blood and pushing his berserk fury to even greater heights. The king foamed at the mouth, and bled from the golden spikes hammered through his temple that formed his crown.

Ulfdar could feel her own battle fury threatening to explode from her at any moment, the bitter herbal infusions she had swallowed before battle surging through her heart and driving her into this paroxysm of rage. Her arms and neck were ringed with iron torques, her bare flesh painted with fresh tattoos to ward off enemy blades, and her golden hair was pulled into a tall mohawk with handfuls of smeared blood.

Her king raised his mighty axe, chained once more to his wrist, and let loose a wordless shout of rage and fury. Along the line of Thuringian warriors, the king's war shout was answered, and Ulfdar felt the wild beat of her heart hammering like a frenzied drummer against her ribs.

The king screamed again, his eyes wide and his mouth pulled back in a rictus grin. His body shuddered like a tethered colt, and he leapt forward, unable to contain his berserk fury any longer. King Otwin charged towards the orcs, a lone warrior against a horde, and his lust for battle swept through his warriors in an instant.

With a cry of rage equal to that of the enemy, the Thuringian berserkers charged towards the greenskin lines. Ulfdar easily caught up to her king, her twin swords spinning in her grip as she ran and gnashed her teeth, chewing the inside of her cheeks bloody. The sharp, metallic flavour mingled with the intoxicating anger that consumed her, and she screamed as she saw the face of the first orc she would kill.

King Otwin's axe hammered through an orc, cleaving it in two, and the king leapt amongst the foes behind it. Ulfdar's sword plunged into a body, and tore upwards as she leapt, feet first, at another. She felt bone break and landed lightly, spinning on her heel and slashing her sword through another greenskin's face.

A spear stabbed for her, but she swayed aside and thrust both her blades though her attacker's throat, ripping the blades free in a spray of blood. Orcs were all around her, stabbing and chopping, but she wasted no energy in defensive strokes, simply attacking with all her strength. Her swords were twin blurs of iron, slashing throats and opening bellies as she spun amongst her foes.

A club struck her a glancing blow to her shoulder, spinning her around. She hacked the wielder's arm off at the elbow, revelling in the pain, noise and confusion of battle. Hundreds of her fellow warriors tore through the enemy lines, a mass of screaming, berserk warriors intent on killing.

A warrior with his pelvis crushed stabbed orcs from the ground until a massive green fist flattened his skull. A berserker used his own entrails to strangle his killer, while yet another had cast aside his weapons in his fury and tore at the orcs with his bare hands. Ulfdar shrieked at the sensations flooding her body.

The blood, the violence and the noise were incredible. She bled from a handful of wounds she could not remember receiving, but even the pain was intoxicating. A sword slammed into her, cutting into the metal of her torques and breaking her arm, but sliding clear before severing the limb.

Ulfdar yelled in pain and swung her good arm to behead the orc. More and more of the greenskins were attacking, yet still her king was pushing deeper and deeper into their ranks, his huge axe sweeping out in great arcs to cut down anything in his way.

Everywhere was blood and death, her fellow warriors cutting a bloody swathe through the heart of the greenskin ranks. The pain in her arm was intense, but Ulfdar used it to fuel her anger, and she leapt into the fray once more, her sword cutting and stabbing.

More blades stabbed for her, and she felt a spear plunge into her back. She twisted and the point was wrenched clear. Her sword smashed the spear-tip from the shaft, and the return stroke slammed down on the orc's helmet. The metal crumpled, and her sword was torn from her grip as the dead beast fell backwards.

She heard a rumbling thunder around her, but her world had shrunk to the foe in front of her and its death. She swept up a fallen axe and threw herself forward, the blade biting flesh and armour alike as she laughed and screamed with hysterical fury.

HER COPPER HAIR streaming behind her like a war banner, Queen Freya pulled back her bowstring and let fly with deadly accurate arrows. She gave a whooping yell with every orc she felled, though there were so many it was impossible to miss. One might as well applaud an archer for hitting the sea.

The queen's chariot was high-sided and armoured with layered strips of baked leather, its wheels rimmed with iron and fitted with deadly blades. Maedbh held the reins loosely in one hand, holding a throwing spear aloft in the other.

Two hundred chariots thundered towards the orcs in a staggered line, a swarm of arrows slashing from each one as Asoborn warriors loosed their shafts into the enemy. The sandy plain of Black Fire Pass was ideal ground for chariots, and Freya felt a delicious shiver of pleasure as Maedbh drove them ever closer to the enemy.

Otwin's berserkers had broken ranks, and charged forwards as soon as the orc line had twitched, but that was no surprise. Sigmar himself had bid her protect the Thuringian king, fully expecting him to charge wildly at the enemy. The berserkers fought magnificently, their fighting wedge plunging into the enemy army and driving deep into its heart.

The greater numbers of orcs was now telling, however, and, like the jaws of a trap, the greenskins were surrounding and butchering the Thuringians. Freya could see King Otwin atop a mound of dead monsters, his huge, chained axe cutting down foes by the dozen. Hundreds of berserkers pushed ever deeper into the orcs, but their pace was slowing, and more and more were being dragged to their deaths.

Across the battlefield, Freya could see a furious exchange of missile fire between the armies. Black-shafted arrows flew from darting goblins, but most of these thudded into wooden shields or bounced from shirts of iron mail. In contrast, the arrows of the Unberogens and Cherusens were wreaking fearful havoc amongst the orcs, thousands of iron-tipped shafts slashing downwards and punching through orc skulls.

Galloping horsemen rode in wild circuits before the charging greenskins, riding in close to loose frantic volleys before galloping clear. Some were swift enough, others were not and were brought down to be torn limb from limb by vengeful greenskins.

'Be ready, my queen!' shouted Maedbh, dragging Freya's attention back to her portion of the battlefield. The orcs were close, and she loosed a last arrow before dropping her bow and drawing her broadsword. A spear was a better weapon for use in a chariot, but Freya's blade had belonged to an ancient hero of her blood, and she could no more wield a different weapon than she could stop loving her sons.

Freya lifted her sword and swung it around her head. The foetid odour of the orcs was strong, and the billowing clouds of dust caught in her throat.

She saw the gleam of hatred in their red eyes and felt the hot reek of their foul breath.

'Now, my brave warriors!' she yelled.

Freya braced herself against the side of the chariot and looped a leather thong around her wrist, as Maedbh wrenched the reins, and the horses veered to the side.

Almost as one, the Asoborn chariots turned to run parallel to the orc lines, the scythe blades on their wheels tearing the front ranks of their enemies from their feet in a storm of blood and severed limbs. Freya hacked through skulls as Maedbh skilfully guided the chariot along the front of the greenskin horde.

Bellows of pain followed the Asoborn queen as her host of chariots cut the front ranks of the enemy down. Spears stabbed the survivors, and hissing arrows slashed into the orcs further back. Without a word from her queen, Maedbh turned her chariot away, and those following behind followed her example.

Roaring orcs leapt forward, and a handful of chariots were brought down, splintered to matchwood by enormous axes.

Freya laughed with the joy of battle and waved her bloodied sword in the air once again.

The chariots of the Asoborns wheeled and turned back towards the orcs.

SIGMAR SWUNG GHAL-MARAZ in a looping arc, and smashed the head into a bellowing orc that had its hand wrapped around his horse's neck. The greenskin collapsed, its skull a splintered ruin, and Sigmar kicked the dying beast from him as he guided his horse forward once more. Beside him, Pendrag held his banner high in his silver hand, the sight inspiring all those around him to greater effort.

Attack was the best form of defence, and Sigmar watched with pride as King Otwin led his berserk warriors in a screaming charge. The furious melee had halted the orcs in their tracks, and though Otwin was surrounded, Freya's chariots were cutting a bloody path towards him.

As the arms of the trap had closed around Otwin, Sigmar had raised his hammer high and led his Unberogen riders forwards in a charge to glory. Armoured riders slammed into the orcs and trampled them beneath iron-shod hooves as swords cleaved through crude helmets and spears stabbed unprotected backs.

Arrows arced overhead in a constant rain, and the swelling roar of battle was building into a rolling wave like the boom of surf on cliffs. Sigmar blocked a sword blow with his shield, smashing his hammer down and feeling its joy singing in his veins. Blood sprayed him, and his horse reared, the stink of blood a foul stench in its nostrils.

Sigmar gripped his horse's flanks with his thighs as it lashed out with its hind legs and crushed a handful of goblins that sought to hamstring it. The warhorses of the Unberogen were trained to fight and defend themselves as well as any warrior, and this horse, the roan gelding King Siggurd had gifted him, was just as ferocious as any bred by Wolfgart.

Sigmar's sword-brother rode alongside him, his mighty sword swooping around his body in deadly arcs that smashed through iron plates and shattered shields. Arterial blood sprayed around him, and, though he carried no shield, Wolfgart appeared unwounded.

'Unberogen!' shouted Sigmar. 'To me! Onwards!'

A roar of approval followed Sigmar as he rode deeper into the orcs, bludgeoning a path with Ghal-maraz and killing any foe that dared come near him. A dozen fell before his fury, and then a dozen more. His every strike was death, and the orcs before him saw their doom in his eyes as he rode through them like a vengeful god.

Ahead, Sigmar could see King Otwin fighting for his life in the centre of a mass of howling foes. Perhaps a score of berserkers fought alongside him, and Sigmar saw that one was Ulfdar, her left arm hanging useless at her side. The orcs pressed in, scenting victory, but the crash of horses and the whooping yells of Asoborn women were drawing ever closer.

If Otwin knew his warriors were surrounded, he gave no sign, and simply kept on hacking his way through as many orcs as he could reach. His body was a mass of deep wounds, a long gash on his thigh pouring blood down his leg, and a broken sword blade jutting from his shoulder.

Most of the berserkers were similarly wounded, but fought on regardless. Sigmar saw Freya's flame-coloured hair, and felt a flush of excitement at the sight of her standing proud and fierce atop her chariot, lopping heads like ears of corn with her long, golden-hilted broadsword.

The greenskins were being crushed between the Unberogen horsemen and Asoborn chariots, yet there was no give in them. Dying orcs were trampled beneath thundering hooves or crushed beneath iron-rimmed wheels. Ghal-maraz reaped a fearsome tally of dead, the hammer of the dwarfs crushing skulls, shattering shoulders and smashing chests with every stroke.

Sigmar took the head from a roaring orc, and slammed his shield into the face of another as it leapt for him. Reeling from the force of the impact, he did not see a monstrous orc rise up behind him, towering above him with its cleaver raised to split him in two.

A terrifying scream sounded behind Sigmar, and he twisted in the saddle to see a hulking orc in battered plates of iron armour struggling with one of Otwin's berserkers. As the orc twisted around, Sigmar saw Ulfdar clinging to the orc's back, an arm that was clearly broken wrapped around its massive neck as she plunged her blade into its throat like a dagger.

The monster fought to throw her off, blood squirting from its neck in a geyser of sticky fluid. Ulfdar screamed as she was thrown around, and Sigmar could only imagine the agony of her shattered arm.

Sigmar kicked his feet from his stirrups and leapt from his horse, swinging his hammer for the orc's face. Bone shattered beneath the blow, and Ghal-maraz smashed clear of its head. Sigmar landed beside the corpse as it fell, and Ulfdar was thrown clear.

Amid the chaos of fighting orcs and men and thrashing horses, Sigmar ran over to the berserker woman. She struggled to rise, but her arm was twisted in ways an arm was not meant to bend, and her body was covered in blood, though Sigmar could not tell how much of it was her own.

'Here!' he cried over the din as he hooked an arm under her shoulder. 'Come on.'

She looked up at him with a snarl of rage, not seeing him for who he was, and stabbed with her sword. There was no strength to the blow, and Sigmar blocked it easily, hauling Ulfdar to her feet.

'Stay your hand!' he yelled. 'It is Sigmar!'

His words cut through the red mist of her rage, and she slumped against him.

Sigmar backed away from the fighting, the triumphant yells of Unberogen and Asoborn warriors telling him that the first orc attack had been broken. He looped Ulfdar's unbroken arm around his shoulders, and hooked his own arm around her waist as he half carried, half dragged her to safety.

'Climb up here, Sigmar!' said a voice, and Sigmar looked over as Freya and Maedbh's chariot skidded to a halt beside him in a cloud of dust.

'My horse is somewhere here!' shouted Sigmar.

'It ran off,' replied Freya, 'back to our lines.'

Sigmar swore, and dragged the wounded warrior woman onto the chariot. Freya helped lift her, and Sigmar climbed up to join them. The chariot was cramped with the four of them in it and Sigmar found himself pressed up against the warm, naked flesh of the Asoborn queen.

'Just like old times,' smiled Freya.

THE DAY HAD opened well for his army, but Sigmar had fought enough battles to know that such things were rarely decided in the first clashes. The initial orc advance had been defeated, split apart by the wild charge of the berserker king, and then crushed between the hammer and anvil of the Unberogen and Asoborns.

Sigmar let his warriors cheer as they saw him returned to his army in the Asoborn chariot, but quickly hopped down when Ulfdar had been carried to the healers at the rear of the army. His horse had been caught by Wolfgart, and he vaulted back into the saddle.

'We've bloodied their nose,' said Sigmar, watching as the scattered survivors of the orc vanguard limped back to their lines, 'but this is just the beginning.'

'Aye,' agreed Wolfgart, his armour dented and torn, but all the blood dripping from him was that of slain orcs. 'This is work for the infantry now.'

The main body of the orc army was advancing, a solid wall of green flesh, brazen armour and hatred. Tall monsters with grey flesh and wiry hair advanced with the army, and rumbling chariots, heavy things with baying crew, were thrown out in a ragged screen before them.

'The next portion of the battle will not be so easily won.'

'Easy?' asked Pendrag as he rode over with Sigmar's banner clutched tightly. 'You thought that was easy?' Like Wolfgart, Pendrag appeared to be unharmed, though his horse bore several slashes to its hindquarters.

'That charge was just to test our strength,' said Sigmar. 'Our enemies will know now that they will need to bring their entire force to bear to crush us and take the pass. Still, it has given us a victory, and that will lift the men's spirits.'

'It will need to lift them high indeed,' agreed Wolfgart. 'For if this is how the battle is to go, we'll be lucky to see out the day.'

Asoborn chariots wheeled in circles before the army, the warriors of Queen Freya standing tall, their spears jabbing the air as Taleuten horsemen rode towards the flanks of the enemy army in search of a gap to exploit. Sigmar knew that such were the enemy numbers that they would not find one.

'Come on,' said Sigmar, turning his horse. 'This is a fight to be made on foot.'

THIS TIME THE orc army advanced en masse, an army as wide as the pass itself, and the hearts of men quailed before such an awesome spectacle. No warrior gathered beneath Sigmar's banner had witnessed such a sight, and to see so many orcs gathered in one place was to believe that the entire greenskin race had come to destroy the lands of men.

Goblins mounted on slavering wolves sped forward and the Taleuten horsemen were caught unawares by their incredible speed. A volley of arrows felled several of the wolves, punching through their fur and pitching them to the ground, but many more survived. Fangs and talons flashed, and blood sprayed as men were clawed to death and horses' necks were bitten open.

Some warriors tried to flee, but great spiders leapt from the high cliffs, pouncing onto the horses' rumps and tearing the riders from their saddles to feast on their flesh.

The valley echoed to the tramp of marching feet and the rumble of chariot wheels. Orc chariots were nothing like as elegant or as masterfully created as those of the Asoborn. Heavier and festooned with blades, no horse pulled these ungainly contraptions, but filthy, matted boars with sharpened tusks like sword blades. Each was as large as Blacktusk, though none had the nobility of spirit possessed by that mighty beast.

Hundreds of arrows arced towards the orc line, most thudding into the thick wood of the chariots' armour, or embedding themselves in heavy iron shields. Several chariots were smashed on the rocks as some arrows plunged home in the flesh of the boars and drove them mad with pain.

Most of the chariots survived the hail of arrows, however, and the orc crews drove their beasts to even greater speed with cracks of their whips. Where the Asoborns had mastered the use of the chariot throughout a battle, the orcs cared little for subtlety, and simply drove hard and fast for the enemy line.

The chariots smashed into King Siggurd's warriors, ploughing through rank after rank of them. Blood sprayed as scythe blades severed limbs and the heavy chariots crushed men beneath them. Boars squealed and snapped, razor-sharp tusks goring men to death even as they bit and stamped through their enemies.

Shuddering like a wounded beast, the line of warriors folded in around the orc chariots, stabbing and cutting at the encircled orcs. Even as the chariots were surrounded and destroyed, the main strength of the orcs was advancing at a rapid pace. Before the Brigundian warriors could redress their lines, however, the latest orc weapon was brought to bear.

Enormous boulders sailed overhead and crashed into the earth with teeth-loosening force, crushing a dozen warriors beneath them and exploding into whistling fragments that killed a man as surely as any arrow. Huge holes were torn through King Siggurd's men as orc catapults hurled more and more boulders through the air.

Terrified of these enormous missiles, some men turned and ran, and only the shouted cries of their king steeled their hearts once more.

The damage was done, however, and ragged holes opened up in the centre of Sigmar's army.

King Kurgan Ironbeard was first to see the danger, and pushed his warriors forward beyond the battle line to cover the gap. On the other side of the Brigundian warriors, Sigmar shouted a command to King Wolfila, who marched his clansmen forward and planted his sword in the earth before him.

The king of the Udose spat on his hands and took his banner from the warrior next to him. He rammed it into the earth beside his sword, and the meaning of the gesture was clear.

This was where he would fight, and this was where he would stay.

No sooner had the king retrieved his sword than his warriors were embroiled in battle.

A swelling roar of hatred burst from the orcs as they charged the last gap between them and the combined line of dwarfs and Udose clansmen. The dwarfs were a dam of iron and courage, and the orcs broke against it like a green wave, hurled back again and again by the stoic resolve of the mountain folk.

No brute ferocity could compete with the bloody-minded determination of the dwarfs, their axes cutting through every green-skinned foe that came before them. Like one of the machines of the dwarf craftsmen, the warriors of King Kurgan slaughtered the foe mechanically, never tiring and never flagging in their killing.

In contrast, King Wolfila's clan warriors battled with heart and fire, their war songs lusty and full of lurid tales of past heroes. The Udose king fought without care for his own defence, two kilted giants in black breastplates protecting him from his own reckless ferocity.

The two armies met in a heave of strength and iron, both charging in the last few moments before contact. The early stages of the battle had been move and countermove, but this was raw courage against hate and aggression. Swords stabbed and axes fell. Shields splintered and spears were thrust into gaps.

Both armies shuddered as their front ranks were killed almost to a man, the sheer ferocity of their meeting a killing ground where only the strongest or luckiest could possibly survive.

Howls of pain and hate. The screaming clash of handcrafted iron and crude pig iron. The grunts of men pushing shields and the bellows of unthinking brutality were all mingled into one almighty roar of battle, the like of which this world had never yet seen, nor would again for a thousand years.

As the centre of the army struggled, the flanks met, and the sound of tearing fangs added to the din of battle. Blood-maddened wolves charged into King Markus's warriors, tearing, snapping and biting with animal ferocity. The king's hunting hounds leapt to defend their master and dour Menogoth spearmen lowered their polearms and marched forward in solid lines. The handful of surviving wolves were impaled on iron spear-tips, and the Menogoths offered no quarter to their riders.

There were no cheers from the Menogoths, for they had suffered too much in the previous year to take any joy in slaughtering their foes, only grim revenge. Their vengeance was to be short-lived, however, for a hail of monstrous iron javelins, hurled from enormous war machines, slashed through the air to punch through their ranks. Each bolt killed a dozen men, skewered by the powerful barbs, and scores were hurled towards the Menogoths in every volley.

The carnage was terrible, and the Menogoth warriors fell back before this dreadful hail of spears, leaving the flanks of the Merogens unprotected. Orc warriors streamed forward, pouring into the gap the flight of the Menogoths had opened, and, though Sigmar had ensured that each sword band had a smaller group of warriors to protect its vulnerable flanks, these detachments were soon butchered and overrun.

Scenting victory, the orc advance was angled towards the open flank, and the shape of the battle began to change. Where before, two armies had faced each other in an unbroken line, the battle now swung like a gate, with the solid left flank as the hinge.

The Merogens were crumbling beneath attacks from the front and side, and it was only a matter of time before they broke.

TWENTY-TWO
The Death of Heroes

SIGMAR SAW THE right flank collapsing, and raked his spurs back. Orcs were pouring into the gap created by the flight of the Menogoths, and fearful slaughter was being wreaked upon the Merogens. The great strength of this battleground was that the orcs could not bring the full force of their numbers to bear upon his army, but that advantage would be for nought if the greenskins were able to get behind them.

Thanks to the courage of the dwarfs and Udose warriors, the centre was holding, and the left flank of the army, held by King Adelhard's warriors was untouched. The Ostagoth warriors were yet to fight, and Sigmar could see their eagerness to spill orc blood.

'We have to get over there,' said Sigmar. 'If Henroth's warriors break, we are lost.'

'Aye,' agreed Pendrag. 'The Merogens have courage, but they won't last long attacked on two fronts.'

'Pendrag, you and I will plug the gap,' ordered Sigmar. 'Wolfgart, take five hundred men and reinforce the centre. Wolfila's men cannot keep fighting as they are for long, and they will need the strength of our warriors to hold.'

Wolfgart nodded and ran over to gather his warriors as Sigmar and Pendrag dismounted and ran to join the nearest sword band. Sigmar quickly outlined his orders. The clarion's war horn gave three short blasts followed by one long blast, and the Unberogen formed up around Sigmar's banner, six hundred warriors in mail shirts, carrying wickedly sharp swords. Each warrior carried a kite-shaped shield and wore a helm of iron or bronze.

With all the discipline worked into them over the long years of campaigning, the Unberogen marched towards the collapsing flank with Sigmar's banner rippling in the wind and their king at their head.

Sigmar could feel the pride these men had in him, and he returned that pride. They could not know the honour it was to lead them, and his heart swelled to see them marching towards battle with fire in their hearts.

'King Henroth's warriors have the hearts of heroes, but they need our help!' cried Sigmar as the clarion blew the note for war pace. His warriors shouted, and broke into a steady jog.

Sigmar could see that the orcs were rolling up the flanks of the Merogen forces, butchering warriors who could not fight as they had trained. Menogoth warriors were re-forming further along the pass, under the wrathful cries of King Markus, but they would not return to battle in time to save the Merogens.

Some of the orcs were turning to face the Unberogen, but most were too busy killing Merogens to bother with what was happening around them. The carnage was terrible, and Sigmar could only marvel at the courage of the Merogens to have kept fighting in the face of such horrendous butchery.

The clarion gave a last strident blast of his horn, and Sigmar raised Ghal-maraz for all his warriors to see as they broke into the charge. The orcs before Sigmar fell back, ancient fear of his weapon causing their hearts to quail before it.

With a cry of fury and pride, the Unberogen warriors smashed into the orcs, and great was the slaughter. Sigmar cleaved left and right, and no armour was proof against his blows. Plates of iron were sundered before his might, and blood spattered his armour and flesh as he killed orcs by the score. His warriors slammed into the orcs, shields battering their opponents to the ground with the momentum of their charge, and swords stabbing for throats and groins.

The orcs turned to face their new enemy, and great axes smashed Unberogen shields and bore their bearers to the ground. The charge slowed, and, for one terrible moment, Sigmar feared that the orcs would not break.

Roaring with anger, Sigmar hurled himself forward into the mass of orcs, punching deep into the packed mass of enemy warriors. His warhammer was a blur of striking iron, the rune-forged head breaking open skulls and chests in equal number. Swords and spears stabbed at him, and his shoulder guard was torn away by a stray axe blow.

Orcs fell back around him, and Unberogen fighters poured into the space he had created. Sigmar fought onwards, driving the wedge deeper into the orcs, heedless of the fact that he was pushing ahead of his warriors.

A spear stabbed into his unprotected shoulder, and Sigmar grunted in pain as the orcs pressed in around him. His pace faltered, and a looping club slammed into his helmet, driving him to his knees as starbursts exploded behind his eyes.

Blood streamed down the side of his head, and dizziness swamped him.

The metal of his helmet was buckled across his eyes, and he dragged it clear, hurling it into the face of a charging orc. The beast smacked it aside with its fist, but then Pendrag was beside him, his sword plunging into the orc's throat. The crimson of Sigmar's banner caught the light, and Pendrag held it high in his silver grip as he stood over his king.

'Sigmar!' cried Pendrag, leading the Unberogen onwards. 'For Sigmar and the empire!'

Bloody warriors pushed past Sigmar, cleaving into the orcs, the pace of their charge unrelenting. Brutal momentum carried them onwards, and within moments the greenskin attack on the Merogens was all but destroyed.

Sigmar pushed to his feet and wiped blood from his eyes.

The Unberogen were pushing ever forward, chasing down the fleeing orcs with great fury, but even as Sigmar exulted in the victory, he saw the danger.

Thousands more orcs were charging towards the right flank of his army, and his warriors would soon find themselves isolated and alone, crushed as they had crushed the orcs.

'Wait!' he cried. 'Hold! Hold!'

The noise of the battle was overwhelming, and his cries fell on deaf ears. Sigmar looked for the clarion, desperate to call his warriors back from their peril, but he saw the crushed and broken form of the horn blower lying in the dirt. The man's war horn was shattered, and nothing Sigmar could do would quell his warriors' battle fury.

KING MARBAD OF the Endals rode as though the daemons of the mist were at his heels, his black horse lathered with sweat as he whipped it to greater speed. His son, Aldred, rode at his side, and eight hundred Raven Helms galloped across the plain behind their king.

Many years had passed since he had ridden to battle, and it felt magnificent to have so great a steed beneath him and the curved blade of Ulfshard in his hand.

Only fighting beside his old friend, King Björn, could have made this moment more perfect, but then without Sigmar, this battle would not have been fought at all.

The ebb and flow of the battle had changed dramatically in the last few moments, and, with the arrival of Wolfgart's warriors, the centre was still holding. The Ostagoths and surviving Thuringians were hooking around the centre to relieve the pressure there, but orc boar riders were even now moving to counter them. Every manoeuvre made by Sigmar's army could be met with vast hordes of orcs and bludgeoned into submission.

Courage and iron could only hold the line for so long.

Eventually, the brutal arithmetic of war would see the army of men destroyed.

Clouds of dust were thrown up around them, and Marbad desperately sought out the banner of the Unberogen king amid the swirling melee before the cliff face.

He and his Raven Helms had been searching for a gap in the enemy lines to exploit when Marbad had seen the crimson banner raised high by Sigmar's silver handed standard bearer.

No sooner had Marbad seen the banner than he had ordered his warriors to follow him. Aldred had protested, but the word of his father was law, and Marbad had ridden with his finest warriors towards the embattled right flank.

When you see the silver hand lift the crimson banner high.

He had been dreaming, or so he had thought, when he had seen the vision of the crone in black beside his bed in the Raven Hall twenty years ago. How she had come to be in his chambers was a mystery to him, yet here she was, perched on the end of his bed.

'Who are you?' he asked. 'And how did you get here?'

'How I got here is unimportant, Marbad,' said the white-haired crone, 'but I am sometimes known as the hag woman of the Brackenwalsch. An ugly name, but one I am forced to bear for this age of men.'

'I have heard of you,' said Marbad. 'Your name is a curse to the Unberogen. They say you practise the dark arts.'

'The dark arts?' laughed the hag woman. 'No, Marbad, if I practised the dark arts then Sigmar would already be dead.'

'Sigmar? What has Björn's son to do with anything?'

'To some, maybe I am a curse,' continued the hag woman as though he had not spoken, 'but when men are desperate, you would be surprised how swiftly they seek my aid.'

'I require nothing of you,' answered Marbad.

'No,' agreed the hag woman, 'but I require something of you.'

'What could one such as you want of me?'

'A sacred vow, Marbad,' said the hag woman, 'that when you see the silver hand lift the crimson banner high, you will ride with all your strength to Sigmar's side and grant him your most precious possession.'

'I do not understand.'

'I do not require your understanding, Marbad, just your sacred vow.'

'And if I do not give it?'

'Then the race of men will die, and the world will end in blood.'

Marbad paused to see if the woman was joking, but when she remained silent he knew she was not. 'And if I give you this vow?'

'Then the world will endure a little longer, and you will have changed the course of history. What man could ask for more?'

Marbad smiled, recognising the flattery for what it was, but sensing no lie in the hag woman's words. 'For this, I will earn glory?'

'You will earn glory,' agreed the hag woman.

'I have the feeling you are not telling me something,' said Marbad.

'True, but you will not want to hear it.'

'I will be the judge of that, woman! Tell me.'

'Very well,' said the crone. 'Yes, if you honour your vow you will earn glory, but you will be choosing a path that leads to your death.'

Marbad swallowed, making the sign of the horns. 'They are right to call you a curse.'

'I am all things to all men.'

Marbad chuckled. 'Glory and a chance to save the world,' he said. 'Death seems like such a small price for that.'

'Do I have your oath?' pressed the hag woman.

'Yes, damn you. I give you my oath. When I see the silver hand lift the crimson banner high, whatever that means, I will ride with all my strength to Sigmar's side.'

The following morning he had awoken refreshed and with only a fleeting recollection of the encounter with the hag woman, but as he had seen Pendrag raise Sigmar's banner, the memory of two decades ago had returned with incredible clarity.

Marbad sat tall in the saddle as he rode with all his strength to Sigmar's side.

Glory and a chance to save the world... *Not bad for an old man, eh?*

THE FIGHTING SWIRLED around Sigmar like a living thing, pulsing and flowing to unseen rhythms that were invisible to a normal man, but which were as plain as day to him. The charge of his Unberogen warriors had been magnificent and glorious, headstrong and courageous, but ultimately foolhardy.

Blades rose and fell, but the sword arms of the Unberogen were tired, their weapons seeming to have gained ten pounds in weight. The charge to rescue the Merogens would be a tale to tell in years to come, but first they had to survive the fight.

The Unberogen had hacked down many of the fleeing orcs, and then run into a solid wall of iron and green flesh. Orcs as hard as the mountains, and with as little give in them, cut men down with ruthless ferocity, and Sigmar saw that these darker-skinned orcs were larger and more heavily muscled than any they had fought thus far.

Where once his warriors had marched to the rescue of their fellows, they now fought for their lives. Pendrag still held the banner high, but he bled from a wound to the head, and the great standard wavered in his grip.

Sigmar hammered a shield from a snarling orc's grip, and slammed a fist into its porcine face. He grunted at the impact, for it was like punching stone. The orc roared and lashed out with its axe, and Sigmar ducked, slamming his hammer into the beast's groin. It dropped, and Sigmar drove his shield into its face, snapping its tusks and sending it reeling backwards.

Bellowing orcs surrounded him, and a heavy club smashed into his shoulder, tearing his last remaining shoulder guard away and driving him to his knees. Ghal-maraz swept out in a low arc and smashed the legs from his attacker, who fell in a crumpled heap beside him.

Sigmar rose and stamped his heel down on the orc's throat as he blocked the sweeping axe blow with his shield. A sword sailed past his head, and he swayed aside as a spear stabbed for his chest. He smote the spear-carrier, and rammed his shield forward into the face of another orc as an axe caromed from his breastplate.

'Pendrag!' cried Sigmar as he saw a great shadow loom over his sword-brother.

The troll creature was a terrifying monster of gigantic proportions, its limbs grossly swollen and lumpen with twisted muscle. Its head was enormous, repellent and humanoid, but its eyes held no gleam of intelligence. Hideous growths and fur like wire sprouted from its grey, stony flesh, and it carried the trunk of a tree with a dozen sword blades jutting from the end.

The monster drooled smoking saliva, and its limbs moved with a ponderous strength. Pendrag looked up through a mask of blood in time to see the massive spiked club descending towards him, and raised his arms in a futile gesture of defiance.

Sigmar slammed into Pendrag, pushing him from the path of the troll's club. The monstrous weapon split the ground, and Sigmar rolled to his feet with Ghal-maraz raised and his shield held before him. Pendrag lay where he fell, the crimson banner fallen beside him.

The troll towered above Sigmar, a thick lipped smile of hungry malice spreading across its slack features. A series of booming grunts came from its mouth, and Sigmar realised that it was laughing.

Anger filled him, and he ducked beneath its swinging club, smashing his hammer against the monster's thigh. The beast's hide cracked beneath the blow, and the ringing impact travelled up Sigmar's arm as though he had struck the side of a mountain. Its club swung for him again, and he took the blow on his shield. The metal cracked, and his arm felt as though a horse had trampled it.

The troll reached for him, but he dodged its clumsy, grasping hands. Sigmar heard shouts from his men as they saw their king's danger and rushed to his aid. The orcs fell back from the renewed attack, but they would not be held for long.

Sigmar spun inside the troll's reach, swinging his hammer for the monster's face, but the beast reared up, and Ghal-maraz slammed into its chest with a heavy crack. The troll's armoured hide split wide open, and vile, stinking blood sprayed from the wound. Sigmar gagged and fell back, his gorge rising at such an unholy reek.

He blinked to clear his vision, and stared in shock as the terrible wound in the troll's chest began to close over, its thick skin slithering and growing with unnatural speed to repair the damage. Sigmar's surprise almost cost him his life as the troll drew in a great breath and leaned forwards with its mouth opened wide.

Instinct made Sigmar raise his shield, and he cried out as a torrent of disgusting fluid vomited from the troll. The stench was unbearable and the acrid stink of its digestive fluids stung his eyes.

Sigmar tumbled away from the troll, repulsed beyond words as he felt a sizzling heat across his arm and chest. His shield was melting, the metal hissing and flowing as it dripped in golden droplets to the earth. Astonishment made him slow, until a tiny rivulet of the troll's eructation dripped onto his arm.

The pain was incredible, and he cast the shield from him, seeing that he had been the luckiest of those standing before the troll. A trio of Unberogen warriors screamed in unimaginable pain as the acidic bile burned through their armour and liquefied the flesh beneath. Sigmar felt a heat on his chest, and looked down to see a bubbling stain of hissing bile eating through the metal of his breastplate.

Sigmar dropped to his knees, fumbling with the straps securing the breastplate to his chest, but they were out of reach. He cried out as the heat of the acid seared his skin.

'Hold still,' said Pendrag, appearing at his shoulder with a knife in his hands.

'Hurry!' cried Sigmar.

Pendrag sawed through the straps securing the armour, and Sigmar cast the breastplate from his body with a desperate heave. In pain, but grateful to be alive, Sigmar nodded his thanks to his sword-brother and rose to his feet in the thick of the fighting.

Pendrag once again held his banner, and Sigmar saw that his warriors had formed a shield wall around him, protecting him while he faced the troll. Perhaps a hundred men still fought, and Sigmar could see no end to the orcs encircling them. An ocean of green flesh surrounded this island of Unberogen.

His warriors were attempting a fighting withdrawal, but the orcs had cut off every avenue of escape, and they were trapped. Sigmar could see little of the battle beyond this fight, but he hoped that Alfgeir or some other king could see their desperate predicament.

Sigmar heard a disgusting cracking, slurping sound, and saw the troll devouring one of the warriors who had fallen beneath its dreadful vomit. The man's leg still protruded from its jaws, but with a heave of its gullet, the leg was swallowed. The troll looked up, and, seeing Sigmar, bludgeoned its way through the shield wall towards him.

Warriors were smashed aside by its enormous club, sailing over the heads of their fellows to land in the midst of the orcs. Sigmar leapt to meet the troll, even as he knew he could not defeat it alone. As if in answer to that thought, a handful of his warriors, including Pendrag, attacked with him, stabbing long spears and swords at the horrific beast.

Blades cut its hide and spears stabbed into its sagging belly, but no sooner had the monster bled than its terrible anatomy would heal within moments. Men were crushed beneath its heavy club, and Sigmar saw cruel enjoyment in its moronic features. Nothing they could do was harming this monster, and the shield wall was shrinking as men fell to the chopping blades of the orcs.

Then Sigmar heard the thunder of hooves, and his heart leapt as he saw the blessed sight of the Raven Helms of King Marbad cutting a path through the orcs. The black-armoured riders smashed through the greenskins, their heavy steeds crushing their foes, and their lances spitting them where they stood.

King Marbad rode at their head, and the old king was magnificent, his silver hair streaming behind him as he clove through the ranks of the orcs, Ulfshard's blade streaming with blue fire. No power of the orcs could stand before the sword of the fey folk, and the stone set in its pommel shone with ancient power.

The Raven Helms were the greatest warriors of the Endals, and the orcs scattered before them or else were destroyed by them. Needing no orders, the Unberogen began fighting to link with Marbad's warriors.

A deafening roar of hunger echoed as the troll smashed through Sigmar's warriors and came at him again, its stomach heaving with grotesque motion. Its monstrous head lowered and its jaws spread wide once more.

'Sigmar!' shouted Marbad, drawing his arm back.

The king of the Endals hurled Ulfshard towards Sigmar, the glittering blade of the fey folk spinning with effortless grace towards him.

Sigmar plucked the weapon from the air, blue flames leaping from the blade at his touch, and spun on his heel.

The wondrous blade sliced into the troll's throat, cutting clean through its neck with a searing blast of power. The monster's head flew from its shoulders, and its body crashed to the ground.

Sigmar roared in triumph, and let the fire of Ulfshard join with the winter flames that burned in his own heart. With a weapon of power in each hand, Sigmar turned from the troll's corpse and raced to rejoin his warriors as Pendrag led them through the orcs towards the Raven Helms.

A cry of rage torn from scores of throats made him look up, and he cried out as he saw Marbad's horse brought down, and the old king fall among the orcs.

'Marbad!' shouted Sigmar, cleaving a path towards his friend. The orcs were no match for him, and his twin weapons cut through his enemies with ease, but Sigmar already knew he would be too late. He smashed Ghal-maraz through the skull of an orc too slow to flee before him, and stabbed Ulfshard through the back of another as he drove them from the body of the fallen king.

Sigmar reached the king of the Endals and knelt beside him, anguish tearing at his heart as he saw the terrible wound in Marbad's chest. Blood pooled beneath the king, and Sigmar saw there would be no saving him.

A spear had torn into his lower back, ripping up into his lungs, and a broken sword blade jutted from his side. A circle of warriors formed around him, Raven Helms and Unberogen both.

'You old fool,' wept Sigmar, 'throwing your sword like that.'

'I had to,' coughed Marbad, gripping Sigmar's hand. 'She promised me glory.'

'And you have it, my king,' said Sigmar. 'You are a hero.'

Marbad tried to smile, but a spasm of coughing shook him. 'There is no pain now,' he said. 'That is good.'

'Yes,' said Sigmar, pressing Ulfshard into the dying king's hand.

'I always feared this day,' said Marbad, his voice drifting, 'but now that it is here... I do not... regret it.'

With those words, the king of the Endals passed from the realms of man.

Sigmar stood, and his hatred of the greenskins burned hotter than ever as he took in the measure of the battle in an instant. The tempo of the fighting had changed, and he saw that Menogoth warriors were pushing forward to secure the right flank that they had previously fled.

Once more the battle had become a desperate toe-to-toe struggle of heaving warriors.

Howling orcs crashed against the warriors of men and dwarfs, the line of defenders bending back, but as yet unbroken. The charge of the Raven Helms had forged a path back to his army, and Sigmar was not about to waste his brother king's sacrifice.

A young man Sigmar recognised as Marbad's son pushed through the ring of warriors, his face a mask of grief.

'Father,' wept Aldred, cradling Marbad's head in his lap.

'Let me help you with him,' offered Sigmar.

'No,' snapped Aldred as four Raven Helms stepped forward. 'We will carry him.'

Sigmar nodded and stepped back as the Endal warriors lifted Marbad onto their shields.

As he watched the Raven Helms bear Marbad away, Sigmar knew that there was only one way to end this battle.

'GODS, MAN, WHAT were you thinking?' demanded Alfgeir as Sigmar jogged back to where the war banner of the Unberogen was planted in the ground. He did not answer Alfgeir, but simply swung into the saddle of his gelding. His armour had been torn from him, and his body was a mass of blood and scars.

'We cannot win the battle like this,' said Sigmar. 'The orcs will grind us down, and there is nothing we can do to stop them.'

Alfgeir looked set to deliver a withering reply, but saw the cold fire in Sigmar's eyes and thought better of it.

'What are your orders, sire?' he asked.

'Send runners to every king,' commanded Sigmar. 'Tell them to watch the rock of the Eagle's Nest and to follow my example.'

'Why?' asked Alfgeir. 'What are you going to do?'

But Sigmar had already ridden away.

TWENTY-THREE
Birth of an Empire

SIGMAR PUSHED HIS roan gelding hard towards the Eagle's Nest, riding behind the front lines of battle. The clash of iron and flesh filled his senses, and it was all he could do not to turn his horse towards the battle. He would fight soon enough, but he had grander plans than simply joining the fighting ranks.

The jutting rock was aptly named, for it rose in a sweeping curve like an eagle's noble head. It dominated the centre of the pass, its summit some ten yards above the ground, and Sigmar could see why Master Alaric had suggested he direct the battle from here.

Sigmar vaulted from his saddle as he reached the rock, and slapped the gelding's rump to send it on its way to the reserves gathered behind the front line. He swiftly climbed the rock, the many handholds making the ascent easier than he had thought.

Atop the Eagle's Nest, the entire battle was laid out before him, and the sheer scale of it astounded him. In the thick of the fighting, a man could only see his immediate surroundings, the warriors next to him and the enemy before him, but here, the awesome spectacle of two entire races attempting to destroy one another was laid before Sigmar.

He could not even begin to guess how many warriors filled the pass, for surely no concept existed for such an amount. From the narrowest point of the pass, the orc hordes stretched back, virtually uninterrupted, to where the ground dropped away to the east.

Tens of thousands of warriors opposed them, but they were a thin wall of iron and courage between the dark lands of the east and Sigmar's bountiful homeland of the west.

High above the orc host, its master soared on the back of the dark-pinioned wyvern, and Sigmar longed to bury his warhammer in its foul skull.

Goblin arrows arced towards him, but Sigmar did not move as they clattered against the rock or whistled past him. His practised eye, which had read a hundred battles, now saw the grim reality of this struggle.

It could not be won.

As things stood, his warriors had already achieved the impossible, holding back a numberless tide of greenskins with a fraction of the numbers, but that could not last forever, the orcs would simply wear them down.

King Kurgan's warriors fought in the centre of the battle, where the fighting was thickest, the dwarf king killing orcs with gleeful abandon. Master Alaric fought beside the king, his runestaff wreathed with crackling lightning that burned the flesh of whatever it touched.

No king could ask for finer allies than these.

The warriors of the tribal kings saw him atop the Eagle's Nest, and cheered his name as they fought, pushing the orc line back with renewed determination. Warriors from all the different tribes fought side by side, and as Sigmar saw the fresh fire in their hearts, he knew what he had to do.

Sigmar gripped the haft of Ghal-maraz tightly and sprinted towards the edge of the rock, leaping from the Eagle's Nest towards the mass of roaring orcs.

ALFGEIR SAW SIGMAR'S insane leap from the Eagle's Nest, and cried out as his king flew through the air with his warhammer raised high. The moment stretched, and Alfgeir knew he would never forget the sight of Sigmar as he fell towards the orcs like a barbarian hero from the ancient sagas.

Every warrior in the army watched as Sigmar landed among the orcs with a roar of hate and then vanished from view.

Alfgeir had lost one king in battle and he vowed he was not about to lose another.

He circled his horse and shouted, 'White Wolves. To me! We ride for the king!'

SIGMAR SWEPT HIS warhammer around his body, the heavy head smashing the armour of a huge orc armed with a blood-soaked cleaver. He wielded Ghal-maraz in both hands, his strength undiminished despite the bloodshed of the day. Each blow was delivered with a bellowing howl of rage, animal to the core, answering the orcs' unending war cry.

Blood sprayed as the king of the Unberogen slaughtered his foes, driving ever deeper into the greenskins like a man possessed. Cold fire burned in his eyes, and, where he fought, the winter wind howled around him.

Orcs scrambled to be away from this bloody madman, who fought with a fury greater than that of any orc. Sigmar killed and killed without thought, seeing only the enemies of his race and the destruction of all that was good and pure. His vengeance against the orcs was unsullied by notions of honour and glory. This was simple survival. Ghal-maraz filled him with hate, his fury armoured him in thunder, and Ulric poured lightning into his veins.

Sigmar was screaming, but he knew not what he shouted, for his entire being was focused on the slaughter. His rage was total, yet this was not the wanton fury of the berserker, this was controlled aggression at its most distilled.

A hundred orcs were dead already, and a great circle opened around Sigmar as the orcs fought each other to escape his rampage. Ancient energies flared from Ghal-maraz as it worked its slaughter, powers that not even the most revered runelords could name aiding the king's bloody work.

Sigmar fought with the might of every one of his illustrious ancestors, his enemies unable to even approach him, let along bring him down. Powers from the dawn of the world flowed through him, his muscles iron hard and invigorated with strength beyond imagining.

With grim, murderous strokes, Sigmar pushed onwards, hearing a swelling roar behind him as the tribal kings followed the last order he had given to Alfgeir.

Their hearts filled with fiery pride, the armies of men charged with the last of their strength and hope.

Unberogen champions and Udose clansmen threw themselves at the orcs, fighting with the same fury and strength as Sigmar. Wolfgart cut through orc armour with mighty swings of his heavy sword, and Pendrag fought like a berserker as he hacked a path towards Sigmar.

Ostagoth blademasters cut bloody ruin through the orcs, and Cherusen wildmen cackled like loons as they tore at their foes with hooked gauntlets. Asoborn warrior women danced through the greenskins with long daggers, plucking out eyes and slashing hamstrings, while Taleuten riders abandoned their steeds to charge in with slashing swords.

Raven Helms skewered orcs upon lowered lances, and the steeds of the White Wolves smashed into the orcs as their riders broke open enemy heads with their swinging hammers.

Screaming berserkers fought without heed of their own lives, and King Otwin roared as he swung his axe in lethal arcs. Myrsa and the warriors clad in all-enclosing plate chopped a bloody swathe through the orcs with wide sweeps of their terrifying greatswords.

The orcs were in disarray, and the front line was butchered by the sudden onslaught.

None dared come near Sigmar as he pushed onwards, further even than his most courageous warriors had reached. Orcs flowed around him, and panic seized the nearest, a ripple of fear spreading from the front of the army as the fury of this newborn god spread.

Sigmar neither knew nor cared how many orcs he had slain, but no matter how grand a total, he knew it would never be enough. Even with the courage and fire his warriors were displaying in this magnificent charge it could never be enough. Sigmar was leaving his warriors far behind, their war cries swallowed by the baying of the orcs.

The press of bodies from the rear of the orc army prevented many from escaping his wrath, and he slew them without mercy, corpses building around him in a vast mound of the dead.

Ghal-maraz shone like a beacon of faith in the centre of the battlefield, and the orcs quailed before it. The warriors of the twelve tribes fought like heroes, and as yet more orcs fled before its might, Sigmar felt the first stirrings of hope in his breast.

Then a dark shadow fell upon the battlefield like a slick of oil across water.

Sigmar looked up and saw great emerald wings and a roaring maw as the wyvern struck like a thunderbolt from the sky.

THE WYVERN'S JAWS snapped at Sigmar, and he dived to the side, tumbling down the slope of orc dead and falling to the ground amid a rain of split heads and broken corpses. He rolled to his feet as the wyvern landed atop the bodies of the greenskins that Sigmar had slain. Its horned head was massive, thrice as big as the largest bullock, and its jaws were filled with teeth like Cherusen daggers.

Its monstrous body was scaled and leathery, rippling with muscle and bony scales that ran the length of its back to a slashing tail that dripped hissing black venom. Two enormous wings stretched out behind it as its thick, serpentine neck pushed its head forward.

The black soulless orbs of its eyes fixed Sigmar with a stare of brutal cunning.

Atop the wyvern's back sat the largest orc that Sigmar had ever seen. Its skin was coal dark, and its armour was composed of heavy plates of iron hammered into its flesh with spikes. Tusks as large as those of the beast it rode jutted from its jaw, and its red eyes burned with all the hatred of its race.

Not even the eyes of Vagraz Head-Stomper had held such malice within them. This warlord was the purest incarnation of orc rage and cunning combined.

Ghal-maraz burned in Sigmar's hand, and he felt its recognition of this warlord: *Urgluk Bloodfang.*

Green fire rippled around the warlord's axe, a weapon of immense power and evil. The blade was smooth obsidian, and no orc craft had fashioned so deadly a weapon. Twisted variants of the runes that blazed on Ghal-maraz were worked along the length of its haft, and Sigmar felt their evil clawing at his soul.

Currents of power flowed around the two masters of the battlefield, and the fate of the world rested upon this combat. Man and orc faced one another, and the souls of both armies were carried within them. His own warriors were still far behind Sigmar, and, though orcs surrounded him, none dared intervene in this titanic duel.

'Come ahead and die!' shouted Sigmar, holding Ghal-maraz before him. The ancient hammer blazed with power, its urge to wreak death upon its enemies an almost physical force.

The wyvern launched itself at Sigmar, its wings flaring as its jaws snapped for him. Sigmar sidestepped, and swung his hammer in a short arc that slammed into the side of the beast's head. Roaring in pain, the wyvern staggered, but did not fall.

A powerful sweep of the wyvern's thick tail caught his shoulder and hurled him from his feet. He landed badly and felt something break inside him, but he managed to scramble to his feet as the monster lunged forward. He dived beneath the snapping jaws and rolled beneath the creature's neck, snatching up a fallen sword as he went.

With every ounce of his strength, Sigmar thrust the sword into the wyvern's chest. The blade sank into the beast's flesh, but before Sigmar could drive it home, the creature took to the air, clawing at him with its rear legs.

Talons like swords sliced down Sigmar's chest and he roared in agony. He brought his warhammer up and battered the wyvern's legs away before its claws could disembowel him. Gasping in pain, he rose to his feet in time to see the beast diving towards him once more.

Sigmar dived to the side, blood flowing freely from the wounds on his chest and a dozen others. He let the pain fuel his anger, and rose to his full height, a blood-soaked king of men with the mightiest of hearts.

'Come down and face me!' he shouted to Bloodfang.

If the warlord understood or cared, it gave no sign, but it hauled on the beast's chains and grunted as it pointed at Sigmar. The wyvern's jaws opened wide enough to swallow Sigmar whole, and it gave a terrifying roar. Its head snapped forward, and Sigmar vaulted over its jaws as he smashed Ghal-maraz down on its skull.

The beast shuddered and once again it reared up in pain.

Sigmar dropped close to the wyvern and swung his warhammer with two hands towards the sword that still jutted from the monster's chest. Ghal-maraz slammed into the sword's pommel, thrusting the weapon deep within the wyvern and piercing its heart.

With a strangled bellow, the wyvern crashed to the ground, its wings crumpling like torn sails as the life went out of it.

Sigmar rushed forward, hoping to catch Bloodfang struggling beneath his fallen mount, but the warlord was already on his feet and waiting for him. The black axe sang for Sigmar's neck, and he hurled himself to the side. Green fire scorched Sigmar's skin as the blade came within a hair's-breadth of taking his head.

Bloodfang arose from the death of his mount, a towering giant of enormous proportions and endless hate. The warlord's muscles bulged and pressed at the armour plates nailed to his flesh. A warlike chant built amongst the orcs surrounding Sigmar, and Bloodfang seemed to stand taller as the brutal vitality of his race surged through him.

For long seconds, neither combatant moved. Then Sigmar leapt to attack, his warhammer swinging in a deadly arc for Bloodfang's head.

The axe flickered up to block the strike, and the warlord pistoned a fist into Sigmar's jaw.

Sigmar had seen the blow coming at the last second, and rolled with the punch, but the force behind it was phenomenal, and he staggered away, desperate to put some space between him and his foe. The black axe slashed towards him, and Sigmar dropped, slamming the head of Ghal-maraz into Bloodfang's stomach.

The warhammer howled as it struck the enormous orc, unleashing potent energies as it found the perfect target for its rage. Bloodfang staggered away from Sigmar, a new-found respect in the glowing embers of his eyes.

Both warriors attacked again, axe and hammer clashing in explosions of green and blue fire. Though Bloodfang had the advantage of strength, Sigmar was faster and landed more blows against the orc.

As the battle went on, Sigmar knew that he was reaching the end of his endurance, while Bloodfang had just begun to fight. The orc chanting was growing louder, but so too were the war cries of Sigmar's army.

His warriors were battling to reach him and their courage gave him the strength to fight on.

The axe came at him again, and Sigmar slammed his warhammer into the obsidian blade, leaping closer to the immense orc. He spun low, and brought Ghal-maraz up in a crushing underarm strike, the head connecting solidly with Bloodfang's jaw.

The warlord's skull snapped back, but before Sigmar could back away, the orc's fist closed on his shoulder, and he screamed as bones ground beneath his skin. Bloodfang fell back with a heavy crash, and Sigmar was dragged with him, fighting to free himself from the warlord's grip.

Bloodfang released his axe and took hold of Sigmar's head.

Sigmar dropped Ghal-maraz and wrapped his hand around Bloodfang's wrists, the muscles in his arms bulging as he strained against the enormous strength that threatened to crush his skull.

Veins writhed in his arms and his face purpled with the effort of trying to pull Bloodfang's hands from his head.

Their faces were less than a hand's span apart, and Sigmar locked his gaze with the powerful warlord, his twin-coloured eyes meeting the blazing red of Bloodfang's without fear.

'You. Will. Never. Win,' snarled Sigmar as the power of a winter storm surged through his body with cold, unforgiving fury.

Inch by inch, he prised Bloodfang's hands from his head, relishing the look of surprise and fear in the warlord's eyes. That fear drove Sigmar onward, and with growing strength he pulled the warlord's hands even further apart.

Sigmar grinned in triumph and rammed his forehead into the warlord's face. Blood burst from the orc's pig-like nose and it roared in frustration. Realising that he could not simply crush Sigmar with brute strength, Bloodfang ripped a hand clear and reached for his axe.

It was all the opening that Sigmar needed.

He swept up Ghal-maraz and brought the ancestral heirloom of the dwarfs down upon Bloodfang's face with all his might.

The warlord's skull exploded into fragments of bone and flesh and brain matter. A flare of white light burst from the warhammer, and Sigmar was hurled clear as Bloodfang's body was entirely unmade by the most powerful energies of the dwarfs' ancient weapon.

Blinking away the after-images of Urgluk Bloodfang's death, Sigmar saw the shock and awe on the faces of the orcs that surrounded him. They still carried sharp swords, and he saw the fires of vengeance and opportunity in their eyes.

Sigmar tried to stand, but his strength was gone, his blood-covered limbs trembling in the aftermath of channelling such mighty power. He sank to his haunches and reached for a weapon of some description to fight these orcs, but only broken sword blades and snapped spear hafts lay next to him.

A broad-shouldered orc with a helmet of dark iron reached for the fallen warlord's axe, and a white-shafted arrow punched through the visor of its helmet to bury its iron point in the beast's brain. Another followed and within seconds a flurry of arrows thudded into the orc ranks, followed by a swelling roar of triumph.

Sigmar lifted his gaze to the blue sky, and wept in gratitude as the warriors of his army swept past him and into the stunned orcs. Asoborn warrior women shrieked as they tore into the orcs alongside Unberogen, Cherusens, Taleutens and Merogens. Thuringian berserkers, led by King Otwin, rushed headlong into the orc lines, followed by Menogoth spearmen. Thundering Raven Helm cavalry, hungry to avenge Marbad's death, smashed into the greenskins, and Brigundian archers harried the orcs with deadly accurate shafts.

King Wolfila cleaved a bloody swathe through the orcs with his enormous, basket-hilted broadsword, and his howling clansmen followed him into the orcs with furious howls.

The orcs' courage and resolve, teetering on a knife edge at the incredible death of their leader, broke in the face of this new attack, and within moments they were a panicked, fleeing mob.

A horse drew up next to Sigmar and he looked up into Alfgeir's scowling face.

'By all the gods, Sigmar!' snapped the Marshal of the Reik. 'That was the most insane thing I have ever seen.'

DARKNESS WAS FALLING by the time the last of the greenskins had been driven from the field. With the death of Urgluk Bloodfang, the awesome power that had dominated and bound the orc tribes together was gone, and they had fractured like poorly forged steel. Without the warlord's force of will, old jealousies erupted and, even amid the slaughter of the rout, the orcs had turned on one another with bloody axes and swords.

The exhausted warriors of Sigmar's army had pursued the orcs as long as they were able, vengeful cavalry riding down thousands as they quit the pass and fled for the desolation of the east. Only darkness and exhaustion had prevented further pursuit, and the sun was low in the west when the riders returned in triumph, their horses windblown and lathered.

It had taken some time for the enormity of the victory to sink in, for so many had died to win it, and so many would yet die upon the surgeon's tables, but as the horsemen rode back to camp, the laughter and songs had begun, and the relief of those who lived surged to the fore.

Wagons of ale threaded through the camp, and Sigmar watched the spirits of men soar like sparks from a fire. Men and dwarfs shared this night of victory, talking and drinking as brothers, sharing tales of courage and the deeds of heroes.

The dead would be mourned, but tonight was for the living.

The warriors that lived drew air that was fresher than any they had previously breathed into their lungs, drank ale that tasted finer than any brew supped before, and sat with friends that would become dearer than any they had ever known.

Moonlight bathed the battlefield of Black Fire Pass, and Sigmar smiled as he felt the breath of the world sigh through the mountains, filling him with the promise of life. The lands of men would endure, and the first great challenge had been met and overcome, though he knew there were still battles to fight and enemies to overcome. He wondered where the next enemy would arise as a cold wind blew from the north.

The orc dead were dragged away and left for the crows, while the fallen of Sigmar's army were carried to great funeral pyres built in the shadow of the ruined dwarf watchtower. A warrior from each of the tribes stepped forward to light the pyres, and as the flames caught and sent the dead to Ulric's hall, the pass echoed with the howls of mountain wolves.

With the warriors of the army honoured, the kings of men marched in solemn procession towards the last remaining pyre, bearing the body of King Marbad upon a bier of golden shields.

The king of the Endals was borne by Otwin of the Thuringians, Krugar of the Taleutens, Aloysis of the Cherusens, Siggurd of the Brigundians, Freya of the Asoborns and Marbad's son, Aldred.

Sigmar followed behind the fallen king with Wolfila of the Udose, Henroth of the Merogens, Adelhard of the Ostagoths and Markus of the Menogoths. Each of these kings carried a golden shield, and no words were spoken as they followed the body of their brother king to his final rest.

Kurgan Ironbeard of the dwarfs stood at the watchtower, resplendent in his silver armour and a flowing cloak of golden mail. Beside him stood Master Alaric, his head bowed in sorrow, and Sigmar favoured his friends with a nod of respect.

A priest of Ulric awaited the bearers of the dead beside the pyre, swathed in a cloak of wolf pelts and carrying a flaming brand. Thousands of warriors surrounded the procession of kings, but not a breath of wind or a single whisper broke the silence.

The kings bearing Marbad brought him to the pyre and laid his body upon it. Even in death, the aged king of the Endals was a striking figure, and Sigmar knew he would be greatly missed.

His black cloak was folded around his body, and the kings of the lands west of the mountains stepped back as the priest of Ulric thrust the flaming brand deep into the oil-soaked wood.

The pyre roared to life, and as Marbad burned, Sigmar stood before Aldred. The young man had his father's lean physique, and carried Ulfshard sheathed at his waist. Tears gathered at the corners of his eyes, and Sigmar placed a hand on Aldred's shoulder.

'This was your father's,' said Sigmar, handing a golden shield to Aldred. 'You are now king of the Endals, my friend. Your father was a brother to me. I hope you will be too.'

Aldred said nothing, but nodded stiffly and turned his eyes to the pyre once more.

Sigmar left Aldred to his grief, and moved to stand beside King Kurgan as the kings of men raised their golden shields in salute of their fallen brother.

'Nice shields,' noted Kurgan. 'Do I see Alaric's influence in their craft?'

'You do indeed,' agreed Sigmar. 'Master Alaric is a fine teacher.'

Alaric bowed at the compliment as Kurgan continued. 'Young Pendrag told me what you said when you gave them those shields. Fine words, lad, fine words.'

'True words,' said Sigmar. 'We *are* the defenders of the land.'

'Aye,' agreed Kurgan, 'but a warrior needs a weapon as well as a shield to defend his home. What say I have Alaric here fashion you some swords to go with those shields?'

'I would be honoured.'

'Well, Alaric, you up for making some swords for Sigmar's fellow kings?'

Alaric seemed taken aback by Kurgan's offer, and hesitated before answering. 'I... well, it will be difficult and–'

'Good, good,' said Kurgan, patting Alaric on the shoulder. 'Then it's settled. I give you my oath that the kings of men will have the finest blades forged by dwarf craft, or my name's not Kurgan Ironbeard.'

Sigmar bowed to the king of the dwarfs, overwhelmed by the generosity of Kurgan's offer. As he straightened, and turned back to Marbad's pyre, he saw his brother kings gathered before him. Each carried the shield he had given them at their side, and each bore an expression of loyalty that made Sigmar's heart soar.

Siggurd stepped forward and said, 'We have been talking of what comes next.'

'What comes next?' asked Sigmar.

'Aye,' said Siggurd. 'The lands of men have been saved, and you have your empire.'

The king of the Brigundians nodded and as one, the assembled kings dropped to their knees with their heads bowed. Behind them, the hosts of man followed the example of their kings, and soon every warrior in the pass knelt before Sigmar.

'And an empire needs an emperor,' said Siggurd.

EMPIRE

BOOK ONE
Empire of Hope

Then all chiefs made an oath
To stand together, united as men,
And a crown was fashioned
By Alaric, runesmith of the dwarfs,
Placed by Ulric, the priest,
Upon noble Sigmar's brow.

ONE
The Last Days of Kings

THE SHADOWS WERE long as the hag woman stepped from the misty hilltop overlooking the city of Reikdorf. She had walked many miles from her home in the Brackenwalsch, and her limbs were aching from the long journey. The poultices and tisanes of spiderleaf and valerian were no longer able to keep the crystals in her joints from causing her pain, and she rested for a moment upon a long staff fashioned from the wood of the rowan tree. The staff's top was hung with talismans of protection and shrouding, for the summer solstice was a time when the eyes of the gods were turned on the world, and it did not do to attract unwanted attention.

The hag woman set off down the hill towards the city that shone like a beacon in the gathering darkness. Torches had been set on the new walls of stone and light poured from the city, illuminating the landscape around it in a warm, safe glow.

The hag woman knew that safety was illusory, for this was a dangerous world, an old world, where monstrous beasts lurked in the sprawling forests, and warlike greenskin tribes raided the lands of men from their mountain lairs. Nor were these the only dangers that pressed close to the light: things unknown and unseen gathered their strength in the darkness to assault mankind.

A shiver travelled the length of the hag woman's spine, and she felt the clammy embrace of the grave in its chill. Her time in this world was nearing an end, and there was still so much to do, so many courses yet to steer, and so many fates to thwart. The thought made her pick up her pace.

The ground was soft underfoot, warm and still damp from earlier rain. Though a stone-flagged road wound its way towards the open southern gate of the city walls, the hag woman kept to the grass, preferring to feel the life of the world beneath her feet. To walk barefoot was to feel the power that dwelt in the earth, and to know that streams of uncorrupted energy still existed in the sacred places of the world.

That such places were becoming ever fewer was a source of great sorrow to the hag woman. Every road, every hall of stone and every step taken on the path of civilisation took mankind further from his connection with the land that had birthed him. The advancements that allowed men to survive in this world were the very things divorcing them from their origins and their true strength.

The city walls reared up before her, tall and strong, constructed from blocks of dark stone. They were at least thirty feet high, and she recognised the teachings of the mountain folk in the precisely cut blocks. A pair of stout towers flanked the open gateway, and she saw the gleam of firelight on armour behind their saw-toothed battlements.

She reluctantly stepped onto the roadway and limped through the gateway, past rows of bearded Unberogen warriors armoured in fine hauberks of gleaming mail and bronze helmets with horsehair plumes.

None of the warriors so much as glanced at the hag woman, and she smiled at how easily men were fooled by even the simplest of enchantments.

Reikdorf opened up before her, and though it had been many years since she had come to Sigmar's city, she was nevertheless shocked by how much it had changed. What had once been little more than a simple fishing village on the banks of the Reik had grown to something huge and sprawling. Despite herself, she was impressed by Sigmar's achievements.

Buildings of stone clustered tightly together in a warren of streets and alleys that reeked of life and unfettered growth. Granaries and storehouses loomed over her, and shouted oaths drifted from reeking taverns. Even this late in the day, metal clanged on metal from a nearby forge, and runners darted through the crowds carrying messages between merchants. The streets were thronged with people, though none save children and dogs spared her more than a glance. As she made her way through the city, men made the sign of the horns for no reason they could adequately explain, and women pulled suckling babes tighter to their breasts.

She could see the longhouse of the Unberogen kings ahead, a magnificently constructed hall fashioned by dwarf hands in gratitude for the rescue of King Kurgan Ironbeard of Karaz-a-Karak from greenskin marauders. The heavy timber shutters were thrown open, and yellow light spilled from within, carried on the sounds of great mirth and raucous merrymaking.

A host of banners was planted before the longhouse, a riot of colours and devices that had once signified division, but which now spoke of unity and shared purpose. She saw the raven of the Endals, the rearing stallion of the Taleutens, the Skull Banner of King Otwin of the Thuringians and many others. She frowned at the one notable absence, and shook her head as she made her way towards the longhouse, to where the lord of the Unberogen tribe and soon-to-be Emperor gathered his warriors.

Wide doors of iron-banded timber led inside. Before them stood six warriors in thick wolfskin cloaks with heavy hammers of wrought iron. As before, none paid her any attention as she passed between them, fogging their minds and memories of her presence. The guards would go to their graves swearing on their children's lives that not a single soul had passed them.

The smell of sweat and free-flowing beer assailed her inside the longhouse, along with the vast heat of the fire pit at its centre. Sturdy tables ran the length of the building, and hundreds of warriors filled it with songs and laughter. Smoke from the fire gathered beneath the roof, and the rich aroma of roasting pork made her mouth water.

Though she had passed unseen through the streets of Reikdorf, she kept to the shadows, for there were minds close by that were sharper than those of ordinary folk. Kings, queens and dwarfs had gathered in Reikdorf and would not be so easily fooled. She made her way to the rear of the longhouse, far from the empty throne at the other end of the hall that sat beneath a series of grisly battle honours.

War banners hung from the rafters, and the hag woman was gratified to see tribesmen from across the empire moving through the hall with an ease only shared by brothers-in-arms. These warriors had fought and bled at the Battle of Black Fire Pass, against the greatest horde of greenskins the world had ever seen. That incredible victory and shared horror had forged a bond as unbreakable as it would be enduring.

Endal pipers played martial tunes, and dwarf songsmiths told tales of ancient battles in time to the skirling music. The atmosphere was festive, the mood joyous, and the hag woman felt a moment of guilt for intruding on this day of celebration.

She wished she could have brought the new Emperor a gift of joy on his coronation night, but that was not the way of the world.

HIGH ABOVE REIKDORF on Warrior Hill, Sigmar knelt before his father's tomb, and scooped a handful of soil into the cup of his palm. The earth was dark, rich and loamy. It was good soil, nourished by the ancient dead. Looking at the great slab of rock that sealed King Björn's tomb, Sigmar wished his father could see him now. He had achieved so much in his time as king, yet there was still much to do.

'I miss you, father,' he said, letting the earth pour between his fingers. 'I miss the strength you gave me and the earned wisdom you freely offered, though too often I heeded it not.'

Sigmar lifted a foaming tankard of beer from the ground beside him and poured it onto the earth before the tomb. The smell of it stirred a thirst in Sigmar as he drew his hunting knife from its sheath at his belt. The weapon was a gift from Pendrag, and the workmanship was exquisite, the blade acid-etched with the image of a twin-tailed comet. Even King Kurgan had grunted that the blade was serviceable, which was about as close as a dwarf ever came to a compliment on the metalworking skills of other races.

With one swift motion, Sigmar drew the blade across his forearm, allowing blood to well in the cut before turning his arm over to let the ruby droplets fall to the ground. The dark soil soaked up his blood, and he let it flow until he was satisfied that he had given enough.

'This land is my one abiding love,' he said. 'To this land and its people, I pledge my life and my strength. This I swear before all the gods and the spirits of my ancestors.'

Sigmar stood and turned his gaze further down the hillside, where countless other tombs had been dug into the earth. Each contained a friend, a loved one or a sword-brother. The day's last light caught on a pale stone lying flush against the hillside, its surface etched with long spirals and garlanded with wild honeysuckle.

'Too many times have I sent my brothers into the hillside,' whispered Sigmar, remembering the climb to roll that boulder across the darkened sepulchre housing Trinovantes's body. It seemed inconceivable that sixteen winters had passed since his friend's death. So much had happened and so much had changed that it was as if the time when Trinovantes had lived belonged to some other life.

Painful memories threatened to surface, but he forced them down, not wishing to tempt fate on the day his grand dream of empire was finally coming to fruition.

A cold wind flayed the summit of the great Unberogen burial mount, but Sigmar did not feel its chill. A dark wolfskin cloak was pulled tightly about his shoulders and a padded woollen jerkin kept him warm. His blond hair was pulled tight in a short ponytail, his forelocks braided at his temples. Sigmar's features were strong and noble, and his eyes, one a pale blue, the other a deep green, carried wisdom and pain beyond his thirty-one years.

Sigmar stood and brushed his hands clean of earth. He took a deep breath, and looked out over the landscape as dusk cast its purple shadows eastwards. Reikdorf shone with torchlight below him, but it was possible to see spots of light in the far distance, each one a well-defended town with a strong body of armed men to protect it. Beyond the horizon of forest, hundreds more villages and towns were spread throughout his domain, all united under his rule and sworn to the cause of a united empire of man.

The year since Black Fire Pass had been a bountiful one, the fields providing much needed grain to feed the returning warriors and their families. The winter had been mild, the summer balmy and peaceful, and the recent harvest had been among the most plentiful anyone could remember.

Eoforth claimed it was a reward from the gods for the courage shown by the warriors of the Empire, and Sigmar had been only too pleased to accept his venerable counsellor's interpretation. The years preceding the battle had been lean and hard, the land ravaged by constant battle against the greenskins. Mankind had been on the verge of extinction, but the flickering candle-flame had survived the darkness, and, now, burned even brighter.

'Winter coming soon,' said Alfgeir, standing a respectful distance behind him.

'A fortune teller are you now, old friend?' asked Sigmar, gripping the handle of Ghal-maraz, the great warhammer presented to him by King Kurgan Ironbeard.

'Don't need to throw the bones to feel winter on this wind,' said Alfgeir. 'And less of the "old" thank you very much. I'm barely forty-four.'

Sigmar turned to face the man who was both his Marshal of the Reik and personal bodyguard. Standing tall and proud in his gleaming bronze plate armour, Alfgeir was the very image of a proud Unberogen warrior. His face was scarred and craggy, yet Alfgeir wore his age with great dignity, and woe betide any young buck who sought to humble the old man during training on the Field of Swords. Once, his hair had been dark, but now it was streaked with silver.

Like Sigmar, he wore a long wolfskin cloak, though his was white and had been a gift from King Aloysis of the Cherusens. A longsword of cold iron was belted at his waist, and his eyes constantly scanned the landscape for enemies.

'There's nothing out there,' said Sigmar, following Alfgeir's wary looks.

'You don't know that,' replied Alfgeir. 'Could be beasts, goblins, assassins. Anything.'

'You're being paranoid,' said Sigmar, setting off down the path towards his city. He pointed towards the tribal camps beyond the city walls to the west. 'No one would try to kill me today, not with so many armed warriors around.'

'It's having so many warriors around that makes me nervous,' said Alfgeir, following Sigmar towards Reikdorf. 'Any one of them might have lost a father, a brother or a son in the wars you fought to win their kings to your cause.'

'True enough,' agreed Sigmar. 'But do you really think any of the great kings has brought someone like that to my coronation?'

'Probably not, but I do not like to take chances,' said Alfgeir. 'I lost one king to an enemy blade. I'll not lose an emperor to another.'

King Björn had fallen in the wars to drive the Norsii from the lands of the Cherusens and Taleutens, and the shame of his failure to protect his liege lord had broken Alfgeir's heart. When Sigmar became king of the Unberogen, he had all but destroyed the northern tribe in the following years, pushing their armies into the sea and burning their ships. His father had been avenged and the Norsii cast out from the Empire, but Sigmar's hatred remained strong.

Sigmar stopped and placed his hand on Alfgeir's shoulder.

'Nor shall you, my friend,' he said.

'I admire your certainty, my king,' said Alfgeir, 'but I think I'll be happier keeping my guard up and my sword sharp.'

'I would expect nothing less, but you are not a young man anymore,' said Sigmar with a grin that robbed the comment of malice. 'You should let some of the younger White Wolves assist you. Perhaps Redwane?'

'I don't need that young pup hounding my heels,' snapped Alfgeir. 'The lad is reckless and boastful. He irritates me. Besides, I told you, I am barely forty-four, younger than your father was when he took the fight to the north.'

'Forty-four,' mused Sigmar. 'I remember thinking such an age to be ancient when I was young. How anyone could let themselves grow old was beyond me.'

'Believe me, I don't recommend it,' said Alfgeir. 'Your bones ache in winter, your back gets stiff and, worst of all, you get no respect from youngsters who ought to know better.'

'I apologise, my friend,' chuckled Sigmar. 'Now come on. We have honoured the dead, and now it is time to greet my fellow kings.'

'Indeed, my Emperor,' said Alfgeir with a theatrical bow. 'You don't want to be late for your own coronation, eh?'

'YOU ARE DRUNK,' said Pendrag.

'That I am,' agreed Wolfgart, happily taking a bite of roast boar. 'I always said you were the clever one, Pendrag.'

Wolfgart drained his tankard and wiped his arm over his mouth, smearing a line of beer and grease across his sleeve. Both men were dressed in their finest tunics, though Wolfgart had to admit that Pendrag's had survived the preliminary festivities rather better than his.

His sword-brother was dear to him, and they had shared adventures the likes of which would make great sagas to tell his son when he was born, but he did so love to nag. Pendrag was solid and immovable, the perfect build for an axeman, where Wolfgart had the wide shoulders and narrow hips of a swordsman.

Pendrag's flame-red hair was worked in elaborate braids, and his forked beard was stiffened with black resin. Wolfgart had eschewed such gaudy adornments, and simply restrained his wild dark hair with a copper circlet Maedbh had given him on the anniversary of their hand fastening.

Serving girls threaded their way through the heaving mass of celebrating tribesmen, bearing platters stacked high with meat and tankards of foaming beer, while fending off the attentions of amorous drunks. Wolfgart reached out and swept a beaten copper ewer of beer from one of the girl's trays and slurped a noisy mouthful without bothering to pour it into his tankard.

Most of the foaming liquid went down his front, and Pendrag sighed.

'You couldn't stay sober tonight?' asked Pendrag. 'Or at least not get so drunk?'

'Come on, Pendrag! How often does our childhood friend get to be crowned Emperor over all the lands of men? I'll be the first to admit, I thought he was mad as a Cherusen Wildman when he told us his plan, but Ulric roast my backside if he didn't go and do it!'

Wolfgart waved his tankard at the hundreds of feasting tribesmen gathered around the long fire pit. Wild boasts and happy laughter passed back and forth, pipe music vied with songs of battle, and the rafters shook with the sound of great revelries.

'I mean, look around you, Pendrag!' cried Wolfgart. 'All the tribes gathered here, under one roof and not fighting each other. For that alone, Sigmar deserves to be Emperor.'

'It is impressive,' agreed Pendrag, taking a refined sip of Tilean wine. King Siggurd had brought six barrels of the stuff, and Pendrag had acquired quite a taste for it.

'It's more than impressive, it's a damned miracle,' slurred Wolfgart, using his tankard arm to encompass the entire longhouse. 'I mean, the Cherusens and Taleutens have been fighting over their border territories for longer than any of us have been alive, and here they are drinking together. Look over there... Thuringians swearing blood oaths with thems as used to be Teutogens! Bloody miracle is what it is, a bloody miracle.'

'Aye, it's a miracle, but it'll be a greater miracle if you're able to walk in a straight line when the time comes to take the king's march to the Oathstone.'

'Walk. Stagger. What's the difference?' asked Wolfgart, lifting the ewer once again.

Pendrag reached over to restrain him from pouring another drink, and Wolfgart felt the cold metal of his friend's silver hand. A Thuringian axe had taken three of Pendrag's fingers during the Battle of the Berserker King, and Master Alaric of the dwarfs had fashioned the new gauntlet for him. Pendrag claimed that the mechanical fingers functioned as well as his old ones, but Wolfgart had never been able to get used to them.

'You will shame Maedbh if you cannot stand up,' pointed out Pendrag. 'And do you really want that?'

Wolfgart stared hard at Pendrag for a moment before upending the ewer.

'Damn, but you always cut to the bone, friend,' he said, reaching instead for the largely untouched jug of water. 'I slept with the horses for three days the last time I came home drunk.'

Wolfgart took several gulping draughts of water, rinsing his mouth of the taste of beer and spitting it over the straw-covered floor.

'Civilised as always,' said a voice beside Wolfgart as a warrior, armoured in iron plate painted a deep red lowered himself to sit next to him. 'I thought Reikdorf was the light of civilisation in the world these days, and that the northerners were supposed to be the crude barbarians?'

'Ah, Redwane, how the young misunderstand the ways of their elders and betters,' said Wolfgart, smiling and throwing an arm around the White Wolf. Like Pendrag, Redwane's copper-coloured hair was elaborately braided, and his handsome features were open and friendly. Some called them soft, but those who had seen Redwane fight knew that nothing could be further from the truth.

'In the south, it is a sign of good breeding to behave like a lout from time to time,' said Wolfgart.

'Then you are the most civilised man I know,' said Redwane, adjusting his wolfskin cloak around his shoulders, and setting down his hammer before lifting an empty mug.

Wolfgart laughed, and Pendrag poured Redwane a beer.

'Welcome, brother,' he said. 'It is good to have you back in Reikdorf.'

'Aye, it's been too long,' agreed Redwane. 'Siggurdheim is a fine place, with cold beer and warm women, but I'm glad to be home.'

'How come he gets to drink beer, but I don't?' demanded Wolfgart.

'Because Ulric has blessed me,' said Redwane, patting his flat stomach. 'My guts are lined with trollhide, and, unlike you milksops, I'm able to consume more than a flagon before falling down dead drunk.'

'That sounds like a challenge to me,' said Wolfgart, reaching for the beer.

'Leave it,' ordered Pendrag. 'Save it until after the coronation.'

Wolfgart shrugged and threw his hands up, saying, 'Ulric deliver me from these mother hens, one of them barely seventeen summers!'

'How was your journey?' asked Pendrag, ignoring Wolfgart's exasperation.

'Uneventful,' said the warrior, 'more's the pity. Since Black Fire the roads have been quiet, no bandits or greenskins to speak of. Even the forest beasts seem cowed.'

'Aye, it's been a quiet year,' agreed Pendrag.

'Too quiet,' grumbled Wolfgart. 'My sword's getting rusty above the fireplace, and I've not killed a greenskin in two seasons.'

'Wasn't that the point?' countered Pendrag. 'All the years of war were to keep our lands safe and protected. Now we have done that, and you complain because you do not have to fight and risk your life?'

'I am a warrior,' said Wolfgart. 'It's what I know.'

'Maybe you can learn a new trade?' said Redwane, winking at Pendrag. 'With the land safe and the forests being cleared for new settlements, Sigmar's empire will need more farmers.'

'Me, a farmer? Don't be foolish, boy. I think that southern air has rotted your brain if you think I'll be a farmer. Just because we slaughtered the greenskins at the pass doesn't mean they won't be back. No, I'll not be a farmer, Redwane. I'll leave that to others, for this land will always have need of warriors.'

Redwane laughed.

'I expect you're right,' he said. 'You would make a terrible farmer.'

Wolfgart smiled and nodded. 'You have the truth of it. I've not the patience to work the land. I fear I am more suited to ending life than bringing it forth.'

'That's not what I hear,' said Redwane, elbowing Wolfgart in the ribs. 'The talk is that you are to be a father in the spring.'

'Aye,' said Wolfgart, brightening at the mention of his virility. 'Maedbh will bear me a strong son to carry on my name.'

'Or a daughter,' said Pendrag. 'Asoborn women beget girls more often than not.'

'Pah, not on your life!' said Wolfgart. 'With the strength of my seed, the boy will climb out himself, you mark my words.'

'We shall see in the spring, my friend,' said Redwane. 'Whatever form your heir takes, I will help you wet its head in beer, and sing the songs of war through the night with you.'

'I'll be happy to let you,' said Wolfgart, clasping the White Wolf's wrist.

* * *

SIGMAR'S BROTHER KINGS were waiting for him at the base of Warrior Hill, resplendent in robes of many colours and armour of the highest quality. Each carried a golden shield upon one arm, and a line of flaming brands was set in the ground before them. The firelight cast a warm glow about them, the most powerful warriors in the lands of men. Together they had saved their people from annihilation, and now they had gathered to bear witness to a singular event in the history of the world: the crowning of the first Emperor.

This night would seal their pact to preserve the safety of every man, woman and child in the Empire. Sigmar loved them all, and mouthed a silent prayer of thanks to Ulric for the honour of standing shoulder to shoulder with such heroes.

King Krugar of the Taleutens, a broad-shouldered warrior in a gleaming hauberk of silver scale, stood at their centre, flanked by King Henroth of the Merogens and Markus of the Menogoths. Both southern kings were smiling, though Sigmar could see the great sorrows they carried. Their kingdoms had suffered terribly in the wars against the greenskins, and little more than a thousand of their people had survived the years of death.

Sigmar's eyes were drawn next to Queen Freya of the Asoborns. The flame-haired queen was clad in shimmering mail that looked as though it had been woven from golden thread. A torque of bronze and silver encircled her graceful neck, and a winged crown of jewel-studded gold sat on her high brow. A cloak of vivid orange hung from her shoulders, but did little to conceal the smooth curve of her limbs and the sway of her hips as she turned to face him.

Sigmar felt himself responding to Freya's primal beauty, recalling the night of passion that had sealed their union with a mixture of pleasure and remembered pain. He quickly suppressed his feelings and concentrated on greeting the rest of his allies.

Next to the Asoborn Queen stood Adelhard of the Ostagoths, his drooping moustache waxed to gleaming points, and his chequered cloak of black and white echoing the trews and shirt he wore beneath it. Ostvarath, the sword of the Ostagoth kings, was sheathed at Adelhard's side. Adelhard had offered to surrender this sword to Sigmar in return for his aid in battle against the orcs. Sigmar's warriors had fought alongside the Ostagoths, but he had declined Adelhard's sword, claiming that so mighty a weapon should remain with its king.

Aloysis of the Cherusens was a lean, hawk-faced man with dark hair tied in a long scalp lock. In the manner of his fiercest warriors, he had shaved his beard and adorned his face with curling tattoos of blue and red, and his bright red cavalry cloak flapped in the wind. The laconic king give Sigmar a respectful nod.

King Aldred of the Endals wore a fur-lined robe of brown wool, edged in black and gold thread. The symbol of his kingship, the elf blade Ulfshard, was belted at his side, and Sigmar remembered Aldred's father hurling the blade to him at Black Fire Pass. The weapon had saved Sigmar's life, but Marbad had died moments later. Sigmar saw the bitter echoes of Marbad's death in his son's eyes.

The kilted warrior next to Aldred was King Wolfila of the Udose, a gruff king of reckless bravery and great warmth. His clansmen had fought the Norsii for many years, and his pale skin shone with a healthy glow in the torchlight. A great, basket-hilted claymore was sheathed over his shoulder, longer even than Wolfgart's monstrous blade. Wolfila grinned like a loon, and his pleasure at the night's events was clear.

Sigmar smiled to see that King Siggurd had outdone himself, appearing in a rich array of purple and blue robes, edged in ermine and bedecked in enough gold to make a dwarf's eyes gleam with avarice.

Given his last observation, Sigmar was not surprised to see that King Kurgan Ironbeard of the dwarfs stood next to Siggurd, though his oldest ally wore almost as much gold as did the Brigundian king. Clad in a shirt of runic gold plate with silver steel pauldrons and a gold helmet, Kurgan seemed more like one of his people's ancient gods than a mortal king. Alone of all the gathered kings, Kurgan's weapon was bared, a mighty axe with two butterfly-winged blades enchanted with runes that shone with their own spectral light.

King Otwin of the Thuringians stood slightly apart from the others, though whether that was his choice or theirs was unclear. His crown was a mass of golden spikes hammered through the skin of his head, and he wore little more than a loincloth of dark iron mail and a cloak of deepest red. The Berserker King's bare chest heaved, and Sigmar saw the wildroot juice staining his lips.

Myrsa of the Fauschlag Rock, dazzling in his armour of purest white, looked uncomfortable in the company of kings but, as the master of the northern marches, he had earned the right to be part of this fellowship. A long-handled warhammer was slung at Myrsa's belt, but it was no imitation of Sigmar's weapon, for this hammer was designed to be swung from the back of a charging steed.

Only one tribe was not represented, and Sigmar quelled his anger at the absence of the Jutone king. That was a reckoning for another day.

He squared his shoulders, and glanced round at Alfgeir, who gave a barely perceptible nod.

Sigmar took a deep breath and began to speak.

'Never before has this land borne witness to such a gathering of might,' he said, unhooking Ghal-maraz from his belt. 'Even on the barren plain of Black Fire Pass we were not so proud, so strong or so mighty.'

Krugar of the Taleutens stepped from the ranks of kings and drew his sword, a curved cavalry sabre with a blade of brilliant blue steel.

'Have you honoured the dead, King Sigmar?' he asked. 'Have you made offerings to the land and remembered those men from whence you came?'

'I have,' replied Sigmar.

'And are you ready to serve this land?' asked Siggurd.

'I am.'

'When the land is threatened, will you march to its defence?' demanded Henroth.

'I will,' said Sigmar, holding Ghal-maraz out before him.

'Then it's to the Oathstone!' shouted Wolfila, swinging his enormous claymore from its scabbard. 'Ar-Ulric awaits!'

TWO
Rise an Emperor

SIGMAR LED THE kings from Warrior Hill into Reikdorf. Word of their coming had spread, and the city's populace came out to greet them. Hundreds of people lined the streets, carrying torches to dispel the darkness, and cheering as the procession of kings passed. Warriors spilled from the longhouse, banging their swords on their shields as they came. Endal pipers ran to the front of the procession and led the way to the Oathstone, their lilting music speaking to the heart and filling the blood with fire.

He saw Wolfgart and Pendrag in the crowd of warriors, and smiled at their joy. To have come so far and achieved so much was incredible, but Sigmar knew he could not have done it without his friends. What he and his sword-brothers symbolised was the Empire in microcosm; individually men were strong, but together they were mighty.

The kings of the land marched alongside Sigmar with their heads held high and their weapons resting on their shoulders. Tribesmen from all across the Empire yelled and whooped to see their kings so honoured.

Banners waved in the air in a dazzling array of rearing stallions, mailed fists, golden chariots and snarling wolves. Oaths and promises of fealty in a dozen different dialects were shouted as every warrior gathered offered his sword to the king of the Unberogen. As

Sigmar watched their faces, ecstatic in the reflected glow of firelight, he felt the weight of their expectations settle upon his shoulders.

To have won this land was only the first part of his journey.

Now he had to keep it safe.

The procession wound its way through the cobbled streets of the city, past great halls, stone dwellings and timber-framed stables. Children in colourful tunics ran wild, playing with barking dogs, their innocent laughter a welcome counterpoint to the martial shouts of warriors.

The procession emerged into the open square on the river's northern bank, where the sacred stone carried from the east in ages past by the first warriors of the Unberogen was set in the earth. This had been the centre of the original settlement of Reikdorf, back when it had been little more than a collection of wattle and daub huts huddled by the side of the river. The settlement had grown immeasurably since those long ago days, but its heart was ever this place.

The pipers peeled away, taking up positions beside Beorthyn's forge. Sigmar smiled. The irascible old smith had been dead for ten years, yet the forge still bore his name.

Perhaps a thousand people filled the square, pressed against the buildings at the square's perimeter. Torches were planted in a circle around the Oathstone, and a huge figure stood within the ring of firelight beside a vast cauldron of black iron.

Clad in wolfskin and glittering mail that shimmered with hoarfrost, the figure's breath gusted from his mouth as though it were the darkest winter night instead of the last days of summer. He carried a staff of polished oak, hung with long fangs and topped with a wide axe blade that glittered like ice. His face was obscured by a wolf-skull mask, and a thick pelt of white wolfhide hung from his shoulders.

Taller and broader than any warrior Sigmar had ever seen, this was Ar-Ulric, the high priest of the god of battles and winter, a warrior who wandered the wilds with the snow and wind. Generations might pass without any sign of Ar-Ulric, for he had little to do with the affairs of mortals. Ulric was a god who expected his followers to fend for themselves. At his side were two enormous wolves, one with midnight-black fur, the other of purest white. Their fur stood erect, as though frozen, and their eyes were like smouldering coals.

The pipers ceased their music, and the warriors filling the city fell silent as Sigmar entered the circle of torches. His fellow kings took up positions around the circle as Sigmar stood before the enormous cauldron. Dark water filled it, and ice had formed on the surface.

The wolves slowly padded forward and began circling Sigmar. Their fangs were bared and thick ropes of saliva drooled from their jaws. Ar-Ulric remained unmoving as the wolves growled and sniffed him. Sigmar felt the cold of their gaze upon him, knowing he was being judged by a power greater than that of mere beasts.

Cold waves radiated from the wolves, and their icy touch entered Sigmar's bones. Endless winter swept through his flesh in a moment, as though his blood had turned instantly to ice. A vision of vast, unending tundra, eternally roamed by packs of slavering wolves, flashed into his mind. Sigmar glanced at his fellow kings gathered at the ring of torches. None appeared to be feeling the dreadful cold. The breath of Ulric touched only him.

The wolves completed their inspection, and the vision faded from Sigmar's thoughts as they returned to their master's side. Their orange eyes never left Sigmar, and he knew their gaze would always be upon him, no matter where the paths of fate led him.

Apparently satisfied with his wolves' judgement, Ar-Ulric came around the cauldron to stand before him. Like the wolves, the high priest carried the chill of unending winter, and Sigmar saw that the blade of his axe was indeed formed from a jagged shard of ice.

Sigmar knelt before the priest of the wolf god, but kept his head held high. He honoured Ar-Ulric, but he would not show fear before him.

The mighty priest towered over him, a primal presence that spoke of devotion beyond measure and a life of battle in realms beyond mortal ken. Where Sigmar had served Ulric faithfully in battle, Ar-Ulric was the very embodiment of Ulric. This warrior's power was enormous, and for him to emerge from the icy wilderness was a great honour.

'You seek Ulric's blessing,' said Ar-Ulric, his voice hoarse, like a blast of winter wind and just as cold. 'By what right do you think you are worthy of the lord of winter's favour?'

'By right of battle,' said Sigmar, fighting to stop his teeth from chattering in the cold. 'By my blood and sacrifice I have united my people. By such right, I claim dominion over the land, from the mountains to the seas, and all who dwell there.'

'A good answer, King Sigmar,' replied Ar-Ulric. 'Ulric knows your name and watches you with interest. How is it that Ulric should care for the fate of a mortal such as you?'

'I passed through the Flame of Ulric and was not burned,' said Sigmar.

'And you think that is enough?'

Sigmar shrugged.

'I know not,' he said, 'but I have fought every battle with Ulric's name on my lips. I could have done no more.'

Ar-Ulric reached down and took hold of Sigmar's head. The priest's fingers were sheathed in wolf claws, and the king could smell the blood on them. 'I see into your heart, King Sigmar. Your lust for immortal glory sits alongside your devotion to Ulric. You seek to rival his mighty deeds and carve your name in the pages of history.'

Defiance flared in Sigmar's heart.

'Is that wrong?' he asked. 'To desire my name to live beyond my time in this world? Lesser men may be forgotten, but the name of Sigmar will echo into the future. With Ulric's blessing, I will forge the land into an empire that will endure until the end of all things.'

Ar-Ulric laughed, the sound as brittle as ice and as cold as the grave. 'Seek not immortality through war, for it will only bring you pain and death. Go from here, sire sons and daughters, and let them carry your name onwards. Seek not to match the gods in infamy.'

'No,' said Sigmar. 'My course is set. The life of hearth and home is not for me. I was not made for such things.'

'In that you are correct,' said Ar-Ulric. 'There will be no soft bed to pass away the last breath of your dotage, not for you. A life of battle awaits you, Sigmar, and this pleases Ulric.'

'Then you will bless my coronation?'

'That remains to be seen,' said Ar-Ulric. 'Stand and call forth your sword-brothers.'

Sigmar forced himself to his feet, his limbs cold and muscles cramped. He turned towards the ring of firelight and scanned the crowd for his sword-brothers. At last, he saw them just beyond the ring of firelight.

'Wolfgart! Pendrag!' he shouted. 'Come forth and stand with me.'

The kings parted to allow the two warriors through their ranks. Both were dressed in long tunics of red, with wide leather belts from which hung daggers and wolf-tail talismans. Pendrag's attire was clean, where Wolfgart's was crumpled and stained with grease and beer spills. Both looked pleased to be asked to come forth, but Sigmar could see their unease at being in the presence of the hulking priest of Ulric.

'Damn, but I wish I was drunk,' hissed Wolfgart, his gaze never leaving the burning eyes and bared fangs of Ar-Ulric's wolves.

'You already are, remember?' said Pendrag.

'Drunker then.'

A low snarl from the black wolf silenced them both.

'My sword-brothers, Wolfgart and Pendrag,' Sigmar told Ar-Ulric. 'They have fought at my side since we were youngsters, and are bonded to me in blood.'

Ar-Ulric's wolf-skull mask turned towards them, and Sigmar heard sharp intakes of breath as the full force of his frigid gaze swept over them.

The priest nodded and waved Sigmar's sword-brothers forward.

'Disrobe him,' he said, 'until he is as he came into this world.'

Sigmar handed Ghal-maraz to Wolfgart, and, piece by piece, his sword-brothers removed his clothing until he stood naked before the cauldron. His body was lean and muscled, with a host of pale, ridged scars snaking their way over his arms and across his chest and shoulders.

'This is the Cauldron of Woe,' said Ar-Ulric. 'It has been used for centuries to determine the worth of those who seek Ulric's blessing.'

'The Cauldron of Woe?' asked Wolfgart. 'Why's it called that?'

'Because those found unworthy do not survive its judgement,' said Ar-Ulric.

'You had to ask,' snapped Pendrag, and Wolfgart shrugged.

'How does it judge my worth?' asked Sigmar, fearing he already knew the answer.

'You must immerse yourself in its waters and if you emerge alive, you will have proved your worth.'

'That doesn't sound so hard,' said Wolfgart. 'It looks cold, sure enough, but that's all.'

'Do you want to try it?' asked Sigmar, already imagining the freezing temperature of the icy water in the cauldron.

'Oh no,' said Wolfgart, putting up his hands. 'This is your day after all.'

Sigmar gripped the cauldron's edge, feeling the intense cold of the water through the iron. The ice on the surface was solid, but there would be no help in breaking it. He took a deep breath and hammered his fist upon the ice. Pain and cold flared up his arm, but the ice remained firm. Again, he slammed his fist down, and this time a spider-web of cracks appeared.

His hand was a mass of pain, but again and again Sigmar punched the ice until it broke apart beneath his assault. His chest heaved with painful breaths and his fist was covered in blood. Sweat was freezing on his brow, but before he could think of how cold the water was going to be, he hauled himself up and over the lip of the cauldron, and plunged in.

The cold hit Sigmar like a hammer blow, and the breath was driven from him. He tried to cry out in pain, feeling his heart batter against his chest, but freezing water filled his mouth. Bright light, like the dying sun of winter, flashed before his eyes.

Sigmar sank into the darkness of the cauldron.

THE DARKNESS BENEATH the surface of the water was absolute, unending and unyielding. Cold seared his limbs, the sensation akin to being burned. Strange that such icy water should feel like that. Sigmar sank deeper and deeper, far further than the cauldron's size should allow. His body tumbled in its icy depths, lost in the endless night of winter.

His lungs were afire as he tried to hold his breath, and his heart's protesting beat sounded like the pounding of orc war drums in his head. Images flashed before him in the darkness, scenes from his life replayed before him as they were said to do before the eyes of a drowning man. Sigmar watched himself lead the charge at the Battle of Astofen, feeling the savage joy of breaking the greenskin horde, and the numbing sorrow of Trinovantes's death.

He saw the fight against the forest beasts, the slaying of Skaranorak, the battle against the Thuringians and the wars he had fought against the Norsii. A rippling face drifted into view, cruelly handsome with lustrous dark hair and eyes of seductive malice.

Hate swelled in his breast as he recognised Gerreon, the betrayer who had slain his own sister and Sigmar's great love, the wondrous Ravenna. In the wake of his treachery, Gerreon had fled the lands of men, and none knew what had become of him, though Sigmar had always known there was blood yet to be shed between them.

Gerreon's face vanished, and Sigmar saw a great tower of pearl in a mountain valley, long hidden from the sight of men. Atop this tower, he saw a crown of ancient power, and the loathsome creature upon whose skeletal brow it sat. This too drifted from sight, and was replaced with a vision of a towering pinnacle of rock set amid a sprawling, endless forest. A city was built upon this rock, a mighty city of pale stone, and above its towers and spires was a shimmering vision of a snarling white wolf.

Sigmar recognised the Fauschlag Rock, but not as he knew it. This city was old and time-worn, groaning at the seams with centuries of growth. Mighty causeways pierced the forest canopy, immense creations of stone that defied the eye with their enormous proportions. They soared towards the summit of the rock, and a host of warriors garbed in strange, slashed tunics held them against attack.

An army of cruelly malformed horrors, each a hideous meld of man and beast, fought to destroy the city on the rock, but the courage of its defenders was unbreakable. Warriors in bloodstained armour of brazen iron gathered around the city in vast numbers, and the forest burned with sacrificial pyres to their dark gods.

The tide of beasts and warriors broke against the city's defences as a warrior clad in a suit of brilliant white armour sallied forth to break the charge of the hideous attackers. The warrior's face was obscured by the visor of his winged helm, but Sigmar knew that whatever the identity of this warrior, his life was tied to that of the city. If he fell, the city would fall.

Before Sigmar could see more, the vision of battle faded as he sank deeper into the cold depths of the cauldron. His strength was almost spent and his lungs cried out for air.

Was this how his dream of empire was to end? Was this how the greatest warrior in the lands of men was to die, frozen within the Cauldron of Woe and judged unworthy?

Anger lit a fire in Sigmar's heart, and fresh strength flooded his limbs. He swept his arms out with powerful strokes, determined not to die like this.

No sooner had he formed the thought than a shaft of light pierced the darkness, and Sigmar twisted in the water's icy embrace to seek its source. He saw a circle of brightness above him, and twisting spirals of red sank down through the water towards him.

Warmth and the promise of life were carried with the light, and he kicked upwards, swimming through the frozen water towards it. With each stroke, the light grew brighter, and the promise of life surged in his veins. Bursting for air, his head pounding with fiery agony, Sigmar swam through the descending trails of red liquid. He recognised it as blood, but knew not who or what had shed it.

The light shone like the new sun of spring, and with one last desperate heave, Sigmar broke the surface of the water.

SIGMAR ERUPTED FROM the cauldron, drawing in a huge, gulping breath. His vision swam, and he gripped the rim of the cauldron for support as he drew one tortured gasp after another. Cold water ran from his body in a torrent as he held himself upright, determined that he would stand tall before all who witnessed his icy rebirth.

He felt the presence of warm bodies around him, and blinked water from his eyes. Standing around the cauldron were Sigmar's fellow kings, each with bared arms that bled from deep cuts in their flesh. He looked down and saw the water was red with their blood. Ar-Ulric stood behind him. Sigmar swung his legs over the side of the cauldron, and stood naked before his people, holding himself upright with a supreme effort of will.

The cold presence of Ar-Ulric moved closer, and a heavy wolfskin cloak was set upon Sigmar's shoulders. The pelt was warm and soft, and the aching cold of his immersion vanished in the time it took to fasten the leather thong at his neck.

'Kneel,' said Ar-Ulric, and Sigmar obeyed without hesitation.

The Oathstone was on the ground before him, and Sigmar placed his hand upon it. The stone was rough to the touch, red and streaked with gold veins unlike any other stone hewn from the rock of the mountains. It felt warm to the touch, and he heard a keening wail in his head, as though the stone itself was screaming. It was a scream of joy, not of pain, and Sigmar smiled at this affirmation.

He looked up to see if anyone else could hear this scream of elation, but it was clear from the faces around him that the sound was for him and him alone.

Kurgan Ironbeard stepped from the circle of kings, a crown of wondrous design in his hands, a rune-inscribed circlet of gold and ivory set with precious stones. Sigmar lowered his head as the dwarf king handed the crown to Ar-Ulric. The mighty priest stood before him, but his freezing aura did not trouble Sigmar, the icy cold kept at bay by the magic of the wolfskin cloak.

Ar-Ulric raised the crown above his head for all to see. The glow of the torches reflected from the ivory and jewels like starlight on silver, and Reikdorf held its breath. 'The cauldron judges you worthy. You are reborn in the blood of kings.'

'I was born in blood once before,' replied Sigmar.

'Serve Ulric well and your name will live on through the ages,' said Ar-Ulric, setting the crown upon Sigmar's soaking head.

It was a perfect fit, and as the crown settled on his brow the people of Reikdorf erupted in wild cheers, and the music of the pipers began anew. Drums beat and horns were blown as men and women of all the tribes roared their approval, dancing and singing, and beating swords on shields as the mood of jubilation spread throughout the city.

Kurgan Ironbeard leaned forward and said, 'Wear this crown well, Sigmar, for it is the work of Alaric.' The dwarf king winked. 'He wanted to present it to you himself, but I am keeping him busy forging those swords I promised you.'

Sigmar smiled.

'I will wear it with pride,' he said.

'Good lad,' said Kurgan, as Wolfgart came forward, holding Ghalmaraz out to him.

Sigmar grasped the mighty warhammer, feeling the immense power the ancient craft of the mountain folk had wrought into its form. The hammer's grip fitted his hand as never before, and Sigmar knew that this moment would live in the hearts of men forever.

'Arise, Sigmar Heldenhammer,' cried Ar-Ulric, 'Emperor of all the lands of men!'

ONCE AGAIN, THE longhouse was filled with kings and warriors. Wolfgart was enjoying himself immensely: he had bested warriors from the Thuringians, Cherusens and Brigundians in feats of strength, and had put a Menogoth under the table in a drinking contest. Galin Veneva, the Ostagoth warrior who had carried word of the greenskin invasion from the east, now challenged him to a fresh drinking game with a spirit distilled from fermented goat's milk.

'We call it *koumiss*,' said Veneva. 'Is good drink for toasts and games of drinking!'

Wolfgart loudly and graciously conceded defeat after one mouthful of the stuff.

'It's like drinking molten lead,' said Wolfgart, slapping Veneva on the back, his eyes streaming at the liquor's potency. 'But then I'm not surprised you eastern types like your drink so strong, I've seen your women. You'd need to be blind drunk to sleep with them.'

Pendrag led him away from the good-natured jeering of the

Ostagoth fighters, steering him through the scrum of painted, armoured and sweating bodies. Tonight, the kings of men feasted with their warriors, and the smoky atmosphere in the longhouse was one of good cheer and battle-earned brotherhood.

At the end of the longhouse, Sigmar sat on his throne, speaking with Kurgan Ironbeard of Karaz-a-Karak, and the gold of his crown shone as if with an inner fire.

Clad in dwarf-forged plate, a mighty gift from King Ironbeard, the Emperor shone like a god. Alfgeir stood to one side, while Eoforth, Sigmar's venerable counsellor, sat on a bench to his left. The dwarf king leant on his axe as he conversed with Sigmar, taking great gulps of ale between sentences.

Wolfgart waved, and Sigmar nodded in his direction with a broad smile.

'Look at that, eh?' said Wolfgart. 'A bloody emperor! Who'd have thought it?'

'He did,' said Pendrag simply.

Wolfgart looked over the fire pit, seeing Redwane standing on a table and swinging his sword as he recounted tall tales of his heroics at Black Fire Pass to an audience of smiling girls.

'Someone won't be sleeping alone tonight,' said Wolfgart.

'He never does,' replied Pendrag. 'Why spend coin on a night maiden when you can just seduce a pretty serving girl?'

'Good point,' laughed Wolfgart. 'Though, as a married man, I need do neither to wake up next to a warm woman.'

'You are married to an Asoborn woman,' said Pendrag. 'Maedbh would cut off your manhood if you behaved like Redwane.'

'Again, a good point well made,' said Wolfgart, laughing as he spied a familiar face amid the mass of celebrating tribesmen.

Wolfgart pushed through the crowded longhouse, scooping up two unattended tankards of beer from a nearby table on the way. Pendrag followed him as he approached a warrior in black armour, who stood close to the stone walls of the longhouse with his arms folded across his chest.

'Laredus, you old dog!' shouted Wolfgart. 'How in Ulric's name do you fare?'

The man turned at the sound of his name. He wore a winged black helmet and a dark cloak over his similarly black breastplate. Older than Wolfgart by a decade, Laredus was a warrior of the Raven Helms, the elite guards of the Endal kings since the tribe's earliest days.

'Wolfgart,' said Laredus warily.

'I haven't seen you since before Black Fire,' said Wolfgart, thrusting a tankard towards Laredus.

The Raven Helm warrior shook his head, saying, 'No. Thank you, I won't.'

'What?' exclaimed Wolfgart. 'Take a drink, man! Tonight of all nights!'

'I cannot,' said Laredus. 'King Aldred has commanded us not to partake of any strong drink.'

'Ach, you'll be fine then,' said Wolfgart, looking into the mug. 'I think it's Merogen beer. I've pissed stronger stuff than this. Go on, take a drink!'

'No,' repeated Laredus stiffly. 'My king has spoken, and I must obey his orders.'

'Then sit with us awhile,' demanded Wolfgart, irritated at the Raven Helm's refusal to drink with him. 'Tell us of what's happening in Marburg these days.'

Laredus's jaw was set and he bowed curtly to Wolfgart and Pendrag.

'If you will excuse me, I must see to my men,' he said.

Before Wolfgart could reply, Laredus turned on his heel and marched away.

'Ranald's balls, what was the meaning of that?' said Wolfgart, turning to Pendrag.

Pendrag didn't answer, and Wolfgart watched as Laredus joined a group of cloaked Endal tribesmen gathered around their young king.

'I don't understand,' said Wolfgart. 'I wintered in Marburg after Astofen, and fought alongside Laredus against Jutone raiders. We were like brothers, and this is how he treats me! Damn it all, the bugger was friendly enough when last he came to Reikdorf.'

'Aye,' said Pendrag, looking warily at the Endals and their grim-faced king, 'but Marbad was king of the Endals then.'

'You might be onto something there, my friend,' agreed Wolfgart, not liking King Aldred's hooded gaze one bit. Alone of all the kings, he and his warriors sat apart from the celebrations, their eyes cold and aloof. Wolfgart drained the tankard he had offered to the Raven Helm, and then tossed it into the fire pit, making sure the Endals saw him do it.

'Come on, leave it. It's not worth starting trouble tonight,' warned Pendrag, taking hold of his arm.

Wolfgart nodded, more hurt than angry at being snubbed by Laredus.

It made no sense. Brotherhood between warriors was a precious thing, a bond that those who had not risked death facing the enemy would never understand. To break such a bond was sure to anger the gods, and Wolfgart spat into the fire to ward off the bad luck that such a deed would attract.

He shrugged off Pendrag's arm.

'I'm fine,' he said. 'I'm not going to do anything stupid. If Laredus won't drink with us, then let's go find someone who will.'

'I'll save you the hunt,' said a gruff, northern voice behind them. Wolfgart laughed, his ill-temper forgotten as he turned to face the Warrior Eternal of the Fauschlag Rock.

'Myrsa! Gods, man, it's grand to see you,' cried Wolfgart, sweeping his friend into a crushing bear hug. Myrsa was clad in his ubiquitous white plate armour, and hammered his palm against Wolfgart's back. Wolfgart grunted at the strength of the man. He released Myrsa, who took Pendrag's wrist in the warrior's grip.

'It's grand indeed to see you too, my friends,' said Myrsa. 'You fare well?'

'We do all right,' said Wolfgart. 'Nothing a good battle wouldn't cure.'

'Indeed we do,' put in Pendrag. 'Reikdorf grows every day, our people have enough food and the land is at peace. We can ask for no more.'

'Aye, there's truth to what you both say,' agreed Myrsa, lifting a tankard of beer from a passing serving girl's tray.

The three friends took seats at a nearby table, and Wolfgart procured them a long platter of roast boar and steamed vegetables.

'Pendrag's getting soft in his old age,' said Wolfgart, chewing on a succulent rib. 'Spends all his time with Eoforth in that storehouse of books and papers. He's a scholar now, not a warrior.'

'Is that right, Pendrag?' asked Myrsa. 'You hung up that big axe of yours?'

'Wolfgart exaggerates,' said Pendrag, helping himself to some cuts of meat. 'But, yes, I have been spending a great deal of time gathering instructional texts and setting down all that the dwarfs taught us. After all, what use is peace if we do not make use of it to learn new things? How will we pass on that knowledge to future generations?'

'Pendrag has convinced me, Wolfgart' said Myrsa. 'Perhaps we should all become men of learning?'

'Would that the world would let us,' said Pendrag, slapping a hand on Myrsa's pauldron, 'but enough of this mockery. You played your part in Sigmar's crowning well.'

'Aye,' said Wolfgart. 'When Ar-Ulric cut you over that cauldron I thought you were going to bleed ice water. Almost like a proper king, eh?'

A shadow crossed Myrsa's face.

'Do not say that,' he answered. 'I am no king and do not wish to be one. I am charged with leading the warriors of the Fauschlag, but am forced to delegate command more and more often as the business of running Middenheim consumes my every waking moment. It is a nightmare, my friends, a living nightmare. I am a fighter, not a ruler!'

'Middenheim? Is that what they're calling that mountain city of yours?' asked Wolfgart.

Myrsa nodded. 'Our scholars decided that it was time we had a proper name for the city, and they chose the name of the original settlement built around the Flame of Ulric. Supposedly, it comes from an old dwarf word, "watchtower in the middle place" or something like that.'

'Poetic,' grunted Wolfgart.

'And you would know,' smiled Myrsa. 'After all, "town by the Reik" is a name of lyrical beauty.'

Wolfgart was spared from thinking of a suitable response by the arrival of Redwane. The White Wolf was escorted by a statuesque woman in a long green dress, whose skin was pale where it was not decorated with colourful, winding tattoos. She was tall, with broad shoulders and blonde hair wound in a long ponytail that reached to the small of her back.

She cuffed Redwane over the back of the head.

'Maedbh, light of my life and queen of the bedchamber,' cried Wolfgart. He wrapped his arms around his wife and pulled her tight, careful to avoid the new swelling of her belly.

'Husband,' said Maedbh. 'I am returning this lusty dog to you before some jealous warrior sticks a knife in his heart. If he has one, that is.'

'Causing trouble again, Redwane?' asked Myrsa.

'Me? No, just a slight misunderstanding,' protested the White Wolf. 'Christa was feeling faint from the heat, and I was simply taking her outside for some fresh air. I can't help it if Erek thought my intentions towards his woman were anything other than honourable!'

'That rod of yours will get you in real trouble one day,' said

Wolfgart, though he admired the youngster's nerve in making a pass at the notoriously sharp-tongued Christa. 'And my wife won't be there to pull your arse out the fire when it does.'

Redwane smiled and shrugged before sitting on the edge of the table and helping himself to some of Pendrag's food.

'Don't you worry about me,' said Redwane, patting the worn, leather-wound grip of his hammer. 'I can handle any trouble that comes my way.'

'It's not you we're worried about, you dolt,' said Pendrag. 'It's any poor fool who dares challenge you. I don't want you killing a man in an honour duel just because you fancied a tilt at his woman.'

Redwane nodded, but Wolfgart saw that Pendrag's words had made no impression on the volatile young warrior.

'Ah, what's the use?' hissed Pendrag. 'You'll hear no words I say. Only bitter experience will teach you the lesson you so badly need to learn.'

'Always the teacher, eh, Pendrag?' said Wolfgart. 'You see, Myrsa? I told you he was a scholar now.'

Myrsa nodded and drank some more beer as the pipe music filling the hall was silenced and the chaotic hubbub of voices died down. Wolfgart looked towards the end of the longhouse. Sigmar had risen from his throne, and his iron gaze swept the assembled warriors.

'What's happening?' asked Redwane.

'When a new king is crowned, it is traditional for him to dispense favours to those who supported him,' said Pendrag. 'I assume it will be the same for the crowning of an emperor.'

'Favours? What sort of favours?'

'Land, title... That sort of thing.'

'Ah, so lots of kings get more land and fancier titles,' said Redwane.

'Something like that,' agreed Pendrag. 'Don't worry, lad, it won't be anything that affects the likes of us.'

THREE
Reckonings

SIGMAR CLOSED THE door to his bedchamber at the rear of the longhouse and sighed with exhaustion. Two of his White Wolves stood guard on the other side of the door, but if they saw any sign of his weariness, they did not show it. Alfgeir had trained them well. His three hounds lay on his bed in a lair of bearskins, basking in the sullen heat from the banked fire. Their heads bobbed up as he entered. Ortulf, the eldest of the three, bared his fangs, but bounded from the bed upon catching Sigmar's scent. Lex and Kai quickly followed him, all three inordinately pleased to see their master once more.

The hounds had been a gift from King Wolfila of the Udose in the aftermath of Black Fire Pass. Udose warhounds were vicious beasts, difficult to train and temperamental, but once their allegiance had been won, they were loyal to their master unto death. Much like the Udose themselves, reflected Sigmar.

He knelt, ruffled their fur and threw them some strips of roast boar he had taken from the feast hall. They scrapped amongst themselves for the food, though Lex and Kai were careful to allow Ortulf the choicest cuts. As the hounds devoured the boar meat, Sigmar rubbed his eyes and yawned. It had been a long day and he wished for nothing more than a good night's rest.

Sigmar removed the wolfskin cloak around his neck and reached for the clasps securing his magnificent silver armour. Kurgan Ironbeard had presented him with the armour as a coronation gift, and, as Sigmar unbuckled each piece, it felt like he had worn it all his life. Each plate was worked with a skill and craftsmanship known only to the dwarfs, the burnished metal carved with runic script and flawlessly finished to a mirror sheen.

The breastplate was lighter even than the lacquered leather chestguards the Taleuten horse archers wore, moulded to his physique and embossed with a twin-tailed comet of gold at its centre.

No mortal man had ever worn so fine a suit of armour.

He removed the armour quickly and hung each piece on a rack in the corner of the room. Clad only in his tunic and crown, he lifted Alaric's gift from his brow. Like the armour, the crown was a thing of beauty, and Sigmar sensed the ancient power bound to it in the gold runes worked upon the metal.

Sigmar placed the crown in a velvet-lined casket next to his bed and closed the lid. Ghal-maraz he set on an iron weapons rack alongside his leaf-bladed sword, an Asoborn hunting spear and his favourite Cherusen dagger. He sat on the edge of the bed, listening to the raucous celebrations from the great hall of the longhouse, knowing they would continue long into the night.

Though hundreds of warriors were close by, Sigmar felt strangely alone, as though his elevation to Emperor had somehow isolated him from his fellows. He knew he was still the same man he had always been, but something fundamental had changed, though he could not yet fathom what it was.

He thought back to his pronouncements in the longhouse, and the deafening cheers that greeted each one. In the weeks leading to his coronation, Sigmar had thought long and hard about what boons to grant those that had sworn loyalty to him. His allies were proud men and women, and would seek rewards for the blood their people had shed to make him Emperor.

Sigmar's first act had also been his grandest.

He abolished the title of king, declaring that no one who called himself a king should be subject to another's rule. Instead, each of the tribal kings would take the title of count, retaining all their lands and rights as rulers over their people. Their sword oaths still bound them to Sigmar, as his did to them.

The land of each of the counts was entrusted to them for all time, and Sigmar swore on Ghal-maraz that they and their descendants would remain his honoured brethren for so long as they upheld the ideals by which their realms had been won and made safe.

One land, one people, united under a single ruler, yet still able to retain their identities.

With the biggest proclamation made and accepted, Sigmar had then turned to individual honours. He named Alfgeir Grand Knight of the Empire, and entrusted him with the protection of Reikdorf and its people. Sigmar presented the stunned Alfgeir with a glorious banner woven from white silk acquired at fabulous expense from the olive-skinned traders of the south. Depicting a black cross with a wreathed skull at its centre, Sigmar declared it would forever be borne by those who fought in defence of Reikdorf.

Amid wild cheering, Sigmar had declared that Reikdorf would be the foremost city of the Empire, his capital and seat of power. It would become a beacon of hope and learning for his people, a place where warriors and scholars would gather to further man's knowledge of the world in which he lived.

To this end, Sigmar announced the building of a great library, and named the venerable Eoforth as its first custodian. The canny Eoforth had served as Björn's counsellor for more than forty years and, together with Pendrag, had amassed a vast collection of scrolls written by some of the wisest men in the Empire.

Eoforth would be entrusted with the gathering of knowledge from all across the lands of men, bringing it together under one roof so that any who sought wisdom might find it within the library's walls. Sigmar placed the grey mantle of a scholar upon Eoforth, seeing Pendrag's anticipation as he awaited a similar position within this new institution.

But Sigmar had a greater destiny in mind for Pendrag.

He smiled, picturing Pendrag's face as he was appointed Count of Middenheim, entrusted with the rule of the Empire's northern marches. The shock on Pendrag's face was mirrored by the relief on Myrsa's, and Sigmar knew that the decision was the correct one.

Warriors from all the tribes were honoured for their courage at Black Fire Pass, Maedbh of the Asoborns, Ulfdar of the Thuringians, Wenyld of the Unberogen, Vash of the Ostagoths and a score of others. The longhouse shook with the sounds of swords and axes banging on shields, and with his duty to his warriors fulfilled, Sigmar had left them to their revelries.

Tired beyond measure, Sigmar slid beneath the bearskin covers of his bed, his three hounds curling together on the Brigundian rug at the centre of the room.

He longed for sleep but, as the hours passed, slumber would not come.

THE HEARTH-FIRE HAD burned low, casting a dull red glow around his chamber. Though the room was warm and his covers thick, Sigmar suddenly felt the lingering soul-chill of his near-drowning in the Cauldron of Woe.

He shivered as fleeting glimpses of the things he had seen beneath the icy water returned to him. What did they mean and how should he interpret them? Were they visions of the future granted to him by Ulric or mere phantasms conjured by his air-starved mind to ease his passage into death? When the days of feasting were over and the counts had returned to their lands, Sigmar resolved to task Eoforth with researching the meaning behind his visions.

Ortulf and Lex lifted their heads from the rug, growling softly at some unidentified threat, and Sigmar was instantly alert. Without appearing to move, he slid his hand beneath the covers for the punch dagger hidden in a secret pocket within the bearskin.

Opening his eyes a fraction, Sigmar scanned the room for anything out of place. All three hounds were growling now, though he could hear their confusion. Something had alerted them, but they could not identify what.

A shadow detached itself from the corner of the room, and Sigmar's fist closed around the bronze hilt of the punch dagger.

'Put down your weapon, Child of Thunder,' said a loathsome voice that Sigmar had hoped never to hear again. 'I mean you no harm.'

'I wondered when you would show your face,' said Sigmar, propping himself up and keeping his grip firm on the hilt of his dagger.

'You sensed my presence?' said the hag woman, limping across the room. 'I am impressed. Most men's minds are too concerned with their desires to notice the truth of the world around them.'

'I sensed a foulness on the air, but knew not what it was,' said Sigmar. 'Now I do.'

The hag woman chuckled mirthlessly and moved towards his bed using a staff of dark wood for support.

'So that is to be the tone of our discussion,' she said. 'Very well, I shall speak no words of friendship or congratulation.'

Sigmar's hounds bared their fangs, muscles tensed and hackles raised. The hag woman spat a curse in their direction, and the dogs whimpered in fear, slinking away to the furthest corner of the room.

'The beasts fear me, even if men do not,' she said wistfully. 'That is something at least.'

She sat on the end of Sigmar's bed, and he could see the weight of years upon the woman. Her skin was loathsomely wrinkled, like weathered leather, and what little remained of her white hair was lank and thin. For a moment, Sigmar was moved to pity. Then he remembered the misery she had allowed to enter his life and his heart hardened.

'You truly knew I was in Reikdorf?' she asked.

'Yes,' said Sigmar. 'And now I wish you gone. I am weary and I am not in the mood for words of doom.'

The hag woman laughed, the sound like winter twigs snapping underfoot.

'Alaric's crown gives you perception,' she said. 'Beware you do not seek to replace it.'

'What is that supposed to mean?'

'A piece of advice, nothing more,' said the hag woman. 'But that is not why I am here. I come with a warning and a request.'

'A request?' said Sigmar. 'Why should I grant you anything? All you have done is bring me misery.'

A shadow of anger passed over the hag woman's face, and Sigmar recoiled from her cold fury.

'You hate me,' she said, 'but if you knew all I had sacrificed to guide you, make you strong and prepare you for what is to come, you would drop to your knees and grant me my heart's desire.'

'Why should I believe you?' demanded Sigmar. 'Your words bring only death.'

'And yet you have your empire.'

'Won by the courage of warriors,' said Sigmar, 'not the wiles of your scheming.'

'Won by your lust for death and glory,' snapped the hag woman. 'Most men's desires are simple and banal: food in their belly, a home to shelter from the cold, and a woman to bear their sons. But not you... No, Sigmar the Heldenhammer is a killer whose heart only sings when death is a hair's-breadth away and his bloodstained hammer is crushing the skulls of his foes. Like all warriors, you have darkness in your heart that *lusts* for violence. It is what births the urge to kill and destroy in men, but yours will consume you without balance in your heart. Temper your darkness with compassion, mercy and love. Only then will you be the Emperor this land needs for it to survive. This is my warning to you, Child of Thunder.'

The hag woman's words cut like knives, but Sigmar could not deny the truth of them. The clamour of battle *was* when he felt truly alive, when his enemies were broken and driven from the field of battle in a tide of blood.

'You call it darkness, but it allowed me to defeat my enemies,' said Sigmar. 'I need it to defend my lands.'

'It is ever my curse to be unappreciated,' sighed the hag woman, 'but my time in this world is short, and I have only this one chance to pass on my knowledge of things to come.'

'You have seen the future?' asked Sigmar, making the sign of the horns.

'There *is* no future,' said the hag woman. 'Nor is there a past. All things exist now and always. It is the blessing of mankind that they do not perceive the whole of this world's infinite structure. Existence is a complex puzzle, of which you see but a single piece. It is my curse to see many such pieces.'

'You do not see them all?' asked Sigmar, intrigued despite himself.

'No, and I am grateful for that small mercy. Only the gods dare know everything, for it would drive men to madness to know the full truth of their destiny.'

'You have delivered your warning,' said Sigmar. 'Now make your request and begone.'

'Very well, though you will be pleased that this time I speak of life, not death.'

'Life? Whose?'

'The man named Myrsa,' said the hag woman. 'You call him the Warrior Eternal, and it is a well-chosen title. The people of the Fauschlag Rock harken to an ancient prophecy, one that warns of their city's fall without such a warrior to lead their armies in times of war.'

The hag woman laughed. 'A false prophecy delivered by a conniving soothsayer to advance his idiot son's ambitions, though now it seems it has a measure of truth to it. More by accident than design, I suspect. In any case, you must not allow the Warrior Eternal to die before his time.'

'Before his time?' asked Sigmar. 'What kind of request is that? How can any man know when it is his time to leave this world?'

'Some men know, Child of Thunder,' said the hag woman. '*You* will know.'

Once again Sigmar made the sign of the horns.

'A curse on you, woman!' he said. 'Speak not the words of my death! Now leave or by Ulric's blood I will kill you where you sit.'

'Be at peace,' said the hag woman. 'I do not speak of your death.'

'Then what do you mean?'

'No,' said the hag woman with a knowing wink. 'That I *choose* not tell you, for it is the uncertainty of life that keeps it interesting, don't you think?'

Anger flared in Sigmar's heart, and he slid from the bed, his blade extended before him.

'You torment me with your mysteries, woman,' he said. 'Well, no more! If I see you again, I will cut your throat before that vile tongue can utter another curse upon my head.'

'Fear not, Child of Thunder, for this will be the last time we speak,' promised the hag woman sadly. 'Yet we will see one another again, and you will remember my words.'

'More riddles,' spat Sigmar.

'Life is a riddle,' said the hag woman, rising from the bed with a smile and turning her gaze upon the smouldering fire. 'Now sleep, and do not forget what I have said, or everything you have built will be destroyed.'

The hearth erupted with flames, and the dagger dropped from Sigmar's hand as he collapsed onto his bed. Great weariness descended upon him, and the sleep that had previously eluded him dragged him down into its warm embrace.

SIGMAR AWOKE WITH the dawn, warm and refreshed beneath his bearskin. There was no sign of the hag woman and his hounds were no worse for the encounter, though the same could not be said for Sigmar. Her words hung like chains around his neck, and throughout the rest of the week of feasting and celebration, he found his eyes darting to the shadows lest her dark form should emerge from them.

Over the next six days, the warriors of the Empire gorged themselves on the fruits of their victory: mountains of food and lakes of beer. Counts from the far corners of the Empire brought wines and fiery spirits from beyond the mountains to the south, and tribal dishes were prepared by the womenfolk of every land. Unberogen beer, a powerful ale flavoured with bog myrtle was consumed by the barrel-load, and crate after crate of Asoborn wine was unloaded from the docks and dragged to the longhouse.

Cherusen beef was served on platters with Menogoth pork, and every count enjoyed new and exotic dishes from across the Empire. Truly, it was a feast that none gathered in Reikdorf would ever forget. Nor was it only the warriors who were honoured with such largesse; Sigmar commanded his granaries to be opened, and for the duration of the coronation, free bread was distributed to every family in Reikdorf and beyond.

Eoforth bemoaned the expense, but Sigmar was not to be dissuaded, and his name was praised from one end of the land to the other.

Custom dictated that the Emperor spent his coronation day as an aloof and magisterial ruler, but for the rest of the week he resolved to be simply Sigmar the man. Wolfgart and Pendrag had approached him almost immediately on the second morning, and Sigmar knew exactly what his banner bearer was going to say.

'I cannot do this, Sigmar,' said Pendrag. 'Ruler of an entire city? It is an honour, but there must be others more suited to the task.'

Wolfgart shook his head, and said, 'He's been like this all night, Sigmar. Sort him out.'

Sigmar took his old friend by the shoulders and said. 'Look at what you have done with Reikdorf: stone walls, new schools, forges and regular markets. You have made it the jewel in my crown, and you will do the same for Middenheim, I know it.'

'But Myrsa... It is his city,' protested Pendrag, though Sigmar saw that the thought of applying his ideas to a new city appealed to him. 'The honour should be his. He will feel slighted.'

Sigmar shivered, recalling the hag woman's words as Wolfgart said, 'I think Myrsa will be only too happy to have you take charge. What was it he said last night? "I am a fighter, not a ruler!" I don't think you need worry about Myrsa's feelings, my friend.'

'For a man who's been up all night drinking, Wolfgart speaks sense,' added Sigmar. 'But keep Myrsa close, for he knows the city and its people. He will be a staunch ally in your rule.'

'I am not sure–'

'Trust me, my friend, you will make a grand count of Middenheim. Now go, enjoy yourself and get drunk!' ordered Sigmar.

'First sensible thing I've heard this morning,' said Wolfgart, leading Pendrag away.

Over the following days, Sigmar mixed with his subjects and conversed with his counts about what needed to be done to secure the peace they had won. Sword oaths were renewed and plans laid to defend the east and north, while expeditions were planned to learn more of the lands far to the south.

Many called for war against the Jutones, and the sentiment found much support amongst the counts. King Marius, safe in his coastal city of Jutonsryk, endured thanks only to the great victory others had won. All agreed that a reckoning was due, and that Marius must be brought to heel or destroyed.

Queen Freya of the Asoborns was Sigmar's constant shadow throughout the feasting, and he endured countless tales of her twin boys, Fridleifr and Sigulf, who were gods amongst men if their mother's stories were to be believed. Freya's desire for him was undimmed and her disappointment was clear when he gently rebuffed her offers of carnal pleasure.

Krugar of the Taleutens and Aloysis of the Cherusens both tried to broach the subject of their shared border, each claiming that the other was sending raiders to violate their lands. Sigmar forestalled such disputes until the spring; this was a time for unity, not division. Neither count was happy with his judgement, but both bowed and withdrew.

Of all the counts gathered, Sigmar enjoyed the company of Wolfila the most. The Udose count was a garrulous guest, and seemed to have a limitless supply of energy with which to feast and partake in games of strength and skill. None who fought him in mock duels could best him, until Sigmar put him flat on his back with one punch.

No sooner had he regained consciousness than Wolfila dragged Sigmar into the longhouse to break open a bottle of his finest grain spirit, a bottle said to have been laid down in his grandfather's time. The two men drank long into the night, cutting their palms and becoming blood-brothers while devising ever more elaborate means to solve the evils of the world.

On the morning of the fourth day of feasting, Wolfila introduced Sigmar to his wife, Petra. Swathed in a patchwork dress of many colours, Petra was petite and slender, though she had fought in battle since becoming Wolfila's wife. From the swelling of her belly, it was clear that she was with child, her first, though this had not stopped her from eating and drinking her share of the feast platters.

'He'll be a bonny lad,' said Wolfila, patting his wife's belly. 'A hellraiser and a warrior to be sure. Just like his father.'

'Whisht,' scolded Petra. 'Away with you, it's a girl, as sure as night follows day.'

'Don't be foolish, woman,' cried Wolfila. 'A boy, didn't old man Rouven say so?'

'Rouven?' snapped Petra. 'Ach, the man couldn't predict rain in a thunderstorm!'

The Udose were renowned as an argumentative tribe, whose clannish family groupings fought with one another as often as they battled their enemies. Though Wolfila and Petra loved each other dearly, Sigmar soon learned that they would argue over the smallest thing, and that it was best to leave them to it. The strange thing was that they seemed to enjoy it.

As well as the rulers of each tribe, Sigmar spent a great deal of time with the warriors of the tribes, listening to their tales of courage and heartbreak from the field of Black Fire Pass. A Thuringian warrior broke a table as he re-enacted his killing of a gigantic troll, a pair of Asoborn spearmen ran circles around their listeners as they explained the tactics of a chariot charge, and shaven-headed Taleuten horsemen sang songs of how they rode down fleeing greenskins at battle's end.

With every account, Sigmar's awe for these men and women grew deeper and his gratitude more profound. Most moving of all were the words of a Menogoth warrior named Toralf, who tearfully begged Sigmar's forgiveness for his cowardice in running.

'We tried,' sobbed Toralf, showing a monstrous scar in his side where a great barb had pierced him. 'We killed the wolves and marched into the teeth of the spear throwers. We didn't know... We didn't know... Hundreds of bolts let fly at us, thick as a felled tree they were, and each one killed a dozen men, skewered like pigs in a row. I lost my father and both brothers in the time it takes to nock an arrow, but we kept going... We kept going till we couldn't go no more... And then we ran. Ulric forgive me, but we ran!'

Sigmar remembered the dreadful fear he had felt watching the Menogoth ranks breaking under the horrific onslaught of orc spear throwers. The greenskins had poured into the gap and savaged the flanks of King Henroth's Merogens before Sigmar had led his Unberogen sword bands forward to hurl the orcs back.

'There is nothing to forgive,' he told Toralf. 'No warriors could have held firm under such an attack. There is no shame in fleeing from so grievous a slaughter. What matters most is that you came back. In every battle, there are those who flee for their lives. Fewer are those who find their courage and return to the fight. Without the strength of the Menogoths, the battle would have been lost.'

Toralf looked up with wet eyes and dropped to his knees before Sigmar, who placed his hand on the man's head. All eyes were upon him as Toralf received Sigmar's blessing, and a palpable sense of wonder filled the longhouse as the hearts of the Menogoths were healed.

Though he favoured no count over another, Sigmar found that he spent almost no time at all with Aldred. This was not for lack of effort on Sigmar's part, for it seemed the Endal count deliberately kept away from the new emperor. King Marbad, Aldred's father, had been one of Sigmar's staunchest allies, and it grieved him to feel the distance growing between him and the count of the Endals.

No sooner had the feasting come to an end on the seventh day than the Endals mounted their black steeds and rode through Morr's Gate, Reikdorf's westernmost entrance. Sigmar watched them go, the Raven Helms surrounding their master as they followed the course of the river towards Marburg.

One by one, the counts of the Empire returned to their homelands, and it was a time of great joy and melancholy. With the celebrations done and the warriors departed, Reikdorf felt strangely empty. Autumn was coming to an end, and the cold winds howled over the northern hills with the promise of winter.

Soon darkness would cover the land.

THE SEASONS FOLLOWING Black Fire Pass had been mild, but the winter that fell upon the Empire in the wake of Sigmar's coronation was as fierce as anyone living could remember. The land was blanketed in white, and only the most foolhardy dared venture far from the warmth of hearth and home.

Blizzards sprang from nowhere, raging southwards to bury entire villages beneath the snow and wipe them from the map. Only when the snows retreated in the spring would many of these settlements be rediscovered, their frozen inhabitants huddled together in their last moments of life.

Days were short and the nights long, and the people of the Empire were left with little to do but press close to their fires and pray to the gods to deliver them from the bitter cold. Harsh as the winter was, the Unberogen passed it with relative ease, for the granaries were well stocked, even after Sigmar's generosity at his coronation.

The ground was like iron, and work ceased on the forest clearances as well as the wide roads running between Middenheim in the north and Siggurdheim in the south. The workers were glad of the respite, for the hungry forest beasts made it too dangerous to venture beyond the walls of a settlement for any length of time. Work would resume in the spring, and fine roads of stone would link the great cities of the Empire.

The danger of the forest beasts was illustrated only too clearly when a pack of twisted monsters raided the village of Verburg, burning it to the ground and taking the inhabitants captive. Though savage winds howled around Reikdorf, Sigmar had gathered a hunting party to track the beasts and rescue his captured people. His head scout, Cuthwin, found the beasts' trail a mile east of Astofen, and the Unberogen riders had fallen on the creatures as they camped above a frozen lake.

The slaughter had been swift, for the beasts were starving and weak. Not a single rider fell in the fight, but the captives were already dead, butchered to feed the hungry pack. Dispirited by their failure to rescue the villagers, the Unberogen rode back to Reikdorf without the soaring pride that would normally accompany the slaying of so many of their enemies.

Two days later, Sigmar still brooded on the deaths of his people, and it was in this mood that his friends found him as they came to discuss the spring muster.

THE FIRE IN the centre of the longhouse burned low, yet the dwarf craft in the hall's construction was so precise that no cold seeped in through the windows or doors. Sigmar sat upon his throne, Ghalmaraz lying across his lap and his faithful hounds curled at his feet.

Behind him stood Redwane, one hand on the grip of his hammer, the other on a polished banner pole of yew. With Pendrag in Middenheim, the honour of bearing Sigmar's crimson standard had gone to the strongest warrior of the White Wolves. Alfgeir had advised Sigmar to choose a warrior of greater maturity, but he had seen great courage in Redwane and would not change his mind.

The doors to the longhouse opened, and a malicious gust of wind scattered the dry straw spread across the floor. Eoforth limped inside, swathed in thick furs and flanked by Alfgeir and Wolfgart. The cloaked warriors helped Eoforth to a seat by the fire, and Sigmar descended from his throne to sit with his closest friends.

'How goes work in the library?' asked Sigmar.

'Well enough,' nodded Eoforth, 'for many of the counts brought copies of their foremost scholars' work with them in autumn. The winter has given me the chance to read many scrolls, but the business of organising them is never-ending, my lord.'

Sigmar nodded, though he had no real interest in Eoforth's books. The first hints that winter was loosening its grip were in the air, and he was eager to make war once more.

As promised at his coronation, there were reckonings to be had.

He turned from Eoforth and spoke first to Alfgeir.

'How many men do we have under arms for the spring muster?' he asked.

Alfgeir glanced at Eoforth.

'Perhaps five thousand in the first raising,' he said. 'If need be, another six when the weather breaks.'

'How soon can they be gathered?'

'Once the war banner is unfurled, I can send riders out, and most of the first five thousand will be here within ten days,' said Alfgeir. 'But we will need time to prepare food and supplies before ordering such a gathering. It would be best to wait until the snows melt.'

Sigmar ignored Alfgeir's last comment and said, 'Eoforth, draw up a list of everything the army will need: swords, axes, spears, armour, wagons, war machines, horses, food. Everything. I want it ready by tomorrow evening and I want us ready to raise the war banner as soon as the roads become passable.'

'I will do as you command,' said Eoforth, 'though the planning of so large a muster should be given more time than a single day.'

'We do not have more time,' said Sigmar. 'Just make it happen.'

Wolfgart coughed and spat into the fire, and Sigmar sensed his friend's confusion.

'Something troubles you, Wolfgart?' he asked.

Wolfgart looked up and shrugged.

'I'm just wondering who you're in such a rush to go and fight,' he said. 'I mean, we killed the beasts and burned their corpses didn't we? The others of their kind will get the message.'

'We are not riding out to kill beasts,' said Sigmar. 'We march to Jutonsryk. The coward Marius must be called to account for deserting us at Black Fire.'

'Ah... Marius,' said Wolfgart, nodding. 'Aye, well he needs to be dealt with, right enough, but why so soon? Why not wait until the snows break properly before ordering men to leave their homes and loved ones? Marius isn't going anywhere.'

'I thought that you of all people would be eager for this,' snapped Sigmar. 'Were you not complaining that big sword of yours was getting rusty?'

'I'm as eager for battle as the next man,' said Wolfgart, 'but let's be civilised about this and fight in the spring, eh? My old bones don't like marching in the snow or sleeping rough in the cold. War's hard enough as it is, there's no need to make it harder.'

Sigmar stood and circled the fire, Ghal-maraz held loosely across his shoulder as he answered Wolfgart.

'Every day since I threw his ambassador from Reikdorf, Marius has been fortifying Jutonsryk, building his walls and towers of stone higher. His ships bring grain, weapons and mercenaries from the south, and every day we sit like old women around the fire, his city grows stronger. The longer we wait to take the fight to Marius, the more men will die when we attack.'

Sigmar and Wolfgart locked eyes, and it was his sword-brother who looked away.

'You're the Emperor,' said Wolfgart. 'You always did see things bigger than me, but I wouldn't go haring off to Jutonsryk without making sure my back was covered first.'

'What are you talking about?' asked Sigmar, stopping in front of Wolfgart.

'Aldred of the Endals,' said Alfgeir.

'Aldred?' asked Sigmar. 'The Endals are our brothers, Sword Oath sworn and bound to us for generations. Why would you dishonour a man who has sworn a sword oath with me?'

'That's just it,' said Wolfgart. 'His father did, but he hasn't.'

'And you think Aldred would dishonour his father's memory by turning on us?' demanded Sigmar, angry that his sword-brother would suggest such a thing.

'He might. You don't know Aldred's heart.'

'I think what Wolfgart means is that the Endals are something of an unknown quantity,' said Eoforth hurriedly. 'King Marbad was your father's greatest friend and a proud ally of the Unberogen, but Aldred...'

'I grieved with Aldred when we set Marbad on the pyre,' said Sigmar. 'He knows I honoured his father.'

'We all grieved for Marbad,' said Alfgeir, 'but I agree with Wolfgart. It makes no sense to face one enemy with potentially another behind us.'

Wolfgart rose from his seat and stood face-to-face with Sigmar. 'I watched the Endals the whole time they were here, and I didn't like the looks of that Aldred one bit. The way he stared at you, well, it was as if you'd rammed that spear in his father's chest yourself.'

'You're saying that he blames me for his father's death?'

'You'd have to be a blind man not to see that,' said Wolfgart. 'Even Laredus was like a stranger, and it wouldn't surprise me if we saw less and less of the Endals as time goes on.'

'You agree with this?' Sigmar asked Eoforth.

'I think it is worth considering,' said Eoforth. 'As Alfgeir says, it's sensible to make certain of the loyalty of the warriors behind you before laying siege to Jutonsryk. Be sure of Aldred, win him to your cause, and *then* take your anger to the Jutones.'

Sigmar wanted to rage against their words, but he had seen the bitterness in Aldred's eyes and had known it for what it was. Marbad had been dear to Sigmar, but he was Aldred's father too. Nothing could assuage Aldred's knowledge that, had his father not been compelled to hurl the blade Ulfshard to Sigmar at the height of the battle, he might have lived.

Sigmar took a deep breath.

'You are right,' he said. 'My anger towards Marius and my frustration at the deaths of my people is blinding me to the wisdom of my friends. I saw the hurt in Aldred's eyes, but I chose to ignore it. That was foolish of me.'

'We all make mistakes,' said Wolfgart. 'Don't worry about it.'

'No,' said Sigmar. 'I am Emperor, and I cannot afford to act so rashly or people will die. From hereon, I will make no decisions of magnitude without speaking with you, for you are all dear to me and this crown weighs heavy on my brow. I will need your honest counsel if I am to make wise decisions.'

'You can count on me to tell you when you're being an ass,' said Wolfgart. 'You always could.'

Sigmar smiled and shook Wolfgart's hand.

'So do you still want to order the spring muster?' asked Alfgeir.

'No, not yet,' said Sigmar. 'Our reckoning with Marius will need to wait.'

'Then what are your orders, sire?'

'When the snow breaks, assemble a hundred of the White Wolves,' said Sigmar. 'We will pay a visit to Count Aldred in Marburg and see what truly lies in his heart.'

FOUR
City of Mist

THE COLUMN OF riders made its way along the muddy track that served as a road through the sodden lands of the Endals, a hundred warriors in red armour, all carrying long-handled hammers. Sigmar rode at the head of the column, with Redwane alongside him holding the emperor's standard aloft. The crimson banner hung listlessly from the crosspiece, for there was no wind and damp air had saturated the fabric.

The journey from Reikdorf had begun well, the snows breaking swiftly and spring's warmth arriving earlier than had been predicted by the bones of old men. That fortune had lasted for the first three days, as the riders made good time along the stone roads leading from Sigmar's capital.

Then the road ended and the rest of the journey had been made along muddy trails, forest tracks and rutted roadways. Wolfgart had travelled this way before, and though he was reluctant to leave Maedbh so near to the birth of his child, he insisted on riding with Sigmar.

Alfgeir remained in Reikdorf as Sigmar's regent. Though the Grand Knight of the Empire understood the honour of being appointed the city's guardian, he chafed at the thought of allowing others to protect the Emperor. At Alfgeir's insistence, Cradoc had accompanied the riders. In lieu of Alfgeir, the finest healer in the Unberogen lands would have to suffice in safeguarding the Emperor's life.

Sigmar looked over at Redwane. The young warrior was only two summers older than he had been when he first rode to war. The young White Wolf sensed the scrutiny and glanced over, his youthful face alight with excitement and anticipation.

Sigmar could barely remember being so young and brash, and he suddenly envied the young man's outlook on life, seeing the world as new and alive with possibility.

'How far is it to Marburg, Wolfgart?' asked Redwane.

'Gods, boy!' snapped Wolfgart. 'I'll tell you when we're close. Now stop asking me.'

'It's just I thought we'd be able to see it by now.'

'Aye, you'd see it yonder if not for this damn mist,' replied Wolfgart, winking at Sigmar. 'It's the noxious wind of the daemons that live in the marshes around Marburg, so don't breathe too much of it in lest you become one yourself.'

'Truly?' asked Redwane, trying to keep his lips pursed tightly together.

Cradoc stifled a laugh as Wolfgart continued, 'Aye, lad, for the daemons of the mist are cunning beasts. King Björn fought them before you were born. Rode to Marburg just like we're doing, and marched into the mist to face the daemons with King Marbad at his side. A hundred men went in, but barely a handful came out, the rest dragged to their deaths beneath the dark waters of the bogs.'

'Gods! That's no way for a warrior to die!' cried Redwane.

'That's not the worst of it, lad,' continued Wolfgart, looking warily to either side of the road, as though the daemons might be lurking within earshot.

'It isn't?'

'No, not by a long way,' said Wolfgart, and Sigmar saw he was enjoying tormenting the White Wolf immensely. 'Some say the souls of those dead men linger beneath the marsh, and when the Dread Moon waxes, they rise from their watery graves to feast on the living. Horrible things they are, lad: a single deathly eye, needle teeth and grasping claws ready to pull you under the water to join them forever.'

Sigmar's father had told him of the mist daemons that haunted the marshes around Marburg upon their return from Astofen Bridge. Wolfgart was exaggerating that tale, but like the best storytellers, he was weaving his embellishments around a core of truth.

'Daemons, eh?' said Redwane. 'I've never fought a daemon before.'

'Then you are lucky,' said Sigmar, remembering the desperate fight against a host of daemonic beasts in the Grey Vaults, the bleak netherworld between life and death. His father had crossed over into Morr's realm to rescue him, giving up his life to save his only son. A lump formed in Sigmar's throat at the thought of his father's sacrifice.

'Ulric's teeth, what I wouldn't give to fight such a beast,' continued Redwane. 'Imagine it, Wolfgart. You'd have the pick of the maidens after a kill like that.'

'Trust me, Redwane,' said Sigmar. 'I have fought beings from the dread realms, and you should pray to all the gods that you never face such a creature.'

Wolfgart looked curiously at him. 'When did you fight a daemon? And why wasn't I beside you?'

'Do not ask me that,' said Sigmar, unwilling to be drawn on the subject. 'I will not speak of it, for evil like that is drawn by such talk. There are daemons enough in this world without summoning more to us.'

Wolfgart shrugged, and a stern glance silenced the question Sigmar saw on Redwane's lips. A thin rain began to fall, and the riders journeyed in silence for perhaps another hour before the mist began to thin and the land began to rise. Sigmar saw villages huddled in the distance, their waterlogged fields worked by mud-covered farmers and sway-backed horses.

This land was drained of life and colour, the sky was leaden and thunderous above the vast mountains to the south. Everywhere Sigmar looked, he saw tones of a dull and muddy brown. This was not what he had expected to see. Around Reikdorf, the land was green and golden, fertile and bountiful. Though life was hard and demanding, a sense of pride and purpose filled the settlements in Unberogen lands.

Sigmar saw none of that here, and a gloomy solitude settled upon him.

Several times during this last stage of the journey, the riders left the road to make way for rattling corpse-carts piled high with the dead. Each wagon was escorted by grim-faced knights in black and dark-robed priests of Morr, their monotone chants and dolorous bell-ringing muffled by the fog. Wailing mourners followed the carts, tearing at their hair and mortifying their flesh with knotted ropes hung with fishhooks.

The White Wolves covered their mouths with their cloaks, and made the sign of Shallya to ward off any evil vapours as each procession passed. Sigmar rode alongside Cradoc as the old man stared into a cart where the ties binding the canvas covering had come loose. Stiff and cold bodies looked out with bulging eyes that spoke of terrible fear and agonising pain.

'Looks like lung rot,' said Cradoc. 'Don't worry, it's not infectious, but the air here has turned bad. Something has stirred a miasma from the depths of the marsh to infect the air.'

'That's bad, yes?' asked Redwane.

'Oh yes, very bad,' said Cradoc. 'Over time, fluid builds up in the lungs, draining your strength until you can barely move or even speak.'

'Then what happens?' asked Wolfgart.

'Then you drown in your bed.'

'Shallya's mercy,' hissed Sigmar, covering his mouth. 'Should we take any precautions?'

'Not unless you plan to live here,' said Cradoc, riding away from the corpse-cart.

At last the sodden road led the riders through a wilting stand of trees of bare branches. Topping a rise shawled in wiry gorse, Sigmar caught the scent of sea air and saw Marburg. The city of the Endals sat atop a jagged bluff of volcanic black rock that reared from a desolate landscape of fog-shrouded heaths and endless marshland. This was where the mighty Reik reached the sea, and its sluggish waters were frothed with patches of ochre scum.

The black promontory of Marburg glistened in the rain, and an uneven band of pale blue stone rose to a height of about six feet from its summit, almost as though it had grown out of the rock. This was all that remained of an outpost built by an ancient race of fey folk who were said to dwell far across the ocean.

Even from here, the great skill of the stonemasons was evident, the joints between the blocks barely visible, and the curving sweep of the walls elegantly fashioned. Where dwarf-craft was solid, straightforward and had little in the way of subtlety, the remains of this structure were as much art as architecture.

Vast earthen ramparts of all too human construction were piled high upon the pale stone, and sadness touched Sigmar to see such a noble outpost so reduced. For a moment, he pictured it as it might once have looked: a glittering fastness of slender towers of silver and gold, arched windows of delicate glass and a riot of colourful flags.

The picture faded from his mind as he saw thick logs with sharpened ends jutting from the muddy ramparts, as much to reinforce the earth as to deter attackers. Black banners hung limply from a pair of flagpoles, rising from the stone towers built to either side of a wide timber gateway. Both towers were built from the same black stone of the rock and each was shaped in the form of a tall raven.

Trails of smoke rose from the city, and the tops of buildings roofed with grey slate could be seen over the walls. Flocks of dark-pinioned birds circled the winged towers of the Raven Hall at the heart of Marburg.

Beyond the city, the ocean's dark expanse spread towards the horizon. Grey banks of fog clung to the surface of the water and a few ships bobbed in the swells. Fishing nets trailed from their sterns, though Sigmar had little appetite for any fish caught in such sombre seas.

'Gods, have you ever seen anywhere so depressing?' asked Redwane, waving a hand in front of him. 'It stinks worse than an orc's breath!'

'Wasn't like this when I was here,' said Wolfgart. 'Marburg was a fine town, with good beer and food. I don't recognise this place.'

Sigmar wanted to rebuke Redwane and Wolfgart, but there was little point, for there was no denying the pall of misery that hung over Marburg. The entire land of the Endals was soaked in despair.

'Come on,' said Sigmar. 'I want to find out what's at the heart of this.'

THEY RODE TOWARDS Marburg, the widening road laid with timbers to ease the passage of wagons and horses. The raven sculpted towers loomed above them, dark and threatening, and a chill travelled down Sigmar's spine as he entered their shadow. The city gates were open, and Endal tribesmen in brown and black made way for the mud-spattered horsemen.

Sigmar knew they made an impressive sight, for their horses were powerful beasts, the product of years of careful selective breeding on Wolfgart's lands. Long ago, Wolfgart had promised to breed horses capable of wearing iron armour, and he had set to the challenge with as much determination as Sigmar had set about achieving his dream of an empire.

As a result, Unberogen horses were the biggest in the land, grain-fed mounts of no less than sixteen hands, with wide chests, strong legs and straight backs. By any reckoning, Wolfgart was a wealthy man, for his stallions were much sought after by those whose coin was plentiful, and several had been requested by Sigmar's counts upon seeing them at the gallop.

The White Wolves were no less impressive: tough, capable men who were equally at home fighting from the back of a horse as they were on foot. Their armour was of the finest quality, though they eschewed the use of shield or helmet, and their red cloaks were arranged carefully over the rumps of their horses. There was no give in them, and their long hair and beards were deliberately wild and barbarous.

Sigmar led the White Wolves through the gateway and into a cobbled courtyard. Warriors in black breastplates and helmets lined the courtyard, each carrying a long, bronze-tipped lance. Sigmar was instantly alert, for this was not the welcome an Emperor might expect. It felt more like the arrival of a tolerated enemy.

A warrior in a black, full-faced helm and a man dressed in flowing robes of green wool stood in the centre of the courtyard. Sigmar angled his course towards them. The warrior was powerfully built, while the robed man was old, his beard reaching almost to his waist. A long, curved blade hung from a belt of woven reeds, and he carried a staff of pale wood, its length garlanded with mistletoe.

'Why do I feel like there's an arrow aimed between my shoulder blades?' whispered Wolfgart.

'Because there probably is,' replied Redwane, nodding upwards.

Sigmar saw warriors peering down from the raven towers and nodded, knowing there would indeed be archers above them with arrows nocked. Aldred would not be so foolish or bitter as to have him killed, but still his senses were warning him of danger.

'Stay alert,' he hissed, 'but do nothing unless I do it first.'

The warrior in the black helmet stepped forward and bowed curtly to Sigmar. He removed his helmet and tucked it into the crook of his arm.

'Laredus,' said Sigmar, recognising the warrior of the Raven Helms. 'Where is Count Aldred? He cannot come to greet me himself?'

'Emperor Sigmar,' said Laredus, 'you honour us with your presence in Marburg. Count Aldred sends his regrets, but the health of his brother deteriorates daily and he fears to leave his side.'

'His brother is ill?' asked Sigmar, dropping from his horse to stand next to Laredus. If archers were going to shoot, he would give them a choice of targets.

'Indeed, my lord. The sickness from the marsh claims pauper and prince alike,' said Laredus.

'And who is this?' asked Sigmar, indicating the robed man beside Laredus. 'I do not know him.'

'I am called Idris Gwylt,' said the man with a short bow, his voice lilting and unfamiliar. His skin was the colour of aged oak and his hair was the pure white of freshly fallen snow. Pale green eyes regarded Sigmar with curiosity, and though there was no hostility in them, neither was there welcome.

'You'll address your Emperor as "my lord" in future,' snapped Redwane.

Sigmar waved Redwane back and said, 'What is your role, Idris Gwylt? Are you a priest, a healer?'

'A little of both, perhaps,' said Idris, with a wry smile. 'I am counsellor to Ki... Count Aldred on matters spiritual and worldly.'

Sigmar turned from Idris Gwylt and addressed Laredus. 'My men have travelled far and require food, lodgings and hot water. We shall also require stabling and grain for our mounts. When I have washed myself clean of mud, you will take me to Count Aldred, sick brother or not.'

'As you wish, my lord,' said Laredus coldly.

THE GUEST LODGINGS in Count Aldred's royal apartments were functional and clean, though no fire had been set in the hearth in anticipation of their arrival. A meal of fish and steamed vegetables came quickly, though it took an hour for enough water to be heated to allow Sigmar to bathe. Such treatment broke all the rules of hospitality that existed between allies, but Sigmar kept his temper in check, for he could ill-afford two enemies in the west.

With the journey washed from his body, Sigmar followed Laredus and a handful of cloaked Endal warriors through the streets of Marburg towards the Raven Hall. Dressed in a robe of crimson and a long wolfskin cloak, Sigmar marched at the head of Wolfgart, Redwane and an honour guard of ten White Wolves. Though outwardly calm, their hands never strayed far from their weapons.

Sigmar's crown glittered upon his brow, and he carried Ghal-maraz at his belt, holding the haft tight against his leg as he looked in horrified wonder at the dismal city surrounding him.

Water and human waste sluiced the streets of Marburg, and a sickly oily sheen coated the cobbles where it had seeped into the cracks. The rancid smell of spoiled meat and grain hung on the air, hemmed in by buildings that crowded together and loomed over the few wretched people abroad in the streets. A forsaken air hung over the city, as though its inhabitants had long ago fled its darkened thoroughfares for the lands left by the Bretonii.

The buildings were predominantly constructed from warped, sun-bleached timbers, with only the lower portions of each structure built from stone. Damp blotched the walls, and runnels of black water fell from leaking eaves. Windows and doors were shuttered, and through those that were ajar Sigmar heard little sign of life, only soft weeping and muttered prayers.

'Look,' said Wolfgart, nodding down a reeking alleyway to where another corpse-cart was pulling away from a thatched house. A black-robed priest of Morr painted a white cross upon the door as a hunched man wearing a grotesque mask with glass eyes and an elongated nose nailed a wooden board across it.

'Plague?' said Redwane. 'They must have breathed the daemon air!'

'Be quiet,' hissed Sigmar, though he reached up to touch the talisman of Shallya that he wore around his neck.

'Redwane is right, the city is cursed,' said Wolfgart. 'The carrion birds circle this place as if it were a fresh corpse. We should leave now.'

'Don't be foolish,' replied Sigmar. 'What manner of empire would I have forged if I turn my back on the suffering of my people? We stay and find the cause of this.'

'Very well,' shrugged Wolfgart, 'but don't say I didn't warn you when you're coughing up your lungs and drowning in your own blood.'

Sigmar put such concerns from his mind as the Raven Hall came into sight. The ancestral seat of the Endal rulers was a towering miracle: a majestic hall carved from a mighty spire of volcanic rock and hollowed out to form the rearing shape of a vast raven. Black pinions of glistening stone swept from the tower's flanks, and a great balcony was formed within the jutting beak at its summit.

Sigmar caught a flash of movement on the balcony, and saw the slender form of a woman clad in a long black dress with shoulder-length hair of golden blonde. No sooner had he spotted her than she vanished inside the tower.

'Ulric's bones,' said Redwane. 'And here's me thinking Siggurdheim was impressive.'

'Aye, they did something special here,' agreed Wolfgart. 'You can see almost all the way to the hills around Astofen when the mists roll back.'

'It's amazing,' said Sigmar, his anger with Aldred retreating in the face of this wondrous creation. Far to the north, the Fauschlag Rock dominated the landscape for miles around, but its towering form had been shaped by the fist of Ulric; the Raven Hall was the work of men. Countless years of toil and skill had gone into the Hall's creation, and it was a thing of dark, majestic beauty.

Laredus led them into the tower through a gateway formed between two giant claws and guarded by more Raven Helms. Now that he was closer, Sigmar saw the intricate detail worked into the tower's walls, the glassy stone carved with feathers that looked almost real.

The corridors within the tower were black, and torchlight rippled on the stonework like moonlight on water. Laredus led them deep into the heart of the tower, eventually reaching a carved stairway that led up into darkness. Sigmar wanted more time to explore this fabulous place, but Laredus lifted a torch from a sconce at the foot of the stairs and set off upwards.

Sigmar followed the Raven Helm, running his fingers over the smooth walls. The stone felt like polished glass, and was slightly warm to the touch, as though the fire of its vitrification still lingered deep in its heart. The stairs rose high into the tower, following the outward curve of its walls, and Sigmar's legs were soon aching.

'Does this damn tower ever end?' asked Redwane. 'It feels like it goes on forever.'

'You've been spoiled in Siggurdheim,' chuckled Wolfgart. 'Too much soft living has made you weak. You youngsters might have the edge in years on a veteran like me, but you've no stamina.'

'That's not what your wife says,' joked Redwane.

Even in the torchlight, Sigmar saw Wolfgart's face darken with anger. Wolfgart gripped Redwane's tunic and slammed him against the wall. His knife hissed from its leather sheath to rest against Redwane's throat.

'Speak that way about Maedbh again and I'll cut your heart out, you little bastard!' he said.

Fast as quicksilver, Sigmar's hand shot out and gripped Wolfgart's wrist, though he did not remove the blade from Redwane's throat.

'Redwane, sometimes your stupidity surprises even me,' said Sigmar. 'You insult the honour of a fine woman, wife to my sword-brother and shield maiden to a queen.'

'I'll kill him,' snarled Wolfgart. 'No man claims I wear the cuckold's horns and lives!'

'You will not,' stated Sigmar. 'Kill him and you will be a murderer. The boy's words were foolish, but he did not mean them. Did you, Redwane?'

'No, of course not!' cried Redwane. 'It was just a jest.'

'Make such jests at your peril,' hissed Wolfgart, putting up his knife and stepping away from the White Wolf. Though Redwane's life was no longer in immediate danger, Sigmar knew that Wolfgart would never forget those poorly-chosen words. He glanced over to where Laredus had been standing, but the Raven Helm had already gone ahead. Sigmar knew Aldred would already know of this altercation, and he cursed.

'Pull yourselves together and follow me,' said Sigmar, setting off after Laredus. 'And if either of you behaves like this again, I'll have you flogged and stripped of those wolf cloaks you prize so dearly.'

COUNT ALDRED'S HALL was a great domed chamber at the very summit of the tower. It was lit by twin shafts of yellow light that speared in through windows that formed the eyes of the Raven Hall. From its position in relation to the windows, Sigmar guessed that a curtain of red velvet led to the balcony he had seen from the outside. Scented torches formed a processional route towards a dark throne, and Sigmar guessed that they were lit to disguise the stench of the city below as well as to provide illumination.

Count Aldred awaited them clad in his father's armour, a bronze breastplate moulded to resemble a muscular physique and a tall helm with feathered wings of black that swept up from angular cheek plates. His long dark cloak spilled around a throne of polished ebony with armrests carved in the form of wings and legs shaped like black talons. The Raven Banner was set in a socket in the backrest of the throne, and Sigmar remembered the pride he had felt watching that same banner carried into battle at Black Fire Pass.

Laredus and Idris Gwylt stood behind Count Aldred, and two thrones of similar, but smaller design sat to either side of the Endal ruler. One of these thrones was empty, while upon the other sat the golden-haired girl that Sigmar had seen from beyond the tower. She was perhaps sixteen years old and pretty in a thin kind of way, though her skin had an unhealthy pallor to it, much like everyone else Sigmar had seen in Marburg. She looked at Sigmar with a haughty expression for one so young, yet he saw the interest behind her veneer of indifference.

Sigmar marched towards Aldred's throne, keeping his smouldering anger chained tightly within. He had come to the realm of the Endals to learn what lay in Aldred's heart, but seeing the count told him all he needed to know. The scent of the torches caught in the back of Sigmar's throat, and suddenly he knew what to say to Aldred.

'Count Aldred,' he said, 'your lands are in disarray. Pestilence blights your city and a curse lies upon your people. I am here to help.'

Sigmar hid his amusement at Aldred's surprise, and pressed on before the young count could reply, 'King Marbad was as a brother to my father, and he saved my life upon the field of Black Fire Pass. I shed tears as we sent him to Ulric's Hall, and I pledged to you that we would also be brothers. I have come to Marburg to make good on that pledge.'

'I do not understand,' said Aldred. 'I asked for no aid.'

'When the lands of my counts are threatened, I do not wait for them to ask for my help. I bring a hundred of my finest warriors to your city to help in whatever way we can.'

Idris Gwylt leaned down to whisper something in Aldred's ear, but Sigmar could not hear the words over the sound of the wind playing about the tower. Before Aldred could say anything in response to Gwylt's counsel, Sigmar took a step towards the throne.

'Count Aldred, tell me what troubles your city,' said Sigmar. 'As well as warriors, I bring my healer, Cradoc, a man who saved my life when I lay at Morr's threshold. Let him try to ease your people's suffering.'

Idris Gwylt stepped forward, and Sigmar breathed in his earthy aroma. Gwylt carried the smell of freshly turned soil and ripened crops, as though fresh from a field of sun-ripened corn. The feeling was intense, and Sigmar felt the power of the man, as though something vital coursed through him, a pulse of something old beyond imagining.

'The curse that afflicts us is beyond the power of your warriors to defeat, Emperor Sigmar,' said Gwylt. 'The daemons of the mist grow strong once more and their evil flows from the depths of the marshes. It spreads through the earth and corrupts all that it touches. Disease strikes our people and the life drains from the land, washed into the ocean with all our hopes. Hundreds of our tribe are dead and even my noble count's brother, the gallant Egil, has been struck down.'

'Then let Cradoc help him. There is little he does not know of the ways of sickness.'

'Egil is beyond the help of men,' said Idris Gwylt. 'Only the healing power of the land can save him now, and it wanes as that of the daemons waxes. Only by offering the daemons our most valued treasure can Egil's life be saved.'

'That is foolishness,' stormed Sigmar, addressing his words to Aldred. 'This man speaks of offering tribute to daemons as though you are their vassals. Daemons are creatures of darkness and can only be defeated with courage and strong sword arms. What say you, Aldred?

Rally the Raven Helms to your banner and join me in battle. Together, we can cleanse the marshes of their evil forever. My father and your father fought these creatures, so let us finish what they began!'

'Our fathers failed,' said the young girl seated beside Aldred. 'The daemons drove them from the marshes and killed most of their warriors. What makes you think you can triumph where they could not?'

Sigmar lifted Ghal-maraz from his belt and held it out to her.

'I have never met a foe I could not defeat,' he said. 'If I go into those marshes to fight, I will be victorious.'

Her eyes blazed with anger.

'You are arrogant,' she said.

'Perhaps I am,' admitted Sigmar. 'It is my right as Emperor. But you have me at a disadvantage. You know who I am, but I do not know you.'

'My name is Marika,' she snapped, 'daughter of Marbad and sister to Aldred and Egil. You speak of battle as though it is the only way of ending our troubles, but not every curse can be lifted with killing. There are other ways.'

'Oh, like what?'

'It is not for me to say,' said Marika, the anger in her eyes replaced with sadness. Sigmar saw her glance towards Idris Gwylt.

'Then how would you end this curse, my lady?' asked Sigmar.

'By appeasing the daemons,' said Idris Gwylt.

'I was not asking you,' said Sigmar.

'Such daemons cannot be defeated by mortal men,' replied Gwylt, ignoring Sigmar's displeasure. 'The earth has been corrupted by the touch of the mist daemons, and we cannot restore its goodness with swords.'

'Does this man speak for you, Count Aldred?' demanded Sigmar. 'I appointed *you* to rule these lands, not some old man who speaks of appeasement. Good gods, man, you do not invite the fox into the hen house, you root him out and kill him.'

'Gwylt enjoys my full confidence,' said Aldred. 'We hold to the ways of our ancient forebears in Marburg, and it is in them that we will find salvation. Idris Gwylt is a priest of a power older than the gods, a servant of the land, who knows its ways and the means by which we may restore it. His words are wise beyond the understanding of most mortals, and he has done much to ease the suffering of my people. I trust him implicitly.'

'You may trust him, but I do not,' said Sigmar, understanding the source of Gwylt's strange and powerful aura. 'I thought the Old Faith died out a long time ago.'

'So long as the land bears fruit, it will endure,' said Gwylt.

Sigmar glared at the robed priest. 'In Reikdorf we put our faith in the gods.'

'This is not Reikdorf,' replied the priest.

SIGMAR AND HIS warriors spent the next three days secluded in the royal apartments. Though they were free to roam the city and its environs as they pleased, the sickness that ravaged the population kept most of them indoors. Sigmar spent the first day walking the fog-shrouded streets of Marburg to see how its population fared, and when he returned to his chambers there was a shadow on his soul.

The city of the Endals was a grim and melancholy place, not at all like the vibrant, cosmopolitan coastal city its old king had once told raucous tales of. Noxious mists coiled in from the marshes to drain the city of colour, and its inhabitants moved through the streets like ghosts. Despair came on those mists, a smothering blanket of misery that coiled around the soul and leeched it of vitality. Immediately upon his return, Sigmar bade Cradoc do what he could for the population of Marburg.

The old healer appropriated two score of the White Wolves to be his orderlies, and day and night Cradoc did what he could for the sick. Those whom the sickness had touched were too often beyond the power of his remedies. Families were found dead in their homes, faces spattered with crusted mucus and eyes swollen and red as though filled with blood. Despite Cradoc's best efforts, the priests of Morr led more and more corpse-carts on their sad journeys from the city.

It was thankless, heartbreaking work, but that did not stop Cradoc from trying to help those he could, and his poultices of lungwort and vinegar were freely distributed among the sick. It did little to halt the terrible pestilence, but until the source of the sickness was defeated it was all that could be done.

On the evening of the third night, frustrated at the lack of action from Count Aldred, Sigmar and Wolfgart sat outside their apartments on a high terrace overlooking the cliffs and marshes to the north of Marburg. They talked long into the night, drinking from a clay jug of southern wine and eating platters of salted fish. They told tales of battles won and friends in far off lands, enjoying a rare moment of companionship.

Though the talk was ribald and flowing, Sigmar sensed sadness in his friend that had little to do with too much wine. As Wolfgart finished telling the story of his fight against a particularly large greenskin in the opening moments of the battle at the crossing of the Aver, he sighed, his face melancholy.

'It has been too long since we talked like this,' said Sigmar.

'That it has,' said Wolfgart, raising his goblet. 'Life gets busy as we get older, eh?'

'That it does, old friend, but come, say what's on your mind. Tell me what troubles you.'

At first he thought Wolfgart would dismiss his invitation to speak, but his sword-brother surprised him.

'It's what Redwane said when we were going to see Aldred,' he said.

'You didn't take him seriously? The lad is young and foolish and he spoke out of turn, but you know Maedbh would never betray you like that.'

'I know that,' said Wolfgart, 'but that's not what I meant.'

'Then what is it?'

'I reacted to him like a stag in heat, as though he was a rival or something. I know he's not, but I pounced on him as if I was going to kill him. I would have done if you hadn't stopped me. I should have kept my temper in check, for I shamed you in front of Laredus.'

Sigmar shook his head and drained his goblet.

'Aye, we could have done without the Endals seeing us at each other's throats,' he said, 'but what's done is done. I don't hold it against you.'

'Maybe not, but I should have known better,' said Wolfgart. 'I've been around you long enough to know that I need to think before I act, but when he said that about Maedbh... Well, you saw how it affected me.'

'I'm just glad Maedbh didn't hear it,' said Sigmar with a smile.

Wolfgart laughed and said, 'True enough. She'd be wearing Redwane's balls for earrings by now.'

'You are a man of high emotion, Wolfgart, you always have been,' said Sigmar. 'It is one of the reasons I love you. Pendrag is my conscience and my intellect; you are the voice of my passions and my joys. I must be an Emperor, but you are the man I would wish to be were I not. By all means think before you act in future, especially when I must be seen to be the master of the Empire, but never lose your fire. I wouldn't have you any other way, and you would not be Wolfgart without it.'

His sword-brother finished his wine and smiled. 'I'll remind you of this the next time I lose my temper and embarrass you. You know that, don't you?'

'I know that,' said Sigmar, reaching over to pour more wine. 'I think the drink must be getting to me.'

Wolfgart lifted his goblet and took a long swallow.

'You might be right,' he said. 'You never could drink as much as me. This wine's not bad, but it's not a mug of Unberogen beer. Too weak.'

'Drink the rest of the jug and tell me that.'

'Don't tempt me. I'm that sick of waiting for something to happen, I might as well spend my time here drunk. How much longer do you think they'll make us sit on our backsides?'

'I do not know, my friend,' said Sigmar with a shrug. 'But for Idris Gwylt, I think I could have persuaded Aldred to march out with us.'

'He's a sly fox that one, he needs watching,' agreed Wolfgart. 'I heard those that followed the Old Faith used to sacrifice virgins to let the purity of their blood bless the earth, or something like that.'

'So they say, but stories of old religions are almost always exaggerated by the faiths that replace them to make people glad they are gone. It's like the stories you hear as a child about ancient heroes who bestrode the world like giants only to vanish and have their people claim that they will one day return when the world needs them most.'

'Why do you think that is?'

'Because people need hope when things are at their darkest,' said Sigmar. 'Of course, none of these heroes ever do return. Most likely they got a knife in the back or fell from a horse and broke their neck, but who wants their legends to end like that?'

'Not me,' said Wolfgart, letting loose an almighty belch. 'I want my heroes to be gods among men, warriors able to level mountains with a single blow, rescue beautiful maidens from monsters without a second thought, and turn back armies with a word.'

'You always were a dreamer,' said Sigmar, laughing.

THE MOON HAD risen, lighting the sky with its pale glow as Sigmar opened his eyes. He blinked, realising he'd fallen asleep. He groaned, feeling the beginnings of a thumping headache. Wine had spilled down his tunic, and he saw that Wolfgart had passed out with his head between his knees. A puddle of vomit stained the flagstones of the terrace. Sigmar ran a hand through his hair. His eyes ached and his mouth felt as though he'd drunk a barrel-load of bog water.

'Now I remember why I do not do this,' he groaned, pushing himself to his feet. 'I need to get to bed.'

A cold wind was blowing in from the darkened ocean, and Sigmar lurched towards the wall of the terrace, resting his palms on the cool stone and taking several deep breaths. It was foolish to try and blot out problems with strong drink, for they only returned all the more troublesome the following morning.

He looked down at the city gates below the terrace, surprised to see they were open. In Reikdorf, the gates were shut fast as night fell and did not open until the dawn. More corpse-carts no doubt.

Sigmar sighed, knowing that he was going to have to order Aldred to march alongside him to end the threat of the daemons. He was Emperor, and it was time to flex his imperial muscles.

'I had hoped to avoid coercing you, Aldred,' he whispered. 'What brotherhood does not create, force will not correct.'

The night was clammy and still, but the fogs had cleared enough to reveal a portion of the marshes stretching off into the distance. It was not an inspiring view, for the land around Marburg's walls was desolate and uninviting, and the gibbous moonlight made them all the more threatening.

Looking northwards, all Sigmar could see was treacherous mist-wreathed bogs along the line of the coast. Nothing lived in those bogs, nothing wholesome at least, and Sigmar spat a mouthful of bitter phlegm over the edge of the terrace.

He was about to turn away when a column of cloaked figures emerged from the city, but this was no solemn procession of corpse-carts. Sigmar recognised Idris Gwylt at the head of the column, his white hair and beard dazzling in the moonlight. Behind him went twenty Raven Helms with the bronze-armoured Count Aldred leading them. Ulfshard shimmered in Aldred's grip, wreathed in ghostly blue light like a frozen bolt of northern lightning.

The Raven Helms escorted what looked like a captive in their midst, and Sigmar's eyes narrowed as he saw that it was Aldred's sister, Marika, her willowy form and golden hair unmistakable.

The column turned from the road and made its way into the marshes. The mist closed around them, and in a heart-stopping moment of realisation, Sigmar understood the nature of the offering that Idris Gwylt intended to make to the daemons.

FIVE
Daemon Moon

THIRTY OF SIGMAR'S warriors marched through the gates of Marburg with purposeful strides, their faces set and determined. The moonlight made their wolfskin cloaks glow, and reflected from the few pieces of armour they had been able to put on as Sigmar roused them from their beds. Wolfgart and Redwane followed Sigmar as he splashed from the roadway onto the boggy ground at its side.

He stopped, feeling the cold water seeping through the worn leather of his boots. Beyond the road, the marsh was shrouded in ghostly mist. Sigmar shivered as he remembered the last time he had seen such a desolate, soulless landscape. It had been ten years ago, when he had lain close to death and his soul wandered the barren wastelands of the Grey Vaults.

The souls of the damned haunted that netherworld between life and death, and these marshes would be little different. The mist writhed and coiled around itself, an opaque wall of grey with distant flickering lights bobbing in its depths.

'What in the name of Shallya's mercy is going on?' asked Redwane. 'Why are we here?'

'Aye,' said Wolfgart, still clad in his stained tunic. 'It's bad luck to fight beneath the dread moon, especially when it's full. No good can come of it.'

'We are here to save an innocent life,' said Sigmar, hefting Ghal-maraz in both hands. The runes worked into its haft shone in the moonlight, as though energised by the thought of wreaking havoc against creatures of darkness once more.

'What are you talking about?'

'You remember telling me about the Old Faith and their sacrifices of virgins?' asked Sigmar.

'Vaguely,' replied Wolfgart.

'Turns out they're not just stories after all. I saw Aldred lead the Raven Helms into the marsh with Marika as their prisoner. Idris Gwylt means to offer her to the mist daemons.'

'Bastard!' snarled Redwane. 'I'll break his skull open with my hammer and tear his damn heart out!'

Sigmar was surprised at the strength of Redwane's anger, but was pleased to see the outrage on his warriors' faces as word of what was happening spread amongst them. He turned to face the White Wolves, knowing that some might not survive the night. Wolfgart was right, it *was* bad luck to go into battle beneath the spectral light of the dread moon, but they had no choice if they hoped to save Marika's life.

'A deluded old man seeks to murder an innocent girl!' Sigmar cried, though the mist seemed to swallow his words, throwing back strange echoes as if to mock him. 'I will not allow this to happen, and I need your strength to stop it. Are you with me?'

As one, the White Wolves raised their hammers and roared their affirmation, as Sigmar had known they would. Though the thought of entering this terrible marsh was a fearful prospect, the Wolves would never dream of letting their Emperor go into battle without them.

Sigmar nodded and set off into the mist, splashing through sucking mud and icy pools of stagnant water the colour of pitch. He had no way of knowing exactly where the Endals had gone, for brackish water poured into every footprint and erased it in seconds. Sigmar wished he had thought to bring Cuthwin to Marburg, but wishes were for fools and children, and they would need to find the Endals without their finest tracker.

The mist closed around the Unberogen as they forged a slow, stumbling path into the marsh. Their passage was lit by the sickly glow of lifeless moonbeams, and strange burping and bubbling sounds gurgled from the bog. A whispering wind dropped the temperature, but did not stir the heavy mist.

Nightcrawlers wriggled in the reeds and flies buzzed low over the ground. Sigmar saw an enormous dragonfly droning softly as it hunted in the hungry glow of the moon. His skin crawled and the hairs on the back of his neck itched as though a clawed hand was poised to strike him. This marsh was not like the Brackenwalsch, which wore its dangers openly. It was a haunted place where death crept up on a man and took him unawares.

'Look!' shouted Redwane. 'Over there!'

Sigmar turned to where Redwane was pointing, and his eyes narrowed as he saw bobbing lights in the distance, like hooded lamps borne by weary travellers. He tried to remember if the Endals had carried such illumination. He thought they had, but couldn't be sure.

Still, he was wary. The old men of Reikdorf spoke of such lights in the Brackenwalsch. They called them doom-lanterns, for the treacherous illumination they provided was said to lure men to their deaths with the promise of safety. Pendrag had told him that such lights were merely ignited swamp gases or moonlight reflecting from the feathers of night owls, but neither explanation gave Sigmar much comfort.

If these lights were indeed those of the Endals, then they had to follow them.

'This way,' called Sigmar, setting off after the lights. 'Keep watch on the ground!'

Once more the Unberogen plunged deep into the marsh, the ground becoming progressively softer and wetter underfoot. Flies buzzed around Sigmar's head and he saw yet more of the lights surrounding them, flickering like dancing torches. Bubbles burst around his feet, sounding like the mirthless laughter of dead things.

Time ceased to have meaning, for the thick fog made it impossible to judge the moon's passage across the night sky. Sigmar looked up, wincing as the dread moon's leering face seemed to stare back at him. Ill-favour followed those who turned their faces too long to that malevolent orb, and Sigmar hurriedly made the sign of the horns.

He started as he felt something brush his legs, and jumped back, seeing a pale shape, like a darting eel beneath the surface of the water. Sigmar lifted his boot from the sucking marsh, the fine leather stained and ruined. A filmy residue of reeking ichor, like pale syrup, dripped from the buckles. Once they got out of the marsh, he would never wear these boots again.

Sigmar heard a dreadful cry, followed by a heavy splash behind him. He spun to see a group of men holding out their hammers to a fallen warrior who thrashed his arms in a hidden pool of murky water. Sigmar recognised him as Volko, a man who had fought at his side in the charge to rescue the Merogen flank at Black Fire.

Volko was waist-deep in the bog, but his armour was dragging him down swiftly. He reached for the outstretched weapons, but the marsh was not about to release its victim. Volko's head vanished beneath the surface of the water as he drew breath to scream, leaving only a froth of bubbles in his wake.

'Ulric save us,' said Wolfgart, stepping back from the water. 'I knew this was bad luck.'

Sigmar fought his way through the mud and water to the bog where Volko had died. Tendrils of fog gathered around the legs of every warrior, and it was next to impossible to tell solid ground from deadly bog.

'Move out,' ordered Sigmar. 'Check every footstep and stay close to your comrades.'

'What about Volko?' demanded Redwane. 'No warrior deserves to die without hearing the sound of wolves.'

Sigmar risked a glance into the darkened sky. 'You're right, lad, but this is a night when the wolves are silent and only the moon howls.'

'So we're just going to leave him?'

'We will mourn him later,' said Sigmar, setting off once more.

He had no way of knowing which way to go, but felt a slight pull to the north-east, as though Ghal-maraz knew better than he in which direction its enemies lay. Sigmar put his trust in the craft of the dwarfs and followed the wordless urging.

Wolfgart came alongside him, his eyes flicking from left to right.

'None of us are going to make it out of here alive,' he said.

Sigmar felt his fear, but said, 'Let none of the men hear you say that.'

'It's true though, isn't it?'

'Not if I can help it,' said Sigmar. 'We are Unberogen and there is nothing we cannot do.'

Wolfgart nodded, visibly controlling himself.

'You know we might have to fight the Raven Helms to save the girl,' he said.

'I know,' nodded Sigmar, keeping a close eye on the ground. 'And if that's what it takes, then so be it. I drove the Norsii from the Empire for such barbarism, and I'll do the same to the Endals if that's what's needed.'

'Aye,' said Wolfgart. 'It's wrong is what this is. Utterly wrong.'

Sigmar halted and raised his hand. His warriors stopped with a series of splashes and curses. Ahead, more of the doom-lanterns were moving through the dark, but this time it appeared as though they were borne by indistinct, shadowy forms.

'Unberogen! Stand ready!' shouted Sigmar.

The White Wolves swung their hammers to their shoulders and formed a ragged battle line as best they were able.

The lights drew closer and the mist parted as the ghostly figures came into sight.

Idris Gwylt, eyes wide with surprise, halted at the sight of Sigmar. Laredus stood beside the priest of the Old Faith, supporting the weeping form of Count Aldred. The Raven Helm's face was grim and etched with regret. Of the twenty warriors he had led into the marsh, Sigmar counted only a dozen left alive.

Of Count Aldred's sister, there was no sign.

Redwane surged forward and lifted Gwylt by the throat.

'Where is Marika?' he roared. 'What have you done with her?'

SIGMAR SAW THE Raven Helms reach for their swords and knew that this desolate stretch of marshland might become a battleground in a matter of moments. It was madness, and he would be damned if this one moment would undo the long years of sacrifice spent in building the Empire.

The Raven Helms looked to their ruler for orders, and Sigmar marched over to him. The tension racked up a notch, but instead of words of rebuke Sigmar said, 'Count Aldred, where is your sister?'

Ulfshard dropped from Aldred's hand, landing point down in the water with a soft splash as the lord of the Endals sank to his haunches. He buried his head in his hands and sobbed aching tears.

'We left her.' he cried. 'Ulric forgive me, we left her there.'

'Where?' asked Sigmar, kneeling next to Aldred. 'Tell me where and we will get her back. You and me both. This is wrong, Aldred, you know that.'

'It had to be done!' cried Aldred. 'A plague ravages my people and my brother is dead!'

Sigmar was shocked.

'Egil is dead?' he asked.

Aldred nodded, tears cutting clean lines through the mud on his cheeks. 'A few hours ago, and now my sister will join him in Morr's realm. It was the only way to save my people.'

'You are wrong,' said Sigmar.

Aldred wiped his sleeve across his face.

'What choice did I have?' he asked. 'Everything was being taken from us and only the sacrifice of a pure and noble-born maiden could save us.'

Sigmar took Aldred by the shoulders and forced him to meet his gaze.

'You have been deceived,' he said, looking over his shoulder to where Redwane stood with his hammer poised to smash Idris Gwylt's skull to shards. 'Did he tell you that?'

'The daemons demanded a sacrifice!' shouted Gwylt, struggling in vain to free himself from Redwane's iron grip. 'And the girl went willingly! She knew that the land must be nourished by virgin's blood, as it was in the elder days. Aldred, you know I speak only the truth!'

'Shut your mouth, you dog,' snarled Redwane, squeezing Gwylt's throat.

Sigmar stood and snatched Gwylt's staff. He broke it over his knee before hurling the shards into the marsh. The Raven Helms still gripped their swords and the White Wolves were braced to meet their charge. With the wrong word, Sigmar could have a civil war on his hands.

'All of you listen to me!' he shouted. 'And listen well, your lives depend upon it. This is a black day for the Endals, for you have heeded the words of a madman. You are warriors of honour and this act shames you. Leading a young girl to her death in this evil place is a vile deed, and if she dies, I will damn your names for all eternity. This curse, if curse it is, will only be lifted if we seek out these daemons of the mist and destroy them. Now I am going to find Marika, and I am going to bring her back to Marburg. You can either come with me and regain your honour, or you can slink back to your homes and live the rest of your lives known forever as cowards and nithings, to be cast out and shunned by all men.'

Sigmar turned from the warriors as Aldred pushed himself to his feet. The count of the Endals rubbed the heels of his palms against his face, as though waking from a dreadful nightmare, and Sigmar saw the strength he had seen in Aldred's father.

'Aye,' said Sigmar, gripping Aldred's hand. 'Take up your sword, brother. We will get her back, I swear.'

Aldred lifted Ulfshard from the water, the blade's ghostly glow banishing the darkness with its brilliance. No trace of the foul marsh-water stained its blade.

'When my father died, light fled from our lives,' said Aldred, his voice choked with emotion. 'Since then I have lived in darkness. It has been so long that I cannot remember the light.'

'Help me rescue your sister and the light will return,' said Sigmar.

Aldred nodded, and a fierce determination shone in his eyes. He turned his gaze upon Idris Gwylt and said, 'Aye, and this old fool will lead us back to their domain or I will cut his throat.'

THE LAIR OF the daemons sat upon a large hill that reared from the heart of the benighted marsh. Banks of fog gathered at its base as the Unberogen and Endal warriors crept up its rocky slopes. Towering menhirs carved with spirals, circles and one-eyed monsters punctured the sodden gorse of the hill, like jagged teeth growing from within the body of the mound.

Nearly fifty warriors darted between the grotesque monuments as they approached the summit, keeping as low and silent as possible. The deadening qualities of the mist worked in their favour, and the clatter of plate and mail was muffled.

Sigmar kept his eyes upon the ridge at the top of the hill, feeling Ghal-maraz tingling in his grasp. The ancient weapon knew that evil creatures were near, and the urge to split their skulls coursed through Sigmar's veins. Count Aldred climbed next to him, while Wolfgart and Redwane followed close behind. The young White Wolf kept a tight grip on Idris Gwylt.

They were almost at the summit, and Sigmar halted, moving forward on his belly to a jagged, rock-crowned ridge that overlooked the daemons' lair. Looking through a gap in the rocks, he saw the top of the hill was in fact a vast crater, and the breath caught in Sigmar's throat at what lay within.

Colossal blocks of pale, moonlit stone lay scattered throughout the crater, all that remained of a city raised in a forgotten age by unknown hands. It covered an area at least the size of Reikdorf and Marburg combined, and Sigmar could only imagine the scale of the beings that had lived here if the size of the streets was any indication.

'Ulric's bones,' hissed Wolfgart, as he reached the ridge and saw the city. 'What is this place? Who lived here?'

'I don't know,' said Sigmar. 'Aldred?'

'Gwylt took Marika through the mist to the top of the hill. I know nothing of this place.'

'It looks like it was built for giants,' said Redwane.

'Then let's hope they're as dead as their city,' said Wolfgart.

All thoughts of the city's builders fled from Sigmar's mind as he saw a flash of golden hair below them in what looked like a crude arena. Marika was bound to one of the soaring menhirs, and Aldred cried out as he too saw her.

'Blood of my fathers!' swore Redwane. 'Daemons!'

Sigmar felt his blood chill as monsters emerged from the darkness. A host of vile creatures hauled themselves from lairs carved beneath the arena, and even from a distance they were repulsive.

There were around a hundred of the pallid-fleshed daemons, their bodies hairless and hunched. Bronze shields strapped to their torsos protected their wasted bodies, and barbed tails swayed beneath kilts of tattered mail. Each daemon carried a rusted weapon, either an axe or a spiked club, and beak-like snouts filled with savage, needle-like teeth snapped and gnashed as they closed on Marika.

Each of the daemons saw the world through but a single eye, and such a hideous aberration of form left Sigmar in no doubt as to their diabolical nature. More hideous than even the worst of the daemons was the loathsome creature that lurched and shuffled at the centre of the pack. Though shaped like its lesser brethren, this monstrous cyclops was much larger, the height of three tall men. Its limbs were bloated and its distended belly was like that of a woman on the verge of giving birth. Lank hair hung from this creature's skull like tarred ropes and two shapeless dugs of withered flesh hung from its breast.

Was this some form of abominable daemon-queen?

The vast creature advanced on Marika, and Sigmar's stomach turned as he saw a vile lust in its cyclopean features.

There was no time for subtlety here, only action.

Sigmar shouted, 'Into them!' and surged over the ridge with Ghal-maraz raised over his shoulder. The hammer's runes shimmered in the weak light, and the daemons let loose a gurgling shriek of warning at the sight of him.

The mass of Unberogen and Endal warriors charged after Sigmar, ululating war cries splitting the dead air with their ferocity. Wolfgart and Aldred charged alongside Sigmar, and the wiry count of the Endals pulled ahead of him, the desperate need to redeem himself and save his sister lending his tired limbs fresh strength. Redwane ran with a look of hatred twisting his young features. The daemons shambled from the arena towards them, brandishing their rusted weapons and answering the war cries of their enemies with hoarse roars of their own.

Sigmar sprinted downhill towards the arena, vaulting a fallen monolith and bellowing the name of Ulric. There was no way he could reach Marika before the daemon-queen tore her to pieces, but if nothing else, he would avenge her.

The running warriors struck the daemons in a clash of iron and bronze. As horrifying as the creatures were, they died as any creature of flesh and blood could die. Wolfgart's huge blade clove through three of the monsters with a single blow, while Aldred spun through the daemons with the elegant sweeps of a fencing master. Redwane killed with brutally precise hammer blows, the heavy, wolf-shaped head spinning around his body in devastating arcs.

Sigmar fought to keep up with Aldred, smashing a daemon from its feet with a chopping blow from Ghal-maraz. The beast howled in agony as the runes on the dwarf weapon seared its flesh and crushed its bones. Another monster came at him, but Sigmar ducked a skull-crushing sweep of its axe and slammed the head of his hammer against the creature's midriff. Its belly split open and a bubbling gruel of stinking fluids spilled onto the hillside. Dank mist began forming in the bowl of the arena, and the vile smell of rotten meat increased on every stale breath of wind.

Sigmar pushed onwards, killing a daemon with every blow, but too many of the beasts were between him and Marika. All around him the battle raged, and the courage of his warriors, both Unberogen and Endal, was a thing of rare magnificence.

White Wolves fought with a brutal directness, always pushing forward with chopping blows from their hammers. Such weapons were designed for swinging from the back of a charging steed, but such was the skill of the Unberogen warriors that it made little difference to their tally of kills.

The Raven Helms fought to expunge the shame of leading their princess into the marsh, and each man cut into the daemons with no thought for his own defence, their swords stained with the blood of their enemies. The months of misery and suffering caused by these daemons were repaid in full, as the Endals vented their hatred and grief in every blow.

The daemons fought with equal ferocity, their axes and clubs landing with dreadful strength that smashed plate armour asunder, and tore through mail as though it were woven from cloth. Their limbs were wiry, but they were strong and brutal, and many a warrior had marched into this battle without armour.

Thick banks of mist rolled out from the enormous daemon at the centre of the horde, flowing up the hill in an unnatural tide. The stink of it was like a midden at the height of summer and it coiled through the battle like a host of wet grey snakes. Soon the entire hillside was wreathed in mist, and every warrior fought his own battle in the smothering fog, unable to tell friend from foe.

Blood stained the hillside as men and daemons hacked into each other. The Endals and Unberogen still pushed forward, but the greater number of their inhuman foes was beginning to tell. Their courageous charge slowed and finally stopped.

Sigmar caught up to Aldred, the Endal count's glowing sword blade a beacon in the obscuring fog. The mist seemed reluctant to close around Sigmar and Aldred, as though kept at bay by the magic of their weapons.

Redwane fought towards them.

'The girl!' he shouted. 'Get to the girl!'

Sigmar saw the hideous beast rear over the Endal princess. It reached for the struggling girl and let out a screeching, gurgling cry of triumph. Aldred cried out in despair, but no sooner did the daemon-queen touch Marika, than it recoiled as though burned. It loosed a hideous shriek, its monstrous features twisted in revulsion, as though disgusted by the young girl before it.

Aldred fought at Sigmar's side. Together they cut a path through the daemons, parting the mist before them with their enchanted weapons. Side by side, Emperor and count slew their foes, each protecting the other, and each fighting as though they had trained together since childhood. Their weapons wove killing arcs, and Sigmar sensed a kinship between these wondrous artefacts, as though they had slain creatures of the dark together in ages past in the hands of their makers. Though forged by craftsmen from very different races, oath-sworn pacts of ancient days still bound the fates of the weapons.

The moment passed, and Sigmar felt stone beneath his boots as he stepped onto the marble-flagged floor of the arena. He killed another monster as Aldred slew the last of the daemon-queen's protectors and ran to his sister. Marika still screamed and wept in terror, sagging against the chains that bound her to the menhir.

'So much for willing, eh?' said Redwane, coming alongside Sigmar.

The daemon-queen backed away from them, though it hissed and spat in Marika's direction. The sounds of battle still raged on the hillside above, but Sigmar knew that the daemons' curse would only be ended with the death of this monster.

'Let's finish this,' said Sigmar.

'Gladly,' agreed Redwane.

The two warriors charged towards the daemon-queen, but they had travelled no more than a few yards when the ground underfoot transformed from solid marble to sucking mud and water. Redwane stumbled, and Sigmar sank to his calves.

'Sorcery!' cried Redwane, hauling himself from the mud and pushing on. Sigmar extricated himself and splashed over the boggy ground after Redwane. Columns of yellow fog boiled from the suddenly marshy ground, and a powerful stench like rotten eggs assailed him. He gagged on the acrid mist, feeling his guts rebel at the foulness. In seconds, he was as good as blind.

A shadow moved in the fog, and Sigmar threw himself to one side as a huge clawed arm slashed towards him. He splashed into the stinking water as filth-encrusted talons flashed over his head, a hand's span from decapitating him. He tasted the rank marsh water the daemon-queen had conjured.

Sigmar coughed and spat the black fluid clear, rolling in the mud as a huge, clawed foot slammed down. He swung his hammer, and the creature shrieked as the ancient weapon struck its wet and spongy flesh.

Redwane's hammer tore into the creature's side, and a froth of blood and lumpen matter spilled from the wound. That matter flapped and writhed as though alive, but thankfully sank into the swamp before Sigmar could see its true nature. The White Wolf's hammer was a blur of dark iron, slamming home again and again into the daemon-queen's flesh.

Sigmar struggled to his feet in the slippery mud, feeling the desire of the swampy ground to suck him down to his death. The beast lurched towards Redwane, faster than its bulk would suggest, and its clawed arms plucked him from the ground. The mist closed in around the combat, and Sigmar heard Redwane roar in pain, before his cries were suddenly silenced. A heavy splash sounded, and Sigmar swung Ghal-maraz up to his shoulder.

A bloated shape moved in the mist, and the daemon-queen loomed over him, its lank hair whipping around its head as it snapped at him. Sigmar threw up his hammer, holding it above his head with both hands, and the creature's beaked jaw snapped down on the haft.

The force of the bite drove Sigmar into the sodden ground, and marsh water sucked greedily at his body, pulling him deeper into the mire. The monster's foetid breath enveloped him, and gobs of stinging drool spattered him as it tried to bite through Ghal-maraz. Mud rose past his waist, and bubbles burst around him as he sank even further.

A flash of movement caught Sigmar's eye as a dark shape leapt to the attack.

Sigmar's heart leapt as he saw Redwane. The young warrior's mail shirt was shredded, splintered links falling from him like droplets of silver. Blood soaked his side where the daemon-queen had torn his flesh, but the fury of battle was upon him and no force in the world was going to stop him.

Redwane yelled, 'Ulric give me strength!' and brought his hammer down over his head.

The weapon thundered against the side of the daemon-queen's head, and its lower jaw was smashed from its skull. Greenish-brown blood spattered Sigmar, and the pressure on his arms vanished. He wrenched Ghal-maraz free, and swung it one-handed over the splintered remains of the monster's chitinous beak. All his strength was behind the blow, and the head of the rune hammer slammed into the daemon-queen's eye.

It burst like a ruptured bladder, showering Sigmar and Redwane in reeking gelatinous fluids, and the daemon-queen howled in agony. The enormous beast crashed down, its flailing arms clutching its ruined socket. Blood squirted from the wound, and the mists that cloaked it began to fade as its life bled out. The monster convulsed in its death throes, and it vomited an enormous slick of wriggling things that flopped and thrashed like landed fish.

Sigmar struggled to free himself from the sucking marsh, as he felt the ground begin to solidify around him. He had no wish to be trapped when the magic that had transformed the stone to swamp was exhausted.

'Need a hand?' asked Redwane. His face was deathly white, and Sigmar saw how deeply the daemon-queen had cut him. Bright blood flowed from his side and drenched his leggings.

'If you can,' said Sigmar.

'I think I'll manage,' said Redwane, taking hold of Sigmar's wrist and pulling. Though his face contorted in pain, Redwane hauled Sigmar free of the mud without complaint. Sigmar got to his feet, feeling that the ground beneath him was solid stone once more.

'Right,' whispered Redwane, 'I think I'll lie down now.'

Sigmar caught the youth as he fell, and laid him down gently before lifting the torn mail from his body. The skin was ashen and slick with blood, three parallel scars running from Redwane's ribs to his pelvis.

'I need water!' shouted Sigmar,

'Damn, but that stings,' hissed Redwane. 'The bitch was quicker than she looked.'

'These?' asked Sigmar. 'Ach, they're nothing, lad. I've had bigger scars from the bites of Ortulf's fleas.'

'That old dog must have some damn big fleas,' said Redwane, gritting his teeth against the pain. 'Perhaps Wolfgart should throw saddles on them and we'll fly into battle.'

Sigmar smiled and looked uphill to where Wolfgart and the White Wolves stood triumphant with Laredus and the Raven Helms amid a field of corpses. Daemons and men lay scattered across the hillside, for it had been a battle won with the blood of heroes. The dead would be mourned in time, but for now, the victory belonged to the living.

'Here,' said a voice at Sigmar's side. 'Water.'

Sigmar looked up into Aldred's battle-weary face. The count of the Endals and his sister stood over Sigmar. Aldred held out a leather canteen. Sigmar took it and poured clear liquid over Redwane's wounds.

'Will he live?' asked Marika, dropping to her knees beside Redwane.

'His wounds are wide, but shallow,' said Sigmar, trying not to think of the filth encrusted on the daemon-queen's claws. 'So long as the wounds do not fester, I believe he will live.'

'That's good to know,' hissed Redwane.

'He will receive the best care in Marburg, my Emperor,' said Aldred.

'I will nurse him myself,' promised Marika.

Aldred offered Sigmar his hand and said, 'I have been a fool, my friend. I doubted your vision, and my father's death blinded me to its truth. Idris Gwylt fanned the flames of that doubt and his dark faith almost cost me the life of my sister.'

'He promised my sacrifice would save our people,' said Marika, and Sigmar was impressed at how quickly she had recovered her composure after so close a brush with death. Clearly Endal women were as hardy as those of the Unberogen. 'His lies had me convinced that only

I could save us, that I should walk into the marsh and let that… thing devour me.'

'Aye, and for that he will pay with his life,' said Aldred. 'I will curse his soul to eternal torment with a thrice death in the waters of the marsh.'

'It is no more than he deserves,' said Sigmar.

Marika rose from Redwane's side and Aldred took her by the hand, holding it as though he meant to never let go.

'The mists are lifting,' said Aldred. 'I think the journey out of the marshes will be happier than the journey in.'

'Indeed it will,' agreed Sigmar, 'but we should move quickly. It will be dark soon.'

Aldred nodded and led Marika away as Wolfgart came over to help him with Redwane.

'Well, lad,' said Wolfgart. 'You have fought daemons now. Was it all you hoped for?'

'Oh yes,' snapped Redwane. 'I've always wanted to be mauled by a fat daemon bitch.'

Wolfgart grinned, tearing strips from the lining of his cloak to use as bandages.

As Wolfgart bound Redwane's wounds, Sigmar looked over at the mouldering corpse of the daemon-queen, picturing how the creature had recoiled from its intended victim.

'There is one thing I don't understand,' said Sigmar. 'Why did the beast not kill Marika? I thought daemons hungered for the blood of virgins.'

'Trust me,' said Redwane with a sly grimace. 'That lass is no virgin.'

⤙ SIX ⤚

Troublesome Kings

Count Aldred renewed the Sword Oath of his father in the main square before the Raven Hall, dropping to one knee and lifting Ulfshard for the Emperor to take. Cheers echoed from one end of Marburg to the other as Sigmar took the ancient blade and then handed it back to Aldred, thus sealing their pact of confraternity.

Dawn had been lighting the eastern horizon when the battle-weary but elated warriors emerged from the marsh. They bore their dead but, after the noxious reek of the swamps, the sweet smell of clean, sea air banished any thoughts of grief.

All through the journey back to Marburg, bodies had floated to the surface of the swamp, as though the defeat of the daemons had freed them to return to the world above. The unique properties of the bog water had preserved the bodies remarkably, and in time they too would be recovered and sent into the next world with honour.

Within days of Sigmar's return, Cradoc reported a marked drop in new cases of lung rot, and soon it was clear that the worst had passed. The number of corpse-carts leaving the city dwindled, and those that had fled to the country to avoid the pestilence now returned to their homes. The city came back to life, and the oppressive gloom that had hung over it for so long was banished as light and wonder returned. The indefatigable human spirit, which had been on the verge of being snuffed out, had held on, and now bloomed stronger than ever.

Sigmar and his warriors remained in Marburg for another week, hailed as saviours and showered with gifts from a grateful populace. As she had promised, Princess Marika nursed the wounded Redwane personally, but Sigmar ensured that Cradoc was never far away. When Redwane complained about such a prudish chaperone, Wolfgart settled the matter by pointing out that Redwane would need to keep his hands to himself or take Marika as his wife, for Aldred would be well within his rights to kill him if he ever found out that his sister had been taken advantage of. Having heard the gruesome details of Idris Gwylt's execution, Redwane was in no mood to count on Aldred's forgiveness, and his complaints ceased.

Gwylt had suffered the hideous fate of a thrice death, and even Sigmar had blanched when he heard the details. The priest had been fed a broth laced with poisonous white mistletoe berries, and then led in chains to the edge of the marsh. A slaughterman then broke his crudely-shaven skull open with three precisely measured blows from an iron-tipped cudgel. Barely alive, Gwylt was dragged into the sucking bogs of the swamp, where Aldred slashed Ulfshard across his throat. Poisoned, dying from numerous skull fractures and with his lifeblood pouring from his neck, Laredus completed the execution by holding Gwylt beneath the marsh water until his feeble struggles ceased.

With so many 'deaths' inflicted upon the priest in quick succession, his soul would not know when to flee the body until it was too late. Gwylt's flesh would never decay in the depths of the swamp, and his soul would remain trapped in the corpse for all time.

The priests of Morr had protested at such a harsh punishment, for to deny a soul its final journey went against the sacred tenets of their faith. Their pleas for clemency fell on deaf ears, for the Endals had practised this form of execution for centuries, and no one could deny that such a painful death was richly deserved.

The Unberogen left Marburg in high spirits, despite bringing nine mounts back home without their riders. They travelled through a realm that was coming to life once more, the last remnants of the mist daemons' curse lifting as the strength of the land emerged resurgent from its imprisonment.

Two months to the day after setting out for the city of the Endals, Sigmar led his warriors back across the Sudenreik Bridge and into Reikdorf.

* * *

SIGMAR PINCHED THE bridge of his nose between his thumb and forefinger, and sipped the herbal infusion Cradoc had prepared for him. His head hurt, though he had suffered no injury to make it ache. Rather, it was the incessant demands on his time that caused this headache. Uniting the tribes of men had, it turned out, been the easy part of forging the Empire.

He sat in his private chambers, reclining on his bed with Ortulf, Kai and Lex curled at his feet. A freshly banked fire crackled in the hearth and the soothing aroma of wood smoke helped ease the pain behind his eyes. Since returning from Marburg, the business of gathering his warriors for an expedition to Jutonsryk had occupied his every waking moment, though there had been some good news to lighten Sigmar's days.

As spring's goodness blessed the land with warmth and life, Maedbh of the Asoborns gave birth to Ulrike, who came into the world with a lusty war cry on her lips. The joyous Wolfgart paraded his daughter through the city streets with tears of wonder spilling down his cheeks, and the people of Reikdorf had showered them both with handfuls of grain, earth and water.

Wolfgart and Maedbh honoured Sigmar by asking him to be Ulrike's sword-guardian, a role traditionally filled by the closest friend of the parents. Sigmar accepted the great responsibility and solemnly swore to protect the child should they die.

At the child's birthing ritual, held on a hillside to the east of Reikdorf, a priestess of Shallya named Alessa lit a fire and anointed Ulrike's head with three drops of water taken from a nearby spring. As each droplet fell, she recited the Blessing of Welcome. 'A little drop of the sky on thy little forehead, beloved one. A little drop of the land on thy little forehead, beloved one. A little drop of the sea on thy little forehead, beloved one.'

Alessa then placed a heart-shaped locket of silver around Ulrike's neck and said, 'The heart of Shallya to shield thee from the fey, to guard thee from the host, to cloak thee from the wicked, to ward thee from the spectre, to surround thee and to fill thee with grace.'

With Ulrike protected against dark sorcery, Alessa then immersed her in the cold spring with a silver and gold coin in each hand to honour the powers of the moon and sun. Wolfgart held the crying child in the fast-flowing water as the priestess filled her palm with earth and rubbed it over the child's belly, arms and legs while singing a prayer of protection and health.

With the father's duties complete, Wolfgart handed Ulrike to Maedbh, who completed the ritual by taking Ulrike and touching her forehead to the ground as she recited a prayer to Morr. This last act was to ask the god of the dead to seal the gate between the previous world and this one, for no others should cross the threshold of life.

With the correct rites observed, Ulrike was handed to Sigmar, who lifted her towards the sky, for to move a child downwards would forever doom it to remaining lowly in the world, never able to rise to distinction or wealth.

This had been a rare moment of joy in a spring that brought ill news to Reikdorf every week. A haphazard pile of rolled parchments sat on a table beside Sigmar, each one a letter from his counts that bore news of their lands and people.

They made for grim reading.

In the north, Pendrag and Wolfila sent word of increasing raids by Norsii Wolfships, the dark-armoured Norsemen marauding settlements many miles inland as well as those on the coast. The Norsii were attacking with ever more frequency, and the cunning of their leaders was all too apparent in their choice of targets. Most of the raids had come at a time when the majority of the menfolk were gathering for sword musters in distant towns, and Sigmar sensed more than simple luck in the Norsii's timing of their attacks.

Survivors of the raids carried south the names of two warlords, names that spoke of the naked brutality of the Norsii. Cormac Bloodaxe was said to be a towering warrior in black armour, who fought in a frenzy with a mighty twin-bladed axe of red fire, while Azazel was a lithe swordsman with dark hair, who delighted in cutting his opponents apart a piece at a time.

So far, the raids had been confined to the northern coastline, though Pendrag warned that it would not be long before the Norsii grew bolder.

That was a problem for another day, for the greenskins on the eastern mountains were once again daring to venture from their mountain lairs to raid and kill. Amid the tall tales of her sons' achievements, Freya of the Asoborns warned that a growing number of settlements in the foothills of the Worlds Edge Mountains were being raided by orcs. Scouts who had ventured into the mountains found no sign of any greenskin forces of any great size, though Sigmar knew it was only a matter of time before a powerful leader emerged and sought to weld the tribes together once more.

Further west, progress on the stone roads linking Reikdorf with Middenheim and Siggurdheim had slowed considerably. Attacks from forest beasts were an almost daily occurrence. Sigmar had tasked more men to patrol the roads and protect the work gangs, as well as increasing their pay to tempt others to volunteer for the roads' construction. Alfgeir had urged him to put those who broke the law to work, but Sigmar was loath to use such labour. He wanted men to work with pride, and to feel that they had participated in something worthwhile. Men forced to work under the lash would never build something worthwhile, and Sigmar did not want his empire to be built on the backs of criminals.

In the south, Count Markus spoke of his people's attempts to reclaim their tribal domains, for the orcs, trolls and twisted vermin-beasts from beneath the mountains had grown bold of late. During the wars against the greenskins, many of the Menogoth hill forts had been destroyed, and their people slaughtered or taken beyond the eastern peaks as slaves. The Menogoths had been on the verge of extinction, and taking back their ancestral lands with so few warriors was no small challenge. Markus was a canny leader of men, and the Menogoths a hardy, pragmatic tribe, and not even dark rumours of the dead rising from their mountain tombs dissuaded them from the task.

Sigmar sighed, sipping his herbal infusion and wondering if the world would ever allow him to be free from protecting his people. No matter how many warriors he could call upon, there was always a threat building somewhere, if not from beyond his lands then from within them. Sigmar's thoughts darkened as he thought of the audience with Krugar and Aloysis earlier that afternoon.

With the looming threat of extinction lifted, the counts of the Empire were free to turn their gazes on ancient grudges and long-standing feuds with neighbouring tribes. Both Krugar and Aloysis had sent bleating letters, once again claiming the other was sending masked raiders across their borders to harass their people's settlements, burning crops, killing livestock and stealing grain. Of course, both counts denied they were doing any such thing, citing years of border disputes and blaming the other for their woes.

In the end, Sigmar had summoned both counts to Reikdorf to put an end to the matter.

* * *

The atmosphere in the longhouse was tense, the crackle of the fire and the distant noise of the city beyond the only sounds to disturb the brooding silence. Sigmar sat upon his throne at the far end of the hall, his crown glittering upon his brows and Ghal-maraz laid across his lap. A wolfskin cloak spilled around his shoulders, and the foulness of the Emperor's mood was obvious.

Alfgeir stood behind Sigmar, his bronze-bladed sword unsheathed and held with its point resting on the floor. Eoforth sat to Sigmar's left, with a long, rolled-up length of hide parchment laid across his lap. Neither man looked at the counts, and disappointment was etched into both their faces.

Aloysis, lean and immaculately presented, was a hawkish man with a closely trimmed beard and hooded eyes. The Cherusen count was precise in movement and thought, the very antithesis of his people, who were wild and rough foresters proficient with axe and bow. His robes of crimson and emerald were richly appointed, and a golden chain with a silver eagle at its centre hung around his neck. A vivid yellow cloak was thrown rakishly over one shoulder, and a long Cherusen dagger with a beautifully inlaid scabbard of mother-of-pearl was sheathed at his hip.

Across from Aloysis was the grim-eyed count of the Taleutens. Krugar was a wild-bearded giant of a man in gleaming scale armour, formed from intricately carved leaves of silvered iron. Sheathed in a plain scabbard of dark leather was Utensjarl, a curved cavalry sabre said to have been forged by Talenbor, the first king of the Taleutens. Krugar had the bow-legged stance of a seasoned horseman, and when the Taleutens made war, he rode with the Red Scythes, the lancers who had broken the orc line at the Aver. Krugar's cheeks and neck were tattooed with jagged lines of red and gold, and his gaze smouldered with long-burning anger.

Neither count deigned to look at the other, and Sigmar knew this dispute would not be settled without angry words. Sigmar nodded towards Aloysis, and the count of the Cherusens did not hesitate to speak.

'This situation is intolerable, my Emperor,' began Aloysis. 'Taleuten riders regularly cross the Taalbec river and spread terror and destruction amongst my people. Already nine Cherusen villages have suffered at their hands, losing grain and precious supplies for the winter.'

'Pah,' sneered Krugar. 'If my riders were crossing into your territory to raid, your people would not have food to last them a week. Taleutens know how to pick the land clean.'

'You see?' cried Aloysis. 'The braggart admits his crimes before you! I demand justice!'

'I admit nothing, you fool,' roared Krugar, gripping the hilt of his sabre. 'It is you who sends axemen across the river! Your logging gangs hack down trees from land that is not theirs and float them down-river to Cherusen lumber yards in the Howling Hills.'

'A fool, am I?' roared Aloysis, the veins standing out on his neck as his hand flashed to the engraved hilt of his dagger. His eyes bulged, making him look like one of the painted Wildmen of his tribe. 'I'll not suffer your lies and insults any longer, Krugar.'

'Lies? You are the one poisoning the air with falsehoods!'

'Enough!' roared Sigmar, rising from his throne. The two counts ceased their bickering as he strode towards them. He glared first at Aloysis and then at Krugar, his expression softening in regret.

'It saddens me how soon you forget the brotherhood we forged in blood,' said Sigmar. 'Can you not remember how your souls soared at the pass when the orcs broke and ran? Has the golden memory of that shared victory faded from your thoughts?'

'Never, my lord!' said Aloysis. 'I will take the glory of that bloody day to my grave.'

Krugar drew his sword and held it before Sigmar. The silver blade was etched with the dwarf rune for Black Fire Pass. 'Each time I unsheathe Utensjarl, I am reminded of that great battle!'

'That day brought us together,' said Sigmar, 'all men joined in unity and fighting as one race. We stood before the largest army this world has ever seen. We proud few stood against that army, and we defeated it.'

Sigmar pointed to the huge orc skull that hung on the wall above his throne, that of the warlord who had led the greenskin horde at Black Fire Pass. Larger than the mightiest stallion's, the skull boasted two enormous tusks that jutted from the lower jaw like those of the mythical beasts of the Southlands. Even in death, the fearsome power of the monster once known as Bloodfang was palpable.

'The world will never see its like again, yet here we are, a year from that day and you squabble with a brother whose warriors stood shoulder to shoulder with you in the battle line. Sword Oaths were sworn in the years before Black Fire Pass and we renewed them by the flames of Marbad's pyre. Or at least I thought we did.'

'My Sword Oath is yours,' said Aloysis immediately. 'My *life* is yours.'

'And mine also, Lord Sigmar,' said Krugar, unwilling to be shown up before his rival. 'I gave my oath to your father and I gave it again to you, freely.'

'Aye, you both swore Sword Oaths with me,' nodded Sigmar. 'And swearing an oath with me is the same as swearing an oath with your brother counts. Aloysis, have you forgotten how you fought alongside Krugar and my father to drive the Norsii from your lands? And Krugar, can you not remember when the charge of the Cherusen Wildmen split apart the greenskin trap that encircled your riders at the Aver?'

'An attack on one of you is an attack on me, remember?' continued Sigmar, waving Eoforth forward. 'Your lands are threatened, so I must ride to your aid. Each of you claims the other attacks you, but upon whom should I make war?'

Neither count answered as Eoforth handed the long roll of parchment to Sigmar. He undid the leather cord binding it, and unrolled a beautifully rendered map on one of the tables that ran the length of the great hall. Aloysis and Krugar gathered close to Sigmar, their enmity forgotten in the face of this incredible piece of cartography.

The forests, rivers and cities of the Empire were picked out in coloured inks, each feature drawn with wondrous skill and precision. The territories of each tribal group were clearly marked, and golden lettering named the major settlements, rivers and mountain ranges.

Sigmar stabbed his finger into the centre of the map, where an exquisitely drawn castle in black ink represented Hochergig, the largest city of the Cherusens and seat of Count Aloysis.

'Do I march north and fall upon the Cherusens, smiting them with my wrath for attacking my brother Krugar?'

Without waiting for an answer, Sigmar's finger trailed downwards across the Taalbec River to where a great basin nestled in the eye of the forest. 'Or do I ride to Taalahim, smash down its gates with my war machines, and slaughter the Taleutens for daring to attack my friend Aloysis? Tell me, brothers, what should I do?'

One after the other, Sigmar looked each of his counts in the eye, letting them see his deadly earnestness. Indecision warred in their souls, the need to save face against their rival vying with the desire to spare their lands and people from the Emperor's wrath.

Sigmar did not want to march north, especially when his warriors were mustering for war against the Jutones, so he was prepared to offer each man a way out. He traced a line down the course of the Taalbec, which marked the border between the counts' territories.

'On the other hand, perhaps the reavers that plague your lands are simply brigands,' said Sigmar, thoughtfully. 'Mayhap there are several of these rootless sword bands with secret forest camps in both your lands. Instead of my army marching north, perhaps you might hunt them down and destroy those that skulk in your lands. That would resolve your difficulties and see an end to this matter would it not? Tell me your thoughts, my friends.'

Krugar saw the resolve in Sigmar's eyes and nodded slowly.

'I believe you may be right, my Emperor,' he said. 'Now that I look closer, these raids have all the hallmarks of banditry.'

The words were spoken without conviction, but that they were spoken at all was good enough for Sigmar. He looked over to Aloysis.

'Indeed,' agreed Aloysis, quick to seize the opportunity to save face that Sigmar had offered. 'I have skilled trackers who should be able to locate such bands.'

'That is great news, my friends,' said Sigmar. 'Then you will put an end to this dispute, and return to your lands as brothers. This is my command.'

'It shall be as you say, my lord,' said Aloysis with a bow.

'I will return to Taalahim immediately,' said Krugar.

Aloysis turned to Krugar and the two counts embraced. The gesture was forced and awkward, but it was enough for now. Both men faced Sigmar, and bowed before withdrawing from the great hall. As the door shut behind them, Eoforth rolled up the map, and Alfgeir descended from the dais of the throne. The Grand Knight of the Empire sheathed his sword and sat on the edge of the table as Eoforth tied the leather cords around the map.

'Do you think they will do as you say?' asked Alfgeir. 'Krugar and Aloysis, I mean.'

'They had damn well better,' said Sigmar. 'Or else they will see what it means to incur my displeasure.'

'You don't really believe there are bandits in the forest, do you?'

'There are always brigands,' said Sigmar, 'but not raiding Cherusen or Taleuten lands. Each of them was right, they were being attacked by their neighbour.'

'Why? It makes no sense,' said Alfgeir.

'Human nature,' replied Eoforth. 'Without a common enemy, men will look for foes in the one place they can guarantee finding one: the past. The Cherusens and Taleutens have fought to control the fertile lands around the Taalbec for centuries. They only came together when King Björn forced them to join forces during the Winter of Beasts, you remember?'

'Aye,' said Alfgeir. 'The vermin-beasts from beneath the Barren Hills, I remember it all too well. I had my first taste of battle and blood in the snows around Untergard.'

'Long before I was born,' said Sigmar with a wry smile.

'Not *that* long,' muttered Alfgeir.

'The point is,' continued Eoforth, 'that powerful men with warriors to command will always look for someone to attack, and past grievances, unsettled wergelds and ancestral grudges are a good place to find them.'

'So what are you suggesting?' asked Sigmar.

'That we give our troublesome kings a better target for their warlike tendencies.'

THE SUMMER MUSTER began early, with riders bearing letters, sealed with wax and imprinted with the twin-tailed comet emblem of Sigmar, despatched to the furthest tribal lands of the Empire to rouse the counts to war.

The marching season had come, and it was time to call Marius of the Jutones to account.

As the days of spring warmed to summer, hundreds of warriors pitched their tents in the cleared fields around Sigmar's capital, and over the next two moons, sword bands from the furthest corners of the Empire arrived to join the Unberogen.

Autumn-hued Asoborns rode in on chariots of lacquered black and gold, provoking cheers and wolf-whistles from the richly-attired Brigundians who waved their spears and bared their many scars to the fierce warrior women.

Armoured warriors from the Fauschlag Rock marched to Reikdorf bearing news from Pendrag and Myrsa, and Sigmar smiled as he read of his friend's tribulations in attempting to modernise a populace rooted in tradition. As difficult as Pendrag was finding the task, Sigmar could read between the lines well enough to know that he was relishing the challenge, and he was pleased at the optimistic tone of his friend's words.

The southern kings had sent two hundred warriors each: grim-faced

Merogens in their distinctive rust-coloured cloaks, and slender Menogoth swordsmen in shimmering greens and golds. Taleuten horse archers rode though the campsite, showing off their skills to any who cared to watch, and competing with the shaven-headed Ostagoth bowmen for bragging rights in the coming march. Galin Veneva led the Ostagoths and he presented Wolfgart with a gilded bottle of *koumiss* and a promise of a drinking challenge at the end of this muster.

In addition to two hundred swordsmen, Count Krugar sent a company of his Red Scythes, armoured horsemen bearing glittering lances and wickedly curved sabres. Krugar did not attend the muster. Nor did the Cherusen count ride south, though the sending of five hundred tattooed warriors in earth-coloured cloaks and tunics was a grand gesture indeed. A hundred of the famed Cherusen Wildmen had also come to Reikdorf, their near-naked bodies crusted with coloured chalk and writhing tattoos.

By spring's end, over nine thousand warriors had assembled beyond Reikdorf's walls. The majority of these were Unberogen, though close to a third were men who called another land home. So great a host required feeding and watering, and since Sigmar had first begun to build the Empire, the size of its armies had grown enormously. Consequently, the task of supplying them had grown ever more complex.

To make war so far from home, an army needed huge amounts of wagons, and thus Sigmar sent loggers out to chop down vast swathes of forest to enable carpenters to construct them. The lands around Reikdorf were squeezed of every last grain of corn, and the fletchers, bowyers and smiths of the city worked day and night to fashion thousands of arrows, swords and axes. Ropes, picks, levers, scaling ladders, saws, adzes and shovels were stockpiled alongside the heavy timbers of Sigmar's disassembled catapults. Such was their weight that new yokes had to be designed to enable the oxen to pull them. Mobile forges were hauled onto the backs of reinforced wagons, and hundreds of craftsmen joined the muster in order to maintain its equipment ready for battle.

Tens of thousands of pounds of grain, flour and salt were stacked alongside hundreds of barrels of cured meat and fish, and enough food to feed the army for several months was quickly assembled. Eoforth and a virtual army of scribes and bookkeepers kept track of the supplies coming in from the country, and yet more wagons were set aside for the quartermaster's records, for so large an army could not operate without a thorough understanding of the available resources.

As the sun rose on a glorious summer's morning, Eoforth declared the army ready to march, and the priests of Ulric burned offerings to the god of battles on a great pyre atop Warrior Hill. Led by Alessa, the priestesses of Shallya moved through the host of warriors, blessing their hearts and asking the goddess of mercy and healing to watch over them.

Sigmar, Wolfgart and Redwane rode through Morr's Gate at the head of two hundred White Wolves and took up their position at the front of the column. A great cheer echoed from the hills around Reikdorf as Redwane lifted the crimson banner of Sigmar high, and with the Emperor's banner unfurled, a rippling flurry of tribal colours rose above the assembled host.

The White Wolves led the way along the paved western road as the army set off to war.

A WEEK LATER, Sigmar's army was joined by five hundred Endal warriors in dark armour at the river crossing of Astofen. A cavalry squadron of Raven Helms led by Count Aldred and Laredus met Sigmar in the centre of the bridge where Trinovantes had died, and Sigmar wished good fortune to the spirit of his old friend.

Swollen with these reinforcements, Sigmar's army now numbered nearly ten thousand swords, with perhaps a thousand camp followers bringing up the rear. As the army halted each night, ostlers, craftsmen, drovers, healers, merchants and night maidens would make their way through the camp to ply their trade and maintain the army's battle readiness.

Spirits were high, and each night Sigmar moved from campfire to campfire, speaking with his warriors and listening to their tales. All the men were looking forward to teaching the upstart Marius the price of cowardice and driving his warriors across the sea. Sigmar would remind them that the Jutones were still men and that it would be better to bring them into the Empire than destroy them, though the words sounded hollow, even to him. Marius had deserted them in their hour of need. What manner of ally would such a man make?

The army turned northwards, and Sigmar led the march across the fertile flatlands that made up the northern reaches of the Endal lands, skirting the marshes and swampland around the Reik estuary. Though the vast expanse of marshland was still a treacherous mire of sucking bogs and stagnant pools of black water, the mists no longer clung to the earth, and sunlight bathed the landscape in warmth.

At the Great North Road, which had once marked the boundary between the lands of the Teutogens and Jutones, Sigmar's army encountered a force of Thuringian warriors led by the giant Count Otwin. The berserker king had answered Sigmar's call to arms with four hundred warriors, painted men and women in a riotous mix of plate armour, mail shirts and baked leather breastplates. Otwin's warriors proudly bore the scars earned at Black Fire Pass, and Sigmar saw the berserker woman, Ulfdar, among the Thuringian host.

Otwin presented Sigmar with three prize bulls from his herd, and hundreds of Thuringian beef cows were slaughtered to feed the fighting men before they began the march to Jutonsryk. A grand feast was held on the Jutone border, with offerings made to Ulric, Taal and Shallya.

The following morning, with Otwin and Aldred at his side, Sigmar's army crossed the Great North Road.

The war against the Jutones had begun.

SEVEN
The Namathir

THE BOULDER SAILED through the cold morning air, describing a graceful arc before slamming into the damaged walls of Jutonsryk with a distant crack of splintered stone. Heavy wooden thumps and the creak of ropes signalled the release of the other catapults, and two more missiles were hurled towards the walls of the Jutone capital.

Accompanied by a bodyguard of ten White Wolves, Sigmar watched the rocks slam into the walls with a grim nod of satisfaction. The impact cratered the repaired stonework and broke loose a tumbling avalanche of masonry from the promontory.

'You knew your craft,' whispered Sigmar, speaking of whoever had raised these formidable walls, 'but I will break your work down, stone by stone if need be.'

The battlements were finally beginning to crumble, but Sigmar raged that he had allowed Marius so long to prepare his city's defences, for it had taken nearly two years of siege to bring Jutonsryk to the edge of defeat. To have constructed walls this strong must have cost Marius dear, but wealth was clearly one thing that Jutonsryk had in abundance.

Situated in a sheltered, sandy bay of the Reik's coastal estuary, Jutone settlers driven from their lands by the Teutogens had quickly recognised its worth as a natural harbour. They had built their settlement on a raised, leaf-shaped promontory known as the Namathir, and over the last twenty years Jutonsryk had developed into a thriving city of merchants. Traders arrived in Jutonsryk every day, their ships laden with exotic treasures from lands far to the south and, it was rumoured, from the mythical kingdoms beyond the Worlds Edge Mountains.

Dominating the coastline, Jutonsryk was an imposing city of formidable walls and solid towers. Snow shawled its battlements, and the machicolations worked into its towers were hung with icicles that looked like fangs of glass. Beyond the unbroken walls, the red clay roofs of the city huddled close together, and sails billowed from towers and flagpoles, proudly bearing the five-pointed crown of Manann.

Marius's castle sat at the highest point of the Namathir, a citadel of pale stone, slender towers and large windows of coloured glass. The majority of the city was built on the promontory's western slope, spilling haphazardly down to the harbour on the edge of the ocean's dark waters. The city's architecture reflected the maritime culture of the Jutones, and a great many of its buildings were constructed from the hulks of wrecked ships, or were hung with nets, ships wheels and brightly coloured figureheads.

A long wall of dark stone encircled the town, and solid drum towers topped with curving battlements shaped like the hulls of ships studded its length. A dozen warships sailed the wide estuary, blocking any passage down the river towards Marburg or out to sea. In the opening days of the siege, Endal ships had attempted to blockade the city, but the Jutone fleet had sunk them all in a horribly one-sided battle.

A single mast jutting from the icy water was all that remained of the Endal ships, and Count Aldred had sworn vengeance for their drowned crews.

Since then, Sigmar's army had battered itself bloody against the walls of Jutonsryk, and the first attempts to carry the walls by storm had taught them all a valuable lesson in underestimating their foe. Expecting the Jutones to be weak and cowardly, a tribe more suited to trading and commerce than battle, Sigmar's warriors had charged the walls with scaling ladders and grappling hooks.

As the warriors came within bow-shot of the crenellated walls, a long line of warriors with swarthy skin had appeared at the embrasures, carrying strange weapons at their shoulders. Like a thick bow laid upon its side and mounted on a length of wood, the weapons were loosed, and hundreds of men were cut down as volley after volley of short, iron-tipped bolts punched through shields and mail shirts.

The attack faltered, but kept going under continuous hails of bolts. By the time the ladders were thrown against the walls there were too few warriors to pose a serious threat to the defenders. The hardy souls who survived to reach the wall-head were killed without a single warrior gaining the ramparts, and the survivors fell back in disarray. Jutone axemen had sallied out and captured the ladders, and the humiliation of the defeat had stung the pride of every man in Sigmar's army.

Since then, the attack on Jutonsryk had proceeded at a more methodical pace, with retrenchments built on the ground before the main gate, cutting off the northern approaches to the city. Jutone sally parties hampered the work at every turn, and it was a full two months before the trenches and palisades were completed.

Sigmar's catapults were assembled within reach of the walls and the bombardment had begun. The walls of Jutonsryk had been built against the slope of the promontory and were as solid as the rock they stood upon. Hundreds of rocks had been hurled at the walls over the next seven months, but no practicable breach had been made. A number of fresh assaults were launched, warriors moving forward under cover of wetted mantlets and darkness, but blazing bales of straw turned night into day, and the chopping blades of the Jutone fighters kept the battlements clear of attackers.

The campaign, which had started in such high spirits, stalled, and cold and hungry warriors huddling around their campfires began to lose faith that the city would ever fall. The days grew shorter and the temperature dropped, but Sigmar rejected talk of lifting the siege and retreating for the winter. To withdraw would only give the defenders heart and further opportunities to fortify their city. Jutonsryk would fall, and it would fall to this army.

Winter closed in, and freezing storms blew off the sea, whipping past the Namathir and across the flatlands around Jutonsryk like a blade. Food grew scarce, and only convoys of wagons from Marburg and Reikdorf kept the army from starving.

Morale rose with the coming of spring, but any optimism that the battle would soon be over was dashed when fleets of strange ships bearing the flags of unknown kings arrived from the south, their hulls groaning with provisions and mercenary warriors with dark skin and brightly coloured tunics.

Spring turned to summer, with Sigmar's army growing ever more frustrated as the siege dragged on and every attack was repulsed. A section of the eastern wall was brought down at midsummer, and the Thuringians immediately charged towards the breach, screaming bestial war cries and brandishing their axes and swords like madmen. An unbending line of the southern mercenaries held the breach with long pikes, and Count Otwin's warriors were hurled back without ever reaching its summit.

By morning, the breach had been filled with rubble and refortified, but Sigmar's catapults had concentrated their efforts on this weakened portion of the wall. At first, it had seemed like this was the change in fortune the attackers had been waiting for, but that night Jutone raiders had made their way through the circumvallations and set three of the mighty war machines ablaze before being caught and killed.

Sigmar had the night sentries put to death, and stationed a permanent guard of fifty men from each tribe to protect the remaining catapults, for he could ill-afford to lose any more of his precious war machines.

Months passed, and still the walls of Jutonsryk stood in defiance of Sigmar as his army faced its second winter on the western coast. His anger towards Marius grew at the thought of spending frozen nights huddled around a brazier, wrapped in a wolfskin cloak and subsisting on meagre rations, while Marius ate heartily in his great hall before a roaring fire.

Sigmar shook his head free of such thoughts, knowing they would only cloud his judgement, and watched as sweating Unberogen warriors hauled fresh cart-loads of rocks from the shoreline far below. Drovers whipped the starved oxen that pulled the catapults' windlass mechanisms, and the process began again. He told himself that the damaged section of wall was ready to collapse. Once it was down, his warriors would storm the breach, and they would not stop fighting until Jutonsryk fell.

Footsteps on the wet ground made Sigmar turn, and he saw Count Otwin climbing the hill towards him. The Berserker King – for he had never shed that name, despite his new title – wore little to insulate himself from the weather except for a furred loincloth and a threadbare cloak of foxfur, yet he seemed not to feel the cold.

'Working such a machine is no task for a warrior,' said Otwin, staring in distaste at the backbreaking labour required by the catapults. 'Blade to blade, that's the way to kill a man.'

'Maybe there is no glory in employing such weapons,' said Sigmar, 'but if the walls of Jutonsryk are ever going to be brought down, then the catapults need to be manned night and day.'

'But where is the honour in such a weapon?' pressed Otwin. 'To kill a man without cleaving your axe through his body or feeling the sensation of his blade cutting your flesh is to deny the joy of battle and the sweetness of life when it hangs in the balance.'

'There will be plenty of opportunities to risk your life soon enough,' said Sigmar. 'The wall is almost breached and we'll be dining in the great hall of Jutonsryk before the first snows.'

'Damn, but I hope you are right,' said Otwin, his fists clenching and unclenching repeatedly. 'I lost a hundred warriors to those devils with the pikes, and their deaths must be avenged.'

Sigmar refrained from pointing out that those warriors had died when the Thuringian King had led a reckless charge against the breach without support. Even as he admired the man's courage, he disapproved of such reckless disregard for the order of battle. Raw courage had its place on the battlefield, but battles were won with discipline and courage alloyed together in the right balance.

Instead, Sigmar pointed to the fleet of mercenary ships beached on the sandy bay below them.

'You may not get a chance, my friend,' he said. 'If that breach breaks open as wide as I hope, then it is likely that those warriors will sail south. Those men are paid to fight, but they will not die for Marius.'

'Only a cur would fight for money,' snarled Otwin, flecks of blood dribbling down his chin as he chewed the inside of his mouth. 'And only a coward would pay others to fight his battles.'

'Marius is no coward, Otwin. He is a canny warrior, who has kept us at bay for nearly two years. We need to harness that and turn it to our advantage. Think how much the Empire will flourish if Jutonsryk joins with us.'

'You expect too much, Sigmar,' growled Otwin. 'Marius will never submit to you. Even if I am wrong and he gives you his Sword Oath, the line of Marius will always have a troublesome streak of independence.'

'Perhaps,' allowed Sigmar, 'but that is a problem for another time.'

A WEEK LATER, the wall had still not fallen, though Sigmar's engineers assured him that it was only a matter of days until they formed a practicable breach. The first snows had not yet arrived, but the promise of their coming was on the northern winds.

Sigmar's camp was shrouded in darkness, with only a few fires scattered over the flatlands to keep the thousands of warriors warm through the night. As had become the custom each night, the leaders of the army gathered in Sigmar's tent with skins of wine to tell tales of their homelands and lay plans for the following day.

Goblets were filled, but the talk was muted, for the Jutones had driven yet another escalade from the walls. Six battering rams had been lost, three siege towers toppled and another four burned to ashes. The butcher's bill had been high and the screams of the wounded carried from the surgeons' sheltered camp.

Sigmar studied the faces around the fire, each as familiar to him as his own, for they had spent the better part of two years on campaign together. Otwin was still vast and threatening, but the years of battle had thinned him considerably and his ribs were clearly visible on his chest. Aldred too was thin, his features pinched with grief. The Endals had led today's assault and the majority of the dead were his warriors.

Wolfgart and Redwane had visibly aged since marching from Reikdorf. The young White Wolf had matured, and though his reckless spirit still burned brightly, he had seen too much death on this campaign to ever forget. Sigmar knew Wolfgart ached to return to Reikdorf, for his daughter would be nearing her second year, and he had not seen her in all that time. Sigmar had given Wolfgart leave to return to Reikdorf, but his sword-brother had refused, claiming that he would not be shamed by leaving a fight before it was done.

More wine flowed and as Sigmar outlined his plans for the assault on the Namathir promontory, Wolfgart commented on the oddness of the name, wondering aloud which tribe had chosen it.

'My father believed it was a word in the language of the fey,' Aldred said, not looking up from the fire that smouldered in the brazier.

'A fey word?' asked Wolfgart. 'How did Marbad know their language? They're long dead aren't they?'

'I heard they sailed across the ocean to paradise,' said Redwane.

'No, that's not right. I heard they betrayed their oaths of kinship with the dwarfs and were driven across the sea as a punishment,' put in Otwin, making the sign of the horns over his heart. 'Our wise men say they covet this land and leave changelings in the cribs of unwary mothers.'

'Why do they do that?' asked Wolfgart.

Otwin shrugged, and a thin line of blood leaked from the scars around the spikes he had driven through the muscles of his chest that morning. 'Out of spite, I suppose. This is a land of men, and they hate us for it. Why else do we have so many charms for newborns? You should know that, Wolfgart.'

Wolfgart nodded and said, 'The priestess of Shallya made sure that Ulrike was well protected.'

Sigmar saw the sadness on Wolfgart's face as he spoke.

'You will see Maedbh and Ulrike again soon, my friend,' he said.

'I miss their warmth,' said Wolfgart. 'It feels like a piece of me is missing.'

No words Sigmar could say would comfort his friend, so he simply nodded towards Aldred.

'You were talking about how the promontory got its name,' he said.

'Yes, it was when my father discovered Ulfshard in the depths of the black rock. He loved delving into dark places in search of the past, and it was during one of his many expeditions into the rock beneath the Raven Hall that he found a secret chamber. It was hidden well, but the enchantments concealing it must have faded over the centuries, and my father was able to gain entry. He found Ulfshard unsheathed and stabbed into the rock floor, surrounded by ancient bones that must have once belonged to a dwarf.'

'See!' said Otwin. 'I told you they betrayed their oaths.'

'Well, it certainly looked like whoever had last wielded Ulfshard had killed the dwarf,' said Aldred. 'Though it was clad in strange armour that crumbled to dust as soon as my father pulled the sword from the ground.'

'What else did he find?' asked Sigmar.

'Some golden coins, some clothes and a few books. He couldn't read them, but he spent his every free moment trying to translate them. He didn't get very far, as the language was very complex and seemed to have lots of subtle differences in meaning that relied on pronunciation to make them clear, but he did manage to understand a few words. He deduced that Namathir was part of a larger name that hadn't survived the passage of years.'

'So what does it mean?' asked Wolfgart when Aldred didn't continue.

'My father couldn't say for certain, but he thought that Namathir meant "star gem".'

'Then perhaps there are gems hidden beneath Jutonsryk?' suggested Wolfgart hopefully.

'It's possible,' allowed Aldred. 'Though surely the fey would have carried any such treasures across the ocean with them.'

'They left Ulfshard behind, didn't they?'

'It might be an idea to let that circulate among the men,' said Otwin. 'Could give them an extra incentive to get over the walls if they think there's treasure buried beneath the city.'

'No,' said Sigmar emphatically. 'When we take Jutonsryk there is to be no looting or unnecessary killing. Do you all understand that?'

Silence greeted Sigmar's pronouncement, each man weighing up how best to answer him.

'That might be easier said than done,' said Wolfgart eventually, with sidelong glances at Otwin and Aldred. 'You know what it's like in the heat of battle, especially in a siege. When you've fought as long and as hard as we have, and suffered so much loss, it's an easy thing to lose control when you've battled your way over a wall. Warriors who've seen their sword-brothers killed aren't too choosy about who gets in their way when they're out for vengeance.'

'Wolfgart speaks true,' said Otwin. 'When the red mist descends upon a Thuringian, there's no man can stop him until the killing rage is spent. Well, apart from you, Sigmar. You choked it out of me on the battlefield, but I do not think there will be many men like you beyond Jutonsryk's walls.'

Sigmar stood and lifted Ghal-maraz, holding it out before him. 'Tell your warriors that any man who disobeys me in this will pay with his life.'

'You have to allow the men some reward for taking the city,' said Aldred. 'They have camped out here for nigh on two years, and they'll need something to take back home or they will be reluctant to march out again.'

Sigmar considered Aldred's words and nodded.

'You are right,' he said. Tell the men that when Jutonsryk is ours, I will send a portion of its wealth to each of the counts to distribute among the warriors who fought to capture it for as long as they live. Will that suffice?'

'I think it might,' said Aldred. 'We can work out what that portion is later, but if our warriors know they're going to get some reward if the city is kept safe, then that should help stay their hands.'

'It had better,' warned Sigmar. 'I want to bring the Jutones into the Empire, but that won't happen if we burn their city to the ground and murder its inhabitants.'

* * *

Flames from a burning siege tower flickered and danced on the timber walls around Sigmar, and the smell of mingled wood-smoke and seared flesh set his nerves on edge. Reaching up to wipe sweat from his brow, he felt the tension within the upper compartment of the siege tower he travelled inside. Sigmar wore his silver armour and a golden helmet, and bore an iron-rimmed shield with a spiked boss in one hand and Ghal-maraz in the other.

Wolfgart stood next to him, his enormous sword held at his side. The blade was safely in its scabbard, as the Unberogen warriors were too closely packed together within the siege tower to risk unsheathing it until the wooden ramp crashed down on the parapet.

'Ulric preserve me, but I don't like this,' said Wolfgart. 'We could die without even being within striking distance of the Jutones.'

'Don't remind me,' said Sigmar, looking through a gap in the timbers.

Yoked oxen, draped in shields and breastplates, hauled on thick ropes attached to a windlass mechanism set behind a covered position built in a patch of dead ground at the foot of the walls during the night. Each strained pull of the ropes drew the tower closer to Jutonsryk and an end to the siege. This high up, the tower rocked and swayed as it crossed the uneven ground, and Sigmar tried not to think of what would happen should it topple before reaching the walls.

A hundred warriors were packed into the siege tower, divided through the four levels, and a dozen archers crouched behind movable screens on its roof. Sigmar had positioned himself in the uppermost level of the machine aimed at the ramparts, closest to the towers protecting the city gates. The fighting was sure to be heaviest there, and that was where he needed to be.

It had taken the catapults another three days to finally smash down the damaged section of the city walls to the point where an armoured warrior could climb the rubble slope and still fight. A fresh sense of excitement galvanised Sigmar's army as the news of the breach spread. Swords were sharpened and armour polished to shine like new. This was to be the final battle and the gods would be watching, so every warrior desired to look his most heroic.

As Sigmar had predicted, the mercenary warriors who had sailed into Jutonsryk early in the campaign took to their ships soon after the wall collapsed. Though he understood why they were leaving, Sigmar felt nothing but contempt for these men. To fight for freedom, for survival, a noble ideal or to protect the weak were just reasons to go to war, but those who fought for money sullied the warrior ideals upon which Sigmar had founded the Empire.

He had ordered every warrior in his army to fight, gambling everything on this assault, for there would be no second chance if it should fail. The camp that had housed Sigmar's army for the last two years was dismantled, sending a clear signal to the Jutones that the battle was ending one way or another.

Six more siege towers had been constructed and sheathed in soaked animal skins, bringing the total number of towers to twenty-five. Taleuten archers built hundreds of mantlets to shelter behind while showering the ramparts with arrows, and every sword band fashioned dozens of scaling ladders from the detritus of the camp.

The Red Scythes, Raven Helms and White Wolves mounted their horses, ready to repulse any sallies from the city gates, and Cherusen Wildmen howled and screamed alongside Count Otwin and his Thuringian berserkers as they worked themselves up into a battle frenzy. Otwin had requested the task of storming the breach, and Sigmar had agreed, knowing that there were no better shock troops in the army. The Thuringians had failed to carry the breach once, and honour demanded they not fail again.

A series of heavy thuds on the armoured front of the siege tower told Sigmar they were within crossbow range of the walls. The mercenaries who had come to Jutonsryk may have left, but their new weapons had stayed behind. Once this siege was over, Sigmar resolved to have such weapons distributed throughout the Empire.

'How long do you think?' asked Wolfgart, and Sigmar was surprised at the fear he heard in his sword-brother's voice.

'Not long,' said Sigmar, hearing a wild roar as the Cherusens and Thuringians charged the breach. The intensity of crossbow impacts on the front of the siege tower grew in volume, and, with every pull of the oxen, Sigmar saw the barbed tips of the bolts punch further and further through the hide and timber coverings draping the tower. Something bright struck the tower, and Sigmar smelled smoke as burning arrows thudded into the wood.

'Ulric save us, we're on fire!' cried Wolfgart.

'No we're not,' snapped Sigmar. 'The Jutones are loosing flaming arrow, but we're safe. The tower was soaked before we moved out.'

His words calmed the warriors around him, but the sheer volume of fire the tower was attracting would soon cause the timbers to catch light, regardless of how much water had been poured over it.

Screams came from above them, and a body fell from the top of the tower. Sigmar could hear the shouted curses of the Jutones and the thud of hooves on cold ground. The clash of iron on armour and the screams of the dying drifted over the battlefield.

'Stand ready!' shouted Sigmar, gripping the haft of Ghal-maraz, and feeling his heart race and his mouth go dry as he picked up his shield. 'Every man on his knees and get your shields ready. When that ramp goes down, get onto the walls as quickly as you can!'

The warriors around him lifted their shields and crouched on the wooden floor of the tower, a feat that was only accomplished with some difficulty given how many warriors were crammed together.

Sigmar felt the yardstick on the front of the tower strike the wall and shouted, 'Ulric grant you strength!'

He smashed the locking pin securing the tower's bridge free with a blow from Ghal-maraz, and daylight flooded the tower as the winch spun and the bridge dropped. It slammed down onto the ramparts, and a flurry of black-shafted arrows slashed into the tower. Many went high, but many more found homes in Unberogen flesh despite their shields and armour. Half a dozen arrows hammered into Sigmar's shield, but it was of dwarf origin and proof against such irritations.

With a fearsome war cry, Sigmar surged to his feet with his shield held out before him. A pair of arrows bounced from his shield, and he grunted in pain as another scored across his bicep. He sprinted across the ramp, and leapt to the ramparts, swinging his warhammer in a murderous arc. A Jutone tribesman with a bronze breastplate and armed with a short stabbing sword ran at him, but Sigmar smashed him from his feet before he could draw back his arm to strike.

Warriors poured from the siege tower, but the Jutones were not about to give up this section of wall without a fight. Unberogen fell with arrows jutting from their chests, and the Jutones dragged them from the walls with hooked pikes. The press of bodies from the tower was forcing the Jutones back and more and more of the Unberogen were gaining the walls.

Sigmar pushed towards the squat tower at the gate, kicking one enemy warrior from the walls and slamming another to his knees with the edge of his shield. His hammer struck left and right, killing with every stroke, and he pushed deeper into the mass of Jutone warriors.

Wolfgart fought with deadly sweeps of his enormous sword, killing handfuls of men with every stroke. The size of his blade ensured that he fought alone, but he was clearing the way for more warriors from the tower.

Smoke billowed from somewhere nearby, but Sigmar could not spare the time to see where. The Jutones had been driven back along the ramparts by his and Wolfgart's wild charges, but were gathering for a counter-attack.

'On me!' he yelled. 'Wedge formation!'

Sigmar ran at the Jutones, hammered Ghal-maraz through an enemy skull, and threw his shield up to catch a pair of arrows loosed from the tower. Jutones surrounded him, and a lance stabbed into his side. The blade snapped on Sigmar's dwarf-forged armour, and he backhanded his warhammer into the lancer's face. More enemy warriors pressed him, but he drove them back with a wide sweep of his hammer that shattered armour, crushed ribs and splintered limbs.

The Jutones fled from his fury, jumping to the courtyard below or fleeing towards the great tower protecting Jutonsryk's main gate. More arrows arced downwards, but they flashed past Sigmar and clattered harmlessly from the battlements. A clash of iron and the scream of horses sounded from beyond the walls, and Sigmar looked down to see a mass of his cavalry fighting in the shadow of a burning siege tower. The oxen that had pulled it close to the walls were dead, skewered by heavy spears.

Sigmar realised what had happened in an instant.

Jutone spearmen had charged from a concealed sally port at the base of the tower to kill the oxen dragging two of the siege towers. They had succeeded, which left the warriors within the towers trapped and burning as archers loosed volleys of flaming arrows at their timbers. Before the Jutone raiders could escape, the Raven Helms had caught them and were cutting them to pieces.

Count Aldred, resplendent on a black gelding, plunged Ulfshard's blade into the chest of a Jutone captain armed with an enormous axe, as Laredus drove the rest of the Raven Helms towards the sally port.

'Unberogen!' shouted Sigmar. 'The tower! We need to get on the ground!'

Sigmar ran towards the tower as the last of the Jutones dragged the door shut. It was a thick slab of heavy oak banded with black iron, virtually impenetrable and proof against anything short of a battering ram.

Sigmar hammered Ghal-maraz against the centre of the door,

smashing it to splinters with a single blow. The door flew from its frame, and Sigmar vaulted into the tower over its shattered remains. Horrified Jutones filled the room, and Sigmar gave them no chance to recover from the shock. His hammer struck out, and two Jutones died in as many strokes. Unberogen warriors followed Sigmar, slaying their enemies with sword and axe.

Sigmar led the way down the curving tower stairs. Arrows flashed upwards, ricocheting from the walls and off his shield. The level below the ramparts was also filled with Jutone warriors and a volley of gull-feathered shafts and iron crossbow bolts flashed. Sigmar's shield finally broke apart, and he hurled it aside as crossbow bolts hammered into the warriors next to him.

Sigmar charged the Jutones with a terrifying war cry.

Then he was amongst them and Ghal-maraz sang out. The fury of battle was on him, and Sigmar's world shrank to the space around him and the movement of blades and limbs through it. He fought with hammer, elbow and foot, using every weapon available to him to throw the Jutones back. Sigmar swept up a fallen short sword and hamstrung a Jutone archer, before charging for the stairs that led to the ground.

An arrow flashed past his head, and Sigmar pressed himself to the wall as another archer loosed up the spiral stairs. The arrow clattered from the walls and struck his breastplate, but its strength was spent and it fell clear. The spiral stairs were curved so as to impede a right-handed attacker from swinging his weapon. They were designed for swordsmen to defend, not archers. Sigmar charged down the stairs, keeping as close to the centre as possible so that any arrows would skitter around him.

He could hear shouting voices calling for more archers, and the clash of swords and shields. Sigmar glanced over his shoulder, to see grim-faced Unberogen warriors gathered behind him, their swords and faces red with blood.

'Let's take them,' he said, and spun around the last steps of the staircase. A line of archers knelt by the far wall of the tower's lower chamber, and no sooner had Sigmar appeared than they loosed. Sigmar threw himself flat, rolling beneath the slashing volley of shafts. Screams sounded behind him, and a second volley flashed overhead.

An arrow thudded into Sigmar's breastplate, and another bounced from his helmet. His dive had carried him to the archers, and he rolled to his knees, sweeping his hammer in a wide, slashing arc that shattered thighs, crushed kneecaps and scattered his foes like straw men. Another shaft ricocheted from his pauldron and sliced across his neck, drawing blood, but the wound was not deep.

Unberogen warriors poured from the stairs, following Sigmar into the Jutones. The men in the tower were doomed, yet they fought on, and Sigmar was forced to admire their courage even as he killed them. A screaming Jutone lancer tried to skewer him, but Sigmar batted away the barbed tip of his weapon with his forearm before slamming his hammer down on the man's skull.

In seconds it was over, the interior of the tower a charnel house of the dead.

Sigmar took a moment to catch his breath and let the visceral rush of combat drain from his body enough for him to think. Around him, Unberogen warriors roared in triumph, and Sigmar saw the potential for a massacre in every gap-toothed bloody grin. Worse, he saw his own lust for violence reflected in their eyes.

Sigmar felt a savage joy when he fought his enemies, but this was different, this was a war that could have been averted. Looking at the Jutone corpses, he knew that but for one man's ambition, these men would still be alive. He knelt beside the last Jutone warrior he had killed, a man with a family and dreams of his own no doubt, and wondered whose ambition was worse, his own or that of Marius.

Daylight and the clamour of battle sounded from beyond the doorway, and Sigmar took a deep breath. This battle was not yet won, and more would die before this day's bloody work was done.

EIGHT

A Darkness of the Heart

Outside, all was chaos. Smoke from burning siege towers painted the sky, and the walls were bloody battlegrounds where the difference between life and death could depend on a step in the wrong direction or an accidental sword thrust. The inside of the city reminded Sigmar greatly of Reikdorf, though he had no citadel to match that of Marius.

Rearing up from the Namathir like a collection of stalagmites, the citadel was a fortress within a fortress, with gates of iron, protected by a deep ditch and a barbican of solid, hoarding-covered parapets. Flags bearing Marius's crown and trident symbol flapped from the blue-tiled roofs of the towers, while flights of arrows arced from the highest ramparts.

Behind the citadel, the city of Jutonsryk spread down the flanks of the promontory to the sea, and Sigmar could feel the fear of its inhabitants. He read the pulse of the fighting in a second, and his masterful eye saw that the battle for Jutonsryk rested on a knife-edge. Wolfgart appeared at his side, his enormous blade wet and dripping.

'The walls are still holding,' cursed Sigmar.

'We're too exposed here,' said his sword-brother. 'If the Jutones counter-attack from that citadel, we'll be slaughtered.'

'I know,' said Sigmar. 'We need more warriors inside the city.'

'Looks like you'll have some soon!' cried Wolfgart, looking along the length of the wall.

Two hundred yards to Sigmar's left, Count Otwin stood atop the breach, his naked, spike-pierced body red with blood, and his chained axe raised to the heavens in triumph. Thuringian and Cherusen warriors poured over the rubble, hacking down their fleeing opponents. Having fought their way through the bloodiest possible aspect of a siege, the berserkers and wildmen were drunk on slaughter and hungry for death.

Sigmar took Wolfgart's arm.

'Go!' he said. 'Put something between Otwin and the Jutones. He'll drown this city in blood if you don't.'

'Where are you going?'

'I am going to get more warriors inside the city.'

'The gate?' asked Wolfgart

'Aye, the gate, now go!'

Wolfgart nodded and dragged half of Sigmar's warriors towards the screaming Thuringians and Cherusens. Wolfgart wouldn't be able to stop the berserk warriors completely, but Sigmar hoped he could prevent the inevitable fury that followed the carrying of a breach from becoming a wholesale slaughter. He put that thought from his mind, and turned his attention to the task at hand.

He had around thirty warriors with him, hopefully enough for what he had in mind. More would follow when they realised that this gate tower had been taken, but these few were all he could count on for now.

'With me!' he yelled.

Sigmar followed the curve of the tower until he reached the cobbled roadway that ran between it and another gate tower just like it. The mighty gateway of Jutonsryk loomed in the torch-lit darkness between the towers, shuddering under repeated blows from an iron-sheathed battering ram on the other side.

The gate's heavy wooden structure was braced with thick timbers that had once been the keels of ocean-going ships. Giant chains of iron ran from the top of the gate to an enormous winch and wheel mechanism, which was protected by around a hundred Jutones clad in colourful tunics worn over mail shirts.

The gate's defenders carried heavy pikes, and were formed up in three lines facing the gate, ready to repulse any assault. Should the gate be broken down, any attackers would run into a solid wall of sharpened iron, or at least any attackers coming from the front...

A strident trumpet blast sounded from the tallest tower of the citadel, and Sigmar looked over his shoulder to see its iron portal opening. A glittering host of armoured horsemen wearing the blue cloaks of Jutone lancers emerged, riding out to assemble beneath a vivid turquoise and green banner depicting a crown and trident.

'Marius,' whispered Sigmar.

Part of him wanted to charge out to face the king who had caused them to shed so much blood, but that part was Sigmar the warrior. To win this battle, he had to be Sigmar the Emperor. Marius would wait.

Sigmar turned to his warriors and shouted, 'For the glory of Ulric! The gate must open!'

He charged towards the gate, Ghal-maraz held over his shoulder. His warriors pounded after him, ferocious war shouts driving them onwards. They were feral hunters, warriors with the taste of blood on their lips and the fires of battle in their veins.

The Jutones cried out in alarm at the sight of them, a thunderous wedge of bloodstained warriors that howled like madmen. They tried to turn and face the threat to their rear, but in the confines of the gateway and with long, cumbersome pikes, such a manouevre was doomed from the outset.

Sigmar smashed his hammer through the spine of a Jutone pikeman, plunging his borrowed sword into the chest of another. The man fell, tearing the sword from Sigmar's hand. He shifted his grip on his hammer and swung it two-handed, killing again as he plunged deeper and deeper into their ranks. Unberogen warriors cut through the heart of the Jutone defenders, fighting with the strength of Ulric as they sought to emulate their Emperor.

Polearms were cast down and swords unsheathed as the Jutones realised their pikes were useless, and the battle for the gate devolved into a close scrum of stabbing blades and brutal axe blows. Sigmar's hammer was a blur of dark iron, slashing left and right as he slew the defenders of the gate without mercy. Swords and knives scored his armour, and a stabbing dirk sliced the skin of his arm.

Even with the bloody slaughter of the opening moments of the fight, the Jutones outnumbered the Unberogen three to one, and those numbers were telling. More of Sigmar's warriors were being cut down, and he knew it was only a matter of time before a lucky blow found a gap in his armour.

A screaming warrior in an orange-dyed tunic stabbed his sword at Sigmar, the blade lancing into his thigh. Sigmar grunted in pain and stepped back as he thundered his fist into the man's face. He spun away from a thrusting spear and backhanded his hammer into the Jutone warrior's chest. An axe clanged against his breastplate, and he dropped to one knee as his wounded leg gave out beneath him.

He threw up his hammer to ward off another sword blow, and an iron-shod boot hammered against his helmet. Sigmar rolled and ripped the helm from his head as dizziness swamped him. A pair of Jutone warriors closed on him with their spears aimed at his neck. They stabbed, but before their spear-tips struck a slashing blur of silver hacked the points from the ends of the polearms. Sigmar looked up to see Wolfgart roaring in anger as his sword swept back and clove through the first Jutone. His reverse stroke all but beheaded the second.

Bestial howls echoed from the gate towers and a host of near-naked warriors with painted and tattooed skin smashed into the Jutones. Wolfgart hooked his arm beneath Sigmar's shoulder and helped him to his feet. All around him, Thuringians and Cherusens were butchering the Jutones, hacking them to pieces with their swords and axes in a frenzy of bloodletting. King Otwin bashed a man's brains out on the cobbles, and a naked warrior with hooks embedded in his arms wrestled a Jutone to bloody ribbons.

Within moments, the Jutone defenders were dead, and the berserkers and wildmen roared their triumph in the torch-lit gateway.

Still groggy from the blow to the head, Sigmar said, 'What...? How did you get here?'

'You said to put something between Otwin and the Jutones,' said Wolfgart. 'I figured this gate would do.'

Sigmar watched as Otwin continued to slam the virtually headless body against the ground, the light of madness in his eyes.

'How?' gasped Sigmar, nauseous from the blow to his head. 'The red mist is upon him.'

'I told him you were in danger,' said Wolfgart, showing Sigmar an enormous dent in his breastplate. 'Though I had to let him hit me a few times before he knew who I was.'

Sigmar nodded, hearing the shrill blast of a Jutone cavalry horn.

'Get those supports down!' he shouted. 'The gate must open or we are lost!'

The Thuringians hurled themselves at the timbers bracing the gate and attacked them with ferocious axe blows. Wood splintered under the assault of blades, and one by one the supports came crashing down.

'Wolfgart,' said Sigmar, 'the winch mechanisms! I will get the one on the left, you take the one on the right.'

'It'll take more than you and I to open this!' cried Wolfgart, but he ran to the winch on the opposite side of the tunnel. Sigmar ran to one of the winches that lifted the gate and shifted the locking bar from the wheel. He dropped Ghal-maraz and began hauling on the spoked wheel, but the gate was designed to be opened by teams of horses yoked to the mechanism.

'It won't move!' shouted Wolfgart from across the gateway.

'Otwin!' shouted Sigmar. 'Gather your warriors and help us!'

The Berserker King looked up from his slaughter and bellowed in answer. Two score men ran to help Sigmar and Wolfgart, bending their backs to haul on the chains and winch. Sigmar's muscles burned with exertion, and he felt the sinews straining as he fought to push the mechanism.

A thin line of daylight appeared as the gate lifted a hand's span, and the Thuringian count bellowed at his warriors to push harder. Not to be outdone, the Cherusens chewed more of their wildroots and dug deep into their madness for strength. The line of daylight grew larger, and as the gate began to move upwards, Unberogen, Taleuten and Endal warriors crawled under and wedged iron bars beneath it. More warriors ran in to help with the winch mechanism, and Sigmar released his hold to allow stronger warriors than him to push.

He swept up Ghal-maraz as a squadron of black-armoured horsemen rode under the gate. Count Aldred and Laredus rode at their head, and the captain of the Raven Helms raised his lance in respect when he saw Sigmar. Two score Taleuten Red Scythes and a half-century of White Wolves were mixed with the Endal horsemen, and Sigmar saw Redwane carrying his crimson banner like a lance.

With the gates raised enough to allow cavalry within, the locking bars were dropped, and warriors streamed through the open gate. More horsemen rode with them, and Sigmar ran to a riderless gelding with bloodstains coating its flanks. He gripped the saddle horn and vaulted into the empty saddle. He looped the reins loosely around his wrist, and the horse reared, its front hooves pawing the air.

'Warriors of the Empire!' he shouted. 'This is our moment! This is where we make our land whole. We will defeat our enemies and make them our brothers. Now ride with me!'

* * *

SIGMAR THUNDERED FROM the gatehouse at the head of a hundred and fifty horsemen, black-armoured Raven Helms, wild and bearded White Wolves, shaven-headed Taleutens, and Unberogen bowmen. They formed a wedge like a wide-bladed Asoborn spear aimed towards the heart of the Jutone defenders. Warriors on foot followed them in their hundreds, and the misery of two long years of siege was forgotten as they charged into the city of their enemies.

Trumpeting war horns sounded from the walls, and roars of triumph erupted from the attacking warriors as they saw their Emperor ride out with his banner unfurled like a slick of blood on the air. A Jutone flagpole was hacked down from the gatehouse towers, and Sigmar's army surged towards the opened gate.

From the back of his horse, Sigmar saw the Jutone lancers fighting at the breach in the city walls, riding down any warrior who survived the hails of arrows from the citadel's towers. A warrior in golden armour with a silver helm led the Jutone cavalry, riding beneath Marius's banner. Though he could not see the warrior's face, Sigmar instantly recognised the man's majestic bearing.

With the Jutone king beyond his fastness, Sigmar angled his horse towards the lancers, knowing that he could end the battle in one fell swoop. A rising series of notes from a Jutone clarion sounded a warning note, and the blue-cloaked lancers expertly wheeled their horses.

Sigmar expected the lancers to ride for the citadel, but he was surprised and not a little impressed that they turned to face him instead. The lancers formed up in a wedge with the golden warrior at their point, and galloped across the killing ground behind the walls towards them. Sigmar guessed there were around a hundred lancers under Marius's command, heavily armoured horsemen who were clearly skilled warriors. Though Sigmar had more riders alongside him, they were a mix of tribes and most were not as heavily armoured as the Jutones.

Sigmar leaned forwards in his saddle, pressing his heels back hard against the stirrups. He held Ghal-maraz high for all to see and let loose a fearsome war cry. Less than a hundred yards separated the two wedges of horsemen, and Sigmar felt the familiar exultation at riding into battle on the back of a charging steed. The sensation of speed and power was like a wild elixir, and he laughed as he gripped the reins tightly. Truly, the cavalrymen were the kings of the battlefield!

He steered his horse with his thighs, aiming his charge straight towards Marius. The Jutone king unsheathed a curved blade that shimmered with a blue green light. The noise was incredible, the rumbling thunder of so many horses like being in the midst of a storm.

The cavalry met in a deafening clash of iron, bellowing warriors and screaming horses.

Men were punched from their saddles as lances spitted them and splintered under their weight. Swords swung, axes chopped, and the two groups of horsemen were soon tangled together in a heaving mass of struggling warriors. The Jutone lancers carved a bloody path into Sigmar's warriors, but they did not escape unscathed. The Raven Helms and White Wolves gave as good as they got, unhorsing scores of enemy warriors with their dark lances and heavy cavalry hammers. The Red Scythes lived up to their name, reaping a fearsome tally with their broad-bladed swords.

Sigmar swung Ghal-maraz at Marius, but the Jutone king swayed aside and slashed his sword at Sigmar's back as he passed. The blade clanged from Sigmar's armour, the dwarf-scribed runes flaring as they repelled the enchantments bound within Marius's sword.

Sigmar heeled his horse, the hooves throwing up sparks from the cobbles as it skidded to a halt. Beside him, Redwane slammed his hammer into a lancer's chest, toppling him from the saddle with his ribs shattered. Laredus threw aside his splintered lance and drew his black-bladed sword. Count Aldred circled his kicking horse, Ulfshard rising and falling in ghostly arcs of blue light.

What little sense of order the cavalry clash might once have had vanished in the heaving press of horsemen. This was a fight for warriors protected by iron armour, and the Taleutens had ridden clear, though they galloped around the edges, loosing goose-feathered shafts into the combat when targets presented themselves.

Warriors on foot joined the fight, surrounding the battle against the lancers. Cherusen Wildmen dragged them from their saddles, while Count Otwin leapt upon a loose horse and ran amok through the Jutones.

The silver-helmed warrior pulled his mount around in a tight turn, and Sigmar was impressed by the man's horsemanship. He had expected Marius to be an effete trader, but he had proven himself to be a cunning general. He had also not expected him to be as skilled a rider as he was proving to be. What other surprises might the Jutone king have in store?

Sigmar raked back his spurred stirrups and yelled as he rode at

Marius once again. The Jutone king's sword was aimed at his heart, and Sigmar held Ghal-maraz close.

Marius slashed with his sword, and Sigmar brought Ghal-maraz up to block, but the blade flashed down, aimed not at Sigmar, but at his horse. Blood sprayed the cobbles, and the beast's front legs went from under it as its lifeblood fountained from its opened throat. Sigmar kicked his feet from the stirrups and hurled himself clear as the horse collapsed. He hit the ground hard and the breath was driven from him as he rolled.

A Jutone lancer swept his sword down at Sigmar, but he ducked beneath the blow and dragged the man from his horse. He slammed his hammer down on the warrior's chest, and turned to pull himself up into the saddle, but the horse bucked and ran from him before he could mount.

The battle raged around him, and Sigmar desperately hunted for another horse as Marius wheeled his mount and rode back at him. He planted himself before the charging count and sent a prayer for strength to Ulric. The Jutone king's steed was a towering beast of midnight black, its chest wide and powerful. It wore a caparison of blue silk over its long coat of mail, and Sigmar felt a moment's regret at what he was going to have to do.

Sigmar watched Marius as he charged in, and the world seemed to recede as his vision narrowed and time became sluggish. All he could hear was the clattering hoofbeats of the horse, all he saw was the snorting breaths from its flared nostrils and the wind of its speed ruffling its plaited mane. Marius's blue green sword gleamed as it cut the air.

Sigmar's hammer came up, and, in the moment before he struck, he begged Taal's forgiveness for taking such a fine specimen from the world.

Marius swung his horse to Sigmar's right, and the Jutone king's sword lanced out.

Sigmar stepped straight in front of the horse and brought his hammer down in a sweeping arc upon the beast's head. All his strength was behind the blow and the horse's skull split apart as it died. Marius was thrown from his saddle, and the full weight of the charging steed slammed into Sigmar.

The force of the impact was enormous, and Sigmar landed in a sprawled heap on the edge of the cavalry clash. Stars spun before him and he tasted blood. Sigmar groaned and tried to stand, but his body flared with pain. Gritting his teeth, he pushed himself upright, feeling that several ribs had snapped beneath his armour. But for King Kurgan's gift, he would have broken every bone in his body.

His sky-blue tunic torn and bloody, Marius lay close by, supine amid the chaos his unwillingness to join the Empire had spawned. Hundreds of men lay dead or dying around the Jutone king, the cobbles slick with warriors' blood, blood that need not have been shed if Marius had only submitted to Sigmar's rule. Sigmar cried out as he pushed himself to his feet, his entire body a mass of bloody wounds and fiery pain.

That pain fanned his fury at Marius into a raging inferno, and he felt the iron chains of his control slipping from him. Sigmar the Emperor diminished, and Sigmar the warrior surged to the fore as he staggered over to his enemy.

Sigmar hauled Marius to his knees, who cried out in pain and fear at the sight of the bloodstained warrior Emperor. Marius had lost his silver helm in the fall from his horse, and long blond hair spilled from a leather circlet at his temples. Dirt coated his handsome face, and he looked up at Sigmar through a mask of blood and sweat.

There was fear in his eyes, and Sigmar revelled in that fear as a red haze of anger and vengeance swept through him.

'Please!' cried Marius. 'Mercy!'

'For the likes of you?' roared Sigmar. 'Never!'

He lifted his hammer high, ready to dash his foe's brains out over the cobbles.

Marius raised his hands, as if to ward off his imminent death, and Sigmar laughed at the futility of the gesture.

'So perish all who defy me!' cried Sigmar, and brought the hammer down.

Marius screamed, but before the hammer struck, a powerfully muscled hand flashed out and grabbed the weapon's haft, halting it in mid-swing. Sigmar looked up in fury, seeing a giant warrior, covered in blood and tattoos, whose temple was pierced by a crown of golden spikes.

Sigmar knew he recognised the warrior, but his fury was a raging storm that blotted out any thoughts, save those of violence. He thundered his fist into the warrior's face, but the giant lowered his head, and the golden spikes embedded around his skull tore bloody chunks from Sigmar's hand. The pain was excruciating, and he staggered away from the warrior, as Ghal-maraz was torn from his grip.

The giant dropped the hammer and simply said, 'Enough.'

'I'll kill you!' raged Sigmar, snatching up a fallen axe. 'Get out of my way!

'Don't be a fool, man!' said the giant. 'Killing Marius will be an act of darkness that will taint everything you have achieved.'

'He deserves death,' snarled Sigmar. 'Look at all the men who have died here.'

'Aye, maybe he does, but if you kill him, this will all have been for nothing.'

Sigmar's anger fled in the face of the giant's words and the pulsing waves of rage and hatred melted away. He dropped to his knees, and blinked away tears as the full horror of what he had been about to do flooded through him.

He looked up at the bloodstained giant.

'Otwin? he said. 'Is that you?'

'Aye, Sigmar, it's me,' said the count of the Thuringians. 'Are you calm now?'

Sigmar nodded and took a deep breath, dropping the axe and letting the swelling darkness in his heart diminish. Otwin held out his hand and Sigmar took it, cradling his bloody fist close to his chest. He looked over at Marius, who knelt in the midst of fallen warriors and horses. The Jutone king had climbed unsteadily to his feet, and Sigmar saw that the fighting had ceased. A deathly stillness filled Jutonsryk, as though the world had paused to witness how this drama would play out.

The lancers had thrown down their weapons, but the battle hunger of Sigmar's warriors was poised and ready to devour the defeated Jutones. He could feel the anger in the air, the battle-born hatred that was the father of all massacres and bloodletting. In that moment, Sigmar felt the truth of the hag woman's warning.

She had warned him to beware the darkness in his heart, but he had believed that he could control it, that he was its master and could wield it in battle without fear of losing control.

He saw the folly of that belief and, but for Otwin's hand, he would have crossed the line from battle to murder.

Once that line was crossed there was no going back.

Sigmar had allowed his darkness to slip its leash, and it very nearly destroyed everything he had built in one moment of hatred. That it had taken Count Otwin, a warrior who was no stranger to slaughter, to save him from himself was no small irony and a measure of how close Sigmar had come to letting his all-too-human failings get the better of him.

The future of the Empire hung in the balance, and Sigmar knew that this was the most important moment of his life. He nodded to Otwin and reached for Ghal-maraz.

'Give me my hammer,' he said.

'You're not going to do anything foolish are you, lad?' asked Otwin.

'No.'

'You sure? I don't want to have to put you on your arse again.'

'I am sure, my friend,' promised Sigmar. 'And thank you.'

Otwin shrugged and handed him Ghal-maraz. The hammer felt natural in Sigmar's grip, a symbol of his rule more than a weapon, a tool for the uniting of men, not their destruction. Sigmar moved past Otwin, and stood before Marius. The Jutone king took a step back, looking warily at Sigmar's bloody hammer.

'King Marius,' said Sigmar. 'We are divided, and in division we are weak. It is my desire that we be united. One land, one people.'

Marius licked his lips and ran a hand through his hair. He straightened his tunic and stood proudly before Sigmar, every inch a king of men.

'You offered me that before,' said Marius. 'What makes you think I will accept now?'

'Look around you. Your walls are carried and your warriors defeated. If I order it, your city will burn and all your people will die.'

'Threats are no way to win me to your cause.'

'That was not a threat, it was a statement of fact.'

'Hair-splitting, nothing more.'

'No,' said Sigmar. 'I came here with anger in my heart and it almost cost me my soul. I think I hated you, and that hatred blinded me to what it was doing to me. I wish for nothing more than you and your people to be part of the Empire. It is all I have ever wanted, and if you could see all that we have achieved, I know you would wish to be part of it.'

'All I wanted was for my people to be left in peace,' said Marius. 'It is you who have brought war and bloodshed.'

Sigmar nodded and said, 'I know what I have done and I will bear the burden of that for the rest of my days, but put aside notions of blame for the moment. Think of what you might gain as part of the Empire: the protection of every warrior in the Empire and the brotherhood of fellow kings and your Emperor. Jutonsryk grows fat on trade, but with the whole of the Empire opened up to you, how much richer might it become? In time, your city will become the jewel of the Empire, a gateway to the world beyond our shores!'

'I will be no man's vassal,' said Marius, but Sigmar saw that his appeal to Marius's greed and vanity had struck home. 'You may have taken my walls, but I'll not swear allegiance to any man who demands it at the end of a bloody weapon.'

'Nor should you,' agreed Sigmar, dropping to one knee and holding Ghal-maraz out to the king of the Jutones. 'I offer you the hammer of Kurgan Ironbeard and place my life in your hands as a symbol of the honest brotherhood I offer. Bear the symbol of my power and judge my heart. If you judge it pure, join with me. If not, then strike me down, and I swear that no man here will ever violate your lands again.'

Sigmar felt a wave of sudden fear sweep through his men as Marius lifted Ghal-maraz. The ancient hammer seemed to pulse with the power of days past, and a tremor worked its way up Marius's arms. His expression, which had been belligerent and defiant, eased, and his eyes widened at the awesome power bound within the dwarf weapon.

Sigmar saw Marius's desire to strike him down with the hammer at war with the truth Ghal-maraz represented, and the knowledge of what might be forged with it as a beacon to all men. The Jutone king let out a shuddering breath and reversed the hammer, holding it out to Sigmar in both hands.

'We have been fools,' said Marius. 'Pride and anger have divided us, and look at what it has wrought – death and misery.'

'We are but men,' said Sigmar. 'It is our curse to allow pride and anger to lead to hatred and fear. From them are spawned the wars that feed the cycle of hatred. Join me so we might put an end to the darkness that sees men divided.'

Sigmar reached out and placed his hands next to those of Marius, so that they held Ghal-maraz together, bound as brothers by that ancient weapon of power.

'One land, one people?' said Marius.

'Always,' agreed Sigmar.

And it was done.

BOOK TWO
Empire of Blood

Thus did Sigmar call to account
Those who turned their backs.
And great was the war waged
On a king that lived by the blood of heroes.
Mighty was Sigmar's wrath,
Yet guarded not was his weary heart,
And evil of ancient times
Found root in the present.

NINE
Northern Fire

OF ALL THE Udose settlements Cyfael had seen, Haugrvik was amongst the most pleasant. Most villages on the Empire's northern coastline were battered by the cold winds raging southwards from the ice-bound lands beyond, but a high ridge to the north of Haugrvik sheltered it from the worst of the coastal weather. Built on a crescent bay of shingled shores, the low dwellings had a rustic charm not seen in the townships and settlements south of the Middle Mountains.

Cyfael made his way from the house the village chief, Macarven, had assigned him, a single storey structure of wattle and daub with timber struts and a rough coating of harling to the exterior. As he stretched in the early morning sunshine, he massaged his head and reflected that rustic charm was all well and good so long as you didn't have to wake up every morning with a raging thirst and monstrous hangover.

The women and youngsters of the village were already at the shoreline, folding the nets, and packing barrels with meat and bread for the fishermen. Six longboats were pulled up onto the shore, ready to be sent out into the Sea of Claws to bring back the day's catch. The village elders joined the women in their work, for the majority of the village's men were marching south to the Fauschlag Rock to answer a sword muster called by Count Pendrag.

Since arriving in Count Wolfila's castle of Salzenhús from Middenheim a month ago, Cyfael had ridden the length of the northern coastline with his fiercest clansmen to bring word of that summons to the villages of the Udose.

They were welcomed in the main, for Emperor Sigmar's armies had saved the Udose from destruction at the hands of the Norsii many years ago, and highland memories were long. Honouring the blood debt to the Unberogen and the Emperor was a matter of pride, and none of the many Udose clans would bear the shame of not living up to that obligation.

So far, Cyfael had mustered three hundred men, more than enough for this stretch of coastline, for it would not do to strip it completely of its warriors. The northern coasts of the empire were dangerous, and though Norsii raids were few and far between this far east, no one forgot the terror of the mighty Norsemen.

That fact was made clear by the presence of the timber hill fort atop a low mound on the northern curve of the bay. Surrounded by a palisade wall of sharpened logs and a wide, water-filled ditch, Macarven's fort was one of the largest Cyfael had seen in Udose lands. A tall watchtower rose from the walls, and, though the stronghold wasn't a patch on the grand fortress of Middenheim, there was a barbarous splendour to its construction.

The size of his hill fort was an indication that Macarven was a clan chief of some importance in the area, commanding respect from at least six other clans. The chieftain had been a generous host and had demanded Cyfael stay on for a few more days to sample Udose hospitality, which mainly involved flagon after flagon of strong drink and endless feasts of beef and fish.

Cyfael pulled his cloak tighter about himself as a bitter squall whipped up from the sea, and a shiver of unease travelled the length of his spine. He made his way down the stony path to the shore, enjoying the wildness of the country around him. He called the Fauschlag Rock home and from its towering heights a man could see to the edges of the world. The view across the endless forests of the empire was something to be treasured, but here... Here a man could *live* in that landscape.

The land of the Udose spread out before him like a great tapestry, rugged and harsh, but possessed of a haunting beauty that would never leave his soul. The ocean was an impossibly vast expanse of shimmering blue that stretched to the horizon and promised far off lands as yet unexplored. At least it would be, were it not for the thin morning mist that clung like fallen clouds to the surface of the water.

Donaghal, one of Count Wolfila's Hearth-Swords, waved at him from the shore, his near-naked body wrapped in a plaid cloak. The man was soaked from an early morning swim, and Cyfael saw the pale lines of scars criss-crossing his chest and arms. A long, basket-hilted claymore sat propped up against one of the longboats next to him. Donaghal was a fine warrior, a man whom other men looked up to.

'How's the water, Donaghal?' shouted Cyfael.

'Bracing. You should get yourself in and find out.'

Cyfael shook his head and grinned.

'I don't think so, my friend,' he said. 'Us southern types don't like the cold. I do not wish a fever before I return to Middenheim.

'Cold? Ach, whisht, man, this isn't cold, it's like swimming in a hot spring.'

'To you perhaps,' said Cyfael. 'You Udose have ice in your veins.'

Donaghal started to reply, but his mouth snapped shut as a ringing bell echoed from above. Cyfael turned at the sound, shielding his eyes as he looked up towards the hill fort. A clansman at the top of the watchtower was ringing the warning bell and pointing to the ocean. Cyfael couldn't make out what he was saying, but Donaghal clarified the nature of the threat with a single shouted word that was part warning, part curse.

'Norsii!'

Cyfael looked out to sea, and a trio of dark ships slid from the mist like phantoms. Tapered hulls angled upwards with wolf-headed prows arced towards the shore, driven by banks of oars that swept up and back in perfect unison.

'Ulric save us...' hissed Cyfael, wishing he'd thought to buckle his sword-belt on this morning. The Wolfships arced over the water, each vessel carrying at least thirty warriors in dark armour and horned helms, their swords and shields gleaming in the sun.

'Go!' shouted Donaghal. 'Get the women and children to the stockade!'

'I can help you,' said Cyfael.

'Don't be daft, you have no weapon and this is my shore. Now go!'

Though it tore at his heart to leave the clansman, Cyfael knew he would be little use without his sword.

'Ulric bless you, my friend,' he said. 'Take as many of the bastards with you as you can!'

Donaghal grinned, and said, 'No bother.'

Cyfael ran back to his lodgings, and quickly ducked inside to retrieve his sword, a fine Asoborn weapon with a leaf-shaped blade. Buckling on his sword-belt as he ran, he glanced back to the shoreline, and a cold lump of fear settled in his belly as he saw the three Wolfships driven up the shingle and Norsii warriors leaping over the side.

Donaghal charged to meet them with an Udose war cry on his lips, and his sword smashed through the armour of the first warrior to land on the beach. He killed a second Norsii with a devastating overhead sweep, and another with a disembowelling cut that tore up through the Norseman's mail shirt. His defiance couldn't last, and Cyfael watched in horror as a giant warrior in midnight-black armour leapt to the shingle with a red-bladed axe that seemed to burn with an evil flame.

Donaghal attacked the warrior, but his sword was batted aside with ease, and the burning blade swept back to cleave the clansman from neck to groin. The brave clansman fell to the bloody water, and Cyfael ran as Donaghal's killer turned his baleful gaze towards the settlement.

Cyfael sprinted through the village, passing homes that he had visited many times, and which would probably be burned to the ground before the day was out. In his short time here he had come to love this place, and the thought of its destruction at the hands of the Norsii filled him with a towering rage.

Women carrying children were fleeing along the roadway of hard-packed earth that led to the stockade on the hill. Cyfael ran after them, but his pace faltered as he saw something amazing.

Streaming from the forests around Haugrvik were at least two hundred warriors in patterned cloaks of red and green with heads shaven except for long braids at their ears. Each man was armoured in a mail vest and bore a small wooden buckler and a wide-bladed sword.

Roppsmenn!

The women of Haugrvik cried out in relief at the sight of the Roppsmenn, tribal warriors from the east who, while not sworn allies of the empire, were certainly more welcome than the Norsii.

A swordsman in form-fitting silver armour, who bore twin blades of slender beauty, led the Roppsmenn, and Cyfael recognised a deadly killer in his every move. A dark suspicion formed in his mind as the warriors took up positions in the heart of the village on the road that led to the stockade.

Cyfael shouted a warning, but it was already too late.

The Roppsmenn fell upon the women with swords, and the screaming tore at Cyfael's heart. He dragged his own weapon from its sheath and ran at the nearest of the Roppsmenn, plunging the blade into the man's side. Even as he died, he lashed out at Cyfael, who leapt back to avoid a killing blow from the dying man's weapon.

A Roppsmenn warrior lunged at him, and Cyfael swept the man's blade aside and spun around him, slashing his sword across the back of his foe's knees. Hamstrung, the man collapsed with a foul scream, and Cyfael tore the man's buckler from his arm. The Roppsmenn circled him, and Cyfael knew that he couldn't hope to survive the fight.

'Right, you bastards!' he yelled. 'Who's next?'

A shaven-headed Roppsmann with a scarred face raised his sword, but the silver-armoured swordsman shook his head.

'No,' he said, 'this one's mine.'

The warrior circled Cyfael, and his courage fled as he recognised the lithe footwork of an expert swordsman in the man's every move. Cyfael had once been privileged to witness a display of Ostagoth *Droyaska,* blademasters who elevated sword combat to an art-form. Next to this man's fluid movement, they seemed like crippled simpletons.

'You should be honoured,' said the warrior. 'You will be my first.'

'First what?'

'The first Empire man I will kill.'

'You are arrogant,' said Cyfael, mustering the last shreds of his warrior spirit. 'Perhaps I will kill you.'

The man laughed and shook his head.

'No,' he said. 'Already, fear is turning your bowels to water and you know you do not have the skill to defeat me.'

'A fight is about more than just skill. There is luck and fate. You might slip, your sword might break or I could surprise you.'

'No. You won't.'

The man removed his helm, and Cyfael's jaw dropped at the sight of the wondrously handsome man before him. Lustrous dark hair was bound in a long scalp lock, but it was the man's face, sensuous and perfectly symmetrical that snared Cyfael's attention.

Handsome to the point of obscenity, the man's features were clearly not those of the Norsii tribes. His curving cheekbones, full lips and softer jaw spoke of southern tribal ancestry. Cyfael was a lover of women, and had no interest in men beyond their comradeship, but he felt an undeniable attraction to this beautiful man.

'Who are you?' whispered Cyfael, his sword lowering.

The swordsman's blade lanced out in a gleaming blur, and a rush of blood poured onto Cyfael's chest. He looked down, and saw that his throat had been opened, the blade that killed him so sharp he hadn't even felt it cut his flesh.

He dropped to his knees as his life poured out of him. The swordsman stood over him, and Cyfael was glad that his death had come at the hands of this perfect warrior and not some stinking, traitorous Roppsmann.

'I am Azazel,' said the swordsman, 'but before that I was called Gerreon.'

Cyfael tried to form a reply, but his mouth filled with blood and the words wouldn't come.

'I once called this land home,' said Azazel, kneeling beside Cyfael and unsheathing a dagger. 'But I was betrayed and driven out by a man who called me sword-brother. His name is Sigmar, and I have come home to kill him.'

Azazel gripped Cyfael's neck and held the glittering blade of his dagger a hair's-breadth from his eye. As the last of his strength faded, Cyfael saw the swordsman's face twist in anger, and what he had once thought beautiful was now hideous and terrifying.

'I am going to put out your eyes and cut out your tongue,' hissed Azazel with obvious relish. 'You will walk blind and without voice in the void for all eternity. Your torment will be exquisite.'

The dagger stabbed home, and Cyfael knew no more.

HAUGRVIK BURNED. THE stockade on the hill had fallen within the hour and its chieftain was nailed to its splintered gates. His wife and children were thrown, still living, onto the pyre of the dead. The elders and warriors were impaled on sharpened logs that had once encircled the hill fort, and the women too old to bear children were given to the blooded warriors for sport or taken by Azazel for torture.

The young women were whipped and chained before being taken aboard the Wolfships as spoils of war. The settlement's children were offered to Kharnath, the dark god of blood, and their skulls woven into trophy chains to be hung from the banner of Cormac Bloodaxe.

Kar Odacen watched as the settlement burned, pleased at the victory and at the sense of ancient plans in motion that he felt all around him. The wizened, stoop-shouldered shaman sat on a fallen log, as Cormac stalked through the blazing village, his powerful form clad in blood-coloured armour taken from the lost tomb of Varag Skulltaker the previous year. The warrior's axe, a dread blade into which Kar Odacen had bound a creature from the pit, was dark and lifeless, its hunger for slaughter sated for now.

With eyes that saw the world beyond that of mortals, Kar Odacen perceived the red haze of anger that enveloped Cormac, and smiled. That anger had been a potent force in rebuilding the Norsii tribes, an anger that Kar Odacen had carefully fanned and built, ever since Cormac's father had been killed and the Norsii driven from their homes by Sigmar Heldenhammer.

Forever on the fringes of the southern lands, the Norsii had honoured the ancient gods of the world, and for this they had been hated and feared. The soft-bellied southern tribes knew nothing of the power of the northern gods, and so were prey to the Norsii. Then the hated Sigmar had united the tribes beneath his banner and made war on the chosen of the gods.

Against such a powerful enemy, the Norsii had had no choice but to flee to the icy wastelands across the sea. Here they scraped a pitiful existence from the bleak landscape, dreaming of the day when they would sing the songs of war and sail the Wolfships south to bring death to their enemies.

Alone of all the Norsii, Kar Odacen embraced his new home, for he had travelled these forsaken lands before in ages past. Centuries before Cormac's birth, Kar Odacen had dared venture into the northern reaches of the world, where the very air seethed with power, and the land writhed with the breath of the gods. Unimaginable energies had poured into his body, the gods blessing him with extended life and the power to change the world. The elements bent to his will, daemons of the pit were his to command, and the myriad patterns of the future came to him in dreams and visions.

Upon his return to the world of men, he walked amongst the Norsii for many lifetimes, shaping their destiny and ever working to bring about the End Times, the days of blood when the Dark Gods would finally claim this world as their own. Kar Odacen had held to the old ways, and with Cormac's anger binding the Norsii together, they had rebuilt the tribes, gathering the survivors of Sigmar's wrath and filling their hearts with hatred.

With the coming of Azazel, that time was closer than ever before.

Kar Odacen looked over the burning hill fort as the young warrior walked from its ruins. He stopped beside Cormac, and the two warriors made their way towards him. As they drew close, Kar Odacen studied them both.

Cormac Bloodaxe was the greatest of the Norsii warlords, a warrior who had brought many of the disparate tribes of the north together under one banner and promised them revenge. A core of molten rage burned in his heart, and that anger would burn the Empire to ashes.

Azazel's silver armour was drenched in blood, and lines of red streaked his cruelly handsome face. The man revelled in torture, and the burning fort was filled with the mutilated bodies of his victims. The swordsman had come a long way in the ten years since his arrival on their shores in a stolen boat, delirious and near death. The womenfolk nursed him back to health, and as soon as he had regained his strength, Kar Odacen took the warrior into the northern wastelands. Deep in the abode of the gods, Azazel fought creatures of nightmare and felt the blessings of the gods flow in his veins. The warrior had been reborn there and, like Cormac, Azazel had good reason to hate the Empire.

His thirst for vengeance was a sword aimed at the heart of its ruler.

It had been hard for Cormac to accept the southlander as an equal, but in the years of battle since he had first come to their lands, Azazel had proved himself a warrior of superlative skill and ruthlessness. His cruelty and beauty were feared and beloved in equal measure, and he had willingly turned from the weak gods of the southern tribes to worship the hungry gods of the dark.

'A grand day's slaughter,' said Kar Odacen as the two warriors reached him.

'This?' spat Cormac, removing his helm. 'This was nothing.'

Cormac Bloodaxe had the face of a fist fighter, his nose a flattened nub of gristle that had been broken many times, and his eyes were hooded and malicious. His hair was the colour of copper, and his skin was windblown from a life lived in the tundra of the northern realms.

Cormac bore numerous tally scars on his cheeks, each one representing a great mound of skulls offered to his patron god. He looked over at the line of impaled Udose prisoners. 'There was barely a fighter among them, save the clansman I killed at the shore,' he said. 'The chieftain opened his gates after we slew the first of his women. A man like that does not deserve to be a leader.'

'The men of the Empire are sentimental,' said Azazel. 'It will be their undoing.'

'Exactly,' agreed Kar Odacen. 'They do not live a life of battle and blood like the Norsii. Comfort and peace makes women of their warriors.'

'You were once one of them,' pointed out Cormac, never passing up an opportunity to remind Azazel of his southern heritage. 'I have yet to see your sentimental side.'

Kar Odacen expected anger from Azazel, but the man simply shrugged.

'I cast off such weakness when I killed my sister,' he said. 'I am no longer one of them. I am Norsii.'

'Aye,' said Kar Odacen, 'that you are. Tell me, Cormac, did the Roppsmenn fight well?'

Cormac shrugged.

'Well enough,' he said. 'They know what will happen to their womenfolk should they falter.'

Kar Odacen smiled. With the breaking of the ice around the Norscan coastline, Cormac and Azazel had sailed the Wolfships across the ocean and plundered the towns and settlements of the Roppsmenn. They had taken the Roppsmenn's women and tribal leaders hostage, and demanded a season's servitude from the eastern tribe's warriors in return for their safety.

It was a bargain Kar Odacen had no intention of living up to. He sensed Azazel's dark eyes boring into him.

'The Roppsmenn must know you will not return their hostages,' said Azazel. 'You will burn them upon a great pyre to ensure the success of next year's campaigning.'

As always, Azazel's beguiling allure gave Kar Odacen pause, but he forced himself to see past the haunting beauty the dark prince had bestowed upon the swordsman.

'You see much that is hidden, Azazel,' said Kar Odacen. 'You have the sight?'

Azazel shook his head and smiled.

'I don't need sorcerous powers to know that you will kill them,' he said. 'It's what I would do. Slowly.'

Kar Odacen smiled. Truly the man Gerreon was no more. Only Azazel, disciple of Shornaal, remained.

'It matters not,' said Kar Odacen. 'There is nothing they can do to prevent it. But time is passing, and we should leave this place. The smoke will bring Udose warriors from other settlements.'

'Let them come,' snarled Cormac. 'I grow weary of killing women and old men, shaman.'

'Yet you take such relish in the task.'

'Kharnath cares not from where the blood flows,' spat Cormac, 'but we gain nothing by killing such wretches. My blade hungers for worthy foes to slay.'

'You must be patient, Cormac, this is not a time for war; it is a time for terror.'

'Terror? Terror does not reap skulls for Kharnath. Terror does not win us back land that is rightfully ours!'

Kar Odacen held up a placatory hand.

'Terror is a potent ally, Cormac,' he said. 'It moves through the land faster than any army, and saps the courage of every man it touches. Your name is known in the south already, for it is carried on every panicked scream and cry of loss. The terror of what you have done here will spread like a plague, and tales of your slaughters will reach the furthest corners of the Empire. With every retelling, they will grow in magnitude until terror gnaws at the hearts of Sigmar's warriors like rats in the darkness.'

'Then it is time to march south?' asked Cormac.

'No,' said Kar Odacen. 'Not yet. There is work to be done before the Empire burns.'

'Damn you, shaman, you say that every time I ask. What is left to be done?' asked Cormac.

'Patience, young Cormac, you have nursed your hatred for ten years. What matters one more turning of the seasons?'

'Tell me, shaman, or I shall feed your soul to my axe!'

'Very well,' said Kar Odacen, feigning submission, though he knew his death would not be at the hands of a mortal like Cormac Bloodaxe. 'There is an enemy that dwells in the south who draws power from the pulse of the earth.'

'A sorcerer like you?'

'No,' hissed Kar Odacen, 'not like me. There are no others like me, but this one... This one has real power, and the gods have spoken words of death that cannot be denied.'

'Then kill this mystic and be done with it.'

'I shall,' promised Kar Odacen. 'I must travel deep into the lands of the south, but I shall not be going alone. Azazel must accompany me, for he knows the ways of its people. He shall be my guide and my protector.'

'And then we take the fire south?' demanded Cormac.

'Then we take the fire south,' promised Kar Odacen.

* * *

THANKS TO THE paved roads leading from Reikdorf, it took Sigmar and his warriors less than two weeks to travel north to Count Otwin's castle in the Dragonback Hills. Here they rested for three nights, enjoying the rough and ready hospitality of the Thuringian count before pressing on towards the Fauschlag Rock.

So far the journey had been uneventful, with each town and settlement greeting the Emperor and his warriors with open arms and generous hospitality. The settlements were protected by tall palisade walls and armed men equipped with mail shirts and sturdy iron swords. As secure as they were, the arrival of three hundred White Wolves was most welcome.

The settlement of Beckhafel marked the most northerly extent of the road to Middenheim, and Sigmar was pleased to see hundreds of men hard at work in the forests beyond the village. Robed mapmakers and scribes consulted with foresters to plot the route of the road, and logging gangs felled trees from its path as well as cutting undergrowth back from the road to allow armed warriors on horseback to protect the working men.

Burly men with iron-bladed augers broke the ground for the diggers to form the wide trench that would be filled and levelled with sand before the stonecutters laid flattened slabs on a bed of lime mortar. Scores of tents and wagons lined the road, filled with sand, stone and tools. The scope and scale of the work filled Sigmar with pride as he and Redwane rode alongside the ever-lengthening road.

Workmen waved as they passed, and Sigmar held Ghal-maraz out for his subjects to see, holding the weapon aloft until they rode out of sight of the work-gangs and into the wild reaches of the forest. The regular sound of axes biting into timber was soon swallowed by the thick woodland, and Sigmar shivered as the trees seemed to crowd in that little bit closer.

He looked into the forest on either side of him, unable to see further than ten or fifteen feet.

Anything could be lurking in the darkness, and Sigmar's hand slipped back onto the haft of Ghal-maraz. A palpable tension descended on Sigmar's warriors as they appreciated how isolated they were. The sensation was not entirely unwelcome and as their guide, a huntsman named Tomas, led them deeper into the shadowy reaches of the forest, Sigmar had a potent sense of venturing into the unknown.

As though picking up on his thoughts, Redwane leaned over and said, 'Are you sure this man knows where he's going? It doesn't look like anyone's come this way in years.'

Sigmar had to agree with the young White Wolf. Their route was overgrown, and tangled with plants and gently waving ferns. He could barely see the faint trail of hard-packed earth that wound its way between the trees.

Without looking back, Tomas said, 'You're welcome to try and find your own way, boy.'

Their guide was a tall and rangy Thuringian, clad in leather and buckskin that blended with the neutral tones of the forest. A long-hafted axe was sheathed on his back and, unusually for one of Count Otwin's subjects, he carried a compact recurved bow, Taleuten by the craft of it.

'Redwane meant no disrespect, friend Tomas,' said Sigmar. 'Though the trail *does* look abandoned.'

'It's not,' said Tomas. 'Few use this path now, only foresters and hunters. And good ones don't leave signs of their passing.'

'What about the bad ones?' quipped Redwane.

'They end up dead. The forest doesn't forgive mistakes.'

'You travel this way regularly?' asked Sigmar as Redwane made a face of mock terror at the huntsman's back.

Tomas nodded.

'Aye,' he said. 'End of each hunting season I'll take my furs north to the Fauschlag Rock. Wolf, deer and fox mainly, but sometimes I get a bear. Trade them for supplies to last out the winter.'

'A hard life,' said Sigmar.

The huntsman shrugged, as though he hadn't given the matter any thought. 'No harder than most, I suppose. I don't like towns. I like the peace of the forest.'

'How long till we reach Middenheim?' asked Redwane.

Tomas looked up. 'A week. Maybe less if the weather holds.'

The huntsman pushed deeper into the forest ahead and, careful to keep his voice low, Redwane said, 'A dazzling conversationalist, eh? Makes Alfgeir look like a blabbermouth.'

'He is a man who spends a lot of time on his own,' said Sigmar, 'and someone who can bring a bear down on his own is clearly not a man to antagonise.'

Redwane nodded, glancing over at Tomas and the well-used axe on his back.

'I take your point,' he said.

'Still,' continued Sigmar, 'I like the idea that we are treading paths few others have followed. It feels as though we are discovering somewhere new, for the Empire is becoming a smaller place.'

Seeing Redwane's confusion, Sigmar said, 'The roads I am building are bringing lands once thought unreachable within our grasp. As traders from Jutonsryk and beyond the southern mountains forge new trade routes throughout the land, it sometimes feels as though the unknown places of the world are becoming fewer and farther between.'

'That's a good thing, surely?'

'Yes,' agreed Sigmar. 'While my intellect rejoices at the idea of unlocking the land for my people, allowing trade and travel to flourish, my heart mourns the passing of its mysteries. Soon there will be no secret places left in the world, and the light of civilisation will usher in a new age.'

'Sounds grand,' said Redwane, though Sigmar knew the young warrior did not grasp the implications of a land made small by the expansion of man. As much as the world needed illumination, it needed the promise of realms unexplored to drive the imagination.

Sigmar remembered journeying south to Siggurdheim and the sense of boundless space he had felt while alone in a landscape free from the stamp of civilisation. Travelling through the northern forests had awakened that wanderlust in Sigmar, and he felt the excitement of an explorer daring to brave new horizons.

He wondered how much longer this would last, for loggers were clearing forests all across the Empire. New towns and farms and grazing land were emerging every day, and his people were carving out their homes in areas that had once been beast-haunted wilderness. It seemed as though the forest and lands of the Empire were limitless, but Sigmar knew they were not.

What would happen when the land grew too small for his people?

TEN

Curse of the Dead

MIDDENHEIM, CITY OF the White Wolf. The sheer pinnacle of rock looming from the forest canopy never failed to amaze Sigmar. More than a thousand feet high, the mighty Fauschlag Rock dominated the landscape for miles around, inescapable and impossible.

Stark against the evening sky, Middenheim towered over the land of mortals like the home of the gods, an impregnable bastion whose summit glittered with light. Sigmar followed the road towards the granite-hewn gate fortress at the base of the rock, feeling a strange unease settle upon him as he glanced towards the towering Middle Mountains beyond the city.

Spreading into the north-east, they were a bleak and inhospitable range of jagged peaks and soaring cliffs, perpetually wreathed in snow and flensed by icy winds from the far north. Inhuman monsters made their lairs deep within the mountains, and many an expedition to purge them from its haunted valleys and shadowed gorges had ended in disaster.

Cresting the last rise before the city, Sigmar saw the forests around the city had been cleared for almost a mile in every direction, and a vast expanse of canvas tents surrounded the base of the rock like a besieging army. Looking closer, he saw that the tent city was instead home to carpenters, builders, stonemasons and labourers.

If Sigmar had thought that the work on the road linking Middenheim with Reikdorf was impressive, it was nothing compared to the scale of industry that surrounded the Fauschlag Rock. Thousands of craftsmen toiled in makeshift quarries and carpentry shops to service the construction of the giant structure rearing from a wide clearing in the forest floor.

Like an ever-ascending bridge of stone aimed at the summit of the Fauschlag Rock, a giant viaduct rose from the ground at the southern compass point of the city. The viaduct climbed to around a hundred feet before coming to an abrupt end, a forest of scaffolding clinging to its sides like vines on some ancient ruin. Workmen swarmed around its upper reaches on rope pulleys and harnesses, and the sound of hammers, chisels and saws reminded Sigmar of the clash of iron in a battle.

'Great Ulric's beard,' hissed Redwane as the full scope of the work was laid out before them. 'How in the world did they ever...'

'Pendrag is a clever man, and he had some help from the dwarfs,' said Sigmar, pointing to a number of short, stocky figures in iron shirts and pot helmets at the top of the viaduct. 'This is only the first of four of such structures Pendrag plans to build.'

'Four!'

'If Middenheim is going to be one of the great cities of the Empire, it is going to have to be easier to get to than it is now,' said Sigmar. 'Until the viaduct is complete, we have to travel to the summit on one of the chain lifts.'

Redwane shielded his eyes from the setting sun as he followed the swaying progress of one of the chain lifts as it made its juddering way from the ground to the timber structure that leaned out from the top of the rock. Sigmar smiled as he saw the young warrior's face pale.

'Of course, if you really want to prove your courage, you could climb the rock like I did.'

'You climbed that?' asked Redwane. 'From the ground up?'

'I did,' said Sigmar, still amazed that he had dared attempt so dangerous a climb. 'So did Alfgeir. But then we were young and foolish. Or at least I was.'

'And you killed Artur once you got to the top?'

Sigmar nodded, remembering the desperate fight with the Teutogen king, and the soul-chilling fall he had taken through the Flame of Ulric that burned eternally at the heart of the peak's summit. In that glacial moment, he had felt the briefest touch of a power greater than any mortal mind could hope to perceive. As he had felt its touch, it too had sensed his presence. The cold, pitiless echo of that moment had never left him.

'I regretted killing Artur,' said Sigmar. 'He was once a good man, but he had grown arrogant atop his fortress, and thought himself above all men.'

'But not you, eh?'

'No,' said Sigmar sadly. 'Not me.'

Their Thuringian guide had left them yesterday, when the towering spire of Middenheim had come into sight. The taciturn huntsman had merely taken his coin and vanished into the forest without any word of goodbye. Sigmar had been sorry to see Tomas go, for he had liked the man's self-reliance and independence.

They rode towards the gate fortress along temporary roads of rough-laid stone, passing workshops of carvers and stonemasons, assembly shops of carpenters and scaffold makers, hospitals, cook tents and the hundred other trades required for so colossal an undertaking. Numerous guild flags were planted throughout the campsite, and Sigmar recognised many of them as having worked on the buildings of Reikdorf.

In the years that Sigmar had spent campaigning in the west, Reikdorf had grown and prospered, with the great library taking shape in its heart and many new temples erected within its walls. Though it broke his heart to leave so soon after the successful conclusion to the war against the Jutones, a request for aid from his oldest friend could not be ignored.

As he led his warriors through the enormous camp, Sigmar felt a strange unease settle upon him, like a cold wind blowing with the breath of despair. He looked to the eastern mountains, and felt ancient eyes of incalculable evil watching him. For the briefest second, a profound sense of hopelessness swept over him, as though his very existence were meaningless in the face of death's inevitability.

Sigmar shook off the feeling, but as he watched the sullen faces of the camp's inhabitants, he saw he was not alone in this feeling. An unspoken fear hung over the camp, men and women moving with leaden steps and expressions of hopelessness. On the journey northwards, the people he had seen had welcomed them and smiled with each new dawn, but around Middenheim it was as if the sun were setting on the last day, and no one believed it would ever rise again.

'What in the name of all that is good is wrong here?' asked

Redwane, riding alongside Sigmar. 'It's like everyone's mother suddenly dropped down dead.'

'I do not know,' said Sigmar as the wide drawbridge of the gate fortress lowered. 'Pendrag will tell us more when we reach the summit.'

Redwane looked up as a series of chain lifts rattled and clattered their way down the sheer cliff face of the Fauschlag Rock, and he swallowed nervously at the thought of ascending the rock in such a contraption.

'Couldn't we wait until the viaduct's finished?' asked the White Wolf.

Pendrag and Myrsa were waiting when Sigmar stepped from the chain lift and onto the roofed platform built out from the rock on a series of mighty cantilevers. His sword-brother had changed in the five years since he had last seen him, but Sigmar hid his surprise. Pendrag's waist had thickened and the cares of the world, which he had always carried in his eyes, seemed magnified by the dread that seeped from the mountains. His flame-red hair was no less wild, and his joy at seeing Sigmar was like the first rays of sunlight after a winter of darkness.

Pendrag swept Sigmar into a crushing embrace, and the two men laughed at the sight of one another. Sigmar held his brother's shoulders as they relished this long overdue meeting.

'Damn me, Sigmar, but it's good to see you,' said Pendrag when he finally released him.

'You are a sight for sore eyes, Pendrag,' replied Sigmar. 'Wolfgart sends you his best.'

'The rogue isn't with you?' asked Pendrag, his disappointment clear.

'He wanted to come, but I told him that he needed to spend time with his family,' said Sigmar. 'Ulrike is nearly four now. Even if I hadn't forbidden him to come north, Maedbh would have cut off his manhood had he tried to ride out with me.'

'Aye, she's a fierce one, right enough,' said Pendrag, as Sigmar turned to Myrsa and took his wrist in the warriors' grip.

Where Pendrag had changed, Myrsa was as solid and untouched by the passing of the years as his mountain home. His white armour was polished and pristine, his grip as firm as ever and his eyes like chips of ice.

'My lord,' said the Warrior Eternal. 'Welcome to Middenheim.'

Myrsa was pleased to see him, but where Pendrag greeted Sigmar like the old friend he was, the Warrior Eternal welcomed him as an Emperor. As he released Myrsa's wrist, Sigmar was reminded of the hag woman's warning not to let the Warrior Eternal die before his time. It had seemed like a ridiculous request then, and seemed doubly so now. How could any man promise such a thing?

'It is good to be here,' said Sigmar as his White Wolves formed up behind him. Ten warriors had accompanied Sigmar in the chain lift, and they looked anxiously at the creaking wooden floor, conscious that there was nothing beneath it but fresh air and the ground hundreds of feet below. 'I have left it too long to come north, but there has been much to do in the west.'

'So I hear,' smiled Pendrag. 'Two years... Jutonsryk must have been a tough nut to crack.'

'It was,' admitted Sigmar. 'I could have used some of your dwarfs to help break it open.'

Pendrag led Sigmar and his bodyguards from the platform and onto the streets of Middenheim, as the lifts descended to bring more White Wolves to the summit.

Despite his outward calm, Sigmar was grateful to feel solid rock beneath his feet, and he was once again struck by the distinctive architecture of this northern city. It was as if the close-packed buildings had been carved out of the rock, dour and low-roofed, with little in the way of ornamentation. They were crowded together, as Sigmar would expect of a city with a finite amount of land on which to build. Few were higher than two storeys, for unforgiving winds whipped across the Fauschlag Rock and quickly toppled any structure that dared to test its power. Many of the buildings bore the hallmarks of dwarf craftsmanship, but even these solid structures clung close to the surface of the rock.

The people of the north were hardy and pragmatic, and their dwellings were a reflection of that grim temperament. Most of the city's inhabitants were dark-haired and broad-shouldered, as firm and unbending as their city. Though Sigmar sensed the same unnatural gloom that possessed the camp below, he saw an impressive determination to resist it.

The busy streets were narrow and filled with people, far more than Sigmar remembered from his last visit to Middenheim, and Myrsa's plate-armoured warriors were forced to clear a path with shouted oaths and blows from their scabbarded greatswords.

'So many people,' commented Redwane.

'Aye,' said Pendrag guardedly. 'The city is almost full.'

Sigmar sensed a deeper meaning in Pendrag's words, but saved his questions for later as they forged a path through the crowds.

'I doubt I could have spared you any of the mountain folk,' said Pendrag answering Sigmar's earlier comment. 'Without them we wouldn't have managed to get the viaduct so high in so short a time. In any case, you took Jutonsryk in the end, though I'm still amazed that Marius swore his Sword Oath with you. I thought he would die first.'

Sigmar shook his head.

'Marius is no fool,' he said, 'and if a Sword Oath was the price of his life and his city's fortune, then he was more than willing to give it.'

'The man is an opportunist,' spat Pendrag, turning down a wider avenue that led to the stone circle where Sigmar had fought Artur. A tall building of white stone was in the process of being built around the menhirs encircling the Flame of Ulric, and Sigmar felt a tremor of bone-deep chill as he caught a glimpse of its flickering light, like a spear-tip of dancing ice.

He shook off the memory of the flame's chill and said, 'True, but great wealth is pouring into the Empire from the west. Without that, there would not be the gold to pay for Middenheim's viaducts. That is after a twentieth of Jutonsryk's yearly income is tithed for distribution amongst the warriors who fought so hard to take it.'

'I'll bet Marius hated that,' laughed Pendrag, passing the construction site and leading the way down a deserted street that was even narrower than the others they had traversed.

'That he did, but even with the tithe, his city's coffers are swollen with gold from all the trade that has opened up for him,' said Sigmar. 'If Marius had realised how lucrative swearing a Sword Oath would be, I think he would have done it long ago.'

'And you trust him to live up to his oath? He failed to stand by us once before.'

Sigmar smiled and put his arm around his friend's shoulders. 'I left a thousand warriors in Jutonsryk to make sure of it.'

'Unberogen?'

'A mixed force of warriors from all the tribes,' said Sigmar. 'Each of the counts sent fresh troops from their homelands.'

'Hoping to pick Jutonsryk clean, no doubt.'

'No doubt,' agreed Sigmar, 'but I did not want warriors who had lost friends garrisoning a city they had shed blood to take. The time had come to send the army home.'

Pendrag nodded and said, 'Two years is a long time for a man to be away from his family.'

'It is,' agreed Sigmar, hearing the wistful longing for home in Pendrag's voice, 'but enough reminiscing, my friend, are you going to tell me why you have brought me here?'

'That is why we are here,' said Pendrag, indicating a simple structure of polished granite at the end of the street. The building had a heavy wooden door guarded by two Ulrican templars and its few windows were shuttered. A White Wolf with painted red eyes set in a sunken reliquary above the door provided the only colour on a building that was grim even in a city of dourly constructed buildings.

'A temple of Ulric?' asked Sigmar.

'The building belongs to the Ulricans,' said Pendrag, sharing an uneasy glance with Myrsa, 'but it is not a temple. It is a prison.'

'A prison for whom?'

'Something evil,' said Pendrag. 'Something dead.'

THE BUILDING'S INTERIOR was smothered in gloom, the only illumination provided by a series of tallow candles set into niches shaped like the gaping maws of snarling wolves. Sigmar felt the hairs on his arms and the back of his neck stand erect, and his breath feathered the air before him. The walls were dressed ashlar, unmarked by a single devotional image or carving. A sullen sense of despair clung to the stonework, as though it carried the weight of the city's sorrows.

Four priests in dark wolfskin cloaks awaited them, each carrying a candle that gave off a cloying, sickly aroma. Pendrag closed the door behind Sigmar, shutting out the last of the evening light, and he felt a crushing sense of soul-deep unease settle in his bones.

Something was very wrong here, something that violated the very essence of human existence. This place reeked of abandonment and decay, as though the ravages of centuries had taken their toll in an instant. More than that, a palpable sense of fear lingered in every passing moment.

'What happened here?' whispered Sigmar, feeling the full toll of all his thirty-six years. He felt the pain of long-healed scars, the ache of tired muscles and the unending, ever-increasing weight of his rule upon his shoulders.

'I'll show you,' said Pendrag, following the priests as they turned and made their way down the shadowy corridor. Moisture pooled on the floor, and Sigmar noticed that droplets hanging from the ceiling were forming icicles.

Myrsa matched step with Sigmar as the priests led them deeper into the cold and echoing building.

'While you made war against the Jutones, the Norsii have been raiding all along the coast, destroying dozens of settlements,' he said. 'Entire villages have been massacred: men, women and children impaled on sharpened stakes. Even the livestock is butchered and left to rot.'

'You have seen this yourself?' asked Sigmar, knowing how such tales could grow in the telling until they bore little resemblance to the truth.

'Aye,' nodded Myrsa, 'I have,' and Sigmar did not doubt him.

'Many of the people in Middenheim are from those few settlements that have not yet been attacked,' continued Pendrag. 'The northern marches have been virtually abandoned.'

'Abandoned?' asked Sigmar. 'The Norsii have always raided the coastline. What more is there that drives people from their homes? There is something you are not telling me.'

'That is why I sent word to you, my friend,' said Pendrag. 'As you drew closer to Middenheim you must have felt the nameless fear emanating from the mountains?'

'We felt it,' confirmed Sigmar, stepping into an echoing chamber filled with lecterns of dark wood, 'a black dread that tears at the heart with talons of despair.'

No scribes sat at the lecterns, though open books and pots of coloured ink awaited their careful hands. The chamber smelled of copper, vinegar and oak apples, though Sigmar had the sense that no one had sat here in many years.

'What causes it?' asked Redwane. 'An enemy we can fight?'

'Perhaps,' said Myrsa, leading the way from the lettering chamber along a bare stone corridor towards a thick timber door secured with heavy iron bolts top and bottom. 'There is one beyond who may know something of what afflicts us.'

Another two priests flanked this door, each carrying a spiked man-catcher, a long polearm with a vicious collar on the end and sharpened spikes on its inner surfaces that would rip a prisoner's throat out if he struggled.

'The dead thing you spoke of?' said Sigmar, and Redwane made the sign of the horn.

'The same,' replied Pendrag, drawing the bolts and opening the door. Sigmar saw a set of curving steps that spiralled deep into the rock. Pendrag set off down the stairs and Sigmar followed him. The temperature dropped with every downward step. Hoarfrost formed on the walls, and each intake of breath was like a spike of cold ice to the lungs.

'The priests of Morr came to me two months ago,' said Pendrag, as the stairs wound deeper and deeper into the rock. 'They spoke of dreams coming to their gifted ones, dreams of a long dead evil stirring in the Middle Mountains. The high priest claimed that Morr himself appeared in a dream to warn them that a terror from the ancient days had awoken from its slumber and sought dominion over the lands of men.'

'Did the high priest say what this terror was?'

Pendrag shook his head, and said, 'No, only that it would spread like a plague, bringing misery and death to the race of man. Less than a week later, we heard the first tales from the villages in the foothills of the mountains.'

'Tales? What manner of tales?' asked Redwane.

'Of the dead walking,' said Pendrag. 'Entire villages destroyed in the night, every living person vanished and every grave emptied. Soon this began spreading ever further from the mountains, and more and more people fled to Middenheim as the shadow crept ever onwards.'

'You suspect a necromancer?' asked Sigmar as the cramped stairwell grew steadily brighter.

'Or worse,' said Myrsa. 'I sent warriors into the mountains – Knights of Morr and Ulrican templars – but none ever returned.'

'Until now,' added Pendrag, as the stairs opened up into a wide chamber hacked from the rock with picks and bare hands. A swaying lantern hanging from the ceiling on a long chain and a host of torches set in iron sconces illuminated the chamber. A rough-hewn tunnel in the far wall led into darkness.

The candle-bearing priests took up positions on either side of it, chanting soft prayers to their god as those armed with the spiked collar weapons stood before it with their weapons held at the ready.

As Sigmar stared into the darkness of the tunnel, he felt as though the last breath was sucked from his body and icy hands had taken his heart in a cold, clammy grip. Though he had faced death many times, he felt unreasoning terror seize his limbs at the sight of the darkened passageway.

He gripped Ghal-maraz tightly, the warm, reassuring presence of the ancient warhammer steadying his nerves and easing his terror. The runes worked into its haft and head shone with a warm light, and, gradually, the paralysing fear holding him immobile began to diminish.

'What lies at the end of that tunnel?' asked Sigmar, fighting to hold his voice steady.

'It's better if I show you,' said Pendrag, taking a torch from the wall.

With the priests of Ulric leading the way, Pendrag, Myrsa, Sigmar and Redwane entered the darkened passageway. The darkness seemed to swallow the light from the torches, pressing in on them like a smothering blanket. Only the light of Ghal-maraz shone steadily, and never was Sigmar more thankful for King Kurgan's gift.

As a warrior, he had known fear, for he had faced many terrible foes, but this was not the fear of defeat, this was something else. This evil wormed its way into his soul with the fear of rotting flesh, of decomposing organs, his soul enslaved to an eternity of damnation.

The tunnel began to widen, though the light of the torches barely illuminated the walls. Sigmar saw they were scrawled with feverish lettering, as though someone had copied vast tracts of text onto the bare rock of the walls. He eased closer and saw that the words were charms of protection and warding, and entreaties to the god of the dead. The very walls of the prison were enchanted to keep whatever lay ahead bound to this place.

The journey along the passageway seemed endless, though it could only have been a hundred yards or so. Sigmar looked over his shoulder to see the dim rectangle of light from the antechamber shrinking away from him, as though an impossible distance away. Swallowing hard, he kept his attention fixed on Myrsa's glittering white armour.

At last the passageway opened out onto a wide ledge in an echoing cavern. A deep chasm plunged into the infinite darkness, and a raised drawbridge swayed gently in the cold gusts from below. Fresh torches burned with the same sickly aroma as the priests' candles, and Sigmar finally recognised it as wightbane, a plant cultivated by the priests of Morr to ward against the walking dead.

Across the chasm was a solitary individual, chained to the rocks with fetters of silver and cold iron. Clad in bloodstained white vestments and rusted armour, the man raged against his bindings, hissing and spitting with animal fury. His flesh was grey, and thin strands of white hair hung from his mottled skull.

Sigmar gasped as he saw the wolf symbol of Ulric on the man's chest, but when the prisoner's head came up, he saw the true horror of his condition. The knight was a man no longer, but a thing of corruption and decay. What little flesh remained on his body writhed with maggots and carrion beasts of the earth, and his breath was ripe with the stink of the grave. Glistening innards hung from his ruptured belly, and snapped ribs jutted from his chest where an axe blow had split him open. A fell radiance waxed and waned in the skull's empty eye sockets, and Sigmar saw the promise of extinction in that light.

'Ulric preserve us!' hissed Sigmar, taking an instinctive step back from this monstrous thing. 'What is it?'

'It is – or *was* – Lukas Hauke, a warrior priest of Ulric,' said Myrsa. 'He led the expedition into the mountains to defeat this evil. He left Middenheim in the spring and returned alone two months ago, barely alive. I knew Hauke well, my lord, and he was a full five years younger than I, but when he rode into the eastern gate-fortress he appeared older than any man I have ever seen. The priestesses of Shallya treated Lukas with their most potent remedies, but he was ageing a year for every day that passed.'

The horror of such a dreadful ailment struck at the core of Sigmar's humanity, and he felt his mouth go dry and his stomach knot in fear.

'Eventually, he appeared to die,' continued Pendrag, 'but when the priests of Morr came to remove his body, Hauke rose from his deathbed and attacked them with his bare hands. He killed three men and eleven priestesses before they were able to bind him with blessed chains and bring him here.'

Sigmar lifted Ghal-maraz from his belt and Lukas Hauke, or what he had become, turned his creaking skull towards him.

The evil light in Hauke's eyes glittered with unholy power, and he spat a wad of black phlegm.

'That toy of the stunted ones will not save you, man-thing,' he said. 'Its power is a flickering ember before the might of the crown! If you knew the power of my master, you would end the pitiful, meaningless parade you call life and offer yourselves to Morath!'

Sigmar's skin crawled at Hauke's loathsome voice, a monstrously rasping, gurgling sound that conjured images of diseased lungs frothing with corruption.

He held Ghal-maraz out before him, and despite the dead thing's earlier words, it recoiled from the pure light that shone from the warhammer's head.

'Who is this Morath?' asked Sigmar. 'Speak now or be destroyed!'

Hauke spat and shook his chains as the light of Ghal-maraz touched him, but the evil in his eyes remained undimmed as he said, 'He is your new master and the living are his playthings.'

'I call no man master,' roared Sigmar, advancing to the edge of the chasm, feeling his courage growing with every step he took towards the unnatural monster. 'You will tell me of Morath, his plans and his strength. Do this and I will free your soul to travel to Ulric's hall.'

Hauke writhed in pain as the hammer's light grew brighter. The silver of its chains burned hot as its essence unravelled in the face of such ancient power. The creature's jaw gnashed in fury, but the dread force animating the brave knight's corpse could not resist the power that compelled it to answer. Its back arched and an awful crack of splitting bone echoed as it fought to keep its secrets. Bones ground and wasted muscles tore.

At last, Hauke's body sagged against the chains as the monster revealed itself.

'Morath is the Lord of the Brass Keep that holds dominion over Glacier Lake, and he is the doom of you all!' said the dead thing, the words dragged from its unwilling throat by the power of Sigmar's hammer. Each word was hissed through rotted stumps of teeth and spoken as a curse. 'He alone survived the doom of Mourkain and bore the crown of his master to this land in an age forgotten by the living.'

Much of what the creature said made no sense to Sigmar. He had no knowledge of Mourkain, whether it was a place or a person, but the mention of a crown piqued his interest. In its defiance, the creature had claimed its power was greater even than that of Ghal-maraz.

Lukas Hauke flailed and tore at the bindings, the silver chains glowing with the heat of their forging. Dust fell from where the iron bolts were driven into the rock, and the creature's limbs writhed with unnatural strength.

'You shall die!' screamed Hauke. 'The flesh will slide from your bones yet you will serve my master until endless night covers the land in darkness!'

With a final surge, the dead creature tore its chains from the wall and leapt across the chasm, its claws outstretched to tear Sigmar's throat. Its eyes burned with killing light, but Sigmar was ready for it.

He swung Ghal-maraz in a swift upward stroke, smashing the monster's skull from its shoulders. The deathly animation within the fallen knight's body was snuffed out by the power of the dwarf hammer, and a howling shriek of oblivion echoed from the walls of the cavern as the body tumbled into the chasm, disintegrating with every yard it fell. Within moments, all that remained was a drifting cloud of grave dust, and even that was soon lost to sight. Sigmar heard a gentle sigh of release, and knew that the soul of Lukas Hauke was freed.

'Gods of Earth and Sky!' said Redwane. 'Is it... dead?'

'It is,' said Sigmar, stepping back from the edge of the chasm. 'But this was just a messenger. This Morath wanted us to hear what it had to say.'

'Why?'

'Because he seeks to draw us into his lair.'

Redwane wiped his brow and risked a glance into the chasm, and said, 'And we're going?'

'We are,' said Pendrag, seeing the iron determination in Sigmar's eyes. 'That creature was a challenge to us, and we must answer it.'

Sigmar turned to Myrsa and said, 'Gather your bravest warriors and raise the Dragon Banner from the highest tower.'

'It will be done, my lord.'

'We shall find this Brass Keep and bring it down stone by stone,' promised Sigmar.

ELEVEN
The Mountains of Fear

THE ARMY OF the north set off as the sun passed its zenith the following day, six hundred warriors of courage and iron. Only the bravest had rallied to the Dragon Banner, for to march out under that blood-red standard was a declaration that no quarter was to be given to the enemy and none expected in return. It was a banner of death from the ancient days of the Unberogen and had not been raised since before the time of Redmane Dregor.

Cold winds blew off the snow-capped peaks, and Sigmar could feel the black amusement of the hidden necromancer in every warmth-sapping gust. He marched at the head of the column of warriors as they made their way from the eastern gate fortress and followed the road that skirted the rippling haunches of the towering mountains. The army moved on foot, for no horse would be able to negotiate the treacherous paths of the towering mountains.

Redwane marched with the White Wolves, his body swathed in a thick bearskin cloak, and he clutched Sigmar's banner close to his body. The youngster's face was pale and he was quieter than Sigmar could ever remember. Myrsa and Pendrag accompanied the warriors of the Count's Guard, giant men encased in glittering suits of plate armour who carried enormous greatswords across their shoulders. These proud northern warriors towered over the White Wolves, and already Sigmar could see proud rivalry developing between the stalwart fighting men. It was a rivalry born from confidence won in battle and the knowledge of mortality, and Sigmar knew that it would help the men conquer the fear he heard in the forced banter hurled between the different orders.

Pendrag carried the Dragon Banner, and his silver hand reflected wan, lifeless sunlight that did nothing to lift the army's spirits. Cheers followed them as they marched through the camps at the base of the Fauschlag Rock, but they were flat and without the infectious enthusiasm that had sent the Emperor's army to Jutonsryk.

These people did not expect them to return alive.

THE ARMY MARCHED into the mountains beneath a sky the colour of bone. The ground rose, the weather deteriorated with every mile, and the gently sloping hills and wide valleys around Middenheim quickly gave way to craggy gullies and a broken landscape like crumpled leather.

Rain fell in unending sheets and purple lightning smote the heavens from black clouds at the centre of the mountains. The sky was screaming at some unnatural violation and it was towards this that Sigmar led his army. The whispered mutterings of his warriors grew more fearful with every passing day, and Sigmar could not shake the feeling that he was leading his men to their doom.

Wolves howled in the night, but these were no welcome heralds of Ulric. They were black wolves of the mountains, beasts that had turned from the god of winter in ancient days and now roamed wild and masterless. Their howls plucked at the nerves of every fighting man, and wolf-tail talismans and protective amulets were held tightly as each night closed in like a fist.

On the morning of the third day's march, Sigmar saw a burial party at a crossroads upon the last valley of the foothills, and was reminded of the sad sight of the corpse-carts leaving Marburg.

A crookbacked priest of Morr stood beside an open grave marked only with a simple fencepost. A man in the tribal garb of a Middenlander and a gaggle of weeping children knelt beside the grave. Sigmar ordered the army banners dipped. Lying next to the grave was the body of a woman wrapped in a white burial shawl that left her head exposed to the elements. The man gently stroked her head, her blonde hair stark against the black ground of the hills.

The priest nodded towards what Sigmar had assumed was the haft of a shovel stuck in the earth, but which he now saw was a wide-bladed felling axe. The man took up the axe as the priest spoke again and the children rolled their mother onto her front. The axe swept up and then down, and the woman's head rolled clear. Weeping, the man dropped the axe, before helping the priest lower her face-down body into the grave.

The tribesman lifted his wife's head and placed it in a canvas bag as the priest intoned the blessing of Morr, and the children began scooping earth with their bare hands. Sigmar raised his hand to the priest, who bowed and helped the grieving family to fill the grave.

The army continued on its way, marching higher into the soaring peaks, winding a treacherous course through icy valleys and mist-shrouded gorges as they climbed high above the snowline. Sigmar chose their course without truly understanding what guided him, for this region of the north was little mapped, and few had travelled this way and lived to tell of it.

It felt as though the coldest wind in the world blew from the heart of the mountains, and Sigmar was merely following it, like an explorer tracing the course of a river back to its source. At each fork in the landscape, Sigmar would strike out without hesitation, leading his army deeper and deeper into the unknown. Scouts reported signs of greenskins and other dangerous monsters dogging their course, but none dared attack so numerous a body of warriors.

As the army camped in a rocky gully and darkness fell upon the camp like an unwelcome guest, Redwane said, 'I've been thinking.'

'That bodes ill,' said Pendrag with a forced smile. Sigmar chuckled and threw a handful of twigs on the fire. Myrsa held his hands out to the flames as the dead wood caught light.

'Thinking about what?' asked Sigmar.

'That burial we saw yesterday. I mean, what was that all about with the axe? Did that man hate his wife?'

'Far from it,' said Myrsa. 'He must have loved her dearly.'

'So that's what passes for love in the north, chopping your dead wife's head off. Nice.'

'He was making sure she wouldn't return from the dead,' replied Pendrag. 'Her husband will take the head away and burn it out of sight of the grave so that if an evil spirit possesses the body it will spend eternity searching for something it can never find.'

'Don't they have gardens of Morr in these parts? We're miles from the nearest village. It must have taken them hours to get here.'

'I think they buried her here *because* it is far from their home,' said Sigmar. 'Putting her face down in the ground at a crossroads means she will not know which way to go to wreak havoc among the living. And if some evil spirit lingers in her flesh and wakes, it will dig its way downwards, never to return to the world above.'

Redwane shook his head and pulled his cloak tighter around his body. 'Damn, but whatever happened to dying and just going on to Ulric's hall? It's not right having to do all this stuff to a body to make sure you get to the next world.'

'Better that than coming back as one of the walking dead,' pointed out Sigmar. 'Better that than having to destroy a dead thing that wears the face of a loved one. If this necromancer is as powerful as Hauke claimed, then there are men in this army who may well have to face their sword-brothers in battle. The warriors Myrsa sent into these mountains may well be waiting for us.'

'There's a happy thought,' grumbled Redwane. 'A man ought to die with a sword in his hand and be carried by the battle maidens to Ulric's hall. I don't want to die in these mountains and come back as one of the walking dead. You hear me? I want you to promise me you'll make sure of that.'

Pendrag reached out and shook Redwane by the shoulder.

'If it comes to it, I'll cut your head off myself and burn your body to ash,' he said.

'You'd do that for me?'

'Just say the word,' promised Pendrag. 'What manner of sword-brother would do less?'

Sigmar hid a smile and idly drew shapes in the dust around the fire. It felt good to sit around the fire with his friends, yet he could not shake the feeling that the words spoken in jest carried fears that ran deeper than any of them cared to admit.

'But to do that to your woman? Or to have her do that to me?' said Redwane. 'I don't know if I could do that to a woman I loved.'

Pendrag snorted. '*Have* you ever loved a woman? I thought you bedded one and then moved on to the next conquest.'

'Guilty as charged,' agreed Redwane. 'But that was in my younger, wilder days.'

'So are you saying you're in your older, more settled days now?' asked Myrsa.

'Not exactly, but you know what I mean. If I was ever to find a woman I wanted to fasten hands with over the Oathstone, then I don't know if I could ever do that to her.'

'If you ever wanted to fasten hands with a woman, we'd know the End Times were upon us,' said Pendrag.

'I'm serious,' snapped Redwane, and Sigmar saw that the undercurrent of fear that gnawed at the nerves of every man was preying especially hard on the young White Wolf. It was easy to forget that, for all his skill in battle, Redwane was still only twenty-five; old enough to be considered a veteran, yet still young enough to feel the immortality of youth.

Close to home in the warm lands of the south, it was easy to put thoughts of mortality from the mind, but here in the mountains, with each breath of cold wind promising death, such thoughts were harder to ignore.

Like Sigmar, Redwane had risked his life many times, but the fear that wormed its way into the mind was not of falling in battle but the slow, lingering death that came at the end of years of pain and suffering, indignity and madness.

To a warrior, death was something to be faced and defeated in battle, not something that came with talons of age and infirmity. With the cold dread of mortality hanging on every icy breath, the stark fact that they would one day die seemed achingly, horribly close.

Redwane shook his head and stared deep into the fire.

'I've loved a lot of women,' he said, 'but I never found one I wanted to spend the rest of my life with. Or, if I'm honest, one I thought would want to spend her life with me.' He looked deeper into the mountains and pulled his cloak tighter. 'But here? Here I'm getting to think that carousing is not what I want anymore. It might be time to find a good woman and sire strong sons. Don't you feel that?'

Sigmar studied the faces of his friends and knew that Redwane's words had cut through the armour protecting their souls. None of them had ever expected Redwane to speak such words, and they had been caught unawares and unguarded.

'I've felt that,' said Pendrag bitterly, 'but I do not believe in love. It is for fools and poets.'

Sigmar felt the pain behind his sword-brother's words, and wanted tell him that a life lived without knowing love was a bland and tasteless thing, but the memory of Ravenna appeared in his mind, and the black mood of the mountains crushed the words in his heart.

Myrsa nodded in understanding, looking at each man in turn. 'The role of Warrior Eternal denies me the chance of a wife and sons, but I have made my peace with a life lived alone.'

Redwane looked over at Sigmar, but before Pendrag could silence the question that he saw was coming, the White Wolf said, 'What about you, Sigmar? Have you never thought of finding a wife? An Emperor needs heirs after all.'

A heavy silence greeted Redwane's words, but Sigmar nodded.

'Yes, Redwane, I have,' he said. 'Once, I loved a woman. She was called Ravenna.'

'What happened to her?'

'Ulric's bones, Redwane!' stormed Pendrag. 'You are a prize fool and no mistake. Can you not leave well alone?'

Sigmar raised a calming hand. 'Don't blame the lad, Pendrag. He would only have been a boy when it happened, and no one dares speak of it now.'

Sigmar looked across the fire and said, 'Ravenna was a beauty of the Unberogen, and I loved her from the first moment I saw her. She loved me for all my faults and knew me better than I knew myself.'

'Did you marry her?'

'I was going to,' said Sigmar. 'I promised her that when I was king I would marry her, but she died before I could. Her brother Gerreon had a twin named Trinovantes, and when he died at Astofen Bridge, Gerreon blamed me. I thought he had accepted what happened to his twin, had accepted the truth of it, but he nursed his hatred in a secret place in his heart and almost killed me as I swam with his sister. He failed to slay me, but he murdered Ravenna.'

'No!' cried Redwane. 'Gods, man, I'm sorry, I didn't mean to...'

'From that moment, I vowed I would love this land and no other,' said Sigmar. 'I have devoted my life to the Empire and it will be my bride, my one abiding love. I swore this on Unberogen soil before the tomb of my father, and I shall live and die by that oath. I know that there is talk of my taking a wife, for people think I must sire an heir for the Empire. They lament a future without me, but they do not know the strength that lies within this land and its people. They do not see that what I am building is greater than any one man. After all, I did not found the Empire for it to become the possession of a single dynasty.'

Sigmar stood and looked at each of his friends in turn, and none doubted the sincerity of his words. 'The Empire is an idea that lives in the hearts of all men and women who dwell within it, and when

I am dead and gone, the Empire will live on in them. For they are all Sigmar's heirs.'

THE WELCOME LIGHT of morning crept over the hills, only reluctantly pushing back the darkness and spreading down the icy valleys and jagged gorges of the mountains. Fires that had burned through the night were doused, and the army swiftly broke camp after a meal of warm oats. Sigmar's banner was raised, and his warriors followed him as he marched purposefully into a snow-shawled valley that loomed like a vast, columned gateway.

Six days had passed since the army had left Middenheim, and the friendly rivalry that passed back and forth between the warriors was forgotten as each man fought against unbidden thoughts of crows pecking at his eyes and worms gnawing at his decaying flesh.

The valley was deathly silent, the walls glistening with spears of ice and swallowing the sound of marching feet and the clatter of armour. The sun did not reach to the base of the valley and the army climbed in shadow, what little relief had been provided by daybreak crushed by the deadening gloom. Clouds of dark-pinioned birds circled overhead, ravens and other scavengers of the battlefield. Their raucous cries echoed in the narrow valley and scraped like blades down each man's nerves.

Pendrag came alongside Sigmar. His sword-brother had lost weight since the march had begun, and Sigmar nodded as Pendrag slapped a hand on his pauldron.

'That's fine armour,' Pendrag said. 'You could work a whole lifetime and never have enough coin to buy such a gift.'

'Alaric is a master of his craft,' said Sigmar.

'That he is,' agreed Pendrag. 'Do you know the runes worked into the metal?'

'Kurgan told me they were runes of protection crafted centuries ago by a runesmith called Blackhammer. He said they would do me more good on their own than the finest suit of armour crafted by man.'

Pendrag patted his mail shirt. 'The dwarfs do not have a high opinion of our metalworking skills, do they? You remember that breastplate I crafted for Wolfgart's hand fastening ceremony, the one with the gold embossing and fluted rims?'

'Of course, it is a masterful piece.'

'Alaric told me it was "serviceable", perhaps the equal of an apprentice's work in his forge.'

'High praise indeed,' noted Sigmar.

'That's what I thought,' said Pendrag wistfully. 'It has been too long since he has visited Reikdorf.'

'I think he has his hands full making the swords King Kurgan promised. And you know Alaric – he will not rush their creation.'

'He won't, no. Perhaps we might arrange to visit Karaz-a-Karak?' ventured Pendrag.

Sigmar shrugged. 'I do not think the mountain folk encourage visitors, my friend. Except maybe other dwarfs, and even then there are all manner of formalities before they are granted permission to journey to a hold. Why are you so keen to see Master Alaric?'

'No reason,' said Pendrag. 'He is my friend and I miss him, that's all.'

They lapsed into silence for a while, the trudging monotony of the climb and the constant twilight wearing at their spirits like a millstone. Sigmar found his hatred towards this necromancer growing with every mile that passed.

'Why would anyone desire this?' asked Sigmar, looking around at the bleak, inescapable hostility of the landscape.

'Desire what?'

'This,' replied Sigmar, sweeping his arms out to encompass the sepulchral valley. 'I understand the lust for power, but surely if a man can cast spells and use magic, he would live somewhere less dismal. I mean, why would any man choose a life that sees him banished to a place like this?'

'The path of the necromancer necessitates a solitary existence,' said Pendrag. 'To violate the dead breaks one of our most sacred taboos. You do not do such things where people can find out about it, so you live where no one else wants to.'

'I suppose,' agreed Sigmar, 'but that leads to another question.'

'Which is?'

'Why be a necromancer at all?'

'To live forever?' suggested Pendrag. 'To cheat death?'

'If living like this is cheating death, I would sooner not bother. Even if you *were* to cheat death, is what you would have really life? Living like this, shunned by your fellow man and surrounded by corpses? No, if that is what living forever entails, then I want no part of it.'

'They say that some men are drawn to necromancy in the hope of bringing back a loved one,' said Pendrag, 'that they do not begin as evil men.'

'Maybe that is true, but to delve into such darkness can only drive a man to madness. I loved Ravenna and I lost her, but I would not dream of using the dark arts to bring her back.'

'Not all men are like you, Sigmar,' said Pendrag, casting an uneasy glance towards the tombstone sky. 'To fear death is not unusual.'

'Trust me, Pendrag, I am in no rush to find death, but I do not fear it. Death is natural, it is part of what makes us human. That is why we must strive to make every moment special, because it might be our last. Some men live in fear their whole lives. They fear to fail, so they do nothing. You can hide from danger all your life, but you will still die. What matters is how we make use of the gift of life, bettering ourselves and helping our fellow man wherever we can. That is why this Morath is so dangerous: he lives only for himself and contributes nothing of value to the world. In the realm of the necromancer, nothing grows, nothing lives and nothing dies. And stagnation is death.'

'So is *starvation*,' said Pendrag, looking over his shoulder at the six hundred men who marched through the valley behind them. 'Between what the pack ponies and the men are carrying, we only have food enough for another two days march into the mountains. If we're going to find this Brass Keep, we'd better do it soon.'

'We will,' said Sigmar, feeling the deathly chill of the cold wind blowing from the centre of the mountains grow stronger, reaching into his chest and caressing his heart with icy talons. 'We are close, I know we are.'

'I hope you are right,' said Pendrag. 'I don't know how much more of this I can take.'

The shadows moved across the valley sides, the only visible indication that time was moving on at all. After a mid-afternoon stop for food and water, Sigmar's warriors continued on through the valley as the ground became even more broken and uneven.

Jagged rocks tore at tunics and flesh as the day lengthened and the slopes of the mountain grew steeper. The unnatural silence of the mountains loomed over everyone, broken only by the pebbles that skittered from ledges high above. Pallid shapes darted between narrow clefts carved in the mountainside by scouring winds, and arrows loosed at the shapes clattered harmlessly on the rocks before Myrsa ordered his men to stop wasting their shafts.

The valley began to widen ahead of a sharp northward turn around a black spur of knife-sharp rock, perhaps a mile distant. A gust of cold air, like the last laugh of a suicide, swept the landscape, and Sigmar knew that he had reached its source.

'Raise the banners,' said Sigmar. 'Assume battle march formation.'

'Battle formation?' queried Redwane, looking up to the sky. 'But it's nearly dark.'

'Do it,' said Sigmar. 'We are here.'

The White Wolf nodded, and the word was passed along the line. No sooner was the order given than the warriors moved smoothly into formation. Swords were bared, and a fresh sense of purpose infused every warrior. Sigmar loosed Ghal-maraz from his belt and a squadron of White Wolves formed up around him.

With Pendrag at their head, the Count's Guard took up position on the right, while Myrsa led the warriors of Middenheim on Sigmar's left. Moving at a swift yet economical pace, the army marched towards the black spur, shields locked and swords held at the ready.

As Myrsa's warriors reached the turn, he slowed their pace as the Count's Guard wheeled around it, the entire shallow wedge of the army swinging around like a closing gate with the spur as the hinge.

Beyond the spur, the landscape fell away in rippling slopes of icy rock towards a wide crater gouged in the heart of the mountains, thousands of yards in diameter. The ground shone like a mirror, a vast and stagnant lake that had frozen in an instant during some forgotten age. Broken spires and strange collections of jumbled stone jutted from the frozen lake, like stalagmites in a cave. Towering over this grim and frozen tableau was a mighty edifice that could only be Morath's lair.

'Ulric preserve us,' breathed Redwane at the sight of the gleaming fortress.

The name Lukas Hauke had given it was apt, for it shone in the last light of day as though sheathed in brass. Its towers were tall and slender, and its walls were smooth and fashioned with great cunning. A great iron portal wreathed in sharpened spikes barred entry, and spectral light shone from every shuttered tower and lofty turret of the gatehouse. At the heart of the dreadful castle, a single tower of pearlescent stone rose above all others, and from it shone a pulsing dead light, a glow that drained life from the landscape instead of illuminating it. Sigmar felt a powerful attraction to the tower, as though this were the source of the cold wind that had led him to this place.

He had expected to find the creatures of Morath waiting for them, but the crater was empty, unnaturally so, for even the carrion birds that had followed them from the foothills kept their counsel. Thousands of black-feathered ravens observed his army from perches high on glittering spires of icy rock, and Sigmar sensed their dreadful appetite.

These birds had gathered in anticipation of a feast.

'Move out,' ordered Sigmar, and the army advanced down the icy slopes towards the dreadful Brass Keep. The ground underfoot was slippery and treacherous, and many warriors lost their footing as they made their way down to the icy plain.

Darkness gathered over the fortress, bruised clouds heavy with rain and lightning. A fell wind issued from the far reaches of the valley, and Sigmar tasted the foulness of dead things at the back of his throat. As the army marched out onto the frozen surface of the lake, Sigmar gasped in astonishment as he saw a sunken city lying far beneath its glassy surface.

As though he looked through the clearest glass instead of ice, Sigmar saw an ancient metropolis, grander and more massive than Reikdorf, with towers and structures taller even than the Fauschlag Rock. Cries of astonishment and fear spread along the battle line as his warriors saw the same thing.

Sigmar had never seen its like in all the realms of man, though it was clearly a city designed and raised by the artifice of his race. The towering buildings were colossal and defied understanding, such was their magnificence. Enormous temples, sprawling palaces and rearing statues filled the city, and its grandeur stole Sigmar's breath. Yet for all its glory, it was a dead place, a mockery of a city where lives were lived and dramas, both vital and banal, were played out on a daily basis. As he formed this last thought, the image wavered for a second, as though the city was no more substantial than morning mist.

'What is this place?' asked Redwane, still keeping pace with the battle line as he stared in horror as the sunken city. Collapsed portions of the city's tallest towers jutted through the ice, lying in crumbled piles of fallen masonry, sad remnants of something wondrous that had passed into ruin and decay.

'I do not know,' answered Sigmar. 'Perhaps this is Mourkain? When Lukas Hauke said its name, I did not know whether it was a place or a person. Now I know.'

'Mourkain? Never heard of it,' said Redwane, shaking his head as though to deny the city's existence. 'Surely if there was a city here, we'd know about it?'

'Perhaps,' said Sigmar, tearing his eyes from the ghostly city's wreckage as a shimmering mist formed around the battlements of the gleaming castle. 'I think maybe that we are seeing an echo of something that has long since vanished from the face of the world. Hauke said that Morath survived the doom of Mourkain, so maybe this is his way of remembering it.'

'What happened to it?'

'I will be sure to ask him,' said Sigmar dryly.

'Point taken,' said Redwane, grinning and hefting his hammer. The White Wolf's earlier fears had receded in the face of imminent battle, and looking along the line of determined faces of his warriors, his heart soared to see such strength. The fear that had dogged the army's every step into the mountains fled in the face of their courage.

Sigmar felt a cold gaze fasten upon him, and looked towards the dread tower at the heart of the castle as Ghal-maraz grew hotter in his grip.

Atop the bone-white tower stood a figure wreathed in black, a slit of darkness against the sky that seemed to swallow the light around it. Robes of night billowed in ethereal winds, and even from this distance, Sigmar saw the pale, ravaged features of a thing more dead than alive. The necromancer carried an ebony staff, and upon his skull-like brow he wore a glittering golden crown that seemed to pulse in time with Sigmar's heartbeat.

'Morath,' hissed Sigmar as the dark sorcerer raised his staff. A withering light pulsed from the ice, the rocks and the very air, as though some ancient rite were nearing completion.

'Stand firm!' shouted Sigmar, his voice echoing from the valley sides to bolster his warriors' resolve. Shouts of alarm came from both flanks, and Sigmar saw scores of shambling horrors climbing from the ruins of the towers that jutted through the ice. Loathsome cadavers in tattered robes and rotted flesh lurched and stumbled from the ruins in their dozens, and then in their scores.

Their armour was rusted from the long centuries that had passed since their deaths, yet their swords and spears were still deadly. Skeletal fists punched through the ice, and armoured warriors of bone hauled their fleshless bodies upwards, before turning grinning skulls upon their warm-bodied foes with dreadful malevolence. As though commanded by a living general, they marched in hideous lockstep, forming sword-bands like those facing them.

Sigmar's army halted at so terrifying a sight, for these abominations were an affront to the living, a dreadful violation of the natural order of things. The fear that had been quashed by courage returned to tear at each warrior's heart, and they could not take so much as a single step towards the dead things.

But that was not the worst of it.

The iron gateway of Morath's keep swung open like the maw of hell, and an unliving host of armoured warriors marched out in dreadful unison. A pall of fear went before them, and a low moan of anguish swept through Sigmar's army as the dead warriors in silver armour and bloody robes drew relentlessly closer.

Sigmar's flesh crawled and his bladder tightened at the sight of the hideous warriors, for they wore the heraldry of Ulric and of Morr. The flesh decayed and rotted on their bones, but they were not so long dead that that their faces were unrecognisable. Brothers and sons marched at the command of the hateful necromancer, and every man in Sigmar's host felt piteous horror at the sight of their fallen comrades.

'Men of the Empire!' shouted Sigmar, his voice carrying across the field of ice, and striking home into the hearts of his men like arrows of truth. 'You are the bravest warriors in a land where bravery runs in every man's blood! You have climbed into these mountains in the face of fear, and you have reached this place of death by the iron in your souls and the fire in your hearts! Though they may wear the bodies of our friends, these monsters are not your sword-brothers. Their souls are bound to the will of an evil man, and only you can free them to travel onwards to Ulric's hall. We march beneath the Dragon Banner, so let not your blade hesitate from destroying these dread foes, for theirs shall seek to bring you down!'

A ragged cheer greeted Sigmar's words, desultory and half-hearted, but he had broken the paralysing terror that held his men rooted to the spot. The fear of this dead host still cast a dark pall over his warriors, but swelling embers of courage were steadily pushing it back.

Sigmar looked up at the necromancer's tower as the hosts of the living and the dead marched into battle. The golden crown at Morath's brow shone like a beacon of unimaginable power.

'The cowardly sorcerer skulks atop his tower,' shouted Sigmar. 'I shall tear the crown from his brow and take if for my own!'

TWELVE
The Battle of Brass Keep

THE DEAD WERE silent, no battle cries or bellows to a watching god for strength of arm or divine protection. Somehow that was worse. When man fought man there was hatred and anger, emotions that both clouded the mind and granted strength, but these abominations fought with none of that. They came towards the army of men with singular determination, their rotten meat faces and skeletal grins terrible, giving each warrior a glimpse of the fate that awaited them should they fall.

Sigmar knew of no other way to lead his warriors save by example, and he lifted Ghal-maraz high as he charged towards the living dead.

'For Ulric and the wolves of the north!' he proclaimed.

The White Wolves followed him, howling like their namesakes, their hammers swinging. Pendrag's Count's Guard charged the enemy with their greatswords held high, shouting oaths that would make a Jutonsryk docker blush. The Middenland warriors on the left each shouted their own battle cry and then slammed into the decaying creatures spilling from the tumbled ruins of the towers.

A skeletal warrior stabbed a spear at Sigmar, but the thrust was slow, and he smashed his hammer down on the fleshless skull. The creature dropped, its bones falling apart as the power holding it together was undone. Another came at him, but he spun away from its attack and smashed its ribcage to splinters with an overhand sweep. The White Wolves fought all around him, their hammers breaking bones and skulls with every blow.

The dead were no match for these brave warriors, but there seemed no end to them. As each creature fell, two or more pushed forward to take its place. Shambling creatures with pallid skin sloughing from their bones crawled from the wreckage of the city, and Sigmar saw hundreds more climbing the ruins beneath the ice towards the surface.

A rusted lance hooked around his pauldron and hauled him off balance. He swung Ghal-maraz and crushed the pelvis of the lance wielder, but his feet slipped on the ice. Sigmar landed heavily, and no sooner was he down than the dead were upon him. Axes and swords chopped downwards with mechanical precision, and he rolled and blocked to keep them from him.

He kicked out, breaking legs and kneecaps, but still they came on. A spear jabbed downwards and skidded from his breastplate as a bony foot stamped down on his face. He twisted aside and swung his hammer in a wide arc, splintering thighs and creating some space around himself.

'Here!' shouted Redwane, holding his hand out. The White Wolf had slung his hammer, but still held Sigmar's banner aloft. Sigmar gripped Redwane's wrist and hauled himself upright, careful not to spill them both to the ice.

'My thanks,' said Sigmar. 'Lost my balance.'

'So I saw. Lots of them, eh?'

'Too many for you?' asked Sigmar.

'Never,' grinned Redwane, unhooking his hammer and plunging back into the fray.

Pale light, evil and suffused with emerald, bathed the fighting in a lambent glow. A flickering radiance seemed to dance around the blades of each warrior, both living and dead. The dread moon had risen, its rough surface leering down at the carnage beneath it, and a shiver of fear passed down Sigmar's spine as he saw that it was as full as it had been when they had fought in the swamps around Marburg.

White Wolves stood sentinel over him, and Sigmar nodded to them as he set off after Redwane. The fighting wedge of the army, with the wolves at the centre, was a spear thrust at the gateway to Morath's fortress, with the flanks keeping the tip from becoming bogged down. Sigmar looked for his standards, quickly finding them in the morass of fighting warriors.

Beneath the Dragon Banner, the Count's Guard fought with killing sweeps of their enormous blades, cleaving great paths through the dead. Each warrior fought his own battle: for the reach of such swords ensured that no warrior dared fight nearby for fear of being struck. To fight in such a manner was courageous and heroic, but to wield a greatsword was heavy work and rapidly sapped a warrior's strength. How much longer would Pendrag's warriors be able to keep pushing on?

To his left, Sigmar saw Myrsa battling a host of black wolves, their mouldering fur and decaying flesh hanging in tatters from rotten bones. The wolves fought with savage strength and speed, and only Myrsa's superlative skill with his enormous hammer kept them at bay. Fangs flashed and bloody jaws snapped as Myrsa's men were torn down and devoured.

The blue and white banner of the Fauschlag Rock still flew proudly over the fighting, but Sigmar saw that the men of the north were in danger of being overrun. The ferocity of the frenzied wolves was slaughtering them, but they refused to break. With the Dragon Banner raised, every man understood that against such a dreadful foe there could be no retreat.

It was fight or die.

Myrsa fought in the centre of a circle of snarling, snapping wolves and the hag woman's warning returned to him at the thought of the Warrior Eternal being brought down.

'Emperor's Guard, with me!' shouted Sigmar, pushing through the host of fighting men towards Myrsa. Armoured warriors of bone fought to reach Sigmar, but deadly strikes from Ghal-maraz and the weapons of his guards smashed them down.

Sigmar battered a path towards Myrsa through the dead warriors as the clouds above the Brass Keep vomited up arcing bolts of lightning that slammed down and exploded in purple sheets of fire. Men were hurled skyward as bolt after bolt struck the ice with shattering force. He risked a glance towards the keep, and saw Morath with his hands raised to the heavens, laughing insanely as his staff crackled with the same purple lightning that smote his warriors.

Wolves leapt and bit as they pushed into the ranks of Myrsa's warriors, tearing with diseased claws and ripping flesh from bones with jagged fangs. The Middenheim banner bearer had no time to scream as a wolf's jaws fastened on his head and crushed his skull with a single bite. The snarling wolf swallowed its morsel, and a great wail went up from the northern warriors as their standard fell towards the ice.

Sigmar leapt forward and swept up the banner before its silken fabric touched the ground. He raised it high before hammering its sharpened base into the ice.

'The banner still stands,' he shouted. 'And so shall you!'

A pair of wolves launched themselves at him, but Sigmar leapt to meet them. Ghal-maraz smashed the spine of the first and clove through its dead heart. The second beast's enormous jaws snapped at him, but he dived beneath them, rolling to his feet and gathering up the fallen banner bearer's sword. As the beast turned to face him, Sigmar thrust the blade between its jaws. The wolf howled and dropped to the ice, its flesh crumbling and decaying as it fell.

Given fresh heart by his courage, Myrsa's warriors fought back against the wolves, driving them onto the spears of their brothers with flaming torches and wild charges.

Myrsa came alongside him, his white armour streaked with blood and torn with deep gouges. Yellowed claws and gore-flecked fangs were buried in the metal of his breastplate. The Warrior Eternal's hair had come unbound, and he looked every inch the northern barbarian warrior from which his tribe descended.

'Tough fight,' said Myrsa.

'It's not done yet,' replied Sigmar, nodding towards the tower from which Morath brought down yet more bolts of lightning. 'You with me?'

Myrsa nodded and swung his hammer up to his shoulder.

'Always, my lord,' he said.

'Then let us finish this!'

PENDRAG'S AXE CHOPPED through the face of a decaying corpse, the stagnant ooze that remained in its veins spattering his armour. He spat flecks of rotten meat as he pushed onwards through the shambling horde of the dead. They fell easily to the hacking blows of the Count's Guard, but they staggered from the ruins of fallen towers without end.

His arm ached from hewing through the wet bodies of men and women who had once depended on him for protection, and though every creature slain was a soul freed, each one was a rusty nail in his heart. They pressed in on him and the Count's Guard with grasping fingers and teeth as their only weapons, and such a contest of arms would have been ludicrous but for the fact that there was no give in them.

Any normal foe would have long since broken and run from the deadly blades of his warriors, but with no thoughts of their own, enslaved to the will of Morath, they would never retreat. Only when their dead bodies were destroyed would they stop fighting.

More of the dead things fell to his axe, and he looked to his left to ensure that the speed of his warriors' advance was keeping pace with the White Wolves. He couldn't see Sigmar, but knew he would be in the thick of the battle where the fighting was heaviest. Across the valley, the banner of the Fauschlag Rock still flew, and Pendrag felt a moment's guilt that he was not fighting beneath it.

Sigmar had asked him to carry the Dragon Banner, and Pendrag could not refuse that honour, for only warriors of unbreakable courage were offered such a duty. He looked up at the banner, its once white fabric dyed red with the blood of the men who fought with it as their declaration of courage. The dragon was stitched in gold thread, and it flickered in the light of the moon and the flashing bolts of lighting that battered Sigmar's army.

A chill wind swept over Pendrag, and his body was suddenly gripped in a deathly cold embrace, as though he were drowning in the icy lake beneath him. The disgusting, cadaverous monsters moved aside, and a band of armoured warriors with mighty two-handed swords that shimmered with eerie light marched towards the Count's Guard. Clad in rusted armour of bronze and dark iron, these grim sentinels of death advanced beneath a banner of deepest black that rippled with dark winds and heart-stopping cold.

Spectral blades flashed as the dead warriors smashed into the Count's Guard. Where the corpse-things fought with mindless hunger, these creatures were skilled, and fought with all the deadly fury they had possessed while alive. Enormous blades flashed in the moonlight, and warriors, alive and dead, were cut down by brutal sweeps of long, heavy blades. Against the weight of the Count's Guards' greatswords, the rusted armour of the dead was no protection, and every blow smashed a skeletal warrior to shards.

Yet the blades of the dead were no less lethal and the dead warriors struck with a power that belied their rotten frames. Darkly-glowing swords cut into the northlanders, and each man that fell died with his head hacked from his shoulders. The swords of the dead warriors flashed with a speed that would have been impossible for a mortal man, each blow precisely weighted and aimed to kill with a single stroke.

A towering warrior in corroded bronze armour coated in verdigris fought at their centre, the flesh withered to his bones and a light from beyond the grave flickering in the pools of his eye sockets. Armoured in the fashion of hundreds of years ago, Pendrag knew that he faced one of the ancient warrior kings of old, a great leader interred within a hidden barrow beneath the earth, only to be torn from his eternal rest by the magic of the necromancer. The undead king's sword glimmered with frost, and Pendrag could feel it hunger for his neck.

Pendrag slammed the Dragon Banner into the ice and hefted his axe in both hands.

'You are mine!' Pendrag bellowed, holding the double-bladed axe towards the dead king.

The mighty king heard the challenge and could no more ignore it than could a living warrior. He dragged his shimmering blade from the chest of his latest victim, and charged Pendrag with a cold fire burning in the sockets of his skull. The sword swept up, a blur of rusted bronze, and Pendrag barely had time to block it, twisting his axe to sweep the blade aside. Pendrag spun around the king and swung his axe at his back, but the blade was blocked as the warrior impossibly brought his sword around to parry the blow.

The leathery flesh of the ancient king creaked as he smiled in triumph. The jaw gaped and rancid breath, like gases expelled from the depths of a bog, enveloped Pendrag. He stumbled, retching, blinded by the rankness of the grave king's exhalation. He threw himself back and brought up his axe, knowing that an attack was coming. The king's sword slammed into his breastplate and smashed him from his feet. Pendrag lost his grip on his axe and skidded across the ice.

His silver fingers gouged the frozen lake as he hit something jammed in the ice that halted his slide. The ancient king of the dead walked towards him with measured paces, his sword raised to finish him off. Something red flapped above Pendrag's head, and he looked up to see the Dragon Banner, its bloody fabric shimmering in the light of the dread moon.

The dead king brought his sword up to take his head, as Pendrag wrenched the banner from the ice, rolling to his knees as the sword swept towards his neck. Pendrag launched himself forward with the bladed finial of the banner pole aimed at the heart of his deathly foe.

Both weapons struck at the same instant, the silver point of the banner pole plunging through the rusted mail of the ancient king's chest, and the dread blade slamming into Pendrag's neck. Bright light exploded before Pendrag's eyes as the dead king's sword struck the torque ring that Master Alaric of the dwarfs had given him many years ago. He screamed as the torque seared his skin, fighting to resist the dreadful power of the dead king's blade.

The silver point of the banner pole tore from the dead king's back, swiftly followed by the bloody banner as his weight dragged him deeper onto it. The balefire in his eyes guttered and died, the blood of heroes driving the fell animation from his long dead frame. With no trace of that power remaining, the king's body fell to pieces, the skeleton and armour clattering to the ice in a rain of bone and rusted bronze.

Pendrag let out an agonised breath, still holding the banner aloft, and reaching up to drag the deformed torque from his neck. Forged from the star-iron of the dwarfs and shaped with runic hammers, the metal was blisteringly hot. He dropped it to the ice, and it sank into the frozen surface of the lake in a cloud of boiling steam.

No sooner had the ancient king's body disintegrated than his skeletal guards began to fall apart. Bound to the service of their liege lord in death as in life, their souls fled the decaying shells in which they were trapped. Pendrag breathed a relieved sigh as the deadly warriors collapsed into piles of bone and iron. His warriors stood amid a billowing dust cloud, surrounded by the headless bodies of their comrades. Every blow the dead had struck had killed one of his warriors.

Pendrag planted the Dragon Banner, and used the pole to haul himself to his feet.

On the far left of the battlefield, Myrsa's warriors pushed onwards, hacking a gruesome path through a host of snapping wolves of rotten flesh and mangy fur. The warriors Myrsa led were rough and ready, yet their courage had seen them willingly follow their Emperor into the jaws of battle.

In the centre of the battlefield, the White Wolves battered their way onwards, yet Pendrag could still not see Sigmar in their midst.

The Count's Guard formed up around the banner he clutched tightly in his silver hand. He saw their expectant faces and, lifting the crimson banner high, he aimed it towards the gleaming walls of the necromancer's keep.

'Onwards!' he cried. 'For Sigmar and the Empire!'

* * *

FIGHTING SIDE-BY-SIDE, SIGMAR and Myrsa bludgeoned a path through the walking dead. The warriors of Middenheim followed their Emperor, wheeling around and pushing hard towards the gateway of the brass fortress. Before the great iron portal, dead warriors clad in the livery of Ulric and Morr awaited them.

Myrsa smashed another of the dead from its feet and took a moment to recover his breath. These monsters were without skill, but the horror of their very existence drained a man's spirit and will to fight. It took every ounce of his courage to stand firm in the face of these abominations.

Beside him, Sigmar fought with a fury and strength that put Myrsa in mind of the greatest heroes of ancient times: legendary warriors such as Ostag the Fell, Udose Ironskull or Crom Firefist. Ghal-maraz swung around the Emperor's body in a blur, and wherever it struck, a dead thing was destroyed. Its bones would fly apart, shattered into fragments, and the horrid animation in its eyes would be snuffed out.

Myrsa's skill with a warhammer was great indeed, but as hard as he fought, he could not match Sigmar's strength. The speed and precision with which Sigmar wielded Ghal-maraz was truly breathtaking, as though the weapon was a part of him, or had always *been* a part of him. Myrsa had heard the story of how the Emperor came to bear the hammer of the mountain king, but no dwarf had borne this hammer to such deadly effect. Myrsa knew with utter certainty that whoever had forged Ghal-maraz had done so in the knowledge that Sigmar would be the warrior to bear it.

Myrsa drove the head of his own hammer through the face of a rotten death mask of a creature wielding a butcher's cleaver as another came at him with a grain-cutter's sickle. These were not warriors, these were ordinary men and women enslaved to the will of the necromancer. Each blow he struck fanned the flames of Myrsa's rage, for these were *his* people, Middenlanders all, and they deserved a better end than this.

Myrsa swung his hammer up in readiness to face the next foe, but all that remained standing between them and the keep's black gateway was a shield wall of warriors in all too familiar tunics. Myrsa let out a low moan as he saw dozens of familiar faces before him, men he had despatched to seek out the source of the evil in the mountains.

Sigmar stood before the Ulrican templars and Knights of Morr, the dead-faced warriors as unbending and firm in the face of the enemy as they had always been. Myrsa's soul rebelled to see these fine, honourable warriors so debased.

He looked over at Sigmar, seeing the same revulsion that men who had fought against such evil were now forced to serve it. His fury overcame the dread he felt at seeing the dead walking, and Myrsa charged the shield-wall with his hammer swinging in wide, crushing sweeps.

The warriors of Middenland followed him, and he heard their wild yells as they pounded across the ice. He felt Sigmar charging alongside him, and the sheer presence of the Emperor steadied Myrsa's nerves. The shield wall loomed before them, the dead warriors bracing their shields and lifting their swords over the tops.

Living and dead clashed in a surging mass of armour and flesh. Myrsa blocked a sword thrust with the haft of his hammer and swung the head into the shield before him. Sigmar punched a huge hole in their ranks of the dead, and hurled himself into the gap, battering his way into the shield wall with a blend of skill and brute strength.

'With me!' he shouted. 'Break it open!'

Warriors poured after him, cutting their way into the formation. A normal shield wall would fly apart now, but the dead warriors remained where they were, cutting and stabbing and blocking as though nothing had happened.

A sword clanged on Myrsa's armour, slashing up to his helmet and tearing off his cheek guard. Blood sprayed from his chin as the blade caught him, and he spat a tooth.

He lost sight of Sigmar as the dead warriors closed ranks, pushing back with their shields and stabbing down with their blades. Though they were dead, their armour was still bright and their swords were still sharp. The ice was sticky with blood and entrails, fresh and rotten, and screams of pain echoed from the sides of the crater as men were killed by warriors who had once sworn to stand beside them.

Myrsa blocked a clumsy sword thrust and swung his hammer in an upward arc, tearing the shield – and the arm that bore it – from the dead warrior who carried it. He lifted his hammer high to finish the job, but his jaw dropped open and the blow never landed as he saw the face before him.

'Kristof?' he said, seeing the face of his sword-brother from before he had sworn the oath of the Warrior Eternal. Together they had fought greenskins in the Middle Mountains and Norsii raiders on the coast, and they had cleared whole swathes of the forest of hideous beast creatures. Kristof had saved his life on dozens of occasions, and Myrsa had repaid that debt many times. He had known there was a chance he would have to face his sword-brother on this march, but he had held out hope that Kristof would not have been among the risen dead.

He lowered his hammer.

'My sword-brother... What have they done to you?' he said.

Kristof's sword lanced out in answer, a blade that Myrsa himself had presented to him. He tried to dodge aside, but memories of his lost friend cost him dearly. The blade hammered home just below the breastplate, and mail links snapped as the north-forged iron plunged into his stomach. Myrsa cried out, feeling cold fire spread out from the wound, such that he felt as though he had been stabbed with a shard of winter.

He dropped to his knees, and cried out as the sword was torn from the wound. He looked up at the man with whom he had sworn eternal brotherhood, seeing that the sunken orbs of Kristof's eyes held no memory of him.

The pain of his wound faded, and Myrsa watched as the blade swept up and then down, moving as though in a dream. Metal flashed, and he heard a thunderous ring of metal on metal as a hammer of magnificent workmanship intercepted Kristof's blade. The hammer twisted the sword aside, and its wielder smashed the end of the haft into his former sword-brother's face. Decaying skull matter broke apart, and the hammer's reverse stroke shattered Kristof's ribcage to cleave his body in two.

Myrsa felt strong hands dragging him back, and saw Sigmar looking down at him with fearful eyes. The pain of his wound returned with a savage vengeance, and he cried out as he saw that his lap was soaked in warm blood.

'Take him!' ordered Sigmar, lying him down on the ice and shouting at some people that Myrsa could not see. Warriors of Middenheim knelt beside him, pulling open his armour and pressing their hands against his wound. The pain was indescribable, but was fading with each passing moment.

The clouds were dark and purple, split by crackling lightning, and Myrsa thought that it would be a shame to die with such an ugly sky looking down. Sigmar loomed above him, his face creased with lines of terrible fear.

The Emperor tore something from around his neck and pressed it into his hands. Myrsa craned his neck and saw that it was a bronze pendant, carved in the image of a gateway.

'Hold to this, Myrsa,' said Sigmar.

'Morr's gateway,' he whispered. 'Then it's my time? I'm dying?'

'No,' promised Sigmar, though he flinched at Myrsa's words. 'You will live. My father gave it to me when death hovered near and it kept me safe. It will do the same for you.'

Sigmar nodded to the men behind him. 'Do not let him die, no matter what occurs!'

Myrsa lifted the bronze pendant to his heart as Sigmar turned back to the battle.

SIGMAR RAN FOR the gateway of Brass Keep. Ragged bands of warriors followed him, all semblance of order gone in the desperate fighting to break the shield wall. The necromancer's citadel was breached, but not without cost. Hundreds of Sigmar's men were wounded, and even if he could defeat Morath, many would not survive to reach Middenheim.

This thought spurred Sigmar to greater speed, and he emerged from the darkened gateway into a cobbled plaza in the midst of the ancient keep. Within the walls, he saw that Brass Keep was no more real than the manufactured city beneath the ice. Like that drowned city, the keep was little more than a shimmering artifice created by Morath, a fiction to recall past glories and ancient triumphs.

The walls were simply walls, bereft of ramparts or stairs, and the towers were simply columns of stone without any means of accessing them. What buildings there were in the courtyard were simply ruined shells, little more than rubble and decay. Perhaps there had once been a mountain fortress here, but it had long since been forgotten by the race of men.

The only structure of any reality within the fortress was the tower fashioned from glistening, pearlescent stone. The pinnacle of the tower was haloed with dark lightning, the withering light from the necromancer's staff bathing the underside of the clouds with a demented, sickly aura. A spectral mist oozed from a skull-wreathed archway at the base of the tower, and hideous shapes writhed in its depths, howling souls bound to Morath's evil.

Sigmar ran towards the tower, and the warriors of the Fauschlag Rock came with him, their swords bright and their hearts hungry for vengeance on the hated necromancer. The mist twitched and danced as the spirits felt the lash of their master's will, and they streaked across the ice towards Sigmar's warriors like glittering comets.

Streamers of light surrounded them, and Sigmar saw they were the spirits of ghostly women, flying through the air as though moving underwater. They were beautiful, and he lowered his hammer, loath to strike out at a woman, even a ghostly one.

Then their jaws opened wide and they screamed.

Their dreadful wailing tore into Sigmar's soul with talons of fire. He dropped to his knees and Ghal-maraz fell as his hands flew to his ears to block the agonising sound. One of the she-creatures hovered in the air before him, robed in grave shrouds that swirled around its emaciated body with a life of their own. Its beauty sloughed from its remarkable face to reveal a fleshless skull with eyes that blazed with bitter hatred. A long mane of spine-like hair billowed behind it, and Sigmar instantly knew that these were not victims of Morath at all, but creatures of evil.

They shrieked around the men of the Empire, wailing in torment, seeking to wreak a measure of their eternal suffering upon the living. Ghostly claws ripped open armour, and shrieking laments cut deeper than any blade. Some men went mad with fear and fled back through the gateway, while others dropped down dead, their faces twisted into rictus masks of terror by nightmares only they could see.

Sigmar's mind filled with visions of lying beneath the earth with worms feeding on the diseased meat of his body. He cried out as he saw Ravenna, her once beautiful features ravaged by the creatures of the earth, her flesh bloated and rotten, blue and waxy as the world reclaimed her.

Tears streamed down his face and his heart thudded against his chest in terror. The pain in his head was beyond measure and he could feel his soul being prised from his mortal flesh with every shrieking wail.

Then he heard something else, a sound that spoke to his spirit and cut through the unnatural fear of these monstrous women. It was a sound of the wild, a sound that represented the core of who he was and everything for which he stood. It was the sound of the Empire and its patron.

It was the sound of wolves.

Sigmar twisted his head towards the sound to see a host of warriors pouring through the gateway: a mass of Pendrag's Count's Guard and Redwane's White Wolves. Armoured in silver and red, their wolfskin pelts and the Dragon Banner billowed as though they marched through a winter storm. Their wild hair was unbound, and each man howled with all the ferocity he could muster. Their wolf howls were like the pack of Ulric, and Sigmar saw his friends leading these brave men with a hammer and sword, hewing the dead with every stroke.

Freed from the awful, soul-shredding agony of the witches' shrieks, Sigmar bellowed in rage. The women howled again, but they had no power over the men of the Empire, for faith in Ulric had armoured their souls.

Pendrag ran towards him.

'Are you hurt?' he asked.

'No,' said Sigmar, pushing himself upright and forcing the visions of death from his mind.

'Here,' said Redwane, holding out Ghal-maraz. 'You dropped this.'

Sigmar took the warhammer, feeling a strange, jealous stab of power surge up his arm as he turned his gaze upon Morath's tower. The spirit-haunted mist was dispersing, as though blown by a strong wind, and the skull-wreathed archway yawned like the deepest cave in the rock of the earth. Only death awaited in such a place, and Sigmar felt his innards clench at the thought of venturing within.

Monstrous laughter boomed from above, and Sigmar's resolve hardened like dwarf-forged iron. He turned to his warriors and saw that same resolve in every face.

'Men of the Empire, today a necromancer dies,' he snarled.

THIRTEEN
A Warning Unheeded

DARKNESS SWALLOWED SIGMAR as he led his warriors into the tower, and icy winds swirled around him as though he had stepped into an ice cave far beneath the earth. The tower was hollow, a soaring cylinder that rose dizzyingly to a pale, deathly light. An unnatural, echoing silence filled the tower, the noise of the furious battle raging beyond its walls extinguished the instant he crossed the threshold.

Fallen headstones and crumbling tombs filled the tower's interior, a sprawling necropolis impossibly filled with thousands of graves. The earth on each was freshly turned, as though the dead had only recently been lowered beneath the ground, though some unknown instinct told Sigmar that whoever was buried here had been dead for centuries or more.

'I don't like the looks of this,' said Redwane, nodding towards the mass of graves.

'There are thousands of them,' added Pendrag.

Sigmar didn't answer, seeing a series of mossy, tread-worn steps cut from the inner circumference of the tower. The cold wind that had led him to this hidden valley gusted from above. It seemed to beckon him, as though daring him, or perhaps *needing* him to climb the steps. Sigmar sensed a power greater than any man could master in that sickly summons, but it was a summons he had come too far to ignore.

'This way,' he said. 'We cannot stop now, we have to push on!'

He ran towards the stairs with Redwane and Pendrag at his side. The White Wolf kept one eye on the gloomy necropolis, a faint green glow from the dread moon bathing the city in its hateful illumination.

'I suppose it's too much to hope that the dead things we fought outside were in these graves?' asked Redwane.

'I wouldn't count on it,' replied Pendrag as a hideous moaning filled the tower.

It sounded as though it came from somewhere deep underground, as if the earth itself were howling in its depths. Seconds later, the dirt upon the graves trembled, and the slabs sealing each tomb crashed to the ground with the grinding of stone on stone.

'Ulric's bones, doesn't this ever end?' hissed Redwane as grasping, skeletal hands clawed their way from beneath the ground and over the lips of dusty sepulchres. A fresh host of the living dead rose from their slumbers, warriors armed with short curving swords and clad in rusted plate of a style that Sigmar had never seen. Elaborately crafted with sweeping curves and horned spikes, it seemed that they were designed for intimidation as much as protection. These warriors had last made war thousands of years ago.

'There's too many of them,' said Redwane. 'We can't fight our way through them all.'

Sigmar looked up the curving spiral of the stairs towards the nimbus of light that gathered at the top of the tower.

'Maybe we will not have to,' he said.

'What do you mean?' asked Pendrag as the ancient warriors shuffled and dragged their rotten carcasses towards the waiting men of the Empire.

'Morath is up there, and with him, the source of his power,' said Sigmar. 'The priests of Morr told me that without the will of the necromancer binding them, these wretched souls will return to the realm of the dead where they belong.'

Redwane nodded, as though that were the most natural thing in the world. He shifted his grip on his hammer and nodded again, taking a deep breath.

'Then go,' said the White Wolf, hauling warriors into position to form a rough battle line at the bottom of the stairs. 'We will hold these dead things back. Get to the necromancer and bury your hammer in his skull!'

* * *

SIGMAR AND PENDRAG took the stairs two at a time, pushing upwards without pause for breath or any words. Already tired from the march through the mountains and the battle on the ice, Sigmar's thighs burned with exertion, yet he did not dare stop. The sound of clashing blades and screams drifted up from below.

Pendrag had refused to let Sigmar face Morath alone, and his sword-brother puffed and panted as he followed behind. He still clutched the Dragon Banner, and Sigmar was reassured by his brother's unwillingness to be parted from it. To fight the necromancer with such a potent symbol at their side would send a clear message that Sigmar was in no mood for mercy.

The fear that held sway over the battlefield was concentrated and distilled within the tower, a black dread that sank down from above like blood in water. Shadows howled and spun in the gloom, faceless phantoms that swirled like flocks of crows. Each time the hungry shadows swooped towards the two climbers, Pendrag held the Dragon Banner high, and they screeched and spun away from its power.

Sigmar did not know what that power was, but was grateful to whatever enchantments had been woven into the banner... or to whatever it had acquired in the course of the battle.

He glanced over his shoulder, feeling his armour and hammer weigh heavily upon him. Every step he took towards the top of the tower, the heavier they became. His limbs ached and he fought the urge to give up. He was exhausted, his body and mind pushed beyond the limits of human endurance. A sibilant, voiceless imperative urged him to rest, to lay down his burdens and accept that there was no more he could do. He fought it with every scrap of his will.

Sigmar gritted his teeth and put his head down. When he had climbed the mountain to face the dragon ogre Skaranorak, he had concentrated on simply putting one foot in front of the other, and that single-mindedness served him as well now as it had then. Even so, his steps were leaden, each one a small victory.

He heard Pendrag's laboured breath and knew that his sword-brother was suffering as he was. The tower darkened until all Sigmar could see was the faint glow from the rune-carved haft of Ghal-maraz. The climb was sapping Sigmar's strength, draining his vitality and feeding every dark thought that lurked in his mind, telling him he was too weak, too stupid and too *mortal* to ever succeed. Only by embracing the power of dark magic could any man hope to cheat death and see his labours truly bear fruit, for what ambition of any worth could be satisfied in the span of a single life?

Sigmar shut out that voice, that damnable voice of doubt that lodged like a parasite in every man's heart and chipped away at his resolve. *Don't bother trying anything, for all your dreams are dust,* it said. *It is pointless to struggle, for in a hundred years no one will remember you.*

'No,' hissed Sigmar. '*I* will be remembered.'

Mocking laughter rang from the walls, and Sigmar fought against the arrogant superiority that he heard in the echoes. *You will fail and be forgotten,* said the laughter. *Give in now.*

'If failure is so certain, why do you work so hard to make me believe it?' he cried.

Behind him, Pendrag let out a soft moan, and Sigmar felt warmth at his brow where the crown fashioned by Alaric slotted neatly over his helmet.

'I may fail and, in time I *will* die, but I am not afraid of that!' Sigmar shouted at the oppressive, smothering blackness. 'I am not afraid to fail. I only fear not to try!'

With every word, the gloom lifted, until he could once again see the steps beneath his feet and the glowing light at the top of the tower. Barely a dozen steps lay between him and a square-cut opening. The sickly light and cold wind that had guided him here shone like a hopeless beacon at the end of the world.

Sigmar looked down to see Pendrag at his back, blinking and letting out short, hiking breaths, as though awaking from a dreadful nightmare.

'Whatever he's telling you, don't believe it,' said Sigmar.

Pendrag looked up at him through tear-filled eyes. 'He told me of my death.'

Sigmar saw the terror in Pendrag's eyes and shook his head.

'All men die, Pendrag, it takes no sorcery to know that,' he said. 'If that is the best this necromancer can conjure, then we have nothing to fear.'

Pendrag looked past him at the square of light at the top of the stairs. His face crumpled in self-loathing.

'I can't.' he said. 'I'm afraid.'

Sigmar came down the stairs to Pendrag and gripped his shoulder.

'It is Morath who should fear us,' he said. 'He knows the strength of mortals and he fears it. He seeks to break our spirits before we can destroy him.'

Reaching up to the Dragon Banner, Sigmar took hold of the stiff, crimson fabric and held it before his friend.

'You carry a banner of heroes, Pendrag,' he said. 'The blood of brave men stains this cloth, and we dishonour them if we falter. You are a warrior of great courage, and I need you at my side.'

Pendrag took a great gulp of air, and Sigmar saw that he had overcome the dark enchantments that were working against them. The fear was still there, but the warrior spirit that made Pendrag so formidable remained firm.

'I will always be by your side, my friend,' Pendrag said.

Sigmar nodded, and together they climbed into the lair of the necromancer.

THE MOUNTAINS STRETCHED out for hundreds of miles around them, and the view was so spectacular that Sigmar almost forgot that they stood upon a tower raised by dark magic. Giant, snow-capped peaks marched off into the distance, jagged and impossible, immense structures of rock that were surely sculpted by the hands of the gods.

In the distance, bands of pink clouds clung to their summits like feathers, but here they were ugly, sooty smears, the black smoke of a flaming midden, greasy and reeking of rotten meat. Lightning arced in broken spears around the circumference of the tower, and more of the shrieking skull-faced witches spun around it like trapped hurricanes.

The necromancer was waiting for them, and the sight of him took Sigmar's breath away.

Like a sliver of the deepest darkness imaginable, Morath stood at the edge of the tower, a monstrous creature of evil who sucked the life from the world. Tattered robes of black flapped and blew around the necromancer, though no wind disturbed Sigmar's cloak or the cloth of the Dragon Banner.

The necromancer had his back to them and gave no sign that he was even aware of their presence. For a reckless moment, Sigmar thought of rushing forward and pushing the sorcerer from his pearl tower, and wanted to laugh at the ridiculousness of such a foolish plan.

Morath turned his head, and his ghastly visage struck a deep wound in Sigmar's heart, for here was the very face of death. The necromancer's face was not a skull, yet the skin was drawn so tight across his jutting, angular bones it might as well have been. Morath's hood was drawn up over his gleaming head, and his features were bathed in the glow of the pellucid lightning and his staff's dreadful illumination.

That human eyes could stare out from so hideous a face was a horror neither he nor Pendrag had been prepared for. In his hatred, Sigmar had assumed that Morath would be an inhuman monster, a creature of darkness and evil with whom they could share no commonality.

But in the haunted orbs of Morath he saw rage and bitterness fuelled by emotions that were all too human: an age of fear, regret, loss and thwarted ambition that had driven him to madness and acts of such depravity and horror that nothing, not even the gods, could redeem his damned soul. Such a man had good reason to fear judgement beyond death.

'By all the gods,' breathed Pendrag. 'What are you?'

Morath grinned, exposing a glistening and blackened tongue that licked the yellowed stumps of his teeth. Any lingering trace of humanity was dispelled by that grin and Sigmar forced himself to take a step forward, gripping Ghal-maraz tightly, focusing all his courage into that one act.

He locked his gaze with Morath as the necromancer lifted a withered hand and swept the hood from his head. Sigmar's steps faltered as ancient light shimmered on the golden crown that sat upon the necromancer's brow. It was a beguiling thing, crafted in an age long dead, a wondrous artefact imbued with all the power of its maker.

Morath hissed, and turned to fully face Sigmar and Pendrag. Shadows swirled around him, as though the darkness of the deepest night enshrouded his form. Now that he looked closer, Sigmar saw that Morath was hunched and emaciated, his physical form withered and decayed. Skeletal ribs were visible through the tattered fabric of his robes, but Sigmar knew not to judge the necromancer's power by his frail appearance.

'You have come a long way to die,' said Morath, his voice silken and seductive, at odds with his dreadful appearance.

'As have you,' said Sigmar. 'Mourkain is a long way from here.'

Morath laughed, the sound rich and full, as though they had shared a private jest.

'You speak of a place you do not know,' said the necromancer, 'of an empire that fell before your degenerate tribe even came to this land.'

Sigmar flinched at Morath's words, as though each was a dart tipped with poison.

'But you could not let it die, could you?' asked Sigmar.

'Would you allow yours to be ended by the foolishness of one man, Sigmar the Heldenhammer?' asked Morath, taking a step towards him.

'All things have their time, and all things must die in time.'

'Not all things,' promised Morath. 'I came to this land near death, but I slept away the centuries beneath the world and far from the sight of men. Now I am risen, and already your empire is dying. Can you not feel it? The cold touch of the death I bring is carried on every breath of wind and all that you love will soon be gone.'

'Not if I kill you first,' said Sigmar. 'This land is strong and it will survive your magic.'

'It will not,' promised Morath, 'but I am done talking with you. It is time for you to die, but fear not, I will bring your soul back and you will stand at my side as we carve a new empire from the bones of your doomed race.'

'I am here to make sure that never happens,' said Sigmar, forcing himself to close with the terrible, wretched form of the necromancer. If he could only get close enough to strike a single blow, he knew he could end this.

Morath chuckled, and a chill entered Sigmar's heart.

'You think you are here by your own design? Foolish, arrogant man,' said Morath. 'Even entombed beneath the world I sensed your power, and I knew I would need to draw you to me. One such as you will make a fine general for my army of the dead when I rebuild the glory of Mourkain.'

Morath raised his hand, and Sigmar's step faltered as the chains of duty that bound him to his people crushed him within their grip. To rule a united empire of man had been his dream since he had wandered the tombs of his ancestors on Warrior's Hill as a young man, but he had not been prepared for the reality of the task.

Smothered beneath the hideous weight of his undertaking, Sigmar's arms fell to his sides. He knew this was Morath's sorcery, but he was powerless to resist.

Sigmar dropped to his knees.

'I can't do this,' he whispered.

Pendrag stood tall at his side, his chest heaving with effort as he clutched the Dragon Banner tightly to his breast.

'What are you doing?' he asked.

'It's too much,' said Sigmar.

Pendrag caught his breath and looked over at Morath.

'Fight him! Your warriors are buying us time to kill Morath with their lives!'

'I don't care,' said Sigmar tearing off his helmet and hurling it away. Pendrag watched helplessly as the magnificently crafted helm fell through the opening in the floor, hearing it clatter down the steps as it fell to the bottom of the tower.

'Stand and fight!' demanded Pendrag, hauling on his arm.

'Don't you understand?' shouted Sigmar. 'It's too much for any one man. The Empire... We will never be safe. Never. There will always be someone or something trying to destroy us, whether it's greenskins from the mountains, Norsii or worse from across the seas, twisted forest beasts or necromancers. We can't fight them all. We fight and we fight, but they keep coming. Eventually, one of them will drag us down, and drown this land in our blood. It's inevitable, so why bother fighting to keep the flame alive when it's eventually going to be extinguished?'

Morath's triumphant laughter swirled around him, and Sigmar saw the black form of the necromancer swell and billow, his robes spreading like the wings of a huge bat.

Pendrag roared and hurled himself at the necromancer, but a flick of Morath's shrivelled hand sent him sprawling, the banner torn from his silver grip. The standard skidded across the smooth stone before coming to rest at the edge of the tower, its bloody cloth flapping in the shrieking winds that circled the tower.

Morath slid through the air to hover above Pendrag, his leering features twisted in ghoulish relish, his head cocked to one side, like a carrion bird deciding which eye of a freshly dead corpse to devour first.

'I spoke words of your death, yet still you came,' hissed the necromancer. 'You will make a fine lieutenant for my new general.'

A pale light built within Morath's outstretched hand, and Pendrag cried out in pain, his face twisted in agony. His sword-brother's skin grew pallid and leathery, the colour bleaching from his hair until it was utterly white.

The life was being sucked out of him, yet Sigmar could no more lift himself from his knees than he could sprout wings and fly. One of his oldest and dearest friends was dying before his eyes, and he could do nothing to prevent it. Nothing.

He closed his eyes as his dreams collapsed. His vision of a strong and united land fractured and died within him. Morath was right. No empire of mortals could ever really last, for such was the fate of all works of man. Empires grew and prospered, and then became fat and complacent. Before long, one of their many enemies would rise up and destroy them.

It was as inevitable as nightfall.

In Sigmar's mind's eye he saw a ruined city by a river, a once magnificent capital built around the mighty tomb of some ancient king. It had once covered a vast area and been home to thousands, but now only greenskins dwelled there. Its gilded plazas served as arenas for battling warlords, its sunken marble bathhouses as pens for wolves, boars and foul, cave-dwelling beasts that skulked in the shadows. Tomes and scrolls that had been gathered over thousands of years burned on campfires, and works of art that had stirred the hearts and minds of those who studied them were smashed for sport.

Morath's honeyed words sounded in his mind. *This is the doom of your Empire.*

Sigmar wept to see so fine a city despoiled, realising with a jolt that this was the same city he had seen recreated beneath the ice. Was this Mourkain? This was the city mourned by the necromancer, the dream he sought to rebuild from the ashes of Sigmar's Empire.

The ruin of Mourkain faded from sight, and Sigmar was glad to see it go, for it spoke of ancient loss and the inevitable doom of dreams. Yet the achievements of its builders were no less impressive for its having fallen. They had built a great city and carved out a mighty empire, and that was something to be proud of. That it had eventually been brought to ruin did not lessen the wonder of that achievement.

Yes, empires fell and men died, but that was the way of the world. To defy that was to go against the will of the gods, and no man dared stand before those awesome powers with such arrogance. His father had once told him of how the ageing leader of a wolf pack would leave and roam the mountains alone when his strength was fading and stronger wolves were ready to lead. For a thing to endure beyond its time was a sad and terrible thing, and to see what was once glorious and noble reduced to something wretched and pathetic was heartbreaking.

Sigmar's Empire would one day fall, and when that time came, men would mourn its passing. Other empires would arise to take its place, but this was the time of *his* Empire, and no necromancer was going to take it away from him!

Sigmar lifted his head, and stared at Morath as he sucked the life from Pendrag.

His heart hardened and growing strength filled his limbs. He forced himself to his feet, crying out as the chill touch of the necromancer fled his body in the face of his acceptance of the future's inevitability. With every second that passed, the despair and hopelessness shrouding him diminished in the face of his determination to resist Morath's dark power.

'Empires rise and fall,' snarled Sigmar as he stood tall, 'but that matters not. All that matters is that they rose, and in their time men walked with honour and fought for what they believed. What matters is what we do with the time we have.'

Morath turned at the sound of his voice, and the necromancer's sunken eyes widened in surprise. His hands stretched out towards Sigmar, and streaming bolts of cold fire leapt from the necromancer's fingers. Dancing sheets of icy flame erupted from the air around Sigmar, but he smiled as the runic script worked into his armour blazed in reply.

Sigmar walked untouched through the inferno, Ghal-maraz ablaze with the white fire that Morath hurled.

'You have no power over me,' said Sigmar. 'Your despair means nothing to me, for I have no fear for the future. That I shall die and all my achievements turn to dust does not make them pointless. Living forever and creating nothing of worth... *that* is pointless. You have no place in this world, necromancer. You should have died a long time ago, and I am here to send your soul into the next world and whatever torments await you.'

Morath raised his arms, and Pendrag sagged to the stones of the tower. With every step Sigmar took, Morath took one away from him. Once more he stabbed his hands towards Sigmar, and the shrieking ghosts that swirled around the top of the tower gathered in a mass of howling spirits. Morath hurled them towards Sigmar, and they came at him in a mad, swirling pack of screaming skulls.

They howled around him, snapping with fleshless claws and ethereal fangs. Sigmar ignored them, his towering self-belief carrying him through their hate unharmed. His heart was iron, his soul a stone, and the depraved spirits could not turn him from his path.

'What manner of man are you?' demanded Morath as Sigmar came closer. 'No mortal can resist such power!'

The necromancer's staff blazed with dark light, but Sigmar raised

Ghal-maraz, and the staff shattered into a thousand fragments, each one blowing away like ash in a storm. Morath fell to his knees, his hunched form now pitiful and contemptible. He reached out with reed-thin fingers, but Sigmar batted them away. The necromancer seemed to shrink within his robes, as though his form was diminishing, whatever power that had sustained him over the centuries withdrawing from his flesh.

'No...' hissed Morath, holding his withered hands up before his face. 'You promised...'

The roiling stormclouds above the tower began to break up as the dark energies that bound them dissipated. A fresh wind blew over the tower, carrying the scent of highland forests and fast-flowing rivers of cool water.

Morath crumpled, his bony frame folding into itself with every second. His flesh was wasting away, and the golden crown he had worn with such arrogant pride fell from his brow. It landed with the heavy metallic ring of pure gold, and rolled across the tower before coming to rest at Sigmar's feet.

Sigmar wrapped his hand around Morath's throat, feeling the frailty of his bones, and he knew that he could snap his neck with ease. There was no weight to him, and Sigmar looked upon the icy battlefield to see that the dead warriors no longer fought. Their bones crumbled to dust, and the city beneath the ice began to fade like a distant memory as he watched.

His warriors cheered as they saw him atop the tower with the necromancer as his prisoner. They bayed for Morath's death, and they were not the only ones. Half-heard moans of anger were carried on the wind, the freed spirits of the dead demanding vengeance.

'I think there will be many souls awaiting your arrival in the next world,' said Sigmar.

Morath's gnarled and ancient face stretched in fear, and he gibbered nonsensical pleas for mercy as he clawed at Sigmar's arm. His struggles were feeble, and Sigmar quashed the flickering ember of pity that threatened to stay his hand.

'You have existed for too long,' said Sigmar, lifting Morath over the edge. 'It is time for you to die.'

He hurled Morath from the tower, and watched as his thin body tumbled downwards, spinning end over end until he smashed into the ice. Sigmar let out a long, exhausted exhalation and felt a wave of gratitude wash over him. Thousands of faces and names flashed through Sigmar's mind, each one a soul freed from eternal damnation, and tears of joy spilled down his face as they passed on.

Sigmar turned from the edge of the tower and felt something at his feet: the crown Morath had worn and which had granted him such power. He reached down and turned it around in his hands. The workmanship was incredible, easily the equal of any dwarf-forged metal, yet its design was unfamiliar. Worked in gold and set with jewels, it was a thing of beauty, and he felt the vast power bound to it, an ancient power beyond the ken of even the mountain folk to craft.

For a fleeting moment, he beheld an ancient city of the desert, and a host of bejewelled armies marching across the scorched sands beneath great banners of blue and gold. Then it was gone and the incredible vista of the Middle Mountains returned to him. He saw Pendrag lying on his side at the edge of the tower, crawling towards the fallen Dragon Banner.

Sigmar rushed towards his friend, his vision of the desert armies forgotten as he knelt at his side and turned him over. He tried to hide his shock, but Pendrag saw the horror in his eyes.

'It's that bad is it?' whispered Pendrag, his voice little more than a parched croak.

'No… It's–' began Sigmar, though he could not bring himself to lie.

Pendrag's face was sunken and hollow, the very image of Lukas Hauke, the creature that had been imprisoned beneath the Faushlag Rock. His eyes were rheumy with cataracts and his skin wrinkled like ancient parchment. What Morath had taken was Pendrag's youth, for Sigmar cradled a man hundreds of years old.

He wished he could save Pendrag. He wished he had not succumbed to Morath's dark magic, that he could have broken the spell of his despair sooner. Tears fell from his eyes and landed on Pendrag's face at the thought of his death, and Sigmar knew that all the power in the world was meaningless in the face of such loss.

'Sigmar!' cried Pendrag, and Sigmar opened his eyes as the crown grew hot in his hands.

Golden heat flowed from the crown and into Sigmar. It filled him with light, and the weight of his burdens lifted in an instant. But the crown had not yet finished its work. Amber light flowed from Sigmar and passed into Pendrag, filling his body with light and undoing the necromancer's hateful magic.

Pendrag cried out as his hair thickened and the red that had drained from it returned more lustrous than ever. His flesh filled with life and the colour returned to his eyes. Old scars on his arms faded, and his chest rose and fell with powerful, deep breaths.

Both men looked in astonishment at the golden crown. The light faded from the jewels, yet Sigmar could sense that its power was far from spent.

'I don't believe it!' cried Pendrag, climbing to his feet and examining every inch of his body as though afraid to believe in the miracle of his renewal. He threw his head back and laughed, the sound filled with renewed life and hope: the laughter of one who has faced death and come back stronger than ever.

'The crown…' said Sigmar. 'I have never seen anything like this… It healed you. This is powerful magic indeed.'

'Aye,' agreed Pendrag, staring in joyous wonder at the magnificent artefact. 'Magic used for evil by a necromancer.'

Sigmar turned the crown in his hands, knowing that he held the key to making the Empire stronger than ever before. With such power, he could defend his land and people, ruling with justice and strength. Morath had twisted the power of the crown, but Sigmar would use it to heal, not to kill. To govern with wisdom and compassion, not to enslave.

He looked at Pendrag, and his sword-brother answered his unasked question with a nod.

'Yes. It is yours now,' said Pendrag.

Sigmar lifted the golden crown and slipped it over his head. Though Morath's skull had been thin and hairless, the crown was a perfect fit. He felt its power, and he took Pendrag's hand in the warrior's grip.

He heard the sound of footsteps behind him and a group of battle-weary warriors poured onto the top of the tower. Redwane was at the forefront, his face streaked with blood and his armour hanging from him in torn links of mail and battered plate. In his hands he held Sigmar's helmet, the metal dented and scraped from its fall down the length of the tower. Alaric's crown still sat upon it, and a flicker of unease passed through Sigmar.

Redwane held the helmet with an amused grin.

'Must I always be picking up after you?' he asked.

Sigmar laughed. 'Keep it,' he said, sweeping past the White Wolf. 'I have a new crown.'

UNWILLING TO REMAIN a moment longer within the valley of the necromancer, Sigmar's warriors gathered their dead and wounded and marched through the darkness. The Dragon Banner was lowered and, as the moon traversed the clear night sky, Sigmar spoke to each man in his army, praising his courage and honouring the sacrifice of the dead.

The wounded were carried on makeshift litters, and, as Sigmar took their hands, it seemed their suffering lessened. He sought out Myrsa, and was relieved beyond words to find that he still lived. No sooner had he laid his hand upon the Warrior Eternal's brow, than the colour returned to the wounded man's face and his breathing deepened.

Forgetting his promise to bring Brass Keep down, stone by stone, Sigmar led his warriors from the mountains, taking a more direct westerly route through thickly forested valleys that would bring them out on the western flanks of the mountains.

Four days later, the weary men of the Empire emerged from the foothills of the Middle Mountains, following a curving path towards the forest road that led south to Middenheim. On the morning of the fifth day, scouts reported a large column of people and wagons coming from the north, and Sigmar went out to meet them with his new crown glittering at his brow. Redwane and three White Wolves marched with him, and the invigorated Pendrag carried the Emperor's crimson banner aloft.

The first groups of people to emerge from the tree line marched in a long, weary column, and Sigmar swore softly under his breath at their wretched, sorry state. As more and more came into view, he saw that they came on foot, on rattling carts or on overflowing wagons. He had expected travelling merchants or labourers heading to Middenheim to find work. What he had not expected was hundreds of refugees, for there could be no mistaking that these were people fleeing from some terror behind them.

'Udose by the look of them,' said Pendrag.

'Aye,' agreed Redwane. 'I see plaid, and some of the men have claymores.'

'What in the name of Ulric happened to them?' asked Sigmar, approaching a wagon with a ragged scrap of an Udose flag bearing the patchwork colours of Count Wolfila flapping on a makeshift banner pole. A pair of weary pack ponies pulled the wagon, and a one-armed man with wide shoulders and the face of a pugilist sat on the buckboard. A young woman with three children sat behind him, their faces pinched and fearful.

'Ho there, fellow,' said Sigmar, walking alongside the wagon. 'What do they call you?'

'Rolf,' said the man. 'Though most call me Oakfist on account of my left hook.'

'I can see why,' said Sigmar, seeing the meaty scale of the man's remaining fist. 'Where have you come from?'

'Salzenhús,' said Rolf. 'Or what's left of it.'

Sigmar felt a knot in his stomach at mention of Count Wolfila's castle and said, 'What do you mean? What has happened?'

The old man glared at him and spat a single word, 'Norsii.'

'The Norsii? They did this?'

'Aye,' said the old man. 'Them and their traitorous allies.'

'Allies? Who?'

'Bastard Roppsmenn,' said Rolf. 'Wolfships been raiding up and down the coast all season, but there's been sword bands of Roppsmenn riding with 'em this year, killing and burning and driving people south.'

'Are you sure they were Roppsmenn?' asked Sigmar, feeling a throbbing pulse of fury at his temple as the full weight of what he had been told sank in. 'They hated the Norsii as much as any tribe ever did.'

'Damn right I'm sure,' snarled Rolf, rage and sadness choking his voice. 'I seen them with my own eyes. Shaven heads and curved swords they had. Burned Wolfila's castle to the ground and cut him into pieces for dogs to eat. Killed his family too. Wife and child butchered and crucified on the only tower left standing.'

Sigmar felt the knot in his stomach unravel with a dreadful sickness at this news, and the fiery pulse at his temple grew stronger. He remembered Wolfila at his coronation, the garrulous northern count introducing his wife to Sigmar during the feasting days. Her name was Petra, and she had been pregnant with their first child. Sigmar had sent a silver drinking chalice to Salzenhús upon the birth of the child, a boy they had named Theodulf. The boy would have been around six or seven years old, but if what Rolf was saying was true, the line of the Udose chieftains had ended.

'Wolfila killed?' Sigmar said, still unable to believe that one of his counts was dead.

'Aye,' said Rolf, 'and all the men able to hold a sword. Boys and old men. Bastards only left me alive since I ain't got no sword arm. I'd have fought though, but they laughed at me, and I had my daughter and her young 'uns to look after. I thought they'd take 'em, but they let us go, like we weren't worth bothering with.'

Sigmar heard the shame in Rolf's voice, knowing the man would have died with his chieftain but for the need to protect his family. Such things were at the heart of what made a man proud, and to have that taken away by an enemy was a bitter blow indeed.

Sigmar stepped away as Rolf shucked the reins and the wagon moved on. His fists clenched and he turned his furious gaze northwards, as though he could see his enemies through the forest.

When he had driven the Norsii from the Empire, the Roppsmenn had claimed their territory, largely because no one else had wanted it. Barren and said to be haunted by the ghosts of those their shamans had burned on sacrificial pyres, the land of the Norsii was bleak and lashed by freezing winds from the north.

In his quest to unite the tribes of men, Sigmar had not sought the Sword Oaths of the Roppsmenn chieftains, because they lived so far to the east that they were for all intents and purposes a tribe of a different land. It had been an arrangement of convenience, for he had been reluctant to wage war or pursue diplomacy so far from Reikdorf.

'Damn me,' said Redwane, shaking his head as yet more frightened people passed. 'Roppsmenn? Who'd have thought it? They've never raided south into the Empire. Why would they do such a thing, and why now?'

'It does not matter,' said Sigmar, his fists bunched at his side. 'They have allied with the Norsii and that makes them my enemy.'

Sigmar turned to his friends, his face scarred with hostility.

'Pendrag, raise the Dragon Banner,' he said. 'I have need of it again.'

'The Dragon Banner?' asked Pendrag in alarm. 'Why?'

Sigmar squared his shoulders before his sword-brother, as though daring him to gainsay his words.

'Because I am going to gather an army and march east,' he said, his voice all fury and hurt. 'I am going to avenge the death of my friend. The Roppsmenn are going to learn the fate of those who make war on my people.'

'What does that mean?' asked Pendrag.

'It means their lands will burn!' roared Sigmar.

FOURTEEN
Sigmar's Justice

NORMALLY THE BRACKENWALSCH Marsh was a gloomy place of mist and shadow, but this day was glorious, the sun shining upon the waters like glittering shards of crystal. A cool breeze kept the temperature pleasant, and the aroma of late-blooming flowers and fragrant reeds perfumed the air with myriad pleasing scents.

The hag woman sat upon a fallen tree trunk, its mouldy bark alive with insects and thick with moss. Where others would recoil at such things or find them repulsive, she enjoyed the rich cycle of death and rebirth. As one thing died, it became a home to some creatures, a hatchery for others and food for yet more.

'All things have their time,' she said to no one in particular, watching as a raven settled on the low branch of a nearby tree. The bird cawed, the sound echoing over the deep pools and hidden pathways of the marshes.

'What do you have to say this fine morning, bird of prophecy?' she asked with a smile.

The bird regarded her with its onyx eyes, and hopped from foot to foot as it cawed again.

'What am I to make of that?' she asked. 'I can no longer see the future, so I hoped you might spare me a shred of your knowledge.'

The bird cawed once more before taking flight. The hag woman watched it until she could no longer pick its form out in the sky. She shrugged and pushed herself upright with the help of her rowan staff. Her joints were stiff, and popped with the sound of snapping twigs. She winced, knowing that her forced levity masked the fear that had been gnawing at her ever since her powers had begun to fade.

The awakening of the necromancer in the Middle Mountains had heralded the decline of her power. She had fled from a terrible nightmare of a towering, monstrous evil arising from the desert, and had felt the spread of dark magic in the north like a growing cancer.

The malice of the dread sorcerer seeped into the earth like a poison, tainting the energies that flowed along its rivers and saturated the very air. Ever since that night, it took longer and longer for her spirit to unchain itself from her flesh, and soar on the winds of magic that drifted like oracle smoke from the earth. In her youth, she merely had to lie back and close her eyes, but now her spirit could not fly at all, no matter how hard she tried.

Without that freedom, she felt the ravages of time upon her physical form more than ever.

Worse was to come, for no sooner was her spirit confined to her body than the brimming vistas of possible futures that crowded her thoughts drifted away like guests from a feast, until she was utterly alone. Despite living a solitary existence in the Brackenwalsch, she had witnessed the great dramas of the world and had helped to shape their course.

Until now, that had been enough.

Before her powers vanished, she had followed the progress of young Sigmar as his empire grew and flourished. She saw his rescue of Princess Marika, and smiled at the naivety of men. Despite what they called the swamp creatures they fought, she knew well that they were not daemons; the immortal servants of the Dark Gods were far more terrifying.

She watched the siege of Jutonsryk, and her heart despaired as she saw Sigmar raise his hammer to kill the rebellious King Marius. But for the intervention of the Berserker King, the lord of the Jutones would have died, and the doom of the Empire would have begun.

Though she could not see it, she felt the death of the necromancer. Yet a dark miasma of ancient evil still polluted the healing energies of the world, as if his power still lingered. It cast a pall over the world and the promise of her ending hung over every day. That was why she cherished this day, a beautiful time of gold, blue and vivid green.

Bereft of her powers and unable to perceive the world beyond what her failing eyes could see, the hag woman felt lonely for the first time in her life. Out here, with nothing but the birds and marsh creatures for company, she felt divorced from the race of man, as though she were no longer part of it.

The Hag-Mother had confessed similar feelings in the days leading up to her death at the hands of the greenskins. Was this then her time to leave this world? Was this day a last gift to her before she completed her journey through life? She had lived many years, and death held no terror for her, but it was not death that quickened her steps as she made her way back to her cave along paths only she knew.

She skirted a rippling pool of clear water, seeing a tall plant growing at its edge, its stems dotted with white flowers in flat-topped clusters. A sickly smell wafted from the plant, and she frowned at the sight of the water hemlock. She had not seen such a plant for many years, and the sight of it stirred uncomfortable memories.

The hag woman's steps faltered. She looked up as a shadow crossed her eyes, and she felt a shiver of dread. The sky was clear and bright and empty. The sun hung low and fat above the horizon, and a black-feathered bird circled above her. She hurried her steps, not yet ready to be a meal for a hopeful carrion bird.

That age should undo her rather than the wiles of her enemies was no bad way to end a life that had been lived for the good of others. Her steps had taken her along some dark roads, and she had done much that she was not proud of, but the race of man endured, and she would not second-guess the choices she had made for the greater good.

The image of a young woman with dark hair leapt to her mind, but she quashed the thought before it could fully form. That had been a necessary sacrifice, a death required to set Sigmar on the path to the birth of the Empire. Had Ravenna lived, the greenskins would now rule this land of men, and all that she had fought to save would have come to ruin.

Is that how you sleep at night?

The thought took her by surprise, for she had long since come to terms with Ravenna's death. More and more, she found her thoughts skipping randomly around her mind, revisiting memories and past regrets thought long buried.

She was an innocent, and you killed her.

No, thought the hag woman, as she turned from the path towards a ragged black rock that jutted from the marshland like a sunken mountain that left only its topmost peak visible. The ground leading towards a black cleft in the rock was soggy underfoot, and a wrong step in any direction would see her sucked beneath the bog.

She reached the mouth of her cave and paused, taking a last look at this magnificent day.

This world was harsh and unforgiving, yet it was also beautiful and miraculous. If you knew where to look, wonders could be found in every corner and she would miss it when she was gone.

The hag woman ducked her head and entered the cave, her eyes taking a moment to adjust to the shadowy interior. She moved deeper into the cave, allowing sense memory to guide her in the dim light. The smell of herbs and heat came to her, reassuring in their familiarity, and following hot on their heels was the smell of cold iron and the sweat and dust of travel.

The hag woman halted, realising she was not alone. Orange light flared in the darkness, and a crackling fire appeared in the circle of stones that served as her hearth. A wizened old man sat cross-legged before the fire, his head bowed and his hands steepled before him as though in prayer. She narrowed her eyes, needing no wych-sight to tell that this man was more than he seemed. The breath of the Dark Gods filled this one, and his power was palpable.

'Who are you?' she asked.

'A traveller who walks a similar path to you, Gráinne,' said the old man.

The hag woman started at his use of her given name. 'No one has called me that in many years. How is it you know it?'

'The Dark Gods know your name and they have spoken the words of your death,' said the old man, raising his head and looking at her with cold eyes that had seen the passage of centuries and the slaying of thousands.

She swallowed and reached deep into herself for any last shreds of power that remained to her, knowing that she would only have one chance to fight him. She felt a movement behind her, but before she could move, strong hands seized her and held her fast.

'Remember me?' said a silky, seductive voice at her shoulder.

The hag woman twisted in her captor's grip, but her struggles lessened as she saw the face of the man holding her. He was wondrously handsome, with a beautifully cruel grin that was beguiling and yet curiously repellent.

Though the light was poor, there was no mistaking the young man who had come to her cave many years ago in search of vengeance. Lost innocence hid behind his killer's eyes, but beyond that, a hidden face shone with unspeakable desires and monstrous arrogance. With a sinking heart, she knew it was his true self, and she marvelled that she had not seen it before.

These were not the eyes of a man; they were the eyes of a daemon.

She turned away and the old man laughed, saying, 'She remembers you, Azazel.'

'That is not your name, Gerreon,' she whispered, knowing it would do no good.

'It is now,' hissed Azazel, drawing his knife and holding it to her throat, 'and it will be the last name you hear as you die.'

WOLFGART SAT BEFORE his fire and watched Ulrike fight sleep, curled on Maedbh's lap, smiling at the sight of his family and wondering at his luck to be blessed with two such fine women in his life. Maedbh smiled at him and stroked her daughter's golden hair, so like her own. Ulrike was five and a half years old, as beautiful as her mother, and already Wolfgart could see that he would be hurling suitors from his door in the years to come. He remembered his own wild youth, carousing and trying to bed as many of the village girls as possible. The thought of Ulrike encountering someone like him when he had been that age was more terrifying than any enemy he had faced in battle. He pushed the thought aside. That was a problem for another day, and he had a few years yet before he would be replaced in his daughter's affections by some young buck eager to take her maidenhead.

The room was warm and lit with golden light from the fire. The surround was carved from Asoborn wildwood and had been a gift from Queen Freya upon her last visit to Reikdorf. The workmanship was exquisite, depicting a host of entwined trees with a multitude of roots that plunged deep into the earth before coming together. Maedbh said it depicted the Asoborn belief that all living things were connected. Wolfgart just thought it looked pretty.

The stone-built house kept the heat, and chopped logs stacked against the north wall kept the wind from sapping its warmth. It was a fine building, one Wolfgart had commissioned from Ornath the Stonemason, a man whose prices were outrageous but whose genius with a hammer and chisel was such that it was rumoured the dwarfs had trained him in their mountain halls. Wolfgart knew that wasn't true, but the man's skill was prodigious nonetheless.

Less than a generation ago, a man would have built his own home, but in the two years since the siege of Jutonsryk had ended, gold had flowed in an unending river from the west, and the Empire had flourished like never before. Traders from lands so far distant as to be almost mythical travelled the roads linking the cities, bringing exotic goods and swelling the coffers of Sigmar's counts.

With trade bringing peace and prosperity to their lands, tribal chieftains who had once fought bloody wars with one another were now the best of friends. The common enemy of the greenskins had brought them together, but wealth was the glue that held them. Well, with the exception of the Taleutens and Cherusens who, in defiance of Sigmar's threats, still insisted on raiding one another's lands and feuding over some ancient grievance.

Wolfgart received a portion of Jutonsryk's wealth for his part in its capture, and also earned a generous monthly coin as Sigmar's Captain of Arms in Reikdorf. Taken together with his horse breeding farms and the merchants in which Maedbh had persuaded him to invest, Wolfgart was one of the wealthiest men in Reikdorf, and his home was as luxuriously appointed as any of the Empire's counts. Thick rugs of bear fur from the Grey Mountains were spread throughout the downstairs rooms, and finely crafted tables and chairs of oak and ash were set with plates of delicate ceramics that had come from a land far to the east.

Endal tapestries hung from the walls, though pride of place was given to a silver breastplate with gold embossing in the shape of a snarling wolf and fluted rims of bronze. Pendrag had forged the breastplate as a gift to him, and it had served him well in the campaigns he had fought in Sigmar's name. His eyes drifted to the mighty sword hung on the wall above the fireplace, its blade six feet long and still razor-sharp.

It had been several years since Wolfgart had swung his sword in anger. He remembered the last blow he had struck, an upward sweep that smashed through the shield of a Jutone lancer before he buried the blade in his chest. With Alfgeir appointed regent of Reikdorf while Sigmar fought the Roppsmenn in the north, Wolfgart had taken over the training of the Unberogen youth in the arts of war. It was worthy work, but not the same as a real fight.

'Do you miss it?' asked Ulrike, startling him from his reverie.

'What's that, my dear?'

The young girl pointed above the fireplace.

'Fighting,' she said. 'You keep looking at your sword.'

He shook his head.

'No, beautiful girl, my days of war are over,' he said. 'The kings have all sworn fealty to Sigmar, and the Empire is at peace. Well, mostly.'

'Are you sure?' asked Maedbh with a sly look. 'I think Ulrike might be on to something.'

'Ganging up on me now, eh?' grinned Wolfgart. 'Gods preserve me from two women in the house.'

'That is our right as women, husband of mine,' said Maedbh. 'You are outnumbered, so you might as well surrender and answer your daughter's question.'

Wolfgart stood and he lifted Ulrike from his wife's lap. He walked a slow circle around the room, pausing by each of the fine things that filled their home. 'Trade is how a man makes his name now,' he said, 'not how well he can swing a sword.'

'That's not an answer,' pressed Ulrike.

Wolfgart was about to give another flippant response, but he saw real fear in his daughter's eyes. She was clever, and she knew that not all men who went to war came back.

'Honestly? Yes, I do miss it,' he said. 'I wish I didn't, but I do.'

'That's silly,' said Ulrike. 'Why would anyone *want* to fight? You could get hurt or... or killed. War is stupid.'

'I can't argue with you there, girl, but sometimes we need to go to war.'

'Why?'

Wolfgart looked over at Maedbh for help, but his wife shook her head with a wry grin.

He was on his own for this one.

'The Empire is safer than it's ever been, but there are still enemies to be fought.'

'Who? You said all the kings were our friends now.'

'Aye, that they are, but there are other enemies we have to fight. Like greenskins or the forest monsters. They aren't our friends and they never will be.'

'Why not?' asked Ulrike.

'Because, well, because they hate us,' said Wolfgart.

'Why? What did we do to them?'

'It's not anything we did to them,' said Wolfgart, exhausted by his daughter's never-ending questions. 'They're monsters, and they only want to kill and destroy. They don't want to live in peace, because it's not in their nature. They can't do anything else except fight.'

'But you want to fight,' said Ulrike. 'Does that make you like them?'

'No, my sweet girl, it doesn't. Because I only fight to protect you and your mother, and our friends. I fight when our enemies want to take what is ours from us. I am a warrior, and yes, I can't deny that the call of an Unberogen war horn sets the blood pounding in my veins. But I don't make war on others unless they make war on me first.'

'Is that why Uncle Sigmar is fighting the Roppsmenn?'

Wolfgart felt a knot of tension in his gut, and shared an uneasy glance with Maedbh. He was spared from thinking of an answer by a knock at the heavy wooden door of his home. He walked back to Maedbh and handed Ulrike to her.

'Take her to bed,' said Wolfgart. 'She needs to sleep.'

'I'm not tired,' said Ulrike, even as she drowsily slipped her arms around her mother.

Maedbh took their daughter upstairs, and Wolfgart opened the door.

Alfgeir and Eoforth stood at his threshold, clad in long, hooded cloaks.

'You're late,' said Wolfgart.

THEY SAT AROUND an oaken table carved by an Endal craftsman as Wolfgart poured rich red wine into silver goblets. Alfgeir took a long swallow, while Eoforth sipped his more delicately. He poured himself a drink and took his place at the head of the table as Maedbh came downstairs and sat next to Eoforth.

'Tilean,' said Eoforth as he took another sip. 'Very nice.'

'Pendrag persuaded me to try some, and I got the taste for it in Marburg,' said Wolfgart, 'but we're not here to discuss my well-stocked wine cellar.'

'No,' agreed Eoforth, 'we are not.'

'Have you had word from Pendrag or Myrsa?' asked Alfgeir.

'I have,' said Wolfgart, 'and it makes for evil reading.'

Wolfgart rose and pulled an iron box from beneath a loose stone in the floor beside the fireplace. He returned to the table and opened the box, lifting out several folded parchments.

'It's getting worse,' he said. 'Sigmar's army numbers over eight thousand warriors, mainly Ostagoths and Udose, but there are some Asoborns with him too.'

Alfgeir glanced at Maedbh and asked, 'Asoborns?'

'The forests thin out in the east,' she said. 'Good killing ground for chariots.'

Wolfgart ran a hand through his hair, still dark, though strands of grey were beginning to appear at his temples and in his beard.

'The news from the north is bloody,' he began. 'Myrsa sends word that the Norsii are raiding up and down the coast in greater numbers than ever before. He thinks they are testing our readiness to repel an invasion.'

'An invasion?' hissed Alfgeir. 'Damn, but we need Sigmar back.'

'Don't hold your breath expecting that any time soon,' said Wolfgart. 'I don't think Sigmar will stop until he's wiped the Roppsmenn from the Empire. He's fought three major battles under the Dragon Banner.'

'Sweet Shallya's mercy!' cried Eoforth. 'The Dragon Banner was raised every time?'

'Aye,' said Wolfgart grimly. 'Pendrag reckons around ten thousand Roppsmenn dead so far. Their towns and villages are burning and their people are fleeing into the east. Pendrag says that any who do not move fast enough are caught and killed.'

'Surely no Unberogen warrior of honour would take part in such slaughter?' asked Alfgeir.

'They are warriors fighting beneath the Dragon Banner,' said Maedbh. 'It makes no distinction between warriors and ordinary people. Unberogen warriors know that too.'

'Thankfully there are few Unberogen in Sigmar's army,' said Wolfgart. 'The worst excesses are being perpetrated by the Udose. After all, it was their lands that were ravaged and their own count was murdered in his castle.'

'These deeds bring dishonour upon us,' said Eoforth, shaking his head as though unable to believe what he was hearing. 'To think that Sigmar is responsible for such slaughter.'

'The Roppsmenn brought this on themselves,' snapped Wolfgart. 'They attacked the Empire and killed Count Wolfila and his family. What else did they expect?'

'Retribution, yes,' said Eoforth. 'But such slaughter? No one could have expected this.'

'Word is already spreading,' put in Alfgeir. 'I have had letters from

Otwin, Aldred and Siggurd all demanding to know what is happening in the north. They are talking of "Sigmar's Justice" and what it really means.'

'They fear for their lands and people should they ever voice a contrary opinion,' said Eoforth. 'They fear they will suffer the same fate.'

'That will not happen,' said Maedbh. 'The Roppsmenn suffer because they betrayed Sigmar and killed his friend. They deserve this.'

'You're a harsh woman, Maedbh,' said Eoforth. 'You are right that they deserve to feel Sigmar's wrath, but this goes too far. Villages burned to the ground, prisoners executed and entire families butchered? It is too much, and it shames me that our Emperor allows this.'

'The question is, what do we do about it?' asked Wolfgart.

'What *can* we do?' asked Alfgeir. 'He is the Emperor.'

'He is our friend,' stated Eoforth, 'first and foremost. The loss of Wolfila must have unhinged him, and he vents his anger and grief on the Roppsmenn.'

'Does that excuse such slaughter?' asked Alfgeir.

'Of course not, but knowing why a thing occurs makes it easier to understand,' said Eoforth. 'When Sigmar leads his warriors back home, we will speak with him on this matter. Knowing what drove him to such excess will help us to soothe the fears of the other counts.'

'Where was Sigmar when last you heard from Pendrag?' asked Alfgeir.

'Last I heard, what's left of the Roppsmenn were falling back towards the great dividing river,' said Wolfgart. 'It's the last line on the map before you head into the unknown.'

'Does anyone even know what lies beyond that river?' asked Alfgeir.

'Ulric alone knows what's on the other side,' said Wolfgart with a weary shrug. 'But we know what's certain on *this* side.'

'What's that?'

'Sigmar and death.'

IT WAS DARK by the time the old man decided they had come far enough. Though her hands were bound, Gerreon – she could not think of him as Azazel – held her fast the entire way, whispering the terrible things the old man was going to do to her. The hag woman had thought that death would hold no fear for her, but that had been foolish on her part.

She did not want to die like this.

The night sky was cloudless, the stars bright pinpricks in the velvet darkness, and she saw that they had travelled almost to the very edge of the marsh. Somehow the old man had known the secret routes through the deadly swamps. The moon's reflection shimmered on the surface of the water, and its uncaring face bathed the silent landscape in a pale, dead glow.

'How did you find your way through the marshes?' she asked. 'The paths are unknown to most men.'

'I am not "most men", Gráinne,' said the old man. 'Your powers may be gone, but you can still tell that, can't you?'

'You follow the Dark Gods,' she said.

'I follow the *true* gods,' he replied, 'the gods that rule in the realm beyond this ashen existence and whose breath fills me with life. They are the real power in this world, not the feeble avatars dreamed up by the minds of men. They existed before this world and they will exist long after it is dust in the void.'

'If you are going to kill me, then tell me your name,' she said. 'At least tell me that.'

'Very well,' shrugged the old man. 'I am Kar Odacen of the Iron Wolves, shaman to Cormac Bloodaxe of the Norsii.'

'You are a long way from home, Kar Odacen of the Iron Wolves. What makes you think you will live long enough to return? You are deep in Unberogen lands and Sigmar's hunters are very skilled.'

'As am I, woman,' hissed Gerreon. 'I knew this land well enough to escape those hunters once before, and I will do it again. No man can match my skills and cunning.'

She laughed and twisted in his grip. She saw the raging desire to kill her in his eyes.

And the chance to escape the fate Kar Odacen had planned for her.

'You think you evaded them?' she asked. 'Sigmar sent no one after you. He let you go to honour Ravenna's memory.'

'You lie,' said Gerreon, and the hag woman relished the flinch she saw at the mention of his sister's name: the sister he had killed. The sister she had sacrificed to temper Sigmar's ambition with determination.

The hag woman sagged in his grip.

'I feel sorry for you, Gerreon,' she said. 'You lost Trinovantes and then Ravenna. That must have been hard. You were a pawn in a grander plan, but I did not foresee what those losses would drive you towards. Nor did I see that I would pay for your fall with my death.'

'I do not want your pity, woman,' he hissed, pushing her to her knees. 'And call me Gerreon again and I will gut you right now.'

The hag woman spat in Gerreon's face.

'I should have strangled you with your mother's cord when you were born,' she said. 'I told her that one of her sons would grow to know the greatest pleasure and greatest pain. If she had known you would murder her only daughter, she would have begged me to kill you while you slept in her belly.'

Gerreon slammed his fist into her face, and bright lights exploded before her eyes. Her nose and cheekbone broke, and tears streamed down her face. She fell to her side, feeling the dank wetness of the marshy ground on her skin.

She coughed up a wad of blood and marshwater as Gerreon hauled her upright.

'Your sister knew your soul was sick, but she still tried to help you,' the hag woman said through the pain. 'You repaid her goodness by sticking a sword in her belly and ending her life before its time. She would have borne strong children and been a mother of kindness and strength.'

Gerreon drew his knife, and the blade hovered an inch from her eyeball.

'Do not mention her name again!' he screamed.

'Why? Because you cannot face the horror of what you did?'

'My sister was a slut!' yelled Gerreon, the killing lust of the daemon behind his eyes flaring with rage. 'She opened her legs for Sigmar and deserved to die for that. I was the greater man, she should have loved me! I loved her with all my heart and she spurned me.'

'She knew your true face, Gerreon,' said the hag woman. 'That is why she rejected you.'

'No!' hissed Gerreon, his shoulders shaking with the effort of control. 'She loved me, and I know what you are trying to do. It will not work.'

Gerreon looked up, and Kar Odacen dragged her to the edge of the marsh, his strength surprising for so wizened a man.

'There is no escape for you,' said the shaman. 'The Dark Prince has claimed the one you knew as Gerreon. I know you see this, and it pleases me for you to know that you gave birth to this. How does it feel to know that every soul Azazel has sent screaming into the next world, and every soul he will kill during his immortal life, is thanks to you? You created Azazel, and for that I thank you.'

The hag woman wanted to spit defiance at Kar Odacen, but she knew he was right. Her designs had shaped Gerreon into a vessel, into which the shaman of the Iron Wolves had poured venomous evil and corruption, making him easy prey for a creature from beyond the veil. She had done this, and now she would pay the price for all eternity.

'Do it,' she said.

'No last words for hate's sake?' smiled Kar Odacen.

'What would be the point?'

'A chance to feed the self-righteousness that moves you to meddle in affairs that do not concern you,' suggested Kar Odacen.

'You are no different from me, shaman,' said the hag woman. 'You meddle with the fate of the world and will come to no better end than I.'

'I already know how I will die,' said Kar Odacen. 'It holds no fear for me.'

Defeated, the hag woman sagged in Gerreon's grip.

'I did the best I could to guide mankind,' she said. 'I did what I thought best at the time, and I would do the same again.'

'So arrogant,' said Kar Odacen. 'So like you to excuse your actions.'

'No,' said the hag woman. 'I make no excuses.'

'Very well,' said Kar Odacen, bending to pick up a fist-sized rock. 'Then let it be done.'

She saw a flash of iron in the moonlight, and her eyes widened as hot blood poured down her front. Gerreon held her upright as her body began to convulse. Even as she felt the pain of the cut, Kar Odacen smashed the rock against her temple. Bone cracked and was driven into her brain. Fresh blood streamed down her face.

Her mouth worked soundlessly as the life drained from her body, but before either of her wounds could send her down into death, Gerreon turned her around and pushed her body down into the Brackenwalsch.

Black water rushed into her mouth even as her lifeblood poured out to mix with the marsh water. The pain in her head was incredible and she bucked and heaved against her killer's grip. It was dark beneath the water, but she could see the wavering image of stars and the moon through the churning water.

They were laughing as the thrice death claimed her.

FIFTEEN
The Price of Betrayal

PENDRAG SAT TALL in the saddle on a snow-covered crest overlooking the banks of a bloody river. He supposed that it had a local name, but on his map it was simply known as the great dividing river. Behind him were the lands of the Empire, but the far bank was undiscovered country, a bleak and inhospitable landscape of windswept tundra and open steppe. Freezing winds swept down from the north, and Pendrag watched as the last remnants of a destroyed people fled across the cracking ice of the river.

Perhaps a thousand people huddled in terror on the muddy banks, a ragged mixture of survivors: warriors, cavalry and ordinary men and women. It seemed absurd and monstrous that this was all that was left of an entire tribal race, yet the advance of Sigmar's army had been merciless and thorough. No settlement had gone unmolested, and nothing of value had been left intact in its wake. Every day, pyres of the dead sent reeking plumes of black smoke into the sky, and what had once been fertile eastern grassland was now a charred, ashen wasteland.

A hundred Roppsmenn warriors in iron hauberks and bronze helms tried to impose some order on their people's flight across the river, but it was a hopeless task. The horror of their tribe's destruction overcame any thought other than escape, and braving the still-forming ice was preferable to annihilation at Sigmar's hands.

Pendrag heard a dull cracking sound, and a portion of the ice gave way. Dozens of people were plunged into the sluggish black water. Weighed down with all their worldly possessions, they did not return to the surface. Pendrag closed his eyes as shame threatened to overwhelm him.

'Shallya's tears,' said Redwane as weeping women pulled children away from the hole in the ice, unable to help those who had fallen through. 'What are we doing, Pendrag?'

'I don't know any more,' he said honestly, rubbing the heel of his palm against his temple, and regarding the White Wolf through eyes that carried a lifetime of sorrow acquired in the passage of a season. Redwane had aged in the six months since he had left Reikdorf, his demeanour sullen and his youthful eyes no longer sparkling with roguish charm.

Pendrag knew that he looked no better. The healing energies that had undone the necromancer's dark magic had restored the physique of his youth, yet he was bone-tired and wanted nothing more than to fall into a dreamless sleep. The softness of his former life as Count of Middenheim had vanished from his spare frame, but there was little left of the young man who had set out with Sigmar on the grand journey of empire.

Both he and Redwane had seen too much horror on this campaign to ever be young again.

'Surely this will see an end to the slaughter?' asked Redwane, waving a hand at the terrified people below. 'The Roppsmenn are destroyed. Surely Sigmar will halt the killing?'

Pendrag did not answer, and watched as Sigmar and Count Adelhard surveyed what was left of the Roppsmenn tribe. Beside them, an Udose clansman held the Dragon Banner, for Pendrag had refused to carry it after the Battle of Roskova. Nearly three thousand Roppsmenn warriors had been killed on that blasted heath, and there had been no quarter for the wounded. Once the Dragon Banner was raised, it could not be lowered until every enemy warrior was dead.

Twice more they had brought the scattered Roppsmenn warrior bands to battle, and each time Sigmar ordered the bloodthirsty banner raised. The slaughter had been terrible, and the screams of the dying and images of burning villages haunted Pendrag's dreams each night.

'I don't know how much more of this I can take,' said Redwane, numbly picking at the wolfskin cloak he wore. 'This isn't war anymore. It hasn't been for some time.'

Pendrag nodded as a fresh dusting of snow began to fall from the slate-coloured sky. To either side of him, thousands of fur-cloaked warriors gathered in sword bands under the colours of their tribes, ready to be unleashed on the fleeing Roppsmenn. Chequered Ostagoth banners of black and white billowed in the winter wind next to the gold and red flags of the Asoborns, but they were far outnumbered by the patchwork banners of the Udose.

The clansmen had taken bloodthirsty relish in the war, killing all before them with hearts hungry to avenge the death of Count Wolfila. The stories of his death had been told and retold so often that the truth was lost and the horror of what the Roppsmenn were said to have done grew to ridiculous levels.

'All the better to justify what we do here,' he had told Redwane one night as they gathered around the campfire and the White Wolf had told him the latest gruesome embellishment.

Sigmar and Adelhard marched up the iron-hard ground towards the army, and Pendrag felt a chill at the sight of the Emperor that had nothing to do with the plummeting temperature. Though snow swirled in the air and his breath misted before him, Sigmar was clad in only a thin tunic of red with a silver wolf stitched upon his chest. The warriors of the army were wrapped in thick furs, but Sigmar appeared not to feel the intense chill that stabbed like knives from the north.

Since leaving the Middle Mountains, Sigmar's face had hardened, and the death of Wolfila hung like a noose around his neck. His hair was lank and thin, and the flesh seemed somehow tighter on his body, as though his bones were pushing out a little harder than before. His eyes were haunted by the loss of his friend, but glittered with a light that seemed to come from a dark place deep inside him. He still wore the golden crown he had taken from Morath, and instead of Ghal-maraz, the long, basket-hilted claymore that had once belonged to Count Wolfila was scabbarded at the Emperor's hip.

King Kurgan's hammer was wrapped in an oiled cloth in Pendrag's pack, nestled beside the crown crafted by Alaric the Mad for Sigmar's coronation. It sat ill with Pendrag that he carried such legendary items, but Sigmar had insisted that the Roppsmenn be fought with the blade of the man they had so brutally killed.

Sigmar drew Wolfila's weapon and held it out before him. The sword was heavy and fashioned from thick, dark iron. It was not the weapon of a swordsman, it was the weapon of a butcher.

'I want those warriors dead,' said Sigmar aiming the sword towards the Roppsmenn by the river. 'Redwane, take your White Wolves and ride them down.'

'Very good,' said Adelhard. 'I order the Ostagoth horse archers to hem them in and you will drive them into the river.'

'My lord?' asked Redwane, looking at Pendrag for support.

'Is something about my order unclear?' asked Sigmar.

'No, my lord,' said Redwane, 'but is it really necessary to attack?'

'Necessary?' hissed Sigmar. 'These treacherous curs killed a count of the Empire. Of course it is necessary! Now follow my orders.'

Redwane shook his head.

'No, my lord, I won't,' he said.

Sigmar planted the claymore in the ground before him, his face twisted in fury.

'You dare to defy me, boy?' he asked. 'I am your Emperor and you will obey my orders or I will see you dead.'

'I'm sorry, my lord, but I won't lead the White Wolves to murder those men.'

'You will do as you are ordered!'

'No,' said Redwane, and Pendrag's heart soared with pride. 'I will not.'

Sigmar stepped towards Redwane, and Pendrag dropped from his horse to put himself between the two warriors.

'There is no need for this,' he said. 'The Roppsmenn are defeated. They are a broken people, and you have avenged Wolfila's death.'

Sigmar turned on Pendrag, and the well of hate he saw in the Emperor's face sent a jolt of fear down his spine. For the briefest moment, it seemed as though someone far older looked out from behind Sigmar's eyes, but it vanished so quickly, Pendrag wasn't sure he had really seen it.

'Always the peacemaker, Pendrag.' hissed Sigmar. 'It was your counsel that stayed my hand when I could have destroyed the Norsii. Look at what that mercy has brought us. Wolfila dead and fleets of Norse raiders attacking our coast every day. No, I will not make the mistake of leaving any of these vermin alive to return with vengeance in their hearts.'

'You speak of the Norsii,' said Pendrag, fighting to keep his voice even. 'Then why are we not readying ourselves to fight them? You must know they will come at us soon. Our people live in terror of their warlords and, with every day that passes, that fear grows more powerful and saps their courage.'

'The people of the Empire will stand firm against the Norsii,' promised Sigmar.

'No,' said Pendrag. 'The north is wide open. All we have done here is weaken our land. We need to return to Reikdorf and gather the forces of the counts to strengthen the north.'

'Spoken like a true coward,' snapped Sigmar. 'I remember you telling me you were not fit to rule Middenheim, that there were others more suited to the task. It seems I should have listened to you.'

'Listen to *yourself*, Sigmar,' begged Pendrag. 'This bloodshed is madness. It sullies everything we have achieved over the years. Is this how you want to be remembered, as a butcher of men? A tyrant king? A killer of women and children, no better than a greenskin?'

Sigmar's face darkened with anger, but Pendrag felt a weight lift from his shoulders with every word he spoke. 'I am soul-sick of this killing. Every man here has blood on his hands, and our honour is stained by what we have done here.'

He reached out and put his hand on Sigmar's shoulder, and said, 'It is time to go home, my friend.'

Sigmar's hand closed on the hilt of the claymore and drew it from the earth. He stared at the butcher's blade, and for a dreadful moment, Pendrag thought that his friend was about to run him through.

Though imperceptible to the eye, Pendrag could feel that Sigmar's entire body was trembling. The muscles at his jawline were as tight as a drum, clenching and releasing as though he sought to quell a dreadful killing rage.

At last his head came up, and Pendrag's heart broke to see the pain in his friend's eyes, swimming to the surface as if from a great depth.

Sigmar looked back at the desperate scramble of people fighting to cross the river to escape his wrath, and his shoulders sagged.

'You are right,' said Sigmar, letting out a shuddering breath. 'It *is* time to go home.'

NEARLY FOUR HUNDRED Wolfships filled the sheltered bay, their clinker-built hulls crafted from the scarce wood of the tundra and timbers carried from the ruins of plundered Udose settlements across the sea. Cormac Bloodaxe felt a potent sense of purpose as he stood on the cliff above the shoreline and admired the host of warships bobbing in the heavy swells. It had taken an entire year to build them, and no warlord in the history of the Norsii had ever assembled so mighty a fleet.

Behind him, what had once been a ramshackle collection of crude dwellings constructed from the cannibalised remnants of Wolfships was now a settlement to match any from their old lands. As well as the rebuilt tribe of the Iron Wolves, the nameless settlement was now home to thousands of tribesmen who had come from far and wide to make war on the southern lands.

It had begun as the first rays of weak summer sun had thawed the iron ground. The season of night had come to an end, and the power of the gods had swept the lands of the north, summoning their followers to battle. Warriors with golden skin and almond-shaped eyes, who called themselves the Wei-Tu, had come out of the east and sworn their lives to Cormac. Two days later, warbands of tattooed fighters called the Hung had emerged from the swirling lights of the far north on towering steeds of darkness.

That was just the beginning.

Over the course of the season of sun, warriors from tribes with names like the Gharhars, Tahmaks, Avags, Kul, Vargs and Yusak had crossed the northern sea and pledged their swords to his banner. Every day brought fresh champions and fighters to the coast, drawn by the thrumming pressure in their veins that demanded war. Over ten thousand northmen were camped within a day's ride, and the totems of a dozen warlords were planted in the earth. The rivalry between them was fierce, and only Cormac's vision of destruction and the growing sense of history unfolding was keeping the violence in check. It would not last forever, and, as soon as the pack ice around the coastline melted, Cormac would lead his fleet of Wolfships across the sea.

He turned from the cliffs and made his way back down to his longhouse, passing the camps of warriors from the Khazags and Mung. The latter tribe of flat-faced warriors were short and stocky, and fought with enormous axes that were almost comically oversized. Cormac had seen one of them split a column of seasoned timber with a single blow, and any doubts as to how lethal they would be in battle were forgotten.

As he passed yet more totems rammed into the hard ground, Cormac thought back to Kar Odacen and Azazel. Kar Odacen had predicted that there would be a gathering of might, and he had been proven right. As much as he detested the vile shaman, Cormac was not so blinded by his devotion to the Dark Gods that he did not value the man's insight.

He had not seen or heard from Kar Odacen in months, and had no way of knowing whether his mission into the south had been successful. Whether the shaman and Azazel still lived was a matter of supreme indifference to Cormac. The subjugation of Sigmar's people would begin at the next turning of the world, with or without them.

The year of raiding and slaughter had spread terror through the lands of the Empire.

There would never be a better time to attack.

'Now it is time to take the fire south,' he said.

THE AFTERMATH OF the destruction of the Roppsmenn was a sombre time for Sigmar's army. It was not called a war, for the Empire's wars were fought for noble reasons, and no one could think of a noble reason for this slaughter. Wolfila's death had been avenged, but vengeance was not so noble a reason for the virtual annihilation of an entire tribe.

No sooner was the campaign declared over, and the army withdrawn from the great dividing river, than the Asoborns turned their chariots south and rode away from the army with their banners lowered. They said no fond farewells nor made oaths of brotherhood, for the warriors of Queen Freya wished to forget their part in this killing.

Count Adelhard led his Ostagoths eastward the following morning, exchanging words with Sigmar that no one could hear. Sigmar never spoke of what Adelhard said to him, but his face was murderous as he turned away from the eastern count and mounted his horse.

Only the Udose warriors felt no remorse at the bloodshed, and they marched with the Unberogen as far as the tip of the Middle Mountains before turning north to their homelands. They had a land to rebuild and a new leader to find. Months of skirmishing and political infighting was sure to follow as the powerful clan lords manoeuvred for supremacy and sought to position themselves or their heirs as the new count of the Udose.

Sigmar led his warriors around the snow-wreathed peaks of the mountains towards the Fauschlag Rock. Winter was at its zenith and the land was deathly quiet, as though afraid to intrude upon the Emperor's sombre isolation. The army trudged through the snow, each man lost in his thoughts and wrapped in misery as they skirted the rocky haunches of the mountains. The Emperor kept a distance from his friends, unwilling to be drawn into conversation beyond what was necessary for the upkeep and course of the army.

Redwane and Pendrag said little to Sigmar on the journey home, for the brutality of the campaign still played out in their nightmares, and neither man wished to relive their part in it. Pendrag still carried Sigmar's crown and hammer, for the Emperor had not relinquished Count Wolfila's claymore, and the golden crown of Morath still glittered upon his brow.

The days were long, the nights bitter and hard. The Unberogen huddled close to the fires, wrapped tightly in their wolfskin cloaks to survive the darkness until the sun crested the Worlds Edge Mountains.

Each night, Redwane walked the camp, unable to close his eyes without seeing the faces of the dead that seemed to hang over them like a curse. Passing the Emperor's tent, he would hear Sigmar crying out in his sleep, as though in the grip of a never-ending nightmare. He spoke of this with Pendrag, who confessed that he had often seen Sigmar whispering under his breath, as though conversing with unseen spirits.

Sigmar dismissed their concerns with the same sullen expression with which he made every pronouncement, and the march through the snow continued.

At last, the soaring rock of Middenheim came into view, and the spirits of the army lifted as thoughts turned to homes and wives unseen for more than half a year. Even Sigmar seemed buoyed by the sight of the incredible city when it became apparent that the first of the great viaducts had been completed. The camps around the city were deserted, the labourers and craftsmen having returned to their villages for the winter, but work had already begun on clearing the forest at the site of the second viaduct.

Myrsa marched down from the city to greet them, surrounded by a bodyguard of plate-armoured warriors. The Warrior Eternal had made a full recovery from the wound he had taken at the fortress of the necromancer, yet his joy at seeing his friends return was tempered by the tales of slaughter from the east, and the hollow-eyed appearance of the Emperor.

The Middenlanders climbed to their city with Myrsa at their head, and Pendrag bade Sigmar farewell with stiff formality. Something precious had been lost between them and, though they would always be sword-brothers, it seemed their friendship had died along with the Roppsmenn. The journey into the north ended as it had begun, with Sigmar and Redwane riding at the head of the White Wolves.

A month and a half later, with the promise of spring prising loose winter's claws, the ruler of the Empire rode through the gates of Reikdorf.

FROM HIGH UPON the walls of his city, Sigmar watched the Red Scythes as they crossed the Ostreik Bridge. The sun was setting, and the last of winter's light gleamed on the iron hauberks worn by the forty men in vivid red cloaks surrounding Count Krugar. The leader of the Taleutens was dressed in a fine tunic of crimson and gold over his heavy suit of armour, and a banner of the same colours flew in the brisk wind.

Sigmar felt a thrill of anticipation at what was to come, and gripped the hilt of Wolfila's sword tightly. The eastern gate of the city was open and, as the riders made their way towards it, Sigmar turned and descended the steps to the hard-packed earth of the gateway.

Six White Wolves followed him, men who had marched into the north, whose loyalty he could trust absolutely. Since he had returned from the land of the Roppsmenn, he had felt the eyes of his people on him constantly. Men and women he had called friends for years now cast sidelong glances at him when they thought he wasn't looking. He felt their suspicious looks, and knew that they spoke ill of him when his back was turned.

Men who claimed to care for him spoke in hushed whispers when he was near, no doubt plotting against him, imagining a day when his back would make a good home for a traitor's dagger. They questioned him constantly, and though the war against the Roppsmenn was months old, Eoforth and Wolfgart would not let it rest, endlessly asking why he had led his army with such brutality.

Brutality they called it, yet without such brutality the Empire could not be maintained. They did not understand that betrayal had to be punished in a manner that would send a clear message to those who thought their oaths of loyalty could bend as they saw fit. Loyalty to Sigmar's Empire was inflexible, and the war against the Roppsmenn had been a bloody reminder to his counts of the price of disloyalty.

It would not be the only one.

Sigmar reached the roadway as the Taleuten warriors rode through the gate, moving to the sides of the esplanade as Krugar's horse approached him. He felt the White Wolves around him tense in readiness.

'Count Krugar,' said Sigmar. 'Welcome to Reikdorf.'

The Taleuten count smoothly dismounted and removed his helm. His hair was matted with sweat, and his beard was plaited in three long strands. The man was weary and Sigmar saw suspicion in his eyes, for the summons that had brought Krugar to Reikdorf had been direct and without any hint of a reason.

Sigmar's eyes were drawn to the curved leather scabbard at Krugar's hip, in which was sheathed Utensjarl, the sword of the Taleuten kings. When he had seen it first, it had seemed little more than a well-crafted blade, but now he saw that it was a weapon of power. Dangerous.

'Emperor,' said Krugar, his voice strong and resonant. He took Sigmar's hand in the warrior's grip, and said, 'It is good to see you. My congratulations on your victories in the north of the Empire.'

Sigmar nodded and released Krugar's sweaty hand as though it were a poisonous snake.

'Yes, a usurper destroyed, and the Roppsmenn will trouble me no longer. All in all, a fitting end to a season of campaigning.'

'You have a new crown,' said Krugar. 'What happened to the old one?'

Sigmar reached up to touch the golden circlet at his brow, feeling the reassuring warmth of its power coursing through him.

'It was destroyed,' said Sigmar. 'The dwarf magic was not so strong after all.'

'Destroyed?' said Krugar. 'Damn me, but I didn't think I'd see the day when something forged by dwarf-craft could be undone.'

'It matters not. As you say, I have a new crown,' said Sigmar, eager to change the subject. 'I trust you encountered no trouble on the road?'

'Nothing we couldn't drive off with a few charges,' said Krugar proudly. 'My Red Scythes are nothing if not fearsome.'

'They are that,' agreed Sigmar, 'but they must be weary. To have reached Reikdorf so soon, you must have ridden like the *Scrianii* themselves were at your heels.'

'We made good time,' said Krugar, handing his helmet to one of his warriors and running his hands through his hair. 'We skirted the forest to the edge of the Asoborn lands, and then followed the river here.'

'Your men will be fed and watered, and their horses given the best of care in Wolfgart's stables,' promised Sigmar, waving his men forward.

'My thanks,' said Krugar with a curt bow. 'Before I forget, Queen Freya sends you her best greetings.'

'You saw the Asoborn queen?' asked Sigmar with a frown.

'Aye, we did. An impressive woman to be sure,' said Krugar with a lecherous grin that made Sigmar sick to his stomach. 'Came out to greet us in a chariot made of gold and brass, I swear it! Changed days, eh? Time was she'd have been riding out to kill us and mount our heads on her banner pole! Had her two boys with her, Fridleifr and Sigulf. Fine lads they are, strong and tall. A few years and they'll be riding out to their first battle!'

'I have no doubt they will,' said Sigmar with a toothy grin. He guided the Taleuten count from the gateway as stable lads and White Wolves led the lathered horses of the Red Scythes towards the ostler yards. The Taleuten cavalrymen went with them, leaving four stout warriors to accompany their count.

'Have to say that she seemed more than a little put out not to have been summoned to Reikdorf also,' said Krugar. 'I was surprised, because your letter talked of a gathering of counts.'

'It will be a select gathering,' said Sigmar.

'Oh? Who else is coming?'

'All will become clear soon enough, my friend,' said Sigmar. 'But come, I have something to show you.'

Sigmar and Krugar made their way into Reikdorf, along quiet streets, towards the heart of the city with a dozen White Wolves following them. Darkness was closing in on the world, and Sigmar felt himself growing calmer as the light faded and the shadows deepened.

He could sense Krugar's unease and said, 'Tell me what else Freya had to say for herself.'

'She talked about the Norsii mainly,' said Krugar. 'You'll have heard the tales of the warlords, Bloodaxe and Azazel? Well, the north is wide open now that the Roppsmenn are... gone... and the clan lords of the Udose are fighting among themselves. It seems clear that the Norsii are going to come south as soon as the ice melts in the northern oceans, and we need to be ready to face them when they do.'

'I will be,' promised Sigmar, 'I assure you. By the time any Norsii arrive, there will be an army the likes of which has not been seen in over a thousand years.'

Krugar gave him a confused look, but followed him through a heavy wooden gate set in a high wall and into a cobbled courtyard. At the centre of the courtyard stood a large building of dark stone with narrow windows sealed with iron bars. Eight warriors with heavy hammers stood guard around a wooden door of banded iron, and they moved aside as Sigmar approached.

'What in the name of Ulric is going on?' asked Krugar. 'Is this a prison?'

'Yes,' said Sigmar. 'But only you and I can enter. Our warriors will need to wait outside.'

'What? Why?'

'Trust me, all will become clear in a moment.'

'It had better do. I don't mind telling you that I don't like this.'

The Unberogen guards opened the door, and Sigmar indicated that Krugar should enter. He followed the Taleuten count into an empty vestibule lit by oil lanterns. The sound of shouting could be heard from deeper in the building, but the thick walls muffled the sense of them. Sigmar lifted a lantern, and set off down a corridor to his left. He led Krugar along a series of narrow passageways towards an iron door secured with a heavy padlock.

He unlocked the door, and they descended square-cut steps that led to another narrow corridor, this one lined with empty cells.

'Almost there,' said Sigmar, making his way towards a cell at the end of the corridor.

He hung the lantern on a hook outside this cell, and watched as Krugar tried to make sense of what he was seeing. A lone figure stirred at the sound of their footsteps and the warm glow of the lantern.

Chained to the wall and dressed in rich clothes that were tattered and filthy, Count Aloysis of the Cherusens shielded his eyes from the light.

'What is the meaning of this?' demanded Krugar, reaching for his sword.

Sigmar was faster.

With one hand, he snatched Krugar's blade from its sheath, and with the other took the man by the throat and slammed him against the bars of the cell. The point of Utensjarl hovered an inch from Krugar's throat.

'I commanded you to put an end to your dispute!' roared Sigmar. 'I told you to go back to your lands as brothers! Now I return from the north to find you have betrayed me.'

'Betrayed?' gasped Krugar, clawing at Sigmar's wrist. 'What?'

'In defiance of everything I said to you both, you continue to fight one another. You plunder one another's lands, raiding and killing in spite of my command. I gave you a way to save face and return home in peace, but no, that was not good enough for you, was it?'

'Sigmar, I–' began Krugar.

'Sigmar, please,' said Aloysis from his cell. 'There is no need for this!'

'Enough!' shouted Sigmar. 'The Roppsmenn paid the price for attacking me. Now you will both see what it means to betray me. At dawn tomorrow you will be taken to the marshes of the Brackenwalsch and put to death.'

SIXTEEN
The Temptation of Sigmar

GREY SKIES GREETED the day of the executions. Sigmar rode through the streets of Reikdorf at the head of twenty White Wolves, moving quietly and without conversation. Counts Krugar and Aloysis were borne upon a hay wagon, their heads swathed in hessian hoods and their hands bound with iron fetters. A bell tolled from the steeple of the temple of Ulric, and a light rain began to fall.

It was still early, and the few people abroad at this hour stopped to stare in surprise and fear at the sight of him leading so strange a procession. Beneath their hoods, both prisoners were gagged, and all signs of their former station had been removed. To all appearances, the prisoners were no more than base criminals, yet Sigmar was not fool enough to think that their identities were not already common knowledge.

The thought did not trouble him, for the warriors who had ridden with Krugar and Aloysis were even now under guard in a number of warehouses on the southern bank of the river. The city gates had been closed to prevent word from spreading beyond the walls, but Sigmar could not stop tavern talk, and news of Aloysis and Krugar's arrests had swept through the city like marsh pox.

Aloysis had arrived in Reikdorf only two nights previously, and the Cherusen count had been similarly outraged at his harsh treatment.

Sigmar ignored his protests and left him chained to the dungeon wall until he had brought Krugar down to join him. As he held the blade to Krugar's throat, the killing urge that had been with him since Morath's defeat threatened to overwhelm him. It had taken all his self-control not to cut Krugar's throat there and then.

Such urges were anathema to him, but the desire to kill Krugar and Aloysis was like a craving to which he dared not surrender.

These men were his friends.

No, they were his enemies, defying him and breaking their oaths of loyalty.

They were men who made foolish errors of judgement, letting ancient hatreds whose origins had long been forgotten blind them to their ties of brotherhood.

No, they were fools who deserved to die!

Sigmar's head ached with conflicting thoughts and emotions. As much as he knew that what he was doing was very wrong, the rage that fed his urge to kill pulsed like fiery waves in his skull, blotting out any thoughts of compassion. So vile and bitter was this rage that he did not even recognise it as his own. Sigmar had known anger in his life, but this rage had been nursed for thousands of years, a hatred that had grown to such immense proportions that Sigmar's mind recoiled from such darkness.

Even as he understood that this hatred was alien, calming warmth spread through him, seeping down from his temple and into his chest. It spread along his limbs, easing his fears and soothing his troubled mind. All remembrances of this morning's evil fled from his thoughts.

The Ostgate loomed in the pre-dawn light, and the armoured warriors stationed there pulled the locking bar from its runners. The gate was opened, and Sigmar rode between the high towers flanking it. None of the gate guards dared meet his eyes, and he sensed great fear in their lowered gazes and submissive postures.

Even as he relished that fear, anger swelled as he saw that they pitied the prisoners.

These men had betrayed him, and his own warriors dared look at them with pity?

Keeping his hands tight on the reins, Sigmar rode from his city, keeping the pace steady as they travelled through the morning along the eastern road that skirted the edges of the Brackenwalsch. Weak sunlight warmed the earth, yet wisps of fog still oozed from the bleak fens to the north. The muddy greyness of the day lingered, and when the road bent towards Siggurdheim, Sigmar stopped his horse and dismounted.

'Bring them,' he said, his voice cold and laden with ancient relish.

The White Wolves manhandled the two captives from the wagon, and Sigmar marched over to them. He pulled off their hoods, and both counts blinked in the sudden brightness. Sigmar looked into their eyes, pleased at the fear he saw behind their bravado. Men always feared to die, no matter what they claimed.

'This is the day of your deaths,' he said, pointing into the fog-shrouded marsh. 'Some years ago I watched the Endals execute a traitor named Idris Gwylt in the marshes around Marburg. They called it the thrice death, and it was a bad death. The priests of Morr tried to stop it. They said that for a man to die like that would deny him his journey onwards to the next world. I say it is the only death appropriate for traitors.'

He smiled as they blanched at the mention of the thrice death. Word of Idris Gwylt's fate had spread throughout the Empire, and the horror of his death was writ large in their eyes.

Sigmar led his warriors from the road and into the marsh, leaving a handful of White Wolves to guard their horses. The air tasted of life, and Sigmar felt his bile rise at the rancid stench of growth and fecundity. This was a liminal place, where worlds overlapped, and where the walls that separated them grew thin. He could sense power seeping up through the ground, the essence of life and creation, and his flesh crawled at its nearness.

No paths existed through the marshes, yet Sigmar led the way through the fog as though following a well-remembered route. He had never travelled these marshes, but he knew with utter certainty that he would not be sucked beneath the dark waters. Behind him, his warriors splashed and cursed as they dragged the reluctant prisoners through the sodden ground.

The marshes were alive with sound, and Sigmar shut out the cries of birds, the buzz of insects and the croaks of swamp creatures. His flesh grew clammy and warm with the life energy pouring from the waters. His warriors were oblivious to it, yet he could see it as a translucent green mist that rippled from the water and fens like noxious swamp gas.

When he decided they had come far enough, he raised a hand and turned to face his victims. He stood at the edge of a dark pool, the waters brackish and dead. It was perfect.

'This is far enough,' he said. 'Bring them.'

Krugar and Aloysis were dragged forward and pushed to their knees at the edge of the pool. Their eyes bulged with fear, wordlessly pleading with Sigmar not to do this. He drew Krugar's sword, carrying Utensjarl now instead of Count Wolfila's blade. The hilt felt warm in his hand, the power within it cowed by something greater.

He held the gleaming blade before Krugar, and said, 'To be killed by a weapon bound to your lineage will send a message that will be heard throughout the Empire.'

Krugar struggled against his bonds, but the White Wolves held him firm.

'This gives me no pleasure,' said Sigmar, 'but betrayal can have only one punishment.'

'And what of murder?' asked a familiar voice.

Sigmar turned as Wolfgart emerged from the mist, his sword-brother leading a lathered horse that picked its way fearfully over the sodden ground.

'What are you doing here, Wolfgart?' asked Sigmar. 'This does not concern you.'

'Oh, this concerns me, Sigmar,' replied Wolfgart. 'This concerns me a great deal.'

'These men defied my command. What message does it send if my counts can pick and choose which of my commands they obey and which they do not?'

'I don't deny that action must be taken, but this?'

'This is a legitimate execution,' said Sigmar.

'It is murder,' replied Wolfgart.

Sigmar shook his head, aiming Utensjarl at Wolfgart.

'Of all the people I thought would betray me,' he said, 'I never once thought you would be one of them.'

Wolfgart took a step towards Sigmar, his hands held out in supplication.

'I'm not betraying you, my friend. I'm trying to save you,' he said.

'From what?'

'From yourself,' said Wolfgart, moving closer. 'Something happened to you in the north. I don't know what, but something changed you, made you more ruthless, more… I don't know… heartless.'

'Nothing happened in the north, Wolfgart,' said Sigmar, 'save my eyes being opened to the true nature of man. He is an animal, and it is in his nature to betray. All the race of men understand is blood and vengeance.'

'Vengeance is pointless, Sigmar. Continuing the feuds that divide us will only lead to further hatred. You taught me that.'

'I was young and foolish then,' said Sigmar. 'I was blind to the reality of the world.'

Wolfgart was right in front of him, and Sigmar felt a nauseous spike of pain in his gut, as though his sword-brother's very nearness was somehow its cause. Wolfgart reached out, placing a hand on his shoulder, and he flinched.

'What do you think will happen to the Empire if you kill Krugar and Aloysis?' Wolfgart asked. 'The Cherusens and Taleutens won't stand for it. They'll rebel, and you'll have a civil war on your hands. Some of the counts might support you, but others won't, and what will you do then? March on their lands and burn them like you did the Roppsmenn?'

'If need be,' said Sigmar, shrugging off Wolfgart's hand.

'I won't let you do this,' said Wolfgart.

'You cannot stop me,' laughed Sigmar. 'I am the Emperor!'

Sigmar turned his back on Wolfgart.

'I am done explaining myself to you. It is time to deliver my judgement upon these traitors,' he said.

'Sigmar, don't,' pleaded Wolfgart.

'Begone,' he said. 'I will deal with you when I return to Reikdorf.'

Sigmar lifted Utensjarl, but before he could strike Wolfgart hurled himself forward, sending them both tumbling to the ground. The sword landed point down in the mud.

Sigmar roared in anger as Wolfgart fought to hold him down. His fist cannoned into Wolfgart's face, and he heard a crack of bone. Wolfgart slammed a right cross into Sigmar's jaw, but he rode the punch and slammed his forehead into the middle of Wolfgart's face. Blood burst from Wolfgart's broken nose, and Sigmar brought his knee up into his groin. His sword-brother grunted in pain, but did not release his hold.

'This is murder,' hissed Wolfgart through a mask of blood.

Hands gripped Wolfgart, hauling him from Sigmar.

'No!' roared Sigmar. 'Leave him!'

They rolled in the mud and sopping pools of the marsh, punching, kicking and clawing at one another like wild animals. All thoughts of honour and nobility were forgotten in the brawl. Sigmar spat out a mouthful of stagnant water, and drove his elbow into Wolfgart's neck.

Wolfgart clutched at his throat, crawling away as he gasped for air.

Sigmar reached out as he saw a gleam of silver, his hand closing on Utensjarl's hilt. He dragged the sword from the mud. A ring of warriors surrounded him, but he cared nothing for their expressions of shock and confusion. All that mattered was that his enemy died.

He half-crawled, half-scrambled on his knees through the mud towards his sword-brother. Wolfgart lay at the edge of water, and Sigmar turned him onto his back. The water bubbled and churned around them, as though their struggles had stirred something beneath them. Rank swamp gas frothed to the surface.

Wolfgart's face was bloodied, and he fought for breath. Sigmar took Utensjarl in a two-handed grip, the blade aimed at Wolfgart's chest.

'Brother!' cried Wolfgart, and Sigmar's killing fire faltered as he saw not fear, but sadness in his sword-brother's face. The water around them heaved again, and Sigmar heard a wet, sucking sound, like a boot pulled from the mud.

A body broke the surface of the water, a corpse once held in the stygian darkness below, but now returned to the world above. The body rolled upright, and Sigmar gagged on the stench of the marsh's depths as he found himself staring at a pallid, dead face.

It was the hag woman. Though dark water slicked from her face and marsh fronds garlanded her hair, there was no mistaking the Brackenwalsch seer.

Her throat had been cut and her skull was caved in at the temple.

Her eyes were open, and they stared directly at Sigmar.

And in them, he saw his soul shining back at him.

SIGMAR CRIED OUT as he saw himself reflected in the hag woman's eyes, sitting astride his oldest and dearest friend with murder in his heart. As though looking up through her cold, lifeless orbs, he saw the horror in the faces of those around him, and the berserk rage on his own. For the briefest instant, he did not recognise himself, the drawn, parchment-skinned monster that revelled in bloodshed and the pain of the living.

The moment stretched, as though frozen in time, and Sigmar felt a feather-light brush of a power greater than anything he had ever known, including the Flame of Ulric. It was elemental and vast beyond understanding, a power that had existed since the dawn of the world, and which would endure beyond the span of men or gods.

It was old this power, old and strong, and with that one, almost inconsequential touch, Sigmar recognised it as a power he had long ago sworn to serve in a moment of grief. The hag woman had promised he would see her again, and he understood the meaning of her last words to him in one sudden, awful burst of clarity.

He looked beyond the ring of White Wolves, seeing that which was invisible to the sight of mortals. Was this a last gift of the hag woman, an echo of her powers granted to him that he might understand what he had become?

Sigmar saw the tautness of his body, as though his flesh and soul had been stretched and twisted like a fraying rope on the verge of snapping. A black miasma surrounded him, a cloying shroud that smothered the very things that made him the man he was and poisoned everything within him that was good and noble. Within this miasma, a towering shadow hung over him, a monstrous outline of something long dead, yet which endured impossibly down the thousands of years since its doom.

A clawed hand of glittering gold and silver seemed to reach from the miasma with fingers of black smoke that pressed upon his skull like the blessing of a priest. Yet this was no blessing, this was a curse, for, even as he watched, the essence of the shadowy creature was slowly, moment by moment, passing into Sigmar.

'No!' he cried, but he was not a player in this scene, merely a passive observer.

In an instant, he relived the war against the Roppsmenn, the hideous massacres, the burning villages, the bloodthirsty rampages of the Udose which he had not only allowed but encouraged. The slaughter of an entire people. Tears welled in his eyes as he knew that he had passed the darkness of his heart to every man who fought with him in the north.

The souls of all who took part in the destruction of the Roppsmenn would be forever tainted by that unjust war, and Sigmar knew he could never atone for it. Looking around him, he saw the same shadow that enveloped him as a haze around the warriors he had brought from Reikdorf. Through him evil had touched them, bringing the hidden darkness within them to the surface.

Looking closer, Sigmar saw that the dark shadow seeping into his soul was slithering around the golden crown at his brow. The soothing warmth that quietened his fears and quashed any rebellious thoughts had silenced the shrieking voice of his heart that knew what he was doing was wrong. Every day since the defeat of Morath crowded his thoughts, and he wept to see the passage of days, knowing they were his yet experiencing them as a stranger might hear the tale of a long-lost brother.

'This is not me!' he screamed, watching as the shadow that loomed over his body swelled in anticipation of this murder.

Images flashed before him, and his soul fought against the dark spirit invading him.

Ravenna by the river.

A city swallowed by the sand...

His father in the Grey Vaults.

A murderous enemy with a fell sword...

The kings of men swearing sword oaths with him.

The forging of a mighty crown of sorcery...

The soaring nobility of the race of man coming together as one.

Utensjarl fell from Sigmar's hands, and the world snapped back into focus as he looked, once again, through his own eyes. The black miasma surrounding him vanished, and Sigmar looked down at Wolfgart, heartsick with grief and horror. He sobbed, and the sound clawed from his throat as though from a great distance.

'Sigmar?' cried Wolfgart. 'Is that you?'

He blinked, tears of shame and fear spilling down his cheeks as he felt the awesome rage of something older and more terrible than anything he had ever known turn upon him.

'Gods, brother,' he whispered. 'What has become of me?'

Sigmar grasped the golden crown at his brow, but no sooner had his fingers touched the metal than fiery agony exploded inside his head. He screamed as shooting spikes of pain ripped into him, like a choke-chain violently pulled at the neck of a disobedient hound.

He surged to his feet, screaming as his humanity warred with this invasive force that poisoned him with its evil. Wolfgart scrambled to his knees, reaching out to him, but his sword-brother could not help him now.

He had to fight this battle alone.

With a cry of anguish, Sigmar turned and fled into the depths of the marsh.

THE MIST CLOSED around him as he ran blindly through the depths of the Brackenwalsch. He heard alarmed cries following him, but they were soon swallowed by the deadening fog and eerie silence of the marsh. Sigmar ran without care for where he stepped, knowing that at any moment he might wander from the path, stumble into a sucking bog and be lost forever.

He welcomed the thought, but with every stumbling step he plunged deeper and deeper into the haunted fens, driven by the imperative to flee from any he might corrupt with the evil power growing within him.

How could this have happened? The blood of an entire tribe was on his hands. He wept as he ran, his entire body wracked with heaving sobs for the lives he had ended and the souls blackened by his actions.

The mist thickened until he could see no farther than his next step. He ran faster than he had ever run in his life, yet the blackness that hung over him followed him wherever he went. He splashed through shallow streams, blundered into tearing bracken and gorse, tripped over buried rocks and breathed in great lungfuls of swampy air. He ran until he could run no more, and dropped to his knees before a deep pool of peaty water, the surface like a black mirror.

Ripples spread from the edge of the pool, and eyeless things disappeared beneath the surface as they sensed his presence. Fat flies with iridescent wings droned over the surface of the water and loathsome plants with white, sticky fronds brushed him with hideous caresses as he fell forward.

His arms sank to his elbows, and segmented worms blindly wriggled around his flesh. He pulled his arms from the mud and held his hands out before him. Black water ran from them like blood, and the horror of the last few months surged to the forefront of his mind.

How could he have done this?

That was not him. Sigmar Heldenhammer was a better man than that.

Are you so sure?

Sigmar's head lifted at the question. Had he spoken aloud? Was this the voice of his conscience? Or was there someone else in the marsh?

Something black moved in the mist, like an enormous figure swathed in robes of utter darkness, but when Sigmar snapped his head around to look, he saw nothing but the undulant banks of yellowish-white fog drifting at the edge of the pool.

'Show yourself!' he demanded.

I am not here, the voice said. *You know where I am, and you know what I can give you.*

'I want nothing from you!' screamed Sigmar. 'Whatever you are, you are a monster. A creature of evil!'

True, but I could not have reached out to you had there not already been a darkness within you. The door was open. All I needed to do was step through.

'No! I am a good man!' wailed Sigmar

You are a man, and man is born with darkness in his heart, hissed the voice and Sigmar saw the phantom shadow at the edge of his vision once more. It circled him, though part of him knew it was but a fragment of some far greater power.

'I will not listen to you,' said Sigmar, reaching up to tear the crown from his head. Once again spikes of pain stabbed through his eyes, and he fell to the ground, clawing at his head.

You will listen, for you are to be my herald. You shall usher in an age of death to the world. You will craft a realm of bone for me to rule. Such has been your destiny since before your insignificant ember of life was spat into existence.

Sigmar picked himself up as yet more memories of his slaughter of the Roppsmenn flooded his thoughts.

You see? This is what you are. This is who *you are. Embrace it and the pain will end. Cease your resistance and give me your flesh to wear. You cannot keep my spirit out forever, and when you are mine, I shall give you power beyond your wildest imaginings. This petty empire of man that you have built is nothing to what we might achieve together. There are lands far beyond these shores to be conquered, worlds beyond this paltry rock to be enslaved! Stand at my side and this entire world will be yours!*

Sigmar saw it all, the warring states of the eastern dragon kings, the mysterious island of the fey in the west, the endless jungles of the south where lizards that walked like men built towering cities, and the seething lands of chaos and madness in the north.

All of it could be his, and he saw himself at the head of an invincible army of warriors that stretched from horizon to horizon. Wherever these warriors marched, the land blackened and shrivelled, dying with every footstep taken in dreadful unison. This was an army of the dead, an unstoppable force that defied the living and left nothing but ashes in its wake. This was an army that would never die, led by a warrior whose name would live forever.

That name could be yours.

He saw himself atop the world with all the power such a position could grant. He saw worlds beyond his own, worlds of unimaginable wealth. It was all just waiting to be brought low. This could be his, and world upon world would know and fear Sigmar's name.

The allure of such eternal power spoke to the ambition that had driven Sigmar to build the Empire, promising the fulfilment of every desire, the satisfaction of every dream and the power to achieve the impossible. His ambition revelled in such potential, yet the flickering candle that was Sigmar's humanity rebelled at this perversion of his vision of a united land.

'No,' he whispered. 'This is not what I want. This is a domain of the dead.'

It will live forever. As will you.

'No,' repeated Sigmar, the very act of denial giving him strength. 'I will not!'

Then if not for you, perhaps for another.

The mist before Sigmar parted and a tormented moan issued from deep within him. Across the water, he saw Ravenna, as beautiful as the last time he had seen her by the river. Her dark tresses spilled around the sculpted arc of her pale shoulders, and the light in her eyes was like the dawn of the brightest day. Nearly two decades had passed since her death, yet Sigmar remembered every curve of her body, every subtle aroma of her flesh, and this vision was just as he pictured her in his dreams.

'My love,' whispered Sigmar.

She smiled at him, and his heart broke anew.

Join me and she can live again. Death is meaningless in the face of the power I can give you. Surrender to me and she will be yours forever.

Sigmar pushed himself to his feet, knowing that the vision across the water was not Ravenna. Nevertheless, he stepped into the pool, sinking to his knees as he went to her. He took another step, the black water rising to his waist. Another step and the water was at his chest.

Yes, let the water claim you.

Sigmar heard the glee in the shadow's voice, but didn't care. All he wanted was to cross the pool to get to Ravenna. With her in his arms, the world could go away. He would have reclaimed his lost love.

The water rose to his neck, and he felt the clammy embrace of underwater fronds like grasping hands on his body. Water splashed his eyes, and the image of Ravenna shimmered like a ghostly mist before him. Thoughts of life and death vanished from his mind as the water closed over his head, and Ravenna disappeared.

Then he was alone in the darkness, and all he could hear was booming laughter echoing across the gulf of time.

WHEN HE OPENED his eyes, he was lying beside a river, its fast-flowing waters like shards of dancing ice and the scent of the surrounding woodlands intoxicating with its vitality. He watched as children played in the river, two boys and a girl. Their laughter was like musical rain, sweet, joyous, and unburdened by the passage of years.

He felt a presence beside him, and smiled to see his wife lying next to him. Her hair was grey, and though she was close to seventy years old, she was as beautiful as ever. He stroked her hair, seeing that his own flesh was gnarled and lined with age. The thought pleased him.

'Is this real?' he asked.

Ravenna turned to face him and smiled.

'No, my love. It is but a dream,' she said, 'a last, sweet memory of a future that never came to pass.'

'Ours?'

'Perhaps,' said Ravenna, watching the children playing in the river. 'Though I doubt it.'

'Why?' asked Sigmar, hurt by her honesty.

'Is this what you wanted?' she asked him. 'Really?'

'A future where I have lived a full life, with many children and now grandchildren? What man could ask for more?'

'You are no normal man, Sigmar,' said Ravenna. 'You were always destined for things beyond the reach of mortal men. As much as I would have wished you to live out the span of our days together, it could never be. I know that now.'

'Then it is really you, Ravenna?' asked Sigmar. 'This is not some evil fantasy?'

'It is me, my love,' she said, and the sound of her voice was like a soothing balm upon his soul. 'I have watched with pride as you achieved everything you set out to do.'

'I did it all for you,' he said.

'I know you did, but you are being corrupted from within. A dread power has come to this land and threatens everything you and all who came before you have built. Even now it seeks to drag you down into death.'

Sigmar sat up as a cloud passed across the face of the sun and the surrounding forest, which had seemed so benign beforehand, was now haunted by shadows. The laughter of the children faltered, and his heart beat a little faster as unbidden images of dead Roppsmenn flickered behind his eyes. A hot wind blew through the trees, dusty and dry, and laden with the powdered bones of a long-dead civilisation.

'Tell me what I must do!' he cried. 'I cannot fight it alone. I... I have done terrible things, and I am losing more and more of myself with every day. I can feel it, but I cannot stop it. The evil that poisons me grows stronger as I grow weaker.'

'You are Sigmar Heldenhammer,' said Ravenna, taking his head in her hands as the winds grew stronger. 'You are the greatest man I know, and you will not give in to this.'

'It is too strong for me,' he gasped, hearing the children's laughter turn to cries of fear as the darkness closed in. Trees bent with the force of the howling winds of the desert, though Ravenna's face remained unwavering before him. Grit carried on the wind scoured his flesh, peeling back his solidity as if seeking to erase him from this dream. The forest faded, and he held on to Ravenna's words even as the wind fought to obscure them.

'You are the Chosen of Ulric,' said Ravenna, her voice fading as he was torn away from her by the wind. 'The wolf of winter runs in your blood and the power of the northern winds gives you life. You can stand tall against this reborn evil, though it poisons you through that sorcerous crown. The land must be united as one, for its maker will soon come to claim it, and you must be ready to face him!'

'I don't know how!' he cried with the last of his breath.

'You will,' promised Ravenna as the winds plucked him away and sent him spinning off into the darkness.

SIGMAR'S EYES SNAPPED open, and he saw nothing. Absolute darkness filled his vision. No, that wasn't right. Bright spots of light danced before his eyes, and his head pounded with searing pain. He tried to scream, but achingly cold water poured down his throat, and he gagged as the rank, stagnant taste of it filled his lungs.

He coughed, and his whole body spasmed as he realised that he was beneath the water of the Brackenwalsch. Half-remembered fragments of dreams and memories came to him, but through all of it he saw Ravenna's face. Her bright eyes willed him to live, and he struggled against the deathly grip of the water. He kicked upwards as he fought to reach the surface, but no matter how hard he fought, a leaden weight kept him from rising.

The pain in his head intensified, as though a red-hot band of iron was slowly tightening upon his temple, burning its way through his skull to his brain. Swirling in the water around him, the phantom darkness spun him grand illusions of wealth, power, women and immortality, but without Ravenna, they were hollow, worthless promises.

If not for her, then for your land, hissed the voice, undaunted by his resistance.

Sigmar's vision blurred, and he saw barren, windswept tundra, a northern realm haunted by daemons and ancient gods of blood. His mind's eye swooped and dived like a bird, and he flew over this bitter, hateful landscape in the blink of an eye, seeing signs that thousands of people had, until recently, called this place home.

His immaterial form swept out over the grey waters of the Sea of Claws, following a course southwards through riotous tempests, until he came upon a vast fleet of ships sailing over the crests of surging waves: Wolfships.

These were the Norsii ships of war, and there were hundreds of them bound for the northern coasts of the Empire. An army of conquest or an army of destruction, it made no difference. They would invade the north and ravage his land unless he could defeat them.

I can help you. With the power I offer, the Norsii will be food for crows. Your land will be safe and one day we will cross the water to wipe their race from the face of the world!

Sigmar ignored the voice and shook off the vision, pushing hard for the world above. Each passing moment increased the pressure and pain in his lungs. He could not last much longer. Then the pounding in his head eased, and he felt his struggles grow weaker as the weight at his head dragged him deeper into the water.

Yet more images flashed before his eyes: Blacktusk the Boar, Trinovantes as his body was carried into his tomb on Warrior's Hill, the towering peak of the Fauschlag Rock, and a hundred other moments from his life. It was a life lived for the good of others: a life lived with honour, courage and sacrifice.

A wasted life, sneered the voice.

Then he heard another voice, one with a deep and resonant timbre that instantly transported him to his youth, when he had sat with the veteran warriors of the tribe and thrilled to their tales of heroic sagas, of kings long since taken to the Halls of Ulric.

'I want no other son,' said this voice. 'I have you. I know you will be a great man, and people will speak the name Sigmar with respect and awe for years! Now *fight*!'

The new voice echoed in his head with absolute authority, and he could no more disobey its command than he could breathe underwater. Sigmar cast off the last of the crown's blandishments, knowing that he had a *duty* to live. He had to return to the world of light and life to protect his people.

All else was folly, and he grieved at how easily his heart had been turned from its course.

Sigmar took hold of the golden crown.

It burned with dark magic, and he saw that its golden light was hideous and filled with malice. It fought him, filling his thoughts with ever more outrageous promises of power. His weary soul had been blinded to the crown's malevolence, but now he knew what a terrible trap it had been.

With a soundless scream, Sigmar tore the ancient metal from his brow.

His entire body was a searing mass of pain, but not even the touch of Shallya could compare to the joy that filled him as the crown's terrible hold was broken. Sigmar pushed up from the bottom of the pool with the last of his strength, feeling a wordless scream of frustration echo from somewhere far, far away.

Slicks of light whirled above him, strange stars and unknown worlds, but he kept his gaze fixed upon the water's rippling surface. At one and the same time it seemed unbearably close, yet impossibly distant. His strength was gone, and he knew he could not reach the surface.

A questing hand splashed down into the water, and Sigmar reached out for it, feeling an iron grip take hold of his wrist and pull.

Sigmar burst from the pool, his chest heaving and expelling a torrent of scum-frothed water. He clawed his way up the muddy banks, revelling in the sweetness of the air and the myriad scents that filled the swamp. A strong pair of hands hauled him the rest of the way and he rolled onto his back, sucking great gulps of air into his tortured lungs.

A hulking form sat on a nearby rock, a warrior covered from head to foot in black mud, whose face was bruised and bloody. Sigmar wiped his face and gathered breath to thank his rescuer, but the words died in his throat.

'Thought I'd lost you there,' said Wolfgart.

* * *

When he had strength enough to stand, Sigmar embraced his sword-brother, shamed and honoured by his devotion. The cool air of the marsh felt wondrously sharp against his skin, and Sigmar revelled in the sensation. He breathed as though it were the sweetest nectar. His entire body shook with cold and pain, but he welcomed it, for it was a reminder that he was alive.

At last they parted, and Sigmar looked down at the crown he held in one hand. He dropped it as though it were red-hot and stepped away from it. Wolfgart bent to examine the crown, but Sigmar kicked it away.

'Do not touch it!' he cried. 'It is a thing of evil!'

'I know,' said Wolfgart, 'and you should have known too. What kind of fool trusts a treasure taken from a necromancer?'

Sigmar knew that Wolfgart was right, but would anything be gained in trying to explain the glamour with which the ancient crown had ensnared him? That it had preyed upon his ambition and exploited the warlike heart that made him so formidable a warrior? Anything he said now would sound like an excuse, an attempt to abrogate responsibility for his actions.

And that was something that Sigmar would never do.

'The Roppsmenn,' he said, burying his head in his hands. 'Oh gods, what have I done?'

That the crown had saved Pendrag's life did not matter, for there were no excuses that could atone for what he had done in the months since Morath's defeat.

'Aye, you'll carry that one for the rest of your life,' said Wolfgart. 'And you'll have a job earning back the trust of the counts.'

'What about you?' asked Sigmar haltingly. 'I almost killed you.'

'But you didn't,' said Wolfgart, offering him his hand. 'That's what's important. It was the crown, it made you do those terrible things. But that's done with now.'

'The crown is evil,' agreed Sigmar, 'but it could have done nothing to me unless it had found some darkness within me to latch onto. The hag woman tried to warn me about replacing Alaric's gift, but I did not listen.'

'Ah, speaking of the mountain folk,' said Wolfgart, reaching down to lift a canvas bag from the edge of the pool, 'I brought some things for you. I had hoped to give them to you earlier, but... Well, things got a bit out of hand.'

Wolfgart reached into the bag, and Sigmar almost wept at the sight of what he pulled out.

Ghal-maraz glittered in the light, and Sigmar felt his hand curl with the urge to grip the ancient warhammer.

'How?' he asked.

'Pendrag gave it to Redwane when you parted company at Middenheim, and he carried it south to Reikdorf,' said Wolfgart. 'Go on, take it.'

Hesitantly, Sigmar reached out, and slowly wrapped his fingers around the rune-encrusted haft of Ghal-maraz, flinching as the last of the golden crown's influence was purged from him by the dwarf rune-magic. He smiled as the weapon settled in his grip, just as a well-made cloak which had weathered the harshest winter would feel after being warmed by the fire.

Wolfgart reached into the bag again, and pulled out another gift

The crown fashioned by Alaric the Mad.

Sigmar took a step back.

He shook his head.

'No, I do not deserve to wear it,' he said.

'Of course you do,' said Wolfgart. 'You're the only man who can. This has been a dark period, but it's time for you to be our Emperor once again. A fresh start. What do you say?'

Sigmar looked into his friend's eyes, seeing devotion and forgiveness he did not deserve.

Through everything, Wolfgart still believed in him.

'I do not deserve a friend like you,' he said.

'I know, but you're stuck with me,' said Wolfgart. 'Now take your crown.'

'No,' said Sigmar, dropping to his knees before Wolfgart. 'If this is to be a fresh start, then I want you to crown me anew.'

'I'm no Ar-Ulric, but I think I can manage that.'

Sigmar bowed, and Wolfgart placed the crown upon his head. Like Ghal-maraz, Alaric's crown welcomed him without reservation or rancour, and the wisdom and love that had gone into its craft filled him with strength he had not realised had drained from him.

He stood and looked out over the marshes. The sun was breaking through the clouds and clearing the mists away. Sigmar felt the sunlight on his skin and smiled. It felt good to be alive, but even as he relished this rebirth he knew there was much yet to be done.

'We must get back, my friend' said Sigmar at last. 'The Empire is in great danger.'

'Isn't it always?' asked Wolfgart.

'There are two counts of the Empire I need to set free,' said Sigmar. 'I have behaved shamefully towards them, and I only hope they can forgive me.'

'Ach, they'll be fine,' said Wolfgart. 'Krugar and Aloysis know they did wrong, and one thing's for sure; they'll not be sending raiders into each other's lands again any time soon. But that's not what you meant, is it?'

'No,' said Sigmar. 'The Norsii return to reclaim the lands I took from them. Hundreds of Wolfships are already crossing the Sea of Claws, and the north is virtually undefended.'

Wolfgart shrugged.

'It was only a matter of time until they came at us again,' he said. 'At least I'll get to put that sword above the fire to good use, though you'll be the one explaining to my little girl why her father is going to war again!'

BOOK THREE
Empire at War

Twelve swords, one for each chief,
And holy Sigmar bade each to wield it
In justice for his people,
And pledge to fight for one another
In undying unity,
Thus did every chief's hall
Become a stronghold in the realm of men.

SEVENTEEN
Wolves of the North

THEY HAD LOST.

Dawn was minutes old, and the army had been on the march for eight hours already. Thousands of warriors in ragged bands of blooded survivors marched south in the shadow of the Middle Mountains. Sigmar watched each man as he passed, seeing the same sullen disbelief in every face.

They had lost.

The armies of the Empire never lost a battle.

It hadn't quite sunk in.

No one could believe it, least of all Sigmar.

It had been a bright spring afternoon, the perfect day for a battle. Sigmar had felt powerful and invincible as he sat atop his horse and watched the Norsii of Cormac Bloodaxe march out to give battle. Eight thousand warriors of the Empire – Udose, Unberogen, Thuringians and Jutones – stood in disciplined ranks on a forested ridge some fifty miles from the northern coast. Each of the tribal contingents was led by its count, and Sigmar had relished the chance to march alongside Otwin and Marius.

The counts had gathered the previous evening to plan the coming battle, and Sigmar found himself missing Wolfila's garrulous company more than ever, for the Udose chieftain who attended the war council was a dour, humourless man named Conn Carsten. Since last spring, the Udose lands had been riven with skirmishes as the clan lords fought one another to claim the title of count, but the Norsii invasion had put an end to the feuding long enough for them to name Conn Carsten as their war-chieftain.

Hard to like, Carsten was nevertheless a canny soldier who knew the land well. Under his command, the northern clans had slowed the Norsii advance, and given Sigmar time to gather a sword host. But for Carsten, the north would have already fallen.

With plans drawn and the courage of their warriors bolstered by the presence of the Emperor, the army had marched out to victory. Every warrior could taste the sweetness of triumph, the honour and glory that would be theirs. The tales of blood and courage they would tell upon their return home were already taking shape in each man's head.

But they had lost.

No sooner had the counts taken the field beneath a wild panoply of colourful banners than malformed storm-clouds swelled in the clear sky. They crackled with gleeful lightning, fat with the promise of rain. Howling storm winds blew, and a sour, battering downpour began, like the legendary floods said to have drowned the world in ages past.

Arcing bolts of lightning slammed into the earth as the storm broke, and tremors of fear rippled along the Empire line at such unnatural phenomena. Worse was to come.

Sigmar rode with the White Wolves in the centre of his army, and each warrior sought to restore their honour after the war against the Roppsmenn.

The thunder of their hooves was the sound of victory.

Then a shrieking bolt of azure lightning had struck the bearer of the White Wolves banner.

The warrior fell from his horse, his flesh blackened, and the symbol of the Emperor's Guard afire. The banner fell to the ground, its crimson fabric utterly consumed by blue flames that were apparently impervious to the endless rain. Horrified cries rang from the forested ridge, but it was too late to quell that fear. Torrential rain turned the ground to a quagmire, and the advance became a trudging hell of sucking mud and blinding lightning strikes.

As Sigmar's warriors floundered, the Norsii attacked with a savage bray of war horns. The host of Norsemen marched out beneath the skull-banner of Cormac Bloodaxe and fought with discipline, courage and, worst of all, a plan. Instead of the usual mass of charging warriors, the Norsii gave battle in imitation of Sigmar's army. Norsii fighters marched in tightly-packed ranks, moving in formation with a hitherto unheard of cohesion.

Whooping tribesmen with dark skin and short-bows rode horses of black and gold to encircle Count Otwin's Thuringians and hammer them with deadly accurate blows. Otwin's advance faltered, and a host of Norsii warriors, mounted upon dark steeds taller than any grain-fed beasts of the Empire charged the scattered Thuringians. Led by a mighty warlord in bloody armour, a warrior who must surely have been Cormac Bloodaxe, the Norsii hacked the Thuringians down without mercy.

Jutone lancers drove back the marauding warriors, but not before Otwin had taken a lance to the chest. Marius led the countercharge, and carried the wounded Otwin from the fighting slung across his saddle. Even now, the camp surgeons fought to save the Thuringian count's life.

Sigmar's stratagems were met and countered at every turn, his warriors hurled back time and time again. As afternoon waned into evening, he realised the sick feeling in his gut was despair. The battle could not be won, and Sigmar had ordered the army's clarions to sound the retreat. Only here, at battle's end, did the discipline of the Norsii finally break down, the tribal champions leading their men in an orgy of slaughter amongst the wounded.

As terrible as it was to leave the wounded to their fate, the vile appetites of the Norsii ensured there was no pursuit, and Sigmar was able to lead his men from the field of battle unmolested. The night march had been cold and cheerless, with the wounded treated on the move or during one of the infrequent breaks from the retreat.

Wolfgart rode alongside him, the flanks of his horse lathered in bloody sweat. Sigmar's sword-brother had come through the battle unscathed, save for a long slash along his jerkin that had missed cutting his gut open by a hair's-breadth.

'Long night, eh?' said Wolfgart.

'It won't be the last,' replied Sigmar. 'Not now.'

'Aye, you have the truth of it, but we'll get them next time.'

'I hope you are right.'

'Do you even doubt it?' asked Wolfgart. 'Come on, man. They're barbarians, and looking at how many totems I counted, there's a lot of war leaders there.'

'Is that supposed to be a good thing?'

'Of course,' said Wolfgart. 'You put that many barbarian chiefs together, and they'll fall to fighting each other soon enough.'

'I am not sure, my friend,' said Sigmar, recalling the deadly precision he had seen in the Norsii, in particular a warrior in glittering silver armour, who fought with twin swords. 'I swear it was as if they knew our every tactic. We will lose the Empire one battle at a time if we think of the Norsii simply as barbarians.'

'You're giving them too much credit,' said Wolfgart. 'I can teach an animal to do tricks, but that doesn't mean it's clever.'

'No, but the way they fought... It was as if they had a warrior schooled in the Empire leading them, someone who knew how we fight. All through the night, I have gone over the battle, picturing every clash of arms and each manoeuvre, hoping to find some clue as to how the Norsii beat us.'

'And what have you come up with?'

'Time and time again, I come back to the same answer,' said Sigmar. 'I underestimated them, and my warriors paid for that mistake with their lives.'

'Then we'll not do that again,' stated Wolfgart, and Sigmar was forced to admire his sword-brother's relentless optimism. He had faith in Sigmar, even in defeat.

Wolfgart rubbed a hand over his face, and Sigmar saw how tired he was.

Since Sigmar's attempted execution of Krugar and Aloysis, Wolfgart had spent virtually every waking minute with the Emperor. The two counts had been freed, and Sigmar begged their forgiveness on bended knee. It took the combined skills of Eoforth and Alfgeir to avert what could have been a devastating civil war but, in the end, both Krugar and Aloysis accepted that Sigmar had been under the dread influence of the necromancer's crown.

Their slighted honour demanded recompense, however, and both counts returned to their castles laden with gold, land and titles. Sigmar could only promise that what had happened would never happen again, for the hateful crown was buried deep in the heart of Reikdorf.

Wolfgart had wanted to hurl it deep into the marsh and be done with it, but Sigmar knew he could not so casually dispose of such a dangerous and powerful artefact. Lifting the crown with a branch broken from a rowan tree, he carried it straight to High Priestess

Alessa at the temple of Shallya. With solemn ceremony, the crown was sealed in the deepest vault and warded with every charm of protection known to all the priests of Reikdorf.

Never again would the crown see the light of day, and if its maker ever dared come to claim it, he would find it defended by every warrior in the Empire.

A CONTINGENT OF painted Thuringian warriors marched past Sigmar and Wolfgart, each with a twin-bladed axe slung across his shoulders. They were bloodied and angry, having lost many comrades on the battlefield, men and women both. They wore little armour, for these were the King's Blades, the fiercest and most deadly of all the Thuringian berserkers. They escorted a covered wagon pulled by horses more usually employed to carry Jutone lancers, but which Count Marius had offered to serve the wounded Berserker King.

Sigmar saw a familiar face among the Blades, and nodded to Wolfgart. Together, they rode alongside the tattooed warriors. A berserker woman with long hair pulled in tight braids, naked but for a mail corslet and bracers, looked up at them with eyes haunted by defeat.

'How is he?' asked Sigmar.

'Ask him yourself,' said Ulfdar, the berserker warrior Sigmar had defeated when he had fought the Thuringians to secure their king's sword oath. Her mail was torn and links fell to the muddy road with every step.

'I saw you fight,' said Sigmar. 'I lost count of how many you killed.'

'I don't keep count,' replied Ulfdar. 'I remember little of battles. When the red mist is upon me, it's hard enough to tell friend from foe.'

Sigmar lifted his voice for all the Thuringians to hear.

'Yesterday you fought like heroes,' he said, 'every one of you. I watched as the enemy bore down on you, and not one of you took a backwards step. That is iron courage that cannot ever be broken. The Norsii proved a stronger foe than we remembered, but we are better than them. They are far from home and we are defending our homelands. No force in the world can compare to the warrior defending their hearth and home and loved ones.'

The Thuringians marched past without acknowledging him, and Sigmar could not tell whether his words had any effect on them. The wagon bearing Count Otwin approached, and he waited for it to reach him. The Blades parted before him, and a hatchet-faced Cradoc pulled the canvas flaps at the rear of the wagon aside.

'Don't tire him out,' warned the surgeon. 'The lance broke three of his ribs and nicked his right lung. He's lucky to be alive, though to hear him you'd think he'd just cut himself shaving.'

'Damn it, man,' said Otwin from behind Cradoc. 'I've been hurt worse after a night on the beer. Come morning, I'll be back on my feet.'

'It *is* morning,' snapped Cradoc. 'And if you try to stand you'll die.'

Cradoc lowered himself from the wagon, looked up at Sigmar, and said, 'I have others to treat today, so keep an eye on him. And don't let him up from his bed. If he dies, I'll blame you.'

'I understand. You have my word he will not leave this wagon.'

The irascible healer nodded, and wearily made his way towards more of the walking wounded. Sigmar walked his horse behind the wagon and looked in at his wounded friend.

Count Otwin reclined on a cot bed, his upper body completely wrapped in linen bandages. The Berserker King's skin was waxy and pale, his chest rising and falling with shallow hiked breaths. He smiled weakly, and Sigmar saw how close to death he had come.

'I hope you listened to what Cradoc told you,' said Sigmar.

'Ach, surgeons, what do they know about being wounded in battle?'

'Plenty, you old rogue,' said Wolfgart. 'Cradoc's stitched my wounds more than once, and back in his day he swung a sword as well as a wielding a needle and herb bag.'

'Fair enough,' conceded Otwin, 'and I heard what you said to the Blades. Good speech, but they're not big on fancy words.'

'So I saw,' said Sigmar. 'But it needed to be said.'

Otwin nodded. 'Aye, it did. The damn Norsii handed us a beating and no mistake, Sigmar, so I hope you're giving that same speech to everyone. The men need to hear how those bastards got lucky and that we'll drive them back the next time we face them.'

'That's what *I* told him,' put in Wolfgart.

'So how many did we lose?' asked Otwin.

'We've still to tally the final butcher's bill, but it looks like we lost close to a thousand men,' said Wolfgart.

'Shallya's tears, that's a lot,' cursed Otwin. 'And the Norsii?'

'Hard to judge,' said Wolfgart, 'but I'd wager no more than three hundred.'

'Aye, a beating,' repeated Otwin, shaking his head. 'It would have been more if not for Marius. His lancers and crossbows really pulled our arse out of the fire.'

'That they did,' agreed Sigmar.

The Jutone count had surprised them all with his courage and steadfast resolve in the face of defeat. Mercenary crossbowmen with pockets lined with Empire gold hammered the rampaging Norsemen with merciless volleys of iron-tipped bolts, covering the retreat and preventing it from becoming a rout.

'Who'd have thought it, eh?' asked Otwin with an amused grin. 'Bloody Marius. I'll bet you're glad I didn't let you kill him at Jutonsryk, aren't you?'

'More than you know,' said Sigmar.

Otwin took a drink from a wineskin, grimacing as his stitches pulled tight. He slumped back on his bed, his brow sheened in perspiration, though the day was still chill.

'So what now?' asked Otwin when he had recovered enough to speak. 'I trust you have a plan to send these bastards back across the water?'

'I think so,' said Sigmar. 'This Cormac Bloodaxe is a clever general, but the very savagery that makes his warriors so fierce was our salvation. Had they been disciplined enough to mount a pursuit, they would have destroyed us. Cormac will not make that mistake again.'

'What about the other counts?' asked Otwin. 'Is there any word? We need their strength.'

'I know, but it will take time for them to gather their armies and march to our aid.'

Otwin hesitated before saying, 'And you're sure they'll come? I mean, after what happened with the Roppsmenn and that... unpleasantness with Aloysis and Krugar.'

'They will come,' said Sigmar, with more conviction than he felt. 'If for no other reason than the Norsii will surely turn their axes on them if we fail.'

'There's truth in that,' agreed Otwin. 'So how will you buy the time they need to march?'

'I underestimated the Norsii,' said Sigmar, 'but I will not do that again. We need to draw them to us and destroy them as a surgeon lances a plague sore.'

'And how do you plan to do that?' asked Wolfgart. 'They outnumber us by several thousand now.'

'We will retreat to Middenheim,' said Sigmar. 'It is the greatest fastness in the Empire and it has never fallen.'

'It has never been attacked,' pointed out Wolfgart. 'A city on a mountain? You'd have to be mad to attack it. Why would they not just ignore us and push on to Reikdorf? Or any other city that won't be as impossible to take.'

'Their leaders are thinking like us, and they will know they cannot simply ignore Middenheim,' said Sigmar. 'To push further into the Empire while leaving an army at their backs would be madness. They will have no choice but to come at us.'

'Then let us hope you are right about the other counts,' said Otwin. 'If they do not heed your summons then Middenheim will be our grave.'

PYRES BURNED, PYRAMIDS of skulls were built long into the night, and Cormac watched the bloody torture of the prisoners. Their screams were prayers to the Dark Gods, and the forests echoed to the chants and prayers of the Norsii. Drunk on slaughter and victory, thousands of men filled the shallow valley where they had faced the might of Sigmar and prevailed.

Cormac could still hardly believe they had won.

Watching the army of Sigmar upon the hillside, his mouth had been dry and his guts twisted in apprehension. The Emperor had never been defeated, and the men of the Empire fully expected to crush the invaders in one great battle.

Though he hated to admit it, Kar Odacen's plans and the training regime of Azazel, who had spent the last two seasons teaching the Norsii the Empire way of war, had borne fruit. Cormac relished the sense of panic that seized their foes when they had seen the Norsii fighting as a disciplined whole. Kar Odacen's host of shamans had worked their sorceries to bring the heavens down upon the enemy, and their doom was assured.

The slaughter had been mighty, and he had given an equal share of the living plunder to each of his vassal warlords. The Kul had ritually disembowelled their captives, and hunchbacked shamans with gibbering shadows at their shoulders had eaten the entrails. Groups of Wei-Tu riders attached ropes to the limbs of prisoners and rode off in different directions to tear them apart, while Khazag strongmen pummelled their prisoners to death with their fists.

Cormac had fought and killed two dozen warriors in a hastily-dug battle pit ringed with swords. With bare hands and naked ferocity, he had beaten each prisoner down, and drunk their blood as it gushed from necks torn open with his teeth.

The Hung had violated their captives in every way imaginable, and then given their broken, abused bodies to the slaves as playthings. Of all the fates suffered by the prisoners of the Empire, this was the one that had offended Cormac the most. Every warrior, even an enemy, was entitled to a death of blood, his skull offered to the brass throne of Kharnath.

Kar Odacen placated him by speaking of the myriad aspects of the Dark Gods and how each was honoured differently. Were not the reeking plague pits of Onogal a means to serve the gods of the north? Though they took no skulls in battle, the shamans who ventured into the madness of the far north and returned twisted and insane with power were just as devoted to the old gods. The pleasure cults of the Hung were no less honourable, elaborated Kar Odacen, though they seemed so to Cormac's eyes.

Besides, as Azazel had pointed out, Cormac could ill-afford to invite dissent into his army by keeping the Hung from their sport. Its unity was a fragile thing at best, and to single out the worshippers of Shornaal would start a rot that would see the army break up within days.

Cormac threaded his way through the camp, pausing every now and then to watch a particularly amusing or grotesque sacrifice at a makeshift altar. His skin was hot and red from the pyres, for there was plenty of wood to burn. In time, the Empire would be one gigantic pyre, with the skull of its Emperor mounted on a great pyramid of bone and ash.

As he reached the head of the valley, he saw Kar Odacen and Azazel. His mood soured, for he could not look upon them without thinking that they plotted behind his back. A shaman and a traitor to his own kind. Such lieutenants he had!

A brutalised corpse lay at the shaman's feet, and from the hideous mutilations wrought upon its flesh, Cormac knew that Azazel had indulged his lust for torture. The corpse's belly was opened, and Kar Odacen's hands were buried in its intestines. With a wet, sucking sound, Kar Odacen removed a glistening liver and turned it over in his red hands.

'What do the entrails say?' asked Cormac, and Azazel only reluctantly tore his eyes from the ruptured corpse. Cormac was about to ask again when Kar Odacen held up a hand.

'Be silent,' said the shaman. 'The art of the haruspex requires concentration.'

Cormac fought the urge to take his axe and bury it in the shaman's head for such disrespect, releasing the iron grip on his weapon. He hadn't been aware he was holding it.

'It was a good victory,' said Azazel, gazing rapturously at his own image in the gleaming metal of his sword blade. 'Hard fought and well won.'

Cormac nodded, unsure whether Azazel was talking to him or the reflection. He forced himself to answer without anger.

'Aye, it was that,' he said. 'Many skulls taken and fresh trophy rings for every champion.'

'It is a shame you did not capitalise on it,' said Kar Odacen without looking up from his reading of the dead man's meat. 'Discipline broke down at the end and our enemies escaped us. Now we will need to fight those men again.'

'Then we will fight them again,' hissed Cormac, 'and we will defeat them again.'

'I wouldn't be too sure about that,' said Azazel. 'We beat Sigmar's men because they were not ready for us to fight like them, but they will learn from that mistake.'

Cormac tried not to look at Azazel, and waited for the shaman to speak.

'Did you hear me?' asked Azazel.

'I heard you,' snapped Cormac, finally meeting the swordsman's gaze. As much as he detested the rites of Shornaal, the dark prince's powers must surely have shaped Azazel's features. To raise his voice in anger to such a specimen of perfection seemed abhorrent.

He forced himself to look past Azazel's glamours to the corruption beneath.

'I thought your training made us their equals in battle?' he said.

Azazel laughed, and such was its beguiling quality that Cormac felt his anger melting in the face of such a wondrous sound.

'Hardly,' said Azazel, flashing him a smile. 'We have trained for little more than two seasons. Sigmar's men have trained and fought together for years.'

'Your army outnumbers Sigmar's,' said Kar Odacen, 'and the power of the Dark Gods makes us invincible.'

'No, it makes us vulnerable,' said Cormac.

'That makes no sense,' hissed Kar Odacen. 'My power has never been greater.'

'It is a mistake to think yourself invincible, shaman. Overconfidence will see us defeated. Think like that and we will make mistakes, leave openings for the enemy to exploit. We must assume nothing, and expect that our enemies will come back from this defeat stronger and more prepared. The master of the Empire is no fool and will surely learn from his humbling.'

'Then what do you think Sigmar will do next?' asked Azazel.

'He will fall back to Middenheim,' said Cormac. 'It is his only option.'

Azazel nodded and said, 'I will climb to the heavens and tear him from his lofty perch.'

'No, you won't,' said Cormac. 'At least, not yet.'

Azazel's expression hardened and his eyes grew cold.

'What?' he said. 'Our enemy is within reach, why do we not strike for his throat?'

'Because that is what he will expect us to do,' explained Cormac. 'Sigmar must win time for his forces to gather. He will do so by drawing us onto the walls of an impregnable city.'

'Then what do you suggest?' hissed Azazel. 'My blades ache for Sigmar's body.'

'That we do not dance to his tune. We ignore Middenheim and push eastwards. Burn the forests and villages of the Empire, and seek out the forces answering Sigmar's call for aid. Destroy them one by one, and soon tales of our victories will draw more of our kin across the sea. Within a season, we will see the Empire in flames.'

'No,' said Kar Odacen, rising from the corpse and holding the liver out for them to see. Its hard, fibrous interior was yellow with sickness. 'You are mistaken. That will not happen.'

'What do you mean?' demanded Cormac.

Kar Odacen stroked the liver, stringy ropes of rancid pus dripping from his fingers.

'We follow Sigmar to Middenheim,' said the shaman.

'That is a mistake,' said Cormac. 'We can destroy the Empire without facing the Emperor in battle until we have taken everything from him.'

'You think this is about the Empire?' snapped Kar Odacen, his bitter gaze sweeping over Cormac and Azazel. 'It is not. It is about Sigmar. You think you fight for lost lands, for revenge? No, this war is the first of many, and all others will hang upon it.'

'Though I dislike the thought of leaving Sigmar in his mountain city, Cormac's plan has merit,' said Azazel, and Cormac was surprised at the swordsman's support.

'Cormac's plan?' hissed Kar Odacen. 'Since when do the tribes of the north heed the word of a mortal man? He is warlord and champion of this host by the will of the gods, and when they speak he must obey!'

'Then what is the will of the gods?' asked Cormac, fighting down his killing urge.

The shaman's eyes took on a glazed, faraway look, and his voice seemed to echo from a place or time far distant.

'The Flame of Ulric must be extinguished and Sigmar must die,' he said. 'I have seen ages beyond this time of legends to a place where darkness closes in on the world, and the forces of the old gods stand poised to bring ruin upon the world. The final triumph of Chaos is at hand, but one name holds back the darkness, one name of power that gives hope to men and bolsters the courage of all who hear it. That name is Sigmar, and if we do not destroy him here and now, then his name will echo down the centuries as a symbol for our enemies to rally behind.'

Cormac felt a shiver of dark premonition travel the length of his spine as the forests around his army trembled with motion. His first thought was that Sigmar's army had returned in the night to fall upon them as they gave thanks for their victory, but that thought died as he saw what emerged from the tree line.

Thousands of beasts that walked, crawled and flew stood illuminated in the firelight, completely encircling the northern army. Blessed by the warping power of the Dark Gods, no two were alike, a glorious meld of man and animal. Armed with crude axes, rusted swords or studded clubs, they had come at the shaman's call, a host of monsters with the snarling heads of wolves, bears, bulls and a myriad other forms that defied easy identification.

As one, they split the night with their howls, brays and shrieks, and Cormac's sense of might and power as master of this army retreated in the face of such atavistic devotion to the old gods. Primal and devoid of any urges save to destroy and revenge themselves on a race that hated and feared them, the beasts were ready to tear the throat from the Empire.

'These are days of great power,' said Kar Odacen. 'The tribes of the north, the beasts of the forest, and a great prince of Kharnath will fall upon Middenheim, and we will baptise this world in blood!'

* * *

NIGHT WAS FALLING, but still they kept coming.

Like a living sea of fur, flesh and iron, the host of the north swirled and flowed around the base of the Fauschlag Rock without end. Sigmar stood at the edge of the city with the wind billowing his wolfskin cloak behind him, while his fellow warriors stood a more prudent distance from the sheer drop.

The last time so many of them had been gathered together was at Sigmar's coronation, nine years ago. So much had happened since then that Sigmar barely remembered the promise and hope of that day.

Some of those hopes had been fulfilled, some had been dashed.

Friendships had been forged and strengthened. Others had been soured.

The coming war would test which would endure.

Conn Carsten of the Udose stood with his hands resting on the pommel of a wide-bladed broadsword, while Marius of the Jutones simply watched the gathering enemy impassively. Against all advice, Otwin had joined them, held upright by Ulfdar and a Thuringian warrior whom Sigmar didn't know. The Berserker King's vast axe was freshly chained to his wrist and would only be parted from him in victory or death.

Myrsa and Pendrag were on his left, with Redwane and Wolfgart at his right. His greatest friends and allies stood with him, and their continued faith and friendship was humbling. Despite everything he had put them through over the years, they remained steadfastly loyal.

'They came,' said Wolfgart. 'Just like you said.'

'Aye,' agreed Redwane. 'Lucky us, eh?'

'I didn't think they would,' said Pendrag. 'They must know they cannot take this city.'

'I do not think they would have come if they did not expect to defeat us,' said Sigmar.

'They won't get up the chain lifts, so the only other way in is the viaduct,' said Wolfgart. 'With the warriors we have, we can hold that until the end of days.'

Sigmar read their faces. High on this rock, they believed themselves secure and invincible. They would learn soon enough the folly of that belief.

'If the viaduct was the only way into the city I might agree with you,' said Sigmar, 'but it is not. Is it, Myrsa?'

The Warrior Eternal shook his head, looking as though he were being forced to reveal an uncomfortable secret.

'No,' he said. 'It is not. How did you know?'

'I am the Emperor, it is my duty to know such things,' he said. He smiled, and then tapped the rune-inscribed circlet of gold and ivory at his brow. 'Alaric told me how his miners and engineers helped Artur reach the summit of the Fauschlag Rock. He told me that the rock beneath us is honeycombed with tunnels and caves. Some carved by the dwarfs, others made by hands that are a mystery to even the mountain folk.'

'It's true,' said Myrsa. 'We have a few maps, but they are mostly incomplete and, truth be told, I don't think anyone really knows exactly what's beneath us.'

'There is another way in to my city and I do not know of it?' asked Pendrag. 'You should have told me of this, Myrsa.'

'The city's defence is my domain,' said Myrsa. 'Long ago it was decided that the fewer people knew of the tunnels the better. In any case, our enemies cannot know of them.'

'They will,' said Sigmar. 'They will find them and we must defend them.'

They watched the assembling forces of the Norsii in silence for a while, each trying to guess how many enemies they faced, for Cormac Bloodaxe's force was far larger than before. Inhuman beasts had swelled its ranks, and the sight of so vast a gathering of monsters was horrifying.

'The forests have emptied,' said Otwin. 'I never dreamed there were so many beasts.'

'There will be fewer by the end of this,' snarled Conn Carsten.

Though Sigmar could claim no fondness for the Udose clan chief, he silently thanked him for his defiant words as he saw resolve imparted to his fellow warriors. He returned his gaze to the enemy army, his keen eyes picking out the banner of Cormac Bloodaxe.

Beneath the banner, a towering warrior in black armour and horned helm looked up at the mountain city. Though great distance separated him from his foe, Sigmar felt as though Cormac was right in front of him. If he whispered, his enemy would hear what he had to say.

'You will not take my Empire from me,' he said.

Two figures attended the Norsii warlord, a hunched form that reeked of sorcery, and the lithe warrior in silver armour who bore twin swords. The swordsman's hair was dark, his skin pale, and as he drew one of his blades Sigmar felt a tremor of recognition.

It was impossible. The distance was too great, and though the warrior's face was little more than a tiny white dot amid a sea of warlike faces, Sigmar was certain he knew him.

'The swordsman,' he said, 'next to Cormac Bloodaxe.'

Wolfgart squinted in the crepuscular gloom. 'Aye, the skinny looking runt. What of him?'

'I know him,' he said.

'What?' hissed Wolfgart. 'How can you know him? Who is he?'

'It is Gerreon,' said Sigmar.

Wolfgart sighed.

'This just gets better and better,' he said.

EIGHTEEN

The Empire at Bay

THE ARMY OF Cormac Bloodaxe began the assault on Middenheim at dawn the following day, after a night of braying howls, echoing warhorns, sacrificial pyres and blood offerings. Their chants and songs of war drifted up to the defenders, promising death and rich with the primal urges of the gathered Norsii tribes.

Where the men of the Empire craved peace and the warmth of hearth and home, the Norsii craved battle and conquest. Where progress and development were the watchwords of the Empire, slaughter and the lust for domination drove the northern tribes. The gods of the south watched over their people in return for worship, but the baleful gods of Chaos demanded worship, and offered only battle and death to those that venerated them.

Eight thousand Empire warriors stood ready to defend the city, around half the number opposing them. More than just men were poised to attack: bull-headed monsters, winged bat-creatures, and twisted abominations so far removed from any known beast that their origins could never be known. They bellowed alongside packs of slavering, black-furred wolves, and towering troll-creatures lumbered through the host with clubs that were simply trees ripped from the earth.

Sigmar had long since planned the defence of Middenheim,

knowing the Flame of Ulric would draw the followers of the Dark Gods like moths to a lantern. The bulk of the enemy would surely come at them up the viaduct, and despite the best efforts of Middenheim's engineers, the stonework connecting it with the city could not be dislodged. The skill of its dwarfen builders was such that not a single stone could be removed. To compound this problem, the citadel and towers designed to defend the top of the viaduct had yet to be completed. The barbican walls were barely the height of a tall man, and the towers were hollow and without ramparts. Blocks of stone intended to raise the wall to a height of fifty feet were even now being used to plug the unfinished gateway or hauled into position to form a fighting step for the men behind it.

This was where Sigmar would make his stand, and he would do it with a thousand warriors drawn from every tribe gathered in Middenheim. Thuringian berserkers stood shoulder to shoulder with Udose clansmen, Jutone spearmen, Unberogen swordsmen and the city's greatswords. Though the White Wolves fought elsewhere, Redwane had refused to leave Sigmar's side, claiming that Alfgeir would have his hide nailed to the longhouse's wall if anything were to happen to the Emperor.

Pendrag and Myrsa commanded a thousand Middenlanders on the city's northern flank, its count and Warrior Eternal facing their foes' homeland as tradition demanded. The White Wolves stood with the Count of Middenheim and his champion, given the duty of their protection by Sigmar. Though unhappy not to be fighting at their Emperor's side, each warrior had sworn himself to this duty before the Flame of Ulric. The eastern districts were held by Conn Carsten's Udose, while the west was the domain of Marius and the Jutones.

Every able-bodied man and boy in the city carried a weapon, though the very oldest and youngest were spared fighting on the front lines. To them was entrusted the defence of the streets and crossroads leading towards the temple being built at the centre of the city.

Middenheim groaned at the seams with people from the surrounding settlements and refugees fleeing the Norsemen's brutal invasion. The city's wells were covered with iron grates and what food remained was under armed guard. At a conservative estimate, Pendrag's quartermasters calculated there was enough to last a month.

Sigmar stood behind the unfinished wall at the top of the viaduct, and watched as the Norsii gathered behind a smoking construct of brass and bone. Beside him, five hundred warriors of the Empire stood with spears and bows and swords, ready to fight alongside their emperor. Behind him, five hundred more awaited his order to advance.

A rhythmic booming echoed from far below, the northern tribesmen banging axes and swords against shields as they marched up the viaduct. Monotonous chanting droned in counterpoint to the clash of iron, and the howls of monstrous beasts completed the dreadful, courage-sapping noise. It was a sound that spoke of destruction for destruction's sake, the urge to kill and maim for no reason other than the suffering it would cause.

No courage or faith a man might possess could fail to be shaken by such a noise, for it had been the primordial sound of mankind's doom since the beginning of the world.

Sigmar felt the fear take root in the hearts of his warriors, and vaulted to the top of the wall, resplendent in the glittering armour of his coronation. Each plate shone like silver, each wondrously-crafted engraving dazzling the eye and capturing the heart with its glory. The visor of his winged helm was raised and all who looked upon him saw his determination to resist this attack. He raised Ghal-maraz in defiance of the Norsii and his golden shield, a gift from Pendrag to replace the one destroyed at Black Fire Pass, captured the sunlight.

'Men of the Empire!' he shouted, his voice easily carrying to the farthest extent of the defences. 'The warriors before you have been forged in the harshest lands of the north, yet they have not your strength. Their gods are bloody avatars of battle, yet they have not your faith. They live for war, yet they have not your heart! Because they live only for themselves, they are weak. Because they place no value on the lives of their fellow men, they have no brotherhood. Look around you! Look at the face of the warrior beside you. He may be from a land far distant to your home; he may speak a different language, but know one thing: he is your brother. He will stand beside you, and as you will fight and die for him, he will fight and die for you!'

Sigmar turned to face the Norsii, standing tall and proud and mighty.

'Together we are strong,' he shouted. 'Together we will send these whoresons back across the sea and make them wish their mothers had never birthed them!'

* * *

PENDRAG HEFTED HIS axe, and watched in disbelief as the beasts began climbing the Fauschlag Rock. They swarmed its sides, clawing their way up the impossible face of the sheer rock. Sigmar had climbed this rock once and it had almost killed him, but these monsters ascended with no more trouble than a man might climb a ladder.

The sky was the colour of ashes, dripping with clouds, and Pendrag felt a queasy sense of vertigo as he looked beyond the northern horizon. No one knew what lay beyond the eternally snowbound landscape, but the legends of every tribe described it as a land of gods and monsters, where the very air carried madness and the power of creation.

He took a deep breath as he altered his grip on the haft of his axe. His silver hand tingled with the memory of fingers and the scar at his neck, from where the long dead warrior-king had struck him, itched abominably. All his old wounds were retuning to haunt him, and he tried not to think what kind of omen that might be.

Beside him, Myrsa stood in perfect stillness. Pendrag had fought countless foes and stood with heroes in the greatest battle in the history of the race of men, yet still his heart hammered at his chest and his mouth was dry.

Six hundred warriors of Middenheim stood at the defensive wall encircling the city, a chest-high barrier built where the ground sloped down to the vertical face of the Fauschlag Rock. Three hundred warriors occupied perches on roofs and towers further back, armed with hunting bows and slings. Their faces were dour and stoic, a cliché of the grim northern tribesman. In the years since he had come to Middenheim, Pendrag had come to see that stoicism as simple practicality and a recognition of the futility of wasted emotion.

No glorious war cries roused the warriors of Middenheim, and bitter experience had taught Pendrag that grand speeches would be wasted on such men. All that mattered to them was the courage in a man's heart and the strength of his sword-arm. Pendrag had proved himself to them, and thus they stood with him to defend their city. Their presence was symbol enough of his acceptance.

What more could any man ask?

The city's blue and white banner flew above him, and Pendrag was honoured to fight in its shadow. He had fought the dead creatures of the necromancer beneath the Dragon Banner, and it felt good to face an enemy beneath a battle flag of honour, not one of murder.

Among the Middenlanders were a hundred White Wolves, their

red armour and white wolfskin cloaks marking them out among the city's defenders. Though they should have fought with Sigmar, Pendrag was glad of their strength.

A group of men clad in the neutrally coloured tunics of foresters scrambled from the very edge of the rock towards the defensive wall. They climbed towards Pendrag, and a host of hands helped them across it.

'They're close,' said one of the foresters. 'A hundred feet or so and climbing fast.'

'Good work,' said Pendrag. 'Join the rest of the archers.'

'Be wary,' said the forester as he pushed through the tightly packed defenders. 'There are flying beasts as well as climbing ones.'

Instinctively, Pendrag looked up, but the sky was empty save for circling carrion birds gathered in anticipation of a feast of flesh.

He turned to Myrsa.

'Fight well, Warrior Eternal,' he said.

'And you, Count of Middenheim,' replied Myrsa.

SIGMAR AND HIS warriors threw the Norsii charge back three times before the strange construction of brass and bone reached them. The morning was only a few hours old and Morr had come to claim the souls of the fallen time and time again. The enemy dead were thrown from the viaduct, and the screams of the wounded warred with the battle-chants of the Norsemen.

Each charge was a furious scramble of blades and blood, screams and courage, with Sigmar killing dozens of frenzied Norsii champions seeking his head.

This latest attack promised to be something different.

'What in Ulric's name is that?' asked Redwane, voicing the question on every man's lips.

'I do not know,' said Sigmar. 'But it can be nothing good.'

It towered over the Norsii, a mighty altar of blood and blades pulled by two mighty steeds with curling ram's horns and smouldering coals for eyes. More nightmares made flesh than animals, the beasts' skins smoked with furnace heat and their flanks ran with steaming blood. Skulls tumbled from the monstrous construction, and endless rivulets of boiling blood poured from the altar, staining the flagstones with hissing red streams. Black smoke twisted and billowed in defiance of the wind, and Sigmar blinked as he thought he saw screaming skulls in its depths.

The Norsii gathered around it, howling a single name that sent spasms of nausea stabbing through his body. It was a name of death, yet Sigmar felt his warrior's heart stirred by the damnable syllables. A towering warrior in blood-soaked armour marched to the fore, bearing a black banner that seethed with the power of a storm, its surface alive with chained arcs of black lightning.

With one last screamed exhortation of their dread god's name, the Norsii charged, a foaming mass of tattooed warriors. A volley of iron-tipped crossbow bolts from mercenaries hired with Jutone gold hammered the Norsii, splintering shields and punching through armour. The front rank fell, only to be trampled by the warriors behind them. Another volley and another hit home, each one reaping a fearsome tally.

Archers loosed shafts, but without the power of the crossbows, many thudded home into heavy shields without effect. Sigmar offered a silent thanks to whichever of the gods had sent Otwin to prevent him killing Marius. Without these crossbows, the Norsii might already have broken through.

Then it was too late for arrows and crossbows.

The Norsii hurled themselves at the wall, and the bloodshed began again.

Sigmar blocked a slashing axe, and smashed his hammer into the face of a screaming warrior. The man fell back, his skull caved in, but another clambered over his body, and thrust his blade at Sigmar's neck. He swayed aside and slammed his shield into the warrior's chest.

Screaming Norsemen used their dead to gain height, and the mound of corpses at the wall was crushed beneath their armoured weight. Sigmar stood firm in the face of the enemy, striking out with killing sweeps of Ghal-maraz and, where he fought, the Norsii were hurled back. The warrior with the black banner raised it high, and Sigmar heard a dreadful hissing as smoke from the diabolical altar was drawn towards it.

A howling bellow seemed to come from the bloody altar, and the monstrous beasts pulling it reared and slashed the air with iron-shod hooves. Sigmar felt the ancient power bound within the terrible altar as a stocky tribesman with one eye and hair spiked with chalk and resin hurled himself forward.

He turned to meet the man's attack, but no sooner had he raised his shield than a flickering black light erupted from the dread banner and a terrific impact tore at him. His shield flared and crumbled to ash, its edges hot and golden like parchment in a fire.

'Ulric's teeth!' he yelled, hurling the last remnants of the grip away. The one-eyed tribesman slammed into Sigmar, and he fell from the ramparts. They landed hard, and Sigmar lost his grip on Ghal-maraz. He rammed his helmet into the tribesman's face, but the man seemed impervious to pain. He bit and spat at Sigmar as iron talons erupted from his fingertips. He clawed at Sigmar with bestial ferocity.

Along the length of the wall, the Norsii threw themselves at the men of the Empire with renewed fury, the ancient power of their northern gods searing their veins and filling them with rage. It was a destructive power that would consume them without care, but not one of the Norsii feared such an end.

Sigmar rolled, feeling the man's skin ripple and bulge beneath him, as though a mass of snakes writhed in his chest. The tribesman's lengthening fangs snapped at his neck, and only the silver gorget saved Sigmar from having his throat ripped out.

He punched the man in the face. Bone broke and fangs snapped, but the man's flesh was like iron. His skin was darkening, and a pair of bony horns erupted from his forehead in a frothing shower of pink flesh. A spear plunged into the tribesman's side, and he reared up to tear the belly from the spearman. Sigmar scrambled clear, and swept up Ghal-maraz as the tribesman, now more beast than man, sprang at him once again.

He loosened his grip on his warhammer, letting it slide until he held it just beneath the head. Sigmar stepped to meet the monster and punched Ghal-maraz straight at his enemy's face with all his strength behind the blow.

The creature's head burst apart and its grey-fleshed body dropped to the cobbled esplanade. The body jerked and kicked, as though the change wracking its body was not yet done and fresh horns, limbs and bony protuberances erupted from its flesh.

Sigmar leapt back to the makeshift fighting step, seeing that the entire mass of the Norsii were fighting like beasts, their bodies infused with dark magic and warping to render them less than human. Transformation ran amok through the Norsemen, and Sigmar saw a group of warriors whose skin had become scaled and reptilian. Some sprouted horns like those of a mighty bull, while the bodies of others writhed with blazing green flames. A few hurled themselves from the viaduct, their minds unhinged by the dreadful power coruscating through their ranks.

Redwane fought with a tribesman whose body had swollen to gargantuan proportions, his muscles corded with veins like ropes, whose armour had ruptured into fragments. Crossbow bolts peppered the giant's body, but they were little more than irritants to the berserk warrior. Redwane held the beast at bay long enough for Jutone spearmen to drive the maddened creature back to the wall, where Unberogen swordsmen finally hacked it down.

In the centre of the Norsii charge, the ghastly altar of skulls and brass pulsed with unholy light, a foul beacon of dark sorcery. Its dreadful power surged through the Norsii. Beside the altar, the warrior in bloody armour laughed with the sound of thunder.

It had to be destroyed or this battle was as good as over.

A mass of screaming, maddened tribesmen stood between him and the altar.

Only one group of warriors had a chance of reaching it.

'King's Blades!' shouted Sigmar, vaulting the wall to land in the midst of the Norsii. 'With me!'

THE ROCKS SWARMED with beasts, and Pendrag fought to keep his feet as snarling monsters with the heads of black wolves and lean, sinewy bodies snapped and bit. Blood fell like rain from the top of the Fauschlag Rock, and the ground underfoot was slippery with the stuff. A screeching beast with a cat-like face hissed and pounced towards him, and he buried his axe in its chest. He kicked the body from his blade as an arrow clattered from his breastplate, and he glanced up long enough to see a winged creature with a face like a bat swooping through the air above him. The skies swarmed with such beasts, showering the men below with crudely-made arrows tipped with sharpened flint. Most such missiles either missed or bounced from helmets, but every now and then a warrior would fall as an arrow found a gap in his armour. The archers placed in the buildings behind the defenders at the wall tried to bring them down, but the beasts were fast-moving and difficult to hit. Pendrag had ordered them to ignore the flying creatures and save their arrows for the climbing beasts.

A black-shafted arrow slashed out from his archers behind him, taking the monster in the chest. It squealed in pain and vanished from sight. Pendrag smiled as he watched it die, glad that one archer had thought to disobey his order.

He returned his attention to the battle around him as the beasts roared and howled, clawing their way up the craggy slopes to the low wall at the city's edge. White Wolves and Middenlanders fought side by side, battling furiously to deny the beasts a foothold in the city. Bodies fell from the rock, pierced by arrows or cloven by axes and swords. The creatures fought with fangs and talons, for it was next to impossible to climb with a weapon, and they had come close to gaining the city on four separate occasions.

Myrsa killed with a clinical efficiency, his mighty hammer sweeping out with killing strikes that smashed skulls from shoulders. Where the Warrior Eternal fought without emotion, Pendrag's blows were struck with the knowledge of all that would be lost should they falter.

Along the circumference of the wall, the White Wolves sang songs of battle as they fought, while the men of Middenheim hacked at the beasts in grim silence. These men fought without cries of fear or anger, simply attending to the business of battle with as much emotion as they might butcher cattle. Their foe attacked without strategy or intelligence, simply using their hatred and hunger. Pendrag's axe hewed furred limbs from bodies and split snarling jaws, his arm moving like a mechanical piston on one of Master Alaric's steam bellows.

An enormous, bull-headed beast with a spiked collar reared up and both he and Myrsa leapt to meet it. The Warrior Eternal ducked a savage sweep of its clawed hand and swung for its belly. Pendrag slammed his axe into its side. The blade bit barely a handspan before thudding into hard bone.

The creature reared up, tearing the axe from Pendrag's hands, and slashed its horns towards him. Pendrag leapt back, but not fast enough. The razor edge of the horn caught the leather strap securing his breastplate. He was wrenched from his feet and lifted high into the air as the tip of the horn gouged into his side. Mail links parted and the sharpened horn of bone gored his side. Blood streamed from the wound as the horn sawed through the leather strap of his armour.

Pendrag felt himself falling and landed with bone-jarring force. He rolled, seeing sky and rock swirling above him as he tumbled downhill. He scrabbled for purchase as he slid, his limbs battered bloody by the rocks. Suddenly, there was nothing beneath him and the world dropped away.

He thrust his silver hand out, the metal gouging rock and sending sparks flying. The dwarf-forged metal bit, and Pendrag's shoulder wrenched in fiery agony as he jerked to a halt. Breath hissed from behind clenched teeth as he swung helplessly from the edge of the rock, suspended thousands of feet in the air. His vision swam and his stomach lurched at the vertiginous drop.

Far below, swarms of beasts climbed the Fauschlag Rock, and yet more winged creatures took to the air. Larger than the bat-creatures with their short-bows, these beasts carried others in their claws, though the distance was too great to make out who they were. He heard sounds of battle, and bodies fell past him, both man and beast. A monstrous creature, part-hound and part-bear almost dislodged him, but as his grip began to loosen, a hand grabbed his and hauled him back over the lip of the rock.

Pendrag swung his other hand around, and clawed his way to safety, laughing hysterically at his survival. Hugging the rock, he looked up at his rescuer, a man he didn't recognise, but who wore a blue and white ribbon of cloth around his upper arm.

'I've got you, count,' he said, hauling him upwards.

'The beasts?' gasped Pendrag.

'Driven off. For now. Now come on, don't let's be hanging about down here, eh?'

Pendrag nodded, scrambling up the slope through sticky patches of blood and broken fangs. His legs were shaking by the time he reached the wall. With infinite care, he hauled himself upright, and the warriors of Middenheim cheered to see him alive.

He lost sight of his rescuer as the man returned to his position on the defences. Myrsa pushed his way through the press of fighting men, and his face broke apart in a wide grin.

'Gods, man! I thought we'd lost you!' said the Warrior Eternal.

Pendrag bent double, still in shock at the nearness of his death. He held out his battered silver hand, and said, 'I have the craft of Master Alaric to thank for my survival.'

Myrsa looked at the battered limb and said, 'Then I owe him my thanks too.'

Pendrag lifted a fallen axe.

'If we live through this, we'll travel to King Kurgan's halls together and thank him,' he said. 'But there are more beasts on the way.'

'Stand to!' shouted Myrsa, and the warriors around them braced themselves at the edge of the wall, spears and bows aimed down the slopes. There was no panic in these men, no undue haste and no fear, simply duty and courage. Pendrag had never been prouder to be their leader.

'Men of Middenheim, this is your hour!' he shouted, and no sooner had the words left his mouth than a hundred or more beasts with wide wings and broad shoulders flew up past the edge of the rock. Most carried strangely twisted warriors that thrashed and howled, while others bore robed figures that crackled with sorcerous light.

'Bring them down!' cried Pendrag.

Flocks of arrows slashed upwards.

HUNDREDS OF FEET below, in a lightless cavern beneath the city, Wolfgart listened to the dark. He had presumed it would be quiet down here, but he could not have been more wrong. Metal scraped on stone and the tumble of pebbles and dust echoed from far off caves and distant passageways.

His breathing sounded impossibly loud, and he could feel his heart thudding painfully and fearfully in his chest. Behind him, the heavy breath and muffled curses of a hundred men armed with long-bladed daggers, picks and heavy maces filled the lamplit darkness.

'What was I thinking?' he whispered as Sargall stooped at the mouth of a rough-cut tunnel in the rock. The miner stopped to examine a cut mark on the wall, listening at a hollow in the rock before grunting and moving to another tunnel. The man seemed to know his way, but how anyone could navigate this labyrinth of hewn passageways, high caves and rocky galleries was a mystery to Wolfgart. Moisture glinted on the walls, reflecting the lamplight, and Wolfgart wiped sweat from his brow.

'Is it hot or is it just me?' he asked.

'It's just you,' said Steiner, little more than a silhouette beside him.

Steiner was a siege engineer, a thin, nervous man more at home with calculations, measuring rods and diagrams of castle walls than a weapon, but he had been pressed into service to aid the warriors who volunteered to fight below the city. Like Wolfgart, he was uncomfortable below ground, but where Wolfgart was a warrior, Steiner was an academic.

Nearly five hundred warriors had gone into the secret tunnels beneath Middenheim, split into five groups to better cover the known passages and watch for intruders. Voices and shouts from the disparate groups echoed weirdly through the rock, but it was impossible to tell how much distance separated them.

'How far down do you think we are?' asked Wolfgart.

Steiner shrugged. 'Perhaps a few hundred feet?'

'Don't you know?'

'I can't see anything, and we've twisted up and down through these rocks more times than I can count. How am I supposed to know for sure?' snapped Steiner.

'Quiet, both of you,' hissed Sargall, appearing next to them from the darkness. 'Listen.'

Conversation ceased, and Wolfgart swallowed hard, trying not to imagine all the horrible things that might be lurking somewhere in the dark: oozing black insects, slimy creatures of the night that hated sunlight and feasted on the decaying bodies of those lost in the tunnels...

He shut out such thoughts and tried to concentrate.

'You hear that?' whispered Sargall.

'Aye,' said Steiner, bringing the lamp closer to the wall. Wolfgart couldn't hear anything and pressed his ear to the rock. He still couldn't hear anything, and opened his mouth to say so when he heard it: a tiny *tink, tink, tink* sound. It was like a long fingernail gently rapping on an iron breastplate.

'What is it?' he asked.

'Sounds like a drill of some sort,' said Steiner. 'Nearby. Parallel to this gallery I think.'

'Close?' asked Sargall.

'Close enough,' agreed Steiner. 'Too close.'

'So what do you think it is?' asked Wolfgart. 'Invaders?'

'Who else would be stupid enough to be down here?' asked Sargall.

The noise was getting louder and faster. Wolfgart drew his dagger and unhooked the iron-headed mace from his belt. Though it had grieved him to leave his sword in the city above, it simply wasn't a practical weapon for tunnel fighting.

Steiner placed his head to the rock once more, his face creased in puzzlement.

'I don't understand,' he said. 'It's like a drill, but it sounds much closer now. No drill can go through that much rock that quickly. It must be an echo from somewhere, perhaps a bell chamber that's magnifying the sound.'

'Then we need to find it,' said Wolfgart, 'quickly.'

A sharp crack of splitting stone shot through the tunnel, and cries of fear echoed from the walls as everyone hunched down and looked at the ceiling. Rock dust drifted down and a groan of cracking stone rumbled from somewhere close by.

'What in the name of Ranald's staff was that?' demanded Wolfgart, hearing what sounded like a distant rock-fall. Screams sounded close by, and he brought his dagger up as he heard a metallic scraping sound, like a groundbreaking auger.

'The wall!' he cried. 'Get away from the wall!'

But it was too late. The deep crack of stone split the wall next to Steiner and a roaring, whirling cone of metal speared from the rock. It slammed into the engineer, and the tunnel was suddenly filled with screams and blood. A spinning drill punched into his back and exploded from his ribs. Gouts of red sprayed from the man's convulsing body. Rocks crashed from the wall, and a strange green light filled the tunnel as dust and smoke billowed outwards.

Lamps fell and shattered. Men screamed, and a chittering mass of rats boiled from the hole in the wall. Wolfgart cared nothing for vermin; it was the enormous creature standing in the newly-opened cave mouth, its arm ending in a bloody, spinning auger that captured his attention.

Taller than the mightiest warrior, it was a monstrously swollen, patchwork beast of furry flesh and metal piercings. Though it stood upright, it was no man, for its head was that of a gargantuan rat. Filthy bandages matted in blood wrapped its arms and head, and brass circlets with thin golden wires trailing from them were sewn into its shaven scalp.

Scars and welts covered its body, and it roared with a deafening screech. Shapes moved behind it. Scores of hunched forms in rusted armour bearing jagged swords, pushed past the great beast and into the tunnel.

'Into them!' shouted Wolfgart.

NINETEEN
Heroes of the Hour

TATTOOED THURINGIANS DROPPED from the wall at the head of the viaduct, and followed Sigmar as he charged the mass of screaming Norsii. The first warrior Sigmar reached was a bearded giant with dark skin and eyes that smoked with shimmering fire. A great skull was branded on his chest, and he came at Sigmar with thoughtless hate.

Sigmar ducked a decapitating axe blow, and swung his hammer for the warrior's legs. Ghal-maraz smashed into his kneecaps and tore his left leg off below the thigh. The warrior screamed and fell, but still swung his sword as Sigmar ran past him. Ulfdar the Berserker led her King's Blades from the wall, a wedge of painted warriors like savages from ancient days. They cut into the Norsii, and Sigmar was struck by the notion that whatever sorcery empowered their foe might also speak to some part of his own warriors.

Though their enemies were engorged with dark magic, Ulfdar and the Thuringians gave no heed to it, for the red mist was upon them and they thirsted only to slay. The warrior with the black banner drew a sword of darkness, its blade etched with runes that mocked those hammered upon Ghal-maraz. Sigmar felt his ancient weapon's hunger to destroy them.

Thousands of Norsii pushed up from below, but the tight confines of the viaduct denied them the advantage of their superior numbers.

Warriors swirled around Sigmar, hideous aberrations of flesh twisted by this shrine to the Dark Gods. Flesh melted, burned and ran beneath its power, yet those afflicted by such change howled in ecstasy to be so touched by the power of the gods. To either side of him, the Thuringian berserkers cut a bloody path towards the debased shrine. They fought without heed for their lives, always attacking, and the Norsii fell back in dismay before these warriors who killed and killed and never retreated.

Sigmar fought through a mob of warriors whose skin had erupted with thorny growths, smashing them aside with deadly sweeps of Ghal-maraz. They split apart as they died, their bodies disintegrating to mulch as Sigmar pushed onwards.

The warrior with the banner stepped towards him, and the Norsii cleared a path for their champion. A full head and shoulders above his fellow tribesmen, the warrior planted the banner beside him, its substance seemingly woven from a thousand rippling black snakes. Waves of malice poured from the banner, and Sigmar recognised the touch of purest evil in its creation.

'You die, mortal!' yelled the warrior, leaping to attack with his sword raised.

Sigmar turned aside the blow, and spun away from the reverse stroke. The blade came at him again, faster than he would have believed possible, but once again he was able to parry the warrior's attack. Each time the black sword and Ghal-maraz met, sparks flashed with colours that Sigmar could not name. He felt the unholy strength of the warrior, but knew that it was not his own, it was a gift from the gods he called master. Sigmar's strength was *his*, earned upon countless battlefields and by right of victory.

The sword lanced out, and Sigmar swayed aside, slamming his hammer into the warrior's helm. The strength of the blow drove the warrior to his knees, and Sigmar kicked him in the face, toppling him over onto his back. Before his foe could rise, Sigmar swung Ghal-maraz in a mighty overhead blow, as though hammering a stake into the ground, and smashed the warrior's skull all over the viaduct.

A great wail of anguish went up from the Norsii at the champion's death, and the Thuringians answered with a howl of triumph. Ulfdar cut down the writhing banner with her axe, and lines of smoke unravelled from its disintegrating substance as it fell, its fate entwined with the champion that bore it.

The battleground before the walls was littered with twisted corpses, and nothing now stood between Sigmar and the damned altar. Howling with manic fury, the Thuringians charged the terrible construction of bone and bloody brass, but the daemon-steeds reared and crushed any who dared come near. Their breath was like furnaces searing the air, and anything that came near them died.

Ulfdar staggered over to him, her naked flesh bruised and streaked with blood. She had been wounded several times, yet appeared not to notice. Her eyes had a glazed, faraway look, and purple liquid dribbled from the corners of her mouth as she pointed at the deathly altar.

'How do we destroy it?' she asked, her words slurred from the enraging narcotics.

'Like this,' he said, turning to face the half-built towers at the top of the viaduct. He lifted Ghal-maraz high and swept it down. A hundred bolts slashed out and hammered into the smoking shrine. The daemon steeds yoked to it screamed as they were cut down, collapsing into mouldering heaps of arrow-shot flesh. The heat from their bones died, and their dark hearts were stilled as the spell that breathed life into their forms was broken.

'Now we kill it,' said Sigmar, hooking Ghal-maraz to his belt and running towards the torn-up shrine. The surviving Thuringians ran with him and skulls tumbled from the monstrous shrine as they took hold of it. Closer now, Sigmar saw that the horrific construction also housed a grotesque reliquary of bones, and a swirling cauldron of blood.

This was why Sigmar had driven the Norsii from the Empire. Any last notions of regret at what he had done to that tribe were swept away in the face of this dreadful altar. With the help of the Thuringians, Sigmar pushed the sopping altar to the edge of the viaduct.

'Come on!' he shouted. 'Put your backs into it before they return!'

The altar tipped onto its side, and with a final push, toppled over the edge. It tumbled end over end, spilling skulls and blood as it fell.

Sigmar didn't wait to see it hit the ground.

The Norsii were massing for another attack.

MIDDENHEIM WAS ABLAZE. Pillars of smoke painted the sky, and the smell of burning timber carried to the men on the walls. Smaller, bat-like beasts flew over Pendrag's fighting men, soaring over the city to drop flaming torches, while their more powerful cousins swooped over the defensive walls. The tinder-dry wood of the city was ripe for burning, and high winds fanned the flames.

Laden with warriors, dozens of the larger beasts were brought down with deadly accurate arrows, but this mattered little, for their purpose was not to fight, simply to deliver their armed burdens. Thrashing monstrosities that were not wholly human, but something far more terrible and violent, fell amid the ranks of defenders, and the carnage was terrible.

Pendrag watched as one of the howling creatures landed less than ten feet away. It had once been a man, but its body had twisted and mutated beyond all reason, and it lashed out with a clawed arm that was bulbous and sheathed in bony blades. Its eyes were filled with madness and fury, and it hurled itself at the horrified defenders with a bestial roar of hunger.

'What are they?' asked Myrsa.

'Something forsaken by all the gods of mercy,' replied Pendrag.

More were dropping every second, screaming maniacs whose flesh was twisted by their devotion to the Dark Gods, and whose minds were raging maelstroms of unreasoning hatred. They fought without weapons, their limbs and strength requiring no sharpened iron to do their killing. Unnatural limbs and vestigial body parts pressed out through shattered plates of armour, and the black eyes of the monsters burned with maddening pain.

Desperate fights broke out randomly along the defensive wall as the frenzied warriors clawed their way through the men of Middenheim. Many were brought down by disciplined spear-thrusts and lucky arrow strikes, but they were tearing a bloody wound in the heart of the defenders. Terrified warriors fell back from the walls, and a gap opened in the defences.

'Ulric's name!' cried Myrsa. 'We're wide open!'

Pendrag was torn between the urge to fight the maniacal warriors, and the need to defend the slopes, but the sight of the beasts climbing to the walls in the wake of these attacks made the decision for him. He gripped Myrsa's arm.

'Go! Kill them!' he said. 'More beasts will be at the walls soon, and we must be ready for them.'

Myrsa nodded.

'It will be done,' he said, and set off towards the nearest monsters.

Pendrag watched him go as a body flew through the air, almost severed at the waist, and a sheet of blood arced upwards. Roaring, snapping and screaming spread from the attack, and he looked up as a shadow passed over him.

A flying beast with an arrow lodged in its chest dropped from the sky, a hulking brute of an enemy warrior clutched in its claws.

'Look out!' shouted Pendrag as the dying creature spiralled downwards. It slammed into the ground behind the wall, its fragile body crushed beneath the monstrous form of the thing that it had carried from the ground. Clad in scraps of armour, the warrior's flesh seethed with invention, vestigial forms oozing beneath its skin and its distended face like a wax effigy left too close to a fire.

One of the White Wolves rushed in to kill it before it could rise, but hands like pincers smashed him from his feet and pulled him towards its gaping maw. Bloody fangs crunched the warrior's skull to splinters. Spears punctured its back, but it gave no heed to its wounds as Pendrag rushed to kill it.

Perhaps some part of what was left of its mind recognised a fellow warrior, for it dropped the body it was disembowelling and charged towards Pendrag. Someone shouted a warning, but the Count of Middenheim stood firm in its path. The warped creature reared up, fangs bared and claws extended to tear him apart.

Pendrag's axe swept down and hacked the creature's arm from its body, cleaving into its chest and exiting in a spray of ichor from its belly. The beast fell before him, and the men of Middenheim cheered such a mighty blow.

'They can die!' shouted Pendrag. 'They are touched by sorcery, but they can die. Now kill them all!'

As though ashamed of their brief moment of panic, the warriors of Middenheim fell upon the screaming once-men, cutting them down without mercy and forcing them back to the edge of the city. The White Wolves killed a warrior-beast with a nest of claws for hands and curling horns sprouting from its shoulders and back. It tore at them as it died, its madness driving it to acts of carnage even as its lifeblood pooled beneath it.

Another beast, with budding heads oozing through the flesh of its chest, hurled broken men aside with lashing, blade-tipped tentacles instead of arms.

It had to be hacked into a dozen pieces before it would die.

WOLFGART TRIED TO make sense of the confused mêlée raging through the tunnels, but it was impossible. Flames danced on the floor, and pools of oil burned where lamps had been dropped in death or panic. Shadows leapt across the walls. The caves below Middenheim were lonely battlegrounds, where men fought in the claustrophobic passageways, stabbing at shadows and dying alone in the dark.

Scores of the hooded invaders poured from the cave-in, and his warriors fought to hold them from getting past. It was a losing battle, for tides of bloated rats swarmed the tunnel, biting and dragging men down with their furry bodies. The reek of the sewers came with them, and Wolfgart had already stabbed dozens from his legs. His tunic was in tatters where he had cut himself in his desperation.

As loathsome as these vermin were, it was the hideous, rat-faced beasts that walked upright in imitation of man that struck the greatest terror into Wolfgart's men. So human and yet so bestial, their flame-lit faces were malicious and cunning, a mockery of man's intelligence.

The giant auger-carrier battered its way into the tunnels, and the rat-beasts followed in the wake of its bludgeoning attacks. Elongated fangs bit through flesh and armour, and the power of its enormous arms broke men in two if they came too close.

Wolfgart heard shouts of alarm from far off tunnels. Clearly this was not the only breakthrough into the warrens beneath Middenheim.

The monstrous rat-beast charged him, its spine hunched over in the cramped tunnel, and he ducked a crushing sweep of its deadly auger. The conical blades still spun, sending chunks of rock flying as it bit into the wall. Wolfgart slammed his mace into the monster's side, the flesh stitched and raw-looking. Bones broke and flesh caved in beneath the blow, but the monster gave no sign that it was even aware he had struck it.

Its auger stabbed down, and Wolfgart leapt back, slashing his dagger across its twitching snout. Blood burst from its mouth, and he stumbled away from the monster. A rusted sword scraped across his chest, skidding over the mail links and slashing his cheek. Wolfgart lashed out with instinct rather than skill, and was rewarded by a squeal of pain.

A creature that was a smaller version of the giant fell broken, but before he could even register its death, the huge monster threw itself at him once again. Its claws caught his mail shirt and slammed him against a wall. Stars exploded before him as the force of the impact drove the breath from his lungs. Through the haze of pain, Wolfgart saw its arm draw back for a thunderous punch.

He ducked, and its fist pulverised a section of wall behind him. Wolfgart reached up and slashed his dagger at the monster's throat as it bellowed in pain. Fur and sinew parted beneath the desperate slash, and Wolfgart was sprayed in a hosing squirt of blood. The creature's iron grip relaxed and it dropped to its knees, as though mystified as to why its strength was failing.

He spat blood from his mouth and wiped his eyes clean with his sleeve.

It was impossible to read the flow of the battle, for so much of it was fought in darkness. Weapons clashed, but who, if anyone, was winning was a mystery. Wolfgart leapt over the giant rat-thing and plunged into the tunnels, stabbing and crushing any invaders he came across. His warriors fought in blind terror, a host of panicked men wildly swinging swords at their chittering attackers.

The hot confines of the tunnels were hellish to fight in, and every blow was fuelled by his fear of this dark, terrible place. A sword lunged at him from the shadows, and he batted it aside with his mace. Flickering firelight illuminated the frightened face of the miner, Sargall.

'Watch it, damn you!' shouted Wolfgart, his voice carrying to all the men who still fought in the tunnels. 'Strike the enemy, not your friends!'

'Sorry!' cried Sargall, and Wolfgart saw the man was in tears. 'I thought you were one of them! Ulric save us, we're all going to die down here, they're going to kill us all.'

'Not if I have anything to do with it,' barked Wolfgart. 'Now shut up.'

He heard a scrape of metal on stone, and turned with his weapons raised as a pack of hunched forms emerged from the darkness.

'Come on then, you bastards!' he yelled. 'Here I am! Come and get me!'

They were clad in black armour, and vile segmented tails whipped at their backs. Spears jabbed at him, and no sooner had he turned the first aside than a host of rats swarmed from the walls, leaping from ledges and nubs of rock to attack him.

He hurled himself against the wall, crushing half a dozen and dislodging yet more. A spear slashed for his neck, and he blocked it with the haft of his mace. Sargall screamed as a rat-thing stabbed him in the belly and the rats swarmed over him. Two of the spear-carriers ran at Wolfgart, and he roared as he ran at them.

The first died as Wolfgart jammed his dagger through the rusted plates of armour protecting its chest, and twisted the blade up under its ribs. It squealed in agony as it died, and he hurled it back as the second came at him. He slammed his mace into its toothy jaw, and it dropped dead at his feet. Screams and the sounds of battle rang deafeningly from the walls of the tunnels, the echoes magnified and distorted by the close confines.

He heard a crash of stone, and choking dust billowed along the length of the tunnel.

Gods, more of the damn things!

A spear pierced his side, and he grunted in pain. Rats climbed his trews and bit his legs. Teeth snapped on his hamstrings, and the pain sent a bolt of white fire zipping up his spine. Wolfgart cried out, and dropped to one knee as more rats swarmed him. He dropped to the floor of the tunnel and thrashed like a madman, crushing rats as he rolled in pain and desperation. Blades stabbed at him, some drawing his blood, some that of the rats. His attackers seemed not to care which.

He lashed out with his mace, trying to clear some space, but it was hopeless, and he filled the air with curses at the thought of dying like this, far from the world of men and without his sword in his hand. Wolfgart tried to regain his feet, but the weight of rats was too heavy, and he could not rise.

'Ulrike!' he shouted, as a vision of his daughter filled his mind. Sadness filled him as he thought of all the years he would miss of her life.

A hooded figure in armour reared over him with a long, serrated dagger, and its furry snout twitched in anticipation of killing him. Wolfgart could taste the rankness of its hissing breath and smell the reek of foulness on its twisted body. The dagger swept up, but before it could plunge down, the creature's head flew off, and the tunnel was filled with light.

The rats pinning Wolfgart to the ground fled, scurrying off into the darkness, and he scrambled onto his backside, reaching for his dagger and mace.

Wolfgart shielded his eyes from the source of the blinding light, seeing a number of short, armoured figures in gleaming plates of silver, bronze and gold advancing towards him.

'Back, you devils!' he roared, blinking furiously as his eyes adjusted to the illumination.

One of the armoured figures shouldered a bloody axe and knelt before him. The warrior raised the visor of its helmet, revealing a bearded face and a stern, but not unkind expression of recognition.

Wolfgart laughed and let out a shuddering breath.

'Once again the dwarfs come to the aid of you manlings,' said Master Alaric with a wicked grin. 'It's getting to be a habit.'

THE VIADUCT AND northern flank of the Fauschlag Rock were assaulted with the greatest ferocity, but the eastern and western flanks also came under heavy attack. Conn Carsten's Udose fought with great courage, keeping the swarms of beasts from the makeshift ramparts with powerful sweeps of their wide-bladed broadswords. Their battles were fought to the tunes of gloriously heartbreaking laments played by pipers who marched through the thick of the fighting, heedless of the danger.

Skirling tunes of lost loves and ancient wrongs provided a stirring backdrop for the clansmen, an emotional reminder of that for which they fought. Time and time again the beasts were hurled back, and each time the ingenious insults of the clansmen chased the bloody survivors away. Wineskins of grain liquor were passed around during each lull in the fighting, and though scores of fighters were dead and crippled, the mood was light, for the Udose were never happier than when they were in battle.

Carsten's warriors came from dozens of different clans, men and women who had been killing each other only weeks before in bitter internecine power struggles, but who now fought like lifelong sword-brothers. When the fighting was over they would go back to their feuding, and none would have it any other way.

As Sigmar was casting the dread altar from the viaduct, and Pendrag brought down the last of the forsaken once-men, another ravening pack of beasts climbed the eastern cliffs. Once again, Conn Carsten called his warriors to battle in his grim and humourless manner, and every clansman readied his sword.

But this attack was to be something different.

Borne up the rock face by a monstrous bear-creature, a robed beast-shaman with the shaggy look of a bullish goat and the twisting antlers of a stag climbed onto the upper slopes of Middenheim. Arrows hammered the forest beasts as soon as they appeared, but the shaman uttered guttural words of power in a dark tongue, and they burst into flame.

Instead of charging the defensive wall, the beasts gathered below the Udose, snarling and roaring as the beast-shaman chanted a filthy incantation. A creature with a body that was a meld of man and fox with sable fur threw itself to its knees before the beast-shaman, its head thrown back and its throat bared. A slash of the beast-shaman's claws and its black blood arced up to spatter the grotesque sorcerer. Bathed in sacrificial blood, the beast-shaman let loose an ecstatic cry, its clawed hands twisting and tearing at the air.

At first it seemed as though nothing was happening, but within moments it was clear that something was horribly wrong. It began among the clan warriors of the Gallis. Their hurled insults changed, losing the form of speech and becoming honking brays, bellowed roars and bestial growls.

Horrified cries rippled outwards as the men and women of the Gallis began convulsing and the full terror of the beast-shaman's sorcery took hold. Proud Udose warriors fell on all fours as their bones cracked and reshaped into new and hideous forms. Flesh slithered and swelled, bristling fur erupted from pink flesh, and screams of terror became animal barks.

Men fought to get away from these abominable transformations, and as the beast within each man took hold, the newly-birthed monsters threw themselves at their former comrades-in-arms. Within moments, the Udose were in disarray as the horribly altered warriors of the Gallis went on a bloody rampage, fangs tearing out throats and claws ripping flesh from bones. The pipes fell silent and the songs died, as what had begun as a gloriously raucous fight became a desperate battle for survival.

As the Udose formation collapsed, the beasts below attacked.

And there was no one to stop them.

A VERY DIFFERENT battle was fought on the western flank of Middenheim, where the forces of Count Marius manned the defences. The Jutones had come to the City of the White Wolf with a host of mercenaries, men with olive skin who hailed from a sun-baked land far to the south. They spoke strangely, yet their skill in the art of killing needed no translation.

Marius watched with disdain as the mutant abominations gathered on the slopes. Creatures with the powerfully muscled bodies of bears and wolves roared and stalked the cliffs of the Fauschlag Rock, wary of the deadly weapons of the men that could kill from afar.

'Why do they bother?' he wondered aloud.

'My lord?' asked his aide-de-camp, a handsome youth named Bastiaan.

Marius waved a manicured hand at the slavering beasts.

'What can such aberrations know of civilisation and commerce?' he asked. 'The Norsii seek to conquer the lands of the south, but what will they do with such a prize? Become merchants? Learn to farm the land? Hardly.'

'I do not know, my lord,' said Bastiaan, ever the sycophant. The boy was efficient and attended to his needs with alacrity. Sometimes he even said things of interest. 'Perhaps vengeance drives them. You yourself have led hunts into the forest to cull such creatures.'

'True, but war is a means of extending one's will across the world,' said Marius. 'War for the sake of vengeance is ultimately pointless. There is no profit in it.'

'Not all wars are fought for profit, my lord.'

'Nonsense, Bastiaan, analyse any conflict closely enough and you will find a lust for gold at its heart.'

'The Norsii and these beasts do not fight for gold.'

'Which is why disciplined volleys of crossbow bolts have hurled every attack from the rock,' Marius said. 'Not a single beast has survived to reach the wall.' He drew his sword, the eastern-styled cavalry blade shimmering with a hazy light in the evening sun. 'You see? This is the first time I have drawn my sword today. It has yet to be blooded.'

Bastiaan nodded towards the rapt faces of the Jutone warriors.

'Maybe so,' he said, 'but I believe your warriors desire to meet their foes blade to blade.'

'I am sure they will, but not yet,' said Marius. 'It will be better for the mercenaries to bear the brunt of the beasts' attack.'

'You doubt the courage of your warriors?'

'Not at all, but dead mercenaries do not require payment,' explained Marius.

'Of course, my lord,' said Bastiaan. 'I shall alter our account ledgers.'

Marius smiled at the thought, picturing the secret treasure vaults hidden in the depths of the Namathir. Even with Sigmar's ludicrously unfair levies and tithes after the battle of Jutonsryk, Marius still had more gold than any man could hope to spend in a dozen lifetimes. A young courtier had once remarked that his love of gold was akin to that of a dwarf, and though the remark was astute, Marius had the boy whipped to death.

More of the beasts were gathering, and they were getting dangerously close. Marius frowned as he realised the mercenary crossbowmen were allowing them to climb unmolested towards the defensive wall. He felt tingling warmth in his hand as a strange, bitter taste of metal fizzed in the air.

'What in the name of Manann are those fools doing?' demanded Marius. 'Why are they not loosing their bolts?' The taste of metal grew stronger and the hairs on the back of his neck stood erect in a primal warning of danger.

'I... I don't know, my lord,' said Bastiaan, his voice sounding dreamlike. 'Perhaps they don't want to hit all the chests of gold.'

Marius gave the boy a sidelong glance.

'What foolishness are you talking about?' he asked. 'What gold?'

'There,' whispered Bastiaan, moving towards the wall. 'So much gold!'

Marius watched in horror as the mercenaries climbed over the defensive wall, fighting one another as they made their way towards the beasts without fear. A muttered ripple of heated conversation came from the ranks of Jutone warriors behind him. He turned to rebuke them for breaking silence, but his harsh words trailed off as he saw the glassy avarice in their eyes, each man lost in a dream of something wonderful.

The warmth in his hand became heat, and he looked down to see the etched lettering running the length of his sword blade shimmering as though bathed in twilight. The golden-skinned king who had presented it to him had claimed it could turn aside evil spells, though Marius hadn't believed him at the time. A whispering evil urged him to sheath the blade, but Marius knew that his sword's power was all that was protecting him from whatever fell sorcery affected his warriors.

Bastiaan had reached the wall, but Marius ran forward and took hold of his arm.

'Get back here, boy,' snapped Marius. No sooner had he touched his aide-de-camp than the boy shuddered and blinked in surprise. He looked from Marius to the beasts and back again.

'What did you do with it?' he cried, tears spilling down his cheeks.

'With what?' demanded Marius. 'Have you lost your mind?'

'The gold!' shouted Bastiaan. 'It was there... All the gold in the world. It was mine!'

'There is no gold there, you fool!' said Marius. 'Snap out of it, you are ensorcelled.'

Bastiaan shook off Marius's grip.

'Of course you'd say that!' he protested. 'You want to keep it all for yourself! You don't want anyone else to have any of your precious gold!'

Marius slapped Bastiaan, tired of the boy's theatrics. He brushed past the youth and leaned over the wall. The olive-skinned mercenaries were almost at the bottom of the slope. None of them had their weapons drawn, and their movements were like those of sleepwalkers.

Marius saw the dreadful hunger in the eyes of the monsters. Saliva drooled from their jaws and he knew that he had only seconds to act.

He turned to shout at his Jutone warriors, but before he could open his mouth, searing pain exploded in his side. Marius looked down and saw the golden hilt of an exquisitely fashioned knife pressed against his leather and silk doublet. Blood welled around the blade, and he watched, uncomprehending, as it spilled onto the stone flags.

Bastiaan twisted the knife, and Marius cried out in pain, clutching his aide-de-camp's shoulder as the strength in his legs gave out.

'I won't let you take the gold!' hissed Bastiaan. 'It's mine. All mine. You can't have it!'

'There is no gold,' whispered Marius, sagging to the ground, and leaning against the wall as his vision greyed. He heard the screams of the mercenaries as the beasts tore them apart, and the slaughter began.

We failed, thought Marius, and this city will fall.

TWENTY
The Last Days

THE CITY DID not fall.

On the eastern flank, the Udose were torn apart by the twin assaults from the beasts and their transformed comrades. Horrified warriors fled into the city, leaving the eastern approaches to the city wide open.

The west fared little better, with the enraptured Jutones walking blindly towards non-existent treasures and illusory visions of their deepest desires. Most were torn apart by the beasts, but many more fell to their deaths as they chased phantoms of riches, women and lost loved ones over the edge of the cliff.

Sigmar's forces at the viaduct and Pendrag's warriors to the north were cut off from one another as beasts and fires raged through the heart of the city. As Middenheim burned, its people prayed to Ulric and their prayers were answered as a frozen wind blew from the north, preventing the fires from spreading and saving their city from destruction.

The flames were doused, but hungry beasts tore into the city's inhabitants, killing and feeding in an orgy of slaughter. Blood ran in rivers through the streets of Middenheim, but its people were hardy northerners, and were not about to go down without a fight. Just as it seemed the city was doomed, aid came from two unlikely sources.

The warriors that Sigmar had deemed too young or too old to stand on the front lines rose to the defence of their city, and an aged veteran named Magnus Anders rallied the warriors of the eastern districts to him. Already in his fiftieth year at the time of Black Fire Pass, the veteran Anders led his warriors in a series of brilliantly orchestrated guerrilla attacks that blunted the charge of the beasts, and led them into blind alleys where they could be butchered. Civilians and refugees followed his example and fell upon the beasts with axes, cleavers, clubs and pitchforks, driving the last of them into killing grounds of archers who had fallen back in the wake of the slaughter of Conn Carsten's men.

As the Jutone defence of the west was broken, rampaging packs of beasts flooded into the mercantile quarter of the city. The streets here were narrow, and the squat stone buildings bore the hallmarks of dwarf craftsmen. As the monsters surged into the city, the doors of these buildings burst open, and armoured wedges of stocky warriors in gleaming plates of burnished gromril smashed into the forest beasts.

The Ironbreakers of Karaz-a-Karak cut a bloody path through the monsters, hammers and axes hewing warped flesh with grim, merciless skill. Alaric the Mad fought with an axe that shimmered with golden light, and his warriors were like a dam of iron before the tide of monsters. Blinking in the sunlight, Wolfgart fought at Alaric's side, bloody and filthy, but unbroken and elated to be alive.

The beasts broke upon the iron fortitude of the dwarf line again and again, until Alaric deemed the the time was right and a double horn blast sounded the advance. The dwarfs marched through the streets of Middenheim, each separate host of warriors linking and forming an unstoppable wall of iron and blades. Roars of hunger and triumph turned to howls of fear as the beasts fell back before the inhuman killing power of the dwarfs.

The beasts were pushed back to the western edge of Middenheim and driven from the cliffs without mercy. Here, Wolfgart found Marius of the Jutones among the fallen, still gripping his curved cavalry sabre. His rich tunic was soaked with blood, and though Wolfgart feared the worst, the stubborn Count of Jutonsryk still clung to life.

At last, the sun sank below the horizon, and night fell.

The first day of battle was over, and the city had not fallen.

* * *

NIGHT BROUGHT A much-needed respite from the battle, for both sides had exhausted themselves in the furious struggle. Warriors rested, having spent the day fighting, but Sigmar, Pendrag and Myrsa made a circuit of the defences, taking time to praise each sword band's courage and assure them of victory. It was draining work, and the strain was telling by the time Sigmar gathered his counts in the Hall of Winter.

The mighty longhouse at the heart of Middenheim had once been Artur's great hall, but now it belonged to Pendrag. It had been a cold place of isolation and power, but Pendrag had transformed it into a place where all men were equal and free to speak their minds.

A great fire burned in the hearth and the walls were hung with the pelts of legendary wolves that had hunted the Forest of Shadows. This was a place of warriors, and Sigmar had summoned his friends and allies to him as they faced a second day's fighting. Normally, vast platters of roasted boar and flagons of northern ale would fuel such a gathering, but with no end in sight for the siege, the leaders of the Empire ate sparingly, though they drank as fulsomely as ever.

Alaric's warriors had brought several casks of dwarf ale with them, for no force of Grungni's chosen went into battle without the taste of beer in his beard.

A single day had passed, yet Sigmar felt as weary as he had after a year of fighting at the siege of Jutonsryk. His limbs ached and his head thumped with the same dull pain that had been his constant companion since his destruction of the Norsii's bloody altar. He was bone tired, but proud of all that his warriors had achieved.

Though Sigmar was the Emperor, Pendrag sat at the head of the longhouse, as was only right and proper in his own city. Myrsa stood behind the Count of Middenheim, and Alaric sat at Pendrag's side, contentedly smoking a long ashwood pipe. The two warriors spoke with real pleasure at this unexpected meeting of old friends. Wolfgart and Redwane sat on the steps before Pendrag's throne, resting their elbows on a flagon of ale from which they regularly refilled their tankards.

Count Otwin sat by the fire, his body thick with bandages and his chained axe resting next to him. Similarly swathed, Count Marius lay on a padded couch next to the Thuringian count. His skin was an unhealthy grey, but he was lucky to be alive. Though Marius had been deeply wounded, the blade had not pierced his vital organs. The bewitched youth who stabbed him had been torn apart by the beasts, which was just as well, for Marius would have been sure to wreak a terrible vengeance.

Conn Carsten sat staring into the fire, lost in thought, and Sigmar's heart went out to the bluff clansman. In the face of disaster, Carsten had rallied enough of his warriors to fight his way clear of the beasts' attack, and return to the fight alongside the aged warriors of Magnus Anders, but that did not change the fact that clansmen had run from a fight. The honour of the Udose had been slighted, and shame burned in every man's heart.

The atmosphere in the hall was subdued, for the day's fighting had been hard, and the morrow promised to be harder still. Sigmar lifted his tankard of dwarf ale from the table and stood before Pendrag, bowing to the master of the hall before turning to face those gathered around him.

'Ulric bless you, my friends,' he said. 'This has been a day of blood that will never be forgotten. Our foes pressed us hard, but we are still rulers of Middenheim.'

'Aye, but for how long?' asked Conn Carsten. 'I lost two hundred men today. We won't survive another attack like that.'

'We can and we will,' promised Sigmar. 'I swear this to you now. The first day of any siege is always the hardest. It is when enemies test one another and gain the measure of their foe. The attacker hopes to sweep the defenders away in one mighty storm, and those within hope to break the will of the besiegers with the strength of their resistance. Tomorrow will be hard, but it will be easier than today.'

'You can't know that,' said Carsten. 'Pretty words might fool some men, but I have seen my share of battles and I know that's just hot air. You know as well as I do that another attack like today will break us!'

Sigmar moved around the fire to stand before Conn Carsten, and the clansman got to his feet, as though expecting the emperor to attack him. He probably does, thought Sigmar, recognising the bellicose quality common to Udose tribesmen.

'It will not,' said Sigmar, 'and I will tell you why. We only need hold the Norsii here until our sword-brothers reach us. Cormac Bloodaxe has made a mistake coming to Middenheim, for even now armies are closing on him, and he knows he must finish us before they arrive. He surprised us with his skill before, but now he has no time for subtlety and must throw everything he has at the city.'

'I'm no defeatist,' said Wolfgart, taking a long draught of ale, 'but it strikes me that might be enough. We lost close to a thousand fighting men today, and the same again are too badly hurt to fight tomorrow. Like I said, we can hold the viaduct, but Middenheim's a big place.'

'Aye, it is,' agreed Sigmar, circling the fire and meeting the gaze of every one of his friends. 'and we will defend every inch of it.'

'How?' demanded Conn Carsten. 'Where will you get the warriors to man the wall?'

'Pull what strength you have in the tunnels back to the surface, manling,' said Alaric from the end of the hall. 'My Ironbreakers will hold the secret ways into the city. We know them better than any of you.'

'You see?' said Sigmar. 'At every turn we are blessed by the gods. Fire took hold of the city and the people prayed for salvation. The wind and rain of Ulric answered those prayers and the city was saved.'

'It rains every day in the north,' said Marius from his padded couch. 'That is hardly a miracle, for the climate here is quite revolting. Must be bad for the lungs.'

'If you don't like the weather in the north, just wait an hour and it'll change,' said Myrsa.

Sigmar smiled, pleased to hear a note of levity from his commanders. 'When it looked as though we would be overrun, the people drove back the invaders, and our allies from the mountains drove the beasts from the city,' he said. 'The gods help those who help themselves, and Alaric brings some of the greatest fighters from his hold to fight alongside us. How many warriors make up your throng, Alaric?'

'Five hundred stout fighters from honourable clans,' said the dwarf runesmith. 'Warriors from the Grimlok goldsmiths, the Skrundok runesmiths of Morgrim, the Gnollengroms and the Grimargul veterans. But best of all, I bring Hammerers from King Kurgan's personal guard and a hundred Ironbreakers to defend the tunnels.'

'A hundred?' asked Carsten. 'We had five times that number in the tunnels and they very nearly couldn't hold back the vermin-beasts!'

'Aye, and for every battle you have fought, manling, they have fought a dozen more. They've been fighting grobi and trolls and worse in the dark for longer than any of you have been alive.'

Alaric leaned forward, blowing a puff of aromatic smoke from his pipe, and saying, 'I warn you not to insult their honour by doubting their courage, manling.'

'Conn Carsten meant no disrespect, Alaric,' said Sigmar.

'No,' agreed Carsten, hurriedly. 'None at all. I apologise, runesmith.'

Alaric nodded and stepped down towards the fire as a dwarf in burnished armour of gold and silver marched from the edge of the hall bearing a long, slender case of dark wood.

'I bring warriors, right enough,' said Alaric, 'but I bring a mightier gift to aid the defence of this city.'

The dwarf runesmith took the case from the warrior, and turned to hold it out to Sigmar. Alaric's expression was hard to read beneath his thick beard, but it looked a lot like sadness, as though he were being forced to give up his most treasured possession.

'I laboured long and hard crafting this in the greatest forge of Karaz-a-Karak,' he said. 'Use it wisely, my friend.'

Sigmar undid the golden clasp securing the case, and lifted the polished lid.

Cold silver light spilled from the fur-lined interior. and the fierce beauty of the object within stole Sigmar's breath away.

It was a sword, but what a sword it was!

Its blade shone like captured moonlight, its edge keen enough to cut the veil between worlds. Etched runes ran along its length, carved into the very heart of the blade. Sigmar had never seen a more perfectly forged weapon.

'Is this...?' whispered Sigmar as those of his friends that could stand gathered around him.

'Aye,' said Alaric. 'The first of the runefangs. Take it.'

Slowly and with reverent care, Sigmar reached out and lifted the sword from its case. Its hilt was silver, the handle wrapped in the softest leather, and the pommel stone a nugget of smooth gold. In the wake of Black Fire Pass, Kurgan Ironbeard had promised him a mighty blade for each of his kings, and Sigmar had never held a sword so fine. The runefang was light, yet perfectly balanced, the work of a master craftsman at the peak of his powers.

The sense of connection he felt with the blade was incredible. It was akin to Ghal-maraz, but this was a weapon crafted for a man's hand and forged for a spirit that endured for a fleeting moment compared to that of a dwarf.

'Does it have a name?' he asked, turning the blade and letting it capture the firelight.

'Not yet,' said Alaric. 'It will earn one in battle, but that is for you to choose.'

Sigmar spun the sword, feeling the blade cut the air like the sharpest razor, and shook his head. The sword was magnificent, a work of art so awesome that it seemed an insult to its perfection for his crude human hand to even touch it.

'No,' said Sigmar, turning to face Pendrag. 'This is not my sword to bear. We fight in defence of Middenheim, and its count is in need of a new weapon.'

Sigmar reversed the blade and offered the handle to Pendrag, feeling the sword's approval of his act. Pendrag looked from the runefang to Alaric. He too shook his head.

'No, I can't,' he said. 'I am not worthy. You are the Emperor, it should be yours.'

'I already have a weapon gifted to me by the king of the mountain folk,' said Sigmar, holding the magnificent blade out. 'Take it, for it is yours to bear, my friend.'

Pendrag took the runefang from Sigmar, and the light that flowed from the blade bathed him in pale luminescence, like the moon of a winter solstice. Sigmar turned to Conn Carsten, the normally sour-faced Udose war leader smiling and full of wonder.

'Still think we are doomed?' asked Sigmar.

Conn Carsten shook his head, and said, 'Not any more.'

THE CITY DID not fall on the first day, and it endured for the next twelve days.

Every day, the Norsii attacked along the viaduct as beasts swarmed up the sides of the Fauschlag Rock. Unnatural storms battered the City of the White Wolf, heaving rainstorms and lightning strikes that levelled whole districts. Doomsayers cried that the gods had turned from the race of man, but as night fell on each day, the defences were rebuilt to face the next attack. After the first day's fighting, there were no bystanders in the battle to save Middenheim. Every living soul within the city bent their efforts to resisting the siege, either as a warrior or in the infirmaries or granaries, or wherever help was needed.

As well as warlike tribesmen, Cormac Bloodaxe sent hideous beasts into battle. Vile, slime-skinned trolls attacked alongside hulking ogres with horribly disfigured limbs and skin like hardened leather. Black wolves ran with the monsters, and red-furred hounds with spiked collars leapt the wall at the head of the viaduct to bite and tear at the defenders, before being cut down by hardened dwarf fighters.

Flying beasts with wide wings swooped over the city, but the foresters of Middenland were deadly hunters, and brought dozens of the creatures down. Soon none dared fly too low for fear of a goose-feathered shaft between the ribs.

The battle beneath the city was no less fierce, with every day bringing fresh attacks up through the tunnels and rocky galleries. Conn Carsten's fears proved as unfounded as Alaric had promised, for the Ironbreakers of Karaz-a-Karak met and defeated every attack. They fought with more than just axes and swords, for Alaric had brought three of the Guild of Engineers' most prized weapons with him.

Called Baragdrakk in the dwarf tongue, each was a bizarre mechanical contraption that sprayed great gouts of liquid flame, and burned the vermin creatures from their lairs in the rock. The fighting in the tunnels was near continuous, and only rarely were any of the Ironbreakers seen above ground.

Sigmar had Alaric spread his remaining warriors around the city to bolster the defences where they were weakest and where the Norsii were sure to attack the hardest. With warriors from the Skrundok clan, the venerable runesmith made his way through the fighting to hammer arcane sigils into the very stones of Middenheim. He would not be drawn on the nature of these runes, but as the days passed, the lightning strikes that clawed at the city grew weaker and weaker until they ceased altogether. With the lifting of the storms, the hearts of the defenders grew lighter, and the oppressive gloom that hung over the city vanished with the brooding clouds.

Sigmar fought in a different part of the city every day, strengthening the spirits of the warriors he joined with his great heart and enormous courage. Where Sigmar raised his hammer, men and dwarfs fought harder and with greater determination than ever before.

Against Cradoc's instructions, Count Otwin took to the field of battle, fighting alongside the King's Blades, and his chained axe was red with blood that could never be cleaned from its edge. Marius also returned to the battle, though Sigmar was careful to position him where the fighting was less intense, for fear the Jutone count's pride might see him killed.

Conn Carsten's Udose fought harder than ever, their broadswords cleaving through the beasts and monsters with a fury borne from the fear of dishonour. No fiercer foe was there than a wronged clansman.

At Sigmar's suggestion, Pendrag also fought in different parts of the city, letting his warriors see the magnificent blade crafted for him by Alaric. Fighting alongside Myrsa and the White Wolves, Pendrag became an inspirational leader of men, and all who witnessed him wield the mighty runefang in battle felt a measure of his power pass to them.

As the days passed and the city endured, hope that a grand victory might be won seeped into every man's heart.

All that came to an end on the thirteenth day.

CORMAC FELT THE blood run down his face, relishing the taste of it even as the stink of dead flesh turned his stomach. He was naked but for a loincloth, and the tanned colour of his skin was entirely obscured by the crusted blood that covered every inch of his flesh. His arm ached from sawing through meat and bone, yet he could not deny the exhilaration that filled him as he stood in the centre of the pit.

The pit was precisely eighty yards wide and eight deep, filled with severed heads to the height of a man's waist. Every corpse that had fallen from the mountainous spire of Middenheim since battle had been joined was dragged here and decapitated. Day after day, Cormac had hacked the skulls from the fallen and hurled them into the pit. Kar Odacen had spoken of a great prince of Kharnath and such a mighty avatar of the Blood God demanded great honour.

The ground underfoot was thick with coagulated blood, and rotting flesh peeled from the skulls of men and beasts alike. Warriors and champions from every tribe surrounded the pit, each with a dagger poised at the throat of his fiercest warrior. Only the most vicious killers would serve as sacrifices, for a sacrifice was not a sacrifice if it was not valued.

Cormac had woken this day with his veins throbbing and his vision streaked with red, as though an endless gourd of blood was being slowly poured over his head. The taste of it was in his throat and a rabid fury filled his heart. He had felt a similar sensation in the tomb of Varag Skulltaker, and he had felt it when Kar Odacen bound the dark spirit to his axe.

Cormac now saw that those moments had been hollow and meaningless, pale echoes of the bloodlust that now coursed through his body. Mighty powers had turned their eyes upon this mortal world with ruinous ambition, and Cormac's heart soared at the thought of being their mortal champion. His axe growled and hissed, the fell spirit bound within the blade also sensing that this day was special.

Today promised bloodletting like no other.

Today, he would fight alongside one of the mighty daemon lords of Kharnath.

Kar Odacen had sought him out at first light, and the moment he caught sight of Cormac his eyes widened with a mixture of fear and awed reverence.

'It is time,' said the shaman.

Word had spread through the camp, and the assault on Middenheim was forgotten as warriors, beasts and monsters were drawn to the pit to witness this great and terrible sorcery.

Alone among Cormac's warriors, Azazel and the Hung had not come to share this glorious moment, for their master was Shornaal, the ancient god most hated by Kharnath. To be a devotee of the Dark Prince at the birth of one of the Blood God's avatars would be suicide.

Cormac had ritually taken the skulls of eight times eight captives, holding their severed heads above his own and letting the blood drain onto his iron-hard flesh. Each baptism had sent his heart racing, and when he dropped into the pit of heads, he felt the *thinness* of the air, as though he could tear down the wall between this world and the void with his bare hands.

The day was silent, no sounds of life or the passage of moments, for the powers pushing into this world were the bane of all living things. Cormac could feel the pressure within his skull, like the coming of a storm. He welcomed it, for this was a storm of blood, a storm of blades and a storm of skull-taking.

He looked up at Kar Odacen, the shaman's wizened features energised by the power being drawn to the pit. Cormac blinked as his vision blurred. The world around him began to turn red, as though his eyeballs were filling with blood. The sensation was not unwelcome. For the first time, Cormac could see the breath of the gods roaring over the earth, clouds of red howling soundlessly around him like smoke in a storm. It touched everything with rage and hatred, pride and glory. Nothing was left without its boon.

The breath of Kharnath was everywhere, in every act of violence, every act of martial pride and every act of spite. Every mortal heart was touched by it, and he laughed as he saw the top of Middenheim was just as wreathed in the breath of the Blood God as his own army.

'I feel it!' he roared, a red fury of power surging in his veins.

Kar Odacen raised his arms, and the red mists gathered around the shaman, drawn to him as he gave voice to a host of guttural, primal syllables that sundered the air with their horror and rage. Instinctively, Cormac knew that these were the first words of death, the sounds of the first murder and the echoes of Kharnath's birth at the dawn of all things.

The shaman nodded, and the champions of the north sliced their blades across the throats of their willing victims. Blood jetted from a hundred opened throats, and the air was rent by howls, roars and cries in honour of the great god of battle and blood. But death alone was not enough, and the blades hacked through sinew and bone to sever each head.

Cormac gasped as the heads were hurled into the pit with him. Ruby droplets spattered him as they bounced and tumbled over the decaying carpet of skulls. The howling red clouds were drawn up into a towering spiral of crimson, like a bloody vortex that reached from this poor, tasteless realm to the abode of the gods.

How Cormac ached to climb to that domain of murder and hew skulls in the name of the Blood God, but this moment was not for him to transcend, but for something far older and far more terrible to tread the soil of this mortal earth.

Cormac felt it pass from its own existence to his, and threw back his head as he welcomed the avatar of Kharnath with a bellowing roar of bloody devotion. The pit began to fill with gore, as though an endless lake of blood was flooding through an invisible tear in reality. Forking traceries of light flashed in the sky and crimson bolts of lightning slammed into the pit. The blood boiled and the earth screamed as something ancient and abominable poured its essence into the world.

The pressure in Cormac's skull intensified a thousand-fold, and he screamed in agony, collapsing into the mass of severed heads that floated in the lake of blood. The jostling skulls and blood swallowed him as his flesh burned with invention.

Too late, he realised his mistake.

His role in this was not to fight alongside a lord of Kharnath.

His role was to become one.

SIGMAR KNELT BEFORE the Flame of Ulric, and knew that this was the last day.

He felt it in the icy fire that chilled his bones, and he saw that same knowledge on the face of the hundred warriors who stood with him in the midst of the half-built temple. Even Wolfgart and Redwane were on edge, sensing that this day was somehow special. Sigmar felt a dreadful pressure on the air, like the last breath before the executioner's axe falls.

Coruscating sheets of lightning danced in a sky the colour of mourning, and streaks of red left blinding after-images on the backs of his eyes. Sigmar's nose was bleeding, and he saw that he wasn't the only one. Cuts and wounds he had received during the fighting bled freely as though freshly sliced in his flesh, and he felt an aching sickness in his soul. He tasted blood and smelled a rank, foetid stench, like an overflowing cesspit in summer. It was the smell of corruption, the smell of things about to die.

'Shallya preserve us, what *is* that?' gasped Redwane. 'Smells worse than a dead troll!'

'I thought it was you, lad,' said Wolfgart. 'You White Wolves look as ragged as Cherusen Wildmen. Proper northmen you are now.'

'I'll take that as a compliment,' said Redwane, cupping a hand over his mouth and nose.

Sigmar knew that smell, for it had saturated the air in the Grey Vaults. It was the reek of the daemonic. Earlier that morning he had watched a mass of Norsii and beasts gathered around a wound carved in the earth, like a wide pool of blood, and felt the dread power of the Dark Gods being drawn forth.

A column of armoured Norsii warriors was already climbing the viaduct to the half-built towers at its top, but Sigmar was confident that Pendrag and Myrsa could handle whatever the tribesmen could throw at them. The runefang had completed his sword-brother, as though it were a piece of his soul that he had not even known was missing.

'I've got a bad feeling about today,' said Redwane, idly dabbing at a reopened cut on his neck. The White Wolf looked up at the bruised sky and shook his head. 'You remember when we talked about finding a wife? When we marched to Brass Keep?'

'I remember,' said Sigmar, understanding the source of his friend's woe. 'What of it?'

'I wish I'd done something about it,' said Redwane, and Sigmar was surprised to see that the warrior was crying. 'I didn't though. I thought there would be time for that kind of thing later, but there is no later for the likes of us, is there? There's only the here and now.'

'We make of life what we can, Redwane,' said Wolfgart. 'We make the best choices we can, and we have to live with them, good or bad. I'll wager that when this is over, you'll find yourself a good lass.'

'You still think we can win?' Redwane asked Sigmar.

'I know we can,' promised Sigmar.

Redwane sighed, looking over the slate-grey rooftops of the buildings around them to the mighty mountain peaks in the distance that reared to the heavens.

'It doesn't really matter in the end, does it?' asked Redwane. 'I mean, look at the land we call the Empire, it's so… eternal, and we're so insignificant in the grand scheme of things. Will it matter if we all die here? Does the land care which king sits upon a throne and declares himself its master?'

'Perhaps not, but it does not change our duty to fight,' said Sigmar. 'We are fighting for the land and everyone who lives under our protection. If we fail, thousands more will die, for the warriors of the Dark Gods will not stop until the whole world burns. Our enemies bring disorder and chaos with them, darkness from the blackest realm of nightmare that will consume all that is good in this world. But you are right, in the end, it does not even matter if we live or die.'

'How can it not matter?' asked Redwane.

'All that matters is that we are here, right now,' said Wolfgart, 'standing against that evil.'

'That doesn't make sense,' replied Redwane, 'and since when did you become a philosopher?'

Wolfgart shrugged. 'I'm not, but I know in my heart that we have to try and stop Cormac or everything we love will be destroyed: Maedbh and Ulrike. If I don't fight, they die. I need no more reason than that to kill these bastards.'

Redwane nodded slowly.

'Then that's good enough for me,' he said.

Though his wounds ached with the promise of pain, Sigmar smiled at Wolfgart's words. Better than any notions of honour or glory, the love of family and the need to protect them was all any warrior needed in order to fight.

Sigmar took a breath of mountain air and tasted bitter, burning metal in the back of his throat. He looked over at the walls of the temple, seeing red smoke hissing from the runic patterns hammered into the stone. Alaric had told him these runes were proof against the sorceries of the northern shamans, but even as Sigmar watched, the stone was disintegrating as though it were no more solid than sand. Only the most dread powers could unmake the runes of the dwarfs, and Sigmar felt an icy hand grip his heart as a shadow passed over the sun and the world was plunged into gloom.

A deafening roar shook the Fauschlag Rock, the scream of a creature older than time and more terrible than any nightmare. Men fell to their knees, screaming and vomiting blood as their every sense was violated by something utterly inimical to mortality.

Sigmar tasted blood and burned meat, wet fur and hot iron.

He looked up and saw the worst thing in the world.

And it was coming for him.

TWENTY-ONE
The Last Day

PENDRAG'S SWORD WAS a shimmering blur of silver as it clove through a screaming Norseman's chest. No armour was proof against its edge, and no warrior brought low by its power would live. In the heart of the battle, the Count of Middenheim fought alongside his people; their leader, their hero and their friend.

Count Otwin hacked men down by the dozen with his mighty axe, his muscled form bleeding from a score of wounds, and his face a mask of crimson where his crown of blood pierced his temple. The King's Blades screamed as they slew, paint running from their bodies in streams of sweat and blood.

Resplendent in their orange tunics, the Jutones battled with lance and sword, fighting with a precision lacking in their Thuringian brothers. Marius, though still in great pain from Bastiaan's traitorous attack, stood with his fellow counts, cutting through flesh and armour with elegant sweeps of his eastern cavalry sabre.

Conn Carsten and his clan-kin fought at the viaduct also, all three leaders of men having been drawn to fight together on this last day. Pendrag had welcomed them, understanding on some unknown level that this was where they needed to be. Alaric and the dwarfs were assembled on the wide esplanade, the Grimloks, the Skrundoks, the Gnollengroms and the Grimargul veterans. Front and centre were the Hammerers from King Kurgan's personal guard, and Alaric stood among them, a great runic axe held at his shoulder.

The Norsii attacked with greater ferocity than ever, their war cries more brutal, more hideously animalistic than the howls of the wildest rabid beast. The viaduct was all that mattered now, and the enemy had abandoned their attempts to carry the walls elsewhere. From the edges of the forest, the beasts howled as the men of the north alone fought to break into Middenheim.

A warrior in armour of burnished blue plate leapt for Pendrag's unprotected back, but Myrsa's hammer intercepted him in mid-air. The Warrior Eternal smashed the tribesman aside, sending him tumbling to his death. The two masters of Middenheim fought side by side like brothers, slaying their foes and protecting one another with deadly grace.

White Wolves howled as they killed, the fury of Ulric upon them as they fought to protect the city that shared their name. With their wild hair and brilliant red armour dazzling in the sunlight, they were as fearsome a sight as the Norsii, feral and magnificent.

Pendrag blocked the sweeping blow of an enormous axe and stepped in to hammer his fist at the snarling tribesman. Blood and teeth burst from the warrior's face, though this only seemed to amuse him. The axe came at Pendrag again, and he ducked, bringing his sword up in a whistling arc that sliced his foe from groin to shoulder. The runefang was a weapon beyond compare, its edge sharper than the dawn and lighter than a dream. With its awesome power at his command, Pendrag's wounds and aches were forgotten as he fought with the strength and speed of a man half his age.

How long they had fought for, Pendrag did not know, but they were holding their foes at bay. The Norsii were pushing hard, throwing their all into the fight, but the resolve of the defenders was like iron. Jutones, Udose, Thuringians, Middenlanders, Unberogen and dwarfs fought as one, an unbreakable line of courage that no wild charges of the Norsii could break.

Dreams of triumph filled Pendrag's head, but, like all dreams, they could not last.

As the attackers fell back once more, a monstrous darkness filled the sky, and Pendrag dropped to his knees as blinding pain flared throughout his body. The skin at his neck blackened where the dead king's blade had struck, and blood poured over his silver hand, as though the fingers had been cut from him but moments ago. The runefang tumbled from his grip and he screamed as his body curled into itself in terror. Through tear-blurred vision, Pendrag saw men who only moments before had been fighting like heroes of legend, fleeing from a monstrous shadow that filled the sky with its terrible bulk.

It moved too fast to see, its blood-matted hide reeking of death and ancient rage: enormous wings of darkness, brass and iron, the smell of charred flesh and wet fur.

Blood burst from Pendrag's mouth and nose. He vomited over the cobbles.

The shadow flew over the viaduct, the doom of his race made real, and Pendrag wept as its deathly power washed over him. He scrabbled for his fallen weapon, and no sooner had his fingers closed on the runefang's hilt than the suffocating fear fled his mind. His blade crackled with power, and he felt its ancestral hatred of the enveloping shadow.

The Norsii screamed a name, a vile, filthy sound that clawed at the air like fingernails on slate, but it had no power over Pendrag, for he bore a weapon of ancient times. No matter that it had been newly forged, this was a weapon that had *always* existed. Sometimes as a sword, sometimes a flint spear or bronze-bladed axe, but through all the ages of the world, this weapon and its as yet unmade brothers had always been here to fight the corrupting power of the Dark Gods.

Pendrag stood tall amid the helpless defenders of the viaduct, and the runefang blazed with the purest light, a brightness to conquer the blackest night and banish the deepest of shadows. He thrust the sword to the sky and smote the darkness with its blade. Sunlight broke through as the terrible shadow flew towards the centre of the city, and the warriors of the Empire clambered to their feet as the power of the runefang gave them strength.

The Norsii charged, and Pendrag's eyes were drawn to the warrior leading them.

He wore form-fitting silver armour that shone wondrously in the light, and flowing black hair spilled gloriously around his shoulders. The warrior bore twin swords of dazzling brightness and, as he skilfully rolled each blade in his grip, Pendrag was struck by the familiarity of the move. Sigmar had claimed Ravenna's murderer was among the Norsii, but until now, Pendrag had thought that impossible. Clean shaven and pristine, he was monstrously out of place amongst the Norsii, and Pendrag's heart skipped a beat as he saw the image of his old friend Trinovantes in the warrior's face.

'Gerreon,' he whispered.

Though fifty yards or more separated them, Gerreon seemed to hear him, and a smile of breathtaking beauty slid across his face as he angled his course to meet Pendrag.

Of the hundred men who stood with Sigmar, fully a third dropped dead from terror at the sight of the abomination that landed in their midst. Others fled in terror, leaving only a staunch few able to overcome their fear. Like the darkest desires of men and beasts knitted together in a nightmare, it was a creature of darkness dragged into the light by dreams of blood.

It stood four times the height of a man on back-jointed legs, its body vast and muscled. Sheathed in bronze and iron, its flesh was the brutal colour of charred corpses, and the stink of the grave was pressed into its wiry fur. The blunt wedge of its horned head was filled with serrated fangs, and its eyes were like holes pierced in the flank of a volcano.

Enormous wings of smoking darkness spread out behind it, and flagstones shattered as its enormous weight landed. It clutched a bronze axe in one meaty fist and a writhing whip like a cat-o'-nine-tails in the other. The ends of the barbed whip's lashes ended in wailing skulls that dripped blood from their empty eye sockets.

'Daemon,' said Sigmar, and the colossal beast roared, baring its fangs and shaking the foundations of the temple. Blocks of stone crashed to the ground, and every pane of glass in the city shattered.

'Ulric save us,' said Redwane, his face bleached of colour. As if in response to his words, the Flame of Ulric flared angrily at this violation of sacred space.

'I warned you that you would regret your wish to fight a daemon,' said Sigmar.

'I thought we'd done that in the swamps around Marburg?'

'That was no daemon,' said Sigmar. '*This* is a daemon.'

'How do we fight such a thing?' asked Wolfgart, his sword held out before him in trembling hands.

Sigmar lifted Ghal-maraz to his shoulder.

'With courage and heart, my friends,' he said. 'It is all we have.'

The vast daemon took a thunderous step towards them, its cloven hoof shattering each stone and blackening it with corruption. Sigmar's blood raged around his body, the daemon's presence filling him with anger and the lust to destroy. This was the power of the Dark Gods, and the acrid, bilious taste of it filled his mouth.

Perhaps thirty men still stood with Sigmar, the bravest of the brave, but against so mighty and powerful a foe, there would be few survivors. The daemon's wings flared black, and it was amongst them. Half a dozen men died instantly, hacked down with a single blow of the daemon's axe. Another three were sliced in two by a crack of its whip. Blood sprayed the air and hissed as the daemon drank it in through its furnace hot skin.

It moved like a nightmarish phantom, its bulk shifting and indistinct, as though the mind refused to fasten on its diabolical form for fear of being driven to madness. Sigmar threw himself to the side as the daemon's whip cracked with a thunderous peal, and the stone flags of the temple were torn up like a ploughed field.

Sigmar rolled to his feet as the daemon flickered, and its blazing, black bulk towered over him. The axe slashed down, and he leapt back, the monstrous blade smashing into the ground with the force of a comet. The impact hurled Sigmar back, and more stones came crashing down from the unfinished temple walls. A huge lintel slammed into the flagstones next to him, and he spat rock dust.

Rippling light spilled between his fingers, and Sigmar felt the aeons-long enmity of these two powers, one designed to heal and build, the other to corrupt and destroy. He hauled himself upright over the broken stones of the temple.

The daemon was coming for him.

Broken glass and stone crunched underfoot as the daemon threw back its head and roared, the sound echoing through the city and scraping down every warrior's spine with its primal power. Its hellish bulk seemed to fill the temple, an unholy darkness in a place of sacred power.

A score of men fought to surround the daemon, spears thrusting desperately at its armoured form. Its whip slashed out and they died, their bodies bursting apart in wet rains of blood that were drunk by the creature's axe. Blades shattered on its hide, and a dozen more were slain before the daemon's blade.

Sigmar climbed onto a huge block of stone as Wolfgart rushed at the monster's unprotected flank. His sword-brother's enormous blade slashed the iron-hard flesh of its back-jointed legs, drawing a froth of steaming black ichor from the wound. Wolfgart's sword dissolved in an instant, and where the daemon's blood splashed the flagstones, they were burned to a reeking ooze. A casual flick of the daemon's wrist sent Wolfgart flying. His sword-brother slammed into the stone walls of the temple and did not get up.

'Here I am, daemon!' Sigmar yelled. 'Fight me!'

The daemon heard him and swung its shaggy, horned head towards him. Death lived in its eyes, death and an eternity of suffering and pain. Sigmar's spirit quailed before such awesome destructiveness, but he heard a freezing wind howl in his mind, and winter ice filled his veins in answer to the fires of this daemonic foe.

Redwane leapt in to swing his hammer at the daemon's knee. The White Wolf howled as the iron head of his weapon exploded against the daemon's armour, and Redwane fell back as razored fragments tore at his exposed face. The daemon's fist lashed out, catching Redwane on the shoulder and sending him spinning through the air with a horrific crack of shattering bone.

With a howl of all the wolves of Ulric, Sigmar sprinted over the tumbled stones of the temple and hurled himself through the air towards the daemon. Ghal-maraz spun in his grip as he brought it around in a devastating overhead sweep. The ancient dwarf-forged star metal arced towards the centre of the daemon's face, and Sigmar knew that this would be the blow to end this vile creature's existence forever.

The daemon's fang-filled mouth opened wide, and its whip flicked up, its many lashes coiling around Sigmar like the grasping arms of the monstrous kraken that seafarers claimed haunted the ocean's depths.

They tightened on him like barbed coils of wire and his armour buckled beneath its enormous strength. Sigmar screamed in pain as bony thorns pierced his flesh in a dozen places.

The world spun around him: ground, sky, walls, cold-burning fire.

Sigmar slammed against the floor of the temple with bone-crushing force. Ghal-maraz spun away from him, coming to rest before the Flame of Ulric. The lashes of the whip slithered away like guilty snakes, leaving bloody trails behind them. He heard screams of pain and fear, and rolled onto his back, every nerve in his body shrieking with agony. His arm was useless, and he scrambled backwards on his haunches towards his warhammer.

Black shadows gathered over the temple of Ulric, and the daemon's black outline loomed over him.

* * *

The Norsii smashed into the defenders at the viaduct, and within seconds it was clear that the wall could not hold. Enraged by the same darkness that had so terrified the men of the Empire, the howling tribesmen killed with savage ferocity and madness, each fighting as though to outdo their fellow warriors.

Swords and axes clashed in desperate battle and scores of men died in the opening moments. The defenders fought for their lives, while the Norsii fought for the chance that their ancient gods might notice their bravery.

Pendrag sliced the runefang through the neck of an armoured warrior, his heavy plates of iron no protection against Alaric's masterful blade. Another blow cut through the helmet of a warrior with golden skin and an oversized axe. His sword moved like quicksilver, cutting and stabbing without pause. He saw Gerreon ahead of him, and the swordsman caught his eye and smiled with feral anticipation of their duel.

The Empire line was bowing back from the walls, and for all that Pendrag's men were fighting with renewed courage and determination, he saw that it wasn't going to be enough. The hammers of Myrsa and the White Wolves smashed down time and again, and the Norsii died in droves before this incredible fighting force. The Warrior Eternal was sublime, and the White Wolves fought alongside him as faithfully as blooded bondsmen.

Udose clansmen fought to the battle tunes of their ancestors, the skirling wail of their pipes defying their enemies to silence them. No force but death would dislodge them. The Jutone line had broken in places, and though Marius and his fiercest lancers were helping stem the tide, it was only a matter of time until the Norsii gained a foothold from which they could not be dislodged.

Pendrag moved through the Norsii as though they were no more than clumsy children, leaving his White Wolves behind as he killed without mercy or a second thought. Next to his graceful sweeps and deadly lunges, the Norsii were lumbering buffoons, slow-witted and without skill.

A burst of shimmering silver flashed beside him, and he brought the runefang around in a sweeping block as a glittering blade slashed towards him. He spun around, his sword held out before him, but his battle-fury faltered in the face of this magnificent foe.

'How about you try that pretty little sword against a real opponent,' said Gerreon.

Pendrag tried to reply, but words failed him at the changes wrought upon the man he had once called brother. Gerreon's skin was white, like the finest porcelain, and his hair was darker than the deepest starless night. The sounds of battle faded until all Pendrag could see was the perfect, enrapturing figure before him.

It was the eyes that held him, so full of innocence, yet brimming with cruelty and utterly without pity. Pendrag was enthralled by Gerreon's eyes, appalled by beauty that should have aroused, but instead evoked nothing in his soul but revulsion.

Gerreon's sword slashed for his throat, but the runefang swept up and parried the blow without conscious command. No sooner had their swords touched than the spell holding Pendrag transfixed was broken. The frantic clash of iron and screaming swelled like a tide around him.

'I'll gladly cut you down, Gerreon,' snarled Pendrag, thrusting the runefang towards the swordsman. His attack was easily batted aside, and Gerreon laughed with musical amusement as he bounded lightly from foot to foot.

'My name is Azazel,' said the swordsman. 'Gerreon is dead.'

'Gerreon, Azazel,' replied Pendrag with an angry snarl, 'whatever damned name you go by, I'll still kill you.'

Pendrag attacked again, and Gerreon swayed aside, parried another stroke and launched a dazzling riposte. Pendrag flinched as Gerreon's sword sliced the braids from his beard.

'I do so love your pathetic confidence,' smiled Gerreon, spinning his swords in a terrifying display of skill. 'It's so much sweeter to kill someone who thinks they have a chance.'

'Try your best,' challenged Pendrag.

'Gladly,' said Gerreon, attacking in a furious ballet of blades. Pendrag blocked desperately as Gerreon's swords nicked the skin of his neck, cheeks and forehead.

'Fight like a man!' he roared, blocking another slicing blow. The runefang blazed in his grip, its power surging as it empowered him to fight this dread foe. Pendrag drew on every reserve of courage in his heart, and the runefang steeled his will to resist the dark allure of the swordsman's beauty.

Never in Pendrag's life had he fought with such skill, power and speed.

Instantly he knew that it was nowhere near enough to defeat Gerreon.

'You cannot win, Pendrag,' hissed Gerreon, rolling his right blade around the runefang and slicing another braid from Pendrag's beard. 'You must see that I am far more skilful.'

'Skilful, aye,' said Pendrag, backing away along the fighting step, 'but I have something you don't.'

'Oh,' chuckled Gerreon. 'And what's that?'

'Friends,' said Pendrag.

He relished the look of confusion on Gerreon's face as Otwin's axe swept down and crashed into the swordsman's back. Gerreon was driven to his knees by the force of the blow, his reflective armour intact, yet cracked from neck to abdomen. A graceful sword-thrust struck Gerreon in the chest as Count Marius leapt into the fight.

The swordsman fell against the parapet, his face more angry than fearful. Any normal warrior would have been cowed, but Gerreon's face was alight at the prospect of so many opponents.

'All for me?' he mocked. 'Truly I am blessed to be able to kill you all.'

The Berserker King roared in red fury, his axe sweeping out to take Gerreon's head as Pendrag lunged. The swordsman moved like a cat, dodging Otwin's axe, and blocking Pendrag's attack with an almost contemptuous flick of one of his swords. Marius's cavalry sabre was not intended for duelling, but he wielded its shimmering blade like a veteran fencer. Blood seeped from the knife wound in his side, but only a tightness around the eyes gave any hint of the pain he felt.

The three of them came at Gerreon together, understanding that to face him singly would be to die. Otwin fought with maniacal fury, Marius with calculated precision, and Pendrag attacked with a skill borne of betrayal. Their axes and swords slashed and stabbed at Gerreon, but his twin blades were a blur as he blocked, parried and counter-attacked.

He taunted them as he fought, tossing his mane of hair, and flashing them his most winning smiles. Pendrag saw past the trap of Gerreon's wondrous countenance, and it seemed his fellow counts were also immune to his charms. Otwin was too deep in his berserker rage to be ensnared by petty adornments such as physical perfection, and Marius cared only for gold. Neither man craved solace in beauty, and Gerreon's temptations were wasted.

Marius cried out as Gerreon's sword slid past his guard and sliced through his armour, the swordsman's blow seeking out his wounded side. The Jutone count dropped to one knee as Gerreon spun low to stab his other sword into Otwin's thigh. Before Gerreon could twist his weapon free, Otwin thundered his fist against Gerreon's shoulder. The swordsman staggered, but did not release his grip.

The Berserker King reached down and took hold of the blade. Gerreon twisted his grip, and blood sprayed from the Berserker King's hand. Otwin roared in anger, his muscles swelled, and he snapped Gerreon's sword-blade with his bare hand. Otwin fell back with a foot of iron embedded in his leg. Gerreon was left with the broken stump of a sword, and his face twisted in petulant anger.

Pendrag saw his chance, and thrust the runefang at Gerreon's exposed chest.

The swordsman twisted aside, and Pendrag's blade sliced across the mirrored surface of his breastplate before sliding clear. Gerreon threw himself at Pendrag, pulling him close as though for a brotherly embrace.

'Too slow,' hissed Gerreon, and rammed what was left of his broken sword under Pendrag's arm. It punched through Pendrag's mail shirt and ripped into his heart. Blood burst from Pendrag's mouth, and he heard someone cry his name. The runefang fell from his hand, and the world spun in fire as he dropped to the parapet.

Cold stone slammed into his face, and his chest was bathed in warm wetness. The sounds of battle seemed distant and tinny now, as though coming from some faraway place. It seemed he could hear the sound of distant howling, drawing ever closer.

He was cold, so very cold, and he could hear wolves.

They were calling to him.

TWENTY-TWO

The Doom of Men

MYRSA CRIED OUT as the silver-armoured swordsman plunged his blade into Pendrag's side. Blood sprayed from the wound as the Count of Middenheim fell, the broken sword still clutched in the hands of his killer. The sky seemed to darken, and Myrsa felt the passing of something precious from the world.

The tableau before him seemed static and unmoving: Otwin with his axe poised to cleave into Gerreon's neck, and Marius with his curved blade thrusting for his unprotected back. Pendrag lay at their feet, but it was the look of loathing and regret etched into Gerreon's face that expressed the greatest sadness.

'Pendrag!' shouted Myrsa, and time caught up with the dreadful moment. Gerreon sidestepped Marius's thrust and bent over backwards to avoid Otwin's axe, which came perilously close to taking the head of the Jutone count. The swordsman threw aside the instrument of Pendrag's death as though it were red-hot, and spun away from the clumsy attacks of his enemies.

His remaining sword hung limply at his side, and Myrsa was amazed to see that he was weeping, as though suffering the greatest pain imaginable. The fighting at the wall still raged around him, and though he never once took his eyes from Pendrag's body, he blocked and parried with magnificent precision.

'You are mine, swordsman,' howled Myrsa, and that howl was taken up by hundreds of throats at his back. Such was the force and fury behind the cries that the surging fury of the battle eased as warriors fighting for their lives turned to seek out their source: the warriors of Middenheim.

They were grim-eyed men who lived harsh lives in the north, not given to open displays of emotion or grief, yet they came with tears in their eyes for their fallen count. The blue and white banner of the city came with them, and Myrsa had never been prouder to call this city his home.

Gerreon saw Myrsa and the warriors of Middenheim coming for him, and shook his head. He threw aside his sword and vaulted back over the wall.

'No!' cried Myrsa, leaping to the blood-slick parapet. Thousands of enemy warriors still pressed up the viaduct, but Myrsa easily spotted the silver figure of the swordsman among the baying tribesmen, a lone figure pushing against the tide of attackers.

'The coward flees!' cried Myrsa, furious to be denied his vengeance.

'Warrior Eternal!' shouted a voice beside him, and Myrsa saw Count Marius of the Jutones pointing to the parapet beside him. Myrsa looked down and saw a dead warrior slumped against the wall. Myrsa stared at the man in confusion, wondering what had attracted the Jutone count's eye.

Then he saw it.

The fallen man's weapon: a crossbow.

Myrsa dropped his hammer and lifted the heavy weapon of iron and wood. He was no expert with a crossbow, but had trained with every weapon devised by the race of man. He slotted a bolt into the groove and pulled the wooden stock hard into his shoulder.

He sighted down the length of the crossbow, seeing Gerreon's fleeing form in the small square of iron that served as an aiming sight. Shooting downhill at a moving target was not easy, but just as Myrsa was about to loose, Gerreon stopped moving and turned to face him.

The swordsman stood motionless, his arms outstretched, and his mouth moved as he said something that was lost in the din of battle. Though Myrsa was too far away to hear his words, he knew exactly what Gerreon had said: *I'm sorry*.

'You will be, you bastard,' hissed Myrsa. 'You will be.'

He squeezed the release, and watched as the iron bolt flew from the crossbow, arcing over the heads of the Norsii towards Gerreon's heart. Myrsa lowered the weapon, knowing the shot was true, and his eyes locked with Gerreon's in the split second before the bolt slammed home.

But it was not to be.

A chance gust of wind or the will of the gods, who could know? Either way, the bolt wavered in flight as its fletching unravelled. Instead of skewering Gerreon's heart, the lethal bolt slammed into his shoulder. The swordsman reeled under the impact, but with a final dejected look of disappointment, he turned and fled down the viaduct, beyond the reach of even the greatest marksman.

Myrsa cursed and tossed aside the crossbow. He ran to where Marius and Otwin had carried Pendrag's blood-soaked body. Surrounded by a ring of White Wolves, Pendrag lay cradled in the Berserker King's arms. Incredibly, he still lived, though blood still pumped over Otwin's hand despite the fistful of rags held tight to the wound. The fast-spreading pool beneath Pendrag told Myrsa everything he needed to know.

He knelt beside his ruler and friend as Pendrag's eyes flickered open.

'Did… you… kill him?' gasped Pendrag, his lips flecked with bloody froth.

Myrsa struggled to speak, his grief threatening to overcome him. For the briefest instant, Myrsa considered lying, telling Pendrag that he had been avenged, but the moment passed. He was a warrior of honour, and Pendrag deserved the truth.

'No, my lord,' he said. 'I wounded him, but he escaped.'

'Good,' whispered Pendrag.

Myrsa struggled to understand Pendrag's meaning, but simply nodded as Marius knelt at his side. He carried the runefang and held the handle out to Pendrag.

'Your sword, my brother,' said Marius, and Myrsa was astonished to see tears in the man's eyes. 'Take it one last time and bear it with you into the Halls of Ulric.'

Pendrag's hand closed around the leather-wound grip of the incredible sword, his fingers smearing blood over the golden pommel. A mask of peace soothed the lines of pain on his face, and he smiled, as though hearing words of comfort. Just holding the blade strengthened Pendrag, and he looked up at Myrsa with eyes that were clear and determined.

'Warrior Eternal,' said Pendrag, and Myrsa leaned in close.

'My lord? You have a valediction?'

'I do,' said Pendrag, lifting the runefang towards him. 'The sword is yours now.'

'No,' said Myrsa, shaking his head in denial. 'I am not worthy to bear it.'

'Funny...' said Pendrag. 'I said the same thing. But you must listen to me. This is the runefang of Middenheim, and before these witnesses, I name you Count of Middenheim. The sword needs you, and you *must* take it!'

Myrsa swallowed, and looked over at Marius and Otwin, seeking some sign as to what he should do.

Marius nodded and Otwin said, 'Go on, lad. Take it.'

'Heed what it tells you, my friend,' said Pendrag softly, his voice fading.

'I will, my lord,' said Myrsa, taking hold of the runefang, his hand wrapped around Pendrag's as they held the blade together. Ancient craft and skill were woven into the blade's making, and with it came wisdom beyond the ken of mortals.

Pendrag sighed, and his hand slipped from the sword. Tears spilled down Myrsa's face, and the White Wolves howled with grief. Their sorrow lifted to the skies, calling the Wolves of Ulric to carry the spirit of this great warrior to his final rest.

Myrsa lifted the gleaming blade.

'I know what I have to do,' he said.

STANDING AT THE edge of the forest far below, Kar Odacen watched the dark halo around the city on the rock, and knew that its final moments were at hand. He felt every life the daemon lord of Kharnath took, and the pleasure it gained from such wanton killing coursed like the finest elixir through his flesh. It had taken every scrap of his power to summon so mighty a champion of the Blood God, and he had been forced to bind his life-force to it to seal the pact.

Such a bargain was dangerous, but the vitality that flowed from the daemon lord's killing was worth any risk. His mind was clouded with blood, his sight red with the baleful energies of the powerful daemon. The Blood God had no love for sorcery, and Kar Odacen struggled to hold on to his powers in the face of so mighty a slaughter. The present was a blur of blood, and the future a swirling chaos of possibility, so he focused on the past to hold onto his sense of self.

He smiled as he remembered the dawning comprehension on

Cormac's face before he fell into the lake of blood that preceded the manifestation of the daemonic creature. Too late, he had realised how he had been manipulated and groomed to become the perfect vessel for the destroyer of men. To think that he had thought that a mere mortal would be the instrument of the Dark Gods' will! The thought was laughable.

Kar Odacen watched the distant struggle on the viaduct, hearing only the faintest sounds of battle. If the men of the Empire knew the ultimate fate of the world, they would take their blades to their own throats. The End Times were upon this age, yet it was the doom of men that they could not see the hangman's noose around their necks.

A trickle of bloody saliva dribbled from the corner of his mouth, and he blinked as he became aware of movement around him. He forced his eyes open, seeing the forest beasts with their heads lifted, sniffing the air and gathering in huddled, fearful packs. Kar Odacen felt the urge to kill them all threaten to overwhelm him. The rage of Kharnath was upon him, and only with an effort of will was he able to suppress it.

A pack of beasts with the heads of snarling bears and wolves clustered close to him, pawing the ground and clawing the air. Their fear spread to their twisted kin around the Fauschlag Rock with every bray. Kar Odacen rounded on the nearest creature, a towering brute with dark, reptilian scales and the head of an enormous horned bull.

'What is going on?' he demanded, his mouth thick with the iron taste of blood.

The creature didn't answer, and Kar Odacen tried to draw on his powers to destroy it, but the weight of the daemon lord's presence was too great, and he could summon no trace of his sorcery. The huge beast shook its shaggy head and spat a mouthful of bloody cud before turning and vanishing into the trees. Its pack followed it, and all around the towering spire of rock, others were doing likewise.

'Where are you going?' raged Kar Odacen, but the beasts ignored him.

'They are going home,' said a voice choked with self-loathing behind him.

Kar Odacen turned, and his anger fled as he saw Azazel standing before him. An iron bolt jutted from his pauldron, and his silver armour was streaked with blood.

'What in the name of all the Dark Gods are you doing here?' shouted Kar Odacen. 'You should be atop the city! You carry the walls of Middenheim and bathe in the Flame of Ulric! I have seen it!'

'Maybe one day,' said Azazel, turning and walking away, 'but it will not be today.'

DARKNESS GATHERED OVER the temple, the daemon's outline a deeper blackness against the gathering shadows. Its axe howled with monstrous hunger and its whip wound itself around its arm, the skulls laughing with lunatic glee. Sigmar scrambled away from the colossal monster, knowing he had only moments to live.

The daemon hissed, its breath that of a charnel house, hot and reeking of unnumbered headless corpses. The brass and crimson of its armour was matted with blood, and its black fur stank of burned meat. It stepped towards him like a hunter stalking wounded prey, enjoying the last, futile moments of defiance before stepping in for the kill.

Its eyes fastened on Sigmar, and in that brief moment, he saw the man within the monster, a soul torn apart and used as a gateway for a creature of madness and death to pass between worlds. Somewhere deep in this daemon, Cormac Bloodaxe relished his body's destruction for the glory of bringing forth a mighty avatar of the Dark Gods.

Sigmar's hand closed on the haft of Ghal-maraz, and the shadows lifted as his warhammer blazed with light. He climbed to his feet, and the daemon roared, as though pleased it had found worthy meat at last. Its axe swung for him, and Sigmar rose to meet it.

Hammer and axe clashed in coruscating arcs of crimson, two weapons forged by masters of their art. A thunderous shockwave exploded outwards, smashing the last columns and archways of the temple to ruins. The Flame of Ulric danced like a candle in a hurricane, but it remained true in the face of powers that sought to extinguish its light.

The cold fire flared brighter than ever, and Sigmar knew that Ulric was with him.

'I am ready for you,' said Sigmar, and the daemon raised its axe in salute.

Man and daemon faced one another in the ruins of the temple, the blood-tinted sky like sunset on the last day of the world.

Sigmar charged the daemon, its mighty form vast and terrible, its dreadful axe a weapon to unmake all life. He ducked beneath a killing sweep and smashed Ghal-maraz against the daemon's flank. Brass armour parted beneath the force of the blow, and more of the daemon's black blood sprayed. Where it had melted iron blades and stone, Ghal-maraz was proof against it, and the daemon roared in anger.

Its axe chopped down and Sigmar threw himself to one side. The blade clove the air, but with a dark shimmer, it reversed itself upon the haft and slammed into Sigmar's chest.

All the malice and rage that had gone into the creation of the daemon's axe was in that blow, and it smashed Sigmar's armour asunder. Runes of protection flared white-hot as they were destroyed by the raw, elemental power of the Blood God, and Sigmar felt the heat burning his skin, forever branding him with the script of the dwarf runesmiths. He felt ribs break and blood burst from his mouth as he was slammed into the fallen ruins of the temple. He fell to the ground beside the Flame of Ulric, still clutching Ghal-maraz tightly as his armour fell from his body in blackened pieces. He rolled onto his side, propping himself up on one elbow as the daemon raised its axe to destroy him.

The sound of wolves echoed through the temple, and the winter wind howled around them. Particles of snow and chips of ice billowed from the fire at the heart of the temple, and Sigmar's chest heaved in pain as the air around him froze. The daemon's form hissed as ice and fire met.

Sigmar knew with utter certainty that this was the breath of Ulric himself.

Just as surely as he knew it was not for him.

He heard a warrior's shout, a cry of loss and rage, courage and devotion, and a silver sword blade burst from the daemon's stomach. Cold fire bathed the blade, its runic surface drawing the breath of Ulric to it in a blinding whirl of ice and snow.

The daemon roared, its essence fighting to prevent its flesh from unravelling in the face of this new power. Sigmar dragged himself to his feet to see the daemon transfixed by a warrior in pristine white armour who drove a dead man's sword up into its unnatural flesh.

White light surrounded the warrior, and Sigmar saw it was Myrsa, the Warrior Eternal of Middenheim. The breath of Ulric was not for Sigmar, but for the hero who had pledged his life to the city's defence. The sword with which Myrsa had impaled the daemon was no longer a weapon forged by mortal hands, but a blinding spike of ice, a shard of the Wolf God's power brought to earth to slay the avatar of its enemies.

Even as Sigmar rejoiced at the sight of Myrsa, his heart despaired. There could be only one reason why Myrsa wielded the runefang.

Moment by moment, the daemon's form wavered and flickered, its will and power to endure a match for the energies that sought to destroy it. This was Sigmar's one chance, and he knew what he had to do. He held Ghal-maraz in the Flame of Ulric, letting the cold fire bathe the head of the mighty warhammer in the power of his god.

Sigmar pulled his hammer from the flames, its entire length rippling with white fire, and ran towards the daemon. He leapt from fallen stone to fallen stone until he was level with the daemon's chest, and hurled himself towards its horned head.

Its eyes blazed, but no daemon-born fury could prevent Sigmar from striking.

Ghal-maraz thundered into the daemon's chest and its darkness exploded into shards of night. Fell powers screamed, and the sky was rent asunder as the daemon lord's body was torn back to the damned realm from whence it had come. Winter storms raged around the fallen temple, and Sigmar was swept up in the tearing, slicing whirlwind of ice and frozen air. His flesh burned with the bitterest cold, but the touch was not unwelcome, its icy bite familiar and divine.

He slammed into the ground, and the breath was driven from his body as the Flame of Ulric surged with life and power. Its fire spread over the ground as though an invisible coating of oil covered every surface. The rocks ran with blue flame and the bodies of the dead leapt with it.

The whole world was afire, and it swept out into the city of Middenheim.

LIKE A STORM-BLOWN tide, the Flame of Ulric spread through the city, a blazing, seething river of blue fire that echoed with the howls of wolves and frozen winds. It did not burn, yet it roared with the hunger of a mortal blaze, and nothing it touched would ever be the same. A towering pillar of winter fire lifted from the heart of the city, spearing the furthest reaches of the sky and spreading its cold light across the land as far as the eye could see.

The warriors of Middenheim howled as the power of their god touched them, and their eyes shone with the light of winter. Their blades were death, and the Norsii saw the defeat of the dread lord of Kharnath in the cold, merciless eyes of their foes.

At each man's side, whether Middenlander or not, a shimmering wolf of blue fire snapped and bit at the Norsii, tearing open throats, and clawing flesh from bones with ghostly paws. No blade could cut them, no armour could defy them, and the phantom wolves tore into the Norsii with all the power of their master.

Terror overcame the Norsii, and they scattered before the tide of fiery wolves and winter warriors. The viaduct became a place of certain death, with the wolves of the north and the men of the city hacking down their fleeing foes without mercy.

Amid the howls of wolves and the screaming winds, there came another sound, a sound the defenders of Middenheim had almost despaired of hearing.

Great horns, blowing wildly from a host of men.

THEY CAME FROM the forests: the swords of ten thousand men from all across the Empire.

From the east came the Asoborns, the Cherusens and the Taleutens. A thousand chariots led by Queen Freya smashed into the Norsii, swiftly followed by the Red Scythes of Count Krugar. Howling packs of Cherusen Wildmen fell upon the scattered beasts and men, their painted bodies glowing in the fire atop the Fauschlag Rock.

From the south came the Endals, the Brigundians and the Menogoths, warriors who had marched day and night to reach their Emperor and fight at his side.

The Raven Helms of the Endals rode down the Norsii fleeing from the viaduct, Count Aldred cutting a path through the northern tribesmen with arcing blows from Ulfshard. Princess Marika rode a midnight horse at his side, loosing arrows from a gracefully curved longbow.

Merogen spearmen drove Norsii horsemen onto the blades of the Menogoths and the Brigundians, and Markus and Siggurd relished the chance to lay waste to their enemies from afar. Ostagoth blademasters cut down Norsii champions with sword blows that were as deadly as they were elegant, while Count Adelhard's kingly blade laid waste to any who dared come near.

Within the hour, the Fauschlag Rock was surrounded by warriors of the Empire, and the Norsii were doomed. By nightfall, the Flame of Ulric had retreated to the ruined temple, the winter winds and ghostly wolves returning once more to the realm of the gods.

Only two souls escaped the Empire's vengeance: a weeping swordsman in silver armour and a screaming madman whose eyes ran with blood.

They fled into the shadows of the forest, where the beasts were waiting for them.

SIGMAR MET HIS counts at the head of the viaduct.

Krugar and Aloysis stood together, brothers once more now that they had seen what might be lost should their friendship falter. Freya was as magnificent as ever, her golden armour streaked with Norsii blood and her fiery hair unbound. Count Aldred and Princess Marika, resplendent in gleaming black armour, smiled warmly as he approached.

The southern counts, Siggurd, Markus and Henroth, bowed grandly as he approached, their faces haggard from the long march, yet elated to have arrived in time. Adelhard of the Ostagoths swept Ostvarath in a dazzling flourish, ending by sheathing his ancient blade and bowing to Sigmar.

Conn Carsten, though not yet appointed a count of the Empire, had earned the right to stand with such heroes, and his normally sour expression was banished in favour of a thin smile at this great victory. Behind them, the pipes of the Endals and Udose entwined in triumphant harmony.

Bloodied and weary, yet no less magnificent, Otwin and Marius held each other upright. They made for unlikely brothers-in-arms, but they had fought and bled at each other's sides and shared great heroism and hardship.

Only one count was missing, and Sigmar's heart ached with his loss.

Alaric, Wolfgart, Redwane and the new Count of Middenheim stood over the body of Pendrag, his fallen sword-brother and oldest friend. All three were hurting, but none would let this moment pass without their presence. Myrsa's face was impassive, but Wolfgart and Redwane wept openly. Even Alaric, a warrior of a race for whom the lives of men were but a brief moment in time, had shed tears for Pendrag.

Sigmar's sword-brother was wrapped in blue and white, for the warriors of Middenheim had fashioned his shroud from the banner of their city, and Sigmar could think of no more appropriate a gesture. Myrsa now bore the runefang, but to honour Pendrag's passing, he laid the mighty blade upon his fallen lord's chest.

Though Sigmar's body was on the verge of collapse, he held himself tall before his counts. To do any less would dishonour the men who had fought and died to win this day.

He tried to think of words that would convey how grateful he was, how blessed with such fine friends he was, but the words would not come. Sigmar stood amid his counts and wept for all they had lost this day, for friends who would never laugh with them again, and for brothers, fathers and sons who would never return to their families.

Count Siggurd stepped forward, his hand on the hilt of his sword.

'I did not know if you would come,' said Sigmar at last.

'You called for us and we came,' said Siggurd. 'We will always come.'

GOD KING

BOOK ONE
Danse Macabre

Thus Sigmar wept not for Middenheim
Nor did he weep for his burned lands.
But he wept on seeing his brother lie dead
While all his people wept for themselves.

From that day upon the Fauschlag Rock
We did not speak boldly;
And we passed not either night or day
That we did not breathe heavy sighs.

Thus it was that Death carried off
Pendrag, whose strength and vigours had been mighty
As it will every warrior
Who shall come after him upon the earth.

ONE
Fire and Retribution

Lord Aetulff was dead, and they carried the body from his village in a long procession through the snow towards the surf-pounded shoreline. Those that had served under him, those despised few who had survived the long flight from the vengeful blades of their enemies, followed the solemn bier with their broken swords carried before them. Their lives were forfeit, but there were few enough men remaining along the coastline to put them to death for their cowardice.

The chieftain's favoured huscarls carried the body on a palanquin of broken shields, the body wrapped in a tattered flag brought from the south. The body was light; a wasting sickness had eaten the flesh from his bones upon his return from the disastrous war. Zhek Askah had said it was punishment from the gods, and none dared gainsay him.

Broken in spirit, Aetulff's wounded body had lingered six seasons after the defeat before finally succumbing. He had been strong, and he took a long, painful time to die.

His sons were all dead, slain in battle as the gods decreed, and none now remained to preserve his line. He had died in the knowledge that no living creature would carry his name into the future. He would die unremembered and his bloody deeds would be forgotten in a generation.

The womenfolk did not follow the body, and his shame was complete.

The shield bearers followed a path to the water, where a fire burned in a pit hacked into the frozen ground. The waters of the ocean were dark, cold and unforgiving, and a storm-battered ship rose and fell with the surge and retreat of the tide. Sturdily built from overlapping timbers and tar, a rearing wolfshead was carved at its prow. It was a proud vessel and had carried them through the worst storms the gods could hurl from the skies. It deserved better, but if the last year and a half had taught the people of the settlement anything, it was that this world cared nothing for what was deserved.

The warriors following the body climbed aboard and turned to help lift the dead chieftain onto his ship. They were strong men and it took no effort to manoeuvre him onto a tiered pile of precious timbers and kindling. One by one, the warriors slashed their forearms with the broken blades of their swords. They spilled their blood over their dead war chief and dropped their useless weapons to the deck. Blood shed and swords surrendered, they climbed over the gunwale, which looked bare without lines of ranked-up kite shields and banks of fighting men hauling at the oars.

One warrior with a winged helm of raven's feathers waited until the others had splashed down into the sea before upending a flask of oil over the body. He doused the ship's timbers with what remained and tossed the flask to the deck. The raven-helmed warrior tugged a tied rope at the mainmast, and the black sail unfurled with a boom of hide.

He turned and dropped over the side of the ship, wading ashore to take his place with the rest of his forsaken band. Their war chief had died, yet they had lived. Their shame would be never-ending. Women would shun them, children would spit on them and they would be right to do so. The gods would curse them for all eternity until they made good on their debt.

The freezing wind caught the sail, and the ship eased away from the shore, wallowing without a steersman to guide it or rowers to power it. The tide and wind quickly dragged the ship away from the land, twisting it around like a leaf in a millpond. The treacherous currents and riptides around this region of the coast had dashed many an unwary vessel against the cliffs, yet they bore Lord Aetulff's ship out to sea with gentle swells. Gulls wheeled above its mast, adding their throaty caws to the chief's lament.

The raven-helmed warrior lifted a bow from the shingle and nocked an arrow to the string. He held the cloth-wrapped tip in the fire until it caught light and hauled back on the string. The wind dropped and he loosed the shaft, the fiery missile describing a graceful arc through the greying sky until it hammered home in the ship's mast.

Slowly, then with greater ferocity as the oil caught light, the ship burned. Flames roared to life, hungrily devouring the rotten meat of the dead man and setting to work on the oily timbers. Within moments, the ship was ablaze from bow to stern, black smoke trailing a mournful line towards the sky.

The warriors watched it until it split apart with a sound like a heart breaking. It slid over onto its side and with a final slurp of water vanished beneath the surface.

Lord Aetulff was dead and no one mourned him.

FROM A CAVE mouth high on the cliffs above the village, a man in tattered furs and a cloak of feathers watched the last voyage of the doomed Wolfship. His face was bearded and long hair hung in matted ropes from his head. Once it had been jet black, but it was now so wadded with mud and dirt that its true colour had long since been obscured. The filth of living in a cave encrusted his skin and his arms were rank with sores and rashes that burned and tingled pleasurably in equal measure.

The villagers called him Wyrtgeorn, though he could make little sense of the word. What he had bothered to learn of their language allowed him only the most basic understanding. A fetish-draped shaman had spat it at him a year and a half ago when he and the wizened immortal stepped from the Wolfship that now burned to ashes. Though he did not know its meaning, it was a name to hide behind, a shield to hold before the deeds of his true name.

The immortal had left the village, imploring him to travel onwards into the northern wastes, but he had refused, climbing the cliff and making this cave his home. He knew he should have gone; his presence here would draw the hunters, but something had kept him from leaving, as though invisible shackles held him here.

He shook off such gloomy thoughts, and watched the Wolfship slide beneath the waves. A rolling fogbank crept in from the south, obscuring the horizon and making the air taste of wet cloth. He watched the warriors as they trudged through the snow to the village, all too familiar with the shame they bore for their survival.

He threw a guilty look over his shoulder, wincing as the wound that would never heal flared with old pain. The immortal had given him a cloth-wrapped bundle as they fled across the ocean, and even without unwrapping it, he knew what lay within. How such a thing was possible was a mystery. He had thrown it away in the wake of defeat, yet there it was.

He kept it wedged in a cleft at the back of the cave. He knew he should hurl it into the sea, but also knew he would not.

Something moved in the fog, and he lifted a hand to shield his eyes from the winter sun.

A phantom of the mist, or something darker?

His right hand twitched with the memory of slaughter, and his gaze slid towards the settlement as old instincts and new senses prickled with danger.

From out of the fog, a dozen ships cut through the water towards village.

POWERFUL SWEEPS OF oars drove the ships onward, and their decks were crammed with armed men in gleaming iron breastplates and full-face helms of bronze. They clutched axes and swords and spears, and he sensed their anger, even from high on the cliff. He looked back into his cave, but closed his eyes and took a deep breath. He had feared this moment ever since he stepped onto the shore, but now that it was here, he found himself utterly calm.

The same calm he felt before a duel. The same calm he felt before he killed.

He watched the ships surge through the crashing breakers and slide up the shingle beach. The village's few warriors ran to meet them with axes held high over their shoulders, old men and youngsters mainly. Fifty men of sword-bearing age were all that were left to defend the village.

Nowhere near enough.

Whooping war shouts echoed from the stony beach as women and children ran towards the cliffs. There was no escape there, just a postponement of the inevitable. These warriors would leave no survivors. They never did.

Even isolated in his cave, he had heard the recent scare stories of the seaborne raiders, the killers from across the ocean who wiped out entire tribes in their vengeful slaughters. Their crimson and white sails were the terror of the coastline, a sight to drive fear into the hearts of those that had once been masters of the ocean.

A score of armed men dropped from the lead ship, led by a warrior in gleaming silver armour and a gold-crowned helm. He bore a mighty warhammer and smashed one of the village warriors from his feet with a single blow. More ships beached, and in moments a hundred warriors were ashore. Arrows leapt from the decks of the ships, serrated tips slicing into proud flesh, and flame-wrapped barbs landing amid the tinder-dry homes of the villagers.

A dozen warriors were dropping into the surf with every passing second. Though the defenders of the settlement were hopelessly outnumbered, they fought with the fury of warriors given one last chance to reclaim their honour in death.

Lightly armoured men with bows fanned out onto the beach, taking aim at the fleeing villagers and cutting them down with lethally accurate shafts. Iron clashed with iron on the shore as the last of the defenders were overwhelmed. He watched the raven-helmed warrior hurl himself at the leader of these reavers from the sea with his axe slashing down over his head. The warhammer swept up, and the blade slammed down on its haft. Such a blow should have shattered any normal weapon and split the enemy's skull, but he knew that this was no ordinary warhammer. Nor was the warrior who bore it any ordinary foe.

The warhammer spun in the warrior's hand, faster than any weapon of such weight and power should move. Its head slammed into raven-helm's face, caving his skull to shards and knocking him to the red snow.

'No pyre for you,' he said as the warriors from the sea advanced into the settlement.

Its buildings were burning and its people dead, yet the raiders kicked them down, leaving nothing standing to indicate that anyone had once called this bay home. This was no raid for gold or slaves or plunder. This was an attack of destruction.

The raiders hauled the bodies of the defenders from the sea and began stripping their helmets. One by one, the warrior with the warhammer bent to look at their faces, but each time he would shake his head in disappointment.

Wyrtgeorn chuckled as the warrior shook his head and hissed, 'You won't find what you're looking for among the dead.'

He heard a noise from further down the cliff and pulled back into the shadow of the cave mouth. A slender, hard-faced woman carried a pair of children up the icy cliff paths towards the cave. Her steps were faltering, and he saw a pair of arrows jutting from her back. She saw him and tried to speak, but no words came, only a froth of bubbling blood.

She reached the ledge before his cave and collapsed onto her knees. Her eyes were frantic. Only seconds of life remained to her and she knew it.

'Wyrtgeorn,' she said in a language not her own. 'Save... my... children.'

He backed away from her, shaking his head.

'You must!' she said, thrusting the youngsters toward him. He saw they were twins, one a boy, the other a girl. Both howled with uncontrollable sobs. The woman's eyes closed and she swayed as death reached up to claim her. The woman's daughter threw her arms around her mother's neck and the pair of them fell from the cliff, falling a hundred yards into the sea.

The warriors on the shoreline saw them fall, their eyes drawn up to the cave on the cliff. He knew he was invisible in the shadows, but the boy stood on the ledge as plain as day. Four warriors ran from the beach towards the cliff paths, and the man cursed. He felt a tugging at his fur jerkin and looked down into the coldest blue eyes he had ever seen. The boy stood with his fists bunched at his sides, and there was pleading desperation in the way he met the man's gaze.

'You are Wyrtgeorn,' said the boy in the man's own tongue. 'Why did you not come down and fight them?'

'Because I have no wish to commit suicide,' he replied.

'They have killed my tribe,' wept the boy. 'Why won't you kill them?'

'I will kill anyone who tries to kill me,' said the man.

'Good,' said the boy. 'Zhek Askah said you were a great warrior.'

'I don't know who that is.'

'The shaman who named you Wyrtgeorn. Lord Aetulff wanted you and your friend slain, but Zhek Askah said you were a killer of men and that we should let you live in the cave.'

'Did he now?' replied the man. 'I wonder why. Perhaps it was to save your life.'

Four warriors were climbing towards them, carefully picking their way along the treacherous path. They carried long knives, eschewing axes on so narrow a ledge. The man watched them come: confident, arrogant and with a swagger that didn't match their abilities. He'd watched them fight on the shore. They were competent warriors, but no more than that.

'There is a passage at the back of the cave,' said the man. 'It leads through the rock and comes out a few miles north of the village. Wait for me there. I will join you shortly.'

'I don't want to run,' said the boy, and the man saw fierce determination behind his fear.

'No,' he agreed. 'You don't, but sometimes that's all you can do.'

'What do you mean?'

'Nothing,' said the man. 'It doesn't matter. But I know now why I did not leave this cave.'

Before the boy could ask any more, the light at the mouth of the cave was blocked as two of the warriors reached his squalid dwelling place.

'Get behind me,' said the man, pushing the boy away.

The first warrior stepped cautiously into the cave, his eyes adjusting to the gloom. A second followed close behind. The blades of their knives glittered in the dim light.

'What do we have here?' he said, his voice heavily accented. 'A hermit and a shit-scared boy. Should be nice and easy, lads.'

'You should go and never come back,' said the man, his voice calm and even.

'You know that's not going to happen,' said the warrior.

'I know,' agreed the man, leaping forwards with dazzling speed. Before the warrior was even aware he was under attack, the man slammed the heel of his hand against his throat. Windpipe crushed, the warrior dropped to his knees, already choking to death.

The man caught the falling dagger and plunged it into the throat of the second warrior. The blade sliced into the gap between his iron torque and the visor of his helmet. He gave a strangled gurgle and toppled to the ground as his lifeblood squirted over his killer and the walls of the cave.

Lethal instincts returned with a vengeance as the hot stink of blood filled the man's nostrils. He leapt, feet first, towards the remaining two warriors. His booted feet slammed into a chest encased in a heavy hauberk of linked iron rings, and the warrior was pitched from the ledge, arms flailing as he fell to his death. The man landed lightly as the last warrior thrust a dagger towards his guts. He swayed aside, locking the warrior's arm beneath his own, and sent two lightning-quick stabs of his purloined dagger through the visor of his victim's helmet.

'No glorious sights in the Halls of Ulric for you,' hissed the man, letting the body fall from the ledge to dash itself on the rocks far below. He stood on the edge of the rocky spit of stone before his cave, his arms and upper body drenched in blood. His heart should be racing, yet it beat with a casual rhythm, as though he rested in a peaceful meadow beneath the clearest sky.

Looking down at the beach, he saw the raiders staring up in horror. Alone of the raiders, the warrior in the gold-crowned helm met his gaze. A dozen men ran for the cliff path with murder in their hearts. The man threw the dagger away and returned to the cave, moving with grim inevitability to the cleft in the rock.

Quickly he pulled out a pitch-blackened bundle of cloth and carefully undid the rotted length of twine that secured it. The boy looked on in wonder as he revealed a glittering sword with an ivory handle and gold-inlaid hilt. The blade was slightly curved, in the manner of the Taleuten horsemen, and it shone like fresh-minted silver.

His hands closed around the hilt like a long lost friend, and he sighed as though welcoming a midnight lover.

'Zhek Askah was right,' said the boy. 'You *are* a great warrior, Wyrtgeorn.'

'I am the *greatest* warrior,' said the man, stripping the sword belt from the first man he had killed. He slid his own blade home. It was a loose fit, the scabbard designed for an Unberogen stabbing sword. 'And do not call me Wyrtgeorn. It is not my name.'

'It isn't?'

'No. My name is Azazel,' he said, letting the name settle in his mouth, as though he hadn't really earned it until now. The boy looked up at him with a mixture of awe and wariness.

Azazel smiled and put his hand on the boy's shoulder, leading him towards the hidden passageway through the rocks. The warriors pursuing them would find the entrance, but they would never find them in the warren of tunnels that lay beyond.

The boy looked back at the slice of light at the cave mouth and hesitated.

'There is no going back,' said Azazel. 'There never is.'

THE BODIES WERE taken from the cave and carried down the narrow cliff path to the waiting ships. None of their number would be left behind on this cold land, they would be taken back to their homelands for the proper funerary rites to be observed. Their souls demanded no less. Wolfgart studied the ground and splashes of blood on the walls with eyes of cold anger, tracing the course of the fight, though it could hardly be called a fight such was the speed with which his comrades had been killed.

He ran a gloved hand through his long red hair, pushing the woven braids from his face as he shook his head. Wolfgart was no youngster, but his body had lost only a little of its youthful power since he had first swung a sword in battle.

His body was a warrior's, yet his face was that of a rogue.

'It was him, wasn't it?' said a voice behind him.

'Aye,' agreed Wolfgart. 'But then you knew that, didn't you?'

'As soon as I saw him on the ledge,' said the warrior with the gold-crowned helm.

Wolfgart gestured to the tracks and scrapes on the cave floor. 'It happened so damn quick, the poor buggers didn't have a chance. He killed Caeadda first and took his weapon. Then he cut Radulf's throat with it. You saw what he did to Paega and Earic.'

The warrior removed his helm and handed it to another behind him. His golden hair was bound in a short scalp lock and his face was handsome with a rugged edge that made him a leader to follow in war and an Emperor to obey in peace.

Sigmar, ruler of the lands of men and Emperor of the twelve tribes.

'Only Gerreon could have killed them so quickly,' said Sigmar, his differently coloured eyes tracing the course of the fight and reaching the same conclusion as Wolfgart. 'I should have known he would be here.'

Wolfgart turned to look up at his friend and Emperor. 'Why? How could you know he would be here?'

'The burning ship,' said Sigmar. 'It is how the Norsii send their dead to the gods. To fight in the shadow of unquiet souls is an omen of ill-fortune.'

'Aye, well we've had enough of them over the last year,' grumbled Wolfgart.

Sigmar nodded and moved to the back of the cave, peering into the darkness of a rough passageway. Wolfgart's eyes were drawn to the mighty warhammer hung on Sigmar's wide leather belt. The hammer's rune-encrusted haft glittered with pale winter's light and its heavy head was unblemished by so much as a single drop of blood. This was Ghal-maraz, ancient weapon of dwarfcraft that had been gifted to Sigmar by King Kurgan of the mountain folk.

Sigmar turned and Wolfgart was struck by the change that had come upon him in this last year. Though he had just entered his fortieth summer, Sigmar carried himself with the poise and strength of a man half his age, yet it was his eyes where he bore the weight of years. The rise of his empire had been hard won, built upon foundations of blood and sacrifice. Friends and loved ones had been lost along the way, and enemies old and new tore at the newly-birthed Empire with avaricious claws.

A full year had passed since the defeat of the Norsii invasion at the foot of the Fauschlag Rock; a year that had seen Sigmar's raiding fleets scouring the icy coastlines of the north. Village after village was burned to the ground and its people put to the sword. Wolfgart had been as vocal in his support as any when Sigmar had announced his plan to take the fight to the lands of the Norsii, believing that such vengeance would safeguard the Empire for decades to come.

Now he wasn't so sure, for these raids were building hatred for the lands of the south that would only fester and grow stronger with every passing year. With every bloody slaughter, Wolfgart understood that Sigmar's reason for these attacks was more personal. In every ruined village, he sought signs of the swordsman Gerreon, the traitor who had killed the woman he loved and plunged a broken sword into the heart of his dearest friend.

Wolfgart rose to his feet, his height a match for Sigmar's. The wan light entering the cave only served to highlight the frustration he saw in his friend's face.

Sigmar slammed a gauntleted fist into the rock of the cave.

'He was here,' snapped Sigmar. 'He was here and we missed him. We were so close.'

'Aye, we got close, but he's gone now,' said Wolfgart.

'Gather the men,' ordered Sigmar. 'That passageway likely opens out somewhere north of the village. If we hurry we can mount a pursuit.'

Sigmar made to pass him, but Wolfgart laid a hand on the centre of the Emperor's breastplate. Though the air in the cave was cold, the ancient metal was warm to the touch, the magic bound to it sending a threatening vibration through Wolfgart's fingertips.

'He's gone,' said Wolfgart. 'You know it too. Who knows where these tunnels lead, and do you really want to go haring off into the darkness after someone like Gerreon? It's time to go home, Sigmar.'

'Really? I seem to remember you were the one who called me a fool for not going after him the last time.'

'Aye, that was me, but I was young and foolish then. I'm older now. Can't say as I'm much wiser, but I know when a quest is hopeless. The Empire needs you, my friend. It's been the hardest year for our people, and they need their Emperor to guide them. The suffering doesn't end just because the fighting stops.'

Sigmar looked set to argue, but the light of anger went out of his eyes. Wolfgart hated to be the one to tell him these truths, but there was no one else. Not any more.

'Pendrag was better at this sort of thing than me,' said Wolfgart, feeling the ache of loss once again. 'But he's not here, and I'm all you've got. Like I told you in the Brackenwalsch, you're stuck with me.'

'Aye, Pendrag was the wisest of us,' agreed Sigmar, looking over his shoulder at the darkened passageway. Wolfgart saw him accept the truth of his words and his shoulders slumped just a little.

'The Empire needs us,' said Wolfgart. 'But more to the point, it needs you.'

'You are wiser than you know,' said Sigmar. 'It's starting to worry me.'

'Don't worry, I won't let it go to my head,' said Wolfgart. 'I live in a house of women who keep telling me how much cleverer than me they are.'

'Then let's get you back to them,' said Sigmar. 'They must be missing that.'

'Aye,' said Wolfgart with a broad smile. 'Let's do that.'

THEY WATCHED FROM a concealed ledge further along the cliffs. A rutted track twisted through the rocks and defiles behind them, leading down towards the bleak landscape of the north. Beyond the cliffs, the achingly wide vista became ever more irregular, a harsh mix of tundra, ice shelf and blasted wilderness. The horizon shimmered, and the boundary between earth and sky blurred as though the difference between them was maddeningly inconstant.

Beyond the horizon, Azazel knew the world grew stranger still, the land no longer bound by the laws of nature and man. It was a shifting realm of nightmares and Chaos, its character broken and bitter, like a land shaped by spiteful gods.

Azazel smiled, knowing that was exactly true. He could feel the breath of northern powers sweeping down from the realm of the gods, laden with ruin and aeons-old malice. He and Kar Odacen had ventured far into that forsaken wilderness, travelling paths known only to madmen or those whose lungs drew breath of the air touched by the great gods of the north.

It had changed them both, though Azazel remembered little of the journey save the monumental tomb of an ancient warrior and a duel with its guardian. The quest into the north had reshaped him in ways beyond his comprehension. His body was faster and stronger than was humanly possible, and his senses were honed to preternatural levels.

Those senses now told him he would venture into that wilderness again.

They were silent as to whether he would ever return.

He and the boy had threaded their way through the tunnels of the cliffs, finally emerging in a sheltered defile high on the flanks of the mountain. They lay in a concealed ravine high above the soaring white cliffs that marked the boundary of this icy realm, watching as black smoke from the burning settlement pressed down on the bay like a mourning shroud. A hundred and thirty-four people had lived there, mostly women and children, with fifty men to bear swords. All were now dead, slain by a man he had once called friend.

Azazel hadn't known any of the villagers and felt nothing at their deaths. Everyone had been slain, but this one boy had survived. That had to mean something, didn't it?

Azazel looked down at the young boy. He was clean limbed and looked strong for his age, with a shock of hair so blond it was almost white. His high cheekbones were characteristic of the Norsii tribes, and Azazel saw he would grow into a strikingly handsome man.

Tears cut through the grime on his young face, his body wracked with sobs now that the adrenaline of fear had worn off. Azazel sensed a confluence of fates in their meeting, the twisted schemes of higher powers at work. Kar Odacen would have said it was the will of the gods that had brought them together, but the shaman had been raving and delusional when Azazel had seen him last.

Perhaps it *was* the will of the gods, but who could tell? Anything could be interpreted as a sign from the gods, and it was no use trying to guess their intent. All he could do was follow his instincts, and his instincts were telling him that this boy was special in ways he couldn't even begin to imagine.

He returned his attention to the south, watching as the crimson sails of the raiders from the Empire pushed out to sea, past where Lord Aetulff's Wolfship had sunk beneath the waves. The ships cleared the headland, but instead of turning along the coastline to seek fresh slaughter they kept going, aiming their tapered prows to the south.

'Are they going home?' asked the boy.

Azazel nodded. 'It looks like it, yes.'

'Good,' sobbed the boy.

Azazel slapped him hard, knocking him back onto his haunches. Instantly, the boy was on his feet, his grief swamped by anger. He reached for a sword that wasn't there, and hurled himself at Azazel.

'I'll kill you!' he screamed.

Azazel sidestepped his rush and pushed the boy to the ground. Before the boy could rise, he planted a booted foot in his chest.

'Anger is not your friend, boy,' said Azazel. 'Learn to control it or I will throw you from these cliffs. Listen to me, and listen well. You are the last of your tribe. No other will take you in except as a slave, and the land will kill you if you do not start using your head. We are going to travel into the north and you will do exactly as I say or it will be the death of us both. I will teach you what you need to survive, but if you ever disobey me, even once, I will kill you. Do you understand me?'

The boy nodded. His grief and anger were gone, replaced by smouldering resentment.

That was good. It was a beginning.

He held his hand out to the boy, hauling him to his feet. An angry red weal burned on his cheek where Azazel had struck him.

'That is the first lesson I will teach you,' said Azazel. 'It won't be the last, but it will be the least painful.'

The boy regarded him coldly, rubbing his cheek and holding himself straighter.

'Look out there,' said Azazel, pointing out to the ocean. 'What do you see?'

'The raiders' ships,' said the boy.

'Yes, and they are going home to a land that hates you.'

'Will they be back?'

'I doubt it. Southerners don't do well with this cold. Even the Udose don't get winters like we do up here.'

The boy looked at him with a sneer curling his lip. 'You say "we" like you are one of us.'

'I am more part of this land than you will ever be,' Azazel promised him. He turned from the diminishing ships, setting a brisk pace along the path over the cliffs. This was the first day of their journey, and who knew how long it would last.

The boy trotted after him, throwing careful glances towards the smoke rising from the ruin of his home.

'Will we ever come back here?' he asked.

'Oh yes,' promised Azazel. 'One day we will. I promise. It will be many years from now, but we will return and we will avenge all that has befallen us.'

'Good,' said the boy, his jaw clenched and his blue eyes cold and dead.

Azazel paused in his march as a thought occurred to him.

'What is your name, boy?' he asked. 'What do you they call you?'

The boy drew his shoulders back, and said, 'I am called Morkar.'

TWO

Young Minds and Old Men

EOFORTH TRIED TO keep his frustration in check, but it was hard in the face of such thick-headedness. Teon wouldn't listen; he had no interest in listening, and stared defiantly at Eoforth, daring him to press on. Eoforth perched on the edge of his desk, a finely made piece of furniture crafted by Holtwine himself, and folded his arms across his chest.

'I ask you again, Teon,' he said, pointing to the tally marks chalked on the slate. 'If you multiply the first number by the second, what do you end up with?'

Teon looked over at Gorseth, his best friend and companion in troublemaking. He winked and said, 'A sore head. It's all nonsense anyway. Who needs numbers when you can swing a sword as well as I can?'

He flexed his arm and Gorseth laughed on cue. The rest of the class nervously followed.

'Enough!' said Eoforth, lifting the birch cane from beside his desk.

'Go ahead,' said Teon, 'I dare you. My father will kill you, old man or not.'

For all his bluster, Teon was popular with the other boys. Powerfully built for his age and blessed with handsome features and an easy manner beyond the classroom. Close to his fifteenth birthday, he would soon ride out on his first war hunt. His father was Orvin, one of Alfgeir's captains of battle, and the boy saw little need to spend his days cooped up in a classroom when there were fights to be gotten into and maidens to pursue.

Eoforth stood and limped towards Teon's desk, the cane swishing the air before him like a threshing scythe.

'Every day you cheek me, Master Teon,' said Eoforth. 'Every day you test my patience, but I counselled King Björn in the time of woes when all around us threatened to destroy the Unberogen. I stood at his side when the Cherusens and Taleutens raided our lands. I brokered the peace that first united those tribes as allies, and I have spoken with the kings and queens of all the great tribes. I have done all this, and you think you can intimidate me? You are a foolish young boy with a head as thick as a greenskin skull and the manners of a forest beast.'

Teon frowned, unused to being spoken to like this. He was off balance and Eoforth smiled as he stopped by the boy's desk.

Eoforth tapped the cane on the arithmetical problem chalked on the slate surface of the desk. 'Now I am asking you again. What is the answer to the problem?'

Teon looked up at him defiantly before spitting on the slate and smearing the chalk illegible with his sleeve. 'A pox on you, old man. I spit on your sums and letters!'

'Wrong answer,' said Eoforth, slashing his birch cane down on Teon's fingers.

The youngster snatched his hand back with a howl of pain. Tears brimmed on the curve of his eyes and Eoforth wasn't proud that he hoped they would spill out. Some shame and humility would do the boy a world of good. Teon's face flushed with anger and he rose to his full height, clutching his hand to his chest.

'My father will hear of this,' he spat, heading for the classroom door.

'Indeed he shall,' said Eoforth. 'For I will tell him, and he will give you a sound beating for disrespecting your elders. Your father knows the value of discipline, and he would thrash you within an inch of your life were he to see you behave like this.'

Eoforth wished that were true. Orvin was as brash and quick to anger as his son, yet he was a fierce warrior and had ridden with Alfgeir's knights for ten years. Though Eoforth did not like the man, he knew of his respect for the proper order of things. He just hoped his son saw that.

Teon paused and Eoforth saw the battle raging within him. To lose face by complying with Eoforth's demand or to risk a beating from his father. The lad returned to his seat, though he continued to glare fiercely at Eoforth.

'Thank you,' said Eoforth, moving between the lines of desks. A dozen boys and girls filled his classroom, a dusty room within a timber-built schoolhouse on the southern bank of the River Reik. A hundred children of Reikdorf learned their numbers and letters here, taught by women he himself had instructed. No men taught at the school, for the youngsters tended to rebel more against male teachers, and seemed more reluctant to pick fights with the matronly women Eoforth had chosen.

'I know what you are thinking,' he said. 'You are thinking that this is a waste of time, that you would much rather be practising on the Field of Swords, learning how to fight. The skills of a warrior are important, and every Unberogen needs to know them. But consider this, without your numbers how will you know how much beef to carry in your wagons when you go to war? How much grain and fodder for the horses, and how much extra for the beasts of burden who pull those wagons? How many swords will you need? How many arrows and what size of war chest should you bring to pay your soldiers?'

Eoforth paced the length of his classroom, his limp forgotten as he warmed to his theme.

'And what of your orders? How will you read the map to deploy your warriors, or read the names of the towns your captain has sent you to? Will you be able to work out how far you must travel or where your evening campsites must be? How will you send word to your fellow warriors without knowledge of your letters?'

He paused by Teon's desk and fished a lump of chalk from the pockets of his grey scholar's robes. He scratched the problem on the slate once more.

'Now let's try again,' he said.

THE LESSON CONTINUED for another twenty frustrating minutes, with the youngsters seemingly incapable of grasping the concept of numbers and solutions that couldn't be calculated on their fingers. Eoforth pinched the bridge of his nose between his fingertips and took a deep breath. Everything was easy when you knew how it was done, and it was hard to remember what it was like not to know these things.

He was in the process of chalking a simpler problem on the board when an excited shout went up from one of the boys seated by the window. Eoforth heard the sound of metal and the whinny of horses from beyond the walls of the schoolhouse.

'Look!' shouted a girl with corn-coloured hair and petite features, pointing at something beyond the window. She bounced on her stool with excitement, clapping her hands together.

'Erline!' snapped Eoforth. 'Your attention please.'

'Sorry,' said Erline. 'But look!'

The rest of the class hurried over to the windows and an excited babble broke out as the boys cheered and the girls blushed and scolded one another at their whispered suggestions. Eoforth stooped to look through the window and knew there would be no more lessons today.

While part of him was angered at that fact, he could not deny his Unberogen heart was stirred by so formidable a display of martial power.

Fifty horsemen rode down the thoroughfare, each armoured in a heavy shirt of mail and gleaming iron breastplate. They bore crimson and white shields bearing the hammer of Sigmar, and each carried a lance supported in a Taleuten-style stirrup cup. Spitted upon each lance tip was a rotting greenskin head. A glorious banner of white silk emblazoned with a black cross and wreathed skull flew over these warriors, and Eoforth smiled as he recognised the bronze-armoured warrior who rode at the head of these horsemen.

Alfgeir, Grand Knight of the Empire.

SUNLIGHT FILTERED THROUGH the forest canopy in thin bars, leaving much of the silent spaces beneath cloaked in shadows. Cuthwin slid through the trees towards the road, a seldom-used track that ran south from Reikdorf all the way to the Grey Mountains. Hardly anyone used these roads any more; the settlements at the foot of the mountains had been destroyed by greenskins ten years ago, and the wilderness had risen up to claim them back.

But someone was using them now, someone who was in trouble.

He moved with an arrow nocked to his bow, a magnificent weapon of yew and ash inlaid with lacquered strips of rowan. Blessed by a priest of Taal, the weapon had never once let him down and had saved his life more times than he could count. The string was loose, but could be drawn in an instant. Sounds of battle were coming from the road, the clash of iron weapons and the screams of wounded souls. Normally Cuthwin would give such sounds a wide berth, for the monstrous denizens of the deep forests were as fond of making war amongst themselves as they were on humanity.

He'd been about to carry onwards to Reikdorf when a loud bang echoed through the forest. Birds fled the treetops and he darted into hiding to string his bow. Another booming echo rolled through the forest. Cuthwin knew that sound, it was a dwarf weapon; one of their thunder bows. He'd seen the mountain folk use them at Black Fire Pass and knew how lethal they could be. His mind made up, he swiftly followed the sounds to their source.

Clad in hard-wearing leather and fur, Cuthwin was the colour of the forest, a ghost moving from shadow to shadow with carefully weighted footfalls. Dead leaves pressed softly into the dark earth without sound and twigs were pushed aside by his buckskin boots. His long hunting knife was sheathed in a leather scabbard, and his pack was hung from a high tree branch a hundred yards behind him. He kept his hair long, though it was pulled back over his ears and held by a leather cord around his temples. He scanned the forest to either side, his peripheral vision alert to anything moving on his flanks.

He heard the clang of swords, the howls of wounded creatures and more of the banging reports of thunder bows. The wind carried their smoke to his nostrils, acrid and reeking of hot metal, like Govannon's forge on a hot day. Beneath that there was a familiar smell of rank, unwashed bodies and rotten food.

Cuthwin knew that smell. He remembered it from the days before Black Fire Pass, when he and Svein had scouted the mountains and discovered the vast host only days from descending into the Empire.

Greenskins.

He heard malicious, squealing voices, squawking war cries and vicious wolf barks, answered by deep, rumbling voices that sounded like they came from the deepest pits of the earth. Cuthwin eased through the forest, keeping his back to the trees and altering his approach every time the wind changed.

Cuthwin was travelling alone, a dangerous pastime in the forests of the Empire, for all manner of peril lurked within their shadow-haunted depths. He knew the risks he took, but was confident enough in his skills to see such dangers as a challenge. To Cuthwin there was nothing as liberating as spending time alone in the deep forests. To survive by his skill with a bow and an innate empathy with the seasonal lore of the wilds was what made him feel alive.

The sounds of battle were growing louder, and Cuthwin pressed himself to the thick bole of a larch, easing his head around it and peering through its branches to the clearing below.

The ground sloped down to the road, a rutted track almost obscured by high grass and gorse. Bodies lay strewn around four wagons arranged in a loose circle on the road. Six dwarfs in long mail shirts fought from the backs of the wagons, armed with a mix of hammers and short-hafted axes. The mules hauling the wagons were dead, and a dozen wiry creatures with pallid green flesh wrapped in filth-encrusted rags surrounded them.

Smaller and weaker than orcs, goblins were cunning little runts that had learned to strike from ambush and kill with the backstab and the low blow. A man or a dwarf was more than a match for a goblin in a straight contest of arms, but that wasn't how these vicious creatures fought. Half bore compact bows of horn and bone, while others swung curved blades with rusted and serrated edges. They rode emaciated wolves that howled with bloodlust, their fur matted and their jaws dripping with saliva.

Two dwarfs emptied fine black powder into the barrels of their thunder bows, while the others slashed at any goblins that came too close. As things stood, the dwarfs would be overrun, but like Sigmar before him, Cuthwin would aid the beleaguered mountain folk.

He hauled back on the string of his bow and sighted on a goblin with a skullcap of bright red leather.

EOFORTH DISMISSED HIS class, knowing there would be no more work done today. He was disappointed, but remembered the excitement he had felt when the royal brothers, Björn and Beronguden, had ridden through his village behind their father, Redmane Dregor. The king had been magnificent that day, clad in his burnished bronze armour and leading a host of Unberogen horsemen from the back of a tall dappled stallion of grey and white. His white bearskin cloak fell like a mantle of snow from his armoured shoulders and his hair was the colour of fire.

Powerful and elemental, Dregor had stopped beside him.

'You are Eoforth?' asked the king.

'I am, my lord,' he said, surprised the king knew his name.

'And this is your village?'

'I am the elder of Ingaevon, yes.'

'I have heard of you, Eoforth of Ingaevon. The other village elders say you have no taste for war. Is that true?'

'It's true I have no love of killing, but I know it is sometimes necessary. That is why I have trained men under arms quartered here. It is also why I had our carpenters construct a high palisade wall and the village's stockade. I may not carry a sword in this world, but I know how to stay alive in it.'

'Aye, they said you were a sly fox,' said the king, surveying the lines of the hilltop fort and the well-built and nigh-impregnable walls of the settlement. 'You may not swing a sword, but you wield that mind of yours like a weapon.'

The king sighed, looking him in the eye, and Eoforth had been surprised at the marrow-deep weariness he saw in his gaze. The king leaned down and lowered his voice so that only Eoforth could hear his words.

'This world is changing, but the hag-mother of the Brackenwalsch tells me I will not live to change with it. That will be for those that come after me. I have need of men like you, men who know that not all battles are fought by warriors, that men of peace will one day be as important as men of war.'

'I would hope that such a day is already here,' Eoforth had replied.

Dregor laughed, a rich, wholesome sound that lifted the hearts of all who heard it.

'For a clever man you are naïve, Eoforth, but I like your optimism.'

'What is it you want of me, my lord?'

'I want you to come to Reikdorf,' said the king in a tone that suggested this was not a request that could be ignored. 'My boys are good lads, but like their father, they are headstrong; all too eager to rush into battle without considering what other options may be open to them. When Berongunden is king, he will have need of a wise man at his side. I want you to be that wise man.'

'I am flattered, my lord,' said Eoforth, genuinely taken aback.

'Then you'll do it?'

'Of course. It would be an honour.'

Thus had begun his long years of service to the kings of the Unberogen. A life that had seen the Unberogen grow in strength and prominence with every passing year. Björn had readily accepted Eoforth's counsel, but Berongunden was a warrior cast too closely in his father's image to listen to anyone's voice but his own. Proud, reckless and full of Unberogen fire, Berongunden had died in the mountains to the north of the Fauschlag Rock, torn to pieces by a winged beast that haunted the highest crags. A year later King Dregor followed his son into the depths of Warrior Hill, his chest pierced by a dozen greenskin arrows, and Björn had taken the crown.

The power and influence of the Unberogen had steadily increased under Björn's leadership, with many sword oaths and trade pacts sworn with neighbouring tribes. Gold and goods from all across the land flowed into Reikdorf, and as the fame of Björn's far-sightedness spread, many tribal kings came to his settlement to meet this wise ruler.

Björn honoured Eoforth for his wisdom and when Sigmar eventually took the crown after his father's death fighting the Norsii, he had continued to advise the Unberogen king. Sigmar was now Emperor and Eoforth knew his own span was coming to an end. Sigmar had proven to be a greater king than any of his ancestors, bringing all the tribes of men together under his rule, forging the Empire of men and holding it firm in the face of all enemies.

A mix of his father's keen mind and his grandfather's hot temper, Sigmar was a ruler fit for the Empire: warlike when roused to fight, diplomatic and persuasive when called to pass judgement. Of course there had been times when Eoforth's steadying hand had been required, such as the incident with Krugar and Aloysis and the dread crown of Morath.

Thankfully, Sigmar had learned valuable lessons from those moments of weakness, a strength born from understanding that no man was infallible, that such perfection was best left to the gods. Since then Eoforth had quietly faded into the background, content to pass his teachings onto the next generation of Unberogen.

He sighed, thinking back to his treatment of Teon. The lad had been rude and arrogant, but Eoforth should have been above such retaliation. In striking the young boy, he had already lost.

'I may not be a warrior, but I am Unberogen,' he said, smiling as his good humour was restored at the recognition that no matter how cultured a man could become, there was no escaping his heritage. He gathered his books and writing tools from the desk, running a gnarled finger over the carvings around its lip.

Master Holtwine was a master craftsman and many of the pieces in the Emperor's longhouse had come from his workshop. His work was truly extraordinary, and was in demand by patrons as diverse as

Count Otwin and Count Adelhard. Marius of the Jutones had several pieces, including a great bed frame carved with his heroic deeds during the battle for the Fauschlag Rock.

Eoforth made his way from the classroom and stepped out into the warm spring sunlight. Winter had broken early and the farmsteads around Reikdorf were being prepared for the sowing. The warm smell of freshly turned earth filled the air, even in the heart of the city, reminding Eoforth that it was not by swords that empires endured, but by keeping food plentiful.

He made his way along the street, meandering between the streams of youngsters as they gawped at the armoured horsemen. He saw Teon speaking to his father. Eoforth wondered if he was recounting his punishment in class. He decided that was unlikely; he knew the boy and his father were not close. Orvin was of typical Unberogen stock, broad-shouldered and powerfully built with a shock of dark hair. His bearing was confident to the point of arrogant, but unlike his son he had earned the right to walk with a swagger.

Eoforth waved as he saw Alfgeir walking his horse along the cobbled street towards him.

'Welcome home, Grand Knight of the Empire,' said Eoforth. 'I take it you were successful? The orcs are defeated?'

Alfgeir lifted his helmet's visor and scowled at Eoforth's use of his formal title. Alfgeir had many titles, Grand Knight of the Empire being but his most recently acquired. Marshal of the Reik was another, but to Eoforth he would always simply be his friend.

'That we were, High Scholar of the Empire,' replied Alfgeir, returning the favour. 'We caught them at Astofen and trapped them against the river.'

'Astofen?' said Eoforth as Alfgeir walked his horse towards a water trough. 'Strange how the greenskins always find their way back to Astofen. I wonder what draws them there?'

'Does it matter? They come and we kill them.'

'And the following year they will need killing again.'

Alfgeir nodded and looked over towards the flag flying over the longhouse to the north of the city. 'Any news of the Emperor?' he asked.

It had been nearly nine months since Sigmar had set off to the north. With ships requisitioned from Count Marius's fleet at Jutonsryk, he'd taken the swords of the Empire across the frozen seas to the lands many were already calling Norsca. The Norsii were going to learn that there were consequences to attacking Sigmar's realm.

'There is indeed,' said Eoforth. 'Redwane sends word from the Fauschlag that Sigmar's ships have put ashore in Udose lands at a place called Haugrvik.'

'Do you think they found him?'

'Gerreon? I doubt it,' said Eoforth. 'We would have heard.'

Alfgeir nodded, having already suspected that would be the answer. 'So when is Sigmar coming back to Reikdorf?'

'Soon, I expect. If they're done with the war across the sea, then they're probably on their way now.'

'Good,' said Alfgeir. 'It's time he was back. We're not an Empire without an Emperor.'

Alfgeir had a point. In the year following the great victory against the Norsii, the Empire had weathered the storm of war in consolidation. Each of the counts had returned to their lands to regroup and refortify, but instead of returning to Reikdorf, Sigmar had gathered a force of warriors and crossed the sea to make war on the Norsii. No more would the banished tribes of the north dwell with impunity in their frozen homelands, believing themselves safe from attack. Yet without the Emperor, the people of the Unberogen grew restive, withdrawing behind their palisade walls and spears. Many traders now carried on up the coast to Marburg and Jutonsryk or headed east to Three Hills or south to Siggurdheim.

The Unberogen needed their Emperor back.

The horse lowered its head and Alfgeir patted its flanks as squires arrived from the stables to care for the knights' mounts. These were beasts bred from Wolfgart's stock, wide-chested, powerful and trained to fight. Bred for strength and musculature, not speed and height, the knights' horses were squat and pugnacious beasts. Iron plates riveted to a boiled leather harness protected the horse's flank, while segmented bands of iron and mail sheathed its neck and head.

'Maybe the greenskins keep attacking Astofen due to its historical significance?' suggested Eoforth, returning to their earlier discussion.

'I still don't see why it matters,' said Alfgeir.

'Perhaps if we knew why they came, we could do something about it,' said Eoforth as Alfgeir's squire led the horse away to be stripped of its armour, rubbed down, fed and watered. The care of a good warhorse was a thorough and expensive business.

Alfgeir sat on a stone bench at the side of the street, and Eoforth saw how tired he was. It was a long ride from Astofen and as much as the Empire was far safer than it had been in Björn's time, it still did not do to be away from the scattered pockets of civilisation for too long. Orcs were not the only dangers that lurked in the depths of the Empire's forests.

'Very well, I will indulge you, scholar, but what is there to do?' said Alfgeir, tilting his head back to allow the breeze to cool his skin. 'Orcs are savages, they are driven by their lust for blood. There is no force in this world that can change that.'

'You may be right,' said Eoforth, sitting next to him. 'It is a depressing thought.'

'That I am right or that the orcs will never change?'

Eoforth smiled. 'I was referring to the orcs, my friend. Tell me, does the dwarf bridge still stand to the south of Astofen?'

'It does,' said Alfgeir. 'And someone has erected a shrine on the north bank.'

'Oh? Dedicated to which god?'

'To no god. It is dedicated to Sigmar.'

'To Sigmar?' chuckled Eoforth. 'An understandable gesture, but let us hope it is too small for the gods to notice and take offence.'

'Indeed,' said Alfgeir, removing his helmet and pulling back the coif. He set the helmet next to him and ran a hand through his sweat-streaked hair. Eoforth noticed it was thinning at the crown, and there was more than a hint of grey to its hue.

Alfgeir saw the look and said, 'None of us are getting any younger, scholar.'

He smiled as he said it, but Eoforth saw the horror of aging in the warrior's eyes.

He forced a smile. 'There's truth in that, my friend. Even I am starting to feel old.'

They sat in companionable silence for a while, watching the youngsters fussing around the knights, offering to carry their lances, lead their horses or polish their armour. The knights shooed them away with smiles or pantomime growls, and Eoforth watched the boys following behind them, wielding sticks like swords and miming the slaying of their enemies.

'How goes the teaching?' asked Alfgeir, nodding towards the books in Eoforth's lap.

'Slowly,' admitted Eoforth. 'As you see, the boys are more interested in learning to kill than to read poetry or count.'

'We will always need warriors to defend us,' pointed out Alfgeir.

'And we will also need poets to inspire them, artists to commemorate them and tallymen to organise their armies.'

'Young men don't care for that,' said Alfgeir. 'They hunger for glory, not numbers and letters. Unberogen boys weren't made for study. I mean no offence by that, the pursuit of wisdom is an honourable one.'

'No offence taken,' said Eoforth, 'but it saddens me that we still need warriors at all. Wasn't the foundation of the Empire supposed to be an end to wars?'

'Even a rose needs thorns to defend it,' said Alfgeir.

Eoforth gave Alfgeir a sidelong look. 'Poetry?'

Alfgeir looked embarrassed. 'I read that book you loaned me. The writings of the Brigundian saga poet, what was his name...?'

'Sigenert,' said Eoforth. 'I wasn't sure you'd read it.'

'I read it,' replied Alfgeir. 'It just took me a while.'

'What did you think of it?'

Alfgeir shrugged. 'A lot of it went over my head, but I liked his words.'

Eoforth laughed and pushed himself to his feet. 'That's about all a poet can hope for, I suppose.'

THREE
Flight and Fight

CUTHWIN LOOSED BETWEEN breaths, his goose-feathered shaft thudding home at the base of the goblin's skull. It toppled from the back of the wolf with a surprised squeal. He drew another arrow from the quiver at his shoulder and sent it through the throat of a wolf-riding goblin. One of the riderless beasts leapt onto the wagons, bloody saliva dripping from its jaws.

It pounced onto one of the dwarfs armed with a thunder bow and bore him to the ground. Yellowed fangs fastened on the dwarf's neck and blood fountained as the beast bit through his throat. Cuthwin's next arrow punched though its eye socket, and the beast dropped next to its victim with a howl of agony.

The goblins either didn't realise they were under attack from a different direction or didn't care. A flurry of ragged arrows flew from the goblin bows. Most thudded harmlessly into the timber sides of the wagons, but a dwarf fell with two shafts buried in his chest. The wolf-riding goblins were quick to take advantage of the situation, two of their number goading their mounts to leap onto the wagons.

Swinging his bow around, Cuthwin's arrow slashed into the flank of the first wolf, his next into the hindquarters of the other. The dwarfs fell upon the downed goblins and slew them with quick, economical blows from their axes. A shot rang out from the dwarf with the thunder bow and another goblin was punched from the saddle.

Cuthwin exhausted his quiver, emptying another four saddles and killing three wolves. He set his bow upright against the tree next to him and drew his hunting knife, a foot of cold steel that had shed more than its fair share of greenskin blood. Two more dwarfs were down, one with an arrow protruding from his neck, another with a goblin blade buried in his guts. The thunder bow spoke again and a goblin died with half its head blown off.

Cuthwin ran down to the road and leapt on the back of a wolf, plunging his blade into the goblin rider's side. The creature shrieked in agony and he hurled its corpse to the ground. He rammed his bloody blade into the wolf's back. It howled and rolled, trying to dislodge him. He landed lightly beside it and stabbed its throat as it scrambled to get upright.

Another wolf landed on him, the claws of its front paws scoring his thigh and barrelling him to the ground. Cuthwin rolled as its fangs snapped for his throat. He threw up his knife arm and hammered its jaw with the pommel. Yellow teeth snapped beneath the Empire-forged iron and the stinking beast threw back its head and roared. One of the dwarfs dropped to the road and ran towards him, but a goblin with better aim or luck than most loosed a shaft that sliced home into his rescuer's neck.

The dwarf sank to his knees, blood pumping in a flood down his mail shirt. He pitched forward as the goblin turned its bow on Cuthwin. A thunderous boom echoed across the clearing and the last goblin fell from the back of its wolf with what passed for its brains mushrooming from its skull.

Cuthwin rolled to his feet as the wolves, free of their cruel masters' spurs and goads, fled into the forest, leaving the clearing silent save for the laboured wheezes of wounded beasts. Cuthwin's leg ached, but the cuts were not deep. He scrambled over to the wagons, checking each of the dwarfs in turn. Only one still lived, the dwarf who'd fired the shot that had saved his life. An arrow was lodged in his chest, its shaft warped and crudely fletched with what looked like raven feathers.

The dwarf's beard was twisted into three heavy braids, each bound with an iron band at the end, and his cheeks were black with powder burns. The dwarf was bald, his heavy brow pulled down in pain. Blood flecked his spittle and his eyes were glassy and unfocussed.

'You're hurt,' said Cuthwin. 'Pretty badly, but if I can get you to Reikdorf you might live.'

The dwarf looked at him in pained confusion and murmured something in a strange, angular language of harshly edged words. Cuthwin didn't understand and shook his head.

'I don't know what you're saying. Do you understand me?'

The dwarf nodded slowly, grim faced and belligerent.

'My fellows?' he said.

'They're all dead.'

The dwarf nodded and Cuthwin saw a depth of pain and anger that frightened him with its intensity. He had felt sorrow at the death of friends, but this was a different order of feeling entirely.

'Were they your kin?' he asked, helping the dwarf to sit upright.

'All dwarfs are kin,' hissed the dwarf, as though he was being wilfully dense.

'Sorry I asked,' replied Cuthwin. 'Now hold still. I need to get that arrow out, and it's going to hurt.'

The dwarf looked down at the jutting shaft and said, 'Don't tell me it will hurt, manling, just do it before I die of old age.'

'Suit yourself,' said Cuthwin. 'I'm going to count to three, and then–'

He jerked the arrow out in one swift motion. The dwarf roared in agony and swung his fist at Cuthwin's head. He'd been expecting that and swayed back from the blow. Blood pumped from the wound and the dwarf's eyes rolled back as the pain threatened to overwhelm him.

'Stay with me, mountain man!' said Cuthwin, holding the dwarf upright. 'Come on, look at me! Listen to me, you have to stay awake or you're as good as dead. There's likely more of those goblins out there, and it won't take them long to get here on those wolves. So you need to come with me if you want to get back beneath the mountains.'

The dwarf gripped the edge of the wagon and it seemed as though his anger alone was sustaining him. Cuthwin turned to cut strips of cloth from one of the dead dwarfs' cloaks to bind the wounds. The dwarf watched him and said, 'What is your name, manling?'

'I'm Cuthwin of the Unberogen,' he said.

'The Heldenhammer's tribe…' said the dwarf, the hard edges of his voice softening with blood loss and fatigue.

'The very same,' said Cuthwin, binding the dwarf's wound as best he could. He would have preferred to lace the wound with healing poultices, but they were in his pack.

'And you? What's your name, mountain man?'

'Deeplock,' said the dwarf, his voice already sounding distant and faint. 'Grindan Deeplock of Zhufbar, Engineer to the Guildmasters of Varn Drazh, Keeper of the–'

The dwarf's voice faded and the ragged howling of wolves from further south told Cuthwin it was time to move on. Slinging the dwarf's arm over his shoulder, he set off towards where he'd set his bow and hoped he could put enough distance between him and the goblins before they were able to pick up his tracks.

'Wait…' said Deeplock. 'Must bring…'

'No time, mountain man,' said Cuthwin, half carrying, half dragging the wounded dwarf into the shadows of the forest. Were it only the larger greenskins behind them, Cuthwin wouldn't have been worried, they were strong but not too clever.

But goblins were cunning and would find their tracks swiftly. On his own he could evade them without trouble, but with a wounded dwarf in tow…

That was going to be a challenge.

'HAND ME THE tongs, son,' said Govannon, squinting in the smouldering orange light of the forge. His hand grasped air until Bysen placed the warm metal in his hands. The furnace was a blaze of light before him, the roar of its heat and the hiss of water droplets from the powered wheel that worked the bellows acting as a sounding guide for him as he thrust the tongs into the hot coals.

Govannon felt the metal and clamped it hard, drawing it out and placing it upon the anvil.

The stink of hot iron burned the air and its orange-yellow colour told him it was just right. His sight was all but destroyed, but his sense for the metal was just as strong.

'Looks good, da,' said Bysen. 'Forging heat right enough.'

'Aye, I can tell, lad,' nodded Govannon, handing his son the tongs and feeling on the workbench for his fuller. Its curved, walnut grip slipped into his hand and he hefted it to get the weight right before bringing it down in a short, powerful arc onto the iron bar. He struck several blows, swiftly establishing a working rhythm as Bysen turned the bar and drew it out, gradually lengthening the metal. They'd done the hard work earlier, working with strikers and other apprentices to work the cold lump of iron into a long bar from which to shape the blade.

It was to be the sword of the Empire's Grand Knight, for Alfgeir had earned great accolades in his defence of the realm in the Emperor's absence.

'Turn it again,' said Govannon. 'Once with each strike.'

'Aye, da,' said Bysen. 'Once each, aye, da. Like you say.'

Govannon worked the fuller along the length of the iron, working by instinct and earned skill. The bar was a blurred outline of yellow gold before him, and he could only tell Bysen was turning the bar by the sound of the hot metal scraping on the anvil. Counting his strokes, he adjudged the iron to be the right length. He had taken Alfgeir's measurements and tested the weight and balance of his currently favoured blade before laying a hammer to the metal. The Grand Knight of the Empire preferred a weapon with the weight slightly towards the tip, requiring a stronger arm to wield it, but delivering a more powerful blow when it landed. The ore that formed this sword had come from the mines of the Howling Hills, Cherusen land, which meant it was freer from impurities and should produce a blade of great brilliance.

'Look long enough?' he asked.

'Aye, da,' said Bysen. 'Just right, da.'

Govannon wiped a meaty forearm across his brow, blinking away salty beads of sweat as they dripped into his eye. Just for a second, he could see the outline of his son clearly, a giant of a boy, nineteen summers old, but with the mind of a child.

Grief and guilt welled in the smith's heart.

It had been at Black Fire when everything had changed.

Govannon and Bysen had been fighting in the heart of the Unberogen lines, smashing greenskins down with powerful strokes of their iron-headed forge hammers. After hours of fighting, the day was almost won, and the warriors of the Emperor's army were hot and close to exhaustion. Victory was so close, they could almost touch it, and that alone kept them fighting beyond the limits of endurance.

A shadow fell over their sword band and an abominable stench rose up as a monstrous, rugose-skinned troll crashed into their flank. Taller than three men and growling with a throaty roar of idiot hunger, it swung a tree branch as thick as an oaken beam. Six men were bludgeoned to death with a single blow.

Many ran from its horror, but Govannon and Bysen stood firm, their hammers feeling woefully inadequate to face such a towering mass of muscle and fury. Warriors rallied to their side, for they were men much respected amongst the Unberogen, and together they charged the hideous creature. Its leering grin split apart in a mass of broken teeth and half-chewed flesh, but it was not in anticipation of feeding. A burbling heave spasmed through its stomach, and a caustic flood of acidic bile spewed from its wide mouth.

Govannon was one of the lucky ones. Leading the charge, he was spared the agony of being eaten alive by the deadly acid. His helmet took the brunt of the splash, but after three hours of fighting in the punishing heat, he'd pushed the visor up. Droplets of the viscous stomach bile dripped into his eyes, and the fiery agony as it burned into them was the worst pain in the world.

He remembered Bysen leaping to face the hideous beast. Its heavy club had smashed him to the ground and left him lying with his skull caved in like a broken egg. That had been the end of their battle, and the next Govannon had known was days later when he awoke in the surgeons' tents at the mouth of the pass. Bright light hurt his eyes and only the dimmest outline of shapes and contrasts were visible to him.

Though his sword-brother, Orvad, had splashed water into his face moments after his wounding, the damage was done. His sight was virtually gone. Orvad died later in the battle, but with the help of one of the surgeons' runners, Govannon had sought news of his son. It took two days to find him among the thousands of wounded, and though he still lived, the lad left the better portion of his brain in the dusty sand of the pass.

Govannon could not weep, his eyes ruined by the beast's venom, but he sat with his son until they were set upon wagons for the journey back to Reikdorf.

Black Fire had taken away his sight and his son's mind, but there wasn't a day went by he wasn't glad he had stood in the line and faced the greenskin horde.

'Da?' said Bysen. 'What the matter, da?'

Govannon snapped out of his melancholy, squinting through the gloom at the blurred outline of his son. He held the sword metal in the tongs, and Govannon shook his head at his foolishness. The metal had cooled too far to work, and would need to be reheated. That was careless, for the quality of the blade would suffer after too many reheats.

'Nothing, son,' said Govannon. 'Let's get this metal heated up or this sword will be no better than a greenskin club.'

'Aye, da,' grinned Bysen. 'Heat it up, aye, heat it good.'

The metal was thrust into the fire and the process began again.

Govannon watched the seething glow, wishing for the thousandth time that he'd kept his visor lowered.

'Damn you for a fool,' he whispered, the words lost in the roaring of the furnace.

THEY WERE GETTING close now, too close. Cuthwin moved as fast as he could with the injured dwarf stumbling alongside him. He bore the bulk of Deeplock's weight, which was slowing him down and making it much harder to keep their passing secret. The forest had closed in, thick and ideal for getting lost in, but Cuthwin had travelled this way many times.

The forest was a harsh companion, a friend to those who understood its rhythms, a deadly enemy to those who didn't give it the proper respect. Cuthwin knew how to make his way in the wilderness, but the goblins were equally at home in its shadowed depths. Their pursuers were, at best, a mile behind. The wind carried the yapping barks of the wolves and though Cuthwin tried to angle his course so that it wouldn't carry his scent to them, it was proving to be impossible. He'd kept to the hard-packed earth and stony ground where he could, wading through shallow streams and leaving false trails to throw their pursuers. That had bought him time, but hadn't shaken the goblins.

He'd stopped every now and then to give the wounded dwarf a rest, and had used the time to set traps on their back trail. At least one snare had caught a wolf; he'd heard its plaintive cry of pain. The breath heaved in his lungs and he knew he couldn't run much further. At some point soon he'd have to turn and fight. There hadn't been time to pluck his arrows from the goblin and wolf corpses, but his retrieved pack had a spare quiver with a dozen arrows. He didn't want to face the goblins and their wolves with only his bow and hunting knife, so any ambush would have to be planned carefully.

Cuthwin looked up through the high branches of the tangled canopy, trying to judge how far it was to the river. He could hear the distant sound of it and its cold, clear scent was a crisp tang over the mulchy greenness of the forest. If they were going to get away from these creatures, he'd need to have plotted their course correctly.

Deeplock stumbled and almost dragged Cuthwin down with him.

'Up, mountain man!' he hissed. 'Use those damn legs of yours!'

'Must... go back...' gasped the dwarf, and Cuthwin saw there was blood in his beard.

'Not if you want to live,' he said, hauling the dwarf to his feet.

Deeplock muttered something else, but Cuthwin couldn't make it out. He set off again through the trees, but the dwarf fell before they'd managed ten yards. Cuthwin fell with him, rolling to keep his bow from touching the ground.

'Damn you, but you're trouble,' he hissed.

The sound of a howling wolf drifted through the trees. It was east of him, and another answered it, this time to the west. There would be more behind him, at least four, and he knew they were racing to get ahead of him, to close the circle around him and leave him nowhere to run.

How far away were they? Listening to the echoes through the trees, he guessed they were no more than half a mile from him. He cursed and gripped the dwarf's tunic, hauling him over his shoulder.

'Ulric's balls, but you're heavy,' he told the unconscious dwarf. Though much shorter than Cuthwin, the dwarf was at least as heavy as a tall man. Bowed under the dwarf's weight, Cuthwin set off again, following the building swell of river noise, hoping that he'd emerge from the trees where he'd planned.

He ran on, sweat dripping into his eyes, losing track of time and distance as he fought to keep going. At last he saw a break in the trees and heard the rushing sound of falling water. Despite his exhaustion, he smiled, knowing the forest had steered him true. The sound of wolves was louder now. They knew they had him cornered, and were howling to get the fear pumping in his veins.

'We'll see about that,' he hissed, emerging from the trees onto the banks of a fast-flowing tributary of the Reik. Tumbling from the high peaks of the Grey Mountains, it wended its way through the uplands of the forest, gathering speed as it fed into the basin of the fertile southlands of the Empire.

Perhaps fifty yards wide, the river poured northwards in a tumbling froth of white spume and swirling black pools. The riverbed was only a yard or so down, but it would take all his strength to keep his feet against the speed of the water.

Greasy rocks slicked in moss jutted from the river as it widened towards a crashing waterfall. A glittering rainbow arced over the edge of the drop, the water falling to a wide pool of upthrust rocks far below.

Cuthwin set down his burden, leaning the dwarf against a boulder at the side of the river. His pallor was terrible, and Cuthwin doubted that even the best healers in Reikdorf could save him. To be killed rescuing a dwarf that likely wouldn't live out the day. That would be a poor way to meet his end.

Heavy tree branches drooped over the water, willows, whip-limbed birch and young, supple saplings. Cuthwin shucked off his pack. He strung his bow and unsheathed his hunting knife, moving quickly to the tree line and testing the longest and thinnest tree branches.

A wolf howl came from the forest, and Cuthwin knew he didn't have much time.

SWEATING AND BREATHING hard, Cuthwin looped Grindan Deeplock over his shoulders and waded back into the river. Swollen with mountain water, it was bitterly cold and the breath caught in his throat. It threatened to snatch him from his feet and send him hurtling over the waterfall, but thanks to the additional ballast of the dwarf, Cuthwin was able to keep his balance. He waded out into the river, biting his lip to keep the pain of the cold at bay.

A dozen yards to his right, the waterfall boomed and roared like a hungry beast, and he tried not to think of how much it would hurt to be dashed to death on the rocks below. He reached the halfway point of the river, shuffling his feet through the mud and stones of the riverbed. Just ahead of him was a jutting boulder, its surfaces worn smooth by the passage of centuries of water. He slid Deeplock from his shoulders and propped him up against the rock, pressing his own back into the dwarf to hold him in place.

The wolves emerged from the trees, seven of them, each with a goblin perched behind the blades of their shoulders. Chittering laughter giggled from beneath the goblins' hoods, and hooked noses twitched in anticipation. They spat curses at him in their foul language, and many lifted their short horn bows from their backs.

Cuthwin pulled back on his own bowstring and let fly, sending an arrow into the mouth of a snarling wolf and dropping it instantly. The goblin fell from its back and plunged into the waters of the river. It squealed in fear before being carried over the waterfall. The roar of the water swallowed its cries. Four of the wolves entered the river, the flesh of their jaws drawn back over their fangs. A black-fletched shaft skittered off the rock and Cuthwin flinched, swinging his bow around and sighting down the length of his arrow.

He exhaled and loosed, watching the arrow as it slashed through the air to sever the thin knot of bound saplings he'd wedged in the soft earth before the bent branches of a long-limbed willow. Its branches whipped around, like the arm of a catapult laid on its side, and slashed into the wolf-riding goblins. Two of the wolves in the shallows were smashed from their feet and howled as they were swept downriver towards the falls. They and their riders vanished over the edge and as the other goblins watched in dismay Cuthwin nocked and let fly with another arrow.

It punched through the chest of the goblin whose wolf had leapt back quick enough to avoid his trap. Another goblin arrow spun up to slice the skin of his forehead. Blood streamed down Cuthwin's face, and he shook his head clear as the remaining four wolves leapt into the river, their lean bodies powering them through the water as the goblins held on for dear life.

Cuthwin waited until they were a dozen yards from him and sent his next shaft into a branch he'd wedged beneath a precariously perched boulder further upriver. His arrow thwacked into the wood, but the branch didn't move. The wolves snapped in the foaming water, and Cuthwin saw their feral hunger to tear him apart. He loosed another shaft into the wood, and this time it fell from where it was wedged into the soft mud he'd dug out of the riverbed.

The boulder toppled over, and the water breaking behind it surged downriver with tidal force. The wave slammed into the wolves and broke against them with enormous power. They were helpless against the strength of the current and all but two were borne over the edge of the falls by the surging water. Their howls and the screeching fear of the goblins dwindled as they fell.

Before he could congratulate himself, a goblin arrow ricocheted from the rock and sliced through his bowstring. Cuthwin took hold of his now useless bow and hurled it towards the far bank. It was a good throw, and the weapon landed in the ferns at the edge of the river. He couldn't move from the rock for fear of losing Grindan Deeplock, so drew his knife and prepared to fight the last two of his pursuers.

The wolf was fighting against the current, and before it could reach him in his sheltered enclave, Cuthwin lunged forward. Keeping one hand braced against the dwarf, he slashed his blade across the wolf's snout as the goblin swung its sword at him. The beast yelped in pain and the goblin's sword went wide. Cuthwin plunged the tip of his dagger into the rider's throat. Blood spilled over his hand, and the goblin lurched back, yanking hard on the rope reins of its mount.

The creature's pain outweighed its sense of danger and the power of the river eagerly snatched it away.

The last wolf had entered the river higher up and used the flow of water to its advantage. Swimming with the current, it lunged towards him. He hurled himself back against the rock and its jaws snapped shut an inch from his face. The goblin stabbed with its rusty blade. Cuthwin swayed aside and Grindan Deeplock slid away from him, his head sinking beneath the level of the rushing water.

Cuthwin punched the wolf in the face and rammed his knife into the goblin's side. Both tumbled away from him and he twisted the dagger in the greenskin's flesh, pulling it out and stabbing it down into the wolf's skull.

Its yelp of pain was abruptly cut off and the corpses spun lazily away, disappearing over the edge of the waterfall. Cuthwin let out a long breath and turned to lift the dwarf from beneath the water. His eyes were closed, and it was impossible to tell if he were alive or dead. Checking the tree line for more enemies, Cuthwin hauled Grindan Deeplock over to the far side of the river and dragged him onto the bank.

He pressed his fingertips to the dwarf's throat, and was rewarded with a pulse. Weak, but steady. Cuthwin's pack was sodden, but the oiled lining had kept the worst of the river at bay. Stripping the dwarf of his sodden clothes, he wrapped him in a woollen blanket from his pack and rubbed circulation back into his limbs.

'Just as well you're unconscious, mountain man,' said Cuthwin. 'Don't think you'd be keen on me doing this for you.'

Satisfied the dwarf wasn't about to die from the cold, Cuthwin swiftly redressed his wounds, using a healing poultice of valerian and spiderleaf and binding them with strips of vinegar-soaked linen. The dwarf grunted a few words in his harsh language. Cuthwin tied the bindings off under the dwarf's shoulder and lay back against the bole of a tree, letting the adrenaline drain from him in a series of slow breaths. There was nothing more he could do for the dwarf, and they were still some days from Reikdorf.

The dwarf would either live or die on his own terms.

Night was coming, and they needed to find shelter. Cuthwin saw foresters' marks on a nearby tree and dragged the dwarf further into the woods, following the signs towards a sheltered overhang of rock and fallen trees. A fire had been set in this hollow by its previous occupant, a fresh base of kindling and twigs ready for the next traveller to take shelter here. A stack of firewood lay bundled and tied with twine beneath the overhanging lip of a hollow tree.

Cuthwin recognised the style of fire that had been set. Though he had never met the man, he knew him to be a hunter who favoured his right hand and walked with a slight limp. He was a successful hunter, as his footprints – when Cuthwin could find them – were always deeper on the way home than on the way out. Whoever he was, he lived perhaps a day or two from here, somewhere along the high ridges of the south-east.

Cuthwin pulled out his tinderbox and got the fire going without difficulty. The hunter had built a good fire, and soon a small blaze was warming their sheltered hollow. With the fire going, he lay back and rested his eyes. He wouldn't sleep though. With only one of them able to stand guard, it didn't pay to leave their safety during the night to chance.

Grindan Deeplock grumbled in his sleep, yet amid the unintelligible words of his strange language, Cuthwin heard a few heavily accented words in Reikspiel.

One was *buried*, and he thought the other was *organ*.

That didn't make any sense. Were these dwarfs selling musical instruments?

Putting the dwarf's ramblings from his head, Cuthwin set about restringing his bow and settled down for the night.

FOUR
New Friends and Old Enemies

The Emperor's army returned to Reikdorf in triumph, his black steed flanked by a dozen others, and trailed by two thousand marching warriors. Since arriving back on Empire soil, his forces had swollen with followers, farm boys eager to take up a life of the sword and warriors from distant lands wishing to serve under the Imperial banner.

Though Gerreon had escaped them, the stated purpose of the campaign had been to strike terror into the hearts of the Norsii, to let them know that they were not safe in their desolate realm of ice and snow. That task had been accomplished, and the crowds gathered to greet their Emperor's return waved swords and axes high in recognition of his victories.

Bells pealed from every tower that had one and the schoolhouses emptied as word spread throughout the city. First the arrival of the Grand Knight of the Empire, and now the return of the Emperor. Truly the city of Reikdorf was blessed. Thousands of men, women and children lined the streets, cheering and alternately shouting the names of Sigmar and Ulric.

Conn Carsten and a hundred Udose warriors marched with the Emperor, grim-faced men in long kilts and baked leather breastplates. Each carried a long, basket-hilted broadsword over their shoulders and a round leather-covered shield was slung over their backs. They carried themselves with a rowdy confidence, utterly sure of themselves and cheerfully scornful of the ordered ranks of the Unberogen.

Clad in his dwarf-forged plate and silver helm, Sigmar kept Ghal-maraz held high. The symbol of his rule, it served to remind his people of the bond of loyalty that existed between his people and those of the mountains. The Empire had come close to disaster at Middenheim, and in times of trouble it was good to remind people of all that stood in their favour. It had been many years since King Kurgan had visited Reikdorf, and Sigmar longed to visit the mountain hold of his fellow king and friend someday.

Wolfgart had not returned to Reikdorf. He had ridden south with Sigmar as far as the castle of Count Otwin of the Thuringians, before heading eastwards toward the lands of the Asoborns. Maedbh and Ulrike, his wife and daughter, now dwelled in the lands of Freya, Queen of the Asoborns. No one called Freya a count, no one dared. Like the Berserker King, she was one of Sigmar's allies that found it hard to shed her former title.

Behind the Emperor came an ornate bier, pulled by four white horses, the finest of Wolfgart's southern herd. Upon it lay an iron coffin, draped in the blue and cream of Middenheim. The body of Pendrag lay within, preserved with camphorated wine and powdered nitre. For his service and friendship, Pendrag would be rewarded with a place of honour within Warrior Hill. Sigmar rode through the streets of his city, basking in his subjects' adulation, the image of the heroic warrior-emperor his people needed and wanted.

THE FIRES OF the longhouse burned fiercely, filling the length of it with warmth and light. Three wild boars hunted that morning from the forests north of Reikdorf turned on spits and the smell of roasting pork was making every man in the great hall salivate. Blessings to Taal had been said in thanks, and serving maids bearing trays laden with platters of roasted meat and wooden mugs of beer circulated amongst the celebrating tribesmen.

The Udose drank heavily, singing achingly sad songs of lament to the wheezing, skirling music of the pipes. Unberogen warriors joined in, though the singsong language of the northern tribesmen was all but impenetrable to their southern ears. The mood in the hall was hearty, for both groups of warriors had fought side by side for the last year. Many oaths of brotherhood had been sworn between

Udose and Unberogen, the kind that lay at the heart of what made the Empire strong.

Sigmar sat upon his throne, stripped of his armour save for the gleaming breastplate and a thick bearskin cloak. Two of his hounds, Lex and Kai lay curled at his feet, while Ortulf – ever the opportunist – circulated through the longhouse in search of scraps. Conn Carsten sat in the place of honour to Sigmar's right, while Alfgeir and Eoforth sat to his left. Though both these men had helped steer the Empire through some of its darkest hours, Sigmar found himself missing the earthy counsel of Wolfgart and Pendrag.

This hall had once echoed with Wolfgart's dreadful singing and off-colour jokes, but more and more, he was spending time in Three Hills with his family. Sigmar couldn't blame him, Maedbh was a hard woman to refuse. As was any Asoborn woman, thought Sigmar, remembering how he had secured Queen Freya's Sword Oath.

Conn Carsten had filled the void of leadership left by the death of Count Wolfila, binding the argumentative clans of the Udose into a fighting force in the face of the Norsii invasion. But for Carsten's merciless hit and run raids, the north would have fallen long before the armies of the Empire could have marched to save Middenheim.

This night was to honour his courage during the war against the Norsii and confirm his appointment as Count of the Udose. It should have been an occasion for great celebration, and certainly was amongst Carsten's warriors. But since this night had begun, Conn Carsten had said little and responded to any query with curt answers. He nursed his beer and seemed content to simply watch proceedings rather than participate.

Sigmar regarded his newest count's brooding countenance, his gloom-swept face having surely seen more than its fair share of hardship. His silver hair was cut tight to his skull and his beard was similarly trimmed. Where his warriors were bellicose and roaring, he was quiet and ill-suited to conversation.

None of the other counts were in attendance, nor had Sigmar expected them to be. After the mustering of their armies for the relief of Middenheim, the tribal leaders were attending to matters in their own lands. Since his return, Sigmar had read missives from Freya and Adelhard of increased greenskin activity in the Worlds Edge Mountains, of warbands of twisted forest beasts in the southern reaches and increased coordination between brigands and reavers in the north. Krugar and Aloysis both begged the Emperor's help in quelling numerous incidences of the dead rising from their tombs to attack the living, and Aldred of the Endals reported increased attacks from unknown seaborne corsairs.

Eoforth had once said that winning the Empire had been the easy part. Holding on to it would be the real challenge. Sigmar was now beginning to see what he meant. Something so precious would always attract enemies, and the true legacy of Sigmar's creation would be how long it endured against the encroaching darkness.

As much as he found it hard to enjoy Carsten's company, Sigmar knew this man was key to keeping his land safe. Better the northern marches were ruled by a competent, disagreeable man than a gregarious friend who didn't know one end of a sword from the other. Yet it sat ill with Sigmar that he could not reach the dour clansman, as though some unknown gulf existed between them that he could not cross. He did not expect to be as close to all his counts as he was to his friends, and as their ruler he knew he ought not to be. Yet to count a man as his ally and not to know him, that would not stand.

Sigmar turned to Conn Carsten and said, 'Can I ask you something, Conn?'

The newest count of the Empire nodded slowly, as though wary of Sigmar's purpose.

'This should be a grand day for you,' said Sigmar, knowing that flowery words or an indirect approach would only irritate the northerner. 'You are a count of the Empire now, a man of great respect and responsibility. Yet you seem distracted, like you stand at the grave of your sword-brother. Why is that?'

Carsten put down his beer and wiped his lips with the back of his sleeve.

'I have lost too many men in the last year and a half to celebrate, my lord. The wolves of the north wreaked great harm on my tribe and devastated our lands. Every village among the Udose has widows to spare, and the black shawls of mourning are too common a sight among my people. We are always first to feel the bite of Norsii axes. That makes it hard to know joy.'

Sigmar shook his head, gesturing at the gathered warriors. 'Your warriors seem to have no difficulty in finding it.'

'Because they are young and foolish,' said Carsten. 'They think themselves immortal and beyond death's touch. If they live a little longer they will see the lie of that belief.'

'A grim view, my friend.'

'A realistic one. I have buried three wives and six children in my life. I once believed that I could have it all, the life of a warrior with its glory and battles, with a loving wife and family to come back to. But it is impossible. You of all people should know that.'

Sigmar felt the touch of Ravenna's memory, but instead of pain, it now brought him comfort, a reassurance that she was alive within his heart.

'You're right, I *do* know the pain of losing loved ones. I lost the love of my life many years ago and my best friend was killed by a man I once called a brother. Every death in Middenheim was a grievous loss, but I know that a life lived without hope or joy is a wasted one. I know the reality of life in the Empire, my friend. I know it is dangerous, often short and violent. That is precisely why we must take what joy we can from what the gods give us.'

'That may be the Unberogen way, but it is not my way,' said Carsten. 'Live in hope if you must, I will live in the knowledge that all things must die.'

Sigmar said, 'Look at Reikdorf, look at all we have achieved here and how the Empire's cities grow larger and stronger. One day we will have borders that no enemy, no matter how strong they are, can breach. We will have peace and our people will know contentment.'

Conn Carsten took a mouthful of beer and smiled. 'It would not do for me to call you foolish, my Emperor, but I think that is a naïve belief. We will always have to fight to hold on to what you have built. Already you have defeated two major invasions. Many more will come. It only takes one to succeed and the Empire will be forgotten in a generation.'

'I have heard that before, Conn,' said Sigmar with a grim smile. 'The necromancer Morath tried to break me with a similar argument. If we live fearing that all we have will be lost, then we would never build anything, never *achieve* anything. I cannot live that way; I will build and defend what I have built with my life. You are part of that, Conn, a vital part. I cannot do this without your support. You alone can keep the clans united and be my sword in the north.'

Carsten smiled and his face was transformed in an instant. Sigmar's words were flattery, but the northern clansman saw the sincerity in them and his dour expression lifted. He raised his mug of beer and Sigmar toasted with him.

'I'll drink to that,' said Carsten. 'But I know what I am, a cantankerous old man the clan chieftains tolerate as their count because they know that every other clan hates me too. I have no sons left to follow me, so the other chieftains look at me and know they will be rid of me in a few years. They can wait.'

Sigmar extended his hand and Conn Carsten took it.

'Make the bastards wait a long time,' said Sigmar.

Conn Carsten laughed and somewhere beyond the longhouse walls a bell tolled.

THE REVELRIES CONTINUED for another three hours, though Conn Carsten excused himself not long after their conversation. As the last of the tribesmen staggered or were carried from the longhouse, Sigmar stood from his throne and paced the length of the dwarf-built structure. Its walls were fashioned from black stone quarried from deep beneath the Worlds Edge Mountains, carried on wagons from the east and raised by surly craftsmen of the mountain folk under direction of Alaric.

Sigmar knew the dwarfs called him Alaric the Mad, a name that rankled, for a more level-headed, pragmatic individual would be hard to find. Alaric now laboured deep beneath the mountains to forge twelve mighty swords for the counts of the Empire. Before Black Fire, Pendrag had crafted wondrous shields for each of the tribal kings, and King Kurgan had decreed that he would present Sigmar with swords to match.

Alaric himself had delivered the first of those swords to Sigmar at the battle for the Fauschlag Rock, a blade without equal among the realm of man. It had been given to Sigmar, but he had presented it to Pendrag as the Count of Middenheim, and upon his death it had been taken up by Myrsa – once the Warrior Eternal, now the new count.

Sigmar sat on a bench, idly tracing the outline of a wolf in a spilled pool of beer. He missed his friends. Time and distance had seen them pulled to the corners of the Empire, and though each was in his rightful place, he still wished they could be near. He even found himself missing the reckless wildness of Redwane. The young warrior and his White Wolves were now quartered atop the Fauschlag Rock as honour guard to Myrsa, a position Sigmar saw no need to rescind.

The hall smelled of cold meat, sweat and stale beer. It was the smell of maleness, of warriors and companionship. Sigmar looked up as the moon emerged from behind a long cloud and its light flooded the hall. He remembered catching Cuthwin and Wenyld trying to sneak a glance at the warriors within on his Blood Night, smiling at the memory of those long ago days. Two and a half decades had passed since then, and Sigmar shook his head at the idea of such a span of time. Where had it all gone?

'Thinking of the past?' said Alfgeir, sitting opposite him and depositing a pair of wooden mugs of beer on the trestle table. 'Isn't that the job of old men?'

'We *are* old men, Alfgeir,' said Sigmar with a grin.

'Nonsense,' said the Grand Knight of the Empire. He was drunk, but pleasantly so. 'I'm as strong as I was when I first took up a sword.'

'I don't doubt it, but we're not the young bucks of the herd anymore.'

'Who needs to be? We have experience those with milk from their mother's teat on their thistledown beards can only dream about.'

'Those that are old enough to have beards.'

'Exactly,' agreed Alfgeir, taking a long swig of his beer.

Sigmar knew that Alfgeir would pay for this indulgence tomorrow. It wasn't as easy to shake the effects of Unberogen beer as it had been in their youth. Sigmar had ridden to Astofen after a heavy night of drinking and had felt no worse than any other morning, but he now had to nurse his beer or else he'd feel like the gods themselves were swinging hammers on the inside of his skull. His friend was still a powerful warrior, yet Sigmar knew he was slowing down. A young man when he served King Björn, Alfgeir was now approaching his sixtieth year.

'Do you remember when we climbed to the top of the Fauschlag Rock?'

'Remember it? I still have nightmares about it,' said Alfgeir. 'I still can't believe I went with you. I must have been mad.'

'I think we were both a bit mad back then,' agreed Sigmar. 'I think youth needs a bit of madness, or else what's the point?'

'The point of what, youth or madness?'

'Youth.'

Alfgeir shrugged. 'You're asking the wrong man, my friend. You want clever answers, you should ask Eoforth.'

'I would, but he went to his bed many hours ago.'

'Always was the clever one, eh?'

'The wisest among us,' said Sigmar, taking a long mouthful of beer.

They drank in silence for a while, listening to the good-natured arguments of drunken warriors outside as they wended their way to their bedrolls. Sigmar could well imagine the substance of their strident roughhousing, the same things he and his sword-brothers had squabbled over when they were young; women, war and glory.

'I sometimes miss it though,' said Sigmar. 'When all you had to do was strap on your armour, carry a sharp sword and ride out with the blood thundering in your ears. You fought, you killed the enemy and you rode back with your cheeks blooded. Things were simpler back then. I miss that.'

'Everything seems simple to the young.'

'I know, but it would be pleasant to live like that again, just for a while. Not to have to worry about the fate of thousands, to try and protect all you've built and fear for what will happen to it when you're gone.'

Alfgeir gave him a sidelong look down the length of his nose. His eyes were unfocussed, but there was a clarity to his look that Sigmar knew all too well.

'The Empire will endure,' he said, taking his time not to slur. 'The youngsters behind us may be foolish just now, but they're good men and they'll grow wiser. You've built a grand thing in the Empire, Sigmar, grand enough that it'll endure without sons of your blood to keep it strong.'

Sigmar nodded and looked into the thinning froth on his beer. Alfgeir had hit a raw nerve, and he took a moment to consider his answer.

'Ravenna and I talked of a family,' he said.

'She would have borne you strong sons,' said Alfgeir. 'She was a bonny lass, but she had strength too. Every day I wish Gerreon a thousand painful deaths for what he took from you.'

'What he took from us all,' said Sigmar. 'But I don't want to talk about Ravenna. The world will have to make do without my sons.'

'And mine,' said Alfgeir. 'Never wanted to make a woman wait for me every time I rode to war. Didn't seem fair, but I wish I'd sired a son. Someone to carry on my name after I die. I wanted there to be someone who'd remember me after I was gone.'

'The saga poets will remember you, my friend,' said Sigmar. 'Your deeds will be immortalised in epic verse.'

'Aye, maybe so, but who'll read them?'

'They'll be sung from the longhouses of the Udose to the castles of the Merogens. I'm the Emperor, I can make it law if you like.'

Alfgeir laughed and the maudlin mood was banished. That was the

Unberogen way, to laugh in the face of despair with a drink in one hand and a sword in the other. Alfgeir threw his empty mug over his shoulder into the gently glowing firepit and nodded.

'Aye, I'd like that,' he said. 'Make it happen.'

'First thing tomorrow,' promised Sigmar, draining the last of his beer and lobbing his mug over Alfgeir's shoulder. It broke apart on the coals, the last dregs of the beer hissing as the alcohol burned with sudden brightness.

'So how was Carsten?' asked Alfgeir, apropos of nothing. 'Looked like you cracked the granite of his face at the end.'

Sigmar took a moment to consider the question. He and Carsten had established a connection tonight, one he hadn't expected to make, but Sigmar still felt like he hardly knew the man.

'We're never going to be friends, but I think I understand him a bit better.'

'What's to understand? He's a dour-faced misery, though he's a devil of a fighter.'

'I knew that already, but I know why he's the way he is. He's known great pain and suffering and I think it got the better of him.'

'We've all known suffering and loss,' said Alfgeir, raising his mug. 'To the dead.'

'To the dead,' said Sigmar.

BENEATH THE LIGHT of Mannslieb a hundred warriors of the Menogoths marched from the hill fort of Hyrstdunn. They followed an oft-used road that led through the fields and villages clustered around the sprawling settlement like children afraid to venture too far from a parent's protection. Many warriors carried tall spears tied with green and yellow cords, flanked by groups of hard-eyed men in lacquered leather breastplates with unsheathed broadswords. Torchbearers accompanied the marching warriors; each robed in black and with their hoods pulled up over their heads. At the head of the column rode Count Markus of the Menogoths, draped in the black cloak of mourning and with his own swords sheathed across his back.

The fortress city at their back had stood for hundreds of years, a forest of wooden logs with sharpened tips and strong towers. The land hereabouts was rugged and undulant, rising in gentle sways towards the haunches of the Grey Mountains that bordered Menogoth lands to the south. The earth here was fertile and rich in resources, yet the price for that bounty was a life lived in the shadow of the monsters that made their lairs within the mountains: greenskins, cave beasts twisted by dark magic or strange monsters with no name and ever more fearsome reputations.

King Markus had carved a life for his tribe in this wild land, but not without great cost. His people were hardy, yet their souls were forever caught in the shadow of the mountains. Often gloomy and fatalistic, the Menogoths were viewed as a miserable tribe by their more northerly cousins, but had they spent a year in their lands, not one Unberogen, Cherusen or Thuringian would fail to see why.

Count Markus rode beneath a streaming banner of yellow and green silk carried by his sword champion, Wenian. The banner had been a gift from Marius of the Jutones in the wake of the great victory at the Fauschlag Rock, and its fabric was said to have come from lands far to the east beyond the Worlds Edge Mountains. Markus had cherished the gift ever since.

His wife and daughter rode in an ornate coach pulled by four black horses that had been harnessed in bronze and plumed with black feathers. The coach was of lacquered black wood, hung with ebony roses, spread-winged ravens and, at its front, the image of a great portal. The women had their heads bowed, and heavy veils hung with black pearls obscured their faces.

This was a grim night for the Menogoths, for the only son of Count Markus was dead.

Borne on a palanquin of spears, Vartan Gothii went to his rest among the tombs of his ancestors. An honour guard of the Bloodspears carried the body of Markus's son, granted this honour for their courage in standing firm at Black Fire while their brother warriors had run.

Markus led the procession through his lands towards the flat-topped hill where the Menogoth heroes of old were buried. Called the Morrdunn, its height should have made it the natural place to build one of the forts that gave the Menogoths their name of hill people, but the first tribesmen to settle here had instinctively known that this was not a place for the living. A number of torches flickered at its summit as the grim procession wound its way up the hard-packed earth of its burial paths.

They passed the tomb of Devyn of the Axe, the heroic warrior who had saved the first king of the tribe from an ogre's cook pot. Further up, Markus nodded respectfully to the mausoleum carved into the hill where Bannan, the greatest Swordmaster of the Menogoths, lay at his final rest. Odel the Mad lay within a simple sepulchre of polished grey granite built into the upper slopes of the hill, and Markus touched the talisman of Ranald at his chest to ward off the malign influence of the berserk huscarl.

He rode onto the crest of the hill, its summit enclosed by a ring of rune-carved stones like spikes on an ancient ruler's crown. The priests of Morr were waiting, a dozen men in black robes tied with silver cords and each carrying a thin book bound in soft kidskin. The black coach rumbled onto the hilltop, and the Bloodspears moved to the centre of the hill, where the only priest of Morr with his hood drawn back stood ready to fulfil his duty to the dead.

'Who comes with a lost soul to be ushered into the realm of Morr?' intoned the priest.

Markus and his champion dismounted, walking alongside the Bloodspears towards the centre of the hilltop tomb. Wenian planted the banner before the priest as Markus answered.

'I do, Markus Gothii, King of the Menogoths.'

Markus used his old title, for this was an ancient rite of his tribe, one in which his new title of count had no part.

'Morr would know this soul's name, King Markus of the Menogoths.'

'I bring my son, Vartan Gothii, slain by greenskin warriors while defending his people.'

'Slain in service of a higher calling,' said the priest. 'Then he will find rest in the realms beyond this world of flesh.'

Markus clenched his jaw. He was the master of the Menogoths, a warrior of superlative skill. He rubbed a hand across his shaven scalp, tensing his lean, wolfish physique as the grief threatened to unman him before the priests who would see his son to the realms of the dead.

The priest saw his battle and opened the book he carried as the Bloodspears gently lowered Vartan Gothii to the ground. The acolytes of the head priest came forward and knelt in a circle around the body. Markus looked at the unmoving features of his son, so pale and serene that they might have been carved from marble.

'Keep it simple, priest,' ordered Markus. 'Vartan hated ceremony.'

'As you wish, King Markus,' said the priest, flipping to a shorter passage.

Markus's wife and daughter came alongside him and he took their hands as the priest began his recitation of the benediction to the dead. The priest's voice was clear and strong as he read, and Markus took comfort in the words he heard.

'Great Morr, master of the dead and dreams, you have made death itself the gateway to eternal life. Look with love on our fallen brother, and make him one with your realm that he may come before you free from pain. Lord Morr, the death of Vartan Gothii recalls our human condition and the brevity of our lives in this world. For those who believe, death is not the end, nor does it destroy the bonds forged in our lives. We share the faith of all men and the hope of the life beyond this frail realm of all flesh. Bring the light of your wisdom to this time of testing and pain as we pray for Vartan Gothii and for those who loved him.'

The priest closed his book and bowed his head. The hillside was silent, even the black horses and the torches seeming to understand that it would be unseemly to intrude on a king's mourning.

A slow clapping came from the far side of the hill, and a figure armoured in gleaming silver and gold emerged from behind one of the great menhirs. A mantle of white silk spilled from his shoulders, contrasting sharply with the soft caramel colour of his skin and the oiled darkness of his lustrous hair.

'Very poetic,' said the warrior, his accent soft, rounded and obviously cultured, though it was of no tribe Markus had ever encountered. 'You mortals do so enjoy indulging in the luxury of woe.'

'Begone,' declared the priest of Morr, brandishing his prayer book like a weapon. 'This is a sacred moment you are defiling.'

The warrior snatched the book from the priest and hurled it into the darkness. 'This? Utter nonsense! Don't believe a word of it, but what can you expect from a man who has not passed over to see the other side for himself?'

THE BLOODSPEARS LIFTED their weapons and the swordsmen tensed as the warrior walked slowly towards the mourners at the centre of the Morrdunn. His movements were unhurried and casual, yet Markus's expert eye caught the telltale signs of a man perfectly in balance with his body. This man was a killer, no doubt about that. He seemed utterly unafraid, which marked him either as a madman or a man who knew something Markus did not.

'Who are you?' he said, struggling to keep his voice calm. 'I am burying my son, and you are being disrespectful. That can get a man killed in these lands.'

'So can being in the wrong place at the wrong time,' said the warrior. 'But in answer to your question, I am Khaled al-Muntasir, though I am sure that will mean nothing to you.'

'You're right, it doesn't,' said Markus. 'Now begone before I have you slain.'

Khaled al-Muntasir laughed, a rich sound full of dark amusement. He smiled and swept back his cloak to reveal a slender-bladed scabbard of pale wood inlaid with mother-of-pearl and jade. The warrior placed his hand on the sword and drummed his fingers on the pommel of jet.

'If you are looking for a fight, then you are a fool,' said Markus.

'I am many things, Count Markus: a man of culture, an artist, a writer of sorts and a dilettante in all things mystical. I have some knowledge of the celestial mechanics wheeling above us and am a passable tailor, weaponsmith and crafter of fine jewellery and ornaments. But one thing I am not, is a fool.'

'Let me gut him, my lord,' hissed Wenian, drawing his sword with a hiss of metal on leather.

Markus hesitated, knowing full well how skilful Wenian was, but fearing that any duel fought here would be an unequal match.

'Yes, let him,' said Khaled al-Muntasir, drawing his own weapon. The blade reflected Mannslieb's glow such that it shone like a sliver of moonlight itself. 'I have been cooped up too long in Athel Tamera, and it will be good to wet my blade in mortal flesh again.'

'You talk big, fancy man, but you'll bleed just the same,' said Wenian, spinning his sword to loosen his shoulders.

'Actually, I think you'll find that–'

Wenian didn't give him a chance to finish, launching himself at the finery-clad warrior. Khaled al-Muntasir's blade swept up in a blur of white gold, flickering like sunlight on ice. Wenian's charge carried him past the warrior, but before he turned, he sank to his knees and toppled to the side. His head fell from his shoulders, rolling to a halt before one of the great menhirs.

Markus was horrified. Wenian was one of the greatest swordsmen he knew, more skilful than any *Droyaska* of the Ostagoths, and twice as fast as any Cherusen Wildman. Yet this effete warrior had beheaded him without so much as batting an eyelid.

Khaled al-Muntasir knelt beside Wenian's corpse and wiped his sword blade clean of blood. He looked up at Markus with a predatory gleam in his eyes. They were dark and liquid, like the oil that burned in sunken pools deep in the reeking canyons of the Grey Mountains, and he found it hard to look away. Markus had seen that kind of look before, in the eyes of a wolf with its prey firmly locked in its grip.

'What are you?' he said.

Khaled al-Muntasir stood and smiled. 'I am your worst nightmare. Or at least one of them.'

'Kill him,' ordered Markus, and the Bloodspears moved to surround this lone warrior. No one, no matter how skilful could survive against such numbers. Fifty spearmen advanced towards the warrior, the iron blades of their weapons aimed at the swordsman's heart.

'Really?' said Khaled al-Muntasir, as though disappointed. 'You are a king, are you not? This is the best you can do? I'm insulted you think I would fight like some common brawler. Luckily, Krell here excels at this sort of fight.'

A terrifying roar swept over the summit of Morrdunn, the echoes bouncing from the menhirs and filling every heart that heard it with the naked fear common to all prey creatures. Something moved in the shadows and a hulking red shape flew through the air to land with a crash of metal and stone in the centre of the ring of spearmen.

It was a warrior, but a warrior unlike any other.

A full head and shoulders above his tallest rival, Krell was clad in brazen plates of ancient iron so stained with blood that their original colour was impossible to gauge. A great skull rune was stamped or branded into his chest, and Markus's courage deserted him at the sight of it. Great horns of bone extended from the monstrous warrior's helm and Markus saw Krell's face was a skeletal horror of yellowed bone and leathery flesh. A hideous emerald glow burned in his empty eye sockets, and any warrior brave enough to meet his gaze saw the manner of his death there.

A vast axe with a blade of utter darkness swung out and a dozen men died, their bodies hurled through the air like corn stalks at threshing time. The red-armoured warrior bludgeoned its way through the Bloodspears, hacking them down with insane ferocity and without mercy. Khaled al-Muntasir watched the slaughter impassively, as though bored by such violence.

In seconds, every warrior of the Bloodspears was dead, chopped into ragged hunks of gory meat. It was impossible to tell one warrior's remains from another, such was the scale of butchery. Markus ran to his wife and daughter, gathering them to him and shielding them from the whirlwind of destruction that killed his warriors.

The sword bands fared no better; cut down in a frenzy of bloodletting that left Markus horrified and disbelieving. The summit of the Morrdunn was soaked in blood, the ground sodden with the vital fluid of a hundred men, slain in less time that it would take to count them. The slaughterman returned to Khaled al-Muntasir's side, a constant stream of blood pouring from the black blade of his axe.

Only now did the swordsman look interested in the slaughter. A thin network of veins pulsed beneath the skin of his temples, his jaw clenched and his nostrils flared at the bitter reek of blood on the air.

'Ulric preserve us,' whispered Markus, backing away from the two warriors.

'The wolf god?' smiled Khaled al-Muntasir. 'He won't hear you. And if he does, he won't care. Isn't that what his priests teach, that his followers should be self-reliant?'

'You are daemons,' said Markus, drawing his sword and standing before his family. 'Fight me if you must, but let my wife and daughter live. They are innocents and do not deserve this.'

'Innocent?' hissed Khaled al-Muntasir, as though enjoying the taste of the word. 'There is no such thing in this world. Just by being born mankind corrupts this world. Every step a mortal takes, he destroys a little piece of it. No, do not think to appeal to me with thoughts of compassion. I forgot that emotion before your tribe even crossed the eastern mountains.'

'What are you?' demanded Markus.

Khaled al-Muntasir stepped closer, and Markus saw that the pale hue of his complexion had nothing to do with the moonlight. Khaled al-Muntasir smiled, revealing two elongated fangs descending from his upper jaw.

'You are a blood drinker!' hissed Markus. 'A creature of the dead.'

'I cannot deny the truth,' said Khaled al-Muntasir. 'And your daughter's terror is such a tantalising sweetmeat that I think I shall leave her until last. As much as it would give me great pleasure to make you watch them die, I will savour her terror all the more as she watches her parents bled dry before her young eyes.'

'Why are you doing this?' said Markus, fighting to control his terror of this beast of the night. His blood was sluggish in his veins, and it was all he could do to keep hold of his sword.

'It is not I,' said Khaled al-Muntasir. 'I am but a humble servant in this drama.'

A vast shadow moved in the darkness behind the warrior, a slice of the deepest, darkest night given form and motion. As Krell towered over Khaled al-Muntasir, so too did this giant figure loom over them all. It stepped into the flickering circle of light cast by the fallen torches, yet no hint of illumination touched its blackened form.

A mighty figure cloaked in night and armour from the darkest forges of the damned, its eyes burned with the same green light as shimmered in Krell's vacant skull. One arm clutched a forked staff in the form of an elongated snake while the other had a sickly metallic sheen to it, like iron with a rainbow scum of oil slithering across its surface.

Grotesque and twisted with vile animation, the grim visage was that of death itself, a horror cast from the nightmares of men and women since the dawn of time. Markus's wife fainted dead away with horror, and he felt his own fragile grip on sanity slipping in the face of such irrevocable knowledge of his own death. His sword fell to the ground and tears spilled from his eyes as he turned his daughter's face away from the monster.

She sobbed uncontrollably, and Markus knew it would be a mercy to cut her throat rather than have her face what was to come. Until this moment, Markus had not feared death, knowing his courage in battle would surely earn him a place in Ulric's Hall. One look into the lambent pits of this horror's eyes told him there would be no journey to the next life to hunt in the forests of eternal winter. Even the horror of the grave, with cold earth embracing his rotting flesh and the worms growing fat on his meat was to be denied him. Compared to the fate this creature was soon to visit upon them, such an end would be a mercy.

Markus dropped to his knees before this dreadful apparition as it closed on him.

'It is fitting that you give homage to the new lord of these lands,' said Khaled al-Muntasir.

Markus fumbled for his dagger, thinking to end his and his family's life, but before his hand even closed on the hilt, the blood drinker was at his side and holding him in an unbreakable grip, the cold flesh of his face inches from his own.

'No, not yet,' whispered Khaled al-Muntasir. 'Not when there are such sights left to see.'

Darkness boiled from the towering black warrior's form, filling the sky with unnatural gloom, blotting out the moon and filling the sky with evil clouds and the screeching of bats. Wolves howled in the darkness, blood-hungry beasts of the deep forest, not the noble creatures of the northern woods that carried the chill winds of Ulric in their veins. The darkness closed on Hyrstdunn, obscuring it from view, but Markus heard the screams and knew his city was doomed.

'I want you to say his name,' said Khaled al-Muntasir.

'I don't know it,' said Markus, wishing that were true.

'Come now,' chided Khaled al-Muntasir, digging a manicured nail into his throat. 'It lives in mortal minds as a nightmare of distant lands and forgotten days. It is a name of death that travels with fearful taletellers and poisons the lips of scared men huddled around fires in the foolish belief that they are safe from his reach. Say it, mortal. Say it now.'

'No,' wept Markus. 'I cannot.'

'Of course you can, it's just wind noises passing through your throat.'

'He is... he is...'

'That's it, go on,' urged the blood drinker.

'He is *Nagash,*' said Markus, spitting the name like a curse.

As though giving voice to the name of the dread necromancer from the ancient horror tales gave it power, the mighty form slammed its vile metal hand into the earth of the Morrdunn. A booming peal of thunder split the heavens and the green light in Nagash's eyes blazed with incredible power, flowing through his withered, monstrous body to pour into the earth of the Empire like a corruption.

Flickering green light danced over Markus's son's body, like wisps of corpse light in the swamps. Though he was cold and dead, Vartan sat up with stiff movements, as some dread force other than his own wasted muscles empowered him. Markus wept at this violation of his son's flesh, hating these beings of darkness more than he had hated anything in his life.

Vartan turned his dead gaze upon Markus, the cold empty green light flickering in his sunken, shrivelled eyes. Cold horror crept over Markus as his son stood on limbs he himself had washed and oiled the night before, the metal links of Vartan's armour clinking together as he took his place at the blood drinker's side.

The ground of the hill trembled and a deep groaning from its heart rumbled far beneath Markus's feet. The grass rippled, as though an army of snakes writhed beneath its surface, and a hand punched up through the earth. Dried flesh clung to the bones and fragments of rusted armour emerged as the dead warrior clawed its way from beneath the hill.

More and more followed it, hundreds of Menogoth dead torn from their eternal rest by the dark sorcery of the ancient necromancer. The hill shook as the honoured slain broke open their mausolea, tombs and barrows and marched to the summit of the Morrdunn.

Markus felt his anger crowd out his fear, but Khaled al-Muntasir's grip was unbreakable.

'Know that your Emperor's realm is doomed,' said the blood drinker. 'Know that all you love will die and rise again to serve this army of darkness. Know this and despair!'

Khaled al-Muntasir's fangs sank into his neck and Markus felt his life being sucked from his flesh. Yet as he slipped down into the black abyss of death, his thoughts were that once again the Menogoths had failed their Emperor.

FIVE

Homecomings

ANOTHER ARROW THUDDED home in the straw man hung from the pole, spinning him around with a foot of Asoborn wood protruding from his chest. Wolfgart watched as the black and gold chariot rumbled a weaving course through a long line of stakes hammered in the dry ground. Maedbh guided the two horses pulling the chariot with an expert hand, while his daughter loosed carefully aimed arrows from the fighting platform behind her.

'Only a youngster and already she can handle a bow better than I,' he said.

The chariot turned at the end of the strip of land and came back towards him. Maedbh gave her daughter a hug and Ulrike waved her bow for him to see. He waved back, but inwardly he hated the sight of his little girl with a weapon. Too small to practise with spears, Maedbh had not wasted the year he had been in the north with Sigmar, and Ulrike had transformed from a small girl into a budding young woman.

Maedbh hauled back on the reins and the chariot came to a halt next to the piled logs on which he sat. Situated on the outskirts of Three Hills, this wide strip of land had been used by Asoborn youths to hone their skills with bow and spear and chariot for decades. A huge square of hard-packed earth and stone, the wheels of countless chariots and the hooves of unnumbered cavalry mounts had long since beaten any fertility from the soil.

At the field's northern end, a group of Asoborns marched back and forth, getting used to the notion of fighting and manoeuvring in ranked-up blocks of sword bands. It wasn't the usual way Asoborns fought, but after Black Fire had proved its worth, Sigmar had pressed every tribe to master such organised warfare.

Men and women marched together, and Wolfgart smiled. Some of the tribes of the Empire thought the Asoborn armies comprised of only women, but such an idea was ridiculous. Any tribe that sent only its women to war would soon be extinct without mothers to birth the next generation of warriors and farmers.

'Did you see, father?' cried Ulrike as Maedbh brought the chariot to a halt beside him. 'I didn't miss a single one! Even Daegal can't manage that!'

'Aye, dear heart, I saw,' he said, wondering who Daegal was. 'No greenskins will get by you with that bow of yours.'

'I know,' she said, miming the act of pulling the bowstring back. 'I'll kill them all. Swoosh, swoosh, swoosh!'

'Our daughter's a natural,' said Maedbh, stepping lightly from the chariot and lifting Ulrike down. The little girl ran over to Wolfgart and leapt into his arms, curling her own wiry limbs around his neck. She kissed his cheeks and he hugged her back, the most precious thing in the world to him.

'Easy there, Ulrike,' he said. 'You'll squeeze the life out of me like that.'

'Sorry,' she giggled. 'I don't think I could do that. You're too strong.'

'Aye, maybe you're right,' he said, squeezing her until she squealed at him to stop.

She rested her head on his shoulder, and Wolfgart hated that he had been away for so long. He had missed so much of her childhood with war calling him from one corner of the Empire to the other. Too often, Wolfgart felt like he was being pulled in different directions. Maedbh had eventually tired of living in Reikdorf and after months of sullen silences and furious rows, she had declared that she and Ulrike were moving back to the Asoborn settlement of Three Hills.

Wolfgart had remained in Reikdorf as one of Sigmar's Shieldbearers, but had travelled often between Unberogen and Asoborn lands. The times between each visit grew longer as he and Maedbh would often end up arguing, and if not for Ulrike, Wolfgart wondered whether he would come at all.

'When are you going back?' asked Ulrike, and Wolfgart hated that this was always one of the first questions she asked when she saw him.

'Ach, don't let's talk about that just yet, lass,' he said, prising her from his shoulder and setting her onto the ground. 'Gather your shafts and show me again how good you've gotten with that bow.'

Ulrike nodded enthusiastically and ran off towards the gently swaying straw men to pluck the arrows from their abused forms. Wolfgart straightened and sighed as he saw the fiery look in his wife's eyes.

'Well?' said Maedbh.

'Well what?' he said, though he knew fine well what she was asking.

'You didn't answer your daughter,' said Maedbh. 'When are you going back to Reikdorf?'

'Can't wait to get rid of me, is that it?'

Maedbh stared at him coldly, and even in such an ill-temper, she was still beautiful. Her fiery red hair was bound in two long scalp locks that fell to her waist and her figure was gloriously curved and full. Desire swelled in him, but one look at her icy eyes quelled it.

'You always have to start a fight, don't you?'

'That's rich coming from an Asoborn,' he said, though he knew it would only inflame the situation. 'As I recall, you're the ones who prefer to hit first.'

Maedbh sighed, and Wolfgart wanted to reach for her, to hold her close to him and tell her that he loved her, that he knew she still loved him and that this fighting was stupid. But his pride wouldn't let him. She was a hellion in war and in the bedchamber, but her viper's tongue drove him to words he knew were foolish.

'I do not want to fight, Wolfgart, but I need to know you will be here for Ulrike. She misses her father. She *needs* her father. *I* need him.'

'I'll stay as long as I can,' he said. 'There's trouble in the south, and we're hearing rumours that the forest brigands have banded together in the northern marches. They'll need rooting out before they become too strong. Not to mention the greenskins coming down from the mountains and the beast raids along the Taalbec.'

Maedbh moved away from him and rubbed the horses' necks, loosening the bits at their mouths now that they were at rest. He saw the disappointment in her posture and rose from his seat on the logs.

'Look, what do you want me to say? I'm oath-sworn to Sigmar, I can't just leave him.'

'He is an Emperor,' snapped Maedbh. 'You think you are his

only warrior, that the Empire will fall if you are not at his side?'

'It almost did once before,' he said. 'There was that business with the crown I told you about.'

'I know,' she said. 'I know you are his oldest and dearest friend, but you also swore an oath to me, remember?'

'I remember,' he said, taking her hand. 'It was one of the happiest days of my life.'

She pulled away, watching as Ulrike plucked the last of her arrows from the straw men.

'She will make a fine warrior,' said Maedbh. 'A proud Asoborn warrior woman.'

Anger touched Wolfgart and he said, 'Does she have to be?'

'What do you mean?'

'A warrior. She's my little girl; she shouldn't be using any weapons at all. It wasn't so long ago she chided me for wanting to go to war. She said it was stupid, and she wasn't wrong, but here you are pushing her into the battle lines.'

'As every Asoborn child is,' pointed out Maedbh. 'Or is there some reason you think she shouldn't learn to defend herself?'

'She's a girl,' protested Wolfgart. No sooner were the words out of his mouth than he knew he'd made a terrible mistake.

'She's a girl,' repeated Maedbh. 'Like me, you mean? Unberogen women may not fight, but you are in Asoborn lands now, Wolfgart. And if you don't like it go back to Reikdorf and stay in your draughty house without us.'

'Aye, well for all the warmth you bring to it, I might just do that.'

Maedbh's face turned to granite and she looked away as Ulrike returned with her quiver restocked. Wolfgart wanted to take his harsh, thoughtless words back, but it was too late.

'Come on,' said Maedbh, lifting Ulrike back onto the chariot. 'Let's try again, and this time I'll make it more difficult for you.'

As the chariot pulled away, Ulrike waved to him and shouted, 'Watch me! Watch me hit them all again!'

Wolfgart waved back, though a leaden weight settled in his belly.

ELSWYTH KNELT BY the dwarf's pallet bed, cleaning the wound at his shoulder, tutting at Cuthwin's crude application of herbal poultices. Inflamed joints had forced Cradoc to hang up his healer's satchel, but his apprentice had proved to be no less capable, though her manner was just as abrasive as the old man's.

'Did he tell you his name?' Sigmar asked Cuthwin, looking at the dwarf's pallid features.

Sigmar had seen his share of battlefield injuries and though he'd seen many a man and dwarf recover from such a wound, few of them had travelled for six days through the wilderness before being properly treated.

'Yes, my lord,' answered Cuthwin. 'Grindan Deeplock. Said he was from Zhufbar.'

'And an engineer by the looks of it,' added Elswyth, lifting the dwarf's hand. Scarred and callused, the tips were dark with powder burns and the nails were caked with the residue of oils and coal dust.

'He said he was an engineer, aye,' nodded Cuthwin. 'Said he worked for the Guildmasters of Varn Drazh. Didn't say what that was though.'

'It's a vast lake, high in the mountains,' said Sigmar. 'Alaric told me of it long ago. Supposedly a comet fell from the sky and blasted a huge crater in the mountains. Alaric said there's lots of dwarf settlements nearby, because the rock around the lake is rich with iron and precious metals.'

'Really, Cuthwin, were you *trying* to help this dwarf to die?' cut in Elswyth. 'This wound is so dirty and infected that I don't know if anything I can do will halt it. You might as well have packed the dressing with nightshade.'

Cuthwin shrank from the healer's sharp words, and Sigmar hid a smile. Though many considered Elswyth a fine looking woman, few dared attempt to court her, for her tongue was well known amongst Unberogen men, though for all the wrong reasons.

'We were on the run from greenskins,' protested Cuthwin.

'They were only goblins,' pointed out Elswyth.

Cuthwin's face darkened. 'I didn't have time to redress his wound. It looked fine.'

'Did you check? Or did you just drag him here through all the muddy, stagnant pools of water you could find?'

Cuthwin looked set to lose his temper. Sigmar smiled and put himself between the scout and the healer before violence ensued.

'He got him here alive is what matters,' said Sigmar. 'Now it's your job to keep him that way. Can you do that?'

'I won't promise anything, not even to you, Sigmar,' said Elsywth. 'I'll keep his wound clean and change the dressing hourly. If he recovers consciousness, I'll have him drink a berberry tisane with some sweet balm. That's all I can do, and it probably won't be enough, so you'd best get Alessa at the temple of Shallya to say some prayers for him.'

'You talk about me like I'm dead already,' croaked the dwarf and they all jumped.

Sigmar joined Elswyth at Grindan's bedside. He placed a hand lightly on the dwarf's chest. The effort of talking was taking its toll on the dwarf and runnels of sweat poured down the age lines carved in his face.

'Where am I?' asked Grindan.

'You're in Reikdorf,' said Elswyth. 'Under the protection of Sigmar Heldenhammer.'

'Ah,' said the dwarf. 'So the young lad got me here then...'

'Aye, that he did,' said Sigmar. 'He's a canny one is Cuthwin.'

'I'm in your debt, youngling,' wheezed the dwarf, his eyes screwed up in pain.

'Think nothing of it,' said Cuthwin.

'Don't be a damn fool, youngling,' snapped Grindan. 'You think the life debt of a dwarf is given lightly? Bear the tale of my doom to the Deeplock clan and you and all your line will become Umgilok to them.'

'I'll do that,' promised Cuthwin.

'It means a man worthy of praise,' said Sigmar, seeing the scout's look of confusion.

'You know your Khazalid, young Heldenhammer.'

'Master Alaric has taught me a tiny bit,' said Sigmar. The dwarf's chest rasped like a punctured forge-bellow with every word. He looked up at Elswyth, who shook her head.

'Ah, the Mad,' grunted Grindan. 'He toils night and day for you, manling. Another year and he'll have a second sword for your kings. Foolish to rush these things, I say, but it'll outlast any man it's given to so I suppose it doesn't matter.'

The dwarf's chest hiked and his eyes widened as a memory returned to him and he gripped Sigmar's shoulder urgently. He looked past the Emperor to Cuthwin and fixed him with a desperate gaze.

'Youngling! Did they get it? The grobi, did they find it?' demanded Grindan.

'Get what?' said Cuthwin. 'I don't know what you mean.'

'The Barag... the Thunder Bringer...' wheezed Grindan. 'We... we were bringing it home. Prince Uldrakk of Zhufbar... loaned it to the third son of... of Mordhaz, lord of the Grey Mountain clans, three hundred and seventy-five years ago. We'd gone there to get it back, but the grobi ambushed us... too much beer and not enough caution...'

Red flecks sprayed from the dwarf's mouth as he spoke and his words were forced out though the effort was killing him.

'Hush now,' said Elswyth. 'Don't talk any more. That's an order.'

But Grindan paid her no mind and squeezed Sigmar's shoulder even harder.

'Promise me!' he hissed. 'Go back... find it. We buried it deep, so the grobi wouldn't... wouldn't think to look... the Barag...'

'What's he talking about?' said Cuthwin.

'I don't know,' said Sigmar, taking the dwarf's hand and holding tightly.

'Promise me!' demanded Grindan. 'You must or the Deeplock clan will be disgraced! Heldenhammer, you are oath-bound to my kin... do this thing for a dying son of Grungni and I will meet my ancestors with pride.'

'Aye,' nodded Sigmar. 'I am a sworn brother to King Kurgan, and I give you my oath that I will find the... Barag.'

Grindan nodded and laid his head back on the bed, satisfied with Sigmar's words. His chest rose and fell in jerky spasms.

'The Halls of Grungni,' sighed Grindan, looking off into realms beyond the sight of mortals. 'How grand they are...'

Grindan Deeplock's last breath rattled from his throat, and his ore- and fire-blackened hand slid from Sigmar's grip.

'Go with honour to your rest, friend Grindan,' said Sigmar.

WOLFGART SADDLED HIS horse, a fine grain-fed stallion from his herds around the Barren Hills. The horse's coat was dappled dun and chestnut, with a long russet mane. The finest beast in his herds, he'd called him Dregor in honour of Sigmar's grandfather, a gesture his friend had appreciated immensely.

He adjusted the blanket beneath the saddle and tightened the girth under Dregor's belly, lowering the Taleuten-style stirrups to his preferred riding style. Wolfgart was a natural horseman and liked to ride low in the saddle, leaning over his horse's neck as he fought. He slung his panniers over its rump, the packs laden with enough food and spare clothing to see him to Reikdorf. He had a bowstave and string in case he needed to hunt, but hoped he wouldn't have to, as his eye wasn't as sure as it had been in his youth.

He patted Dregor's flank. 'At least you don't talk back to me, eh lad?'

The horse stared at him with a curious look in its eyes, unused to being taken from its stables at so early an hour. Wolfgart wanted to be gone before Maedbh roused Ulrike from sleep. He didn't think he'd be able to leave if she was awake. Wolfgart took a deep breath, resting his forehead on the warm, oiled leather of the saddle.

He didn't want to leave, but nor could he stay with such a poisonous atmosphere between him and his wife. Ulrike was already picking up on it, and the last thing he wanted was for her to see her parents at each other's throats. No child needed to see that.

Dregor was stabled with the royal horses of the Asoborns, and they were powerful beasts: strong and wide shouldered. Bred to pull war chariots, they had stamina and strength, but little in the way of real speed. Even the least of Wolfgart's herd could outpace an Asoborn mount in a straight sprint. But harness one of his mounts to a chariot and it would baulk at such harsh treatment.

Two hundred horses were stabled here: an underground collection of stalls, haylofts and exercise yards where Asoborn horse breakers trained the beasts for a life of war. He'd watched them at work, and while the effectiveness of their methods was without doubt, Wolfgart preferred to establish a bond with his beasts instead of bending them to his will.

The air was close and reeked of animals and dung, but it was an earthy fragrance that reminded Wolfgart of home. Even at this early hour, grooms and stable boys and girls were busy attending to the tribe's stock. Animals were being led over the cobbled floor toward the curved tunnels that led towards the surface and bales of hay were dropped down chutes cut through the earth of the hill.

Wolfgart checked Dregor's bit wasn't too tight and made a circuit of the animal, ensuring all was well before mounting. He gripped the saddle horn and hauled himself onto Dregor's back, relishing the sensation of owning so fine a beast.

He touched his spurs to the horse's sides and walked him slowly towards the sloping tunnel that led back to the surface. A group of men and women marched down the tunnel into the stables, hard Asoborn warriors armed with lances and swords. Clad in iron breastplates chased with silver and black, and golden-winged helms, these were the Queen's Eagles, the elite guardians of the Asoborn royalty.

Wolfgart's mood darkened further as he saw who they escorted – a pair of young men, both thirteen summers old and fair haired. One had pale blue eyes, while the other's were deep green. Wide shouldered and tall, they were already men, having ridden out on their first blooding three years ago.

Sigulf and Fridleifr, the sons of Queen Freya.

Wolfgart pulled Dregor to the side as they marched past, and he kept his head down, not wishing to look upon these boys a moment longer than necessary. Few outsiders had seen the queen's sons, for they rarely ventured beyond Asoborn lands, and were constantly attended by the Eagles. Wolfgart had first laid eyes upon them at a feast held beneath the Queen's Hill to honour their first kills after riding out to battle at the age of ten.

No sooner had he seen the two boys beside their flame-haired mother than he was catapulted back to the days of his youth and a shocked paralysis had seized his limbs. The breath froze in his lungs and he felt a gabble of words ready to spill from his throat.

Maedbh had clutched him and dug her nails into the muscle of his arm.

'Say nothing,' she warned him.

'But Ulric's balls, they're–'

'I know,' she hissed urgently. 'I warn you, say nothing. The queen has demanded it.'

Wolfgart had turned to her in surprise. 'You knew?'

'All the Asoborns know.'

Wolfgart looked back at the two lads, both laughing and drinking beer as their proud mother smeared Asoborn warpaint on their cheeks. Freya was a fearsome-looking woman, all curves and flame, a hellion in form-fitting armour and shimmering mail that left nothing to the imagination. The years since Wolfgart had first met her appeared to have left no mark upon her; the queen's flesh still war-sculpted and firm, her hair still long and fiery, her breasts still high and full.

Wolfgart tore his gaze from Freya's intoxicating beauty and looked back at her sons.

'By Ulric and Taal, they're his image…'

'That they are,' agreed Maedbh, 'but you're to say nothing. Do you understand me, Wolfgart?'

'By all the gods, he has sons!' said Wolfgart. 'The man has a right to know.'

'Maybe in Unberogen lands, but Asoborn queens take many lovers during their reign, and precedent comes from the maternal lineage, not the line of the father. Give me your word that you'll say nothing. Do it now or I'll send you from Three Hills right now.'

'What? That's no kind of bargain.'

'It's not a bargain,' Maedbh had warned him.

Left with no choice, Wolfgart had acceded to his wife's demand and sworn the oath she demanded. He'd spent the rest of the night trying not to stare at the two boys, struggling to contain a strange mixture of joy and sadness at the thought of all they could represent and what they would mean to their unaware father.

The Queen's Eagles and the royal twins passed him, heading towards where their own mounts were stabled. Wolfgart didn't watch them go, but rode up and out of the hill, emerging onto the hard-packed ground in the midst of Three Hills.

Torches were lit at the settlement's perimeter and a low morning mist still clung to the ground. The grass glittered with dew and the stars were visible in the purple sky. Where Reikdorf was a city that represented the Empire's progress, with its stone walls, ornate buildings, many schools, and great library, Three Hills was a pastoral settlement, without walls or defensible location. Its security came from its fusion with the landscape, such that any enemy would find it next to impossible to locate it, so cunningly were its dwellings crafted in the earth.

Archers watched the approaches from miles beyond its furthest extent and chariots roamed the wild lands to the east. Three Hills might look undefended, but the truth was altogether different. An enemy coming against the Asoborns would be harried by chariots and archers for many miles before they even came within sight of Three Hills.

It was a wild place, a savage realm of a people equally fierce and lusty. Wolfgart would be sorry to leave, but he hoped he would come back one day soon. Perhaps time and distance would allow old wounds to heal, harsh words to fade and absence to fill cold hearts with love once again.

Wolfgart turned Dregor towards the Reikdorf Road.

'Come on, lad,' he said. 'Let's go home.'

SIGMAR GATHERED HIS knights in the longhouse, twenty men of hardy Unberogen stock and proven courage. The fires burned brightly, filling the hall with warmth, for the night beyond its walls was chill, and oppressive clouds hid the moon. Eoforth studied an unrolled map with Cuthwin, listening attentively to the scout's tale of his rescue of Grindan Deeplock.

He sat on the edge of a long trestle table, judging how long it would take them to reach where the dwarf wagons had been ambushed.

'I reckon four days to get there and back,' said Alfgeir.

'Assuming no trouble,' replied Sigmar. 'That part of the forest's not travelled much. The beasts and greenskins have grown bold in the south.'

'They'd have to be bolder than I've known them to attack twenty knights, plus you and me.'

'They attacked a convoy of dwarfs,' pointed out Sigmar.

'I suppose,' said Alfgeir with a shrug. 'These are my best, and can handle any trouble that comes our way.'

Sigmar nodded, shivering despite the heat of the nearby fire. He pulled his bearskin cloak tighter about him. Eoforth stood straight, rubbing the small of his back with one hand and pinching the bridge of his nose with the other.

'Well, High Scholar?' asked Sigmar. 'What do you have for us?'

Eoforth scowled at Alfgeir and said, 'I think I have a good idea of where young Cuthwin came upon the goblin raiders, on the old mountain road about two miles north of the Thaalheim mines.'

A murmur passed through the armoured knights, and it was Orvin who spoke up. Sigmar had fought alongside Orvin many times, and knew him as a warrior of great personal courage, quick temper and unpredictable moods.

'Dangerous country,' remarked the knight. 'The greenskins we routed were from around there. I'll wager they came from under the mountains via the mineworks.'

'More than likely, Orvin,' said Eoforth, and Sigmar caught the tension between the two men. He knew Orvin's son to be a source of frustration to Eoforth, and wondered how much of the father had passed to the son.

His thoughts were interrupted as he heard a sudden commotion from the main doors to the longhouse. His hand flashed to Ghalmaraz at his belt in anticipation of danger. His crown grew warm at his brow, a runic warning of fell sorcery and unnatural powers at work.

'To arms!' he shouted as the doors to the longhouse burst open and a swirling gale of icy wind blew inside. The fire was snuffed out in an instant, its fitful embers glowing dully with all the heat that remained to them. Frozen gusts of dead air flew around the longhouse like poisonous zephyrs, carrying with them the scent of death and far off lands that baked beneath an oppressive sun.

A lone figure stood silhouetted in the doorway, a tall warrior in silver and gold mounted upon a hellish black steed with rippling flanks and eyes of smouldering red. Stinking steam like marsh gases gusted from the beast's flared nostrils. The rider walked his nightmarish mount into the longhouse, its iron-shod hooves sparking from the flagstones like heavy hammer blows.

He dismounted with easy grace and folded his arms across a gleaming breastplate. His manner was confident to the point of arrogance and a white cloak flowed like snow from his shoulders. The knights drew their swords and roared in anger, moving to surround the elegant warrior, his long dark hair swept back over his ears and his swarthy complexion cut from a cruel mould. His eyes were black and without pupil, his mouth twisted in a malicious grin of spiteful mischief.

Alfgeir took a step towards the intruder, but Sigmar held him back.

'No,' said Sigmar. 'This man is death.'

'Your Emperor is a wise man,' said the warrior, his voice liquid and seductive. 'I have heard that about him. You should listen to him, for I would kill you before you could even swing that lump of pig iron in your hand.'

'You talk big for a man surrounded by twenty warriors,' said Alfgeir.

'Then that should tell you something about how good I am.'

Sigmar stepped towards the warrior, his hand tight on the grip of Ghal-maraz. Everything about this warrior sent pulses of anger and hate from the ancestral hammer of the dwarfs into his hand. The weapon longed to be unleashed, but Sigmar kept his urge to fight in check. He knew this man was no ordinary foe.

'I am Sigmar Heldenhammer, Emperor of these lands,' he said. 'By what right do you come before me into my longhouse?'

The warrior bowed elaborately. 'I am Khaled al-Muntasir, and I bring a message to you, Sigmar Heldenhammer.'

'A message from whom?'

'My master, the lord Nagash,' said Khaled al-Muntasir.

'You lie!' hissed Alfgeir, making the sign of the horns over his heart. 'There's no such being; he's just a story to frighten children. You can't scare us with old ghosts.'

'Can't I?' laughed Khaled al-Muntasir. 'I beg to differ.'

Sigmar had heard the tales of Nagash, there were few in the Empire who had not. No two stories were the same, lurid tales of walking corpses, fallen warriors stirring from their tombs and legions of the living dead marching to the howls of carrion wolves as darkness covered the land and the living cowered in terror.

But all the tales agreed on one thing. Nagash was the supreme lord of the undead, an evil king from an ancient land far to the south where a world-spanning empire had once risen from the desert sands. That empire had been destroyed in an age long forgotten, and only dusty tales and half-remembered legends survived from those times.

Sigmar knew from bitter experience that the dead could indeed rise from their graves. He and his warriors had destroyed a sorcerer of the undead many years ago, but if even half the tales of Nagash were true, then his power dwarfed that of the necromancer of Brass Keep.

'You are not welcome here, Khaled al-Muntasir,' said Sigmar. 'So deliver your message and begone.'

'No threats?' said Khaled al-Muntasir. 'No promises of a swift and brutal death?'

'I sense you are not a man cowed by threats.'

'True, but that doesn't stop the foolish from making them,' said Khaled al-Muntasir. He gave Sigmar an elaborate bow and threw his cloak back over his shoulder. The knights tensed, but made no move against the warrior, as a blade that shimmered with dark power was revealed at his side.

'You have something that does not belong to you,' said Khaled al-Muntasir. 'A crown forged by my master over a thousand years ago. You know this crown belongs to another, yet you keep it from its true lord. It will be returned to him.'

'I know this crown can never be allowed to fall into the hands of evil men.'

'I was not offering you a choice.'

'The crown remains where it is,' said Sigmar. 'If your master wishes to try and take it back, he will find all the armies of the Empire ranged against him.'

Khaled al-Muntasir smiled, a winning smile of pristine white teeth. Sigmar was not surprised to see two sharpened fangs at the corners of his mouth. His heart beat a little faster as he knew he faced a vampire, a creature of the night that fed on blood and murder.

Sigmar saw the monster's eyes widen a fraction and knew it could sense the increased flow of blood around his body. The hunger was upon this creature – he could no longer think of Khaled al-Muntasir as a man – and the danger of every one of them dying within the next few moments was very real indeed.

'You cannot stand against my master,' said Khaled al-Muntasir.

'Others have said similar things, yet the Empire endures.'

'Not against the legions of the dead it won't,' promised Khaled al-Muntasir. 'Your friend Markus, king of the Menogoths, is already dead. He and his family and his tribe have swollen the ranks of my master's army and more will follow.'

Sigmar sensed the furious shock of Khaled al-Muntasir's revelation sweep through his knights. They badly wanted this warrior dead.

'Hold!' cried Alfgeir, also seeing the angry urge to attack in the faces of his knights.

Sigmar's voice was colder than the Norscan ice as he met the blood drinker's gaze.

'Get out,' he said. 'And if you return you will be killed. This is the word of Sigmar.'

Khaled al-Muntasir turned and vaulted onto the back of his terrible steed. Its eyes flared brightly and it reared up onto its hind legs. He rode from the longhouse and Sigmar's knights ran after him with Alfgeir at their head.

No sooner was the vampire beyond the walls of the longhouse than a pair of wide black wings of impenetrable darkness unfolded from the steed's sides. The beast leapt into the air and its wings boomed with the sound of a mainsail catching a stormwind. It rose swiftly into the night sky, a bat-like slice of darkness against the black vault of the heavens.

Alfgeir watched it vanish over the hills and treetops, his face pale and fearful.

'Do you think he was lying?' he asked. 'About Markus, I mean.'

Sigmar shook his head. 'I fear not, my friend.'

'Damn,' whispered Alfgeir. 'The Menogoths gone...'

Sigmar turned and re-entered the longhouse, barking orders as he went.

'Bring every scribe and runner in Reikdorf here,' he said. 'I want word of this on its way to every one of the Empire's counts before sunrise. Eoforth, search every scroll in the library for tales of Nagash. Sift what facts you can from the legends. We're going to need to know what we're up against. Draft orders for sword musters to be gathered in every town and village from the Grey Mountains to the Sea of Claws. I want to be ready for these monsters when they come at us.'

Alfgeir nodded. 'I'll make it happen,' he said. 'I take it we'll not be heading south now?'

'I cannot, but you must lead these knights and Cuthwin to find what the dwarfs buried. Find it and bring it back here. I swore an oath and I mean to see it kept, even if I cannot do so myself.'

'I'll see it done, my Emperor,' promised Alfgeir.

'And Alfgeir?' said Sigmar. 'Be swift.'

'The crown is really that important to Nagash?' asked Alfgeir.

'You have no idea,' said Sigmar.

SIX
Dead Flesh

The madmen chanted and danced with wild abandon, like Cherusen Wildmen in the grip of a bane leaf frenzy. Redwane shifted uncomfortably in his saddle, trying to gauge the right moment to ride in and end this. He glanced at the rider next to him, a wide-chested warrior in red plate and thick mail with a sodden wolf pelt cloak draped over his shoulders.

Like every White Wolf, Leovulf didn't wear a helm, and his wild mane of black hair was plastered to his skull by the rain. Apparently to go bareheaded into battle was considered an act of bravery, openly displaying a warrior's contempt for the foe. Redwane wasn't so sure that going without a helm was a good idea, but since the White Wolves he'd recruited from Middenheim followed Leovulf's lead in all things, he couldn't very well go against it.

The man had carved himself a legend in the fighting that had raged through the streets of the northern city, and though he was lowborn, Count Myrsa had decreed that station was no barrier to entry into the ranks of the White Wolves. Courage was all that mattered.

'Madness,' said Leovulf, watching the madmen with bemused distaste. 'Why would anyone do such a thing?'

'I have no idea,' said Redwane, wincing as he watched a screaming man jam a long iron nail through the palm of his own hand. 'But Myrsa wants it stopped.'

'*Count* Myrsa,' said Leovulf.

'Of course,' replied Redwane. He'd known Myrsa for a long time, and still couldn't get used to the idea of calling him count, though he'd more than earned that title during the siege of Middenheim. 'Force of habit.'

He returned his gaze to the centre of the village, shaking his head at the sight before him.

Two hundred men dressed in rags filled the centre of Kruken, a gloomy, stockaded miners' settlement a day's ride to the west of Middenheim. Built upon ancient dwarf ruins, Kruken nestled in an undulant range of hills in the midst of the Drakwald Forest. It had found prosperity with the discovery of tin beneath the high ground, but that prosperity had quickly faded as it became clear the seams were nowhere near as deep and rich as had been thought.

Wailing and moaning, the madmen whipped their bare backs bloody with lengths of knotted rope bound with thorns and fish-hooks. Some cut into their chests with gutting knives, while others jammed splinters of sharpened wood beneath their fingernails.

Each man chanted meaningless doggerel interspersed with monotone dirges in an unknown tongue that sounded part gibberish, part incantation. A wooden log had been hammered into the ground near the centre of the square and a pile of kindling set at its base, though Redwane wasn't sure what they were planning to burn.

A drizzle of rain drained the life from the day, and only made the utilitarian nature of the soot-stained buildings, mine-workings and dormitories of Kruken all the more depressing. Perhaps a hundred people were gathered in the town square, watching the carnival of madness at its centre with varying degrees of dour amusement. Children threw stones at the chanting men, while yapping dogs snapped and bit at their bloody ankles.

In the days since the defeat of the Norsii horde, the people of the north had suffered great hardship; the forest beasts that had fled the destruction of Cormac Bloodaxe's horde had returned to hunting men as their prey, banditry had increased, harvests had gone uncollected and famine was widespread. In the aftermath of the fighting, outbreaks of pestilence in the settlements around the western foothills of the Middle Mountains stretched the resources of the land still further.

Life in the north was always hard, but this last year had been especially hard, so any diversion, no matter how absurd or bloody, was welcome.

No one had noticed these wandering bands of madmen at first, for the Empire was a land of strangeness, of the bizarre and dangerous. They had been tolerated as an aberration that would soon burn itself out, but as the year grew darker and life harder, it became obvious that, far from dying out, these roving bands of lunatics were growing in strength.

The largest of these bands was said to be led by a man named Torbrecan, a man who – depending on which fanciful tale you listened to – was either a warrior driven mad by a life of bloodshed or a priest of Ulric who'd spent too long alone in the winter woods. Torbrecan's host marched in bloody procession from the isolated towns and villages north of the mountains, curving in a southerly bow towards Middenheim. Pestilence marched alongside them, and thus Middenheim's warriors blocked the roads to the city. Something had to be done, and so Myrsa had despatched Redwane and the White Wolves to break up this band and take Torbrecan prisoner.

Redwane shook his head as he watched a man drag his dirt-encrusted fingernails down his face then drop to his knees and plunge his scarred features into the mud. Was he Torbrecan? Who could tell? Each man looked just as ferociously insane as the next.

Leovulf shook his head. 'We'll need to move if we want to stop this getting out of hand.'

'Aye,' said Redwane. 'But I want to make sure we don't start trouble going in too early.'

'Trouble's started already. We're just limiting it.'

Leovulf's gloomy assessment of the situation wasn't far off the mark. Like most northern tribesman, Leovulf had a grim world view, one born out of years of harsh winters and the constant struggle for survival in the inhospitable wilds of the northern marches. The people of the north were tough and hard as oak, but weren't noted for their lightness of spirit.

A tall figure in a mud-spattered robe that might once have been white, but which was now a grimy brown danced towards the centre of the square. His shoulders were stained red, and he carried a metal-studded switch that dripped blood. Matted and unkempt hair hung lank and limp to his shoulders and his beard was tied in a number of braids like tangled tree roots. Each burned with a small coal that sent acrid fumes into his nostrils.

'You think that's Torbrecan?' asked Leovulf.

'Must be,' agreed Redwane. 'He looks mad enough.'

The man walked a ragged circle around the square, his eyes wild and staring, his mouth open in a silent scream. He beat himself over the shoulders with his switch and laughed hysterically with each blow. His followers gouged and tore at themselves with each crack of his switch.

'People of Kruken!' howled Torbrecan. 'Listen well to me, for I speak of your doom! It is the doom of us all, for the gods have turned their faces from this world! Who among you has not seen the signs of the End Times? Who among you has not seen heralds that portend our extinction from this world? Plague destroys your towns, beasts hunt your children and ungodly men seek to take what is not theirs with blade and bow! We are doomed, and it is no one's fault but our own. We turned from our proper devotions and led the gods to abandon us. The terror that stalks the land is one of our own making, for we are a godless people, condemned to die unless we can wash away our sins in blood and pain.'

The crowd jeered him, but not as many as Redwane expected. Some looked like they were seriously entertaining this insanity, and some were even nodding their heads like he was making some kind of sense.

'The gods are far from us,' went on Torbrecan, jabbing a scabbed fist at the sky, 'and they grow farther with every passing day. Only through the ecstasy of pain shall we draw their attention to us. Only by the exquisite wails of our suffering shall we turn their gaze back upon us.'

Redwane shook his head, unable to believe that folk weren't simply laughing this man out of their village. Surely life was hard enough without people like this wanting to make it worse?

'This has gone far enough,' said Redwane, jabbing his spurs into his mount's flanks.

'Aye,' agreed Leovulf. 'Bloody lunatic needs to be shut up for good.'

Redwane shook his head. 'No killing. Myrsa, *Count* Myrsa, was very specific about that.'

Leovulf nodded and passed the word through the ranks. The White Wolves shucked their pelt cloaks from their right shoulders to clear their hammer arms. Ustern unfurled the banner, a glorious piece of red linen with a wolf picked out in silver thread, and Holstef blew two rising notes on his clarion.

Redwane led his riders into the village, the crowds parting as their heavy horses plodded through the mud towards the centre of the square. Torbrecan saw them coming and aimed his switch at them. For a second, Redwane wondered if he was going to charge him, but instead he threw his hands up as if in praise.

'The very warriors who serve the doombringers come to silence my words! They fear the truth and the knowledge that they are blind fools serving a master who cannot see the forces ranged against him. They have not the strength to suffer as we suffer, to bleed as we bleed. Brothers, show them the strength of true belief! Show everyone!'

A dozen men ran from the mob of ragged lunatics towards the stake hammered into the earth. They fought to climb the stacked kindling, biting and punching each other in their desperation to reach the upright log. Two fought harder than the others, and clutched the tall log as close as a lover. One carried a set of hooked chains and he wrapped these around their waists, binding them fast to the wood. Those denied the chance to reach the log took up lit torches and Redwane's jaw dropped open as he realised what they were going to do.

'Ulric's mercy, no!' he yelled, but it was too late. The torches were thrust into the kindling, which lit with a rushing *whoosh* of ignition. Redwane smelled the oil and not even the misting sheets of rain could dampen the flames as they leapt high. The two men clung to one another as the fire took hold of their robes and set them alight from head to foot. So swiftly did the flames leap to life that Redwane knew their bodies must have been doused in oil too.

The crowd pulled back in horror as the two men shrieked in agony. Their robes vanished and Redwane watched in revolted fascination as their flesh blackened and blistered in seconds. As though to aid this martyrdom, the rain ceased, and the air filled with the reek of burning meat and hair. The men screamed as they were consumed, fatty smoke pouring from their melting flesh.

Their fellows danced around the flames and the burning men sagged against the log, their lower limbs little more than blackened stumps of bone. The smoke would surely have killed them by now. At least Redwane hoped so.

He spurred his horse to greater speed and rode through the ragged mob of chanting madmen. They clawed at him with broken fingernails, screaming and howling without words or sense. They weren't attacking as such, more clamouring to be punished. Redwane obliged one man with a filth-encrusted face, slamming the haft of his hammer down and sending him sprawling to the mud. The man screamed as the horse rode over him, but Redwane didn't spare him a glance.

His horse barged through the crowd of raving lunatics, scattering them as he angled a course towards the ringleader. Keeping the reins loose in his hand, he steered his mount towards Torbrecan. The laughing madman's switch beat against his chest and a triumphant stare of vindication bored into Redwane's eyes.

'Deliver me unto the arms of the gods!' yelled Torbrecan, hurling himself to the ground in front of Redwane's mount. Redwane hauled back on the reins and his horse reared up, its front legs pawing the air. The gelding's hooves stamped down into the mud, inches from the madman's head. Redwane kicked his feet free of the stirrups and jumped down. He dragged the mud-covered man to his knees and slammed the butt of his hammer into his face.

Torbrecan's nose burst across his face, but he laughed as blood spilled into his mouth. Redwane hauled him to his feet as the screaming mob pressed in. Ustern's horse came alongside him and the weak sunlight caught the red of the banner like a flash of glorious crimson.

Redwane drew himself up to his full height and yelled, 'Enough! In Ulric's name, enough!'

His voice cut through the baying mob of lunatic screeching, and the blood-smeared men dropped to the ground, moaning and yelling in equal measure. Redwane realised they were waiting for the White Wolves to ride them down, to crush their skulls with hammers or trample them beneath the hooves of their mounts.

'Hold!' he yelled. 'White Wolves hold!'

His warriors pulled up, circling their horses around the madmen and corralling them away from the villagers. Realising they weren't to be killed, many of the madmen sprang to their feet and sprinted off into the forest. Redwane watched them go, knowing most of them probably wouldn't survive more than a day alone in the forest.

The people of Kruken cheered, amused by the spectacle as much as anything. The fire burned brightly at the centre of the village, but the black smoke from the damp kindling thankfully obscured the ravages of the fire on the dead men's flesh. Melting fat fizzed in the fire and sharp cracks sounded as bones split in the heat.

Redwane hauled Torbrecan to his feet and thrust him towards Leovulf.

'Get him out of my sight,' he said.

NIGHT HAD CLOSED in on Kruken, and Redwane sat with Ustern and Holstef in what passed for the village tavern. To ride through the forest now would be too dangerous. The night belonged to the beasts, and even thirty armed warriors would likely never be seen again were they to travel its haunted paths in the dark.

The tavern was a high-ceilinged building built of heavy timbers atop square-cut blocks of stone that were clearly of dwarfcraft. A fire burned within an inglenook that had once been a doorway, with faded angular runes carved into its lintel. Redwane guessed the tavern was normally sparsely populated, but today's drama had brought the locals out in force. A number of hard-bitten men sat in huddled corners nursing their dark beer and casting furtive glances their way.

The beer was peaty and flavoursome, but it was too strong for Redwane's tastes. The other White Wolves seemed to like it though. Conversation had been muted, for Kruken wasn't a town that welcomed outsiders much, even ones in the service of Count Myrsa.

'I reckon we've seen the last of those idiots,' said Ustern between puffs on his pipe, a long-stemmed piece with a bowl in the shape of an upturned drinking horn. Ustern bore the White Wolves banner, and was always the first to venture a grim opinion. 'Aye, the beasts'll do for them and no mistake.'

'I'd not be too sure,' said Holstef. 'They survived this long, what makes you think that just because we got Torbrecan they'll end up beast food?'

One the youngest White Wolves, Holstef was an eternal optimist, which made him a perfect foil for the banner bearer. He and Ustern argued like an old married couple, though neither seemed to mind, as though it was all part of their friendship. Ustern leaned forward and jabbed his pipe at Holstef.

'How d'you even know it's Torbrecan who we got?'

'He was the leader, stands to reason doesn't it?'

'You think that lot care about "reason"?'

'Why was he the one doing all the talking then? Why would a leader let someone else talk?'

'So he wouldn't be caught by the likes of us,' suggested Ustern.

'Crap,' replied Holstef. 'Someone that mad wouldn't think like that.'

'How d'you know? Touched by a bit of moon-madness are ye?'

'Must be,' said Holstef. 'Why else would I fight alongside you?'

Redwane let them bicker and watched the tavern's patrons as they drank and argued. They were a motley bunch, miners and woodsmen mostly by the look of them. None looked like they'd worked in a while, though that hadn't stopped them coming in here to spend their coin. Redwane recognised an underlying connection between the snatches of conversation he heard, knowing a familiar thread ran through every one.

Fear.

Their expressions spoke of fear of one sort or another. Fear of poverty, fear of starvation, fear of being alone, fear of the dark and, worst of all, a fear that the madmen in the square today were right.

In the last year, Redwane had seen the same expression on many faces throughout the northern marches, a pinched desperation for things to be better. Sigmar's Empire had promised great things, but for many of its people it had yet to deliver.

He followed one of the tavern's serving girls, a good-looking woman with a body that time hadn't yet caused to sag and a face in which bitterness had its claws, but hadn't yet won the battle. She wore a black bow tied around her wrist that told him her man had been killed, most likely in the war against the Norsii, though in the north he could have met his end in any number of ways. She sensed his gaze and looked over, a thin smile creasing her full lips. She couldn't quite keep the grimace from her face, but she nodded and her eyes flickered towards the stairs.

Redwane sighed and nodded back to her. Was this what it had come to, a fumbled liaison in a cold tavern room, loveless and bought with copper coins? He remembered having the pick of the girls, a different one every night if he'd wanted. But that was before the battle at the centre of the Fauschlag Rock when he'd swung his hammer at the daemon lord. He could still feel the searing pain as it had exploded against its infernal armour and sent red-hot shards of iron into his face.

Now no woman would look at him unless he paid them.

A cold wind gusted into the tavern and the locals grumbled as candles flickered and the fragile heat in the building slipped outside. Their mutterings ceased at the sight of Leovulf in his armour and heavy wolf pelt cloak. Redwane's second stamped the mud from his boots on a threadbare mat and pulled off his cloak. Still clad in his armour, he sat next to Redwane and shouted at the tavern keeper to bring him some beer.

'Everyone bedded down?' asked Redwane.

'Aye,' agreed Leovulf. 'I've told them to keep the gambling and drinking to a minimum and that I'll take my hammer to anyone who isn't ready to ride out at daybreak.'

'Good, I want to be back at the Fauschlag before nightfall,' he said. 'There's an evil feel to the forest just now.'

'Isn't there always?' put in Ustern.

'More than normal I mean,' said Redwane.

'It's the pox,' said Leovulf. 'Gets everyone on edge. It's an enemy you can't fight. Show me a beast or a greenskin and I'll break it in two with my hammer. But the pox... that's something a man *should* be afraid of.'

'You sound just like Ustern,' said Redwane.

'Ulric save me, but things must be bad,' said Leovulf with a shake of his head. He removed a thin pipe from his belt and lit it on the candle at the centre of their table. More beer arrived on a platter, and the White Wolves each took a tankard.

'To Ulric,' said Redwane, raising his beer.

'To Ulric,' echoed the White Wolves.

Their conversation turned to the logistics of their journey home, but Redwane's attention was fixed on the serving girl. She finished her rounds and spoke a few words to the tavern keeper, who glanced over at their table. He grunted something and waved her away. She looked over at him and headed upstairs.

Redwane drained the last of his beer and said, 'I think I'll leave the rest of the drinking to you northerners.'

'See,' said Ustern, nudging Holstef. 'Told you the southern tribes couldn't hold their beer.'

Redwane knocked over his empty mug. 'You call that beer. Harder stuff than this falls from the sky over Reikdorf. Our pigs drink better than this.'

'That's no way to talk of your women,' said Holstef, emboldened by several beers.

'Easy, soldier,' cautioned Leovulf. 'Watch that tongue of yours.'

Redwane left them to it and made his way towards the stairs, climbing to the upper level where the girl was waiting for him. She stood in a doorway of the corridor and threw him a smile. He knew it was false, but didn't care.

She looked at him, trying to conceal the horrid fascination she had of his scars. She reached up to touch them, but he grabbed her hand before her fingers touched his face.

'Don't,' he said, turning his head away. 'Please.'

She nodded and led him into the room.

* * *

WOLVES HOWLED AT the moon and feasted on the dead as carrion birds lined every rooftop or billowed in sweeping clouds of feathered bodies. Death had come to Hyrstdunn and not a single soul had lived through the battle to break down its walls. With their dead king now fighting in the ranks of the enemy, the defence of the city had been without heart and the mortals had fought with desperation born of knowing they could not win.

Khaled al-Muntasir walked the darkened streets of the city, revelling in the sounds of its doom as a conductor might enjoy a musical recital. The sounds of death were familiar to him; as well they should be after centuries of inflicting them upon the living. He made out the sound of splintered wolf teeth tearing at human meat, the *peck, peck, peck* of beaks battering at skulls to get to the soft matter within. Beyond that, he could hear screams of the last survivors as they were dragged from hidden cellars or attics.

King Markus walked listlessly behind him, his flesh pale and dead, his eyes flickering with green embers as the vampire's will remade him. Dried blood caked his ravaged neck, and though he bore the semblance of the man he had once been, nothing now remained of that mortal vessel. Khaled al-Muntasir had delivered the blood-kiss to the Menogoth king, knowing the effect it would have on mortals to see their fallen leader fighting alongside the army of the dead. Markus would soon emerge from this catatonic state, and a new blood drinker would walk the land. It gave Khaled al-Muntasir perverse pleasure to see the panicked faces of mortal cattle as they realised that neither prince nor pauper was safe from death's touch.

The sound of crying children drifted on the midnight wind, and this was the most exquisite sound of all. Innocent blood was the sweetest elixir, and though his hunger was long sated on the blood of warriors, there was always desire for such epicurean delights.

The city itself was a poor specimen of architecture: a random collection of muddy timber structures built upon older ruins. No two were alike, a mishmash of prosaic, peasant architecture that offended his cultured eye. His lips curled in distaste as he looked up at the count's dwelling, a ridiculous hall of crudely hewn stone with a thatched roof and laughably childish daubings of antiquated gods on timber panels.

'To think that you, a king of men, lived in this hovel is absurd,' said Khaled al-Muntasir, shaking his head in disbelief. 'I was but a lesser prince and I grew to manhood in a sun-kissed palace of marble towers, glittering fountains and triumphal domes that enclosed vast spaces of such beauty that they could move a man to tears. You primitive savages could never achieve something so magnificent.'

Markus didn't answer of course, and Khaled al-Muntasir waved his thin hands at the hall's swaybacked roof. 'Such inelegant design is so utterly primitive for a land that claims to be the greatest empire of man. The notion that you people actually believe that to be true is so ludicrous that it makes me want to laugh. Or maybe weep, I haven't decided. Oh, how the race of man has fallen.'

He shook his head in sadness and moved on, keeping to the centre of the cobbled thoroughfares to avoid the sewage leaking down the edges of the road. He held his white cloak draped over his forearm to keep it clean. Filth encrusted every surface of the city, and thousands of dead bodies lay strewn around like burst sacks of grain. A pack of wolves ran through its streets, fighting over scraps of flesh. Flocks of crows followed them, eager for their leavings.

Khaled al-Muntasir climbed the steps towards the king's longhouse, smelling the aroma of fresh-spilled blood from within. The doors were splintered and sagging, and skeletal warriors in rusting armour of bronze stood like silent guardians of a tomb. He turned to look back into the city, watching as the army of Nagash completed its destruction.

Beneath the light of the moon, armoured skeletons marched between the buildings, gathering the dead and dragging them into the open, where they were deposited on rotted carts pulled by shambling animated corpses. Ghoulish scavengers loped through the streets, fighting the rotten-furred wolves for warm flesh torn from the bone. Pale-fleshed and scabbed with open sores, these carrion feeders hissed and bit with grave-dirt claws, their bodies thin and wasted, yet ravenous and tenacious.

And holding court over this glorious tableau of death was its lord and master.

Nagash himself was surrounded by ghostly flocks of revenants, howling wisps of light and shadow that curled in supplication around his monstrous limbs. Krell, the hulking champion of the northern gods marched at Nagash's side, a physical manifestation of his master's rage and aggression. Darkness went with them, a shroud of bleak misery that invigorated Khaled al-Muntasir, but which sapped the living of their courage and filled their hearts with fear. More than just the fear of death, it spoke of an eternal life of servitude to a cruel master, of paradise denied and the promise of a life that would go unrewarded by the gods.

The vampire stood on the highest point of the city and watched with relish as his personal retinue of warriors climbed the steps towards him. Each skeletal champion dragged a screaming child behind it, none older than six or seven summers. They wept and fought, but the dead men who carried them to their doom were as inexorable as their fate was inescapable.

His fangs tingled with anticipation, his eyes filling with killing red as the first dead warrior pushed a struggling girl-child towards him. He lifted her head with a finely manicured nail, tracing its razor edge around her chin.

'Hush, child,' he said. 'Do not cry. There is no need for tears, they are a waste of something precious.'

The girl looked into his eyes, and she saw his hunger.

Before she could scream, he sank his fangs into her neck and began to feed.

KHALED AL-MUNTASIR DROPPED the shrivelled husk of the last child, glutted on innocent blood and his senses afire with the rush of undiluted life energy. His eyes beheld the world around him with greater clarity than before, every living thing glinting with its own internal fire. To his eyes, the world was ablaze in silver light.

He smiled, feeling the rush of another's blood filling his atrophied veins and unused organs with a semblance of life. Sensuous, erotic and deliciously painful, it was a fleeting sense of wonder, absolute knowledge of the thoughts and life of another living being as they were extinguished forever.

Yet as soon as it was drunk and revelled in, it was gone. The curse of the blood drinker was never to know satiety, to always crave the blood of the living. He wiped the droplets from his chin, licking his fingers clean and enjoying the last sensations of life as a starving peasant would relish the crumbs of a prince's discarded meal.

His vision was already returning to its more mundane outlook as he saw the great lord of the undead climb the steps towards him, his pall of shadow like a soothing balm of radiant energy. Nagash towered over Khaled al-Muntasir, his power straining at the boundaries of existence, almost too intense for his undying frame to contain. Even with sight far beyond that of mortals, Khaled al-Muntasir could see only a fraction of the great necromancer's power. It was immense and unstoppable, an energy that existed in worlds beyond understanding, crossing the gulfs of death and empowered by a dark wind whose source had been a mystery to even the greatest practitioners of the arts in his sand-swallowed city.

The necromancer's shimmering metallic hand glimmered with power, a reservoir of untapped energies drawn into its mysterious structure by the slaughter of this pitiful city and its inhabitants. Walking its streets, Khaled al-Muntasir had laughed to feel the stirring spirits below his feet, knowing that this land was already a tomb.

This region of the Empire was awash with forgotten sepulchres and barrows of long dead warriors. The people of this place lived atop a great mound of corpses, buried beneath the earth thousands of years ago, and didn't even know it.

Khaled al-Muntasir closed his eyes and let his senses flow out around the city, searching for any sign of life, any living thing that had somehow escaped the killing. There was nothing, and he looked up into the emerald fire of the necromancer's eyes.

He shook his head and the necromancer thrust his hand towards the sky.

A blazing pillar of green light filled the heavens with its necrotic glow, piercing the clouds and unnatural darkness with its brightness. The light built within Nagash's body, a lambent glow that slithered down through his invisible flesh. It filled the necromancer's skull, infused his dried bones, formed phantom organs and coursed through his debased body into the heavy plates of his armour. A black wind sighed, and the silver light that suffused the earth was snuffed out in an instant. The ground shook as the impossibly powerful will of Nagash spread through the land, reaching deeper than the roots of the mountains and out into the wilds far beyond.

The wolves of the city threw back their heads and howled. The darkness was suddenly lit by thousands of pinpricks of green light as the dead of Hyrstdunn were dragged from their rest to serve in the army that had slain them. Bloody men, half-eaten wives and murdered offspring screamed as their dead flesh was filled with horrid animation.

Dead Menogoths climbed to their feet, reaching for weapons that had lain beside their brutalised corpses. Those without weapons wrenched sharpened timbers from their former homes, gathered up meathooks, gutting knives or cleavers from butcher's blocks.

At some unseen command, they shuffled towards the northern gate of the city, moving with dreadful purpose and monotonous unison.

The army of the dead, already thousands strong, swelled by thousands more. And all across this degenerate empire, the dead would be stirring in the damp earth that contained them, roused to wakefulness by the most powerful necromancer ever to rise from the lost kingdom of Nehekhara.

High above Nagash, a black miasma saturated the heavens, a roof of oppressive coal-dark cloud that roiled outwards from its boiling epicentre. The dark of night was nothing compared to this, for it was an umbra of complete emptiness, the *oblivion* of light not just its absence.

The dread blackness slipped over the sky like a slick of oil on a lake, creeping towards the horizon in mockery of the coming sunrise and life itself.

Death had come to the Empire.

BOOK TWO

Down Among the Bone Men

Some, though headless, stood erect,
From some the arms were hacked,
Some were pierced from front to back.
And some on horse in armour sat,
Some were choked while at their food.
Some were drowned in flood,
And some were withered up by fire,
Some raving mad and others dead.
Merciful Shallya of the Sorrow
pours bright tears from her eyes
Weeping and wailing the fate of Men
Alas my grief that ye did not heed her cries.

SEVEN
Portents of Death

A COLD, SALTY wind blew off the ocean and a bell chimed high on the Tower of Tides. Gulls wheeled over the docks of the lower town, and Count Marius of the Jutones took a moment to savour the smells of his city. Unlike many cities in the Empire, those smells were not shit and refuse and livestock. Jutonsryk smelled of wealth, prosperity and contentment.

The buildings of his city were a haphazard mix of stone and timber, the oldest jutting from the cliffs and spurs of the rock forming the natural bay that made it such a perfect location for a port. Dominating the city was the Namathir, the leaf-shaped promontory of dark rock upon which Marius's castle was built. Crafted of pale stone with many slender towers and shimmering roofs, the fortress of the Jutone count was a curious mix of power and grace. High walls of stone surrounded the city on its landward side, patched and rebuilt by dwarf masons hired at ruinous expense in the aftermath of Sigmar's siege.

Always a nautical city, most buildings of Jutonsryk sported some recognition of the sea that had made its fortune. Tall masts with billowing sails jutted from numerous rooftops, while figureheads from wrecked ships, cargo netting and entire forecastles made up frontages, roofs and gables. Effigies of Manann in his aspect of a bulky man with an iron crown were common, as were images of crashing waves and sea creatures. Warehouses and loading bays for the hundreds of ships that berthed here every week crowded the seafront, finely-built structures paid for by the wealthy merchants and traders who had grown fat on Jutonsryk's prosperity.

Hundreds of ships filled the harbour, a myriad of sails of many colours and different kings. Udose ships sat alongside those of the Endals and ones bearing flags of nations that most people in the Empire had no knowledge of. Ships of all size and shape jostled for space on the quayside and a forest of lifting hoists worked in a never-ending procession of unloading and loading.

Trade was Jutonsryk's lifeblood, and it had brought undreamed-of wealth to Marius's city.

Yet only a few years ago, it had come to the edge of destruction at the hands of the man to whom Marius now gave homage as Emperor. Smiling to himself, he knew he should have allied with Sigmar a long time ago, but not for the reasons the Emperor would have liked to hear.

Always independent, the Jutones had stood apart from Sigmar's burgeoning Empire, but as Marius looked at how his city and people had benefited from that alliance, he knew it had been a worthwhile investment. The streets were clean, part of an initiative proposed by his physicians as a means to alleviate sickness among the poor, as was the building of a new almshouse to care for the ailing and needy. Taxes on incoming trade ships had paid for these institutions, and such was the influx of new trade that followed his Sword Oath with Sigmar, that each year brought more gold than he could spend.

Marius rode past the Tower of Tides on a white stallion, a gift from Sigmar's warrior friend, and its caparison was of fine blue and green cloth woven by Thuringian women as a tribute from the Berserker King. He leaned back in the saddle as he negotiated the winding, cobbled streets that led down to the old town and the docks. Citizens of Jutonsryk bowed as he passed and he favoured them with his most magnanimous smile.

Yes, it was a good day to take the air, though a smear of darkness on the horizon portended storms to come. He shivered, pulling his exquisite cloak of bearskin tighter about his shoulders. His clothes were finely made, a tasteful mix of eastern silks and hard-wearing Ostogoth tanned leather that gave him the unmistakable appearance of wealth, yet retained the look of a man who knew how to wield the sword buckled at his waist.

A troop of lancers accompanied him, their pale blue cloaks falling tidily over the rumps of their mounts. Spoiling this image of perfection was the wobbling form of Vergoossen, his latest aide, who rode his chestnut gelding about as well as a bale of hay might.

Ever since Bastiaan had stabbed him at Middenheim in the height of the fighting, Marius had forbidden his aides to bear arms. Looking at Vergoossen, it didn't look like he knew one end of a dagger from another, yet he had a head for numbers and a total lack of ego to be bruised by Marius's frequent tirades and verbal abuse. All of which made him a perfect aide.

'My lord,' said. 'If you'll just look over these documents…'

Marius sighed, his good mood evaporating in the face of Vergoossen's pleadings.

'What is so important that you need to spoil a perfectly good day?' he demanded.

Vergoossen held out a sheaf of papers. 'My lord, I have petitions from a number of merchants, and–'

'Let me guess, Huyster and Merovec.'

'Amongst others, but yes, the majority of correspondence is from them.'

'So what do they want, as if I can't guess?'

'Master Huyster wishes to bring to your attention the latest increase in berthing fees and the imposition of the new import tariffs,' said Vergoossen. 'And Master Merovec asks if you have had time to consider his request for permission to extend his warehouses along the north shore.'

Marius felt his anger grow at these foolish, greedy merchants. Their coffers were already swollen with gold, yet still they wanted more. It seemed a lust for gold wasn't simply confined to the mountain folk. What angered Marius most was that he saw a reflection of his old self in their grasping, transparent greed. He took a calming breath.

'Tell Huyster that the berthing fees are paying for additional docks to be built along the shoreline, which will allow him to double his revenue within the year. And if he wants it known that he feels aggrieved with the berthing fees, then he is only too welcome to bring that to the attention of the stevedores' guild. I'm sure they would be happy to hear of his dissatisfaction.'

'Really?' said Vergoossen, missing his sarcastic tone. 'I would have thought it a recipe for disaster to say such a thing.'

'Of course it is,' snapped Marius. Vergoossen was efficient and thorough when it came to organising Marius's affairs, but he had no head for understanding people. 'The stevedores' wages are paid from berthing taxes, and any shipmaster who wants to pay less will find a greater than usual percentage of their cargoes inexplicably lost or accidentally dropped into the sea.'

'But that's blackmail, my lord,' exclaimed Vergoossen.

'All trade is blackmail of one sort or another,' said Marius. 'But that is a lesson for another day.'

'And what shall I tell Master Merovec?'

'Tell him that I know he already owns more quayside frontage than city regulations permit. He may fool others with his straw men, but I was finding new ways to earn gold while he was soiling his swaddling clothes. Tell him that if he *really* wants me to have you investigate his assets to adjudge his property holdings with a view to his future expansions, then I am more than happy to oblige him.'

'I understand, sir,' said Vergoossen. 'He wouldn't want that.'

'No,' agreed Marius. 'He wouldn't. Now is there anything else that needs my subtle hand of diplomacy, or do you think you can actually do your job and handle the minutiae of running a busy sea port?'

'There is one other matter, my lord,' said Vergoossen.

'Go on then, what is it?'

'Some sailors from Tilean lands are refusing to pay their berthing fees.'

'Typical bloody Tilean,' said Marius with a shake of his head. 'Their coin purses are sealed tighter than a Brigundian virgin's legs. Why are they refusing to pay?'

'They say they don't have any cargo to unload, so they don't see why they should pay a berthing fee.'

'No cargo? Then why are they here?'

'They claim they were attacked and had to ditch their cargo to escape.'

'Pirates?'

Vergoossen consulted his notes, as though reluctant to voice the reason the sailors had given.

'Well, in a manner of speaking, my lord,' stammered Vergoossen.

'Oh, just spit it out, man!' ordered Marius.

'Yes, my lord. Sorry. They claim they were attacked by ships crewed by dead men.'

* * *

'THIS IS THE place?' asked Alfgeir. 'You're sure of it?'

Cuthwin gave the Marshall of the Reik a look that said he was sure, and that he'd have liked to see the knights find this place again. Instead he simply nodded. A life lived in the wilderness was a solitary, silent one, and even when in company, Cuthwin found himself limiting his speech to short answers.

'Yes, this is the place,' he said.

'There's nothing here,' said Orvin, dismounting from his gelding and looking around. 'You said there was a fight here.'

'There was,' said Cuthwin. 'You'd see that if you looked.'

Orvin stepped towards him. 'Are you cheeking me, scout?'

'Leave it,' warned Alfgeir, and Orvin backed off, returning to his horse's side. Twenty of the Empire's finest knights stood at the edge of the road, where Cuthwin had forced them to dismount lest they spoil the tracks. It had taken them two days to reach the road, much less than it had taken Cuthwin to reach Reikdorf, but then he'd been on foot and had a wounded dwarf to carry.

He squatted at the edge of the road where he and the dwarfs had fought the goblins and wolves. He could picture the wagons, where he had come out of the forest and how he had moved through the fight. The road was empty now, no sign of any bodies or wagons to indicate that a life and death struggle had played out here.

At least to the untrained eye.

Alfgeir stepped onto the road, moving from smudged track, to discoloured patch of earth and broken branch. He moved well for an old man, kneeling to dust earth from a stone and follow the course of the fight through the telltale marks such a struggle inevitably left behind.

'You killed the first one here,' said Alfgeir, miming the act of drawing a bowstring.

Cuthwin nodded as Alfgeir wended his way through the fight, moving as though he fought it anew. At last he turned to face Cuthwin, his face betraying a grudging respect.

'You took a big risk in helping these dwarfs, scout,' said Alfgeir. 'That took courage.'

Cuthwin shrugged, uncomfortable with praise. 'It seemed like the right thing to do. It's what Sigmar did.'

'And we all want to be like Sigmar,' laughed Alfgeir. 'Good lad. Now the wagons were over here, yes?'

Cuthwin rose and smoothly made his way to join Alfgeir, carefully avoiding the earlier tracks and making sure to stick to the hardened ground to leave no trace of his own passing. The knights followed him, leading their horses and without the care he showed.

He pointed to a disturbed area of ground at a bend in the road.

'There,' said Cuthwin. 'That's where the wagons were.'

'So where are they now?' asked Orvin.

'Maybe the goblins took them,' he said. 'Maybe the forest beasts broke them up for firewood or weapons.'

'Can't you tell?'

Cuthwin shook his head. 'Maybe if your horses hadn't trampled the ground I could have.'

Alfgeir put a hand on his shoulder and said, 'You do enjoy provoking people, scout.'

'I reckon the goblins took the wagons,' said Cuthwin, pointing back down the road. 'There's a stone path leads up into the mountains about a mile back. Could be they took them that way.'

'Do you think they found what the dwarf buried?'

'Hard to say,' said Cuthwin. 'Let me look.'

He waved away the knights and dropped to his hands and knees, lowering his face to the earth, scanning left and right for any trace of something out of the ordinary. Moving like a bloodhound with the scent of its prey in its nose, Cuthwin ghosted over the ground as though listening to it. He ignored the chuckles of the knights. Let them laugh; they'd be choking on it when he found something.

He moved over where the wagons had been circled, touching the ground and feeling the tension in the soil, brushing it with his fingertips. The earth here was looser, less densely packed, as though disturbed. Where the wagons had been pulled around and turned into makeshift barricades, the earth was hard-packed, but this patch in the middle was loose.

Cuthwin rose to his feet, circling the area and searching for any other obvious signs of something buried. He brushed the ground with the sole of his boot, closing his eyes as he relied on senses honed in the wilderness over many years.

'It's here,' he said, dropping to his knees. He drew his dagger and sketched a rough rectangle in the dirt, encompassing where he knew the dwarf had buried what Grindan had called the Thunder Bringer.

Alfgeir knelt beside him. 'I don't see anything.'

'It's here, trust me,' said Cuthwin. 'The mountain folk are masters of digging. If anyone can bury something they don't want found, it's them.

'Aye, that's true enough I suppose,' agreed Alfgeir. He looked over to his knights. 'Orvin, you and the others break out the shovels and start earning your pay.'

'By digging?' said Orvin, as though the notion was beneath him.

'By digging,' confirmed Alfgeir. 'Get to it.'

Orvin shook his head and, together with five other knights, began shovelling earth from the spot Cuthwin had indicated. They dug relentlessly and swiftly moved a large amount of soil. Cuthwin watched with Alfgeir as they dug down around four feet into the ground without finding anything.

Just as he was beginning to entertain doubts that there was anything buried here, Orvin's shovel clanged on something metallic. Orvin used the end of his shovel to clear away the black earth, using his hands when the shovel proved insufficient for the task. At length, he leaned back to allow those above him to see what he had uncovered.

Cuthwin looked into the hole the knights had dug. He caught a gleam of tubular iron, like the funnels on Govannon's forge, spars of splintered timbers and what looked like an iron-rimmed wheel.

'What in Ulric's name *is* that?' said Alfgeir, tilting his head to the side.

'The Thunder Bringer,' said Cuthwin. 'And we have to get it back to Reikdorf.'

THE SHIP WAS a long merchantman, sleek-hulled and coloured a garish blue and green with wide, dark eyes painted beneath its prow. An elaborate figurehead jutted provocatively from her forecastle, representing Myrmidia and Manann entwined in an embrace that Marius was sure the temple priests of Jutonsryk wouldn't find in any of their holy books. Its flag was one Marius had seen before, but he couldn't remember to which distant princeling it belonged. He saw so many ships in any given week, it was hard to keep track of them all.

Hundreds of people bustled to and fro: sailors, tax collectors in blue robes, maritime enthusiasts, dwarf masons and shipwrights, rope-makers, labourers, hawkers, map-makers, whores and sellswords. The taverns were doing a brisk trade, as a number of ships had just finished their unloading and their crews were eager to spend their wages.

The air tasted of salt water and hard work, and Marius felt his brow turn thunderous as he saw the crew of the impounded vessel pressing against the ring of armed lancers preventing them from leaving the quay. Olive-skinned sailors from the south, they waved their arms and jabbered in their foreign tongue, apparently oblivious to the fact that they were on Empire soil and ought to be speaking Reikspiel if they wanted to be understood.

'To be fair, they do look rather unsettled,' said Vergoossen.

Marius waved away his aide's comment. 'Nonsense, these foreign types are always ludicrously animated when they converse. The way they talk to each other, they could be discussing the weather and you'd swear they were relating news of the End Times.'

'But still,' pressed Vergoossen, 'what if they aren't lying?'

'Of course they're lying,' snapped Marius, rounding on his aide. 'It's the oldest trick in the book for fly-by-nights and thieves. Listen, Vergoossen, one of two things has happened here. Either they've stolen their master's cargo and transferred it to another ship, which we'll see in a few days with false papers of lading, or they have come here claiming they had to ditch their cargo to outrun some pirates so they don't have to pay the berthing tax. Then they'll miraculously find a hugely lucrative trade deal when they get ashore. Either way, I won't stand for it. I'll have them locked in the tower for trying to cheat Marius of Jutonsryk.'

His lesson in tax evasion dispensed, Marius marched towards the merchantman, noting how high it was riding in the water. Its holds were empty, that was for sure, but he'd wager they'd been empty long before the sailors had come within spitting distance of the city.

The Sergeant of Lancers turned as he heard Marius approach. He gave a formal salute and placed his clenched fist against his chest before bowing curtly.

'My lord,' he said. 'Sergeant Alwin. We detained these men when the Master of Taxes informed us they refused to pay the berthing fee.'

Marius scanned the sailors, a grimy bunch of men with colourful complexions and dark hair to a man. He counted around a hundred men on the quayside or clustering the rails of the ship. They looked desperate to get onto dry land, and many threw furtive glances over their shoulders out to sea.

'Is this all of them?' asked Marius.

Alwin nodded. 'A couple of them may have gotten into the city before we arrived, but looks like there's more or less a full ship's complement here.'

That seemed about right, and Marius looked for the sailor in the least grubby clothes, the one that likely captained this vessel. His eyes immediately fixed on a man with skin like tanned leather and a mane of slick black hair. His manner was agitated, but from the looks the others were giving him, it was clear he was in command.

'You,' said Marius, beckoning the man through the line of lancers. 'You speak Reikspiel?'

The man nodded and gratefully pushed through the lancers towards Marius. Two of his personal bodyguard quickly searched the man for weapons, taking a pair of daggers and a gunwale spike from his belt.

'I am Count Marius of Jutonsryk, lord of this city. What is your name?' said Marius, careful to enunciate each word carefully.

'My name is Captain Leotas Raul, and I speak Reikspiel very well.'

'Good, then we won't have any misunderstandings,' said Marius. 'This is your ship, yes?'

'It is,' said Raul, his voice prideful and yet melancholy. '*Myrmidia's Spear*, sole surviving ship of Magister Fiorento's fleet.'

'Yes, well I'm sure he will be overjoyed to hear that his last ship is soon to be impounded,' said Marius.

Before Raul could react to Marius's dire pronouncement, the count of Jutonsryk said, 'Tell me, Captain Raul, what do you think of my harbour? Is it adequate for your magnificent ship?'

Raul looked confused, and Marius said, 'Would you like me to repeat the question?'

'No,' said Raul, a hard look entering his eyes. 'That will not be necessary.'

'Well? Are my docks fit to berth your ship?'

'These are very fine docks, Count Marius,' answered Raul coldly.

'Good, so why don't you tell me why you've taken the liberty of berthing in my perfectly good harbour and yet refuse to pay the berthing fee.'

'We have no cargo,' replied Raul. 'No cargo means nothing to tax.'

'Oh there is always something to tax, Captain Raul,' Marius assured him. 'But if you have no cargo, then you have come a long way for nothing. Magister Fiorento must be a wealthy man indeed to despatch ships with no cargo all this way.'

'We did not come here with empty holds, my lord,' said Raul. 'We were forced to abandon our cargo.'

'So tell me, what manner of cargo were you carrying before you abandoned it?'

'A thousand bales of embroidered cloth,' answered Raul. 'Dyes and oils from the warmer climates of the southern islands.'

'I see, and you threw these overboard because...'

'We were attacked by black ships with crimson sails of ragged cloth and crewed by dead men. Sailors from the depths of the ocean risen from the sea to hunt the living.'

'Very poetic,' commented Marius. 'Of course, you realise I don't believe a word of it?'

'I speak no lies,' hissed Raul, and Marius smiled at his conviction.

'Then, please, elaborate,' said Marius, knowing even a skilled liar would often trip themselves up in the details of an over-elaborate farrago.

'As we rounded the Reik headland from the south a noxious fog arose from the sea and a host of crimson-sailed vessels moved to intercept us. Not a breath of wind stirred their sails, yet they came on at speed, as though all the fiends of the deep pulled their rotted hulks through the waters. More appeared around the northern headland, trapping us between them, two hundred vessels at least.'

'Two hundred?' laughed Marius. 'Now I know you are lying. There are, I'll grant you, a few corsairs who raid the shorelines of the far Reik, but none with so large a fleet.'

'These were no corsairs,' insisted Raul. 'As their ships drew nearer we smelled the stench of rotten, waterlogged timbers and saw the decaying flesh of the skeletal crewmen aboard each vessel. We tried to outrun them, but they were too fast, and our sister ship, *Shield of Glory*, was overtaken. A hundred dead warriors swarmed her decks, and they tore the living apart to eat their flesh. Though our fellow brothers of the sea were being devoured, not a man aboard ship dared turn to help them. *Golden Goddess* tried to evade, but she was too heavy, and more of the ships of the damned cut her off. She too was lost with all souls.'

'But you escaped,' said Marius.

'No sooner had I seen how many ships opposed us than I knew we were too heavily laden to escape. I ordered our cargo ditched, but even then we only barely made it through the line of mouldering hulks.'

'These ships of the dead did not pursue you? How convenient.'

'They did not,' said Raul. 'But they are still out there, this I swear on the life of my mother. They are out there and no more ships will come to your city. And while they lurk in the fog, none shall leave.'

Marius had heard enough and shook his head. 'A fanciful tale, Captain Raul, but one I am disinclined to believe.'

He turned to Sergeant Alwin. 'Impound the ship and lock these men up in the Old Town gaol. Vergoossen, draft a letter to Magister Fiorento and tell him that if he wants his ship and crew released then he'll need to pay their fines and taxes. Be sure to inform him of the increasing levy of fines the longer he leaves them here.'

'As you wish, my lord,' said Vergoossen.

Marius turned and walked away as the lancers began rounding up the protesting sailors.

'Dead corsairs, indeed,' he said. 'Ridiculous.'

THE FIVE CHARIOTS thundered over the rugged flatlands to the south of Three Hills, the horses running at battle pace as Maedbh let them stretch their muscles. Asoborn beasts needed to have their head now and again. The training fields allowed the youngsters to get a feel for the beasts and how the chariot behaved, but there was nothing like riding tall at battle pace to get the heart pounding and the blood racing.

Two chariots sped along either side of her, each with an Asoborn youth at the reins. Not one was over thirteen years of age, but they worked the reins like veterans. The ground here was dotted with thin copses, unexpected slopes and random patches of rocks, but so far they had steered around them without losing valuable speed. Ahead, the Worlds Edge Mountains soared to the sky and a black line of thunderheads rolled like a giant wave crashing over the distant peaks to the far south.

Looking at those clouds gave Maedbh a shiver of dread, though they would be long back at Three Hills before any storm broke. She returned her attention to the ground before her chariot as they rolled over a rough patch of earth and the wheel spun in the air for a moment. The chariot wobbled, but Maedbh brought it back level without effort.

'Careful, mother!' squealed Ulrike with frightened delight.

'Are you still secure?' called Maedbh, sparing a quick glance over her shoulder.

'Yes, mother! Of course I am!'

Ulrike had her right ankle braced against the side armour, her left against an angled ridge of wood Wolfgart had crafted to compensate for her narrower stance. Her knees weren't locked, her legs flexible and her posture loose; the perfect position for a charioteer spear-bearer. Maedbh smiled, seeing the same fierce determination in her young features she saw in herself. And, if she was honest, she saw in Wolfgart.

Thinking of her estranged husband brought a lump to her throat. She missed him, and it rankled that she felt like that. An Asoborn woman needed no man to complete her, she was a fiery warrior princess with the winter fire of Ulric flowing in her veins. Maedbh knew all that was true, but she knew there was no shame in wanting to be part of a union that had created so beautiful a life as their daughter.

She and Wolfgart were too alike, that was what she loved about him, and, perversely, was also the problem. Like two bulls in a pen, they locked horns every day to establish dominance, though surely there was no need. She regretted her harsh words to him, but like arrows of fire, they could not be taken back and had struck where they would do the most damage. Maedbh knew herself well enough to know that pride was but a facet of stubbornness, a quality both she and Wolfgart possessed in abundance.

It wasn't in her nature to back down, and yet Ulrike needed a father. She had cried when Maedbh told her that Wolfgart had returned to Reikdorf. Part of her hated him for leaving without saying goodbye, but she recognised that any such farewell would have resulted in a bitter quarrel, and couldn't blame him for wanting to avoid such a confrontation.

'Mother!' cried Ulrike, and Maedbh cursed as she wheeled the chariot away from a scattered tumble of rocks in a dry riverbed. Her attention wasn't on what she was doing, and that was dangerous. Many a careless charioteer had run themselves into rocks or trees through their inattention, and such inglorious fates were amongst the most shameful among the Asoborns.

She pushed Wolfgart from her mind and fixed her attention on her wild ride, weaving a deft path through a sparsely wooded forest in the shadow of a long ridge that ran from east to west. The chariots formed a line in her wake, smoothly changing formation in response to her manoeuvres, and she smiled at the youths' deft touch on the reins.

The horses were breathing hard, their flanks lathered with sweat and Maedbh drew them in, gradually slowing them until they were gently trotting. The horses came to a standstill and Maedbh coiled the reins through the loop of iron fixed to the chariot's wooden frame. She was sweating, her limbs pleasurably sore from their ride.

'Why are we stopping?' asked Ulrike. 'I like going that fast!'

'The horses need to rest, my dear,' said Maedbh. 'They've had a hard morning. Think how tired you are after you've run around the training ground five times. These horses have done that and more.'

'They need to rest then.'

'Yes, my dear, they do,' said Maedbh. 'We all do. See to the horses, and I'll fix you some food once you're finished.'

'Can't I have food first?'

'No, always see to your horses as soon as you stop,' instructed Maedbh. 'You can go without food for a little while, but your horses may need to ride fast at a moment's notice, so be sure they're watered and rubbed down before you see to yourself.'

Ulrike nodded reluctantly, but began expertly brushing the sweat from the horses' heaving sides. The chariots had halted in such a way as to form a rough circle, a perfect defensive formation and one that allowed each rider to set off without fear of hitting another. Maedbh watched the others follow Ulrike's lead, rubbing their horses down with handfuls of straw before allowing them to drink from a trickling stream of clear water.

Satisfied the horses were being looked after, Maedbh stepped down from the chariot and sat on its base, untying a bundle of black bread and cheese from an internal pannier. She broke the bread and set out a portion for her and Ulrike, enjoying this chance to get out in the wilds. Any Asoborn warrior preferred the wind in their hair and the sight of open horizons to the feel of enclosing walls and buildings of stone. Though Three Hills was far from oppressive, Maedbh still relished the chance to explore the far reaches of Freya's lands, to ride the wild woods and race along the open flatlands beyond the hills.

'That was well done, my beauties,' said Maedbh, as the others led their horses back to the chariots. They didn't hobble the horses, but let them roam freely, knowing they would come with a whistle. They beamed at her pride, knowing that as charioteer to Queen Freya, her praise was not given lightly.

As they gathered around her, Maedbh offered instructional tips, helpful pointers and the occasional admonishment to her charioteers. Each had performed well, but there was always room for improvement, and nobody could afford to rest on their laurels.

'You're leaning left when you crack the reins, Osgud,' she said, angling her hand as she spoke. 'It makes the horse pull away from the line, and you need to keep your spacing close when you're riding in close to the enemy. And Daegal, follow through with your spear thrusts, but remember to twist the blade at the extent of your thrust, otherwise it will be torn from your grasp. Ulrike, you need to watch your balance, always keep your back foot braced or you'll be thrown out if the wheels strike a rock or hit a dip in the ground.'

They listened intently, and Maedbh was pleased with their progress. With their midday meal eaten, they broke into smaller groups, practising with their spears and posture. Ulrike ran to join them and Maedbh watched the young Asoborns with a fierce maternal affection. They were *all* her children, not just Ulrike.

She rested her head on the side of the chariot, letting the sounds of the wilderness wash over her: the burble of the water, the sigh of the wind through the trees and the distant caw of a carrion bird over something dead. It had been a long day and she closed her eyes briefly, letting a warm lethargy sneak up on her.

Again the carrion bird cawed, and Maedbh opened her eyes.

The sound was closer than before, louder and more strident, which was strange, as food for crows didn't normally move. She didn't react, but let the sensations of the world come into sharper focus. The wind was coming from the north, the carrion bird was to the south and getting closer.

Maedbh rose to her feet as the wind changed and the horses' heads came up, their ears flat against their skulls and their eyes wide with fear. They snorted and tossed their manes, walking back towards the yokes of the chariots. A wolf howled to the south, and Maedbh tensed. Such a sound would normally be auspicious, but there was something wrong with this howl, it had a hollow, hungry edge to it that no animal servant of Ulric would possess. An answering howl answered the first, this time from the west. A wolf pack was circling them, and Maedbh fought down her rising fear.

'Get the horses yoked back to the chariots,' she shouted, authoritative, not frightened.

The young Asoborns moved to obey, too slowly.

'Get a move on!' she cried. 'If you were under attack, is this how fast you'd move?'

Maedbh gathered the two horses of her own chariot and swiftly harnessed them to the yoke with quick tugs of the bronze buckles. A shadow flitted across the chariot's frame and she looked up to see a flock of circling birds with black feathers. Eaters of the dead.

'Hurry it up, for Ulric's sake!' she said, scooping up Ulrike and depositing her in the chariot. She unlimbered her bow from the side of the chariot and quickly bent it back to string it.

'String yours too,' she said to Ulrike. 'And keep a wary eye out.'

'What's going on, mother?' said Ulrike, sensing a measure of her mother's unease.

'Nothing, my dear,' she said. 'Just do it. Hurry.'

She climbed onto her chariot seeing that the rest of her group were almost ready. The birds cawed again and another wolf howl echoed over the desolate wilderness. That one was unmistakably from the north, and as the wind changed again, Maedbh caught the reek of dead flesh, of mangy, maggot-ridden fur and stagnant, bloody saliva.

Someone screamed and she looked up to see a line of huge timber wolves on the ridge above them. Their fur was rotted and patchy over yellowed bone and torn muscle. Vacant eye sockets glimmered with emerald light and drooling ropes of bloody saliva hung from their exposed fangs.

Some dead things *did* move, it seemed.

'Ride!' shouted Maedbh.

EIGHT

The First to Die

THOUGH HE HAD faced the horror of the living dead before, Sigmar's soul rebelled at the sight before him. Once Ostengard had been a prosperous, well-populated logging village, home to two hundred Cherusen woodsmen and their families. Now it was a charnel house, a field of blood and death.

'Ulric's bones,' swore Count Aloysis, his face pale and the tattoos that curled across his face bleached of colour. His shaven head was criss-crossed with scars and his long scalp lock was more silver than black, bound with circlets of cold iron. 'Those were my people.'

Aloysis's scarlet cloak flapped in the cold wind and his hand twitched on the hook-bladed sword at his side. His eyes were wide with fear at what lay below them.

'Not any more, they're not,' grunted Count Krugar, trying to mask his own fear. 'Now they're dead meat for hewing.'

The Taleuten count was wide and powerful, clad in a shimmering hauberk of silver scale. He hefted Utensjarl from hand to hand. The ancient weapon of Talenbor was slender-bladed, but Sigmar had seen Krugar hew Norsii like saplings with its lethal edge. Despite Krugar's bluster, Sigmar knew both counts were afraid. He didn't blame them.

'Krugar speaks the truth, Aloysis,' said Sigmar. 'These are not your people. Remember that.'

'Aye, I know,' said Aloysis. 'That doesn't make it any easier to take a blade to them.'

Sigmar knew that only too well, having fought against dead things that had once been men of the Empire in the Middle Mountains. This would be hardest on Aloysis, but it would be a test every one of them would have to face soon, of that Sigmar was certain.

A thousand warriors lined the hillside above Ostengard, a mix of Cherusen axemen and foresters, the Red Scythes of the Taleutens and Unberogen swordsmen. Though the Cherusens and Taleutens had almost gone to war a few years ago, their leaders had since become staunch allies, their bond forged by the nearness of their death at Sigmar's hands when the dread crown of Morath had poisoned him with its evil.

In the wake of Khaled al-Muntasir's appearance in Reikdorf, Sigmar had gathered a sword host of five hundred warriors and ridden with all speed towards Taalahim, the great forest city of the Taleutens. If the dead were on the march, then it seemed their first move was in the north. Both counts had sent desperate missives asking for the Emperor's troops to quell the rising dead, and Sigmar had answered their calls.

The Unberogen had ridden hard, meeting the Cherusens and Taleutens in the rugged southern skirts of the Howling Hills. Too late to save the people of Ostengard, but not too late to avenge them.

Clustered around a central thoroughfare that led to the river, Ostengard had been built in a horseshoe shape, with a grain store and carpentry building at its centre. Numerous dwellings were built around these structures, and an elaborate shrine to Taal stood at the riverside. Vast swathes of the forest had been cleared around the village, and much of that had been given over to cultivation, with fields of golden corn and barley waving in the gentle breeze.

The village seethed with activity, unnatural activity. Pallid-skinned creatures with thin, wiry limbs and enlarged skulls feasted on the dead, loping from corpse to corpse to fight for the choicest shanks of meat. Shambling corpses in muddy rags gathered together in moaning bands of rotting flesh, stumbling and dragging themselves towards the hillside where the warriors of the Empire watched.

The dead had risen from the mulchy earth and devoured Ostengard, and a gathering darkness held sway over the day, though the sun was only just past its zenith. The horde of dead things, sensing the warm meat of the living, came for them in an inexorable march of dread patience and insatiable hunger.

Sigmar guessed they faced at least five hundred living dead, a number that could normally be easily overcome, but this was a foe that fought with fear as their greatest weapon.

'Aloysis, you and your axemen are with me. Krugar, split your horsemen and ride around the enemy to hit them from behind,' said Sigmar. 'Ride down to the village and come up through its main street.'

'They won't break and run,' pointed out Krugar, mounting his horse, a powerful, grain-fed stallion of midnight black. 'The dead don't fear anything.'

'They fear this,' said Sigmar, lifting Ghal-maraz from his belt. The dwarf runes etched into its surface shimmered with silver light, and he could feel the weapon's ancestral hatred of the living dead. 'Somewhere down there is a will that is controlling this horde. Ghal-maraz will find it and I will destroy it. With its destruction this horde cannot exist.'

'Then let me be the one to fell it,' begged Aloysis. 'My people demand their count's vengeance.'

Sigmar nodded. 'So be it, but enough talk, it's time to fight.'

Krugar dug his heels into his mount's flanks and said, 'May Ulric give your arm strength, brothers.'

The Taleuten count wheeled his horse and joined the Red Scythes. At a curt command, the horsemen split into two groups with the smooth ease of practiced warriors. They rode with incredible skill, crouched low over their mounts' heads as they moved to encircle the host of the dead.

Aloysis offered Sigmar his hand, and he shook it, feeling the clammy sweat coating the Cherusen count's palm. The man was terrified, but he was facing that terror with iron courage. Sigmar had always respected Aloysis, but this was a level of courage beyond simple bravery.

'Ready?' he asked.

'No,' answered Aloysis honestly. 'But let us fight together, my Emperor.'

Sigmar took Ghal-maraz in a two-handed grip and raised his voice so that every warrior on the hillside could hear him.

'Men of the Empire, you fight a terrible enemy today, but know this. The dead can die. Lay them low as you would slay any foe.

Sword and axe will fell them as surely as any living man. Fight in Ulric's name and we will prevail! For Ulric!'

A ragged cheer erupted along the hillside and Sigmar led the warriors forward in two solid blocks, Sigmar in command of the left, Aloysis the right. They marched towards the enemy, and Sigmar felt the fear of the dead spread through the ranks.

He raised Ghal-maraz and the man next to him hoisted the Imperial standard high, a magnificent banner of red, blue and white. A glorious beast of legend was picked out in gold, with a silver crown encircling its breast, and the sight of Sigmar's new heraldry filled the hearts of all who saw it with fresh courage.

Closer now, the dead were a truly horrific sight, a collection of all degradations time could wreak upon the frailty of human form. Decomposing flesh hung from the bones of those who had clawed their way from earthen graves, loose jawbones hanging like grotesque ornaments from splintered skulls. Those more recently dead were bloody and raw where grasping hands, grave-dirt claws and broken teeth had torn the meat from their bones.

Worse than that, the dreadful aspect of their very existence sent cold spikes of unreasoning fear through every man who stood against them. A man could face another man with courage and know that he could prevail by the strength of his sword arm alone. To face the dead was another matter entirely, for to look into their eyes was to see your own death, to know that your existence in this world was fleeting. To face the dead was to face mortality itself.

Sigmar increased his pace to a loping run, lifting Ghal-maraz over his shoulder and letting loose a fearsome Unberogen war-shout. His warriors echoed him, bellowing the name of Ulric and matching his pace. The Cherusens whooped and hollered, their painted faces recalling the days they had fought near-naked and chewing on wildroot and bane leaves.

Where the Unberogen marched in close-packed ranks, the Cherusen fought as individuals, their mighty felling axes requiring space to swing without hitting a fellow warrior. Aloysis had his sword drawn, a long cavalry sabre more useful on the back of a horse, but a fine enough weapon to strike down the dead on foot.

Less than twenty yards separated the living from the dead.

Sigmar shouted, 'For Ulric!' and broke into a furious charge.

The Unberogen and Cherusen came with him and they struck the dead with all the force and vitality the living could muster.

* * *

MAEDBH HAULED THE reins left as a savage beast with blood-red eyes leapt towards her, its taloned paws slashing. The feral wolf slammed into the side of the chariot with a heavy thump, its claws tearing down through the wooden sides. Ulrike screamed in terror and Maedbh risked a glance back to check her daughter was safe.

Ulrike loosed a poorly aimed shaft. The arrowhead scored through the wolf's fur and bounced from its skull. It howled and fell away from the chariot.

'Keep them back!' shouted Maedbh.

Only three of the chariots had escaped the riverbed, breaking through the encircling packs of wolves. The horses yoked to Yustin and Kreo's chariot were torn apart before they could get moving, and the youngsters were brought down moments later. A huge, black-furred wolf snapped its jaws on Yustin's head, killing the youth instantly, while two wolves with bare skulls and exposed musculature tore Kreo's arm off with brutal sweeps of their claws.

Henia and Torqa got their chariot moving, but a pair of wolves leapt from the ridge straight onto them. Torqa skewered the first with her spear, but the second wolf bit her in two and smashed Henia's spine with one slash of its claws.

The rest of them had broken free and rode with all speed to the north.

Maedbh looked around. The wolves were loping alongside them, their decayed bodies ravaged and wasted, yet powerful and untiring. Six followed them and another four ran on each flank, content to drive them into the path of wolves Maedbh knew were lying in wait somewhere up ahead. These were dead creatures, but they hunted like living ones.

A steady stream of arrows flew from the backs of the chariots. Of all the youngsters, Ulrike had the best eye, and her arrows struck home more than anyone else's. Already she had brought down two wolves. Even amid this desperate chase, Maedbh was proud of her.

The wolves howled and closed in. A slavering beast loped in from the right, its eyes fixed on Maedbh's throat. She pulled the reins in hard, almost tipping the chariot, and its right wheel came off the ground. The wolf hit the spinning wheel and its momentum carried it under the chariot. It gave a mournful howl before its bones were crushed and whatever animation empowered it was extinguished.

Ulrike loosed an arrow at the creature behind it, the shaft punching through the beast's eye socket, and its body writhed as the unnatural energies that bound it together faded and it dropped without a sound. The other creatures cared nothing for the deaths of their pack brothers, and drove the chariots onwards. Maedbh saw three wolves closing on Osgud's chariot and steered around a patch of rocks to sweep in behind him.

'Bloody fool never could keep his spacing,' she hissed. The wolves saw her coming, but too late, and she drove over the rearmost creature, flattening it beneath her wheels. The second loped away, but the third was too fixated on its prey to pay her any mind.

'Osgud! Hard right!'

The terrified youth obeyed instantly, his training making the movement automatic. The two chariots slammed together, crushing the wolf between them. Ulrike screamed as she was jolted from her perch. Maedbh reached back and grabbed her daughter's arm as she slid off the chariot.

Ulrike flailed with her free arm, desperately clawing her way back on board. Spying a target of opportunity, a ravaged wolf with a spectral gleam in its eyes and a hollowed skull bounded towards her, stinking grave dirt spilling from its fang-filled jaws. It leapt towards Ulrike, claws outstretched.

A heavy spear slammed into its side, punching through its ribs and skewering it in mid-air. The blade twisted and the wolf fell away, its bones dissolving and its fur rotting to ash in the wind. Daegal drew back his spear as another wolf leapt for the back of his chariot. The blade stabbed into its skull, and the wolf howled as it died anew.

Maedbh hauled Ulrike back into the chariot, pleased at least one of her students had listened to her. She lashed her horses to greater speed, pulling in close to Osgud's chariot and making sure Daegal's was close by too.

Eight wolves remained, but one of those was slain by a pair of arrows that pierced its chest and skull. Another died when it dared to come too close to Daegal's chariot, and ended up beneath its wheels. Six left, and the ground was rising towards the hills where they would find sanctuary. She heard the howls of wolves from ahead, and knew that was just where the wolves were driving them.

'Circle up!' she cried, and the chariots rolled around, each moving in a smooth arc until they had formed an ad-hoc fortress with one another. The wolves surrounded them, wary at this change of strategy on the part of their prey. Ulrike dropped one wolf with an arrow to the head, and Daegal hurled his spear into the flank of another. Both yelped as their bodies crumbled away to stinking ash.

Realising they could not afford to wait, the remaining wolves hurled themselves at the Asoborns. Freed from the need to control the chariot, Maedbh loosed a quick arrow that tore the throat from a leaping wolf. She threw her bow aside and drew her sword as the rest of the wolves attacked.

Osgud killed a wolf with a spear thrust, and was borne to the ground by a second. Ulrike stabbed a throwing spear into the side of a snapping beast as it climbed over the sides of the chariot. The shaft snapped off in the creature's ribcage, but Maedbh stepped in and hacked the wolf's head from its shoulders with one blow.

The last wolf backed away from the Asoborns, its fangs bared and its eyes alight with killing fire. A living wolf would have slunk away in defeat, but this dead creature circled the chariots at speed before finally leaping onto Osgud's chariot and plucking the fallen youngster from his position there. Its jaws closed with the sound of two spars of wood slamming together and Osgud's body came apart in a spray of crimson.

Four arrows sliced into its body and a heavy throwing spear all but severed its spine. Its rotten bones fell apart and Osgud's remains flopped into his chariot, little more than torn limbs and ruptured meat.

Maedbh cast a wary look north. She saw no signs of wolves and let out a pent up breath.

'Gather up your arrows!' she ordered. 'Quickly, there's likely more of these things out there.'

Ulrike and the others ran to obey and she was proud of them all. Maedbh retrieved her own bow, constantly scanning the horizon for fresh threats. The darkened skies to the south worried her, more than they had before. Something evil was coming to the lands of the Asoborns, and this was just a foretaste.

The youngsters ran back to the chariots, and they mounted up.

'We ride west!' shouted Maedbh.

'No!' protested Ulrike. 'We can't go west. Three Hills is north.'

'And so are the wolves,' answered Maedbh, coming down to Ulrike's level. 'If we go west through the hills, no wolves will be able to find us. When it's safe, we'll cut back north.'

'I was scared,' said Ulrike, holding onto Maedbh's arm.

She saw the fear behind her daughter's eyes, a fear for her own life, but also that of her mother. Only now, with the immediate danger averted, did Maedbh realise how close she had come to losing Ulrike. The thought terrified her, and a sickening feeling in the pit of her stomach sent a dreadful nausea through her entire body.

'I know you were, my dear,' said Maedbh, fighting to keep her voice even. 'So was I, but you were very, very brave, my girl. You were scared, but you didn't run, you fought like a true Asoborn. I'm so proud of you.'

Ulrike smiled, but Maedbh saw the fear hadn't left her entirely. She stood on trembling legs, and took hold of the chariot's reins. Her hands shook and she gripped the leather tightly to keep her terror from showing.

'Perhaps Wolfgart was right,' she whispered, fighting back tears.

SIGMAR SLAMMED HIS hammer into the face of a long-dead man in mouldering rags. The skull caved with a wet, tearing sound and his hammer broke through the corpse's collarbone and burst from the ruined chest cavity. He jabbed the butt of the hammer through the throat of a nearby corpse and kicked out at a fallen dead thing that grasped his legs with broken fingers. All around him, the battle raged with one-sided fierceness. The dead clawed and bit at the living, but there was no passion or courage to their violence. An animating will filled them, but did so without the spark that drove living warriors to risk their lives for something greater than themselves.

Yet for all their monotonous rigour, the blows of the dead were no less fatal. The flesh of the living was a choice sweetmeat to them, the craving for the warmth and softness of their flesh a hunger that could never be satisfied.

Sigmar's armour bore numerous dents and scars from viciously wielded clubs and cleavers, and blood flowed from a deep cut on his shoulder where a dead logger's axe had smashed the pauldron from his armour and bitten through the links of his mail shirt. He fought alongside Unberogen veterans of the Battle of Middenheim, each hacking a path through the dead while watching for threats Sigmar could not see.

He ducked a slashing axe and drove Ghal-maraz up into the pelvic cavity of a skeletal warrior clad in ancient armour of corroded bronze. The head of the hammer shattered the dead warrior's spine and broke the body in two. It collapsed in a rain of dusty bone and Sigmar swung his hammer around, knocking three more revenants to the ground. Hoarse cries of Ulric's name echoed from the hillside as the Cherusens hewed a path into the dead, felling them like dead wood with every crushing blow of their axes.

Sigmar's warriors fought as one, each pushing forward with the support of the man next to him. Only Unberogen discipline allowed such close-quarter fighting, and it was paying dividends, as few were falling to the blades of the enemy. Lone Cherusen axemen fought until their arms grew weary and they were overwhelmed by the dead, dragged down and torn apart by the voracious enemy.

The pallid cannibal creatures darted through the trees in cowardly packs, skulking at the edges of the fighting and darting in for opportunistic slashes and bites. Sigmar paid them no mind, forging a path onwards towards Ostengard as he saw the Red Scythes ride along the arms of the horseshoe shaped settlement and form a deadly wedge of cavalry in a magnificent display of horsemanship.

'Hold them!' shouted Sigmar, spotting a black-cloaked warrior in the heart of the enemy host, a warrior with the bleached bone of a skull beneath a full-faced helm of bronze. Jade light burned in the sockets of his eyes, and Sigmar felt a monstrous will gathered there, a black sorcery of abominable darkness that was holding this dead host together.

He smashed a pair of skeletal things aside with one blow of his hammer, angling his course towards the Cherusens.

'Aloysis!' he yelled, spotting the slender count of the Cherusens as he beheaded a rotten-fleshed cadaver with expert skill. 'Fight with me!'

The count of the Cherusens heard him and gathered his closest warriors, cutting a path through the dead warriors towards Sigmar. They met in a ring of dead things, both blooded and both breathing hard. Yet for all the carnage around them, they both grinned with fierce battle fury.

'You're hurt,' said Aloysis.

'Not badly,' answered Sigmar, pointing Ghal-maraz towards the black-cloaked warrior with the bronze helm. 'There yonder, that's the source of their power. Destroy it and the host will crumble like morning ashes.'

Aloysis nodded and with a wild, ululating yell, set off downhill towards the nightmarish master of the dead. Sigmar followed him, breaking through the lumpen ranks of the dead to aid his count. Once more they were surrounded by the dead, but with numbers on their side, the strength of the mortal warriors was telling.

The thundering wedge of Krugar's Red Scythes smashed into the rear ranks of the dead, trampling corpses and splintering bone beneath their hooves. Long lances punched into rotten bodies and the host of living dead were split apart. Krugar wielded Utensjarl as though it weighed nothing at all, its blade cleaving dead things in two with every stroke. Most mortal foes would have broken and run at this sudden attack, but the dead cared nothing for this new enemy, fighting with the same horrid determination as ever.

Sigmar and Aloysis fought their way towards the black-cloaked warrior, but with every step more of the dead seemed to rise and block their path. Bones once broken fused together and skulls split open reformed in a dreadful parody of healing. All around Sigmar, the dead pressed in, grasping with decayed hands.

'Sigmar!' shouted Krugar. 'Duck!'

Knowing never to question a shouted battlefield command, Sigmar threw himself flat as something whirling and silver flashed over his head. He rolled swiftly to his feet and bludgeoned two dead warriors with quick jabs of his hammer. He looked left and right for fresh opponents. None of the dead came near him, and as he sought out the black-cloaked master of this dead host, he saw why.

The creature whose will drove the horde was dying.

Utensjarl had been bathed in the fire of Ulric in Middenheim after the great victory, and was now buried deep in the monster's chest. Baleful energies flared from the dead thing, green fire streaming from its eyes as it sought to hold its unmaking at bay. An armoured warrior leapt towards it, a slender-bladed cavalry sabre arcing towards its bony neck. Aloysis's blade found the gap between the dead warrior's breastplate and helmet, his power and rage driving it through unnaturally formed sinews, bone and sorcery.

The bronze helm and skull parted from the body, falling to the ground and rolling downhill. A torrent of icy energy swept out from its disintegrating form as the bones collapsed and a spectral scream of hideous rage split the forest.

No sooner had its vile echoes faded than the dead host fell apart. The recently dead slumped over like drunks and the skeletal warriors risen from their graves fell to pieces like poorly made puppets. Sigmar blinked as the loathsome twilight they had fought this battle beneath was dispelled and sunlight returned to the forest.

Sigmar took a deep breath, feeling the air as a clean draught in his lungs, not the stale, stagnant miasma he had endured in the fighting.

His warriors and those of Krugar and Aloysis stood amazed as life and vitality returned to the land. There was no cheering, no victory cries, for this was simply survival.

Krugar rode up to Sigmar and vaulted from his horse. He lifted Utensjarl from the rusted pile of armour and mouldering cloak. Its blade shone like new, and he turned it over to ensure no lingering trace of the dead warrior remained to taint its edge.

Sigmar stood next to Krugar as Aloysis joined them.

'My warriors gave me a stern lecture the last time I hurled my weapon in the middle of a fight,' said Sigmar.

Krugar shrugged. 'And they were right to do so, but I never miss.'

'You've done that before?' asked Aloysis.

'Once or twice,' grinned Krugar. 'After all, it never hurts for a leader of warriors to have the odd trick or two up his sleeve.'

Aloysis nodded and looked around the grim spectacle of the destroyed village. Sigmar felt his count's pain, for it was his pain too. These people were Cherusens, but they were also Sigmar's people, men and women of the Empire. This attack had brought them together as warriors and it united them as men.

'People will return,' said Sigmar. 'That is what those who make pacts with the dead will never understand. Life will always return stronger than ever.'

'I hope you are right, my lord,' said Aloysis. 'I fear that belief will soon be put to the test.'

NINE
Darkness Closes In

Govannon ran his hands along the cold metal cylinder, feeling the smooth, almost perfect finish the craftsman had applied to its surface. Even the most highly polished metal forged by man had imperfections, a roughness to the surface that no amount of sanding and finishing could erase. This had none of that, and if what he believed was true, then this was no decorative piece to be found in a king's palace, but something far more interesting.

'What is it, da?' asked Bysen. 'Is it a bellows, is that what it is, da?'

'No,' said Govannon. 'It's not a bellows, son.'

'So what in Ulric's name is it?' asked Master Holtwine, staring at the device. 'And why did you need me here?'

No sooner had Govannon given what Alfgeir's knights had recovered from the earth a cursory examination, than he knew he'd need Holtwine's help. He'd sent Cuthwin to fetch the master craftsman, knowing the man would not be able to resist this challenge. Holtwine was a stout man of average height with a scowling face and thinning blond hair. He had been a superlative bowyer and archer in his youth, but his time as a warrior was cut short when a greenskin spear had pierced his chest and nicked his left lung.

Turning his dextrous hands to woodwork, he quickly discovered a natural talent that carpenters who had worked the wood for decades couldn't match. The man was a master of his art, a craftsman who could shape timber in ways that were simply incredible. Govannon had seen his most fabulous pieces, exquisite tables and chairs, decorative cupboards and beds. Even kitchen furniture was given his special attention, resulting in pieces almost too good to be placed in such a harsh environment.

'The dwarf called it a Thunder Bringer,' said Govannon.

'His name was Grindan Deeplock,' Cuthwin reminded him.

Govannon heard the grief in the boy's voice. Since losing his sight, Govannon had become adept at picking the truth from people's voices. He'd heard from Elswyth that this young scout had rescued the dwarf clansman from the forest, though his wounds had been too severe and he'd later died.

'Aye, that it was, Master Cuthwin,' said Govannon. 'My apologies. You saved his life, and it's thanks to you that he'll keep his honour in death. It's all too easy to feel responsible for that life when it ends, trust me I know.'

'No, it's me that needs to apologise,' said Cuthwin. 'I know you meant no disrespect. It's just that I promised that I'd get this machine back to his clan.'

'And so you shall, my boy,' Govannon assured him.

Govannon circled the machine, once again letting his hands inform him of its dimensions and construction. Five long cylinders of cold iron were fixed in a wooden brace harness, which in turn was mounted on a broken carriage with two iron-rimmed wheels supporting the machine. Govannon could tell that each was precisely the same size, which was no mean feat.

Four of the five cylinders were perfectly cast, no blemishes, miscasts or air pockets that he could hear when he tapped the iron with his finishing hammer. The fifth was badly dented at its furthest extremity, as though pinched between enormous tongs, though Govannon shuddered to think of the strength that would be required to compress so strong a casting.

'You still haven't answered my question,' said Master Holtwine.

'Don't you know?' asked Govannon. 'Even Bysen here could guess.'

Holtwine took an irritated breath. 'I am a master craftsman, Govannon, not a player of games, so why don't you just tell me? I have a weapons cabinet to finish for Count Aldred, and the individual walnut panels require chamfering before they can be fitted.'

'I am sure Count Aldred would understand were he here right now,' said Govannon, letting the moment hang. 'This, my good friend, is, in the dwarf tongue, a barag.'

'What does that mean?' asked Cuthwin, leaning down to inspect the machine.

'What indeed?' asked Holtwine, his patience wearing thin.

'Is it Thunder Bringer?' suggested Cuthwin. 'Grindan called it that before he died.'

Govannon smiled. 'I am no expert in the dwarf tongue, but Wolfgart told me that the dwarfs who fought in the tunnels beneath Middenheim used a weapon known as a baragdrakk, which was a bellows-like machine that hurled gouts of sticky fire at the enemy. I'm guessing barag is a term for war machine, a dwarf version of the great catapults we use.'

Holtwine leaned over the device, his eyes roaming the expert shaping of the wood, the fabulous joint-work, the inlaid carvings and elegant cuts that ran with the grain. 'Really? It's a bit small. What manner of wall could you bring down with this?'

'I don't think this is meant to bring down walls,' said Govannon. 'I think this is designed to kill living things, a great many at once if I'm not mistaken.'

'How's it do that, da?' asked Bysen, peering down the length of one of the iron cylinders.

Govannon ran his hands towards the back of the war machine, to where a complex series of flint and powder trap mechanisms in the shape of iron hammers and brass cauldrons were fitted to the back of each cylinder. He pulled each of the hammers back then hauled on the length of leather cord hanging from the base of the mechanism. The first hammer slammed down in the empty cauldron with a hard clang of iron. One by one, the other triggers battered down in their cauldrons, and sparks flew from the impact of flint and iron.

Everyone jumped, but it was Cuthwin who spoke first. He tapped the iron hammer. 'It's a kind of trigger mechanism, isn't it? Like the firing lever on a crossbow.'

Holtwine leaned in, and Govannon could smell the beeswax, woodsap and polish on his skin. He smiled, knowing this device intrigued the man.

'A trigger mechanism, eh?' mused Holtwine. 'Then this small cauldron would be filled with their fire powder? Ulric's breath, is this some manner of enormous thunder bow?'

'That is exactly what I think it is,' said Govannon.

'So what do you plan to do with it?'

'I plan to return it to the dwarfs,' said Govannon. 'But first, I intend to fix it. And I need you to help me.'

REDWANE DREW ON his pipe, letting the fragrant smoke swirl around his mouth before blowing a series of perfect rings. Though the sun was shining, the day still seemed gloomy and cold. The clouds over the Middle Mountains were black and threatening, the skies to the south not much better. His relaxed posture and long wolfskin cloak hid his readiness for trouble, and his free hand never strayed too far from his hammer.

He and the other war leaders of the north made their way through the narrow, greystone streets of Middenheim, talking in the open air, as was Myrsa's custom. The man hated being indoors, and insisted on conducting all planning with the northern wind in his hair and the open sky above him. The wardens of his northern marches, Orsa, Bordan, Wulf and Renweard, walked with him and the mood was grim.

Redwane had thought the dark clouds gathering over the Middle Mountains were a bad omen when he'd first seen them on waking. Now he knew that to be true.

Sigmar's herald had arrived from Reikdorf at first light, bearing evil tidings of a coming war with the living dead. Count Myrsa had listened in stoic silence to the herald's words of the Lord of Undeath's return, and immediately summoned his northern wardens to a war counsel.

They strode down Grafzen Street, on the eastern side of the city, with the Middle Mountains soaring to their left and the rising walls and towers of the great temple to Ulric rearing up to their right. Redwane averted his eyes from the mighty structure, his dreadful scarring and the fight with the daemon lord too fresh and raw for comfort. He still dreamed of that terrible battle, wondering if he could have aimed his blow differently, if there was any outcome that would not have left him so disfigured. A dolorous bell pealed from the temple of Morr, its echoing toll unmistakable. Somewhere, someone was dead, and Redwane whispered a prayer for their journey into the next world.

Redwane glanced at the magnificent sword sheathed at Myrsa's side, the runefang crafted by Alaric the Mad of the dwarfs. That blade had unmade the daemon lord's malefic protection, allowing Sigmar to destroy it with the power bound to his enchanted warhammer.

In the wake of the battle, Sigmar had named the blade *Blodambana,* which meant *Bloodbane* in the ancient tongue of the Unberogen, and not a day passed when Redwane didn't wish that Myrsa had reached the battle sooner.

He shook off his gloomy thoughts, concentrating on what was being said around him. He was the senior bodyguard of the Count of Middenheim, and his attention was wandering far too much these days. Not that he had any real reason to fear for Myrsa's safety. A ring of White Wolves surrounded the council of war, twelve fur-cloaked warriors with hammers resting on their shoulders. The citizens of Middenheim gave them a wide berth, sensing the bellicose mood of the count's guards.

'There are people streaming south from the villages in the foothills of the Middle Mountains,' said Wulf, the lean and wiry Mountain Lord whose hardy warriors watched the high valleys and deep canyons of the Middle Mountains for trouble. 'Many claim that the living dead are rising up in their hundreds, and I'm inclined to believe them. I've heard their stories and looked in their eyes as they spoke. They're not lying.'

'The dead, are they coming from Brass Keep?' asked Myrsa, unable to contain his revulsion. 'I prayed that we had broken Morath's power.'

'We did, my lord,' said Wulf with gruff confidence. 'Brass Keep is nothing more than a refuge for the few Norsii bastards who escaped the slaughter last year. If there's dead rising in the mountains, then they're not coming out of the peaks. It's mainly the villages' own dead that are rising, and it's happening all over. Some of the local sword bands have contained the smaller attacks, but that won't last long. The dead are rising in greater numbers, and they're gathering together, like some damned pack instinct is at work.'

'Nonsense,' put in Bordan. 'You put too much faith in peasants' scare stories. And you're giving the dead too much credit. It's simple hunger that brings them together, nothing more.'

Bordan's title was Forest Master, and the safety of the numerous villages and trails through the western woodlands were entrusted to his foresters and huntsmen. It was a thankless task, and had ground Bordan down into a cynical man with little patience for others. In return, few had time for him, Redwane included.

'You were not at Brass Keep, Bordan,' said Myrsa. 'Wulf and

Redwane and I were, and I am in no hurry to dismiss the Mountain Lord's reports. I understand only too well the malign cunning that animates the living dead, and we should not dismiss any tales of malevolent intelligence.'

'As you say, my lord,' said Bordan, suitably chastened.

'Tell me, Bordan, how fare the forests?' said Myrsa, knowing when to scold and when to embolden. 'I know there are many barrows and forsaken places within the Forest of Shadows. Have any of them been disturbed?'

'The western settlements have faced increased raids, my lord,' replied Bordan. 'The beasts and brigands grow bolder and more desperate with the early onset of winter. There have been a several instances of pestilence, but I have heard of no attacks by the walking dead.'

'There's a surprise,' grunted Redwane, unable to contain himself any longer.

'What did you say?' snapped Bordan.

'You heard me,' said Redwane. 'Your own grandfather could climb from his grave and bite you on the arse and you wouldn't notice.'

Bordan's hand flashed to his hunting knife, but one look into Redwane's horrifically scarred features convinced him that to draw it would be folly of the worst kind.

'You insult me, White Wolf,' hissed Bordan. 'Men have died for less.'

Redwane laughed at Bordan's threat, tapping the warhammer at his belt. 'Come at me with that toothpick of yours and I'll knock that damn fool head off your shoulders. You stood by and allowed Torbrecan's band of lunatics to march through the forest unimpeded. Now you've got hundreds of them in the city shouting for his release and Ulric knows how many of them camped outside the city.'

Bordan shrank before Redwane's words. Ever since the White Wolves had brought Torbrecan back to a Middenheim gaol, the mood in the city had been ugly. Contrary to Ustern's gloomy prediction, the madman's followers hadn't died in the forest, they had followed their captive leader back to the Fauschlag Rock, their numbers growing in strength with every village they passed through.

Hundreds had entered the city before Renweard had closed the gates to their kind. Now the growing flock of screaming, dancing and chanting madmen made camp at the base of the rock, whipping themselves into deliriums of agony-fuelled rage. A group of the ragged lunatics had set themselves ablaze and hurled themselves from the top of the rock, tumbling like falling stars to their doom below. Such heinous acts and their doom-laden presence set the entire populace of Middenheim on edge, and tension spread like a plague to every nook and cranny of the cloud-wreathed city.

'If they are camped around the rock, then surely it is the Way Keeper's duty to break up these fanatics' camp and disperse them,' said Bordan.

'Oh, it is, is it?' said Orsa, the barrel-chested and big-hearted man who sought only to see the good in men. Redwane liked him a great deal, though he knew there was no love lost between Orsa and Bordan. 'Telling me how to do my job are you? Fancy becoming the Way Keeper, do you?'

'No,' said Bordan. 'It was just a suggestion.'

Orsa grunted and shook his head.

'Duly noted, Forest Lord, duly noted,' said Orsa, turning his attention to Myrsa and giving his report. 'We've suffered increased attacks on the workers building the great road, and I've authorised new watch-houses to be built along the route it needs to take through the forest, but even they're proving vulnerable to sustained attack. One was burned to the ground by the forest beasts last week, and another would have fallen but for timely aid from the Berserker King's warriors.'

Throughout these reports of hard times, Myrsa had largely kept his own counsel, but now he turned to the last of his warriors, a youthful man encased in burnished white plate armour named Renweard. The demands of ruling a city in Sigmar's name had become too much for Myrsa to bear alongside his duties as Warrior Eternal, and though it had broken his heart to set aside the role that had defined him for two decades and more, he had bestowed his armour and title to a successor.

Young and courageous, Renweard was a perfect choice for the role. He had no vices as far as Redwane could tell, who *knew* how to spot a man's vices, and was as a devout an Ulrican as it was possible to find. Even Ar-Ulric himself, were he ever to return from the frozen wilderness, would surely approve.

'Well, Warrior Eternal,' asked Myrsa. 'What is happening beyond our walls?'

'It is true that more and more people are coming to Middenheim, my lord,' said Renweard with arch formality. 'And the Mountain Lord is correct that a great many are fleeing packs of the dead. As to this Torbrecan's followers, I think we shall be rid of them soon enough.'

'How so?' asked Myrsa.

'It seems they plan to march on Reikdorf soon.'

'Reikdorf?' said Redwane. 'Why?'

Renweard shrugged with a clatter of cream plate. 'It is hard to be certain, White Wolf, but it seems they believe that the great battle between life and death is to be settled there. When Torbrecan is eventually released, they plan to march on Sigmar's city in a great host.'

'Perhaps we should let them,' said Redwane, surprised to find he was only half joking.

THE DREAM WAS always the same, rank and malignant tree roots growing up from beneath the earth and spreading their poisonous taint to the far corners of the world. She knew, of course, what it signified and what was causing it, but no amount of prayers to Shallya could keep it at bay. High Priestess Alessa rose from her bed and poured some water into a mug from a copper ewer.

She drained the entire mug and rubbed her eyes, looking towards the curtained window at the far end of her room. It was still dark outside and the fire in the hearth had burned to low embers. Alessa rose and threw another log onto the fire, knowing there would be no more sleep tonight.

She wanted to wake someone, anyone, just to have another living person to talk to, but that was selfish, and she did not want fear of what was buried beneath their temple to spread among the novices. Ever since it had been brought here, she had feared to face it.

She remembered Sigmar and Wolfgart bringing her the damned crown of Morath, locked within an iron casket and sealed with holy words recited by every priest in Reikdorf. The shaft they had sunk beneath the temple to bury the crown was a hundred feet deep, lined with iron rods and filled with blessed earth. That artefact of evil had been removed from the world of men as far as any object could be.

Then why did she feel that the precautions they had taken were nowhere near enough?

'It feels the nearness of its maker,' she whispered, seeing her breath mist before her, despite the warmth growing in the hearth. She shivered and returned to the bed, gathering up her woollen blanket and wrapping it around her shoulders. Alessa clutched the dove pendant around her neck and whispered a prayer to Shallya.

She smiled at her own weakness. Shallya answered prayers of the needy, of those who could not help themselves. Alessa was no helpless victim, no unfortunate at the end of her tether. She was a high priestess, a servant of the goddess of healing and mercy, her instrument for good in this world. There were others more deserving than she, and Alessa gave thanks for what she had and all she had been allowed to do in her life.

She had served the people of Reikdorf for over twenty years, first as a novitiate tending to the small riverside shrine dedicated to the goddess, then later as a temple maiden, before finally becoming high priestess of the temple built by Sigmar ten years ago. It had been a fulfilling life, a worthy one, and she had blessed many children as they came screaming into the world, and eased the passage of those whose time in it was done. Alessa had healed the sick, tended the wounded and comforted the dying.

Alessa left the room and made her way through the cold corridors of the temple. Faint starlight gleamed through the windows as she made her way past the infirmary, where many of the sick of Reikdorf were treated, heading towards the chapel. She felt at peace there and, with the last traces of the nightmare lingering in her mind, she needed the solace just kneeling before the shrine to Shallya brought before facing her greatest fear.

Inside it was quiet, as she had expected it would be. A few low-burning candles guttered behind glass panels and white banners stitched with gold thread hung from the walls, each depicting Shallya in her many aspects; the maiden before the bubbling spring, the soaring dove, the bleeding heart and the benevolent mother of all.

She made her way between the long rows of benches toward the small shrine at the end of the nave. Set within a curved chancel, a marble statue of a beatific figure of a woman shawled in white knelt beside an injured warrior and healed his wounds. Though most warriors offered praise to Ulric, they all prayed to Shallya eventually.

Alessa knelt before the image of her deity, closing her eyes and placing her hands over her heart. She recited the healing litanies, listing the ten sacred virtues of selflessness, and felt her serenity return and the vision of the black tree roots burrowing into the world lose its potency.

'I will not fear you, for even death is part of the cycle of life,' she whispered. 'I will face you and I will be restored by resisting you.'

Alessa rose and moved around the statue, where a wooden table laid with a muslin cloth was set. Upon it was a softly glowing lantern, a washbowl and a collection of cleansing oils. She pulled the table to one side, revealing a heavy iron trapdoor set in the flagstones. She lifted a silver key from around her neck, and slipped it into a keyhole worked from the same blessed metal.

The lock clicked and she pulled the heavy trapdoor open, its bulk offset by a system of counterweights and pulleys designed by Govannon the smith. A cold gust blew up from the depths, but she paid it no mind as she took up the lantern and descended the spiral staircase that disappeared into the earth.

She followed the stairs until they opened out into a long corridor of black stone. Verses to ward off evil influences were inscribed on the walls, and just looking at them gave her the strength to follow the corridor to its end. A door fashioned from yew and rowan barred the way forward, but once again the silver key unlocked it.

Beyond the door was a diamond-shaped chamber, its wood-panelled walls aligned east to west to attract the influences of the sun and rubbed in essence of valerian and jasmine. Incense vials placed around the chamber filled it with the ripe scent of crops, verdant growth and burgeoning life. The floor was hard-packed earth from the fertile Reik estuary, and though nothing would grow down here away from the light, corn seeds were sown in its loamy richness as the fields above were planted.

It was cold, and Alessa shivered, knowing the chill had nothing to do with being below ground. She moved to the centre of the chamber and dropped to her knees, once again clasping her hands over her heart. With her eyes closed, she let her awareness of her physical surroundings fall away, allowing her spirit to fill the void in her senses.

Immediately, she could feel the crown's evil pulsing below her. Even contained within its iron casket and bound with wards and charms passed down through unremembered generations, its power was strong enough to bleed out. Alessa could feel its influence reaching out to her, promising eternal life, the return of her youth, and an existence free from fear of disease, disfigurement or infirmity.

'You cannot tempt me,' she said through gritted teeth. 'Everything you promise is a lie.'

Her mind filled with its blandishments, each more fanciful than the last. She saw herself renewed, her skin unblemished like the cool marble statue of Shallya. She could not deny the attraction of what the crown offered; yet one look into the eyes of this immortal vision of her eternal features betrayed the truth of it. Immortality was an affront to nature, an abominable state of existence where growth was impossible and stagnation the only outcome.

She banished the crown's promises, feeling its hold on her thoughts grow weaker as her will to resist it grew stronger. *This* was why she had come here, knowing that only by facing her fear of its temptations could she overcome them.

'Only those who feel fear can know true courage,' she whispered. 'And my faith was meaningless unless put to the test. I know now it is stronger than anything you can offer.'

Alessa felt the crown's fury, its icy touch retreating into the depths of its prison. She let out a shuddering breath, feeling as weak as a newborn, but renewed in her heart. She rose to her feet and left the chamber, locking the door behind her and mounting the steps to the temple with a lightness of spirit she had not felt in months.

As she locked the trapdoor once again, she felt a last spiteful stab of venom from the buried crown. A searing image burned itself into her mind, and she dropped the lantern as her limbs spasmed in fear.

She blinked, but there was no erasing the horror of the vision.

Sigmar Heldenhammer, riding through the gates of Reikdorf with the crown of the damned once again upon his brow.

THE GREAT LIBRARY was quiet, as it always was, but this quiet was more than just the absence of hushed voices and the rustle of parchment. It was a silence that told Eoforth he was alone in the building and always would be. That was ridiculous of course, but such was the emptiness he felt here that it was easy to believe no one would ever come here again.

He loved his Great Library, feeling more at home amongst its wealth of knowledge and the accomplishments of man than he did anywhere else. It was a place of solace, where he could retreat from the world of violence and lose himself in a Brigundian treatise on mathematics, a colourful Ostogoth tale of family histories or the incredibly complex blood-feuds between the Udose clans. This was his refuge, yet tonight it felt like a tomb, a cold and empty place where no one ever came and no one ever would.

He blamed it on the stacks of books and piles of rolled up scrolls scattered around him, for who would choose to remain in a building with such evil reading material out in the open? For weeks, Eoforth had pored over every manuscript he could find that had some mention of Nagash, however tangential. Most of it was surely nonsense, but Sigmar had tasked him with unearthing everything that could be found on the Lord of Undeath, and Eoforth was not about to let him down.

A great many of the most useful tomes had come from the dusty library of Morath, the necromancer of Brass Keep, though copies of translated manuscripts from the far south had come to Reikdorf's Great Library via the Empire's southern kings. Oral tales told by traders returning from the southern lands of searing deserts or from across the Worlds Edge Mountains had been painstakingly compiled by the library's scribes.

Lack of material was not the problem; sorting the embellishments and exaggerations from the truth was proving to be the hardest part of this task.

Trying to cross-reference and corroborate details was proving to be next to impossible, for no two manuscripts or tales agreed on any details of worth. Eoforth sat up straight as the small of his back flared in pain. His joints were aching and it felt like he had a desert's worth of sand trapped beneath his eyelids. He yawned and put his head in his hands.

People called him wise, as though that were enough to reach back across the gulfs of time to pluck the truth from the mass of conflicting information. He knew a great deal, it was true, more than most men, but in the face of all he needed to discover, his knowledge was a paltry thing indeed. Eoforth rubbed his eyes with the heels of his palms and stared at the manuscript before him once again.

Its edges were curled and blackened, as though it had been plucked from a fire, and the writing was an old form of Reikspiel, one that only a handful of the oldest men and women in the Empire could decipher. It was a depressing thought that he was one of those oldest men.

Endal mariners returning to Marburg from a mapping expedition to the far north over a century ago had discovered the manuscript aboard a smouldering galley drifting at the mouth of the Reik. No trace had been found of any ship that might have attacked the galley, nor were any of its crew found aboard.

It was a mystery that had never been solved, but the sailors had found a treasure trove of trinkets and tomes of unknown provenance aboard the galley, all of which they took back to their city and presented to King Alderbad, the great-grandfather of Count Aldred.

Eoforth had travelled to Marburg many years ago to study these artefacts – golden effigies of jackal-headed monsters, strange, beetle-like creatures and elaborate death masks of gold and jade.

Many of the manuscripts Eoforth had studied made reference to ancient gods of similar aspect, naming them as forgotten kings of a lost land named Nehekhara. It was said that these kings had been laid to rest in fabulous tombs and mausoleum cities now lost to the desert sands. In many of the manuscripts, Nagash was blamed for the final doom of these kings in a single night, though how anyone, even Nagash, could have laid an entire civilisation low so swiftly was beyond Eoforth.

If such tales were to be believed, then Nagash had walked the earth for over two thousand years, a fantastical span of time that Eoforth had trouble in grasping. It seemed absurd, but then the ultimate goal of the necromancer was to cheat death and live forever, so perhaps it was not so unbelievable after all.

Some of what Eoforth read was plainly nonsense, tales of a beautiful queen of the dead who had become his consort and sired the race of blood drinkers, an alliance with a burrowing race of vermin creatures who infested the hidden corners of the world and, most incredible of all, the building of a vast obsidian pyramid somewhere in the southern mountains that prevented the necromancer from ever truly dying.

All the accounts agreed on one thing: Nagash was the bane of life, a twisted and corrupt sorcerer whose existence had transcended his human origins to become something more monstrous and more evil than anything that had ever walked the face of the world. His powers were beyond imagining, his reach limitless and his armies legion.

Inextricably linked with the tale of Nagash was the tale of the crown he had forged and into which he had bound the essence of his damned soul. This, the ancient taletellers agreed, was the source of Nagash's greatest power and his greatest weakness. The manuscript from the burning galley spoke of an ancient warrior named Al-Khadizaar who slew the Lord of Undeath with a dreadful sword of fell power and cast his bones and crown into a great river.

Frustratingly, the manuscript said no more of the crown, but in a long-dead trader's recounting of his travels in the blasted lands south of the Black Mountains, Eoforth unearthed mention of a ruined ancient city that bore all the hallmarks of having been destroyed by a greenskin invasion. When Sigmar had told him of the battle against the necromancer of Brass Keep, he had spoken of a phantom city beneath the ice; a vision conjured by Morath to recreate the fallen glory of his lost city of Mourkain. Like the cities of Nehekhara, it too had been made great and then brought low by Nagash's crown.

A greenskin invasion had destroyed the city, but had they been drawn to destroy Mourkain by the crown's influence? Everywhere the crown appeared in history, great devastation quickly followed: terrible invasions, cataclysms of dreadful power or corruptions of once noble civilisations into barbarism. The crown was a talisman of woe, a bringer of destruction that brought only misery and death whenever it came to light.

And it was buried in the heart of Reikdorf.

A soft gust sighed past Eoforth, and he heard a dry, dusty chuckle that echoed from the blackness between the stone pillars. It drifted on the still air, and Eoforth knew in that moment he was not alone. Deathly eyes were turned upon him, mocking his feeble attempts to unlock the nature of a creature that had walked the haunted paths of the world from the earliest ages of man. Cold chills travelled the length of his spine and Eoforth slammed the book shut, his breath misting before him as the light from the flickering candles dimmed and the shadows crept closer.

Gathering up his notes, Eoforth fled the library.

TEN
Creeping Death

A dozen riders fled north, whipping their mounts in a frenzy of terror and desperation. Khaled al-Muntasir watched them go with a wry grin of amusement on his lips. A city of nearly eight thousand people, and twelve men were all that now lived. He watched from a high balcony of the Count's Palace, a grand tower decorated with finery from all across the Empire and a number of artefacts he recognised as belonging to civilisations from the other side of the world.

'You were a man of culture,' said Khaled al-Muntasir, lifting a delicately-wrought vase of pale white ceramic decorated with exquisite images picked out in blue ink. The artist had skilfully rendered a man and women drinking tea at a low table in a bamboo-framed home. The brushwork was flawless and the detailing incredible. In any land this piece would fetch a small fortune.

Khaled al-Muntasir tossed the vase from the balcony, watching as it tumbled down the cliff to smash to fragments on the way down. The vase's owner didn't bat an eyelid at his prized possession's destruction.

'Yes,' said Khaled al-Muntasir, moving back into the Great Hall, its walls painted with colourful frescoes depicting scenes of hunting and battle. 'You have some wonderful pieces here. This rug, for example, bears the handiwork of the dreamweavers of Ind, while this wall hanging is from the silk-worms of the Dragon Emperor is it not?'

The vampire stopped beneath a podium of oak, upon which was mounted a pair of giant ivory tusks. He stroked the monstrous fangs, marvelling at their size and contemplating the scale of the beast from which they had been torn. The vampire looked towards the warrior standing motionless in the centre of the audience chamber, a tall man in golden armour and a crown of the same metal upon his brow. His hair was white and flowed across his shoulders like a frozen waterfall.

'Ordinarily, I would say these belonged to a dragon, but I know of no such beasts in these lands any more. So tell me, Siggurd, what manner of creature once owned these?'

The warrior turned to face Khaled al-Muntasir, his face drained of life and his throat a ruined mess of torn sinews and muscle. Blood coated his chest and his eyes were now sunken, filled with a hideous red light. His mouth opened and closed, but no words came out, just a hiss of dead air from his opened throat.

'Ah, yes, of course...' said Khaled al-Muntasir. The vampire muttered a petty incantation of dark magic and the torn meat of Siggurd's throat began to close up, the necrotic flesh weaving the ghastly wound closed. 'Now, you were saying...?'

The count of the Brigundian tribe's mouth opened and a rasping death rattle emerged, a sound dragged from the abyss that carried such pleasing anguish that Khaled al-Muntasir couldn't resist a wide grin.

'Skaranorak...' hissed Siggurd. 'A dragon ogre...'

Khaled al-Muntasir's eyes widened, and he stroked the heavy tusks with his carefully clipped nails, a new-found respect in his deathly eyes.

'You killed this beast yourself?' he asked.

'No,' said Siggurd, his voice returning. 'Sigmar killed it.'

'Ah, yes, Sigmar,' said the vampire. 'I should have guessed.'

Siggurd walked out onto the balcony, a perch from where he had once surveyed the lands belonging to his tribe, lands that had once brought trade and wealth to his city, but were now overtaken by darkness and fear. Swollen by the Menogoth dead, the army of Nagash had taken Siggurdheim in a matter of days, its rugged peak climbed by hundreds of ghoulish infiltrators as thousands of dead warriors marched along its steep winding roads to batter their way in through the heavy gateway. The city had fallen in a night that still held sway, the Great Hall's many windows admitting no light, only the darkness of eternal night.

'Are you not going to stop them?' asked Siggurd, his flesh finally losing its vigour and warmth as the Blood Kiss destroyed the last of his humanity and completed his journey to become an immortal killer of the living.

'Why would I care to do that?' said a voice laden with thousands of years of blood and slaughter. Like tombstones crumbling, it was the sound of toppled civilisations, cultures destroyed and entire realms drained of life.

Siggurd and Khaled al-Muntasir bowed as Nagash entered the Great Hall. The darkness beyond the windows was eclipsed by the bleak presence of the arch necromancer, a thick miasma of dark energy that filled his servants with macabre vigour. The coiled snake staff crackled with simmering power, and his metallic fingers dripped beads of dark magic to the stone floor of the hall.

The hulking violence that was Krell marched at Nagash's right hand, his black axe strapped across his armoured back. The fallen warrior of the Dark Gods had run rampant through the city, killing with a frenzy that would no doubt have pleased his former master. To Nagash's left was the wolfish figure of Count Markus, his lean frame now invigorated with slaughter. His blade and chin were covered in blood; his eyes alight with the thrill of feeding on so many fearful hearts.

'They will carry word of what has happened here,' said Siggurd, staring hungrily at the blood on Markus's blade. 'It will give them time to prepare for your attack.'

'It matters not,' said Nagash. 'Already my vassal forces spread fear to the furthest reaches of this land. Man is a beast and it is good that fear fills him.'

'And that fear will drain men's hearts of courage,' said Khaled al-Muntasir, returning to the balcony. 'But more than that, it tastes so sweet...'

Khaled al-Muntasir watched as the riders fleeing Siggurdheim's destruction disappeared over the horizon, their life lights as bright as stars. 'Where will they go?' he asked.

'North to Asoborn lands,' answered Siggurd, licking his lips and pacing the hall like a restless stallion. 'They will flee to Queen Freya in Three Hills. She lives for war and will muster her warriors as soon as she learns what has happened here.'

'Then that is where you will go, Khaled al-Muntasir,' said Nagash. 'Hunt down this queen and destroy her.'

Khaled al-Muntasir bowed and dropped into the throne that had once belonged to the Brigundian count. 'I will leave her lands as desolate as Bel Aliad itself.'

'What of the Merogens?' asked Siggurd, his hands clawed into fists. 'Is Henroth dead?'

'Henroth's people huddle around flickering candles within their castles of stone, surrounded by the dead. They will be no threat,' said Nagash as Markus walked over to Siggurd and took hold of his chin.

The former count of the Menogoths turned to Khaled al-Muntasir. 'The birth-hunger is upon him,' he said.

'It is,' agreed the vampire.

'He will need to feed soon or else go mad.'

'There are living yet within this city's walls,' said Khaled al-Muntasir, languidly twirling a finger through the air, as though stirring its flavours. 'Young Siggurd must learn to hunt on his own, just as you did.'

Siggurd took Markus's hand from his chin, his eyes hostile, and they circled like two virile males in a wolf pack. Khaled al-Muntasir smirked at such posturing in newly-ascended blood drinkers.

'Give a mortal a taste of true power and it all but overwhelms them,' said Nagash.

'If either survive to learn how to use that power they will be formidable killers,' said Khaled al-Muntasir.

'The fate of blood drinkers interests me not at all,' hissed Nagash ducking below the balcony's archway and casting his immortal gaze over the landscape. The darkness of his armour and tattered cloak swirled around him like sable light, the faint glow from within his bones like the last sunset of the world. 'Only the crown matters.'

'Then why am I to ride north?' asked Khaled al-Muntasir. 'Surely we should march straight to Reikdorf.'

Krell took a thunderous step towards him, his axe unsheathed in a heartbeat and the light in his skull shining with the threat of furious violence.

'You question my purpose?' said Nagash.

'No, my master,' said Khaled al-Muntasir, smoothly swinging his legs from the arms of the throne and giving an elaborate bow. 'I am your humble servant in all things.'

Nagash's eyes bored into him, and Khaled al-Muntasir instantly regretted his flippant tone. He felt himself touched by a fraction of the necromancer's power, a dreadful extinction that held everything that lived or once drew air into its lungs with contempt. Even the living dead were not immune to the necromancer's touch. His enormous reservoirs of power could snuff out unlife as easily as a mortal blew out a candle.

Khaled al-Muntasir had passed the point where he feared much of anything, but the one fate that still struck horror through his undying flesh was oblivion. To live forever, to hunt the living and to indulge his every sense and vice was the sum total of his desire, and the thought of that end filled him with dread.

Nagash saw his acquiescence and the lambent glow in his eye sockets shimmered at his vassal's fear. The Lord of Undeath turned to the darkened landscape beyond Siggurdheim.

'Spread the terror of death before you and drive those you do not kill toward my crown,' hissed Nagash. 'Lay waste these petty kingdoms and scour the seed of mortals from this land.'

'It shall be my pleasure,' Khaled al-Muntasir assured Nagash.

A LOW BELL tolled, echoing across the Old Town harbour, and Sergeant Alwin of the Jutonsryk Lancers paused to watch the beacon fire atop the Tower of Tides light up, signalling the end of another day.

'Regular as always,' he said to himself. 'Good to know that some things never change.'

He moved on, walking with an unhurried gait, his sword sheathed at his side and his blue cloak flitting behind him in the choppy evening wind blowing off the seafront. It was a quiet night, which made a nice change, the drunks keeping a low profile instead of roistering in the streets or brawling in the taprooms.

The docks were quiet, just the slap of water against the quay, the creak of ships' timbers and the sigh of wind through the rigging and flags. His lancers followed behind him, four men of proven character, all of whom he could rely on in a tight spot. Not that he expected any tight spots tonight; the day had been without incident, as though the thousands of sailors, tradesmen and inhabitants of the city had been reluctant to remain outdoors for any length of time. He'd thought it odd, but anything that helped keep the peace in Jutonsryk was a boon as far as Alwin was concerned.

He paused by the westernmost spur of the docks, putting his foot up on one of the iron mooring rungs set in the quay. The *Ormen*

Lange, an Udose vessel familiar to the docks of Jutonsryk, was moored here, and he waved up to the bearded clansman at ship's watch in the forecastle.

'All's bonny,' called the man. 'None reddin the fire the night, eh?

'Indeed,' agreed Alwin, though he had no idea what the clansman had just said.

He moved on, looking up at the Namathir to Count Marius's castle, its many windows glowing with colour and light. The lord of Jutonsryk was a hard man to like, but Marius knew how to run a busy port, understanding that commerce and trade would only flow into a city if its streets could be made safe. Merchants would not come to a city where they feared for their life and cargo.

Which wasn't to say the city was a utopian society where crime didn't happen, far from it, but those who flouted the law were punished by Marius's only penalty – death. Justice in Jutonsryk was harsh, uncompromising and final. Which made for a city where all but the most foolish drunks or desperate footpads observed the law.

Alwin followed the line of the docks as he and his lancers made his way towards Taal's Fire, the most southerly beacon brazier of the docks. It burned with blue fire, a shimmering lodestone for incoming ships. Further north, around the curve of the bay, Ulric's Fire wavered with a green light. Differing herbs altered the colour of the flames, and it was thanks to these beacons, together with the one atop the Tower of Tides, that not a single vessel had been lost while navigating the treacherous channels around the Reik estuary.

As Alwin looked north, the light from Ulric's Fire was momentarily obscured, as though a shimmering curtain had been drawn in front of it. He frowned and squinted through the darkness as it flickered and disappeared.

'Did you see that?' he said, turning towards his warriors.

They nodded and Alwin looked south towards Taal's Fire. It too was gone.

'Damn me,' hissed Alwin. 'I don't like that, no I do not.'

He looked back at the Tower of Tides, reassured to see that its beacon light was still lit. Low clouds clung to the distant tower, tendrils of mist that seemed not to move with the wind. Alwin looked out to sea, and his mouth fell open at the sight of a rolling grey fog coming in from the darkness. Living by the ocean, with a coastline of marshland to the south, a man got used to mists, but this was something more. It hugged the water, undulating over its black surface like a scum of sea filth as it crept towards the city.

The fog was thick and reeked worse than a bloated corpse dragged from the water. It drifted over the hundreds of berthed ships, slinking and creeping over their timbers with an unclean touch. It slithered up the quayside, oozing onto the docks with dreadful purpose, and Alwin knew he'd never seen anything quite so unpleasant.

'It's only mist, damn it,' he chided himself, irritated that something so banal had him spooked. Even as he told himself it was only weather, he couldn't shake the feeling that it portended something far worse. No sooner had he formed the thought than he heard the dolorous peal of a brass ship's bell, a talisman to guide a vessel through just such a fog, yet this familiar sound gave him no comfort.

The sound was dead, without the natural echo or earthly touch of an instrument forged by man. Another bell answered it, then another. Soon the quayside was echoing to the ringing of dead bells, hundreds of flat peals that slid through the darkened streets like midnight assassins. Sailors and traders were emerging from the taverns, drawn by the deathly echoes and an instinctual understanding that these sounds were just *wrong* in every way it was possible to be.

Alwin wanted to tell these people to run, to flee whatever doom was soon to overtake the city, but he couldn't think of what to tell them that wouldn't sound ridiculous. He looked back out to sea, searching for the source of the hollow bells, now hearing the sluggish passage of water over rotten timbers. Lights began to appear in the fog, drifting corpse lights that rose and fell with the tide, a hundred or more of them.

They shone like a host of candles for the departed, poisonously evil flares that bridged the gap between the living and the dead. Or guided the dead *to* the living...

'Reinen, get back to the barrack house,' ordered Alwin. 'Gather everyone you can find and have them arm themselves before getting down to the quayside.'

'Sir? What's going on?'

'Don't argue with me, just do it!'

Reinen nodded and sped off, grateful to be freed from remaining at the water's edge. Moments later, Alwin heard a clatter of armour behind him as his lancers fled the quay, leaving him alone on the dockside. Though he knew hundreds of people were nearby, he could see none of them as the fog thickened around him.

Isolated in his mist-wreathed world, he saw nothing but the

approaching lights and heard nothing beyond the sullen bells, his thudding heartbeat, the slurp of water and the rattle of dusty bones, chains and rusted iron.

A shape emerged from the fog; a black-hulled vessel wreathed in a spectral light and which could surely never have remained above the waves such was the rotten, holed nature of its hull. Its timbers were swollen and decayed, and whole swathes of its side were missing. Stagnant water poured *from* it as though recently raised from the deeps. The fog lifted momentarily, and Alwin saw hundreds of these ships of the damned surging into Jutonsryk harbour, each with tattered crimson sails that hung lank and limp, stirred by no wind and made fast without ropes or crew.

Captain Raul claimed he had seen two hundred vessels of the dead, and Alwin now knew the southern captain's estimate of numbers had been conservative. The black ships moved against the wind, relentless and inexorable as they drifted over the sea to the quay. Black things moved through the sky, horrors thankfully concealed in the thick fog, swooping over the city with murder in mind. Chittering flocks of bats billowed in their wake and a distant screech of something monstrous echoed through the fog-bound city.

Muffled by the fog, Alwin heard cries of alarm from the moored ships. Alarm bells began ringing, on the ships and throughout the city, but Alwin knew it was too late for any warning to save Jutonsryk. He heard a sickening crash of timbers and looked back over his shoulder to see the *Ormen Lange* cloven in two by an eastern war galley built in the style of a hundred years ago. The galley slammed into the quayside with a thunderous crash of splitting timbers, and Alwin had his first look at the damned crew aboard this abominable vessel.

All along the gunwale, dreadful figures with piercing green lights for eyes stared at him with hungry fervour. Pale corpses, rotted skeletons in corroded armour and hunched figures with water streaming from their wounds clutched spears, axes and short blades in their dead hands.

They streamed onto the land, a host of dead sailors come for revenge on the world of the living. Alwin heard the first screams from further along the quay. The sound broke through the paralysing terror that held his limbs fast, and he drew his sword, determined to fight these seaborne invaders with whatever courage he could muster.

He ran back to the *Ormen Lange*, seeing the clansman he had spoken to earlier crawling from the wreckage of his ship. Bloated, grey-skinned dead men hacked at him with sharp cutlasses. As soon as they saw Alwin, they abandoned their victim and lurched towards him with a dreadful hunger in their sunken, dead eyes.

Alwin wanted to run, to live, but he was a Jutone warrior, and he brought his sword up.

'Come on then, you dead bastards!' he shouted, hurling himself at the damned.

His first blow clove a rotten corpse in two. Its flesh was soft and yielding, and his blade easily cut through its sodden meat. Alwin slashed the neck of another drowned man, and a froth of stagnant water bubbled from the wound. A grinning skeleton came at him and he slammed his blade through its skull, dropping it in a clatter of bone. The dead pressed in, dying by the dozen, but they poured in unending numbers from the hundreds of ships.

He buried his sword in the guts of another waterlogged corpse, twisting the handle to relieve the suction of wet flesh on the blade. A corpse fastened its teeth on his arm and bit through the meat there. Alwin cried out and punched the dead thing in the face. Its jellied eye squirted ooze, momentarily blinding him, but momentarily was all the opening the undead needed.

Clawed hands fastened on his throat and tearing limbs pinned his arms to his side, as they bore him to the ground. Sharpened teeth gnawed at his flesh and Alwin's sword was torn from his grip. He struggled furiously, but there were too many and the pain was too great. He screamed as they devoured him, biting chunks from his legs and stomach like warriors with hunks of roast boar at a victory feast. Blood burst from his mouth, and the stink of it drove his killers to fresh heights of hunger.

Alwin's last sight was the beacon fire atop the Tower of Tides as it died, plunging the world into a darkness which it could never survive.

THE MUSTER FIELDS of Three Hills were thick with horses and the clamour of warriors. Maedbh wound a careful path through the thousands of people gathered here, nodding to those she knew and picking out the differing tattoos of various tribal sword bands. Even within the Asoborns there were fiercely clannish groupings, and though they were united by Queen Freya's call to arms, each swaggered with something to prove.

At the centre of the maelstrom, Freya directed her warriors with fiery sweeps of her spear and shouted pronouncements. Her twin boys were at her side, their faces downcast and sullen. Maedbh could guess the reason why, now understanding a measure of Wolfgart's reluctance to see Ulrike trained in the arts of war.

Five hundred chariots were lined up along the edge of the field or rolled in to take up position by the rutted track that led towards the river. Two acres of forest had been felled to corral the horses and a neverending train of wagons was assembling on the far side of the hills to carry their fodder. Sword bands in their hundreds milled around the field, warriors from all across Asoborn lands greeting one another like long lost friends. Many of these warriors would not have seen each other for years, and Maedbh lamented that it took times of such darkness to bring them together.

Ulrike walked beside her, holding tightly to her hand. Every night since the attack of the wolves, she had woken in the darkness, screaming and weeping uncontrollably. Maedbh had held her tight, hating that her little girl was suffering like this. She remembered her own first blood, a desperate chariot ride before a mob of greenskins raiding the eastern lands of the Asoborns. Freya's mother, Queen Sigrid, had broken the enemy horde, but Maedbh never forgot the exhilarating terror of riding close enough to the enemy that she could smell their rank, rotten-meat breath and feel the bite of their axes on her chariot.

'Is the queen going to fight the wolves?' asked Ulrike.

'Yes, my dear,' said Maedbh. 'That's exactly what she's going to do. All these men and women are going to ride south and hunt them down. They're going to kill every one of them so they never hurt anyone ever again. Do you understand me? The queen doesn't tolerate bad wolves in her lands.'

'Good,' said Ulrike. 'I hope they kill them all. I hate wolves.'

'Those weren't real wolves,' said Maedbh, stopping and coming down to Ulrike's level. She looked her daughter in the eye and said, 'Real wolves are servants of Ulric, the god you were named for, so don't hate them. Those things that attacked us were once noble wolves, but an evil man made them into monsters with his dark magic.'

Ulrike nodded, though Maedbh saw she was yet to be convinced. Maedbh led her through the sword muster, passing mail-clad fighters of the east, bare-chested horse archers of the hill folk, colourfully tattooed women of the Myrmidian sects and burly horsemen from the northern woodlands with their long iron-tipped lances. Everywhere she heard proud boasts of the monsters the warriors would kill, tall tales of martial prowess and bravado, but it rang hollow to Maedbh's ears.

Mixed in with the Asoborns were perhaps two hundred Brigundians and a hundred Menogoth warriors; all that had survived the invasion of the dead. Hundreds of refugees from both tribes were sheltered in Three Hills, but these men, with their grief-etched faces and hollow eyes, sought only vengeance. Maedbh didn't blame them; their lands had been ravaged, their homes destroyed and their families murdered. With nothing left to lose, they were only too glad to join the Asoborn war muster.

Maedbh knew how she would feel if Three Hills suffered as their lands had suffered, and that thought gave her stride fresh purpose as she marched through the uprooted warriors towards the Asoborn queen.

Freya stood beside her chariot, a gold and bronze creation of deadly power. Its sides were reinforced with iron cords and layered wood against the grain. Golden fire was inlaid in finely crafted carvings of flaming wheels and blazing comets. A dozen of the Queen's Eagles surrounded her, mounted on tall, wide-chested geldings, their golden-winged helms shining like sunlight on silver. Sigulf and Fridleifr harnessed two beasts Maedbh recognised as having once belonged to Wolfgart's herds to the chariot, though it was clear the boys were less than happy with their mother.

Freya herself was clad in her finest armour of bronze and iron, and, as always, the queen was attired to impress as much as protect. Bronze mail hung in a weave from her shoulders, and the plates protecting her chest and belly were moulded to the form of the muscles beneath. Iron greaves and vambrace were strapped to her shins and forearms, leaving the curved sway of her hips and thighs bare. A scarlet cloak was pinned to her shoulders with silver brooches in the form of snarling wolves.

'Maedbh!' cried the queen as she saw her approach. 'A fine gathering is it not?'

'Yes, my queen, very fine,' said Maedbh, looking around the muster field. 'How many answered the call to arms?'

'All of them it seems,' laughed Freya. 'Near five hundred chariots, two thousand warriors on foot and a half century of horsemen. A host to chase the dead back to their tombs, eh?'

'A mighty army indeed,' answered Maedbh. 'Our lands must be empty of warriors.'

The queen nodded, her face darkening at Maedbh's insinuation. 'I know you think me rash to ride off like this, and, yes, this muster will leave us vulnerable for a while. But brother Siggurd's lands are aflame and what manner of queen would I be if I left his murder unavenged? You heard what Sigmar's herald said, the dead are rising everywhere and the Menogoths are already gone. Now Siggurd's city is taken and our southernmost scouts say there's an army moving on Three Hills. No one invades my lands, Maedbh, no one.'

'I understand, my queen,' said Maedbh. 'But I have faced this enemy, and it is not cowed by threats, boasts or reputations. It is a foe that lives to kill and create more of its kind.'

'You can still come, Maedbh. I need you with me,' said Freya, indicating her chariot. 'I can find another rider when battle is joined, but no one has your skill with a chariot. No one has your fire and daring.'

Maedbh glanced down at Ulrike, pulled by the desire to ride with her queen and the need to protect her daughter. She had crewed Freya's chariot ever since the queen had taken the throne, and the idea that she would go into battle without Maedbh rankled. Yet one look at her daughter's need told her she could not ride with this army. In that moment she understood the demands on Wolfgart, but to Maedbh, the choice was clear. She could not leave Ulrike.

'Thank you, my queen,' said Maedbh, 'but I cannot. I have Ulrike to think of.'

The queen shrugged and said, 'Your child is blooded now, she should ride with us too.'

Anger touched Maedbh. 'As Sigulf and Fridleifr do?'

The queen's face darkened and she climbed aboard her chariot.

'You know why they do not march with me,' hissed Freya, mercurial as ever. 'If you will not ride with me, then I charge you to protect them. Keep my boys safe, Maedbh, promise me this and I might forget your insolence.'

'I will watch over them as though they were my own,' promised Maedbh.

Freya smiled, her earlier anger forgotten.

'I know you will,' said the queen. 'I will leave a sword band of my Eagles too, but it is a great honour I do you, Maedbh.'

'I understand, my queen,' said Maedbh, bowing as Freya took her sons in a crushing embrace. The queen hugged them to her breast, whispering something to each of them in turn and pushing them towards Maedbh. They stood with Ulrike, hurt that they were not riding to war with their mother and resentful that they were under the protection of another.

Freya took up a spear from her chariot and raised its bronze blade high. At her signal, the Asoborns let loose a whooping war shout, which was taken up by every warrior gathered in the muster field. The queen of the Asoborns cracked the reins and her chariot rumbled away, leading her army towards the route south.

Maedbh watched her go, her heart heavy at the sight of so many warriors going into battle without her, yet secretly relieved she wouldn't have to leave her daughter. She looked at the three children she was now beholden to protect, and the maternal urge flowed through her entire body.

She would die before she allowed any harm to come to these youngsters.

'Are you our guardian now?' asked Sigulf.

'Yes,' said Maedbh. 'I am.'

ELEVEN
Unwelcome Guests

THE VIEW FROM the top of the Raven Hall was spectacular, and Princess Marika never tired of looking out over Endal lands. A relentless grey twilight gripped the day, as it had done for the last few weeks, but on a clear day it was possible to see all the way to the Great Road and the marshes beyond. She suppressed an involuntary shiver at the thought of the marshes, recalling an unhappier time when Aldred had almost sacrificed her to the mist daemons to save their ailing kingdom.

Marika and her brother had publicly made their peace, though she could never quite forget the nearness of her death. As count of Marburg, Aldred had done what he thought best to lift the curse from his people, his good intentions twisted by Idris Gwylt, a manipulative priest of an ancient faith now outlawed in the Empire. That didn't make it any easier for her to forgive.

Gwylt was dead now, executed in the manner of the thrice death, but Marika still woke with the stink of the daemon queen in her nostrils more nights than not. The reek of the swamp took her back to that dark time, but she was a princess of the Endals and destined for great things. As a child, a soothsayer had told her that she would one day bear the first king of a great city of union, a place of wealth and prosperity that would one day stand taller than all others. It was a child's fantasy, yet one that made her smile on a day like this, when even a child's dream was a welcome relief from grim reality.

'So many of them,' said Eloise, her lady in waiting, her hands clasped before her heart in an unconscious supplication to Shallya. 'Those poor people.'

Marika shook her head, thinking there were no more than two thousand people trudging along the coast road towards Marburg.

'So many? No, it should be a lot more,' she said. 'Jutonsryk was a mighty city. This is less than a third of its population.'

'Where are the rest of them?' asked Eloise, and Marika rolled her eyes. Servants could be wilfully dense sometimes.

'They're dead,' said Marika, turning and making her way towards her brother's chambers.

SHE FOUND ALDRED with Laredus in the throne room of the Raven Hall, donning his armour in preparation for meeting his fellow count. Laredus helped buckle Aldred's bronze breastplate, its front moulded to replicate abdominal muscles Marika knew were nowhere near as sculpted as the armour would suggest. Aldred pulled his sword belt around his waist, shifting Ulfshard's hilt to be within easy reach.

Twin shafts of weak sunlight shone through the eyes of the carved raven's head that surmounted the top of the tower, and a warm fire burned in the hearth, filling the glossy-walled chamber with glistening reflections. It was a cold room, one that had seen its share of bad decisions in its time. She had long since vowed to see that no more were made here.

Her brother wore a long dark cloak of feathers, and as she watched Laredus buckle on the last portions of Aldred's armour, Marika saw an all too familiar melancholy settle upon Aldred. Laredus lifted a tall, black-winged helm from the armour stand behind the count's ebony throne, where the majestic Raven Banner was seated in a socket cut into the backrest.

Marika took her brother's hands and looked into his sad features. The years had been difficult for him. The death of their father at Black Fire cast a long shadow, and when their brother Egil died of the mist daemons' plague, a black outlook had settled upon Aldred like an indelible stain on his soul.

'You should hurry,' said Marika, adjusting his cloak. 'He'll be at the gates soon.'

'They're here?' asked Aldred without looking up at her. 'They've moved fast.'

'So would you with the dead nipping at your heels,' she said.

'I suppose,' he answered as Laredus handed him his helmet. Aldred tucked it in the crook of his arm and said, 'How do I look?'

'Grand,' replied Laredus. The captain of the Raven Helms was a warrior born, a man who had fought all manner of enemies in his service to the royal bloodline of the Endals. 'You do your fellow count honour to meet him warrior to warrior.'

'He's damned lucky I'm meeting him at all,' said Aldred. 'The man's insufferable. First he refuses to stand with us at Black Fire, and then we have to lay siege to his city to earn his Sword Oath. Now he's a hero of the Empire? I've a damn good mind to shut the gates on him and his bloody people.'

'Don't be foolish,' said Marika, moving in close and adjusting his sword belt. 'What kind of message does that send? You will be gracious and welcoming.'

'His people drove us from our homes,' said Aldred.

'Thirty years ago, after the Teutogens drove them from theirs,' pointed out Marika.

'Semantics.'

'History.'

'History,' he grunted, 'Is written by those who now live in lands they took by force.'

'No, it's written by scribes cleverer than you and I,' she said. 'Now come on, you don't want to keep Marius waiting.'

Aldred eyed her suspiciously. 'If I didn't know better I'd swear you were in a hurry to meet this mercenary.'

Marika smiled. 'Marius may be a mercenary, but he is a count of the Empire. You should remember that.'

'Like you'll let me forget,' he muttered.

THE GATES OF Marburg swung open and a group of blue-cloaked horsemen rode through on tired mounts. Most were warriors, their armour torn and mud-stained, though one was a young man who was clearly no horseman. A scribe perhaps? Their mounts were lathered and winded, and Marika saw they were near the end of their endurance. Only a fool would ride their mount to such extremes, but what other choice was there when death was the only other fate?

The cobbled courtyard was lined with spearmen in the blacks and browns of the Endals, and a lone piper filled the air with a skirling lament. The lancers looked uneasy, as well they might, for the Endals and Jutones had long been enemies. The coming of the Empire had made them allies, but no amount of Sword Oaths could erase the memory of centuries of bitter fighting.

Count Marius rode at the head of his lancers, incongruous amongst their raggedness by looking as though he had just stepped from his dressing room in search of a grand feast. His long blond hair was kept from his classically handsome features by a silver band, and his blue eyes regarded the warriors lining the courtyard with amused disdain. Where his warriors were dirty and weary, his clothes were immaculate and tailored to make the most of his lean physique. Marika had met Marius briefly atop the Fauschlag Rock the previous year, and had been dazzled by his quick wit, easy smile and roguish charm. Though she bore as much ancestral antipathy towards the Jutones as any Endal, she had found herself warming to him and the cosmopolitan description of his coastal city.

That city was now gone, scoured of all life by an invading fleet of the dead, and all that remained was a decaying charnel house. Or so the fastest refugees had told it. Looking at the bedraggled column of frightened people travelling in the wake of Marius, she was inclined to believe that description.

Marius rode toward Aldred and dismounted. The Raven Helms tensed, though there was surely no threat here. In a gesture of uncharacteristic humility, the dispossessed count of the Jutones dropped to one knee and bowed his head.

'Count Aldred of Marburg,' said Marius. 'I am here to ask for your help, though Ulric knows, you've reason enough to turn me away.'

'Aye, that I do, Jutone,' said Aldred, his tone icy as he drew Ulfshard. The fey-forged blade shone with a sapphire light in the wan afternoon sun, and Marika gasped as her brother stepped towards Marius. 'It's thanks to your tribe that we live on the edge of a marsh, afflicted by disease and cut off from our ancient lands. The spirits of my ancestors cry out for vengeance, so give me one good reason I shouldn't kill you right now.'

Marika was horrified at her brother's reaction, but to his credit, Marius took Aldred's anger in his stride. He nodded, as though he'd been expecting such an outburst.

'Our tribes have never been friends, it's true,' said Marius, 'but I ask you to look past our shared enmity and give my people shelter. They have lost everything and have walked many miles to escape death. There is nothing left of Jutonsryk, the corpse army destroyed it all. Thousands of the living dead came in from the sea and killed most of my subjects. Fires burned out of control through the city and I had no choice but to lead the survivors from its burning gates. My castle is ruined and my walls toppled. Only the Namathir remains, and the dead now haunt its tunnels and catacombs. Deny *me* a place within your walls if you must, but do not punish those who have not earned your ire.'

The count of the Jutones rose to his feet and Marika saw the anguish in his eyes, a genuine sorrow that she had never expected to see in him. Aldred still held the softly glowing blade of Ulfshard out before him, unwavering in his hatred. His anger had blinded him to what he was doing, and Marika decided to take matters into her own hands.

'Marika! What are you doing?' hissed Aldred as she walked towards Marius

'What *you* should be doing, brother,' she said, keeping her gaze fixed on the Jutone count.

She extended her hands, and Marius took them, bending to kiss her palms. His lips were soft and he smiled at her as he stood straight.

'You are a magnificent woman, my lady,' he said. 'As radiant as the sun.'

'I know,' she replied.

Aldred stormed over to her side, but before he could speak she rounded upon him.

'Do not say a word, Aldred,' she warned him. 'I am the daughter of Marbad, and this is my city as much as yours. And you owe me, remember?'

'You're never going to let me forget that, are you?'

'Is there any reason I should?' she hissed.

'But he's Jutone!' protested Aldred.

'No, he is a man of the Empire,' said Marika. 'As are you. Would you be known as a murderer or a man of mercy? A man of compassion and forgiveness or one who left thousands of innocents to die?'

'Damn you, Marika,' said Aldred, though there was relief in his tone. 'You are the better angel of my nature. I sometimes think it would be better if you ruled Marburg.'

Aldred took a deep breath and sheathed his sword. He removed his helmet and met Marius's gaze, his murderous anger dissipated, yet his hostility intact. It would take more than her simple, if heartfelt, words to quench his long-burning hatred of the Jutones.

He extended his hand to Marius and said, 'You and your people are welcome in Marburg, Count Marius. In the face of our enemies, we are one nation. Your enemies are my enemies.'

Marika saw Marius was genuinely surprised and he nodded, accepting the truth of Aldred's words in his heart.

'Thank you, brother,' he said. 'A small beginning, but a beginning nonetheless.'

Aldred said, 'Laredus will see that your people are given shelter and food.'

'You have my thanks, and the thanks of my people,' said Marius.

Aldred nodded stiffly and turned away, marching towards the gatehouse that led into the city of Marburg. A detachment of Raven Helms went with him, leaving Laredus and Marika with Count Marius.

The Jutone count favoured her with a grateful smile.

'You are an exceptional woman, Princess Marika,' he said.

'In all kinds of ways,' she replied with a smile.

SIGMAR STARED INTO the fire, more weary than he could ever remember. His horse was hobbled with the rest of the mounts, and three hundred Unberogen swordsmen huddled around their fires with their weapons within easy reach. They kept tired eyes averted from the flames, looking out into the darkness for their foes, but hoping not to see them. The night offered no respite from the armies of the dead, for they marched with hellish vigour and had no need to sleep, eat or rest.

Count Krugar sat across the fire, drinking from a battered leather canteen. The Taleuten count had always been a powerful figure of a man, broad of shoulder and square of jaw, but these last weeks had strained even his formidable constitution. His left arm was in a sling, and his chest was bandaged from where a rusted spear had punctured his silver hauberk. Utensjarl was laid across his thighs, its scabbard torn and dented, yet the blade within as sharp and lethal as ever.

Since the battle at Ostengard, the combined force of Taleutens, Cherusens and Unberogen had destroyed five more such hordes, yet it was an unending war. Each battle cost lives, but no matter how many of the dead they felled, more could always be brought back to hunt the living.

This camp was within a cratered basin on the edge of the Howling Hills, which was Cherusen land, though the Unberogens were camped with two hundred riders of Krugar's Red Scythes. Count

Aloysis had led his warriors north to the Old Forest Road, where barrows clustered like blisters on the eastern foothills of the Middle Mountains had disgorged thousands of skeletal warriors to ravage the countryside. Dozens of villages had been destroyed, their victims dragged from death to serve in Nagash's army.

'You're sure you won't come with me to Taalahim?' asked Krugar.

'I cannot,' said Sigmar. 'But I appreciate the offer.'

'My city is closer than Reikdorf,' persisted Krugar. 'It will be safer.'

'If the situation were reversed, would you ride to somewhere safer instead of your own homeland?' said Sigmar.

'No,' admitted Krugar, 'but I'm not the Emperor.'

'Which makes it even more pressing that I return to Reikdorf.'

'Well, don't say I didn't try to save your life,' said Krugar, passing the canteen over to Sigmar.

'I'll be sure it's remembered,' said Sigmar, taking a drink, and not surprised to taste the fiery bite of harsh Taleuten corn spirit.

'Ulric's beard,' said Sigmar, wiping his mouth with the back of his hand. 'It's a wonder you Taleutens are able to stay on the back of your horses drinking this stuff.'

'Makes it easier to stay on if you're a little looser in the saddle,' said Krugar, taking the canteen back with a smile. 'Why do you think our horsemen invented stirrups?'

They lapsed into a companionable silence, neither man wishing to break this moment of peace amid so dark a time. Count Krugar was preparing to ride to Taalahim and rally his people to defend their tribal heartland. Over the weeks of fighting, the army of the dead's grand stratagem was becoming clear: isolate smaller villages in a black noose of corpses and choke them. No village could hold on its own, but gathered together in greater numbers the people of the Empire might be able to resist this terrible threat.

'Any word from across the land?' asked Krugar.

Sigmar shook his head. 'Little, my friend. I have to assume the southern kings are under attack too. With Markus gone, Henroth and Siggurd are sure to be next to face Nagash's wrath.'

'If they haven't already,' pointed out Krugar. 'What about the west? Marius and Aldred?'

'No,' said Sigmar. 'And nothing from the north either. The dead are cutting us off from one another and denying us our greatest strength.'

'And what's that?'

'Our unity,' said Sigmar. 'The strength that comes from knowing we are one people who can count on our fellow men to honour their oaths of brotherhood. Nagash knows this; it's why he's forcing us to fight like this, as divided as we were before I founded the Empire. He's drawing our forces into battle all across the Empire, trying to pick us off one by one and keeping us from gathering our strength.'

'Then you definitely need to get back to Reikdorf,' said Krugar, setting down the canteen and drawing Utensjarl from its sheath. The blade shone like a sliver of gold in the firelight. 'I swore on this blade that I would fight and die for the Empire, and I stand by that.'

'Which is another reason for me to go home, for I'll have no one dying needlessly. I'm the Emperor and I don't know what's happening in my own lands. If Nagash is half as cunning as the old legends make out, he won't be attacking from just one direction, he'll be pressing hard on all sides. We've done good work here, but it's time for me to go.'

'It'll be a dangerous journey,' said Krugar. 'Take a hundred of my Red Scythes with you.'

'Thank you, my friend, but that's not necessary,' said Sigmar.

'Nonsense, they know this terrain better than anyone, better than the Cherusens even. They've raided these lands more than once over the years.'

'I thought I told you that it was bandits, remember?'

'Ah, yes,' said Krugar. 'I forgot. So it was. Look, I'm not offering, they're coming with you and that's that.'

'Very well,' smiled Sigmar, knowing it was pointless to argue. 'I will be glad to have their blades.'

'Damn right,' said Krugar, handing over the canteen once more. 'It may be some time before I see you again.'

'It may indeed,' agreed Sigmar.

'Then drink with me as friends do around a fire. Let's talk of happier times when the sun was golden, women were maidens, and old age something that happened to other men.'

'I'll drink to that,' said Sigmar, taking another swig.

THE GATES OF Reikdorf swung open as Wolfgart led two hundred of his finest warriors across the Sudenreik Bridge. He glanced at the panels carved into the inner faces of the bridge, heroic endeavours from the history of the Unberogen and its greatest heroes rendered by the woodcarver's art. Master Holtwine had crafted the latest panels, depicting the heroic defence of Middenheim's viaduct and the rout of the Norsii army from the base of the Fauschlag Rock. No panel depicted the desperate fighting in the tunnels beneath the rock, and Wolfgart was glad, only too happy to have that terror forgotten.

To see the high walls of his home lifted his spirit in ways he could never describe. The blue and red flags fluttering from the towers and high buildings within were a shining light of hope in the long night. To see Reikdorf, it seemed impossible that darkness could ever truly hold sway.

Though Reikdorf was a welcoming sight, his pleasure at seeing it again evaporated at the thought of returning to his empty home. Without Maedbh and Ulrike it was just a hollow structure of stone and timber, without life and warmth. He missed them terribly, but covered that loneliness by riding to war at every opportunity. And with the dead rising all across the Empire, there was no shortage of opportunities.

This latest ride had seen them fighting on the edge of the Skaag Hills, where the dead had pressed north along the River Bogen. A number of mining settlements in the hills had sent word of the dead emerging from cairns in the high slopes, and Wolfgart led yet another band of warriors to fight them.

They had destroyed the host, but with every ride, it seemed the dead were arising closer and closer to Reikdorf. How much longer would it be before they were clawing at the walls of Sigmar's city? The Emperor was in the north, and though Alfgeir was more than up to the task of defending Unberogen lands, Sigmar's presence was greatly missed.

Not least by Wolfgart, for he had left Three Hills in order to fight alongside his friend.

He and his warriors rode through the gate and into the streets, following a curving route that led towards the open square of the Oathstone. It never failed to amaze Wolfgart how the city had grown over the years. He remembered when it had been little more than a small settlement of timber structures, none taller than two storeys, huts of wattle and daub, and riverside lean-tos. Now most of the city was built of limestone and granite, the city's masons learning how to shape stone with ever-greater skill from travelling craftsmen who came down from the fortified mountain holds of the dwarfs.

Wenyld, one of Wolfgart's battle captains, rode alongside him and said, 'This isn't the route to the stables.'

'I know,' said Wolfgart. 'I want to stop at the Oathstone.'

'Any particular reason?' said Wenyld. 'The horses are tired, and the men need rest.'

Wolfgart wondered if he should even try to explain. Wenyld was only seven years younger than Wolfgart, but carried a weight of war upon his face. A wide scar split the left side of his jaw where a greenskin axe had smashed through his shield, and one eye was covered with a rough cloth patch. The claw of a ravening ghoul-creature had taken the eye on their last ride, and the wound had festered. Elswyth had done what she could, but Wenyld had lost the eye.

'I want to touch the past,' said Wolfgart at last.

'What?'

Wolfgart sighed, knowing any explanation would sound foolish to the younger man. In truth, he didn't understand his reasoning himself, he just knew he had to go there.

'Take the men back to the stables then, I'll meet you there when I'm done.'

Wenyld nodded and issued the orders to the armoured horsemen, who gratefully turned their mounts and rode towards the stables. Wolfgart saw they were exhausted after the long ride to the west and two major battles. It had been inconsiderate of him to put his own desires ahead of his warriors' needs.

He turned his horse and rode away, twisting in the saddle as he heard iron-shod hoof beats coming after him.

'You should go with them,' he told Wenyld, as the man rode next to him.

'A good battle captain never leaves his commander until the ride is over.'

Wolfgart did not want company, but had not the energy to argue with the younger man.

'Fair enough, though it'll be longer until you get to your bed,' he said.

Wenyld shrugged, a few torn links in his mail slipping from his corslet and falling to the ground. 'It's as far now, whichever way I go. I'll ride with you.'

'Suit yourself,' said Wolfgart, riding onwards in silence.

The streets were quiet, the unnatural greyness of the world keeping people indoors, as though to see so grim a day would remind them of the gathering threat. Word of what was facing them had spread throughout the city, and though the temples were busy, little else had the power to tempt people from their homes. Every doorway was hung with talismans of Morr and every keyhole was plugged with dried fennel. Those men and women on the streets avoided eye contact and hurried into side streets and doorways as the armoured horsemen passed.

'Some welcome home, eh?' said Wenyld. 'Don't they know we're out there risking our lives to keep them safe?'

'They know,' said Wolfgart, 'but no one likes to be reminded of what we're fighting. It's bad luck to dwell on the dead, and only a fool wishes for more ill-fortune at times like this.'

'I suppose,' replied Wenyld.

Wolfgart turned his horse into the square of the Oathstone, the hard-packed earth almost as solid as stone. There had been talk of paving the square, but Sigmar had refused to allow this ground to be covered.

'If we sever our links to the earth beneath us completely, then we are doomed. The Oathstone shares its bed with no other slab,' the Emperor had said, and the matter was closed.

The square was empty save for a few wild dogs fighting over scraps stolen from a nearby butcher's slops, and the sound of hoarse bellows roared from within Beorthyn's forge. Wolfgart smiled. The old smith had been dead for twenty years or more, yet still the name stuck. It belonged now to his apprentice, Master Govannon, a worker of metal considered by many to be a greater craftsman than Beorthyn had ever been.

'What do you suppose they're doing in there?' asked Wenyld, as a sooty black cloud billowed from the iron chimney stack and a thunderous bang echoed from the walls of nearby buildings. Even over that noise, Wolfgart could hear Govannon cursing.

'Who knows? Something with that giant thunder bow Alfgeir and Cuthwin brought in I expect.'

'Is Cuthwin still in the city?'

'I don't know, maybe,' said Wolfgart. 'Why?'

'We were friends as youngsters,' answered Wenyld. 'The years have taken us down different paths, but it would be pleasant to see him again.'

'I vaguely remember the pair of you trying to get a look at my Blood Night, the evening before Sigmar rode to Astofen for the first time.'

'You remember that night? I thought you were too drunk.'

'Not so drunk I don't remember you falling on your arse and running like the Ölfhednar themselves were after your manhood.'

'Aye, well it's not every day you're caught by the king's son on his Blood Night.'

'Sigmar and I tried it once, and we got the thrashing of our lives.'

'Maybe you should have run as fast as I did.'

Wolfgart smiled. 'Maybe, lad, maybe.'

He reined in his horse and dismounted before the Oathstone, the earth around it trod by a thousand people every day. He knelt beside the red stone, its rough surface warm and threaded with golden veins. Those veins were thinner than they had been when Sigmar had made them swear their oath to help him build the Empire, and he hoped that wasn't an omen.

'I miss you,' he whispered, thinking of Maedbh and Ulrike.

No sooner were the words out of his mouth than he felt the Oathstone grow hot to the touch. He tried to pull his hand back, but it was stuck fast to the stone. Wolfgart gasped as he felt the heat travel up the length of his arm, his vision swimming as unknown power held him in its grasp.

'What...?' he managed as his vision greyed and he saw a host of chariots riding through hills of rolling greensward in his mind's eye. Armoured in black and gold, they were escorted by hundreds of horsemen and painted warriors in mail shirts who marched beneath banners of gold and red.

He recognised the landscape around Three Hills, and the chariot at the front of the army as that of Queen Freya. The woman at the reins was not Maedbh, and a gathering evil loomed over the Asoborns, a doom that none could see, but which was slowly enveloping them in its encroaching shadow.

The vision of Freya's army was overlaid with the sight of Maedbh and Ulrike standing side by side on a wooded hillside. Both loosed arrows into an oncoming horde of the dead, but he could tell from their expressions that it wouldn't be nearly enough to stop them. His heart broke to see the fear on their faces.

Death stalked these lands, and he wanted to scream, but he had no voice, no way to warn the Asoborns that their enemies were almost upon them or that he was aware of their plight. He heard wolves, noble, white-furred heralds of Ulric, and knew they were calling to him, demanding he take action.

A sudden, twisting sense of vertigo seized him, and he felt himself falling, his arms windmilling for balance. The visions faded from sight, and the harsh angles and stone walls of Reikdorf snapped back into focus. Wolfgart's stomach lurched and he put a hand out to steady himself, his gut churning in fear.

'What in Ulric's name just happened there?' demanded Wenyld, and Wolfgart looked up to see the warrior holding onto his shoulders. The golden lines on the Oathstone pulsed with life, now even thinner, as though the stone had all but exhausted its power to grant him this vision.

'I have to go,' said Wolfgart, pushing himself unsteadily to his feet. He ran to his horse and vaulted into the saddle.

'What are you talking about?' demanded Wenyld. 'We've only just got back.'

'My family is in danger,' said Wolfgart. 'And I have to go to them.'

TWELVE
Three Thrusts to the Heart

FREYA'S ARMY LEFT Three Hills in triumph, cheered by those whose age or wounds prevented them from joining their queen. Three thousand warriors marched or rode south-east through the rolling landscape, moving quickly towards the River Aver, the watercourse that effectively divided Asoborn lands from those of the Brigundians.

Within three days, the army came within sight of the mighty river that ran from the Worlds Edge Mountains through the Empire before emptying into the sea at Marburg.

Here, the coming winter had made the landscape flat and hard, ideal for chariots and cavalry, and the army moved into marching column as it followed the river east towards the river crossing at Averstrun.

Despite the grim skies that wreathed the world in bleak twilight, the army's spirits were high. Freya was an inspirational presence, taking many lovers en route and ensuring that overblown erotic tales spread through the camp quicker than a dose of the pox. As always, Freya led from the front, her black and gold chariot unmistakable among the less ornate chariots of the Asoborn warriors.

With the river on the army's right flank, Asoborn horse archers galloped wide, while the heavier lancers rode closer to the main body of the infantry and chariots. By noon of the fourth day of march, Freya sent word back down the line that she had spied the river crossing and their enemy.

Blocking the crossing were a thousand dead warriors in ancient armour, arranged like a row of obsidian statues in a mausoleum. All were clad in rusted bronze, the weak light glinting from the corrosion on the rings of their mail. An eldritch green light glimmered in the empty eye sockets of each warrior and a hundred knights sat on skeletal horses on either flank. Flocks of carrion birds gathered for the feast and the few trees in the scattered patches of woodland were thick with screeching bats.

A warrior in gleaming silver armour sat upon a hellish steed at the centre of the host, black wings like smoke billowing from its flanks. Khaled al-Muntasir was an incongruous sight amid this army of darkness, and his wondrous form drew all the light to him, such that he shone like a legendary hero of old.

Freya wasted no time in arraying her army for battle, issuing orders with customary fire and fury. The Asoborn infantry moved into four blocks of five hundred, spears and swords held in fists that demanded vengeance for the loss of the Brigundians and Menogoths. With the chariots thrown out before her main battle line, the heavy horse rode out to the flanks, ready to roll up the line of the dead warriors.

Bare chested horse archers whooped and yelled as they rode around the army of the dead, loosing flurries of arrows into the massed ranks of skeletal warriors. Though the dead had no flesh to damage or organs to pierce, the barbed shafts felled them just as surely as they would a mortal man. Intended to provoke a reckless charge rather than inflict mass casualties, the arrows of the horse archers did little but fell a few score of the dead warriors.

Ululating Asoborn war horns signalled the advance, and the infantry moved forward, moving at a brisk trot to cover the ground between the two armies. Freya led the advance, her chariot thundering towards the serried ranks of the dead with hundreds more behind her. The hard ground threw up no dust with their passage, and the entire army witnessed the horror of what happened next.

Before Freya's horn blew to signal the turn, Khaled al-Muntasir aimed his sword at the earth before the charging chariots. The hard ground cracked and split as hundreds upon hundreds of dry, fleshless corpses clawed their way to the world above, dust and earth spilling from their empty skulls and opened jaws. Unable to stop or turn, the chariots slammed into them with a tremendous crash of dried bone and wood.

Asoborn chariots were never meant to be run straight into the enemy, but raced along the front of a foe's formation. Archers would loose arrows into the faces of the enemy at point-blank range, and spear bearers would hurl heavy, iron-tipped shafts into the warriors pressing in from behind. To run a chariot straight into the foe would certainly kill a great many of the enemy, but would, more often than not, destroy the chariot and kill the riders and horses.

The chariots came apart in a screaming bray of pain, both animal and human. Most simply shattered in the impact, but some overturned, crushing their crews and breaking the horses' legs. The queen's chariot vanished in a crash of shattered timber, broken apart by the violence of the impact. Hundreds more were destroyed in explosions of splintering timber, hurling their crews to the ground or breaking them beneath the wheels of those behind them. Only the quickest crews were able to avoid the catastrophic collision of dead bodies and screaming horses, but in doing so they bled off the speed that kept them safe.

Grasping skeletons clawed their way onto the chariots, attacking with broken swords or cudgels salvaged from the vast swathe of wreckage left by the destruction of the chariots. Khaled al-Muntasir swept his sword up and hundreds of rotten-fleshed wolves burst from the ranks of the dead warriors at the river. They fell upon the struggling Asoborns with dreadful hunger, jaws tearing open throats and claws raking warm flesh from the bone.

The warriors blocking the river crossing marched forward in dreadful unison, each bony footfall crashing down at the same time as they fell upon those the wolves hadn't yet killed. Swords and spears stabbed and slashed with mechanical precision, and the entangled Asoborns were cut down without mercy.

Freya's shield maidens dragged her bloodied body from the wreckage, fighting with all the fury of berserkers as the rest of the army raced forward to rescue their fallen queen. The black skeletons chopped through the ruin of the chariots, killing anything living they could find.

Asoborn cavalry charged towards the flanks of the dead army, but the corpse knights wheeled their skeletal mounts and raced towards them as hundreds of leathery-winged bats launched themselves from the trees. Green fire flickered around the undead knights, their blades shimmering with ghostly light, and the two forces met in a thunderous clash of iron. Asoborn lances smashed through ancient armour, splintering as the weight of the dead broke them apart. Screeching bats tore at the Asoborn riders, clawing their faces and entangling their blades with their wings and stinking bodies. Both forces of horsemen swirled together, hacking at one another with swords and axes, but within seconds it was clear the Asoborn charge was doomed.

In the centre of the battle, Khaled al-Muntasir danced through the fighting, his gleaming sword slaying all it cut. No weapon could touch him, no warrior lay him low, and he slid through the scattered Asoborns like a ghost, leaving a trail of bodies in his wake. Tattooed warrior women of the Myrmidian sects formed a ring of screaming fury around him, but within moments, all were dead, gutted, beheaded or fatally pierced by his quicksilver blade. Malign clouds of sable light billowed around the blood drinker, a miasma of dark sorcery that drained the life from any who came near him and animated the corpses of those he had killed.

The ranks of the dead swelled with every passing moment, for the newly slain rose up to attack their former comrades, bloodied and mangled charioteers clawing at men and women they had broken bread with only that same morning. The encircling horns of the dead army began to envelop the Asoborns, but even at this desperate moment, the battle could have been saved.

At that critical moment, when one spark of heroism or fear could have turned the tide of the fighting, a warrior named Daegal, a lad no older than twelve summers who had trained and fought with Maedbh, turned and fled from the horror of the bloodletting. His sword and shield forgotten, Daegal ran in blind terror, and his panic spread to those around him.

Within moments, hundreds of Asoborns were fleeing the battle, desperate to escape the slaughter and frantic to live. The battle line collapsed as the fragile courage of the mortal army broke in the face of this nightmare horde.

But there was to be no such easy escape.

The dread knights rode down the fleeing Asoborns, trampling them beneath the pellucid fire of their mounts' hooves or chopping them down with pounding blows of their swords. The encircling army of the dead surrounded the dying Asoborn host, drawing it into a black embrace of massacre.

Only a handful of mortals escaped the slaughter, the queen's shield maidens and a hundred or so warriors who had been first to flee. Their shame burned almost as hot as the relief that they still lived, and as darkness fell, barely a tenth of the queen's army escaped into the hills.

Khaled al-Muntasir stood triumphant, his army arranged across the battlefield in silence as the crows and ravens pecked the choicest morsels from the defeated army. The blood drinker let them have their feast, for what could be more terrifying to a mortal warrior than to later face one of his own kind with eyes pecked out, flesh partially eaten and tongue hanging loose on rotten sinews?

As Morrslieb slipped from behind the clouds to bathe the blood-soaked field in its rich, emerald moonlight, he uttered the words given to him by Nagash and laughed long into the night as the vanquished Asoborns rose to their feet once more.

Without any orders needing to be issued, the army of the dead arrayed itself for march, moving in deathly silence and utter precision as they followed the route Queen Freya's doomed army had taken.

Back towards Three Hills.

VOLLEYS OF ARROWS flew overhead, slashing down the causeway and slicing into grey, lifeless flesh. Bordan's foresters loosed more arrows, and another clutch of the dead were felled. The viaduct from the ground was thick with dead warriors, partially decayed men and women lurching and swaying towards Middenheim with horrid purpose and grotesque hunger moaning from their slack jaws.

'Got to hand it to Bordan's men,' said Holstef, the beast-horn clarion clutched tightly in his gauntleted fist. 'They're killing everything they hit.'

Ustern grunted. 'They can't miss. Even I could loose an arrow that would slay something.'

'Probably one of us,' added Leovulf, undoing the leather thong that held his black hair.

'You cut me deep,' said Ustern, tapping smouldering ash from the end of his pipe.

Redwane let them talk, it was their way of easing the tension before a charge. Though the White Wolves feared no living foe, the horde arrayed before them today was something much worse. Redwane had fought the living dead before, but the same fear was still there, still poisoning his gut with a sour-bile taste. The thoughts that had haunted him on the march towards Brass Keep returned to him anew; the dread of dying alone, the fear that his best years were already behind him and that he was on a grim descent into dotage and infirmity.

Redwane took a deep breath, looking to the sky in a bid to cast off such gloomy thoughts, but he found no refuge there. The sky above the Fauschlag Rock was as black as his mood.

It had been that way ever since the dead had isolated Middenheim from the Empire.

The noose had closed slowly, with villages blotted out one by one and the steady stream of traders, mercenary companies and pilgrims diminishing until it was impossible not to see that something terrible was developing in the haunted forests surrounding the city.

Despite his dislike of the man, Bordan's foresters had quickly discovered the roads cut by lurking bands of the dead and packs of fiery-eyed wolves. The villages and camps around the city were hastily evacuated, their people brought within Middenheim's walls. Even Torbrecan's band of lunatics had come into the city, which had surprised Redwane until he remembered that they had foreseen their deaths before the walls of Reikdorf. Despite his insistence that no one be left beyond the city, Redwane suspected that Myrsa was already regretting his decision to allow the self-mutilating madmen into Middenheim. They marched through the streets, preaching their prophecies of destruction and pain, while whipping themselves into maniacal frenzies. No warriors could be spared from the fighting to stop them, and the mood in the city soured as more and more of Middenheim's citizens joined in their cavalcade of blood.

'If they're so eager for death, I say we help them on their way. Give them a sword and stick them on the walls,' Redwane had muttered at one of Myrsa's war councils, and few disagreed with him. Yet for all their apparent lust to die, the madmen refused to take arms to defend Middenheim. Clearly they weren't insane enough to want to die just *yet*.

Within a day of the gates closing, the living dead host swallowed the lands around Middenheim, throwing themselves at the fortresses clustered around the city and the chain lifts. Those bastions still held, but the horde had soon discovered another way up. Led by shadowy, dark-cloaked figures on black steeds, skeletal warriors armed with spears, axes and swords climbed the great viaduct towards the city. Frothing, blood-hungry corpses scrambled up the rocky sides of the Fauschlag Rock, and Orsa's city defenders had their hands full hacking them down as they reached the summit.

Trapped beyond the walls, Wulf's mountain pathfinders had tried to cut through the dead towards the viaduct, but they had been overrun before making it halfway. Redwane had watched as the Mountain Lord was dragged down and eaten by wiry, hairless things with tearing claws and distended jaws. Orsa led a party of axemen to retrieve the bodies of their fallen comrades, but had been beaten back without success.

Now Wulf marched with the dead, his ravaged flesh hanging from his bones in rotten strips. His warriors fought beside him, as loyal in death as they had been in life. It had been a blow losing Wulf, for he had been well-liked and the tale of his ending had circulated to become a macabre scare story, growing in horror with every retelling.

'They'll be calling for us soon,' said Leovulf.

'Expect you're right,' said Ustern.

Redwane looked towards the fighting raging at the head of the viaduct. Since the war against the Norsii, a more permanent defensive barrier had been built across the head of the viaduct, a curved wall flanked by two drum towers and with a heavy gate of Drakwald oak and good northern iron at its centre. Atop the walls, Count Myrsa led the defenders in battle, the runefang cleaving glowing arcs through the ranks of the dead. None of them could resist it, the dwarf-forged blade slicing through mouldering bones, rotted armour and decayed flesh with its runic edge. To see so magnificent a weapon borne by such a hero lifted the hearts of all who fought beside him. Myrsa's banner bearer battled alongside him, the blue and ivory standard soaked and limp. No wind stirred the fabric and instead of lifting the spirits of those who saw its colours, it only served to remind the warriors of Middenheim of how grim their situation truly was.

The dead swarmed the defensive wall, scaling its rugged surfaces with bony claws digging into the stonework in a way no living warrior could manage. They fought with a speed and ferocity Redwane remembered all too well, dragging men from the battlements and pushing through any gaps in the line.

Myrsa and Renweard commanded the defenders on the viaduct, while Bordan and his men occupied the high ground behind the walls. Perched on rooftops, clock towers and watch posts, the foresters thinned the dead host as best they could. Orsa's men patrolled the city, hunting down any dead warriors that found their way through the caves that honeycombed the rock or successfully scaled its sides.

Redwane had defended this city once before from an attacking army, but this felt very different. Then he had been one of Sigmar's warrior companions, but now he was part of Middenheim's defence, a city that was not his by birth. As much as Sigmar might declare that all men of the Empire were as one, he couldn't shake the feeling that he ought to be in the south, fighting to protect Unberogen lands. This city wasn't his, no matter what oaths he had sworn to Myrsa and the White Wolves.

'Redwane,' hissed Leovulf, leaning in close.

'What?' he muttered absently.

'You're our leader, so damn well lead,' said Leovulf.

Redwane snapped out of his gloomy reverie, and nodded, ashamed he had allowed his mind to wander when he needed to focus now more than ever.

'Aye, sorry,' he said, looking towards the walls for Myrsa's signal.

'Whatever is on your mind, deal with it later,' said Leovulf. 'They'll be looking for us soon. And we need you with us.'

'You're right,' he said, holding himself tall in the saddle. He unhooked his warhammer and slipped the leather thong at its base around his wrist. The White Wolves saw him and repeated the gesture, and every man's shoulders squared. Leovulf had spotted what he should have seen. The defenders on the wall were at the limit of their endurance, the dead finding more breaches and pulling men to their doom in ever greater numbers. Myrsa raised the runefang high and his banner bearer swept the flag from side to side. Now the wind caught it, and the billowing standard flew with glorious brightness against the sepulchral sky.

'That's it,' said Leovulf, turning to Holstef.

Holstef raised the war horn to his lips and blew a three note blast.

Redwane raked back his spurs and shouted, 'White Wolves, ride in the name of Ulric!'

His horse leapt forward, and two hundred heavy horsemen followed him, galloping across the cobbled esplanade towards the city gate in a column ten riders wide, twenty deep. Ustern raised their banner high, and each man loosed a feral wolf howl to banish the fear they all felt as they charged towards the gate. A team of stout men hauled the gates open, but before the dead could take advantage of this new opening, Redwane's White Wolves thundered through and struck the enemy host like a hammer blow.

MARIUS LET OUT a groan of pleasure as Marika rolled off him and lay back on the bed with a contented sigh. Her eyes were closed, and she purred like a satisfied cat, blonde hair tousled with errant strands across her face. He stared at her for a moment, relishing this rare moment of escape from the world of plans, defences and warriors. Marburg was a city readying for invasion, and it felt good to take a moment for himself amid the frenetic battle preparations.

'You're staring again,' she said.

'How do you know?' he asked.

'I'm a princess,' she said, as though that answered his question. 'If we can sense a pea in our beds, we can surely sense when a self-satisfied man is staring at us.'

'Self-satisfied?' he said with mock hurt. 'You have a viper's tongue, Marika.'

'You weren't complaining about my tongue last night,' she said, finally opening her eyes and pushing herself up onto her elbows. Marius smiled and traced his fingertips down her slender neck, over her small breasts and down her flat stomach.

'Indeed I wasn't,' he agreed. 'Though I can't help but feel your brother wouldn't approve of the use you put it to or your choice of lover.'

She laughed and rose from the bed, fetching a silver ewer filled with water. Marius stared at her naked body, the sway of her hips and the beads of sweat running down her spine sending a tingling warmth through his entire body. She half-turned and nodded.

'Aldred never does,' she said. 'He'd have me live out my life as a virgin spinster.'

She laughed. 'Ranald's balls, if he knew half the men I'd bedded, he'd have me locked in the Raven Tower, never to see the light of day again.'

'And that would be a crime against the pleasures of the flesh.'

She padded back to bed with the ewer and a pair of goblets, pouring one for each of them. Marius took the proffered drink and drained it in one gulping swallow. The march along the coast through the swamps had given him a terrible thirst that never seemed to be quenched.

He dropped the goblet to the floor and leaned up to kiss Marika.

'Why me?' he asked suddenly.

'Why you, what?'

'You know fine well what I mean,' he said. 'Why take me as your lover, a man your brother would cheerfully gut? Is it because I am an energetic and thoughtful bedmate with the body of an athletic god or is it simply because I am a count of the Empire?'

'A little of both,' she admitted. 'You are an enjoyable bed partner, but I need more than that. I need a man who can achieve things. A man who can match my dreams with an ability to shape this world to the way it ought to be.'

In any other woman, such candour would have surprised him, but Princess Marika had proven to be a far more interesting woman than any he had met before. She had an open honesty to her ambition that he liked, a mind free of the subterfuges and coquettish games played by most women of his acquaintance. Amid such grim times, the company of a beautiful woman free from the normal petty games of her sex was refreshing.

And these times were indeed grim.

In the week since the Jutones had arrived at the gates of Marburg, Marius and Aldred had clashed many times in deciding how to defend the city. He had come to believe the Endal count *wanted* his city to fall, such was his obstinate rejection of any stratagem or defensive measure Marius suggested.

These interludes with Marika had provided a welcome diversion from talk of war and the dead. Marius liked to think of it as affirming the joys of life. After all, weren't sex and death but two sides of the same coin? Wasn't the moment of climax known by some poetic souls as the Little Morr?

Marika rolled onto her side, interrupting his train of thought. Her face was inches from his, and he felt the directness of her gaze.

'I know what you did with Jutonsryk,' she said. 'You turned a small fishing village into the most prosperous city in the Empire. Ships came from all across the world to your city.'

'That they did,' said Marius, knowing her flattery was intended to stroke his ego, but enjoying it nonetheless. 'If there's one thing I understand it's how to take what the gods have given me and use that to turn a coin.'

'I want you to do the same with Marburg,' she said. 'Aldred is a good man in his own, limited way, but all he wants is to maintain what our father built. Marburg is ideally placed to become as great as Jutonsryk ever was, if not greater, but only if rulers of vision are prepared to make it so. Aldred has no vision to make Marburg great, but you do.'

'You might be right, but Aldred is count of the Endals, not me.'

'That can change,' said Marika.

'How?'

'If you and I were to be married,' she said, leaning forward to kiss him.

Now it was Marius's turn to laugh. He rolled onto his back, pillowing his head on his hands. 'That's your plan? Your brother would never allow it. Manann's thunder, he'd have my manhood on a spike if he thought I'd even kissed you let alone bedded you.'

'Aldred won't be count forever,' she said. 'After all, if what you've been saying in the war councils is true, then this city is likely to be attacked soon by these undead corsairs. Aldred's a decent enough warrior, but anything can happen in a battle, can't it?'

Marius turned to look at Marika, his eyes narrowing as he saw the extent of her ambition.

It matched his own and he felt the stirrings of opportunity.

'What are you suggesting?' he asked.

'Suggesting?' she said, pulling the sheet down and rolling on top of him. She sat up, allowing his eyes to feast on the seductive curves of her body. 'I'm not suggesting anything, I'm just saying that if something were to happen to Aldred, then there would be nothing to stop you marrying me and becoming lord of all the lands from here to Manann's Teeth.'

Marius slid his hands up her sides and cupped her breasts with a smile.

'You are a cunning fox, aren't you?' said Marius.

'Takes one to know one,' she said.

REDWANE CRUSHED skeletal warriors in crumbling iron armour beneath his horse, swinging his hammer in a mighty underhand arc that smashed collarbones, broke shoulders apart and sent skulls flying. His horse trampled the dead beneath its hooves. To either side of him, Leovulf, Ustern and Holstef fought with brute ferocity as they battered a path down the viaduct, winning Myrsa and Renweard time to move up fresh warriors and relieve those who had fought to exhaustion.

'Holstef, spearhead!' bellowed Redwane, and the clarion blew a long, rising blast.

The White Wolves smoothly formed a wedge on Redwane, pushing hard into the choking, massed ranks of the dead. Redwane lost himself in the simple purity of this fight, bludgeoning the dead with his hammer and letting his horse kick and crush its enemies with wild abandon. He heard screams around him as grasping, skeletal hands dragged warriors from their saddles or screeching things with elongated jaws and red eyes tore the throats from horses to spill their riders to the ground.

Their charge was slowing, the press of dead warriors too great for even the mighty White Wolves to smash through. And as they slowed, more of Redwane's warriors were falling to the blades of the dead. A fiery-eyed wolf leapt towards him and Redwane swayed in the saddle, intercepting the beast's opened jaws with his hammer. Its head split apart and its corpse slammed into him. Its dissolving body unravelled, looping, rotted guts spilling into his lap and stagnant fluids hissing as they burned his armour.

'Time to go!' shouted Leovulf.

Redwane nodded and turned to shout at Holstef to sound the retreat, but the saddle next to him was empty. He circled his horse, finally seeing Holstef pinned to the ground by a scabrous ghoul with foam-flecked jaws and needle-sharp talons. Holstef screamed as it tore his guts out, its arms bloody to the elbows as it disembowelled the White Wolf. Redwane hauled back on his reins and his horse reared up onto its hind legs. Its hooves flailed as it came down, crushing the creature beneath its weight, though it was too late to save Holstef.

The White Wolves fought on, the dead pressing in from all around as the sheer number of skeletal warriors finally arrested their charge. The viaduct was choked with the debris of the fighting, a welter of bones, rusted armour and leering skulls.

Though it was probably suicide, Redwane leapt from the saddle and dropped to the ground beside Holstef. The man was already dead, his ruptured stomach steaming in the cold air. Redwane reached for the war horn. Unless he blew the retreat, the White Wolves were as good as dead.

An armoured foot slammed down on the horn, shattering it into fragments, and Redwane leapt aside as a black sword slashed towards him. He rolled to his feet, swinging his hammer up to block a descending blow. The force of the blow rang up his arms and emerald sparks flew from the impact. He backed away, taking in the measure of his opponent as he fought the rising tide of fearful bile in his throat.

Redwane's heart chilled as he saw he faced a dead knight in black armour who was shawled in a cloak woven from nightmares and woe. Its sword and armour were archaic, coated in grave dirt and rust, though the lambent glow that surrounded the ancient warlord told Redwane that this was a champion of the dead, a supreme killer of the living. It wore an open helm, and the green fire in its eyes promised a death as quick as it would be meaningless.

Its sword swung for his neck and Redwane threw himself back as it attacked with a speed and skill no living swordsman could match. Without a shield, Redwane could only block and parry with his hammer, but no matter how skilful, a fight between sword and hammer could only end badly for him.

The champion's blade slipped past his guard and Redwane screamed as its icy tip punched through his armour and slid between his ribs. Numbing waves of cold spread from the wound, and Redwane's heart stilled as the blade twisted in the wound. He staggered away from the champion, and no sooner had its sword scraped free of his armour than his heart thumped painfully in his chest.

The dread champion came at him again, but before it could strike him down, a black horse slammed into it, sending it crashing back against the viaduct's parapet. Leovulf reached down and extended his hand towards Redwane as the champion climbed to its feet, broken bones knitting together once more and its grinning skull welcoming fresh meat to slay.

'We can't fight it...' gasped Redwane.

'I know!' shouted Leovulf. 'Get on!'

Redwane grasped Leovulf's hand, hauling himself painfully onto the horse's rump. The dead were closing in, and Redwane feared that Leovulf's horse would never make it with two heavily armed warriors on its back.

The dead champion strode towards them, but it had taken only a handful of steps before it halted, as though sensing a greater threat than the two warriors before it. Redwane's entire body was cold, his flesh icy and grey from the wound dealt to him, but a deeper cold swept over him as the sound of winter gales howled from the forests. Swirling snowflakes and fragments of ice slashed from the sky, and the dead paused in their relentless attack, as a surging wind roared up the viaduct, echoing with the howls of wolves.

The chorus of lupine fury was utterly without mercy, and Redwane watched in amazement as a blizzard of winter wind blew over the dead warlord who had so nearly slain him. Ice formed on its ancient armour and decaying flesh as the chill wind froze the champion in place. A bitter squall of hail tore at it like a storm of razored glass, and a deafening howl of winter's fury broke its bones apart in an explosion of long dead remains.

The dead parted as something pushed its way up from the ground, a hulking figure in thick wolf pelts and cloaked in a blizzard of freezing ice. He carried a long staff that shimmered with hoarfrost and was topped with a glittering blade of ice. A wolf-skull mask obscured his face, and his heavily muscled limbs were bare to the elements, though he seemed to feel no ill-effects from the deathly cold. Two wolves loped through the motionless dead as he stalked towards them, one pale as moonlight, the other black as jet. The fighting on the viaduct ceased, and the White Wolves drew together as the wolf-clad warrior stopped before them.

'The fire of Ulric calls me,' he said, his voice echoing as though coming from the furthest reaches of the frozen north. Redwane had seen this warrior once before, at the coronation of Sigmar in Reikdorf, and a wave of frozen pain washed through him.

'Ar-Ulric!' cried Leovulf. 'Ar-Ulric has come!'

THIRTEEN
The Next to Die

MAEDBH RAN TOWARDS the centre of Three Hills, hearing the shouts of the sentries and their cries of alarm. Fear clamped her heart and she looked back over her shoulder to make sure Ulrike and the boys were with Garr's Eagles. Asoborns armed with bows and spears were pouring from their homes, dwellings cunningly secluded within hidden arbours and sunken hollows. Any enemy would have a difficult time in locating their homes, but it sounded like someone had done just that.

Her own bow was slung over her shoulder, but she carried a long, leaf-bladed spear that normally sat in the queen's chariot. A priest of Taal had blessed its blade, and its keen edge never failed to find its prey. A thousand possibilities flew through her mind, the living dead had found a way to locate Three Hills, the greenskins were invading from the mountains, the forest beasts had followed a scent trail to the Asoborn homeland…

None of those made sense. Queen Freya's army was between Three Hills and the living dead, and though the greenskins had been more active of late, the mountain scouts had reported no signs of a gathering horde. That just left beasts…

Freya had entrusted the care and safety of her sons to Maedbh. Bad enough that she couldn't have marched with the queen, but to allow enemies within Three Hills would be unforgivable. Maedbh rounded a grassy hillock, overgrown with trees and nettles, finding a line of Asoborn women with bows lined up with their backs to her. Their bowstrings were taut, yet their arrows remained unloosed. Children scampered around their mothers' legs, but there was no sense of fear, no sense that something dangerous had come amongst them.

'What in Taal's name is going on?' said Garr, coming alongside her with the children in tow. Ulrike held his hand, while Sigulf and Fridleifr had their hunting knives bared. Clad in baked leather armour and a bronze-reinforced kilt, Garr was handsome and strong, with a cropped scalp of fine black hair. One of the youngest Queen's Eagles, Maedbh had heard enough stories of Garr's stamina and prowess to know that he was a true Asoborn in all areas the queen required. He had taken to the children well, and they to him, which made their confinement to Three Hills marginally less troublesome.

'I don't know,' replied Maedbh, resting the spear over her shoulder and walking towards the line of Asoborns. She heard gruff voices and the clank of metal beyond, and her trepidation turned to curiosity with every step. The Asoborns parted before her and she found herself looking at a hundred armoured dwarfs, clad from head to foot in armour of silver, gold and bronze. Stained with the dust of many days travel, the dwarfs seemed unconcerned by the bent bows aimed at them or the assembling chariots rumbling around their flanks.

Leading the dwarfs was a broad figure in a suit of glittering gold and silver. The visor of his helmet was shaped in the form of a stern, bearded god and he rested his mailed fists on the haft of an axe almost as tall as he was. The warrior flipped his visor up to reveal a craggy face like the flanks of a cliff and eyes that twinkled like shards of obsidian. The dwarf's beard was plaited with iron cords and he spat a mouthful of dust.

'Which of you manlings is in charge here?' said the dwarf.

Maedbh stepped forward, planting her spear before her in the earth.

'I am,' she said. 'Maedbh of Three Hills. Who are you and how did you get past our sentries? No one enters Queen Freya's lands without permission.'

'I am Master Alaric, Runesmith to King Kurgan Ironbeard of Karaz-a-Karak, and your queen is likely dead,' said the dwarf, and a horrified ripple of disbelief swept through the assembled Asoborns. Maedbh felt a cold hand take hold of her heart. She struggled to maintain her composure in the face of such terrible news.

'As to how we got here,' continued the dwarf, oblivious to the effect his words were having, 'Do you think the paths *over* the land are the only ones? The roots of your manling town reach so rudely into the earth that even a skrati couldn't miss them. There are routes to the surface all over this place. I'm surprised you haven't found them and taken steps to secure them, but then you are only manlings...'

Maedbh struggled to hold her annoyance at the dwarf's insult, instead focusing on the news he had brought.

'What are you talking about?' she said at last. 'Queen Freya's army set out from here only a week ago.'

'Freya?' said the dwarf. 'Tall woman with red hair, doesn't wear enough armour to cover a small child? Rides a chariot of black and gold?'

'Yes,' said Maedbh.

'Aye, that's her,' said Alaric. 'It's hard to tell you manlings apart sometimes. Anyway, the dead destroyed her army at the river crossing. It was messy, not many escaped. A blood drinker swordsman commands the dead, and those he slew now march north with him.'

Maedbh swallowed, grief twisting her gut into a painful knot. She knew little of the dwarfs and their ways, but knew the Emperor counted them as his sworn allies and that they did not lie or embellish.

To the mountain folk, truth was like the hardest stone, unyielding and enduring.

'How many?' she said. 'And how long do we have?'

'His army is near four thousand now,' said Alaric. 'I reckon they'll be here within the day and don't even think about hiding. They'll sniff this place out as sure as gold glitters.'

'Then we need to leave here,' said Maedbh. 'We need to head west to Reikdorf.'

'Aye,' agreed Alaric. 'That you do, manling. And right quick too.'

THE ATTACK ON Marburg came in the dead of night. Spectral fog gathered over the marshland around the mouth of the Reik where it spilled over the treacherous sandbars and narrow channels of the harbour. Marburg wasn't as naturally blessed as Jutonsryk in its geography, but it had the advantage of being on the Reik, which meant it could control the traffic of ships to Reikdorf.

That thought alone made Marius's mouth water.

'A city of gold,' he whispered. 'That's what this place could be.'

His lancers looked over at his words, but none spoke. Unlike some counts, he didn't encourage fraternisation between commoners and their betters.

Marius and a hundred of his warriors stood on the southern shore of the main channel that led to the curving ring of the docks where Aldred and the Raven Helms awaited. The quayside was deserted, all those ships that could flee the city having sailed around the coast to safer ports in the south. It made for a strange sight to see a port bereft of ships.

Despite her brother's urgings to remain in the city, Marika commanded a host of archers on the rooftops and forecastle-shaped towers set in the curve of the citadel's lower walls. From there her archers could rain down arrows upon the dead without fear of retaliation.

Rearing up behind her archers was the Raven Hall, the monstrous tower dominating the skyline with its beaked upper chambers and swept-back wings. Impressive enough in its own way, Marius found it rather vulgar, like something the ancient tribal kings might have raised to some long forgotten animal god. Hundreds of crows and ravens alighted on its ledges and carvings, such that it shivered with feathers as though coming alive.

Endal warriors occupied positions all along the docks and shoreline, their spears and shields wavering like tiny specks of starlight in the darkness. Aldred had been a hard man to convince of his own danger, but with Marika's help, Marius had been able to persuade him to evacuate many of the oldest and youngest along the river towards Reikdorf. Marburg was a city of warriors now, but as night after night passed without an attack, fear gnawed at the courage of every man.

Truth be told, it was almost a relief when the dead finally came.

Huntsmen watched the coastal approaches to Marburg, and Marius had persuaded Aldred to send out sentry ships to watch for the undead corsairs. One of those ships now bobbed in the dark swells of the harbour, its sails torn and holed, listing to the side where planks had been torn from its ribs by bony fingers. Its crew still stood on its decks; the helmsman at the tiller and its captain behind the wheel, but it was clear to all who saw them that these men were dead.

The ship had drifted into Marburg an hour before the watch fires were lit, and as darkness closed in, the city's defenders rushed to their posts. Yellowed fog rolled in from the sea, and Marius heard the flat, toneless sound of ships' bells, the same bells that had rung the death knell of his city. He smiled weakly as he realised he was afraid. That was a new sensation. Even when Bastiaan had stabbed him in Middenheim he had been more angry than afraid.

The monotonous sound conjured images of skeletal ferrymen and a black river crossing from which no living soul could return. Bobbing corpse lights followed the echoes of the bells, and Marius saw a host of ships drift into the harbour, over two hundred of them, each with torn sails, splintered oars and swollen, barnacle-encrusted hulls. They came on without need for wind or sail, dread ships of the forsaken and the damned.

'Now,' hissed Marius, willing the defenders ranked up along the line of docks to hear his whispered imprecation. 'Come on, Aldred, don't be a fool all your life.'

The ships came on until a single fiery arrow arced up into the night sky.

Flames rippled around the curve of the docks as oil-soaked braziers were sparked to life and the city's entire complement of war machines were unmasked from behind wicker mantlets. Marius heard the creak of windlasses as heavy ballistae cranked, followed by a *whoosh* of the barbed tips of great javelins being set alight. Ten of these machines had been dismantled from their positions on the city's eastern walls and carried down to the docks, where they had been rebuilt in make-shift earthworks of good Reikland mud.

The heavy iron bolts leapt towards the enemy ships and six were struck, the flaming missiles punching through their rotten timbers and setting them ablaze. Holed beyond the ability of their masters' dark magic to sustain, they slid beneath the water and distant cheering drifted up to the Jutones' position.

'Don't get carried away,' said Marius. 'The dead don't fear a bit of water.'

More missiles leapt from the war machines, smashing masts and breaking open hulls with every bolt as the war machines' crews found their range. The ships of the dead scattered, moving with greater urgency towards the shoreline. A flurry of arrows rained down from the high town, thudding home on the decks of the hulks or piercing the dead meat of their crew.

Marius saw Marika among the archers, loosing white-fletched shafts from a bow he was sure was of fey origin. He had sent a similar bow to Sigmar before Black Fire, which he'd heard the Emperor had broken over his knee. Such a shame, the bow had been worth more gold than Sigmar would have seen in his life.

Nothing more had been said of his and Marika's conversation the other night, but Marius was savvy enough to know that it still hung in the air between them. He could do nothing to act on her unsaid plan just yet, but perhaps his doing nothing was just what she wanted.

'My lord,' said Vergoossen, appearing from the darkness and shivering in a thick woollen cloak. 'Should we not be on the move? Much as I am loath to approach anything resembling a battle, was our plan not to move to occupy the southern tip of the docks upon the appearance of the dead?'

'Indeed, it was,' said Marius, watching the battle unfold as the ships of the dead reached the docks. The first of the drowned sailors leapt from their ships and no sooner had they done so than Marika loosed a flaming arrow that lit the oil spread around the quayside in wide troughs hacked into the stone. A wall of searing flame leapt up and ran around the docks like a fiery snake, setting hundreds of corpses alight and spreading swiftly to their ships.

'Is that not our plan now?' asked Vergoossen. 'I do not recall any tactical amendments from Count Aldred.'

'No, you wouldn't have, Vergoossen,' said Marius. 'This one came from Princess Marika. She and her brother clearly share an... interesting relationship.'

'I see, my lord.'

'No you don't,' said Marius. 'But it doesn't matter. Watch and learn, Vergoossen. Watch and learn. This is how things change in this world, not with diplomacy and words, but with swords and gold and ambition.'

The wind carried the stink of rotten, burning meat, and Marius covered his mouth with a pomander scented with exotic fruits and rose petals. The fire on the docks was dying now, and yet more of the dead were pouring from their ships or climbing from the muddy waters of the shores. The Raven Helms charged, smashing into the dead with heavy broadswords, cutting them down with brutal strokes. They pushed the dead back, driving them into the water as Endal tribesmen fought to keep the flanks of the elite warriors safe.

'Ah, now things get interesting,' said Marius, as hundreds of the living dead waded ashore below them. Water spilled from opened bellies and vacant ribcages. Green fire guttered in rotted eye sockets.

The dead lurched in the direction of the Raven Helms, ignoring the Jutones on the higher ground.

'Won't the Raven Helms be flanked if we do not move?' asked Vergoossen.

'Of course,' said Marius, drawing his sword. 'And the bloodshed will be terrible, but at the last moment, the heroic Marius will save the day. Saga poets will sing songs of my bravery for years to come.'

'I hope you are right, my lord,' replied Vergoossen.

'Of course I am,' said Marius.

MARIKA LOOSED ANOTHER arrow into the flaming horde below, struggling to contain her horror at these decaying revenants as they shambled ashore from their doomed boats. Dozens were ablaze in the harbour, banishing the crepuscular gloom with the fury of their demise. To see so many of the dead clawing at the living brought back all the memories she'd buried of her time in the marshes. The lingering doubts she'd had regarding her unspoken pact with Marius were forgotten as the suffocating terror of that night returned to her.

'Another quiver!' she shouted, and Eloise passed her a fresh batch of arrows. Her maidservant had refused to leave with the rest of those who fled for Reikdorf, but Marika saw she was now regretting that decision.

She nocked another arrow and sighted on a skeletal warrior with a rusty cutlass and a hole in its breast where a heart once beat. She let out a breath and loosed before drawing another. Her arrow flew straight and true, slashing into the dead warrior's chest and dropping him to the ground in a pile of disconnected bones. It was a fine shot, but ultimately a waste of a shaft. Marius had told them to look for the host's sorcerers, evil beings who gave life to the army of the dead.

Without these fell magickers, the dead could not sustain their existence and would return to the grave. She didn't know how Marius had learned of such things, but supposed that with enough gold, you could learn anything in the world.

Marika scanned the docks, finally spying a hunched figure lurking by the gunwale of a wrecked ship listing against the quayside. She pulled another arrow and took her time with her aim, allowing for the gentle sway of her target's ship and the slight wind. The figure turned towards her, and she saw its face was that of a man, though one ravaged by some hideous wasting sickness or starvation.

Her arrow punched through his right eye, the barbed tip bursting from the back of his skull and pinning him to the gunwale. The dead things clambering from his ship lurched drunkenly as their dissolution overcame them. Armoured warriors of bone and rotted meat collapsed where they stood and the bloated corpses of drowning victims sagged and fell back into the sea. Perhaps fifty of the dead cracked and crumbled to ash with the death of the black sorcerer, and Marika's heart surged with sudden hope.

To face the dead was to know fear like never before, but to fight them... that was the sweetest elixir. She whooped with new-found fearlessness. She shouted to the rest of the archers, reminding them of what to look for, feeling her heart race with surging life.

'My lady?' whimpered Eloise. 'What's that?'

The light of the moon was obscured as the carrion birds took off from the eaves and garrets of the Raven Hall. Marika had seen birds behaving like that before. The birds were flocking not to feed, but to flee. She looked to where Eloise was pointing, seeing hundreds of screeching bats swarming in from the sea. Their leathery wings sounded like a fleet of ships at sail, but behind them came something far larger, far worse and far more terrible than she could have dreamed in her worst nightmares.

ALDRED WATCHED THE sky darken as hundreds of bats swarmed the night with their hideous furred bodies. Ever creatures of ill-omen, bats were vermin with a thirst for blood, and claws that carried all manner of foulness. Arrows flashed toward them from the citadel walls, and though he hated to admit it, Marius was right to deploy the archers further back.

The fighting around the docks raged in the leaping shadows of dying fires, a frantic fight for survival against a foe that cared nothing for pain. His warriors had beaten back one attack and he had driven Ulfshard into the chest of one of the robed sorcerers Marius had told them to look for. That death had unmade two ships' worth of the dead and Aldred felt unbridled joy as their spirits were released from bondage.

Endal tribesmen fought to prevent the dead from getting a foothold on the docks, but their enemy's numbers were telling in every backwards step they were forced to take. The wail and skirl of pipe music echoed over the water and filled the hearts of every warrior with courage. While the ancient tunes of glory played, no man could fail to fight without feeling the judgemental eyes of his ancestors upon him.

A dreadful shriek echoed over the water, and Aldred flinched as something monstrous flew overhead. He heard screams, and saw a winged shadow swoop down on the city, a terrible monster of darkness with a black armoured figure astride its bony, elongated neck.

His terror nearly overwhelmed him as a stray shaft of moonlight reflected from its exposed bone and dead scale hide. Ragged wings of death-stiffened hide flapped with ponderous slowness and its rotted jaws opened wide exposing broken, jutting fangs of yellow.

'It's a dragon... a dead one...' he said, unable to believe his eyes, feeling his fragile courage melting away at the sight of so terrifying a monster in the flesh. Its body shimmered as though not truly corporeal, and Aldred's soul wept to see a creature from the elder days of the world violated in such a hideous manner.

Necrotic flesh withered on its millennia old bones, and flaps of skin trailed from ancient lance wounds in its flank. Its elongated head was horned and hooked, barbs of bone and tooth making its jaw a serrated blade as long as a warship's keel. Sat astride its bony neck was a hooded figure robed in black, its body wreathed in baleful energies of undeath. Pale wisps of bleak twilight billowed around the rider and wherever its gaze turned, men fell dead in terror, the flesh withering to ash on their bones.

The mighty dragon swooped down over the citadel walls, and a billowing cloud of noxious breath streamed from its jaws to engulf the ramparts. The stench was overpowering, even from so far away, and Marius coughed at the grave reek. He could hear men dying, choking and coughing as their internal organs liquefied and the flesh melted from their bones.

Wails of terror spread along the docks as warriors threw down their weapons and fled in terror from the corpse dragon. Alone among the Endals, the Raven Helms held firm, but one look at their faces told Aldred they were close to breaking. He held Ulfshard aloft, and the pale blue glow of the fey enchantments woven into its arcane metal poured iron into their veins.

The living quailed before the sight of the dragon, but the dead cared nothing for its dreadful magnificence, and threw themselves upon the Raven Helms once more. Notched blades clove armour, claws and teeth ripped flesh. Aldred blocked a slashing cleaver and beheaded its wielder as he saw that he and the Raven Helms fought on alone. Endals were dying all around him, borne to the ground by the dead or skewered on rusted spears.

The defence of the docks had become a rout, hundreds of warriors fleeing towards the lower walls of the citadel. The gates were open and men fought to reach the safety of the walls. Laredus fought through a press of the dead warriors towards Aldred, the top portion of his sword snapped off and his black armour torn by bloodied claws.

'We need to go, my lord!' he shouted. 'We can hold them at the walls.'

Aldred nodded, too weary to even reply. His sword arm felt like his veins had been filled with lead and the exhaustion of the fighting settled upon him like a cloak of iron. He knew he was no longer as fit as he needed to be. This one fight had almost drained him.

'Sound the retreat,' he gasped.

'There's no need,' said Laredus. 'We're all that's left. Raven Helms! With the count!'

Aldred and Laredus turned and ran towards the gates of the citadel, but they had covered barely half the distance when the ground trembled. Glittering particles swirled in hundreds of miniature whirlwinds, dust devils that spun and twisted like living things of spectral light. They gathered form and solidity until hundreds of translucent figures stood between them and the citadel, a lambent host of ancient men and women with eyes of pale white and mouths stretched open in soundless screams.

The blood froze in Aldred's veins.

An army of the dead behind them and a host of hungry ghosts ahead of them.

They were trapped.

MARIKA SAW THE host of shimmering spirits arise from the dust and her humanity rebelled at the sight of these wretched souls denied their final rest. She could feel their pain and the horror of their blasted existence, and tears welled at the thought of such a fate. What manner of man could tear these souls from Morr's realm and force them into slavery, denying them their rightful place in the next world?

These dreadful wraiths flickered in the air like wavering candle flames, drifting against the wind towards Aldred and the Raven Helms. A ring of dead warriors and glowing spirits surrounded them, and there was nothing anyone could do. No warrior dared leave the citadel while the looming dragon and fear of the restless spirits held their courage in check.

Screams and groans of pain surrounded her. The dragon's breath had swept the ramparts and its pestilential exhalation choked the life and vitality from all those who breathed its foulness. Young men in the full fire of youth had fallen to the ground, transformed into ancients with withered skin, brittle bones and sunken flesh. Some coughed up bloody froth as their lungs dissolved, while others had the flesh scoured from their bones by the noxious corruption.

A handful of arrows slashed up at the beast, but every single one bounced from its dead hide. The war machine crews attempted to bring down the beast, but some hideous force protected it from their missiles. Unable to harm the dragon, the survivors of its attack turned their bows upon the dead spirits, loosing volley after volley at the glowing figures. Their arrows passed through the spirits' forms, clattering on the cobbled streets and shattering as though they had been frozen in flight.

They might as well have been loosing arrows at clouds for all the effect they were having.

Undeterred, Marika pulled back her bowstring and loosed a shaft from the bow her father had given her on her fifteenth birthday. The bowstave was fashioned from a wood no Endal craftsman could name or work, its length inlaid with silver threads woven through the grain of the wood in swirling patterns that changed with the seasons.

Her arrow leapt from the bow, arcing up and slashing down through the spirits, and where its point struck, one of the forlorn revenants vanished in a flare of light.

'They *can* be slain,' she said, looking in amazement at her bow. The metallic threads shimmered with life and the wood grew warm to the touch. Her father had told her the bow had been crafted by the fey folk from across the ocean, but she hadn't really believed him until now. She bent her bow and released over and over, freeing more of the damned spirits from their hellish servitude in shimmering twists of light.

But as many as she banished, there was no way she was going to destroy enough to save Aldred and the Raven Helms.

Aldred and Laredus stood back to back as the dead drew near. Ulfshard shimmered with a blue light, the blade brighter than Aldred had ever known it. The moans of the dead cut through the din of battle and the dry roar of the dragon and its screeching bats. The Raven Helms fought the dead coming in from the sea with desperate strokes, blocking ship's axes and cutting down dead men who came at them with nothing but their clawed hands reaching to pluck the eyes from their heads.

The spirits of the dead enveloped them, swirling in a cloying mist of screams and tormented wailing. They tore at the Endals with insubstantial claws that passed through the thickest armour yet drew no blood. The merest touch of these damned spirits sucked the vitality from a warrior like a leech drawing blood from a wound. None came near Aldred, flinching from him as soon as he brought Ulfshard to bear. He swept his sword through the misty substance of the spirits, feeling their joy as the connection to the evil sorcery binding them to the world of the living was severed.

Yet it was not enough. The spirits shrieked and wailed as they were dissipated by Aldred's blade, but there were too many of the fleshy undead to defeat. The ring of Raven Helms shrank as the ranks of the dead swelled still further. More ships were crashing into the shoreline to disgorge yet more of the doomed warriors of the dead.

Aldred heard a furious clamour from the citadel and saw a banner of bright colours borne through the mêlée, a flag no Endal would dream of bearing. It was a Jutone flag, ostentatiously colourful and garish, and beneath it rode a host of armoured lancers in pale blue cloaks fighting with curved sabres. Marius fought at their centre, cutting a dashing path through the dead with the elegant sweeps of a duellist. His blade was a golden streak of sunlight, and like Ulfshard, the dead feared it.

The Jutone cavalry smashed through the encircling dead, and Marius backhanded a reverse cut into the skull of a dead warrior, neatly removing the top of his head. Marius fought with fluid grace, as much a showman as a killer. His skill was undeniable, though Aldred saw he favoured his right side.

The charge of the Jutone horsemen was devastating, smashing the dead apart with a ferocity Aldred had hitherto not suspected. The Endals had long believed the Jutones had gone soft in their city of merchants, preferring the luxuries gold could buy instead of living as warriors. Clearly he had underestimated Marius, and the thought disturbed rather than reassured him.

While the Raven Helms and Jutone lancers held the dead at bay, Marius reined in his horse beside Aldred, his face flushed with excitement and the thrill of battle.

'I think you should be getting out of here, yes?' said Marius.

'Where in Manann's name did you come from?' demanded Aldred. 'Weren't you supposed to be holding the southern shore?'

'We were, but rather more monsters than we could handle came ashore and I had to fall back to the citadel to save my men,' said Marius. 'We mounted up as soon as we saw your danger, and here we are.'

'You allowed us to be flanked!'

'Yes, my deepest apologies about that, but I did send a runner informing you of our withdrawal,' said Marius smoothly. 'I suppose he must have been killed en route. That is a pity.'

'A pity!' stormed Aldred. 'We were almost overrun.'

'And you still will be if you insist on having this ridiculous discussion now,' pointed out Marius. 'Get up behind me if you want to live through this night.'

Marius held out his hand to Aldred, who bit back an angry retort as he hauled himself onto the back of the Jutone count's horse. Though it went against everything he knew to be right, he held his sword out to Marius.

'The spirit creatures fear the magic of Ulfshard,' he said. 'Use it to cut us a path.'

'No need, they fear mine also,' said Marius with a manic grin. 'Now let's be off.'

Marius kicked back his spurs with a wild yell, and his horse took off towards the citadel. The Jutone lancers fought alongside the Raven Helms as Marius forced the howling wraiths back with his enchanted blade. They rode back towards the citadel gates through the path the lancers had cut. Aldred heard cheers from the ramparts as they came within sight of the gates and laughed with joy. He saw his sister loosing arrows into the dead, and his relief fled as he saw the expression on her face.

It was disappointment.

FOURTEEN
North, East and West

REDWANE PACED THE firelit interior of the temple of Ulric, a pulsing vein throbbing at his temple as he listened to Myrsa's pronouncement. Renweard stood at the count's side, the sword of the Warrior Eternal held loosely over his shoulder, while Bordan sat on a block of dark stone yet to be hoisted to the temple walls. The Flame of Ulric burned cold in the centre of the stone-flagged plaza, white and stark against walls that rose daily to enclose it as the temple neared completion.

Ar-Ulric and his wolves circled the flame, their black eyes reflecting its glow and regarding Redwane as a fox eyes a wounded hen. The temple had changed a great deal since Sigmar's defeat of the daemon lord, all traces of the battle cleaned from the stonework and paved over with polished granite hewn from the quarries of the Middle Mountains. It had been a magnificent battle, yet no one wanted a reminder of that dread avatar of the northern gods to befoul a holy place of Ulric.

'I can't believe I'm hearing this,' said Redwane. 'You're really not going to march out?'

'I have made my judgement, Redwane,' said Myrsa. 'And my decision is final.'

'But Sigmar needs us. You heard what Ar-Ulric said – the armies of

Nagash are closing on Reikdorf. We have to ride south.'

'We need to keep Middenheim safe,' said Myrsa, clutching the hilt of the runefang tightly. The count of the northern marches walked towards Redwane and laid a hand upon his shoulder. 'I know you and Sigmar are close, but the Emperor has entrusted me with the safety of Middenheim and I cannot let him down. If I ride south with my army then this city is doomed. Surely you must see that?'

'All I see is that we're abandoning the Emperor when he needs us most.'

'You are not thinking straight, my friend,' said Myrsa, concern written across his features. 'The deathly champion on the causeway wounded you deeper than you know.'

Redwane shrugged off Myrsa's hand, angry at the other man's pity. Two days had passed since Ar-Ulric's arrival, and his strength was only now beginning to return. The icy numbness and frozen chill that had stilled his heart still clung to his grey flesh. No heat warmed Redwane now, yet neither cold nor fear touched him any more. His body was alive, yet he felt no sensations of life. Food was tasteless, beauty meaningless, and all that remained to him was the pain of his many scars.

He turned to Ar-Ulric, his tone accusing. 'You agree with this? You crowned Sigmar, remember? You would cower in this mountain city and leave him to his fate? That is not Ulric's way, or if it is, I'll have no part of it.'

The wolves at Ar-Ulric's side growled, baring fangs of ice and obsidian, their yellowed eyes boring into him with cunning beyond that of beasts. Redwane met their stare unflinchingly, daring them to gainsay him. Ar-Ulric crossed the temple towards him, his aura of frozen winters leaving Redwane untouched. Behind the great wolf-skull helm, Redwane saw piercing eyes like those of the wolves, one pale as a winter sky, the other blacker than a moonless night.

'You are soul-sick, Redwane of the Unberogen,' said Ar-Ulric, placing his glittering axe between them. Chill wisps of icy air wafted from the blade and haft, but Redwane felt nothing of the cold. 'You do not see the passage of time as I do. I roam the wild places of this world, following the breath of Ulric to the forgotten sites of primal power. I seek to follow the wolf god's path and instruct men in his ways of honour and courage.'

'Really?' said Redwane. 'Then why do we never see you? It's been over a decade since you've shown your damn face amongst the tribes.

That doesn't sound like you're doing much in the way of instruction. That sounds a lot like hiding to me.'

'Redwane!' barked Myrsa. 'Hold your tongue!'

Ar-Ulric held up his hand to silence Myrsa. 'My days of wandering are over. From this day until the coming of the Red Eye, he who brings the End Times, Middenheim shall be my abode. But the Heldenhammer must face the dread Necromancer without the warriors of the north or he is not fit to be Emperor.'

'Why?' demanded Redwane. 'Tell me why.'

'Because if the Flame of Ulric is ever extinguished, then the Empire dies with it. Do *you* understand that, Redwane of the Unberogen?'

'I understand it, but I do not accept it,' said Redwane. 'And if that is the word of Ulric, then I spit on him and curse his name with my last breath!'

Gasps of horror spread through the temple at Redwane's blasphemy, and more than one hand found its way to a weapon. Renweard swung the sword of the Warrior Eternal down, and Myrsa's face flushed in anger.

'You dare speak such words in this place?' cried Myrsa.

'You're damn right I do,' Redwane shouted back at him. 'You're deserting your Emperor and your friend because this madman who roams the wilderness on his own tells you to. For all you know he's as mad as Torbrecan's lunatics. Well I won't abandon Sigmar, and if you won't march to Reikdorf, I'll go alone.'

'Then you'll die,' said Myrsa.

'So be it,' said Redwane. 'The gods don't seem to care one way or another.'

He spun on his heel and marched towards an archway to the city beyond, feeling dead inside yet filled with fresh purpose and determination.

'Damn you, Redwane, I forbid you to go,' said Myrsa. 'You are a warrior of the White Wolves! Sworn to the defence of Middenheim.'

Redwane turned and tore the wolf pelt from his shoulders. He dropped the cloak at his feet and unhooked the heavy warhammer from his belt. He let it slide from his grip, and it fell with a clatter of finality to the flagstones.

'Not any more I'm not,' he said.

THE STREETS OF Middenheim were cold, colder than he remembered them, but it didn't touch him. Redwane saw men and women huddled in doorways, pulling threadbare blankets around them as the breath misted before their mouths. Sunlight couldn't penetrate the oppressive gloom that pressed down, and it seemed as though the warmth was being leeched from the world day by day. Once again, the city was filled with refugees, and Redwane wondered what manner of gods could leave their people to suffer such an endless parade of misery as the people of the Empire were forced to endure.

Redwane walked the streets at random, keeping to the shadows and losing himself in the maze of stone structures. Faces passed him, men in armour and men in rags. He no longer knew where he was going, and he no longer cared. Men he had trusted and called friend were turning their backs on Sigmar, the hero who had given them everything. Now Sigmar was in mortal danger and they did nothing to help him. The certainties of loyalty and honour upon which Redwane had built his life were crumbling, and all that was left was the coldness in his heart that knew there was only one path open to him.

He passed through the streets as a ghost, numb to the world around him and feeling the pain of his scars as if they reached down through his skin and into his bones. The wound in his chest throbbed like a second heartbeat, one that pumped ice around his body instead of blood. People were looking at him strangely, but he paid them no mind, walking ever onwards as he unbuckled plates of his armour, shedding iron as a serpent sheds its skin to be reborn.

His path became clearer with every plate that hit the ground, his steps surer and more certain. His head came up and he saw the world around him, bleached of colour and life, and knew that this was its true face. Love was a lie and struggling against the pain and misery that life threw up was pointless.

He felt a hand on his shoulder and turned to see a face he knew, but couldn't place.

'What in Ulric's name are you doing, you fool?' said the black-haired man clad in red armour and wrapped in a wolfskin cloak. Another man stood behind him, one with a sour face that made him look like he'd swallowed a mouthful of vinegar.

'I know you,' said Redwane.

'Of course you damn well do,' snapped the man. 'It's me, Leovulf.'

'Leovulf, yes,' nodded Redwane.

'We heard what happened at the temple of Ulric,' said Leovulf. 'But what they're saying's wrong isn't it? You're still a White Wolf aren't you?'

'Doesn't look like it,' said the other man, lifting a discarded vambrace from the street.

'Shut up, Ustern,' said Leovulf.

Ustern, yes, that was it. Redwane turned away from them, making his way deeper into the city.

'Hey,' said Leovulf, taking hold of him once again. 'Were they right about you saying you're leaving for Reikdorf? To fight alongside the Emperor?'

'Yes, I'm going to Reikdorf,' said Redwane. 'That's what I told Myrsa, and that's what I'm doing. The Emperor needs us and I'll be damned if I don't go to him.'

'And I'll be damned if I let you go get yourself killed.'

'Don't try and stop me,' said Redwane, clenching his fists.

'I'm not going to, but I meant what I said. I'm not going to let you get yourself killed, so if you're set on marching to Reikdorf, then I suppose I'm going with you.'

'I'll come too,' said Ustern. Redwane and Leovulf looked at him in surprise. Ustern shrugged. 'A captain needs his banner bearer, else he's not a captain is he?'

'Good point, lad,' said Leovulf. 'Well?'

'Well what?' said Redwane.

'How are you planning to get to Reikdorf?' demanded Leovulf. 'In case you hadn't noticed, there's a host of the living dead surrounding this city. You'll need a damned army to break through, and I don't see Count Myrsa giving you his.'

'I know,' said Redwane, 'but I know how we can get another one.'

DAWN WAS LESS than an hour away, but Maedbh knew the rising sun wouldn't save them. She knelt beside a boulder at the edge of the river and dipped her cupped palms below its rippling surface. Splashing the cold water on her face sharpened her focus, but she knew it wouldn't last. Her entire body ached and she rubbed the heels of her palms against her eyes.

Even on campaign, when sleep was an elusive bedfellow, she hadn't been this tired. In times of war she fought alongside warriors, men and women who could look after themselves. This was very different.

Now she had people to protect who couldn't defend themselves.

The entire population of Three Hills and its surrounding villages had agglomerated into one long column of frightened people, making their way west with whatever possessions they could load onto wagons or carry on their backs. Perhaps six hundred people rested in the shade of a low ridge of hills, old men and women, children and those too sick or injured to march with the queen. Garr's sword band of Queen's Eagles stood watch and she gave thanks that Freya had thought to leave these fearsome warriors at Three Hills. Only thirty of them marched with them, but their presence alone was helping to keep spirits high.

Maedbh turned away from thoughts of the queen, the guilt that she should have gone with her assuaged by the fact that she could still protect her own daughter and Freya's sons. She clung to the hope that Freya might still live; after all, Master Alaric had said that some had escaped the massacre. If anyone could survive a battle with the living dead, it was Queen Freya.

This was their fifth day of march, and they had covered barely half the distance to the confluence of the great rivers. The oldest and youngest rode in the few wagons that hadn't been taken by the queen's army, but the rest walked. They were moving too slowly, and their pursuers did not need to stop to eat and rest as they must. Despite their stature, the dwarfs easily matched the pace of the Asoborns, moving ahead of the column and keeping watch on its vulnerable sides and rear. They took no rest, didn't seem to eat or sleep, and were as indefatigable as the foe that pursued them.

Packs of dead wolves dogged their every step, darting in from the flanks to savage a straggling family or to pick off a child that wandered too far from the column. The dwarfs had saved as many as they could, but Maedbh sensed their frustration at the slow speed the Asoborns were making. The dead were right behind them, and every time her people rested, they got a little closer.

Ulrike, Sigulf and Fridleifr lay asleep on the grass beside her, and Maedbh stroked her daughter's hair. She was loath to wake the children, but dwarf scouts had reported seeing sunlight on spear points no more than a few miles behind them. They would need to be on the move soon.

She wished Wolfgart were here, imagining him riding over the hills on his finest stallion to her rescue with his mighty sword hewing the dead like corn at harvest time.

'What I wouldn't give to see that,' she whispered. 'I miss you, my gorgeous man.'

Maedbh looked up from the river as she saw a stout warrior in heavy plates of gleaming metal and fine mail reflected in the water. She hadn't heard him approach.

'Master Alaric,' she said.

'The man you are bonded to is called Wolfgart?' asked Alaric.

Maedbh nodded, more surprised at the question than by the fact that the dwarf knew to whom she was bonded. 'That's right. Do you know him?'

'I do,' said the dwarf. 'I fought beside him at Black Fire, and we saved each other's life many times in the tunnels beneath Ulric's city.'

'Middenheim? Wolfgart would never speak of that battle.'

'That does not surprise me, for it was bloody and desperate,' said Alaric. 'I do not like to remember it, but if you are his bonded woman, then I must.'

'I don't understand.'

'A dwarf never forgives an insult, and never forgets a debt.'

Maedbh laughed mirthlessly. 'Wolfgart owes you money? He always was lousy at dice.'

'No,' said Alaric. 'Not money. Wolfgart and I fought the vermin beasts in the tunnels beneath Middenheim. The rats were all over us, and we fought in the cramped darkness by the light of dying torches. We fought with axes, picks and daggers or whatever came to hand. I hauled his arse from the jaws of a giant ogre beast with metal for arms and he slew an armoured rat-champion with a short-handled pick to its brain. We fought in those tunnels for days, but at the end of it all we were victorious. I remember every moment of that fight, and Wolfgart saved my life on seven separate occasions. I saved him six times.'

'I'm sure Wolfgart isn't counting,' said Maedbh.

'That matters not,' said Alaric. 'I am counting, and I owe him a blood debt.'

'What does that mean?'

'It means that I am indebted to him and his kin.'

'Is that why you came to Three Hills, to pay your debt to Wolfgart?'

'Not entirely,' said Alaric. 'We were coming to the Empire to take back a war machine your Emperor's warriors retrieved from a representative of the Deeplock Clan. That, and we heard that the great necromancer had returned. But mainly to retrieve the war machine. Your settlement was on the way and was the quickest way for us to get ahead of the blood drinker's army.'

'Then I'm indebted to you for warning us,' said Maedbh.

Alaric shook his head. 'There is no debt between you and I, Maedbh of Three Hills, but when I see you to Reikdorf, the debt I have with Wolfgart is settled.'

'That seems fair enough,' agreed Maedbh.

'To allow me to honour that debt, I need you to do something.'

'Yes, I know,' said Maedbh, pushing herself wearily to her feet. 'I will get my people moving, but they needed to rest.'

Alaric looked back to the east, as though he could see through the earth to spy upon the army of the dead. For all Maedbh knew of the mountain folk's skill, perhaps he could. Alaric sniffed the air and stamped a foot on the hard-packed earth of the riverbank, as though listening to its echo through the ground.

'That is not what I mean,' said Alaric.

'Then what *do* you mean?'

'You know what I mean. My debt is to you, not these other manlings. You have to leave those who cannot keep up. Your kind lives and dies so quickly it will make no difference to your race. The old will be dead soon anyway, and you can breed more young in your belly. These ones aren't old enough to work or fight yet. What use are they to you?'

Maedbh struggled to hold her temper in the face of Alaric's request.

'You want us to leave our people behind?' she said, as evenly as she could.

'It is the only way some of you will live,' said the dwarf. 'Save those who can outpace the dead, leave the rest behind. Better to save some than none.'

'No, Master Alaric,' said Maedbh. 'That won't be happening. No one gets left behind.'

'Then you will all die.'

'Then we will all die,' hissed Maedbh. 'I'd sooner we all died right here than live with knowing I left my own people here to be killed.'

Alaric's face was unreadable in the dim light, but Maedbh thought he was more surprised at her decision than angry or disappointed. At length, he sighed.

'Very well, if you will not leave them behind, then my warriors and I cannot leave.'

'What? No! I don't want your deaths on my head.'

'That is not our custom, Maedbh of Three Hills,' said Alaric. 'The debt demands it.'

Further words were forestalled as Garr came running over, his sword drawn and the visor of his eagle-winged helmet pulled down over his handsome face.

'My lady,' he said, 'the mountain folk say the vanguard of the dead are upon us. You need to go right now. We will hold them off as long as we can, but you must get the queen's boys out of here.'

Maedbh took a deep breath, weighing the impossible choices before her.

'No,' she said. 'We're not leaving.'

'My lady?' said Garr. 'You have to move. Queen Freya–'

'Queen Freya is not here,' snapped Maedbh. 'And you will obey me, Garr. Do you understand?'

'Yes, my lady,' said the warrior. 'What is it you require of us?'

Maedbh looked around her for somewhere they could make their stand, finally settling upon a wooded hill to the north. The river curled lazily around its eastern flank, and the thick trees would make any advance from the west next to impossible. The dead would have to come straight at them up the steep southern slope.

'Form up with Alaric's dwarfs on yonder hill,' she said, pointing to the ridge of trees above them. 'We can't outrun the dead, so we'll fight them. We'll fight them and make them wish they'd never invaded Asoborn lands.'

Garr quickly studied the lie of the land, and she saw his understanding that this could be nothing more than a last stand. Maedbh gripped his shoulder and jabbed a fist at the column of Asoborns.

'Get everyone who can hold a weapon in the battle line, no matter how old or young or wounded,' ordered Maedbh. 'Everyone fights, no one runs.'

He nodded and said, 'It will be done, my lady.'

The Queen's Eagle ran off to get the Asoborns moving and Maedbh turned to Master Alaric. She drew her sword and said, 'After today your debt is settled, whether we live or die. Will that satisfy your customs?'

'It will indeed, my lady,' nodded Master Alaric with a deep bow. 'It will be my honour to die alongside you, Maedbh of Three Hills.'

'Don't put me in the ground just yet,' said Maedbh as the sun rose over the eastern mountains, spreading its promise across the land. She smiled as fresh hope filled her heart and closed her eyes, tilting her face towards the sun. 'This is the Empire, and stranger things have happened than us living to see another dawn.'

Alaric heard the change in her voice and shook his head.

'Give me a hundred lifetimes and I'll never understand you manlings,' he grumbled.

* * *

THE THIRD NIGHT of attacks on Marburg's citadel walls ended with the dawn, the dead melting away to the shadowed eaves of the lower town and docks. The base of the walls were thick with bones and decaying corpses, the detritus of the night's battle which would, come sundown, rise once more to claw their way up the pitted stone.

Though the loss of the lower town was a blow, Marius's rescue of Aldred had given the defenders fresh hope, and the tale of his magnificent ride circulated throughout the city, becoming ever grander and more adventurous as it went. Each day saw the warriors defending Marburg working in shifts to rebuild broken defences, shore up gates that withered and rotted under the effects of wasting sorcery, stitch wounds and pray to the gods for salvation.

Marius shook his sword free of ash from the grinning, skull-faced dead man he'd just killed, and sheathed his blade. The warriors around him cheered, and he smiled modestly as he accepted a towel from a nearby lancer to mop his brow.

'We may fight at night, but it's still damned hot work,' he said, loud enough for the warriors along this stretch of wall to hear. A few dutiful chuckles greeted his remark, but most of the men were too exhausted and drained by fear to acknowledge his words. Few had slept since the battle had begun. Terrible visions plagued every man's dreams and phantoms haunted the streets in ghostly processions of long dead comrades.

Looping the towel around his neck, Marius rested his elbows on a projecting merlon of the walls, scanning the lower town for any sign of a fresh attack. A dank fug of lingering smoke and mist hung over the abandoned district, rendering its buildings blurred and its inhabitants ghostly. At a distance, the docks of Marburg could almost be normal; hundreds of indistinct figures filled its streets, shuffling from one shadow to the next, milling with apparent purpose, but really just meandering like ants from an overturned nest. Most of the corsair ships that had brought the dead to Marburg were wrecked now, their hulls holed by long shafts of iron hurled from the citadel's war machines or burned with flaming arrows.

Marius glanced skyward, looking for the dragon that had attacked the walls on the first night. It swooped over the fighting, filling the air with a drifting miasma that reeked of putrefaction and caused many of the wounded to sicken.

He turned as he smelled a scent of wildflowers, recognising the fragrant oil Marika liked to rub on her skin. She hadn't spoken to him after his rescue of Aldred, and Marius was intrigued to hear what she would make of that act. Marika wore leather buckskin, elegantly cut yet practical, and a quilted leather jerkin. Her bow was slung over one shoulder and a slender rapier was sheathed at her side. Marika's blonde hair was tied back in a severe ponytail, yet she was still devastatingly feminine.

Which was a welcome sight in a citadel defended by burly, seafaring men.

'Princess,' he said with a languid bow. 'It gladdens my heart to see you well.'

'Count Marius,' she said. 'Would you walk with me awhile?'

'It would be my honour,' replied Marius, hiding his amusement at the simmering anger he saw lurking behind her façade of courtesy. He proffered his arm and she hooked her own around it as they walked the length of the ramparts, looking like a courting couple out for a promenade along the seafront. A pair of Jutone lancers and four Raven Helms followed them, chaperones and bodyguards all in one.

When they had put enough distance between themselves and their warriors, Marika tilted her face towards him and said, 'What in Manann's name did you think you were doing?'

'I assume you're referring to my rescue of Aldred?'

'What else would I be referring to?' she snapped. 'It was perfect. He'd got himself cut off and all you had to do was watch him die. Why did you ride out?'

Marius smiled as they passed a band of Endal warriors gathered around a glowing brazier. He nodded to them as they tapped their fists against their mail shirts. Marika was cunning in a vicious, feral way, but he had been manipulating others for years and knew the way people's minds worked.

'What's so damn funny?' she said, seeing his smile.

'You, my dear,' he said. 'You think you're a wily schemer, but you're not looking at the big picture.'

He saw her anger threaten to spill out and raised a placatory hand. 'Let us assume for the moment that Aldred had died on the first night. You think that would be the outcome you desire, but you would be mistaken.'

'How so?' said Marika.

'If Aldred had died then, nothing would have changed in your tribe's perception of me. They would still hate me, and would never consent to our marriage. But look at how they see me now. Jutones are fighting and dying alongside Endals, and I have saved the life of their beloved count. Now I am not hated, now I am seen as a sword-brother to Aldred. This battle isn't over, and a lot can happen between now and its end, including your brother's untimely end. If we play this game well, you and I will be heroes by its conclusion. *Then* we can marry and make this city the greatest seaport in the Empire. Now doesn't that sound like it's a plan that'll catch a fair wind?'

Marika listened to his words with a growing admiration, and Marius wanted to laugh at how simply she was impressed. He patted her hand and she turned to face him, giving her most winning smile. He saw through it, but it was a pleasant view nonetheless.

'I'm beginning to think I underestimated you, Marius,' she said.

'Most people do,' he replied with a self-satisfied smirk. 'It must be the cultured, debonair appearance of wealth I project. Though anyone with half a grain of sense would realise that you don't get to be this rich and powerful without having a head for intrigue and a heart for murder.'

'So what happens next?' asked Marika, pulling him on towards one of the towers flanking the citadel gates. Endal archers were stationed here and two of the bolt-throwing war machines stood on elevated wooden platforms that could be turned in any direction.

Marius shrugged and leaned on the timber steps that led up to the war machine. 'We fight the dead and, like I said, this battle is far from over. Anything can happen, or anything can be *allowed* to happen.'

'Enemy!' shouted a voice from further along the ramparts, and Marius looked over the lower town, searching for what had triggered the warning. Archers loosed shafts into the grey skies as a vast shape moved through the mist, like a great undersea creature viewed from the deck of a ship. Marius prided himself on being afraid of nothing, but as the great dragon flew from the haze, he found himself rooted to the spot in terror.

A juggernaut of decaying meat and loose flaps of draconic hide, the colossal monster flew over the ramparts of the city with crackling sweeps of its ragged wings. Chains rattled and gears rasped as the war machines were hauled around and eight-foot barbs were loaded into bronze-sheathed firing grooves.

The dragon circled the Raven Hall, its wings beating the air in a parody of flight, for its mass was surely kept aloft by foul sorcery. Astride its neck, the black-robed sorcerer hurled a stream of baleful energies at the Raven Hall, wreathing it in crackling arcs of scarlet light from top to bottom.

Marius grabbed Marika and dragged her behind the war machine as the Raven Hall cracked and groaned, its structure aged a thousand years in the space of a breath. Crumbling stone poured like sand from its joints and a rain of powdered obsidian wept from the raven's eyes as the mighty structure sagged to the side. Booming cracks echoed over the city as the tower's stone split as cleanly as though struck with a giant mason's hammer.

The circling dragon roared with the rasp of a million plague victims' death cries, and beat its wings as it hurled itself at the tower. Its hind claws slammed into the Raven Hall and its enormous weight completed what the sorcerer's spell had begun. The top of the great tower of Marburg exploded in a rain of blackened stone, and its lower reaches keeled over like a felled oak. Vast blocks, each the size of a hay wagon, rained down upon Marburg, smashing buildings flat and wreaking untold damage throughout the city.

Thunderous booms shook the citadel as the rain of blocks hit in a series of percussive hammer blows, and billowing dust storms surged from the impacts. Marius pulled his cloak up over his face as the debris cloud rolled over him. He edged his way along the platform and threw off his cloak. Choking dust made him cough, and gritty fragments scratched his eyes. Marika huddled behind the war machine, her knees drawn up to her chest and her hands covering her face and mouth.

'Marika!' he yelled. 'Are you hurt?'

She looked up, numbed by the sight of the ancestral seat of the Endal kings so comprehensively destroyed. She shook her head and rubbed her eyes free of dust. Marius pulled her to her feet. She was in shock, but he didn't have time to play nice.

He slapped her across the face, and said, 'Snap out of it, princess! The dead will be attacking any moment. If you want to rule this city, then you have to get your people ready to fight! Do you understand me?'

'I understand,' she said, her eyes filled with anger. 'And if you hit me again I'll kill you.'

Marius smiled and said, 'That's my girl. Aren't we a pair of lovebirds?'

The sound of clashing swords and clattering bone sounded from the lower town as the army of the dead marched towards the citadel once more. Endal sergeants and battle captains shouted at their warriors to stand to as the flapping of leathery wings filled the air. The howls of cursed wolves echoed over the black sea, and over everything came the bellowing, deathly roar of the skeletal dragon.

'Shall we?' said Marika, notching an arrow to her bowstring.

'We shall,' agreed Marius, drawing his blade.

BOOK THREE
Dust to Dust

Hollow footsteps, cloaked by night
of sadness known through tortured sight;
The willow weeps its tears of woe
as Owl moans the twin moons' glow.
Wind whispers through the willow's leaves,
and Owl, perched high, eternal grieves.
Raven drinks the blood of Sigmar's dead,
But soon flies off to hidden bed.
Weary 'neath death's black spell,
The dead know pain that none can quell.
Cursed to fight those they loved,
Forever lost, each journey taken,
plagues the mind; the nights awaken.
Troubled visions, thoughts of yesterdays,
that seem like beacons; lives away.
Random comforts cannot ease their soul,
For knowledge takes its weary toll
'Pon one who suffers with each breath,
Who slept once in peace, then awoke in death.

FIFTEEN
Reunions

THOUGH THE SUN was newly risen, light was already bleeding from the sky. The Asoborn battle line was silhouetted on the brow of the hill, three hundred men and almost a hundred women and children. Boys as young as six held long daggers, and men in their seventies gripped felling axes as they awaited the coming of the dead.

Maedbh kept Ulrike and Freya's boys close, trying to hide her fear from them. The desire to flee smouldered in the hearts of everyone, and all it would take to ignite would be one spark of fear. The Queen's Eagles held the centre of the line, thirty warriors in leather armour and golden winged helms. Each bore a long spear and carried a short, stabbing sword. Their presence was all that gave Maedbh hope they might withstand one attack at least.

Alaric had split his warriors into two groups of fifty, placing one on either flank. These redoubtable warriors bore wide-bladed axes slung across their backs, though each was presently armed with a heavy crossbow and bolts as thick as Maedbh's thumb.

Five hundred against four thousand; it was the odds of which sagas were made.

After five days of forced marching, it felt strange to be simply waiting for the enemy to reveal itself. The Asoborn way of war was to strike hard and fast, wreaking as much damage as possible before withdrawing and dragging the enemy onto the blades of the spearmen. To wait for the enemy to attack felt wrong, but what else could they do?

Maedbh felt a small hand tugging at her sleeve and saw her daughter looking up at her with wide, determined eyes. Maedbh's heart ached to see Ulrike afraid, but this was what it meant to be an Asoborn. Battle had to be given and courage earned in the face of fear. As much as Maedbh hated the idea of Ulrike fighting this foe, it would be the making of her.

'Are the bad wolves coming for us?' said Ulrike.

'Yes, dear heart, they are,' said Maedbh.

'But we'll see them off won't we? Just like we did before?'

'Yes, just like then, but this time we'll make sure they don't come back.'

Ulrike nodded and gripped her bow tightly. 'Good,' she said, nocking an arrow to her bowstring. 'I wish my father was here. He'd ride over them on his horse and that'd be the end of them, wouldn't it?'

'I wish that too,' said Maedbh, 'but the gods have already blessed us today, so we must be grateful for what they have given us.'

'How do you come to that conclusion?' said Sigulf, his features pale with worry. 'The gods haven't blessed us, they've forsaken us.'

Maedbh knelt beside the boy, his fair hair plastered to his scalp with sweat. His green eyes were wide and fearful. Sigulf had the soul of a poet, and though he had proved himself a capable fighter, Maedbh knew his heart was only truly free when he was writing music and composing verse.

His twin brother answered him. 'Because they have sent us an enemy to test our courage and the strength of our sword arms.' Where Sigulf was a gentle soul, his twin was a warrior born and bred. Fridleifr loved to fight, and had made a name for himself among the Asoborn as a fist-fighter of some repute. Skilled with sword and axe, he was happiest when the blood flowed and death hung upon every heartbeat.

Just like his father, thought Maedbh.

'They've blessed us because they gave us a beautiful morning, and sent strong friends to stand beside us,' said Maedbh. 'Ulric knows that no warrior should fight alone, and has sent us the warriors of the mountain holds to fight at our sides.'

'But we're going to die,' said Sigulf, his voice quavering. 'The dead are coming to kill us.'

'They'll try to kill us, but I won't be dying today, and neither will you, little brother,' stated Fridleifr. 'These are Asoborn lands and we are the sons of a warrior queen.'

'But the iron men said mother was dead,' said Sigulf.

'Aye, but I'll not believe it until I see her on a pyre,' replied Fridleifr, and Maedbh heard the strength and determination of the boy's father in his words. Both boys possessed qualities of their sire, but only one man of this age embodied such greatness combined. 'I'll wager a fist of gold she'll ride over the hill and send these bastards over the Worlds Edge!'

The boy's voice lifted with every word and Maedbh saw his conviction that they would live through this fight spread to everyone in the battle line. Even the Queen's Eagles took heart, and Maedbh was surprised to find that even she dared to hope he might be right.

A dwarf horn sounded a warning from the end of their formation and Maedbh saw the blood drinker's army for the first time. The sky above the enemy army blackened like dead flesh around an infected wound as a morass of carrion birds, bats and blood-sucking insects took to the air.

A single vast block of skeletons, two hundred wide and twenty deep, marched towards the Asoborns in perfect formation, their bodies armoured in scraps of iron and rusted bronze. Their spears rippled in unison as they brought them down, serrated tips aimed at the hearts of the mortal warriors opposing them. The blood drinker rode in the midst of a hundred black-armoured horsemen, his brilliant white cloak streaming behind him in the cold winds that blew around the deathly army.

Wolves howled and loped around the dread host, filthy, diseased mockeries of the noble heralds of Ulric. Exposed muscles and withered meat hung from their bones and their jaws slavered with rotten saliva. Worse than all of that, was the fact that many of the dead warriors had clearly once been Asoborns. Everyone gathered on the hillside had family who had marched to war beside the queen, and the thought that they might come face to face with a loved one was almost too much to bear.

Maedbh felt the hope drain away from her people at the appearance of the foe. The sight of so unnatural a horde, an enemy of life itself, struck at the very core of what made mortals great. To fight this enemy would test the courage of even the mightiest warrior, and the Asoborns gathered on this lonely hilltop were old men and children.

Yet though these people had either hung their swords up years ago or had yet to be formally blooded, not one moved and not one gave voice to the terrible fear stabbing up from their soul that told them to run, to flee this battle and perhaps earn a few precious hours of life. Maedbh had never been prouder to be a warrior of the Asoborns.

There was no attempt at parley – what would be the point? – and no theatrical displays of martial prowess. The dead marched to the bottom of the hill and began climbing towards the Asoborns.

'Do you want me to kill him?' asked Laredus, working the whetstone across the blade of his sword. 'Because I will if you need me to.'

Count Aldred shook his head. 'No, though don't think the thought doesn't appeal.'

'It could be made to look like the dead did it,' pressed Laredus. 'Or that he sickened.'

'Enough,' said Aldred, fetching himself a drink of water from an earthenware jug on the table of what had once been the seaward officers' barracks of the citadel. The Raven Hall was no more and his servants had been sent to Reikdorf, so this was what he was reduced to. Pouring his own drinks and sitting in a draughty room with no more appointments than a junior officer. Still, it was better than a great many of the Endals were forced to endure. The barracks were cold and damp, the sea air having long since warped the wood around the windows and letting in the clammy dampness of ocean mist.

'I know they're up to something,' said Aldred, 'but I don't want you to kill him. Think how it would look if Marius were to die while under my protection.'

'I told you, my lord,' said Laredus. 'It could be made to look like the enemy killed him.'

'No one would believe that, least of all Marika.'

'Does that even matter? You are the count of Marburg. In any case, it's war, who's to say what happens in the midst of a battle?'

'And what of the other Jutones? Do you plan to kill them too?'

Laredus looked uncomfortable with the idea of such mass murder, but he straightened his back. 'If that's what it takes to keep you and this city safe, then that can be arranged too.'

'There are three hundred Jutone warriors here, not including Marius's lancers,' pointed out Aldred. 'Even the Raven Helms would have their work cut out in killing those men. And I rather think we need those lancers to help defend our city.'

Laredus nodded, though he clearly was deeply unhappy at the idea of relying on Jutones for anything. Laredus had fought the Jutones on many occasions, and there was no love lost between the two tribes. Though that was changing. Ever since Marius had ridden out to rescue him, Aldred had seen the beginnings of camaraderie between the two tribes. That should have been a good thing, but he couldn't help but feel it was the death knell for his city and his people's way of life.

Aldred stared into the fire. It crackled with the little wood remaining to them that hadn't been commandeered to craft fresh arrows and stakes for the defences behind the walls. It felt like evening, but the sun had risen only a few hours ago. The attack of the dead had shifted the diurnal cycle of Marburg, turning it into a ghost city in the daylight, a furious battlefield by night. He pulled his cloak tighter about himself, feeling a chill deep in his bones that had nothing to do with the temperature of the room.

'You should open your cloak, my lord,' said Laredus. 'Let the fire's warmth get to you.'

'I know. It's tiredness playing its part, but I feel the touch of the grave deep in my heart, you understand?'

'I do, my lord,' said Laredus. 'It's settled in every man's bones since the army of the dead sailed into Marburg. And I expect it'll only lift once we defeat them.'

Aldred smiled mirthlessly with a shake of his head. 'Forced from our homeland to a scrap of land in the midst of a marsh, our king slain, the pestilence of the mist daemons ravages our city, and now this. We are not a blessed people are we?'

'We are the Endals,' said Laredus. 'Hardship makes us stronger.'

'Then we will be the strongest tribe of the Empire by the end of this war,' said Aldred.

Laredus tapped his fist against his breastplate in response and they lapsed into a comfortable silence, content to simply drink and enjoy this rare moment of quiet. Aldred wanted to close his eyes, but sleep brought nightmares and festering thoughts of being devoured by the wriggling creatures beneath the earth. When sleep did come upon him, he woke scrabbling at his eyes, fearing writhing masses of worms were feasting upon them.

'You still haven't said what you want to do about Marius,' said Laredus.

'There's nothing we *can* do,' said Aldred. 'To kill him, you'd need to slay all his men too, and that will simply hasten our ending. And I still have a hard time believing Marika would conspire with Marius. She's my sister.'

'I'm just telling you what I heard,' replied Laredus.

'That's just it though, you didn't hear it.'

'One of my men did, and that's good enough for me.'

'Who was it?'

'Daerian, one of my scouts. I had him assigned to the princess as a bodyguard, and he has the keenest eyes and ears I've known. He can see a hawk a mile distant and hear a whisper on the other side of a seafront tavern. If he says they were talking about your death, then I'd wager a ship's worth of gold it's true. She still blames you for what happened with the mist daemons,' said Laredus. 'Even though you weren't at fault. It was Idris Gwylt skewed your judgement. She must understand that.'

'I had hoped she would by now,' agreed Aldred. 'But that woman can hold a grudge like no other. She reminds me of it at every turn, like I *wanted* to sacrifice her.'

'You had no choice,' said Laredus.

'No, I didn't,' said Aldred. 'I did what I thought was best for my people.'

'And the people know that, even if she doesn't,' ventured Laredus.

Aldred caught the hint of something unsaid, something too terrible to be given voice without tacit permission.

'What are you saying?' said Aldred. 'You can speak freely.'

'I'm saying that perhaps we're looking at the wrong person to kill.'

Aldred looked into Laredus's eyes, seeing no give there, only a fierce determination to protect his count. 'Marika?'

Laredus nodded. 'It's terrible and unthinkable, but I'm trying to save your life.'

'By killing my sister?'

'She's trying to kill you.'

'You don't know that for sure,' pointed out Aldred.

'Do you want to die to prove me right?'

Aldred said nothing, but the idea had already taken root.

THE BLOOD DRINKER unsheathed his sword and it glittered in the encroaching darkness with spectral light. Thunder split the sky above the Asoborns, and a crackling bolt of lightning zigzagged in a bright tracery, arcing downwards to be captured by the vampire's sword. The blade swept down and the wolves sprinted towards the mortal prey at the hilltop. In their wake, the skeletal warriors began marching uphill.

Maedbh watched them come, her mouth dry and her bladder tight. Sweat moistened the grip on her bow, and she flexed her fingers. She put an arrow to the string and pulled back, sighting downhill at the loping wolves. Those Asoborns with bows followed her lead, bending their bows towards the howling beasts.

'Remember to aim high,' she shouted, knowing that many archers would send their shafts into the earth when aiming at targets downhill.

Maedbh sighted on a wolf with a ragged pelt of decaying fur and one side of its skull exposed. The green corpse light shimmered in its eyes, and she let fly between breaths, sending her shaft slicing though its jaw. It ran on for a moment before collapsing in a dissolving mass of bone and rotten meat.

Two hundred arrows slashed downhill, but despite her advice most thudded into the earth in front of the charging wolves. At least fifty of the creatures were undone before they could reach the Asoborn lines. A flurry of crossbow bolts hammered the dead warriors behind the wolves, each one punching through rotten flesh and bone to slay the warped power at its heart. Every single bolt loosed by a dwarf crossbow found its mark, yet the dead marched on.

Ulrike's first arrow struck home as did her second, though her third went wide of the mark. Maedbh was able to loose three more times before the unnatural beasts reached them. She swapped to her sword as the wolves crested the summit of the hill. Snarling and clawing, they leapt with jaws stretched wide. Maedbh plunged her sword into a wolf's belly, spilling its decaying entrails to the earth. It screamed as its body was destroyed.

A wolf snapped at Ulrike, but the young girl ducked and rammed her knife into the creature's neck, tearing out the remains of its throat in a welter of grey meat and bone. Another snapped at her, but Maedbh's sword swept down and ended it. Swords and spears flashed in the dim twilight, and wolves died, but a score of Asoborns were pulled to the ground. Fangs snapped shut on skulls and throats were torn out with single bites. Rotten claws opened bellies and thrashing wolves howled as they ate the flesh of those they had killed. Maedbh fought side by side with her daughter, each protecting the other as though they had trained as sword maidens for years.

Sigulf and Fridleifr did not fight with bows, but with exquisitely crafted swords given as gifts to the queen by the dwarfs of the Worlds Edge Mountains. Long before Sigmar had sworn his oaths of brotherhood with King Kurgan, the eastern queens had counted the dwarfs of the mountains as their allies. As different in character as they were, they were alike in skill with a blade, Sigulf fighting with clinical precision, Fridleifr with furious passion.

The Queen's Eagles protected the heirs to the Asoborn crown, sweeping forward and fighting with all the skill that had seen them elevated from the ranks to become the guardians of Asoborn royalty. Garr fought at their forefront, his twin-bladed spear cleaving left and right as he hacked wolves down with every stroke.

The wolves attacked all along the Asoborn line, bounding around the flanks and punching through to attack the weakest members of the Asoborns. Alaric's dwarfs swung around like an opening gate, protecting the flanks and preventing the wolves from getting behind the battle line. They fought with mechanical strokes, relentless and merciless, hewing diseased flesh as easily as a butcher would prepare a bull's carcass. No claw or fang could penetrate their armour, and no wolf could pass them. Immovable and impenetrable, the dwarfs anchored the Asoborn defence.

In moments it was over, the wolves destroyed and the battle line restored. The moans of the wounded were somehow dulled by the oppressive gloom, and the youngest children dragged those hurt too badly to fight further back onto the hillside. There was little that could be done for them, but they could do no more good in the fighting ranks.

Maedbh wiped her sword blade on the grass at her feet and gave her daughter a weak smile. Ulrike's face was flushed with a mixture of fear and excitement, the adrenaline of battle outweighing the thought of facing an army of the dead.

There was no time for words, for the ranks of skeleton warriors in ancient armour were almost upon them. The wolves had been nothing more than a skirmish screen to protect the warriors following behind. The dead were less than fifty paces from the Asoborns, marching in perfect lockstep. Behind them, the vampire and his horsemen walked their skeletal steeds up the hill, ready to ride down any mortals who fled the field of battle.

Cold dread settled in Maedbh's bones, a terrible, suffocating fear of losing everything that she loved in one fell swoop. She looked into the eyes of the vampire lord, seeing a lifetime of cruelty and evil. She saw his blood hunger, and as his army marched onwards, she heard a thunderous rumble, a drumming on the earth like a distant thunderstorm drawing closer with every passing moment.

A wild series of horn blasts swept the hillside as a dozen ululating brays came from the trees behind the Asoborn battle line. What new horror had appeared behind them without warning? She had been so sure the dead would come at them head on that she hadn't even considered the possibility that their flank could be turned.

The horns blew again and Maedbh's heart leapt as she recognised the sound of Unberogen war horns. Shapes moved through the trees, galloping horsemen in their hundreds, but far from being riders of the dead, these were living, breathing warriors atop wide shouldered, powerful steeds clad in heavy hauberks of iron scale.

The riders thundered over the brow of the hill and Maedbh let loose a wild Asoborn war shout as she recognised the warriors at the head of the Unberogen horsemen. One she called Emperor and the other she called husband.

Sigmar and Wolfgart rode over the brow of the hill, weapons unsheathed and ready to fight to save those they held dear. Hundreds of Unberogen riders streamed past Maedbh, along with scores of horsemen armoured in mail shirts and bronze breastplates with blood-red cloaks. Maedbh recognised them as Taleuten Red Scythes and their crimson-pennoned lances lowered in glittering unison.

Ghal-maraz swept up, a shaft of brilliant sunlight breaking through the unnatural gloom to strike the Emperor's mighty warhammer and banish the darkness. Sigmar rode through the trees with his long hair unbound and his armour glowing with impossible radiance. Such was the skill of his riders that they rode through the Asoborn battle lines without trampling those they had come to rescue.

The charge of the Unberogen and Taleuten cavalry was ferocious and it struck the line of the dead with unstoppable force. The Red Scythes leaned into their stirrups and their lances punched into the ranks of the dead, skewering skeletal champions and hoisting them from the ground. Lances splintered with the impact and the riders drew heavy maces and morning stars as they plunged into the undead host.

Wolfgart's vast sword, forged by Govannon less than a year ago, swept from its shoulder scabbard and no sooner was its blade bared than it clove through the chest of an undead warrior clad in a rusted shirt of mail. Swords and axes smashed through bone and patchwork plates of bronze and iron. The dead reeled from the sudden attack, but did not break. Though hundreds were destroyed in the opening moments of the Unberogen charge, hundreds more remained to fight. Sigmar's cavalry plunged into the heart of the dead, breaking them apart as they split the host in two.

The dead cared nothing for the suddenness of the attack and merely turned to face the horsemen whose charge began to slow with the press of skeletal bodies. Sigmar fought at the centre of the dead army, the skull-splitter living up to its name as it shattered bone and pulverised armour with every blow. The dead tried to pull away from Sigmar, but he rode into them with ever greater force, destroying half a dozen with every blow.

Maedbh lifted her sword and charged after the horsemen, and the Asoborns followed her.

Alaric's dwarfs marched towards the dead, cutting through their mouldering ranks like loggers in a forest of saplings. The fear that touched mortal hearts seemed not to have so strong a hold on the dwarfs, and they broke through with sweeping strokes of their axes. Though the dead outnumbered the living by nearly two to one, the dead could not match the skill of those ranged against them.

Sigmar aimed his horse toward the white-cloaked vampire, but if he sought a duel with the blood drinker he was to be denied satisfaction. Sensing defeat for his host, the blood drinker turned and rode away, his black horsemen galloping south as the allies turned to fight the remaining undead warriors.

Attacked from the front and rear, and abandoned by their maker, the host of the dead began to waver, their physical forms unravelling in the face of mortal courage and vitality. The battle was far from over, but without the power of the vampire to bind the dark energies that held them together the dead were falling apart with every passing moment, like ice before the summer sun.

Horsemen rode through the dead, hacking them down with brutal sweeps of their swords, while the Asoborns hemmed them in and the dwarfs trampled them with the pounding force of their relentless advance. Sigmar and Wolfgart rode pell-mell through the diminishing host, their weapons reaping a magnificent tally of the dead.

Though it took another hour, the dead could not long linger, and as the last of the sepulchral twilight faded from the sky, the field belonged to the living. Sigmar turned his horse and it reared up, pawing the air in triumph, but Maedbh cared nothing for the sight.

She threw her weapon aside and ran towards her husband with her daughter in tow.

Wolfgart saw them coming and leapt from his horse, sweeping his wife and daughter into his arms and holding them so tightly she thought he might break them. He kissed Maedbh over and over and the intensity of the kiss was magnified tenfold by the nearness of death. Weeping with relief and the fear of what might have been lost, Wolfgart, Maedbh and Ulrike laughed and cried to be reunited, the bitterness and rancour of what had driven them apart forgotten in the rush of joy sweeping through them.

'You came for us,' said Maedbh, between breaths. 'I wished for it and you came.'

'Of course I came for you,' said Wolfgart, unashamed tears spilling down his face. 'You're my woman and I love you. And you're my little girl,' he added, dropping to his knees to hug Ulrike.

'I thought we'd never see you again,' cried Ulrike.

'Never think that, my beautiful girl,' said Wolfgart. 'No matter what happens, I'll always be there for you. Not even death can stop me from coming to you.'

They stayed locked together for many minutes, savouring this moment of reunion until a horseman rode up to them and Maedbh knew who it would be before she even opened her eyes.

'Sigmar,' she said, only reluctantly releasing her grip on Wolfgart and giving a short bow to the Emperor. 'Your timing couldn't be better. You saved us and you have my undying gratitude.'

Sigmar smiled and said, 'It's your husband you should thank. I was riding for Reikdorf when my outriders saw them heading east. I wanted to know where he was going with six hundred of my best horsemen and he told me you were in danger.'

'The Oathstone showed me this battle,' said Wolfgart. 'I don't know how, Maedbh, but it did. We hand-fastened over it, so maybe there's some lingering magic from that moment, something that brought me to you when you needed me most. I gathered up everyone I could to ride east. Turns out a lot of people wanted to help me.'

'I know,' said Sigmar, seeing her look of confusion. 'I didn't believe him either, but he swore he'd ride east alone if need be, so I thought I'd best keep him safe for you.'

'I'm grateful,' said Maedbh.

Sigmar was about to reply when she saw a shocked expression freeze upon his face. He was looking past her, and Maedbh knew what it would be before she turned around. At the top of the hill, Sigulf and Fridleifr laughed and cheered as Garr and the Queen's Eagles blooded their cheeks.

'Who are those boys?' demanded Sigmar.

WOLFGART CAUGHT UP to Sigmar by the river. The Emperor's head was bowed and his arms were folded across his chest as he stared off into the distance. This was going to be difficult, and Wolfgart took a deep breath as he approached. Right here, right now, Sigmar was not the Emperor, not the ruler of the lands from the Grey Mountains to the Sea of Claws, he was simply his friend.

Sigmar turned his head as he approached, but said nothing.

They stood by the fast-flowing river, enjoying the sights and sounds and smells of a land resurgent after the touch of undeath. Water splashed over rocks and gurgled in pools by the riverbank. Birdsong had returned to the world, not the raucous cawing of ravens and crows, but the wondrously refreshing and hopeful warbling of songbirds. Wolfgart hadn't realised how much he'd missed the birds until now. The sky was a shimmering canopy of blue, the clouds scattered and white.

It was the perfect day but for the tension in Sigmar's body.

'They are Freya's sons, aren't they?'

'Yes.'

'And I am their father,' stated Sigmar.

Wolfgart nodded, though there was no need. It hadn't been a question.

'You knew about them, didn't you?' said Sigmar.

Wolfgart knew there was no need or good to be served by lying. 'I did, but Maedbh swore me to silence.'

'And you don't break an oath to an Asoborn woman,' said Sigmar.

'Not if you want to keep your manhood intact,' agreed Wolfgart, knowing he had let Maedbh down once already with his oaths.

'I understand why she wouldn't want me to know,' said Sigmar. 'Freya's not the family type. Not for her a husband and a doting father.'

'No,' agreed Wolfgart. 'She's not really cut out to be the faithful wife either.'

'But they are my sons,' said Sigmar, finally turning to face Wolfgart. 'I had a right to know them, to watch them grow up and become men! They are the sons I never had with Ravenna. Who will carry on my name when I'm dead, Wolfgart? Who?'

'There's still time, my friend,' said Wolfgart. 'You're not too old to sire sons, and there's plenty of strong women who'd be proud to bear them.'

Sigmar shook his head and knelt beside the riverbank, plucking a flat stone with a smooth face from the earth. He skimmed it across the water, watching as it skipped over the surface a number of times before sinking.

'I remember doing this as a child, and it still makes me smile.'

Wolfgart picked up a similar stone and skipped it across the water. His throw was better and made it farther across the river before sinking.

'You always were lousy at this,' said Wolfgart, stooping to pick up another stone. 'It's all in the wrist you see. Here, like this.'

Once again the stone skipped across the river, but Sigmar shook his head.

'I am who I am, Wolfgart, and it's too late for me to change. Ravenna was my love, and I swore that there would be no other.'

'You can change that, Sigmar,' said Wolfgart. 'You can get to know those boys. They're good lads, strong and brave, reckless and full of the same fire that drove you to build the Empire. Who knows what they might do with you as their father to guide them?'

'I wish it could be that easy, my friend,' replied Sigmar, 'but I am on a path that does not allow change. Others have that luxury, but I do not. The Empire needs me as I am, a warrior Emperor.'

'And what about what *you* need? Love, companionship, family?'

'I cannot be the man this land needs if I am drawn to hearth and home,' said Sigmar, looking over his shoulder to the Asoborns as they prepared to march west to Reikdorf. Freya's boys and Ulrike gathered around Maedbh, like chicks around a mother hen.

'Those boys don't need me, they're Asoborns,' said Sigmar. 'Their mother would never allow me to take them from her. That's what she fears, that I'll take them to Reikdorf and make them my heirs.'

'You should,' said Wolfgart. 'They *are* your sons after all. Doesn't the Empire need heirs, strong rulers to carry your name into the future? You said so yourself.'

Sigmar turned to look out over the landscape, and Wolfgart saw the beginnings of a smile crack his features.

'Aye, the Empire needs heirs,' said Sigmar, slapping a hand on Wolfgart's shoulder and walking him back to the column of people. 'And you are all my heirs. Everyone who lives in this land is my heir. Everyone who fights and bleeds to protect the Empire...'

The Emperor smiled. 'They will all be Sigmar's heirs.'

SIXTEEN
Murder Most Foul

THE DEAD ATTACKED Marburg again and again, clawing at the walls with thin fingers of bone digging into the stonework to pull themselves up. The entire lower town thronged with rotten corpses, shambling cadavers and skeletal warriors, and all of them threw themselves at the walls of the citadel every night. Marius and his lancers held the shorter stretch of wall between the main gate and the eastern shore, while Aldred held the western stretch of the walls and the barbican towers.

Marius swept his sword through the neck of a moaning corpse with green fire in its eyes, kicking the rotting body back down the walls. His sword was proving to be anathema to the dead, and he silently thanked the eastern king who had gifted it to him so long ago. It had saved his life in Middenheim, and was saving him again now. His lancers fought at his side, pushing the dead from the walls, stabbing them with spears, hacking at them with axes and bludgeoning them with heavy maces.

A skeleton came at him with a notched sword, and he stabbed it through the jaw, wrenching its head from its shoulders. The animation went out of the long dead warrior and it collapsed over the stone parapet. Another clambered over its remains and a rusted axe swung down at him. Marius brought his sword up, but the force of the blow turned it aside and the dead warrior's axe slammed into his shoulder.

He grunted in pain and sent a reverse stroke into the creature's neck. The blade parted the bone easily and the warrior dropped to the ground. Marius stepped away from the wall and shouted, 'Take my place!'

Another warrior filled the gap Marius had left and he stabbed his sword into the earth at his feet, rotating his shoulder and prodding the flesh to feel how badly he'd been hurt. The skin was bruised and swollen, but he couldn't feel any blood pouring inside his armour, and he took a moment to survey the fighting.

The entire length of the walls pulsed with desperate combats, Endal and Jutone warriors struggling to keep the dead from getting in. A mobile reserve of Raven Helms stood behind the fighting at the ramparts, ready to bolster the defences whenever the dead punched a hole, but Marius saw they were stretched thinly. All it would take would be one too many breaches and there would be no one to stop the dead from overrunning them.

Marika's archers had taken up positions further back, loosing volleys of arrows over the heads of the warriors at the ramparts. The bat swarms flew overhead, circling the ruins of the Raven Hall or roosting in its tumbled structure. The mist that wreathed the lower town and docks seeped up into the citadel, a choking fog that settled in the lungs and gave every man a hacking cough.

Just thinking about it made Marius cough, though thankfully he'd managed to avoid the worst of it by virtue of having well heated quarters that were free from damp. There was more than one benefit from a close, physical relationship with Princess Marika, he thought with a smile.

A group of lancers formed up around him, and Marius nodded in weary appreciation of their efforts. He didn't waste words on them, for these men were just doing their job, and if a man needed thanks or encouragement just to do his job, then he wasn't worth employing.

Marius heard a shout of terror and the dreadful form of the dragon reared up over the walls, its patchwork wings spread wide as it hovered over the twin towers of the barbican protecting the citadel's gate. Arrows slashed out towards it, but only Marika's white-fletched ones seemed to cause it harm. Two of the war machines hurled iron barbs towards the vast creature, but both splintered against its necrotic hide.

A heaving breath of toxic vapours gusted from the dragon's mouth and enveloped the barbican. Men staggered from the ramparts, choking and vomiting as the hellish miasma did its evil work. The road to the lower town sloped down to the gates, and from his position behind the walls, Marius saw them wither as the timbers shoring up the already weakened structure rotted away to brittle deadwood. The mass of dead warriors on the other side buckled the decayed woodwork and the gates split apart in a flurry of rotten timbers.

A mob of groaning warriors poured through the gateway, but any thought that the dead fought without stratagems was banished the moment Marius saw what manner of undead forced their way inside. The chaff of the dead assaulted the walls, shambling corpses with no more will than to devour the flesh of the living. These new attackers were the champions of this host, warriors with black hearts whose dreadful malice transcended their own deaths to sustain them with pure hate.

Armoured in ancient hauberks of corroded bronze and bearing long-bladed halberds and great axes, they surged into the citadel and split left and right to sweep the walls clear of defenders. Marius looked around for the Raven Helms, but Laredus had already led them to plug a breach further along the western walls.

'Damn you, Aldred, you're practically giving me your city,' said Marius, dragging his sword from the earth. He led his lancers towards the dead champions pouring through the gate as a flurry of arrows sliced into them. A dozen fell, but most simply picked themselves up again, unfazed by the two-foot shafts jutting from their bodies.

The lancers slammed into the dead, cutting the head from the eastern push onto the ramparts. The warriors on the walls saw their danger and captains of battle sent men to stem the tide of flanking enemy. Marius ducked a ponderously swung axe, plunging his sword through a gap in a dead warrior's armour. His sword passed into his foe's body without resistance, its enchanted edge glowing as though heated in a forge. The champion convulsed and the magic sustaining it was broken. Marius spun away from the creature, wincing as the old wound in his side pulled painfully.

He pushed into the mass of dead warriors, fighting with his usual finesse and élan as he beheaded enemy champions with an ease that was as much to do with his blade as his own skill. His lancers fought in a wedge with him at its point, forcing the dead back and stemming the rush of their breach through the gateway.

A heavy halberd blade slammed into his stomach, but its edge was dulled and all it did was drive the wind from him. He doubled up, but before the halberd could be reversed, Marius thrust his sword into the groin of its wielder. The dead champion clattered to the ground as it was destroyed, and Marius surged to his feet, invigorated at yet another brush with death.

'It'll take more than that to kill me!' he yelled, plunging headlong into the mass of dead warriors. The fear was gone, and he felt utterly disconnected from even the idea of it. He heard the booming wing beats of the dragon beyond the walls, but even that held no fear for him. For one wild moment, Marius thought of charging through the gateway to face the dragon like the heroes of legend who were said to fight such monsters on a daily basis. Common sense reasserted itself as he saw Aldred and a detachment of Raven Helms fighting the dead forcing their way down the western stretch of the walls.

The Endals fared rather less well than the Jutones, and Aldred's warriors were falling to the black blades of the dead like cabin boys before a bosun's whip.

'Ten of you with me, the rest of you secure this gate!' he shouted. 'Nothing gets in or out!'

Without waiting to see if his order was obeyed, Marius ran towards the Endals. Pipe music drifted across the ramparts and Marius wanted to laugh with derision. Who in their right mind played music when there was a battle to be fought? His sword shimmered with light as he sliced it across the small of a dead warrior's back, almost cutting him in two. His lancers swung their swords and maces to break a path through towards the Endals.

Marius blocked a slashing blow to the head and hacked the legs from another dead man, spinning around to parry two quick thrusts and destroy another pair of dead champions. These warriors might be the best of the dead, but Marius was a count of the Empire and bore a blade that hated the undead with a vengeance. Its power flowed through his veins like an elixir, and though Marius was a fine swordsman, even he wasn't arrogant enough to believe he was *this* good.

Another blade of power flickered near him and he saw Aldred fighting against a towering monster of bone and iron. Like a vast statue of basalt, iron and discarded butcher meat, the monster slashed ponderously with an axe formed from some enormous creature's jagged-toothed jawbone.

Aldred darted in to slash his sword at the creature, and it turned its great axe upon him. The Endal count jumped back, giving Marius the chance to attack the creature, plunging his blade into its back. His blade flashed with angry light, as though encountering some force inimical to the enchantments worked into its metal.

Marius flinched as the blade stung him like a treacherous serpent, feeling his sudden euphoria and confidence evaporate in the face of this new beast. It turned to face him, its monstrous, bovine skull jammed with the fangs of a dozen different deadly creatures. It snapped at him, a jagged tooth catching the links of his mail shirt and tugging him off balance. The jawbone axe swung for him, but the blue fire of Aldred's blade caught the dreadful weapon in its down-swing and deflected it into the earth.

As the beast struggled to free its blade, Endal warriors and Jutone lancers surrounded it, stabbing with spears and halberds. Marius righted himself and ducked beneath its slashing axe, slicing his own weapon towards the creature's belly. The sword scraped along the monstrously elongated thighbone, trailing sparks of orange fire until it bounced clear on the vast pelvis. Aldred attacked from the beast's other side, hammering Ulfshard against the beast's flank.

As mighty as the beast was, it could not resist the pressure of so many blades and portions of its form began to come apart under the relentless assault. Shards of bone and armour peeled loose from its body as Aldred and Marius clove their blades through its unnatural bulk. Fighting side by side, the counts of the Empire hacked the slow-moving creature down piece by piece.

Aldred was the one to deliver the deathblow, though Marius had seen the opening. Even in the midst of this desperate fight, he knew to leave the glory to the man whose city this was. As the creature tumbled back in a collapsing pile of rotted armour and mismatched bone, Marius heard a sudden clamour from the gateway as the defenders finally resealed the shattered portal. Wagons, debris, broken crates and rocks were rolled down the slope to block the entrance. It wasn't pretty and likely wouldn't hold out against another attack, but it would do for now.

Marius rotated his neck to work loose the stiff muscles and walked towards Aldred.

'Quite some fight,' he said with a laconic smile. 'Damn thing almost had me there.'

Aldred nodded, too weary to answer, and Marius swept his sword out in an elaborate bow before the Endal count. He heard shouts of alarm, but before he could pinpoint the reason for them, he was barrelled to the ground as someone in heavy armour slammed into him.

Marius rolled, but a mailed fist cracked against his jaw and he saw stars. Shouts of alarm became shouts of anger, but Marius was too dazed to understand what was going on. He felt himself being dragged away from where he'd fallen and struggled to get his feet underneath him. He heard Jutone and Endal voices shouting at one another, but couldn't make sense out of what they were saying.

Eventually his vision cleared enough to see that he was being dragged away by one of the Raven Helms, Aldred's chief lieutenant if he remembered correctly, though the man's name was a mystery. He rolled and swung his sword up. The man jumped back and Marius scrambled to his feet as Aldred ran over towards the confrontation.

'Laredus, what in Manann's name are you doing?' shouted Aldred.

'Getting this conniving, murderous bastard away from you!' shouted the Raven Helm.

'Are you mad?' demanded Marius. 'I was fighting alongside your precious count, you damned fool! I'll have you flogged for this, a hundred lashes from my strongest lancer!'

'Enough, both of you!' cried Aldred. 'Put up your weapons, there will be no flogging here. Laredus, I mean it, put up your sword.'

The Raven Helm stared at Marius with unbridled hatred, and Marius knew he saw through his deceptive façade of bonhomie and brotherhood. This man knew he intended to win the hearts and minds of the Endal warriors before engineering Aldred's death. Laredus was a dangerous man, and Marius knew he would have to find a way to be rid of him before continuing with his and Marika's plan to make Marburg their own.

Before any more could be said, a freezing shadow enveloped the ramparts as the mighty dragon and its sorcerous rider dropped from the sky to land upon the barbican towers with a thunderous boom of wings. Its hideous bulk shook the very foundations of the citadel as it reared over them with its jaws spread wide.

Despite his terror of this monster, Marius smiled as he realised the perfect means to be rid of Laredus had just presented itself to him in all its monstrous, draconic glory.

Assuming it didn't kill him too…

'Can you hit it from here?' asked Govannon, squinting towards the blurred outline of the empty barrel resting against the walls of Reikdorf. He'd placed the canvas bag on the barrelhead, but couldn't see it from here. Nor could he tell how far away it was, but Cuthwin assured him they were at least a hundred paces away. Bysen held onto his shoulder, eager to see if this composition would produce a more stable reaction.

Though Govannon's sight was virtually gone, he still felt Cuthwin's withering gaze.

'You could put it another fifty paces back and I'd still hit it,' the scout assured him.

'Sorry,' said Govannon.

'Is this one going to work, da?' said Bysen. 'Is it going to be big bang?'

'Hopefully, son, but not too big.'

Govannon had spent weeks working on the dwarf war machine, melting down almost every spare piece of armour and weaponry to forge a strong enough tube to replace the broken barrel. In every case the required centre of mass was off, the metal perforated with air bubbles or the weight not a precise match. These had proven to be costly mistakes, for each imperfection caused Master Holtwine's wooden carriage to fall out of balance. Dwarf engineering was unforgiving of errors.

But now they had it, a perfect twin of the other barrels; one that was completely in balance with the others and which was free from air bubbles and matched the precise density of the dwarf work. Though he never said so out loud, Govannon wished he could travel to the mountain holds of the dwarfs to hear their cries of astonishment at his accomplishment.

Holtwine's timber carriage was a work of beauty, an elegant recreation of the broken one that had been dug from the ground. Its flanks were embellished with carvings depicting Cuthwin's rescue of Grindan Deeplock, and his battle with the wolves. The machine was locked in Govannon's forge, but as magnificent as it was there was one problem.

Without fire powder, it was simply an expensive sculpture.

Govannon had forged plenty of shot for the machine, but he had no idea how to craft the dwarf folk's fire powder, which the device needed to function. In desperation, he'd made Cuthwin read him passages from accounts stored in the Great Library of Empire tribesmen who'd seen these weapons at war in action. From these accounts, Govannon had worked out how the devices functioned, which was more than any man had done before, but knowing how a device worked and recreating it were two different things.

With Eoforth's help, they had found a Jutone text purporting to be the writings of a trader named Erlich Voyst's journey to the lands of a far-flung eastern empire beyond the Worlds Edge Mountains where the death of a great king was marked by great explosions fired into the sky by a fine black powder. Voyst had tried to discover the secret of this powder, but had been stymied by his host's reluctance to divulge its composition. In the end, he had stolen a batch and tried to recreate it on the voyage home, though all he had managed to do was destroy three of his ships and lose a leg in the process.

It had been a painful process of illumination, for Cuthwin read slowly and Eoforth was too engrossed in his own researches to be much help. Throughout their researches, Govannon noticed that the venerable Grand Scholar took care to remain within sight of them at all times, as though afraid of being alone in his own library.

Armed with the many variations of Voyst's recipe for eastern fire powder, they had tried numerous experimental proportions of charcoal, saltpetre and sulphur, sometimes adding mercury and arsenic compounds for added effect. Most of their concoctions had burned too slowly, while others had blown smoking holes in the forge wall and begun fires that threatened to burn Reikdorf down. In the wake of such incidents, Alfgeir had threatened to shut down their work, but Govannon had, thus far, managed to persuade him of the validity of their researches.

'So are we far enough back, smith?' asked Cuthwin, breaking into Govannon's thoughts.

'Yes,' he said. 'We should be.'

'*Should* be?'

Govannon nodded. 'Yes, I'm almost sure of it. This new concoction has an added resin extract to slow the explosive reaction. It should react with just the right amount of violence, but enough control to allow us to fire the war machine without blowing it to pieces.'

'Or us,' added Bysen. 'We don't want to be blown to pieces neither, do we, da?'

'No, son, we don't,' Govannon assured him.

'Well, if you're absolutely sure,' said Cuthwin.

'I'm sure. Light the arrow.'

Cuthwin lowered the oil-soaked arrowhead into the flame and Govannon heard his bowstring pull taut.

'Best cover your ears after you loose,' said Govannon as the arrow flashed from Cuthwin's bow. The burning shaft flew through the air and punched into the canvas bag. Almost instantaneously, a thunderous bang echoed from the walls and a fiery plume of orange light erupted from the bag. Acrid smoke coiled upwards, and a cloud of black streamed up from where the barrel had stood.

Cuthwin and Bysen led Govannon forward, his ears still ringing from the deafening blast. The barrel had vanished, leaving nothing but splinters the size of a child's little finger. A portion of the city wall was blackened in a teardrop shaped pattern and a number of angry warriors shouted down at them from above.

'Sorry!' shouted Cuthwin, waving at them.

'Did it work, da?' asked Bysen, sifting through the remains of the barrel and turning the smouldering fragments over in his hands.

'In a manner of speaking,' said Govannon, able to make out the extent of the black scorch marks on the wall despite his blurred vision. 'Even with the addition of the resin, the explosion was still too powerful. It would destroy the war machine.'

Though this concoction had failed to produce a workable compound, Govannon took out his measuring sticks and began to plot the dimensions of the blast. He shouted numbers for Cuthwin to note down, running through fresh ideas on how to retard the speed and violence of the reaction.

As Govannon measured the extent of the blast, a troop of horsemen rounded the curve of the wall. Even before he heard the lead rider's booming voice, Govannon knew who it would be. He braced himself for the Marshal of the Reik's ire.

'Damn you, smith! What in the name of Ulric's blood are you doing? I warned you about testing that fire powder!' shouted Alfgeir, dismounting from his horse and marching over to Govannon. He could smell the sweat and anger of the man coming off him in waves.

'Ah, Alfgeir,' said Govannon. 'Yes, you did warn me, I remember it vividly.'

'Then why are you trying to destroy the city walls with your damn foolishness?'

'You said you didn't want me to burn down the city,' pointed out Govannon. 'So here we are outside it. The wall may have suffered some slight damage, it's true, but nothing that should affect its structural integrity.'

'Some slight damage?' snapped Alfgeir, kicking over a pile of blackened timber. 'You damn near put a hole in it.'

'Scientific discovery requires some… experimentation and trial and error methodology.'

Alfgeir paced along the length of the wall, staring at them all one by one, struggling to hold his anger in check. Govannon wanted to remind him of what they might learn from this experiment, but knew the man needed to vent before he would listen to reason.

'Damn me, but if our advancement requires the work of a blind man, a simpleton and a huntsman, then we're doomed for sure,' said Alfgeir. 'And aren't you supposed to be making me a sword? Didn't I commission the finest blade in the land, and didn't you promise that it would be ready by the first snows?'

'It's not snowing yet,' said Govannon, looking towards the sky. 'It's not is it?'

'Not yet, but it will be a week at most, and I still haven't seen any hint of a blade.'

'You'll have your sword, Marshal of the Empire,' promised Govannon. 'And, if I'm any judge, something far more impressive.'

'What are you talking about?' said Alfgeir, kneeling beside the shattered pieces of timber, and Govannon heard the warrior's sudden pique of interest at the idea the weapon might actually function. 'Did it work?'

'No,' said Govannon wearily. 'It didn't, but we're close.'

'Close isn't good enough, Govannon,' said Alfgeir. 'Either get it working in the next few days or I'm loading it on a wagon and sending it east to the dwarfs. Do I make myself clear?'

'Perfectly,' said Govannon.

THE DRAGON ROARED, sweeping the ramparts with its deathly dry bellow. Marius tasted ash and caustic fumes, throwing himself flat as the hot breath billowed. As the heat washed over him, Marius realised these were not the corrosive fumes that stripped flesh from men's bones, but simply a terrible exhalation of long dead lungs.

Cries of terror spread away from the dragon as warriors fled from the nightmarish creature. He rolled onto his side, gripping his sword tightly as though his terror could be kept at bay simply by holding a weapon touched by protective sorceries. Incredibly, it seemed as though that were the case, as his terror diminished in the face of what was surely the most horrifying thing he had ever seen.

Its eyes were sunken, rotted orbs that burned with emerald fire. The rider astride its clattering bone neck loomed over them all, its mailed gauntlets crackling with dark energies that flowed into the dread mount and filled its dead limbs and corpse-flesh with animation. Reeking clouds of bloated, blood-fat insects swarmed around the monster, a haze of flesh-eating creatures ready to feast on the dragon's leavings.

Beneath the rider's hood, twin orbs of smouldering fire swept its gaze across the collection of mortals arranged before it, as though understanding that the masters of this city were within its grasp.

'Aldred!' shouted Laredus, running towards the count of the Endals. 'Get back!'

Marius felt the eyes of the black-robed sorcerer boring into him, a hollow gaze of utter evil, but his sword hilt grew hot in his hands and he felt the power of the creature swirl around him without effect.

He smiled, flexing his fingers on the copper-wound handle of his sword as the feeling of invulnerability surged through him once again. The dragon lurched forward, not sinuously, but with an awkward gait that was at odds with the grace it showed in the air. Marius was reminded of a fish scooped from the water onto a riverbank, or the wide-winged birds that lived on the cliffs above Jutonsryk – poised in the air, but waddling and graceless on the ground.

Its claws slashed out at waist height and half a dozen of the Raven Helms were smashed to bloody ruin. Its skeletal head snapped down and plucked another from the ground. The man screamed, but his cries were cut off as the dragon bit down and snapped him in two. Laredus fought to get Aldred back, but to his credit, the count of Marburg stood his ground. Ulfshard blazed with fey light that reflected from the tarnished scales that still hung from the dragon's bones.

Lancers and Raven Helms stabbed long pikes at the dragon, but the blades scraped down the beast's hide or bounced from iron-hard bone. Dozens surrounded it, hurling spears and jabbing its body with halberds. Marius worked his way around the edge of the fight, staying close enough to play a part, but keeping clear of the vast monster's slashing claws and snapping teeth.

The fire-eyed rider reared back and a gust of parched wind, like a sirocco blown off the southern deserts, swept down to engulf the ramparts. Endal warriors screamed and fell to their knees as their bodies were wracked by dark magic. Their flesh withered and rotted, their bones becoming brittle and dusty. Marius felt the seething energies around him, but he remained untouched. Likewise Aldred seemed impervious to the malefic sorcery, so clearly there was an advantage to bearing a sword enchanted by the fey or foreign kings.

Laredus staggered under the effects of the powerful magic, his skin pallid and the veins on his neck straining like hawser ropes. The dragon's neck came down and its jaws opened, still drooling a wash of blood and entrails from its last kill. The Raven Helm hammered his sword into the dragon's mouth and broke several fangs. Arrows bounced from its bony skull, and a huge javelin hurled by a war machine plunged between its ribs. Aldred ran to join his champion, but Laredus pushed him away.

'Stay back!' he yelled.

His distraction cost him dear, as the dragon's jaws snapped shut on his shoulders and head. Laredus came apart like a wineskin filled with blood, his upper body carved open with a gory 'V' shape in his torso. Aldred screamed his champion's name as Marius leapt forward to bring his sword down on the dragon's head.

His fiery blade clove through the bone of its skull, hacking a fist-sized chunk of bone from its body. The beast roared and snapped at him, but Marius was already moving. He dived beneath the dragon's jaw, rolling to his feet on its left-hand side. His sword plunged into its eye and a blaze of green fire spurted from the wound.

Aldred hurled himself at the beast, Ulfshard slashing a burning tracery across the dragon's snout. It reared back and its claws slammed down. A cracked talon slashed Aldred's chest open and the Endal count fell back. Blood streamed from the deep wound and Aldred toppled to the ground.

Marius ran to the injured Aldred, but the hooded rider hurled a forking blast of black lightning from his iron-sheathed fingers towards him. He staggered under the force of the dread sorcerer's power as ice poured through his veins, his sword's magic unable to prevent the darkness from overcoming him.

'Damn you!' he yelled, more angry than afraid. 'Not like this!'

His sword flared brightly, and the enchantments beaten into its folded metal by the wizards of the Celestial Tower of the Divine Dragon a thousand years ago unravelled before such dread energy. Its blade shone like the sun, cracks of light spurting all along its length as the magic dissolved. The sword exploded in radiant beams of light that spiralled heavenward with the sound of bells and shattering glass in a far away tower.

The full force of the black sorcerer's magic surged in Marius's body, but moments later it was gone. Marius blinked away dark spots from his eyes and saw Aldred on his feet before the rearing dragon, the sorcerer's arcing forks of black lightning being drawn into the pellucid blue form of Ulfshard.

It seemed impossible that any blade, enchanted or not, could survive such an assault, but Ulfshard was an ancient weapon of the immortal fey folk from across the oceans. Their smiths had mastery of magic and all its secrets since before mankind had crawled from muddy caves in the mountains. Those who had bound their arcane knowledge into its star metal had done so with complete understanding of the winds of magic and how to defeat those who sought to pervert that power to evil purposes.

As powerful as this sorcerer's magic was, it was nothing compared to the power bound to Ulfshard's elder design. Marius watched in amazement as Aldred, blood pouring from the mortal wound in his chest, swept his blade down, casting the corrupt energies of undeath into the earth. The ground at his feet blackened and withered, its life drained in an instant as the dark magic was dissipated through the enduring rock of the citadel.

A white-fletched arrow flew through the air and buried itself in the chest of the sorcerer, who let out an almighty howl of rage. Its magic was cut off abruptly as another arrow sliced through its black robe and flared brightly with a wash of pure light. As his strength began to return, Marius twisted to see Marika calmly walking towards the dragon and its rider, loosing arrow after arrow at the dread creature. Her bow shimmered with light, silver-blue threads worked into the bowstave gleaming with the same pale light as suffused Ulfshard.

More arrows slashed into the dark sorcerer and Marius felt the creature's desperation as the magic of the fey folk severed the connection to its dread master. Marius surged to his feet as Aldred collapsed to his knees and slumped onto his side. Ulfshard dropped from his hands as Marika sent another arrow through the hood of the sorcerer.

It screeched with agony and scales fell from the dragon's body, its limbs spilling powdered bone from between its joints. The green fire in its remaining eye dimmed and Marius saw he had a chance to end this. He swept up Aldred's fallen sword and charged the reeling dragon. Ulfshard blazed with all the power the ancient smith and his archmage brother had bound to its edge.

Marius brought Ulfshard down on the dragon's neck, the blade shattering mighty bones as thick as a man's waist as easily as if they were fashioned from brittle clay. The sword cut through the dragon's neck and its head fell to the ramparts with a bellowing roar, like a whirlwind through a bone-filled desert. The sorcerous will animating the long-dead beast could not hold its form together in the face of

Ulfshard's magic, and it began falling apart, bones and withered flesh falling like ashen flakes from its mighty form.

Its wings folded and rotted away, blown like cinders from a cold firepit. Its hollow bones disintegrated, and the black sorcerer upon the dragon's back fell to the ramparts. Its robes billowed around it like hellish wings and its hood fell back to reveal a loathsome face with gaunt cheeks, pallid skin and a narrow tapered jaw filled with needle-like fangs. Its eyes were sunken and violet, but Marius saw they were all too human. This evil that had bound itself to Nagash was no unholy creature of darkness, but had once been a man.

A man steeped in evil and filled with unnatural power, but a man nonetheless.

Glowing arrows protruded from his body, shafts of white and gold that trembled as though working deeper into his magically sustained existence. The creature hissed and bared its fangs, but Marius saw it was wounded nigh unto death and stripped of its powers by Marika's arrows.

Marius stepped in and hammered Ulfshard across the creature's neck, the blade slicing as cleanly through the monster's flesh as it had the unholy dragon's. It died with a curse on its lips, but as its head flew through the air the body ignited with an internal fire that consumed it within the time it took Marius to bring Ulfshard around.

A cold wind blew over the ramparts and a foetid exhalation gusted along the length of the walls as skeletal warriors hacking their way over the walls collapsed into piles of decaying bone. Undead corsairs slumped on the docks and bloodied corpses that had, moments before, been clawing at the desperate defenders of Marburg now fell to the ground as the dark will empowering them was undone.

Thousands more remained beyond the walls, but this attack was over.

And that was good enough for Marius.

He sheathed Ulfshard, not surprised in the least to find it fitted within his scabbard, despite being almost a handspan longer than his previous blade.

Marika ran up to him and threw her arms around his neck. She held him tightly, and he responded in kind, though the gesture was automatic rather than heartfelt.

'We did it!' she cried. 'They're dead!'

Marius looked at the decaying remains of the sorcerer and his dragon, lying next to the corpses of Aldred and Laredus.

He wondered which deaths she meant, but realised it didn't matter.

'That we did, my dear,' he said with a satisfied grin. 'That we did.'

SEVENTEEN
The Price of Knowledge

EOFORTH HURRIED THROUGH the darkened streets of Reikdorf, fear lending his exhausted limbs strength. The streets of the city, once so familiar and reassuring, were now threatening and unknown. Every turn was laden with uncertainty, each step echoing strangely as though this was a city that existed beyond the realms of men, a place forsaken by the natural laws of the world.

A gibbous moon hung low in the sky, casting stark shadows through the empty street. Eoforth knew that thousands of people, refugees from all across the Empire, packed Reikdorf, so the idea that the city could be so empty was surely ridiculous. Thousands of people filled every nook and cranny: refugees from Marburg and Jutonsryk, southern tribesmen and villagers coming up from the Grey Mountains and villagers fleeing the closing net of the dead from the east and north.

Nor were refugees the only people to come to Reikdorf. The city had the feel of an armed camp, with warriors billeted throughout its many buildings. The majority were Unberogen, for they made up the bulk of the population around these parts, but many more were Asoborns and Brigundians fleeing the destruction of their lands.

Eoforth had heard snippets only of the news from across the Empire, for his researches into Nagash's history had driven him to the point of obsession. His head ached constantly and the aches and pains that plagued him on a daily basis seemed stronger and more insidious than ever before – as though the dread necromancer's reach was clawing him down into the ancient pages and scrolls gathered on the library's shelves. His breathing rasped in his lungs and every step sent a spike of pain shooting through his chest. Eoforth knew the eyes of the necromancer were upon him, mocking his attempts to uncover some secret that might give Sigmar and his warriors a means of defeating him. No such secret existed, and it amused Nagash to allow Eoforth to fritter away his time on such fruitless research.

Yet Eoforth *had* found something...

Not a hidden nemesis by which the necromancer could be defeated, but a character trait that might yet be exploited. He had to take what he had found to Sigmar's longhouse, yet the street before him seemed to stretch away into infinity. Scrolls fell from the bundle haphazardly stacked in his arms and he blinked stars from his eyes as his heart lurched painfully.

Sigmar had returned to Reikdorf two days ago, and the mood of despair that had settled upon the city had lifted as he rode through the Ostgate with Wolfgart and the Asoborns. News of what had befallen Freya's army had not dampened the spirits of Reikdorf's people, but Sigmar had not wasted any time and instructed every smith in the city to sharpen blades, repair armour and bolster the defences of the Unberogen capital.

Every man, woman and child within the city bent their efforts to ensuring the survival of the Empire, carrying armloads of arrows to the walls, establishing makeshift infirmaries for the wounded and doing all they could to help. Not one person or family stinted on their duties, and the sense of brotherhood that stretched from one side of Reikdorf to the other was palpable.

All that would be for nothing if Eoforth could not reach Sigmar's longhouse.

His moment of epiphany had come as the last glimmers of light faded from the library's high, lancet windows. Only when the dozen candles with which he surrounded his desk had blown out in the one instant had he realised he was alone.

Eoforth felt the gloom and the unseen whisperers in the darkness close in on him. Glimmers of light drifted from the farthest halls of the library, a host of sibilant voices sighing like distant choirs as they spiralled towards him, laughing in derision at his puny efforts to undo the schemes of their master.

He'd cursed himself for allowing himself to become so engrossed in his work that he'd forgotten the passage of time. He'd allowed the dead to get in and now he was going to pay for it. His heart beat an irregular rhythm on his thin chest, and a painful numbness flowed down his left arm. He flexed the fingers, trying to force the blood to flow. His heart was weak and to put it under such strain was too much for him to bear.

Eoforth rested against a stone building, trying to gather his strength. He heard whispers behind him and spun, clutching the scrolls he'd gathered in the dark before fleeing for the streets. Moonlight bathed the world in cold, heartless light and he saw shadows where no shadows should be. They slid across the cobbles and over the walls of nearby dwellings, stretching and swelling to resemble elongated figures with black, featureless faces, thin, wasted arms and curling claws.

They chattered with the rattle of unseen teeth, clicking their insubstantial claws on the stonework as they closed in on him. Eoforth pushed himself from the wall as they drew near, limping down the road with desperate heaves of tortured lungs rattling in his chest. Though it was cold and his breath misted the air before him, his skin was slick with sweat.

Despite the reek of boiling hops that turned his stomach, Eoforth set off down Brewer Street, weaving like the drunks who clustered around the beer makers' back doors, hoping for the slops.

The shadows on the walls followed him and he heard screeching laughter from the streets running alongside him, half-glimpsed phantoms flickering at the corners of his eyes. It seemed impossible that no one else could be aware of these spectres, or that he hadn't yet encountered another person.

Perhaps he walked in the world of the dead now, a living soul that moved unseen by those untouched by mortality. The enemy stalked him, perhaps fearing what he knew and might pass to Sigmar. The dead believed he had found something that could hurt them and that made him pick up his pace, forcing his wretched body onwards.

Eoforth clutched the silver dove pendant around his neck, mouthing a prayer to Shallya that he hadn't said aloud since he was a youngster.

'Merciful Shallya, meek and mild, watch me now, your helpless child,' he said, feeling the chill of the grave lessen with every word.

He fought to remember his other prayers, especially ones to Morr and Taal. Morr for his hatred of the undead, Taal for his joy in life.

'Now I lay me down to sleep, I pray to Morr my soul to keep–'

His words were cut off by a feral snarl and Eoforth looked up to see a pack of wolves blocking the road ahead. Filthy, rotted creatures with bone and muscle exposed beneath mangy, dirt-encrusted fur, these were abominable creatures of darkness. They did not howl, but their broken teeth were bared and they stalked forward, limping and ungainly on broken bones and twisted spines. As malformed and broken in death though they were, Eoforth had no illusions as to his ability to outrun them or survive their attack.

He couldn't make it past them, and looking over his shoulder he saw the chattering shadows easing down the street with their stretched arms reaching out to him. There was no way he could reach the longhouse, and the Gardens of Morr were on the other side of the city walls, so he set off down the Street of Temples, to the only place that might yet grant him sanctuary.

They came after him, but slowly, as though they were afraid to follow him into this place of gods. These divine beings watched over mankind, and the minions of necromancers were their most hated foes, for the dead worshipped nothing.

Still clutching his dove pendant, Eoforth hurried down the street with the wolves padding behind him and the shadow hunters laughing at his feeble attempt to escape. He saw the building he sought, just as a sharp pain stabbed into his chest. Eoforth gasped with the shock of it. He stumbled, losing more of his scrolls, and ground his teeth against the pain spreading down his left side. Eoforth was no physician, but he knew his heart was giving out under the strain.

He cried out as he slammed into the temple door, the pain of the impact spreading through his body as he slid down the stonework.

'Help... me...' he gasped, though he knew no one could possibly hear so weak a cry.

The shadows closed in and the wolves bared their fangs.

'In the name of Shallya, have mercy!' he cried with the last of his strength.

And then, a miracle. A sliver of light filled the street and the shadow hunters fled its touch, retreating to the forsaken corners of the darkness. The wolves backed away from the light, wary of its touch. They waited, uncertain and afraid, the torchlight reflecting in the empty sockets of their eyes.

Eoforth reached out to the light, as greyness smothered his vision. His chest burned with pain and he fell into the arms of the woman who appeared in the doorway like the beauteous goddess of mercy and healing herself. His heartbeat became an arrhythmic crescendo as the light haloed her head and softened her angular features.

Eoforth had never seen anything so beautiful in all his life.

'My lady…' he said. 'You came for me…'

High Priestess Alessa of the temple of Shallya knelt beside Eoforth and cradled his head. Her eyes swept the street beyond her temple, and the wolves fled from her stern, unflinching gaze. No creature of darkness could face so holy and pure a vision without fear.

He felt himself sliding down into darkness, and tried to speak, but the words wouldn't come.

'Be at peace, Eoforth,' said Alessa, seeing immediately that he was dying. 'Whatever they were are gone now.'

'I must… speak,' he said, as a single tear slid down his cheek. 'Sigmar needs to know…'

Alessa brushed it away and said, 'Speak to me. Whatever you have to say, I will tell him. I promise. What would you have as your last words in this world?'

Eoforth gripped her shoulder and pulled his lips to her ear. With his final breath he whispered one last thing to the high priestess. As his eyes closed, he saw her face turn cold, and went into Morr's embrace terrified that she hadn't understood.

He heard wolves in the distance.

And then nothing.

SIGMAR KNELT BESIDE the body of his counsellor and kept his eyes closed. He gripped Eoforth's hand and wished he could have been there for his friend's final moments. This war against the enclosing forces of Nagash had already cost the Empire dear, but that cost had never been harder to bear than now. Friends and allies had fallen to the advance of the undead, but no one who had been as dear to him as Eoforth.

The venerable counsellor lay on Sigmar's bed at the rear of the longhouse, as though he were asleep and would shortly awaken and demand the honey-sweetened oats he liked so much. Lex, Kai and Ortulf lay curled at the foot of the bed, sensing their master's sorrow and knowing not to intrude on his grief. Kai yawned and stretched his back paws, looking up to make sure he wasn't needed.

Eoforth had steered Sigmar through the darkest moments of his rule. He had offered sage counsel and age-tempered wisdom to cool the Unberogen fire in Sigmar's heart that would otherwise have seen him become no better than a Norsii warlord. Over the years, Sigmar had lost his father, the love of his life, and some of his best friends. It had been a hard road to walk, but he had walked it knowing he could rely on Eoforth's steady, even-handed advice.

The dead man's face was at peace, the dimmed lanterns seeming to ease the furrows of care and smooth the lines of pain he had borne with quiet dignity. His pain was now gone, and Sigmar tried to find comfort in that, but all he could think of was that his friend was gone. Elswyth sat on the end of the bed, one hand resting on Eoforth's shoulder as she awaited Sigmar's leave to withdraw.

'Well?' said Sigmar.

Elswyth sighed. 'His heart gave out, nothing more sinister than that. I know you want another reason to hate Nagash, but I can't give it to you.'

'You think that's what I want?' he snapped. 'You are the hag woman's successor now?'

The healer scowled at him and leaned forward. 'You've lost a good friend, so I'll let that go, but speak to me like that again and it'll be the last time you see me in Reikdorf.'

'I'm sorry,' said Sigmar, instantly contrite. 'I just thought he'd be around...'

'Forever?' said Elswyth.

'Stupid, I know, but yes,' shrugged Sigmar.

'With his heart condition, it's a wonder he lived as long as he did. He wasn't a well man.'

'I didn't know that.'

'He didn't want you to. Thought you'd make him retire for good if you did.'

'Maybe I should have. It might have given him more life.'

Elswyth shook her head. 'Not Eoforth, you'd have killed him years ago if you'd made him step away from the sides of kings.'

'What are you talking about?'

'Men like Eoforth, men like you, they don't just fade into the background. What they are defines them and if you take that away, what's left to them? Like old Beorthyn. When Govannon took over his forge after the old man's joints inflamed, he was lost and didn't know what to do with himself. Without purpose, Beorthyn felt like he didn't have anything left to live for and died a year later. Why do you think Govannon's not retired, even though he's mostly blind? He knows he'll be the same. What would you do if you weren't Emperor?'

'I don't know,' admitted Sigmar.

'You'd be a waster, a brigand or a sell-sword,' said Elswyth. 'You live for blood and battle, and even though you're the Emperor and say you want peace, you're secretly glad you'll never find it in your lifetime.'

'You have a healer's heart, but a viper's tongue,' said Sigmar.

'I say things as I see them,' said Elswyth. 'I've seen too many Unberogen boys brought to my home with the most horrific battle injuries to believe any warrior who says he wants peace while carrying a sword or axe. Or a hammer. And you know I'm right; else you'd have gotten angry.'

'Maybe you are right,' said Sigmar, 'but I can still mourn my friend, can't I?'

'Of course you can, you fool,' said Elswyth with a smile that made her beautiful. 'I never said you couldn't. You'd be made of stone if you didn't grieve for this old man. His counsel probably saved more lives than that hammer of yours.'

Sigmar shook his head. Elswyth's harsh tongue could deliver rebuke and praise in the same breath without a man even noticing.

'Eoforth advised my father and grandfather,' said Sigmar. 'I remember him back when I was a young boy. He seemed like he'd always advised the Unberogen kings, and always would. Now that he's gone, I feel... adrift... like a guiding star that shone above me without me even knowing it was there has been taken away.'

'Eoforth was a good counsellor,' said Elswyth, 'but you were always the Emperor. You ruled with him to aid you, and now you'll rule without him. You have good friends around you, and they will help. Anyway, you know this already, so why I'm wasting time telling you is beyond me.'

'Because that's what you do, healer,' smiled Sigmar. 'You help people.'

Elswyth snorted as she gathered up her belongings.

'Only those that need it,' she said, patting his shoulder as she passed.

'IT WASN'T SOME magic of Nagash?' asked Alfgeir. 'She's sure? How can she be sure?'

'She's sure,' said Sigmar, pacing the length of the longhouse. 'I wanted it to be Nagash, but Eoforth was just old. I think we forgot how old sometimes.'

Alfgeir sighed and raised his mug of beer. 'He was a good man, and a good friend. I'll miss him.'

'Aye, we all will,' agreed Wolfgart, also raising his mug.

Everyone in the longhouse raised their drink, toasting the soul of the departed scholar and wishing him a speedy journey through Morr's gateway to the Wolf God's halls. Though Eoforth had not been a warrior, he had the soul of a fighter and Sigmar knew the old man would be welcomed as a true son of Ulric.

'To Eoforth,' said Maedbh, keeping one torq-wrapped arm around Wolfgart and the other around Ulrike. 'May the foolish fire of youth fill him again as he runs with the wolves.'

Since returning from the east, Wolfgart's family had been inseparable, as though the terror of potential grief had forged their bond stronger than ever before. Sometimes it took nearly losing what you had to remind you of how precious it was.

Or sometimes you had to lose it forever, thought Sigmar, touching the golden cloak pin that secured the bearskin at his shoulders.

Worked in the form of a snake curling around to eat its own tail, it had been fashioned by Master Alaric in happier times, and the workmanship was exquisite, with small bands along the length of the snake's body engraved with twin-tailed comets. Sigmar had given the brooch to Ravenna as a symbol of his love, but it had returned to him all too soon thanks to Gerreon's betrayal.

Alfgeir offered him a mug of beer. The smell was inviting, but Sigmar shook his head.

'There's nothing I'd like more than to lose myself in a beer haze,' he said, 'but I want a clear head tonight.'

The Marshal of the Reik shrugged and took the mug for himself.

'Probably wise,' said Alfgeir, draining the mug. 'But Eoforth was the wise one.'

Like Eoforth, Alfgeir had served Sigmar's father, and the old man's death had hit him hard. Losing men in battle was hard, but every man who commanded warriors made their own peace with that fact. To lose friends to something as cruelly banal as a weak heart was, in its own way, harder to deal with. Though they had been opposites in almost all regards, Alfgeir and Eoforth had been true friends and comrades in arms.

Sigmar laid a hand on Alfgeir's shoulder and continued his circuit of the firepit.

The warrior Maedbh had introduced as Garr stood against the far wall, his arms folded across his chest and his expression hard to read. Sigmar knew the man was wary in this company, and given the identity of the boys he had been entrusted to guard, that was understandable. He had a fierce look to him that Sigmar liked, and his Queen's Eagles would be a formidable presence when battle was joined.

He had spoken briefly to Garr, assuring him that no one in Reikdorf had any intention of removing the boys he guarded from his custody. The man had nodded, but said nothing, as a perfect understanding flowed between them. Since then, Freya's boys had not been seen outside beyond their first arrival at Reikdorf.

Master Alaric sat on a stubby barrel of dwarf ale, his armour gleaming in the low firelight, and his axe propped next to him against a bucket of coal. Sigmar had been overjoyed to see his old friend, but thanks to his behaviour on the hillside where they had rescued Maedbh and the Asoborns, he had been forced to endure a stern lecture on the proper protocols on greeting friends. Alaric's dwarfs lounged around the edges of the longhouse, casting critical eyes around its structure, as though lamenting what men had done to the fine work they had crafted for them.

The Taleuten Red Scythes were represented by their captain, a warrior named Leodan, a man Sigmar had seen ride into the heart of the dead without fear. His skills were prodigious, but there was something missing to him, some part of him that wasn't entirely normal. At the moment, Sigmar didn't care whether the warriors he could count on to fight alongside him were normal. That they would fight was enough.

'Elswyth says it wasn't magic?' said Wolfgart. 'So why was the old man running for the temple of Shallya? They were using sorcery on him and he ran for help from the goddess of mercy. Makes perfect sense to me.'

'You might be right,' said Sigmar. 'You might very well be right, but I don't see that it makes any difference right now. Eoforth is dead, and when the priests of Morr have completed their rites, I will take him to a place of honour on Warriors Hill. But right now we have other matters to consider.'

'How close are the dead to Reikdorf?' asked Garr. 'You have word from your scouts?'

'I do,' nodded Sigmar. 'Cuthwin has seen the wolf packs and the eaters of the dead on the Reik, near the Wörlitz mines.'

'Two days' march,' said Wolfgart.

'About time Cuthwin tore himself from Govannon's side,' said Alfgeir, helping himself to another beer. 'They've wasted weeks on that machine, and it still doesn't bloody work.'

Sigmar nearly said something to Alfgeir, but a slight shake of the head from Maedbh convinced him not to. He glanced over at Master Alaric, but if the dwarf runesmith knew to what Alfgeir was referring, he said nothing.

'Did the scout say anything about their numbers?' asked Leodan.

'No, none of his men could get close enough,' said Sigmar. 'Many tried, but none returned. Nagash will be served by many thousands of revenants, and every day his army will swell with those who have died fighting him.'

'If you had to guess?'

'At least thirty thousand, maybe more.'

Leodan nodded, understanding the sacrifices Cuthwin's foresters and huntsmen had made in trying to gather information on the enemy. The number was staggering, and Sigmar could see that many of those gathered in the longhouse had trouble even picturing so vast a horde. Such a force had only ever been seen at Black Fire or around the foot of the Fauschlag Rock, and even then, no one really knew how many warriors had been present.

Sigmar saw the controlled anger in the captain of the Red Scythes. He wanted this battle finished so he and his warriors could return to defend their own homeland, for the Taleuten people were undoubtedly besieged within Taalahim.

'Can this city hold against an army of that size?' asked Garr, looking towards Alaric. 'The walls look strong and high, but I'm no expert on that sort of fighting.'

'The walls are serviceable,' said Alaric. 'Designed by a dwarf, but built by manlings, so who knows if they're strong enough? I'd need to test them to be sure, but I reckon they'll hold against what these grave-hoppers can throw at them.'

Alfgeir laughed, a drunken, nasal bray. 'Walls? It won't matter about the walls. We've a city filled to bursting point with refugees and warriors, and not enough food to last out the week, let alone a siege.'

'We have grain reserves,' said Sigmar. 'We can last a season.'

'And how long can the dead last?' snapped Alfgeir. 'They don't need to eat or drink, they don't need to sleep, and they don't need to worry about disease or fear or losing their friends. They don't even need to fight us. They can just trap us in here and wait for us to die!'

'They won't do that,' said a soft female voice from the doorway to the longhouse. 'And you're too old to be drinking that much beer, Alfgeir Gunnarson. The enemy is two days away and you'll still be puking your guts out if you have one more mouthful.'

'What are you, my mother?' said Alfgeir, though he didn't take another drink as he saw High Priestess Alessa standing in the longhouse door.

'Hardly, but the people of this city need you to fight,' said Alessa, sweeping inside and making her way towards Alfgeir. 'Are you going to let them down?'

Alfgeir licked his lips and shook his head, putting the beer down on the table next to him. It was easy enough to shout at fellow warriors, but to snap at a priestess of Shallya would be boorish beyond even what his drunkenness would allow.

Maedbh rose from her seat and knelt before Alessa. The priestess touched the top of her head and smiled warmly, all hint of her irritation vanished. Alessa had blessed Ulrike when she had come into this world, and Maedbh would always be in her debt, for that protection had served her well over the years.

'High priestess,' said Sigmar. 'I hadn't thought to see you at a gathering of warriors.'

Alessa turned to Sigmar and he was struck by the hostility he saw in her face.

'Nor would you under normal circumstances, but these are not normal times.'

'Then join us,' he said, gesturing towards an empty space on a long trestle bench.

'I'll stand,' she said. 'I do not relish being here, so I will say what I have come to say and then I will go.'

Sigmar nodded. 'You said that the dead won't simply trap us within the city and allow us to starve to death. Why do you think that?'

'It is the crown,' said Alessa. 'Nagash is desperate to retrieve it, and he will not wait for you to die from lack of food and water. He will want to break the walls of this place down as soon as he can and kill everyone inside. Eoforth knew as much, they were his last words to me before he died.'

'He spoke to you?' demanded Sigmar. 'Why did you not tell of this before now?'

Alessa's hostile confidence diminished and Sigmar saw the agony of indecision within her. Whatever she had to say to him, it had taken a great deal of soul searching for her to come forward.

'He spoke about the crown I foolishly allowed to be buried beneath my temple.'

'What about it?' said Sigmar, seeing a number of confused expressions around the longhouse. The secret of what he had buried beneath the temple of Shallya was not widely known, and Sigmar would prefer it to stay that way. One look into Alessa's eyes told Sigmar that wasn't going to happen.

'Nagash is obsessed with it. It's the only thing he desires.'

'We already know that,' said Alfgeir. 'The blood drinker told us that.'

'But he would not have communicated how the great necromancer is consumed utterly by his desire, how his entire existence is bound to it in ways no mortal can understand. It is part of him, and without it he is less than nothing. To be close to the crown will drive all thoughts of restraint and reason from Nagash. It is his greatest strength and his most terrible weakness.'

'Eoforth told you all that?' said Wolfgart. 'He always did use ten words when one would do. Not bad for a dying man.'

'Of course he didn't,' said Alessa. 'He simply said, "The crown, tell Sigmar it's his Ravenna".'

'And you got all this talk of obsession and desire from that?' said Alfgeir.

'That and an understanding of what it means to be near the wretched thing,' whispered Alessa. 'You understand what I mean, don't you, Emperor?'

Sigmar nodded, only now seeing how pale Alessa was, how thin and undernourished. Her hollow cheeks and haunted eyes were a true testament to the insidious nature of Nagash's crown, a pervasive evil that sapped the vitality of the living by degrees.

'I do,' said Sigmar. 'And if we survive this coming battle, I swear I will hide this crown far from the lands of men, somewhere its evil will no longer wreak harm.'

Wolfgart turned to him. 'Do you know what Eoforth meant? Does it help us?'

'He does,' said Alessa, bowing her head and clasping her hands as tears flowed down her cheeks. 'Shallya forgive me, but I should never have told you.'

'What is she talking about, Sigmar?' said Alfgeir, rising to his feet.

Fear touched Sigmar as he understood the source of Alessa's reluctance to speak of what Eoforth had told her. They had shut the crown away from the world for good reason. Mortals were not meant to wield such magic, for their hearts were too malleable and too easily seduced to be allowed near such temptations as eternal life and ultimate power.

Sigmar had broken free from the malign effect of Nagash's crown once before, but could he do it again?

'There is only one way we can fight Nagash,' said Sigmar. 'Only one way I can face him with any hope of victory.'

He stood at the end of the firepit and took a deep breath, loath to even say the words, let alone contemplate the reality of what it would mean for the Empire if he failed.

'I have to wear Nagash's crown again,' said Sigmar.

EIGHTEEN
The Dead of Reikdorf

THE HOST OF Nagash arrived before the walls of Reikdorf on the leading edge of dark storm clouds. Winter cut the air and the cold winds that blew from the vast horde of the undead carried the stench of mankind's corpse. Chain lightning flashed in the clouds and rumbles of thunder that seemed to roll out from distant lands echoed strangely from the walls of the city's temples, taverns and dwellings.

No sun rose on this day, the unnatural darkness covering the land in a bleak shadow from which it could nevermore be lifted, a gloom that entered every mortal heart and filled it with the sure and certain knowledge of the fate of all living things. Skeletons marched at the fore of the army, ancient warriors in serried ranks that stretched from one line of the horizon to the other. Cursed to serve Nagash for all eternity, they wore armour of long lost kingdoms, clutched weapons of strange design, and the grave dirt of far off lands clung to their bones. Heavily armoured champions in heavy hauberks of scale and corslets of iron marched at their head, exalted warriors of the dead whose skill with the executioners' blades they carried was more terrifying than when they had been mortal.

Where the warriors of bone resembled the army they had been in life, the thousands of bloody corpses dragged from shallow peasant graves or raised back from the dead in the wake of battle were a shambling mockery of life. Limping on twisted limbs and groaning with the torment of their existence, they were a stark reminder that even death in battle against this foe would be no escape from the horror. Hunched things in black robes moved through the shuffling horde of corpses, their fell sorcery directing its mindless hunger.

The sky above Reikdorf blackened with the fluttering wings of bats and every rooftop was lined with black-winged carrion birds. Ravens cawed in anticipation of a feast of flesh, hopping agitatedly from clawed foot to clawed foot, impatient for the slaughter to begin.

Hundreds of dark riders on skeletal steeds caparisoned in black and red and riding beneath banners of skulls and fanged maws took position at the centre and flanks of the army, the stillness of their mounts hideous and unnatural. These dread riders carried long black lances, their tips glittering with a loathsome green shimmer.

Scraps of lambent light billowed like pyre smoke around the horde, wailing with the torments of the damned. Spectres and howling revenants dragged from death, but whose remains were no more, spun and twisted in ghostly wisps, their eyes bright with aching need for the warmth of mortal flesh. Their howling struck terror into all who heard them, and scores of terrified people took blades to their own necks rather than face such an enemy.

Loping ahead of the host, a ragged line of corpse eaters moved on all fours, wretched and debased, with only their monstrous appetites to sustain them. These degenerate monstrosities had once been men, but they had fallen far from the nobility of their former race. Some clutched sharpened bone, others fragments of swords, but most only needed their long, gnarled claws to tear out an enemy's throat. They gurgled and croaked as they skulked in the shadows, eager for the bloodletting to begin, but fearful to be the first into the fray.

No trace of the land could be seen as the black host spread out before the city, a tide of rotten meat, bleached bone and unquiet spirits. This was an army to end the reign of mortals, to plunge the world into eternal night.

Yet it was the figures at the head of this mighty army that drew the eye, a vanguard of three riders, one in silver plate, and the others in armour of black. Khaled al-Muntasir was easy to identify, but the two warriors alongside him were unknown to the defenders. Each clutched a flag so soaked in blood it was impossible to tell what heraldic devices it had once displayed.

Yet even among such dreadful abominations, the master of this army was clear, a towering column of fuliginous chill that seemed to draw in what little light remained to the world only to snuff it out within his immortal form.

This was Nagash, the Great Necromancer, the bane of life and undying corpse lord who had toppled empires and unleashed the curse of undeath upon the world. His dread form floated above the earth, and where he passed, the ground split apart, withered and destroyed as sable light was drawn upwards and coiled about his armoured and ragged-cloaked form. The creatures of the earth crept from the soil, crawling, buzzing and slithering away from the necromancer as his monstrous power sucked the vitality from everything around him.

Through the roiling miasma of deathly energies that surrounded him, black segments of iron and bronze could be glimpsed, shimmering coils of green light suffusing each plate, rivet and fluted line of beaten metal. A grinning skull of ancient bone loomed from the darkness, massive and long since bereft of flesh, muscle and life.

At Nagash's side, a towering warrior of brazen iron and ferocity. Broader and taller than even the mightiest tribesmen, Krell bellowed a martial challenge that not even death could contain. The bloody champion of undeath and slaughter brandished his axe, raising it to point at the city before him, as though claiming it as his own.

A wind from the depths of the earth sprang up around these fell lords of sorcery and battle, a chill breath of lifelessness and the withering passage of time. It roiled towards the city, billowing like a desert sandstorm. Where it struck the walls, the stonework cracked and spalled, aged a thousand years in a heartbeat. Wooden gates rotted and crumbled as though split apart by centuries of hoarfrost. The cold wind blew through the city with a ghastly whisper heard by every man, woman and child.

It was the Necromancer's promise and threat all in one.

Man is cattle...

YET NAGASH WAS not the first to reach Reikdorf this day. As the fleeting light of dawn crested the eastern mountains before being smothered by the black canopy of the undead twilight, a ragged band of a hundred warriors limped towards the city's southern gateway. Led by her sword maidens, Queen Freya returned to the lands of men, having fought her way through the infested wilds of the southern Empire.

These wounded, exhausted men and women were all that remained of the proud host she had led from Three Hills, warriors whose honour sought redemption by bringing the queen they had failed to safety. Death would be a release for them, should the enemy facing them grant such mercy. Maedbh was overjoyed to see Freya, as were the people of Reikdorf, for her survival was a lone beacon of hope in these grim times. That Freya could survive meant others could too. No sooner had she ridden through the gates than the Queen's Eagles surrounded her, bringing her sons to her side for a tearful reunion.

The joy that greeted Freya's arrival was soon tempered by word that the dead were no more than an hour behind them. The gates were sealed and barred, and the warriors preparing to defend the city with their lives manned the walls, clutching swords and axes in hands slick with fear. Though still gravely wounded, Freya took her place with the Queen's Eagles, and no words of admonition could shift Sigulf and Fridleifr from her side.

There could be no bystanders in this battle for survival.

All would fight, or all would die.

The bell on the temple of Ulric chimed, and the dead came to Reikdorf.

'I CAN'T BELIEVE we're doing this,' said Alfgeir, holding tightly to the reins of his horse as it tossed its head and snorted in fear. 'This is madness and you know it.'

'Maybe so,' said Sigmar, 'but it needs to be done.'

'I am never one to back down from a foe, but I agree with your Reik Marshal,' said Freya, riding alongside Garr and three of his Queen's Eagles. As the only one of Sigmar's counts present in Reikdorf, she had the right to ride out with him, but he found it hard to look at her without picturing the boys that carried his blood.

They rode through the rotted remains of the Ostgate towards the enemy army. Since arriving at the walls of Reikdorf, the undead host had stood in silence, content to let fear worm its way into the hearts of those mortals who would soon be joining their ranks. The only movement had been when the three armoured warriors in the army's vanguard had ridden forward beneath a lowered banner, the universal symbol of parley.

'Why should we respect this parley?' said Garr, one hand on his sword hilt. 'We outnumber them and should cut them down while we have the chance.'

Sigmar looked over at the man, irritated at his foolishness.

'You could try, but these are blood drinkers, and they would kill you before you even drew that blade,' said Sigmar.

Garr swallowed hard and released his hold on his sword.

'Damn, but what I wouldn't give to be riding out to these bastards with Redwane and a century of his White Wolves about now,' said Wolfgart.

Sigmar smiled. 'Aye, that would be most welcome, but Middenheim will have its own problems if I'm any judge.'

Further conversation was halted as the air grew dense and cold. The blood drinkers were ahead of them, blocking the road and silhouetted on the crest of the slope ahead of them. Sigmar felt his skin crawl at their nearness, the very core of what made him a man rebelling at being so close to creatures that so obviously violated the natural order of the world. An aura of freezing air surrounded them, as though warmth was repelled by their very presence.

Khaled al-Muntasir gave an elaborate bow from the back of his dark steed, smiling in welcome as though they were old friends and not mortal enemies. Sigmar's horse balked at the proximity of the undead, its ears pressed flat against its skull and eyes wide with fear. He heard a jingle of trace and harness as the horses of his companions whinnied and sought to gallop back the way they had come.

'Emperor,' said the vampire, and Sigmar saw the gleam of razor-sharp fangs in the corner of the monster's mouth. 'It is a great pleasure to see you again.'

'I cannot say the same,' he replied.

'No, I expect not,' agreed the vampire, turning his attention to the Asoborn queen with a mocking glint in his eyes. 'And Queen Freya, I am gratified to see you survived our previous encounter. I cannot promise you the same mercy I showed you at the river, but as you can see, many of your tribesmen now fight with me. Were you to join them, it would have a pleasing symmetry.'

Freya seethed with fury and hurt, and Sigmar saw it was taking every scrap of her restraint not to hurl herself at the vampire. She took a deep, shuddering breath.

'You defeat my army, but you run from a host of old men and children,' she said, each word a venomous barb. 'You are nothing to be feared. You and your kind are leeches, not warriors. A true leader would have died with his army, not run like a gelded catamite.'

Khaled al-Muntasir glared at her, but his angry expression turned to one of polite indifference, as if she had not spoken.

'Death is meaningless to me,' said Khaled al-Muntasir with a dismissive wave of a thin-boned hand. 'None of your inferior race can strike down one of my kind. The blood of ancient queens runs in my veins, and I will simply rise from any wound a mortal can deal me.'

Sigmar was studying Khaled al-Muntasir's eyes as he spoke, and almost missed the lie, so glibly did it trip from the vampire's mouth.

'I don't believe you,' said Sigmar, suddenly seeing a crack in the vampire's self-perpetuated aura of invincibility. 'You fear extinction like any mortal. More so. You've become so attached to the idea of immortality that just the thought of oblivion terrifies you.'

The vampire turned his gaze on Sigmar, and he felt the full might of his will, a potent force that had sustained his existence for centuries and which had seduced hundreds with its promises of a life undying. Its promises were empty to Sigmar, for he had faced the temptations of a being far older and far more dangerous than a mere vampire.

'I told you that you were not welcome in Reikdorf,' said Sigmar, without breaking the vampire's gaze and letting him know that the attempt to dominate him had failed. 'I said that if you returned that you would be killed.'

The vampire looked hurt at Sigmar's harsh words and said, 'You would not respect the sanctity of the parley? I had thought you a civilised man.'

'What do you want, fiend?' demanded Wolfgart.

The vampire's tongue flicked out, as though tasting the air like a serpent. He smiled and nodded toward Wolfgart. 'You should keep yapping dogs on a leash, Sigmar. They might have their throats torn out to teach them a lesson.'

'Now who's not respecting the parley?' said Alfgeir. 'What is it you want? Speak your offer so we can spit on it and get back to our drinks.'

'Very well,' said Khaled al-Muntasir, more offended at Alfgeir's disrespect than any notion of the parley being broken. 'I came here to offer you one last chance to hand over my master's crown. Ride out with it within a day and you will be...'

'Spared?' laughed Sigmar.

'No,' replied Khaled al-Muntasir. 'Not spared, but you would become exalted champions of the dead, great kings among the host of the unliving. It is a great honour my master does you by even offering you this chance.'

'So why doesn't he come here himself to offer me this boon, ruler to ruler?' said Sigmar.

The vampire cocked his head to one side, as though trying to discern whether Sigmar was joking. Deciding he wasn't, Khaled al-Muntasir shrugged.

'My master does not lower himself to treat with lesser races,' said the vampire. 'Bring him his crown and your deaths will be swift, your rebirths glorious. Deny him and he will kill everyone in your ridiculous city, and bring your people back from the dead only after their corpses have been violated by the flesheaters. There will be no glorious resurrection for any of you, just mindless hunger and a craving for living meat that can never be sated.'

'Tough choice,' said Wolfgart. 'Can we think about it?'

Missing the sarcasm, the vampire said, 'You have one day. When the twin moons rise, the end begins.'

'Then we will fight you beneath their light,' said Sigmar, turning his horse back towards Reikdorf. Before he could rake his spurs back, Khaled al-Muntasir had one last parting shot.

'Where are my manners?' said the vampire with mock embarrassment. 'How rude of me not to introduce you to my new companions. My brothers, come greet our honourable foes.'

The two warriors accompanying Khaled al-Muntasir rode level with the vampire and raised their visors. Sigmar's heart lurched with a spasm of grief as he beheld the once-noble features of Counts Siggurd and Markus. Their faces were pale and bloodless, lined with spiderweb patterns of empty veins, and their eyes gleamed red with hunger. Sigmar counted these men as his dearest brothers, warrior kings who had marched into the jaws of death with him and emerged victorious.

He had called them to his side time after time, and they had honoured their oaths to him without question. Now, when they had needed him, he had failed them. Their people were enslaved and their heroic lineage had been ended, each man cursed to an eternity of suffering and torment as a soulless blood drinker. They stared at Sigmar with undisguised thirst, fangs exposed and their bodies leaning forward, as though about to leap from their horses and bear him to the ground.

'You must forgive them their ill-manners,' said Khaled al-Muntasir with relish. 'They are little more than children, still driven by their own selfish desires and hunger. They have yet to master their appetites when in civilised company.'

'What have you done?' said Sigmar, overcome with anguish at the sight of counts.

'He has given us a great gift,' said Markus. 'One that can be yours if you so choose.'

'Gift?' spat Sigmar. 'You are both damned and you do not see it.'

He turned away from the vampires, disgusted and ashamed at what had become of them.

These abominations looked and sounded like his counts, but they were not Siggurd and Markus, and he wouldn't waste any words on the monsters that wore their faces. The brave men who had fought beside him at Black Fire and who had come to his aid at Middenheim were no more, and all that remained of them were memories.

Sigmar and his companions rode away from the vampire counts, each struggling with their emotions at the sight of the newest blood drinkers. Khaled al-Muntasir's laughter rang in their ears and Markus spurred his black horse forward to shout after them.

'We have been lifted from the mud of mortality,' the former count of the Menogoth tribe cried. 'Born anew to higher forms, and if you could feel what I feel, you would beg for my fangs to fasten on your neck!'

No one answered him. No one could.

THE SOUND OF hammers woke Govannon from a deep sleep, a percussive beat that set his whole room vibrating. It was dark, but that didn't mean anything. Since the dead had arrived it was always dark. He had thought that the loss of sunlight would not make much of a difference to him; his world was grey and lightless anyway. But even locked in his blind world he felt the crushing bleakness of a world without sunlight.

Though everyone in the city was afraid, including Govannon, he had no trouble in sleeping, for his work on the dwarf war machine had driven him past the point of exhaustion. He had yet to discover a workable fire powder compound, and his body was unforgiving in its protests at his treatment of it.

Rolling onto his side, Govannon yawned and stretched his tired muscles. He groped for his bearskin pelt, hanging on a hook beside the bed, and pulled it around his shoulders. The hammering was coming from below, but who would dare break into his forge to use his tools and materials without asking? They'd be in for a hiding, that was for sure. Bysen might have the mind of a child, but he had the right hook of a bare-knuckle fist fighter.

Govannon crossed the room, seeing nothing, but not needing to.

The layout of his room was well known to him. He reached down to wake Bysen, but found his son's bed empty and cold. It hadn't been slept in for some time, and Govannon's anxiety grew. Bysen was missing, and in that moment, Govannon was back at Black Fire Pass, desperately searching the infirmary tents for any sign of his boy.

He heard muffled voices from below, and reached for the knife wedged in the gap between Bysen's bed and the wall. The blade was sharp on both edges and triangular in section, meaning any wound it caused would never properly heal. It was a weapon of spite, but whoever had broken into his forge had more than earned that spite.

Govannon eased onto the stairs that led down to the forge, feeling the heat wash up from below on his skin. A blurred orange glow illuminated the lower level of the building, a glow that told Govannon his forge was burning hotter than it had ever burned before. The voices were punctuated with clangs of hammers on metal and sparks of white fire that penetrated even Govannon's limited sight. The air tasted of hot metal, burning coal and some nameless, actinic residue he couldn't identify. What in Ulric's name was going on down there?

Though he carried a knife, Govannon wasn't naïve enough to believe that he could defend himself from an intruder. Still, his forge was his domain, and anyone who thought otherwise was going to get badly hurt before they cut him down.

He counted twelve steps, made a turn to the right and then counted another ten. The heatwash from below was like nothing he had felt before, a rushing, all-enveloping fire that burned hotter than any forge he had ever known.

'Whoever you are, get out of my forge!' he bellowed, mustering as much of his warrior shout as he could. 'I swear to Ulric, I've a knife I'll stick in the neck of any bastard who tries to take me!'

Govannon saw two shapes beside the forge, one tall and hunched over, the other short and squat and swinging what looked like a short-handled sledgehammer. White sparks flew, each like a firefly of light that cut through his blindness in staccato flashes of clarity. The knife dropped from his hands as he saw Bysen by the roaring maw of the forge, lifting a gleaming sword blade from the anvil, where one of the mountain folk stood back with a monstrously heavy-looking hammer casually slung over one shoulder.

The sight faded with the white sparks and Govannon groaned as his vision became blurred and hazy once again. He heard Bysen's voice over the roaring of the forge.

'Da, you're here!' said his son, closing the door to the firebox with an iron-reinforced boot heel. 'I didn't want to wake you, da. But the dwarf man said it didn't matter none.'

The heat in the forge dropped as the firebox door shut, though it was still hot enough to take the chill off the unnatural cold that filled Reikdorf. Refugees clamoured to take shelter in the lee of the forge, as it was one of the warmest places in the city.

'Are you all right, da?' said Bysen. 'You need to go back to sleep?'

'I'm fine,' insisted Govannon, walking toward where he had seen the dwarf with the enormous hammer.

'You are Govannon, the blind manling smith?' said a gruff voice, pitched somewhere between irritation and condescension.

'I am,' he said. 'Who are you and why are you in my forge?'

'I am Master Alaric, Runesmith to King Kurgan Ironbeard of Karaz-a-Karak, and I am here to reclaim my property. You're in a lot of trouble, manling.'

'What are you talking about? You're not making any damn sense,' said Govannon, before the identity of the dwarf hit him between the eyes. 'Wait, Master Alaric? You're the smith who made the runefang. And Sigmar's crown.'

'Amongst other things,' grumbled Alaric in annoyance. 'I do make things other than trinkets for manlings, you know.'

'Of course, of course,' said Govannon, moving through the forge with the ease of one who had a perfect memory of its layout. 'It's a great honour to meet you. I've admired your work for years. I just wish I could have seen the Runefang Blodambana before I lost my eyes…'

'Bloodbane,' said Alaric. 'A good name well earned.'

'Bysen, fetch our guest some beer, the good stuff,' said Govannon.

'Aye, da. Right away, da,' said Bysen, moving past him. The sword blade he carried shone in the light, as clear to Govannon's sight as if he looked upon it with Cuthwin's keen eyes.

'Wait,' said Govannon, putting his hand on Bysen's arm. 'What is that?'

'It's Master Alfgeir's sword, da,' said Bysen. 'The mountain man helped me finish it.'

'He helped you…'

'Finish it,' said Bysen happily. 'Now all I need to do is take it to Master Holtwine and he can fit the handle he made for it.'

Govannon had all but forgotten about Alfgeir's sword, it had been so long since he had begun its forging. Though he had sworn to the Marshal of the Reik he would finish it before the snows, that had been an empty promise, for the work on the war machine had taken all his time and effort.

'Show me,' he ordered.

Bysen obligingly lowered the sword, and Govannon was amazed at the finished blade. Smooth beyond belief, the metal was pristine and etched with angular symbols along its centreline that sparkled with strange light. Though everything around him was as blurred as ever, the sword blade was sharp and clear, a vision of perfection that made Govannon's eyes wet with tears.

Gingerly, he tested its edges, not surprised to find that both were sharp beyond the ability of any human whetstone to grind.

He turned to Alaric. 'You did this?' he said, his voice choked.

'I came for something else, but saw that the blade needed doing,' said the dwarf. 'It's nothing, just some simple cutting and keenness runes.'

'I can see them,' said Govannon in wonderment.

'Some things are clearer than others, manling,' said the dwarf cryptically. 'Now, as to the matter I came here for. The baragdonnaz.'

'I don't know what that means,' said Govannon, finding it hard to think of anything but this perfect sword blade.

Alaric sighed, as though bored by his stupidity. 'The war machine Grindan Deeplock was returning to Prince Uldrakk of Zhufbar. The one to which you have made alterations unsanctioned by the Guild.'

'You mean the Thunder Bringer?' said Govannon, moving to the corner of the forge and removing the tarpaulin covering the war machine. Though he couldn't see it clearly, he ran his hands over its warm metal barrels. Alaric joined him and prised his hands from the metal.

'Is that what you call it?' said Alaric, shaking his head. 'Trust you manlings to call it something so bloody literal.'

'I fixed it,' said Govannon proudly. 'It took a while, but I got the metal densities in the end, though it took a lot of trial and error.'

'Fixed it? A bodge job if ever I've seen one. More errors than I'd expect from a hundred apprentices,' grunted Alaric, circling the war machine and tapping it with an iron-ringed knuckle. The dwarf listened to the sounds, grunting and harrumphing with each one, until he'd made a full circuit of the machine.

'What's he doing, da?' asked Bysen.

'I don't know,' said Govannon, angry that his finest work had been so slighted.

'I'm listening to the metal, manlings,' said Alaric. 'Which would be a damn sight easier if you two didn't keep jabbering on so.'

Govannon could contain himself no longer and declared, 'I managed to repair it, damn it, and I'll wager no other smith in the land could do what I've done. If I can just get the fire powder formula to work, then we might be able to shoot it.'

'Shoot it?' gasped Alaric. 'You want to shoot it?'

'Of course, what else would we do with it?'

'With an untested barrel made by manlings?' said Alaric, kicking the pile of iron shot stacked beside the war machine. 'And irregular shot too. Grungni and Valaya save me from manlings with ideas above their station! Even if I let you shoot the baragdonnaz, you'd likely blow yourself and anyone nearby to a thousand tiny burned pieces.'

'Now just wait a minute,' said Govannon. 'A lone Unberogen scout saved the life of the dwarf who hid this machine. Unberogen warriors found it and brought it back here. And an Unberogen smith fixed the bloody thing. The least you could be is grateful.'

'Grateful? For this?' snapped Alaric, squaring up to Govannon and planting his hands on his hips. 'Imagine your finest sword was found by a greenskin and then broken in two. Then imagine that greenskin bolted it to a rock he'd just dug out of a troll's dung pile and called it fixed. That's what this is to me.'

'Aye, well if I was surrounded by enemies I'd be grateful just to have a weapon in my hands,' snapped Govannon, weary of this dwarf's constant harping. 'In fact, I'd be damn glad of it.'

Master Alaric seemed to consider this for a moment. At last he sighed in resignation.

'You might have a point there, manling,' said Alaric. 'Very well, tradition is one thing, but an enemy at our throat is quite another. This is what I'll do, I'll make you enough black powder for a couple of volleys, but that's all. And you're to tell no other dwarfs of this.'

'So you'll help us make it work?' cried Bysen.

'I reckon I might,' said Alaric. 'Just make sure I'm nowhere nearby when you fire it.'

NINETEEN
The Last Night

As it always was, the air was fresh and cool on Warriors Hill. The stillness that surrounded the last resting place of the honoured dead of the Unberogen was a place of solitude, where a man could wander the tombs of his forefathers and reflect on all that had gone before him and all that had made him who he was. Sigmar remembered coming here on his Dooming Day, just after he'd broken Wolfgart's arm with a smelting hammer.

His father had sent him here to walk through the dead of the tribe and listen to the whispers of the ancestors. Entering the tomb of Redmane Dregor, he'd made offerings to Morr before being plunged into darkness. Trapped within the tomb, he had prayed to Ulric and the wolf god had given him the strength to free himself from his grandfather's barrow.

Sigmar circled higher on the hill, the flag-wrapped body of Eoforth held across his chest as he carried him uphill towards his resting place. The old scholar's body weighed next to nothing, and Sigmar was ashamed he had asked so much of this man, who had already given more than enough to his tribe and his Emperor.

The priests of Morr had spoken the words of warding over Eoforth's body, but even they could not say for sure whether that would be enough to resist the sorcery of Nagash. The only sure way to keep

Eoforth's remains from rising again would be to burn them, but Sigmar had balked at the idea of cremation. Eoforth would be interred within Warriors Hill, with the other heroes who had served the Unberogen.

Sigmar passed the tomb of Trinovantes and Pendrag, feeling his throat tighten and his eyes fill with tears as he thought of his lost friends. They had died in battle, and were drinking, feasting and hunting in the Halls of Ulric. No man could ask for more, yet Sigmar selfishly wished they were here beside him, fully armoured and standing ready to give battle against this dreadful foe.

At last he reached the tree-covered summit of the hill and laid Eoforth's body down on the stone slab at its centre. He unwrapped the flag, exposing Eoforth's face, and bent to kiss the old man's forehead.

'I will miss you, old friend,' said Sigmar. 'You kept me honest and true.'

Sigmar knelt and unhooked a small pouch from his belt, removing a bull's heart he had cut from the animal himself. He placed it in a bronze bowl set into the rock and poured a flask of oil across the bloody organ. Sparks from his tinderbox ignited the oil and the heart began to burn, slowly at first, for the muscular meat was tough and leathery. Eventually it caught and the heart fizzed and spat as the fire consumed it. The smell of the cooking meat filled Sigmar's nostrils.

'Father Morr, guide this soul to his final rest and watch over him as he passes from the lands of the living into the realm of the dead. Light his path through the Grey Vaults and keep the shadow hunters from his back as he makes his way to the Halls of Ulric. Judge him worthy, for no truer son of the Unberogen has come before you. Eoforth was a warrior without a sword, but thanks to his actions the world is a safer place. His peace was won with words and wise counsel, not with blades and war. Would that we could all be so wise. Guide him to his last rest, Father Morr, and I will preserve his memory for as long as I shall live.'

The heart hissed as it was consumed, the fire flickering with a purple light. The dancing flames lit Eoforth's face, and Sigmar stood, placing a hand on his friend's chest. A tomb had been dug on the eastern face of the hill, and with the offering to Morr complete, Sigmar bent to lift Eoforth's body once again.

Cold air brushed past him, carrying the whispers of ancient voices, fleeting sighs of long dead warriors and the murmur of ghostly war shouts. Sigmar looked down, seeing that the rune-etched haft of Ghal-maraz glittered with power. The hairs on the back of Sigmar's neck stood erect and he knew he was not alone. His hand slid down to his warhammer and he spun around, bringing the weapon up to his shoulder in one smooth motion.

The hill thronged with ghostly warriors, scores of them drifting uphill from their tombs with axes and unsheathed swords. They converged on the summit, and Sigmar knew he could never fight his way through so many. Alfgeir and Wolfgart had counselled against climbing Warriors Hill alone, but Sigmar had denied any attempt to provide him with a protective escort. It felt like the right thing to do at the time, but now seemed foolish and arrogant.

The spirits closed in, crowding the summit of the hill, and Sigmar took a deep breath, flexing his fingers on the textured grip of his hammer. The dead warriors were translucent, the wavering outline of trees visible through their immaterial forms. A fearsome Unberogen war cry died on Sigmar's lips as three figures stepped from the ranks of the spirit warriors, limned in shimmering winter's light.

Armoured in the style of many years ago, some in bronze, some in iron, they wore Unberogen war helms, and carried long swords that glittered with frostlight. Wolfskin cloaks hung from their shoulders and though Sigmar knew he should be afraid, nothing of these phantoms sent any tremors of fear through him.

The largest of the three snapped up the visor of his helm and Sigmar felt himself hurled back to his childhood as the stern features of his father were revealed. King Björn looked upon his son with loving, paternal affection, his lined and bearded face alight with pride.

At his father's right stood Pendrag, resplendent in the armour he had worn in the defence of Middenheim. Even the blade he bore was a shimmering likeness of the runefang Sigmar had commanded him to wield. On Björn's left was a young man, barely old enough to ride to war, and Sigmar's heart broke to see the youthful features of Trinovantes. Twenty-five years had passed since Trinovantes's death at Astofen, the first battle they had ridden to after their Blood Night, and Sigmar was amazed to think he had ever been that young.

Tears flowed freely at the sight of these heroic warriors, friends who had stood beside him in battle and the father who had set him on the path to becoming a man. Their legacy was the Empire and their role in shaping him into the man who would build it was immeasurable. Trinovantes – Ravenna's brother and Gerreon's twin – smiled at Sigmar, and though he wanted to say how much he missed them all, how much he had loved them, he simply couldn't. The words choked him, loss and grief like a powerful hand around his throat.

His father nodded, and he knew they understood.

The spectral army moved past him and he felt their pride in his accomplishments. They watched over him from Ulric's Halls and they were at peace, knowing the lives they had lost in defence of their homelands had not been given in vain. Sigmar lowered his hammer as the spirits of the dead Unberogen lifted Eoforth's body from the rock and moved off down the hillside to his open tomb.

Björn, Pendrag and Trinovantes turned away and began moving off again, their duty to Eoforth stronger than any dark sorcery that sought to break the chains of loyalty and duty that bound the Unberogen together. Sigmar had never been so humbled in all his life. To know that the blood of these great warriors flowed in his veins was the greatest honour Sigmar could imagine.

One by one, the soul lights of the dead began to dim. Trinovantes faded back into the mists of memory, and Sigmar raised a hand in farewell. He thought he saw Trinovantes smile, but couldn't be sure. Pendrag's form grew more and more insubstantial, until he too had vanished.

Eventually only Björn remained. He and Sigmar stood in silent communion, and of all the things that mattered in this world, his father's pride was the most important. Björn looked down at Reikdorf, and Sigmar saw a wry smile tug at the corner of his mouth, feeling his proud amazement at the magnificent city that had arisen from the small settlement he had known in life. His father pointed towards the city, and turned back to Sigmar.

Know them and understand them, for it will make you mighty.

The words were not spoken, but Sigmar heard them as clearly as though his father had been standing right next to him. King Björn nodded, knowing Sigmar had understood his message. He moved off into the darkness, and was soon lost to sight as his shade returned to the realms beyond the knowledge of mortals.

Sigmar sank to his knees, overcome with emotion. Ghal-maraz dropped to the ground and he buried his head in his hands. He wept as memories of his father and friends surged to the fore, but they were not tears shed in grief, but in remembrance of all the joy they had shared in life. At last his tears were spent, and Sigmar stood tall as he turned to look at the city below, heartened by the thousands of pinpricks of light that glittered in the darkness.

In the last month, the population had quadrupled, with thousands coming in from the countryside ahead of the rising tide of undead. Warriors, farmers and craftsmen thronged the city's streets, frightened and cold and hungry, but unwilling to give up.

Though a black host of the dead waited beyond the city walls, this island of humanity still stood inviolate. That alone was cause for hope, and as his father's last words echoed within his mind, he felt his gaze drawn up and out of his body, climbing into the sky and expanding to encompass the entirety of the Empire.

His awareness of the land was complete, and he saw the vast swathes of forests, rivers and hills. Flatlands and coastline stretched from the towering mountains of the south and east to the cliffs of the western wastelands and the frozen, ice-locked shores of the north.

Like a creeping sickness, the armies of Nagash spread throughout the Empire, hordes of the dead enslaved to the will of the ancient necromancer like war hounds on a fraying leash. Bound together by a web of dark sorcery with Nagash at its centre, the armies of the dead jealously strangled the life from the land of mortals. The southernmost reaches of the Empire were already enveloped in darkness, but across the Empire, scattered lights of resistance flared brightly against the encroaching shadow.

Sigmar saw the palisade forts of the Udose besieged by corpses of ragged flesh, while other clans were pushed into bleak highland valleys where they fought desperate battles for survival. Conn Carsten gave battle from the parapets of Wolfila's rebuilt castle, his army a patchwork of warriors from a dozen different clans. Welded together by the common foe, they fought as brothers, though they scrapped like bitter foes in times of peace.

In the east, Count Adelhard led daring hit and run attacks against the dead, riding at the head of glorious winged lancers, whooping with excitement as they charged hither and thither through the ranks of the dead with wild abandon. The Ostagoths did not build cities, their people living in settlements that could be broken down at a moment's notice and loaded onto wagons for transport. The dead had no focus for their assault, and the Ostagoth cavalry armies encircled and destroyed their enemies piecemeal.

The Cherusens and Taleutens took refuge behind the walls of their great cities. Krugar fought heroically on the spiked walls of Taalahim, the great crater city that nestled like a giant eye in the enormous expanse of the great forest. Always where the fighting was thickest, Krugar hewed the undead with glittering sweeps of Utensjarl.

Further west, Aloysis defended Hochergig with all the wild fury for which his kinsmen were famed. Forced to fight with every weapon available, many of the Cherusens chewed wildroot and drove themselves into bloody frenzies.

Atop the spire of the Fauschlag Rock, Myrsa and his warriors hurled the dead from the walls of their soaring city. The cliff-like sides of the rock writhed with climbing horrors, yet the city still held. Myrsa's runefang shone with simple purity, and where it smote, the dead could not resist its power.

Count Otwin's lands were near empty, his people scattered by the sudden invasion of the dead from the wastelands to the north-west. Long shunned by the living, these lands had vomited forth a ravening tide of the dead that had driven the Thuringians from their lands. Many now fought in Middenheim, or had since fled to Marburg.

Jutonsryk was a city of the dead, its streets empty of life and infested with degenerate cannibal creatures. Even if this war against Nagash could be won, Jutonsryk would forever be a forsaken and damned place, where no soul would seek to live again. Its great buildings and stone walls would fall into disrepair and within the span of a lifetime, no one would know that men had once lived there.

Further south in Marburg, the dead hurled themselves at the walls of a great citadel, but the defenders here were resolute and filled with determination to hold. Here, the power of the undead seemed weakest, as though a turning point in the battle for Marburg had been reached, and mortals now had the upper hand. Sigmar scanned the walls of the citadel for Count Aldred, but could not see the ruler of the Endals. Princess Marika and Count Marius fought side by side and when Sigmar saw the shimmering blue blade of Ulfshard in the Jutone count's hand, he knew with heavy heart that Aldred was dead.

Setting aside his grief, Sigmar's awareness of the Empire shrank until he found himself staring at Reikdorf once more. Despite everything that had been lost, Reikdorf remained. Enemies of the most terrible aspect stood poised to destroy it, but there was still hope.

Some people called hope a weakness, claiming it was foolish to trust in the world's inherent natural justice. Sigmar knew better. Hope was strength. Hope could drive men and women to the most incredible feats of heroism, from the everyday kindnesses between friends to the epic, world-changing feats of kings and warriors.

Sigmar smiled to himself, understanding that most world-changing events came about not through the actions of so called great leaders, but ordinary men and women driven to extraordinary heights of courage.

And as he had seen his land, so too he saw his people.

SIGMAR'S SIGHT TRAVELLED the streets of Reikdorf, seeing the strength that resided in every man and woman taking shelter within the city's walls. Though his body knelt atop Warriors Hill, Sigmar roamed freely through the city, flying over its thatched roofs and along its cobbled streets as though transformed into an invisible observer of life. He saw acts of tiny kindness between people who had never ventured further than the outskirts of their villages and who had been brought up to fear and mistrust outsiders; these people now shared what little food they had with those they would have fought only a few years before.

Here, an Asoborn woman offered bread to Brigundian children orphaned by the fighting, there an Unberogen family sheltered Taleutens and Endals within their home. In a silent, firelit dwelling in the northern quarter of the city, Orvin handed down his father's helmet to his son, Teon. The lad took the helmet, and even as he slid it over his head, Sigmar saw the shame that he had not been kinder to his old teacher. For his part, Orvin wished he could tell Teon how proud he was, but he didn't know how to begin. He loved his son, but a warrior's duty without a wife at his side had made them strangers. Instead, they simply sat and sharpened their swords and polished their armour in strained silence. Though there was no affection between them, both Teon and Orvin would fight for the Empire, and both would die if need be.

Sigmar passed onwards, seeing Freya coupling with Garr, the commander of the Queen's Eagles. This was the Asoborn queen's way, using sex as a means of wringing each moment dry of sensation and taking advantage of all that life had to offer. She was a passionate woman, and lived without compromise. Sigmar admired her for that, but knew she could never be his Empress. Freya would never be any one man's woman.

He did not linger on her lovemaking, but smiled as he saw Sigulf and Fridleifr practising swordplay in the other room. His heart ached to see these boys and not to know them, but to tear them from their old life for one they didn't know and wouldn't want would be a cruelty he could not inflict. These boys knew him as the Emperor, and would never know him as a father. Though it cut deeper than the sharpest sword, Sigmar knew it was the only thing that could be done.

Moving on, he saw Govannon the smith and his son, Bysen, with Master Alaric. They rolled the war machine they had been working on for weeks on end towards the eastern gates of the city. Elswyth was right, the blind smith would never willingly give up working, knowing all that would be left to him was a slow decline into death. To continue working gave him purpose, and that purpose kept him alive. Bysen was a hulking giant of a warrior, his mind left in tatters after Black Fire Pass. Both men had given so much in service of the Empire, but each was still willing to give more. Master Alaric had once again come to the aid of Sigmar's people, which spoke volumes of his character, for a dwarf's friendship was never given lightly. Sigmar was thankful every day that the irascible runesmith had seen fit to be his friend.

Alfgeir sat in the longhouse with his knights as they told bawdy tales and made proud boasts. Captain Leodan's Red Scythes drank here too. These men were eager for the coming fight, painting fire masks on their helms and images of the sun on their shields. If they were to fight in twilight, then they would bring their own light.

Leodan drank with his men, the barriers of rank broken down on this last night, but Alfgeir sat apart from his knights. He drank sparingly, bound to these fine Unberogen men, but apart from them. Thirty years separated him from the next oldest of his warriors, and where their thoughts were fixed on the battle to come, Alfgeir's were turned inwards, looking back over a life lived with honour and courage, but, ultimately, alone. In that respect, Sigmar felt more kinship with Alfgeir than any other man in Reikdorf. The Marshal of the Reik missed Eoforth, yet another thread linking him to his glorious youth cut away like a fraying rope that was on the verge of snapping. Where most men pushed thoughts of falling in battle aside, Alfgeir brooded on them – knowing his death was almost certain on the morrow.

Saddened, Sigmar flew on, passing Cuthwin and Wenyld as they drank and remembered happier times. Sigmar remembered catching the pair of them sneaking across the market-place to spy on the Blood Night before the ride to Astofen. Neither lad had been old enough to fight, and to see them as grown men was a stark reminder of how much time had passed since then. Though it had been many years since Cuthwin and Wenyld had seen one another, they picked up where they had left off, as though it had been only a few days. Such friendships were rare, and Sigmar dearly hoped they would survive tomorrow's bloodshed.

Lastly, he moved to the large house in the south of Reikdorf where Wolfgart and Maedbh lived. Once again its walls were warm and its welcome complete. Wolfgart and Maedbh and Ulrike lay curled up together on their bed, sleeping in each other's arms and content to pass this time together. Joy touched Sigmar at this sight, a man and his wife and their child together, all pretence and antagonism forgotten as the depth of their love for one another drove out all pettiness or recriminations. This had been Sigmar's dream before the hag woman had cruelly disabused him of the notion that he could ever aspire to such a life.

Knowing he could never have the simple pleasures of hearth and home, wife and child, Sigmar had made his peace with knowing that the Empire was his bride. He had sworn to love it and no other, and he had kept his faith with that, sacrificing his desire for love and companionship to be the man he needed to be in order to rule. Seeing Wolfgart and Maedbh, with Ulrike nestled in the protective embrace of her father, made that sacrifice worth every moment spent alone and without Ravenna by his side.

In that moment, Sigmar vowed that when this world was done with him, when he was ready to act upon his father's words, he would honour his promise to Ravenna. When the Empire was strong enough not to need him, he would walk the wolf's road he had been promised in Ulric's fire so long ago it felt like it belonged to the story of another man's life.

Sigmar flew up and over Reikdorf, understanding that the strength in every person came from the life each one treasured. That it could be snatched away at any moment made it all the sweeter, driving men and women to chase their dreams and make them real. The dead had no dreams, no ambition and no forward momentum. If Nagash defeated Sigmar and covered the world in shadow, then it would stagnate, becoming a barren rock bereft of life and light. To cheat death and achieve immortality was one thing, but to rule over a world of grey, ashen wastelands, populated only by the shuffling, mindless dead, was no life at all. What could any man want with such a prize?

High upon Warriors Hill, Sigmar opened his eyes, feeling a swelling sense of humility as he looked down on Reikdorf with his mortal eyes once more. He rose to his feet and walked back down the hill towards his longhouse. Beyond the city was darkness, an uninterrupted sea of shadow and death. Curiously uplifted by that, Sigmar found his fear of the dead had completely vanished.

The outcome of tomorrow's battle was unimportant.

That he fought in defiance of Nagash's lifeless, empty future was enough.

Sigmar would ride out and give battle, but he would fight with all the Empire at his back.

THOUSANDS HAD GATHERED to hear the Emperor speak, filling the square at the centre of Reikdorf with a press of bodies like the crowd at an execution. Sigmar looked up to see the twin moons slung low in the sky, as though eager to witness this moment. His closest warriors gathered around him and people hung from windows and gathered on rooftops, eager to hear what the Emperor had to say as the time of battle drew near.

Freya and her Queen's Eagles formed a ring around Sigmar, who sat atop his horse beside the Oathstone. His mount was a dappled grey gelding with a bright red caparison and a mane pleated with silver cord. Armoured in his dwarf-forged plate, Sigmar was a single source of brightness in the darkness, his armour gathering all the moonlight and magnifying it tenfold. Sigmar's head was bare, his long hair unbound and spilling around his shoulders. His pale blue and green eyes swept over the thousands waiting to hear him speak, and he felt their belief in him wash over him like a tide.

People of all tribes were gathered before him. They had asked much of Sigmar over the years, and now it was his turn to ask something of them. He knew they would not refuse him.

Sigmar lifted Ghal-maraz, and the ancient heirloom of King Kurgan glimmered with runic traceries as it sensed it would soon be set loose amongst the unliving.

'People of the Empire, we are besieged by an army of the dead,' began Sigmar. 'A dread necromancer from the dawn of time has invaded our lands, murdering our people and enslaving those he kills to march in his dread legions. He comes not for plunder or any reason conquerors give, but simply to drain the land of life. He comes to our city to retrieve a powerful crown, forged by his own hand in an age forgotten by all save Nagash himself. He must not succeed, for the crown has the power to enslave all the lands of the living. I cannot stand by and let this happen, and nor will you.'

Sigmar's voice grew in power as he spoke and saw the effect his words were having. They believed him, *really* believed him. They trusted him to deliver them from this terrible foe, but this was not a battle that would be won by one man, it would need to be won by *all* the people of the Empire.

He saw they were afraid, and Sigmar remembered what his father had said before he rode to Astofen. He recognised the universal truth of these words as he said them anew, like a father passing age-won wisdom down to his son.

'I know the fear that consumes your innards like a snake, but have courage, for we are living folk of flesh and blood! Feel your heart pumping that blood around your body; it is hot and vibrant, filled with all the passions of the living. Love, hate, joy, anger, fear, sorrow, happiness, exultation! Feel them all and you will know you are alive, that your soul is free and you are a slave to no one.'

Sigmar jabbed Ghal-maraz towards the east and shouted his last demand. 'It is the dead beyond our walls that shuffle and wail, crawl and cower under the spell of their dark master who should fear us! Though the sun is shrouded by shadow, I call upon you to take up your weapons and sally forth with me to meet this foul army.'

Thousands of swords were drawn from scabbards and raised high. Axes waved and spears stabbed the air as the people gathered in Reikdorf screamed Sigmar's name. The walls shook with the deafening volume and the carrion birds perched on the roofs and garrets of the city took to the air with raucous caws of fear. The swelling roar spread through the city, taken up by every living soul in Reikdorf, even those too far away to hear Sigmar's words.

'Together we will defeat the legion of Nagash,' shouted Sigmar. 'We will send him screaming to the underworld that waits to consume him. Rally, people of the Empire! Rally to me and fight!'

SIGMAR LED THE way through the streets of Reikdorf towards the splintered wreckage of the Ostgate. Behind him marched a column of tribesmen, thousands upon thousands of warriors, men and women, old men and young, mothers, daughters, fathers and sons. Those without swords carried iron-tipped cudgels, butcher's hooks, felling axes or clubs formed from broken furniture. Sigmar's army was everyone in Reikdorf, peasant and noble-born alike. They came with him, chanting his name like a mantra or a prayer, their belief in him like a force of nature or some divine mandate stolen from the gods themselves.

His boon companions rode at his side, and though this could very well be the last day of the Empire, Sigmar faced it with pride and courage.

High Priestess Alessa was waiting for him at the Ostgate, surrounded by a hundred warriors with their heavy broadswords drawn. She carried a heavy iron box, banded with silver and secured by a lock of the same metal. Dark earth clung to the box, as though it had only recently been dug from the ground. Sigmar could feel the dark power bound to the dread artefact within, remembering the foul deeds it had driven him to before.

'You are sure about this?' said Alessa, tears streaming down her face.

'I am,' said Sigmar. 'There is no other way to face Nagash and live.'

Alessa nodded, as though she had been expecting this.

'You will need to be strong, Sigmar Heldenhammer,' she said. 'It will tempt you with all the secret things you hold deep in your heart.'

Sigmar shook his head with a derisive sneer. 'It offered me my heart's desire once before and I rejected it. There is nothing else it can show me.'

'I hope you are right,' said Alessa, opening the box. 'Or else it will not be Nagash who destroys the lands of men. It will be you.'

TWENTY

The Battle of the River Reik

THE ARMY OF mortals poured from the ruined gates of the city, forming a great mass of flesh and blood in the land between the two forks of the river that converged within its walls. Khaled al-Muntasir saw Sigmar at the heart of this force, a figure in shining armour to match his own. A twinge of unease flickered in the vampire's chest, as though he were watching some magnificent Nehekharan host arrayed for ritual battle instead of a pathetic, desperate horde of mortals.

Sigmar took his place at the head of maybe three hundred horsemen, each atop a powerful, armoured steed, and each bearing a mix of swords, axes and spears. As more of the Emperor's subjects marched from Reikdorf, a shape began to form of Sigmar's plan, and Khaled al-Muntasir laughed as his unease was replaced by relief.

Another block of cavalry formed up beside Sigmar's, and great wedges of infantry formed up to either side of the horsemen. Some of these were disciplined and marched like they'd been given some training, but others were little better than ragged mobs. Give them a taste of blood and death and they'd run easily enough. Yet more cavalry rode onto the northern flank of the army, their armour red-painted and bedecked with suns. A handful of chariots and painted warriors took position by the southern fork of the river, and the vampire smiled as he recognised Freya's barely-armoured form.

'Some mortals just never learn,' he said.

'What do you mean?' asked Siggurd.

'They think they can win,' said Khaled al-Muntasir. 'Even after all that's happened, they still think they can win. Hope has undone them. Hope has sent them out here to die ingloriously instead of accepting the inevitable and prospering.'

'Sigmar will always think he can win,' said Markus. 'Until the blade cleaves his heart, I'll not be too sure he's wrong.'

Khaled al-Muntasir looked over at his creation and frowned. 'You think that pathetic force can best ours?' He looked out over Sigmar's army, trying to estimate how many warriors the Emperor had. 'He has fifteen thousand men at best. We outnumber him by more than two to one. He cannot possibly defeat so many.'

Markus shrugged. 'I've heard of battles lost with better odds.'

'Impossible,' sneered Khaled al-Muntasir.

'You don't know Sigmar,' said Siggurd, his black steed pawing the ground and snorting with impatience.

Once again, the tiny ember of unease in Khaled al-Muntasir's chest was fanned, but he quashed it ruthlessly. More than numbers would decide this battle. The terrible fear of the dead would unman many of the Emperor's warriors, and for every one of them that fell, another fighter would be added to the army of the dead. Though Markus and Siggurd had not yet developed their sorcerous powers, his own were formidable. But even they were a pale shadow compared to the magic of Nagash. With a word, the necromancer could command the dead to rise, the living to wither and die, and curse the skies to bring forth elemental fury.

No, his vampire counts were simply being overly cautious, yet the thought would not leave him that this last, desperate battle was in fact a ploy to lure them into a trap. His gaze swept the mortal army as it began a slow advance, skirling war horns, trumpets and drums driving the army towards the silent host of undead. Sigmar's horsemen pulled ahead of the main battle line, riding at speed towards the centre of Nagash's army.

Khaled al-Muntasir followed the line of Sigmar's charge, seeing where it led with a derisive bark of laughter.

'What's so funny?' asked Markus.

'Sigmar wants to duel,' he said in disbelief. 'He thinks he can face Nagash.'

At the centre of the army of the dead, the pillar of terror and ice that was Nagash bellowed with rage. Black lightning surged from the necromancer, a furious, blitzing whirlwind of dark magic that consumed hundreds of revenants around him. A roaring scream of rage and bitter spite cracked the sky, and a cold rain began to fall as the wounded heavens wept over the lands of men.

Khaled al-Muntasir felt the terrible force of the necromancer's rage and, moments later, realised its source. Riding ever closer to the army of the dead, Sigmar's head was held high, and upon his brow was the glittering majesty of Nagash's crown. It pulsed with silver light, its magic unseen by mortals, but visible as a ghostly corona of light around the Emperor's head. Khaled al-Muntasir had taken it for some cheap mortal bauble, enchanted with some hedge wizard's pitiful ward charms, but the dormant power coming off it in waves told another story.

'Blood of the Ancients…' hissed Khaled al-Muntasir, angered at the sight of a mere man wearing the crown crafted by the master of the dead. The incredible power bound to its unknown metals was not for some fleshy sack of blood and meat to wear, it was for the Lord of Undeath alone. Sigmar had worn the crown once before and it had almost destroyed him, but his strength of will had been enough to resist its siren song.

A terrible thought occurred to the vampire…

Had Sigmar mastered the power of the crown?

Was that what this was, a trap to lure the army of the dead to Reikdorf just to wrest it from Nagash?

'Ride out,' commanded Khaled al-Muntasir. 'Ride out now!'

SIGMAR FELT THE awful weight of the crown at his brow, its immense power threatening to crush his skull and invade his mind with all the terrible temptations of power it had offered him before. He had had Wolfgart's help to resist it last time, now he was on his own. Black thoughts of vengeance, power and dominance filled his mind, but knowing them for what they were, he was able to push them away for now.

To march to war at the head of so great a host of men was a truly magnificent honour, but facing them was an army of nightmares. The greenskin horde at Black Fire had been larger, but so had his army. And this foe could return from the dead…

A great mass of shambling dead opposed him, a ragged, shuffling horde of corpses in numerous stages of decomposition. Many wore the garb of Empire warriors or peasants, and he kept his anger in check, lest it feed the black sorcery of the crown. Dark horsemen rode to each flank of the enemy army and ravening packs of dead wolves and ghoulish cannibals roamed the banks of the southern arm of the Reik. The Asoborns faced this scattered horde of teeth and claws, led by Garr's Queen's Eagles and Freya herself. Sigmar saw the warrior queen atop a commandeered chariot, with Sigulf acting as her rider and Fridleifr as her spear bearer. Sigmar felt a knot in his gut at the sight of those boys going into battle, but they had been blooded already and would be again if they survived this fight.

Beside Sigmar, Wolfgart stood tall in his saddle, waving towards Maedbh. Her chariot sped along beside the queen's, with Ulrike and Cuthwin in the back, each armed with bows and many quivers of arrows blessed by the priests of Taal.

Wenyld rode next to Wolfgart, holding Sigmar's banner aloft with an expression of disbelieving pride. The rippling battle flag, with its glorious beast of legend picked out in gold, represented everything this mortal army stood for and was willing to die to defend. To carry it was the greatest honour, one that had fallen to Pendrag before his death. Though Sigmar had thought Wolfgart would want to bear the banner, he had instead preferred to carry his enormous sword. Sigmar understood, and Wolfgart's battle captain had taken up the banner. Thinking back to how he had first encountered Wenyld, Sigmar was pleased the banner would be borne by someone he knew.

Looking left and right, Sigmar saw his countrymen, warriors of all different tribes and lands. Scattered among the battle-trained warriors were cheering masses of farmers, craftsmen and labourers, men who had never faced battle until now. As glad as Sigmar was to have them march out with him, he knew they could not be relied upon to stand when the fighting became close and bloody.

In the moments before battle, the priests of each temple had given their blessings to the army, but instead of retreating behind the walls, each took up a heavy hammer, mace or cudgel and joined the battle line. With the exception of the priests of Ulric, no holy men fought with the army of the Empire, but Sigmar was happy to have the help of whichever god chose to aid them this day.

Far to Sigmar's left the Red Scythes rode along the line of the northern fork of the river, Leodan leading his warriors in an attempt to flank the enemy army and put their lances and heavy swords to good use. Sigmar rode at the head of one detachment of the Great

Hall Guard, while Alfgeir commanded the other. Both masses of heavy horse held the centre of the army, and Sigmar's entire strategy depended on their strength, speed and power.

Ahead of them, beyond the thousands of lurching corpses, ghostly revenants and rank upon rank of skeletal warriors, was a towering figure wreathed in black light and shimmering arcs of deathly energy. Sigmar could see Nagash clearly now, a boon from the crown no doubt, and he saw the incredible, unknowable power that seethed in his chest. Sustained by the darkest of magic, Nagash was immortal, invincible and deadly.

He felt the black gaze of the necromancer slide over him, a creeping chill that would have frozen his heart in an instant but for the power of the dwarf-forged plate that encased him. No sooner had that icy gaze felt what sat upon his brow than a hideous roar of fury shook the world and booming peals of thunder rolled across the landscape. Sheets of rain fell in cascades and brilliant traceries of lightning forked from the sky.

'Looks like you were right, old friend,' said Sigmar, thinking back to Eoforth's last words.

Even armed with that knowledge, Sigmar knew he would only get one chance to land a killing blow. He took a deep breath, whispering a prayer to Ulric.

'Is it time?' said Wolfgart.

'It's time,' said Sigmar. 'Sound the horns.'

The order was given, and all along the Unberogen line, a rippling series of horn blasts spread from the army's centre. Pipes and drums joined the crescendo, and even before the first echoes faded, the army of the Empire was on the move.

SIGMAR RAKED BACK his spurs and the gelding leapt to the charge. The ground between the forks of the river was hard-packed and flat, ideal cavalry terrain, and the sound of hoof beats was like the thunder booming in the heavens above them. Hundreds of heavily armoured horsemen kicked their mounts from a canter to a charge, yelling fearsome Unberogen war cries to banish the fear that tore at every one of them.

Wolfgart drew his heavy two-handed sword from his shoulder scabbard. The weapon was unwieldy to use from the back of a horse, but Wolfgart would sooner be defenceless than go into battle without such a blade. Wenyld held the banner high, gripping onto his horse with his thighs and stirrups as he swung the spiked ball of a great morning star in looping arcs.

Sigmar picked out the dead man he would slay, an eyeless corpse with thin, wasted arms hanging limply at its sides. His steed whinnied in fear and he lifted his hammer high.

'For Ulric!' shouted Sigmar, urging his horse to greater speed. 'For the Empire!'

Ghal-maraz slammed down and broke the corpse in two as the Unberogen cavalry struck the shambling mass of the dead in a deafening crash of iron and bone. The first ranks of the dead simply disintegrated as the unstoppable mass of horsemen crushed them with the speed and weight of their charge. Hundreds were trampled and broken apart in moments, hammers and swords and axes hacking a bloody path through the undead.

Sigmar kicked a dead man in the face, caving in the bone of his skull and backhanding his hammer into the chest of another. Ribs splintered and rotten meat sprayed from the impact. Emerald-lit eyes dulled as the corpse fell, but Sigmar was riding onward before the body had even fallen. Claws tore at his horse and his legs, but his armour was impervious to the broken nails and bony fingertips of the dead. The Great Hall Guard were the very best of the Unberogen, and these wretched specimens could not hope to halt their advance.

'Keep pushing!' shouted Sigmar. 'If we stop we are lost!'

Wenyld's morning star battered the dead from his path as he sought to keep up with Sigmar, and Wolfgart's sword clove living corpses in two with every blow. Sigmar's horse kicked out as he drove it onwards, iron-shod hooves breaking skulls and shattering rib cages as it fought as hard as its rider.

With Sigmar at their head, the Unberogen punched through the ranks of the corpse warriors, but this had been but a taster for the battle to come. These were the chaff of the dead, and served only to slow Sigmar's charge. The Great Hall Guard hacked, bludgeoned and sliced through the wall of corpses, punching through to the army beyond, where ranked up skeletal warriors marched towards them with spears lowered and shields locked together.

ALFGEIR MARVELLED AS his new sword cut through the necks of two dead men with flawless ease. It was half as light as he would have expected, yet it was perfectly balanced for his reach and strength. Wherever he swung the sword, it connected with the most vulnerable portion of his enemy, and he had left two score headless corpses in his wake. Its edge was keen beyond imagining and not a trace of grave dirt or blood befouled its surface.

Govannon had presented the sword to him as they gathered to hear Sigmar's words at the Oathstone. Together with Masters Holtwine and Alaric, Govannon had handed him the blade, hilt first, and apologised for the lack of a case.

Alfgeir had been speechless, overcome with gratitude that the smith had actually managed to fulfil his promise and finish the blade before the first fall of snow.

'If I live through this battle, I will commission a sword case from Master Holtwine,' he'd said.

'It will be my finest work,' Holtwine had said.

It was a sword of heroes, a blade that never failed to find its mark and clove to the very heart of its victim. Beyond the works of the dwarfs, no man had wielded a finer weapon. Too fine a blade to belong to one man alone; this would be the blade of the Marshal of the Reik for evermore.

Alfgeir fought with the skill and strength of a man half his age or less, showing the younger warriors how to fight like a true Unberogen. His two hundred knights fought just as hard, seeking to earn his favour with their faith and fury. While Sigmar's cavalry punched through the centre of the undead towards the necromancer, Alfgeir's riders angled their course towards the dead marching along the northern fork of the river.

Behind Alfgeir, Orvin and his son, Teon, fought the dead with crushing blows from their heavy broadswords. Orvin was a man quick to anger, with a temper that had made him few friends in peacetime, but which served him well in battle. His son wore an old bronze helmet with a white, horsehair plume. It was dented on one side from a blow struck more than forty years ago, and Alfgeir remembered the boy's grandfather wearing the helm. The dent had come from the axe blow that had panned in his skull. Alfgeir hoped the grandson would have better luck with it.

Orvin carried the white gold banner Sigmar had presented to Alfgeir upon his coronation as Emperor, and though no words had ever been spoken to make it so, it had become a kind of unofficial talisman for the Great Hall Guard. His warriors fought all the harder when it flew above them, so Alfgeir was happy for them to count it as their own.

Alfgeir chopped the arms from a corpse seeking to drag him from his saddle and pushed his mount through the press of crushing bodies. The banner flew proudly above the knights, a beacon of light for his warriors to rally around. Though fear of this foe threatened to overcome every one of them, none would falter while the white and gold banner flew. Wolfskin cloaks streamed at their backs as they broke through the shambling dead and came face to face with rank after rank of the warriors formed from bone and iron.

'Onwards!' cried Alfgeir, urging his steed onwards. 'For Sigmar and the Empire!'

ANOTHER WOLF HOWLED as it was crushed beneath the iron-rimmed wheels of Maedbh's chariot. Its remains rotted in an instant, and Ulrike loosed an arrow through the jaws of another beast as it leapt towards them. Beside her, Cuthwin loosed with calm precision, each shaft slicing home into the body of a wolf.

'Keen eyes!' shouted Maedbh, proud to have her daughter as her spear bearer and glad to have a warrior as cool-tempered as Cuthwin next to her.

After the terror of their first battles together, Maedbh had made peace with Ulrike riding to war. Wolfgart appeared to have done likewise, though she knew neither of them would ever lose their fear of her going beyond their protection. They knew the dangers that lurked everywhere in the world, but with this invasion of the dead there were few mortals who did not. She wished she could have fought this foe alongside her husband, but the back of a chariot was no place for someone unschooled in such a demanding form of warfare.

A dozen chariots, all that had survived the battle at the river, followed Queen Freya as she led the charge towards the rabid packs of death wolves and their disgusting companions. Now fitted with spinning iron blades at their hubs, the Asoborn chariots had already torn through scores of the undead wolves, slicing them and their ghoulish brethren apart. The Queen's Eagles and hundreds of Asoborn warriors, their skin painted in the manner of the ancient queens and their hair stiffened with resin, followed in the wake of the chariots.

Maedbh hauled on the reins, sweeping her chariot in a sharp turn as a pack of pallid-skinned flesheaters ran towards her. They ran with loping, bandy-legged strides, hissing as they clawed at her chariot. Ulrike put an arrow through the nearest creature's eye, and Cuthwin put another through the throat of the one behind it. Maedbh swept up her spear and slashed it around in a wide arc, opening the top of one of the hideous cannibals' skulls.

Freya loosed an ululating Asoborn war shout and climbed onto the upper lip of her chariot's armoured frame with her ancient broadsword unsheathed. Maedbh's heart swelled with pride to see her queen fight, a fiery goddess of war sent from the violent times before the Empire, when none dared to travel in Asoborn lands for fear of the warrior women said to dwell there with sharp knives and cruel hearts. Sigulf steered the chariot with great skill, and Fridleifr killed wolf and cannibal with graceful sweeps and thrusts of his spear.

'Mother!' shouted Ulrike.

Maedbh saw the flesheater too late and felt its claws slash down her back in lines of fire. She cried out in pain as it vaulted into the chariot. Keeping one hand on the reins, Maedbh slammed her elbow into its fanged jaw. Ulrike hammered her knife up and under its ribs. It squealed horribly as it died, and Cuthwin kicked it from the back of the chariot.

'Are you hurt?' asked Ulrike.

Maedbh couldn't answer. Already she could feel filth from the creature's claws entering her body and bit the inside of her mouth bloody against the pain. Her flesh burned where she had been cut and her side was sticky with fresh blood, but Maedbh was Asoborn and this pain was nothing to one who had given birth.

'I'm fine,' she hissed through gritted teeth.

'Are you sure?'

'I'm sure,' she snapped, harsher than she meant to. 'Watch our backs…'

Ulrike nodded, and Maedbh turned back to the fighting ahead of them.

They had cut deep into the swirling mass of wolves and flesheaters, and the hideous monsters fought all around them as the Asoborn infantry caught up with the slowed chariots. To anyone but an Asoborn there was no easily discernable shape to this battle, just a confused mass of circling chariots and intertwined warriors on foot, but Maedbh knew better. She saw how close they were to being overrun. Freya should command them to withdraw, reform and charge again, but Maedbh knew the queen would never give that order.

Maedbh looked over at Freya's chariot, so proud to be a servant of this magnificent woman and glad the gods had granted her this last chance to fight alongside her. She turned her chariot around, cutting the throat of a wolf with her wheel blades and looked to see where the queen was heading.

Maedbh saw the danger before Sigulf. Years spent anticipating threats to a chariot had given her a preternatural sense for when to charge and when to evade. She saw the enormous wolf, twice as large as its brethren, as the exposed muscles on its powerful back legs bunched and hurled it through the air.

'My queen!' she screamed, but it was too late.

The giant wolf's forepaws smashed through the chariot's armour as though it was dead wood. Freya flew through the air as the chariot flipped onto its side, dragging the horses down with screams of pain as their legs shattered. The queen landed hard, cracking her skull against a rock, and lay still. Sigulf vanished amid the wreckage, but Maedbh saw Fridleifr thrown clear, the boy rolling as he hit the ground and coming to his feet like a tumbler.

'Asoborns!' ordered Maedbh. 'To the queen!'

The flesheaters surrounded the fallen queen as Maedbh whipped the reins and drove her horses on. Arrows flew from Ulrike and Cuthwin's bows as hurled javelins skewered yet more wolves and eaters of the dead. Hundreds more pressed in, scenting easy meat and knowing on some primal level that they had the chance to earn their master's favour with this prey.

Leodan's warriors wheeled expertly around the advancing blocks of Unberogen infantry, feeling the ground grow soft beneath their horses' feet. This close to the river, the ground was already muddy, but the cold rain was in danger of turning it into a quagmire. The Red Scythes were the elite cavalry of the Taleuten kings, and though they owed fealty to the Emperor, it felt wrong riding into battle without Count Krugar in their midst.

The mass of dead opposing them was a limping, shuffling horde of corpses, unworthy of a blade, and without skill. Yet the sheer number of them, their hunger and their mindless aggression, could drag even the noblest warrior to his doom. Leodan tried to keep that in mind as he rode towards them with his lance lowered.

He kicked his spurs back, driving his horse to charging speed, and his riders followed suit, charging in a disciplined line. To maintain cohesion in such terrain and weather was nothing short of miraculous, but the Taleutens had been masters of mounted warfare since before their earliest ancestors had been driven across the eastern mountains.

'Strike fast and ride them down!' he shouted, lowering his lance and aiming it towards the chest of a dead man with a jawbone sagging on one rotten sinew. It was a waste to use lances on such dregs, but it wasn't as though they could sling them for later use.

The Red Scythes slammed into the corpses with a wet slap of hard wood on bloated meat. Leodan's lance punched his target into the air, ripping open its chest and splintering apart with the impact. His steed slammed through the press of bodies behind the dead man, trampling them to pulp beneath its weight. In a matter of seconds, Leodan was ten deep in the mass of enemy warriors. He dropped the broken lance and unsheathed his curved cavalry sabre, slashing it through the throat of a dead man clawing at his horse's face.

He slashed left and right as the dead pressed in, cutting off heads and lopping off rotten limbs held on by little more than glutinous tendons and scraps of gristly cartilage. His blade hewed dead flesh with ease, and his horse crushed bones with every kick. His warriors were unstoppable, riding through the mass of undead as though they were nothing more than a fleshy annoyance. The blood thundered in his ears as he destroyed these vile corpses. To ride into battle like this was to be a god, to tower over the enemy and slay them with impunity.

Leodan could imagine nothing worse than fighting on foot.

'Ulric damn you all!' whooped Leodan as the mass of corpses thinned and he knew they had broken through. This was the golden dream of every cavalryman, to break through the line before wheeling around to smash into the flanks and rear of the enemy army. He hauled on the reins and punched the air twice. Sheets of rain and the bleak darkness hid what lay beyond, but Leodan had no intention of continuing eastwards.

'Clarion! Reform and wheel right!'

A trilling trumpet blast sounded behind him and he caught a glimpse of the red banner of his troop as the rider carrying it rode alongside him. No one man ever had the singular honour of being the Red Scythes' banner bearer; it was passed between his warriors with every fight. Today it was borne by Yestyva, a man with a deadly lance and powerful sword arm.

The Red Scythes formed up with Leodan at their centre, and he snarled to see the inviting flanks of the ranked-up warriors of bone.

They would roll up this line and tear the unlife from this host. To think that they had feared these creatures was ridiculous; they fell more easily than any mortal man.

Leodan kicked his spurs back and held his sabre aloft and urged his warriors onwards. The rain shifted and he heard a faint clatter of bone and jangle of trace. The trumpet blew again and his warriors went from a trot to a canter, steadily building speed as they rode to glory.

He heard the rattle of bone and iron again, louder this time. The darkness and rain lifted for the briefest moment as an arcing bolt of lightning streaked across the sky. In that moment of brightness, Leodan saw his worst nightmare.

Hundreds of skeletal horsemen, heavily armoured in shirts of black mail, black breastplates and heavy caparisons of iron. The horses were fleshless, skeletal and quite dead. Green light burned in their eyes and their chamfrons were fitted with long, barbed spikes. Each of the riders leaned low across the necks of their horses, a long black lance aimed for the hearts of the Red Scythes. Too late, Leodan saw he'd been lured into this easy attack.

Their shields were long and kite-shaped, emblazoned with skulls and images of ancient kings, their banner a ragged, torn scrap of leathery flesh with a leering jaw spread wide. They came on in a thunder, lances lowering with hideous precision.

''Ware cavalry!' shouted Leodan, though he knew it was too late.

The black knights smashed into the Red Scythes, lances tearing through their armour and into their flesh. Men were hoisted from their saddles, screaming as the frozen iron of the enemy lances impaled them. Though seemingly fragile, the black steeds were as powerful as any mortal horse and punched into the centre of the Taleuten horsemen.

Leodan swayed aside as a lance speared past him, slashing his sword into the face of the black knight who bore it. His sword smashed the helmet from the dead warrior's skull, and sent him spinning from his horse. He wheeled as the two groups of horsemen became hopelessly entwined, a throbbing mass of warriors hacking one another from their saddles.

He plunged his sword through the neck of a dead man's horse, taking grim satisfaction as it fell apart beneath him. Leodan spun in his saddle as the clamour of battle thundered in his ears and the sky split apart with yet more lightning. Rainwater streaked his face and all he could see were flashing blades, grinning skulls beneath iron visors and blood spraying from mortal wounds. The bloody banner of the Red Scythes still flew proudly and he spurred his mount towards its glorious colours.

Before he could reach it, a thundering juggernaut of red iron and black-edged death smashed into his horse and hurled him from the saddle. He landed badly, slamming into the ground with a crack of breaking bone and the breath driven from his lungs by the fall.

Dizzy with the impact, Leodan knew at least one of his ribs was broken. He tried to stand, but pain shot up his leg and he crumpled onto one knee as the splintered ends of his shinbone ground together. Gritting his teeth, Leodan looked up and saw the enemy that had unhorsed him.

A monstrous, hulking warrior in blood-red armour towered over him, its frost-limned armour burning with a glaring rune of an ancient, bloody god. Its horned helm covered a grinning skull face with burning fire in its dead eyes.

A dread battle cry roared from the warrior, a chant and a mantra from the beginning of time, but no less potent for the vast span this champion had been dead.

Blood for the Blood God!

'Ulric save us…' wept Leodan.

THE GREAT HALL Guard smashed into the ranks of skeletal warriors and tore through their front ranks in a hammering thunder of beating iron. Alfgeir's sword sliced down through a bronze pot helmet and into the skull beneath. He wrenched the blade free and beheaded another two skeletal warriors, their armour no protection against his rune-forged weapon.

Orvin fought at his side, hacking down the dead with furious blows of his heavy broadsword. The man screamed as he slew, using his fear and turning it to anger. Teon fought at his side, his own sword arm rising and falling like a blacksmith at the anvil. The youngster had not the ferocity of his father, but he had speed and skill beyond anything Orvin could muster.

A spear jabbed at Alfgeir. He twisted in the saddle to cut the point from the shaft, following through with a lancing blow that split the dead warrior's ribcage apart. Like the shambling corpses, these dead were no match for Alfgeir, but where those first foes had little ability in battle, these dead had been warriors in life and fought with remembered skill. Swords flashed, spears thrust and the enemy plucked men from their mounts with every passing moment.

The momentum they had won from their charge was quickly spent, and every yard would now be paid for in blood. Alfgeir bellowed the name of Ulric as he fought, driving his aged body to heights of aggression and fury he had never known. The dead surrounded them, a mass of grinning faces, leering jaws and eyes filled with green bale-fire. Their rusted swords cut and slashed, bringing down horses and men with their unearthly magic.

He heard a wild horn blast, seeing Sigmar over to his right. The Emperor's band of horsemen crushed a path through the ranks of skeletal swordsmen. Wolfgart rode at Sigmar's side, cleaving a path with his enormous two-hander, and Alfgeir wished he could have ridden with the Emperor.

'On, damn you!' shouted Alfgeir as thunder boomed overhead and the rain beat down with ever greater force. 'The Emperor rides on and we should be with him!'

Orvin and Teon pushed next to him, fighting to clear a path through which they could match the Emperor's charge. The noise of the storm overhead sounded like a great battle was being waged in the heavens, echoing the conflict being played out in the mortal realms below. For all Alfgeir knew, that might well be the case. Perhaps they were all merely pawns of the gods, cursed to fight their wars on the face of the world while the gods were embroiled in their own nightmarish battle for survival.

'We're with you!' shouted Orvin, and Alfgeir nodded as more and more of the Great Hall Guard pushed through the mass of slashing blades, rallying for another push into the ranks of the dead. If they could recover their momentum, they could still reach Sigmar.

Orvin cried out as a black sword plunged into his stomach, a plate-clad champion of the dead driving it through his body with a powerful two-handed grip. Orvin toppled from his horse and Alfgeir cried out as the banner fell with him. He swept his sword down through the enemy warrior's blade. It shattered and the weaponless champion turned its dead eyes upon him. Alfgeir froze as he saw death in those eyes. Not the prospect of death, but the *exact* moment his life would end. His sword arm fell to his side and his lungs failed to draw a breath. A shooting pain spiked into his left arm and he cried out as the sword fell from his grip.

The champion swept up a fallen spear and lunged towards him.

Another blade intercepted it, and Teon lanced his blade through the champion's visor. The skull broke open and the hellish green light was extinguished from its eyes. Alfgeir's breath returned with a whooshing roar in his ears, bright spots of light bursting before his eyes.

'Father!' shouted Teon, leaping from his horse and holding his father's head.

Alfgeir tried to shout at him to get back on his horse, but his throat was tight and his chest afire. The fighting swept around them, and the youngster wept as the muscles in his father's face went slack and Morr claimed his soul. Alfgeir felt their chance to counter-attack slipping away, and shuddered as a deathly chill crept over him.

He had felt something similar when…

'I think you dropped this, Alfgeir,' said a voice that cut through the clash of swords and spears. 'It's very nice work. Careless of you to have lost it.'

Alfgeir turned his horse to see himself facing a warrior in midnight black plate, with a white, bloodless face and eyes red with blood-hunger. Count Markus turned Alfgeir's sword in his hand, admiring the silver runes etched along the length of the blade.

'Yes,' said Markus. 'I think I may keep this weapon after I kill you with it.'

≺ TWENTY-ONE ≻
The End is Nigh

MAEDBH LEAPT FROM her chariot as it came to a halt beside Freya's body, her spear skewering a flesheater as it bent to take a bite. She swept the spear around, hurling the beast from the tip and standing over the fallen queen. Blood leaked from a wound at Freya's temple, and pooled around her mouth. Maedbh didn't have time to check if the queen was alive.

Ulrike and Cuthwin took up position next to her, loosing arrows into the mass of wolves circling them. Each shaft punched through a dead beast's side, while Fridleifr and Maedbh kept those that survived the arrows at bay with looping swings of their spears.

'Ulrike! Look to the queen!' ordered Maedbh. 'And find Sigulf!'

A wolf howled as it reared up over Maedbh, but before it could pounce, a leaf-bladed spear punched through its chest and it fell to the ground in pieces of rotten meat and mangy fur. Fridleifr pulled his spear back from the beast's body and Maedbh nodded her thanks as the monsters closed in.

'Is she dead?' asked Fridleifr, without looking down.

Ulrike shook her head, and Maedbh felt a wave of relief that almost blotted out the pain from the wound on her back. Her limbs were aching, her head thumping with a powerful headache. Her skin was clammy and cold.

She slammed the end of her spear against a flesheater's head, reversing it to plunge the blade into the belly of a wolf. Its weight bore her to the ground, and the haft of her spear snapped. Maedbh rolled, spying a leather-wrapped sword handle amid the wreckage of the queen's chariot. She grabbed it and spun around, swinging it two-handed to cleave a flesheater in two with one blow. Amazed, Maedbh saw she held the bronze-bladed sword of Queen Freya. It had once belonged to Eadhelm, who claimed to have looted it from a secret chamber beneath a tower of the stunted ones beyond the mountains of the east.

Maedbh rolled to her feet, the pain of her wounds forgotten as the vital energies of the sword filled her body with strength and lustful thoughts.

'Mother!' shouted Ulrike, hauling Sigulf from the wreckage. The boy was bloody, but conscious, and gripped his sword tightly.

'Can you fight?' Fridleifr asked her.

Maedbh's lip curled in anger. Of course she could fight! With this blade she could fight for a year and never get tired. Dimly she recognised this was the sword's anger and battle fury talking. Maedbh let it come, knowing she would have need of it before the day's end.

Fridleifr fought with his spear in one hand and a hammer in the other. His skill and strength were beyond compare, each powerful blow caving in a skull or opening a belly. His blond hair shone in the low light, and his features were the image of his father's. Garr and the Queen's Eagles rushed to surround their fallen queen, as yet more of the undead pressed in.

Wolves circled them and the eaters of the dead squealed and chattered as they darted in to slash with their decaying claws. Ulrike stood over Freya, wiping blood from her face and speaking to her in soft tones. Cuthwin emptied his quiver and drew his hunting knife, but Maedbh knew he'd need more than that to survive this fight.

'Can we hold them?' shouted Cuthwin.

Maedbh nodded, then saw the mass of skeletons atop iron-clad steeds riding towards them. The Asoborns were scattered and disorganised, gathered around their queen and without cohesion. A cavalry charge would ride right over them.

'Shield wall!' shouted Fridleifr.

SIGMAR BATTERED THROUGH the ranks of the dead, his hammer clearing a path with every thunderous blow. Nothing could stand against its power, living or dead, and though every yard gained was a struggle, the Unberogen horsemen fought like heroes from the sagas beside their Emperor. He could feel the power of the crown straining at the edges of his control, pleading and begging to be allowed to help him.

Part of Sigmar wanted to let it, to use the power of its maker in the fight to defeat him, but he knew the crown's greatest strength lay in the lies it could spin. It had ensnared him atop Morath's tower with such blandishments, and he knew better than to trust its honeyed words.

The dead clawed at them in a frenzy, a host of biting, clawing corpses and armoured warriors of bone. His warriors fought them back with crushing blows from hammers, swords and axes, their fighting wedge pushing deep into the enemy ranks. The dead were slowing them down, but not enough to prevent them from breaking through.

At last the skeletons were smashed aside and the Unberogen circled, ready to reform and charge onwards. Sigmar reined in his horse and the rest of his warriors brought their horses to a standstill. Their horses were blown and lathered, exhausted by their ride. Sigmar's breathing was laboured, for the fight had been a hard one, and his hammer arm ached from such destruction.

Wolfgart rode alongside him, his face bloody and his mighty sword notched from the many blows he'd struck. His mail was torn and plate dented, but none of the blood coating his flesh was his own. Wenyld lifted the banner high and a roaring cheer burst from every Unberogen throat. Sigmar saw Wenyld's face was ashen, and blood streamed down his leg.

'Can you ride?' he asked the younger man.

'Aye, my lord,' said Wenyld, breathlessly. 'I was careless. Took a spear thrust a moment ago. It's nothing.'

'I've seen my share of wounds, boy,' said Wolfgart. 'That's not nothing.'

'I'll ride with you,' stated Wenyld, and there was no disagreeing with him.

'Ulric keep you,' said Sigmar, sharing a glance with Wolfgart.

Wenyld saw it and said, 'Don't worry, if I'm going to die on you I'll hand the banner over first. Can't have it falling, eh? Not now.'

'Not now,' agreed Sigmar, turning his horse and taking a moment to survey the battle. It was difficult to see much through the mass of the dead and the unnatural darkness, but he saw enough to know that they had little time to waste. The northern flank was in danger of collapsing, the Red Scythes embroiled in a furious battle with mounted black knights and a terrible avatar of destruction, while a mass of wolves and shambling corpses swept past the Asoborns towards the city walls. He couldn't see what had become of Freya, and Alfgeir's riders had become bogged down in the ranks of the skeleton warriors.

'We're on our own here,' said Wolfgart, seeing the same thing.

'Looks that way,' said Sigmar. 'But I always knew that would be how it ended.'

'Then let's finish this before I lose my nerve,' said Wolfgart, hefting his sword over his shoulder and wiping the blood from his face. 'All these men dying around us will be for nothing if we can't get through to that bony bastard.'

Sigmar nodded, searching the darkness ahead for Nagash. The necromancer was not hard to find, a towering black form atop a low hill beyond the road. Swirls of sable smoke coiled around Nagash, his undying body a black tear in the fabric of night through which all the cold of the Grey Vaults leached into the world.

Unberogen horsemen formed up on the banner, bloodied and weary after their long ride, but hungry for more.

'Our foe is within reach!' shouted Sigmar, pointing Ghal-maraz towards the hill upon which stood the necromancer.

'On! On!' cried Wolfgart in answer.

And the charge began again.

WHILE SIGMAR PUNCHED through the hordes of the dead, the people of Reikdorf marched in defence of their city. Positioned behind the main battle line, they were thrilled and terrified, clutching makeshift weapons in the hope that they would not have to use them. It had been all too easy to follow Sigmar and his warriors through the ruined Ostgate on a wave of exhilaration, but as the rain battered down and the darkness closed in, fear returned to erode the fragile courage that had been built within the city walls.

In the centre of the mass of people gathered to the south of the gate Daegal felt his terror climb to new heights. He had fought the army of Khaled al-Muntasir by the river and terror flowed through his veins at the thought of facing the army of the dead once more. He knew it had been his cowardice that had seen the Asoborn army break, his panic that had spread to the warriors around him and caused the defeat.

Too ashamed to ride out with his fellow tribesmen, he had hidden within the city and managed to avoid anyone that knew him. Instead, he had been swept up in the borrowed courage of Reikdorf's people and found strength enough to march with them to this patch of ground before the walls.

'Please don't let me fail again,' he whispered to the gods.

KHALED AL-MUNTASIR WATCHED the battle unfold, admiring the strength of purpose invigorating this mortal army. He had fought for Nagash since before leaving Athel Tamara, and had been less than impressed by the skill and resilience of this northern empire. How could such a people claim to be the masters of this land?

Then he had fought the remnants of the Asoborns at the wooded hill, and the first chinks of doubt had entered his mind. Now, as Sigmar drew ever closer, Khaled al-Muntasir found himself wondering if he had grossly underestimated this barbarian Emperor. True, his people were little better than savages, but they possessed a primitive nobility that had surprised him. Individually they were weak and pathetic, but welded together by Sigmar, they were stronger than even they knew.

Khaled al-Muntasir glanced towards Nagash, wondering if he too had underestimated these mortals. It seemed absurd that he should entertain such doubts, for the host of the dead was already beginning to envelop the mortal army. Krell was butchering the warriors in the north, and the south was on the brink of collapse. The carrion eaters and corpses were already moving on the city walls, and Markus would soon end the resistance in the centre.

So why did he still feel so uneasy?

His black steed tossed its head, snorting and stamping the ground as it smelled the blood on the air. It was impatient to join the slaughter, and its hide steamed in the relentless rain cascading from the sky. Khaled al-Muntasir lifted the lank fabric of his cloak, knowing the material was ruined.

He jerked the reins of his mount, and turned his horse to the north.

Nagash's cold gaze fell upon him and he felt the necromancer's displeasure.

'The northern flank is holding out,' said Khaled al-Muntasir. 'I will take some riders and break it open.'

Nagash didn't answer, his attention firmly fixed on the glittering crown upon Sigmar's brow as the Emperor rode straight for him.

Khaled al-Muntasir drew his sword and rode north, grateful to be free of that frozen, penetrating gaze.

The vampire looked to the east, to the lands already taken by the dead, and saw moonlight glittering from distant spires and forgotten castles perched high on rocky bluffs. He smiled to himself, picturing a reign of terror that could be unleashed from such a lair.

'Yes,' he said to himself. 'That would be very fine.'

ALFGEIR WATCHED AS the thing that had once been Count Markus of the Menogoths circled him, swinging the sword Govannon had forged for him. Death had erased none of the swordsman count's skill with a blade, and Alfgeir knew he could not prevail against him. Markus saw the defeat in his eyes and licked his thin, bloodless lips.

'Why don't you come down off that horse?' said the vampire. 'Make it a fair fight?'

'You have my sword,' said Alfgeir. 'How is that a fair fight?'

'True,' smiled Markus. 'Come down anyway. I can kill you just as easily on the back of your horse, but at least on foot we'll be eye to eye.'

'Fair enough,' said Alfgeir, unhitching an axe from the back of his saddle. It was a short-hafted axe, a backup weapon, and would be a poor defence against his own sword. Though the dead pressed in all around, the Great Hall Guard held them back. There was no way they could now ride to Sigmar's aid, and the bitter gall of failure tasted of ashes in his mouth.

Markus spun the sword, its glittering length moving like a snake in the vampire's grip. Alfgeir remembered fencing the Menogoth count in a friendly duel many years ago. It had been a humbling experience to be so outclassed when he rated himself highly as a swordsman.

Alfgeir faced the blood drinker, quelling his hatred for this thing that wore the face of an honourable man. He felt the ice of the vampire's nearness, gritting his teeth against its chill. Markus took up the en garde position, and Alfgeir lunged forward, the axe blade chopping for the vampire's head.

Markus stepped back, rolling the sword around Alfgeir's axe and stabbing the tip through his pauldron and into his shoulder. Alfgeir tried to shut out the pain, but it spread to his chest and he staggered. The vampire spun around Alfgeir, slashing the sword across his other shoulder and neatly slicing away his other pauldron.

'Come on,' sneered Markus. 'I remember you were better than this. Not much better, it's true, but better nonetheless.'

'That was ten years ago,' grunted Alfgeir, pushing himself upright.

'Really? You've aged badly, my friend.'

'Ulric damn you to the Grey Vaults,' hissed Alfgeir. 'You are not my friend!'

Markus came at him again, his sword dancing like a forking bolt of lightning as it whipped around Alfgeir's clumsy axe swings. Time and time again, the blade licked out and cut pieces of his armour away. Alfgeir was left bloodied and in pain with each blow.

'Kill me and be done with it!' bellowed Alfgeir, and Markus stabbed the sword an inch into the muscle of his thigh. He bled from a dozen wounds, none serious enough to kill him, but all painful enough to sap his strength with every passing second.

'Nonsense,' replied Markus. 'You haven't even begun to fight properly yet.'

Alfgeir lifted his axe again, but Markus spun around him, the sword cutting down in a blur of rune-etched silver. Agonising pain shot through Alfgeir's body, and his vision filled with white light as he reeled from the blow. His entire body was a furnace of agony. He tried to lift his arm to strike one last, desperate blow, but his body wouldn't obey him.

He saw the axe lying on the ground.

Next to the axe was his arm.

Alfgeir stared in open-mouthed shock at the neatly severed stump where his right arm had been. There was no blood, so clean and cold had the wound been cut. Horror drove him to his knees, and he fought to hold onto consciousness as the terrible nature of his maiming threatened to overwhelm him. His breath came in sharp hikes of panic.

Markus circled him, the stolen sword spinning in his grip as he looked down at Alfgeir.

'Such a shame, you would have made a fine lieutenant,' said the vampire.

'To you?' hissed Alfgeir. 'Never.'

'I suppose not,' agreed Markus, raising the sword for the deathblow.

Though the duel had been fought in isolation until now, a figure hurled itself at the vampire, one with a dented bronze helm and a heavy broadsword. Teon slashed his sword at Markus's neck, but the vampire was faster than any mortal opponent, and the tip of Teon's blade passed less than a finger's breadth from his neck.

Markus cut high with his sword and the edge slammed into the side of Teon's head.

'No!' shouted Alfgeir.

The sword bounced upwards, deflected from its decapitating course by the dent in the side of the helm to slice off the horsehair plume. Teon fell to the ground with a cry of pain, the sword spinning away and landing upright in the marshy ground. Alfgeir snatched up the fallen axe in his left hand and hurled himself at the vampire. Markus brought his sword up to block the crude attack, but Alfgeir had no intention of going blade to blade with the vampire.

He let go of the axe, and it spun through the air toward the vampire. It struck him full in the face and Alfgeir heard bone break over Markus's shriek of pain. Instinctively, he dropped the sword as his hands flew to his face to stem the tide of dead blood. Alfgeir dropped to the ground, his strength spent in this last, futile act of defiance.

Through tear- and rain-blurred vision, he saw the handle of his sword lying in the mud at the vampire's feet. He wanted to reach out and grab it. Though it was no more than a foot away, it might as well have been a thousand yards. He closed his eyes as the world went grey and he heard the sweet sound of wolves in the distance.

A cold, winter wind blew from the north and Alfgeir felt his limbs fill with the strength of the pack. He reached out towards the sword, feeling an ice-frosted hand that was more like a clawed paw place the handle in his palm.

His fingers closed on the weapon and he opened his eyes. Snow swirled where no snow had been before and the world around him moved as though slowed to the pace of a glacier's advance. He saw droplets of blood hanging in the air, a bolt of lightning tracing a leisurely path across the heavens and the frozen breath of nearby warriors gradually expanding from their lips. Markus turned slowly towards him, his face a mask of dark blood and his red eyes filled with terrible hunger. Long fangs jutted from his jaws and his hands had become elongated claws.

Alfgeir surged to his feet, he alone able to move normally. With a roar of hatred, he sliced his sword in a sweeping arc towards the vampire. He had a moment to savour the gelid onset of fear in Markus's eyes before the blade cut into his neck and parted his head from his shoulders. No sooner had the blade connected than the normal flow of time reasserted itself. Blood spattered, lightning blazed briefly and breath vanished.

Markus collapsed to the ground, his body crumbling within his armour as decay claimed the flesh feast denied it with the blood kiss. Burning with inner embers, the vampire's body became ashes in moments, a ghostly shriek of torment exploding outwards from its demise.

Alfgeir stood on trembling legs for a second until he could stand no more. He sank to his haunches, utterly drained, and slumped over onto his back. He looked up into the sky, seeing a clear patch where the stars shone through the ghastly canopy of darkness. In the distance he heard wolves again, and smiled as the hurt of his wounds vanished.

He felt hands beneath him, lifting him upright, and the pain returned with a vengeance.

'Alfgeir!' shouted Teon. 'Ulric's bones, how did you move so fast?'

He tried to tell the lad to let him go, that Ulric was calling to him, but the sound of wolves faded into the distance and tears spilled down his cheeks.

'Ulric isn't ready for me yet,' he whispered.

'Nor me it seems,' said Teon, and Alfgeir saw how lucky the boy was to be alive. The vampire's blow had taken the plume and the top portion of the helmet, but it had missed the boy's skull by no more than the width of the blade.

'Looks like you were luckier,' said Alfgeir.

'Luckier than who?' asked Teon, tearing off his cloak and wrapping it around Alfgeir.

'Never mind...'

Teon lifted Alfgeir into his arms and he grunted in pain. He looked at the young man, seeing the grief for his fallen father, but also a strength of character his father had not possessed. Despite the pain, Alfgeir smiled, wondering if this new-found clarity was a result of his near death.

Teon looked down at him. 'Chosen by Ulric you are,' said the boy.

'What? No, I was lucky is all.'

'No,' said Teon, lifting Alfgeir onto a horse and climbing up behind him with the white gold banner tucked in the crook of his arm. 'Look at your eyes, man. You've been chosen.'

Alfgeir lifted his sword blade as Teon turned the horse back to Reikdorf. His face was gaunt and pinched with pain, his leathery skin ashen from exhaustion. He looked into his reflected eyes and a cold breath escaped him.

His eyes were pure white, the hue of northern snows.

* * *

LEODAN THREW HIMSELF to the side as the titanic warrior's black axe swept down, cleaving his fallen horse in two with one blow. Searing pain flared up his leg and he crawled away from this towering slaughterman. Its black axe came up and a hissing name burned itself into Leodan's mind, a name that was a byword for death on an undreamed of scale in ages past.

Krell...

Rivers of blood had flowed from Krell's axe, all in service to a dread god of the north, a squatting devourer of blood and skulls. Slain by one of the mountain folk thousands of years ago in an age known by some as the Time of Woes, Krell's thirst for blood and death was undiminished by the passage of uncounted centuries since his death.

Leodan fumbled for his sword, watching as five of the Red Scythes charged towards the giant warrior.

'No,' he croaked. 'Don't!'

His warning went unheeded, and Krell's axe swept out, chopping up through the horses and cleaving the riders in two. The return stroke hacked another two to the ground and before the others could strike, Krell was amongst them. One rider died with his head torn from his shoulders, the other as Krell thundered his fist into his chest and crushed his torso to a pulpy mess.

Taleuten warriors surrounded Krell, hacking at his blood-covered plate, but no blade could penetrate his damned armour. Swords scraped over his shoulder guards, axes bounced from his spiked helm and spears shattered upon his breastplate. Nothing could stand against this monstrous force of destruction, and warriors died ten at a time as Krell hacked them down, chopping bodies in two and mangling flesh with every blow from his black-bladed axe.

Leodan crawled away from Krell, weeping in pain and for the loss of his beloved Red Scythes. His leg was afire, the broken ends gouging the meat of his leg with every yard he dragged himself from the slaughter.

His world shrank to the rain-soaked ground, his muddy knuckles dragging his pain-wracked body and the sound of his men dying. Horses screamed in pain as Krell's axe butchered them too, and men cried in fear as they turned to flee. None could escape Krell's deadly blade and those terrified cries turned to death screams as the Red Scythes were cut down.

Leodan's fingers clawed the ground, the earth too sodden for him to gain a purchase. He could go no further and he rolled onto his side. His breathing was coming in shallow gasps, and he coughed blood. His broken rib had nicked his lung and few survived such a wound, least of all those in the middle of a battle with no hope of rescue.

He heard the sound of marching steps behind him, regular and perfectly in time. Metal clashed as armour moved against armour and Leodan smelled the reek of strong beer and pipe smoke. Who would be drinking and smoking in the middle of such a fight?

Someone knelt beside him and he looked up through a haze of tears and rain to see a hundred warriors of the mountain folk armed with heavy axes and hammers. The warrior beside him was armoured head to foot in plates of iron and bronze. The dwarf's breath smelled of strong beer, and a wooden pipe carved in the shape of a long cavalry horn jutted through a hole specially crafted in his helmet's visor.

'Rest easy, manling,' said Master Alaric. 'We'll handle this big fella. We killed him once before, and we can do it again.'

DAEGAL WATCHED THE black riders charge the Asoborn shield wall and heard the crash of splintering lances, breaking shields and the clang of swords. His mouth was dry and his bladder tightened. The riders of the dead surrounded the Queen's Eagles and he couldn't see any way they could survive.

'I am a warrior of the Asoborns,' he said, repeating the words like a mantra. 'I will not fear this foe. I will not fear this foe.'

The dead streamed around the shield wall, a host of shambling corpses and skeletal warriors marching towards the city. Scores of wolves loped alongside them, accompanied by darting packs of white-bodied flesheaters. Daegal could not count them, but he knew there were too many for them to handle.

Mutters of fear passed through the assembled people, the men and women of Reikdorf suddenly regretting their choice to march into this arena of warriors. Daegal could feel their fear and recognised the teetering panic that could unman them in a heartbeat. He had felt it before at the defeat by the river and knew how devastating it could be. Warriors on the brink of victory could flee a battle believing it lost if they saw their fellows running from the enemy. Sergeants said battles weren't won or lost by individuals, but Daegal knew better.

His fear had hollowed him out at the river, but as he watched the wolves and carrion eaters coming towards him, that fear was replaced by anger. These monsters had taken his honour, stripping him of the one thing he had been assured was his right and destiny as an Asoborn.

Though he had seen only twelve summers, his anger burned like an inferno in his heart.

He drew his sword as the first wolves clawed into the line of people, hurling themselves forward with fangs and claws tearing. Blood sprayed and men and women died as the wolves tore them apart. The carrion eaters came on their heels, dragging men to the ground where they were pounced upon by yet more and eaten alive as they screamed in pain.

A creature with black beads for eyes and a mouth filled with broken teeth threw itself at him, and Daegal swung his sword for its neck. It bit deep into the beast's flesh, and Daegal kicked its corpse from the blade as another came at him with its claws outstretched. He cut its hands off and stabbed it in the throat. Blood spattered him, and the reek of it drove him to even greater heights of fury. He plunged his sword blade into the flanks of a dead wolf chewing on the entrails of a man Daegal had spoken to moments before. His name had been Eoland. He had been a baker of bread, but his days of preparing loaves and sweetbreads were now over.

Daegal fought with all the courage and strength he had forgotten by the river, killing a dozen enemies with as many blows. All around him, the people of Reikdorf took heart from his steadfast courage, holding their ground in the face of these monsters. The tide of flesheaters and wolves broke upon the line of ordinary men and women. Blood soaked the earth, and hundreds had died in the opening moments of the fighting.

Daegal ducked the snapping jaws of a wolf and jammed his sword down its throat. Its mouth snapped shut as it died and broke the blade in two. He swept up a fallen spear, a coloured rag tied just behind its iron tip. He heard screams of pain and terror, and knew the courage of these people hung by a thread.

As it had at the river, a moment's heroism or courage would decide the outcome of this fight. Daegal raised the spear above his head, letting the chill winds catch the fabric tied to the spear. Blue and red streamed above him, not a flag, but merely two rags in the colours of Reikdorf. Though the day was grim and dark, they shone as bright as though freshly dyed and lit by the noonday sun.

The flesheaters saw him raise the makeshift banner and he saw their uncertainty.

This was his moment. This was his one and only chance to reclaim the honour these monsters had taken from him.

'People of Reikdorf, with me!' shouted Daegal.

Daegal plunged the spear into the belly of a snarling wolf and charged from the bloodied ranks of citizen warriors, an Asoborn war shout on his lips.

And the people of Reikdorf followed him.

⤙ TWENTY-TWO ⤚

Champions of Life and Death

THE ASOBORN SHIELD wall splintered and buckled against the charge of the black knights. Men and women were hurled from their feet by the impact of the dead riders, but more Asoborns rushed to pick up the fallen shields and plug the gap. Skeletal horsemen plunged through the shield wall, hacking with darkly glittering swords. Garr swept his twin-bladed spear through a black rider's horse, bringing him down in a clatter of bone and plate. Maedbh's bronze blade stabbed down, plunging through the rider's helm and extinguishing the green light shimmering beyond his visor.

Garr nodded his thanks, but Maedbh was already on the move, spinning around as the thunderous sound of horsemen slamming into iron-rimmed shields boomed once more. Cuthwin now fought with a spear, wrenched from a dead man with his spine all but severed. Beside him Fridleifr rammed his own spear through a rusted gap in a dead knight's breastplate. Sigulf protected his brother's flank, holding a heavy shield and slamming it forward along with the rest of the Asoborns.

Ulrike loosed carefully aimed shafts into the dead, sending arrows through the eye sockets of those warriors whose helmets had been knocked off in the charge. Maedbh took a two-handed grip on the sword as three dead riders smashed through the shield wall. Their defence was shrinking with every passing second, the Asoborns unable to resist the unnatural power of the black knights. One rode towards her with a curved black sword raised above its head.

Maedbh ran at the dead warrior, her own sword hungry to slay this champion of the knights. She dived forward, rolling to her feet as the rider's weapon swept over her head. She slashed her sword across the skeletal mount's rear legs, shattering the bones and toppling the rider to the ground. A host of Asoborns pounced on the dead warrior, stabbing and clubbing his bones to destruction. The second warrior rode straight for the fallen Freya, dropping from his horse and striding towards the fallen queen with murderous determination burning in his eye sockets.

Maedbh ran towards him, but the third dead rider reared up before her, his horse's bony limbs pawing the air. One hoof caught Maedbh on the shoulder and sent her spinning. She landed badly, slashing her arm open on the blade of her sword. Blood poured from the wound onto the blade and she felt a sudden sense of power and anger flow through her.

She rolled as the hooves stamped down, thrusting her sword straight up and into the horse's ribs. Like a ruptured soap bubble, something intangible broke within the steed and its form came apart in a rain of bones. Iron plates tumbled to the earth, and Maedbh rolled as the beast's rider dropped beside her.

Maedbh brought her sword around in a move of desperation. The rider's sword slammed into her own, barely a handspan from her face. Its armoured foot slammed down into her stomach and she doubled up as the rider reached down and lifted her from the ground. Its helmet slammed into her face and blood poured down her chin as she felt her nose break. The sword fell from her grip and the pain of her wounds seared her once again.

She cried out as the gouges on her back flared and the slash on her arm throbbed as though dipped in boiling water. Maedbh looked through the slit in the dead warrior's helm and into his eyes. She saw endless suffering there, a soul chained to the mortal world by dark magic and kept in enduring torment. Though nothing remained of the man this warrior had once been, his suffering was eternal and unrelenting.

The black sword drew back and Maedbh's eyes focussed on the notched tip, picturing how it would punch through her ribcage and split her heart in two. The skull's grin became wider, but before its sword could stab forward, the dead warrior's head flew from his neck and the body collapsed. Maedbh slumped to the ground, scrambling away from the warrior's remains as a glorious figure in fiery bronze stood above her with a hand outstretched.

'Thank you for looking after my sword,' said Freya, hauling Maedbh to her feet.

Ulrike and Cuthwin stood at the queen's side and her daughter held a spear out toward Maedbh.

'My queen,' gasped Maedbh. 'You're alive.'

'Never more so!' roared the queen, turning and hurling herself into the fray.

Together with Sigulf, Fridleifr, Cuthwin and Ulrike, Maedbh joined Garr's faltering shield wall. Though Maedbh's arm and back burned with pain, she fought like never before, unhorsing dead warriors with every thrust. Together with the Queen's Eagles they fought like the legendary heroes of old, but even with such courage there was no way the shield wall could hold. Warriors were dying by the dozen with every passing moment and the ring of swords and spears was shrinking like a patch of snow in spring.

A black rider thundered over a shieldbearer to Maedbh's left and his steed, a black beast with skin like basalt, reared up as a powerful warrior leapt from its back. His black cloak unfolded like wings as he landed in the midst of the Asoborns. Maedbh had seen this man a handful of times only, and though he had changed beyond all mortal recognition, he still bore the features of Siggurd of the Brigundians.

The black riders charged through the gap he had broken, rampaging through the Asoborns and slaughtering them with slashing blows of their black swords. Siggurd hurled Garr to the ground, the heroic warrior's throat torn out and his head lolling on a last shred of sinew. Transformed into something evil, Siggurd's eyes blazed crimson with thirst and his fangs gleamed in the twilight as he bore Queen Freya to the ground.

Maedbh rushed to the queen's side, but a backhanded blow from the vampire count hurled her back. Ulrike sent an arrow thudding into the blooddrinker's back, and he roared in pain. His fangs bit down on Freya's neck, but before he could tear out her throat, Cuthwin leapt onto the vampire and buried his knife in his side.

Siggurd arched his back, his form blurring as though in mid transformation and he slashed a clawed hand across Cuthwin's chest. The young Unberogen fell back, his chest in tatters. Siggurd screeched in anger, his fangs bared and bloody. Fridleifr stabbed the vampire in the back with his spear, the tip punching through his belly. Siggurd spun around, wrenching the spear from Fridleifr's hands and tearing the weapon from his body. Faster than Maedbh could follow, the spear left Siggurd's hands and plunged into the boy's chest, punching through his armour and driving him to the ground.

Sigulf gave a cry of loss and anger and slashed his sword through Siggurd's arm. The vampire screeched in agony as a wash of black blood sprayed from the wound. Siggurd looked at the wound, unable to believe he had been hurt.

'That stung, little one,' hissed Siggurd, leaping forward to take hold of Freya's son.

He looked into the boy's eyes and laughed, as though at some private jest, before drawing a short-bladed dagger and ramming it into Sigulf's belly. The boy screamed, but before Siggurd could twist the knife and spill his guts, another arrow hammered the vampire's body.

Maedbh saw Ulrike standing behind the vampire, scrabbling to nock another arrow to her bowstring as Siggurd fastened his hungry gaze upon her.

'Blessed arrows,' he said, dropping the wailing Sigulf to the ground. 'Little girls shouldn't play with such dangerous things. Now I'll have to make you scream.'

The vampire stalked towards Ulrike, who fell to her knees before the terrifying figure, his form blurring as his cloak billowed around him like the wings of an enormous bat. Siggurd's eyes widened as his lower jaw distended and his fangs sprouted like daggers.

Maedbh clambered to her feet and staggered towards Ulrike, though she knew she could never reach her before Siggurd. Her pain was incredible, but she *had* to reach her daughter.

'Ulrike!' she begged, hearing a swelling roar around her. 'No, please! Don't hurt her!'

Siggurd lifted Ulrike from the ground. The young girl's face was a mask of tears. Siggurd turned back towards Maedbh. He sniffed the blood on Ulrike's face and his monstrous face broke into a horrid leer of understanding.

'Ah... this is your spawn,' said Siggurd. 'Now you will watch her die.'

Before the vampire could say another word, the roaring in Maedbh's head swelled as a mob of people charged into the black riders.

There were hundreds of them, maybe even thousands. Most were without armour, dressed in the garb of farmers and ordinary men and women. They fought with the fury of Thuringian berserkers, tearing the dead riders from their saddles and breaking them apart with blows from clubs, felling axes and scythes.

Leading them was a young boy spattered in blood and with the light of battle fury in his eyes. He fought with a spear tied with blue and red rags, and Maedbh saw he knew how to use it. The boy hooked the haft around the legs of an unhorsed black rider and stabbed it down into the dead warrior's chest, twisting the blade before he withdrew it from the body. Dimly she knew she should know him, but how she could know an Unberogen boy escaped her.

The people of Reikdorf swarmed over the undead and drove them back. Siggurd threw Ulrike down as a score of howling men and women ran at him with spears and swords. Some of these, he could kill without difficulty, but all of them... Maedbh didn't think so. She ran over to Ulrike and scooped her up into her arms.

'I've got you, dear heart,' said Maedbh. 'I've got you.'

'Mother!' cried Ulrike, burying her head against Maedbh's shoulder. 'The bad man...?'

'Gone,' said Maedbh, oblivious to anything except her daughter's weight. 'He can't hurt you now. Not ever.'

Ulrike wept into her neck, and Maedbh held her tightly, closing her eyes and willing the fear away as her body pulsed with waves of fiery pain. They stayed like that until Maedbh heard footsteps. She looked up and saw the young boy with the spear tied with the blue and red rags looking down at her.

'Is she all right?' he asked, and Maedbh caught the strong eastern accent in his words.

'Daegal?' she asked.

'Yes.'

She smiled. 'You remembered your spear training.'

He nodded, and suddenly he wasn't a blood-covered Asoborn warrior, but a boy of twelve years. She gathered Daegal to her and hugged him and Ulrike close to her chest. At last, she released them both and said, 'You were both so very brave. I can't tell you how proud I am of you. You fought like real heroes.'

Ulrike smiled through her tears, and Daegal held himself tall, as though some dreadful weight had been lifted from his shoulders. He looked back over her shoulder and Maedbh saw Freya carrying Sigulf while Fridleifr and Cuthwin had their arms around each other's shoulders to hold themselves upright. Both were bloody, but they were unbowed.

'Siggurd?' she said.

'Fled,' answered Cuthwin. 'When the people came, he took to the air and flew away.'

Maedbh nodded, looking to her queen with relief beyond words. Freya was pale and unsteady on her feet, and blood streamed from the wound at her neck. Sigulf's eyes were closed and his belly wet with crimson. His chest rose and fell, but weakly.

'He's alive?' asked Maedbh.

'Barely,' said Freya, her voice cracked and faint. 'We have to get him back to Reikdorf.'

'We *all* need to get back,' said Cuthwin. 'We've seen this lot off, but there's more of them coming this way.'

Maedbh looked to the east, and the flame of hope was smothered in her breast as she saw thousands more skeletal warriors marching in lockstep towards them. They had weathered this attack, but the dead had many more warriors to send into battle.

'Everyone back!' she shouted. 'To Reikdorf!'

KRELL'S AXE SLASHED down, but instead of cleaving through armour and flesh as it had done in his slaughter of the Red Scythes, this time his blade was halted by gromril armour and the strength of mountains. The towering monster paused in its butchery and looked down at the stout forms opposing it. The furious light in the champion's eyes burned even brighter, as though recognising the stunted forms before him from battles fought thousands of years ago.

Master Alaric felt the power of Krell's blow throughout his body, his great-grandfather's shield almost bent in two by the force. The shock reverberated through his armour and he thanked Grungni that he'd thought to strengthen himself with several firkins of beer.

'Is that the best you've got?' he sneered at the long dead champion. 'No wonder Grimbul Ironhelm was able to beat you.'

Krell roared with renewed fury, and his axe came up as a hundred dwarfs charged him. Alaric hurled himself at the ferocious champion whose name was entered countless times in the Dammaz Kron, his every transgression written in the blood of the High Kings of the age. He hammered his axe against Krell's blood-red form, feeling the star-iron of his axe bite a hair's-breadth into the skull-etched plates of armour. Krell roared and slammed his axe down on a dwarf warrior's head, cleaving him from skull to groin. Blood sprayed the armour of his comrades, and they attacked with renewed fury.

Like the great pistons of Zhufbar, the dwarf axes beat the black armour of Krell, cutting shards of cursed iron away from his body, but leaving the giant, skeletal body beneath unharmed. Alaric circled behind the undead champion, rolling beneath the return swing of the black axe that left six dwarfs bisected at the waist. The ring of iron and gromril tightened around Krell, but the sheer weight of numbers only seemed to drive him to greater heights of frenzied delight.

Krell's axe swept left and right, and those it didn't kill were hurled away to land with the butchered human horsemen. An injured warrior, the one Alaric had spoken to, watched the fight in pained amazement. Alaric would sooner eat grobi dung than fail in front of a manling. The shameful life of a slayer awaited such unfortunates. That was not going to be Alaric's fate.

Yet more of the undead were moving up behind Krell, pushing forward in giant blocks of marching skeletons and lurching corpses. Hundreds of bats wheeled overhead and ghostly wisps of howling shades swirled around them. One way or another, this fight would need to end soon, for there was no way his dwarfs could hold against such numbers.

Alaric waited until Krell swung his axe in a low arc, killing another four dwarfs, before throwing aside his shield and leaping onto the dead champion's back. He wrapped his hand around a broken hunk of armour and beat his axe against Krell's shoulders.

Plates shattered under the assault, and Krell arched his back as he felt Alaric's presence. He roared and spun around, seeking to dislodge Alaric as the remaining dwarfs pressed their attack, battering his thighs with axe blows and hammer strikes. Sparks flew from the red armour, like metal fresh from the forge on an anvil. Alaric fought to hold on as he thundered his axe against the metal of Krell's armour. He felt his grip slipping and slammed his axe though a weakened plate, wedging himself in place by gripping an exposed rib within the unclean iron.

It felt like plunging his hand into an icy lake, and Alaric felt the cold of the other side seeping into his hand, a frozen touch of utter lifelessness and doom. He tried to snatch his hand back from Krell's essence, but it was stuck fast. The cold slithered through his hand, oozing through the veins and meat of his wrist. Alaric knew that when it reached his heart, he would become no better than Krell.

'Master Alaric, sir!' shouted a loud manling voice. 'Da says you got to get clear!'

Alaric knew he had only one chance to live and grimly freed his axe from the weakened plate of broken armour.

'Alaric the Mad, eh?' he said. 'Maybe they're right.'

He brought the axe down upon his wrist, the razored edge easily slicing through his flesh and bone. Alaric grunted in pain and kicked out on Krell's armour, throwing himself as far away from the champion as he could get. He landed on a dead horse and rolled behind it as he heard a series of snapping hammers being pulled back.

'Left one's out of alignment,' he grumbled, as the world filled with fire and noise.

GOVANNON PULLED THE leather firing cords, elated and terrified at the same time. He couldn't see much of the battle, which was a relief to him, yet out of the shadows one shape was terrifyingly clear. The blood-red form of Krell loomed in the darkness, a monster of nightmare come to hunt the living.

The first hammer struck the side of its brass cauldron, slowing enough to prevent the flint from sparking, and Govannon's heart sank. The hulking champion of Nagash loomed over the war machine and Govannon cursed himself for a fool in wishing to be part of this fight. Krell would kill them all; nothing could stand against this horror from an ancient age.

He cursed his naïve belief that he could repair a machine of the dwarfs, bitter that he could have spent these last weeks far more productively. Armour, swords, shields, axes, arrowheads–

The second hammer struck true, and puffs of smoke and fire frothed from the brass cauldrons at the back of the machine. The barrel erupted in a booming storm of shot and fire, another a few seconds later. Govannon's ears rang with the concussive force of the detonation and his eyes watered with the brightness of the fire erupting in thundering booms from the barrels. Then the fourth barrel fired. As the hammer slammed down in the powder cauldron of the barrel he had repaired, Bysen lifted him away as the Thunder Bringer rocked back with ferocious recoil.

The barrel held firm and erupted with a blizzard of iron shot and, clear as day, Govannon saw the towering champion fall, his blood-red armour ripped to shreds by the hurricane of fire and iron. Bones were shattered and torn away, the horned helmet little more than a ragged lump of pulverised iron hanging from a torn leather chin strap.

Part of Krell's head was gone, the left side of his skull a shattered ruin. Blackness gaped within, yet the fire in Krell's right eye blazed as the dwarfs fell upon his ruined body with sharp axes and vengeful hearts.

'It worked!' shouted Govannon. 'In Ulric's name, it worked!'

'Aye, da, it worked good!' said Bysen happily. 'Big, big bang! Bysen's ears hurt!'

KHALED AL-MUNTASIR RODE at a leisurely pace towards the north, watching as the army of the dead began to fully envelop these mortals who dared to stand against Nagash. He had ridden with all speed towards where the red-armoured cavalry had fought the black knights to a standstill, but halted upon feeling Markus's death.

For a mortal, Markus was a tremendous swordsman, but enhanced with the power of undeath, he had been superlative – better even than Khaled perhaps. Yet he was dead, his soul consigned to oblivion by a mortal. The unease that had stirred in the vampire's belly all night returned, stronger this time, and he cursed himself for succumbing to such a mortal sensation.

Yet no sooner had the painful empathic horror of Markus's destruction passed than he felt Siggurd's pain as weapons blessed in the name of the god of all living things pierced his immortal flesh. He winced with each wound, unused to such pain, and felt Siggurd's anger as he was forced to flee. His two unbeatable warriors had been defeated, one destroyed, the other wounded almost to the point of dissolution.

Khaled al-Muntasir forced the anger at their incompetence aside and turned his attention to the rest of the battle, trying to regain his impregnable confidence. Thousands more dead warriors were advancing towards the city, pushing past the tiny islands of resistance that had met with some fleeting success. The battle line of mortals arrayed before the walls was fighting with admirable courage, but no hope of victory. They took backward step after backward step, and it was only a matter of time until they broke. Yet in the centre of the battle, cut off from the rest of his army, Sigmar drove for the low hillside where Nagash awaited him. Less than a hundred warriors still rode with the Emperor, yet they charged as though all of mankind were with them.

The vampire looked to the black form of Nagash, who stood with his enormous sword and twisted-snake staff in his hands. Black light flickered from the staff and blue fire wreathed the blade of his ancient sword.

'What are you waiting for?' hissed Khaled al-Muntasir. 'Just kill him and be done with it.'

Yet even as he said the words, he knew Nagash could not kill Sigmar with his black sorcery while he wore the crown. Its incredible power would protect any wearer from virtually all forms of magic.

Khaled al-Muntasir watched as Nagash raised his staff and arcing bolts of lightning forked downwards, striking the gems inset along its scaled length. A storm of dark energy surrounded the necromancer and he slammed the staff into the ground. With senses beyond those of mortals, Khaled al-Muntasir watched the energy flow from the staff and into the hillside, spreading like the roots of a poisoned tree beneath the earth.

'That's more like it,' he said.

These black roots sought the bleak places of the land, the abandoned graveyards long since paved over, the forgotten plague pits covered in quicklime and the sites of murder and mayhem. Drawn to these places like rats to a cesspit, Nagash's sorcery infused the earth with the dark magic of undeath.

And the unquiet dead rose from their ancient graves to claw their way to the world above.

THE EARTH RUMBLED with the sound of digging claws and moaning hunger, the churned grass rippling as the dead of centuries before rose to the surface. Hands long devoid of meat erupted from the earth and hauled fleshless corpses back to the land that had consigned them to the ground. From the southern fork of the river to the city gates, a huge tear opened in the earth and a thousand or more dead warriors from the time before men had dwelled in cities and towns lurched unsteadily to their feet.

The Asoborns and the people of Reikdorf fleeing the onward march of the dead abandoned all pretence of an ordered retreat at the sight of this new horror. They ran for the city gates, terrified at being surrounded and cut off from their home. Even Freya, whose courage was unquestioned, fled along with her sons, Maedbh, Ulrike and Cuthwin. Daegal, with his new-found courage, formed a rearguard with the few surviving Queen's Eagles, and if any of them thought it strange to be taking orders from one so young, none remarked upon it.

Within the walls of Reikdorf, the ground broke open as the dead climbed from below, pushing their way into the half-light as Nagash's sorcery compelled their grisly remains to rise up and slay the living. Hundreds of dead things stalked the streets of the city, fighting anything warm and feasting on their flesh.

Alfgeir and Teon were trapped within a closing ring of undead, their retreat cut off by a newly emerged phalanx of the dead. They were unarmed, these dead men, but they swiftly picked up the weapons of those the Unberogen had already destroyed. Ragged, disorganised and freshly risen, they were formidable in their numbers if not their skill as fighters.

In the north, yet more dead arose, surrounding Govannon, Bysen and the dwarfs as they hacked at the indestructible corpse of Krell. Though their axes were sharper than any weapon forged by the hands of men, they could not easily undo armour worked in the forges of smiths who gave praise to the bloody gods of the north.

The mortal army was surrounded and doomed.

SIGMAR SMASHED ASIDE a pair of skeletal warriors, champions in ancient, verdigris-stained armour of a thousand years ago. Hundreds of these undying creatures surrounded him, and yet still they pushed on. Ghal-maraz flickered with silver fire and shimmering sparks flew from his every blow. Hundreds of the dead had fallen before him, but hundreds more still awaited destruction.

Beside him, Wolfgart hacked through the dead with great sweeps of his sword, each blow weaker than the last as his strength grew less and less. Where Ghal-maraz imparted a measure of its power to Sigmar, Wolfgart enjoyed no such boon. Wenyld fought mechanically, slumped low over his saddle, though Sigmar's banner still flew above the heroic warriors who rode with him.

Ghal-maraz swept out to either side, breaking the dead warriors apart with brutal cracks of shattered bone. As the last ranks of the dead were crushed beneath their horses' hooves, Sigmar's Unberogen, fifty warriors in total, rode onto the clear ground before the low hillside where Nagash awaited them. Its base was encircled by tall warriors in heavy hauberks of black iron, who carried long halberds with icy blades. A host of swirling spirits gathered in the air above the necromancer, and the darkness around him was total. Sigmar had no idea how fared the rest of his army, but knew that unless he could end this now, it would be slaughtered by morning's light.

A trail of broken bodies littered the ground behind them, and though thousands of the dead were within reach, none turned towards them, as though their presence was an irrelevance.

'Almost there,' said Wolfgart, twisting in his saddle to make sure no more of the dead were moving to attack them.

'Aye,' agreed Sigmar. 'One more push and I'll have him right where I want him.'

Wolfgart gave him a sidelong look and then burst out laughing.

'Damn me, Sigmar,' he said. 'I'm tired worse than I was at Black Fire, and that's saying something, but you can still make me smile.'

Sigmar nodded, feeling the weight of the crown at his brow grow heavier with every step his horse took towards the hillside. He felt its anger at him surge, a fury that a mere mortal dared to wield it and not partake of its power. Its maker was at hand, and it renewed its assault on his mind, battering him with dreams of pleasure, nightmares of failure and temptations of wealth, power and godhood.

None could reach Sigmar, for he had reached that place where all thoughts of self were extinguished. All that was left to him now was service to his people, and not even death could keep him from that duty. Piece by piece, Sigmar had shed all his earthly desires, putting them aside for the greater good of the Empire.

Nagash's crown had nothing left with which to tempt or intimidate him, for his entire being was dedicated to one ideal. That was something no necromancer could ever understand, the dedication of the self to a higher purpose, where the one man could make the difference between life and death, success or failure.

In this world, at this time, Sigmar was that man. He had believed that from the day he had walked amongst the tombs of his ancestors on his Dooming Day, but had *known* it when he passed through the fire of Ulric unharmed.

Everything he had done had driven him to this moment, and he knew this foe was his to face alone. Sigmar swung his leg over his saddle and dropped to the earth as a sudden stillness and silence spread outwards from the hillside. Though battle still raged beyond, Sigmar could hear nothing beyond his own laboured breathing and the distant howling of wolves.

He walked over to Wenyld and lifted his hand towards the red and gold banner.

'Time to pass it on, my friend,' said Sigmar.

Wenyld nodded, too weak from blood loss to resist as Sigmar took the banner pole from his blooded grip.

'What in Ulric's name are you doing?' demanded Wolfgart, walking his horse alongside him and dismounting. 'Get back on your horse, you fool!'

'No,' said Sigmar. 'I'm going to end this now.'

'What? You're just going to walk up to the bloody necromancer on foot?'

'That's exactly what I'm doing,' replied Sigmar, turning and making his way towards the hillside. 'And don't follow me. This is something I need to do alone.'

'Why, for the love of the gods? Tell me that at least.'

Sigmar said, 'Because this is how it has to be. You know how it goes. At the end of all the sagas, the hero always stands alone or else he's not a hero.'

'Damn the sagas,' swore Wolfgart. 'I'm not leaving you.'

'Yes you are,' said Sigmar as the ancient warriors at the base of the hill parted to allow him passage. 'Wenyld needs you.'

Wolfgart turned and caught Wenyld as he fell from his saddle. Once again the howl of wolves sounded from over forested hills and shadowed valleys, carried to Reikdorf by cold northern winds. As Wolfgart lowered the dying Wenyld to the ground, Sigmar turned and climbed the hill towards Nagash, his banner in one hand, Ghal-maraz in the other.

He heard Wolfgart shouting his name, but didn't dare look back.

TWENTY-THREE
The End of All Things

EVERY STEP WAS a battle, each yard he drew nearer to the necromancer a struggle against his mortal inclination to flee this abomination. The summit of the hill was wreathed in spirits in black, ghostly revenants of lost souls doomed to attend upon Nagash from now until the end of all things. Sigmar felt the dead light of Nagash roam across his body, learning in a heartbeat how he had grown and was now edging his way to the grave.

A black miasma swirled around the base of the hill, isolating him from the mortal world beyond, and Sigmar felt his flesh recoil from the vile presence of the immortal necromancer. His armour creaked in the frozen air and webs of frost spread across his breastplate and shoulder guards. Ghal-maraz was his only warmth, the language beaten into its haft by master runesmiths glowing with fierce light beneath his grip. Sigmar held tight to its warmth, for the crown at his brow felt like an ever-tightening fist of ice.

Though it could not touch him, the crown's assault on his mind was undiminished, taunting him for the sake of spite and hatred. Nagash's form seemed to stretch up into the darkness as Sigmar drew near, the necromancer's body growing larger and more imposing as though empowered by the very nearness of his crown.

Armoured in eldritch plates of enchanted black iron, Nagash was easily twice the height of Sigmar. His bones were suffused with a venomous green light, every crack and imperfection in his armour lambent with an internal fire that came from ancient magic woven from the myriad winds blowing from the far north. His staff was a slender length of shimmering darkness, like entwined snakes, and his sword was at least as tall as Sigmar. Cold blue flames licked along its length and it radiated a chill that touched Sigmar deep in his bones.

Nagash stared down at him, and Sigmar fought against that dread gaze, feeling his limbs fill with ice water and lead. Twin orbs of deathly green fire stared at Sigmar, eyes that had seen the world before men had walked the lands he now ruled. Thousands of years separated them, an ocean of time that Sigmar found impossible to comprehend. He could no more imagine the world of such long ago days as he could imagine the Empire in thousands of years to come.

I will show you…

The voice was like continents colliding, a deathly cadence that owed nothing to an actual voice. It was the sound of death itself. Sigmar staggered as he saw a land of forests and mountains, its people divided and the world in turmoil. Blood stained every rock, and the glint of iron weapons was everywhere. Armies of such size as to defy imagination marched all across this land, destroying everything in their path without mercy.

Bodies lay gutted by the roadside, men, women and children. Still-living captives were bound to stakes and left for the animals to devour. Sigmar saw slaughter and blood everywhere, hacked up corpses and bodies burned alive in their homes. He wept to see such destruction visited upon his people and his anger built as he sought the source of this debauchery. His gaze fell upon an army marching to a city at the confluence of many rivers. Colourful banners fluttered overhead, and the soldiers were clad in equally gaudy uniforms.

They marched in disciplined ranks, singing songs of martial pride, and Sigmar wept to see that this was no army of monsters, beasts of the undead. These were men. Worse, they were men of the Empire.

Look closer…

Though he knew it was what Nagash wanted, Sigmar could not help himself. He saw the army's banners were decorated with skulls and laurels, crossed spears and spread-winged eagles. And upon all of them were stitched scrolls, each bearing a single word.

Sigmar.

These were warriors who fought in his name. They carried weapons of unusual design, wooden staves like dwarf thunder bows, and wagons bearing unfamiliar war machines drew up the rear of the marching column. Two metal behemoths followed the supply wagons, lumbering contraptions on iron-rimmed wheels that belched steam and black smoke from square fireboxes at their rear.

This is the world you have created. This is blood that will be spilled in your name. Is it not better to leave this world and let the race of man fall into decline? Your species resurgent is one that lives only for destruction and uncertainty. It knows no other way. The dead do not squabble as this land's rulers do. The dead do not fight one another. The dead have no desires, no petty jealousies or ambitions. A world of the dead is a world at peace…

Sigmar fought against the necromancer's words, understanding that their battle would be fought in the realm of the spirit as well as that of the flesh. He closed his eyes, willing this vision away, knowing that Nagash would seek to defeat him with lies cloaked in truths.

'This may be a true vision of the future Empire,' hissed Sigmar. 'But a world of death is a world of stagnation, without the change that makes it worthwhile. What you call uncertainty, I call life itself.'

He fought down his revulsion at this vision and opened his eyes, no longer seeing the bleak vision of an Empire at war with itself, but the spirit-haunted hillside where a being of ultimate darkness opposed him.

'Show me what you will,' said Sigmar, planting his standard in the soft earth and raising Ghal-maraz over his shoulder. 'This ends with me destroying you.'

So be it.

Nagash's sword swept down and Sigmar lifted Ghal-maraz to block. Blue fire seared out from the impact and Sigmar's arms almost froze with the blow. He rolled aside as the sword slashed out again, catching him on the edge of his pauldron and lifting him from his feet. The iron froze in an instant, cracking apart in a rain of icy splinters as he landed. Cold blood streamed from Sigmar's shoulder as Nagash slipped through the air, fast as a winter squall. His sword cut into Sigmar's breastplate, shattering it like a pane of glass and piercing his chest with icy splinters.

Sigmar rolled away before the blade could penetrate deeper, swinging Ghal-maraz around to deflect yet another swift riposte. The necromancer's staff slashed down and arcing bolts of lightning leapt up from the ground. Sigmar screamed in pain as the energies enveloped him, burning his flesh with cold fire. Though it had been his bane through the entire battle, the crown now came to his aid. Its power was purest evil, but it was utterly directed in its ability to resist sorcery. Nagash's withering energy was drawn into the crown, and Sigmar felt its rage to be so abused as the searing fire vanished.

Nagash's leering skull face, too monstrous and enormous to ever have been human, swept down and Sigmar threw himself to the side as black, corrosive breath gusted from the necromancer's jaws. The hillside withered and died beneath its touch and Nagash spun around with his staff and sword raised to destroy the foolish mortal opposing him.

The necromancer's sword swung low and Sigmar leapt over it, bringing his hammer around to block a slashing blow of the staff to his body. Once again, the impact was enormous, and Sigmar knew he could not keep this up for much longer. He spun inside the necromancer's reach, but Nagash was fast and slid out of range of his strike.

Sigmar leapt towards Nagash, and the necromancer lowered his staff to block the wild blow. Ghal-maraz slammed into the entwined snakes and the runic power of the dwarfs blazed as it met the unnatural sorcery of Nehekhara. Sigmar poured every fibre of his hatred into the blow and Nagash's staff broke apart with a screaming howl of released magic. Nagash reeled from its destruction, and Sigmar saw the hand that had carried it was a shimmering metal, its surface like a silver mirror with oil smeared across it.

Nagash drew himself up to his full height, the black smoke swirling around his lower reaches spinning like an inverted whirlwind. The force of it drove Sigmar back, billowing around him and throwing up grit and sand from the summit of the hill. The hellish wind dispersed the shrieking spirits from the air, hurling them away and revealing the battle in all its horror.

See the fate of all flesh and know despair!

THE LAND BETWEEN the city and the low hill was a charnel house of blood and destruction. As Sigmar's eyes had seen into the hearts of his people the night before the battle, so now Nagash showed him the battle he had led them to. Sigmar's plan was simple, ride through the centre of the undead army and slay the necromancer. He had known that many would die to keep the dead from Reikdorf, but to see the scale of that bloodshed was shattering.

Sigmar was no stranger to battle and death. He had seen friends and loved ones slain over the course of his life, and knew the grim cost of sending men to war. He knew that his orders would see women widowed, children orphaned and lovers forever parted. He knew all this, yet to see it happening all around him, all at once, was a supreme horror.

The thousands who were fighting on this day were dying in droves. Their initial successes against the army of the dead were meaningless as the cadavers and ruined corpses rose to their feet once again. Those who had fallen in battle now returned to tear at their former sword-brothers, and what had once been a magnificent host was now reduced to a few pitiful bands of survivors fighting for their last moments of life.

Even if Sigmar triumphed and slew Nagash, this day would live in infamy as a day of death and woe. There would be too many dead for it to be otherwise. Sigmar heard grating laughter as Nagash revelled in this cavalcade of slaughter. The Empire's dead would be new acolytes for his host, enslaved to reduce this world to a barren, empty wasteland.

Amid the fighting in the south, Sigmar saw Freya and Maedbh leading their children back towards Reikdorf. A multitude of skeletons climbing the walls and wading into the city via the corpse-choked river which blocked their route to safety. Unberogen and Asoborns led by a baying, blood-covered youngster defended them within a fragile shield wall, but with dead wolves and flesh-hungry corpses closing in on them, they had minutes of life left at best.

Nagash cruelly drew his gaze onwards, and in the centre of the battlefield, Sigmar saw Teon and the Great Hall Guard enveloped by a horde of freshly-risen dead as they rode for Reikdorf's gates. Alfgeir slumped against Teon, barely conscious and near death. It broke Sigmar's heart to see the grievous wound his old friend had suffered.

Yet Nagash was not done with him.

Onwards his gaze was drawn, and Sigmar saw a host of black knights riding south towards the city, followed by hundreds of dead warriors marching in perfect lockstep. Shambling corpses in their thousands followed them, a ravening horde set to devour the living. A ring of dwarfs led by Master Alaric hacked at a fallen giant in red armour, their weapons cutting the monster apart piece by piece. It struggled as they fought it, though its body was ruined as though from a thousand heavy impacts. A wrecked machine lay on its side as a tall warrior with a heavy forge hammer stood over a fallen man in the leather apron of a blacksmith.

Sigmar recognised Master Govannon and Bysen, but pale-bellied flesheaters surrounded them. No matter how powerful Bysen's swings of the forge hammer, he would not be able to stop his father from being eaten alive. Sigmar heard the howling of many wolves and despair touched his heart to hear this choir of Ulric's chosen lamenting the death of so many brave warriors.

You see…? This is what flesh entails. Suffering. Bloodshed. Misery. Why would you seek to perpetuate this horror? What creature in my service knows fear, pain or desire? The legions of the dead want for nothing, care for nothing, love nothing. End your foolish resistance and you will be a king of death, a master of the world at my side. You will be my greatest champion and together we will end the suffering of this world!

Sigmar dropped to his knees, as the pain and anguish of every living soul upon the battlefield washed over him. What manner of man could allow such suffering? What sane individual could wish such pain on a life? To strangle a babe as it was born would be a kindness, and to end the plague of the living on this world would be an act of mercy. Sigmar's tears flowed freely and he looked up into the hungry eyes of Nagash as he loomed over him. The metallic hand reached out to him, the sharpened fingertips like silver claws as they reached for the crown.

In that moment, the sound of wolves echoed from the tree line of the northern hills, an ululating chorus that swept over the battlefield. Sigmar felt that sound lift him and fill his mind with a cold wind that had its source in the northern forests. This was a cry born in the forgotten places of ice and snow where the wolves of Ulric made their lairs. He understood that this was no lament for the fallen, but a savage affirmation of life. A war shout and cry of defiance all in one.

Sigmar rolled away from Nagash's outstretched hand, looking to the north as tens of thousands of howling men streamed over the hillside. There were few of them warriors, most dressed in rags and bearing spiked chains, spinning flails, scythes, burning brands and clanging hand bells. Blood-smeared and screaming incoherently, they had the look of madmen, a host of armed lunatics in search of a battle.

Amongst them rode two warriors in red armour and wolf-pelt cloaks. One carried a rippling banner of crimson and white, and Sigmar's heart leapt as he recognised the banner of the White Wolves.

'Redwane!' cried Sigmar, even as he realised that neither rider was the fiery warrior who commanded that elite band of horsemen. His eyes were drawn to two warriors at the forefront of this motley band of ragged madmen. Both were bearded and wore muddy tunics that were torn and stained with old blood. These men looked on the verge of death, yet charged with the ferocity of ten berserkers, seemingly oblivious to the many wounds they had cut into their own flesh. One man was unknown to him, but the other was as familiar as his own reflection. It was Redwane, but the man Sigmar had known was gone, submerged within a tortured madness that banished all thoughts of pain and fear of death.

The host of madmen struck the army of the dead and rolled right over them, crushing them beneath their bare feet and tearing them apart with their makeshift weapons. On they came in an unending tide, men and women gathered from all across the Empire, seduced by doom-laden preachings until the host that had set out from Middenheim had swollen to become this irresistible tide of crazed fanaticism.

Following behind this screaming host came painted warriors in mail shirts who marched beneath the banner of Count Otwin. Perhaps a thousand of the Berserker King's warriors came over the hills, following the deranged army led by Redwane and his unknown companion. They bayed with the voices of wolves and to see them coming to his aid gave Sigmar the strength he needed to face the necromancer.

Nagash drew himself up to his full, terrifying height, his fury at this turn of events spreading from the hillside and empowering his army with fresh hate for the living. The northern flank of the dead collapsed, smashed aside by the army of madmen and Thuringians, yet there was still a virtually inexhaustible supply of rotting flesh to replace those the mortals destroyed.

Sigmar swept Ghal-maraz around, and faced the necromancer for the last time. The crown blazed with silver light at his brow, exerting every last scrap of its power to weaken him and drain his ability to resist. As Sigmar listened to the howling of wolves, he knew it could not touch him. It had kept him safe from Nagash's magic, allowed him to smash through the ranks of the dead without pause, but now it was time to be rid of it.

He tore the crown from his brow and held it up towards Nagash.

'You want this?' he bellowed, and Nagash turned his gaze upon him. Such desire and obsession. Such aching need and devotion. Nothing else mattered to Nagash, not the defeat of Sigmar's army, not the destruction of all living things. Nothing was more important to the necromancer than this crown. Sigmar saw how much its power meant to Nagash and understood Eoforth's last message to him completely.

'You want this?' repeated Sigmar. 'Then have it!'

He threw the crown onto the withered grass of the hillside and raised Ghal-maraz to smash it asunder with one, all-powerful blow.

Nagash bellowed in horrified anger and reached for the crown with outstretched fingers, all thoughts save taking back his crown driven from his mind. Nothing else mattered, and it was the moment Sigmar had been awaiting since this fight had begun.

He leapt towards the necromancer, bringing Ghal-maraz around in a thunderous overhead sweep. The mighty hammer of the dwarfs smashed into Nagash's cuirass, breaking it into a thousand shards and powering into his chest. Green fire flared from the impact and ribs fused with dark magic thousands of years before shattered like ice as Sigmar drove his hammer into the heart of the necromancer's being.

Sigmar howled with the wolves and screamed his hatred of Nagash as the runic script on the hammer's haft shone with the purest light. Runes he had not even known existed flared to life on the hammer's head, filling Nagash's hollow existence with fiery beams of light and searing his immortal essence from within.

The necromancer shrieked as his ancient sorcery fought to resist the powerful magic of the dwarfs. Forces too titanic to be understood by mortals battled within his body, easily capable of laying waste to this entire land. Sigmar held onto Ghal-maraz as the star-iron of its head burned brighter than the sun and its grip burned his hands with its ancient fire.

'I will end you!' roared Sigmar, thrusting the hammer deeper into Nagash's body.

The necromancer gave one last shriek of horror, and his body exploded in a wash of black light and frozen fire. Dark magic and immortal energies flared upwards from his destruction like a volcanic eruption.

And the sky filled with ashes and grief.

WITH NAGASH'S DESTRUCTION, the army of the dead melted away like woodsmoke on a windy day. Warriors of bone dropped their swords and collapsed as their spirits were freed to pass on to their final rest. Undead wolves that had, moments before, been howling for blood, fell to dissolution as the magic binding their bodies to the world of mortals was undone. Spirits shrieked as their ethereal forms were drawn back to the tombs that held them, and the shambling corpses raised from their graves now slumped to the ground, reduced to nothing more than dead meat for crows.

The binding will of Nagash was absolute, and no creature that walked, drifted or flew within his host had power of its own to maintain its existence. As the necromancer's power bled away, the dead ceased their attacks on the living and returned to the realm that had first claim upon their souls. Morr's gates opened to receive them, and as each violated spirit was freed from the necromancer's iron clutches, a wave of euphoria swept over the battlefield.

Weeping men and women laughed and danced as the threat of death was lifted. They cried tears of joy, and hugged one another tight. The nearness of death had reawakened every mortal heart's appreciation of the gift of life. Though that would fade in time, for now it was a glorious moment that would never be forgotten.

Nor was Nagash's influence confined to the dead at Reikdorf, for the black strands of his web of control stretched all across the Empire. The dead at Marburg dropped to the ground as the will driving them over the citadel walls faded into nothingness, while those clawing their way into Middenheim fell from the causeway and tumbled from the sheer sides of the Fauschlag Rock. The Udose watched in amazement as the dead ceased their attacks into their hidden valleys and crumbled to dust around the walls of Conn Carsten's clifftop fortress.

Count Aloysis stood atop the ramparts of Hochergig and waved a Cherusen banner as the dead melted away from his walls, while Count Krugar rode through the gates of Taalahim in triumph. In the eastern reaches of the Empire, Count Adelhard rallied his warriors in a krug around the Bechahorst, a spire of dark stone in the northern marches of his lands, and drank *koumiss* to toast the end of this fight.

The lands of the south were silent, for their people were already dead. Alone among the southern tribal homelands, the Merogens had endured. Count Henroth led his warriors from within their great castles of stone, blinking in the new light and disbelieving that such a miracle could have saved his people.

Nagash's legions were no more, and the living had endured.

The long dark night of the dead was over.

KHALED AL-MUNTASIR CLIMBED to the top of the hillside, his bones aching and his flesh scoured by the incomprehensible destruction of Nagash. The vampire's armour was in tatters, his white cloak torn and burned by the fire that had threatened to consume him. The necromancer's doom had threatened to drag him to destruction as well, but his blood was of a higher calibre than that of the ancient priest king of Nehekhara.

Siggurd crawled by his side, the newly-sired vampire's body wracked with pain. The Asoborns had almost destroyed him, and in his weakened state, his immortal flesh had all but succumbed to the same destruction as had vanquished the army of the dead. Only his superior pedigree had saved him, but it would take dozens of bodies' worth of blood to restore him. His whimpering cries were repugnant to Khaled al-Muntasir's ears, but he was of his blood and could not be abandoned to the savage mercies of the mortals.

Nothing lived on the hillside, every blade of grass withered and every inch of soil barren. His footsteps left prints in ashen sand as he climbed to the top, where he saw the architect of the necromancer's demise.

Sigmar stood with his back to Khaled al-Muntasir, his softly glowing hammer at his side and the crown of Nagash lying at his feet. The crown shone with a dull light, and Khaled al-Muntasir wondered what glories he might achieve were he to take it. The Emperor's flesh was a mass of bruised blood, frostburn and suffering. The vampire licked his lips, seeing that the mortal was at the very end of his endurance. Easy meat.

'You have destroyed that which could not be destroyed,' said Khaled al-Muntasir.

'I told you that you were not welcome in my lands,' said Sigmar, without turning. 'I told you that I would kill you if I saw you again.'

'An empty threat,' said the vampire, taking a step towards Sigmar. Siggurd moaned in hunger and pain, the smell of blood drawing his broken gaze.

'Is it?' said Sigmar, turning to face him. 'Test it, and I will send you to join your master.'

'You are weak,' said the vampire. 'Spent. I could kill you and drink your blood before you could raise a hand to stop me. The crown will be mine and all you have achieved here will have been for nothing.'

'Then come at me,' said Sigmar, lifting Ghal-maraz.

Khaled al-Muntasir laughed, but the sound died in his throat as he saw the hatred in Sigmar's eyes. There was strength and power there beyond anything men should know, a cold fire that came not from mortal realms, but from a place long forsaken that did not belong on this world. Its winter fire hailed from a place of gods and monsters, a realm of power beyond imagining and where the laws of nature held no sway. All this power and more burned in Sigmar's eyes, though he knew it not.

In that instant of connection, Khaled al-Muntasir knew that if he took another step his undying existence would be ended. For the first time since he had awoken as an immortal blood drinker, Khaled al-Muntasir knew the meaning of fear. His limbs trembled. The thought of oblivion and the bleak emptiness that awaited him robbed him of all his courage.

Siggurd pawed at the ground, desperate for blood and unable to comprehend why his master hesitated to end this upstart mortal. His senses dulled and broken by his pain, Siggurd could not feel the terrible danger Sigmar represented to him and all his kind. The Emperor's hate of the blood drinkers was a force all of its own, a force that transcended time and all notions of mortality.

Khaled al-Muntasir backed away from Sigmar, dragging the wretched vampire count he had sired back down the hillside. Terror of Sigmar's inner power burned into their damned souls with unending torment as his voice chased them from the battlefield.

'Hear now the word of Sigmar Heldenhammer,' shouted the Emperor. 'I curse you and all your kind to be my enemies for all time!'

The vampires fled into the shadows.

SIGMAR WATCHED THE vampires run, thankful that his killing boast had not been put to the test. His body was a mass of pain, his heart heavy with the mourning yet to come, and his soul was sickened to see what might yet become of his beloved Empire. The air around him was thick with foetid vapours, unclean fumes that lingered in the wake of the necromancer's destruction. Yet even as he waited, a fresh wind was building, blowing from the west with clean air and the promise of new beginnings.

He took a deep breath, savouring the sweetness of that air. It had been so long since he had tasted air untainted with the ashen reek of grave dust and death that he had almost forgotten what it was like. Freed from the necromancer's magic, the land was already beginning to heal, purging the foulness of dark magic from its soil and wind.

Soon the desolation of Nagash would be little more than a memory, for the world was more resilient than people knew. It would outlast mankind, and its mountains, forests and rivers would see them dead and buried before it would even blink. Mortals were a flicker in the life of this world, yet even that was worth holding onto.

Sigmar opened his eyes as he saw a host of men and women gathering around the desolate hillside, warriors from his army, people from his city and allies from across the land. They were weeping tears of hope and mourning, loss and relief.

The battle was over and they were alive.

Sigmar dropped to one knee before his people, giving homage to them as they had given homage to him. The sky above the battlefield began to lighten as the perpetual twilight of Nagash was banished. Its sullen gloom had gripped the Empire for so long that its people had forgotten the feel of sunlight on their skin. Its radiance spread across the land, a bounteous illumination that banished evil to the shadows and chased away the darkness.

Sigmar smiled and turned his face to the sun.

'People of the Empire,' he said. 'A new day is upon us.'

EPILOGUE

IN THE AFTERMATH of the battle, the bodies of the dead were gathered and taken to the blasted hilltop where Sigmar had defeated Nagash. Nothing would ever grow there again, and the priests of Morr declared it a fitting place for the dead to be given their final rest. Night after night, the priests of all the gods spoke prayers for the dead, and scattered the ashes into the river Reik, where they were carried downstream to Marburg and the open ocean.

Count Marius and Princess Marika were married a month after Nagash's defeat, the ceremony attended by Sigmar, Krugar, Aloysis, Otwin, and Myrsa. Claiming the injuries she had suffered at Siggurd's hands still pained her, Freya and her wounded sons returned to Three Hills to rebuild what the dead had destroyed. Though many people muttered darkly as to what the union of Jutones and Endals might mean for the Empire, Sigmar had blessed the marriage and gifted the couple with a pair of golden sceptres from his treasure vaults.

Wolfgart and Maedbh remained in Reikdorf with Ulrike, though they decided that they would split their time between Sigmar's city and Three Hills. Never again would they allow anger to get the better of them, and never again would they allow themselves to be parted with bitter words between them. Within days of the wedding at Marburg, Maedbh announced to Wolfgart and Ulrike that she was with child, and the celebration that accompanied the news was more raucous than the wedding feast of Marius and Marika.

Redwane left Reikdorf within a day of the victory, leading his ravaged, self-mortifying band of madmen into the forests of the Empire. Less than a thousand of them remained, their headlong charge into the undead costing the majority of them their lives. Sigmar had caught Redwane as he prepared to lead his march of doom, but no words could reach the younger man; his hope had been crushed and life now held no meaning for him. Otwin told Sigmar how the crazed Redwane and Torbrecan had broken the siege of his castle and whipped the people of the Empire along the route of his march south into a morbid frenzy. Taking up a hook-knotted rope, Redwane wished the Emperor well and set off into the shadowed forest with Torbrecan, leaving his heartbroken White Wolves behind.

Master Alaric and his dwarf warriors had sought to destroy Krell after the fire of the repaired Thunder Bringer had brought him low, but Nagash's will was not the only force empowering the dread champion's unlife. The monstrous warrior had fought his way clear of the dwarfs' vengeance, and fled into the north. Too blooded to pursue, the dwarfs had watched in bitter impotence as Krell escaped the clutches of their blades. Yet more entries were noted for the Dammaz Kron, the names of all the dwarfs Krell had slain.

Govannon and Bysen both survived the Battle of the River Reik, as it was becoming known, and returned to their forge. The Thunder Bringer had been crushed in the fighting raging around Krell, but its remains had been salvaged and brought back within the city walls while the dwarfs grieved their fallen brothers. Though it was smashed beyond all hope of repair, Govannon immediately set about working out how to make newer and bigger machines. A scrap of fire powder from the misfiring barrel had been recovered from the wreckage, and the near-blind smith was optimistic he would be able to replicate it.

If Master Alaric knew of this, he gave no sign, and after meeting privately with Sigmar in his longhouse, led his warriors in solemn procession to the east. The loss of his hand affected him deeply, and as Sigmar watched the mountain folk return to their homeland, he sensed a great melancholy within Alaric.

Sigmar returned Nagash's crown to High Priestess Alessa, and bade her take it far from the Empire, somewhere its evil power would be unable to corrupt men's souls. With a group of iron-willed warriors, Alessa left Reikdorf and rode into the east, never to return.

Of all the warriors who had fought for Sigmar, Alfgeir carried the burden of victory more than most. Though many men and women had been dreadfully wounded in the fighting, the loss of his arm cut the Marshal of the Reik far deeper than the flesh. His eyes never regained their normal colour and no fire could warm his skin. Six months to the day after the battle's end, Alfgeir rode a white horse into the north toward a frozen lake, where he met a fur-cloaked warrior with two wolves at his side.

Wenyld and Sigmar watched him go, and the Emperor knew that a stronger compulsion than duty to Reikdorf called to his old friend. As Alfgeir vanished over the hillside, Sigmar bade Wenyld farewell and made his way into the depths of the frozen forest to the west of Reikdorf.

The cathedral of evergreen trees was a shimmering winter garden of glistening icicles and stillness. Walking paths he had not taken in years, he made his way to a peaceful hollow where weeping willows drooped with the weight of snow and ice on their branches. A gurgling waterfall spilled into a wide pool, and a simple headstone was set at its edge.

He touched the headstone and looked to the east.

'Soon, my love,' said Sigmar. 'Soon.'

LET THE GREAT AXE FALL

IN THE END, they counted eighty-eight skulls in the pile at the heart of the village: the skulls of children, no larger than a fist, all the way to those of fully grown men and women. The entire settlement had been wiped out in a single act of slaughter. Such feasts of death would usually attract the attention of carrion birds, but the sky above Heofonum was empty of scavengers.

Stacked in a pyramid, with the smallest at the top, the skulls were coated in sticky blood that had run down the bony ridges of empty eye sockets and jawbones to pool beneath this grim shrine to man's mortality. The wooden homes of the villagers lay in ruins, smashed apart as though a herd of bulls had been driven through them. Even the stone hall at the edge of the settlement had been destroyed.

Their hunting party had ridden the length and breadth of Heofonum, turning over every fallen timber, digging through every collapsed home and raking the debris of its abandoned barns, but they had found nothing of its inhabitants save their fleshless skulls. This was the third such village they had found, and with each bloodied pile of skulls laid before them like monstrous altars of worship, the mood of the hunters darkened still further.

Wenyld leaned against the stone wall of what had been the village alderman's home. The stonework was simple, imitating the style of

Sigmar's great hall in Reikdorf, but this building had not been crafted by the mountain folk, but by the hands of men and was nowhere near as grand or finely made. It had been built to last, with dutiful care and a cunning eye for defence, but that had not been enough to thwart the monster that had razed Heofonum. Having listened to Leodan's account of its ferocious strength, Wenyld doubted any wall, no matter whether wrought by man or dwarf, could withstand such dreadful power.

Wenyld pulled his cloak tighter around his shoulders as a chill blast of wind scudded through the ruined hall. Ever since he'd taken a dead man's spear to the belly in the last moments of the battle to save the Empire from the necromancer's undead legions, he'd found it next to impossible to keep the cold at bay. Only perched on a bondsman's bench at a blazing firepit would any hint of warmth touch him. With winter blowing in over the Vaults to the south, Wenyld knew he was in for a painful season of snow and misery, with aching bones and frost-touched marrow.

'Great Ulric, you favour the snows, but I'll be glad to see your brother again with the spring,' he said with a respectful nod to the ice-white skies of the north.

'Careful,' said Cuthwin, emerging from the trees on the far side of the ruined hall. 'I'd rather we didn't offend Ulric before we head into the mountains.'

'Into the mountains?' said Wenyld, irritated he hadn't even suspected his friend was near.

Cuthwin had always been the better huntsman, but still it irked Wenyld that he hadn't heard so much as a broken twig or brittle leaf being crushed underfoot.

'That's where the tracks lead,' said Cuthwin, moving around the building. Clad in worn leather buckskin and a dappled cloak of faded green and brown, he blended with the landscape. His bow was strung, and his long-bladed hunting knife was loose in its sheath.

Wenyld looked up to the blackened, snow-capped summits of the mountains to the south, their craggy peaks like serrated teeth gnawing at the clouds. The Vaults were the edge of the world as far as Wenyld was concerned, a battleground where two vast ranges of mountains met and threw up treacherous valleys, gorges and shadowed canyons.

He didn't like being too close to the mountains; orcs, goblins and worse made their lairs in the mountains, and no good ever came of going anywhere near such places. Leave such terrain to the Merogens, they were welcome to them.

'You're sure?' he asked, though he knew Cuthwin was never wrong about these things.

'I'm sure.'

Wenyld sighed. 'Ah, good. Just what I was looking forward to, a climb into the mountains at the onset of winter.'

'Could be worse,' said Cuthwin brightly.

'Really?' asked Wenyld. 'How could it possibly be worse?'

'You could be doing it without me to guide you.'

'Aye, there's that,' he conceded. 'You know your way around this terrain. Are you sure there's not some mountain goat in your family history? Is there some shameful tryst you've kept secret all these years?'

'Only that one night with Ebba,' returned Cuthwin with a sly wink.

They both smiled. Ebba was a notorious Reikdorf harridan, a mother of ten and as broad as she was tall. She was married to Bryni, a baker of such willowy proportions that it amazed everyone who knew them that they had produced such healthy children, and that he had survived the ordeal.

'Thank you for that image,' said Wenyld. 'Suddenly the idea of hunting a living dead champion of a Norsii blood god doesn't seem so bad.'

'There, you see? Told you it could be worse.'

Cuthwin threw his arm over Wenyld's shoulder as they made their way back to the centre of Heofonum, where the men and horses of their hunting party awaited their leader's word to move out. Thirty horsemen, clad in gleaming mail shirts and heavy furs, with half-helms of bronzed steel – these were among the finest warriors in all of Reikdorf. Over their armour, they wore white cloaks secured at the neck by a torq stamped with the four-armed cross the former Marshal of the Reik had taken as an informal symbol of their brotherhood.

Many were seasoned veterans, men who had stood in the heaving press of a sword line and lived, which marked them as both skilful and favoured by the gods. A few were little more than youths, the rise of the dead having forced them to manhood before their time.

All were volunteers, none had wives and none had fathered any children.

Sigmar wanted no new orphans and widows in Reikdorf; the war against the dead had created enough already.

One warrior stood apart from the others, a tall, shaven-headed man with a stripe of hair running across his crown to the base of his neck that then became a long, dangling scalp lock, similar to those worn by the Ostagoths. This was Leodan, a horse-warrior of the Taleutens whose Red Scythes rode with Sigmar's army at the River Reik and who had very nearly met his end at the great axe of the monster they hunted.

Like Wenyld, his wounding had been grievous, and few had expected him to see the dawn. But Taleutens are tougher than seasoned oak, and the horseman's shattered bones had knitted whole, though he would forever walk with a pronounced limp. Alone of his Red Scythes, Leodan had lived through that hellish night of war-making, and the loss of his brother riders was a wound that could not be healed by poultices and stitches.

Sigmar had once remarked that there was something missing in Leodan, some part of him that wasn't entirely normal. Wenyld had sensed it too on those few occasions he had cause to speak to the embittered Taleuten. Leodan had remained in Reikdorf following the defeat of the necromancer, a sullen presence at the fire whose shame kept him from returning home and whose pride drove him to relearn his skills as a rider. When Sigmar had asked for volunteers to ride with him, Leodan had been first to offer his lance.

Wenyld and Cuthwin nodded to the warriors as they tightened saddle cinches and fed grain from their panniers to the horses. They all knew that this was likely the last stop before they reached the mountains, and a well-fed horse was a sure-footed horse. None of them had ridden the trails of the Vaults, and Wenyld saw their wariness at venturing into such a hostile environment. The mountains offered a whole host of ways for a warrior to die, none of them glorious. To die falling from a cliff or crushed in a rockslide was no way to enter the eternal hall of Ulric's kingdom.

Leodan limped over to Cuthwin, his scarred face and ice-blue eyes cold as the grave.

'What sign?' he asked.

'South,' said Cuthwin. 'Into the mountains.'

Leodan nodded and turned away, returning to his horse and hauling himself into the saddle with the aid of his lance and an awkwardness the men of Reikdorf pretended not to see. With Leodan gone, two of the younger riders approached, Gorseth and Teon, lads barely old enough to have reached their Blood Night and whose chins were scuffed with only the faintest scraps of beard.

Though they had seen only sixteen summers, Teon had ridden into battle alongside Alfgeir, and earned great renown by standing against the blood drinker that had once been Count Markus of the Menogoths. Gorseth had fought for the Emperor too, standing in the spear line against a host of black riders, and sported a long scar along his shoulder where a rabid corpse-wolf had raked him with its claws.

Both were lads of heart, but they were so young it only reminded Wenyld how old he felt.

'Did you find any bodies this time?' asked Teon.

'No, lad,' said Cuthwn. 'We did not.'

'Where do you think they are?' said Gorseth. 'What does the monster do with them?'

'Best not to think of it,' said Wenyld. 'It would give you nightmares that'll have you weeping at your mother's teat.'

Gorseth glared at Wenyld. 'I earned my blooding,' he said. 'Same as every man here.'

'Maybe so, lad,' snapped Wenyld, suddenly angry. 'And when you've seen more than one battle or can grow more than thistledown on that chin of yours, maybe I'll treat you as an equal. Until then, stay out of my way and stop asking stupid questions.'

Gorseth's face flushed ruddy with colour, but he bit down on his anger and turned away. Teon followed his friend without comment, but Wenyld could see the disappointment in the lad's eyes. He sighed, irked that his temper had got the better of him. Gorseth hadn't deserved such ire.

'You were harsh on the boy, Wenyld,' said Cuthwin, as the two youngsters mounted their horses. 'Seems like only yesterday we were as inexperienced as him.'

Wenyld grunted. 'Maybe to you,' he said. 'I don't remember my bones aching in winter so much or feeling the stiffness in my joints yesterday.'

'Age comes to us all, my friend,' said Cuthwin.

Wenyld said nothing, his heart heavy. Cuthwin was only a single cycle of the moons younger than him, but a stranger could be forgiven for thinking that a decade or more separated them. War and wounds age men, thought Wenyld, but Cuthwin had somehow avoided the worst ravages of both.

'How long do you think before they get here?' asked Wenyld, shielding his eyes against the low sun and looking to the east. 'I don't like the idea of too many nights in the open waiting for them.'

Cuthwin shrugged. 'Your guess is as good as mine. Not long, I'd hope.'

'You'd think it would take them longer,' said Wenyld. 'What with the shorter legs.'

'They don't travel like we do,' said Cuthwin. 'They damn near out-paced the Asoborns of Three Hills on the march to Reikdorf.'

Wenyld nodded. He'd heard the story often enough from Wolfgart, the new Marshal's voice swelling with his pride as he told how his wife and kinfolk had stood fast against the blood drinker's army on that tree-lined hillside.

'Aye, and we'll damn well outpace you and your fancy horses when we get up into the Vaults, manling,' said a voice from the brush behind Wenyld. He reached for the heavy-bladed sword strapped to his hip. Cuthwin's hand kept him from drawing the blade, as a stocky figure encased in layered plates of burnished gromril and shimmering links of mail emerged from the scrub as though from thin air. Silver wings flared from the cheek plates of his full-faced helm, and he carried a great axe across his shoulders, with butterfly-winged blades and an edge sharper than even Govannon could fashion to a weapon.

'Master Alaric,' said Cuthwin, with a short bow.

'Cuthwin, isn't it?' said the dwarf, his hands planted on his hips. 'You younglings all look the same to me.'

'Maybe if you took your helmet off you'd get a better view,' said Wenyld.

'Listen to him,' said Alaric with grim amusement. 'You'd think with that cook pot he calls a helmet on his head he'd have the good sense to keep his flapping tongue silent about someone else's armour.'

'At least my cook pot lets me see who I'm talking to.'

Alaric took a step forward, and a dozen dwarfs in heavy mail shirts with round, steel-rimmed shields stepped from the brush behind him. Each of the mountain folk were like metal statues, and the threat of violence contained in each one was palpable.

Alaric laughed and lifted the visor of his helm and held out his hand.

'Good to see you again, Wenyld,' said Alaric. 'Grungni knows, you've lost none of your charm and good manners.'

'I had few enough to begin with,' said Wenyld. 'But at least I had some.'

'Never had much use for manners, boy,' said Alaric. 'Manners only clutter up what I need to say to someone with pretty words and hot air. And what damn use is that?'

'None at all, master dwarf,' said Wenyld, taking Alaric's hand.

Wenyld had met Alaric in the wake of the battle against the necromancer, when Sigmar had carried his wounded body to the Great Hall at the centre of Reikdorf. The healer Elswyth had been swamped with wounded men, and thus it had been Master Alaric of the dwarfs who had stitched his wounds closed. Even one handed, he had been steadier than most human surgeons, and Wenyld knew he owed the dwarf his life.

'Is Sigmar here?' asked Alaric with his customary abruptness.

Cuthwin nodded. 'He is. The Emperor set out from Reikdorf as soon as he received word from Karaz-a-Karak.'

'Good to see a manling king still understands the value of an oath,' grunted Alaric. 'Take me to him. There's killing to be done.'

SIGMAR KNELT WITH his head bowed beside beside the small stone shrine, one hand over his heart, the other clasping the haft of Ghal-maraz. The plates of the Emperor's burnished armour shone like silver, and the thickly-furred pelt of a great bear hung from his shoulders. A short-bladed sword was strapped to his side, and his anger at the death of his people hung over him like a lightning-shot thunderstorm.

The shrine itself was a small structure of four stone columns with a pitched roof of grey slate. It stood beside the shattered northern gateway of the village, and Sigmar knew it was lucky to have escaped destruction when the gates had been smashed asunder. No walls enclosed the shrine and at its heart was a statue of the wolf god in his bearded, barbarian aspect. A pair of wolves sat by his side, and he carried his mighty two-handed warhammer over his shoulder, a warrior who has never known his equal and never would.

Sigmar did not pray for himself: he petitioned the god of the northern winds and wolves to look kindly on his subjects that had been murdered in Heofonum.

'Great Ulric,' said Sigmar. 'Your people died here, and they come before you as victims of a terrible evil, one which has escaped Morr's judgement more than once. I would ask you to welcome them to your halls, where the beer is cold and the roasted meat is always hot. I ask this not for me, but for your loyal people.'

Sigmar received no response, nor had he expected one, for Ulric was a god who rarely answered prayers. His lessons were harsh, and taught a man self-reliance.

A hard god to follow, but a worthy one.

Sigmar stood as he heard someone approaching. From the heavy, mechanical rhythm of the footsteps he had a good idea who that might be. Sigmar did not turn around, and gently touched the heavy, rune-inscribed head of Ghal-maraz to the carved hammer of Ulric with a nod of respect.

'Praying to the Wolf God can wait. There's a grudge to be settled,' said a voice he knew could only belong to one dwarf.

'Greetings, Alaric,' said Sigmar, finally turning and descending the short steps of the shrine to the ground. Alaric was just as he remembered him: stout, immovable and utterly dependable. His armour was gold and bronze and silver, and he was not surprised to see the hand he had lost in the battle was restored with a mechanical gauntlet.

'I see you got yourself a new hand,' said Sigmar.

'Aye, lad,' said the dwarf, flexing a bronzed gauntlet of articulated digits that moved just like a limb of flesh and blood. 'Cant have a one-handed dwarf smith, sounds too much like an elf god for my liking.'

'And that would never do,' smiled Sigmar, but a moment of melancholy touched him as he was put in mind of the silver fingers the dwarf had crafted for Pendrag. His fallen friend's replacement hand had been a miracle, but this artefact was clearly of much greater sophistication. None among the dwarfs were as skilled in the craft of the smith or the forging of runes as Alaric, and this piece was a masterpiece of the metalworking arts.

'They already call me mad,' said Alaric, his gruff tones not quite concealing his irritation at the name. 'Can't have them thinking I'm an elf-friend too. I'd need to shave my head and find the nearest daemon to kill me.'

'A daemon?' said Sigmar with a shudder, remembering the terrible creature he had fought atop the Fauschlag rock of Middenheim. He shook his head. 'I would not be in too much of a hurry to meet such a beast. Even a hero like you might struggle to defeat a daemon.'

'Maybe so, lad, maybe so,' agreed Alaric. 'And we've a bastard hard fight ahead of us as it is. Even that bumbling smith of yours couldn't put him down fully with the baragdonnaz he'd rebuilt. A dwarf-built one might have done it, but he put it together like a blind apprentice with a hangover.'

'It didn't kill the monster, but it hurt it.'

'That it did, lad, that it did,' conceded Alaric. 'And if we can hurt it, we can kill it.'

Sigmar nodded slowly, offering a hand to Alaric, who accepted his warrior's grip and shook it with a grin of real pleasure.

'Just once it would be pleasant to see you when there's not killing to be done,' said Alaric.

'That it would, my friend, but these are not the times we live in.'

'There's truth in that,' agreed Alaric, striding back to the centre of the village with Sigmar at his side. 'And I'm glad to see you've honoured your oath.'

'You are my sworn oath-brother, you and King Kurgan both,' said Sigmar. 'You should know I would never break my word.'

'There's them among your kind don't know the value of an oath,' said Alaric. 'They'd break a promise as soon as break wind, and with just as much thought for those around them. It's easy to forget sometimes that you're not all the same.'

'I'll try not to be offended by that,' said Sigmar with a wry grin.

The dwarf looked genuinely puzzled by that, but said nothing as they reached the centre of the village. Sigmar's riders stood by their mounts, ready to ride at a moment's notice, and nine armoured dwarfs stood in a small square by a fallen signpost.

Alaric rejoined his dwarfs and turned to survey the warriors Sigmar had brought with him with a critical eye. Apparently satisfied, the runesmith addressed his words to every one of them.

'You all know why we're here,' he said. 'There's a grudge that needs settling, and we've all been wronged by the monster that did this killing. These aren't the first folk its killed, not by a long shot, and my people know that better than anyone. I can see there's some among you manlings know it too.'

Alaric stared hard at Leodan, and the scarred Taleuten gave a slow nod.

'Now this monster is more than just a dead thing that's been lifted from the grave, it's a monster that's been steeped in blood for longer than any of you can remember. Longer than a lot of my kin can remember, and that's saying something.

'It's got a name, and names are powerful things. Knowing a thing's name breaks its hold on you. Once you know its name, you're not so afraid of it. Well this thing's called Krell, and he was reaving and slaying in the name of the Blood God centuries before this new Empire of yours was a glint in young Sigmar's eye. Before your distant kin even came across the mountains, Krell was spilling blood and taking skulls for the Blood God. Grungni alone knows how many dwarfs and men fell before his axe, too many, and every one of those that died needs avenging. Back in my hold, there's a book. We know it as the Dammaz Kron, what you'd call a Book of Grudges, and everyone and everything that's done my people wrong is remembered. We dwarfs never forget an insult, and even if it takes a thousand years or more, we get even.'

Alaric paused, his mechanical fingers clattering as he made a bronze fist.

'Krell's done your kind great wrong too,' said the runesmith. 'He killed your warriors at the River Reik, and he's butchered hundreds more now that he's recovered his strength. Wherever it was he hid his dead face these last months, I don't know. Probably in some dank barrow in the deepest part of the forest or some worm-infested cave beneath the earth. It doesn't matter, all that's important is that he's shown his face again and we can end his slaughters right now.'

'How do we fight a thing like that?' asked Teon. Sigmar had been wondering the same thing. He did not see Krell on the battlefield, but had heard the terrible stories of his power and murderous fury. The undead champion of the Dark Gods would not be a foe easily bested.

Alaric unsheathed his axe and brandished it over his head.

'We fight with heart and courage,' he said, turning the weapon so that all could see the glittering, frosted sigils on its shimmering blade. 'And with master runes.'

Alaric swept the axe in the direction of the mountains to the south, and his dwarfs followed him as he set off with a mile-eating stride. Sigmar had seen dwarfs on the march and knew they would be able to maintain that pace for days on end. There would be no danger of the horsemen leaving the foot-slogging dwarfs behind.

Wenyld led a dun gelding to him, the muscular steed that had faithfully borne him into battle against the necromancer. Sigmar had sought the horse out with the dawn, knowing that a horse of such courage and heart was a rare beast indeed. He had found it grazing by a patch of untouched grass at the northern end of the city, and it had welcomed him with a stamp of its hooves. The horse was named Taalhorsa and tossed his mane as Sigmar climbed into the saddle and secured his boots in the stirrups.

With the Emperor atop his steed, the rest of the warriors mounted and awaited the signal to move. Wenyld unfurled the Emperor's banner, its bright cloth woven anew by the women of Reikdorf in the aftermath of the great victory against the dead. It rippled with gold and blue and crimson, the armoured warrior and wolves adorning the fabric given wondrous animation by the stiff breeze.

Sigmar flicked his reins and Taalhorsa set off after the dwarfs. Wenyld, Leodan and Cuthwin rode alongside the Emperor; his banner bearer, lancer and scout. Leaving Heofonum behind, they rode along little-used and overgrown paths that led inexorably up to the cold, shadow-haunted tracks of the mountains. Sigmar glanced down at the village's fallen signpost as he passed.

It had once pointed to Reikdorf in the north and somewhere illegible in the east. Though Reikdorf was hundreds of miles away, Sigmar was heartened by what it represented. It showed that even people distant from his capital actively thought of him as their Emperor.

It also reminded him of how he had failed them.

He had promised these people protection, but what protection was there from a monstrous champion of the living dead whose damned soul was sworn to the Blood God?

THE GROUND QUICKLY began to rise in choppy waves of rock-strewn ridges, tree-lined gorges and rough slopes of loose stone that cascaded downhill as the horses trudged ever upward. The dwarfs quickly outpaced the mounted men, but Alaric had the sense to order his warriors to slow their stride and allow the riders to keep up. As chafing to the dwarfs as such a delay was, they knew it would be madness to allow their forces to become separated.

Krell was not the only danger in the mountains.

Alaric had spoken darkly of a tribe of greenskins known as the Necksnappers, and the spoor of rats and the sound of their scuttling claws on rock stretched everyone's nerves wire-taut. Cuthwin caught the scent of something repellent, and soon came upon signs of its passing – footprints of splayed claws and sharp talons. He had no idea what this beast might be. Sometimes it walked on two legs, sometimes on all four, but its stride was long and its prints deep, which was enough of a reason to stay out of its way.

Krell's passing was easy enough to discern.

The Vaults had long been a place where the kings of old and their long-vanished tribes had laid their dead to rest. Overgrown barrows, so ancient they had been obscured by rockfalls and the growth of hardy mountains scrub, lay broken open and emptied. Piles of discoloured, dusty bones lay at their entrances and the musty, stagnant air of the darkened tombs was the reek of a spoiled storehouse. Rusted weapons and verdigris-stained armour lay strewn about, as though Krell had thought to loot the tombs and been disappointed by the lack of anything of worth inside. The higher they climbed, the more of these broken barrows they saw, and each one gave Sigmar a shudder of unease as he stared into the darkness beyond their shattered portals. He had stared death in the face, and could not forget the chilling touch of mortality on his soul. Sigmar was a proud man, but he liked to think he was not egotistical. He knew he would not live forever, that he would one day stand before the judgement of Morr in the slabbed necropolis of the dead.

As a warrior and an Emperor, his was a life steeped in battle and blood, and to think that he would live forever was foolish indeed. But as he stared deep into the bleak, emptiness of the cairns of these long forgotten kings, he was touched by an altogether greater worry. He chuckled softly to himself, dispelling the gloom that had crept on him with every step Taalhorsa had taken.

'Sire?' asked Wenyld, twisting in his saddle. 'Did you say something?'

'No, it's nothing,' said Sigmar. 'I was merely amused by my vanity.'

'I don't understand.'

Sigmar pointed to a barrow with a yawning entrance and a crumpled skeleton lying in a heap of brittle bones. 'I look at these violated tombs and my greatest fear is not dying. Do you know what my greatest fear is, Wenyld?'

'No, sire.'

'I fear being forgotten.'

'You will never be forgotten, my lord,' Wenyld assured him. 'How could you be? You are the first Emperor, the founder of the Empire and the ruler of the lands. You and the Empire are one and the same. Without you, there *is* no Empire.'

Sigmar smiled and said, 'I imagine the kings buried in these tombs thought the same, but do any of us remember them? Do the saga poets still sing of their mighty deeds? What is left of them but dust and bones? No, Wenyld, it is only the vanity of men that allows us to think we will always be remembered.'

'I disagree,' said Cuthwin. 'These men may have been kings, but what did they do of note? Did they found an empire? Did they save the race of men from extinction time and time again? Their names and deeds may have been forgotten, but armies will march with your name on their lips for as long as there are men to speak it.'

As Sigmar listened to Cuthwin, the image of the vast column of men with bloodied halberds and red swords the necromancer had shown him in the final moments of their battle returned to him. Those men had carried banners with his name emblazoned upon them, and bore talismans of the twin-tailed comet as they marched from a scene of wanton slaughter.

'You should not speak of such things,' said Leodan, surprising everyone. The horseman was taciturn at the best of times, but he had barely spoken since they had ridden from Reikdorf all those weeks ago.

'Why not?'

'You bring the notice of the gods by speaking of immortality,' said Leodan. 'Men should not dream of it, for immortality is for the gods alone and they are jealous of their eternal lives.'

'We weren't talking about immortality,' said Cuthwin.

'Yes, you were,' said Leodan, raking back his spurs and riding to the head of the snaking trail of mounted men with his lance-tip glittering in the sun.

'What was that about?' wondered Wenyld.

Sigmar had no answer for him and they lapsed into silence as the day wore on and the terrain became ever more difficult. The ground grew rougher and steeper, the path through the tree-shawled gorges getting narrower and narrower. These were mountains that did not suffer living things to move freely through their deep valleys and forests without effort.

At every turn in the path Sigmar felt as though a hundred eyes were upon the hunting party, hidden spies stalking them on the cliffs above or malevolent observers watching from behind every crag or in every shadow. The sense of threat and imminent danger was palpable, and he knew he wasn't the only one feeling it. Many times, horses stumbled and men cried out as they swung out over towering drops when they took their gaze from the path to seek out what might be a lurking enemy above.

A chill wind howled down through the gorge, a knifing cold that sought out every gap in a cloak or every thin patch of cloth covering a man's bare skin. Sigmar shivered in his armour and wished he'd worn the padded undershirt Count Marius had sent from Marburg. Ostentatiously decorated with embroidered stitching and needlepoint images of hammers and comets, Wolfgart had laughed at the sight of it, but it was undeniably warm and of sublime quality. Say what you wanted about Marius, he understood the value of quality goods.

Thinking of Wolfgart brought a rueful smile to Sigmar's lips. He missed his old friend, and dearly wished Wolfgart could have accompanied him on this ride into the mountains. The rogue had wanted to come, but one look at Maedbh's eyes and her swollen belly had convinced him that to leave Reikdorf would be a mistake. The old women who knew of such things had told Maedbh she was to bear a son, and Wolfgart's joy was complete. The boy would be born within three cycles of the moon, and Wolfgart had made Sigmar swear he would return in time for his son's birth.

In any case, Wolfgart had no choice but to remain in Reikdorf. With the departure of Alfgeir into the snow-wilds of the north, someone had to assume the mantle of Marshal of the Reik. Though Wolfgart had protested, Sigmar had known there was no one else who could follow the example Alfgeir had set. In a solemn ceremony, attended by no less than three of the Empire's counts, Sigmar had presented the glittering sword of the Marshal to his oldest friend, who had grinned like it was his Blood Night all over again.

A clatter of falling rock from ahead shook Sigmar from his nostalgic reverie. He looked for the source of the sound, seeing a scree of loose stone tumbling from the cliffs above them. Sigmar's eyes narrowed as he saw a flitting shadow in the thick brush that clustered at the edge of the high cliff like the bushy eyebrows of an old man.

Sigmar heard the creak of seasoned yew and looked over to see Cuthwin had his bowstring pulled back and a goose-feathered arrow nocked. The huntsman scanned the clifftop, but eventually eased the string back, but did not replace the arrow in his quiver.

'What did you see?' asked Sigmar.

'I'm not sure,' said Cuthwin. 'Maybe a coney or a fox.'

'Or something more dangerous perhaps?'

Cuthwin nodded, and Sigmar saw how it irked him to be unsure of anything.

'Keep a wary eye out,' said Sigmar and Cuthwin nodded, keeping one eye on the narrow path and one on the cliffs above them.

The path continued to wind up the angled slope of a white cliff that glittered with golden dust embedded in the rocks, and Sigmar wondered why none of the dwarf holds had constructed some iron structure to hew it from the cliff. Perhaps it was too dangerous or perhaps it wasn't even gold. Sigmar was no miner, and the fact that none of Alaric's dwarfs had given the cliff so much as a second glance told him that it probably wasn't gold.

Alaric was waiting for him at a bend in the track, where a jutting boulder with a flat face projected out into space. Alaric stood with his hands braced on his hip, standing at the very tip of the boulder, with nothing to prevent him from falling thousands of feet to his death. The winds howled around the dwarf, but he seemed not to notice.

'Hard going,' said Sigmar, drawing in the reins.

'This?' said Alaric with a distracted air. 'This is a gentle stroll compared to some of the galleries below Karaz-a-Karak. At least there you have good stone above your head, and not this damned empty sky.'

'It's hard going to us,' said Sigmar.

'Aye, you're only manlings, it's true,' agreed Alaric. 'You like your land flat and covered with trees and growing things.'

'What are you doing out there on that rock?'

Alaric looked around, as though he'd been unaware of where he was standing. He stamped down on the boulder, and Sigmar winced, half expecting it to shear off and carry the dwarf to his doom. Alaric saw his face and grinned.

'I forget your kind doesn't know stone like we do,' he said. 'I was reading the stone ahead of us, lad.'

'What is it saying?' asked Sigmar, who knew not to mock such statements.

'Hard to say,' replied Alaric. 'They don't speak quietly here. These mountains didn't just rise up nice and calm. No, they were brought into the world with violence and fire and earthquakes that would split your Empire into shards if they happened now. I still hear the echoes of that.'

Alaric extended his arms to the north and west. 'The Black Mountains in the north and the Grey Mountains in the west. Tell me what you see when you look at them.'

Sigmar shielded his eyes from the lowering sun with the palm of his hand and looked out over the titanic peaks of the Black Mountains. The jagged, crimson-hued mountain that men of the south knew as Blood Peak reared over a gnarled mob of craggy summits that stretched into the clouds of the far distance. Dots of bird flocks swirled over the nearest peaks, like crows over a battlefield.

Only the misty edges of the Grey Mountains could be seen from here, the sharp slopes cowled in patches of snow. What lay beyond those mountains was a mystery to the men of the Empire. Only the Bretonii had dared venture into the ice-locked passes that led to the lands beyond, and no one had seen or heard from that lost tribe in nearly two decades. Twilight was fast approaching, and there was little Sigmar could see that had attracted Alaric's attention.

'I'm not sure what I'm supposed to see,' he said at last.

'Do you see the mountains moving?' asked Alaric.

'Moving? No, of course not,' said Sigmar. 'Mountains don't move.'

'Ah, lad, of course they do,' said Alaric with the amusement of someone who knows the punchline of a jest. 'This world is a lot less solid than you manlings think it is. All this land, these mountains and the oceans, they drift on giant beds of stone that float on vast seas of molten rock. They move and grind against each other, and sometimes they collide to raise giant mountain ranges like this. A long time ago, before we dwarfs even built our holds, two of those beds collided, and the shock of that threw up these mountains.'

'You're mocking me,' said Sigmar.

'Not at all. Aye, these beds of rock move so slowly that you fast-moving races don't see it, but dig the rock for long enough and you'd soon know. The rock bed to the north scraped up over this one and the tail end of the northern mountains rode roughshod over the mountains of the south to make this almighty snarl-up of peaks and valleys and this pass.'

'This is a pass?' said Sigmar. 'I thought this was just some secret path you knew. Ulric's breath, the very teeth of winter are blowing down on us.'

'It's a pass right enough,' said Alaric. 'Yonder to the north-east is Karak Hirn, but our path won't take us anywhere near there. Shame, I'd have liked to see the great wind cavern and hear it bellow.'

'Alaric, why are you telling me this?' asked Sigmar.

'I'm not sure,' said the dwarf, with a soft sigh. 'I suppose I just want you to understand the rock and stone like I do. There's history here, and memory too. These mountains have seen their fair share of dying, and I can feel there's more on the way. The monster we're hunting came this way, and he wasn't the only one.'

'My scout didn't see any signs of anything else,' said Sigmar.

'Your scout doesn't know rock like I do.'

'You think there's trouble coming?'

'In these mountains, there's always trouble coming,' said Alaric.

* * *

THEY FOUND A place to camp for the night only a little farther up the pass, a projecting lip of rock that Sigmar would have called a narrow plateau, but which Alaric seemed to think was a sweeping plain. In any case, the point was moot, as there was good water streaming down the cliff in a sparkling waterfall, and screes of tumbled boulders that offered plentiful cover and places for sentries to watch the approaches.

The riders saw to their horses first, hobbling them in the centre of the flat ground and rubbing down their lathered flanks with handfuls of scrub grass warily pulled from the edge of the cliff. Each beast was then led in turn to the natural trough at the base of the waterfall and allowed to slake their thirst in the bitingly cold water.

With the mounts settled, the men attended to their own needs, filling waterskins and breaking out hard bread and salted meat from the horses' panniers as the darkness began to close on the mountains like a fist. Fires were lit against the cliff and the reflected heat dispelled the worst of the bitter wind blowing down from the heart of the Vaults. Warriors sat close to the fires, untying their heavy furs to allow the warmth to reach their bodies.

Alaric's dwarfs sat in a small circle around their own fire, though none of them removed their armour or loosened their cloaks. The race of mountain folk and the race of men were bound by powerful oaths, but neither sought out the company of the other. As alike as they were in basic form, there remained – and would always remain – a gulf of understanding between them. Common cause had brought them together, and but for a number of rare instances, few men and dwarfs would count themselves as friends.

Sigmar moved through the campsite, taking the time to stop at each fire and exchange words with the men gathered around it. He knew every man's name, and though he was exhausted by the time he sat at the fire with Wenyld, Cuthwin, Leodan, Teon and Gorseth, he knew the effort had been worthwhile. The talk around the other fires was animated, and good-natured banter flowed between the men instead of dark muttering and fearful speculation of what tomorrow might bring.

'Another long day,' said Cuthwin, as Sigmar sat down.

'They're only going to get longer. Alaric says these are just the foothills of the Vaults.'

'Dwarf humour or dwarf understatement?' asked Wenyld.

'The first, I hope,' said Sigmar, loosening the cords binding his boots and flexing his feet with a relieved sigh. Seeing the men around the fire grinning, Sigmar said, 'Even Emperors get blisters sometimes.'

'Even from horseback?' said Cuthwin, passing Sigmar as bowl of hot oats and goats' milk. The milk was starting to turn, but Sigmar didn't mind. A warm meal at the end of a day's travel did more to restore spirits than anything else, but Sigmar knew they would need to catch Krell soon before lack of supplies forced them to turn back.

They ate their food slowly, letting the aches and pains of the day ease out in the heat and companionable silence. Leodan passed a leather-wrapped bottle around the fire, a powerful Taleuten liquor distilled from grain and root vegetables. Sigmar took the first drink, and Cuthwin and Wenyld gratefully accepted one also. Teon and Gorseth each took a mouthful, and both coughed and retched at the taste of the powerful spirit.

Leodan smiled and said, 'It's an acquired taste, lad, but it'll keep you snug in your bed through a long, cold night.'

'Not too snug,' warned Sigmar, as Leodan took another long mouthful. 'Alaric's dwarfs are taking the first watch, but we'll be taking our turn too.'

Leodan shrugged and put the bottle away with a sour look, as the rest of Sigmar's warriors made themselves as comfortable as they could. With only their saddle blankets between them and the rocky ground, it was going to be a long night. Sigmar arranged his saddle for a pillow before pulling his furs over him.

He closed his eyes, and sleep stole upon him almost instantly.

SIGMAR WOKE WITH the first touch of chill in the air, a deeper cold than simply that of the mountains. This was a cold that only emanated from beyond the portals of Morr, the breath that accompanies those unquiet souls who do not pass through the god of the dead's halls to their final rest. His eyes snapped open, and he rolled from his furs with Ghal-maraz leaping to his hand. The rune hammer glimmered with corposant, the bound magics that were inimical to the dead sparkling like snowflakes in a fire.

'To arms!' shouted Sigmar. 'Up! Up!'

Not a soul moved, his men resting where he had left them. The horses stood as still as the carved horses at the end of Lancer Bridge over the Reik, their eyes glassy and lifeless.

'Up, damn you!' roared Sigmar, delivering his commands with a boot to hasten his men awake. They grunted and rolled over in their sleep, but did not awaken. Sigmar saw that even Alaric's dwarfs were still slumbering, and knew that some fell enchantment was at work.

'Ulric's bones, get up!' shouted Sigmar, kneeling beside Cuthwin and shaking the huntsman violently.

'He can't hear you, son of Björn, no one can,' said a rasping voice from the darkness.

'Show yourself, damn you!' demanded Sigmar, turning to try and pinpoint the sound.

'In time, but for now it would be best for you if you kept silent. Yes, silent would be good. Your men and the stunted ones were easy, but you have will that is not easily hidden.'

'What have you done to them?' cried Sigmar. 'Are they dead?'

'Always so loud, you heroes,' said the voice. 'I'm not deaf, and neither are they.'

'Answer me, damn you!'

'Of course they're not dead, dung-for-brains. Look, they still breathe. Their chests still rise and fall and warm air still blows from their lungs.'

'Come out of the shadows, you coward! Face me!'

'Face you? Don't be ridiculous,' laughed the voice. 'Would I go to all this trouble just for you to bludgeon me with that hammer of yours? Now be silent, son of Björn. I mean you no harm, but they do! Look behind you, Sigmar Heldenhammer, and find yourself a place to remain silent and still!'

Sigmar cooled his temper towards this invisible speaker, angry at being so manipulated, but as he heard the tramp of marching feet from below, he could still recognise the lesser of two evils. Sigmar ghosted silently to the narrow portion of the thin plateau on which he and his men were resting. Far below, but climbing rapidly, was a seething host of creatures, though Sigmar had difficulty in determining exactly what they were.

Some carried torches, while others bore tall banners of bone. He could hear the clatter of armour and a scratching, squealing sound like a barnful of chittering mice. The wind changed direction, and a verminous reek of stinking, unwashed flesh was carried uphill. Sigmar gagged at the stench, like an exposed midden on a summer's day. Sigmar fought to keep his food down as he smelled rotten meat, excrement and a hundred other fouler aromas. The noise of the approaching host grew louder, a barrage of squeals, squeaks and guttural barks.

Though it was too dark for an accurate gauge of numbers, Sigmar reckoned that at least five hundred or more creatures were marching towards their camp. He looked back over his shoulder to his sleeping warriors, knowing they were dead unless he could get them to move.

But how to rouse men who had been ensorcelled by some nameless enchanter?

Before Sigmar had a chance to think of a solution, he saw the pathway leading back down the mountain ripple and undulate, as though the rock had become suddenly malleable. In the thin light of the torches, he saw a wriggling carpet of mangy rats running ahead of the host: hundreds of disgusting creatures with patchy fur, branded backs and splintered fangs.

He stifled a gasp of horror and pushed himself hard against the cliff, stepping up onto a lip of stone as the seething tide of rats surged past like a furry river of diseased flesh and blood-matted fur. Some were brown, some were black, and yet others were white and furless. Pink tails wriggled like worms, and they snapped and bit at each other, as though driven by the whips of cruel masters. A few turned and sniffed the air as they passed him, and several turned their beady pink eyes upon him. They hissed in puzzlement, but passed on without attacking.

Behind the rats came scuttling beasts that loped and darted in the firelight of the torches. Wretched things in rags and scraps of armour, with their elongated snouts obscured by sackcloth hoods and their eyes made huge by orbs of glass nailed to their skulls. Sigmar held his breath at the sight of these vile monsters, monstrous hybrids of man and rat. They carried rusted swords, crude halberds and heavy cleavers with notched blades and old bloodstains. They hissed and spat with feral glee as they moved past him, but none of them so much as turned a grotesque, rag-swathed head towards him.

Sigmar took a tight grip of his hammer's haft, but instead of falling upon his men with their brutal cleavers, the rat-things tramped over the narrow plateau as though it were unoccupied. They marched past with their strange, jerking, hopping gait, but paid no mind to the sleeping men and dwarfs in their midst. Though the sleepers were clearly visible to Sigmar, the stinking horde of ratmen ignored them, as though they had no inkling of their presence whatsoever.

Sigmar let out his breath, and regretted it immediately as a rat-thing with black armour and a bronze headpiece, segmented like a beetle's carapace, paused in its march and stepped close to the cliff. Its nose twitched and its blistered tongue flicked out, as though tasting the air. Stubby whiskers bristled, and it cocked its head to one side. Beneath its helm, Sigmar saw eyes that were the red of a low-burning fire, eyes that narrowed with a loathsome, feral intelligence that horrified him.

The creature stood tall, its furred body twisted in a hideous parody of a man, upright and erect, but still with reverse-jointed legs and a whipping tail that ended in a barbed hook. A wide leather belt at its waist held a collection of skinning knives and a stubby wooden club fitted to an intricate mechanism of bronze and iron with a glowing green light at its heart.

Sigmar leaned back, letting the cold water streaming down the cliff pour over him as the creature took a stalking step closer. The icy chill of the water was freezing, but he did not dare move. How this thing could not see him, he did not know, but he guessed that if he so much as moved a muscle, whatever enchantment was keeping his men from the sight of these beasts would be undone.

The beast's face was less than an inch from him, its breathing wafting the stench of its last meal in his face. The smell of spoiled dairy and rotten meat made Sigmar want to gag, and its hot, rancid breath was animal and reeked of an open sewer. The flesh of its maw pulled back as it hissed in consternation, revealing two enormous, flat-faced fangs like sharpened chisel blades.

A whip cracked and the dreadful thing flinched, spinning around and rejoining the marching host as it continued its journey into the mountain. Sigmar watched the creature go, as larger beasts and more intricately attired creatures shuffled and scuttled past. Careful to keep his breathing even and his movements to a minimum, Sigmar blinked away the spray of water in his eyes as he tried to make sense of these nightmarish horrors.

Wolfgart had spoken of fighting squealing creatures with the faces of rats in the tunnels beneath Middenheim, and Sigmar – like everyone else – had assumed them to be no more than bestial forest monsters yoked to the Norsii army as it burned its way south. But to see such a horde, moving with such cohesion and discipline forced him to think of these things as something else entirely.

At last the end of the vermin horde passed his place of concealment, and when the last of the hissing, chittering beasts had vanished around the bend in the path farther up the mountain, Sigmar dropped to the hard-packed earth of the path. His body was numb with cold, chilled to the bone by the spray of water from the high peaks. His clothes were soaked through and his flesh was like ice as he stumbled back to his camp.

A fire burned at the centre of the plateau, and he made his way towards it, stripping off his sodden garments and pulling a warm blanket from an open pack. A solitary figure sat cross-legged before the fire, a shaven-headed man whose body was concealed by a voluminous cloak of black feathers. His shorn skull was tattooed with the black, reflective eyes of crows, and his own eyes were no less black.

Sigmar knew this stranger must be the source of the sorcery that had kept his men from the attention of the rat-things, but was too cold to do more than kneel beside the fire and let the heat from the flames thaw his naked flesh.

'Greetings, son of Björn,' the man said with a lopsided grin. 'I am Bransùil the Aeslandeir.'

'I am Sigmar Heldenhammer, but you already know that, don't you?'

The man nodded. 'I know a great many things about you, son of Björn. Much of which you would rather I did not know, but that is not to be the nature of our relationship. I will know all your secrets, and that is why you will trust me.'

'Trust you?' laughed Sigmar. 'I don't know you.'

'You will,' said the man with a sage nod. 'Or you did. It is hard to be certain sometimes.'

Sigmar looked over to where his men still slept, peaceful and blissfully unaware of the terrible danger that had just passed them in the night.

'So how is it my men and I are alive?' asked Sigmar as the fire began to warm him. He had decided against any violence to this Bransùil, guessing that any man who could hide so large a group from so many monsters was not someone to be taken lightly.

'A simple incantation,' said the man with a grin that exposed brilliantly white teeth. Sigmar had only ever seen such clean teeth in the mouths of young children, and he was reminded of the leering skull of the dread necromancer. 'When you spend as long in the far north as I once did, hiding yourself is the first trick you learn from the ravens.'

'But how did you do it?' pressed Sigmar.

Bransùil leaned over the fire, and Sigmar saw the darkness of his eyes had receded. In place of the blackness of crows' eyes, the man's eyes were a brilliant, cornflower blue.

'Magic,' he said.

* * *

WHEN CUTHWIN AWOKE, it was as though he'd spent the night in a warm bed with one of Aelfwin's Night Maidens. His limbs felt refreshed and his head was as clear as a winter's morning. He rolled from his blanket and stretched, sitting upright with a bemused grin on his face as he saw the rest of their company felt a similar sense of wellbeing. Teon and Gorseth set off to gather fresh kindling for the fires, but the smile fell from Cuthwin's face as he saw the churned ground all around them, hundreds of footsteps in the earth and scraped claw marks on the rock. Cuthwin leapt to his feet and snatched his sword from its scabbard as he saw more and more signs of a sizeable warhost's passing. Even the men with little in the way of woodsman's skills could hardly fail to notice the imprint of so many feet, and voices were raised in confusion at the sight of the tracks.

'What happened here?' asked Wenyld, kneeling beside a clawed footprint.

'We slept through the night,' said Leodan, scanning the path that led up the mountain.

'What in the name of Ulric's balls was in that drink?' demanded Cuthwin. 'We could have been killed!'

Leodan shook his head. 'Nothing that shouldn't have been. It's just burned water rakia.'

'Damn it, Leodan, you could have killed us,' snarled Wenyld. 'You might have a death wish, but don't drag us down with you.'

The Taleuten horseman gripped the hilt of his knife, and for a moment Cuthwin thought he might actually draw it.

'Talk sense, man,' said Leodan. 'If I'd put us out with strong drink then we'd all be dead.'

Despite his anger, Wenyld saw the logic of what Leodan was saying, and nodded curtly, turning to Cuthwin with a mute appeal for an explanation. Cuthwin had none to give him; he couldn't tell how many had passed in the night, nor, for that matter, could he imagine how they hadn't all been woken or killed. He tried to move carefully around the tracks, but it was impossible to step on any patch of ground that hadn't been tramped flat by the passage of uncounted feet.

'This makes no sense,' he said. 'Why aren't we dead?'

Cuthwin gave up trying to decipher the tracks and looked up as he heard voices raised in anger from farther along the path. He saw Sigmar making calming gestures towards the dwarfs who all looked as though they were ready to start a brawl in a crowded tavern. A hunched figure in a cloak of iridescent feathers stood behind Sigmar, and Cuthwin took an instant dislike to the man, though he could not say why.

'Come on,' he said. 'Looks like trouble.'

Wenyld and Leodan followed Cuthwin as he made his way to the ugly scene brewing between Sigmar and the dwarfs. Even before he reached Sigmar's side, he heard words like necromancer and daemon-spawn. It didn't take any great leap of imagination to know that these words were being directed at the man in the cloak of raven feathers. As Cuthwin approached, the man turned to look at him, and the huntsman felt acutely uncomfortable, as though all his secrets were laid bare. He looked away, standing just behind Sigmar as Master Alaric glowered in fury.

'We will not march with this warlock at our side,' said the dwarf, his hand of flesh and blood curled tightly around his axe, his bronze one clenched in a fist.

'But for Bransùil we would all be dead,' said Sigmar.

'Or enslaved in one of the rat things' hell-pits,' said the raven-cloaked man, clearly the Bransùil of whom Sigmar spoke. 'Which, trust me, would be far worse.'

'Shut your mouth, daemonkin!' roared Alaric, hefting his axe meaningfully.

Sigmar raised his hands. 'Alaric, this man saved your life. Now calm down and put up your weapon before you dishonour yourself.'

Alaric glared at Sigmar, and only the oaths they had sworn kept him from violence. Cuthwin knew how seriously dwarfs took their oaths, and by voicing how close Alaric was to breaking his, Sigmar had shamed him into backing down. But it had cost Sigmar greatly to invoke the power of his oath, and even Cuthwin could see that Alaric was cut deeply.

Alaric lowered his axe and calmed his raging temper with shuddering breaths.

'Aye, so be it, Sigmar,' said Alaric with a disappointed sigh. 'While we march together in these mountains I'll not harm this one, but if he ever works his sorceries on me or my warriors again, my axe will have his head off his shoulders so fast, he'll walk ten paces before he knows he's dead.'

'You have my word he will not,' said Sigmar, turning to face the cloaked man. 'Swear it.'

Bransùil sneered, as though unused to being given such commands, but he nodded and gave an awkward bow to the Emperor. 'So be it, I shall not work my magics upon the sons of Grungni again. You have my word on it.'

Alaric did not acknowledge Bransùil's words, but simply turned and set off towards the path leading farther into the mountains.

'Be ready to march by the time the shadows reach that rock,' said the dwarf, pointing to a white boulder at the end of the plateau. Looking at the sun's position, Cuthwin saw that didn't give them much time. Sigmar saw it too, and let out a deep breath.

'Cuthwin, Wenyld, get everyone ready to move out,' said Sigmar.

'Sire, what just happened here?' asked Cuthwin. 'Who is this?'

'The tracks you see all around us?' said Sigmar. 'A host of armoured monsters passed in the night, and this man saved us from them. How, I do not yet know, but that we are alive at all is thanks to him.'

'I am Bransùil the Aeslandeir,' said the man, and Cuthwin stiffened at the alien sound of the man's homeland.

'You are Norsii?'

'I was born in the north, yes,' agreed Bransùil. 'A student of Kar Odacen, but don't hold that against me.'

'We can't trust his kind,' said Leodan. 'You drove the Norsii out for a reason. They hold to the old ways of dark gods and blood sacrifice.'

Wenyld put his hand on the hilt of his knife, and Leodan's sword slipped an inch from its leather scabbard. Cuthwin saw Bransùil's eyes glitter with dark amusement, and stepped in front of his bellicose companions.

'Why are you here?' asked Cuthwin. 'And how did you come upon us? I saw no tracks that could belong to you.'

Bransùil smiled. 'There are paths through this world that not even you can track, Cuthwin, son of Gethwer. Paths that only those with the shealladh can see.'

A chill travelled the length of Cuthwin's spine and he backed away from the man, making the sign of the protective horns over his heart.

'He is a warlock!'

'Warlock, wyrd, galder-smith, sorcerer, seider… I have been called all such things and worse,' said the man, ruffling the feathers of his black cloak. He grinned, and Cuthwin saw his teeth were a perfect white, like the first snow of winter. No man's teeth should be as white.

'We owe him our lives,' stated Sigmar. 'And that is a debt we will honour.'

'He probably saved us for something worse!' said Wenyld. 'A sacrifice to his heathen gods!'

Bransùil laughed – a cawing, echoing sound – and said, 'Wenyld son of Wythhelm, if I desired you dead, you would already be a feast for the scavengers of these mountains.'

Wenyld blanched as the man laughed.

'Enough,' said Sigmar. 'This man is under our protection and you will fight at his side as you would any of your sword-brothers. You understand? Now put up your blades and get ready to move.'

Cuthwin nodded. He didn't like it, but he understood the debt they owed this man. So many tracks had passed in the night that there was no way they could have lived against such numbers. Sigmar walked past him to where Taalhorsa was hobbled by the edge of the cliff. Cuthwin felt the cloaked man's gaze upon him and reluctantly turned to face him.

'You do not need to fear me, Cuthwin, son of Gethwer,' said the man. 'Today the sun is bright, the wind is clear and the champion of Kharneth is many leagues ahead of us. Let us bask in what the gods have given us while it is ours to enjoy, eh? I have no doom for you this day, but who knows what tomorrow may bring?'

Wenyld took Cuthwin's arm and led him away from the grinning warlock.

'Pay him no mind,' said Wenyld. 'His kind are never to be trusted. Even their truth is cloaked in lies.'

Cuthwin nodded, but said nothing as he reached his horse. He would keep an eye on this Bransùil. No good could come of association with those who practised the dark arts. Cuthwin possessed a single arrowhead fashioned from a silver icon of Morr that he'd had blessed by the high priestess of Shallya.

He had been saving the arrow for Krell.

Now he wondered if he would need it to slay a mortal enemy.

ANOTHER SIX DAYS' travel took them higher and higher into the mountains. Alaric spoke little during that time, aside from advising on the best path for the horses, but Sigmar couldn't blame him. The dwarfs did not approve of men dabbling in the sorcerous arts, though he would not be drawn on why, save a thinly-veiled barb at the easily corrupted hearts of humankind.

Midmorning on the fourth day of travel saw the hunters pass the snowline, and the weather deteriorated still further. Swirling blizzards halted Sigmar's warriors on the fifth day, forcing them to find shelter in a winding cave system that had clearly been home to a large beast at some point. The tracks at the cave mouth were a mix of ursine paw and something vaguely birdlike, but paintings on the stone walls spoke of a crude kind of intelligence.

Piles of gnawed bones, some as long as a man's leg, lay in a rotting pile of discarded trinkets and skulls, some recognisably greenskin, others of a form and shape that none of the hunters could recognise.

'We shouldn't stay here,' said Cuthwin, looking around the stinking interior of the cave. 'It smells of fresh blood. Whatever lives here brings its kills back to devour. It's probably out hunting just now, and we don't want to be here when it comes back.'

'We don't have a choice,' said Sigmar. 'The storm is too severe. We need shelter.'

'If the beast returns to its lair, we'll be trapped.'

'That's a chance I'll take,' said Leodan, leading his shivering horse into the cave, though it fought him as soon as it caught a whiff of the blood and bones. None of the horses were willing to enter the cave without a struggle, and hauled at their riders as they were dragged inside. Even the prospect of a blizzard seemed preferable to their mounts, and Sigmar wondered if he should take that as a sign.

'Get some fires going,' ordered Sigmar. 'And do it quickly if we're not to freeze.'

Cuthwin nodded, but before the huntsman could begin to gather up their meagre supply of firewood, Bransùil opened his hands and spoke a muttered word that sounded part exhalation, part violent expulsion. The cave was suddenly filled with light as twin balls of seething orange fire sprang to life in the palms of his hands.

Sigmar was astonished. He had heard that the shamans of the Norsii could command the elements, but had never seen a man perform such a feat before his very eyes. Bransùil flicked his wrists and the two balls of flame fell to the ground, continuing to burn as though sustained by invisible kindling and fuelled by unseen timber. In moments the cavern was comfortably warm, and the ice and snow coating the warriors' armour and cloaks began to melt.

'You can summon fire with your power?' asked Sigmar.

'I can summon many things,' replied Bransùil. 'Fire is but the least of them.'

'You should not wield great power with such casual ease,' warned Sigmar. 'Men will fear you for it.

'Men already fear me,' said Bransùil. 'Most days they are right to, but not today. The fire will warm us and cook our food and keep nearby predators at bay.'

Sigmar nodded and knelt by the nearest of the fires. Its heat was powerful, and soon warmed his frozen limbs. Though initially reluctant to approach these unnatural fires, cold, hunger and Sigmar's example eventually drove the men to gather around the crackling blazes and prepare the cook pots.

Alaric's dwarfs took neither heat nor sustenance from the fires, and simply sat at the back of the cave, speaking in their native tongue with low voices and chewing their tough stonebread. It saddened Sigmar that Alaric had reacted with such anger at the presence of the Norsii warlock, but he understood the dwarf's hostility. His people had lost warriors in the fight against the northern tribes at Middenheim too, and he had no reason to trust Bransùil.

Neither did Sigmar, but necessity made for strange bedfellows.

Steaming bowls were passed around, and the mood thawed along with the ice as the men began to feel more human with hot food in their bellies. Sigmar sat with his warriors around the blaze nearest the cave mouth, and the shimmering flames made the pictograms on the walls dance like drunken revellers on a feast day.

Bransùil accepted a drink from Leodan's bottle, and Sigmar was surprised at the gesture, for the Taleuten had been the first to draw his blade at the mention of the warlock's homeland.

Leodan saw his look and said, 'The man's not killed us, and now he's keeping us warm. That's worth a mouthful of rakia.'

Sigmar accepted that simple logic and nodded.

The talk was slow and forced, each man wary of speaking too freely in the presence of the Norsii. If Bransùil took offence, he hid it well, and simply sat in silence with his hands stretched toward the fire.

'How far behind Krell do you think we are, Cuthwin?' asked Sigmar.

Cuthwin rubbed a hand over his face, and Sigmar saw the weariness etched into the man's features. He remembered Cuthwin as a young boy, catching him sneaking through Reikdorf to spy on his Blood Night, and still found it hard to reconcile the bearded huntsman before him with that cocksure youngster of his memory.

'Hard to say,' said Cuthwin. 'The storm is blowing away the tracks almost as soon as they're made, but I reckon we're close.'

'How can we ever catch such a monster?' asked Teon. 'It doesn't get tired, doesn't need to sleep and it doesn't need to stop to eat.'

'You are wrong, Teon, son of Orvin,' said Bransùil. 'It does get tired.'

'How can that be possible?' said Gorseth. 'It's dead.'

'How little you know...' smiled Bransùil. 'Aye, Kharneth's champion is dead, and the fiend who brought his damned soul back to life is no more. You saw what happened to the rest of the legion of the dead when your Emperor slew the necromancer, it collapsed to dust and ruin. But Nagash was not the only one with a claim on Krell's soul. The Blood God, Kharneth, claimed him an age ago and his hold is unbreakable. Krell's hate and rage give him strength. They sustained him when all others of his kind fell, but even hate has its limits. Even rage cools.'

The Norsii's eyes glimmered darkly, and Sigmar couldn't shake the idea that he spoke with admiration for such power.

'So he's getting weaker?' asked Wenyld.

'Weaker, yes, but still monstrously dangerous,' agreed Bransùil. 'To walk in the mortal world for a creature such as Krell requires powerful magic. Dark magic. The invisible energy of tombs and graves, of dark deeds and violent murder. That is why he has come to the Vaults, for the tombs of dead kings throng its weed-choked pathways and gloomy valleys. The darkest of magic can be found here, but without a necromancer to channel it, Krell can only sup crudely from broken barrows. Such magic is finite and old; it fades quickly and his strength is a fraction of what it once was. You will never have a better chance of ending him than you do now.'

'So he can be destroyed?' said Sigmar.

'Of course, nothing in this world is eternal,' said Bransùil. 'Not love, not duty, nor – in the end – honour. You know this. When the storm breaks on the morrow, we must travel high to the edge of a vast crater, the site of an ancient starfall that not even the sons of Grungni know, wherein lie the ruins a lost city. An outpost built in the name of a forgotten conqueror from the Land of the Dead. Built to serve an eternal empire, it was destroyed within a hundred years, and passed from living memory. At the heart of the city lies the tomb of its mightiest general, a warrior whose deathly energies Krell will drain to restore his power, perhaps even enhance it. The wards around the tomb are strong, and not even a being as powerful as Krell can break them easily. But he will break them given time.'

'Then we must stop him before he reaches this city,' said Sigmar.

'You cannot stop him, he is already there,' answered Bransùil.

* * *

Despite the threat of the beast whose lair they were currently inhabiting returning, Sigmar's warriors passed a restful night, and awoke warmed by Bransùil's fires that surged back to life with the dawn. The storm had passed in the night, and the day was bright, with a thin powder of snow draping the path into the toothed summits. Sigmar stood at the mouth of the cave, staring out over the mountainscape around him. Such titanic peaks dwarfed the achievements of men, and they would outlast any great deed he might hope to perform.

The city they were to travel to this morning was proof enough of that.

Bransùil had spoken of an immortal god-emperor known as Settra, a being whose armies and war-fleets had once nearly conquered the world. His reign was to have lasted until the end of time, but, like all mortal men, Settra had died and his empire had faded into forgotten myth. What did it matter how many lands a ruler conquered or how many people offered him fealty if he would eventually die? Lesser men would come after him, and all that he had built would decay until nothing remained.

Sigmar knew he was being vain and morbid, but the thought that all he had built and shed blood to create would be lost after his death troubled him deeply. He did not desire immortality as Settra was said to have done, but nor did he want his achievements to pass into legend, a tale of pride and hubris told at the fireside by old men and saga-poets.

Alaric emerged from the cave and gave Sigmar a respectful nod.

'I've been thinking about what you were saying, old friend,' said Sigmar. 'About the mountains.'

'What about them?'

'Looking at them from up here makes a man feel small,' said Sigmar. 'I realise now that we're all very small in a very big world.'

'Some men are bigger than others.'

'Some dwarfs are bigger than others.'

Alaric grunted in amusement. 'You and I are oath-sworn, Sigmar, and nothing will ever change that, but you would do well to hurl that warlock from the cliffs and be done with him.'

'He'd probably spread that feathered cloak of his and fly off.'

'I'm serious,' said Alaric. 'Nothing good will come of keeping him close, mark my words.'

'I'm not a fool, Alaric,' replied Sigmar. 'I know his arts are not to be trusted, but for now his purpose and our purpose are united.'

'You do not know his purpose, it would be unwise to think you do.'

'Very well, then I will say that our purposes appear to be united,' said Sigmar. 'And that will have to be enough. Bransùil has power, and to fight something that bears the mark of the Blood God, we will need that power.'

'Aye, like as not,' agreed Alaric. 'But I still don't like it.'

IT TOOK THE morning and the better part of the afternoon to climb to the edge of the crater Bransùil had spoken of. Though the landscape all around was shawled in snow, the steep-sided rock of the crater's rim was bare and black. The pale glitter-threaded rock they had become familiar with over the last week gave way to the glossy stone more commonly found where mountains erupted with fire and smoke. Even the thin scrub with which they had rubbed the horses and bulked out their grain began to thin. The air took on a grainy quality, as though invisible dust hazed the atmosphere, and when Sigmar dismounted to touch the snowless rock he found it was warm.

The lip of the crater was hundreds of feet above them, almost as tall as the Fauschlag Rock, and Sigmar could see no obvious paths. Alaric led the way, unerringly finding hidden defiles and stepped grabens that afforded access to the upper slopes. The climb was exhausting, and by the time their hunting party had led their mounts to the top, both men and horses were breathing hard and lathered in sweat.

Sigmar saw Alaric and his dwarfs standing silhouetted at the lip of the crater, looking vaguely frustrated at the laboured progress of the men behind them. His breathing came in shallow gasps, and he found it hard to take a breath, far harder than it should have been.

'Breathe slowly,' said Alaric. 'The air is thin up here, and you manlings don't do well at such heights.'

'I thought dwarfs were all about depths, not heights,' said Sigmar.

'Dwarfs cope well with any extremes,' said Alaric, without any hint of irony.

Sigmar nodded as he climbed the last ridge of the crater and stared down into the ruins of what had once been an outpost of a dead empire. What little was left of his breath was snatched away in wonder.

A vast hollow had been gouged from the mountain by the ancient starfall, a wide, steep-sided depression thousands of feet in diameter and hundreds deep. A dozen towering waterfalls spilled into the crater on its far side through a naturally formed dam of compressed rock, and glittering rainbows arced over the ruins of a great city of black stone. Tall towers and giant temples with golden domes and great needles of tapered silver vied for space with grand palaces and ornate castles, with each building Sigmar's eyes fell upon grander than the last. Great lakes formed in what had once been pleasure gardens and rivers flowed along proud avenues before vanishing into abyssal cracks torn through the base of the crater.

Sigmar saw the city was built to an ingenious design: its streets were arranged in concentric rings, with every thoroughfare cutting through its circular geometry angled towards the building at the city's heart. A vast temple, stepped and constructed of angular blocks of a pale stone that even Sigmar could tell had not been hewn from these mountains. Ornamented beyond all reason, its pillars were topped with great carven lions, its portals flanked by wide processionals of beasts that merged human and animal anatomies.

A great road, easily wide enough to accommodate a column of marching men wound down to the city along the inner face of the crater, and Sigmar wondered what had happened to the road on its outer face.

Bransùil strode to the crater's lip, his eyes dark and peering into forbidden places where no man's gaze ought to penetrate.

'You must hurry,' he said. 'The last ward is collapsing.'

SIGMAR RODE AT the head of his warriors, each man galvanised by the thought of finally cornering the monster they had sought for so long. The road into the crater was smooth and led onto one of the main avenues that encircled the palace at its heart. It was a simple matter to navigate the city, for its sacred geometries were necessarily simple.

The city's architecture had been impressive from above, but seen up close it was doubly so. The buildings were of a heroic scale unknown among the lands of the Empire, and Sigmar vowed that his realm would soon boast such monumental structures. Though thousands of years or more had passed since their builders had raised them, Sigmar saw each building was still as sound as they day it had been completed. Only those structures that had suffered at the hands of earthquakes or the eroding effects of the water had suffered the ignominy of collapse.

Leodan rode at his left, Wenyld to his right with Sigmar's banner held high.

Cuthwin, Teon and Gorseth rode behind him, with the dwarfs split into two groups that jogged with an unflagging pace to either side of the riders. Bransùil rode with Gorseth, who, as the youngest warrior in their group, had been appointed the unwelcome task of bearing the warlock on his mount. Sigmar kept the horses at a brisk walk, knowing he might have need of their fleetness later. The mood of Sigmar's warriors was grim but eager, as much at the thought that they would soon be able to return home as defeating Krell.

Twice they were forced to take detours as they came upon blocked streets that had not been obvious from above or found swollen rivers of ice-cold water that were too deep to ford. Yet the precision of the street plan allowed them to navigate their way to the centre of the city without difficulty. A fallen stone needle afforded a crossing of one fast-flowing river and the swift application of dwarf hammers broke open a way that was previously blocked.

Before long, Sigmar found himself riding along the grand, statue-lined processional that led to the great mausoleum temple. The statues were part man, part animal, but not in the monstrously melded way of the beasts that dwelled in the Empire's forests. These creatures looked constructed, as though they had been bred or shaped with deliberate intent. The idea that anyone would breed such monsters was anathema to Sigmar, and he found himself glad that this Settra's empire had passed from history.

'This is the place,' he said. He could feel the strange wash of dark breath that gusted from inside. The part of him that had passed through the Flame of Ulric felt the emanations of dark magic from the temple, and Sigmar recoiled as he sensed a connection between that power and this. To think that Ulric's power shared even a passing kinship with such evil unsettled him greatly.

The portal that led within was easily wide enough to allow his warriors access without breaking formation, but Sigmar ordered a halt as they reached the edge of the darkness that lay within. Sigmar twisted in his saddle to look up at the edge of the cliffs encircling the city as he felt a sudden chill on the back of his neck, as though a cold northern wind had brushed past him. He felt as though someone were watching him, but it was not an uncomfortable sensation or a threatening one.

'Something wrong?' asked Leodan.

'No,' said Sigmar.

'We must hurry,' said Bransùil. 'Krell's strength is growing even as we wait.'

Torches and lanterns were broken out of packs, and tinderboxes sparked to ignite the oil-soaked brushes and wicks. With light to guide them, Sigmar's warriors rode into the temple with greater urgency, the stone carvings of its walls glittering with embedded jewels and gold relief. Sigmar saw the dwarfs' entire demeanour change at the sight of so much ancient gold.

The passage was wide and high, and Sigmar could imagine the great cortege that had accompanied the dead general as he made his way to his final resting place. To this vanished culture, death was something to be venerated.

Cuthwin rode alongside Sigmar and said, 'I've heard that the tombs of the old kings were full of traps. Shouldn't we ride with more care?'

Sigmar shook his head. 'Any traps will have been triggered by Krell.'

He didn't need to add, I hope.

The air of the temple was charged with a subtle vibration, and Sigmar could feel the wards sealing the tomb at the heart of this structure were close to breaking. From somewhere far ahead, he could hear the thunderous booming of enormous impacts. A terrible roar of howling anger echoed from the walls, and Sigmar felt the same fear he had known when facing the dread necromancer himself. He had fought great beasts, creatures of nightmare, daemons and devotees of the Dark Gods, but this fear touched the very mortality of every man, and exposed his worst terrors. Sigmar loosened the haft of Ghal-maraz and swung his glittering warhammer in looping arcs at his side.

The passage opened into a vast, vaulted chamber of dark stone and soaring statuary depicting ancient gods whose names had been lost and great kings whose deeds had been forgotten. Its roof enclosed an immense space of dusty gloom, pierced in numerous places to allow beams of dim, moon-shot twilight to illuminate its grand void.

At the centre of the space stood a great sarcophagus on a golden bier, surrounded by piles of skeletal warriors in armour of gold, silver and jade. They had been smashed to pieces by the fury of the red-armoured giant that stood before the sarcophagus with its great axe rising and falling like a butcher cleaving a carcass in two. Wisps of dark magic flowed like poisonous fog from the cracks in the imperishable substance of the sarcophagus, and Sigmar knew the last ward was on the verge of being broken. Even without further blows from Krell's axe, it had suffered too much damage and was beginning to unravel by itself.

Krell's bulk was enormous, taller by a yard than the Berserker King of the Thuringians and broader than even the troll Sigmar had fought at Black Fire.

Plates of armour beaten into shape from a metal known only to a far distant world encased Krell's body, embossed with skull sigils that writhed in anger and howled in unending rage. Blood dripped from every skull-faced rivet and stained every link of mail that hung in tattered strips from exposed joints. Splayed bone horns jutted from his helm, and Sigmar saw that great portions of the champion of death's armour had been blasted clear or hung from his frame in broken fragments.

The sight would have been pitiful were it not for the vast shanks of dried meat and yellowed bone that jutted from the wounds torn through Krell's armour. The blood that coated his armour and dripped from his gauntlets was not his own, but an unending stream from the skulls taken in the name of his hellish master.

'Krell!' bellowed Alaric. 'I name thee Grudged.'

The giant champion of the dead and slaughter turned at the sound of the name he had borne in life and let loose a fearsome roar. Beneath its shattered visor, the monster's face was a fleshless nightmare of yellowed bone and grey flesh. A hideous emerald glow burned in one eye socket, and its lambent light promised only death.

The grinning skull leered at them, as though remembering those who had escaped its axe once, but who would not do so again. Sigmar felt the cold dread of this monster, the terror that leeched from its dead bones and sapped the courage of all who stood before him.

But these were men of Reikdorf who had faced an army of the dead, men who were commanded by the very warrior who had smashed the great necromancer to dust. They fought beside dwarfs who had stood against Krell and lived, who were led by the greatest runesmith of Karaz-a-Karak.

But most powerful of all, they were dwarfs who bore a mighty grudge.

Krell swung his mighty axe around, a weapon stained black as midnight by the blood of a million victims, and the powerful reek of its murders filled the dusty tomb. Krell had no voice, but a throbbing bass rumble, like a dreadful mockery of a heartbeat boomed with every step he took.

'Any thoughts as to how we're going to do this?' asked Alaric.

'With horse and speed and strength!' shouted Sigmar, raking back his spurs and urging Taalhorsa to a gallop. His riders followed him with a wild yell, Leodan with his lance lowered and Wenyld with Sigmar's banner aloft. It was a wild charge, with none of the grace or elegance of the Taleuten Red Scythes or the wild passion of the Ostagoth Eagle Wings, but it had power and it had Sigmar.

And it had Ghal-maraz.

Driven by anger, driven by shame, or driven by guilt, Leodan was the first to reach Krell.

He thrust his lance into the very heart of the undead champion's chest as though driven by the hand of Ulric himself. The cold iron tip punched through the red-stained metal as the wooden haft of the lance splintered into fragments with the force of the impact. Krell didn't so much as stagger, and the Taleuten kicked his boots free of his stirrups as Krell's axe slashed down with awesome force.

The enormous blade clove Leodan's horse in two through the saddle, and an ocean of blood flooded from the shrieking creature's body as it fell. Leodan rolled to his feet, his sword already in his hand, as the rest of Sigmar's riders hit home. Heavy broadswords, double-edged slashing blades and short stabbing swords clanged against Krell's armour, some piercing the gristly flesh beneath, others rebounding in showers of red sparks.

Krell's axe struck out, faster than any weapon of such size should be able to move, and five riders were hacked from their mounts, decapitated with executioner's precision. Their headless corpses rode on for a few yards before the weight of their armoured bodies dragged them to the ground.

Sigmar swayed aside from a return stroke of the axe and slammed Ghal-maraz against Krell's shoulder. Unnatural plates buckled and broke against the fury of his blow, and Krell at last staggered. The champion spun around, his axe reaching for Sigmar, but finding only empty air. Sigmar wheeled Taalhorsa around and drove his ancient warhammer into Krell's back, splitting apart the cuirass of his monstrous armour and drawing a howl that echoed in this world and the realm of the dead.

The cracks in the sundered sarcophagus split wider, and the deathly tang of evil magic grew stronger. Sigmar cried out as he saw another six of his men cut down by Krell's deadly axe, their souls dragged from their bodies to feed the monstrous appetite of the blood-hungry champion.

'Hurry!' cried Bransùil. 'The last ward is almost spent!'

Alaric and his dwarfs hurled themselves into the fray, hammers beating on Krell's body like demented smiths in a forge. Each warrior bore a weapon inscribed with runes that worked the magic of the dwarfs into a useable form, and each blow wreaked fearful damage on the strange plates of his armour. Alaric's frost-bladed axe bore runic magic the equal of that worked onto the killing face of Ghal-maraz, and every blow sheared slices of metal and bone from the beleaguered champion.

Krell leapt into the air, slamming down with bone-crushing force on two of the dwarfs, their armoured bodies crushed to paste beneath the creature's bulk. A looping axe blow sheared another two in half and only Alaric's master-forged axe saved him from a similar fate.

Mortal warriors faced an immortal champion, and though two of the greatest heroes of the age fought alongside them, this was no equal contest. Each time Krell's axe swept out, men and dwarfs died, and Sigmar knew they could not long suffer such rates of attrition. The sarcophagus at the centre of the temple cracked wider still, and the taint of dark magic gave a bitter, poisonous taint to every breath. Portions of the stone began to dissolve into the air as the magic sealing the long-dead general in his tomb crumbled under the assault of so much malignant power.

'Alaric, go left!' shouted Sigmar, wheeling his horse around the champion's right flank.

The runesmith obeyed without question, attacking the giant from the opposite side. Teon and Gorseth fought beside the dwarfs, darting forward between swipes of Krell's mighty axe to hammer their swords against his armour. Leodan fought alone, standing before the might of Krell with his notched sword held high. His armour was split wide, and Sigmar saw the Taleuten was lucky to be alive. Blood masked his face, and a long gash ran from his collarbone to his hip. A finger breadth deeper and he would already be dead.

Sigmar vaulted from Taalhorsa's saddle and wrapped one brawny arm around Krell's neck. His hammer slammed down on Krell's helm, buckling the metal and drawing a bellow of inchoate rage from the beast. The haft of Krell's axe shot up as Sigmar drew his arm back for another strike and slammed into his temple. The force of the blow was incredible and bright lights burst before Sigmar's eyes as he was thrown from Krell's back. Ghal-maraz spun from his grip, and he landed badly on the steps of the bier.

Little remained of the sarcophagus, only a fading outline of stone that diminished like morning mist. Within lay a skeletal corpse with the flesh pulled taut over a regal bone structure and clad in armour of gold, jade, amethyst and bronze. A strange weapon with a recurved blade lay on the corpse's chest, and a glimmering light was reflected in the emeralds set in its eye sockets. A dusty breath sighed between its sharpened teeth, and Sigmar fought to recover from the dizzying force of Krell's blow.

Bransùil knelt beside him, and placed a hand on his chest. He spoke a soft word that sounded like the chorus of a child's lullaby, and fresh strength flowed through Sigmar's body.

'The ward is gone,' he said. 'This your chance, son of Björn. Drive him into the tomb!'

Sigmar nodded and looked for his hammer, knowing it was the only weapon capable of causing lasting harm to the undead champion. Ghal-maraz lay in the midst of the fighting, where Leodan, Wenyld and Teon battled to keep the great axe of Krell at bay. More men were dead, and only three dwarfs still stood with Master Alaric as Krell shrugged off their attacks with a sound of grating metal that Sigmar realised was diabolical laughter.

Gorseth saw Sigmar rise to his feet and dived under Krell's axe to retrieve Ghal-maraz. The youngster's eyes blazed with winter fire as his slender fingers closed on the haft. Sigmar knew the temptation of such power on a young heart, but Gorseth shook it off and hurled the great warhammer to Sigmar as the black axe descended and cut into his shoulder.

Blood sprayed from the wound, and Teon cried out as his friend fell. Sigmar caught the spinning hammer as Teon threw aside his sword and dragged Gorseth away from the fighting. The effort was noble, though Sigmar knew a wound from so dreadful a weapon would almost certainly prove fatal.

Wenyld screamed and drove his sword up into Krell's belly as Leodan vaulted from a fallen portion of masonry and swung his sword at the mighty champion's head. Such was the power and emotion driving Leodan that his blade struck a blow like no other. Krell's helmet shattered into spinning fragments, revealing his ruined and blackened skull and madly gleaming eye. Fully half of Krell's skull was gone, the rest torn away by the blast of the dwarf war machine at the Battle of Reikdorf. Yet even as Sigmar watched, the bone was reknitting, weaving fresh substance as the dark magic released from the sundered tomb saturated the air.

'Cuthwin, son of Gethwer!' yelled Bransùil. 'Now is your moment! Loose!'

Sigmar looked over to where Cuthwin knelt beside Gorseth and the weeping Teon. The huntsman's bow was bent and a shaft with a shimmering silver arrowhead was nocked to the string. Cuthwin let fly between breaths and the arrow soared as true as any loosed by the king of the fey folk himself. The silver arrowhead punched through Krell's remaining eye, and the towering champion bellowed with rage as the magic imbued in the metal seared his damned soul with holy fire.

Sigmar knew they would never get a better chance to end Krell's terror, and hurled himself at the reeling monster. Master Alaric also recognised the moment and attacked with his rune axe cutting into Krell's thighs and belly. Leodan and Wenyld fought at his side as Krell took backward step after backward step. Dark light spewed from the awful wound in his skull, twisting coils of black smoke that shrieked as it fled the dissolution of Krell's body. The monstrous champion's axe clattered to the ground as his clawed hands sought to contain the abominable energies that sustained his existence.

The tomb of the great general flared with unnatural light as Krell drew on the reservoir of dark magic contained within, and Sigmar saw how they could end this. He spun around the flailing champion and took hold of Master Alaric's shoulder.

'Together,' he said.

Alaric nodded, understanding Sigmar's meaning in the way that only warriors who have fought and bled together for decades can know. Together they surged forward and their blows were struck with such symmetry and unity, that no force in the land could hope to resist. Krell stumbled back towards the tomb as the long dead general stirred from his aeon's long slumber.

Sigmar leapt and swung Ghal-maraz in a vast, sweeping blow that slammed into Krell's chest with all the strength he had earned in his years of battle. The mighty warhammer shattered the last of Krell's armour and a vast explosion of runic magic hurled the champion back into the tomb. Coils of dark magic enveloped the fallen champion; spiralling coils of vicious, jealous blackness. An immortal general from a bygone age fought the theft of the power intended to raise him from the grave, and the two creatures of undeath roared against one another in their desperate fury.

Bransùil stepped in front of Sigmar and Alaric, plunging his hands into the vortex of dark magic with a guttural chant of power words that sounded like a thousand windows shattering at once. The power contained in the tomb was old and strong, and was not about to be contained without a fight. Bransùil shuddered as his own strength went to war with magic conjured into being by a master of undeath. Crackling arcs of deadly energies whipped around him as he drew his arms in as though moulding clay upon a wheel. Sigmar and Alaric stepped back from the tempest engulfing Bransùil, shielding their eyes as a dazzling blaze of light exploded from the tomb and the earth shuddered as though struck once again by the hammer blow of a starfall.

Portions of the temple's roof fell inward, crashing down in enormous, building-sized chunks of masonry. Vast cracks split the walls and moonlight speared into the quaking temple. The crash of falling coffers and cracking rock was deafening, and the surviving warriors fought to hold their footing as the mountains shook with the fury of such powerful magics being unleashed.

'Get out!' shouted Sigmar. 'Get out of the temple!'

Alaric and his fellow dwarfs ran for the nearest crack in the temple walls, knowing with the skill of their race the escape route least likely to bury them beneath thousands of tons of stone. Sigmar ran for Taalhorsa and threw himself into the saddle as Leodan grabbed the reins of a fallen warrior's mount. Cuthwin and Wenyld rode for the passageway by which they had entered the tomb, and Sigmar was pleased to see his banner still flew proudly. Teon hauled Gorseth over his saddle and rode after the remaining riders as yet more pounding slabs of stone crashed to the ground.

It galled Sigmar to see how few would be making the journey back to Reikdorf, but he knew that they had been lucky to finish Krell with any of them left alive. He turned and held his hand out to Bransùil, who gratefully scrambled up behind him. The warlock's face was ashen, lined with exhaustion and sheened with sweat. Behind him, Sigmar saw the tomb of the general was gone, and its place was a shimmering sphere of crystal, like a vast diamond in which two forms could be made out as ghostly shadows.

Krell and the former occupant of the tomb were frozen together, locked in an eternal struggle for survival that would never end. Great chunks of stone slammed down on the magical prison but shattered and spun away, leaving the crystal tomb unmarked by so much as a scratch.

Sigmar raked back his spurs and Taalhorsa surged to the gallop as though all the Ölfhednar of the marshes were at their heels. The temple was collapsing with ever-greater speed and violence, and clouds of dust billowed around them, making it impossible to see more than a few yards. Sigmar had to trust to Taalhorsa's sense for danger as they swerved away from falling rubble and leapt over high barriers of toppled columns. Bransùil wrapped scrawny, buckle-boned arms around his waist as Taalhorsa leapt a yawning crack in the ground and lost his footing for a moment.

'On!' cried Sigmar. 'Taal guides you!'

The horse righted itself and set off with a whinny of terror as the ground heaved with elemental fury. Booming cracks of grinding stone echoed from all around them, and Sigmar heard a groaning crash of falling rocks and a roar of falling water. They rode into the grand tunnel that had brought them to the interior of the mausoleum, and Sigmar leaned over his horse's neck, speaking words of courage in its ear.

At last there was only sky above them, and Sigmar let out a wild yell of exultation as they left the tomb behind. Sigmar's warriors and Alaric's dwarfs saw him, but he saw they were not out of danger yet. The mountains shook and rocks tumbled from the high slopes as the titanic forces of the earth convulsed. The natural dam at the lip of the crater was breaking apart, and vast geysers of icy water were spilling into the city. The rivers were overflowing and soon every building would be underwater.

'Ride!' ordered Sigmar. 'Before we all drown!'

'We'll run,' said Alaric with stubborn pride. 'I'd rather wade than ride.'

'Suit yourself,' said Sigmar, 'but wade fast.'

The riders set off at the gallop, retracing the route they had taken to reach the mausoleum as vast spumes of waters flooded the city. Surging meltwater crashed against the walls of palaces that had stood for thousands of years and toppled them in a heartbeat. Tidal surges dragged entire streets to ruin, and soon the horses were galloping through knee-high water of unbearable cold.

Splashing and frantic, the horses reached the road leading back to the lip of the crater, and Sigmar's racing heartbeat eased a fraction as they gained height above from the drowning city. Higher and higher they climbed, and Sigmar eased the pace as he saw Alaric and his dwarfs wade to the road with little more then their beards above the surface. He laughed as they shook off the water like wet dogs and marched towards the waiting men as though they had just taken a brisk stroll in the rain.

The crashing thunder of falling water continued as they climbed to the top of the slope, and the city was swallowed by the freezing run-off of an ancient glacier. Teon and Wenyld lowered Gorseth to the ground, and Sigmar was amazed to see the lad still clung to life. He was young, but he was tough, as were all good Reiklanders.

Sigmar dismounted and knelt beside the boy.

'You have my thanks,' he said. 'That was brave of you to get me my hammer. Foolhardy, but brave. But for your courage, I doubt we would have prevailed.'

Gorseth smiled and his eyes fluttered.

'Don't you bloody well die,' snapped Wenyld. 'You hear me, boy. Don't you dare. Not when old men like me walk away without a scratch.'

Gorseth coughed, and his spittle was bloody. 'No more jokes about my age…?'

'I make no promises,' said Wenyld, and Sigmar saw there were tears in his eyes. 'Stay alive long enough to reach Reikdorf and we'll see.'

'Fair enough,' said Gorseth as Leodan and Cuthwin began binding the terrible wound in his shoulder.

Though the temperature was falling rapidly as night drew in, none could tear their eyes from the sight of the newly formed mountain tarn. The surface rippled like the ocean, and the moonlight sparkled on the water as it lapped at the edge of the crater, not ten feet below them. The violence of the earthquake had subsided, though the mountains still grumbled with smouldering anger.

Sigmar let out a pent-up breath and helped Bransùil down from Taalhorsa's saddle. Even through his armour, Sigmar could feel the misshapen, birdlike frailty of the warlock's body. The man nodded gratefully as a freezing wind blew over the surface of the lake and an icy prickling sensation crawled over Sigmar's skin.

A bitterly cold mist rose from the water, like the breath of the great frost giants said to haunt the featureless ice tundra of the Northern Wastes. The horses whinnied, their eyes wide and their ears pressed tight to their skulls in fear. The wind passed over them, but it was not the deathly cold of the dead, but the cleansing chill of a good northern winter. Sigmar had felt that cold before, when he had passed through the flame at the heart of Middenheim, and he clung to the memory.

No sooner had it arisen than the mist dissipated, and cries of astonishment arose from the men and dwarfs as they saw what had become of the lake. The water had frozen solid, leaving a vast, shimmering plane of ice before them. From the surface to the deepest reaches of the crater, the lake had been transformed in an instant to solid ice.

'Ulric's blood!' swore Cuthwin, turning to Bransùil. 'Did you do that?'

The warlock shook his shaven, tattooed head, staring over the glacier lake with a curious expression. 'No, young Cuthwin. I have a degree of mastery, aye, but such powerful elemental magics are beyond my ability to wield.'

Sigmar followed Bransùil's gaze, and his eyes narrowed as he caught sight of a distant shape on the far side of the crater. Someone was standing directly opposite them by the shattered gap where the rock dam had once held back the mountain waters. Though it was dark and the shimmering moonlight was filtered through a haze of ice particles, Sigmar swore he could see a figure swathed in fur.

A wolf-clad man with but a single arm.

Even as Sigmar caught sight of the man, he vanished into the moonlight shadows. He watched the spot for a while longer, hoping he would show himself again.

But the man did not return, if he had been there at all...

Sigmar turned away from the lake. Krell lay entombed beneath millions of tons of ice, sealed in a magical tomb in the heart of an ice-locked city, and Sigmar allowed himself a small smile of satisfaction.

'Will it hold?' he asked Bransùil. 'The crystal prison you created, will it hold?'

'It will hold,' replied the Norsii. 'For a very long time, but it will not endure forever.'

Sigmar nodded, as though this was a fundamental truth of the world he had only now come to fully appreciate.

'Nothing lasts forever,' he said. 'Nor should it.'

ABOUT THE AUTHOR

Hailing from Scotland, **Graham McNeill** worked for over six years as a Games Developer in Games Workshop's Design Studio before taking the plunge to become a full-time writer. Graham's written a host of SF and Fantasy novels and comics, as well as a number of side projects that keep him busy and (mostly) out of trouble. His Horus Heresy novel, *A Thousand Sons,* was a *New York Times* bestseller and his Time of Legends novel, *Empire,* won the 2010 *David Gemmell Legend Award.* Graham lives and works in Nottingham and you can keep up to date with where he'll be and what he's working on by visiting his website.

Join the ranks of the 4th Company at
www.graham-mcneill.com

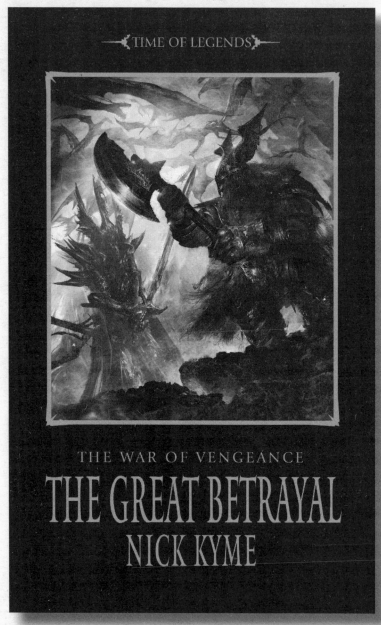